Don Quixote

MIGUEL DE CERVANTES SAAVEDRA was born in Spain in 1547 to a family once proud and influential but fallen on hard times. His father, a poor barber-surgeon, wandered up and down Spain in search of work. Educated as a child by the Jesuits in Seville, the creator of *Don Quixote* grew up to follow the career of a professional soldier. He was wounded at Lepanto in 1571, captured by the Turks in 1575, imprisoned for five years, and finally rescued by the Trinitarian friars in 1580. On his return to Spain, he found his family more impoverished than ever before. Supporting his mother, two sisters, and an illegitimate daughter, he settled down to a literary career and had hopes of becoming a successful playwright, but just then the youthful Lope de Vega entered triumphantly to transform the Spanish theater by his genuis. *Galatea*, a pastoral romance, was published in 1585, the year of Cervantes's marriage to Catalina de Palacios y Salazar Vozmediano. But it did not bring him an escape from poverty, and he was forced to become a roving commissary for the Spanish armada. This venture, which led to bankruptcy and jail, lasted for fifteen years. Although he never knew prosperity, Cervantes did gain a measure of fame during his lifetime, and Don Quixote and Sancho Panza were known all over the world. Part I of *Don Quixote* was published in 1605; in 1613, his *Exemplary Novels* appeared, and these picaresque tales of romantic adventure gained immediate popularity. *Journey to Parnassus*, a satirical review of his fellow Spanish poets, appeared in 1614, and Part II of *Don Quixote* in 1615 as well as *Eight Plays and Eight Interludes*. Miguel de Cervantes died on April 23, 1616, the same day as the death of Shakespeare—his English contemporary and his only peer.

EDWARD H. FRIEDMAN is professor of Spanish and comparative literature at Vanderbilt University. His books and essays include studies of the prose, poetry, and drama of early modern Spain. He is editor of the *Bulletin of the Comediantes* and president of the Cervantes Society of America.

Don Quixote

Miguel de Cervantes Saavedra

Translated by Walter Starkie

With a new Introduction by
Edward H. Friedman

A SIGNET CLASSIC

SIGNET CLASSIC
Published by New American Library, a division of
Penguin Putnam Inc., 375 Hudson Street,
New York, New York 10014, U.S.A.
Penguin Books Ltd, 80 Strand,
London WC2R 0RL, England
Penguin Books Australia Ltd, Ringwood,
Victoria, Australia
Penguin Books Canada Ltd, 10 Alcorn Avenue,
Toronto, Ontario, Canada M4V 3B2
Penguin Books (N.Z.) Ltd, 182–190 Wairau Road,
Auckland 10, New Zealand

Penguin Books Ltd, Registered Offices:
Harmondsworth, Middlesex, England

Published by Signet Classic, an imprint of New American Library,
a division of Penguin Putnam Inc.

First Signet Classic Printing, November 1964
First Signet Classic Printing (Friedman Introduction), February 2001
10 9 8 7 6 5

Library of Congress Catalog Card Number: 00-052643

Printed in the United States of America

Dedicated
to my children
and grandchildren
—W.S.

Contents

PART II

AN INTRODUCTION TO
Don Quixote

Miguel de Cervantes Saavedra (1547–1616) was born in the Spanish university town of Alcalá de Henares. Relatively little is known of the author's early life and formal education. His father was a surgeon who suffered a string of financial reversals, and the family was forced to make several moves. Cervantes spent some years in Seville, a particularly exciting city at the time, and in Madrid, the new capital. He seems to have been involved in a duel in Madrid in 1569, which caused him to abandon his first ventures into the literary domain and to take refuge in Italy. Settling in Rome, he entered the service of Giulio Acquaviva, who would soon be named cardinal. In 1571, Cervantes took part in the Battle of Lepanto, where a Catholic alliance defeated the Turkish enemy in an impressive show of naval force. He was seriously wounded in the conflict and lost the use of his left hand, a sacrifice that he bore with unmistakable pride. Four years later, in 1575, Cervantes embarked for Spain with letters of recommendation for a civil appointment. Unfortunately, Barbary pirates intercepted the galley and transported its Christian captives to Algiers, where Cervantes remained a prisoner for five years. He made a name for himself by virtue of repeated and daring escape attempts. Finally ransomed, he returned to Madrid, where few opportunities awaited him. In 1584, he married Catalina de Salazar, nineteen years his junior. The marriage was not successful, and the couple regularly lived apart. Cervantes resumed his writing career, accepted a number of less-than-distinguished positions in various parts of Spain, and probably served time in jail for accounting irregularities during his service as a tax collector. He never achieved the professional success to which he aspired, but he finally attained recognition as a writer. Cervantes was fifty-eight years old when Part I of *Don Quixote* appeared. The novel would make him famous, but not rich, for his publisher would be the primary beneficiary of the sale of the book.

Although his literary reputation rests primarily on the enormous impact of *Don Quixote,* Cervantes cultivated many genres. He initiated his artistic career as a poet, and in 1585 he published the pastoral novel *La Galatea*. His *Novelas ejemplares,* twelve "exemplary" novellas published in 1613 and highly admired by scholars, cover a broad range of topics and conventions, some tending toward the idealistic and others toward the realistic. Among the most well known of the short novels are *El licenciado Vidriera* (*The Lawyer Made of Glass*), an exploration of madness and human nature; *El coloquio de los perros* (*The Dogs' Colloquy*), a satirical and psychologically fascinating dialogue featuring canine protagonists; *La gitanilla* (*The Little Gypsy Girl*), a shrewd commentary on class consciousness and literary norms; and *Rinconete y Cortadillo* (*Rinconete and Cortadillo*), a response to the roguish antiheroes of picaresque narrative and a portrait of the lower depths of Sevillian society. Cervantes's most sustained poetic composition is the *Viaje del Parnaso* (*Journey to Parnassus*), a view of poetry and poets rendered in a decidedly parodic tone and published in 1614. A frustrated dramatist who never remotely threatened the success of his rival Lope de Vega, Cervantes published, in 1615, eight full-length plays and eight dramatic interludes, or *entremeses,* that had not been presented on stage. Literary history has saved one early play, *La Numancia,* and the *entremeses* from oblivion. Cervantes's final work, a prose epic entitled *Los trabajos de Persiles y Sigismunda* (The Trials of Persiles and Sigismunda), which the writer considered to be his masterpiece, was published posthumously in 1617. Based on Greek romance of classical antiquity, *Persiles* is an ambitious interweaving of lovers' separations, infinite tribulations, travels to exotic locales, episodic digressions, and baroque contrasts and complications. *Persiles* re-creates the past through the recourses of the day. *Don Quixote* is equally reliant on the past, but ends by determining the future of the novel.

Don Quixote belongs to the classical period of Spanish literature, often called the Golden Age, which corresponds roughly to the Elizabethan and Jacobean periods in England. The century and a half from 1550 to 1700 witnessed a tremendous flourishing of the arts in Spain, from early narrative realism to the most ornate baroque poetry, painting, and architecture. Shakespeare and his contemporaries have counterparts in Lope de Vega, Tirso de Molina, and Pedro Calderón de la Barca, among other playwrights, who originated a national theater that has never been equaled. In political terms, Spain under the Habsburg monarchs was the supreme imperial power, the protagonist of the New World encounters, of territorial expansion, and of wars waged against Moslem and Protestant enemies. Religious fervor produced not only holy wars, but a powerful Inquisition aimed at identifying and punishing professed converts to Catholicism ("New Christians") who secretly practiced their former faiths. The growth of urban centers and an early form of capitalism contrasted with the agricultural economy of Spain's large rural areas, which had their own traditions and social structures. This was a time of discovery, rediscovery, and radical change, with a powerful State—at the service of God and of its own inter-

ests—as the dominant authority. For the artist, it was a
contradictory age, of unlimited opportunities and strict
censorship, of reverence for the past and fierce competition to surpass all predecessors. In *Don Quixote,* Cervantes manages to incorporate the broad cultural, social,
and historical panorama into a work of fiction.

Don Quixote is first and foremost a book about books.
Although one probably will tend to think of *Don Quixote*
as a single novel, it was published in two parts, with ten
years between them, in 1605 and 1615. In 1614, a writer
using the pseudonym Alonso Fernández de Avellaneda
wrote a sequel to Cervantes's Part I, and this sequel makes
its way into the "real" Part II. Another factor that the
reader should bear in mind is that in the early seventeenth
century, when Cervantes was creating his masterpiece,
there was really no such thing as the novel as we now
know it. The novel essentially was being invented at this
time, and Cervantes himself was a key player in the game
of creation. Through *Don Quixote,* Cervantes establishes
a model for the novel by writing a novel and by bringing
the writing process, and the gamut of fictional forms of his
day, into the narrative scheme. In effect, *Don Quixote*
tells two interrelated but very different stories: the story
of the misadventures of a man who tries to function as
a knight errant when society has moved beyond its chivalric past and the story of the composition of Don Quixote's story. Cervantes does not simply write a novel
to entertain the reader with an intriguing plot, but he
uses the occasion to make the reader think seriously
about the act of writing and the act of reading.

What are the first stages of these simultaneously told
tales? For the man who was to transform himself into
the knight Don Quixote, the first stage is an obsession
with books. The lesser nobleman, or *hidalgo,* Alonso
Quijano el Bueno is an avid reader. He spends all his
spare time in his library, reading an assortment of books,
but with an overwhelming emphasis on the books of

chivalry. The *libros de caballerías* recounted the adventures of valorous knights who dedicated themselves to lofty goals and to beautiful damsels for whom they were willing to risk everything. These knights went out on the road to face their enemies. Everything about the books of chivalry was exaggerated: the battles were intense, the adversaries were monstrous and disproportionately large, and the course of true love was difficult, filled with years of rejection that deferred the inevitable happy endings. As might be imagined, the language of these episodes was figurative, flowery, and idealistic. The unexceptional landowner from La Mancha in south-central Spain, with little to do but read and dream, fancies himself a knight. When his brain ultimately "dries up" from so much reading, he decides to initiate a journey as the self-fashioned knight errant Don Quixote de la Mancha in order to fight for justice, to protect the defenseless, and to win fame. Thus the action is set into motion.

What about the other level, which relates to the composition of the story? The novel begins with a prologue in which the fictionalized author laments the trouble that he is having in writing a prologue for his manuscript. A friend enters and advises him to write whatever he wants—to make up things and pretend that they come from important sources—and we realize that this discussion of how to write a prologue is itself the prologue, and we also realize that we as readers are going to be very much involved in the process. We will be active—not passive—readers, just as Don Quixote will be an active rather than a passive participant in knightly exploits.

Take into account a visual analogue of this phenomenon. Arguably, the most famous painting of the period is *Las Meninas,* or *The Maids of Honor,* by Diego Velázquez. In the painting, the apparent center is the young princess Margarita. But what happens when we look more closely at the painting? We notice to the left the presence of an artist—Velázquez himself—and his

easel. The painter is at work, and he is facing his subjects, who do not fit into the frame. Or do they? We can
notice in the true center of the painting what seems to
be a mirror, which contains a reflection of the faces of
two people, who happen to be the king and queen of
Spain. Velázquez is painting their portrait, and the princess, her ladies-in-waiting, and the other figures are not
subjects but spectators. The artist does not hide himself,
nor does he forget the observers, who are equivalent to
readers. They are in the picture. On the walls of the
room hang paintings. Like the mirror, the open door-
way at the back right with a standing figure and the open
window at the front right also suggest framed works of
art. Finally, if the mirror in the painting were a real mirror, who would be reflected in it? The spectators, including ourselves when we visit the Prado Museum in
Madrid. Velázquez does not want us to forget our role
in the process, nor does he want us to forget his role
in the process. Without the creator and the consumer,
there is no art object. And people look at art in different ways. They give meaning to what they see, but
this meaning is not necessarily uniform, consistent, or
definitive. Interpretation is, like the door in *Las Meninas,* open. Art that is self-conscious—that is, mindful
of its place as art—can help us to analyze what the
work of art, those who create art, and those who enjoy
looking at art, or who read, are doing.

As in the case of Velázquez, Cervantes has many
tricks up his sleeve, and we note that fact from the
beginning of the novel. In Chapter I of Part I, the narrator makes the point that this is the "true history," *"la
verdadera historia,"* of Don Quixote, but it is not clear
what the protagonist's real name is, what village he is
from, how old he is, and so forth. Cervantes is starting
his story, but he is, at the same time, asking the reader
to ponder how stories (and histories, for the Spanish
historia means both story and history) are made, what

truth is, and how perceptions can vary from person to person. There is always a link between Don Quixote the reader and ourselves as readers.

When Don Quixote embarks on his first sally, he is alone, and the narrator tells us what he is thinking and what is really there. For example, what Don Quixote sees as a castle is, in fact, an inn. It seems that Cervantes had the inspiration to change this format early on, and he sends Don Quixote back home, where he picks up a squire, Sancho Panza. Sancho is not only a humorous character, famous for his proverbs, malapropisms, and comic actions, but he is Don Quixote's foil and partner in dialogue. We no longer need the narrator to interpret for us, for Sancho Panza can argue that the giants are windmills, that the enemy hordes are flocks of sheep, and so on.

Sancho Panza is a rustic character, a poor farmer who can neither read nor write. He is separated from Don Quixote, then, not only by class but by vocation. One man is driven by books, while the other is illiterate. Cervantes appears to be allegorizing the confrontation of the newly developed printing press—and an emerging print culture—with oral tradition and a very different literary past. More important, perhaps, Cervantes shows how Don Quixote and Sancho Panza interact with each other, how each man is affected by contact with the other. Sancho especially learns from the experience. He becomes wiser, craftier, and more assertive as the novel progresses, and in Part II, he is very much in control of the situation. It is commonly noted that Don Quixote represents idealism (the abstract) and that Sancho Panza represents realism (the practical, the concrete), but the novel may stress even more the interdependence and mutual attraction of the two characters, which the noted Spanish critic Salvador de Madariaga called the Sanchification—*sanchificación*—of Don Quixote and the Quixotization—*quijotización*—of Sancho Panza.

In sum, the reader of *Don Quixote* must make a

commitment of sorts to become part of the artistic process. One has to work hard to read Cervantes's novel, but most readers find the effort worth their while. Why is this? In part, perhaps, because the situation remains new, novel in its original sense. No other book is quite like *Don Quixote*. Another significant point is that as readers we enter the story—we come to care about Don Quixote, despite his ridiculous enterprise—while, conversely, we distance ourselves to think about art, historiography, perspective, perception, human nature, sanity and madness, absolute and relative truths, and other fundamental matters. We can relate, as well, to Don Quixote's dreams, exemplified in his transformation of the peasant girl Aldonza Lorenzo into the lady Dulcinea de Toboso, who becomes a symbol not only of idealized love but of humankind's highest aspirations and of the power of the imagination. And we also can enjoy—and marvel at—the beauty, ingenuity, and variety of Cervantes's language.

The language of *Don Quixote* is playful, clever, ironic, poetic, satirical, and profound. As Don Quixote leaves his home—before he has "officially" been knighted and before he has even one adventure, much less a conquest—he envisions himself as the subject of an illustrious history. Don Quixote exalts his mission and the books that inspire his endeavor, whereas Cervantes's narrator exposes and takes satirical aim at the inflated goals and the inflated language. When the knight suffers the wounds, physical and mental, of his altercation with the windmills, he insists that an evil enchanter is responsible for the mix-up. The continual presence of the enchanter (which, interestingly, is the brainchild of Don Quixote's niece) comes in handy. The delusional yet crafty knight has a ready-made excuse for all his misperceptions—his misreadings—of reality. The author forces us to examine and reexamine our concepts of what constitutes reality.

Another challenge to our sense of reality comes at

the end of Chapter VIII of Part I. Don Quixote is immersed in battle with a competitor from Biscay, a province located on the northern coast of Spain, when, to his dismay, the narrator finds himself with no more story to tell. In the next chapter, the narrator discovers a manuscript, written in Arabic, by the chronicler Cide Hamete Benengeli. Since he cannot read Arabic, the narrator must hire a translator, so what we are reading from Chapter IX onward is the edited translation of a document by an Arab historian—a document that insists that it is a true and objective account when, at this historical moment, Christians regarded Moslems as great liars (and vice versa). And, of course, it is inevitable that some things get lost in translation, farther and farther removed from the time of experience. Thus introducing doubt to the veracity of his story, the narrator continues with his tale of Don Quixote's chivalric quest.

During this endeavor the knight meets many people, each of whom adds to the panoramic vision of the novel. A beautiful young country girl named Marcela, for example, seems to step out of the pages of a pastoral romance, a genre that projects a view of the countryside in which shepherds and shepherdesses speak more like men and women of the court than authentic country people. Marcela is no stereotype, however. She is a woman with a mind of her own. When she is pursued by a lovesick gentleman, who eventually dies as a result of her rejection, she adamantly vows to protect her freedom, and in her lengthy discourse she sounds like a precocious feminist. What about the most consequential woman in *Don Quixote,* the lady Dulcinea del Toboso? The immediate response would be that, despite her importance in the narrative, she never appears, since she is a fiction, but neither does her alter ego, Aldonza Lorenzo. (It is worthy of note that in the musical comedy *Man of La Mancha* the character of Aldonza plays a major role.) Don Quixote does describe Dulcinea's breathtaking beauty, and at one point, he observes that she is more real because she is a mental image. Sancho, who knows Aldonza, provides a more earthy description of the farmgirl.

Around the middle of Part I, Don Quixote and Sancho Panza find themselves in the Sierra Morena mountain range, where they intermingle with a number of fascinating characters, who have stories of their own to tell. One is Cardenio, a gentleman who has gone crazy over what he thinks is the treason of his lady and best friend. A highlight of the section is a conversation between Don Quixote and Sancho on the theme of madness, and Cervantes seems to relish having the pot call the kettle black, so to speak. Don Quixote is moved to imitate the penitence of the most famous of the knights errant, Amadís de Gaula—Amadís of Gaul—and by doing so he becomes a madman who has discussed madness and who consciously emulates another madman. Don Quixote returns home from his second excursion in a cage, but there will be more adventures to follow—one month later, according to the novel, and ten years later, according to the publication record.

A prominent feature of the first part of *Don Quixote* is the entry of other characters into Don Quixote's fictional world. Innkeepers take on the role of castle owners, while their wives and employees become grand ladies. On several occasions, Sancho Panza the pragmatist loses his focus as he contemplates the governorship that Don Quixote has promised him as a reward for his service. This theme is intensified in Part II—the 1615 *Quixote*—when it becomes clear that numerous characters have read Part I and can react to Don Quixote even before he has the chance to act.

Cervantes juxtaposes story and history in a striking manner. The scrutiny of Don Quixote's library in Chapter VI is a brilliant exercise in library criticism and an allegory of the Inquisition, which condemned both books and souls. The criminal and galley slave Ginés de Pasamonte in Chapter XXII is a recognizable social type and the author of an autobiography that resembles picaresque narrative. In Chapter XXXII, the characters assembled at the inn engage in a debate on the respective values of fiction and history. The captive's account, which begins in Chapter XXXIX, is a suspenseful tale of rescue, with parallels to the author's imprisonment in Algiers. In Chapter XLVIII, disparaging comments on the state of theater in Spain—made by a canon from Toledo, whom Don Quixote and Sancho meet on the road—appear to be inflected by the failed playwright Cervantes. Some scholars contend that the author of the false sequel wrote the continuation for the specific purpose of chastising Cervantes for having defamed Lope de Vega and his followers.

In contrast to the prologue to Part I, the prologue to Part II is not about prologues, but rather about the false sequel. Cervantes has the chance to condemn the intrusion of the author of the continuation into his literary space. He promises to kill off Don Quixote at the end of his own second part, in order to ensure that no one else will enter this private territory. The early chapters of Part II deal with the reception of the published history. How did people respond to the history? Which components did they like best, and which least? On hearing of the Moslem historian who documented his adventures, Don Quixote becomes worried about the accuracy of the record. He anticipates contemporary authors (and politicians) in recognizing that he is at the mercy of a writer who can put whatever "spin" he wishes on the events. Cervantes introduces a new character, the educated jokester Sansón Carrasco, who is the first person in the text to have read Part I and who devises several plans to cure Don Quixote of his illusions.

Back on the road for his third sally, Don Quixote decides that he would like to pay his respects to Dulcinea in her hometown of El Toboso. Sancho attempts to keep him away from the town, since he earlier had lied to his master about bearing a message to Dulcinea. At this point, we see how Sancho Panza gains control of the situation. He stops three farmgirls riding along on their mounts and announces to Don Quixote that they are Dulcinea and two of her handmaidens. Don Quixote, the creator of his own reality based on fiction, is reduced to replying, "I see nothing, Sancho, but three peasant girls on three asses."

The sly Sancho Panza puts forth the argument that Dulcinea must be enchanted, and Don Quixote declares that his principal mission will be to "disenchant" her. This episode signals a change in Don Quixote, who is increasingly at the mercy of the plots of others. While these plots are based on Don Quixote's previous words and deeds, they ironically cut into his authority within the narrative. He does have his moments, however. One of them is when he is challenged by the mysterious Knight of the Mirrors, whom he defeats. It turns out that the knight is Sansón Carrasco in disguise, and Sansón's generous interest in curing Don Quixote of his madness turns into vengeance for the ignoble loss on the battlefield. Shortly afterward, Don Quixote opens the cage of a real lion to do battle, but the lion is too sleepy to do any harm, and what could have been a catastrophe turns into a moral victory.

Another well-known episode of Part II is Don Quixote's descent into the Cave of Montesinos, where he spends about an hour and a half and returns to tell the story of three days of knightly adventures and visions. Sancho can hardly control his laughter when Don Quixote reports having seen the "enchanted" Dulcinea and her maids of honor, together with noted figures of myth and legend, in the cave. The darkness of the cave obviously arouses Don Quixote's mental juices. Similarly, when he sits in the audience of a puppet show on a chivalric topic, Don Quixote runs on stage to attack the villain and thus to protect the damsel in distress. He ends up paying for the damage to the puppets and the scenery.

Don Quixote and Sancho Panza meet the Duke and Duchess, avid readers of Part I, who invite the knight and squire to their palace and treat Don Quixote with feigned respect. The knight is elated, since "for the first time he felt thoroughly convinced that he was a knight errant in fact and not in imagination, for he saw himself treated in the same way as he had read that such knights were treated in past ages." The Duke and Duchess are connoisseurs of chivalric literature, but even more they are tricksters, and Don Quixote and Sancho become the objects of their mockery and of their elaborate games. The aristocratic couple is willing to spend time and money—and to employ a cast of thousands—to trifle with the mad knight and his uneducated squire. Their most comprehensive plot is to create an "island" for Sancho to govern, a prize that Don Quixote had promised him for faithful service. Before Sancho commences this undertaking, Don Quixote offers him words of wisdom, which in no way hint of madness. Sancho is successful in his judgments—he is called "a new Solomon" by his subjects—and his combination of intuition and common sense serves him well. Nonetheless, the Duke and Duchess have arranged for a series of misfortunes to beset the governor (among them, no food, for fear of poisoning), and Sancho leaves his island in disgust. He meets Ricote, a former neighbor and converted Moslem, and history again mediates the fiction. Sancho and Don Quixote, who has suffered trials of his own in the palace, resume their chivalric itinerary. At an inn, Don Quixote meets two gentlemen who have a copy of the Avellaneda continuation of *Don Quixote,* and Cervantes has the opportunity to malign his imitator. The knight and the squire spend some time with a group of highwaymen, and then make their way to Barcelona, where they once again find the false sequel in a printing establishment. Later Cervantes in-

troduces a character from the spurious text who will
assert, and will certify before a notary public, that the
Don Quixote before him—and not the other—is the
genuine knight. The scenes in which Don Quixote pre-
occupies himself with the illegitimate chronicle of the
other Don Quixote call attention to the interplay of
process and product—of story and storytelling—that
marks Cervantes's bold approach to narrative.

Don Quixote's nemesis, Sansón Carrasco—now the
Knight of the White Moon—reappears and challenges
him to battle. This time, Sansón triumphs, and he
forces Don Quixote to return home and to refrain
from knightly adventures for a period of one year.
Don Quixote undergoes a type of conversion, presented somewhat ambiguously. He decries knight errantry and reassumes his former identity. Is the death
of the protagonist a spiritual conversion or a means
of preventing other writers from keeping him alive?
Readers' opinions vary greatly. But even though Don
Quixote's death is a contested issue, his life—including
his literary afterlife—is not. In every sense, *Don Quixote* and its influence are very much alive. In four
hundred years, the novel and the theory of the novel
have moved in diverse directions, but *Don Quixote*
seems to prophesy and to inform all that is new. Cervantes's novel is amusing, audacious, stimulating, and
multilayered. It is self-referential and evocative, pointing inward to literature and outward to the world at
large. By blending the comic and the serious, it tests
the limits of reading and writing, and it asks readers
to reassess their assumptions about art and life. Tar-
geting the romances of chivalry, Cervantes crosses the
threshold of the modern. Ostensibly rehearsing models
of the past, he provides a template for the future.

—Edward H. Friedman
Vanderbilt University

SELECTED BIBLIOGRAPHY

I. CRITICAL STUDIES

Allen, John J. *Don Quixote: Hero or Fool?* 2 vols. Gainesville: University of Florida Press, 1969 and 1979.

Alter, Robert. *Partial Magic: The Novel as a Self-conscious Genre.* Berkeley: University of California Press, 1975.

Aylward, E. T. *Towards an Evaluation of Avellaneda's False Quixote.* Newark, DE: Juan de la Cuesta, 1989.

Bjornson, Richard, ed. *Approaches to Teaching Cervantes' Don Quixote.* New York: Modern Language Association of America, 1984.

Brink, André. *The Novel: Language and Narrative from Cervantes to Calvino.* New York: New York University Press, 1998.

Close, A. J. *The Romantic Approach to Don Quixote.* Cambridge: Cambridge University Press, 1978.

Cruz, Anne J., and Carroll B. Johnson, eds. *Cervantes and His Postmodern Constituencies.* New York: Garland, 1998.

Dudley, Edward. *The Endless Text: Don Quixote and the Hermeneutics of Romance.* Albany: State University of New York Press, 1997.

Eisenberg, Daniel. *A Study of Don Quixote.* Newark, DE: Juan de la Cuesta, 1987.

El Saffar, Ruth. *Distance and Control in Don Quixote: A Study in Narrative Technique.* Chapel Hill: University of North Carolina Department of Romance Languages, 1975.

El Saffar, Ruth, ed. *Critical Essays on Cervantes.* Boston: G. K. Hall, 1986.

Friedman, Edward H., and James A. Parr, eds. *"Magical Parts": Approaches to* Don Quixote. Special number of *Indiana Journal of Hispanic Literatures* 5 (Fall 1994).

Fuentes, Carlos. Don Quixote; *or, The Critique of Reading.* Austin: University of Texas, at Austin, 1976.

Gilman, Stephen. *The Novel According to Cervantes.* Berkeley: University of California Press, 1989.

Johnson, Carroll B. *Cervantes and the Materialist World.* Urbana: University of Illinois Press, 2000.

—. Don Quixote: *The Quest for Modern Fiction.* Boston: Twayne, 1990.

Madariaga, Salvador de. *Don Quijote: An Introductory Study in Psychology.* London: Oxford University Press, 1961.

Mancing, Howard. *The Chivalric World of Don Quijote.* Columbia: University of Missouri Press, 1982.

Martínez-Bonati, Félix. Don Quixote *and the Poetics of the Novel.* Trans. Dian Fox in collaboration with the author. Ithaca: Cornell University Press, 1992.

Murillo, L. A. *A Critical Introduction to* Don Quixote. New York: Peter Lang, 1988.

Nelson, Lowry, Jr., ed. *Cervantes: A Collection of Critical Essays.* Englewood Cliffs, NJ: Prentice-Hall, 1969.

Parr, James A. Don Quixote: *An Anatomy of Subversive Discourse.* Newark, DE: Juan de la Cuesta, 1988.

Parr, James A., ed. *On Cervantes: Essays for L. A. Murillo.* Newark, DE: Juan de la Cuesta, 1991.

Paulson, Ronald. *Don Quixote in England: The Aesthetics of Laughter.* Baltimore: Johns Hopkins University Press, 1998.

Percas de Ponseti, Helena. *Cervantes the Writer and Painter of* Don Quijote. Columbia: University of Missouri Press, 1988.

Riley, E. C. *Cervantes's Theory of the Novel.* Oxford: Clarendon Press, 1962.

——. Don Quixote. London: G. Allen & Unwin, 1985.

Rivers, Elias L. *Quixotic Scriptures: Essays on the Textuality of Hispanic Literature.* Bloomington: Indiana University Press, 1983.

Robert, Marthe. *Origins of the Novel.* Trans. Sacha Rabinovitch. Bloomington: Indiana University Press, 1980.

Russell, P. E. *Cervantes.* Oxford: Oxford University Press, 1985.

Schmidt, Rachel L. *Critical Images: The Canonization of Don Quixote through Illustrated Editions of the Eighteenth Century.* Montreal: McGill-Queen's University Press, 1999.

Sullivan, Henry W. *Grotesque Purgatory: A Study of Cervantes's* Don Quixote, Part II. University Park: Pennsylvania State University Press, 1996.

Van Doren, Mark. *Don Quixote's Profession.* New York: Columbia University Press, 1958.

Watt, Ian. *Myths of Modern Individualism: Faust, Don Quixote, Don Juan, Robinson Crusoe.* Cambridge: Cambridge University Press, 1996.

Weiger, John G. *The Substance of Cervantes.* Cambridge: Cambridge University Press, 1985.

Williamson, Edwin. *The Half-way House of Fiction:* Don Quixote *and Arthurian Romance.* Oxford: Clarendon Press, 1984.

Williamson, Edwin, ed. *Cervantes and the Modernists: The Question of Influence.* London: Tamesis, 1994.

Ziolkowski, Eric J. *The Sanctification of Don Quijote: From* Hidalgo *to Priest.* University Park: Pennsylvania State University Press, 1991.

Among the most useful general introductions to *Don Quixote* are the studies by Johnson (1990), Murillo, and Riley (1985). For critical studies of the novel, see the bibliography of the Modern Language Association of America, published annually and available online, and *Cervantes,* the journal of the Cervantes Society of America.

II. BIOGRAPHIES OF CERVANTES

Byron, William. *Cervantes: A Biography.* Garden City, NY: Doubleday, 1978.

Canavaggio, Jean. *Cervantes.* Trans. J. R. Jones. New York: W. W. Norton, 1990.

McKendrick, Melveena. *Cervantes.* New York: Little, Brown, 1980.

Canavaggio's book, published in France in 1986, received the Prix Goncourt for biography in 1987.

PART I

TO THE DUKE OF BEJAR,[1]

Marquess of Gibraleón, Count of Benalcázar and Bañares, Viscount of the Township of Alcocer, and Lord of the Towns of Capilla, Curiel, and Burguillos.

Relying on the generous reception and honor that so staunch a princely patron of the liberal arts as Your Excellency grants to all kinds of books, especially those that out of nobility do not debase themselves for the service and profit of the vulgar, I have resolved to publish *The Ingenious Gentleman Don Quixote of La Mancha* under the aegis of Your Excellency's most illustrious name, beseeching you with all the reverence I owe to such greatness to receive it graciously under your protection, so that, although lacking that precious quality of elegance and erudition that usually adorns works composed in the houses of scholars, it may with your backing safely venture to face the judgment of some, who, undismayed by their own shortcomings, are wont to condemn the works of others with more severity than justice. If Your Excellency in your wisdom will bear in mind my good intentions, I trust that you will not disdain the paltriness of this humble offering.

Miguel de Cervantes Saavedra.

[1] The Duke of Béjar, a wealthy patron, was very interested in sport and was so miserly and unappreciative that Cervantes never mentioned him again. Rodríguez Marín compares him to Cardinal Ippolito d'Este, Ariosto's Maecenas, who when the poet had finished reading a canto from his unpublished *Orlando Furioso* to the Court at Ferrara made the following comment: *"Messer Lodovico, dove avete pigliato tante coglionerie?"* (Messere Lodovico, where did you pick up all that tomfoolery?)

PROLOGUE

Idle reader, you need no oath of mine to convince you that I wish this book, the child of my brain, were the handsomest, the liveliest, and the wisest that could be conceived. But I could not violate Nature's ordinance whereby like engenders like. And so, what could my sterile and uncouth genius beget but the tale of a dry, shriveled, whimsical offspring, full of odd fancies such as never entered another's brain—just what might be begotten in a prison, where every discomfort is lodged and every dismal noise has its dwelling?[1] Repose, a quiet corner, fragrant fields, cloudless skies, murmuring brooks, spiritual calm—all contribute their share in making the most barren of muses teem and bring forth to the world such offspring as will fill it with wonder and delight. And if a father should happen to sire an ugly and ill-favored child, the love he bears it claps a bandage over his eyes and so blinds him to its faults that he reckons them as talents and graces and cites them to his friends as examples of wit and elegance. But I, who appear to be *Don Quixote*'s father, am in reality his stepfather and do not intend to follow the usual custom, nor to beg you, almost with tears in my eyes, as others do, dearest reader, to pardon or dissemble the faults you may see in this child of mine. You are no kinsman or friend of his; your soul is in your own body, and you are as much at home in your own house, and master thereof as the king is over his taxes. Moreover, you know the old saying: "Under my cloak a fig for the

[1] According to F. Rodríguez Marín this is a reference to Cervantes' imprisonment in Seville in 1597.

king"—all of which exempts and frees you from every respect and obligation. So you may say what you please
about this story without fear of being backbitten for a bad
opinion or rewarded for a good one.

I would have wished to hand you the story neat and
naked, without the adornment of a prologue or the endless
string of customary sonnets, epigrams, and eulogies that
it is the fashion to place at the beginning of books. For I
must admit that, though the story gave me some trouble to
compose, I found none greater than the writing of this pref-
ace you are reading. Many times I picked up my pen to write
it, and many times I put it down, not knowing what to say.
Once when I was in a quandary, with the paper before me,
my pen in my ear, my elbow on the desk, my hand on my
cheek, meditating on what I should write, unexpectedly a
lively and intelligent friend of mine burst into the room,
and finding me daydreaming, insisted upon knowing the
reason. I did not conceal it, but said that I was thinking about
the prologue I had to write for the history of Don Quixote
and that it worried me to such a degree that I was inclined
not to write one, nor even to publish the exploits of so
noble a knight.

"Have I not good reason to worry about what that ancient
lawgiver, the public, will say when it sees me after all these
years that I have been sleeping in the silence of oblivion,
emerging now with all my years on my back with a tale as
dry as a rush, barren in invention, lacking in style, poor in
conceits, and devoid of all learning and instruction, without
quotations in the margins and notes at the end of the volume, when I see that other books, no matter how fabulous
and profane they may be, are so crammed with sentences
from Aristotle and Plato and the whole mob of philosophers
as to astound their readers and win for their authors a reputation for scholarship and eloquence? And when they quote
Holy Scripture! You are sure to say that there are so many
Saint Thomases and other doctors of the Church, keeping
all the time so portentous a gravity that in one line they will
describe a distracted lover and in the next deliver a Christian
homily, which is a delight and a treat to hear or read. None
of this will be found in my book, for I have nothing to quote
in the margin or to note at the end. Nor do I even know
what authors I follow in it, so as to place their names at the

beginning in alphabetical order, as they all do, commencing with Aristotle and ending with Xenophon and Zoilus or Zeuxis, although the one was a libeler and the other a painter. My book also will be wanting in sonnets at the beginning— sonnets, at least, whose authors shall be dukes, marquesses, counts, bishops, great ladies, or celebrated poets, though were I to ask two or three friends in the trade, I am certain they would give them to me, and of such excellence that they would surpass those of the more renowned poets in this Spain of ours. And so, my dear friend," I continued, "I am determined that *Don Quixote* shall remain buried in his archives of La Mancha until Heaven provides someone to adorn him with the many things he needs, for I find myself incapable of supplying them, owing to my inadequacy and shallowness of learning, and because I am by nature too slack and indolent to go in search of authors to say for me what I myself can say without them. Such is the cause of the daydreaming and perplexity in which you found me, and believe me, there is reason enough for my mood in what I have told you." [2]

No sooner did my friend hear this than he slapped his forehead with his hand and broke into a loud laugh, saying: "Heavens above, brother, I have at last been relieved of a misapprehension I have been in all the years I have known you. I had always thought you were a man of sense and judgment in your actions, but now I observe that you are as far from being so as the sky is from the earth. How comes it that things of so little importance and so easy to remedy can have the power to perplex and trouble so mature a mind as yours, and one so equipped to surmount even greater obstacles and trample them underfoot? This, I assure you, does not spring from lack of ability, but from a surfeit of laziness and a poverty of resource. Shall I convince you that what I say is true? Then listen carefully and you shall see how, in the twinkling of an eye, I can rebut all your arguments and correct all the defects that you say trouble you and drive you into giving up the publication of the history of your famous *Don Quixote,* light and mirror of all knight-errantry."

[2] These are all satirical allusions to Lope de Vega, whose *El Peregrino en su patria* had appeared in 1604.

"Tell me," I replied, "how you propose to fill the void of my fear and bring order to my confused mind."

"The first difficulty you encounter, namely, the sonnets, epigrams, and eulogies that are missing from the beginning and that should be written by weighty and titled personages, can be overcome by your taking a little trouble and writing them yourself. Afterward you may baptize them and put any name you please, fathering them on Prester John of the Indies or the Emperor of Trebizond, who, it is rumored, were famous poets. And suppose they were not, and even if some pedants and bachelors started to snap and growl at you behind your back in the name of truth, do not let that disturb you in the slightest. Even if they prove that you are a liar, they cannot cut off the hand with which you wrote them.

"Now, as to quoting in the margin the books and authors from whom you collected the sentences and sayings you have included in your history, all you have to do is to drag in some trite phrases and tags of Latin that you know by heart, or at least that cost you little trouble to look up—for instance, when dealing with liberty and captivity, to introduce

Non bene pro toto libertas venditur auro[8]

and in the margin cite Horace or whoever said it. If you should deal with the power of death, come in with

Pallida mors aequo pulsat pede pauperum tabernas regumque turres.[4]

If you are writing of friendship and the love that God commands you to have for your enemy, come to the point at once with Holy Scripture, which you can readily do with a tiny bit of research by repeating no less than the Word of God Himself: *Ego autem dico vobis: diligite inimicos vestros.*[5] If you are dealing with the subject of evil thoughts, turn to the Gospel: *De corde exeunt cogitationes malae.*[6] If

[8] "Liberty is not well sold for all the gold in the world." Aesop's *Fables* III, 14.

[4] "Pale Death stalks with equal tread through the cabins of the poor and the palaces of kings." Horace, *Odes* I.IV 13–14.

[5] "But I say to you, love your enemies." Matthew V, 44 and Luke VI, 27,35.

[6] "Evil thoughts spring forth from th~ ~eart." Matthew XV, 19.

on the fickleness of friends, you have Cato, who will supply you with his distich:

> *Donec eris felix, multos numerabis amicos;*
> *Tempora si fuerint nubila, solus eris.*[7]

With these meager scraps of Latin and the like, you may perhaps be taken for a scholar, which is honorable and profitable these days.

"Now, as to notes at the end of the book, you may safely proceed in the following manner: If you mention a giant in your book, see that it is the giant Goliath. In this way, at the cost of next to nothing, you will have an impressive note, for you can write: 'The giant Golias, or Goliath, was a Philistine whom the shepherd David slew with a stone from a sling in the valley of Terebinth,' as is told in the book of Kings in the chapter where you find it written. After this, to prove that you are well versed in the humanities and in cosmography, do manage to work in the mention of the river Tagus, and you will find yourself supplied with another famous note: 'The river Tagus was so called by a king of Spain; it has its source in such and such a spot and dies in the ocean, kissing the walls of the celebrated city of Lisbon; it is reported to have sands of gold,' etc. If you should write about thieves, there is the story of Cacus, which I know by heart; if of whores, there is the bishop of Mondoñedo,[8] who will aid you with Lamia, Lais, and Flora (and that note will give you credit); if of cruel men, Ovid will present you Medea; if of enchantresses and witches, Homer has Calypso, and Virgil, Circe; if of gallant commanders, Julius Caesar will lend you himself in his *Commentaries* and Plutarch will give

[7] "So long as you are wealthy, you will have many friends, but if the skies be overcast, you will be alone." Ovid, *Tristia* I, IX, 5–6.

[8] This refers to one of Antonio de Guevara's *Epístolas Familiares*, which speaks of Lamia, Lais, and Flora. The praise given by Cervantes is ironical. Antonio de Guevara (1480–1545), a celebrated preacher and author, was historiographer to Charles V, and bishop of Guadix and later of Mondoñedo. The *Familiar Epistles* were translated by Edward Hellowes in 1574. His *Libro Auero de Marco Aurelio* (*Golden Boke*, tr. by Lord Berners, 1535) and *Reloj de Príncipes* (*The Diall of Princes*, tr. Thomas North) were celebrated in England.

you a thousand Alexanders. If loves are your theme and you possess a mere two ounces of Italian, you will run across Leon the Hebrew,[9] who will supply you to your heart's content; and if you are not inclined to travel in foreign lands, you have at home Fonseca's *On the Love of God*,[10] which contains all that you or the greatest wits could desire on the subject. Finally all you have to do is to quote these names or refer to the stories I have mentioned in your own, and leave me the task of putting in the notes and quotations, and I swear I'll fill your margins and fill up four sheets at the end of the book.

"Let us now turn to references to authors, which the other books have and yours lacks. Here the remedy is simple: All you have to do is to search for a book that quotes them all, from A to Z, as you say. Then you put this same alphabet into yours. And even though your trick is transparent, owing to the very small need you have to use them, this is of no consequence; and who knows, perhaps there may be someone foolish enough to believe that you have made use of them all in your plain unvarnished tale. And if it serves no other purpose, at least that long catalog of authors will help to give authority to your book at the outset. Besides, no one will take the trouble to ascertain whether you follow your authorities or not, as he has nothing to gain by it. Moreover, if I understand you correctly, this book of yours does not need any of those things you say it lacks, seeing that it is one long invective against the books of chivalry, which Aristotle never dreamed of, Saint Basil never mentioned, and Cicero never dealt with. Nor do the niceties of truth or the calculations of astrology fall within the scope of its fabulous extravagances; nor are the dimensions of geometry concerned with it; nor does it deal with arguments that can be confuted by rhetoric; nor does the book try to preach to anyone by mingling the human with the divine, which is a

[9] Leon the Hebrew (León Hebreo, 1470–1521). His real name was Judas Abravenel, son of Isaac Abravenel, the doctor, counselor of Alfonso V of Portugal and later of Ferdinand the Catholic. After the expulsion of the Jews he took refuge in the court of Ferdinand of Aragon at Naples. His great work *Dialoghi d'Amore* appeared in Rome, 1535. It influenced Cervantes.

[10] Cristóbal de Fonseca (1550–1621). His *Tratado del Amor de Dios* (Salamanca, 1592) was praised by Lope de Vega and Vicente Espinel.

kind of motley in which no Christian understanding should be clothed. All you claim to do is to make best use of imitation in your writing, and the more perfect this is, the better will be what is written. And since this book of yours aims at nothing more than to destroy the authority and influence that books of chivalry have in the world and among the masses, you have no business to go begging for sentences from philosophers, maxims from Holy Writ, fables from poets, speeches from orators, or miracles from saints, but simply to see to it that your sentences are couched in plain, expressive, and well-ordered words, your periods harmonious and lively, setting forth to the best of your ability your intention and explaining your ideas without being intricate or obscure. See to it also that in reading your story, the melancholy man will be stirred to laughter, the merry be encouraged to laugh still louder, the simpleton be not worried, the wise admire your invention, the serious not despise it, nor the judicious reserve their praise. In short, let your aim be steadily concentrated on overthrowing the ill-based fabric of these books of chivalry, abhorred by so many yet praised by many more; and if you achieve this, you will have achieved no little."

I listened in complete silence to what my friend said, and his arguments so impressed me that without question I accepted them, and out of them I chose to make my prologue. And so, gentle reader, you will appreciate the wisdom of my friend and my own good fortune in finding such a counselor at such a time of need, and you will be relieved yourself when you discover how simple and guileless is the nature of the story of the famous Don Quixote of La Mancha, who in the opinion of all the inhabitants of that region of the Plain of Montiel was the chastest lover and the most valiant knight that had been seen in those parts for many a year. I would not exaggerate the service I am doing you by introducing to you so notable and honored a knight, but I would ask you to thank me for making you acquainted with the famous Sancho Panza, his squire, in whom I think I see epitomized all those squirely drolleries that are scattered through the swarm of vain books of chivalry. And so, God grant you health and forget me not. Vale.

Prefatory Verses

URGANDA THE UNKNOWN TO THE BOOK OF
DON QUIXOTE OF LA MANCHA[1]

O book, if this were but your pur-pose,
To reach the wise and virtu-ous,
He won't say, the babbling boo-by,
That your fingers are awry:
But if your loaf is not a-cook-ing,
To cram the maws of all the ass-es,
Look how their fingers they are suck-ing
To show that they are in the know-ing
And ready to gobble the fare you've giv-en.
And as experience demon-strates
That he who may be squatting un-der
A goodly tree finds shade in plen-ty,
You have a lucky star in Bé-jar,
Who brings a royal tree in offer-ing,
With princes as its fruit fes-tooned,
On which a noble duke flourish-es
Who is an Alexander redivi-vus,
And comes to bask within its shad-ow,
For Fortune ever backs the val-iant
And now's the time to tell thè sto-ry
Of the Manchegan cava-lier

[1] These truncated verses (*de cabo roto*) were introduced by
Alonso Alvarez de Soria, the arch-picaroon and ruffian poet who
was executed in 1603. Cervantes met him during his stay in
Seville. The device, which was popularized by Cervantes, consists
in cutting off the last syllable or syllables of every line. Urganda
the enchantress comes from *Amadis of Gaul*.

Whose head by idle read-ing
Was all turned topsy-tur-vy.
Knights, and arms, and lovely la-dies
Drove him into such a dith-er
That he'd vie with mad Orlan-do,
And with doughty arm he'd cap-ture
Toboso's peerless Dulcine-a.
Don't now stamp on your escutch-eon,
I beg you, foolish hieroglyph-ics,
For when every honor is on dis-play,
You'll be marked down and lose the con-test.[2]
But if you're humble in your call-ing,
None will shout in mock-ery:
"Here is the great Don Alvaro de Lu-na!" [3]
"Here is noble Hannibal of Car-thage!" [4]
"Here's King Francis straight from Par-is,[5]
Complaining of his bitter for-tune!"
Since Heaven clearly is not will-ing
To let you shine as word tast-er,
And rival Juan Latino the Nig-ger.[6]
See that you now forswear your Lat-in,
Don't rack your brains for witty sal-lies
And prate no more of philoso-phy,
Lest some pert jackanapes say, gib-ing
Though he ne'er understands a let-ter:
"Why should I be given flow-ers?"
Don't meddle like a busybod-y,
Nor pry into the lives of oth-ers,
Wiser to pass without stop-ping,
Avoiding what's not your con-cern

[2] This is a jibe at Lope de Vega y Carpio, who in the title page of his *Arcadia* (1599) had engraved his coat of arms (nineteen towers) with a motto linking his name with that of the medieval national hero Bernardo del Carpio. Góngora also satirized Lope's pretensions to noble ancestry in a celebrated sonnet.

[3] Alvaro de Luna (1390–1453), favorite of King Juan II, beheaded at Valladolid in 1453.

[4] Hannibal, the Carthaginian general, committed suicide to avoid being handed over to the Romans.

[5] Francis I, King of France, after defeat in the battle of Pavia (1525), was imprisoned in Madrid by Charles V.

[6] An Ethiopian slave of the Duke of Sessa (father of Lope's Maecenas) whose proficiency in Latin earned him that surname. He was Professor of Latin in the University of Granada in 1573.

For he who triggers jokes at ran-dom,
May find them about his ears ere eve-ning;
Better burn the oil at mid-night,
And pave the way to win re-nown;
For he who prints a foolish screed,
Is branded for all eterni-ty
Be warned that it is the height of fol-ly
When living in a glassy man-sion,
To gather pebbles by the hand-ful,
And pepper your nearest neigh-bor.
A wise man should be ever cau-tious
When writing books to let his hu-mor
And his wit run leaden-foot-ed;
For if he writes for silly maid-ens,
He writes for nincompoops and nin-nies.

AMADIS OF GAUL TO DON QUIXOTE OF LA MANCHA

Sonnet

You who my sorrows once did imitate,
When I was scorned and hied me all forlorn,
To Peña Pobre's beetling crags to mourn,
My joy transformed to penance by my fate;
You who of old your pitiless thirst did sate
With saltish tears that flowed from both your eyes;
You who all tins and platters did despise,
And on earth what the earth gave you ate,
Live on secure that for eternity,
At least as long as o'er this earthly sphere
Fair-haired Apollo goads his steeds of day,
Your name for valor shall exalted be,
Your fatherland above all lands appear,
Your learned author, unique, men will say.

DON BELIANIS OF GREECE TO DON QUIXOTE OF LA MANCHA

Sonnet

I smashed, I slashed, I dinged, I did and said
More than did ever mortal errant knight;

Adroit I was, brave, too, and proud in fight,
A thousand wrongs avenged and crusades led;
I'm famed among the living and the dead.
I was as a lover courteous and polite,
All giants I met were dwarfs in my sight;
Each rule in personal combat I kept.
Dame Fortune prostrate at my feet I left;
And by the forelock Opportunity
I willy-nilly forced to do my will.
But though my luck forever soaring swept
Above the crescent moon, your chivalry
And prowess, great Quixote, I envy still.

THE LADY ORIANA[7] TO DULCINEA OF EL TOBOSO

Sonnet

Fair Dulcinea, if I only could
For my own comfort and tranquillity
At thy Toboso Miraflores [8] see,
And London brought to where thy village stood;

Could I my body and my soul adorn
With richest robes and aspirations high,
And see thy gaunt and famous knight draw nigh
With fiery mien rash exploits to perform.

Would that I could so chastely give the slip
To my lord Amadis as thou hast whilom done
With thy love Don Quixote good and true;
With none to envy I would envied be,
And happy too, though always I did moan
And tasted joys without the payment due.

[7] Oriana in *Amadis of Gaul* was visited so frequently by her lover at her castle that her fair reputation suffered. Hence her lamentations in the sonnet.

[8] Miraflores was two leagues from London. Oriana, beloved of Amadis, lived there.

GANDALIN, SQUIRE OF AMADIS OF GAUL, TO SANCHO PANZA, SQUIRE OF DON QUIXOTE

Sonnet

Renowned wight, all hail, when Chance did place
You in the trade of squire, so wise you were,
And yet so cunning, and so debonair,
That you came through your test without disgrace.
No more will spade or reaping hook defy
Knight-errant's emprise, for 'tis now the fashion
For squirish quirks to curb the passion
Of those moon tilters who would assault the sky.
I envy you your Dapple and your name,
And the saddlebags you carry when you ride,
Which are the proof of your wise providence.
Once more, good Sancho, let me hail your fame;
To honor you our Spanish Ovid [9] tried,
Bussing your crown to do you reverence.

FROM DONOSO, A BETWIXT AND BETWEEN POET, TO SANCHO PANZA AND ROZINANTE

To Sancho Panza

Here am I, Squire Sancho Pan-za
Of the Manchegan Knight Quixo-te
I took French leave and hit the high-road,
Thinking it wise to seek my for-tune:
Mum's the word, says Villadie-go,[10]

[9] According to Pellicer, Cervantes calls himself the Spanish Ovid because of the many metamorphoses he introduces into *Don Quixote,* such as the transformation of a gentleman into a knight-errant, a peasant wench into a princess, and a clodhopper into a governor.

[10] Villadiego, a small town near Burgos, gave rise to the proverb *tomar las de Villadiego* (to take the breeches of Villadiego), which originated in the Middle Ages. King Ferdinand III (The Saint), who captured Seville in 1248, issued edicts to protect the Jews. He gave them the town of Villadiego as a place of retreat, but insisted that they should wear breeches of special color as a uniform to distinguish them from the Christians. Ever since, the phrase has been used for running away.

Best policy is strict seclu-sion
As was noted by Celesti-na,[11]
No book I reckon more di-vine,
Were it less nude and unashamed.

To Rozinante

I am the famous Rozinan-te,
Great grandson of famed Babie-ca; [12]
Because I was all skin and bone
They gave me to old Don Quixo-te
I raced my quota like a slug-gard,
Yet by a hoof's breadth never missed my oats,
This trick I owe to Lazari-llo,[13]
When his blind master's wine he stole,
That straw hoax I praised to the skies.

ORLANDO FURIOSO TO DON QUIXOTE OF LA MANCHA

If you were not a peer, you had no peer,
And midst ten thousand peers you might be one!
And where you were, there surely were no peers.
You, victor unvanquished and never vanquished,
Orlando am I, in arms your rival, Quixote,
Betrayed by false Angelica, I roved
O'er distant seas and offered at Fame's shrine
The trophies that Oblivion had spared.
I cannot be your peer, for such a guerdon
To your powers alone is owed, and to your fame,
Even though, like me, your wits too have strayed;
But you may yet become a peer of mine,
If you can humble the high-spirited Moors
And Scythians who challenge us today;
Besides, we're peers in love, in love disconsolate.

[11] A reference to the celebrated work, *La Celestina,* also called *Tragicomedia de Calixto y Melibea* (1499), which marks an epoch in the history of the drama and novel. It was translated by James Mabbe as *The Spanish Bawd* (1530).

[12] The war-horse of the Cid Rodrigo de Bivar.

[13] The first and greatest picaresque novel by an anonymous author (1554). The word *lazarillo* ever since given to the boy who guides a blind man.

THE KNIGHT OF THE SUN TO DON QUIXOTE OF LA MANCHA

My sword with yours, Don Quixote, could not vie,
Rarest of courtiers, you Phoebus of Spain!
Nor my arm with yours, though its aim
Crashed like thunder when days are born and die;
Empires I scorned, and the proud monarchy
Which crimson Orient offered I forswore,
The queenly face of Claridiana fair—
The peerless Aurora of my heart to see,
And absent in her cause the maw of hell
Did tremble at my arm, which tamed its rage.
But you, illustrious Quixote, your great name
Your Dulcinea, through the world will tell,
As you have made her a paragon of this age.

DON SOLISDAN TO DON QUIXOTE OF LA MANCHA

Sonnet

Although by fools bamboozled you have been,
And nonsense has played havoc with your brain,
No one, Sir Quixote, ever dares maintain,
That your actions were ever vile or mean.
Your noble deeds bear witness to your worth,
For your trade was to set the wronged a-right,
Well-drubbèd victim, mournful was your plight
At the hands of rogues and varlets, scum of earth!
If Dulcinea, your fair paramour,
Your fondest hopes of plighted love defrauds,
And no kind thought to your sad suit uncovers,
Let me then bring you comfort in this hour,
Saying that Sancho Panza of all bawds
Is sorriest, she cruel, you worst of lovers.

Dialogue Between Babieca and Rozinante

B. What is amiss, Rozinante, why so lean?
R. Because I toil and moil and never eat.

B. Is there for you no straw nor barley then?
R. Not a mouthful of either from my lord I get.
B. Come sir, you are an uncouth knave, who dare
    To insult your master with your ass's tongue.
R. 'Tis he was ass from cradle to his shroud.
    Do you know why? Watch when he is in love.
B. Is love so foolish?
R.   Of course; it is not wise.
B. You're philosophical.
R.   Because I'm hungry.
B. You blame the squire?
R.   Too scanty that complaint.
    Why shouldn't I blame the author of my woes?
    Why both the squire and lord or seneschal
    Are just as arrant hacks as Rozinante.

CHAPTER I

*Which tells of the quality and manner of life of the
famous gentleman Don Quixote of La Mancha*

At a village of La Mancha, whose name I do not wish to
remember,[1] there lived a little while ago one of those
gentlemen who are wont to keep a lance in the rack, an old
buckler, a lean horse, and a swift greyhound. His stew had
more beef than mutton in it and most nights he ate a hodgepodge, pickled and cold. Lentil soup on Fridays, "tripe and

---

[1] Cervantes was purposely vague in describing the birthplace
of Don Quixote. *En un lugar de La Mancha* is the beginning of
the ballad, "El Amante Apaleado," which was familiar to our
author.

trouble" on Saturdays,[2] and an occasional pigeon as an extra delicacy on Sundays consumed three quarters of his income. The remainder was spent on a jerkin of fine puce, velvet breeches, and slippers of the same stuff for holidays, and a suit of good, honest homespun for weekdays. His family consisted of a housekeeper about forty, a niece not yet twenty, and a lad who served him both in the field and at home and could saddle the horse or use the pruning knife. Our gentleman was about fifty years of age, of a sturdy constitution, but wizened and gaunt-featured, an early riser and a devotee of the chase. They say that his surname was Quixada or Quesada (for on this point the authors who have written on this subject differ), but we may reasonably conjecture that his name was Quixana. This, however, has very little to do with our story; enough that in its telling we swerve not a jot from the truth. You must know that the above-mentioned gentleman in his leisure moments (which was most of the year) gave himself up with so much delight and gusto to reading books of chivalry that he almost entirely neglected the exercise of the chase and even the management of his domestic affairs. Indeed his craze for this kind of literature became so extravagant that he sold many acres of arable land to purchase books of knight-errantry, and he carried off to his house as many as he could possibly find. Above all, he preferred those written by the famous Feliciano de Silva [3] because of the clarity of his writing and his intricate style, which made him value those books more than pearls, especially when he read of those courtships and letters of challenge that knights sent to ladies, often containing expressions such as: "The reason for your unreasonable treatment of my

---

[2] Semiabstinence fare because Saturday was kept as a fast day in memory of the defeat of the Moors in 1212 in the battle of Navas de Tolosa. Others say the phrase *duelos y quebrantos* means "rashers and eggs"—potluck fare in La Mancha, for bacon and eggs were the staple diet of La Mancha in those days. Sancho in Avellaneda's continuation of *Don Quixote* calls an omelet of eggs and rashers "the Grace of God" (*gracia de Dios*). According to the ancient commentator Covarrubias, in La Mancha eggs and rashers fried in honey were called *merced de Dios*. The reason why bacon and eggs received such flattering epithets was because they were the cheapest and easiest food to prepare. Nowadays rashers and fried eggs are called *chocolate de La Mancha*.

[3] Feliciano de Silva, author of the Chronicle of *Don Florisel de Niquea* (1532) and *Amadis of Greece* (1535).

reason so enfeebles my reason that I have reason to complain of your beauty." And again: "The high heavens, which with your divinity divinely fortify you with stars, make you the deserver of the desert that is deserved by your greatness." These and similar rhapsodies bewildered the poor gentleman's understanding, for he racked his brain day and night to unbowel their meaning, which not even Aristotle himself could have done if he had been raised from the dead for that very purpose. He was not quite convinced of the number of wounds that Don Belianís gave and received in battle, for he considered that however skillful the surgeons that cured him may have been, the worthy knight's face and body must have been bedizened with scars and scabs. Nevertheless he praised the author for concluding his book with the promise of endless adventure, and many times he felt inclined to take up his pen and finish it off himself, as it is there promised. He doubtless would have done so, and successfully too, had he not been diverted by other plans and purposes of greater moment. He often debated with the curate of the village—a man of learning, a graduate of Sigüenza—on the relative merits of Palmerin of England and Amadis of Gaul. But Master Nicholas, the village barber, affirmed that no one could be compared with the Knight of the Sun and that if, indeed, any could be matched with him, it was Don Galaor, the brother of Amadis of Gaul, for he had a nature adapted to every whim of fortune; he was not so namby-pamby and whimpering a knight as his brother, and as for valor, he was in every respect his equal.

In short, he so immersed himself in those romances that he spent whole days and nights over his books; and thus with little sleeping and much reading, his brains dried up to such a degree that he lost the use of his reason. His imagination became filled with a host of fancies he had read in his books—enchantments, quarrels, battles, challenges, wounds, courtships, loves, tortures, and many other absurdities. So true did all this phantasmagoria from books appear to him that in his mind he accounted no history in the world more authentic. He would say that the Cid Ruiz Díaz was a very gallant knight, but not to be compared with the Knight of the Burning Sword, who with a single thwart blow cleft asunder a brace of hulking, blustering giants. He was better pleased with Bernardo del Carpio, because at Roncesvalles he had slain Roland the Enchanted by availing himself of the stratagem Hercules had employed on Antaeus, the son of the Earth, whom he squeezed to death in his arms. He praised the giant Morgante, for he alone was courteous and well bred among that monstrous brood puffed up with arrogance and insolence. Above all, he admired Rinaldo of Montalbán,[4] especially when he saw him sallying out of his castle to plunder everyone who came his way, and when beyond the seas he made off with the idol of Mohammed which, as history says, was of solid gold. But he would have parted with his housekeeper and his niece into the bargain for the pleasure of rib roasting the traitor Galalón.[5]

At last, having lost his wits completely, he stumbled upon the oddest fancy that ever entered a madman's brain. He believed that it was necessary, both for his own honor and for service of the state, that he should become a knight-errant, roaming through the world with his horse and armor in quest of adventures and practicing all that had been performed by the knights-errant of whom he had read. He would follow their life, redressing all manner of wrongs and exposing himself to continual dangers, and at last, after concluding his enterprises, he would win everlasting honor and renown. The poor gentleman fancied himself already crowned emperor of Trebizond for the valor of his arm. And thus excited by these agreeable delusions, he hastened to put his plans into operation.

The first thing he did was to refurbish some rusty armor that had belonged to his great grandfather and had lain moldering in a corner. He cleaned it and repaired it as best he could, but he found one great defect: instead of a complete helmet there was just the simple morion. This want he ingeniously remedied by making a kind of visor out of pasteboard, and when it was fitted to the morion, it looked like an entire helmet. It is true that in order to test its strength and see if it was swordproof, he drew his sword and gave it two strokes, the first of which instantly destroyed the result of a week's labor. It troubled him to see with what ease he had broken the helmet in pieces, so to protect it from such an accident, he remade it and fenced the inside with a few bars of iron in such a manner that he felt assured of

---

[4] Rinaldo of Montalbán, one of the most famous of Charlemagne's paladins, is one of the chief characters in Boiardo's *Orlando Innamorato*.

[5] Galalón, or Ganelon of Mayence, a brave soldier of Charlemagne who turned traitor and betrayed Roland at Roncesvalles.

its strength, and without caring to make a second trial, he held it to be a most excellent helmet. Then he went to see his steed, and although it had more cracks in its hoof than there are quarters in a Spanish real and more faults than Gonella's jade, which was all skin and bone,[6] he thought that neither the Bucephalus of Alexander nor the Cid's Babieca could be compared with it. He spent four days deliberating over what name he would give the horse, for (as he said to himself) it was not right that the horse of so famous a knight should remain without a name. So he endeavored to find one that would express what the animal had been before he had been the mount of a knight-errant, and what he now was. It was indeed reasonable that when the master changed his state, the horse should change his name too and assume one pompous and high-sounding, as suited the new order he was about to profess. So after having devised, erased, and blotted out many other names, he finally decided to call the horse Rozinante—a name, in his opinion, lofty, sonorous, and significant, for it explained that he had been only an ordinary hack before he had been raised to his present status of first of all the hacks in the world.

Now that he had given his horse a name so much to his satisfaction, he resolved to choose one for himself, and after seriously considering the matter for eight whole days, he finally determined to call himself Don Quixote. For that reason the authors who have related this most true story have deduced that his name must undoubtedly have been Quixada and not Quesada, as others would have it. Then, remembering that the valiant Amadis had not been content to call himself simply Amadis, but added thereto the name of his kingdom and native country to render it more illustrious, calling himself Amadis of Gaul, so he, like a good knight, also added the name of his province and called himself Don Quixote of La Mancha. In this way he openly proclaimed his lineage and country, and at the same time he honored it by taking its name.

Now that his armor was scoured, his morion made into a helmet, his horse and himself newly named, he felt that

---

[6] Pedro Gonella, according to Clemencín, was the clown of the Duke of Ferrara in the fifteenth century; his horse, all skin and bone, was the theme of many jokes uttered by his minstrel-master.

nothing was wanting but a lady of whom to be enamored, for a knight-errant who was loveless was a tree without leaves and fruit, a body without soul. "If," said he, "for my sins or through my good fortune I encounter some giant—a usual occurrence to knights-errant—and bowling him over at the first onset or cleaving him in twain, I finally vanquish and force him to surrender, would not it be better to have some lady to whom I may send him as a trophy? Then, when he comes into her presence, he may kneel before her and humbly say: 'Madam, I am the giant Caraculiambro, Lord of the Island of Malindrania, whom the never-adequately-praised Don Quixote of La Mancha has overcome in single combat. He has commanded me to present myself before you so that your highness may dispose of me as you wish.' " How glad was our knight when he had made these discourses to himself, but chiefly when he had found one whom he might call his lady! It happened that in a neighboring village there lived a good-looking country lass with whom he had been in love, although it is understood that she never knew or was aware of it. She was called Aldonza Lorenzo, and it was to her that he thought fit to entrust the sovereignty of his heart. He sought a name for her that would not vary too much from her own and yet would approach that of a princess or a lady of quality. At last he resolved to call her Dulcinea of El Toboso (she was a native of that town), a name in his opinion musical, uncommon, and expressive, like the others he had devised.

CHAPTER II

Which deals with our imaginative hero's first sally from his home

Once these preparations were made he was anxious to put his designs into operation without delay, for he was spurred on by the conviction that the world needed his immediate presence; so many were the grievances he intended to rectify, the wrongs he resolved to set right, the harms he meant to redress, the abuses he would reform, and the debts he would discharge. And so, without acquainting a living soul with his intentions, and wholly unobserved, one morning before daybreak (it was one of the hottest in the month of July), he armed himself cap-a-pie, mounted Rozinante, placed his ill-constructed helmet on his head, braced on his buckler, grasped his lance, and through the door of his back yard sallied forth into the open country, mightily pleased to note the ease with which he had begun his worthy enterprise. But scarcely had he issued forth when he was suddenly struck by so terrible a thought that he almost gave up his whole undertaking, for he just then remembered that he had not yet been dubbed a knight, and therefore, in accordance with the laws of chivalry, he neither could nor ought to enter the lists against any knight. Moreover, even if he had been dubbed, he should, as a novice, have worn white armor without any device on his shield until he had won it by force of arms. These thoughts made him stagger in his purpose; but as his madness prevailed over every reason, he determined to have himself knighted by the first person he should meet, like many others of whom he had read in the books that distracted him. As to white armor, he intended at the first opportunity to scour his own so that it would be whiter than ermine. In this way he calmed himself and continued his journey, letting his horse choose the way, believing that in this consisted the true spirit of adventure.

As our brand-new adventurer proceeded, he kept conversing with himself in this manner: "Who doubts but that in future ages, when the true story of my famous deeds is brought to light, the wise man who writes it will describe my first sally in the morning as follows: 'Scarcely had the rubicund Apollo spread over the face of the vast and spacious earth the golden tresses of his beautiful hair, and scarcely had the little painted birds with their tuneful tongues saluted in sweet and melodious harmony the coming of rosy Aurora, who, leaving the soft couch of her jealous husband, revealed herself to mortals through the gates and balconies of the Manchegan horizon, when the famous knight Don Quixote of La Mancha, quitting his downy bed of ease, mounted his renowned steed, Rozinante, and began to ride over the ancient and memorable plain of Montiel.' " [1] (And indeed he was doing so.) Continuing his discourse, he added: "O happy era, O happy age, wherein my famous deeds shall be revealed to the world, deeds worthy to be engraved in bronze, sculptured in marble, and painted in pictures for future record! O thou wise enchanter, whosoever, thou mayest be, whose duty it will be to chronicle this strange history, do not, I beseech thee, forget my good horse, Rozinante, the everlasting companion of my wanderings." Then, as if really enamored, he cried: "O Dulcinea, my princess! Sovereign of this captive heart! Grievous wrong hast thou done me by dismissing me and by cruelly forbidding me by decree to appear in thy beauteous presence. I pray thee, sweet lady, to remember this poor, enslaved heart, which for love of thee suffers so many pangs."

To such words he added a sequence of other foolish notions all in the manner of those that his books had taught him, imitating their language as nearly as he could. And all the while he rode slowly on while the sun rose with such intense heat that it would have been enough to dissolve his brains, if he had had any left. He traveled almost the whole of that day without meeting any adventure worthy of note, wherefore he was much troubled, for he was eager to encounter someone upon whom he could try the strength of his doughty arm. Some authors say his first adventure was that of the Pass of Lápice; others hold it was that of the windmills; but according to my investigations and according to what is written in the annals of La Mancha, he traveled all that day, and at dusk both he and his horse were tired and nearly dead with hunger. He looked around him on every side to see whether he could discover any castle or shepherd's hut where he might rest and find nourishment. He then saw, not far from the road, an inn, which was as welcome to him as a star leading him not to the portals but to the very palace itself of his redemption. So he hastened on and reached it before dark.

Now there chanced to be standing at the door two young wenches who belonged to the category of women of the town, as they say. They were on their way to Seville in the company of certain carriers who halted for the night in that

---

[1] Memorable because the scene of the battle in 1369 in which King Peter the Cruel was defeated by his bastard brother Henry of Trastamara. Henry murdered Peter and became Henry II.

inn. As all our adventurer saw, thought, or imagined seemed
to happen in accordance with what he had read in his books
of chivalry, no sooner did he see the inn than it assumed in
his eyes the semblance of a castle with four turrets, the pinnacles of which were of glittering silver, including drawbridge, deep moat, and all the appurtenances with which such
castles are depicted. And so he drew near to the inn (which
he thought was a castle), and at a short distance from it,
he halted Rozinante, expecting that some dwarf would
mount the battlements to announce by trumpet blast the arrival of a knight-errant at the castle. But when he saw that
they tarried, and as Rozinante was pawing the ground impatiently in eagerness to reach the stable, he approached
the inn door and there saw the two young doxies, who appeared to him to be two beautiful damsels or graceful
ladies enjoying the fresh air at the castle gate. It happened
also at this very moment that a swineherd, as he gathered
his hogs (I ask no pardon,[2] for so they are called) from the
stubblefield, blew a horn that assembled them, and instantly
Don Quixote imagined it was what he expected, namely,
that some dwarf was giving notice of his arrival. Therefore,
with extraordinary satisfaction he went up to the inn and the
ladies. But when they saw a man armed in that manner draw
near with lance and buckler, they started to take to their
heels, full of fear. Don Quixote, perceiving their alarm,
raised his pasteboard visor, and displaying his withered and
dusty countenance, accosted them gently and gravely: "I beseech your ladyships, do not flee, nor fear the least offense. The order of chivalry that I profess does not permit
me to do injury to anyone, and least of all to such noble
maidens as your presences denote you to be."

The wenches kept gazing earnestly, endeavoring to catch
a glimpse of his face, which its ill-fashioned visor concealed;
but when they heard themselves called maidens, a thing so
out of the way of their profession, they could not restrain
their laughter, which was so boisterous that Don Quixote
exclaimed in anger: "Remember that modesty is becoming
in beautiful ladies, whereas laughter without cause denotes
much folly. However," added he, "I do not say this to offend

[2] Even today the peasantry beg one's pardon when mentioning
swine. Proximity to the Moslems, who, like the Jews, abhor pork,
originated this superstition. Cervantes here ridicules the superstition.

you or to incur your displeasure, for my one desire is to do you honor and service." The strange language of the knight was not understood by the ladies, and this, added to his uncouth appearance, increased their laughter and his annoyance, and he would have proceeded further but for the timely appearance of the innkeeper, a man who by reason of his extreme corpulence was of very peaceable disposition. As soon as he saw that uncomely figure all armed, in accouterments so ill-sorted as were the bridle, lance, buckler, and corselet, he felt inclined to join the damsels in their mirth. But out of fear of such a medley of warlike gear, he resolved to be civil, and so he said: "Sir knight, if you are seeking a lodging, you will find all in abundance here, with the exception of a bed, for there are none in this inn." Don Quixote, observing the humility of the governor of the fortress (for such the landlord and the inn appeared to him), answered: "Anything, sir castellan, suffices me:

> My ornaments are arms,
> My pastime is in war."

The host thought he called him a castellan because he took him to be one of the Simple-Simon Castilians,[3] whereas he was an Andalusian, one of those from the Sanlúcar shore, no less a thief than Cacus and not less mischievous than a truant scholar or court page. And so he made the following reply: "If so, your worship's beds must be hard rocks and your sleep an everlasting watching;[4] wherefore you may boldly dismount and I can assure you that you can hardly miss being kept awake all year long in this house, much less one single night." Saying this, he went and held Don Quixote's stirrup, who forthwith dismounted, though with much difficulty, for he had not broken his fast all that day. He then told the host to take great care of his horse, saying that he was one of the finest pieces of horseflesh that ever ate bread. The innkeeper looked him over but thought him not so good by half as his master had said. After stabling him, he

---

[3] A play upon words here. *Castellano* means a castellan and a native of Castile. Also the term *sanos de Castilla* in thieves' jargon meant frank, gullible natives of Old Castile.

[4] The innkeeper caps verses with our knight by continuing the ballad.

returned to receive his guest's orders and found the damsels
(who had now become reconciled to him) disarming him, but
though they were able to take off the back- and breast-plates,
they did not know how to undo his gorget or remove his
counterfeit helmet, which he had tied on with green ribbons
in such a way that they could not be untied. It was necessary
to cut them because the knots were so intricate, but he
would not allow this to be done, and so remained all that
night with his helmet on, and was the strangest and pleasant-
est sight imaginable.

And while he was being disarmed by those lights-o'-love
whom he imagined to be ladies of quality of that castle, he
said to them with great charm:

> "There never was on earth a knight
> So waited on by ladies fair
> As once was he, Don Quixote hight,
> When first he left his village dear:
> Damsels to serve him ran with speed
> And princesses to dress his steed.[5]

"Rozinante, ladies, is the name of my horse, and Don
Quixote of La Mancha my own. I never intended to discover myself until deeds performed in your service should
have proclaimed me, but the need of adapting to my present
purpose the old ballad of Sir Lancelot has made my right
name known to you prematurely. But the day will come
when your ladyships shall command and I obey, and the
valor of my arm make plain my desire to serve you."

The girls, unaccustomed to such flourishes of rhetoric,
made no reply but asked whether he would eat anything.
"Fain would I break my fast," answered Don Quixote, "for
I think that a little food would be of great service to me."
That day happened to be a Friday and there was nothing
in the inn but some pieces of fish, called in Castile pollack,
in Andalusia codfish, in some parts ling, and in others
troutlets, or Poor Jack. They asked him if he would eat
some troutlets, for they had no other fish to offer him. "Provided there are many little trout," answered Don Quixote,
"they will supply the place of one salmon trout, for it is the

[5] These are the opening lines of the ancient ballad from the
Romancero on the romantic story of Lancelot of the Lake, which
Don Quixote adapts to his own case.

same to me whether I receive eight single reals or one piece of eight. Moreover, those troutlets may turn out to be like unto veal, which is better than beef, and kid, which is superior to goat. Be that as it may, let it come in quickly, for the toil and weight of arms cannot be sustained without the good government of the guts." As the air was cool, they placed the table at the door of the inn, and the landlord brought a portion of ill-soaked and worse-cooked codfish and a piece of bread as black and moldy as the knight's arms. It was a laughable sight to see him eat, for as he had his helmet and his visor up, he could not feed himself, and so one of the ladies performed that service for him. But it would have been impossible for him to drink had not the innkeeper bored a cane, and placing one end in his mouth, poured in the wine at the other end. All this he endured patiently rather than cut the ribbons of his helmet.

While he was at his meal, a hog-gelder happened to sound his reed flageolet four or five times as he came near the inn. This was a still more convincing proof to Don Quixote that he was in a famous castle where they were entertaining him with music, that the codfish was salmon trout, the bread of the purest white, the whores ladies, and the innkeeper the governor of the fortress. All this made him applaud his own resolution and his enterprising sally. There was only one thing that vexed him: he regretted that he was not dubbed a knight, for he thought that he could not lawfully undertake any adventure until he had received the order of knighthood.

CHAPTER III

Which relates the pleasant method by which Don Quixote had himself dubbed knight

As he was tormented by that thought, he made short work of his meager, pothouse supper. Then he called for his host, shut himself up with him in the stable, and fell upon his knees, saying: "I will never rise from this place, valorous knight, until your courtesy grants me the boon I seek, one that will redound to your glory and to the advantage of the human race." The innkeeper, seeing his guest at his feet and hearing such words, stared at him in bewilderment, without knowing what to do or say. He tried to make him get up, but in vain, for the latter would not consent to do so until the boon he demanded was granted. "I expected no less from your magnificence," answered Don Quixote, "and so I say unto you that the boon I have demanded and that you, out of your liberality, have granted unto me is that tomorrow morning you will dub me knight. This night I shall watch over my arms in the chapel of your castle,[1] and tomorrow, as I have said, you will fulfill my earnest desires so that I may sally forth through the four parts of the world in quest of adventures on behalf of the distressed, as is the duty of knighthood and knights-errant who, like myself, are devoted to such achievements."

[1] In all the romances of chivalry the *vigilia* (watching over the arms) was an important part of the ceremonial. According to Rivadeneira, the contemporary biographer of Saint Ignatius Loyola, the saint watched over his arms a whole night in front of the image of Our Lady before setting out to found the Militia of Christ. In Smollett's "Sir Launcelot Greaves" there is a parody of this adventure of Don Quixote.

The host, who was, as we said before, a bit of a wag and already had some doubts about his guest's sanity, now found all his suspicions confirmed, but he resolved to humor him so that he might have sport that night. He told the knight that his wishes were very reasonable, for such pursuits were natural to knights so illustrious as he seemed and his gallant bearing showed him to be. He added that he himself in the days of his youth had devoted himself to the same honorable profession and had wandered over various parts of the world in search of adventures; and, moreover, he had not failed to visit the curing grounds of Málaga, the Isles of Riarán, the Precinct of Seville, the Quicksilver Square of Segovia, the Olive field of Valencia, the Circle of Granada, the Strand of Sanlúcar, the Colt Fountain of Córdoba, the Taverns of Toledo, and divers other haunts where he had proved the nimbleness of his feet and the light-ness of his fingers, committing wrongs in plenty, accosting many widows, deflowering sundry maidens, tricking some minors, and finally making himself known and famous to all the tribunals and courts over the length and breadth of Spain.[2] At last he had retired to this castle, where he lived on his own and on other men's revenues, entertaining therein knights-errant of every quality, solely for the great affec-tion he bore them, and that they might share their goods with him in return for his benevolence. He further told him that in his castle there was no chapel where he could watch over his arms, for he had knocked it down to build it anew. However, in case of necessity, he might watch over the arms wherever he pleased, and therefore, he might watch that night in the castle courtyard. Then, the following morn-ing, with God's help, the required ceremonies would be car-ried out in such a way that he would be dubbed a knight so effectively that nowhere in the world could one more per-fect be found. He asked if Don Quixote had brought any money. "Not a farthing," answered the knight, "for I have never read in the stories of knights-errant that they ever carried money with them."

"You are mistaken," answered the landlord, "for although the stories are silent on this matter, seeing that the authors

[2] Cervantes here gives the picaresque geography of Spain from his experience as a wanderer. We have followed Bowle, the pioneer editor of Cervantes (1780), in translating the Azoguejo of Segovia as Quicksilver Square—the celebrated rendezvous of picaroons and Gypsy pickpockets.

did not think it necessary to specify such obvious require-
ments as money and clean shirts, yet there is no reason to
believe that the knights had none. On the contrary, it
was an established fact that all knights-errant (whose deeds
fill many a volume) carried their purses well lined against
accidents, and moreover, they carried, in addition to shirts,
a small chest of ointments to heal their wounds, for in the
plains and deserts where they fought and were wounded,
there was no one to cure them unless they were lucky enough
to have some wise enchanter for friend who straightaway
would send through the air in a cloud some damsel or dwarf
with a vial of water possessed of such power that upon
tasting a single drop of it, they would instantly find their
wounds as perfectly cured as if they had never received
any. But when the knights had no such friend, they always
insisted that their squires should be provided with money
and such necessities as lint and ointments; and when they
had no squires (which was very seldom), they themselves
carried those things on the crupper of their horse in saddlebags so small that they were scarcely visible, for except in
such a case, the custom of carrying saddlebags was not allowed among knights-errant. I must, therefore, advise you,"
he continued, "nay, I might even command you, seeing that
you are shortly to become my godson in chivalry, never
from this day forward to travel without money or without
the aforesaid necessities, and you will see how serviceable
you will find them when least you expect it."

Don Quixote promised to follow his injunctions carefully,
and an order was given for him to watch over his armor in
a large yard adjoining the inn. When the knight had collected all his arms together, he laid them on a stone trough
that was close by the side of a wall. Then embracing his
buckler and grasping his lance, he began with stately air to
pace up and down in front of the trough, and as he began
his parade, night began to close in.

The landlord, meanwhile, told all who were in the inn of
the madness of his guest, the arms vigil, and the knighthood dubbing that was to come. They were astonished at
such a strange kind of madness and flocked to observe him
from a distance. They saw that sometimes he paced to and
fro and at other times he leaned on his lance and gazed fixedly at his arms for a considerable time. It was now night, but
the moon shone so clearly that she might have almost vied

with the luminary that lent her splendor, and thus every
action of our new knight could be seen by the spectators.

Just at this moment one of the carriers in the inn took
it into his head to water his team of mules, to do which would
necessitate removing Don Quixote's arms from the trough.
But the knight, as he saw him approach, cried out in a loud
voice: "O thou, whosoever thou art, rash knight that dost
prepare to lay hands upon the arms of the most valiant knight-
errant who ever girded sword, take heed and touch them not
if thou wouldst not leave thy life in guerdon for thy
temerity." The carrier paid no heed to this warning (it would
have been better for him if he had), but seizing hold of the
armor by the straps, he threw it a good way from him.
No sooner did Don Quixote perceive this than, raising his
eyes to heaven and fixing his thoughts (as it seemed) upon his
lady, Dulcinea, he said: "Assist me, O lady, in this first affront
that is offered to thy vassal's heart. Let not thy favor and
protection fail me in this first encounter." Uttering these and
similar words, he let slip his buckler, and raising the lance
in both hands, he gave the carrier such a hefty blow on the
pate that he felled him to the ground in so grievous a plight
that if he had followed it with a second, there would have
been no need of a surgeon to cure him. This done, he put
back his arms and began to pace to and fro as peacefully as
before.

Soon after, another carrier, not knowing what had happened (for the first still lay unconscious), came out with the
same intention of watering his mules and began to take away
the arms that were encumbering the trough, when Don
Quixote, not saying a word or imploring assistance from a
soul, once more dropped his buckler, lifted up his lance,
and without breaking it to pieces, opened the second muleteer's head in four places. All the people in the inn rushed out
when they heard the noise, and the landlord among them.
As soon as Don Quixote saw them, he braced on his buckler
and laid his hands upon his sword, saying: "O lady of
beauty, strength and vigor of my enfeebled heart! Now is
the time for thee to turn the eyes of thy greatness upon this
thy captive knight, who stands awaiting so great an adventure." These words, it seemed to him, filled him with
such courage that if all the muleteers in the world had
attacked him he would not have retreated one step. The
wounded men's companions, seeing them in such an evil

plight, began from afar to rain a shower of stones upon Don Quixote, who defended himself as best he could with his buckler, but he did not dare to leave the trough for fear of leaving his arms unprotected. The landlord shouted at them to let him alone, for he had told them the man was mad, and as such, he would be acquitted even if he killed every one of them. Don Quixote shouted still louder, called them caitiffs and traitors, and the lord of the castle a cowardly, baseborn knight for allowing knights-errant to be treated in such a manner. "I would make thee understand," cried he, "what a traitorous scoundrel thou art had I but been dubbed a knight. But as for you, ye vile and base rabble, I care not a fig for you; fire on, advance, draw near, and hurt me as much as you dare. Soon ye shall receive the reward for your folly and presumption." Such was the undaunted boldness with which he uttered these words that his attackers were struck with terror. And so, partly through fear and partly through the persuasive words of the landlord, they ceased to fling stones at him, and he allowed them to carry off their wounded, after which he returned to the guard of his arms with as much calm gravity as before.

The landlord did not relish the mad pranks of his guest, so he determined to make an end of them and give him his accursed order of chivalry before any further misfortune occurred. And so, going up to him, he excused himself for the insolent way those low fellows had treated him, without his knowledge or consent, adding that they had been well chastised for their rashness. He repeated what he had said before: that there was no chapel in that castle, nor was one necessary for what remained to be done; that the chief point of the knighting ceremony consisted in the accolade and the tap on the shoulders, according to the ceremonial of the order, and that might be administered in the middle of a field; that he had performed the duty of watching over his armor, for he had watched more than four hours, whereas only two were required. All this Don Quixote believed and said that he was then ready to obey him, but yet begged him to conclude with all the brevity possible, for if he should be attacked again when he was armed a knight, he was determined not to leave one person alive in the castle, except those whom, out of respect for the governor of the fortress and at his request, he would spare. The governor, being warned and alarmed at possible consequences, brought out forthwith a book in which he kept his account of the straw and barley supplied to the carriers, and with a stump of candle, which a boy held lighted in his hands, and accompanied by the two above-mentioned damsels, he went over to Don Quixote and ordered him to kneel. He then read in his manual as if he had been repeating some pious oration. In the midst of the prayer he raised his hand and gave him a good blow on the neck, and after that gave a royal thwack on the shoulders, all the time mumbling between his teeth as if praying. After this he commanded one of the ladies to gird on his sword, which she did with much discretion and aplomb, plenty of which was needed to prevent them all from bursting with laughter at every stage of the ceremonies; but the prowess they had beheld in the new knight made them restrain their laughter. As she girded on his sword, the good lady said: "God make you fortunate, knight, and give you success in your contests." Don Quixote demanded then how she was called that he might henceforward know to whom he was beholden for the favor received, for he was resolved to give her a share of the honor that his valor should merit. And she answered with great humility that she was called La Tolosa and was a cobbler's daughter from Toledo, who lived near Sancho Bienaya Square, and that she would always serve him and consider him her lord wherever she happened to be. Don Quixote replied, requesting her for his sake to call herself henceforth Lady Tolosa, which she promised to do. Then the other lady buckled on his spur and he addressed her in very nearly the same terms as the lady of the sword. He asked her name, and she said she was called La Molinera and was daughter of an honest miller of Antequera. He begged her to take a title and call herself Lady Molinera, at the same time making new offers of service.

Don Quixote could not rest until he found himself mounted on horseback and sallying forth in quest of adventures, and after saddling Rozinante, he mounted, but not before he had embraced his host and said so many extravagant words in thanking him for having dubbed him knight that it is impossible to tell them. The landlord, that he might speed the parting guest, answered him in no less rhetorical flourishes but in briefer words, and without asking him to pay for his lodging, he let him go with a godspeed.

CHAPTER IV

What happened to our knight when he sallied from the inn

It was about daybreak when Don Quixote sallied forth from the inn, so happy, so lively, and so excited at finding himself knighted that his very horse girths were ready to burst for joy. But calling to mind the advice of his host concerning the necessary accouterments for his travels, especially the money and the clean shirts, he resolved to return home to provide himself with them and with a squire. He had in view a certain laboring man of the neighborhood who was poor and had children but was otherwise very well fitted for the office of squire to a knight. With this thought in mind he turned Rozinante toward his village, and the horse, knowing full well the way to his stable, began to trot so briskly that his hoofs seemed hardly to strike the ground. The knight had not traveled far when he thought he heard the faint cries of someone in distress from a thicket on his right hand. No sooner had he heard them than he said: "I render thanks to heaven for such a favor. Already I have an opportunity of performing the duty of my profession and of reaping the harvest of my good ambition. Those cries must surely come from some distressed man or woman who needs my protection." Then turning his reins, he guided Rozinante toward the place from which he thought the cries came. A short distance within the wood he saw a mare tied to an oak and to another a youth of about fifteen years of age naked from the waist up. It was he who was crying out, and not without reason, for a lusty countryman was flogging him with a leather strap, and every blow he accompanied with a word of

74

warning and advice, saying, "Keep your mouth shut and your eyes skinned." The boy answered: "I'll never do it again, master. By God's passion, I won't do it again and I promise in future to be more careful of your flock."

When Don Quixote saw what was happening, he said in an angry voice: "Discourteous knight, it is a caitiff's deed to attack one who cannot defend himself. Get up on your horse and take your lance" (for the farmer, too, had a lance leaning against the oak tree to which the mare was tied) "I will show you that you have been acting a coward's part." The countryman, at the sight of the strange apparition in armor brandishing a lance over him, gave himself up for lost and so replied submissively: "Sir knight, this youth I am chastising is a servant of mine, whom I employ to look after a flock of sheep in the neighborhood, but he is so careless that every day he loses one, and when I punish him for his negligence or rascality, he says I do it because I am a skinflint and will not pay him his wages. Upon my life and soul, he lies."

"Have you the impudence to lie in my presence, vile serf?" said Don Quixote. "By the sun that shines on us I will pierce you through and through with this lance of mine. Pay him instantly and none of your denials. If not, by almighty God who rules us all, I will annihilate you this very moment. Untie him at once."

The countryman lowered his head and without a word untied his servant. Don Quixote then asked the boy how much his master owed him. He replied nine months' wages at seven reals a month. Don Quixote, having calculated the sum, found that it came to sixty-three reals and told the farmer to pay up the money unless he wished to die. The farmer, who was shaking with fear, then answered that on the word of one in a tight corner and also upon his oath (yet he had sworn nothing), he did not owe so much, for they must deduct three pairs of shoes that he had given the boy and a real for two bloodlettings that he had when he was sick.

"That is all very well," answered Don Quixote, "but let the shoes and the bloodletting stand for the blows that you have given him for no fault of his own; if he wore out the leather of the shoes you gave him, you wore out his skin, and if the barber drew blood from him when he was sick, you drew blood from him when he was in good health; so in this matter he owes you nothing."

"The trouble is, sir knight," said the countryman, "that I have no money on me. If Andrés comes home with me, I'll pay him ready money down."

"I go home with him?" said the boy. "Not on your life, sir! I would not think of doing such thing; the moment he gets me alone he'll flay me like a Saint Bartholomew." [1]

"He will not do so," answered Don Quixote. "I have only to command and he will respect me and do my behest. So I shall let him go free and guarantee payment to you, provided he swears by the order of knighthood that he has received."

"Take heed, sir, of what you are saying," said the boy. "My master is no knight; he has not received any order of knighthood. He is Juan Haldudo the wealthy, a native of Quintanar."

"That matters little," answered Don Quixote; "there may be Haldudos who are knights, especially as every man is the son of his own works."

"That's true," said Andrés, "but what kind of works is my master the son of? Isn't he denying me the wages of my sweat and toil?"

"I'm not denying them, brother Andrés," answered the countryman. "Do, please, come with me and I swear by all the orders of knighthood there are in the world to pay you, as I said before, every real down and even perfumed into the bargain."

"I'll spare you the perfume," said Don Quixote. "Give them to him in good, honest reals and I shall be satisfied; but see to it that you carry out your oath. If not, I swear by the same oath to return and chastise you, and I am sure to find you, even if you hide away from me more successfully than a lizard. And if you want to know who it is who gives you this command, learn that I am the valiant Don Quixote of La Mancha, the undoer of wrongs and injuries. So, God be with you, and do not forget what you have promised and sworn, on pain of the penalty I have stated." With these words he spurred Rozinante and in a moment he was far away.

The countryman gazed after him, and when he saw that he had gone through the wood and was out of sight, he turned to his servant, Andrés, saying: "Come here, my boy; I want

---

[1] Saint Bartholomew, one of the twelve apostles and martyrs, who was traditionally supposed to have been flayed.

to pay you what I owe you in accordance with the commands of that undoer of wrongs."

"So you will, I swear," said Andrés; "and you had better obey the orders of that good knight—may he lived a thousand years. He is such a courageous man and such a fair judge that by Saint Roch, if you don't pay me, he'll be back and he'll do what he threatened."

"And I'll swear I will too," answered the countryman, "and to show you my goodwill, I'll double the debt so that I can double the pay." Catching the boy by the arm, he tied him again to the oak and gave him such a drubbing that he left him for dead. "Now, master Andrés," said he, "call out to that undoer of wrongs and you'll find that he won't undo this one. Indeed I don't think I'm finished with you yet, for I've a mind to flay you alive as you feared a moment ago." At last he untied him and gave him leave to go off and fetch his judge to carry out the threatened sentence. As for Andrés, he went off sorely fretful, swearing that he would seek out the valiant Don Quixote of La Mancha and tell him all that happened, and he would make his tormentor pay sevenfold. However, he departed in tears, while his master stayed behind laughing.

Such was the manner in which the valiant Don Quixote undid that wrong.

Meanwhile the knight was quite pleased with himself, for he believed that he had begun his feats of arms in a most successful and dignified manner, and he went on riding toward his village, saying to himself in a low voice: "Well mayest thou call thyself the happiest of all women on earth, O Dulcinea of El Toboso, peerless among beauties, for it was thy fortune to have subject to thy will so valiant and celebrated a knight as is and shall be Don Quixote of La Mancha, who, as all the world knows, received only yesterday the order of knighthood and today has undone the greatest wrong that ever ignorance designed or cruelty committed. Today from the hand of that pitiless foe he seized the lash with which he so unjustly scourged that tender child."

Just then he came to a road that branched into four directions, and forthwith he was reminded of the crossroads where knights-errant would halt to consider which road they should follow. To imitate their example, he paused for a moment's meditation, and then he slackened the reins, leaving Rozinante to choose the way. The horse followed his original intention, which was to make straight in the direction of his stable.

When Don Quixote had ridden about two miles, he saw a big company of people who, as it appeared later, were traders of Toledo on their way to buy silk in Murcia. There were six of them and they carried sunshades. They were accompanied by four servants on horseback and three muleteers on foot. No sooner had Don Quixote perceived them than he fancied a new adventure was at hand. So, imitating as closely as possible the exploits he had read about in his books, he resolved now to perform one that was admirably molded to the present circumstances. So, with a lofty bearing he fixed himself firmly in his stirrups, grasped his lance, covered himself with his buckler, and stood in the middle of the road waiting for those knights-errant to approach (for such he supposed them to be). As soon as they came within earshot, Don Quixote, raising his voice, cried out in an arrogant tone: "Let all the world stand still if all the world does not confess that there is not in all the world a fairer damsel than the Empress of La Mancha, the peerless Dulcinea of El Toboso."

At the sound of those words the traders pulled up and gazed in amazement at the grotesque being who uttered them. Both the tone and the appearance of the horseman gave clear proof of his insanity, but they wished to consider in more leisurely fashion the meaning of this confession that he insisted upon. So one of them, who was a trifle waggish in humor and had plenty of wit, addressed him as follows: "Sir knight, we do not know this lady you speak of. Show her to us, and if she is as beautiful as you say, we shall willingly and universally acknowledge the truth of your claim."

"If I were to show her to you," answered Don Quixote, "what merit would there be in acknowledging a truth so manifest to all? The important point is that you should believe, confess, affirm, swear, and defend it without setting eyes on her. If you do not, I challenge you to try battle with me, ye presumptuous and overweening band. Come on now, one by one as the traditions of chivalry declare, or else all together according to the foul custom of your breed. Here I stand waiting for you, trusting in the justice of my cause."

"Sir knight," answered the trader, "I beseech you in the name of all the princes here present not to force us to burden

our consciences by confessing something we have never seen
or heard, especially when it is so prejudicial to the empresses
and queens of Alcarria and Extremadura. Please show us
some picture of that lady, even if it is no bigger than a grain
of wheat, for a thread will enable us to judge the whole
skein and we shall be satisfied and you yourself happy and
content. I believe that we already are so much on your side
that even if your lady's picture shows that one eye squints
and the other drips vermilion and sulphur, yet in spite of
all, to gratify you, we shall say all that you please in her
favor."

"Drip indeed, you infamous scoundrels!" cried Don
Quixote in a towering rage. "Nothing of the kind drips from
her eyes, but only ambergris and civet in cotton wool. She is
not squint-eyed nor hunchbacked, but straighter than a Gua-
darrama spindle. But you shall pay the penalty for the great
blasphemy you have uttered against so peerless a beauty as
my lady." With those words he attacked the man who had
spoken to him, so fiercely with couched lance that if good
fortune had not caused Rozinante to stumble and fall
midway, the merchant would have paid dearly for his rashness. Rozinante fell and his master rolled a good distance
over the ground. Although he tried to rise, he could not, for
he was so impeded by the lance, the buckler, the spurs, the
helmet, and the weight of the ancient armor. However, as he
was struggling to arise, he kept on crying: "Flee not, cowardly
rabble! Wait, slavish herd! It is not my fault, but the fault
of my horse, that I am stretched here."

One of the muleteers of the company, who indeed was
not very good-natured, when he heard the poor fallen knight
say such arrogant words, could not resist the temptation to
give him the answer on his ribs. So he went up to him, took
the lance, broke it into pieces, and with one of them he so
belabored our poor Don Quixote that in spite of his armor
he thrashed him like a measure of wheat. His masters shouted
to him not to beat him so much and to leave off; but the
fellow was angry and would not stop the game until he had
spent what remained of his rage. Then, running to get the rest
of the pieces of the lance, he splintered them all on the
wretched knight, who, in the midst of all this tempest of blows
that rained on him, did not for a moment close his mouth,
but bellowed out threats to heaven and earth and those
villainous cutthroats (for so they appeared to him). At last

the muleteer became wearied and the traders pursued their journey, carrying with them plenty of matter for conversation at the expense of the poor drubbed knight. And when he was alone, he tried to see if he could get up, but if he could not do so when he was hale and hearty, how could he do it when he was bruised and battered? And yet he counted himself lucky, for he thought that his misfortune was peculiar to knights-errant and he attributed the whole accident to the fault of his horse. But so bruised was his whole body that it was impossible for him to get up.

CHAPTER V

In which is continued the account of our knight's mishap

Seeing that he couldn't stir, he resolved to have recourse to his usual remedy, which was to think of some incident from one of his books. His madness made him remember that of the Marquess of Mantua and Baldwin, whom Carloto left wounded on the mountainside—a story familiar to children, not unknown to youths, celebrated and even believed by old men, yet for all that, no more authentic than the miracles of Mohammed. Now this story, so he thought, exactly fitted his present circumstances, so with great display of affliction he began to roll about on the ground and to repeat in a faint voice the words that the wounded knight in the wood was supposed to have said:

"Where art thou, lady of my heart,
That for my woe thou dost not grieve?

Alas, thou do know'st not my distress,
Or thou art false and pitiless." [1]

In this manner he repeated the ballad until he came to those verses that say: "O noble Marquess of Mantua, my uncle and liege lord." By chance there happened to pass by at that very moment a peasant of his own village, a neighbor, who was returning from bringing a load of wheat to the mill. And he, seeing a man lying stretched out on the ground, came over and asked him who he was and what was the cause of his sorrowful lamentation. Don Quixote, firmly believing that the man was the Marquess of Mantua, his uncle, would not answer but continued reciting his ballad, which told of his misfortunes and of the loves of the Emperor's son with his wife, just as the book relates it. The peasant was amazed to hear those extravagant words. Then taking off his visor, which had been broken to pieces in the drubbing, he wiped the dust off his face. No sooner had he done so than he recognized him and said: "Master Quixana" (for that must have been how people called him when he had his wits and had not been transformed from a staid gentleman into a knight-errant) "who left you in such a state?" But he kept on reciting his ballad and made no answer to what he was asked. The good man then, as best as he could, took off his breast- and back-plate to see if he was wounded, but he saw no blood or scar upon him. He managed to lift him up from the ground and with the greatest difficulty hoisted him on to his ass, thinking that beast an easier mount. Then he gathered together all his arms, not omitting even the splinters of the lance, tied them into a bundle, and laid them upon Rozinante's back. Then taking the horse by the bridle and the ass by the halter, he set off toward his village, meditating all the while on the foolish words that Don Quixote kept saying. And Don Quixote on his part was no less pensive, for he was so beaten and bruised that he could hardly hold himself onto the ass, and from time to time he uttered such melancholy sighs that seemed to pierce the skies that the peasant felt again moved to ask him what was the cause of his sorrow. But it must have been the Devil himself who supplied him with stories so similar to his circumstances, for at that

[1] Cervantes here burlesques the ballad of Baldwin by Gerónimo Treviño, which had been published at Alcalá in 1598.

instant, forgetting Baldwin, he remembered the Moor Abindarráez whom the governor of Antequera, Rodrigo de
Narváez, took prisoner to his castle.[2] So when the peasant
asked him again how he was, he answered word for word
as the captive Abindarráez answered Rodrigo de Narváez,
just as he had read in Montemayor's *Diana*, where the story
is told. And he applied it so artfully to his own case that
the peasant wished he were in Hell rather than to have to
listen to such a hodgepodge of foolishness. This convinced
him that his neighbor was mad, so he made haste to reach
the village and thereby escape being further plagued by Don
Quixote's long discourse. The latter ended by saying: "I
would have you know, Master Rodrigo de Narváez, that
the beauteous Jarifa I have mentioned is now the fair
Dulcinea of El Toboso, for whom I have done, still do, and
shall do the most famous deeds of chivalry that ever have
been, are, or ever shall be seen in the world." To this the
peasant answered: "Take heed, sir, that I am neither Don
Rodrigo de Narváez nor the Marquess of Mantua, but
Pedro Alonso, your neighbor, and you are neither Baldwin
nor Abindarráez, but the honorable gentleman Master
Quixana."

"I know who I am," answered Don Quixote, "and I know
that I can be not only those I have mentioned but also the
Twelve Peers of France and even the Nine Worthies, for
my exploits will surpass all they have ever jointly or
separately achieved." [3]

With this and sundry topics of conversation they reached
the village at sunset, but the peasant waited until it was
dark so that no one would see the belabored knight so sor-
rily mounted. When he thought the time had come, he en-

[2] The loves of the Moor Abindarráez and the fair Jarifa
were a favorite subject of song among Moorish as well as Chris-
tian ministrels of Spain. In 1565 Antonio de Villegas published his
Inventario, which includes his celebrated Moorish novella
Abencerraje y Jarifa. The story was incorporated by Jorge de
Montemayor in the 1561 edition of his *Diana.*

[3] The Nine Worthies were proverbial; they were Jewish,
pagan, and Christian: Joshua, David, Judas Maccabeus, Alexander,
Hector, Julius Caesar, King Arthur, Charlemagne, Godfrey de
Bouillon. A chronicle was written on them by Antonio Rodríguez Portugal (Lisbon, 1530). The Twelve Peers were Charlemagne's celebrated paladins. They were called peers because they
were all equal in valor. Among them were Roland, Oliver, Rey-
naut de Montauban, etc.

tered the village and went to Don Quixote's house, which he found in an uproar. The curate and the village barber, great friends of Don Quixote, happened to be there and the housekeeper was addressing them in a loud voice: "What do you think, Master Licentiate Pedro Pérez" (that was the curate's name) "of my master's misfortune? For the past six days neither he, nor his horse, nor his buckler, nor his lance, nor his armor has appeared. Woe is me! I'm now beginning to understand, and I'm as sure of it as I am of death that those accursed books of chivalry that he continually reads have turned his brain topsy-turvy. Now that I think of it I remember hearing him say to himself many a time that he wished to become a knight-errant and go through the world in search of adventures. The Devil and Barabbas take such books, for they have ruined the finest mind in all La Mancha!" The niece said the same and a little more: "You must know, Master Nicholas" (this was the name of the barber) "that it was a frequent occurrence for my uncle to read those soulless books of misadventures for days and nights on end. At the end of that time he would cast the book from his hands, clutch his sword, and begin to slash the walls. Then, when he was grown very weary, he would say that he had killed four giants as big as towers and that the sweat that dripped off him after his great exertions, he would say, was blood from the wounds he had received in battle. Then he would drink a great jugful of water and become calm and peaceable, saying that the water was a most precious liquor that his friend the great enchanter Esquife had given him. I, however, blame myself for all, for not having warned you of my uncle's extravagant behavior. You might have cured him before things reached such a state, and you would have burned all those excommunicated books (he has many, mind you), for they all deserve to be burned as heretics."

"I agree with that," said the curate, "and I hold that tomorrow must not pass without a public inquiry being made into them. They should be condemned to the fire to prevent them from tempting those who read them to do what my poor master must have done."

All this Don Quixote and the peasant heard. The latter finally understood the infirmity of his neighbor and began to shout: "Open your doors, all of you, to Sir Baldwin and the Marquess of Mantua, who is grievously wounded, and to the Moor Abindarráez, who is led captive by the valiant Rodrigo de Narváez, governor of Antequera."

Hearing these cries, they all rushed out and straightaway recognized their friend. They ran to embrace him, but he had not yet dismounted from the ass, for he was not able to do so. He said: "Stand back, all of you. I have been sorely wounded through the fault of my horse; carry me to my bed and, if possible, call the wise Urganda to examine and cure my wounds."

"A thousand curses," said the housekeeper then. "My heart told me clearly on which foot my master limped. Come on upstairs, sir; we'll know how to look after you here without that Urganda woman. Curses, aye, a hundred curses on those books of chivalry that have driven you to this!"

They carried him to his bed and searched his body for wounds, but could find none. He said he was all bruised after a great fall he had with his horse, Rozinante, when he was fighting ten giants, the fiercest and most overweening in the world.

"Aha!" said the curate. "So there are giants too in the dance. By the sign of the Cross I swear I'll burn the lot of them before tomorrow night."

They questioned Don Quixote a thousand times, but he would give no answer. He only asked them to give him food and allow him to sleep, for rest was what he needed most. This was done, and the curate cross-examined the peasant about the conditions in which he had found Don Quixote. The man told him all, including the extravagant words he had said when he found him and on the way home. This made the curate still more eager to carry out a project that on the following day he actually did, namely, to call his friend Master Nicholas, the barber, with whom he came to Don Quixote's house.

CHAPTER VI

*Of the pleasant and mighty inquisition held by the
curate and the barber on the library of our imaginative knight Don Quixote*

The knight was still sleeping. The curate asked the niece
for the keys of the room where the books, the authors of
the mischief, were kept, and she gave them to him willingly.
They then went into the room, accompanied by the housekeeper, and found over a hundred large volumes very well
bound and others of smaller size. As soon as the housekeeper saw them, she ran out of the room in a great hurry
and returned with a bowl of holy water and a bunch of
hyssop, saying: "Take this, your reverence, and sprinkle the
room, for fear that one of the many enchanters from those
books might cast a spell on us to punish us for our intention
to cast them out of the world."

The simplicity of the housekeeper made the curate laugh,
and he bade the barber hand him the books one by one to
see what they were about, for they might find some that
did not deserve the fire penalty.

"No," cried the niece, "there is no reason why you should
pardon any of them, for they have all been offenders. Better
throw them out of the window into the courtyard, and after
piling them in a heap, set fire to the lot; or else, take them
into the backyard and let the bonfire be lit there, and the
smoke will not trouble anyone."

The housekeeper agreed with her, so eager were the two
women for the slaughter of those innocents; but the curate
would not agree without first reading the titles at least.

The first that Master Nicholas handed to him was *Amadis
of Gaul* in four parts. "There is," said the curate, "some
mystery about this, for I have heard it said that this was

85

the first book of chivalry printed in Spain and that all the rest owe their origin to it. I am therefore of the opinion that we ought to condemn it to the fire without mercy because it was the lawgiver of so sinister a sect."

"No, your reverence," said the barber, "for I have heard that it is the best of all the books of its kind. Since it is unrivaled in its style, it ought to be pardoned."

"That is true," replied the curate, "and for that reason we may grant it life for the present. Let us see the other one lying near it."

"It is," said the barber, *"The Exploits of Esplandian, the legitimate son of Amadis of Gaul."* [1]

"Well," said the curate, "the goodness of the father is not going to help the son. Take it, mistress housekeeper, open the window, throw it into the courtyard, and start the pile for the bonfire that has to be made."

The housekeeper did so with great alacrity, so the worthy Esplandian went flying into the courtyard to await patiently the fire with which he was threatened.

"Let us get on," said the curate.

"This one here," said the barber, "is *Amadis of Greece*, yes, and I believe all on this side belong to the lineage of Amadis."

"Into the yard with the lot of them," said the curate. "Just let me burn Queen Pintiquiniestra and the shepherd Darinel, their eclogues and the bedeviled and tortuous discourses of the author, and I should agree to burn with them my own father if he went dressed as a knight-errant."

"I agree," said the barber.

"So do I," added the niece.

"Since that is agreed," said the housekeeper, "away with them into the courtyard."

They handed them to her, and as there were many of them, she saved herself the trouble of the stairs and threw them out of the window.

"What great bulky thing is that?" asked the curate.

"This," replied the barber, "is *Don Olivante de Laura*."

"The author of that," said the curate, "is the same man

---

[1] Cervantes considered that the first four books of *Amadis of Gaul* alone were worthy to be preserved from the fire. The other twenty-one books devoted to the Amadis' family were mostly composed by French imitators.

who wrote *The Garden of Flowers,* and to tell you the truth
I cannot decide which of the two books is the more truthful,
or rather the less untruthful. All I can say is that he must
go into the yard for a braggart and a nincompoop."

"The next one is *Florismarte of Hyrcania,*" said the
barber.

"Is Sir Florismarte here?" asked the curate. "By my troth,
then he must come to a swift end in the yard, in spite of
his strange birth and fantastic adventures, for his dry and
unsympathetic style deserves no other fate. To the yard
with him and that other one, mistress housekeeper."

"With all my heart, dear sir," she replied, and gaily did
what she was bidden.

"This one," said the barber, "is *The Knight Platir.*"

"That is an old book," exclaimed the curate, "but I don't
find anything in it that deserves mercy. Let him join the rest
without another word." This was done accordingly. Another
book was opened and they noticed that its title was *The
Knight of the Cross.*

"One might pardon the ignorance of a book that has so
holy a title, but then there is a saying: 'The Devil lurks behind the Cross.' Off to the fire with it."

Picking up another book, the barber exclaimed: "This
one is called *The Mirror of Chivalries.*"

"I know that one," said the curate. "There you will find
Rinaldo of Montalbán with his friends and companions,
greater thieves every one of them than Cacus,[2] and the
Twelve Peers with that truthful historian Turpin.[3] To tell
you the truth, I'm for condemning them to nothing more
than perpetual banishment, just because they have a share
in the invention of the famous Mateo Boiardo, out of which
the Christian poet Ludovico Ariosto spun his web.[4] If I
find the latter here and he speaks any other language than

[2] Cacus was a celebrated robber in classical antiquity. See
Virgil's *Aeneid* VIII, 190, and Ovid's *Fasti* I, 543.

[3] Cervantes ironically refers to the Archbishop of Rheims,
Jean Turpin, to whom was attributed, two centuries after his
death, a lying history of Charlemagne and his peers.

[4] Mateo Boiardo, author of the semiburlesque poem, *Orlando
Innamorato* (1486–1495).

his own, I shall treat him with scant respect; but if he speaks his own tongue, I'll place him on my head." [5]

"I have him in Italian," commented the barber, "but I do not understand him."

"It is just as well you do not understand him," replied the curate, "and we should pardon the worthy captain had he not brought him to Spain and turned him into a Castilian, thereby robbing him of much of his native charm. This is what happens to all who translate books of verse into another tongue, for in spite of all the trouble they take and the skill they may display, they will never reach the level of the original. In short, I say that this book and every one we find that deals with these affairs of France should be thrown aside and deposited in some dry well until we see, after further deliberation, what must be done with them, excepting *Bernardo del Carpio*,[6] which is somewhere here, and another called *Roncesvalles*, for they shall pass from my hands into those of the housekeeper and from them into the fire without remission."

The barber concurred in all this, holding it very fit and proper, for he knew the curate was too sound a Christian and too great a lover of the truth to tell a lie for anything in the world. Opening another book, they found it was *Palmerin de Oliva*, and beside it was another called *Palmerin of England*, at the sight of which the curate cried: "Let that olive be cut in splinters at once and burned so that not even its ashes remain. But as for that palm of England, let it be kept and treasured as unique, and a casket be made for it like the one Alexander discovered among the spoils of Darius and dedicated to the preservation of the works of the poet Homer. This book, my dear friend, deserves respect for two

[5] Cervantes here refers to the poor Spanish translation of the *Orlando Furioso* by Jerónimo de Urrea (1556).

The ceremonious gesture of respect when receiving a royal letter or a papal bull was to put it on one's head. There is a proverb referring to this: *Bula del Papa, ponla en la cabeza y págala de plata.* (A papal bull, put it on our head and pay for it in silver).

[6] Legendary character, supposed to be the nephew of King Alfonso the Chaste, who was opposed to Alfonso's vassalage to Charlemagne and joined the Moors of Saragossa. He contributed to the rout of the Carolingian troops at Roncesvalles.

reasons: one, because it is very good in itself, and the other, because it is said to have been written by a wise king of Portugal. All the adventures in the castle of Miraguarda are first-rate and very artfully contrived, the speeches polished and clear, for they observe and interpret the character of the speaker with much propriety and understanding. I say then, subject to your judgment, Master Nicholas, let all the rest perish without any further trial or inquiring."

"No, my good friend," replied the barber, "for this one here is the renowned *Don Belianís*."

"Even he," said the curate, "with his second, third, and fourth part, needs a dose of rhubarb to purge his excess of choler, and we shall be obliged to strip him of all that rubbish about the Castle of Fame and other more glaring follies. So we shall grant them time to put forward their plea of defense, and if they show signs of amendment, mercy or justice shall be accorded them. Meanwhile, friend, keep them in your house, but let no one read them."

"That I shall be pleased to do," replied the barber; and the curate, not being inclined to weary himself by reading any more books of chivalry, bade the housekeeper take all the big ones and throw them into the yard. His demand did not fall on deaf ears, for she had a greater longing to burn those books than to spin the broadest and finest cloth in all the world. So seizing about eight at a time, she tossed them out of the window, and as she took so many of them together, one fell at the barber's feet. He, wishing to see what it was, found that its title was *History of the Famous Knight Tirante the White*.

"Bless my soul!" cried the curate in a loud voice. "Is *Tirante the White* [7] here? Give it to me, friend, for I reckon I have found here a treasure of delight and a mine of entertainment. Here you have Don Kyrieleison of Montalbán, the doughty knight, and his brother Thomas of Montalbán, and the knight Fonseca, and the fight the valiant Tirante had with the huge mastiff, and the witty conceits of the damsel Pleasureofmylife, and the amours and intrigues of widow Repose, and the empress in love with Hippolito, her squire. Truly, my friend, as far as style is concerned,

[7] *Tirant lo Blanch*, published at Valencia in 1490, was translated into Castilian and published in 1511. Menéndez y Pelayo discusses its significance in Vol. I of *Los Orígenes de la Novela*, Introd.

this is the best book in the world. In this book knights eat and drink, sleep and die in their own beds, and make their wills before they die, as well as other things that you will not find in other books of the kind. On that account, I maintain that the author deserves to be praised, for he did not deliberately commit all these follies, which had they been intentional, would send him to the galleys for the rest of his life. Take him home and read him, and you will see that what I have said of him is true."

"So be it," replied the barber, "but what shall we do with the little books that remain?"

"These," said the curate, "are probably not books of chivalry but of poetry."

Opening one he saw that it was Jorge de Montemayor's *Diana*,[8] and thinking all the rest were of the same kind, said: "These do not deserve to be burned with the rest because they do not and will not do the mischief the books of chivalry have done. They are books of entertainment without danger to anybody."

"Oh, sir," cried the niece, "you should have them burned like the rest. For I shall not be surprised if my uncle, when cured of his disease of chivalry, does not start reading these books, and suddenly take it into his head to turn shepherd and roam through the woods and fields, singing and piping, and what is worse, turning poet, for it is said that disease is incurable and catching." [9]

"The girl is right," said the curate. "It would be wise to spare our friend such a stumbling block and danger for the future. And since we are beginning with Montemayor's *Diana*, I am of the opinion that it should not be burned, but only that part cut out relating to the witch Felicia and the enchanted water, most of the longer poems, but let us by all means leave the prose and the honor of being the first book of its genre."

"The next one," said the barber, "is another *Diana*, this one by Salamantino, and here is one more of the same name by Gil Polo."

[8] A pastoral novel by the Portuguese author Jorge de Montemayor (1559). He accompanied Philip II to England in 1554.

[9] This is a prophetic statement referring to Don Quixote after his defeat in Barcelona in the Second Part, when he wished to become a shepherd. Cervantes himself suffered all his life from the pastoral obsession.

"Let the one by Salamantino join and increase the ranks of those condemned to the yard, but Gil Polo's we shall preserve as if it were by Apollo himself. But proceed, good friend, and let us make haste, for it is getting late."

"This," said the barber, opening another, "is *The Ten Books of the Fortune of Love,* by Antonio de Lofraso, poet of Sardinia."

"By the holy orders I have received," cried the curate, "there has never been so humorous or fantastical a book written since Apollo was Apollo, the Muses Muses, and the poets poets. In its own way it is the best and most remarkable book of this kind that has ever seen the light of day, and he who has not read it can be sure that he has never read anything truly delightful. Hand it to me, friend, for I value this find more than if they had given me a cassock of Florentine serge." [10]

He laid it aside with the greatest delight, and the barber continued, saying: "The next are *The Shepherd of Iberia, The Nymphs of Henares,* and *The Unveiling of Jealousy.*"

"There is no more to do," said the curate, "than to deliver them to the secular arm of the housekeeper. Don't ask me why or we shall never finish."

"The next one is *Fílida's Shepherd.*"

"No shepherd is he," said the curate, "but a very clever courtier. Guard him as a precious jewel."

"This big one here is entitled *The Treasury of Divers Poems,*" said the barber.

"If there were not so many of them," said the curate, "they would have been more esteemed. This book ought to be weeded and cleared of certain vulgarities that are to be found amidst its great things. Let it be spared, for the author is a friend of mine and should be respected for other more heroic and elevated works he has written."

"This," continued the barber, "is a book of songs by López Maldonado."

"The author of that book is also a great friend of mine," replied the curate, "and his poems are greatly admired by those who hear him recite them, for his voice is so melodious that he enchants when he chants them. His eclogues are on the long side, though you can never have too much of a

---

[10] The author of this work was Antonio de Lofraso, a native of Alaguer, a town in Sardinia. His ten books were published at Barcelona in 1573.

good thing. Preserve him with the elect. But what is that book lying next to him?"

"*La Galatea* by Miguel de Cervantes," said the barber.

"That Cervantes has been a great friend of mine for many years, and I know him to be more versed in sorrows than in song. His book has some bright ideas; it sets out to do something but concludes nothing. We must wait for the second part he promises, and perhaps with amendment he will attain the full measure of grace now denied him. Meanwhile, until this be decided, keep him as a recluse in your lodging." [11]

"That I shall do with pleasure, my good friend," replied the barber. "And here come three together: *La Araucana* by Don Alonso de Ercilla; *La Austriada* by Juan Rufo, magistrate of Córdoba, and *El Monserrate* by Cristóbal de Virués, a poet from Valencia." [12]

"These three books," said the curate, "are the best in heroic verse ever written in the Castilian tongue and can compare with the most famous in Italy. Let them be preserved as the richest treasure of poetry Spain possesses."

The curate was too tired to look at any more books, and there and then insisted that all the rest be burned, contents unknown; but the barber had already opened one that was called *The Tears of Angélica.*

"I would have shed them myself," said the curate on hearing the title, "if I had ordered such a book to be burned, for its author was one of the most famous poets, not only in Spain, but in the world, and was most felicitous in his translation of some of Ovid's fables." [13]

---

[11] *La Galatea* of Cervantes was published in 1585. Though shortly before his death he again referred to the possibility of writing a second part, he never carried out his promise.

[12] *La Araucana,* an epic poem on the Araucan war in Chile in which Alonso de Ercilla (1533–1594) took part as a soldier. Every night during the campaign he wrote down the incidents of the day in which he had taken part. It has been magnificently reprinted in facsimile by the American hispanist, the late Archer M. Huntington. The poem was published in 1590.

La Austriada (1584) describes the campaign of Don Juan of Austria against the Moriscos of Granada.

El Monserrate (1587) describes the founding of the sanctuary at Monserrate in the ninth century.

[13] He was Luis Barahona de Soto, a soldier as well as a poet and a good friend of Cervantes. The work appeared in 1586.

CHAPTER VII

Of the second sally of our good knight Don Quixote of La Mancha

At this point Don Quixote began to shout at the top of his voice: "Here, here, valiant knights! Now is the time to show the force of your mighty arms, for the courtiers are getting the best of the tourney."

As they rushed out to investigate this noisy hubbub, the scrutiny of the remaining books did not proceed any further, and so it is believed that *The Carolea* and *The Lion of Spain*, with the exploits of the emperor, composed by Don Luis of Ávila, were consigned to the flames unseen and unjudged. No doubt they must have been among the remaining books, and perhaps if the curate had seen them, they would not have suffered so severe a sentence. When they reached Don Quixote's room, they found that he had already risen from his bed and continued his raving and ranting, laying about him with his sword all over the room with slashes and backstrokes, as fully awake as though he had never been asleep. They caught him in their arms and forced him to go back to bed.

After he had calmed down a little, he turned to the curate and said: "Surely, my Lord Archbishop Turpin, it is a great dishonor to us who call ourselves the Twelve Peers to allow the knights-courtiers to carry off the victory in this tourney so easily, when we, the knights-adventurers, have won the guerdon on the three preceding days."

"Hold your peace, dear kinsman," said the curate. "With God's help, fortune may change and today's loss may be tomorrow's gain. Look to your health for the moment; you must be well-nigh in the last stages of exhaustion, if not badly wounded."

"Not wounded," said Don Quixote, "but there is no doubt that I am bruised and belabored, for that bastard Roland has drubbed me with the trunk of an oak tree, out of pure envy, because he saw that I alone can match his prowess. But I would not call myself Rinaldo of Montalbán, if, the moment I rise from this bed, I do not make him pay for it, in spite of all his enchantments. For the present, bring me food, for I know that this is my greatest need; as for revenge, leave that to my care."

They gave him a meal, after which he fell asleep again, leaving them all amazed at his madness. That same night the housekeeper burned all the books she could find in the courtyard and in the house, and some that perished in the flames deserved to be preserved forever in the archives, but fate and the laziness of the inquisitor did not allow it, and thus in their case the saying was fulfilled that the saint sometimes pays for the sinner. One of the remedies that the curate and the barber then prescribed for their friend's infirmity was to wall up the room where the books had been stored so that when he rose he should not find them, for once the cause had been removed, the effect might cease. And they agreed to tell him that an enchanter had whisked books, room, and all away. The plan was carried out with great speed.

Two days later Don Quixote got up, and the first thing he did was to go and see his books, and as he could not find the room in which he had left them, he went up and down and all over the house looking for it. He came to the place where the door used to be and felt the wall with his hands, staring around him on all sides without saying a word. At last he asked the housekeeper where was the study in which he kept his books. The housekeeper, who knew exactly what she had to answer, said: "What manner of study is your worship looking for? There are no studies or books in this house now, for the Devil in person took all away."

"It was not the Devil," said the niece, "but an enchanter who arrived on a cloud one night after you went away from here. He got down off the serpent on which he was riding and went into the room. I don't know what he did in there, but soon after he went flying out through the roof, leaving the house full of smoke. When we looked to see what he had done, we could see no books or room, but we remember very well, myself and the housekeeper, that when the wicked old man was about to depart, he said in a loud voice that owing to the secret enmity he bore against the owner of those books and of the room, he had done damage that would soon be clear. He also said that he was called Muñatón the wizard."

"Frestón was the name he wished to say," answered Don Quixote.

"I don't know," said the housekeeper, "whether he was called Frestón or Fritón; I only know that his name ended in -tón."

"That is true," said Don Quixote. "He is a wise enchanter, a great enemy of mine, and looks upon me with a malicious eye, for he knows by his skill and wisdom that in the course of time I shall fight in single combat with a knight whom he favors, and I shall win, in spite of all his machinations; so, he tries to do me all the hurt he can. But I affirm that he will never prevail over what has been ordained by Heaven."

"Who has any doubts on that score?" said the niece. "But, dear uncle, what have you to do with such quarrels? Is it not better to stay peacefully at home instead of roaming the world in search of better bread than is made of wheat, not to mention that many who go for wool come home shorn?"

"My dear niece," answered Don Quixote, "how far you are off the mark! Before they ever shear me, I'll have plucked and lopped off the beards of all who think they can touch the tip of a single hair of mine."

The two would not make any further reply, for they saw that his anger was rising. As a matter of fact, he remained a fortnight peacefully at home without showing any signs of wanting to repeat his former vagaries. During those days he held many pleasant arguments with his two old friends the curate and the barber. He would maintain that what the world needed most of all was plenty of knights-errant and that he himself would revive knight-errantry. The curate sometimes contradicted him; at other times he would give in to him, for had he not adopted this procedure, he could never have dealt with him.

During this interval Don Quixote made overtures to a certain laboring man, a neighbor of his and an honest fellow (if such a term can be applied to one who is poor), but with very little wit in his pate. In effect, he said so much to him and made so many promises that the poor wight re-

solved to set out with him and serve him as squire. Among
other things Don Quixote told him that he should be most
willing to go with him because some time or another he
might meet with an adventure that would earn for him, in
the twinkling of an eye, some island, and he would find
himself governor of it. With those and other promises,
Sancho Panza (for that was the fellow's name) left his wife
and children and engaged himself as squire to his neighbor.
Don Quixote then set about raising money, and by selling
one thing, pawning another, and throwing away the lot for
a mere song, he gathered a respectable sum. He furnished
himself likewise with a buckler borrowed from a friend, repaired his broken helmet as best he could, and informed
his squire, Sancho, of the day and hour when he intended
to sally forth so that the latter might supply himself with all
that was needed. He charged him particularly to carry saddlebags. Sancho said he would do so and added that he was
thinking of bringing an ass with him, for he had a good one
and he was not used to travel on foot. At the mention of
the ass Don Quixote hesitated a little, racking his brains to
remember any case of a knight-errant who was attended by
a squire mounted on ass-back, but he could not remember
any such case. Nevertheless, he resolved to let him take his
ass, for he intended to present him with a more dignified
mount when he got the opportunity, by unhorsing the first
discourteous knight he came across. He also provided himself with shirts and other necessities, thus following the advice the innkeeper had given him.

After all these preparations had been made, Don Quixote,
without saying farewell to his housekeeper and niece, Panza
to his wife and children, set out one night from the village
without being seen. They traveled so far that night that at
daybreak they were sure that no one would find them, even
if they were pursued.

Sancho Panza rode along on his ass like a patriarch, with
his saddlebags and wineskin, full of a huge longing to see
himself governor of the island his master had promised to
him. Don Quixote happened to take the same road as on
his first journey, that is, across the Plain of Montiel, which
he now traveled with less discomfort than the last time,
for as it was early in the morning, the rays of the sun did
not beat down directly upon them, but slantwise, and so
did not trouble them. Presently Sancho Panza said to his

master: "Mind, your worship, sir knight-errant, you don't let slip from your memory the island you've promised me; I'll be able to rule it well, no matter how big it is."

To which Don Quixote replied: "I would have you know, my friend Sancho, that knights-errant of long ago were accustomed to make their squires governors of the islands or kingdoms they won, and I have resolved not to neglect so praiseworthy a custom. Nay, I wish to surpass them in it, for they sometimes, perhaps even on the majority of occasions, waited till their squires were grown old, and then when they were cloyed with service after enduring bad days and worse nights, they conferred upon them some title, such as count or at least marquess, of some valley of more or less account. But if you live and I live, I may, before six days have passed, even conquer a kingdom with a string of dependencies, which would fall in exactly with my plan of crowning you king of one of them. Do not, however, think this strange, for knights-errant of my kind meet with such extraordinary and unexpected chances that I might easily give you still more than I am promising."

"And so," answered Sancho Panza, "by that token, if I became king by one of those miracles you mention, at least my chuck Juana Gutiérrez would become queen and my children princes."

"Who doubts it?" answered Don Quixote.

"I doubt it," replied Sancho Panza, "for I truly believe that even if God were to rain kingdoms down upon earth, none would sit well on the head of Mari Gutiérrez.[1] Believe me, sir, she's not worth two farthings as queen; countess would suit her better, and even then, God help her."

"Leave all in God's hands, Sancho," answered Don Quixote. "He will do what is best for her, but do not humble yourself so far as to be satisfied with anything less than the title of lord-lieutenant."

"I'll not indeed, sir," replied Sancho, "for a famous master like yourself will know what is fit for me and what I can carry."

---

[1] In La Mancha it is customary for wives to take the surnames of their husbands, so Sancho's wife called herself Juana Panza as well as Juana Gutiérrez. In Part II, however, the author forgets the names he has given her and calls her Teresa Cascajo, and we learn that her father's name was Cascajo.

CHAPTER VIII

Of the valiant Don Quixote's success in the terrifying and never-before-imagined adventure of the windmills, with other events worthy of happy remembrance

Just then they came in sight of thirty or forty windmills that rise from that plain, and no sooner did Don Quixote see them than he said to his squire: "Fortune is guiding our affairs better than we ourselves could have wished. Do you see over yonder, friend Sancho, thirty or forty hulking giants? I intend to do battle with them and slay them. With their spoils we shall begin to be rich, for this is a righteous war and the removal of so foul a brood from off the face of the earth is a service God will bless."

"What giants?" asked Sancho Panza.

"Those you see over there," replied his master, "with their long arms; some of them have them well-nigh two leagues in length."

"Take care, sir," cried Sancho. "Those over there are not giants but windmills, and those things that seem to be arms are their sails, which when they are whirled around by the wind turn the millstone."

"It is clear," replied Don Quixote, "that you are not experienced in adventures. Those are giants, and if you are afraid, turn aside and pray whilst I enter into fierce and unequal battle with them."

Uttering these words, he clapped spurs to Rozinante, his steed, without heeding the cries of his squire, Sancho, who warned him that he was not going to attack giants but windmills. But so convinced was he that they were giants that he neither heard his squire's shouts nor did he notice what they were, though he was very near them. Instead, he rushed on, shouting in a loud voice: "Fly not, cowards and vile caitiffs; one knight alone attacks you!" At that moment a slight breeze arose and the great sails began to move. When Don Quixote saw this, he shouted again: "Although you flourish more arms than the giant Briareus, you shall pay for it!"

Saying this and commending himself most devoutly to his lady, Dulcinea, whom he begged to help him in this peril, he covered himself with his buckler, couched his lance, charged at Rozinante's full gallop, and rammed the first mill in his way. He ran his lance into the sail, but the wind twisted it with such violence that it shivered the lance in pieces and dragged both rider and horse after it, rolling them over and over on the ground, sorely damaged.

Sancho Panza rushed up to his assistance as fast as his ass could gallop, and when he reached the knight, he found that he was unable to move, such was the blow that Rozinante had given him in the fall.

"God help us!" cried Sancho. "Did I not tell you, sir, to mind what you were doing, for those were only windmills? Nobody could have mistaken them unless he had windmills in his brain."

"Hold your peace, good Sancho," replied Don Quixote. "The affairs of war are, above all others, subject to continual change. Moreover, I am convinced, and that is the truth, that the magician Frestón, the one who robbed me of my study and books, has changed those giants into windmills to deprive me of the glory of victory; such is the enmity he bears against me. But in the end his evil arts will be of little avail against my doughty sword."

"God settle it in His own way," cried Sancho as he helped his master to rise and remount Rozinante, who was well-nigh disjointed by his fall.

They conversed about the recent adventure as they followed the road toward the Pass of Lápice, for there, Don Quixote said, they could not fail to find many and various adventures, seeing that it was a much frequented spot. Nevertheless he was very downcast at the loss of his lance, and in mentioning it to his squire, he said: "I remember having read of a Spanish knight called Diego Pérez de Vargas,[1]

[1] Some of the exploits of this Spanish Hercules are told in the ballad on the siege of Jérez in the reign of Fernando III el Santo.

who, when he broke his sword in a battle, tore off a huge
branch from an oak and with it did such deeds of prowess
that day and pounded so many Moors that he earned the
surname of Machuca,[2] and so he and his descendants were
called from that day onwards Vargas y Machuca. I mention
this because I intend to tear from the first oak tree we meet
such a branch, with which I am resolved to perform such
deeds that you will consider yourself fortunate to witness,
exploits that men will scarcely credit."

"God's will be done," said Sancho. "I'll believe all your
worship says; but straighten yourself a bit in the saddle, for
you seem to be leaning over on one side, which must be
from the bruises you received in your fall."

"That is true," replied Don Quixote, "and if I do not complain, it is because knights-errant must never complain of
any wound, even though their guts are protruding from
them."

"If that be so, I've no more to say," answered Sancho,
"but God knows I'd be glad to hear you complain when anything hurts you. As for myself, I'll never fail to complain
at the smallest twinge, unless this business of not complaining applies also to squires."

Don Quixote could not help laughing at the simplicity of
his squire and told him that he might complain whenever he
pleased and to his heart's content, for he had never read
anything to the contrary in the order of chivalry. Sancho
then bade his master consider that it was now time to eat,
but the latter told him to eat whenever he fancied. As for
himself, he had no appetite at the moment. Sancho no sooner
had obtained leave than he settled himself as comfortably as
he could upon his ass, and taking out of his saddlebags
some of the contents, he jogged behind his master, munching deliberately; and every now and then he would take a
stiff pull at the wineskin with such gusto that the ruddiest
tapster in Málaga would have envied him. While he rode
on, swilling away in that manner, he did not remember any
promise his master might have made to him, and so far
from thinking it a labor, he thought it a life of ease to go
roaming in quest of adventures, no matter how perilous they
might be.

They spent that night under some trees, and from one of

---

[2] The verb *machucar* means to pound.

them Don Quixote tore a withered branch that might, at a
pinch, serve him as a lance, and he fixed to it the iron
head of the one he had broken. All that night he did
not sleep, for he kept thinking of his lady, Dulcinea. In this
way he imitated what he had read in his books, where
knights spent many sleepless nights in forests and wastes,
reveling in memories of their fair ladies. Not so Sancho
Panza, whose belly was full of something more substantial
than chicory water. He made one long sleep of it, and if
his master had not roused him, not even the rays of the sun
beating on his face nor the joyful warbling of the hosts of
birds would have awakened him. When he got up he tested
the wineskin once more and found it somewhat flabbier than
the night before. This saddened him, for he thought that
they were not in the way to remedy that loss as soon as
would satisfy him. Don Quixote would not break his fast,
for as we have said before, he was resolved to nurture himself on savory remembrances. They now turned into the road
they had been taking toward the Pass of Lápice, and they
discovered it about three o'clock in the afternoon. When Don
Quixote saw it, he said: "Here, brother Sancho Panza, we
may dip our hands up to the elbows in what they call adventures. But I warn you not to draw your sword to defend me, even if you see me in the greatest danger, unless
you find me attacked by baseborn scoundrels. In that case
you may help me; but if they are knights, you are forbidden
expressly by the laws of chivalry to help me until you are
dubbed a knight yourself."

"Master, I can promise you obedience in this," replied
Sancho, "especially as I am by nature a quiet, peaceable
man with ne'er a wish to thrust myself into noisy brawls.
Nevertheless, when it comes to defending my own person,
I'm not one to pay much attention to such laws, for those
laid down by God and man allow everyone to defend himself against any who would do him wrong."

"I agree," answered Don Quixote, "but in the matter of
helping me against knights, you must restrain your natural
impulses."

"I promise to do so," replied Sancho, "and I'll observe
that injunction as religiously as the Sabbath."

While they were thus talking, two friars of the Order of
Saint Benedict appeared on the road mounted on mules big
enough to be dromedaries. They wore dust masks with spec-

tacles and carried sunshades. After them came a coach accompanied by four or five horsemen and two grooms on foot. In the coach, it was learned afterward, was a Biscayan lady on her way to meet her husband at Seville. He was about to sail for the Indies to take up some important post. The monks were not in her train, but were traveling the same road. As soon as Don Quixote saw them, he said to his squire: "Either I am deceived or this will be the most famous adventure ever seen, for those black, bulky objects over there must surely be enchanters who are abducting in that coach some princess. I must redress this wrong with all my might."

"This will be worse than the windmills," said Sancho. "Take heed, sir, that these are monks and that coach must belong to some travelers. Take heed what you are doing; don't let the Devil lead you astray."

"I have told you before, Sancho," answered Don Quixote, "that you know precious little about adventures. I am telling you the truth and you will now see for yourself." With these words he advanced and stood in the middle of the road by which the monks were to pass. When they had come near enough for them to hear him, he cried out in a loud voice: "Monstrous spawn of Satan, release this instant the noble princesses you carry away in that coach under duress! If not, prepare to meet swift death as just chastisement for your evil deeds."

The monks reined in their mules and stood bewildered both by the appearance of Don Quixote as well as by his words. They then answered: "Sir knight, we are neither monstrous nor satanic, but two monks of the Order of Saint Benedict wending our own way. We do not know whether there are any princesses being carried in that coach by force or not."

"None of those soft words for me; I know you well, accursed knaves," answered Don Quixote. Then, without waiting for any further answer, he spurred on Rozinante, couched his lance, and attacked the first monk with such ferocity that if the latter had not let himself fall from the mule, he would have toppled him on the ground against his will and wounded, perhaps even killed, him. The second monk, when he saw the way his companion fared, clapped spurs into his fine towering mule and began to speed away over the plain faster than the wind itself. Sancho Panza no sooner saw

the monk fall to the ground than he leaped swiftly off his
ass, rushed at him, and began to relieve him of his habit.
But two of the monk's servants came up and asked him
why he was disrobing their master. Sancho replied that it
was his due by law, as spoils of the battle his master, Don
Quixote, had won. The servants, who knew nothing of spoils
or battles, seeing that Don Quixote was at a distance speaking to those in the coach, set upon Sancho, threw him down,
plucked every hair out of his beard, and so mashed and
mauled him that they left him stretched on the ground breathless and stunned.

As for the monk, he straightway got up again on his
mule. He was trembling, terror-stricken and as pale as death,
and no sooner was he mounted than he spurred after his
companion, who stood a good distance away observing the
issue of the encounter. Without waiting for the end of the
whole incident, they continued their journey, crossing themselves oftener than if they had the Devil himself at their heels.

Don Quixote, meanwhile, was talking to the lady in the
coach, to whom he said: "You may, fair lady, now dispose
of your person as you will, for your proud ravishers now
lie prostrate on the ground, overthrown by this mighty arm
of mine. And lest you pine to know the name of your protector, learn that I am called Don Quixote of La Mancha,
knight-errant and captive of the peerless and beauteous Lady
Dulcinea of El Toboso. In return for the service you have
received from me, I demand nought else save that you should
go to El Toboso and present yourself in my name before
my lady and tell what I have done to liberate you."

All that Don Quixote was saying was overheard by a squire
in the retinue of the coach, a Biscayan. When he heard
that the coach was not to pass on but was to return to El
Toboso, he went up to Don Quixote, and taking hold of
his lance, he said to him in bad Castilian and worse
Biscayan: "Away with you, knight, and go to the Devil! By
God who me create, if you no leave coach, me kill you, as
me be Biscayan." [3]

[3] The incorrectness of the Castilian spoken by the Basques
was a standing joke in the sixteenth and seventeenth centuries.
Quevedo said of them: "If you wish to know Biscayan, change
the first to the second person in the verbs." Biscayans were
watchwords of sobriety, honesty, and laconic speech.

Don Quixote understood him very well and with great calmness answered him: "If you were a knight or a gentleman, which you are not, I would by now have chastised your folly and insolence, you vile caitiff."

"Me no gentleman?" cried the Biscayan. "As I be Christian, I swear to God you be liar. Throw away lance, draw sword, and I soon show you how soon you carry water to cat.[4] Me be Biscayner by land, nobleman by sea, nobleman by the Devil, and you lie if else you say."

"Now, quoth Agrages,[5] you will see," shouted Don Quixote. Flinging his lance on the ground, he drew his sword, clasped his buckler, and rushed at the Biscayan with the firm determination of taking his life. The Biscayan, seeing him coming, would have wished to alight from his mule (which was not to be trusted, seeing that it was a hired hack and a sorry one at that), but he had not time to do anything but draw his sword. Luckily for him he was near the coach, from where he snatched a cushion to serve him as shield. Then they fell upon one another as though they were mortal enemies. The bystanders would have wished to stop the fight, but they did nothing, for the Biscayan shouted out in his garbled language that if they would not let him finish the battle, he would kill his lady and everyone else who hindered him. The lady in the coach, bewildered and terrified by what she was seeing, told the coachman to draw aside a little, and from a distance she sat watching the fierce struggle.

The Biscayan in the course of the fight dealt Don Quixote a mighty blow on the shoulder over the buckler, which if it had not been for his armor, would have cleft him to the girdle. Don Quixote, feeling the weight of that colossal blow, cried out in a loud voice: "O Dulcinea, lady of my soul, flower of all beauty! Help thy knight, who, to repay

---

[4] *Llevar el gato al agua* (to carry the cat to the water) means to do something that is difficult and perilous. It was a saying often applied to one who was a victor in a contest. It was derived from a game in which two cats were tied together by the tail, then carried near a pool of water. They had the water between them and the cat that first pulled the other into the water was declared the winner. The Biscayan inverts the phrase.

[5] This phrase from *Amadis of Gaul* became a proverb (*Ahora lo veredes, dijo Agrages*). Agrages was proverbially quarrelsome.

thy great goodness, finds himself in this great peril!" To say this, to grasp his sword, to cover himself with his buckler, to rush upon the Biscayan, was the work of one instant, for he was resolved to risk the fortune of the whole contest on a single blow. The Biscayan, as soon as he saw him coming, perceiving by his ferocious mien his set intention, resolved to do likewise. He stood his ground, covering himself with the cushion, but he could not maneuver his mule either to right or to left, for the beast, being already jaded and unaccustomed to such childish pranks, could not move a step. Don Quixote, as we said before, advanced toward the wary Biscayan, brandishing his sword on high and determined to cleave him in twain. The Biscayan, on his part, waited for him with his sword also raised and protected by his cushion. All the bystanders stood trembling in fearful suspense, dreading the result of those prodigious blows. The lady in the coach and her womenservants were making a thousand vows and offerings to all the statues and places of devotion in Spain that God might deliver their squire and themselves from so great a peril.

But it is most unfortunate that at this critical moment the author of this history leaves the battle in mid air, with the excuse that he could find no more exploits of Don Quixote than those related here. It is true that the second author of this work refused to believe that so curious a history could have been consigned to oblivion or that the wits of La Mancha could have been so lacking in curiosity as not to possess in their archives or in their registries some documents referring to this famous knight.

Relying on this belief, he did not lose hope of discovering the conclusion of this delectable history, and by the favor of Heaven he did find it, as we shall tell in the second part.[6]

[6] The last words of the chapter refer to the original division of Part I of Don Quixote into four parts. Chapter VIII ends the first of the four parts. Cervantes gave up these divisions when he published the Second Part of the novel in 1615 and only kept the division by chapters. He may have decided to give up the original division in order to avoid following Avellaneda, who divided his spurious continuation in three parts.

CHAPTER IX

*In which is decided and ended the stupendous battle be-
tween the gallant Biscayan and the valiant Manchegan*

In the first part of this history we left the valiant Biscayan and the celebrated Don Quixote with naked swords
on high just about to deal two blows of such savagery that
if they had reached home, they would have cleft both knights
asunder from head to foot, splitting them like a pomegranate.
At that critical point this pleasant history stopped and was
left unfinished without our author giving a hint where to
find the missing part. This caused me great annoyance, for
my pleasure from the little I had read of the story was
turned into displeasure when I considered what faint hopes
there were of finding the remainder of so agreeable a tale.
It seemed to me impossible and contrary to reasonable custom that so noble a knight should not have found some
wise man who would have undertaken to write of his unheard-of exploits, a thing that was never lacking in the case
of the knights-errant, who, as people say, sally forth on these
adventures, for all of them always kept one or two sages
ready at hand, who not only wrote of their deeds but also
described their minutest thoughts and most trivial actions,
however much they were concealed; and so excellent a knight
could not have been so unlucky as to lack what Platir and
his peers had in excess. I could not thus bring myself to
believe that such a gallant story could have been left maimed
and mutilated, and I laid the blame on the malice of time,
the devourer and consumer of all things, for either conceal-
ing or destroying the sequel. On the other hand, I believed
that as among Don Quixote's books some had been found
as modern as *The Unveiling of Jealousy* and *Nymphs and
Shepherds of Henares,* his history must be modern too, and

that though it might not be written, it would still be in the memory of the people of his village and the neighborhood. This thought made me anxious and eager to obtain genuine information about the life and marvels of our famous Spaniard, Don Quixote of La Mancha, light and mirror of Manchegan chivalry and the first who in our age and in these our calamitous times devoted himself to the toil and exercise of knight-errantry, to redress wrongs, to succor widows, to protect maidens, so that they could go about mounted on their palfreys with riding whip in hand from forest to forest, from valley to valley, unharmed; for there were virgins in the days of old who, unless raped by some rogue or by some yokel with his casque and ax or by some hulking giant, never slept under a roof all their lives, and yet at the age of eighty went to their graves as spotless virgins as the mothers who bore them. Now, I say that for this and many other reasons our gallant Quixote deserves unending and immemorial praise, and even I should not be denied my share for my toil and trouble in searching for the conclusion of this agreeable story. Though I know only too well that if Heaven, chance, and good luck had not helped me, the world would have remained without the entertainment and pleasure that an attentive reader may now enjoy for almost two hours on end.

The discovery happened in the following manner: One day when I was in the Alcaná or the silk market of Toledo, a lad came up to sell some parchments and old papers to a silk merchant, and as I am very fond of reading even torn papers in the street, I was tempted by my natural inclinations to pick up one of the parchment books the lad was selling. I observed in the book characters that I recognized as Arabic. But although I recognized them, I could not read them, and I went around looking for a Morisco who spoke Spanish to read them to me. It was not difficult to find an interpreter there, and even if I had needed one for a better and older language, I should have found one. In a word, chance offered me one to whom I explained what I wanted, and I put the book in his hands. He opened it in the middle, and after reading a little he began to laugh. I asked him what he was laughing at, and he answered that it was something written in the margin as a note. I begged him to tell me what it was, and still laughing, he replied, "This is what is written in the margin! They say that Dulcinea of El

Toboso, so often mentioned in this history, had the best hand at salting pork of any woman in all La Mancha.' "

When I heard the name of Dulcinea of El Toboso I was startled and amazed, for immediately the thought struck me that these parchments contained the history of Don Quixote. With this in mind I urged him to read the beginning, and this he did, translating the Arabic into Castilian as follows: "History of Don Quixote of La Mancha, written by Cide Hamete Benengeli, Arabian historian." I needed all my caution to conceal the thrill I felt when the title of the book caught my ear. Rushing up to the silk merchant I bought all the lad's parchments and papers for half a real. If he had possessed a tittle of sense and known how eagerly I coveted them, he might easily have demanded and got more than six reals from the sale. I went off immediately with the Morisco to the cloisters of the Cathedral and asked him to translate for me into Castilian everything in those books that referred to Don Quixote, without adding or omitting a single word, and I offered to pay him whatever sum he asked. He was satisfied with fifty pounds of raisins and three bushels of wheat and promised to translate them faithfully and as rapidly as possible. But to facilitate the task and to avoid letting such a prize out of my hands, I brought him to my house, where in little more than a month and a half, he translated it all just as it is here told.

On the first of the parchments a very lifelike picture of Don Quixote's fight with the Biscayan was painted. Both contestants stood in the same posture as the history describes, with swords aloft, the one covered by his buckler, the other by his cushion, and the Biscayan's mule so true to life that one could tell a stone's throw away that it was a hired hack. The Biscayan had at his feet a scroll that read DON SANCHO DE AZPEITIA, which no doubt was his name; and at Rozinante's feet was another that read DON QUIXOTE. Rozinante was vividly portrayed, so long and lank, so shriveled, with so sharp a backbone, and so extenuated, that one saw at a glance how wisely and properly he had been called Rozinante. Near him stood Sancho Panza, holding his ass by the halter, and at his feet was another scroll that read SANCHO ZANCAS, and according to the picture he must have had a portly belly, a short body, and long shanks, and because of this they must have given him the names of Panza and Zancas, for he is called by those two names at different times in the history. There were some other smaller details to note, but they are of small importance and have nothing to do with the faithful telling of this story, and no story is bad provided it is truthful.

Nevertheless, if any objection can be raised against the truth of this history, it can only be because its author was an Arab, for those of that nation are much inclined to lying; and since they are such bitter enemies of ours, we might more readily suppose him to have fallen short of the truth than to have exaggerated. And this is my personal belief, for when he should and could have let his pen run on in indulgent eulogies of so worthy a knight, he seems to pass them over in silence deliberately, thereby acting badly and with malicious intention, for historians are in honor bound to be precise, truthful, and dispassionate so that neither interest, nor fear, nor ill will, nor affection should move them to swerve from the path of truth, whose mother is history, rival of time, storehouse of great deeds, witness of the past, example and lesson to the present, and warning to the future. In this history I know you will find all the entertainment you can possibly desire, and if any good quality is missing, I am certain it was through the fault of its dog of an author rather than through any defect in the subject. In conclusion, the second part, according to the translation, began in this manner.

With their trenchant blades brandished on high the two valorous and raging adversaries seemed to defy heaven, earth, and bottomless hell, such was their courage and their warlike mien. The first to discharge a blow was the choleric Biscayan, and he delivered it with such force and fury that if his sword had not turned in his hand, that blow alone would have sufficed to put an end to this cruel conflict and to all the adventures of our knight. But good fortune reserved him for greater enterprises and turned aside his rival's sword so that, though it struck him on the left shoulder, it did him no other harm than to disarm him on that side, carrying away with it a great part of his helmet and half an ear, all of which in hideous din clattered to the ground, leaving him in a pitiful plight.

Heavens above! Who on earth could adequately describe the fury that flushed the heart of our Manchegan hero when he saw himself thus treated? It is enough to say that it was such that, raising himself again in his stirrups and grasping his sword more tightly with both hands, he brought it down with such force upon the Biscayan, hitting him full on both his cushion and his head, that it was as if a mountain had crashed upon him: blood began to stream from his nose, mouth, and ears, and he reeled as if he were going to fall backward from his mule, as no doubt he would have had he not clutched her neck. Then he lost his stirrups, then let go his arms, and the mule, frightened by the terrible blow, began to gallop across the fields and after a few plunges threw her master to the ground. Don Quixote, meanwhile, stood calmly looking on, and as soon as he saw him fall, he leaped off his horse, ran swiftly toward him, and setting the point of his sword between his eyes, ordered him to yield or else he would cut off his head. The Biscayan was so stunned that he could not answer a word; and it would have gone hard with him, so blind with fury was Don Quixote, had the ladies of the coach, who up to now had been terrified spectators of the fight, not come up and begged the knight earnestly to grant them the grace of sparing their squire's life.

Don Quixote replied with stately gravity: "Truly, lovely ladies, I am most willing to grant what you ask me; but it will only be on one condition, that this knight shall promise me to go to the town of El Toboso and present himself before the peerless Lady Dulcinea, that she may do with him what she pleases."

The frightened and disconsolate ladies, without considering what Don Quixote demanded and without inquiring who Dulcinea was, promised that their squire would do whatever he commanded. "Then," said he, "on the faith of that pledge, I will do him no other hurt, though he richly deserves it."

CHAPTER X

Of the pleasant conversation between Don Quixote and and his squire, Sancho Panza

While all this had been going on, Sancho Panza, who had been somewhat roughly handled by the grooms, had got up and had stood attentively watching Don Quixote's combat. He kept beseeching God in his heart to give his lord victory so that he might win some island of which he might be governor, as had been promised him. Seeing that the contest was now over and that his master was about to mount Rozinante, he ran to hold his stirrups, and before he mounted, he knelt before him, and taking him by the hand, he kissed it, saying: "Be pleased, my good master, Don Quixote, to grant me the government of the island that in this terrible battle you have won. However big it is, I feel myself able enough to govern it as well as the best in the world who has ever governed islands."

To which Don Quixote replied: "Take heed, brother Sancho, that this adventure and others of this kind are not adventures of islands but crossroads, in which nothing is gained but a broken head or the loss of an ear. Have patience, for adventures will come whereby I may make you not only governor but something yet higher."

Sancho gave him hearty thanks, and after kissing his hand again and the skirt of his habergeon,[1] he helped him to mount Rozinante, and he himself, getting up on his ass, followed his master, who rode on at a brisk pace without taking leave of the ladies in the coach or saying another

---

[1] To kiss the skirt of the habergeon or mailed shirt, according to the code of chivalry, was a token of respectful affection.

word to them and entered a wood nearby. Sancho followed him as fast as his ass could trot, but Rozinante went so fast that, finding himself left behind, he had to shout to his master to wait for him. Don Quixote did so, bridling Rozinante until his wearied squire overtook him.

"I'm thinking, sir," said the squire as soon as he came up, "that the wisest course for us would be to retreat to some church, for as you've left the man you fought in a parlous state, I shouldn't wonder if they tipped the wink to the Holy Brotherhood [2] and we'll be nabbed. Mark my words— before we get out of prison we'll have to sweat our tails out."

"Hold your tongue," said Don Quixote. "Where have you ever seen or heard that a knight-errant was brought before the judge, no matter how many homicides he may have committed?"

"I know nothing about 'omecils' " [3] replied Sancho, "nor did I ever commit one against anyone. All I do know is that the Holy Brotherhood does have something to say to those who fight in the country; I'll have nought to do with t'other."

"Set your mind at peace, friend," answered Don Quixote; "I will deliver you from the Chaldeans,[4] not to mention the Holy Brotherhood. But tell me now, have you ever seen a more valiant knight than I on the face of the earth? Have you read in history of any other that has or ever had more courage in fighting, more spirit in resisting, more dexterity in wounding, or more agility in felling his foe?"

"To tell the honest truth, your worship, I've never read any history, for I can't read nor write; but I'll dare wager that I've never served a more daring master in all the days of my life; and may it please God that we don't pay for this boldness in the place I've mentioned. Now I'd like to beg your worship to let me dress that ear of yours, which is losing a power o' blood. Here I have some lint and a little white ointment in my saddlebags."

[2] An old institution revived by Ferdinand and Isabel in 1476, for the purpose of suppressing highway robbery and the lawlessness of the turbulent nobles. It spread all through Spain and made the road safe for travelers. It was a kind of constabulary.

[3] Sancho thinks *omecillos* is equivalent to *homicidios*.

[4] The Moors were often called Chaldeans by the ancient Spaniards.

"There would have been no need of that," said Don Quixote, "if I had remembered to make a vial of the balsam of Fierabrás; with just one drop of it both time and medicines would be saved."

"What vial and what balsam is that?" asked Sancho Panza.

"It is a balsam the recipe of which I have in my memory, and whoever possesses it need not fear death nor consider any wound mortal. Therefore when I have made and given it to you, you have nought else to do when in any battle you see me cleft in twain (as often happens) but deftly to take up the part of the body that has fallen to the ground with the greatest nicety before the blood congeals and put it up again on the half that remains in the saddle, taking great pains to fit it exactly in the right place. Then you must give me just two sips to drink of the balsam I have just mentioned, and you will see me become as sound as an apple."

"If that is so," said Panza, "I renounce from now on the government of the promised island, and all I want in payment for my many good services is for you, sir, to give me the recipe of that precious balsam. I'm certain that an ounce of it must anywhere fetch more than two reals, and I don't need any more to enable me to spend my life with credit and comfort. But tell me, does it cost much to make it?"

"For less than three reals you may make three gallons of it," answered Don Quixote.

"As I am a sinner," answered Sancho, "what is your worship waiting for? Why don't you make it and show me how to do so?"

"Hush, friend," replied Don Quixote. "I intend to teach you greater secrets than this and bestow greater benefits upon you also. For the present let me set about dressing my own wounds, for this ear of mine pains more than I would wish."

Sancho took out of his saddlebags some lint and ointment, but when Don Quixote saw that his helmet was broken, he almost lost his senses. Clapping his hand to his sword and raising his eyes to heaven, he said: "I swear solemnly by the Creator of all things and by all that is written in the four Holy Gospels to lead the same life as was led by the great Marquess of Mantua when he swore to avenge the death of his nephew Baldwin, vowing not to eat bread from a tablecloth,[5] nor sport with his wife, and other things which though I cannot now remember them may be taken as included, until I have exacted full vengeance on him who hath done me such outrage."

When Sancho heard this, he said: "Take heed, your worship. If the Biscayan knight has done what you ordered him to do and presented himself before Lady Dulcinea of El Toboso, then he has paid what he owed. He deserves no other penalty unless he commits a new fault."

"You have spoken well and hit the mark truly," answered Don Quixote; "and therefore, I annul the oath insofar as it concerns further vengeance, but I make it and confirm it again to lead the life I have said, until I capture by force another helmet as good as this from some other knight. Do not, Sancho, think that this is mere smoke of straw on my part. I have a precedent to guide me, for the very same thing happened in the case of Mambrino's helmet, which cost Sacripante so dear." [6]

"Throw those oaths to the Devil, master," replied Sancho. "They do a great deal of damage to a man's health and conscience. Tell me now: what shall we do if we don't butt into a man armed with a helmet? Must you keep the oath in spite of so many hardships, such as sleeping in our clothes, roughing it out on the heath, and a thousand other idle penances that the old lunatic the Marquess of Mantua swore to observe and that you now want to revive? Remember, sir, that armed men don't go gallivanting over these roads, but muleteers and carriers who don't wear helmets and have probably never heard of them all the days of their lives."

"You are mistaken in that," said Don Quixote, "for we shall not have been on these crossroads two hours before we see more men-at-arms than rode against Albraca to win Angélica the Fair." [7]

"So be it," said Sancho. "God's will be done! May all turn out for the best and may the time come for winning

---

[5] This was the sign of penance and mourning as described in the ballads of the Marquess of Mantua and the Cid, and in the romances of chivalry.

[6] Cervantes makes a slip; it was not Sacripante but Dardinel de Almonte it cost so dear. See Ariosto, *Orlando Furioso*, canto XVIII.

[7] This refers to Boiardo's *Orlando Innamorato*.

that island, which is costing me so dear. Then let me die, for all I care."

"I have already told you, Sancho, not to worry on that score, for even if there is no island, there is always the kingdom of Denmark or of Sobradisa which will fit you like a ring on the finger, and you ought to be all the more pleased, as they are both on terra firma. But let us leave this to its proper time, and now see if you have anything for us to eat in your saddlebags. Then we must go in search of some castle where we can lodge this night and make the balsam I told you about, for I swear to God this ear of mine is hurting me greatly."

"Here is an onion, some cheese, and a few crusts of bread," said Sancho, "but these are not delicacies for so brave a knight."

"How little you understand!" answered Don Quixote. "You must know, Sancho, that it is the pride of knights-errant to remain for a whole month without eating, and when they do, they eat only what is ready at hand. You would know this if you had read as many books as I have. In all the books I have delved into I have never found that knights-errant ate, unless by mere chance or at some costly banquets prepared in their honor. The rest of the time they lived on the flowers of the fields, and although we know that they could not live without eating or without performing all the other functions of nature, because they were men like ourselves, yet it is clear that roaming as they did most of their lives through forests and uninhabited wastes without anybody to cook for them, their daily fare must have been coarse country food such as you offer me. Therefore, friend Sancho, do not be troubled about what pleases me, and do not try to make a new world or lift knight-errantry off its hinges."

"Pardon me, sir," said Sancho. "Seeing that I can neither read nor write, as I've said before, I've not yet understood the laws of the knight's profession, but from this day on I'll provide my saddlebags with every kind of dried fruit for you, who are a knight; and for myself, who am not one, I'll lay in store poultry and more substantial fare."

"I do not say, Sancho," replied Don Quixote, "that knights-errant are obliged to eat nothing but those dried fruits you mention; I only say that their ordinary nourishment had to be of such a kind, together with certain herbs they found in the fields, which were as well known to them as they are to me."

"It is a good thing," replied Sancho, "to know those herbs, for I feel we'll need to use that knowledge some day."

He now brought out what he had in his saddlebags, and the two ate their meal in peace and good comradeship. But wishing to look for a lodging for the night, they quickly finished their dry and scanty repast, mounted, and hastened to reach a village before nightfall. But both daylight and their hopes failed them near the huts of some goatherds, so they resolved to spend the night there.

Although Sancho was grieved at not being able to reach the village, yet Don Quixote was more joyful than ever to sleep in the open, for he thought that every time this happened he was performing an act that confirmed his title of knighthood.

CHAPTER XI

Of what happened to Don Quixote with certain goatherds

He was welcomed most cordially by the goatherds, and Sancho, having tethered Rozinante and his ass as best he could, followed the scent of certain pieces of goat's meat that were sizzling in a pot on the fire. Though he longed that very instant to taste and see whether they were ready to be transported from the pot to his belly, he did not do so, for the goatherds themselves took the pot off the fire, spread some sheepskins on the ground, and swiftly laid their rustic table, to which with words of good cheer they invited the two to share potluck. Six of them that belonged to the fold sat in a circle on the skins, having first with rough courtesy invited Don Quixote to sit himself on an upturned trough. Don Quixote took his seat, but Sancho remained standing to serve him with the cup that was made of horn. Seeing him standing, his master said to him: "That you may see, Sancho, the true worth of knight-errantry and how certain those who exercise it are to arrive swiftly at positions of honor and esteem in the world, I want you to sit by my side in the company of these good people and become one with me, your master and natural lord. I want you to eat out of my plate and drink out of my cup, for the same may be said of knight-errantry as of love, that it makes all things equal."

"Many thanks for your favor," replied Sancho, "but I must tell your worship that provided I have plenty to eat, I can eat as well and better on my feet and by my lonesome than if I was perched up on a level with an emperor. To tell you the honest truth, what I eat in my own corner without fuss and frills tastes far better, though it's nought but bread and onion, than turkey at tables where I have to chew slowly, drink but a sip, wipe my mouth often, neither sneeze nor cough even when I'm dying to do so, nor do other things that a man is free to do when he's alone. So, dear master, let these privileges that you wish to give me as a servant and follower of knight-errantry, which I am because I'm your squire, be exchanged for something that'll be of more use and profit to me, for though I'll consider these as having been well received, I hereby renounce them from today until the end of the world."

"For all that," said Don Quixote, "here you will have to sit, for God exalteth the humble"; and taking him by the arm, he forced him to sit next to him. The goatherds did not understand this gibberish about squires and knights-errant, so they just ate, held their peace, and stared at their guests, who with great relish and good humor devoured pieces as big as one's fist. After the meat course was finished, the goatherds spread on the skins a great quantity of parched acorns and half a cheese, which was harder than if it had been made of cement. The horn, meanwhile, was not idle, for it went the rounds so often (now full, now empty), like the bucket of a waterwheel, that it easily emptied one of the two big wineskins hanging in view of the company. When Don Quixote had satisfied his appetite, he took up a handful of acorns, and gazing at them earnestly, held forth in the following manner: "Happy times and fortunate ages were those that our ancestors called golden, not because gold

(so prized in this our Iron Age) was gotten in that happy
era without any labors, but because those who lived then
knew not those two words *thine* and *mine*. In that holy age
all things were in common, and to provide his daily sustenance all a man needed to do was to lift up his hand and
pluck his food from the sturdy oaks that generously invited
him to gather their sweet, ripe fruit. The clear fountains and running brooks offered him bountifully their refreshing waters. In the clefts of the rocks and in the hollow
of trees the busy, provident bees fashioned their republic,
offering without interest the fertile harvest of their fragrant
toil to every hand. The robust cork trees, inspired by their
own courtesy alone, divested themselves of their broad light
barks, with which men began to cover their houses built on
rough stakes, using them only as a defense against the inclemencies of heaven. All there was peace, all friendship,
all concord. The heavy share of the curved plow had not
dared to open and expose the compassionate bowels of our
first mother, for she without compulsion offered through all
the parts of her fertile and spacious bosom whatever could
nourish, sustain, and delight the children who possessed her.
Then did the innocent and beauteous young maidens trip
from dale to dale and hill to hill with braided locks or
flowing tresses, wearing just enough clothing to conceal modestly what modesty seeks and has always sought to hide.
Their adornments were not like those now in fashion among
people who value so highly Tyrian purple and silk fretted in
countless patterns; but being decked in some green dock
leaves interwoven with ivy, they surely outshone our court
ladies of today who wear the rare, outlandish inventions
that idle luxury has taught them. In those days amorous
conceits found simple and unaffected expression in the very
form and manner in which they were conceived, without
any artificial circumlocutions to enhance their value. Neither
fraud nor deceit nor malice had yet interfered with truth and
plain dealing. Justice was then contained within her proper
bounds; she was untroubled and unbiased by favor or self-
interest, which today so belittle, disturb, and persecute
her. Law was not yet left to the personal interpretation of
the judge, for then there were neither judges nor causes to
be judged. Maidens and innocence went about, as I have
said, alone wherever they pleased without fear or danger
from the unbridled freedom and lustful desires of others;

and if they did lose their honor it was only because of their
own natural inclinations. But now, in this detestable age of
ours, no damsel is safe even though she were hidden and
shut up in some new labyrinth like that of Crete, for even
there the amorous pestilence would enter through some
cranny or through the air, owing to the zealous plotting of
some rascal, and drive them to perdition despite their seclusion. Therefore, as times went on and wickedness increased,
the order of knight-errantry was instituted to defend maidens,
to protect widows, and to rescue orphans and distressed
persons. I belong to this order, brother goatherds, and I
thank you for the entertainment and good cheer you are
giving me and my squire, for though it is a law of nature
that every man is obliged to favor knights-errant, yet since
you have received me and feasted me without being aware of
this obligation, it is only reasonable that I should give my
warmest thanks to you."

Our knight uttered this long harangue (that might well
have been spared) simply because the acorns they gave him
reminded him of the Golden Age and put him in the humor
of making that unprofitable discourse to the goatherds. They
listened to him in wide-eyed astonishment without answering
a word. Sancho, too, was silent, munching acorns and frequently paying visits to the second large wineskin that was
hanging from a tree to cool. As for Don Quixote, he took
more time over his speech than he did over his supper. When
he had finished, one of the goatherds said: "Your worship
may be sure that you are heartily welcome; we wish to entertain you by asking one of our fellows, who will presently
join us, to sing for you. He is a bright lad and very much in
love, and above all, he knows how to read and write and
how to strum the rebec as it should be."

No sooner were the words out of the goatherd's mouth
than they heard the sound of a rebec, and presently there
appeared a handsome young man of about twenty-two years
of age. His companions inquired if he had supped, and when
he answered yes, the goatherd who had offered the music
said: "Since that is so, Antonio, you might give us the pleasure of hearing you sing a little in order that this distinguished
guest of ours may see that even in the mountains and forests
there are some who know something about music. We have
told him of your talent, and we wish to prove the truth of
all we have said. So do sit down, I pray, and sing the love

song that was composed for you by your uncle, the priest, and that is so popular in the village."

"I shall be glad to oblige," answered the youth, and without further ado he sat down on the trunk of a fallen oak, and tuning his rebec, he began presently to sing in a pleasantly modulated voice the following:

ANTONIO

Already, fair Olalla, I have won
Thy heart, and I can claim thee as my prize,
Though neither thy lips nor thy sparkling eyes
Are yet aware that we two are as one.

Thy will, wit, and good sense will assure my fate,
And in them my love's triumph I can see;
How could a man e'er be unfortunate
If he dares to proclaim his love for thee.

Yet sometimes I have seen thee frown, alas,
And give my ardent soul a cruel shock;
Then thy soul was transmitted into brass,
And thy white bosom into hardest rock.

But though I feel o'ercome by thy disdain,
Thy sharp reproaches and constant delays,
Hope unexpected comes to ease my pain,
And now the border of her robe displays.

Let my faith in the balance of thy mind
Be justly weighed, for it has never yet
Diminished, though disfavor it did find,
Nor can it grow though thou dost favor it.

If love be courtesy, as shepherds say,
And I can on thy gentleness rely,
I trust that even if thou dost delay,
My hopes will win their guerdon by and by.

And if unfailing services can tame
The hardest heart and render it benign,
Then all that I did for thee, in this game
Will win me victory and make thee mine.

For to appear more pleasing in thine eyes,
I always dress myself with studious care,
And even on Mondays—note with surprise—
My Sunday clothes thou wilt then see me wear.

For love and ostentation partners are
On Life's highroad, and so I always try
To dress myself with neat and scrupulous care,
And so cast all my glamor o'er thy eye.

I shall not mention how oft I did dance
And sing beneath thy casement in the dawn,
When thou didst listen as one in a trance,
And raucous cocks proclaimed the rising morn.

I shall not here recount the rapturous lays
Which I so often chanted to thy fame;
Though they were always truthful, yet their praise
Roused envious tongues to blacken my good name.

Teresa of the Berrocal one day,
When I was praising thee said out of spite;
"Thy doxy is an angel, dost thou say?
She is an ape, we say, a positive fright!

Thanks to her tricksy fripperies and wit,
And all her graces that are counterfeit;
Thanks to false ringlets, she the hypocrite,
The wary god of Love himself might cheat."

I swore she lied, and this did so offend
Her cousin that he gripped me for a fall;
How we then wrestled and how it did end
Thou knowest, my beloved doxy, all.

I do not count thy favors, fairest maid,
To gratify a lecherous desire;
My love is chaste, and pure the vow I've made
To cherish thee with love's abiding fire.

The Church possesses silken cords that tie
Consenting hearts in bondage all their lives;
If only, fairest, this yoke thou wilt try,
Thy swain's thy captive for eternity.

If thou wilt not, I'll make a solemn vow
By all the holiest saints I'll not forsake
These grim sierras where I'm living now,
Unless myself a capuchin I make.

With this the goatherd ended his song, and although Don
Quixote entreated him to sing another, Sancho would not
allow it, for he was more inclined to sleep than to listen to
songs. "Your worship," said he, "had better consider where
you are going to rest this night, for the labor that these good
men perform all day does not allow them to spend the night
listening to singing."

"I understand you, Sancho," replied Don Quixote, "for I
perceive clearly that your visits to the wineskin require payment in sleep rather than in music."

"We all of us enjoyed the taste of it, thanks be to God,"
answered Sancho.

"I don't deny it," replied Don Quixote. "Go and lie down
where you please. As for me, it is better for a man of my
profession to watch than to sleep; however, it would be a
good thing, Sancho, if you could dress this ear of mine again,
for it pains me more than it ought."

Sancho did as he was told, and one of the goatherds, seeing the wound, told the knight not to worry about it, for he
would give him a remedy that would cure it. And picking
a few rosemary leaves from the bushes that were about, he
bruised them, mixed a little salt with them, and having applied them to the ear, he bound it up, assuring him that he
needed no other medicine, which indeed proved to be true.

CHAPTER XII

The story a young goatherd told those that were with Don Quixote

While this was going on another youth arrived—one of those who brought the provisions from the village. "Friends," he cried, "do you know what is happening in the village?"

"How should we know?" replied one of them.

"Well, you may as well know that this morning the celebrated shepherd-student, Chrysostom by name, died, and there's a rumor that he died for love of that she-devil Marcela, wealthy William's daughter, the girl who wanders about these parts dressed as a shepherdess."

"For Marcela, you say?" asked one.

"Yes, for her," replied the goatherd, "and the best of it is that he has directed in his will that he's to be buried in the fields like a Moor at the foot of that rock where is found the spring beside the cork tree, because the report goes—and they say they had it from his own lips—that it was there that he saw her for the first time. And he has left other orders too, and such queer ones that the curates of the village say they mustn't be carried out; and it's right they shouldn't be, for they sound paganish to me. But to all this his closest friend, Ambrosio the student, who used to go about with him dressed like a shepherd too, replies that everything must be done exactly as Chrysostom had ordered. The whole village is in an uproar about the matter, but from what folks are saying, all in the end will be done just as Ambrosio and his friends, the shepherds, wish. Tomorrow they are coming to bury him with great pomp and ceremony where I said; and upon my word, it will be a sight worth seeing. I, for one, won't miss it, even if this means not getting back to the village tomorrow."

123

"We'll all do the same," answered the goatherds, "and cast lots to see who must stay and mind the goats."

"You are right, Pedro," said one, "though there's no need to go to that trouble, for I'll stay behind for all of you. And put it down to kindness on my part or get the notion that I'm not eager to see the goings-on, but the fact is that a splinter ran into my foot the other day and it keeps me from walking."

"We thank you all the same," replied Pedro.

Don Quixote asked Pedro to tell him who the dead man was, and who the shepherdess. Pedro replied that the only information he had was that the dead man was a wealthy gentleman from a village in those mountains, who had been studying at Salamanca for many years and had returned at the end of his course to his village with the reputation of being very learned and well read. They said he was especially versed in the science of stars and aware of what the sun and the moon were doing up there in the sky, for he would tell them exactly when there would be a clips of the sun and moon."

"It's called *eclipse*, friend, not *clips*, that is, the obscuration of those two greater luminaries," said Don Quixote. But Pedro paid little attention to such trivialities and went on with his story: "He likewise used to predict whether the year would be fruitful or stale."

"*Sterile*, you mean, friend," interrupted Don Quixote.

"Sterile or stale, its all the same in the long run," replied Pedro, "and I'll add that, following his advice, his father and his friends, who believed him, became very rich, for they always did what he told them when he said: 'This year sow barley, not wheat,' or 'Now it is time to sow chick-peas and not barley,' or 'The next year will be a bumper crop of olive oil, and the three years to follow not a drop will there be.'"

"This science is called astrology," said Don Quixote.

"I don't know what it's called," answered Pedro, "but I know that he knew all this and more too. Well, to come to the main point, not many months passed after his arrival from Salamanca when one day he appeared dressed like a shepherd with his crook and his sheepskin. The long scholar's coat he used to wear as a student had been put away, and with him was his great friend Ambrosio, his companion in his studies, who likewise was dressed as a shepherd. I had forgotten to tell you that Chrysostom, the deceased, was a great hand at writing verses, so much so that he used to write the carols for Christmas Eve and the plays for Corpus Christi, which the lads of our village used to act and which everybody said were tip-top. When the villagers saw the two all of a sudden dressed up as shepherds, they were dumbfounded and could not guess what had driven them to make so strange a transformation. About this time Chrysostom's father died, and he was left with a considerable amount of property, in goods as well as land, and large flocks and herds, in addition to plenty of money. Of all this wealth the young man became the dissolute owner, and indeed he deserved every penny of it, for he was a very good fellow, as charitable as they make them, a friend to all honest men, and his face was like a blessing. By and by we all understood that he had changed his dress for no other reason than to be able to roam about these desolate wilds after that shepherdess Marcela, whom our lad mentioned a while ago and with whom Chrysostom had fallen in love. And now I must tell you, for it is only right you should be informed, what manner of person this young baggage is, for perhaps—though there's no perhaps about it—you'll never hear the like of this in all the days of your life, though you live longer than Sarna."

"Say *Sarah*," replied Don Quixote, unable to bear the goatherd's blunders.

"Sarna [1] lives long enough," answered Pedro, "and sir, if you mean to go pulling me up at every word I say, we shan't get finished in a twelvemonth."

"Forgive me, friend," said Don Quixote. "I had to tell you because there is such a difference between *Sarna* and *Sarah;* but you have answered rightly, for the mange lives longer than Sarah. So, continue your story and I will not interrupt again."

"I was saying, my beloved sir," said the goatherd, "that in our village there lived a farmer even richer than Chrysostom's father, whose name was William, to whom God gave, over and above his wealth, a daughter. Her mother, the most respected woman in all these parts, died in giving her birth. I fancy I can see her now, with that face of hers that had the sun on one side and the moon on the other. What a good housewife she was and what a friend to the poor! I'm sure for that reason alone her soul must at this very moment be enjoying the sight of God in the other

[1] *Sarna* means the mange.

world. Her husband, William, died of grief at the death of so good a wife, leaving their daughter, Marcela, young and rich, in the care of one of her uncles, a priest and the vicar of our village. The child grew up to be so beautiful that she reminded us of her mother, who had herself been a beauty, but people thought the daughter to be even lovelier. And so it came to pass that when the girl reached the age of fourteen or fifteen years, every man who saw her blessed God for making her so fair, and most men fell madly in love with her. Her uncle guarded her with great care and rarely let her out of his sight, but in spite of this, the fame of her loveliness spread far and wide, and for that reason and because of her great wealth, not only our own villagers but also those from many leagues around kept begging, pressing, and plaguing her uncle to give her in marriage. But he was a good Christian, and though he wanted to speed up her marriage, as she was of age, he would not do so without her consent—not that he had any designs on delaying the marriage in order to reap profit from managing the girl's estate. And I may remark that this was said in praise of the worthy priest in more than one village circle. For I must inform you, sir errant, that in these small villages people poke their noses into everything and gossip about everything, so you may be as well assured as I am that the vicar who obliges his parishioners to speak well of him must be superlatively good, especially in the villages."

"That is true," said Don Quixote, "but do go on, for the story is a very good one, and you, my worthy Pedro, tell it charmingly."

"May the Lord's grace never fail me, that is all that matters. To continue, you must know that although the uncle described in detail to his niece the qualities of each one of her many suitors, urging her to select and marry according to her taste, the only answer the girl gave was that she did not wish to marry yet and that being so young, she did not feel capable of bearing the burden of matrimony. Since the uncle considered her excuses reasonable, he ceased pressing her and waited until she should become more mature and knew how to choose the company she liked, for he said, and rightly too, that parents ought not to marry off their children against their wills. But lo and behold, when everyone least expected it, the dainty Marcela came out one day dressed like a shepherdess, and in spite of her uncle and the entire

village, who tried to dissuade her, went off into the fields
with the other shepherdesses of the place and began to tend
her own flock. And now that she came out in public and
her beauty was there for all to see, I could not tell you how
many rich youths, gentry and peasantry, have dressed up
like Chrysostom and roam through the countryside courting
her. One of them, as I've told you, was our dear departed,
who, they said, from loving turned to worshiping her. Don't,
however, think for a moment that because Marcela adopted
that free and unfettered life with its lack of privacy, she has
given any occasion, or even the hint of one, that might imperil her modesty or virtue. On the contrary, she is so watchful of her own honor that not one of her many suitors has
boasted, nor has the right to boast, that she has ever given
him the slightest hope of obtaining his desire. Although she
does not ignore or avoid the company of shepherds but
treats them in a friendly and courteous manner, if one of
them starts showing his intentions, even though it be with a
proper and holy proposal of matrimony, like a flash she
flings him off as with a catapult. And by this behavior she
does more mischief in this land than if the plague had entered it, for her charming manner and beauty win the hearts
of all who try to love and serve her, but her scorn and brutal
frankness drive them to despair. So, they don't know what
to say to her, but loudly call her cruel and unkind and other
similar things that clearly show her character. If you, sir,
should remain here awhile, you would hear these hills and
dales echo with the laments of those unfortunates who follow her. Not far from here there is a place where there are
some two dozen tall beeches, and every one of them has
Marcela's name cut on its smooth bark, and above her name
sometimes a crown is carved, as if her lover intended to declare more plainy still that Marcela wears and deserves
the crown of all human beauty. Here sighs one shepherd,
there another moans, over yonder you hear songs of love,
near at hand despairing dirges. One spends all the hours of
the night seated at the foot of some oak or rock, and there,
without closing his tearful eyes, rapt and bemused in his
own dreams, the sun finds him next morning; another, sighing without rest or truce and lying prostrate on the burning
sand in the sultry heat of the noontide of summer, sends up
his lamentations to the merciful heavens; and over one and
over the other, and over all of them, the lovely Marcela

triumphs, free and unconcerned. And all of us who know her are waiting to see how her haughtiness will end, and who will be the fortunate man who shall succeed in taming so sinister a nature and in enjoying such an unblemished beauty. As all I have told you is the truth, I am convinced that what our lad has said about the cause of Chrysostom's death is likewise true. So I advise you, sir, not to fail to turn up at his funeral tomorrow. It will be well worth seeing, for Chrysostom had many friends, and it is not more than half a league from here to the spot where he told them to bury him."

"I shall make it my duty to be there," said Don Quixote, "and I thank you for the pleasure you have given me by telling me such an entertaining story."

"Oh," replied the goatherd, "I don't know even half of the things that have happened to Marcela's lovers, but perhaps tomorrow we may run across some shepherd on the road who will tell us more. For the present you would be wise to go and sleep under cover, for the night air may hurt your wound, though the herbs they have put on it are so effective that you'll have no trouble."

Sancho Panza, who had already consigned the goatherd and his never-ending talk to the Devil, begged his master to go into Pedro's hut to sleep. This Don Quixote did, and spent all the rest of the night thinking of his lady, Dulcinea, in imitation of Marcela's lovers. As for Sancho Panza, he laid himself down between Rozinante and his ass and slept—not like a lover rejected, but like a man soundly drubbed.

CHAPTER XIII

In which is concluded the story of the shepherdess Marcela, with other matters

Scarcely had day begun to show itself on the balconies of the East when five of the six goatherds got up and went to awaken Don Quixote and to tell him that if he still intended to go and see the famous burial of Chrysostom, they would bear him company. Don Quixote, who desired nothing better, got up and ordered Sancho to saddle the horse and the ass at once. He did so rapidly, and with the same dispatch they all took to the road. They had hardly gone a mile when from a crossroad they saw advancing toward them some six shepherds dressed in black skins, their heads crowned with garlands of cypress and bitter rosebay. Each of them had a thick staff of holly in his hand, and with them came also two gentlemen on horseback, handsomely equipped for traveling, accompanied by three servants on foot. On meeting, the two parties saluted one another courteously, and when each asked where the other was going, they discovered that they were all bound for the burial, so they journeyed together.

One of those on horseback said to his companion: "I think, Señor Vivaldo, that we can count as well spent the hours we shall delay in attending this notable funeral, for notable it cannot fail to be if we may trust the strange accounts these herdsmen have given us of the dead shepherd and the murderous shepherdess."

"I agree with you," replied Vivaldo, "and I would delay not one day, but four, rather than miss the sight."

Don Quixote asked them what they had heard about Marcela and Chrysostom, and the traveler answered that early that morning they had met the shepherds, and seeing them in such mournful attire, had asked them why they were so dressed. Then one of them had explained and related the strange behavior and beauty of a shepherdess called Marcela, the loves of her many suitors, and the death of that Chrysostom to whose burial they were going. In short, he had told them all that Pedro had told Don Quixote. This conversation ended but another began, for he who was called Vivaldo asked Don Quixote what made him go armed in such fashion in so peaceful a country. To which the knight answered: "The exercise of my profession does not allow or permit me to do otherwise. Ease, luxury, and repose were invented for soft courtiers, but toil, unrest, and arms alone were designed and made for those whom the world calls knights-errant, of whom I, though unworthy, am of all the least."

When they heard this they all considered him a madman, but to be sure of it and to discover what kind of madness his was, Vivaldo asked him what he meant by knights-errant.

"Have your worships not read," answered Don Quixote, "the annals and histories of England that record the famous exploits of King Arthur, whom in our Castilian tongue we commonly call King Artús? There is an ancient and widespread tradition about him throughout the kingdom of Great Britain that this king did not die, but by art of enchantment was changed into a crow, and that in the course of time he will come back to reign and recover his kingdom and scepter. For which reason it cannot be proved that any Englishman, from that time to this, ever killed a crow. In this good king's reign there was instituted that celebrated order of chivalry, the Knights of the Round Table, and there also occurred the amours of Sir Lancelot of the Lake and Queen Guinevere, recorded without the ommision of a jot and in which that honorable Lady Quintañona served as go-between and confidante, whence arose that ballad so widely known and often sung in our Spain:

> Never was there gallant knight
> So waited on by ladies fair
> As the bold Sir Lancelot
> When from Britain he arrived.

And so on that sweet and delectable chronicle of his amours and his mighty deeds. Ever since those days that order of chivalry has been spreading from hand to hand throughout many and divers parts of the world. And famous for their exploits therein were the valiant Amadis of Gaul with all his sons and grandsons, to the fifth generation, the brave Felixmarte of Hyrcania, the never-enough-to-be-praised Tirante the White, and he whom almost in our own times we have seen and heard and talked with, the invincible and valorous knight Sir Belianís of Greece. This then, sirs, is to be a knight-errant, and what I have spoken of is the order of chivalry, in which, as I have already said, though a sinner, I have been professed, and what the knights I mentioned have professed, I profess too. And that is why I am going through these lonely wastes and deserts in quest of adventures, deliberately resolved to offer my arm and my person to the greatest perils fortune may present in aid of the weak and those in need."

This speech enabled the travelers to convince themselves that Don Quixote was out of his wits and gave them an inkling of the particular kind of madness that troubled him. And they were amazed as were all those who for the first time came to know of it. Then Vivaldo, who was both shrewd and cheerful, to relieve the boredom of the short journey that had still to be made before reaching the burial place, sought to give the knight an opportunity of continuing his vagaries; so he said to him: "It seems to me, sir knight-errant, that your worship has adopted one of the severest professions on earth, and I believe that even that of the Carthusians is not so severe."

"It may be as severe," replied Don Quixote, "but whether it is as necessary in the world, I'm within two fingers' breadth of doubting. For to tell the truth, the soldier who carries out his captain's orders does no less than the captain who gives the command. I mean that holy men, in all peace and tranquillity, pray to Heaven for the welfare of the world, but we soldiers and knights carry out what they ask for, and we defend it with the strength of our arms and edge of our swords, not under shelter but under the open sky, exposed as target to the intolerable beams of the sun in summer and to the piercing frosts of winter. Thus are we ministers of God upon earth, and the arms by which His justice is executed here. And whereas the affairs of war and all things concerning it cannot be put into operation without sweating and toiling and moiling, it follows that men whose profession

is war have undoubtedly a more arduous office than those
who in tranquil peace and quiet are praying God to help the
weak. I do not mean to say nor even think that the state of a
knight-errant is as good as a cloistered monk's; I only wish to
infer from my own sufferings that it is certainly a more painful and more cudgeled one, more hungry and more thirsty,
more miserable, ragged, and lousy, for there is no doubt that
knights-errant of old suffered many hardships in the course
of their lives. And if some rose to be emperors by the valor
of their arms, they paid dearly for it in their blood and sweat;
and if those who did rise to such heights had been without
the assistance of enchanters or sages, they would have been
defrauded of their desires and cheated of their hopes."

"I agree with you," replied the traveler, "but there is one
thing among many others that seems to me very wrong in
knights-errant. It is that when they are about to embark on a
great adventure in which there is manifest danger of losing
their lives, never at the instant of attack do they remember
to commend their souls to God, as every Christian in such
danger is obliged to do. Instead they commend themselves
to their mistresses with as much fervor and devotion as if
they were their god, a practice that seems to me to smack
somewhat of heathenism."

"Sir," replied Don Quixote, "this cannot be otherwise,
and ill would fare the knight who acted differently, for in knight-
errantry it is customary that the knight who embarks on any
great feat of arms should have his lady before him and turn
his eyes softly and amorously upon her, as if thereby he
were begging her favor and protection in the hazardous enterprise he is undertaking. And even if no one hears him, he
is bound to mutter certain words between his teeth, commending himself to her with all his heart; of this practice we
have innumerable examples in the histories. And we should
not infer from this that they omit to commend themselves
to God, for they have time and opportunity to do so in the
course of their task."

"Nevertheless," answered the traveler, "one point still
troubles me, and it is that I have often read of two knights
starting off by bandying words. Then little by little their
anger kindles; they wheel their horses around, take up a good
piece of the field, and without more ado, charge one another
at full speed, commending themselves only to their ladies in
the midst of the charge. And the usual ending of their meet-

ing is that one of them tumbles over his horse's crupper, speared right through by his opponent's lance. As to the other, it also happens that if he did not hold on to his horse's mane, he could not help crashing to the ground. I don't see how the dead man could have had the time to commend himself to God in the course of such a rapid action. It would have been better if the words spent on commending himself to his lady during the charge had been reserved for his duties and obligations as a Christian. Moreover, I believe that not all the knights-errant have ladies to whom they commend themselves, for they are not all in love."

"That is impossible," answered Don Quixote. "I say that it is impossible that there could be any knight-errant without a lady, because it is as proper and natural for them to be in love as for the sky to have stars. I can warrant that there has never been a knight-errant without amours in any history ever written, for the mere fact of being without them would prove that he was not a legitimate knight but a bastard who has entered the stronghold of chivalry not through the gate, but over the fence, like a thief and a robber."

"Nevertheless," said the traveler, "if I remember correctly, I have read that Sir Galaor, brother of the famous Amadis of Gaul, never had a particular mistress to whom he could commend himself, and yet was not the less esteemed and was a very valiant and famous knight."

"Sir, one swallow does not make a summer," replied Don Quixote. "Besides, I know that that Sir Galaor was secretly very much in love. Indeed his habit of paying court to all the damsels who attracted him was a natural inclination that he was unable to keep in check. Finally, it is very well established that he had only one whom he had made sovereign of his heart and to whom he used to commend himself very often and secretly, for he prided himself on being a very secretive knight."

"Then, if it is essential that every knight-errant should be in love," said the traveler, "I may then fairly assume that your worship is so, since you are of that profession. And if your worship does not pride himself on being as secretive as Sir Galaor, I beg of you with all earnestness on behalf of all this company and of myself to inform us of the name, the country, the quality, and the beauty of your lady, for she would consider herself happy to have all the world know that she is beloved and served by such a knight as your worship seems to be."

Here Don Quixote breathed a deep sigh and said: "I am unable to affirm whether my sweet enemy is pleased or not to have the whole world know that I serve her. I can only say, in answer to your courteous question, that her name is Dulcinea; her country El Toboso, a village in La Mancha; her quality at least that of a princess, since she is my queen and mistress; her beauty superhuman, for in her are realized all the impossible and chimerical attributes of beauty that poets assign to their ladies; that her hair is gold; her forehead the Elysian fields; her eyebrows rainbows; her eyes suns; her cheeks roses; her lips corals; pearls her teeth; alabaster her neck; marble her bosom; ivory her hands; and her complexion snow; and those parts that modesty has veiled from human sight are such, I think and trust, that discretion can praise them, but make no comparison."

"Her lineage, race, and family we should like to know," said Vivaldo.

To which Don Quixote answered: "She is not of the ancient Roman Curtii, Caii, or Scipios; nor of the modern Colonnas and Orsinis; nor of the Moncadas and the Requesenes of Catalonia; nor yet of the Rebellas and Villanovas of Valencia; of the Palafoxes, Nuzas, Rocabertis, Corellas, Lunas, Alagones, Urreas, Fozes, and Gurreas of Aragón; of the Cerdas, Manriques, Mendozas, and Guzmans of Castile; of the Alencastres, Pallas, and Meneses of Portugal; but of El Toboso of La Mancha, a lineage that though modern may yet give noble birth to the most illustrious families of future ages. Let no one contradict me in this except under the conditions that Cervino put beneath the trophy of Roland's arms:

> *Let none these arms remove*
> *But he who dares Orlando's prowess prove."*

"Although my line is the Cachopines of Laredo," replied the traveler, "I shall not presume to compare it with that of El Toboso of La Mancha, though to tell the truth, such a surname has never reached my ears till now."

"How, not reached you!" cried Don Quixote.

All the rest listened with close attention to the two as they conversed, and even the goatherds and shepherds observed that Don Quixote was completely out of his wits. Sancho Panza alone took all his master said for Gospel truth, knowing who he was and having been acquainted with him from his birth. And if he were to doubt anything, it was all that about Dulcinea of El Toboso, for no such name or such princess had ever reached his ears, although he lived near El Toboso. As they went along conversing, they saw coming down through a gap between two high mountains about twenty shepherds, all dressed in black skins and crowned with garlands, which, as they found out later, were some of yew and some of cypress. Six of them were carrying a bier covered with many sorts of flowers and boughs, and one of the goatherds at this sight exclaimed: "Those yonder are bearing the body of Chrysostom, and the foot of that mountain is the place where he directed them to bury him."

They hastened on and reached the spot just when the others had set the bier on the ground, and four of them with pickaxes were digging a grave next to a hard rock. They greeted one another courteously and then Don Quixote and his companions went to look at the bier, on which they saw a dead body, clothed like a shepherd and evidently about thirty years old, covered with flowers; and dead though he was, they could see that in life he had been a handsome youth of gallant bearing. Around him on the bier were some books and many papers, open and sealed.

And all those present, onlookers, gravediggers and the rest, kept so strangely silent that one could have heard a pin drop, until one of those who had borne the dead man said to his neighbor: "Look carefully, Ambrosio, and see if this is the spot of which Chrysostom spoke, since you wish that all the directions he left in his will be carried out to the letter."

"This is the place," answered Ambrosio, "for here my unlucky friend often told me the tale of his misfortune. Here it was, he told me, that he saw for the first time that mortal enemy of the human race; here it was too that he first declared to her his passion, which was as honorable as it was ardent; here also it was that Marcela for the last time scorned and rejected him, so that he put an end to the tragedy of his wretched life; and here in remembrance of so much misfortune he wished to be consigned to eternal oblivion."

Then turning to Don Quixote and the travelers, he continued: "This body, sirs, which you gaze upon with eyes of pity, was the dwelling place of a soul in which Heaven had

lodged an infinite share of its riches. This is the body of
Chrysostom, who was a man unique in talent, singular in
courtesy, unmatched in kindness, a phoenix in friendship,
generous beyond measure, grave without haughtiness, gay
without vulgarity, and in short, the first in all the art of
goodness, and second to none in all the ways of misfortune. He loved, and was hated; he worshiped, and was
scorned; he wooed a savage; he strove to soften marble; he
pursued the wind; he cried to the wilderness; he served ingratitude; and his only reward was to become death's prey in
the midst of life's course, for he was led to his doom by a
shepherdess whom he strove to immortalize in the memory of
men, as those papers you are gazing at could prove if he had
not commanded me to commit them to the flames, as we are
committing his body to the earth."

"Then you would deal with them more harshly and more
cruelly than their owner himself," said Vivaldo. "It is neither
just nor proper to carry out a man's bequests when his orders
stray from all reason; nor would it have been right in Augustus Caesar himself if he had consented to put into operation what the divine Mantuan ordered in his will.[1] Therefore, Ambrosio, although you entrust your friend's body to
the earth, you should not give his writings to oblivion. For
if he gave such an order as one aggrieved, you should not
be so lacking in wisdom as to comply, but rather, by giving
life to these papers, to keep Marcela's cruelty alive forever
to serve as an example to mankind in days to come so that
they may shun and avoid such pitfalls. For I already know,
and so do all who have come here, the history of your love-
stricken and ill-fated friend; and we know of your friendship and the occasion of his death and the wishes he made in
his last hours. This lamentable story may enable all to judge
the magnitude of Marcela's cruelty, of Chrysostom's love,
and of your sincerity as friend; and from it too all may learn
the fate of those who gallop with loose rein down the path
that reckless love opens before their eyes. Last night we
heard of Chrysostom's death and that he was to be buried
in this place, and so out of curiosity and compassion we
turned out of our direct road and agreed to come and see

[1] When he was dying, Virgil ordered his friends to burn his
Aeneid because he had not finished polishing it. His friends, however, following the dictates of Augustus, refused to carry out the
wishes of the poet.

with our own eyes what had aroused our pity when we heard of it. Now, in return for our compassion and our spontaneous longing to find, if it were possible, a remedy, we beseech you, wise Ambrosio—at least I do, for my part—that instead of burning these papers you will let me take some of them away."

Then, without waiting for the shepherd's answer, he stretched out his hand and took some of those that were nearest him. Seeing this, Ambrosio said: "Out of courtesy, sir, I will consent to your keeping what you have taken, but it would be vain to think that I shall not consume the rest."

Vivaldo, who longed to see what the papers contained, opened one of them at once and saw that its title was "A Song of Despair." Upon learning this, Ambrosio said: "That is the last piece the unlucky man wrote, and to show, sir, to what a pass his misfortunes brought him, read it aloud, for you will have time enough for that while they are digging the grave."

"That I will do most gladly," said Vivaldo; and as all the bystanders were equally curious, they gathered around him in a circle, and he read in a clear voice the poem that follows.

CHAPTER XIV

Containing the despairing verses of the dead shepherd, with other unexpected happenings

THE SONG OF CHRYSOSTOM

Since thou wouldst have me publish, cruel maid,
Thy harsh resolve and unrelenting rigor
From man to man and nation unto nation,
I'll beg grim hell my grieving soul to aid,
Lending my voice such a tone of lamentation
That my own natural voice shall be transformed.

And lest my chanting lack the note of vigor,
It shall by hell's infernal voice be warmed,
And all thy murd'rous deeds and my sad dole
I'll mingle with the blood of my racked soul,
And force all lovers' ears to hear my toll.
So hearken, and that flinty heart of thine
To discordant sounds and fiendish howls incline,
That well up from the depths, and gushing free,
Bring to my pains ease, but despite to thee.

The lion's roar and the blood-curdling howls
Of ravenous wolf, the fearsome sibilant hiss
Of scaly serpent, and malignant ghoul's
Demoniac laughter, and the ominous croak
Of lonely raven, the obstreperous rage
Of storm-tossed sea, the pitiless rampage
Of the new-conquered bull, the mournful coo
Of widowed turtledove, the envious owl's
Monotonous hooting, and the mighty yell
Of the entire black company of hell:
Let all uniting with my tortured soul
Make the whole welkin ring with such a dole,
As to strike terror in men and confuse,
For these ferocious pangs that I am feeling
Oblige me drastic untried modes to use.

The mournful echoes of this grim confusion
On Father Tagus' sands shall not resound,
Nor the famed olive groves of Bétis reach:
Here my woes I shall scatter with profusion,
And with my tongue dead living words I'll preach,
'Midst lofty crags and caverns in the ground,
Or in some hidden vale, or distant strand
Untrodden by the feet of human kind,
Or where the sun has never shown his beam,
Or where with venomous brood the Nile doth teem.
For though the echoes indistinctly sound,
My wrong and thy matchless malignity,
Amidst this lonely and deserted land,
By favor of my niggard destiny,
Shall wing their way to the wide world around.
Disdain's a killer, and, whether false or sound,
Suspicion patience chokes; but a jealous eye
Will smite a deadlier blow; long absence life

Deranges; nor against Oblivion
Are we guarded by firm hopes of renown,
For Death inevitable is the close.
Yet I live on, who suffered all these woes—
O miracle unheard of—I'm alive,
Jealous, disdained, absent, and well assured
Of all doubts which I've patiently endured;
Sunk in oblivion I my fire revive.
But amidst my torments never do my eyes
Catch glimpses of the shadowy hope I prize,
Nor, since I despair, do I hope allow,
But rather to accentuate my throes,
To live without her for all time I vow.

I wonder can I feel both fear and hope
At the same instant, or is't well to do so,
When there is far more cause for me to fear?
Have I the power, when bitter jealousy
Obstructs my gaze, to close my eyes, when I
Am forced to see it through the thousand scars
That bleed in my heart? Who would not ope wide
The gates and let despair come charging in,
When he sees Disdain naked and unashamed,
And all suspicions endorsed as the truth—
O cursed conversion—limpid truth herself
Transformed into a cheat: To thee I cry,
Tyrant of love's realm, savage Jealousy,
In mercy clap thy manacles on me;
Thou, Disdain, tie my hands with twisted rope.
Woe's me, victorious thou dost remain,
My sufferings thy memory have slain.

At last I die, and since I lost all hope
Of more luck in death than in life I have,
I shall keep loyal to my fantasy;
I'll say that he who loves most wins success,
And that the freest heart is still Love's slave,
Beholden to her ancient tyranny.
I'll swear that she, my constant enemy,
As fair a soul as body doth possess,
That her unkindness is what I deserve,
For only by the ills he sends upon us
Can Love his empire in just peace preserve,
So in this fancy, lacking grace and hope,
My wretched term to which I am consigned

By her slights I'll shorten with this tough rope,
Bequeathing my corpse and soul to the wind
Without a wreath, a palm, or prayer to find.

Thou whose unreasoning scorn was the cause
That spurred me on to violence against
My youth, and to quit this life I now loathe,
Since by notorious signs thou art aware
How deep the wounds that now consume my soul,
And how cheerfully I have faced thy scorn;
If, haply, one day thou discoverest
That I'm so worthy of thy sympathy
As to dim the blue heaven of thy eyes,
When of my death thou hearest, shed no tears,
For I refuse to let thee win the prize
Of my stricken soul, but rather gaily laugh,
Proclaiming that my death did make thee glad.
Yet, why am I so foolish as to teach
Thee, knowing that thy greatest glory lies
In hastening so quickly my sad end?

Come Tantalus from hell's profound abyss,
Come, for it is high time; come Sisyphus
Loaded with his oppressive stone; let Tityus
Bring his grim vulture that doth never sleep,
Nor Ixion delay with his resolving wheel,
Nor the three doomed sisters ever toiling:
And let then all transfer their mortal pain
To me at once; and in a doleful strain
(If funeral rites I have the right to claim)
Chant obsequies o'er a corpse that lacks a shroud.
And let hell's grim three-headed porter come,
And a thousand monsters and chimeras swell
In counterpoint the descant of despair.
No graver or more solemn pomp is due
To any devoted lover on his bier.
Song of despair, I beseech thee, do not grieve
Now that my tortured heart thou art to leave,
But rather since the cause whence thou didst spring
Grows still more fortunate by my sad end,
E'en in the tomb thou must shun sorrowing.

Chrysostom's song pleased those who heard it, though
Vivaldo said that it did not seem to him to agree with what
he had heard of Marcela's modesty and goodness, for

Chrysostom complained in it of jealousy, suspicions, and neglect, all to the detriment of Marcela's good name and reputation. But Ambrosio, as one who knew his friend's most intimate thoughts, replied: "To satisfy your doubts, sir, I must tell you that when the unfortunate man wrote this song, he was absent from Marcela, from whom he had voluntarily withdrawn to see if absence would have its usual effect upon him. And as there is nothing that does not vex the absent lover and no fear that does not haunt him, so Chrysostom was tormented by imaginary jealousies and suspicions as frightening as if they were real. So Marcela's goodness, therefore, is as genuine as fame proclaims it, and but for cruelty, a little haughtiness, and much scorn, envy itself cannot justly find fault in her."

"Such is the truth," replied Vivaldo. He was about to read another of the papers that he had rescued from the fire when he was interrupted by a miraculous vision (for so it seemed to be) that suddenly appeared before their eyes. On the top of the rock in which they were digging the grave there appeared the shepherdess Marcela looking even more beautiful than she had been described. Those who until then had never seen her gazed at her silently in wonder, and even those who were accustomed to see her were no less amazed. But no sooner did Ambrosio catch sight of her than he cried out indignantly: "Have you, by chance, come here, O fierce basilisk of these mountains, to see if the wounds of this wretch whom your cruelty has slain will bleed afresh at the sight of you? Or have you come to gloat in triumph over your ruthless work? Or to look down from that height like another pitiless Nero upon the blaze of burning Rome? Or in your arrogance to trample on this luckless corpse as did Tarquin's ungrateful daughter her father's?[1] Tell us quickly why you are here, or what you most desire, for as I know that Chrysostom during his life was unfailingly obedient to you, I'll see to it, though he be dead, that all who called themselves his friends shall obey you."

"I have not come here, O Ambrosio," replied Marcela, "for any reason you have mentioned, but rather in my own defense and to prove to all how wrong they are to blame

[1] According to Hartzenbusch, the allusion here is to Servius Tullius, not Tarquin the Proud, the last king of Rome.

me for the death of Chrysostom. So I entreat every one of
you who is present to listen to me, for it will not take me
much time or many words to convince all sensible men of
the truth. Heaven, you say, has made me so beautiful that
without your being able to help it, my beauty compels you
to fall in love with me, and in return for the love you show
me, you say, and even claim, that I should be obliged to
love you. Through the natural instinct with which God has
endowed me I know that everything beautiful is lovable; but
I do not understand why, merely because she arouses love,
a woman who is loved for her beauty is bound to love the
man who loves her. Besides, it may happen that the man
who loves the beautiful may be ugly; and ugliness being
loathsome, it would be ridiculous for him to say: 'I love you
because you are beautiful; you must love me though I am
ugly.' But even suppose that the beauty is equal on both sides,
the inclinations need not necessarily be the same, for not all
beauties arouse love, and some who charm the eye do not
win the heart. If every beauty inspired love and won hearts,
men's fancy would become vague and bewildered and not
know where to stop, for as beauty is infinite, desire must likewise be infinite. Also I have heard it said that true love cannot be divided, but must be free and uninhibited. If this is
so, as I believe it to be, why do you ask me to surrender my
will under pressure for no other reason than that you say you
love me? But suppose Heaven had made me ugly instead of
fair, should I then have the right to complain that you did not
love me? Moreover, you must consider that I did not choose
to be beautiful. My beauty, such as it is, was given by
Heaven to me as a favor, without my asking or choosing it;
and just as the viper deserves no blame for the poison nature
gave her, though she kills with it, so I cannot be blamed for
being beautiful. For beauty in a modest woman is like distant
fire or a sharp sword; the one does not burn, the other does
not cut, the man who does not go near it. Honor and
modesty are ornaments of the soul without which the body,
beautiful though it be, should not be so esteemed. Now, if
modesty is one of the virtues and the fairest ornament of the
body and soul, why must the woman who is loved for her
beauty lose it to gratify the desires of a man who, for his
pleasure alone, tries with all his strength and ingenuity to rob
her of it? I was born free, and to live free I chose the
solitude of the fields. The trees of those mountains are my

companions; the clear waters of these brooks are my mirrors; with the trees and the brooks I share my thoughts and my beauty. I am the hidden fire and the distant sword. Those whom my looks have captivated, my words have undeceived. If desires are fed on hopes, as I gave none to Chrysostom or any other, it can justly be said that it was his own stubbornness, not my cruelty, that killed him. And if it is charged that his intentions were honest and that therefore I was bound to respond to them, my reply is that when on that very spot where now you are digging his grave he declared to me the goodness of his purpose, I told him that mine was to live in perpetual solitude and that the earth alone should taste the fruit of my chastity and the spoils of my beauty. If, in spite of all this discouragement, he chose to defy hope and to sail against the wind, why wonder that he is drowned in the gulf of his infatuation? If I had encouraged his hopes, I should have been false; if I had gratified him, I should have acted against my better feelings and resolutions. He persisted, though undeceived; though not hated, he despaired. Judge then whether it is right that I should pay the penalty for his afflictions! If I have deceived anyone, let him complain; if I have broken my pledge to anyone, let him despair; if I encourage anyone, let him presume; if I should give in to anyone, let him boast of it. But let me not be called cruel or murderous by those whom I have never promised, deceived, enticed, or encouraged. Heaven until now has not willed that I love by destiny, and it is vain to think that I shall love by choice. May this general warning serve for the particular benefit of everyone who woos me, and henceforth let it be understood that if anyone dies on my account, he dies not out of jealousy or from rejection, for she who loves no man cannot make any man jealous, and discouragement must not be taken for disdain. If anyone calls me a wild beast and a basilisk, let him forget me as a mischievous and evil being; if he calls me ungrateful, let him give up serving me; if strange, let him not know me; if cruel, let him cease following me; for this wild beast, this basilisk, this ungrateful, strange, and cruel being, will not seek, serve, know, or follow them in any way. If Chrysostom's infatuation and headstrong passion killed him, why should my modesty and reserve be blamed? If I preserve my purity in the company of the trees, why should he want me to lose it in the company of men? I, as you know, have wealth of my own and do not covet that of others. I am free and have no taste for subjection; I neither love nor hate any man. I do not deceive this one nor court that one; I do not trifle with one nor keep another on tenterhooks. I find my recreation in the modest company of the shepherdesses of these villages and the care of my goats. My desires are bounded by these mountains, and if they soar beyond them, it is to contemplate the beauty of the sky, steps by which the soul journeys to its first abode."

When she had stopped speaking, she turned around without waiting for a reply and plunged into the thickest part of the nearby woods, leaving all as much impressed by her good sense as by her beauty. And some (those wounded by the powerful shafts from the radiance of her lovely eyes) made as though they would follow her, not profiting from the frank warning they had heard, but Don Quixote, now believing that here was an opportunity for putting in operation his chivalrous theories of succoring damsels in distress, put his hand on the hilt of his sword and exclaimed in clear, resounding tones: "Let no man, of whatever race or condition he be, dare to follow the beauteous Marcela, on pain of incurring the full fury of my indignation. She has shown by clear and ample arguments that she has had little or no blame in the death of Chrysostom and that she is far from yielding to the advances of any lover. Therefore, it is right and proper that instead of being followed and persecuted, she should be honored and esteemed by all good men in the world, for she has demonstrated that she is the only woman living with such pure intentions."

Whether it was because of Don Quixote's threats or because Ambrosio entreated them to conclude the debt they owed to his friend, not one of the shepherds stirred or moved from the place until the grave had been dug, Chrysostom's papers burned, and his body buried in it, not without many tears from the bystanders. They closed the sepulcher with a heavy stone until such time as a slab could be prepared, which, as Ambrosio said, would be inscribed with the following epitaph:

Here the frozen body lies
Of a simple shepherd swain.
Luckless he died of disdain,

Hounded to death by cruel rigor
Of a beautiful, scornful maid;
A victim by whom Love's empire
Widens its tyranny.

Then they strewed flowers and branches upon the grave, and after consoling their friend Ambrosio, bade him farewell. Vivaldo and his companions did the same, and Don Quixote took leave of his hosts and the travelers, who pressed him to accompany them to Seville, which was the very place for finding adventures, since in every street and behind every corner there, they were to be met with more than elsewhere. Don Quixote thanked them for their advice and their evident intention to do him a favor, but said that for the present he could not go, nor ought to go, to Seville until he had cleared all those mountains of thieves and robbers of which, according to reports, they were full. The travelers, perceiving his good intentions, did not try to press him further, but once more bidding him farewell, left him and pursued their journey, in the course of which they did not fail to discuss the story of Marcela and Chrysostom, as well as the follies of Don Quixote. He, on his part, resolved to go in search of the shepherdess Marcela and offer her all the service in his power. But it turned out otherwise than he expected, as will be told in the course of this true history, of which the second part ends here.

CHAPTER XV

In which is related the unfortunate adventure that overtook Don Quixote on his encounter with some heartless Yanguesans

The sage Cide Hamete Benengeli relates that as soon as Don Quixote had taken leave of his hosts and of all those who had been present at the shepherd Chrysostom's burial, he and his squire rode into the same wood that they had seen the shepherdess Marcela enter. And when they had wandered through it for more than two hours, looking for her in vain, they halted in a meadow, rich in fresh grass, near which ran a delightful and refreshing stream that invited and even compelled them to stop and spend there the sultry hours of the siesta, which were already becoming oppressive. Don Quixote and Sancho dismounted, and leaving Rozinante and the ass loose to crop the grass that was there in plenty, they ransacked the saddlebags, and without any ceremony, master and servant ate the contents in peace and good fellowship.

Sancho had neglected to hobble Rozinante, for he knew that he was so gentle and little wanton that all the mares in the stud at Córdoba could not provoke him to any indecorous act. But fate or the Devil, who is not always asleep, so ordained that a troop of Galician mares, belonging to some carriers from Yanguas, happened to be grazing in the same valley. It is the custom of those carriers to take their siestas with their team in spots where grass and water abound, and where Don Quixote happened to be was very well suited to their purpose. Now it happened that Rozinante was smitten with the desire to solace himself with their ladyships the mares, and as soon as he got their scent, he changed his natural accustomed pace into a brisk little trot, and without taking leave of his master, he went off to pay his respects to them. But they, as it seemed, were more eager to feed than to respond to his advances, and received him with their hooves and their teeth in such a manner that in a moment his girths were broken and he became naked, minus his saddles. But the worst of all was that the carriers, perceiving the violence he was offering to their mares, rushed over with staves and so belabored him that they knocked him flat on the ground in a wretched plight.

Then Don Quixote and Sancho, who had seen the drubbing of Rozinante, rushed up puffing and blowing, and Don Quixote said to Sancho: "From what I see, friend Sancho, those are not knights but base scum of a vile race. I say it, because you may help me to take due revenge for the outrage that has been done to Rozinante before our eyes."

"What the devil kind of revenge are we to take," answered Sancho, "when they are more than twenty and we no more than two, perhaps no more than one and a half?"

"I am equal to a hundred," replied Don Quixote, and without another word he clapped hand to his sword and flew at the Yanguesans. Sancho Panza, excited by the example of his master, did likewise. With his first blow Don Quixote slashed a leather jerkin one of the carriers wore and wounded him grievously in the shoulder. The Yanguesans, seeing themselves so rudely handled by two men only when they were so many, seized their staves, and hemming in the two of them, began to lay on with great fury. In fact, the second thwack brought Sancho to the ground, and the same fate befell Don Quixote. His dexterity and courage availed him nothing, and as fate would have it, he fell at the feet of Rozinante, who had not yet been able to rise. From this we may learn how unmercifully staves can batter and bruise when they are wielded by wrathful rustics. Seeing the mischief they had done, the Yanguesans loaded their beasts as speedily as they could and continued their journey, leaving the two adventurers in evil plight and worse humor.

The first to come to his senses was Sancho Panza, who, finding himself close to his master, said in a feeble, plaintive voice: "Master! Master!"

"What is it, brother Sancho?" answered Don Quixote in the same feeble and doleful tone.

"I wish, if it were possible, that you would give me a

couple of sups of that balsam of Vile Blas,[1] if you have it ready to hand; perhaps it will be as good for broken bones as for wounds."

"If I only had it here, woe is me, we should want nothing; but I swear to you, Sancho, on my word as a knight-errant, that before two days pass, unless fortune forbids, I will have it in my possession, or my hands will have lost their cunning."

"In how many days, sir," said Sancho, "do you think we shall be able to move our feet?"

"For my part," said the drubbed knight, Don Quixote, "I cannot say exactly, but I take on myself the blame for all, for I should not have drawn my sword against men who are not knights as I am. Therefore, I believe the god of battles has allowed this chastisement to fall upon me as a punishment for having transgressed the laws of chivalry. Wherefore, brother Sancho, take heed of what I tell you, for it mightily concerns the welfare of us both; and it is this: When you see such rascally rabble do us harm, do not wait for me to draw my sword upon them, for I will not do it on any account, but put your hand to your sword and chastise them at your own pleasure; and if knights come to their assistance, I shall know how to defend you and attack them with all my power, for you have already perceived by a thousand signs and actions how far the strength of my invincible arm extends." So arrogant had the poor gentleman become since his victory over the valiant Biscayan.

But Sancho Panza did not much relish his master's advice and he replied: "Sir, I am a peaceable, sober, quiet man and can let pass any injury whatsoever, for I have a wife and children to maintain and bring up. Therefore, let your worship be advised (since it cannot be a command) that I will on no account clap hand to my sword either against peasant or knight. And from this time on, I pardon, in the name of God, whatever insults have been or shall be offered against me, whether by high or low, rich or poor, noble or commoner, without any exception whatsoever."

His master, hearing these words, answered: "Would that I had enough breath to be able to talk easily, and the pain I feel in this rib were less, that I might make you understand, Sancho, the mistake you are making. If the wind of fortune, up to now so unfavorable, should change in our favor and

---

[1] Sancho says Feoblas (*feo* Blas—ugly Blas) for Fierabrás.

swell the sails of our desires so that we should safely and surely reach our haven in one of those islands I have promised you, what would become of you if after conquering it I were to make you its lord? You would ruin all by not being a knight, nor wishing to be one, and by having neither valor nor will to avenge your injuries or defend your lands. For you must know that in newly conquered kingdoms and provinces the natives are never totally subdued, nor do they so favor their new lord that he must not fear an attack, for they are always inclined to try their luck, as they say, and change the state of affairs. Therefore the new lord should have knowledge enough to govern and courage to defend himself."

"In this trouble that has fallen on us," answered Sancho, "I wish, master, I were furnished with the brain and courage you talk of; but I swear on the faith of a poor man that I'm more fit for plasters than palaver. Try, sir, and see if you can rise. We'll help Rozinante, though he doesn't deserve it, for he was the chief cause of all this mauling. I'd never have believed the like of Rozinante—why, I thought he was as chaste and peaceful a fellow as I am myself. Well, it must be a true saying that it takes a long time to get to know people, and that there's nothing certain in this life. Who would ever have said that after those mighty slashings you gave that wretched knight-errant, this great hurricane of thwacks would have followed up so fast and clattered upon our shoulders?"

"Yours, indeed, Sancho," replied Don Quixote, "must have been made for such squalls, but mine, which were nursed in fine linen and cambric, naturally are more sensitive to the pain of this misadventure. If I did not imagine—why do I say imagine?—if I did not know for certainty that all these discomforts are the accompaniments of the profession of arms, I should be ready to die this moment of pure vexation."

To this the squire answered: "Sir, if these mishaps are what a body reaps from knight-errantry, would you mind telling me whether they occur very frequently or only at set times? For I'm thinking that after a couple of such crops we'd be little or no use for a third unless God in His infinite mercy doesn't give us a hand."

"You must know, friend Sancho," answered Don Quixote, "that the life of a knight-errant is subject to a thousand perils and mischances, yet equally they may possibly become kings and emperors, as experience has shown of various knights with whose histories I am thoroughly acquinted. And I could tell you now, if my pain would let me, of some who by their might of arms alone have climbed to the high degrees I have mentioned, though those same knights found themselves, both before and after, in various calamities and misfortunes. For the valorous Amadis of Gaul once fell into the power of his mortal enemy, Arcalaus, the enchanter, who, it is well attested, when he held the knight prisoner, tied him to a pillar in a courtyard and gave him over two hundred lashes with the reins of his horse. There is also an anonymous author of no small credit who says that the Knight of the Sun was caught in a certain castle though a trapdoor that gave way beneath his feet, and found himself after his fall bound hand and foot in a deep cavern underground. There they administered to him what is called an enema of snow water and sand, which nearly finished him off; and if a certain sage, a great friend of his, had not rescued him in that sore extremity, things would have gone very hard with the poor fellow. So among such goodly company I may well pass, for they endured greater affronts than we are suffering now. For I would have you remember, Sancho, that wounds inflicted with instruments that are by chance in the hand do not disgrace a man, and this is expressly laid down in the law of the duel: if a cobbler strike another with the last he holds in his hand, though it is of wood, it shall not therefore be said that the man who is struck has been cudgeled. I say this in case you might think that because we have been sorely mauled in this encounter we remain disgraced, for the arms these men carried and with which they pounded us were no other than their staves and not one of them, so far as I can remember, carried rapier, sword, or dagger."

"I hadn't a chance," replied Sancho, "to look at them closely, for I'd no sooner laid hand on my blade than they made so many crosses on my shoulders with their sticks that they knocked the sight out of my eyes and the strength from my feet, and laid me in the gutter where I'm lying now. It doesn't bother me in the least to deliberate whether the beating was disgraceful or not, but the blows, which will remain as deeply impressed in my memory as they are on my back, really hurt."

"For all that, brother Panza," answered Don Quixote, "let

me tell you that there is no remembrance that time does not efface, nor pain that death does not end."

"But what greater misfortune can there be," replied Sancho Panza, "than one that waits for time to efface it and death to end it? If this mishap of ours were one of those that could be cured with a couple of poultices, it wouldn't be so bad, but I'm beginning to see that all the plasters in a hospital wouldn't be sufficient to give it a turn for the better."

"No more of this, Sancho," answered Don Quixote. "Make the best of a bargain; that is what I mean to do. Let us see how Rozinante is, for I think the poor beast got by no means the smallest share of our misfortune."

"There is no need to wonder at that," said Sancho, "since he too is a knight-errant. What does amaze me, though, is that my Dapple has got off scot-free while it has cost us a few ribs."[2]

"Fortune always leaves one door open in disasters in order to give them relief," said Don Quixote. "I say this because this little beast will now make up for the loss of Rozinante, and carry me from here to some castle where my wounds may be cured. Furthermore, I shall not consider myself disgraced by such a mount, for I remember having read how good old Silenus, tutor and guide of the merry god of laughter, when he entered the city of the hundred gates,[3] rode comfortably on a very fine ass."

"He very likely went mounted as your worship says," answered Sancho, "but there's quite a difference between riding astride and being slung across like a sack of garbage."

"Wounds received in battle," replied Don Quixote, "rather confer honor than take it away. So, friend Panza, give me no more back talk, but do as I have told you. Mount as best you can and set me on top of your ass however you please, and let us leave here before night comes and overtakes us in this wilderness."

"Yet I've heard your worship say," said Panza, "that it is quite the thing for knights-errant to sleep in wilds and

[2] There is a play on words: *sin costas* (without court costs) and *sin costillas* (without ribs).

[3] Clemencín notes that Cervantes here confuses Thebes of Boeotia, the fatherland of Bacchus, with Thebes of Egypt, which had the hundred gates.

deserts most of the year and that they think themselves lucky to do so."

"That is when it cannot be helped," replied Don Quixote, "or when they are in love. Indeed I have known of knights who stayed on a rock exposed to sun and shade and all the rigors of heaven for two years without their ladies knowing of it. Such a knight was Amadis, who took the name Beltenebros and dwelt on the Bare Rock for eight years, or eight months, for I am not very sure of the reckoning. At any rate, there he stayed doing penance for some displeasure Lady Oriana had caused him. But let us drop the matter and hurry, Sancho, before another disaster like Rozinante's befalls the ass."

"That would be the devil and no mistake," said Sancho. And delivering himself of thirty groans, sixty sighs, and a hundred and twenty damns and curses on whoever had brought him there, he hoisted himself up, but paused halfway, bent like a Turkish bow, unable to straighten himself. Yet in spite of his aches, he managed to harness the ass, who had taken advantages of the day's excess of liberty. He then lifted up Rozinante, who, had he possessed a tongue to complain with, would certainly not have been surpassed by squire or master. Finally, Sancho arranged Don Quixote on the ass, and tying Rozinante to his tail, led the ass by the halter, proceeding as best he could toward where he thought the highway lay.

He had hardly gone more than a couple of miles when Fortune, who was guiding their affairs from good to better, directed him to the road, whereon he spied an inn, which to his grief and Don Quixote's joy must needs be a castle. Sancho argued that it was an inn, and his master that it was no inn, but a castle. The controversy lasted so long that they had time to arrive there without finishing it, and Sancho entered, without further investigation, followed by his team.

CHAPTER XVI

Of what befell our imaginative gentleman in the inn he supposed to be a castle

The innkeeper, seeing Don Quixote slung over the ass, asked Sancho what ailed him. Sancho answered that it was nothing, only that his master had fallen from a rock and had bruised his ribs somewhat. The innkeeper's wife, unlike those that are usually engaged in that trade, was by nature kind-hearted and would grieve at the misfortune of her neighbors, so she immediately began to minister to Don Quixote. She made her young daughter, a very good-looking lass, help her to heal her guest. There was also serving in the inn an Asturian wench, broad cheeked, flat pated, snub nosed, asquint of one eye and not very sound of the other. It is true that the comeliness of her body made amends for other defects. She was not seven hands high from her feet to her head, and her shoulders, which burdened her somewhat, made her look down at the ground more than she would have wished. This bonny maid assisted the daughter of the house to prepare for Don Quixote a makeshift bed in a loft that had in days gone by served for straw. Here, too, lodged a carrier, whose bed was a little distance away from that of our knight, and although it was only made up of the pack-saddles and covering of his mules, was much better than that of Don Quixote, which consisted only of four rough planks on two uneven benches; a mattress no thicker than a quilt, full of knots that from their hardness might be taken for pebbles had their rents not betrayed that they were made of wool; a pair of sheets like the leather of an old target; as for the coverlet, if anyone wished to count the threads of it, he could not have missed one in the reckoning.

In this wretched bed Don Quixote lay down, and then the landlady, with the help of her daughter, plastered him from top to toe, while Maritornes (for so the Asturian wench was called) held the candle for them. The landlady, as she was plastering Don Quixote, noticed how black and blue he was in places and said that the bruises seemed to be more the result of blows than of a fall.

"They weren't blows," said Sancho, "but the rock had many sharp ends and knobs on it, every one of which left behind a bruise." He also added: "Please, lady, leave over some of those pieces of tow, for somebody will be sure to need them; and as for myself, I tell you my back, too, is hurting me a bit."

"In that case," answered the landlady, "you too must have fallen."

"I didn't fall," said Sancho Panza, "but with the sudden fright I took on seeing my master fall, my body aches as if they had given me a thousand thwacks."

"That might well happen," said the landlady's daughter. "I myself have often dreamed that I was falling from some high tower without ever coming to the ground; and when I did awake, I have found myself as bruised and shaken as if I had really fallen."

"That's the point, lady," answered Sancho Panza. "I didn't dream at all, and I was more awake than I am this minute, yet I find myself with no fewer bruises than my master, Don Quixote."

"What's this gentleman's name?" asked Maritornes, the Asturian.

"Don Quixote of La Mancha," answered Sancho Panza; "he's a knight-errant and one of the finest and strongest that the world has seen these many years."

"What is a knight-errant?" asked the wench.

"Are you so green in the world that you don't know?" answered Sancho Panza. "Know then, sister, that a knight-errant is something that, in two words, is cudgeled and an emperor. Today he is the most wretched and most needful creature in the world, but tomorrow he will have two or three crowns of kingdoms to give to his squire."

"How is it then," said the landlady, "that you haven't an earldom at least, seeing that you're the squire of this good gentleman?"

"It's early yet," answered Sancho, "for it's only about a month since we have been gallivanting in search of adventures. Up to the present we haven't bumped into any adventure worth the naming, but perhaps we look for one thing and light on another. But, believe me, if my master, Don Quixote, recovers from this wound or fall and I be not crippled by it, I wouldn't barter my hopes for the best title in Spain."

Then, Don Quixote, who had been listening attentively to this conversation, sat up in his bed as best he could, and taking the landlady by the hand, said: "Believe me, beautiful lady, you may call yourself fortunate in having harbored my person in your castle. For I am such a person that if I say little about myself, it is because men hold that self-praise debases a man; but my squire will tell you who I am. Let me just say that I shall forever keep engraved in my memory the service you have done me, and I shall be grateful to you as long as I live. Would to high heaven that love had not enthralled me and subjected me to its laws and to the eyes of the beautiful ingrate whose name I whisper to myself, else would the eyes of this beauteous damsel here bereave me of my freedom."

The landlady, her daughter, and the good Maritornes stood bewildered by the words of the knight-errant, which they understood as well as if he had spoken in Greek, although they realized that they were compliments and offers of service. Not being accustomed to such language, they gazed at him wonderingly and thought he must be a far different kind of man from those now in fashion. And so, thanking him in their rough pothouse phrases for his offers, they left. The Asturian Maritornes ministered to Sancho, for he needed her care no less than his master.

Now, the carrier and she had agreed to spend the night together, and she had given him her word that as soon as the people in the inn were all quiet and her master and mistress were asleep, she would come to him and satisfy his desires as much as he pleased. And it is said of this good-natured wench that she never gave her word without keeping it, even though she had given it in the woods without any witness, for she prided herself of being of gentle birth and thought it no disgrace to be in service at an inn. In fact, she would maintain that misfortunes and unhappy accidents had brought her to that state.

Don Quixote's hard, narrow, niggardly, and rickety bed stood first in order in the middle of the dilapidated, starlit loft, and next to it Sancho had placed his own, consisting only of a rush mat and a coverlet that seemed to be rather of napless linen than wool. Beyond those two beds was that of the carrier, made, as we have said, of the packsaddles and the trappings of his two best mules, though he owned twelve. Sleek, fat, and goodly beasts they were, for he was one of the rich carriers of Arévalo, according to the author of this history, who makes special mention of him because he knew him very well, and it is even hinted that he was some relation of his.[1] Be that as it may, Cide Hamete Benengeli was a very careful historian and exact in details, as can be seen by his not omitting these various points, petty and trivial though they were. This may be taken as an example by those grave historians who give us such brief and inadequate accounts of events that we hardly get a taste of them, and out of carelessness, malice, or ignorance, leave in their inkhorns the most substantial part of their work. A thousand blessings on the author of *Tablante de Ricamonte*[2] and on the writer of that other book that relates the deeds of Count Tomillas—with what minute details do they describe everything!

Now, this carrier, after he had visited his mules and given them their second feed, laid himself down on his packsaddles and waited patiently for the coming of his most punctual Maritornes. Sancho was already plastered and in bed, but though he tried to sleep, he could not do so owing to the pain in his ribs. Don Quixote for the same reason had both his eyes wide open like a hare. All the inn was sunk in silence, and there was no other light but that of a lantern that hung in the middle of the gateway.

[1] Cervantes here seems to suggest that the muleteer was himself a Moor, one of those who outwardly had been converted to Christianity. Before the total expulsion of the Moriscos in 1609 they were much employed as carriers and muleteers in Andalusia and La Mancha. According to Pellicer, Spain lost by the expulsion of the Moors four or five thousand carriers who transported merchandise from Seville to Madrid.

[2] *The Chronicle of the Noble Knights Tablante de Ricamonte and Jofre, Son of Count Donason,* by an anonymous author, published at Toledo in 1531. Count Tomillas is a secondary character of *The History of Henry Son of Oliva, King of Jerusalem, Emperor of Canstantinople,* Seville, 1498.

This wonderful stillness and our knight's thoughts, which unceasingly reverted to the adventures described at every step in the books, the authors of his misfortune, brought to his imagination one of the strangest follies that can be conceived. He fancied that he was now in a famous castle (for, as we have said, all the inns where he lodged seemed to him to be castles) and that the landlord's daughter (daughter of the lord of the castle), captivated by his gallant presence, had fallen in love with him and had promised to lie with him that night for a good space of time without her parents being any the wiser. Then taking as Gospel truth all this fancy that he had created, he began to feel anxious as he reflected on the perils that his honor would suffer, but he resolved in his heart not to be guilty of the least infidelity to his lady, Dulcinea of El Toboso, even though Queen Guinevere herself with her duenna, Lady Quintañona, should appear before him.

While he lay thinking of these follies, the hour came (that was unlucky for him) when the Asturian wench, faithful to her promise, entered the room. Clad in her shift, barefoot, with her hair trussed up in a fustian net, she stole in with soft and wary steps, feeling her way toward her carrier. But scarcely had she reached the door when Don Quixote heard her, and sitting up in his bed, despite plasters and pain, stretched his arms to receive his fair damsel; but the Asturian, crouching and holding her breath, kept groping her way in search of her lover. Suddenly, she encountered Don Quixote's arms, who seized her first tightly by one of her wrists and then, pulling her toward him (not a word did she dare to utter), made her sit down on the bed. Then he felt her shift, and though it was of sackcloth, he thought it was made of the finest and most delicate lawn. She wore on her wrists bracelets of glass beads, but he fancied they were precious pearls from the Orient; her hair, which was almost as coarse as a horse's mane, he took to be threads of the most glittering gold of Arabia, whose brightness obscured that of the sun; her breath, reeking of last night's stale meat salad, seemed to him to shed a sweet and aromatic fragrance: in short, he transformed her in his fantasy into the likeness of that princess of whom he had read in his books, who came thus adorned to see the grievously wounded knight, being overcome with love for him. And such was the infatuation of the poor gentleman that neither touch,

nor breath, nor other idiosyncrasies of the good damsel undeceived him, though they would have made anyone else,
except a carrier, vomit. He thought he held in his arms the
goddess of beauty herself, and clasping her fast, he began
to court her in a low, tender voice, saying: "I wish, fair
and noble lady, I were in a state to repay so great a boon
as thou hast given to me by disclosing thy beauty; but
Fortune (never weary of persecuting the virtuous) has seen
fit to lay me in this bed, where I lie so bruised and battered
that, even though I were ready to satisfy my wish, it would
be impossible for me to do so, for there is still a more
invincible obstacle, namely, the faith I have plighted to the
peerless Dulcinea of El Toboso, sole mistress of my hidden
thoughts. Had this obstacle not intervened, I should not be
so doltish a knight as to let slip the happy opportunity thy
great bounty has bestowed upon me."

Maritornes all this while sweated in mortal fear at finding
herself locked in Don Quixote's arms, and without attending
or even hearing what he said, wriggled silently to free herself.

The carrier, whose lustful desires had kept him awake,
as soon as he heard his moll enter through the door, listened attentively to all that Don Quixote said. Full of
jealous suspicions lest the Asturian wench might play him
false, he crept toward Don Quixote's bed and stood still,
waiting to see the outcome of the knight's discourse, which
he could not fathom. When he saw the wench struggling to
get free and Don Quixote trying to detain her, he no longer
relished the jest. So, he raised his fist and discharged such
a terrific blow on the lantern jaws of the enamored knight
that he bathed his whole mouth in blood, and not content
with this, he mounted upon his ribs, and using his feet like a
trotting horse, paced up and down from one end to the
other. The bed was unsteady and its foundations were not
the strongest; so, being unable to endure the additional
load of the carrier, it collapsed to the ground with such a
crash that it woke up the innkeeper. He at once suspected
that it was one of Maritornes' nightly skirmishes, seeing
that she did not answer when he called her. Nursing this
suspicion, he rose, and lighting a lamp, went toward the
place where he had heard the scuffle. The wench, seeing
her master coming and knowing that he had a ferocious
temper, was scared out of her wits and rushed for safety

to the bed of Sancho, who was now asleep, where she rolled herself up like a ball.

The innkeeper came in, shouting: "Where are you, whore? I'll swear these are your doings."

Just then Sancho awoke, and feeling such a bulk on top of him, he fancied he had had a nightmare and began to lay about him on all sides with his fists. Not a few of those blows descended upon Maritornes, and at last, stung by sheer pain, she cast aside all decorum and paid him back with such stiff interest that she soon roused him from sleep. And he, finding himself pummeled in that manner by one whom he could not see, raised himself up as best he could, caught hold of Maritornes, and the two of them began the most obstinate and droll skirmish in the world. The carrier, perceiving by the light of the innkeeper's lamp the dismal condition of his lady, left Don Quixote and ran to her assistance. The landlord did likewise but with different intention, for his was to chastise the wench, thinking that she was certainly the sole cause of all this harmony. And so, just as the proverb says: "The cat began to bite the rat, the rat began to gnaw the rope, the rope began to bind the stick," so the carrier drubbed Sancho, Sancho Maritornes, Maritornes Sancho, and the innkeeper Maritornes. All of them minced it with such expedition that they gave themselves no rest. And the best of all was that the innkeeper's lamp went out, and as they were in the dark, they flogged one another so unmercifully that wherever a blow fell it left its bruise.

There happened to be lodging that night at the inn one of the officers of the Holy Brotherhood of Toledo. No sooner did he hear the strange noise of the conflict than he seized his short rod of office and the tin box containing his warrants and groped his way in the dark into the room, calling out: "Stop in the name of justice; stop in the name of the Holy Brotherhood!"

The first object he encountered was the battered Don Quixote, who lay senseless, face up, on his demolished bed. Catching hold of his beard as he groped about, he kept crying out incessantly: "I order you to assist the cause of justice", but seeing that the person whom he held fast moved neither hand nor foot, he concluded that he was dead and that the people there were his murderers. Suspecting this, he raised his voice and shouted: "Shut the inn door and let nobody escape; they've killed a man here."

These words startled the whole company, and each combatant stopped the fight at the exact point at which the shout had caught him. The innkeeper retired to his chamber; the carrier to his packsaddles; the wench to her straw bedding; and only the luckless Don Quixote and Sancho were unable to move from where they lay.

The officer let go Don Quixote's beards, and wishing to search for the criminals and arrest them, he went out to get a light; but he could not find any, for the innkeeper had purposely extinguished the lantern when he retired to his chamber. And so, the officer was forced to go the fireplace, where after much time and trouble he managed to light another lamp.

CHAPTER XVII

In which are continued the countless troubles that befell Don Quixote and his squire in the inn that, to his sorrow, the former took for a castle

By this time Don Quixote had come out of his trance, and in the same sad tone in which the day before he had called to his squire when he lay stretched in the valley of the pack staves, he again called to him, saying: "Sancho, my friend, are you asleep? Are you asleep, friend Sancho?"

"How can I sleep, blast it?" said Sancho, groaning and grumbling. "I swear all the devils in hell have been after me this night."

"You may certainly think so," answered Don Quixote, "for either I know nothing or this castle is enchanted. For you must know— But you must swear to keep what I am going to tell you secret until after my death."

"Yes, I swear," answered Sancho.

"I ask you to swear," said Don Quixote, "because I refuse to take away the good name of anyone."

"I tell you I'll swear," said Sancho again, "and I'll keep my mouth shut until after your death, and please God I may be able to let it out tomorrow."

"Have I done you such injury, Sancho," asked Don Quixote, "that you should wish to see me dead so soon?"

"It isn't for that," answered Sancho, "but because I am all against holding things for long. I don't want them to rot in my keeping."

"Whatever the reason," said Don Quixote, "I put still greater trust in your love and courtesy. I must tell you that last night I had a most extraordinary adventure. Briefly it was as follows: A little while ago I was visited by the daughter of the lord of this castle, who is the most talented and beautiful damsel to be found over a great part of the earth. What could I not tell you of the charm of her person? What of her sprightly intelligence? What of those other hidden things I shall let pass untouched and unspoken, to keep the faith I owe to my lady, Dulcinea of El Toboso? Only this I shall tell you, that whether because Heaven was envious of the great bliss that luck had put into my hands, or perhaps (and this is more probable) because, as I have said, this castle is enchanted, just as we were in most sweet and amorous conversation, an invisible hand, joined to the arm of some monstrous giant, gave me such a buffet on the jaws that my mouth was bathed in blood, and not content with that, so bethumped me that I am now in a worse state than yesterday, when, owing to the indiscretions of Rozinante, the carriers did us the outrage you know about. Wherefore I conjecture that the treasure of this damsel's beauty is kept by some enchanted Moor and she is not reserved for me."

"Nor for me either," said Sancho, "for more than four hundred Moors have so whacked me that the drubbing with the staves was nought but tarts and fancy cakes in comparison. But, sir, tell me something. Would you call this a good and rare adventure, seeing that we're left in such a pickle? It wasn't quite so bad for you, sir, for you hugged in your arms that incomparable beauty; but what did I get except the ruddiest drubbing I'll ever have in all my mortal life? Curses on myself and on the mother who bore me! I'm no knight-errant and I never mean to be one; yet in all our mishaps the lion's share of trouble always falls to me."

"So you have been beaten, too?" said Don Quixote.

"Plague on my race, haven't I told you I was?" said Sancho.

"Do not grieve, my friend," said Don Quixote. "I will presently make the precious balsam that will cure us in the twinkling of an eye."

At this moment the officer of the Holy Brotherhood, having lit his lamp, entered to examine the person he imagined to have been murdered. And as soon as Sancho saw him approach in his shirt, with a nightcap on his head, a candle in his hand, and an ugly expression on his face, he asked his master: "Is this by chance that Moorish enchanter who's out to punish us again in case something was left over?"

"He cannot be the Moor," answered Don Quixote, "for enchanters never let themselves be seen by anyone."

"If they don't let themselves be seen, they let themselves be felt," said Sancho. "If not, let my shoulders bear witness."

"Mine might also," answered Don Quixote, "but that is not sufficient evidence to make me believe that this man whom we see is the Moorish wizard."

The officer when he found them chatting so calmly together paused in amazement. Yet it is true that Don Quixote still lay flat on his back unable to stir from bruises and plasters. The officer then approached them and said roughly: "Well, how goes it, my good fellow?"

"I would speak more respectfully were I such as you are," answered Don Quixote. "Is it the custom in this country, blockhead, to address knights-errant in such a way?"

The officer, finding himself thus badly treated by one of so sorry an aspect, flew into a rage, and lifting up his lamp with all its oil, he hit Don Quixote on the head, leaving him badly bruised. Then, as all was dark again, he retired.

"Surely, sir," said Sancho Panza, "this is the wizard Moor; he must be keeping the treasures for others, and for us nought but blows and lamp smacks."

"It is ever so," answered Don Quixote, "and we must not take any notice of these devices of enchantment, nor must we be angry or vexed with them, for as they are invisible and fantastical, we shall not find anyone on whom to take vengeance. Rise, Sancho, if you can, and call the warden of this fortress and try to get him to give me a little wine, oil, salt, and rosemary to prepare the healing balsam of which I have desperate need at this moment, for I am losing much blood from the wound that the phantom gave me."

Sancho arose, not without aching bones, and crept in the dark to where the innkeeper was. On the way he met the officer, who was waiting to hear what had become of his enemy, and said to him: "Sir, whoever you are, do us the favor of giving us a little rosemary, oil, salt, and wine; we're in sore need of some to cure one of the finest knights-errant in the wide world. He is lying in a bed over there sorely wounded by a Moorish wizard who is in the inn."

When the officer heard this, he took Sancho Panza for a man out of his wits, but as the day was now beginning to dawn, he opened the gate of the inn and called the landlord, telling him what the fellow wanted. The landlord provided what was needed, and Sancho carried it back to Don Quixote. The latter was lying with his hands on his head, groaning with pain from the blows with the lamp, which, however, had only raised two fairly big bumps; what he had supposed to be blood was only the sweat running down his face as a result of his agony in his recent adventure.

Don Quixote took the ingredients, mixed them all together into a compound, and then boiled them a good while until, as he thought, they had reached the exact temperature.

He then asked for a vial to hold the mixture, but as there was not one in the inn, he resolved to put it into a tin cruse or oil pot that the landlord gave him as a present. He, furthermore, recited over the cruse more than eighty paternosters and as many Ave Marias, salves, and credos, accompanying every word with a cross by way of blessing. These ceremonies were witnessed by Sancho, the landlord, and the officer. As for the carrier, he had gone off peaceably to the business of looking after his mules.

No sooner had Don Quixote made the mixture than he resolved to test on himself the power of his precious balsam (for so he really thought it to be), and so he swallowed a good quantity of what remained in the pot after the cruse had been filled. No sooner had he drunk the potion than he began to vomit so violently that his stomach was emptied of every particle of food. Owing to his retchings and rumblings, he fell into a plentiful sweat, and so he ordered them to cover him up well and leave him alone. They did so, and he remained asleep for more than three hours. When he awoke and found himself so much relieved in body and

so much the better of his bruises, he took himself to be
cured and believed he had really compounded the balsam
of Fierabrás. With that remedy in his possession he would
be able henceforth to encounter without fear all brawls, battles, and quarrels, no matter how perilous they might be.

Sancho Panza, likewise, considered his master's cure a
miracle and begged him for leave to swallow what remained
in the pot, which was no small quantity. Don Quixote consented; so he took the pot in both hands, and with good
faith and better will, he tossed down very little less than
his master had done. It happened, however, that poor
Sancho's stomach was not so delicate as his master's, so before he could vomit, he was racked by so many bouts of
writhing, retching, and kicking, with such cold sweats and
swoonings, that he truly thought his last hour had come,
and in his agony he cursed the balsam and the rogue who
had given it to him. Don Quixote, seeing him in that pitiful
state, said: "I am sure, Sancho, that all this trouble has befallen you because you haven't been dubbed a knight, for
I am sure that this liquor can only do good to those who
are professed."

"If you knew that, sir," replied Sancho, "may God blast me
and all mine if I can understand why you let me drink it!"

By this time the beverage began to work to some purpose, and the poor squire discharged so swiftly and copiously at both ends that neither the rush mat on which he had
thrown himself nor the blanket with which he covered
himself were of the slightest use to him. He sweated and
sweated in such a paroxysm of strains and stresses that not
only himself but all present thought he was on the verge of
death. This dreadful hurricane lasted nearly two hours, at
the end of which he found himself not cured like his master, but so shaken and shattered that he could hardly stand.

Don Quixote, as has been said, found himself relieved and
cured, and was eager to set off at once in quest of adventures. He thought that every moment he delayed there
meant depriving the world and those in need of his favors
and services. His confidence, too, was strengthened by his
implicit faith in his balsam. So, full of this determination,
he himself saddled Rozinante, put the packsaddle on his
squire's beast, and helped Sancho to dress and mount his
ass. Then, getting on horseback, he rode over to the corner

of the inn and seized a pike that stood there to serve him as a lance. All the people that were staying in the inn, over twenty in number, stood staring at him. The innkeeper's daughter was also staring at him, and Don Quixote kept gazing at her fixedly, and from time to time he breathed forth so doleful a sigh that it seemed he had plucked it from the bottom of his heart. All, however, or at least those who had seen him plastered the night before, thought that the sighs must have been caused by the pain in his ribs.

When both were mounted and at the door of the inn, he called to the innkeeper and said in a grave and solemn tone: "Many and mighty are the favors, sir governor, I have received in this castle of yours and I shall remain deeply grateful for them all the days of my life. If I can repay you by avenging some affront you may have suffered from some proud miscreant, remember that my sole function is to help the weak, to revenge the wronged, and to punish traitors. Ransack your memory, and if you find anything of this sort for me to do, you have but to utter it and I promise you by the order of knighthood that I have received to procure satisfaction to your heart's content."

The innkeeper replied with equal gravity: "Sir knight, I have no need that you should avenge any wrong, for I know how to take what revenge I think fit when one is done to me. I only want you to pay me the score you have run up this night in the inn, both for the straw and barley of your two beasts and your supper and your beds."

"So this is an inn, then," exclaimed Don Quixote.

"So it is, and a mighty respectable one too," replied the innkeeper.

"All this time I have been deceived," answered Don Quixote, "for I really thought it was a castle, and not a bad one. But since it is indeed an inn and not a castle, all that can be done now is to ask you to excuse any payment, for I cannot break the rule of the order of knights-errant, of whom I know for certain (since I have never read anything to the contrary) that they never paid for lodging or anything else in the inns where they stayed. For the good entertainment that is given them is their fair reward in consequence of the sufferings they endure, seeking adventures both day and night, winter and summer, on foot and on horseback, in thirst and hunger, in heat and cold, exposed to all the inclemencies of heaven and the troubles of earth."

"All that has very little to do with me," answered the innkeeper. "Pay me what you owe me, and forget your fairy stories and chivalries; my only business is to get what I'm owed."

"You are a blockhead and a bad innkeeper," answered Don Quixote; then, clapping spurs to Rozinante and brandishing his lance, he sallied out of the inn without opposition; and without turning to see whether his squire followed him or not, he was soon a good way off.

The innkeeper, seeing him depart without paying, hastened to collect from Sancho Panza, who said that since his master had refused to pay, he would not pay either, for being the squire of a knight-errant as he was, the same rule and reason held good for him as for his master in the matter of not paying anything in taverns and inns.

The innkeeper became very irritated by this and threatened that if he did not pay him, he would get it from him in a way he would not like.

Sancho replied that by the law of chivalry that his master had professed he would not pay a farthing, even if it cost him his life, for he would not be responsible for the loss of the good old tradition of knight-errantry, nor would the squires of the future have cause to rebuke him for breaking so just an enactment.

But poor Sancho's ill luck so ordained that among the crowd there happened to be at the inn at this time four wool combers from Segovia, three needlemakers from the Colt Square in Córdoba, and two natives from the marketplace of Seville—all of them merry fellows, full of mischief and fond of practical joking. As if they were all fired with the same impulse, they came up to Sancho, and pulling him down off his ass, one of them rushed in for the innkeeper's blanket and hurled him into it. But looking up and seeing that the ceiling was somewhat lower than they needed for their job, they resolved to go out into the yard, whose limit was the sky. There they placed Sancho in the middle of the blanket and began to toss him up in the air and make sport with him as they would with a dog at Shrovetide.

The cries of the wretched, blanketed squire were so loud that they reached the ears of his master, who, pausing for an instant to listen, believed that some new adventure was at hand, until he realized that the shrieks came from his squire. Straightaway turning his horse, he rode at a painful gallop to the inn gate, and finding it closed, he rode around the wall to see if he could find anyplace where he might enter. But he scarcely reached the wall of the inn yard (which was not very high) when he saw the wicked sport they were playing with his squire. He saw him go up and down in the air with such grace and agility that if his anger had allowed him, I believe he would have burst out laughing. He tried to climb the wall from his horse, but he was so bruised and broken that he could by no means alight from his saddle; and so, from his horse he began to utter such fearsome curses against those who were tossing Sancho that one could not set them down in writing.

Nevertheless, in spite of his threats, the others did not stop their laughter or their labor, nor did the flying Sancho cease his lamentations mixed now with threats, now with prayers. But all were of no avail, for they carried on their merry game until at last they stopped from sheer fatigue and let him go. They then brought him his ass, and mounting him on it, they wrapped him in his cloak. The kindhearted Maritornes, seeing him so exhausted, thought it best to give him a pitcher of water, which, that it might be cooler, she fetched from the well. Sancho took it, and as he was lifting it to his mouth, he stopped on hearing his master's voice calling to him, saying: "Sancho, my son, drink no water; drink it not, my son, for it will kill you. Behold, here I have the most holy balsam"—he showed him the pot of liquor—"two drops of this will certainly cure you."

At these words, Sancho, giving his master a squint-eyed look, replied in a louder voice: "You must have forgotten that I am no knight, or else perhaps you want me to spew up what remains of my guts after last night's bit of work. Keep your liquor to yourself and in the Devil's name leave me alone."

As he finished saying these words, he began to drink, but at the first gulp, finding it was only water, he would not swallow any more, and he asked Maritornes to bring him some wine, which she did willingly and paid for it with her own money, for indeed it is said of her that although she followed that trade, she had some faint glimmerings in her of a Christian.

As soon as Sancho had finished drinking, he dug his heels into his ass, and as the inn gate was wide open, he rode out, highly pleased at not having paid anything and at getting his own way, even at the expense of his usual creditors, namely, his shoulders. The innkeeper, it is true, kept his saddlebags in payment of what was due to him, but Sancho was so flurried when he departed that he did not miss them.

The innkeeper wanted to bar the door firmly as soon as he saw him out, but the blanketeers would not allow it, being the kind of people who would not have given two farthings for Don Quixote, even if he had been one of the knights-errant of the Round Table.

CHAPTER XVIII

In which an account is given of the conversation that took place between Sancho Panza and his master, Don Quixote, with other adventures worth recording

When Sancho reached his master, he was so exhausted and faint that he could hardly sit on his ass. Don Quixote, seeing him in this state, said to him: "Now I do believe, my dear Sancho, that yonder castle or inn is without doubt enchanted, for those who so cruelly made sport with you, what else could they be but specters and beings from another world? I am sure of this because, when I was by the wall of the inn yard watching the acts of your sad tragedy, I was unable to climb on it, nor was I able to alight from Rozinante; so, I must have been enchanted. For I swear to you on my honor that if I could have mounted or alighted, I would have avenged you in such a manner that those bragging rascals would remember the jest forever, even though to do it I should have had to disobey the rules of chivalry. For, as I have often told you, they do not allow a knight to take up arms against one who is not one, unless in defense of his own life and in cases of urgent and extreme necessity."

"I, too, would have avenged myself if I could have,

whether I was dubbed a knight or not," replied Sancho, "but I could not. And yet I believe that those who amused themselves with me were no phantoms or enchanted beings, but men of flesh and bone as we are, for one was called Pedro Martínez, and another Tenorio Hernández, and the innkeeper's name, I heard, is Juan Palomeque, the Left-handed. So, sir, your not being able to jump over the wall of the yard nor get off your horse did not depend on enchantment but on something else. In fact, what I can gather clearly from all this is that those adventures that we are after will bring us in the end so many misadventures that we won't know our right foot from our left. The best and wisest thing for us to do, in my humble opinion, is to go back to our village, now that it's reaping time, and look after our own affairs, and not go wandering from pillar to post and going from Ceca to Mecca, as the saying goes." [1]

"How little you know of knighthood, Sancho!" answered Don Quixote. "Be quiet and have patience, for a day will come when you will see with your own eyes how fine a thing it is to follow this profession. Now tell me: what greater contentment can the world offer, or what pleasure can equal that of winning a battle and triumphing over one's enemy? Undoubtedly, none."

"It must be so," answered Sancho, "but I don't know. I only know that since we have been knights-errant, anyhow since you have been one (no need to count me among so honorable a band), we have never won a battle, except that with a Biscayan, and even then you came out minus half an ear and half a helmet. Since then, it has been nothing but cudgels and more cudgels, blows and more blows; then, as an extra, I get tossed in a blanket, and it was done by enchanters, from whom I can't take revenge, so I'll be damned if I know what is that pleasure of triumphing over an enemy that you talk of."

"That is my trouble and it should be yours also, Sancho," answered Don Quixote. "But henceforth I shall try to provide myself with a sword made with such art that no kind of enchantment can touch him that wears it. Perhaps Fortune may bring me a sword like that of Amadis, when he

---

[1] Ceca was the name of the great mosque of Córdoba, which was looked upon as nearly equal in sanctity to Mecca. *Andar de ceca en meca* (to go from Ceca to Mecca) is still said of gad-abouts.

called himself Knight of the Burning Sword, which was one of the best weapons ever worn by a knight, for it not only cut like a razor, but there was no armor, however strong or enchanted, that could withstand it."

"It will be like my luck," said Sancho, "that even when you find such a sword, it will, like the balsam, only serve those who are knights, while poor squires will still cram themselves with troubles."

"Do not be afraid of that, Sancho," replied Don Quixote. "Heaven will yet deal more liberally with you."

Such was the conversation of master and squire as they rode on when suddenly Don Quixote saw a large, dense cloud of dust rolling toward them. Turning to Sancho, he said: "This is the day, Sancho, on which shall be clearly seen the good that fate has in store for us; this is the day, I say, on which I shall show the might of my arm and on which I intend to do deeds that shall be written in the books of fame for succeeding ages. Do you see that dust cloud, Sancho? Know then that it is churned up by a mighty army composed of sundry and innumerable people who are marching this way."

"If so, there must be two armies," said Sancho, "for here on this side there is as great a cloud of dust."

Don Quixote turned around to look at it, and seeing it was so, he rejoiced, for he fancied that there were indeed two armies coming to fight each other in the midst of that spacious plain. For his imagination at all hours of the day and night was full of battles, enchantments, adventures, follies, loves, and challenges as are related in the books of chivalry, and all his words, thoughts, and actions were turned to such things. As for the clouds of dust he had seen, they were raised by two large flocks of ewes and rams that were being driven along the same road from opposite directions, which, because of the dust, could not be seen until they came near.

So earnest was Don Quixote in calling them armies that Sancho came to believe it and asked: "Well, what are we to do?"

"What?" said Don Quixote. "Why, favor and help the distressed and needy. You must know, Sancho, that the army marching toward us in front is led by the mighty emperor

Alifanfarón, lord of the great island of Trapobana; [2] the other, which is marching at our back, is the army of his foe, the king of the Garamantans, Pentapolín of the Naked Arm, for he always goes into battle with his right arm bare."

"Why do these two gentlemen hate each other so much?" asked Sancho.

"They are enemies," replied Don Quixote, "because Alifanfarón is a furious pagan and is in love with the daughter of Pentapolín, a beautiful, graceful lady and a Christian. Her father refuses to give her to the pagan king unless he abandon first the false religion of Mohammed and turn Christian."

"By my beard," said Sancho, "Pentapolín does right, and I'll help as best I can."

"Then you will do your duty," said Don Quixote, "for it is not necessary to be dubbed a knight to engage in battles such as these."

"I understand," replied Sancho, "but where shall we tie this ass that we may be sure of finding him after the scuffle is over? I think it was never customary to go into battle mounted on such a beast."

"That is true," said Don Quixote. "What you must do is to leave the ass to his own devices. Let him take his chance whether he get lost or not, for after winning this battle we shall have so many horses that even Rozinante runs the risk of being exchanged for another. Now listen to me carefully while I give you an account of the principal knights in the two approaching armies. Let us withdraw to that hillock over there to get a better view of the two armies."

They did so, and standing on the top of the hill, they could have discerned the two flocks that Don Quixote had converted into armies had their eyes not been blinded by the clouds of dust. But seeing in his imagination what did not exist, he began to say in a loud voice: "The knight you see yonder with the yellow armor, who bears on his shield a crowned lion couchant at a damsel's feet, is the valiant Laurcalco, lord of the Silver Bridge. The other with armor flowered with gold, who bears on his shield three crowns argent on an azure field, is the fearsome Micocolembo,

[2] Cervantes in most of these high-sounding names gave free reins to his skill at inventing fantastic names. Trapobana is Taprobana, the ancient name given to the island of Ceylon. "The utmost isle Taprobane."

grand duke of Quirotia. The other, with gigantic limbs, who
marches on his right, is the undaunted Brandabarbarán of
Boliche, lord of the Three Arabias. He is wearing a serpent's
skin and bears a gate as a shield, which, fame says, was one
of those belonging to the temple that Samson pulled down
when by his death he took revenge on his enemies. Now
turn your eyes to this other side, and there you will see, in
front of this other army, the victorious and never vanquished Timonel of Carcajona, prince of New Biscay, who
comes clad in armor quartered azure, vert, argent, and or.
He bears on his shield a cat or on a field gules with a
scroll inscribed *Miau,* which is the beginning of his mistress'
name—according to report—the peerless Miaulina, daughter
of Alfeñiquén, duke of Algarbe. The other, who weighs
down and oppresses the back of that powerful and spirited
charger, with armor as white as snow and a white shield
without a device, is a novice knight of the French nation
called Pierre Papin, lord of the baronies of Utrique. The
other pricking with iron heel the flanks of that nimble zebra
and carrying for arms the azure cups is the doughty duke of
Nerbia, Espartafilardo of the Wood, who bears on his shield
the device of an asparagus plant, with a motto in Castilian
which says: *My fortune trails.*"

So he went on, naming many imaginary knights in each
squadron as his fancy dictated and giving extemporaneously to
each his armor, colors, devices, and mottoes, for he was completely carried away by his strangely deluded imagination.
He continued without a pause: "That squadron in the front
is composed of men of various nations: Here are they who
drink of the sweet waters of the famous Xanthus; moun-
taineers who tread the Massilian fields; those who sift the
pure and fine gold of Arabia; dwellers on the celebrated
cool shores of clear Thermodon; those who drain in various
ways the golden Pactolus; the Numidians, unreliable in their
promises; Persians, famous for their bows and arrows;
Parthians; Medes, who fight as they flee; Arabs, with their
movable houses; Scythians as cruel as they are fair; Ethio-
pians with pierced lips; and countless other nations, whose
faces I recognize and behold, although their names I do not
recollect. In that other squadron come drinkers of the crystal
waters of the olive-bearing Betis; men who burnish and polish their faces with the liquor of the ever-rich and golden
Tagus; men who enjoy the health-giving waters of the divine

Genil; dwellers in the Tartessian plain with their abundant
pastures; men who enjoy the Elysian fields of Jérez; men
of La Mancha rich and crowned with golden corn; men clad
in iron, survivors of the ancient Gothic race; bathers in the
Pisuerga, famous for its mild current; men who graze their
flock on the broad pastures of the winding Guadiana, famous for its hidden current; men who shiver with the cold
of the wooded Pyrenees and among the white snows of the
lofty Apennines; as many as all Europe contains and en-
closes."

By God! How many provinces did he name! How many
nations did he enumerate, giving to each, with wonderful
speed, its peculiar attributes, so absorbed and wrapped up
was he in all that he had read in his lying books! Sancho
Panza hung on his words without uttering one. Now and then
he turned his head to see whether he could perceive the
knights and giants his master named. Seeing none, he said
at last: "Master, I'll commend to the Devil any man, giant, or
knight of all those you mentioned who is actually here. At
least I do not see them. Perhaps all may be enchantment
like last night's specters."

"Why do you say that?" said Don Quixote. "Do you not
hear the neighing of the horses, the blaring of the trumpets,
and the rattle of the drums?"

"I hear nothing," answered Sancho, "but the bleating of
sheep and lambs." And so it was, for now the two flocks
were close at hand.

"The fear you are in," said Don Quixote, "allows you
neither to see nor to hear correctly, for one of the effects
of fear is to disturb the senses and make things seem different from what they are. If you are so afraid, stand to
one side and leave me alone, for I alone am sufficient to
give the victory to the side that I shall assist." With these
words he clapped spurs to Rozinante, and with lance couched,
rode down the hillside like a thunderbolt.

Sancho shouted at him: "Come back, master, come back!
I swear to God that those you are going to charge are only
sheep and lambs. Come back! Woe to the father who begat
me! What madness is this? Look! There is neither giant,
nor knight, nor cats, nor arms, nor shield quartered or entire, nor azures true or bedeviled. Sinner that I am, what are
you doing?"

Don Quixote, however, did not turn back, but charged on,

shouting as he went: "Ho! You knights who fight under the banners of the valiant emperor Pentapolín of the Naked Arm! Follow me, all of you, and you will see how easily I will take vengeance for him on his enemy, Alifanfarón of Trapobana."

With these words he dashed into the midst of the flock of sheep and began to spear them with as much courage and fury as if he were fighting his mortal enemies. The shepherds and herdsmen who came with the flock shouted to him to stop, but seeing that words were of no avail, they unloosed their slings and began to salute his ears with stones as big as one's fist. Don Quixote took no notice of their stones but galloped to and fro, crying out: "Where are you proud Alifanfarón? Where are you? Come to me, for I am but one knight and wish to try my strength with you, man to man, and take away your life for the wrong you do to the valiant Pentapolín." At that instant a smooth pebble hit him in the side and buried two ribs in his entrails. Finding himself in such a bad way, he thought for certain that he was killed or sorely wounded, and remembering his balsam, he took out his cruse and raised it to his mouth to drink. But before he could swallow what he wanted, another pebble struck him full on the hand, broke the cruse to pieces, carried away with it three or four teeth and grinders out of his mouth, and badly crushed two fingers of his hand. And such was the force of those two blows that the poor knight fell off his horse onto the ground. The shepherds ran up to him, and believing that they had killed him, they collected their flocks in great haste, carried away their dead sheep, which were more than seven, and departed without further inquiry.

All this time Sancho stood on the hillock watching his master's mad escapade and tearing his beard and cursing the unlucky hour and moment when he first met him. But seeing him lying on the ground and the shepherds out of sight, he came down the hill, went up to his master, and found him in a very bad way, although not quite unconscious. So he said to him: "Did I not tell you, sir, to come back, for those you went to attack were not armies, but flocks of sheep?"

"That rascal of an enchanter, my enemy, can counterfeit and make men vanish. Know, Sancho, that it is a very easy matter for such men to make us see what they please, and this malignant persecutor of mine, envious of the glory that

I was to reap in this battle, has changed the squadrons of enemy into flocks of sheep. Now, for my sake, Sancho, do one thing to undeceive yourself and see the truth of what I am telling you. Get up on your ass and follow them softly, and you will see that when they have gone a little distance away, they will return to their original shapes, and ceasing to be sheep, will become grown-up, mature men as when I described them to you at first. But do not go now, for I need your assistance. Come and see how many of my teeth are missing, for I do not think I have a single one left in my mouth."

Sancho went so close that he almost thrust his eyes into his mouth, and it was precisely at the fatal moment when the balsam that had been fretting in Don Quixote's stomach came up to the surface; and with the same violence that a bullet is fired out of a gun, all that he had in his stomach discharged itself upon the beard of the compassionate squire.

"Holy Mary!" cried Sancho. "What has happened to me? The poor sinner must be at death's door, for he's puking blood at the mouth." But reflecting a little, he was soon convinced by the color, smell, and taste that it was not blood, but the balsam that he had seen him drink; and so great was the loathing he felt that his own stomach turned, and he emptied its full cargo upon his master, and both were in a precious pickle. Sancho rushed to his ass to take something out of his saddlebags to clean himself and his master, and when he did not find them, he was on the verge of losing his mind. He cursed himself again and vowed in his heart to leave his master and return to his home, although he would lose his wages for service and his hopes of becoming governor of the promised island.

Don Quixote had now risen, and keeping his left hand to his mouth lest the rest of his teeth fall out, with the other he took hold of Rozinante's bridle (who had not stirred from his master's side, such was his well-bred loyalty) and went over to his squire, who stood leaning against his ass with his cheek upon his hand, looking like the picture of a man lost in thought.

The knight, seeing him in that mood and so full of melancholy, said to him: "Learn, Sancho, that one man is not more than another unless he achieves more than another. All those storms that fall upon us are signs that soon the weather will be fair and that things will go smoothly, for it is not possible for evil or good to last forever. Hence we may infer that as our misfortunes have lasted so long, good fortunes must be near. So, you must not vex yourself about my mischances, for you have no share in them."

"How not?" replied Sancho. "I suppose him they tossed in a blanket yesterday was not my father's son? And the saddlebags that are missing today with all my chattels is someone else's misfortune?"

"What, are the saddlebags missing, Sancho?" asked Don Quixote.

"Yes, they are missing," answered Sancho.

"In that case, we have nothing to eat today," said Don Quixote.

"Very true," said Sancho, "if these fields are barren of the herbs that your worship says he knows all about and with which unfortunate knights-errant like yourself generally supply their wants."

"Nevertheless," answered Don Quixote, "at the present moment I would rather have a quarter-loaf of bread or a cottage loaf and a couple of heads of salted pilchards than all the herbs that Dioscorides describes, though his book be illustrated by Doctor Laguna.[8] But, good Sancho, get up on your ass and follow me, for God, who provides for all, will not desert us, especially being engaged, as we are, in His service. He does not abandon the gnats of the air, nor the worms of the earth, nor the tadpoles of the water, and He is so merciful that He maketh His sun shine on the good and the evil and He causeth the rain to fall upon the just and the unjust."

"Your worship," said Sancho, "were fitter to be a preacher than a knight-errant."

"Knights-errant, Sancho," said Don Quixote, "knew, and ought to know, somewhat of all things, for there have been knights-errant in past ages who were as ready to make a sermon or a speech on the king's highway as though they had taken their degrees at the University of Paris; whence

[8] Andrés de Laguna (1499–1560), author of *Pedazio Dioscorides Anazarbeo*, was physician to Pope Julius III and Charles V and Professor at the University of Alcalá de Henares. His translation of Dioscorides was published at Antwerp in 1555 and dedicated to Philip II. His annotations doubled the size of the original work. See M. Bataillon: *Erasme et L'Espagne* (Paris, 1937) for the influence of Dr. Laguna on the Erasmian movement in Spain.

it may be inferred that the lance never blunted the pen, nor the pen the lance."

"Well, may it turn out as you say," answered Sancho. "But let us be gone and endeavor to get a lodging tonight; and I pray to God we may find a place where there are no blankets, blanketeers, specters, or enchanted Moors; and if there are, may the Devil keep the lot of them."

"Ask that of God, my son," said Don Quixote, "and lead me where you please, for on this occasion I will leave the choice of lodging to you. But give me your hand and feel with your finger how many teeth and grinders I have lost on this right side of my upper jaw, for there I feel the pain."

Sancho put in his finger, and feeling about, asked: "How many grinders did your worship have before on this side?"

"Four," answered Don Quixote, "besides the wisdom tooth, all of them whole and sound."

"Mind well, master, what you say," answered Sancho.

"I say four, if not five," said Don Quixote, "for in all my life I have never had a tooth or grinder pulled from my mouth, nor has any fallen out or been destroyed by decay."

"Well then, on this lower side," said Sancho, "you have only two grinders and a half, but on the upper, not even half a one, for it is as smooth as the palm of my hand."

"Woe is me," cried Don Quixote, hearing these sad tidings from his squire. "I would rather they lopped off an arm, provided it were not my sword arm; for you must know, Sancho, that a mouth without grinders is like a mill without grindstone, and a tooth is far more to be prized than a diamond. But all this must be suffered by those who profess the stern order of chivalry. Mount, friend, and lead the way, for I will follow you at what pace you please."

Sancho did so and proceeded to where he thought it possible they might find a lodging without leaving the highway, which was the most direct way. As they slowly continued their journey, Sancho, seeing that the pain in Don Quixote's jaws gave him no rest, tried to entertain him and divert his mind by anecdotes. And some of the things he said will be told in the next chapter.

CHAPTER XIX

Of the sensible conversation between Sancho Panza and his master, and of the adventure with a corpse, with other famous happenings

"In my opinion, master, all those mischances that have befallen us lately have been a punishment for the sin committed by your worship against the rule of your knighthood by not keeping the vow you made not to eat bread off a tablecloth, nor lie with the queen, and all the rest of the things you swore to keep until you got that helmet of Malandrino, or whatever they call the Moor, for I don't remember."

"You are quite right, Sancho," said Don Quixote, "but to tell you the truth, it had passed my memory. And you can also be sure that you had your blanketing because you did not warn me in time; but I shall make amends, for in the order of chivalry there are ways of settling everything."

"Did I then swear anything?" asked Sancho.

"It does not matter that you did not swear," said Don Quixote. "It is enough that I consider you not very clear of complicity. In any case, there is no harm in providing a remedy."

"If that's so," said Sancho, "be careful, your worship, not to forget this as you did the oath, or perhaps the phantoms may take it into their heads to play their pranks on me again, and even with your worship if they find you so unruly."

While they were chatting thus, darkness overtook them, and they were still on the highway without having found a place where they might rest until morning; and what was more serious, they were dying of hunger, for by losing their saddlebags they were deprived both of larder and journey rations. And to complete their distress, they had an adventure, or something that was uncommonly like one.

The night grew darker but they still plodded dolefully on, for Sancho hoped that, as they were on the king's highway, they would be sure to discover an inn within a couple of leagues or so. All of a sudden the ravenous squire and his hungry master saw coming toward them along the same road a great number of lights resembling a multitude of moving stars. Sancho stood aghast at the sight of them, and Don Quixote himself felt uneasy. The former pulled at the halter of his ass, the latter at the reins of his horse, and both stood peering earnestly in front of them and wondering what it could be. They saw that the lights were advancing toward them and that as they approached nearer and nearer, they became bigger and bigger. At the sight of them Sancho began to tremble like one with quicksilver poisoning, and Don Quixote's hair stood on end. However, recovering somewhat, he said: "Sancho, this doubtless must be a very great and most perilous adventure, where I shall need to show all my might and valor."

"Woe is me!" answered Sancho. "If this turns out, as it seems, to be another adventure of ghosts, where am I to find the ribs to last it out?"

"No matter how many ghosts press on," said Don Quixote, "I will not allow them to touch a thread of your garments; for if they made game of you on the other occasion, it was because I was unable to jump over the wall of the yard, but now we are in open country, where I can parry with my sword at will."

"What will you do if they enchant and benumb you as they did the last time?" said Sancho. "What good will it do us to be in open country then?"

"In spite of all, Sancho," replied Don Quixote, "I beseech you to keep up your courage, for experience will prove to you how great mine is."

"I will, if it please God," answered Sancho.
Both then turned to the side of the road and began to gaze again earnestly at the moving lights, wondering what they could mean. After a short while they perceived many per-

sons robed in white.[1] At the dread sight, Sancho Panza's courage was completely annihilated, and his teeth began to chatter like one who is suffering from ague; and his quivering and chattering increased when they saw distinctly what it was, for they perceived about twenty persons in white habits, all on horseback, with lighted torches in their hands. After them came a litter covered over with black, which was followed in its turn by six persons in deep mourning, whose mules also were in black down to the ground. It was quite plain that they were mules and not horses owing to the slowness of their pace. Those in white robes kept muttering to themselves in low, plaintive tones.

This strange vision, appearing at such an hour and in such a desolate spot, was quite sufficient to strike terror into Sancho's heart, and even into that of his master. As for Sancho, he had pitched away all notions of courage. Not so his master. His imagination, on the contrary, immediately suggested that this must be one of the chivalrous adventures he had read about. He imagined that the litter was a bier on which was carried some dead or sorely wounded knight, whose revenge was reserved for him alone. So, without delay he couched his spear, seated himself firmly in the saddle, and with great spirit and courage took up his position in the middle of the road by which the white-robed procession must pass. When he saw them draw near, he raised his voice, saying: "Halt, knights, whoever you are; halt and give me account of yourselves, whence you come, and whither you are going, and what it is you are carrying on that bier. For, as it appears, either you have done injury to others, or others to you. In either case, it is necessary that I should know the truth that I may chastise you for the evil you have done or avenge you for the wrongs you have endured."

[1] This adventure is based upon an incident that took place in 1593. On December 14th, 1591, the great saint and poet Saint John of the Cross died in his monastery at Ubeda from a pestilential fever. In 1593 his body was secretly conveyed by night to Segovia by way of Madrid. Before reaching the village of Martos on a hill near the road, a man suddenly appeared, who called out, "Where are you carrying the body of the saint? Leave it where it was!" This caused such fear in the bearers that their hair stood on end. They thought that it was the Devil himself who appeared to them. St. John was born at Fontiveros in 1542, not Segovia, and died at Ubeda, not Baeza. Martos was one of the places where Cervantes collected stories in the years 1591–3.

"We are in haste," answered one of the men in white. "The inn is far off, and we have no time to answer your questions." Then spurring on his mule, he pressed forward.

Don Quixote was greatly enraged at this answer, so he laid hold of his bridle and said: "Halt, and answer my questions with greater civility; if not, I challenge you, one and all, to battle."

Now, the mule was nervous, and as soon as he touched the bridle, she started so violently that, rising on her hind legs, she unhorsed the rider. One of the footmen, seeing the man in white fall on the ground, began to revile Don Quixote, and he, being now thoroughly enraged, without more ado couched his lance and ran full tilt at one of the mourners and threw him to the ground sorely wounded. Then, turning on the rest, it was amazing to see with what speed he attacked and laid them low. It seemed, in fact, as if wings had sprouted on Rozinante at that instant, so nimbly and arrogantly he moved.

All the men in white were timorous and unarmed, and they gave up the skirmish in an instant. They began to run over the plain with their lighted torches, looking like the masqueraders who run up and down on a carnival night. As for the mourners, they were so wrapped and muffled in their trailing skirts and trains that they could not stir, so that Don Quixote, entirely safe, drubbed them all and drove them off the road against their will, for they thought he was no man but a devil from hell, striving to snatch away the corpse they carried in the litter.

Sancho, meanwhile, had been watching the fight, amazed at the boldness of his master, and he said to himself: "This master of mine is surely as strong and brave as he says."

A torch lay burning on the ground beside the man whom the mule had overthrown, by the light of which Don Quixote saw him, and going up to him, he placed the point of his lance to his throat and ordered him to surrender on pain of death. To which the prostrate man replied: "I have already surrendered more than enough, for I cannot stir. One of my legs is broken. I beseech you, sir, if you are a Christian gentleman, not to kill me, for that would be a great sacrilege, as I am a licentiate and have received minor orders."

"Well, then," said Don Quixote, "what devils brought you here if you are a churchman?"

"What indeed," answered the fallen man, "but my own misfortune."

"A worse one is in store for you," said Don Quixote, "if you do not satisfy all my demands."

"You shall be satisfied, sir," answered the licentiate. "You must know, sir, that though I said first that I was a licentiate, I am in fact only a bachelor of arts, and my name is Alonso López. I am a native of Alcobendas, and I come from the city of Baeza with eleven other priests, who are those that ran away with the torches. We are traveling to the city of Segovia as escorts to the corpse lying in the litter. It is that of a gentleman who died in Baeza and was buried there till now. And we are carrying his bones to his tomb in Segovia, his birthplace."

"Who killed him?" asked Don Quixote.

"God," replied the bachelor, "by means of a pestilential fever he caught."

"In that case," said Don Quixote, "Our Lord has delivered me from the task of avenging his death, if any other had slain him. Since he fell by the hand of God, there is no other remedy but silence and a shrug of the shoulder, for I should have done the same if He had been pleased to kill me. I would have your reverence know that I am a knight of La Mancha, by name Don Quixote, and my office and profession is to go through the world redressing injuries and making crooked things straight."

"I cannot understand what you mean by that," said the bachelor, "for from straight you have made me crooked, by breaking my leg, which can never be straightened as long as I live; and the injury you have redressed is to leave me so injured that I shall remain so forever. It was indeed a very great misadventure of mine to meet you, who are looking for adventures."

"All things," answered Don Quixote, "do not happen the same way. The trouble, sir bachelor, Alonso López, was caused by your coming as you did, by night, arrayed in those surplices, with burning torches, chanting and clad in mourning, so that you really seemed to be something sinister from the other world. I thus could not but fulfill my obligation to attack you, and let me tell you, I would have attacked you even if you had been, as I truly thought from the start, the devils themselves from hell."

"Since my fate so ordained it," said the bachelor, "I beseech you, sir knight-errant, who have done me such an injury, to help me to get up from under this mule, for my leg is caught between the stirrup and the saddle."

"I might have gone on speaking till tomorrow," said Don Quixote. "Why did you wait so long before telling me your trouble?"

He then shouted to Sancho Panza to come, but the latter turned a dead ear, for he was busily employed ransacking a sumpter mule that those good gentlemen had loaded down with things to eat. Sancho made a bag of his cloak, and having crammed it full to the brim, he loaded his ass. This done, he gave heed to the shouts of his master and helped to release the bachelor from under the mule. He mounted him on his mule and gave him his torch, and Don Quixote bade him follow in the wake of his companions and to beg their pardon for him for the injury that he had done them, for it had not been in his power to have done the contrary.

Sancho said to him also: "If those gentlemen wish to know who the champion is who routed them, you may say that he is the famous Don Quixote of La Mancha, otherwise called the Knight of the Rueful Figure." [2]

When the bachelor had gone, Don Quixote asked Sancho what had moved him to call him the Knight of the Rueful Figure at that time more than any other. "I'll tell you," answered Sancho. "It was because I stood observing you for a while by the torchlight which that unlucky man was carrying and truly you make about the ruefulest figure I've ever seen in my life. This must be due either to your weariness after the fight or to the loss of your teeth."

"That is not the reason," said Don Quixote. "But the learned man who has been entrusted with the task of writing the history of my deeds must have deemed it proper that I should take some appellation as the knights of old have done; for one called himself the Knight of the Burning Sword; another, Knight of the Unicorn; this, Knight of the

---

[2] Shelton translates *caballero de la triste figura,* Knight of the Ill-favored Face. According to Rodríguez Marín the phrase *Triste figura* meant grotesque or eccentric figure. We prefer to translate the phrase as Rueful Figure, remembering the phrase of Alexander Pope:

> piteous of his case
> Yet smiling at his rueful length of face.
> *The Dunciad* II,142.

Damsels; that, Knight of the Phoenix; one, Knight of the
Griffin; another, Knight of Death; and by those names and
designations they were known over all the surface of the
earth. And so I say that the learned man I have just mentioned must have inspired your mind and tongue to call me
the Knight of the Rueful Figure, as I mean to call myself
from this day on; and to make this name fit me better, I am
resolved, when an opportunity occurs, to have a most rueful
figure painted on my shield."

"You need not spend time and money, sir, in getting this
figure painted," said Sancho. "All you have got to do is to
show your own face to the onlookers. Without any other
image or picture they'll be sure to call you the Knight of
the Rueful Figure. And let me say, sir, by way of a jest, that
hunger and the loss of your teeth give you such a dismal
face that you may well spare us the rueful picture."

Don Quixote laughed at Sancho's wit; nevertheless, he
resolved to call himself by that name as soon as he could get
his shield or buckler painted accordingly, and he said: "As
I see it, Sancho, I have incurred excommunication for laying
violent hands on sacred things *juxta illud si qui suadente
diabolo*,[8] etc., though I am well aware that I did not lay
hands on them, but this lance of mine. Moreover, I had no
notion that I was attacking priests or Church property,
which, like a good Catholic and faithful Christian that I am, I
respect and adore; I was convinced they were phantoms
and specters from the other world. But if it comes to this, I
remember what happened to the Cid Ruiz Díaz when he
broke the chair of that king's ambassador in the presence of
His Holiness the Pope, who excommunicated him for it.
And yet the good Rodrigo de Vivar behaved that day like a
very noble and valiant knight."

And hearing this, the bachelor departed, as we have said,
without saying a word. Don Quixote wished to see whether
the corpse in the litter consisted merely of bones, but Sancho would not let him, saying: "Sir, you have finished this
adventure with less injury than any others I have seen. These
people, though overcome and scattered, may perhaps reflect that they have been routed by one person alone, and
growing ashamed of themselves, they may rally their ranks

---

[8] "Wherefore if any, persuaded by the devil." The canon comes
from Gratian, *Decretum aureum*, causa XVII, quaestio IV.

and return to give us plenty of trouble. The ass is as he should be; the mountains are at hand; hunger presses; we have nought to do but retire at a decent pace, and as the saying goes, 'To the grave with the dead, and the living to the loaf of bread.'" Then, driving on his ass, he begged his master to follow him, and Don Quixote, thinking that his squire was right, followed him without a word. After traveling a short distance between two small mountains, they found themselves in a large and sheltered valley, where they alighted. After Sancho had unloaded his beast, they both threw themselves down on the green grass, and sharpened by the sauce of hunger, lunched, dined, had their afternoon snack and their supper all at the same time; and they gorged themselves with more than one cold patty that the dead gentleman's chaplains (who rarely fail to provide themselves with plenty) had brought with them on the sumpter mule. But there was another misfortune that Sancho considered the worst of all, namely, that they had no wine, nor even a drop of water to drink. And moreover, they were parched with thirst. Sancho, however, perceiving that the meadow they were in was covered with green and tender grass, said what shall be told in the next chapter.

CHAPTER XX

Of the adventure, never before seen or heard of, achieved by the valorous Don Quixote of La Mancha, with less peril than any ever achieved by any famous knight in all the world

"This grass here, master, convinces me that there must be some fountain or brook nearby that moistens it and keeps the plants so fresh, so we should move on a bit further in the hopes of running across some spot where we can quench this terrible thirst of ours. Why, it's even more painful than hunger itself."

Don Quixote agreed, and taking Rozinante by the bridle, and Sancho his ass by the halter, after he had placed upon him the remnants of the supper, they began to plod forward through the meadow, groping their way, for the night was pitch dark and they could see nothing. They had scarcely gone two hundred paces when they heard a great noise of water, as if it fell headlong from some high, steep rock. The sound cheered them greatly, and they stopped to listen from where it came. But suddenly they heard another loud noise that drowned straightaway all their joy, especially Sancho's, who was by nature timid and fainthearted. They heard, I say, regular thuds, mingled with the rasping of irons and chains, which, accompanied by the furious roar of the water, would have struck terror into any heart less brave than Don Quixote's. The night, as I have said, was dark, and they happened to enter a grove of tall trees whose leaves, rustling in the gentle breeze, made a low, whispering sound so that the loneliness of the place, the darkness, the noise of the water, the rustling of the leaves, all caused horror and fright, especially as they found that neither the thuds ceased, nor the wind slept, nor morning approached. In addition to all this, they had not the remotest idea where they were.

But Don Quixote, stouthearted as ever, leaped upon Rozinante, seized his buckler, brandished his spear, and said: "Friend, I would have you know that I was born, by Heaven's grace, in this Age of Iron to revive in it the Golden Age. I am he for whom are reserved all great perils and valorous feats. I am he who shall revive the deeds of the Round Table, the Twelve Peers of France, and the Nine Worthies, and consign to oblivion the Platirs, Tablantes, Olivantes, and Tirantes, the Knights of the Sun and the Belianises, and all that herd of famous knights-errant of olden days, by performing in this age in which I live such prodigies, wonders, and such feats of arms as shall eclipse the most glowing they ever achieved. Mark well, trusty and lawful squire of mine, the darkness of this night, the strange silence, the dull, confused murmur of the trees, the dreadful noise of the water we came in search of, which seems to precipitate itself headlong down from the steep mountains of the moon, the constant thumping of the blows that wounds and hurts our ears. If all of those things together, and each by itself, are enough to strike terror, fear, and amazement into the heart of Mars, how much more in one who is not accustomed to such adventures? Yet all that I describe to you serves but to rouse and awaken my courage, and causes my heart to burst in my bosom with longing to encounter this adventure, however great it may be. Therefore, tighten Rozinante's girths a little, and God be with you! Wait here three days for me, and no more. If I do not return in that time, you may return to our village, and from there, for my sake, to El Toboso, where you must say to my incomparable Lady Dulcinea that her captive knight died attempting exploits that might make him worthy to be called hers."

When Sancho heard his master say these words, he began to weep piteously and said: "Master, I do not know why you wish to undertake this dangerous adventure. It is now night; no one sees us here; we can easily turn aside and slip away out of the zone of peril, even though we should not drink for three days, and since no one sees us, there will be no one to mark us down as cowards. Furthermore, I have many a time heard the priest of our village (whom your worship knows very well) say in his sermons that 'he who seeks danger perishes therein.' So, it is not right to tempt God by undertaking such a monstrous exploit, out of which you cannot escape, except by miracle. It ought to be enough for you that Heaven saved you from being blanketed as I was and rescued you safe and sound from the hosts of enemies who escorted the dead man. And even if all this is not enough to soften your heart of stone, let yourself be moved by the thought that as soon as you have left me, I shall, because of fear, hand over my soul to whoever pleases to take it. I left my country, wife, and children to come to serve you, believing that I should rise to be more, not less; but as covetousness bursts the bag, so it has torn my hopes, just when they were most lively and I was expecting that unlucky and accursed island that you have so often promised me. Instead of all that, I find that you are now ready to leave me all forlorn in this desolate spot, far from a human soul. For God's sake, master, don't do me such a wrong, and if you will not give up this enterprise, put it off at least until morning. For according to the bit of science I learned when I was a shepherd, dawn is hardly three hours off, seeing that the Horn's mouth is above our heads and shows midnight in the line of the left arm." [1]

"How can you, Sancho, see where this line is made or where this mouth or top of the head may be when the night is so dark that not a single star appears in the sky?"

"Yes, that is true," said Sancho, "but fear has many eyes and sees things underground and much more in the sky. And besides, we may now assume that dawn is not far off."

"Let it be as little off as it pleases," answered Don Quixote. "It shall not be said of me, now or in days to come, that tears or prayers prevented me from doing my duty as a knight. So I pray you, Sancho, keep silent, since God, who has filled me with courage to attempt this unseen and terrible adventure, will take care to watch over my safety and console you in your sadness. What you must do now is to tighten the girths of Rozinante and remain here, for I will quickly return, alive or dead."

Sancho, seeing that his master's mind was made up and that his tears, entreaties, and prayers were of no avail, determined to use his wits and see if he could, by hook or by crook, make him wait until daybreak. And so, when he was tightening the girths of the horse, he softly and without being observed tied the halter of his ass to both Rozinante's legs in such a way that when Don Quixote wished to depart, he could not, for his horse was not able to go a step but by jumps.

Sancho Panza, seeing the success of his trick, said: "Look, sir, how Heaven has been moved by my tears and prayers and has decreed that Rozinante shall not be able to go a step. If you insist on urging, spurring, and whipping him, it means angering Fortune, and as the saying goes, 'kicking against the pricks.' "

This threw Don Quixote into a state of desperation, and yet the more he spurred Rozinante on, the less would he move. At last, without noticing that the horse's legs were tied, he thought it best to remain quiet until dawn or until Rozinante would move on. Having no idea that Sancho was the cause of the trouble, he said to him: "Well, Sancho, since Rozinante is unable to move, I am content to wait

---

[1] Ursa Minor resembles in shape a curved hunting horn. The hour was calculated by facing the horn and stretching the arms horizontally so as to represent a cross. The time was indicated by the relative position of the horn to the arms.

here until the smile of Dawn, though I weep to think how long she will be in coming."

"No need to weep, sir," answered Sancho. "I'll tell you stories from now till daylight, unless you wish to dismount and snatch a little sleep in the green grass after the fashion of knights-errant so that you may be all the fresher in the morning for the unimaginable adventure."

"Who talks of dismounting and sleeping?" said Don Quixote. "Am I one of those knights who rest in times of danger? Sleep, you who were born to sleep, or do what you please, for I will do what I think becomes my profession."

"Don't be angry, good master," answered Sancho. "I didn't mean that." Then, drawing near to his master, he placed one hand on the pommel of his saddle and the other on the back of it, and he nestled up against the knight's left thigh, not daring to stir from him the breadth of a finger, so frightened was he by the thuds that still continued to sound in regular succession.

Don Quixote then bade him tell a tale for his entertainment as he had promised, and Sancho replied that he would if his fear of the noise he heard would let him.

"But in spite of it, I'll do my best to tell you a story, and if I manage to tell it and be not interrupted, you'll find it the best story in the world. So, pay attention, sir; I'm going to begin. There was what there was, may the good that's coming be for all, and the harm for him who goes looking for it— And take note, your worship, master mine, that the beginning that the old folks put to their tales was not just as they pleased, but was a sentence of Cato, the Roman incenser, that says: 'Evil to him who goes looking for it.' That fits us now like a ring on a finger, meaning that your worship should stay mum and not go searching for trouble anywhere, but for us to go back by another road, since nobody forces us to follow this one, where so many fearful things are keeping us in a continual dither."

"Go on with your story, Sancho," cried Don Quixote, "and leave the road we are to follow to me."

"I say then," continued Sancho, "that in a village of Extremadura there was once a goatish shepherd (I mean that he tended goats), and this shepherd, or goatherd, as my story goes, was called Lope Ruiz, and this Lope Ruiz fell in love with a shepherdess, who was called Torralba, which shepherdess called Torralba was the daughter of a rich flock master, and this rich flock master——"

"If you tell your story, Sancho, that way," said Don Quixote, "and repeat everything you have to say twice over, you will not finish in two days. Speak connectedly and tell it like an intelligent man, or else say nothing."

"My way of telling it," replied Sancho, "is the way they tell all stories in my country, and I don't know any other way of telling it. And it isn't fair for your worship to ask me to pick up new habits."

"Tell it as you please then," answered Don Quixote, "and since it is Fate's will that I can't help listening, go on."

"And so, my dear master," Sancho continued, "as I've said, this shepherd fell in love with Torralba, the shepherdess, who was a buxom, rollicking wench, a bit mannish, for she had a slight moustache—I fancy I'm looking at her this moment."

"Did you know her, then?" inquired Don Quixote.

"No, I didn't know her," replied Sancho, "but the fellow who told me this story said it was so certain and genuine that when I told it to anyone else, I might affirm and swear that I had seen it all. So, as the days went and the days came, the Devil, who never closes an eye and entangles everything, so contrived matters that the love that the shepherd had for the shepherdess turned to hatred and ill will, and the reason was, according to gossip, that she caused him a number of little jealousies, such as exceeded the limit and trespassed on the forbidden; and so much did the shepherd hate her from then on that to avoid seeing her anymore, he resolved to leave the country and go where his eyes would never see her. Then Torralba, when she found herself scorned by Lope, immediately fell to loving him more than she had ever loved him before."

"That," exclaimed Don Quixote, "is natural in women: to scorn those who love them and to love those who hate them. Go on, Sancho."

"It came to pass," said Sancho, "that the shepherd carried out his resolve, and driving his goats before him, took the road along the plains of Extremadura to cross into the kingdom of Portugal. As soon as Torralba heard of this plan, she followed him at a distance, on foot and barefoot, with a pilgrim's staff in her hand and around her neck a scrip that contained, so they say, a piece of looking glass, a broken comb, and some kind of little bottle of face cream; but whatever it was the lass carried, which I'm not worrying about for the moment, all I say is that the shepherd, the story tells, came with his flock to cross the river Guadiana, which at that season was swollen and almost overflowing; and at the spot he came to, there was neither a boat nor anyone to ferry him or his flock to the other side, at which he was mighty vexed, for he saw Torralba drawing near, and she was sure to bother him a great deal with her tears and whining. However, he went searching about till at last he saw a fisherman who had a boat by him, but so small that it could hold only one man and a goat. All the same he spoke to him and arranged with him to carry himself and his three hundred goats across. The fisherman got into the boat and carried one goat across, returned and càrried another, and came back again and carried over another— Now keep an account, sir, of the goats the fisherman is carrying over, for if one should slip from your memory, the story will end and it will be impossible for me to tell you another word of it. I'll go on, then, and say that the landing place on the other side was very muddy and slippery, which delayed the fisherman a good deal on his ferrying back and forth; all the same he came back for another goat, and another, and another——"

"Reckon that he has ferried them all over," said Don Quixote, "and stop coming and going in that manner or you will not finish getting them all over in a year."

"How many have gone over so far?" inquired Sancho.

"How the devil do I know?" replied Don Quixote.

"There you are! Didn't I tell you to keep a good count? Well, the tale is ended, thanks be to God, for there's no use in going any further."

"How can that be?" replied Don Quixote. "Is it so important to the tale to know how many goats were carried over so exactly that if one is missing, you cannot go on with the story?"

"No, sir, by no means," replied Sancho, "for when I asked your worship to tell me how many goats had passed and you replied that you didn't know, at that very instant I forgot everything, but you can bet there were some good and amusing things in it."

"So the story is finished, then?" asked Don Quixote.

" 'Tis as finished as my mother," said Sancho.

"I must say," replied Don Quixote, "you have told me the most original tale, story, or history one could imagine, and such a way of telling and ending it has never been, or will ever be, seen in a lifetime, although I expected no less from your nimble wit. Mind you, I'm not surprised, for probably those unceasing thuds have rattled your brain." [2]

"Very likely," answered Sancho, "but I know that as far as my tale is concerned there's nothing more to add, for it ends where the mistake in the counting of the goats begins."

"Let it end where it will," said Don Quixote. "And now let us see if Rozinante can move." He dug his spurs once more, and the horse gave a few leaps and stood still, so firmly was he tied.

At this point, either the chill of dawn that was just breaking, or something laxative he had eaten for supper, or as seems most probable the natural course of things gave Sancho the inclination and desire to do what no one else could do for him; but he was in such a state of fear that he dared not stir a hair's breadth from his master. Nevertheless, it was quite impossible even to think of not fulfilling his needs. So, in the interest of peace, he adopted the following solution. Very gently he moved his right hand from the crupper of the saddle, and neatly and noiselessly loosened the running knot that alone held up his breeches so that, when it was undone, they fell down and held him like fetters. Next, he raised his shirt as best he could and bared to the air both buttocks, which were not of the smallest. This done (which he thought was all he needed to relieve himself of his griping anguish) another greater problem presented itself: he was afraid that he could not relieve himself without making some report or noise. So, he began to grind his teeth and contract his shoulders, holding his breath as much as he could. But in spite of all these precautions, he was so unlucky as in the end to make a little noise very different from the thudding that was causing him such terror. Don Quixote heard it and said: "What is that noise, Sancho?"

"I don't know, sir," he answered. "It must be something

---

[2] Don Quixote speaks ironically. This unending story is a very ancient one, and we have heard variants of it today from goatherds in the Sierra Morena. In Andalusia, according to Rodriguez Martin, it is told of turkeys; and in Chile such stories for children are collected under the title *Cuentos Chilenos de nunca acabar*.

fresh, for those adventures and misadventures never begin for nothing."

He tried his luck again, and with such success that he relieved himself without any more noise or disturbance of the burden that had caused him such discomfort. But as Don Quixote's sense of smell was as keen as his hearing, and as Sancho was clinging so close to him, it was impossible for some of the smell, which ascended almost perpendicularly, not to reach his nose, and no sooner did it get there than he went to its rescue, and holding his nostrils between two fingers, observed in nasal tones: "You seem to be very frightened, Sancho."

"Yes, I am," answered Sancho, "but how is it that your worship notices it now more than ever?"

"Because now more than ever you smell, and not of amber," replied Don Quixote.

"That may be," said Sancho, "but I'm not to blame, but your worship, who drags me out at such unearthly hours and into such out-of-the-way places."

"Move two or three paces away, friend," said Don Quixote without taking his fingers from his nose, "and pay more attention to your person in the future and to the respect you owe me. It is my great familiarity with you that has led to this contempt."

"I'd like to wager," replied Sancho, "that your worship thinks I have done something I shouldn't with my person."

"The less said,[3] the better, friend Sancho," replied Don Quixote.

In this manner master and squire passed the night, and Sancho, when he saw that morning was near, cautiously untied Rozinante. As soon as Rozinante felt himself free, though he was by no means a mettlesome steed, he revived and began to paw the ground, for (by his leave be it said) he was a stranger to all curveting and prancing. Don Quixote, noticing that Rozinante moved, took it for a good sign and an omen that he should attempt the tremendous adventure.

And now the dawn had risen and the surrounding objects appeared distinctly, and Don Quixote saw that he was among some tall chestnut trees that cast a very dark shadow. He

---

[3] *Peor es meneallo* (it is worse to move it about) is a variant of the proverb *peor es hurgarle* (it is better to let sleeping dogs lie) used by Lope de Vega and others.

perceived that the hammering did not cease, but could not discover what caused it, and so without delay he gave a taste of his spurs to Rozinante and turned back again to bid Sancho farewell. He ordered him to wait there for him three days at the most as he had ordered before, and that if he did not return by then, to take it for certain that it was God's will that he should end his days in that perilous adventure. He again repeated to him the message that he had to take to Lady Dulcinea and assured him that he need not be anxious about the reward for his services, since before leaving his village he had made his will, in which he would find himself gratified as regards his wages in proportion to the time he had served. But if God rescued his master safe and sound from the coming danger, he might reckon himself absolutely sure of obtaining the promised island.

At this point Sancho began to weep again at the pitiful words of his master, and he determined not to leave him until the completion of this adventure.

Because of Sancho Panza's tears and his honorable resolution, the author of this history concludes that he must have been of good stock or at least of Christian lineage. Don Quixote was somewhat moved by the tears of his squire, but not enough to weaken in any degree his resolve; and so, hiding his feelings as best he could, he rode forward toward the place from where the noise of the water and of the thuds seemed to proceed. Sancho followed him on foot, leading by the halter his Dapple, his constant companion in good and evil fortune. Having gone a good distance through those shady chestnut trees, they came to a little meadow lying at the foot of some rocks, down which a mighty cataract of water descended. At the foot of the rock were some huts, so roughly built that they seemed more like ruins than habitable dwellings, from whence came the din and clatter that still never ceased.

Rozinante shied at the noise of the water and the hammering but Don Quixote quieted him and cautiously drew near to the huts, commending himself devoutly to his lady and beseeching her to favor him in this mighty enterprise; and by the way, he also prayed to God not to desert him. Sancho never left his master's side but stretched out his neck and looked between Rozinante's legs to see if he could discover the cause of all his fears.

When they had gone about another hundred paces, they

turned a corner, and before their eyes was the true and un-
doubted cause of that hideous and terrible noise that had kept
them all the night in supreme suspense and fear. It was
(do not, kind reader, take it too bitterly to heart) nothing
worse than six fulling hammers whose alternate strokes produced that terrifying sound of thuds.

When Don Quixote saw what it was, he stood mute and
ashamed. Sancho looked at him and saw how he hung down
his head upon his breast with all the appearance of one who
is abashed. Don Quixote looked at Sancho and saw that his
cheeks were swollen with laughter, with evident signs that he
was in danger of bursting. Don Quixote's melancholy was not
so great that he could help smiling at the sight of Sancho;
and Sancho, when he saw his master smiling, burst out with
such force that he had to put his hands to his sides to prevent them from splitting. Four times he ended and four
times he started again, all with the same impetus as the first.
Don Quixote now began to wish him in hell, especially when
he heard him say in a mimicking manner: "I would have you
know, friend, that I was born in this Age of Iron to revive
in it the Golden Age. I am he for whom are reserved all
great perils and valorous feats." And he went on repeating
the greater part of what Don Quixote had said when they
first heard the dreadful sounds.

Don Quixote, seeing that Sancho was mocking him, became
so enraged that he lifted up his lance and gave him two
such whacks on the shoulders that if he had caught him on
the head, the knight would have saved himself from paying
his wages, unless it were to his heirs.

Sancho now saw that his jests were reaping a bitter harvest,
and afraid that his master might go further, he said very
humbly: "Please, good master, I swear I was only joking."

"Though you may be joking, I am not," replied Don
Quixote. "Come here, Master Merryman. Do you imagine that
if those fulling hammers had been some perilous adventure, I
would not have shown the required courage to undertake and
achieve it? Am I (being as I am a knight) to distinguish
noises and to know which are those of mills and which are of
giants? Especially if (which is indeed the truth) I have never
seen any in my life, as you have—pitiful clodhopper that you
are, who were born and bred among them. Turn those six
hammers into giants and cast them at me, one by one or all

together, and if I do not turn them all with their heels up, then mock me as much as you please."

"Say no more, kind master," said Sancho, "I confess I carried the joke too far; but tell me, sir, now that we are at peace—and may God bring you safe and sound through all adventures that befall you as you've come out of this one —the terrific fright we've been in, isn't it worth laughing at and worth the telling too? At least the fright I had, for I'm only too aware that your worship doesn't even know what fear or fright is."

"I do not deny," answered Don Quixote, "that what happened to us is worth laughing at, but it is not worth telling, for not everyone is intelligent enough to put things in their proper place."

"Your worship, at any rate, knew how to put his lance in proper place when he pointed straight at my head and hit my shoulders, thanks be to God and to my swiftness in skipping aside. But let that be; all will come out in the wash, for I've heard it said, 'He likes thee well who makes thee cry.' Besides, when the gentlemen scold their servants, they generally give them a pair of breeches later, though I don't know what they generally give them after a beating, but who knows, perhaps knights-errant afterward give islands or kingdoms on dry land."

"The fall of the dice," said Don Quixote, "may decide that every word you say will come true. Overlook what has happened since you are sensible enough to know that a man's first impulses are beyond his control. But henceforth mind one thing: You must abstain and curb your desire for so much talk with me in the future, for never in any of the innumerable books of chivalry I have read have I found a squire who talked to his master as much as you do to yours. Indeed I look upon this as a great fault in you and in me: in you for showing me so little respect, in me for not making myself more respected. Take Gandalín, the squire of Amadis of Gaul, who was count of the Firm Isle. We read of him that he always spoke to his lord cap in hand, with bowed head and body bent, in the Turkish fashion. Then what about Gasabal, Don Galaor's squire, who was so quiet that to indicate the marvelous perfection of his silence, only once is his name mentioned in all that great and truthful history? From all that I have said, Sancho, you must infer that it is necessary to make a distinction between master and man, gentleman and servant, knight and squire. So from now on we must treat one another with more respect, without giving ourselves rope, since for whatever motive I may be enraged at you, it will always be the pitcher that gets the worst. The favors and benefits I have promised you will come in due course, and should they not come, your wages at least will not be lost, as I have told you already."

"What your worship says is all very well," said Sancho, "but I should like to know, in case the time for favors never comes and I have to fall back upon wages, how much it was that the squire of a knight-errant made in those times, and if they settled by the month or by the day, like builders' laborers."

"I do not believe," replied Don Quixote, "that squires ever worked for wages, but only for favors, and if I have assigned some to you in the sealed testament that I left at home, it was to provide against what might happen, for I do not yet know how chivalry will turn out in these disastrous times of ours, and I do not wish my soul to suffer for trifles in the other world, for I want you to realize, Sancho, that there is no state more perilous than a knight-errant's."

"That is true," said Sancho, "since the mere sound of the hammers of a fulling mill was enough to trouble and alarm the heart of so valiant a knight as your worship, but you may be confident that henceforth I shall not open my lips to make fun of your worship's doings, but only to honor you as my master and natural lord."

"If you do that," answered Don Quixote, "your days will be long on the face of the earth, for next to our parents we are bound to honor our masters as we would our fathers."

CHAPTER XXI

The noble adventure and rich prize of Mambrino's helmet, and other things that befell our invincible knight

About this time it began to rain, and Sancho would have entered one of the fulling mills for shelter, but Don Quixote had taken such a loathing to them on account of the recent joke that he would not go in. Turning to the right, they struck into another road like the one they had taken the day before. Soon after, Don Quixote espied a man on horseback who wore on his head something that glittered like gold. Scarcely had he seen him when he turned to Sancho, saying: "I am sure, Sancho, that there is no proverb that is not true, for all proverbs are maxims drawn from experience, the mother of all knowledge; especially that one that says: 'When one door shuts, another opens.' I say this because, if Fortune closed the door upon us last night in our quest by deceiving us with the fulling mills, she now opens wide another leading to a better and more certain adventure. If I do not succeed in this, the fault will be mine, and I shall not excuse myself this time by laying the blame on my ignorance of fulling mills or on the darkness of the night. I say this because, if I mistake not, there comes toward us one who wears on his head the helmet of Mambrino,[1] about which I took the oath you know of."

"Take heed, sir, what you say, and more what you do,"

---

[1] This enchanted helmet was originally forged for the Saracen king Mambrino. It was captured by Rinaldo. See Ariosto's *Orlando Furioso*, XVIII, 157–3, 1, 25.

said Sancho, "for I should prefer not to meet any more fulling mills that would hammer and mash us out of our senses."

"Devil take you," replied Don Quixote. "What has a helmet to do with fulling mills?"

"I don't know," answered Sancho, "but if I might speak as much as I used to, I would give you such reasons that you should see that you were mistaken in what you say."

"How can I be mistaken in what I say, you hair-splitting traitor?" asked Don Quixote. "Tell me! Do you not see that knight riding toward us on a dapple-gray steed with a helmet of gold on his head?"

"What I see and make out," replied Sancho, "is nought but a man on a gray ass like my own, carrying on his head something that shines."

"Well, that is Mambrino's helmet," said Don Quixote. "Stand aside and leave me alone with him. You shall see how, in order to save time, I will end this adventure without speaking a word, and become master of the helmet I have so long desired."

"I'll take jolly good care to stand out of the way," replied Sancho, "but God grant, I repeat, it may turn out all marjoram and not fulling mills." [2]

"I have already told you," said Don Quixote, "not to think of mentioning the fulling mills again; otherwise—by God—I will hammer the soul out of your body."

Sancho then held his peace, fearing that his master would carry out the threat that he had uttered so forcibly.

Now, the truth of the matter concerning the helmet, the horse, and the knight that Don Quixote saw was as follows: In that neighborhood there were two villages, one of which was so small that it contained neither shop nor barber, but the larger had both; so the barber of the larger village served also the smaller. It now happened that in the latter there lay a sick man needing a bloodletting, and another who wished to have his beard trimmed, for which purpose the barber came, bringing with him his brass basin. And by chance, as he traveled it rained, so to save his hat, which must have been a new one, from staining, he put the basin on his head, and

[2] A reference to the proverb *Quiera Dios que orégano sea y no se nos vuelva alcarabea* (please God it will be marjoram and not turn out to be caraway seed).

the basin, being recently scoured, glittered half a league off. He rode upon a gray ass, as Sancho said, and that was the reason why Don Quixote took him to be a knight with a helmet of gold riding on a dapple-gray steed, for everything he came across he with great ease adapted to his extravagant notions of chivalry. And when he saw the unfortunate rider draw near, without halting to parley he ran at him with lance couched, spurring Rozinante to a full gallop, with the intention of piercing him through and through. And when he came close to him, without checking his furious pace he cried out: "Defend yourself, base caitiff, or hand over to me of your own free will what so rightly belongs to me."

The barber, so unexpectedly seeing this wild apparition dashing against him, had no other way of avoiding the thrust of the lance than to fall off his ass onto the ground. But no sooner did he touch the earth than he sprang up nimbler than a deer and scampered over the plain faster than the wind, leaving the basin on the ground behind him. With this Don Quixote was satisfied and said that the pagan had been a wise man, for he had imitated the beaver, who, when closely pressed by hunters, tears off with his teeth that which he knows by instinct to be the object of pursuit. He then ordered Sancho to take up the helmet, and the latter, lifting it up, said: "By God, the basin is a good one and is worth eight reals if it is worth a farthing." He gave it to his master, who placed it on his head and turned it about from side to side in search of the visor. Seeing that he could not find it, he said: "Doubtless the pagan for whom this famous helmet was first forged had a very big head, and the worst of it is that half the helmet is missing." When Sancho heard him call the basin a helmet, he could not restrain his laughter, but then, suddenly remembering his master's anger, he stopped laughing at once.

"What are you laughing at, Sancho?" said Don Quixote.

"I laugh," answered the latter, "to think of the great head the pagan owner of this helmet had; it is for all the world like a barber's basin."

"If you want to know my views," replied Don Quixote, "I say this piece of the enchanted helmet must have fallen by some strange accident into someone's hands who did not know its great worth. So not knowing what he was doing, and seeing it was of pure gold, he melted down one half and made of the other half this object, which seems, as you say, to be a barber's basin. But to me, who know what it really is, its transformation makes no matter, for I will have it repaired at the first village where I can find a smith in such a way that it will not be surpassed or even equaled by the one that the god of smiths himself made and forged for the god of battles. Meanwhile I shall wear it as well as I can, for something is better than nothing, all the more as it will suffice to protect me against a blow from a stone."

"Yes, it will suffice," said Sancho, "if they do not shoot from a sling, as the two armies did when they knocked out your worship's grinders and broke the pot containing that blessed beverage that made me spew up my insides."

"I do not mind having lost the balsam," said Don Quixote, "for, as you know, Sancho, I have the recipe for it in my memory."

"So have I, too," answered Sancho; "but if I ever make it or try it again in my life, may that be my last hour on earth. Besides, I do not intend to put myself in the way of needing it, for I intend to keep myself with all my five senses from being wounded or from wounding anyone. As to being tossed again in a blanket, I say nothing, for it is difficult to prevent such mishaps; and if they do come, there's nothing to be done but hunch your shoulders, hold your breath, close your eyes, and let yourself go where luck and the blanket will take you."

"You are a bad Christian, Sancho," said Don Quixote. "You never forget an injury once done to you, though you should realize that truly generous and noble souls pay no heed to trifles. Did you end up with a lame foot, a broken rib, a cracked skull, that you cannot yet forget that joke? For when you examine it carefully, it was only a jest and a pastime, and if I had not taken it as such, I should have gone back there long ago and have done more damage in avenging you than the Greeks did for the rape of Helen, who, if she had lived in our days and my Dulcinea in hers, would not have had such a great reputation for beauty as she has." Here he heaved a sigh and wafted it to the skies.

"Let it pass as a joke then," said Sancho, "since it can't be avenged in earnest, but I know what is a joke and what is in earnest, and I know too that they will not slip from my memory any more than they will from my shoulders. But leaving all this aside, tell me, sir, what we are to do with this dapple-gray steed, that looks so like a gray ass, which that poor devil Martino [3] left behind ownerless when he was unsaddled by you? By the way he kicked up the dust and took to his heels, he doesn't intend to come back for it, and by my beard I tell you the dapple beast is a good one."

"I am not accustomed," said Don Quixote, "to ransack those I vanquish, nor is it the practice of knighthood to take from them their horses and leave them on foot unless the victor lost his own in the fight. In such a case it is lawful to take that of the enemy as won in fair fight. Therefore, Sancho, leave the horse or ass, or whatever you wish to call it, for when the owner sees that we have departed, he will come back for it."

"God knows I would like to take him," answered Sancho, "or at least swap him for mine, which I think is not as good. The laws of knighthood must for sure be strict if they don't even allow the swapping of one ass for another. But I would like to know whether I might exchange a bit of the harness."

"I am not quite sure of that," said Don Quixote, "and as it is a matter of doubt, until I get information on the matter I will allow you to exchange them, provided your need is extreme."

"So extreme," answered Sancho, "that if they were to harness my own person, I could not need them more."

Saying this, he made the *mutatio carparum*,[4] as the saying goes, and decked out his ass with a thousand fineries, making him look much better. They breakfasted on what remained of the rations they had plundered from the sumpter mule and quenched their thirst in the millstream, but without turning their faces toward the fulling mills, such was the hate they bore them for having scared them. Now that all anger and melancholy had disappeared, they mounted, and without choosing any particular road (for it was very much like knights-errant not to select a specific one) they followed wherever Rozinante's will wished, for he was a guide to his master as well as to the ass, who always plodded along in

---

[3] He means Mambrino.

[4] This is a reference to a custom in Rome, where the cardinals and prelates of the Curia changed their hoods and cloaks of fur for those of silk at Whitsuntide.

love and good fellowship wherever he led the way. However, they soon returned to the highway, which they followed at random without forming a plan.

As they were riding along, Sancho said to his master: "Sir, would your worship give me leave to talk a little? For since you imposed that harsh command of silence on me, several things have been rotting away in my stomach, and there's one perched on the tip of my tongue this instant that I don't want to go bad on me."

"Out with it," said Don Quixote, "and be brief in your arguments, for nothing long-winded entertains."

"I say then, sir," replied Sancho, "that for the last few days I've been thinking how little is to be gained from gallivanting after adventures such as your worship seeks in these wilds and at these crossroads, for even when the most dangerous ones are won and concluded, no one can see or hear about them, and so they have to remain in eternal silence to the detriment of your worship's good intentions and of what they deserve. So it seems to me it would be better—saving your worship's better judgment—for us to go and serve some emperor or other great prince who is waging some war. In his service your worship might show the worth of his person, his mighty strength, and greater understanding. Then, once this lord whom we'd be serving saw this, he'd be bound to reward each according to his merits, and in that case there's bound to be someone to put down in writing your worship's deeds for everlasting remembrance. As for my own exploits, I'll hold my tongue, for they must not go beyond the limits laid down for squires, although I will point out that if it is the custom of chivalry to write up the deeds of squires, I don't think mine will be left out."

"You are not far wrong, Sancho," replied Don Quixote, "but before reaching that stage a knight must wander through the world, as though on probation, in quest of adventures in order to win such a name and fame by achieving a few that when he goes to the court of some great monarch, he will be already well known by his deeds. And as soon as boys see him ride through the city gates, they will follow and surround him, shouting: 'Here is the Knight of the Sun,' or of the Serpent, or of any other device under which he may have performed his great deeds. 'Here,' they will say, 'is that knight who vanquished in single combat the great giant Brocabruno, of mighty strength, the knight who freed the

great Mameluke of Persia from the long enchantment in
which he had been held for nearly nine hundred years.' Thus
from mouth to mouth they will continue to proclaim his
deeds until all of a sudden, at the clamor of the boys and the
rest of the people, the king of that kingdom will appear
at the windows of his royal palace. No sooner does he see the
knight than he recognizes him by his armor or by the device
on his shield, and then he is sure to cry out: 'Halt! Let my
knights ride forth, as many as are in my court, to welcome the
flower of chivalry who is approaching.' All will ride out at
his command, and the king himself will come halfway down
the stairs, embrace him very closely, welcome him, kiss
him on the cheek, and lead him by the hand to the chamber
of his queen. There the knight will find her with the princess,
her daughter, who is sure to be one of the loveliest and most
accomplished damsels to be found anywhere in the wide
world, however hard you search. After this she will gaze into
the knight's eyes and he into hers, and each will appear to
the other somewhat more divine than human; and without
knowing the why or the wherefore, they will be imprisoned
and entangled in the inextricable net of love, experiencing
great anguish in their hearts, for they know not how they
should speak in order to reveal their feelings and desires.
From there he will, no doubt, be conducted to some richly
furnished room in the palace, where after relieving him of
his armor, they will bring him a rich mantle of scarlet to
wear, and if he is a goodly sight in his armor, he will be
handsomer still in his doublet. Now that night has come,
he will sup with the king, queen, and princess, during which
he will never take his eyes off her, gazing at her undetected
by the bystanders, and she will do the same with the same
caution, for as I have said, she is a most discreet damsel.

When the tables are removed, suddenly there will enter by
the hall door an ugly little dwarf, followed by a beautiful
lady escorted by two giants, to introduce a certain adventure,
so contrived by a very ancient sage that the knight who triumphantly achieves it shall be declared the best in the world.
The king will then command all those present to attempt it,
but none of them will conclude it successfully except the
stranger knight, to the great enhancement of his fame. At this
the princess will be overjoyed and consider herself happy and
well requited for having set her fancies in so high a quarter.

"Now, by good fortune this king or prince, or whatever he is, has a very stubborn war on with another as powerful as he, and the stranger knight (after he has spent some days in his court) will request permission to go and serve him in the said war. The king will grant it with great goodwill, and the knight will courteously kiss his hands for the privilege. And that same night he will take leave of his lady, the princess, through the railings of a garden that adjoins her sleeping chamber, through which he has already on many occasions conversed with her, owing to the help of the duenna, a damsel much trusted by the princess as confidante. He will sigh; she will swoon; the damsel will fetch water and be greatly distressed because morning is nearly there, and she will fear for her lady's honor if they be discovered. At last the princess will come to herself and give her white hands through the railings to the knight, who will kiss them a thousand times and bathe them with his tears. The two will come to an arrangement as to how they are to acquaint each other with their news, good or bad, and the princess will implore the knight to stay away as little time as possible, and he will promise her with many oaths. Once more he will kiss her hands and bid her farewell with such sorrow as will almost end his life. From there he withdraws to his chamber, flings himself upon the bed, but cannot sleep for the agony of parting. He rises early in the morning and goes to take leave of the king, the queen, and the princess. When he has bid farewell to the royal pair, they tell him that the princess is indisposed and cannot receive a visit, and the knight believes it is from grief at his departure. His heart is pierced and he very nearly betrays his sorrow. The princess' confidante is present and has to note every detail. She goes off to bear the news to her ladyship, who receives her with tears and tells her that one of her greatest afflictions is not to know who her knight may be and whether he be of king's lineage or not; the damsel assures her that such courtesy, gentleness, and valor as he displays cannot exist in any but a royal and illustrious person. The princess is at length consoled; she strives to be cheerful so as not awaken her parents' suspicion, and at the end of two days she appears in public. The knight has already gone off; he fights in the war; he defeats the king's enemies; he captures many cities; triumphs in many battles; returns to court and sees his lady in the usual place; it is agreed that as a reward for his services he shall ask her father for her hand in marriage, but the king will not consent because he does not know who he is. In spite of that, either by abducting her or in some other way, he marries the princess, and her father in the end considers it a most fortunate arrangement, for it transpires that the knight is the son of a valiant king, of what kingdom I do not know, for I do not think it is on the map. The father dies; the princess succeeds him; in short, the knight becomes king. Now comes the moment for bestowing favors on his squire and on all who have helped him to climb to his high state. He marries his squire to one of the princess' damsels, no doubt to the one who was the duenna in their amour and is the daughter of a very important duke." [5]

"That's all I ask," said Sancho, "a fair field and no favors; those are the terms I stick to, for it's all bound to turn out like that to the letter now that your worship has adopted the name of the Knight of the Rueful Figure."

"Of course, Sancho," replied Don Quixote, "for in that way and by the very steps I have described to you, knights-errant rise, and have risen, to be kings and emperors. All we want now is to look around and discover some king, Christian or pagan, who is at war and has a beautiful daughter; but there will be time enough to think of that, seeing that, as I have told you, we have first to gain fame in other parts before going to court. There is also something else missing, for assuming that we find a king with a war and a beautiful daughter and that I have won incredible fame through all the universe, I don't see how it can be made out that I am of royal lineage, or at least second cousin to an emperor; and the king will not want to give me his daughter until he is quite certain on this point, whatever may be the merit of my famous deeds. So that I am afraid by this defect I shall lose what my arm has richly earned. It is true that I am a gentleman of a well-known house, of possessions and properties, and that my life according to the ancient law was assessed at five hundred pounds' fine,[6] and it may happen that the learned man who writes my history will so clarify my

[5] All the preceding description is a brilliant résumé in Cervantes' words of the essential characteristics of a romance of chivalry.

[6] This is a reference to the ancient Gothic code of the *Fuero Juzgo*. *Hidalgos de devengar* were nobles who, if they were insulted by inferiors, had the right to claim a fine of 500 *sueldos*. The *sueldo* was worth two cents.

parentage and descent as to prove me fifth or sixth in line from a king. For you must know, Sancho, that there are two kinds of lineages in the world: those that trace their descents from princes and monarchs, whom time has gradually reduced to a point, like a pyramid upside down; others that derive their origin from common folk and ascend step by step till they arrive at being great lords. So that the difference lies between those who were and are no longer and those who are but once were not; and I might after investigation turn out to be one of those who had a great and famous origin, which should satisfy the king, my father-in-law to be. If it does not, the princess will have to love me so much that she will take me as her lord and husband in spite of her father, even though she knows for certain that I am the son of a water carrier. And if she does not, then it is a question of abducting her and carrying her off wherever I please, for time or death will put an end to her parents' displeasure."

"Yes," Sancho said, "it reminds me of what scapegraces often say: 'Never ask as a favor what you can take by force,' though it were more to the point to say: 'A leap over the hedge is better than good men's prayers.' I say this because if the king, your worship's father-in-law, will not come up to scratch and hand over my lady, the princess, to you, there is nothing to do but, as your worship says, to carry her off and hide her. But the fly in the ointment is that until peace is made and you can enjoy your kingdom nicely and comfortably, the poor squire may go whistle for this reward of his unless the duenna, who is to be his wife, runs away along with the princess, and he shares his misfortune with her until Heaven ordains otherwise, for his master, I suppose, would be able to give her to him at once in lawful marriage."

"There is no one who can prevent that," said Don Quixote.

"Well, since that is so," replied Sancho, "we have only to commend ourselves to God and let fortune take what course it will."

"God grant it," answered Don Quixote, "as I desire and you require, and let him be a rogue who thinks himself one."

"Amen in God's name," said Sancho, "for I'm an old Christian, and that's enough blue blood for a count."

"And more than enough," said Don Quixote. "But even if you were not, it would not matter, for if I am king I can easily confer nobility upon you without any purchase or service on your part; and if I make you a count, there you are, a gentleman; let them say what they will, for they will have to call you your lordship whether they want to or not."

"You can leave it to me," said Sancho. "I'll be as well able to support my tittle as the best of them!"

"*Title* you must say, not *tittle*," said his master.

"As you wish," replied Sancho, "I say that I shall know how to carry off the business with flying colors, for I once was beadle of a brotherhood, and the beadle's gown looked so smart on me that everyone said I had presence enough to be the warden of the same brotherhood. What will it be then when I'm togged out as a duke or dressed up in gold and pearls in the fashion of a foreign count? I bet they'll come a hundred leagues to see me."

"You will look well," said Don Quixote, "but you will need to shave your beard often, for you have it so thick, tousled, and unkempt that unless you use a razor every two days at least, they will see what you are a gun shot away."

"What more have I to do," said Sancho, "but to take a barber and keep him in the house on wages? And if more's needed, I'll make the fellow walk behind me like a grandee's groom."

"How do you know that grandees carry their grooms behind them?" asked Don Quixote.

"I'll tell you," answered Sancho. "Some years ago I spent a month in the capital, and there I saw a very little gentleman out for a stroll, who, they told me, was a great grandee, and a man followed him on horseback, turning everywhere he turned just as if he were his tail. I asked why that man did not ride close to the other but always went behind him, and they answered that he was his groom and that it was the fashion for grandees to carry such behind them. And ever since, I know it so well that it's stuck in my memory."

"You are right, I must agree," said Don Quixote, "and so you may take around your barber with you, for fashions did not all come in together, nor were they invented at once, and you may well be the first count to carry your barber behind you. Indeed trimming a beard is a more intimate service to render than saddling a horse."

"Leave this barber business to me," said Sancho, "and let your worship's job be to try to become a king and make me a count."

"So it shall be," answered Don Quixote.

And raising his eyes, he saw what shall be told in the next chapter.

CHAPTER XXII

Of the liberty Don Quixote gave to a number of unfortunates who were being borne, much against their will, where they had no wish to go

Cide Hamete Benengeli, the Arabian and Manchegan author, relates in this most grave, high-sounding, precise, pleasant, and imaginative history that after the conversation between the famous Don Quixote of La Mancha and Sancho Panza, his squire, which is reported at the end of the twenty-first chapter, Don Quixote raised his eyes and saw coming, along the road he was taking, about a dozen men on foot strung together like beads on a great iron chain. The chain was fastened around their necks and they were handcuffed. With them were two men on horseback, and two others followed on foot. The horsemen had firelocks, and those on foot pikes and swords.

As soon as Sancho Panza saw them he said: "Here's a chain of galley slaves, men forced by the king, going to serve in the galleys."

"How! Men forced?" answered Don Quixote. "Is it possible that the king forces anybody?"

"I don't say that," answered Sancho, "but they are people condemned for their offenses to serve the king in the galleys."

"Then it is a fact," replied Don Quixote, "however you put it, that these men are being taken to their destination by force and not by their own free will."

"That is so," said Sancho.

"Then," said his master, "here is the opportunity for me to

carry out my duty: to redress grievances and give help to
the poor and the afflicted."

"I beg you, sir," said Sancho, "to consider that justice,
which is the king himself, does no violence to these men, but
only punishes those who have committed crime."

By this time the chain gang came up, and Don Quixote in
very courteous words asked those in charge to be good
enough to inform him why they conducted people away in
that manner. One of the guardians on horseback replied
that they were slaves condemned by His Majesty to the galleys and that there was no more to be said, nor ought Don
Quixote to desire any further information.

"Nevertheless," answered Don Quixote, "I would like to
hear from each one of them individually the cause of his
disgrace." To this the guardian on horseback answered:
"Though we have here the register of the crimes of all these
unlucky fellows, this is no time to produce and read them.
Draw near, sir, and ask it from themselves. No doubt they'll
tell you their tales, for men of their sort take delight in boasting of their rascalities."

With this leave, which Don Quixote would have taken
for himself if they had not given it, he went up to the gang
and asked the first man for what crimes he found himself in
such straits. The man answered that it was for being in love.

"For that and no more?" cried Don Quixote. "If men are
sent to the galleys for being in love, I should have been
pulling an oar there long ago."

"My love was not of the kind your worship imagines," replied the galley slave. "Mine was that I loved too much a
basket of fine linen, which I embraced so lovingly that if the
law had not taken it from me by violence, I should not of
my own free will have forsaken it even to this present day.
I was caught in the act, so there was no need for torture. The
case was a short one. They gave my shoulders a hundred
lashes and in addition three years' hard labor in the *gurapas*,
and that's an end of it."

"What are *gurapas*?" said Don Quixote.

"*Gurapas* are galleys," answered the convict, who was a
young man of about twenty-four, born, as he said, at
Piedrahita.

Don Quixote put the same question to the second, who
returned no answer, for he seemed too downcast and
melancholy to speak. But the first one spoke for him and

said: "Sir, this gentleman goes for being a canary bird—I mean a musician or singer."

"Is it possible," said Don Quixote, "that musicians and singers are sent to galleys?"

"I should say so, sir," replied the galley slave. "There's nothing worse than to sing under torture."

"Well," said Don Quixote, "I, on the contrary, have heard it said: 'Who sings in grief, procures relief.' "

"Down here it's the exact opposite," said the slave, "for he who sings once, weeps the rest of his life."

"I do not understand it," said Don Quixote. One of the guards then said to him: "You know, sir, among these unsanctified folk 'to sing under torture' means to confess on the rack. They put this poor sinner to the torture, and he confessed his crime of being a rustler, which means that he was a cattle thief; and because he confessed, he was condemned to the galleys for six years, with the addition of two hundred lashes that he carries on his shoulders. He's always sad and pensive, for the other thieves bully, abuse, and despise him because he confessed and hadn't the courage to say a couple of *nos*. For as they say, 'A *nay* has as many letters as a *yea*,' and it is good luck for a criminal when there are no witnesses and proofs and his fate depends on his own tongue. In my opinion there's much truth in that."

"I think so also," said Don Quixote, and he passed on to where the third slave stood, and put to him the same question as to the others. The man replied quickly and coolly, saying: "I'm off to their ladyship the galleys because I wanted ten ducats."

"I will give you twenty with all my heart to free you from that misfortune," said Don Quixote.

"That," replied the slave, "would be like one who has money in the middle of the sea and yet is perishing of hunger because he has nowhere to buy what he needs. I say this because, if I'd had the twenty ducats your worship offers me at the right time, I would have greased the lawyer's palm with them and so sharpened my advocate's wit that I would now be strolling about in the marketplace at Toledo instead of being trailed along here like a greyhound. But God is great; patience is enough."

Don Quixote passed on to the fourth, who was a man of venerable appearance, with a white beard reaching below his chest. No sooner was he asked the reason for his being there than he began to weep and would not answer a word; but the fifth convict lent him a tongue and said: "This honest gentleman is off for four years to the galleys after having appeared in the usual procession dressed in full pomp and mounted." [1]

"That means, I suppose," said Sancho, "carried to shame in view of the whole people."

"You have said it," answered the galley slave, "and the offense for which they gave him this punishment was for having been an ear broker, and a body broker too. What I mean to say is that this gentleman goes for pimping and for fancying himself as a bit of a wizard."

"If it had been merely for pimping," said Don Quixote, "he certainly did not deserve to go rowing in the galleys, but rather to command them and be their captain. For the profession of pimp is no ordinary office, but one requiring wisdom and most necessary in any well-governed state. None but wellborn persons should practice it. In fact, it should have its overseers and inspectors, as there are of other offices, limited to a certain appointed number, like exchange brokers.[2] If this were done, many evils would be prevented, which now take place because this profession is practiced only by foolish and ignorant persons such as silly women, page boys, and mountebanks of few years' standing and less experience, who, in moments of difficulty, when the utmost skill is needed, allow the tidbit to freeze between their fingers and their mouth and scarcely know which is their right hand. I should like to go on and give reasons why it is right to make special choice of those who have to fill such an important office in the state, but this is not the place to do it. Some day I will tell my views to those who may provide a remedy; at present I only wish to say that the sorrow I felt at seeing your gray hairs and venerable countenance in so much distress for pimping has entirely vanished when I learn that you are a wizard; though I know well that there are no

---

[1] Those condemned for witchcraft or wizardry were dealt with by the Holy Office. They were mounted on mules with face to the tail and led in procession through the streets accompanied by a noisy crowd. They wore a *coroza* or paper miter, carried a lighted candle, and were flogged through the streets.

[2] Don Quixote's ironical praise of pimps is echoed by a number of sixteenth-century authors, including Lope de Vega and Moreto. See also: Cervantes, "The Man of Glass" in *The Deceitful Marriage and Other Exemplary Novels* (Signet CT157).

sorceries in the world that can affect and force the will, as some simple people imagine. Our will is free and no herb nor charm can compel it. What such gullible wenches and lying rascals do is to mix some potion or poison that drives men crazy, claiming that it has the power to rouse love; whereas I maintain that it is impossible to force a man's will."

"That is true, sir," said the worthy old man; "and indeed I was not guilty of witchcraft; as for being a pimp, I couldn't deny it, but I never thought there was any harm in it, for all my intention was that the whole world should enjoy themselves and live together in peace and quiet without quarrels or troubles. But my good intentions could not save me from going to a place from which I have no hope of return, laden as I am with years and so worried with a bladder trouble that does not give me a moment's rest." He now began to weep as before, and Sancho felt so sorry for him that he drew from his purse a four-real piece and gave it to him as alms.

Don Quixote passed on and asked another what his offense was. He answered with much more pleasantness than the former: "I am here because I played a little too much of a game with two cousins of mine and with two other sisters who were not mine. In short, I carried the game so far with them all that the result of it was the increasing of my kindred so intricately that no devil could make it out. It was all proved against me; I hadn't a friend, and I hadn't a groat; my neck was in the utmost danger; they gave me six years in the galleys; I concurred: it's fair punishment for my guilt; I'm young; if only my life lasts, all will turn out for the best. If you, sir, have anything about you to relieve us poor devils, God will repay you in Heaven and we will have care on earth to ask God in our daily prayers to give you as long and prosperous a life and health as your kind presence deserves."

This convict was dressed in a student's habit, and one of the guards told Don Quixote that he was a great talker and a fine Latin scholar.

Behind all these came a man about thirty years of age, of very comely looks, except that he had a slight squint. He was differently tied from the rest, for he wore a chain to his leg so long that it wound around his whole body. He had, besides, around his neck two iron rings, one of which was fastened to the chain, and the other, called a keep friend or friend's foot, had two irons that came down from it to his waist, at the ends of which were fixed two manacles. These held his hands locked with a great padlock so that he could neither put his hands to his mouth nor bend down his head to his hands.

Don Quixote asked why this man was loaded with more fetters than the rest. The guard answered that it was because he had committed more crimes than all the rest put together and that he was such a desperate rascal that, though they carried him fettered in that way, they were not sure of him but feared that he might give them the slip.

"What crimes did he commit," said Don Quixote, "that have deserved no greater penalty than being sent to the galleys?"

"He is going for ten years," said the guard, "which is the same as civil death. I need only tell you that this man is the famous Ginés de Pasamonte, alias Ginesillo de Parapilla."

"Master commissary," said the galley slave, "don't go so fast and don't let us start defining names and surnames. Ginés is my name, not Ginesillo, and Pasamonte is my family name, not Parapilla as you say. Let every man first look to himself and he'll do a good deal."

"Keep a civil tongue, mister out-and-out robber," answered the commissary. "Otherwise we'll shut you up, whether you like it or not."

"I know," answered the galley slave, "that man goes as God pleases; but one day someone will know whether my name is Ginesillo de Parapilla or not."

"Don't they call you that, you lying trickster?"

"They do," answered Ginés, "but I'll make them stop calling me by that name or I'll shear them where I don't care to mention in company. And now, sir, if you have something to give us, hand it out and good-bye, for you tire us with your inquiries about other men's lives. If you want to know mine, I am Ginés de Pasamonte, whose life has been written by these very fingers of mine."

"He speaks the truth," said the commissary. "He himself has written his own history—as good a one as you could wish, and he pawned the book in gaol for two hundred reals."

"Aye, and I intend to redeem it," said Ginés, "even if it stood at two hundred ducats."

"Is it so good?" said Don Quixote.

"It is so good," answered Ginés, "that it means trouble for

Lazarillo de Tormes [3] and for all that has been written or ever shall be written in that style. I assure you it deals with truths and truths so attractive and entertaining that no fiction could compare with them."

"What is the title of the book," asked Don Quixote.

"The Life of Ginés de Pasamonte," answered Ginés himself.

"Is it finished yet?" asked Don Quixote.

"How can it be finished," answered Ginés, "when my life isn't finished yet? What is written tells everything from my birth down to this last time I was packed off to the galleys."

"Then you have been there before?" said Don Quixote.

"To serve God and the king," answered Ginés; "on the last occasion I was there for four years, and I know already the taste of hard tack and the lash. I'm not too sorry to return there, for I'll have an opportunity to finish my book. I've still many things to say, and in the galleys of Spain there's more than enough leisure, though I don't need much for what I have to write because I know it by heart."

"You seem to be a clever fellow," said Don Quixote.

"Aye. And an unlucky one," replied Ginés, "for bad luck always pursues genius."

"It pursues knaves," interrupted the commissary.

"I've already told you, sir commissary," answered Pasamonte, "not to go so fast. The lords of the land didn't give you that rod to mistreat us but to guide us and take us where His Majesty has ordered. If not, by Heaven— But enough! Perhaps one day the dirty work that was done in the inn may come out in the wash; in the meantime mum's the word, and let every man live well and speak better. Now let us move on, for we've had too much of this diversion."

The commissary raised his rod to strike Pasamonte in answer to his threats, but Don Quixote intervened, asking him not to ill-treat the convict since it was only fair that one who had his hands so tied should be somewhat free with his tongue. Then, turning toward the gang, he said: "I have gathered from all you have said, dearest brethren, that although they punish you for your faults, yet the pains you suffer do not please you, and that you go to them with ill will and against your inclination. I realize, moreover, that per-

[3] The first of the picaresque novels (Burgos, 1554).

haps it was the lack of courage of one fellow on the rack, the want of money of another, the want of friends of a third, and finally the biased sentence of the judge that have been the cause of your not receiving the justice to which you were entitled. Now all this prompts and even compels me to perform on your behalf the task for which I was sent into the world, and for which I became a knight-errant, and to which end I vowed to succor the needy and help those who are oppressed by the powerful. But as it is prudent not to do by evil means what can be done by fair, I wish to entreat these gentlemen, your guardians and the commissary, to be kind enough to loose you and let you go in peace, for there will be plenty of men to serve the king on worthier occasions; it seems to me a harsh thing to make slaves of those whom God and nature made free. What is more, gentlemen of the guard," added Don Quixote, "these unfortunate creatures have done nothing against you yourselves. Let each man be answerable for his own sins; there is a God in Heaven who does not fail to punish the wicked nor to reward the good. It is not right that honest men should be executioners of others when they have nothing to do with the case. I ask this boon of you in a peaceable and quiet manner, and if you grant it, I shall give you my thanks. If, on the other hand, you will not grant it willingly, then shall this lance and sword of mine, wielded by my invincible arm, force you to do my bidding."

"This is a pleasant jest," answered the commissary. "You have ended your ranting with a fine joke. Do you want us to hand over to you those the king has imprisoned, as if we had the authority to let them go or you to order us to do it? Go your way, good sir, and a pleasant journey. Settle the basin straight on your pate, and don't go looking for a cat with three legs."

"You are a cat, a rat, and a knave," answered Don Quixote. Without another word he ran at him so fiercely that, not giving him time to defend himself, he struck him to the ground badly wounded by his lance. It was lucky for the knight that this was the one who carried the firelock. The guards were astounded at this unexpected event. But they recovered themselves, and the horsemen drew their swords, the footmen clutched their pikes, and all of them threw themselves upon Don Quixote, who quietly waited for their attack. No doubt he would have been in great danger if the slaves, seeing a chance of liberty, had not broken the chain by which they were tied together. The confusion was such that the guards, first trying to prevent the galley slaves from getting loose, then defending themselves against Don Quixote, who attacked them, did nothing to any purpose. Sancho, for his part, helped to release Ginés de Pasamonte, who was the first that leaped free and unfettered upon the plain. The latter then set upon the fallen commissary and relieved him of his sword and firelock, with which, aiming first at one and then at another, although he never fired it, he cleared the plain of guards, for they all fled no less from Pasamonte's firelock than from the showers of stones that the liberated slaves flung at them.

Sancho was much worried by all that had happened, for he had a shrewd suspicion that the guards who had fled would report the matter to the Holy Brotherhood, who would raise the alarm and sally out in pursuit of the criminals, and he said so to his master, begging him to leave that place at once and hide themselves in the neighboring sierra.

"That is all very well," answered Don Quixote, "but I know what we should do now." Then he called all the galley slaves, who were now running hither and thither in a riotous mood and had stripped the commissary to the skin, and when they had gathered around him in a circle, he addressed them as follows: "It is the duty of well-bred people to be grateful for benefits received, and ingratitude is one of the most hateful sins in the eyes of God. I say this, sirs, because you know what favor you have received from me, and the only return I wish and demand is that you all go from here, laden with the chains from which I have just freed your necks, to the city of El Toboso. There you are to present yourselves before Lady Dulcinea of El Toboso and tell her that her Knight of the Rueful Figure sent you there to commend his service to her. You are to tell her, point by point, the details of this famous adventure, and when you have done this, you may then go whichever way you please and good luck be with you."

Ginés de Pasamonte answered for all the rest, saying: "That which you demand, sir, is impossible to perform, because we must not travel the roads together, but go alone and separate so that we may not be found by the men of the Holy Brotherhood, who will be sure to come out to search for us. What you can do, and ought to do, is to change this service and duty to the Lady Dulcinea of El Toboso into a cer-

tain number of Ave Marias and credos that we shall say for
your worship's intention. And this we may do by night or by
day, resting or on the run, at peace or at work; but if you
think that we are now going to return to the fleshpots of
Egypt—to our chains, I mean—and start off on the road to
El Toboso, you might as well imagine that it's already nighttime, whereas it is not yet ten o'clock in the morning. To expect this from us is like expecting pears off an elm tree."

"I vow then," said Don Quixote in a rage, "sir whoreson,
Don Ginesillo de Parapilla, or whatever you call yourself, that
you will go alone, with your tail between your legs and the
whole length of chain on your back."

Pasamonte, who was a truculent fellow (he now understood
that Don Quixote was not very sane, seeing the foolish thing
he had done by setting them free), would not stand being
abused in this manner; so he winked at his companions, and
they from a distance began to rain a shower of stones on
Don Quixote, whose buckler gave him scant cover; and poor
Rozinante paid no more attention to the spur than if his flanks
were made of bronze. Sancho took cover behind his ass and
thus sheltered himself against the squall of stones that burst
about them. Don Quixote was less able to shield himself
against the countless stones that hit him with such force that
at last they stretched him on the ground. Scarcely had he
fallen when the student Ginés jumped upon him, and taking
the basin from his head, gave him three or four blows with
it on the shoulders and then struck it repeatedly on the
ground, almost breaking it into pieces. They then stripped
him of a tunic he wore over his armor, and they would have
seized his hose too had they not been hindered by his greaves.
They took Sancho's cloak, leaving him in his underclothes,
and after dividing among themselves the rest of the spoils,
each went his own way, with more thought of escaping the
Holy Brotherhood than of dragging their chains to Lady
Dulcinea of El Toboso.

All that remained were the ass, Rozinante, Sancho, and
Don Quixote. The ass pensively hanging his head, shaking his
ears every now and then as if he thought the storm of stones
was not yet over. Rozinante prostrate lying beside his master
on the ground; Sancho in his underclothes, trembling at the
thought of the Holy Brotherhood; and Don Quixote, in the
dumps at finding himself so ill-treated by those for whom he
had done so much.

CHAPTER XXIII

Of what happened to the famous Don Quixote in the Sierra Morena, one of the rarest adventures in this truthful history

Don Quixote, finding himself in so bad a way, said to his squire: "Sancho, I have always heard it said that to do a kindness to rogues is like pouring water into the sea. If I had listened to your advice, I might have avoided this trouble. But now that it is over, we must be patient and take warning for another time."

"If your worship takes warning, you may call me a Turk. But as you say, you might have escaped this mischief if you had followed my advice. Now listen to me, and you will avoid a still greater danger. For let me tell you, it is no use blathering about chivalry to the Holy Brotherhood. They do not care two straws for all the knights-errant there are in the world. Already I'm fancying I hear their arrows whizzing about my ears." [1]

"You, Sancho, are naturally a coward. However, to prevent your saying that I am obstinate and never followed your advice, I will take your counsel this time and hide myself from the terrors you fear so greatly. But it must be on one condition: that you never tell anyone that I withdrew from this danger through fear, but to comply with your en-

[1] Officers of the Holy Brotherhood carried crossbows; they were permitted to execute robbers caught in the act and to hang their bodies on trees.

treaties. If you say otherwise, you lie, and once and for all I denounce you as a liar every time you say or think it. Do not say another word, for at the mere thought that I am withdrawing and flying from some peril, especially from this, which seems to show some faint shadow of danger about it, I am inclined to stand my ground here and singly await the onslaught not only of the Holy Brotherhood, whose name you utter in terror, but also of the brethren of the Twelve Tribes of Israel, the Seven Maccabees, Castor and Pollux, and all the brothers and brotherhoods there are in the world as well."

"Master," answered Sancho, "to withdraw is not to run away, nor is it wise to stay when there is more peril than hope, and it's a wise man's duty to protect himself today for tomorrow. Though I'm only a rough clodhopper of a fellow, I've a smattering of what is called good conduct. So, don't repent of having taken my advice, but mount Rozinante (if you are able; if not, I'll give you a hand) and follow me. I've a shrewd notion that for the present we'll need our heels more than our hands."

Don Quixote mounted Rozinante without another word; and Sancho leading the way on his ass, they entered the neighboring Sierra Morena. Sancho's intention was to pass through it and get out at Viso or Almodóvar del Campo and hide themselves for some days among those rocky wastes so as to escape the notice of the Holy Brotherhood. He was encouraged in this course by finding that the provisions carried on his ass had escaped from the skirmish with the galley slaves—a thing that he looked upon as a miracle, considering what the slaves had taken away and how zealously they searched for booty.

They arrived that night in the heart of the Sierra Morena, where Sancho determined to spend the night, and indeed, as many days as their food would last. They bivouacked between two rocks among a number of cork trees. But destiny, which, according to the opinion of those whose lives are not illuminated by the light of true faith, arranges and adjusts all things its own way, so ordained that Ginés de Pasamonte, the celebrated trickster and robber whom Don Quixote by his valor and folly had released from his chains and who also feared (and rightly so) the Holy Brotherhood, also resolved to hide himself among the same mountains, and his luck and his fear led him to the very spot where Don

Quixote and his squire were hiding. Moreover, he arrived just in time to recognize the two of them and to let them sleep. And as the wicked are always ungrateful, and necessity drives men to evil deeds, and present advantage obliterates all future considerations, Ginés, who was neither grateful nor good-natured, determined to steal Sancho Panza's ass. As for Rozinante, he did not fancy him, for he did not consider him either pawnable or salable. While Sancho slept on blissfully, Ginés stole his ass,[2] and before dawn he was so far distant as to be past finding.

The rosy dawn arose bringing joy to the earth but only grief to Sancho Panza, for he found himself without his ass. And finding himself deprived of him, he began to utter the saddest and most pitiful lamentations in the world. At the sound of his cries Don Quixote awoke and heard him say: "O child of my bowels! Born in my own house, plaything of my children, comfort of my wife, envy of my neighbors, relief of my burdens, and lastly, support of half my person, for with the twenty-six maravedis that you earned daily, I paid half my expenses!"

Don Quixote, when he heard this lament and learned the cause of it, comforted Sancho as best he could and begged him to be patient, promising to give him a note for three out of the five ass foals he had left at home. Sancho was comforted by this promise, dried his tears, moderated his sobs, and thanked Don Quixote for the favors he had done him.

And as they advanced further into the mountains, Don Quixote felt glad at heart, for those places seemed to him suitable for the adventures he was in search of. He reminded himself of the marvelous incidents that had happened to knights-errant in similar wild places; and his mind was so entirely wrapped up in these things that he thought

---

[2] In the stealing of the ass there is an oversight of Cervantes, for later in the chapter he speaks of Sancho still in possession of Dapple, while farther on he again refers to the theft. In the first edition he omitted the paragraphs describing the theft of Dapple by the bandit Ginés de Pasamonte down to Don Quixote's promise to give Sancho the note for the three ass foals. He made the correction in the second edition of Cuesta. Professor Schevill believes that the author, after completing the first edition, wished to introduce the incident of the theft and wrote an additional sheet to be added to the manuscript, but then forgot to arrange with the printer for the changes.

of nothing else. As for Sancho, his only concern (now that he thought himself out of danger) was to cram his belly with the remnants from the clerical spoils; so he trudged along after his master, burdened with all the things that his ass should have carried, but as he walked he took out of the wallet one piece of food after another and shoveled it into his paunch. While he was thus engaged, he would not have given a maravedi for any adventure in the world.

Just then he raised his eyes and saw that his master had stopped and was trying to lift with the point of his lance some object that lay upon the ground. He hastened to see whether he wanted his aid, and reached his side just as he was lifting up a saddle cushion with a portmanteau fastened to it. The latter was half rotten, in fact falling to pieces, but so heavy that Sancho had to dismount to lift it up. Don Quixote ordered him to see what was in the portmanteau and Sancho obeyed him as quickly as he could. Although it was shut with a chain and padlock, Sancho could see through the tears and holes what was in it, namely four fine holland shirts and other linen garments, both unsoiled and of delicate material, besides a handkerchief containing a little heap of gold crowns. No sooner did he find the latter than he exclaimed: "Blessing on Heaven, which has given us an adventure worth something!" After further searching he found a little memorandum book richly bound. Don Quixote asked him for this, but bade him keep the money for himself. For this favor Sancho kissed his hands, and taking all the linen out of the bag, he rammed it into his provision wallet. When Don Quixote saw this, he said: "I think, Sancho (it cannot be possible otherwise), that some traveler must have lost his way in the mountains and run across thieves who slew him and buried him in this desolate spot."

"That is impossible," said Sancho, "for if they had been robbers, they would not have left this money here."

"True," said Don Quixote; "I cannot imagine what can have happened. But wait a moment; let us see if there is anything written in this little memorandum book by which we may discover what we want to know." He opened it, and the first thing he found in it was the rough copy of a sonnet, but written in a most legible hand, which he read aloud to Sancho. It ran as follows:

Now that I'm doomed to anguish and despair,
Love has forsworn all knowledge of my plight;
Does he now glory in his tyrannous might,
Or is it my sin or some past affair?
If Love's a god, and all of us are sure
The gods are merciful, who cast this spell
That in my crazed heart sounds its doleful knell
And grief that I no longer can endure?
If I should blame thee, Chloe, I should lie,
For in thee grace abounds, nor could a taint
Of evil in thy radiant soul be found.
My life now fades, and I must shortly die;
As I can't find the cause of my complaint,
Only a miracle could cure my wound.

"We cannot learn a thing from that poem," said Sancho, "unless by that clue we can get to the thread of the matter."

"What clue is there here?" said Don Quixote.

"I thought," said Sancho, "your worship mentioned a clue."

"I said Chloe," replied Don Quixote; "and that, no doubt, is the name of the lady of whom the author of this sonnet complains. He must be a reasonably good poet, or I know little of the art."

"So your worship," said Sancho, "knows how to write poetry too."

"And better than you think," answered Don Quixote, "as you shall see when you take a letter, written in verse from beginning to end, to my Lady Dulcinea of El Toboso; for I must tell you, Sancho, that all or most of the knights-errant in the olden days were great troubadours and great musicians too, for these two accomplishments, or graces, as I would rather call them, are connected with lovers-errant, though it is true that the verses of the knights of old have more spirit than elegance."

"Read some more, sir," said Sancho, "for we may yet find something that will satisfy us."

Don Quixote turned the page and said: "This is prose and looks like a letter."

"An ordinary letter, sir?" inquired Sancho.

"From its opening," replied Don Quixote, "it looks more like a love letter."

"Then read it aloud, your worship," said Sancho. "I very much enjoy this love business."

"With pleasure," said Don Quixote, and reading it aloud as Sancho had requested, he found that it ran as follows:

"Your false promise and my certain misfortune drive me to a place whence the news of my death will reach you sooner than the words of my complaints. You have abandoned me, ungrateful one, for one who possesses more, but is not worthier than I am. Yet, if virtue were as highly esteemed as wealth is, I should neither envy any man his fortune, nor mourn my own misfortune. What your beauty raised up, your deeds have destroyed; the one made me believe you were an angel, the others convince me you are a woman. Be at peace, causer of my war, and may Heaven grant that your husband's deceptions be forever hidden, that you may not repent of what you have done, nor I take the vengeance that I do not want."

When he had finished reading the letter, Don Quixote observed: "This letter tells us less about the writer than the verses, except that he is some rejected lover."

Turning over the leaves of the book, he found other verses and letters, some of which he could read, others he could not; but they all consisted of complaints, lamentations, suspicions, likes, dislikes, favors, slights, some of them pompous, others mournful. While Don Quixote was examining the book, Sancho ransacked the portmanteau without leaving a corner in it or in the saddle cushion that he did not scrutinize; nor was there a seam he did not rip, nor a flock of wool he did not pick. Such was the covetousness that the golden treasure of a hundred crowns had aroused in him! And though he found no more, he considered himself over and above rewarded for the blanketing, the vomiting of the balsam, the benedictions of the staves, the buffets of the carrier, the loss of the saddlebags, the theft of his cloak, not to mention the hunger, thirst, and fatigue he had endured in his good master's service.

The Knight of the Rueful Figure was eager to know who was the owner of the portmanteau, concluding from sonnet and letters, the money in gold, and the fine linen that it must belong to some noble lover who had been driven to desperate straits by the disdain and ill-treatment of his mistress. But as there was no one in this rough, uninhabitable spot to satisfy his curiosity, he ambled on aimlessly, taking any road that Rozinante chose (he always chose those he found passable), firmly convinced that among these rocky wastes he would meet with some strange adventure.

As he rode on he saw a man on top of a neighboring knoll, leaping from rock to rock and tuft to tuft with amazing agility. He seemed to be half naked, with a thick, black beard, his hair long and matted, his feet unshod, and his legs bare. He wore breeches of tawny colored velvet, but so torn to rags that his skin showed in places. His head, too, was bare, and although he ran by with all haste, as we said before, yet the Knight of the Rueful Figure was able to note all these details. And although he tried, he could not follow him, because Rozinante was too feeble to travel over those rough places, especially as he was by nature slow-footed and phlegmatic. Don Quixote then made up his mind that this man was the owner of the saddle cushion and the portmanteau, and he resolved to go in search of him, even if he should have to spend a whole year in the mountains to find him. So he ordered Sancho to dismount and take a shortcut by one side of the mountain while he went the other, in the hope that perhaps they would come across the man who had vanished so suddenly.

"I cannot do that," replied Sancho, "for as soon as I leave you, sir, fear seizes hold of me and fills me with a thousand different terrifying fancies. Let me say, once and for all, that in future I don't stir a finger's breadth from your presence."

"So be it," replied he of the Rueful Figure. "I am well pleased that you wish to avail yourself of my courage; it will not fail you, even though the soul in your body deserts you. Follow me step by step or as best you can, and use your eyes as lanterns; we shall go around this hill, and perhaps we may meet the man we saw, who beyond doubt is the owner of the portmanteau."

Sancho replied: "Surely it would be far better not to look for him at all, for if we find him and he turned out to be the owner of the money, there is no doubt that I'll have to give it back to him. It would be better, without taking this futile trouble, to let me keep it faithfully until the true owner turns up; perhaps by that time I shall have spent it all, and in that case the king will hold me guiltless."

"You are mistaken, Sancho," answered Don Quixote, "for now that we suspect who the owner is, we are obliged, henceforth, to look for him and restore him his money. And even if we do not go in search of him, the strong presumption we have of his being the owner makes us as guilty as if he really were the owner. So, Sancho, my friend, don't let this search give you pain, and think how relieved I shall be to find him."

With these words he clapped spurs to Rozinante, and Sancho followed him on foot, carrying (thanks to Ginesillo de Pasamonte) his load on his back. When they had gone around part of the mountain, they found in a stream a dead mule, half devoured by dogs and pecked by crows—a discovery that confirmed their belief that the man who had fled from them was the owner of the portmanteau and saddle cushion. As they were looking at it, they heard a whistle like that of a shepherd, and there appeared on their left a great number of goats, and behind them, near the top of the mountain, was the goatherd, an aged man. Don Quixote shouted to him to come down to where they stood; and the goatherd shouted back, inquiring what had brought them to that lonely place that was seldom or never trodden by any but the feet of goats, wolves, or other beasts that prowled about those places. Sancho answered that they would tell him everything if only he would descend. The goatherd came down and said as he approached: "I'll bet you are looking at the mule lying stiff in the gap yonder. He's been lying in the very spot for six months. Tell me, now, has either of you run into his master?"

"We have met nobody," replied Don Quixote, "but we discovered a saddle cushion and a small valise, which we found lying not far from here."

"I too found that same one," said the goatherd, "but I wouldn't pick it up, nor go near it. I was afraid some bad luck might fall on me, and I be held for thieving; for the Devil's a sly one, to be sure, and a man may hit his foot on something that makes him stumble and fall, never knowing the why or wherefore."

"That's what I say," replied Sancho. "I too found it and I wouldn't go within a stone's throw of it. There I left it and there it stays as it was; I don't want a dog with a bell on it."

"Tell me, my good man," said Don Quixote, "do you know who is the owner of these things?"

"All I can say," said the goatherd, "is that it will be

now six months ago when a fine handsome young fellow
came to a sheepfold that is around nine miles from where
we're standing this instant. He was riding that same mule
that is dead there and with the same saddle pad and trunk
that you say you found but never touched. He asked us
which was the most hidden part of the mountain, and we
told him it was here where we are standing; and that's the
honest truth, for if you go three miles further on, you would
likely never find your way out. Indeed I'm wondering how
you found your way here, for there is no road or path that
leads to this place. When the young fellow heard our answer, he turned his bridle and headed in the direction we
showed him, leaving us all taken by his good looks and wondering at his questions and at seeing him ride hell for
leather toward the mountains. Not a glimpse did we get of
him for many a day until all of a sudden he got in the way
of one of the goatherds. Without saying a word he jumped
on the goatherd and punched and kicked him. Then he
went after the baggage ass and took all the bread and cheese
he carried. Then, with unbelievable swiftness he went back
into the mountains. When we heard of this, the goatherds
went in search of him, and we spent almost two days in
the most remote places in the mountains looking. In the
end we found him hiding in the hollow of an old cork tree.
He came out meek as a lamb, his clothes in ribbons, his
face all skinned and scorched by the sun. We hardly recognized him; but his clothes, which we had noticed before,
though then already torn, made us realize that it was he
for whom we were looking. He greeted us cordially and
told us in few and well-selected words not to wonder at seeing him act in that manner, for thus he was carrying out
the penance given him for his many sins. We begged him
to tell us who he was, but there was no way of getting a
word out of him. We asked him also to tell us where we
would be able to find him whenever he needed food, for
we would gladly bring it to him. We also said that if this
didn't suit him, he should at least ask for it without stealing
it from the goatherds. He thanked us for our offer, begged
our pardon for the past assault, and promised from then on
to ask for food in God's name without troubling a soul.
As to where he lived, he said that all he had was what chance
offered when night overtook him. He ended his speech with
such sad moaning that, as we listened to the poor fellow,

our hearts might well have been of stone if we hadn't followed suit, considering how he was when we saw him on the first occasion and what he was now; for, as I have said, he was a handsome, gentle lad, and if I may judge from the niceties of his speech, he must be someone wellborn and of courtly stock. And though we are all country folk, we could see at a glance what kind of a man he was. But being in the best part of his conversation, he shut up and stood dumb and nailed his eyes to the ground while we held our breath, wondering where the poor lad's fit would end and feeling very sorry for him. And from what he did with his eyes, at times staring fixedly at the ground a long while without stirring an eyelid and at other times shutting them as he tightened his lips and arched his eyebrows, we easily guessed that a fret of madness had taken hold of him; and in a flash he showed us we were right, for in a fury he sprang up from the ground where he had thrown himself and set upon the first he found nearest to him with such fury that if we had not pulled him off, he would have battered and bitten him to death. And all the while he kept howling: 'Treacherous Fernando! You'll now, this instant, pay for the wrong you did to me! With my hands I'll tear out that wicked heart of yours that is filled with every crime, especially with fraud and trickery!' To these he added other curses against that Fernando, treating him as traitor and perjurer.

"At last we rescued our fellow from him with no little difficulty, and he, without saying another word, raced away to hide himself among the briars and thickets so that it was impossible to follow him. So we gather that his fret comes upon him at times and that someone whom he calls Fernando must have done him such a grievous wrong as to reduce him to this pitiable state. All this has been confirmed since then, for he has come out many times into the path, sometimes to beg the goatherds to give him a bite of food, at other times to seize it from them by violence. And when his madness lies on him, he won't accept food, though the herds offer it freely, but prefers to snatch it from them with blows. Yet when he is in his senses, he asks for it courteously and politely, for the love of God, and accepts it with thanks and not without tears.

"And to tell you the truth, sirs," proceeded the goatherd, "yesterday we agreed, I and four lads—two of our fellows

and two friends of mine—to search for him till we find him,
and then take him willingly or by force to the town of
Almodóvar, which is about eight leagues from here. There
we'll have him cured, if his disease is curable, or we'll find
out who he is when in his senses and whether he has relatives to whom we may give notice of his trouble. This, sirs,
is all I can tell you of what you have asked me; and you
may be sure that the owner of the articles that you found
is the same man whom you saw racing by so naked and nimble." (Don Quixote, incidentally, had already told him that
he had seen that man leaping from rock to rock.)

Our knight was amazed at what he had heard from the
goatherd, and as he was more eager than ever to know who
the unhappy madman was, he resolved to carry out a plan
he had already been debating within himself to search the
whole mountain, leaving no corner or cavern unexplored
until he should find him. But fortune favored him more than
he expected, for even as he was speaking to the goatherd,
the young man appeared in a neighboring gorge of the
sierra, descending toward them and muttering to himself unintelligible words. His clothes were such as have been described, only that, as he drew closer, Don Quixote noticed
that he wore a leather jerkin, that, though torn to pieces,
still retained the perfume of amber. From this he guessed
that the young man was a person of quality. As the youth
drew near, he greeted them in a harsh voice but with great
courtesy. Don Quixote returned the salute with equal politeness, and alighting from Rozinante, with graceful demeanor
went to meet him, and clasping him in his arms, embraced
him as though he had known him for a long time.

The other, whom we may call the Ragged One of the Sorrowful Figure, as Don Quixote was of the Rueful Figure,
after allowing himself to be embraced, drew back a little,
and laying his hands on Don Quixote's shoulders, stood gazing at him as if he wished to ascertain whether he knew
him. He was, perhaps, no less amazed at the figure, demeanor, and armor of Don Quixote, than the knight was
at him. In the end, the first to speak after the embrace was
the Ragged One, and what he said will be told in the next
chapter.

CHAPTER XXIV

The adventure in the Sierra Morena continued

The history relates that Don Quixote listened with the utmost attention to the ill-starred knight of the sierra, who addressed him as follows: "Truly, sir, whoever you may be, for I do not know you, I thank you with all my heart for your courtesy toward me and I wish I were in the position to repay you for your gracious welcome, but my fortunes give me nothing to offer in return for your kindness but the longing to respond."

"My wish to serve you is so great," said Don Quixote, "that I had decided not to leave these mountains until I had discovered you and learned from you whether any remedy could be found for the pain which your strange way of life shows you to suffer; and if so, I would have searched for it with might and main. But should your misfortune happen to be one of those that close all doors to any kind of remedy, I intended to share your grief as best I could, for it is still some comfort to find someone to help you share your burden. If my good intentions merit some kind of courtesy, I beg you, sir, by all the grace that I see is in your nature, and I jointly conjure you, by what in this life you have loved or do love most, to tell me who you are and what has brought you to live and die like a brute beast in these solitudes—a dwelling place so unsuitable to your rank if I may judge from your person and attire. And I swear," added Don Quixote, "by the order of chivalry that I received, though an unworthy sinner, and by the profession of knight-errant, that if you gratify me in this, I will serve you with all the energy that it is my duty to

exert, either by overcoming your troubles, or if that cannot
be, by joining you in lamenting them, as I have promised."

The Knight of the Wood, hearing the Knight of the Rueful
Figure talk in this manner, kept staring at him from head to
foot; and after gazing at him again and again, he said: "If
you have anything to eat, give it to me for God's sake, and
after I have eaten, I will do all that you ask in return for
the kindness you show me."

Sancho straightaway drew from his wallet, and the goatherd from his scrip, provisions that satisfied the Ragged
One's hunger; but he ate what they gave him like a distracted
person and with such ravenous speed that he made no interval between one mouthful and the next. Indeed he rather
devoured than ate, and during his meal neither he nor the
others, who watched him, spoke a word. Having ended his
repast, he made signs to them to follow him, which they did,
and he led them to a little green field behind a rock nearby.
When they arrived, he threw himself down on the grass and
the rest did likewise. Not a word was spoken until the
Ragged One, having composed himself, said: "If it is your
pleasure, gentlemen, to hear in a few words the story of my
immense misfortunes, you must promise not to interrupt the
thread of my sad story, for the moment you do I shall stop
telling it."

These words of the Ragged One brought to Don Quixote's
mind the story that his squire had told him, when he had
failed to keep count of the goats that had crossed the river
and the story remained unfinished. But to return to the
Ragged One, he continued: "This warning I give you because I wish to pass over briefly the tale of my misfortunes,
for no sooner do I bring them to mind than I seem to add
others, so the less you question me, the sooner I shall finish
telling them. Yet, I shall not omit anything of importance,
as I wish to satisfy your curiosity in every respect."

Don Quixote, in the name of all, promised not to interrupt him, and with this assurance the Ragged One began his
story thus: "My name is Cardenio; my birthplace, one of
the finest cities of Andalusia; my lineage, noble; my parents, rich; and my misfortune so great that it must have
been mourned by my parents and felt by my relations,
though their wealth could do nothing to lighten it, for riches
are of little avail in the calamities imposed by destiny. In
that city there dwelt a heavenly damsel whom love had

crowned with all the glory I could ever desire: such is the
beauty of Luscinda, a lady as wellborn and rich as myself,
though more fortunate and less constant than my honorable
thoughts deserved. This Luscinda I loved and adored from
my earliest years, and she loved me with that innocent affection that was natural at her tender age. Our parents knew
of our attachment and were not sorry to see it, for they
saw that it could end only in a marriage sanctioned by our
birth and wealth.

"As we grew in years, so did our mutual love increase till
Luscinda's father felt obliged, for the sake of prudence, to
deny me admission to his house, thus imitating the parents
of that Thisbe whose praises so many poets have sung,[1]
and this denial added flame to flame and love to love, for
though they imposed silence on our tongues, they could not
impose it on our pens, which usually reveal more freely than
do tongues the secrets of the heart, since many a time the
mere presence of the beloved one disturbs and silences the
staunchest heart and boldest tounge. Alas, how many letters
did I write to her! What sweet and virtuous answers did I
receive! How many songs did I compose, how many love
verses wherein my soul declared its love, described its passion, cherished its memories, and indulged its fancies! Then
finding myself sorely troubled and being consumed with
longing, I resolved to put into operation what seemed to
be the most suitable plan for winning my longed-for and
merited prize, which was to ask for her as my lawful wife
from her father, which I did. He answered that he thanked
me for the desire I showed to honor him and to honor myself with his beloved one, but that, my father being alive, it
was by right his business to make that request. For if it
were not done with his goodwill and pleasure, Luscinda was
not the woman to be taken or given secretly.

"I thanked him for his kindness, and feeling there was
reason in what he said, I hastened to my father to tell him
of my desires. When I entered his room, he was standing
with a letter open in his hand, and before I could speak, he
gave it to me, saying: 'By this letter, Cardenio, you may
learn the wish the Duke Ricardo has to do you a favor.' This
Duke Ricardo, as you surely know, gentlemen, is a grandee

[1] Pyramus and Thisbe, Babylonian lovers. Ovid, *Meta-morphoses* Bk. IV.

of Spain whose dukedom is situated in the richest part of Andalusia. I took the letter and read it, and it was so very kind that it seemed to me wrong if my father did not do what he asked. For he wanted me to be a companion—not a servant—to his eldest son and offered to advance me in life in accordance with the good opinion he had of me. On reading the letter I was struck dumb with consternation, and still more when I heard my father say: 'Cardenio, you must be ready to leave in two days and to do what the duke wishes. You should thank your stars that such a future lies open to you.' And he added to this his fatherly advice.

"The day of my departure arrived. I spoke one night to my dear Luscinda and also to her father, begging him to wait a few days and not to give her in marriage until I knew what Duke Ricardo's plans for me were. He promised and she confirmed it with a thousand vows and swoonings. At last, I arrived at the home of Duke Ricardo, who received and treated me with great kindness, but the one who rejoiced most at my coming was his second son, Fernando, a young man who was noble, gallant, very comely, and of a loving disposition. In a short time he became so intimate a friend of mine that it was the subject of general comment; and though the elder son treated me with much favor, it did not compare with the affection lavished upon me by Don Fernando. Now, since friends communicate all their secrets to one another and my feelings for Fernando were deeply sincere, he told me all his thoughts and desires and confided to me a love affair of his own that caused me much anxiety. He had fallen in love with the daughter of a farmer who was his father's vassal. Her parents were rich, and she herself was so beautiful, modest, wise, and virtuous that no one who knew her could decide which of those qualities she most excelled in. In any case, the charms of the fair farmer's daughter so inflamed the heart of Fernando that he resolved to promise her marriage in order to triumph over her chastity, for he knew that she could not be conquered by any other means. Prompted by my friendship, I tried by all the arguments and the examples I could think of to dissuade him from his purpose, but finding it in vain, I resolved to tell the story to his father, Duke Ricardo. But Don Fernando, who was clear-sighted and shrewd, suspected my intentions, for he feared that I should not, owing to my position as faithful servant, be able to keep back from my master a

matter that was so prejudicial to his honor. So, to put me off
the scent he said that he could find no better way of banish-
ing the remembrance of her beauty than by leaving home
for a few months. Therefore his plan, he said, was for both of
us to go back to my father's house on the excuse of seeing
and buying horses in my native city, which is famous for
producing the best in the world.

"No sooner did he make this suggestion than, swayed by
my own love, I gave my entire approval to his plan because
it gave me so good an opportunity of seeing once more my
dear Luscinda. I therefore encouraged him and begged him
to put it into operation as soon as possible, for absence
would tell in the end in spite of the strongest inclination. I
found out afterward that when he made his proposal to me
he had already, under the title of husband, enjoyed the
favors of the maiden and was only waiting for an opportunity to divulge the truth with safety to himself, for he was
afraid of what the duke, his father, would do when he should
hear of his escapade. Now, love in most young men is not
love but lust, and as its ultimate end is pleasure, it ceases
once that end has been attained; and what appeared to be
love must disappear because it cannot pass the limits assigned to it by nature, whereas true affection knows none
of such limitations. . . . . I mean to say that no sooner
had Don Fernando enjoyed the farmer's daughter than his
desires weakened and his amorous impulses cooled. If at
first he had pretended that he would absent himself in
order to get rid of passions, he now endeavored to go away
to avoid fulfilling his promises. The duke gave him leave and
ordered me to go with him.

"We arrived at my native city, and my father entertained
him according to his rank. I again saw Luscinda. My love for
her revived (though indeed it had never grown cold), and to
my sorrow I told Fernando all about it, for I thought that
by the laws of friendship it was not right to hide anything
from him. I described Luscinda's beauty, charm, and
wit in such glowing terms that my phrases stirred in him
a desire to see a damsel enriched with such rare virtues.
To my misfortune, I gratified his wish and showed her to
him one night by the light of a candle at the window where
we were wont to speak together. He saw her in her light
dress, and such was her beauty that he immediately forgot
every fair lady he had seen hitherto. He was struck dumb,

he lost his senses, he was entranced and so deeply in love as you will see in the course of my sad story. And what inflamed his passion (which he hid from me) was that he happened to see a letter she had written asking me to beg her father again to give consent to our marriage. So sensible and full of tenderness was the letter that when he had read it he said that Luscinda possessed in her person all the beauty, grace, and understanding of the rest of womankind.

"It is true, I confess, that though I admitted the justice of Fernando's praise, it troubled me to hear those praises from his lips, and I began to fear and with reason to suspect him, for at every moment of the day he wished to talk of Luscinda, and he would start the conversation himself, even if he had to drag her in by the hair. This aroused in me a certain amount of jealousy, not that I feared any change in Luscinda's goodness and fidelity, yet my fate made me deeply apprehensive despite all her assurances to the contrary. So, Don Fernando continued to read the letters I sent to Luscinda and those she wrote to me, on the excuse that he took great pleasure in our wit; and one day it happened that Luscinda asked me to give her a book of chivalry of which she was very fond, entitled *Amadis of Gaul.* . . ."

Don Quixote had hardly heard him mention a book of chivalry when he cried: "If you had told me, my good sir, that your lady, Luscinda, was a reader of knightly adventures, you need not have said anything else to make me understand the high quality of her mind, for I would not believe it to be as excellent as you, sir, have described it if she had lacked that taste for such delightful reading. So, do not waste any more words describing her beauty and worth, for now I assert that, owing to her devotion to such books, Lady Luscinda is the fairest lady and most accomplished woman in all the world. But I could have wished, sir, you had sent her with *Amadis of Gaul* the worthy *Don Rugel of Greece,* for I know that Lady Luscinda would be delighted with Daraida and Garaya, with the conceits of the shepherd Darinel, and with those admirable lines in his bucolics, sung and declaimed by him with such charm, wit, and freedom. But a time may come when you can remedy this omission; and this you can do whenever you are minded to come to my village, for there I can give you more than three hundred books that are the solace of my soul and the entertainment of my life, though now I remember that I have none, thanks to the malice of wicked and envious enchanters. Pardon me, sir, for having broken our promise not to interrupt your story, but when I hear anything said about chivalry, I can no more refrain from speaking of them than the sunbeams can help giving warmth or the moonbeams moisture. Therefore, forgive and proceed, for that is more to the purpose."

While Don Quixote had been delivering this harangue, Cardenio held his head down, apparently sunk in deep thought, and although Don Quixote twice requested him to go on with his story, he neither raised his head nor answered a word. But at the end of a long pause, he looked up and said: "I cannot get it out of my head, nor can anyone in the world persuade me to the contrary—indeed he who believes otherwise must be a blockhead—that Master Elisabat, that arrant rogue, was the paramour of Queen Madásima." [2]

"That is not true, I swear," answered Don Quixote in great rage. "It is the height of calumny, or rather villainy, to say so. Queen Madásima was a very noble lady, and it is not to be presumed that so high a princess would grant her favors to a quack, and whoever states the contrary lies like a rogue, and I will make him understand it on foot, on horseback, armed or unarmed, by night or by day, as he likes best."

Cardenio stood gazing fixedly at Don Quixote, for now the mad fit was on him and he was in no condition to continue his story; nor would Don Quixote have listened to him, so irritated was he by what he had heard about Queen Madásima. What a strange thing it was to see him take her part as though she had been his true and natural princess! Such was the power those accursed books had over him. And Cardenio, who was now raving, when he heard himself called a liar and a rogue in addition to other opprobrious epithets, took exception to the jest, and seizing a stone that lay close to him, he threw it with such force at Don Quixote's chest that he knocked him over on his back. Sancho Panza, seeing his master so roughly handled, set upon the madman with his clenched fists, but the Ragged One with one blow laid him at his feet, after which he stood on him and kicked him to his heart's content. The goatherd,

[2] Elisabat is a surgeon in *Amadis of Gaul* who performs miracle cures. Queen Madásima roves through forests and deserts with Elisabat and they sleep together without any scandal to her good name.

who tried to defend him, suffered the same fate. When the madman had vanquished and drubbed them all, he departed calmly and peaceably and disappeared in the mountain scrub. Sancho rose, and in such a rage to find himself so mauled and kicked without cause that he ran at the goatherd to be revenged on him, saying he was at fault for not having warned them that this man was subject to mad fits at times; for had they known, they would have been on their guard.

The goatherd answered that he had told him, and if he had not paid attention to his warning, it was not his fault. Sancho Panza replied; the goatherd did likewise; and the dispute passed from words to blows, for they caught hold of one another's beards and punched away with such fury that if Don Quixote had not pacified them, they would have battered one another to bits. Sancho, still holding the goatherd fast, kept saying: "Leave me alone, Sir Knight of the Rueful Figure, this fellow is a yokel like myself. He's not dubbed a knight; so, I may safely get my satisfaction for the wrong he has done me by fighting with him hand to hand like a man of honor."

"That is true," said Don Quixote, "but know that he is not in any way culpable for what has happened." Having pacified them with these words, he again asked the goatherd if it would be possible to find Cardenio, for he was most eager to know the end of his story. The goatherd repeated what he had said at first, namely, that he did not exactly know his haunts, but that if they wandered about these parts, they would be sure to meet him, sane or mad.

CHAPTER XXV

Of the strange things that happened to the valiant knight of La Mancha in the Sierra Morena, and of the penance he performed there

Don Quixote took leave of the goatherd and mounted once again on Rozinante; he commanded Sancho to follow him on his ass, which he did most unwillingly. They traveled at a slow pace, entering little by little into the thickest and roughest part of the mountains. Sancho Panza was dying to converse with his master, but wanted him to begin talking first so that he might not disobey his orders. At last, being unable to endure such prolonged silence, he burst out: "Please, sir, give me your blessing and permission to depart. I want to go home to my wife and children with whom at least I shall be allowed to chat and gossip to my heart's content. If you, sir, want me to bear you company through these lonely places day and night without letting me open my lips when the whim takes me, you might as well bury me alive. If fate allowed beasts to speak as they did in the times of Aesop, it wouldn't be so bad, for I'd be able to talk to my Dapple as much as I please and in that way I could bear my mishaps. But it is tough luck, and not to be borne in patience, for a man to roam all his life in search of adventures without meeting anything but kicks, blanketings, brickbats, and punches, and all the while to have to keep his mouth sewed up, not daring to say what's on his mind as if he were dumb."

"I understand you, Sancho," answered Don Quixote. "You are dying for me to take off the embargo I have laid on your tongue. Consider it revoked and say what you please, on condition that this revocation lasts only while we are traveling through these mountains."

"So be it," said Sancho. "Let me talk now, for what's to come God alone knows. So now, taking advantage of my license, I ask what your worship meant by standing up so sturdily for that Queen Magimasa, or whatever her name is? And what on earth did it matter whether that abbot was the boyfriend or not? If you had let that pass, seeing you weren't his judge, I'm sure the madman would have continued his story, and we could have avoided the stoning, the kicks, and more than half a dozen backhanders."

"Truly, Sancho," said Don Quixote, "if you knew as well as I do how honorable and high-minded a lady Queen Madásima was, I am sure you would agree that I was very patient not to smash to pieces the mouth that uttered such blasphemous words; for it is grievous blasphemy to say or to think that a queen would lie in sin with a surgeon. The true story is that Master Elisabat was very prudent and full of sound judgment and served the queen as her tutor and physician. But it is folly deserving of the severest punishment to imagine that she was his mistress, and to show you that Cardenio did not know what he was saying, you must remember that when he said it he was out of his senses."

"So say I," replied Sancho, "no one ought to take the words of a madman seriously, and if good luck hadn't given your worship a helping hand, and the stone had hit you on the head instead of the chest, we should have found ourselves in a nice pickle for standing up for that lady of mine, God damn her! And imagine, Cardenio would be let off as a madman."

"Every knight-errant," said Don Quixote, "is bound to stand up against everyone, sane or mad, in defense of the honor of all women, whoever they may be, and all the more for queens of such high renown as Queen Madásima, for whom I have a particular regard on account of her good qualities; not only was she very beautiful but also very wise and long-suffering in her countless misfortunes, and the counsels and the company of Master Elisabat were of much profit and comfort to her, enabling her to bear her troubles with prudence and patience. This is what drove the ignorant and evil-minded rabble to think and say that she was his mistress, but they lie, I say again, and I'll repeat two hundred times more that all who think or say so are liars."

"I don't say so or think so," answered Sancho. "But better let sleeping dogs lie, and may they stew in their own juice for all I care; and if they were living in sin or not, they'll have rendered their account to God for it by now. I come from my vineyards, I know nothing; I'm not one to go pimping and prying into other people's lives. Who buys and lies, his purse will rue the price; what's more, naked I was born, and naked am I now; I neither lose nor win; what they were, what do I care? Many expect flitches of bacon when there's not even a hook to hang them on. Who can put gates to the open? Why, even God Himself is not spared."

"God bless my soul!" cried Don Quixote. "What a nonsensical rigmarole, Sancho! What has what we were discussing to do with the proverbs you string together? On my life, Sancho, do be silent, and in the future spur on your own ass and cease meddling with what does not concern you. Let your five senses convince you that whatever I have done, do, or shall do is very reasonable and is in accordance with the laws of chivalry, which I know better than all the knights-errant that ever professed them in the world."

"Master," replied Sancho, "is it a good rule of chivalry that we should go wandering up and down through these mountains after a madman, who perhaps, when he is found, will take it into his hand to finish what he began—not his story, but the breaking of your head and my ribs?"

"Peace, I say once again, Sancho!" said Don Quixote. "For you must know it is not only the wish to find the madman that brings me into these wastes, but because I intend to carry out an adventure that will win me everlasting fame and renown over the whole face of the earth. And it shall be such that I shall set the seal on all that can make a knight-errant famous."

"Is it a dangerous adventure?" asked Sancho Panza.

"No," replied the Knight of the Rueful Figure, "though the dice may turn up blank instead of sixes, yet everything depends upon your diligence."

"My diligence?" said Sancho.

"Yes," said Don Quixote, "for if you return quickly from the place where I intend to send you, my penance will soon be over, and my glory will then begin. I do not want to keep you any longer in suspense, waiting to hear how my discourse will end, and so I shall explain the meaning of my words. You must know, Sancho, that the famous Amadis

of Gaul was one of the most perfect of all knights-errant.
I was wrong to say one; he was alone, the first, the unique,
the lord of all who in his age were in the world. A fig for
Don Belianís and for all who said they equaled him in
anything! I swear they are mistaken. Moreover, I say that
when any painter wishes to win renown in his art, he endeavors to copy the originals of the most illustrious painters
he knows, and this rule holds good for all the crafts and
callings of any importance that serve to adorn the republic.
And so what he who would win the name of prudent and
patient must do, and does, is to imitate Ulysses, in whose
person and labors Homer depicts for us a lively picture of a
patient and long-suffering man, just as Virgil shows in the
person of Aeneas the virtue of a dutiful son and the wisdom
of a brave and expert captain. They do not portray them or
describe them as they were but as they should have been,
to give example by their virtues to the men to come after
them. In this way Amadis was the North Star, the morning
star, the sun of all valiant knights and lovers, and all of us
who fight under the banner of love and chivalry ought to
imitate his example. This being the case, Sancho, my friend,
I consider that the knight-errant who copies him most
nearly will come nearest to attaining the perfection of chivalry. Now, one of the ways in which this knight most clearly
showed his wisdom, virtue, valor, patience, constancy, and
love was when, disdained by Lady Oriana, he retired to do
penance on Peña Pobre, after changing his name to Beltenebros, a name assuredly significant and suitable to the life
that he had voluntarily chosen.[1] Therefore, as it is easier
for me to imitate him in this than in cleaving giants, beheading serpents, killing dragons, routing armies, shattering fleets,
and dissolving enchantments, and because these wilds are
so suitable for the purpose, I have no reason to let this

[1] This is a reference to the most striking adventure of Amadis.
It was the old hermit who urged the knight to assume the name
Beltenebros, which would symbolize his person and his anguish.
Cervantes closely imitates the penitence of Amadis. The latter
had conquered Firm Island and set out for the court of Sobradisa,
which vas ruled by the youthful Queen Briolanja. This made
Oriana jealous, so she sent her page Burín to Amadis with a
letter full of complaints. Hence the anguish of the lovesick knight,
who withdrew immediately to do penance in the deserts and
forests.

opportunity pass that now so conveniently presents me the forelock."

"What is it then your worship intends to do in this remote spot?" asked Sancho.

"Have I not told you already," replied Don Quixote, "that I mean to copy Amadis of Gaul by acting here the part of a despairing, mad, and furious lover; at the same time following the example of Orlando when he found by a spring evidences that Angélica the Fair had dishonored herself with Medoro, and was so grieved that he went mad, rooted up trees, troubled the waters of the clean springs, killed shepherds, destroyed flocks, fired their huts, demolished houses, dragged off mares, and committed a hundred thousand extravagant deeds worthy of eternal renown. And although I do not intend to imitate Orlando, or Roland, or Rotolando (for all these names he bore) accurately in all the mad things he did, said, or imagined, I shall outline them as best I can in what appears to me most essential. Perhaps I shall content myself by imitating Amadis alone, as he by his tears and sorrows won as much fame as the best without committing any mischievous follies."

"I am sure," said Sancho, "that the knights who went through these penances were provoked and had some reason for doing so; but what cause have you, sir, for going mad? What lady turned you down? What signs have you discovered that her ladyship, Dulcinea of El Toboso, has committed any foolishness either with Moor or Christian?"

"That is just the point of it," said Don Quixote; "and that is where the subtleness of my plan comes in. A knight-errant who goes mad for a good reason deserves no thanks or gratitude; the whole point consists in going crazy without cause, and thereby warn my lady what to expect from me in the wet if this is what I do in the dry. Moreover, I have sufficient cause in my long absence from my peerless lady, Dulcinea of El Toboso, for as you heard that shepherd Ambrosio say the other day, he who is absent feels and fears every ill. So, Sancho, my friend, do not waste more time in advising me to give up so rare, so happy, and so unparalleled an imitation. Mad I am, mad I shall remain until you return with the answer to a letter that I mean to send by you to my lady, Dulcinea. If the answer is such as I deserve, my penance will end; if not, I shall go mad in good earnest, and being mad, I shall feel nothing. Thus, whatever way she replies, I shall escape from the conflict and toil in which you leave me. If it is good news you bring me, I shall enjoy them, being in my right mind; and if they are bad, I shall not feel them, being mad. But tell me, Sancho, have you kept safely the helmet of Mambrino? I saw you lift it from the ground when that ungrateful rogue tried to break it to pieces but could not, showing how firmly it was tempered."

To which Sancho replied: "In God's name, Sir Knight of the Rueful Figure, I cannot keep my patience listening to some of the things you say, and I sometimes think all you tell me of knighthood, of winning kingdoms and empires, of giving away islands, and of doing other favors and great deeds is nothing but wind and lies. For to hear you saying that a barber's basin is Mambrino's helmet and not to find out your mistake in over four days makes me wonder if your brain isn't cracked. I'm carrying the basin in my bag, all battered and dented, and I intend to take it home, repair it, and soap my beard in it some day when I return to my wife and children."

"I swear, Sancho, by the same oath that you swore by just now," said Don Quixote, "that you have the shallowest understanding that any squire has or ever had in the whole world. Is it possible that in the time you have been with me you have not yet found out that all the adventures of a knight-errant appear to be illusion, follies, and dreams, and turn out to be the reverse? Not because things are really so, but because in our midst there is a host of enchanters, forever changing, disguising, and transforming our affairs as they please, according to whether they wish to favor or destroy us. So, what you call a barber's basin is to me Mambrino's helmet, and to another person it will appear to be something else. And it was rare foresight on the part of the wise man, my ally, to make it appear to others a basin, whereas it really and truly is Mambrino's helmet, because, being of such great value, all the world would persecute me in order to take it away from me. But since they think it is nothing but a barber's basin, they do not trouble themselves to get it, as was apparent in the case of the man who tried to break it and left it lying on the ground, for I swear that had he known what it was, he would never have left it behind. Take care of it, friend, for just now I do not need it. In fact, I must strip off my armor and remain as naked as when I was born, that is, if I decide to follow Orlando in my penance rather than Amadis."

As they were conversing, they arrived at the foot of a lofty mountain that stood like a mighty hewed rock apart from the rest. At the foot flowed a gentle rill that watered a meadow so green and so fertile that it was most pleasing to behold. It was planted with many wild shrubs and flowers that made the whole area very peaceful. This was the place the Knight of the Rueful Figure selected as the spot where he would do his penance, and seeing it, he cried out in a loud voice as if he were out of his mind: "This is the spot, O Heavens, that I select to bewail the misfortune into which you yourselves have plunged me. This is the spot where the moisture from my eyes shall swell the waters of this little stream, and my unending sighs shall stir incessantly the leaves of these mountain trees in testimony of the pain that my tortured heart is suffering. And you, rustic gods, whoever you may be, who dwell in this inhospitable place, listen to the plaints of this unlucky lover whom long absence and some fancied jealousy have driven to mourn among these rugged rocks and to complain of the cruel temper of that ungrateful beauty, the sum total of human beauty! And you, wood nymphs and dryads, who are accustomed to haunt the thick mountain groves, may the nimble and lustful satyrs, who crave in vain your favors, never trouble your sweet repose that you may help me to lament my evil fate, or at least be not weary of listening to it! O Dulcinea of El Toboso, day of my night, glory of my sorrow, cynosure of my path, star of my fortune, may Heaven grant you in full measure all the boons you pray for. Consider now the place and the condition to which your absence has reduced me in return for the guerdon my fidelity deserves! O lonely trees that henceforth must be the companions of my solitude, gently sway your branches as a token that my presence does not offend you! And you, my squire, agreeable companion in my enterprises, in prosperity no less than in adversity, fix well in your memory what you will see me do here that you may recite it to the one and only cause of it all."

So saying, he alighted from Rozinante, and stripping him rapidly of saddle and bridle, gave him a slap on his haunches, saying: "He who gives you liberty lacks it himself. O steed, as famous for your feats as luckless in your lot! Go where you please, for you bear written on your forehead that neither the Hippogriff of Astolfo nor the renowned Frontino that cost Bradamante so dear was your equal for speed." [2]

When Sancho heard all this, he could not help saying: "God's peace be with the fellow who saved us the trouble of unharnessing my ass, for he surely would have had plenty of slaps and speeches in his honor. But if the ass were here, I wouldn't allow him to be unharnessed by anyone, for there's no reason for it. The general questions put to people in love or in despair did not apply to him any more than to me, who was his master when it pleased God. But in truth, Sir Knight of the Rueful Figure, if my departure and your madness are in earnest, it would be well to saddle Rozinante again that he may make up for the loss of my ass and save me time in coming and going, for if I do the journey on foot, I don't know when I shall arrive or return, for, to tell the honest truth, I am mighty poor on my legs."

"As you will," said Don Quixote; "but you must not go away for three days yet, for I want to have time to let you see what I am saying and doing for my lady's sake, that you may tell her about it."

"What more have I to see," said Sancho, "than what I have already seen?"

"How little you know about it!" said Don Quixote. "Why, I have yet to tear my garments, scatter my armor about, and bang my head against these rocks, and other similar things that will amaze you."

"For the love of God," said Sancho, "take care how to go knocking your head against the rocks, for you may run up against so nasty a one that your plan of penance will come to an end. It is my opinion that if you think that knocks on the head are necessary and that without them this penance cannot be carried out, you should content yourself, seeing that this business is all sham and make-believe, I repeat, should content yourself with striking your head against water or some soft thing like cotton, and put the onus on me. I'll tell my lady that I saw you banging your head against the point of a rock that was harder than a diamond."

"I thank you, friend Sancho, for your good intention," answered Don Quixote, "but I want you to realize that all these actions of mine are not for mockery but very much in

[2] Don Quixote's farewell to Rozinante resembles Ruggiero's address to his renowned charger Frontino in *Orlando Furioso*, canto VI. From the same canto of Ariosto comes the amusing hyperbole of comparing Rozinante to the dread Hippogriff of Astolfo.

earnest, for if it were otherwise, I should be breaking the rules of chivalry that forbid me to tell a lie on pain of being an apostate; and if I do one thing instead of another, it is the same as telling a lie. And so, the knocks on the head must be real hard knocks without anything imaginary about them. It will be necessary, therefore, to leave me some lint to cure them, since fortune deprived us of the balsam."

"It was worse to lose the ass," answered Sancho, "for with him we lost the lint and everything; but please, sir, don't remind me of that cursed medicine again. The very name of it turns my soul, not to mention my stomach, inside out. As for the three days that you allow me for seeing your mad frolics, I beg you to count them already gone by; I'll take all for granted and judged, and I'll tell wonders to my lady. Now write the letter and send me swiftly on my way, for I'm longing to come back and deliver you from this purgatory where I'm leaving you."

"Purgatory you call it, Sancho," said Don Quixote. "Call it rather hell, or worse, if anything can be worse."

"When one's in hell," replied Sancho *"nulla est retentio,* as I've heard say."

"I do not know," said Don Quixote, "what *retentio* means." [3]

"Retentio," answered Sancho, "means that he who is once in hell never does get out again, nor can he. But it'll be the reverse for you, sir, or something will be wrong with my feet, that is, if I have the spurs to ginger up Rozinante. Once I get safe and sound to El Toboso and into the presence of Lady Dulcinea, I'll tell her such a tale of the mad, foolish frolics (for they're no better) that you have done and are still doing that I'll make her as soft as a glove, even though I find her tougher than a cork tree. And as soon as I get her sweet and honeyed answer, I'll be back as swift as a witch on a broomstick and deliver you from this purgatory that seems to be hell, which it is not, for there is hope of getting out of it, whereas there is none, as I have said, for those in hell; and I don't think your worship will contradict me."

"It is true," said Don Quixote. "But how shall we manage to write the letter here?"

"And the order for the ass foals," added Sancho.

[3] He means that from hell *nulla est redemptio.*

"All shall be included," said Don Quixote, "and since we have no paper, we should write as the ancients did on leaves of trees or on tablets of wax, though it will be as hard to find wax as paper. But now that I come to think of it, there is Cardenio's book. I will write in that and you must see that it is copied out upon paper in good round hand at the first village where you find a schoolmaster or sacristan to transcribe it for you. But don't have it transcribed by a notary, for their writing is so garbled that Satan himself would not make it out."

"What about your signature?" said Sancho.

"The letters of Amadis were never signed," replied Don Quixote.

"That is all very well," said Sancho, "but the order for the foals must be signed, for if it is copied out, they'll say the signature is false, and then I'll remain without my ass foals."

"The order for the foals will be signed in the diary," said Don Quixote, "and when my niece sees it, she'll make no difficulty in executing it. As for the love letter, you must end it thus: 'Yours till death, the Knight of the Rueful Figure.' It does not matter if it is written in a strange hand, for as far as I can remember, Dulcinea can neither read nor write nor has she ever seen my handwriting. For our love for each other has always been of the platonic kind, never going beyond an occasional modest glance at each other; and even that was so rare that I can truly swear that during the twelve years I have loved her more than the light of these eyes of mine, which the earth must one day consume, I have not seen her more than four times. In fact, I even doubt if she ever noticed me gazing at her—such was the reserve and seclusion in which her father, Lorenzo Corchuelo, and her mother, Aldonza Nogales, brought her up."

"Oho!" cried Sancho. "The daughter of Lorenzo Corchuelo! Is she Lady Dulcinea of El Toboso, otherwise called Aldonza Lorenzo?"

"That is she," said Don Quixote, "and she deserves to be mistress of the universe."

"I know her well," said Sancho, "and I assure you she can pitch the iron bar as well was the strongest lad in our village. God save us! Why, she's a lusty lass, tall and straight, with hair on her chest, who can pull the chestnuts out of the fire for any knight-errant now or to come who has her for his lady. God, what a woman she is! What a pair of lungs she has, and what a voice! I've heard it said that one day she climbed to the top of the church belfry to call her father's plowmen, who were working in a fallow field, and though they were more than half a league off, they heard her as plainly as if they were at the foot of the tower. And the best of her is that she's not at all coy, for she's a great hand at courting, always joking with the boys and making game of everyone. Now I'm telling you, Sir Knight of the Rueful Figure, that you not only may and ought to go daft about her, but you'd be right to despair and hang yourself, for everyone who hears of it will say you did very well, even though the Devil himself carried you away. I wish I was gone, if only to catch a glimpse of her, for it's many a day since I saw her, and I'm sure she's changed by now. There is nothing that spoils a girl's face more than to be always working in the fields, exposed to sun and wind. To be frank with your worship, I've been mistaken up to this, for I thought really and truly all this while that Lady Dulcinea was some princess with whom you were in love, or at least some person of such great qualities as to deserve the rich presents you have sent her, as the Biscayan, the galley slaves, and the many others, for there must have been as many presents as there were battles that you won prior to the time I became your squire. But when all is said and done, what good can it do Lady Aldonza Lorenzo —I mean, Lady Dulcinea of El Toboso—to have the vanquished whom you send, or may send, falling upon their knees before her? For perhaps at the time they arrive she may be carding flax or threshing, and they would be all mortified at the sight of her, and she would laugh or maybe poke fun at the present you sent her."

"I have told you, Sancho, many times before now," said Don Quixote, "that you are too great a prattler. Yet although you are obtuse, your remarks sometimes sting. But to bring home to you how foolish you are and how wise I am, I want you to listen to the following little story: There was once a widow, beautiful, gay, free, rich, and by no means a prude, who fell in love with a brawny, rollicking, young lay brother. His superior got wind of it and one day said to the fair widow in a brotherly, reproving tone: 'I am astonished, Madam, and not without good cause, that a woman so noble, so beautiful, and so rich should have fallen in love with such a coarse, ignorant hobbledehoy as so-and-so, when we have in this house so many masters of arts, graduates, and divinity students among whom you could pick and choose as you would pears, saying this one I like, this other I like not.' But she answered with much grace and aplomb: 'You are much mistaken, my dear sir, and you must be very old-fashioned if you imagine I have made a poor choice in so-and-so, ignorant hobbledehoy as he may appear to you, seeing that for all I want of him, he knows as much philosophy as Aristotle and more.' And so, Sancho, for what I want of Dulcinea of El Toboso, she is as good as the greatest princess in the land. And it is not true that all those poets who praise ladies under names they choose so freely really have them as mistresses. Do you think that the Amaryllises, the Phyllises, the Sylvias, the Dianas, the Galateas, and all the rest of which the books, the ballads, the barber shops, the comic theaters, are full, were genuinely ladies of flesh and blood and the mistresses of those who celebrated their charms? Certainly not.[4] Most of them were invented to serve as subjects for verses and to enable the poets to prove themselves lovers or capable of being such. I am therefore content to imagine and believe that the good Aldonza Lorenzo is lovely and virtuous; and the question of her lineage is of little importance, for no one will investigate that for the purpose of investing her with any order, and for my part I consider her the greatest princess in the world. For I want you to know, Sancho, if you don't know it already, that two things above all others arouse love. They are great beauty and a good name, and these two things are to be found in Dulcinea to a surpassing degree. In beauty she has no rival, and few can equal her in good name. And, to conclude, I believe that everything is as I see it, neither more nor less, and in my imagination I portray her as I wish her to be both in beauty and in quality. Helen does not rival her, nor does Lucretia come near her, nor any other celebrated woman of antiquity, whether Greek, barbarian, or Latin. And let everyone say what he pleases, for though the ignorant may reprove

[4] Although Cervantes, the author of *La Galatea,* was all his life obsessed by the pastoral literary convention of his day, he at times follows Shakespeare in ridiculing the Arcadians, as in this passage and the anecdote of the young widow. Platonic love in Cervantes was not always angelic as we saw in the scene with Maritornes in Chapter XVI. Voltaire, who frequently reread *Don Quixote,* comments sarcastically: *"Don Quichotte qui adorait Dulcinée du Toboso dans les bras de Maritorne."* Voltaire, *Oeuvres complètes,* Ed Moland, Vol. XXIV, p. 173.

me for this, I shall not be condemned by men of critical judgment."

"I say that your worship is always in the right," answered Sancho, "and I'm an ass. Now I haven't a notion what on earth put the word ass in my mouth, for one shouldn't mention rope in the house of the hanged; but give me the letter and good-bye, for I'm off."

Don Quixote took out the notebook, and turning aside, began with much deliberation to write the letter. And when he had finished it, he called Sancho, saying that he wished to read it to him so that he might learn it by heart, in case he were to lose it on the way, for with his bad luck anything might happen. To which Sancho replied: "Write it, your worship, two or three times there in the book, and give it to me, and I will carry it very carefully. But it's sheer folly to think that I could carry it all in my head, seeing that my memory's so bad that I often forget my own name. Yet, read it to me all the same, sir; I'll enjoy hearing it, for it is sure to be every bit as good as print."

"Listen," said Don Quixote, "to what it says."

LETTER FROM DON QUIXOTE TO DULCINEA OF EL TOBOSO

Sovereign and most eminent Lady,

One wounded by the barb of absence and pierced to the heart's core, to sweetest Dulcinea of El Toboso, sends the health he himself lacks. If thy beauty despise me, if thy worth act not to my advantage, if thy scorn be reserved for my anguish, although I am long inured to suffering, I shall ill support this affliction, which, besides being violent, is of such long duration. My good squire, Sancho, will give thee ample account, O beautiful ingrate, most beloved enemy, of the state to which I am reduced for thy sake. Should it be thy pleasure to favor me, I am thine; if not, do what thou wilt, for by ending my life I shall satisfy both thy cruelty and my desires.

Thine until death,

The Knight of the Rueful Figure.

"By the soul of my father," cried Sancho, "it's the loftiest thing I've heard in all my life. Bless my heart if your worship doesn't put there everything you had in mind to say! And how well the Knight of the Rueful Figure fits into the signature! Why, your worship is the Devil himself; I swear there's nothing you don't know."

"It is necessary," answered Don Quixote, "to know everything in the profession I follow."

"Come now," said Sancho, "will your worship please stick the order for the three ass foals on the other side of the leaf and sign it very plain that people may recognize your hand at first sight?"

"With pleasure," said Don Quixote. And when he had written it he read it out to Sancho.

"At sight of this my first note for ass foals, dear lady, my niece, give order that three out of the five I left at home in your keeping be delivered to Sancho Panza, my squire. Which three foals I order to be delivered in payment for the like amount received of him here; and this, with his acquittance, shall be your discharge. Done in the heart of the Sierra Morena, the twenty-second of August of the present year."

"That's well done," said Sancho; "now you've only to sign it."

"It wants no signing," said Don Quixote. "I need only to put my flourish, which is the same thing and is sufficient not only for three but for three hundred asses."

"I trust your worship," replied Sancho. "Now let me go saddle Rozinante, and be ready, sir, to give me your blessing, for I intend to start immediately without staying to see the crazy frolics you are going to play, but I'll say I saw you do so many that she'll want no more."

"At least I should like you to see me stripped, Sancho, and cutting a dozen or two mad capers; I'll do them in less than half an hour, and when you have seen them with your own eyes, you can safely swear to any others you may care to add, but you will not, I promise you, tell her of as many as I intend to perform."

"For the love of God, dear master, don't oblige me to see your worship naked. That will depress me so that I shan't be able to stop crying, and I've such a pain in the head from the weeping I did last night for the ass that I'm in no fit state for a fresh attack of tears. And if your worship wishes me to see some of his mad capers, do a couple of them all dressed up—but short ones and such as are of most consequence. Though really, between you and me, I don't need anything of the kind, and as I have already said before, the sooner I'm off, the sooner I'll return with the news your worship desires and deserves. And if not, let Lady Dulcinea watch her step, for if she doesn't reply as she should, I give you my solemn oath that I'll kick and thump a fair answer out of her belly. Wouldn't it be a disgrace for a famous knight-errant like your worship to go mad without the why or wherefore, for a— Let the good lady not drive me to say the word, for, by God, I'll out with it and scatter it broadside by the dozen, no matter if it should spoil the market. I'm rather a good hand at that. She doesn't know me; if she did, I swear she'd give me a wide berth."

"Why, Sancho," said Don Quixote, "you evidently are no saner than I am."

"I'm not so mad," replied Sancho, "but I've a hotter temper. However, let that be and tell me, sir, what are you going to eat until I return? Are you going to take to the road like Cardenio and steal your food from the shepherds?"

"Don't worry on that score," replied Don Quixote. "Even if I had it, I shouldn't eat anything but the herbs and fruits that these meadows and trees provide. The essential point in this enterprise of mine lies in fasting and putting up with other hardships. So, farewell."

"But," said Sancho, "does your worship know what I'm afraid of? It is that on my return I may not be able to find my way back to the place where now I leave you, it is so hidden away."

"Observe the landmarks carefully, and I'll try not to stray from this place," replied Don Quixote. "And I'll even take the precaution of climbing these highest crags to look out for you on your return. But the best way to avoid missing me or going astray yourself will be for you to cut some branches of the broom that are so plentiful about here. Strew them at intervals here and there as you go until you reach the open country. These will serve as landmarks and signs by which to find me when you return, just like the thread in Theseus' labyrinth."

"That I shall do," answered Sancho Panza, and cutting some twigs, he asked his master's blessing, and not without many tears on both sides, took his leave. Mounting Rozinante, whom Don Quixote earnestly commended to his care, begging him to care for him as he would for his own person, he took the road to the plain, scattering the broom twigs at intervals as his master had advised. And so he went on his way, though Don Quixote still urged him to stay and see him perform at least a few of his mad tricks. But he had not gone a hundred paces when he came back and said: "I think you were quite right, sir, and that it would be just as well if I watched one of your mad tricks. I could then swear with an easy conscience that I've seen you doing them, though I've seen you do a mighty big one by staying here."

"Did I not tell you so?" said Don Quixote. "Wait but a moment, Sancho; I will do it as quickly as you can say the credo."

Then, stripping off hastily his breeches, he remained in nothing but skin and shirt. Then, without more ado he cut a couple of capers and did two somersaults with his head down and his legs in the air, displaying such parts of his anatomy as drove Sancho to turn Rozinante's bridle to avoid seeing such a display. So, he rode away fully satisfied to swear that his master was mad. And so, we shall leave him to go on his way until his return, which was speedy.

CHAPTER XXVI

A continuation of the subtle pranks played by Don Quixote, the lover, in the Sierra Morena

To return to the account of what the Knight of the Rueful Figure did when he found himself alone, the history says that after he had ended his tumblings, or somersaults, with his upper parts clothed and his lower parts naked, and after he had seen Sancho depart without caring to see any more of his capers, Don Quixote climbed to the top of a high rock and there set himself to reconsider a problem that he had thought much about on several occasions without ever reaching a definite decision. This was to decide whether it would be better and more advantageous to imitate Orlando in his outrageous frenzies or Amadis in his melancholy moods. So, talking to himself, he said: "If Orlando was as good a knight and as valiant as they all say, why wonder? After all, he was enchanted, and no one could kill him except by thrusting a long pin into the sole of his foot, and so he always wore shoes with seven iron soles. But these tricks were of no avail against Bernardo del Carpio, who knew of them, and strangled him in his arms at Roncesvalles. Leaving in abeyance the question of his bravery, let us consider his loss of wits, which it is certain arose from the evidence he discovered beside the fountain and the tidings that the shepherd brought him of how Angélica had slept more than two siestas with Medoro, a little curly-headed Moor and page to Agramante. If he believed that this was true and that his lady had done him this wrong, it is not to be wondered that he went mad. But how can I imitate him in his madness without a similar cause? For I dare swear that my Dulcinea of El Toboso has never in her life seen a Moor in Moorish dress and that she is today as her mother brought her into the world, and I should do her a grave injury were I to imagine otherwise and go crazy after the manner of Orlando the Furious.[1] On the other hand, I know that Amadis of Gaul, without ever losing his wits or committing crazy actions, won an unparalleled reputation as a lover, for, as history relates, when he found himself slighted by his lady, Oriana, who had ordered him not to appear in her presence until such was her pleasure, he simply retired to the Peña Pobre in the company of a hermit, and there he wept to his heart's content until Heaven came to his aid in the midst of his greatest tribulation. Now if this is true—and it is—why do I now take the trouble to strip myself stark naked, give pain to these trees that have done me no harm, and trouble the clear water of these streams that must give me drink when I am thirsty? Long live the memory of Amadis, and let him be the model, as far as may be, of Don Quixote of La Mancha, of whom shall be said what was said of that other one: that if he did not achieve great things, he died attempting them. If I am not rejected and scorned by Dulcinea of El Toboso, let it suffice, as I have said, that I am absent from her. So then, to work! Deeds of Amadis, come to my memory and teach me where I must begin if I am to imitate you. I remember now that most of the time he spent praying and commending his soul to God. But what shall I do for a rosary, for I have none?"

Then he thought of a way of making one. He tore a long strip of his shirt, which was hanging down, and made eleven knots in it, one fatter than the rest, and this served him for a rosary all the time he was there, during which time he recited a million Ave Marias. But what worried him a great deal was that there was no hermit to be found thereabouts to hear his confession and administer consolation. He entertained himself, however, by pacing up and down the little meadow, by writing and carving on the barks of the trees, and by tracing on the fine sands a great number of verses, all adapted to his sad state and some in praise of Dulcinea. But the only ones that were discovered complete and could be

[1] The meaning here is that Dulcinea never saw a Moor in his Moorish dress because, though there were many in Toboso, they were disguised as Christians. Clemencín states that there were many Moors in La Mancha at the time.

deciphered after he was found were the following:

> Ye trees, plants, bushes in this dell,
> Growing so big, so green, so tall,
> If you delight not when I tell
> My holy plaints, then hear my fall;
> Let my sorrows disturb you not,
> Though I'm sure you ne'er did see, ah!
> Man more luckless, or a lot
> Sadder than that of Don Quixote
> As he weeps for his Dulcinea
>
>   of El Toboso.

> It's here, it's here, the very place
> Where the constant lover hides,
> When he shuns his lady's face;
> Though why on earth he here abides,
> Or how, he cannot even tell me.
> Love now keeps him on the trot,
> For a wicked rogue is he, ah!
> So the tears o'erflow the pot
> Of the doleful Don Quixote,
> As he weeps for his Dulcinea
>
>   of El Toboso.

> Upon adventures he is bound,
> And would be roaming through the woods,
> But now the lonely wastes he curses,
> For misadventures he has found,
> When Love in one of his cruel moods
> Laid his whip upon him hot.
> No soft or gentle thongs had he, ah!
> And they hurt his tend'rest spot.
> So fall the tears of Don Quixote,
> As he weeps for his Dulcinea
>
>   of El Toboso.

The addition of *of El Toboso* to the name of Dulcinea roused the hearty laughter of those who found the verses here referred to because they conjectured that Don Quixote must have imagined that if when he named Dulcinea he did not add *of El Toboso*, the poem would not be understood, and such was the truth as he later confessed. Many others he wrote, but as has been said, only these three stanzas could be deciphered or were found complete. In this and in sighing and in calling upon the fauns and satyrs of these woods, on the nymphs of the streams, and on the damp and doleful echo to respond, console, and listen, he occupied himself, and in searching for herbs on which to feed himself until Sancho's return. And if the latter had delayed three weeks instead of three days the Knight of the Rueful Figure would have become so emaciated that the mother who bore him would not have recognized him.

However, now it is proper to leave him to his sighs and versifying and relate what happened to Sancho Panza on his journey as envoy. The squire, after turning into the highway, took the road that led to El Toboso and arrived the next day at the inn where the mishap of the blanket had befallen him. He no sooner saw it than he imagined that he was once again flying through the air, so he determined not to enter the inn, although it was then dinnertime and he had a mighty appetite for some warm food, as his diet had been confined to cold meat for many days past. This longing made him draw near to the inn, but he was still in some doubt as to whether he should enter it or not. As he stood wondering, there came out of the inn two persons who recognized him at once, and the one said to the other: "Tell me, Master Licentiate, is that horseman over there not Sancho Panza, who went off with Don Quixote to be his squire?"

"It is," said the licentiate, "and that is our Don Quixote's nag." No wonder they knew him so well, for they were the curate and the barber of his village, who had made the search and formal process against the books of chivalry. So, wanting to hear news of Don Quixote, they went up to him and said: "Friend Sancho Panza, where have you left your master?"

Sancho Panza recognized them at once and resolved to conceal the circumstances and the place of retreat of his master. So he answered that his master was detained in a certain place by affairs of great importance that he swore by the two eyes of his head he could not disclose.

"No, no, Sancho Panza," said the barber, "that story will not do. If you do not tell us where he is, we must imagine (as we do already) that you have robbed and slain him, for you are riding his horse. So, find us the horse's owner or there'll be a quarrel."

free from the fits that so often drove him crazy. Seeing the

"There's no reason to threaten me," answered Sancho. "I'm not the kind who robs or kills anybody. Let every man's luck kill him or God who made him. My master is enjoying himself doing penance in the midst of those mountains."

He then rapidly and without pausing a moment told them in what state he had left his master, the adventures that had befallen them, and how he was carrying a letter to Lady Dulcinea of El Toboso, the daughter of Lorenzo Corchuelo, with whom the knight was up to his ears in love.

Both of them were astonished at what they heard. Although they already knew the nature of Don Quixote's madness, yet every new detail they heard caused them fresh amazement. They asked Sancho Panza to show them the letter he was carrying to Lady Dulcinea of El Toboso. He said that it was written in a book and that he was ordered to get it copied out at the first village he came to. The curate then said that if he would give it to him, he would copy it out in good hand. Sancho then thrust his hand into his bosom to search for the little book, but he could not find it, nor would he have found it if he had searched till doomsday, for he had left it with Don Quixote. The knight had not given it to him, and he had forgotten to ask for it.

When Sancho failed to find the book, he turned as pale as death, and rapidly feeling all over his body, he saw clearly that it was not to be found. Without more ado, he clutched hold of his beard and with both his hands tore out half his hair and gave himself half a dozen blows on his nose and mouth and bathed them all in blood. When the curate and barber saw this, they asked him what was the matter that he should treat himself so roughly.

"What is the matter?" replied Sancho. "Why, I've let slip through my fingers in one instant three ass foals, and each of them was like a castle."

"How is that?" replied the barber.

"I've lost the little book," answered Sancho, "in which the letter to Dulcinea was written and a bill signed by my master in which he ordered his niece to give me three colts out of the four or five he had at home." With that he went on to tell them of the loss of the ass.

The curate comforted him by telling him that as soon as they had found his master they would make him renew the order upon paper according to law, for those written in a memorandum book would not be accepted as valid. This comforted Sancho, and he said he did not mind having lost the letter to Dulcinea, for he could almost say it by heart, and so they might write it down when and where they pleased.

"Say it then, Sancho," said the barber, "and we will write it down." Then Sancho stood still and began to scratch his head, trying to remember the letter. He stood first on one leg and then on the other, and looked first at the ground, then at the sky. Then, after biting off half the nail of one finger and keeping his hearers for a long time in suspense, he said: "God help me, sir, may the Devil take anything I remember of the letter, though I am sure that at the beginning it said: 'High and suffering Lady!' "

"I am sure," said the barber, "it did not say *suffering* but *superhuman* or *sovereign* lady."

"So it did," said Sancho. "Then, if I'm not mistaken, it went on, if I'm not mistaken: 'the layman, sleepless and wounded, kisses your hand, ungrateful and most unknown beautiful one'; and then it said something about health and sickness that he sent; and so it scampered along until it ended with: 'Yours till death; the Knight of the Rueful Figure.' "

They were both much amused at Sancho's good memory and they praised it much, begging him to repeat the letter twice so that they too might learn it by heart and write it down in due time. Three times Sancho repeated it, and three times he added three thousand more follies. Then he told them other things about his master, but not a word did he say about being tossed in a blanket in that very inn that he now refused to enter. He told them also how his master, as soon as he had received a good dispatch from his Lady Dulcinea, would set to work to become emperor, or at least king (for so it was arranged between them), and it was a very easy thing for him to become one, such was his courage and the strength of his arm. And when this came to pass, his master would arrange a marriage for him (by then he would be a widower at least) with a maid of honor of the empress, heiress to a large, rich estate on the mainland, without any islands, female or male, for he was not interested in them any more. Sancho said all this foolishness with so much gravity, wiping his nose from time to time, that the two were still more amazed at the vehement nature of Don Quixote's madness, which had swept along in its wake the senses of that poor ignorant fellow. They did not, however, wish to weary themselves trying to convince him of his foolishness, as it didn't harm his conscience, and they thought that if they left him as he was, he would amuse them by his nonsense. So they told him to pray for the health of his master, since it was very possible and feasible for him to become in time an emperor, as he had suggested, or at least archbishop, or something equally important.

To which Sancho replied: "Sir, if by a turn of fortune my master should take it into his head to become an archbishop instead of an emperor, I'd like to know here and now what archbishops-errant usually give their squires."

"Generally," replied the curate, "they give them a benefice, a simple parish, or some sextonship that brings them in a tidy fixed sum, besides the altar gifts, that usually amount to as much again."

"But for that," answered Sancho, "the squire would have to be unmarried and at least know how to serve Mass; and if this be so, my luck's out, because I'm married and don't know the first letter of the *ABC*! What will happen to me if my master should fancy being archbishop instead of emperor, as is the use and custom of knights-errant?"

"Don't worry, friend Sancho," said the barber; "we'll entreat and advise your master and even put to him as a point of conscience that he must be an emperor and not an archbishop. In any case, that will be easier for him, seeing that he is more of a soldier than a scholar."

"So it appears to me," answered Sancho, "though I must say he's clever enough for anything. What I intend to do is to pray to Our Lord to land him in places where he'll do the best for himself and reward me as well."

"You talk like a wise man," said the curate, "and you will act like a good Christian. But we must now discover a way of rescuing your master from that useless penance you say he is doing. So, let us go into the inn to arrange our plans and, incidentally, to get our dinner, for it is now time." Sancho told them to go in, but said that he would prefer to wait for them outside and that he would tell them another time the reason why. He begged them, however, to bring him something nice and hot to eat and some barley for Rozinante. They went into the inn, and after a while the barber brought him out some meat.

After much discussion between the curate and the barber on the best means of accomplishing their purpose, the curate thought of a plan exactly suited both to Don Quixote's humor and to their purpose; it was that the curate should dress himself up as a damsel-errant and the barber should do the best he could to equip himself as her squire. In that disguise they would go to the place where Don Quixote was undergoing penance, pretending that she was an afflicted and distressed damsel, and would beg a boon that he as a valiant knight-errant could not refuse to grant; and this should be a request that he should follow her wherever she should lead him, to redress an injury inflicted on her by a wicked knight. Besides this, she was to pray him not to command her to take off her mask nor to inquire of her condition until he had secured her justice against that wicked knight. He was certain that Don Quixote would consent to do all he was asked, and by this stratagem they would get him away from that place and carry him home, where they would try to see if his strange madness could be cured.

CHAPTER XXVII

Of how the curate and the barber carried out their plan, with other things worthy of mention in this great history

The barber approved of the curate's notion, so they resolved immediately to carry it out. They borrowed a gown and a headdress from the innkeeper's wife, leaving with her in exchange the curate's new cassock. The barber made for himself a great beard out of the tail of a pied ox into which the innkeeper used to stick his currycomb. The landlady asked them what they wanted these things for, and the curate told her briefly all about Don Quixote's madness and that the disguise was necessary to bring him away from the mountain where he was at the moment. The innkeeper

and his wife then realized that the madman was their
former guest, the maker of the balsam and the master of
the blanketed squire. So they told the barber and curate all
about him without omitting what Sancho had been so eager
to conceal. Meanwhile, the landlady dressed the curate up in
a manner that could not be excelled. She made him put
on a skirt with stripes of black velvet, each a span in width,
all slashed, and a bodice of green velvet, trimmed with
white satin, both of which might have been made in the days
of King Wamba.[1] The curate would not consent to wear
a woman's headdress, but put on a little white quilted cap
that he used as a nightcap. Then he tied one of his black
taffeta garters around his head and with the other made a
kind of mask and fixed it on in such a way that it covered
his face and beard very neatly. He then covered his head
with his hat, which was so large that it served him as a
sunshade, and wrapping his cloak around him, he seated
himself upon his mule sideways like a woman. The barber
mounted also, with a beard that reached to his waist, of a
color between sorrel and white, resembling the one we mentioned before, which was made out of the tail of a pied ox.

They took leave of all, not forgetting the good Maritornes,
who promised, though a sinner, to say a whole rosary that
God might give them success in so arduous and Christian a
business as that which they had undertaken. But no sooner
had they left the inn than the curate had a sudden notion
that he was not doing right in dressing up as a woman and
that it was unbecoming for a priest to go about in such a
costume, even though the motive was good. So, he told the
barber his scruples and asked him to change clothes with
him, for he said it was more fitting that the barber should
be the afflicted lady, whereas he would act the part of the
squire. In this way his priestly dignity would be safe, and if
the barber did not agree, he was determined not to go on
any farther, even if the Devil ran away with Don Quixote.

Sancho now came up, and when he saw the two of them
dressed in such manner, he nearly burst his sides laughing.
The barber let the curate have his way, and after exchang-
ing their costumes, the latter began to tutor the former as
to how to act his part and what words to say to Don
Quixote in order to persuade him to accompany them and

---

[1] The last of the Gothic kings of Spain, 672–82.

leave the place he had chosen for his futile penance. The barber replied that without any prompting he would play his part to a nicety, but he refused to put on the gown until they came near Don Quixote's retreat. So he folded it up, and off they went under the guidance of Sancho Panza, who told them about the madman they met in the sierra but kept a discreet silence about the portmanteau and its contents, for though a fool, the fellow had a spice of covetousness.

The next day they arrived at the spot where Sancho had strewn the branches to mark the place where he had left his master. When he saw them he told them that this was the entrance to the mountain pass and that it was time for them to dress up in their disguise, if that was necessary for the delivery of his master. For they had told Sancho before that their disguise was of the greatest importance in the task of rescuing his master from the wretched life he had chosen, and they solemnly warned him not to tell the knight who they were. They also said that if Don Quixote asked, as they were sure he would, whether he had delivered the letter to Dulcinea, he was to say that he had done so; but as she could not read, she had sent her answer by word of mouth, commanding her knight, on pain of her displeasure, to return to her at once on an affair of great importance. By this plan they were sure they could bring him back to a better way of life and give him the possibility of soon becoming emperor or king, for there was nothing to fear about his becoming an archbishop. Sancho listened to all this talk and stamped it clearly on his memory, and thanked them warmly for promising to advise his master to become emperor and not archbishop, for he was convinced that when it came to bestowing favors on their squires emperors could do more than archbishops-errant. He also suggested that it would be best for him to go in advance to find him and deliver his lady's answer, for perhaps that alone would be enough to bring Don Quixote away from the mountains and they would then be spared all their trouble. They agreed with Sancho and resolved to wait until he came back with news of his master. Sancho then went off into the mountain gorge and left them in a pleasant spot by a tiny stream of clear water shaded by overhanging rocks and trees.

It was the month of August when in those parts the heat

is very great, and it was about three in the afternoon; all
this made the spot more pleasant, inviting them to pass the
time there while they waited for Sancho's return, as they
did. The curate and the barber were resting in the shade
at their ease when they heard a voice that although not accompanied by any instrument sounded very sweetly and
melodiously. The song astonished them, for they did not
think this was a likely place in which to find so good a
singer, and although there were reports that shepherds with
unusually beautiful voices were to be found in the woods
and fields, these were due to poetic license rather than the
honest truth. Greater still was their surprise when they discovered that the words of the song were not the verses of
uncouth shepherds but of polished gentlefolk, as was clear
from the following lines:

> What changes all my joys to pain?
>
>   Disdain.
>
> And what increases agony?
>
>   Jealousy.
>
> What racks and tries my patience?
>
>   Absence.
>
> In my case no respite I sense,
> Nor for my sorrow remedy,
> Since my hopes are slain by three,
> *Disdain, Jealousy, and Absence.*
>
> Who through my heart the arrow drove?
>
>   Love.
>
> Who to my misery consents?
>
>   Providence.
>
> Who doth my glory underrate?
>
>   Fate.
>
> If this is so, my soul must wait
> On Death in such a baleful blight,
> Since for my ruin three unite,
> *Love, Providence, and Fate.*
>
> Who can cure my distress?
>
>   Madness.
>
> What can Love's freedom e'er arrange?
>
>   Change.
>
> Who my forlorn hopes bettereth?
>
>   Death.
>
> If this is so, what waste of breath
> To try to banish all my woes,
> For there are no cures for Love's throes:
> But *Madness, Change, and Death.*

The hour, the season, the solitude, the voice, and the skill of the singer thrilled the two listeners, who remained still in the hope of hearing more. But as the silence continued for some time, they determined to go in search of the musician with such an enchanting voice. Just as they were about to do so, however, the same voice held them again by its spell, singing the following sonnet:

Sonnet

O holy friendship that with nimble wing,
Leaving thy phantoms on this earth below,
With blessed souls in Paradise communing,
Up through the Empyrean halls dost go,
From thence, at thy pleasure, we are assigned
Just peace, her features covered with a hood,
But often all is but deceit we find
Tricked out in colors of the good.
Abandon heaven, friends; do not permit
Foul fraud thus openly to masquerade
In thy robes and all honesty defeat,
For if thou lets't him in thy mask parade,
Once more grim chaos will engulf our world
And all of us to anarchy be hurled.

The song ended in a deep sigh, and they listened attentively in the hope of hearing more, but the music changed into sobs and heartrending lamentations, so they went in search of the unhappy person whose voice was no less beautiful than his complaints were mournful. They had not gone far, when in turning the corner of a rock they saw a man of the same figure that Sancho had described when he had told them the story of Cardenio. The man did not show astonishment when he saw them, but stood still with head bent upon his breast in a pensive posture; and after glancing once in their direction, he did not raise his eyes off the ground. The curate, who was a well-spoken man (being already acquainted with his misfortune, for he had recognized him from the description), went up to him and in a few kind words begged him insistently to abandon that wretched kind of life lest he should meet with the greatest of all misfortunes, which was to perish in that lonely spot.

Cardenio at the moment was in his right mind and quite free from the fits that so often drove him crazy. Seeing the two dressed so differently from those who frequented those lonely parts, he could not help being surprised, especially when he heard them speak of his affair as if it were common knowledge (for the words of the curate gave him this impression); and so, he replied: "Whoever you may be, good sirs, I see clearly that Heaven, which takes care to assist the good and often the bad, sends to me, unworthy as I am, even in these desolate wastes so distant from the common haunts of men, kind people who would persuade me to depart with them and dwell in some better place. But though with cogent arguments they point out how irrational is the life I lead, they do not know, as I do, that by running away from my present wretchedness I shall fall into still greater misery. They must take me for a fool, or even worse, for a lunatic. And no wonder, for I am so intensely conscious of my misfortune and my misery is so overwhelming that I am powerless to resist it and am being turned into stone, devoid of all knowledge and feeling. I become aware of this when people show me the traces left by me when these terrible fits master me, but I can only lament in vain, curse my evil destiny, and excuse my outrageous deeds by telling the cause of them to all who wish to listen to me. For sensible men when they learn the cause will not be surprised by its effects. Although they are unable to offer me any relief, they will, at least, not condemn me, and their anger at my outrageous conduct will turn to pity for my misfortunes. If you, gentlemen, have come with the same intention as the others, before you start your persuasive reasonings I entreat you to listen to the story of my misfortunes, for when you have heard it, you will perhaps spare yourselves the trouble of trying to offer consolation for sorrow that admits no remedy."

The curate and the barber, who wanted nothing better than to hear the cause of his misfortune from his own lips, asked him to tell his story and promised that they would do nothing by way of remedy and consolation but what was agreeable to him. Upon this, the unhappy gentleman began his piteous story almost in the same words and style in which he had told it to Don Quixote and the goatherd a few days before, when owing to Master Elisabat and Don Quixote's punctiliousness in defending the dignity of knight-errantry, the tale was left unfinished. Fortunately on this occasion Cardenio had no mad fit and was able to tell it to the end. And when he reached the point about the letter that Don Fernando found in the book of *Amadis of Gaul*, he said he remembered it well and it was as follows:

LUSCINDA TO CARDENIO

Each day I discover in thee qualities that drive me to hold thee dear; and therefore, if thou wouldst desire to have me discharge this debt of mine, without serving a writ on my honor, thou mayst easily do it. I have a father who knows thee and loves me dearly. He, without forcing my inclinations, will grant whatever thou mayst justly wish for, if thou really dost value me as much as thou sayst and I believe.

"It was this letter that moved me to ask for Luscinda again in marriage; it was this letter also that kindled Don Fernando's desire to ruin me before my happiness could be complete. I told Don Fernando how Luscinda's father expected mine to ask for her hand and that I dared not speak to my father about it for fear he would refuse his consent, not because he was ignorant of the quality, kindness, virtue, and beauty of Luscinda, for she had sufficient to ennoble any other Spanish family, but because he did not wish me to marry so soon, or at least not until he had seen what Duke Ricardo would do for me. Finally, I told him that I dared not reveal it to my father because I was full of vague apprehensions and a sad foreboding that my desires would never be accomplished.

"Don Fernando then offered to speak on my behalf to my father and persuade him to ask for Luscinda's hand. O ruthless Marius! Cruel Cataline! O criminal Sulla! O perfidious Galalón! O traitorous Vellido! O vindictive Julian! O covetous Judas! Cruel, vindictive, and perfidious traitor, how had this poor wretch injured you, who so frankly revealed to you the secrets and the joys of his heart? How did I offend you? What words did I utter or what counsels did I ever give that were not all intended for your honor and advancement? But why, unhappy wretch, do I complain? It is certain that when the stars in their course rain disaster, they come rushing down with such unbridled fury that no power on earth can stop, no human ingenuity avert, their onslaught. How could I imagine that Don Fernando, a noble gentleman, indebted to me for my services, certain to triumph wherever his amorous fancy listed, would feel the rankling urge, as I might say, to deprive me of my one and only lamb, who was not yet mine? But setting aside these vain and futile reflections, let us take up the broken thread of my unhappy story.

"Don Fernando, thinking that my presence was an obstacle to his false, wicked design, resolved to send me to his elder brother on the plea of borrowing some money from him to pay for six horses that he had bought on the very day he offered to speak to my father. This he had done with the sole object of getting me out of the way (in order that he might carry out his damned plan). Could I forestall such treachery? Could I even suspect it? No, surely not; on the contrary, with the greatest goodwill I offered to go immediately, and I was delighted at the excellent bargain he had made. That night I spoke with Luscinda and told her what had been arranged between Don Fernando and myself, and I assured her that all would turn out well. And she, no more suspecting the treachery of Don Fernando than I did myself, begged me to return speedily, since she believed that our wishes would be accomplished as soon as my father made the marriage proposal. I know not what it was, but as she spoke, her eyes filled with tears and a lump in her throat prevented her from uttering another word, though she seemed to have more to say. This emotional tension that I had never observed in her before disturbed me, because hitherto, whenever by luck and my connivance we had met, we always rambled on merrily, without mingling tears, sighs, jealous recriminations, suspicions, or fears with our conversation. I would always chant a paean to my happiness, thanking Heaven for giving her to be my love, praising her beauty, and admiring her worth and understanding. She would praise in me the qualities that she, my lover, considered worthy of the highest praise. Then we would amuse each other with a hundred thousand childish trifles, such as the gossip of our neighbors and our friends, and the greatest freedom I permitted myself was to take, almost by force, one of her lovely white hands and to press it to my lips as best I could, despite the narrowness of the bars that separated us. But on the night before the sad day of my departure she wept, moaned, and sighed, and then fled, leaving me filled with confusion and dread at these new and unusual signs of sorrow and tenderness in Luscinda. But not to destroy my hopes, I attributed all this to the force of the love she bore me and to the sorrow that absence causes true lovers. Finally, I departed, sad and pensive, my mind full of fancies and suspicions, without knowing what I suspected or imagined—clear omens pointing to the tragic misfortune that awaited me.

"I reached the town where I was sent and delivered my letters to Don Fernando's brother, who received me well but did not dispatch me at once. Much to my disgust he bade me wait eight days in a place where the duke, his father, should not see me, for his brother had written to him to send a certain sum of money without his father's knowledge. This was all a trick of the false Fernando, for his brother had no lack of money with which to send me home at once. I was very much tempted to disobey this order, for it seemed to me entirely impossible to live so many days away from Luscinda, especially as I had left her in such distress. Nevertheless, like a good servant I obeyed, though I felt that it was to my disadvantage. On the fourth day after my arrival, however, a man came in search of me with a letter that by the address I knew to be Luscinda's, for the writing was hers. I opened it, not without alarm, knowing that it must be some serious matter that would make her write to me in my absence, seeing that she rarely did so when I was present. I asked the bearer, before I read the letter, who had given it to him and how long he had taken to make the journey. He replied that passing by chance at midday through a street in the city, a very beautiful lady had called to him from a window. Her eyes were full of tears and she spoke hurriedly, saying: 'Brother, if you are a good man, as you seem to be, I pray you take this letter to the person named in the address, for both are well known, and if you do this, you will perform a Christian act. And in case you want money to do it, take what you find wrapped up in this handkerchief.' 'With those words,' the messenger went on, 'she threw out of the window a handkerchief in which were wrapped a hundred reals, this gold ring that I am wearing, and the letter that I have given you. Then without waiting for my answer, she left the window, though first she saw me take the letter and the handkerchief and I made signs that I would do what she bade me. And seeing how generously I was paid for my trouble and learning from the envelope that the letter was for you, sir, whom I know very well, and moved as well by that lovely, tearful maiden, I determined not to trust any other messenger but to deliver it with my own hands. And so I have made this journey, which you know is some fifty-four miles, in sixteen hours.'

"While the good-natured messenger was speaking, I stood trembling with the letter in my hand, until at last I took courage and opened it and read the following words: 'The promise Don Fernando gave thee that he would persuade thy father to speak to mine, he has kept more for his own gratification than thy own interest. Know then that he has asked me in marriage, and my father, carried away by his rank and position, has accepted this proposal with such alacrity that the marriage is to be solemnized two days hence, and with such privacy that only God and a few of our own family are to witness it. Imagine my feelings! Consider if thou shouldst not return at once. Whether I love thee or not, the end of this affair will prove. God grant this may reach thy hand before mine is compelled to join his that keeps his promised faith so ill.'

"Such were the words of her letter, and they caused me at once to set out on my journey without waiting for the end of Don Fernando's business, for I knew now that it was not a matter of buying horses but the pursuit of his own pleasure that had led Don Fernando to send me to his brother. The fury I felt toward Don Fernando, joined to the fear I had of losing the jewel I had won by so many years of patient love, lent me wings, and I arrived at my native city as quickly as though I had flown, just in time to see and speak with Luscinda.

"I entered the city secretly and left my mule at the house of the honest messenger who had brought my letter, and fortune was then so propitious to me that I found Luscinda at the grating of the window, the constant witness of our loves. Luscinda recognized me and I recognized her, but not the way that two lovers should meet. But who is there in the world who can boast that he fathoms and thoroughly understands the confused thoughts and variable condition of a woman? None, I am sure. As soon as Luscinda saw me, she said: 'Cardenio, I am attired in wedding garments, and in the hall there waits for me the traitor and my covetous father with other witnesses who shall see my death rather than my marriage. Be not troubled, dear friend, but try to be present at this sacrifice. If my words cannot avert it, I carry hidden about me a dagger that can avert more determined forces, for it will put an end to my life and thus give thee a proof of the love I have ever borne thee.'

"I answered her hurriedly and distractedly, for I was afraid I might lose the opportunity of answering: 'May thy actions, lady, prove how truly thou hast spoken. If thou dost carry a dagger, I carry a sword to defend thy life or to kill myself should fortune be against us.' I do not think she could hear all those words, for I perceived that she was called away in haste, for the bridegroom awaited her. Here the night of my despair closed in, the sun of my joy went down. The light of my eyes was quenched and there was no sense in my mind. I was unable to bring myself to enter her house, nor even had I the power to move. But realizing how vitally important it was that I should be present for whatever might happen in that crisis, I pulled myself together as best I could and went into the house, for I knew well all the entrances and exits; and moreover, owing to the confusion of the whole household, nobody noticed me and I managed to place myself in the recess formed by the window of the hall, which was covered by two pieces of tapestry drawn together. From there I could see all that went on in the hall without anyone seeing me. Who could describe the throbbings of my heart as I stood there, the thoughts that raced through my mind, the reflections that assailed me? So many and of such a nature that I cannot, nor should I, tell them. Enough to say that the bridegroom entered the hall wearing his ordinary dress. His groomsman was a first cousin of Luscinda, and no one else was in the room but servants of the house. In a little while Luscinda came out of her dressing room, accompanied by her mother and two of her maids, adorned as her quality and beauty deserved and courtly pomp could afford. My agony of mind gave me no time to note what she wore. I was only able to note the colors, which were crimson and white, and the glitter of the jewels and precious stones in her headdress and on every part of her robes. They were, however, surpassed by the singular beauty of her fair golden hair, in the glory of which the brilliance of the jewels and the blaze of the four torches in the hall seemed to be lost. O memory, mortal enemy of peace of mind! What good to me is it now to re-

call the incomparable beauty of my adored enemy? Would
it not be better, cruel memory, to portray for me what she
did there so that, goaded on by so outrageous an injury, I
may strive, if not to avenge myself, at least to rid myself
of my own life? Do not grow weary, gentlemen, of hearing
these digressions of mine, for my tale of woe cannot be
briefly or lightly told, since every incident in it seems to me
to need a long explanation."

To this the curate replied that not only were they not
weary of hearing his tale, but that they welcomed the details that could not be passed over in silence and merited
as much attention as the main part of the story.

"Then," continued Cardenio, "when they were all assembled in the hall, the parish priest came in, and having taken
each by the hand, asked: 'Do you, Lady Luscinda take Lord
Don Fernando, here present, for your lawful husband as
our Holy Mother the Church commands?' I thrust my
head and neck out of the tapestry and with attentive ears and
troubled soul listened for Luscinda's reply, expecting from
it the sentence of death or a fresh lease on life. If one had
only dared at that moment to come out and cry: 'Luscinda!
Luscinda! Beware what thou dost! Consider what thou owest
me! Remember thou art mine and cannot be another's! Take
warning that this *I do* means instant death for me! Ah,
treacherous Don Fernando, robber of my glory, death of my
life! What do you want? What claim can you make? Consider that, as a Christian, you cannot achieve your desire,
because Luscinda is my wife and I am her husband.' What
a madman I am! Now that I am far away from the danger,
I say what I should have done, but did not do. Now that
I have allowed my precious jewel to be stolen, I am cursing
the robber on whom I might have taken vengeance if I had
been as ready to act then as I now am to complain! In
short, since I was such a craven coward and idiot, are you
surprised that I now die of shame, repentance, and insanity?

"The priest stood waiting a long time before Luscinda
gave her answer, and when I thought she would take out
the dagger to stab herself or raise her voice to utter one
word of truth for my good, I heard her say in a faint and
languishing voice: 'I do.'

"Then Don Fernando said the same, and giving her the
ring, the knot was tied. But when the bridegroom approached
to embrace her, she put her hand to her breast and fell
fainting in her mother's arms.

"It only remains to tell in what a state I was when in that *I do* I heard all my hopes cheated, Luscinda's words and promises false, and myself forever debarred from receiving what I lost in that one instant. I was totally confused, abandoned, I thought, by Heaven, made an enemy of the very earth that sustained me, denying me air for my sighs and water for my tears; only the fire intensified to such a degree that I was consumed by rage and jealousy. The whole household was in an uproar when Luscinda fainted, and her mother, unfastening her bodice to give her air, found in her bosom a folded piece of paper, which Don Fernando seized and went aside to read by the light of a torch. When he had read it, he sat down in a chair, laying his hand upon his cheek like a man lost in thought, not attending to any of the remedies that were being applied to his spouse to bring her back to her senses.

"When I saw that all the household was in confusion, I ventured forth, not caring whether I was seen or not, but determined, if seen, to do so desperate an act that the whole world would understand the just indignation that was seething in my breast by chastising the false Don Fernando and the fickle, swooning traitress. But my fate, to reserve me for greater misfortunes, if there can be greater, ordained that at that instant I had complete use of my reason, which has since failed me. So, instead of taking vengeance on my worst enemies (it would have been easy to do so, seeing that they were so ignorant of my presence), I determined to take it on myself and execute on myself the penalty they so richly deserved, and even with greater severity than I should have used on them had I killed them on the spot, for death that is sudden ends all pain at once, whereas that which is long drawn out with tortures still slays but never brings life to an end.

"At last I left that house and went to the one where I had left my mule. I had it saddled, and without taking leave I mounted and rode away from the city, like another Lot, not daring to turn my head to look behind me. When I found myself alone in the open country, concealed by the darkness of the night, its silence tempted me to give vent to all my sorrows without fear of being overheard or recognized, and so I raised my voice in malediction after malediction of Luscinda and Don Fernando, as if I could by such means avenge the wrong they had done me. I called her cruel, ungrateful, false, faithless, and above all mercenary, since my enemy's riches had so blinded her love for me that she had transferred her affections to one with whom fortune had dealt more lavishly. But amid this tempest of maledictions and reproaches I found excuses for her, saying that it was not surprising that a maiden shut up in her parents' house and brought up to obey them in everything should have wished to comply with their wishes, seeing that they gave her for husband a gentleman so noble, so wealthy, and so accomplished that had she not been willing to accept his suit, they would have thought her mad or suspected her of having pledged her affections elsewhere, which would have reflected gravely on her honor and good name. Then I would argue that had she told them I was her husband, they could have seen that she had not made such a bad choice that they could not have excused her, since before Don Fernando became a suitor they could not reasonably have wished for a better match for their daughter than myself. She might, I reflected, easily have said, before being finally driven to give her hand to Don Fernando, that I had already given her mine. I should then have been ready to support all she might think fit to invent for the occasion. And so I came to the conclusion that faint love, foolishness, social ambitions, and desire for grandeur had made her forget the words with which she had deceived, encouraged, and backed up my fervent hopes.

"With such disturbing thoughts I plodded on through the rest of the night, and at daybreak I came to one of the passes in these mountains through which I wandered for three days more without road or path until I halted in some meadows lying I know not on which side of these mountains. There I asked some herdsmen where lay the most lonely spot in these mountain ranges. They told me it was in this direction; so, at once I made my way here, resolving to end my life, but when I reached this pass my mule fell dead of weariness and hunger or, as I rather believe, to rid herself of so useless a burden as myself. So I remained on foot, physically exhausted, starving, without even the slightest intention of looking for help. I do not know how long I lay on the ground in this state, but at length I got up without any feeling of hunger and discovered some goatherds beside me. They, no doubt, had satisfied my needs, for they told me how they had found me talking so wildly that I evidently must have gone out of my mind. And since then I feel that I am not always well in the head and at times so worn out and deranged that I behave like a lunatic, tearing my garments, crying aloud in this wilderness, cursing my fate, and vainly repeating the beloved name of my enemy. On these occasions my only wish and object is to wear out my life in lamentations. When I come to my senses, I am so battered and bruised that I can hardly move. My usual dwelling place is the hollow of a cork tree, which is large enough to shelter my wretched body. The cowherds and goatherds who live in these mountains, moved by charity, sustain me by leaving food for me by the paths and on the rocks where they think I may pass and find it. And even when I am out of my mind, a natural instinct makes me recognize my food and arouses in me the desire to take it and eat it. At other times, they tell me when they meet me in my sane moods, I rush out into the paths and take from the shepherds by force, although they would give them to me willingly, the provisions they bring up from the villages to the folds. In this manner do I spend what remains of my miserable life, waiting until Heaven may be pleased to bring it to an end or drive out of my memory all thoughts of the beauty and treachery of Luscinda and the injury done to me by Don Fernando. If Heaven should do this without depriving me of life, I shall turn my thoughts toward some worthier course; if not, I have no alternative but to crave its infinite mercy for my soul. As it is, I feel neither the courage nor the strength to drag my body out of this strait in which of my own free will I have chosen to place it. This, gentlemen, is the melancholy tale of my misfortunes. Do you think I could have told it with less emotion than I have shown? Do not trouble yourselves to advise or persuade me to adopt such remedies as reason may suggest for relief, for they will produce no more effect than a medicine prescribed by some famous physician for a patient who rejects it. I wish to have no health without Luscinda, and since it pleases her to be another's when she is, or ought to be, mine, let me devote myself to misery, though I might have been the devotee of happiness. By her fickleness she sought to make my perdition irrevocable, and I shall gratify her wishes by my own destruction. And future generations shall learn that I alone lacked what other wretches possess in abundance, for they may derive consolation from the very certainty that no relief is possible, whereas in me this is the cause of greater anguish and evil, for I do not believe that they will even cease with death itself."

Here Cardenio ended the melancholy story of his love, and the curate was about to say some words of comfort when he was prevented by a voice that came to his ear saying in mournful tones what will be told in the fourth part of this narrative, for at this point the wise and considerate historian Cide Hamete Benengeli brought the third to an end.

CHAPTER XXVIII

Which deals with the quaint and aggreeable adventure that befell the curate and the barber in the Sierra Morena

Most happy and fortunate was the age in which the bravest of knights, Don Quixote of La Mancha, was launched into the world, since through his noble determination to revive and restore to the world the lost and almost defunct order of knight-errantry, we may enjoy today, in an age devoid of cheerful entertainment, not only the delights of his own truthful history, but also the tales and episodes it contains. In some ways these are no less delectable, imaginative, and truthful than the history itself, which, following its carded, twisted, and reeled thread, now relates that just as the curate was about to comfort Cardenio, he was prevented by a voice that came to his ear, saying in mournful tones: "Please God I may find here a spot that can serve as a secret sepulcher for this body of mine whose weary load I bear so unwillingly! Yes, here will be the place if the solitude these hills promise does not deceive me. Alas, how miserable I am! Yet, I am happier in the company of these rocks, which will allow me to tell my sorrows to Heaven, than in that of any human being on earth, from whom I can expect neither counsel in my perplexities, comfort in my sorrows, nor remedy in my afflictions."

The curate and all those with him heard these words distinctly, and thinking that the person who uttered them must be close at hand, they rose and began to search. Hardly had they gone twenty paces when they saw behind a rock a youth sitting under an ash tree. He wore a peasant's dress, but as he was bending down to wash his feet in a stream that flowed past, his head was turned away from them. They drew near so silently that he did not hear them, for his whole attention was absorbed in the task of bathing his feet, which gleamed like two pieces of pure crystal amid the pebbles of the running brook. They wondered at their whiteness and beauty, for they seemed not to have been made for treading the furrows or following the ox and plow, as his dress seemed to suggest. So, seeing that they were not yet observed, the curate, who went in front, made signs to the others to crouch down and hide themselves behind a rock from where they could watch what he was doing. The youth was clad in a gray-colored cape of two folds, girded closely around his body with a white towel. His breeches, gaiters, and hunting cap were also of gray cloth. His gaiters were pulled halfway up and exposed his bare legs, which were as white as alabaster. After bathing his delicate feet he wiped them with a handkerchief that he took out of his cap, and in doing so he raised his head and showed to those who were looking at him a face of such incomparable beauty that Cardenio said in a low voice to the curate: "Since this is not Luscinda, it can be no human creature." The youth then took off his cap, and as he shook his head, a mass of hair that the sun might have envied fell about his shoulders. They then perceived that he who seemed to be a peasant boy was a delicate woman, and the most beautiful that the two of them had ever seen, and Cardenio likewise would have concurred had he not gazed upon Luscinda, for he afterward declared that the beauty of Luscinda alone could rival hers. Her long golden hair fell down in such profusion that it not only covered her shoulders but concealed all her body, except her feet. Then she combed her hair with her hands, and if her feet in the water looked like pieces of the purest crystal, her fingers, as they moved amid her locks, resembled flakes of driven snow. The three onlookers were now impatient to find out who she was, and they resolved to show themselves. At the sound they made in approaching, the lovely damsel raised her head and thrust aside her tresses to see what it was that had startled her. No sooner did she perceive them than she rose hastily, and without waiting to put on her shoes or tie up her hair, hurriedly snatched a bundle that lay nearby and started to run away full of alarm; but she had not run six paces when her delicate feet, unable to bear the roughness of the stones, stumbled, and she fell to the ground.

The three ran to her assistance, and the curate was the first to speak to her, saying: "Stay, madam, whoever you are; those you see here have no wish but to help you. There is no reason for you to run away from us. In any case, your feet would not allow it, nor would we."

To this she made no reply, being ashamed and bewildered. So they went up to her, and the curate, taking her by the hand, continued: "Madam, your hair reveals to us what your costume would conceal. This is a sure proof that it can be no slight cause that has hidden your beauty in such an unworthy disguise and brought you to this lonely place where we fortunately have found you. Let us, if not dispel your miseries, at least offer you our advice and counsel in your distress, for no affliction except death can be so desperate that one should refuse to listen to words of comfort that are given in all goodwill to those who suffer. So, dear lady or dear sir, whichever you prefer, dismiss the fears that the sight of us has caused you and tell us of your good or evil fortune so that we three may be of assistance to you, either all together or singly."

While the curate was speaking, the disguised damsel stood like one in a daze, gazing at them without moving her lips or saying a single word, like some village rustic when he is suddenly shown some strange new sight. But after the curate had said more to the same effect, she gave a deep sigh and said: "Since the mountains cannot conceal me and my disheveled hair betrays my secret, it would be foolish for me to disguise my words any further, for if you believe them, it would only be through courtesy rather than for any other reason. Therefore, gentlemen, I thank you for the offer you have made, which obliges me to comply with your request, though I am afraid that the tale of my misfortunes will arouse your grief as well as your compassion, for you will not find medicine to cure them or advice to comfort me. Nevertheless, as I do not wish to fall in your esteem, now that you have discovered me to be. a woman and see me, young, alone, and in these clothes, circumstances that taken singly or all together are enough to ruin any honest reputation, I shall tell you something of my misfortunes, though I would far sooner draw the veil of silence over them."

All this she said in such a sweet voice and in so sensible a manner that they were still more charmed by her and they again begged her to tell her story. To this she replied by putting on her shoes, binding up her hair, and seating herself upon a rock with her three hearers around her. Then, brushing away a few tears from her eyes, she began in a calm, clear voice the story of her life.[1]

"In Andalusia there is a certain town from which a great duke takes his name, which makes him one of our grandees, as they are called in Spain. He has two sons. The elder is heir to his estates and apparently to his good qualities; the younger, heir to I know not what, unless it be to Vellido's treacheries [2] and Galalón's lies. To this nobleman my parents are vassals of humble degree, but still so rich that if nature had bestowed upon them birth equal to their wealth, they should have nothing more to desire and I should not now be in this wretched state, for their want of rank is probably the cause of all my misfortunes. It is true that they are not so baseborn that they would have to be ashamed of their lineage, but they are not so highborn that I would stop blam-

---

[1] Rodríguez Marín as the result of his researches in the archives of the towns of Andalusia suggested that the stories of Cardenio and Dorotea refer to real events that occurred in the life of Cervantes. Cardenio, he maintained, was a scion of the Cárdenas family from Córdoba; Don Fernando was Don Pedro Girón, younger son of the first Duke of Osuna; Dorotea was Doña María de Torres, who was seduced by Don Pedro. The events described took place in the years 1581 and 1582, five or six years before Cervantes became a commissary in Andalusia. Don Pedro did not marry Doña María de Torres, but followed his father to Naples, where the latter was appointed viceroy. Don Pedro died a bachelor in 1583. See *Don Quixote*, ed. F. Rodríguez Marín (Madrid, 1912), Vol. III, pp. 52–53.

[2] Vellido Dolfos, the assassin of King Sancho during the celebrated siege of Zamora, became the prototype of treachery.

ing their humble condition for my disgrace. They are but farmers, plain, honest people, without any mixture of ignoble blood, of the kind called old rusty Christians who by their wealth and handsome way of living are by degrees acquiring the name of gentlemen. But what they valued above rank or riches was having me for their daughter, sole heiress of their fortune; and I was always treated by them with the greatest indulgence and affection. I was the mirror of their eyes, the staff of their old age, and the sole object, even considering Heaven, of all their hopes. And as I was the mistress of all their affection, so also was I mistress of their farm. It was I who engaged and dismissed the servants; I kept the account of all that was sown and reaped; the produce of their oil mills, their winepresses, their cattle and sheep, their beehives; in a word, of all that a rich farmer like my father could possess I was both steward and mistress, and I performed my duties to their entire satisfaction. The spare hours that were left after having attended to the overseers, the foremen, and the laborers I spent in occupations that to maidens are as pleasant as necessary, such as sewing, spinning, and lace-making; and if I ever left these tasks, to refresh my mind I would read a devout book or play the harp, for experience has taught me that music calms a troubled mind and eases the wretchedness that springs from the spirit. Such was the life I led in my father's house, and if I have described it in such detail, it has not been out of ostentation or to show that I am rich, but to prove how little to blame I am for having fallen from that happy state I have described into the wretched one I find myself at present.

"In these many tasks I spent my life in such seclusion that I might have been a cloistered nun, unseen, as I thought, by anyone except the servants of the house, for when I went to Mass it was so early in the morning and always accompanied by my mother and our maidservants and I myself so heavily veiled and guarded that my eyes saw no more ground than the space where I set my feet. Nevertheless, the eyes of love, or rather of idleness, sharper than those of a lynx, discovered that I had attracted the interest of Don Fernando, the younger son of the duke whom I mentioned to you."

No sooner did she mention the name of Don Fernando than Cardenio's face changed color, and the curate and barber, noticing it, feared that he would break out into one of his fits. But he remained quiet, fixing his eyes attentively

on the maiden, suspecting who she was, while she, without
noticing Cardenio's excitement, continued her story.

"No sooner, then, had Don Fernando seen me than he
was smitten with a violent passion, as his behavior soon
showed. To shorten the account of my many misfortunes, I
shall pass over in silence the devices Don Fernando employed
to declare his love: he bribed all my servants, he gave gifts to
my relations; every day was a festival in our street; at night
no one could sleep on account of his serenades. Innumerable letters from him came, I know not how, into my hands,
full of amorous declarations and protestations, and fewer
words than promises and vows. All of which, nevertheless,
far from softening my resistance, rather hardened it, as if
he had been my mortal enemy; not that his gallantry and constant pleading displeased me, for I confess that I·felt flattered
by the attentions of a gentleman of his high rank. Besides, we
women, no matter how ugly we are, always love to hear men
call us beautiful. However, it was my virtue that opposed all
those temptations and the continual admonitions of my parents, who had already clearly perceived the intentions of
Don Fernando, for he had not cared whether the whole
world should know it. My parents told me that they trusted
me with their honor and good name, for they relied on my
virtue and prudence. At the same time they begged me to
reflect on the inequality between myself and Don Fernando
because from this I would realize that his intentions (whatever he might say to the contrary) were directed toward his
own selfish pleasure rather than to my advantage, and that
if I were willing to turn a cold eye upon his proposal, they
would shortly arrange a match for me with anyone I liked
from our town or from the neighborhood, for their great
wealth enabled them to do so. With their promises and assurances I strengthened my resistance and refused to give
Don Fernando any answer that could encourage even his
most distant hopes of reaching his desires.

"All my modest behavior, however, which he no doubt
took for disdain, only inflamed his lustful appetite (for that
is the name I wish to give the goodwill he showed toward
me). If he had truly loved me, you would never have heard
this tale of mine, for there would have been no occasion
for me to tell it. At length, Don Fernando heard that my
parents were going to make a match for me so as to put an
end to his hopes of possessing me, or at least so that I should

have more guards to protect me. And this suspicion drove
him to behave in the way I shall now describe. One night I
was in my room with the door well bolted and only my
maid present, when all of a sudden, in spite of all my precautions, in the lonely silence of my retreat, I could not
imagine how, I found him standing before me. The sight of
him gave me such a shock that my eyes went blind and I
lost the power of speech. I was unable to shout, nor do I
think he would have let me do so, for he came up to me at
once, and taking me in his arms (for I was so confused, I
repeat, that I had not the strength to defend myself), began
to plead and protest in such a way that I wonder how falsehood can have so much ability as to give lies the semblance
of truth. The traitor backed up his arguments with tears and
his intentions with sighs. I, a poor simple girl, alone among
my people, inexperienced in such things, began, I know not
how, to believe his falsehoods, though his tears and sighs did
not move me to anything more than pure compassion. When
I recovered somewhat from my fears, I said to him with more
spirit than I thought I possessed: 'If instead of being in your
arms I were in those of a fierce lion, and if I could free myself from them only by doing or saying something to the
prejudice of my honor, it would be no more possible for me
to do or say it than it is to alter the past. Even though you
clasp my body in your arms, I hold my soul safe and secure
in the purity and innocence of my thoughts, and how different they are from your sinful ones you shall see if you
use violence to carry them any further. I am your tenant,
not your slave, and your noble blood has not, nor ought to
have, the right to dishonor and insult my humility, and I
consider myself, a country girl and a farmer's daughter, as
good as you, a gentleman and lord. Your violence will be of
no avail; your riches will be worthless; your words will not
deceive me, nor your tears and sighs wring my heart. If I
were to find any of those things I have mentioned in the
man selected by my parents to be my husband, I would conform, and his will would be mine. Indeed, sir, if it were not
for my honor I would of my own free will grant you, though
without pleasure, what you are trying to gain by force. I say
this that you may not for a moment imagine that anyone
but my lawful husband can gain anything from me.'

   " 'If that be all, lovely Dorotea' " (for that is this unhappy
woman's name), "cried the treacherous man, 'here I pledge

you my hand; and let all-seeing Heaven and that image of Our Lady that you have here witness the agreement.'"

When Cardenio heard her say that her name was Dorotea, his agitation began again, and he was confirmed in his first opinion. Not wishing, however, to interrupt the story and anxious to hear how it would end, though he had almost guessed already, he merely said: "Then Dorotea is your name, lady? I have heard of another of the same name whose misfortunes are similar to yours. Continue, for the time will come when I may tell you things that will startle you as well as arouse your pity."

Dorotea was intrigued by Cardenio's words and by his strange, tattered clothing and asked him to tell her at once if he knew anything about her affairs, for if Providence had given her one blessing, it was the courage to face any disaster that might befall her, being certain that nothing could increase her present sufferings.

"I would certainly not fail to tell you, lady," replied Cardenio, "what I have in my mind if what I think be the truth, but so far there has been no occasion, nor would it interest you to know it."

"Very well," answered Dorotea. "To continue my story: Don Fernando, taking up the holy image that was in the room, called upon it to witness our betrothal and pledged himself by the most solemn vows to become my husband, though I begged him to mind what he was doing and to consider how angry his father would be at finding him married to the daughter of one of his own tenants. I told him not to allow my beauty, such as it was, blind his judgment, for it was not enough to excuse his error, and that if he wished to prove his love for me by a kind action, he should let my fortunes run their course as befitted my birth, for such unequal marriages are never happy and the joys that are theirs at the outset are short-lived. All these arguments I pressed on him, and many that I do not remember, but they were all in vain and did not deter him from his purpose, for he was like a man who is so eager to clinch a bargain that he brushes aside all the troublesome conditions he is bound to meet.

"At the time I did give brief thought to the matter, saying to myself: 'I shall not, after all, be the first whose marriage has raised her from low to high state, nor will Don Fernando be the first whom beauty or blind love (which is more prob-

able) has prompted to choose a bride of humble station. As
I am doing nothing that has not been done before, I should
be wise to accept this honor that Fortune offers me, for even
if his desire only lasts until he has had his way, I shall be
his wife in the eyes of God. If, on the other hand, I dismiss
him with scorn, I am now well aware that he will, when it
comes to that, use violence, with the result that I shall be
dishonored and blamed by everyone. And there will be no
one to know how innocently I have been involved in this
terrible situation, for what arguments of mine could ever
be convincing enough to persuade my parents and others
that this gentleman entered my room without my consent?'

"All these questionings and answers crowded into my
mind at the same instant. Also by this time Don Fernando's
vows, the witnesses he invoked, the tears he shed, and finally
his graciousness and handsome appearance began to incline
me toward a course that, though I was not aware of it, was
to end in my disaster. Indeed all these when accompanied
by so many genuine demonstrations of true affection on his
part would have sufficed to conquer any heart, even one as in-
dependent and as coy as mine. I called my maid to act as
joint witness on earth with those in Heaven. Don Fernando
repeated and confirmed his oaths, invoked new saints as
witnesses, and called down on himself a thousand curses in
the future if he did not fulfill what he promised. His eyes
again began to fill with tears, and he sighed more deeply. He
now clasped me more firmly in his arms, which had never let
me go, and when my maid left the room, I ceased to be a
maid, and he became a perfidious traitor.

"Day followed on the night of my misfortune, but not so
rapidly as I think Don Fernando desired. For once man's
appetite is satisfied his greatest desire is to escape entrap-
ment. I say this because Don Fernando hastily departed, and
with the help of my maid, who had let him into the house,
even before daybreak he was in the street. On taking leave
of me he promised me (though with less vehemence and passion than when he entered) that I could trust his word and
his good faith, and as greater confirmation of his word he
took a valuable ring off his finger and put it on mine. And
so he went away and I remained, whether sad or glad I do
not know. But I can truthfully say that I was desperately
anxious and almost crazed at this new turn of events. Yet,
either I had not the heart, or I forgot, to scold my maid for

her treachery in hiding Don Fernando in my room, for I was not yet sure in my mind whether what had befallen me that night had been good or bad. I told Don Fernando as he left that, as I was his, he could come to see me other nights in the same way, until he should fix a time for the marriage to be announced publicly. He came on the following night but never again, and for more than a month I tried in vain to see him in the street or at church, for I learned that he was in town and out hunting most days, a sport of which he was very fond.

"I know by bitter experience what I suffered during those melancholy days and hours and I began to doubt and even to disbelieve Don Fernando's word of honor; and I also know that it was then that I scolded my maid for her part in the affair, for I had omitted to do so before; and I know what efforts it cost me to control my tears and to compose my face for fear that my parents might inquire what was making me unhappy and I should be obliged to tell them lies. But then came a moment when all polite considerations and all restraints of honor and caution came to an end, for I lost my patience and blurted out all my secret thoughts. This was when I heard in town some days later a rumor that Don Fernando had married in the neighboring city a damsel of extraordinary beauty and of very noble parentage, though not so rich that her dowry could justify so great a match. Her name was said to be Luscinda, and various surprising things were supposed to have happened at her wedding."

When he heard Luscinda's name, Cardenio shrugged his shoulders, bowed his head, bit his lips, and knitted his brows, and soon a flood of tears poured from his eyes. But all this did not make Dorotea pause, and she continued her story by saying: "When this sad news reached me, my heart, instead of freezing, blazed up in such rage and fury that it was all I could do to prevent myself from dashing into the streets to proclaim the treacherous wrong that had been done me. But my fury abated for a time when I devised a plan that I put into execution that very night. I borrowed this apparel from a shepherd in my father's service; I disclosed to him all my misfortunes and begged him to accompany me to the city where I understood my enemy sojourned. At first he rebuked me for my foolish hardiness and found fault with my plan, but seeing that I was determined, he offered to accompany me, as he said, to the end of the world. I packed up in a linen pillowcase a woman's dress, some jewels, and some money, against any eventuality; and in the silence of that night, without saying anything to my treacherous maid, I left my home, accompanied by my servant and by my anxieties, and set out on foot for the city. Although I could not prevent what had been done, I was determined at least to face Don Fernando and ask him how his conscience had allowed him to act in such a way.

"The journey took two and a half days, and when I reached the city, I inquired for the house of Luscinda's parents. The first man whom I asked told me more than I wanted to hear. He pointed out the house to me and informed me of all that had taken place at their daughter's betrothal. It was so talked about in the city that everywhere people gathered in groups to discuss it. He told me that on the night of the betrothal, after the bride had given her consent, she had fallen into a deep faint and that when the bridegroom had loosened her dress at the breast to give her air, he had found on her a letter, written in her own hand. In it she declared that she could not be the wife of Don Fernando because she was already Cardenio's, who, according to what the man said, was a noble gentleman of that same city. And the letter added that if she had said yes to Don Fernando, it was only so as not to disobey her parents. Finally he told me that the letter let it be understood that she intended to kill herself at the end of the ceremony and gave her reasons for taking her own life. All this, they say, was confirmed when they found a dagger in some part of her clothing. And when Don Fernando had seen all this, believing that Luscinda had mocked and insulted him, he attacked her before she recovered from her swoon, trying to stab her with the same dagger they found, and he would have succeeded if her parents and those present had not prevented him. It was said that Don Fernando fled immediately and that Luscinda did not recover from her faint till the next day, when she told her parents that she was the true wife of that Cardenio I mentioned. I learned also that this Cardenio was said to have been present at the wedding and that when he saw her married, which he never believed could happen, he fled in despair from the city, leaving a letter declaring the wrong that Luscinda had done him and his determination to go where men would see him no more. All this was public knowledge throughout the city, and nothing else was talked of; and gossip increased when it was known that Luscinda was missing from her parent's house and from the city, for she could not be found anywhere, and that her parents had almost lost their reason and did not know what they could do to find her. This news raised my hopes, for I was better pleased not to have found Don Fernando than to find him married, for it now seemed that my chances of redress were not entirely ruled out, and I flattered myself that perhaps Heaven had laid that impediment on this second marriage in order to make him realize the duty he owed to the first and to convince him that, as a Christian, he was under a greater obligation to his soul than to the things of this world. I turned all these things over in my mind and derived a little consolation, though no comfort, by inventing faint and distant hopes to sustain the life that has become hateful to me.

"While I was in the city, not knowing what to do, since I could not find Don Fernando, I heard one day a public crier announcing that a large reward would be paid to anyone who would find me and describing my age and the very dress I wore; and I heard that it was rumored that the lad who came with me had abducted me from my parents' house. It cut me to the heart to discover how low my reputation had sunk, for I had not only lost it by coming away, but even worse, by my choice of so base and unworthy a companion. No sooner did I hear what the crier had to say than I left the city with my servant, who even then began to give tokens of faltering in the loyalty he had promised me, and that night through fear of being discovered we sought refuge in the thick woods of these mountains.

"But, as the saying goes, one evil calls another, and misfortunes never come singly. So it was in my case, for no sooner had we found ourselves alone in this wilderness than my worthy servant, who had hitherto been faithful and trustworthy, tried to take advantage of the opportunity that lonely spot appeared to offer him; and incited by his own rascality rather than by my beauty, he dismissed all regard for God or respect for his mistress and talked to me of love. When I rebuked with bitter and severe words his obscene intentions, he discontinued his pleas, by which he intended at first to take advantage of me, and started to use force. But merciful Heaven, which seldom or never fails to succor virtuous intentions, so favored mine that in spite of my feeble strength I was with ease able to force him back over the edge of a precipice; whether I left him dead or alive, I do not know. Then I fled with more speed than might have been expected from my exhaustion after the fight and I made for these mountains with no other thought or plan than to hide from my father and anyone he might send for me. I do not know how many months I had been here with this intention when I discovered a herdsman who took me as his servant to a village in the heart of these mountains, and I have served as shepherd all this time, trying always to be out in the country to conceal this hair of mine, which now so unexpectedly has betrayed me. But all my diligence and all my care have been of no avail, for my master got to know that I was not a man and had the same wicked notions as my servant. But as Fortune does not always discover an immediate remedy for every trouble, I found no precipice or cliff to throw my master down as I had my servant. And so, I thought it simpler to leave him and hide in these wilds again than to try my strength or my entreaties against him. So, I repeat, I took to the mountains once more to seek a place where, undisturbed, I can implore Heaven with sighs and tears to take pity on my plight and to give me grace and strength to escape from it, or else to end my life in this wilderness without leaving any memory of this unhappy woman, who has so innocently given cause to speak evil of her in her own and other lands."

CHAPTER XXIX

Which deals with the pleasant device that was adopted to rescue our love-sick knight from the severe penance he had imposed upon himself

"This, gentlemen, is the true story of my tragedy. Consider now and judge whether the sighs you overheard, the words you listened to, and the tears you have witnessed have not been more than justified. Now that you are acquainted with the nature of my misfortune, you must see that all consolation is in vain, for there is no possible cure. All I ask as a favor (which you could easily grant) is that you advise me where I can live safely without the terror of being discovered by those who seek me. Although I know that my parents love me so deeply that they would welcome me with open arms, I am so ashamed at the mere thought of appearing in their presence, so changed from the daughter they had known, that I would prefer to banish myself forever from their presence than look them in the face, and read in their thoughts their disillusion. For they will believe that I have lost the honor they had the right to expect of me."

Saying this, she lapsed into silence, and her face flushed with a color that plainly showed the shame and anguish of her heart. Those who had listened to her were moved with pity and wonder at her misfortunes. Then, just as the curate was about to offer her consolation and advice, Cardenio anticipated him, saying: "Are you then, lady, the fair Dorotea, only daughter of the rich Clenardo?"

Dorotea was startled to hear her father's name spoken by so tattered and woebegone a creature, for, as we have already said, Cardenio was in rags.

"Who are you, friend," she asked, "who knows my father's name? For if I remember rightly, I have not mentioned it in all the story of my misfortune."

"I am that unhappy Cardenio," he answered, "whom, as you yourself said, Luscinda declared to be her husband. And I, too, suffer because of the evil deeds of that man who betrayed you. You see me now reduced to nakedness and misery, deprived even of human pity, and what is worst of all, minus my reason except when Heaven pleases. I, Dorotea, am he who witnessed Don Fernando's outrages and waited to hear that *I do* with which Luscinda declared herself his wife. I am he who did not have the courage to see the end of her fainting fit or what became of the letter that was found in her bosom, for my soul could not endure so many disasters at once, and so I cast to the winds all patient reflections and left my home, leaving a letter with a guest of mine to deliver to Luscinda. I came to this wilderness with the intention of ending my days here, for from that moment I loathed life as a mortal enemy. But Fate has refused to end my existence and has merely deprived me of my reason, perhaps to preserve me for my good fortune in meeting you. If your story is true, however, as I am confident it is, it may be that Heaven has in store for us a fairer issue from our disaster than we expect. For since Luscinda is mine and cannot marry Don Fernando, as she has openly declared, and as he is yours, we may yet hope that Heaven will restore us what is our own, for it yet exists and is not alienated or destroyed. Since we have this consolation then, which is not based on far-distant hopes or extravagant fancies, I implore you, lady, to pluck up fresh courage as I intend to do, and let us both mold our thoughts to the expectation of better fortune, for I swear on the word of a Christian gentleman that I will not forsake you till I see you Don Fernando's wife, and if I fail to convince him by my arguments to acknowledge all he owes to you, then I will use my gentleman's privilege and challenge him for the wrong he has done you. And I shall not remember the injuries he has done me, but leave them to Heaven to avenge while I devote my energies to avenging yours on earth."

Dorotea was amazed at Cardenio's speech, and not knowing how to express her gratitude for such generous offers, tried to kiss his feet, but Cardenio would not allow her. The curate then replied for himself and for her, approving of Cardenio's generous determination. He particularly begged, urged, and persuaded them to accompany him to his village, where they might provide themselves with such things as they needed, and while they were there, they could take measures to search for Don Fernando, or to restore Dorotea to her parents, or to do whatever should appear most expedient. Cardenio and Dorotea thanked him and accepted his offers of assistance.

The barber, who had hitherto been listening in silent amazement to all that had taken place, then made a courteous speech, offering with no less goodwill than the curate to help them in every way he could. He also told them briefly what had brought the curate and himself there, and expatiated on Don Quixote's extraordinary madness, explaining that both of them were waiting for the knight's squire, who had gone in search of him. Then Cardenio suddenly remembered, as in a dream, the quarrel that had taken place between him and Don Quixote, and he described it to them, although he was unable to say what was the cause of the dispute.

At this moment they heard shouts and recognized them as coming from Sancho Panza. As he had not found them in the place where he had left them, he was shouting their names at the top of his voice. They went out to meet him and asked after Don Quixote. He replied that he had found him naked except for his shirt, lean, yellow, and half dead with hunger, sighing for his lady, Dulcinea. And though he had told him that she had commanded him to leave that spot and come to El Toboso, where she was waiting for him, he had answered that he was determined not to appear before her beauteous presence until he had achieved feats that might make him worthy of her favor. If this went on much longer, Sancho continued, there was danger that his master might never become an emperor, as he was in honor bound to be, nor even archbishop, which was the least he could be; therefore, they should consider what could be done to get him away from there. The curate told him not to worry, for they would get him out from there if they had to carry him. He then told Cardenio and Dorotea of the plan they had devised for Don Quixote's cure, or at least for restoring him to his home. Dorotea then said she could play the distressed damsel better than the barber, especially as she had with her a dress in which she could perform it most naturally. She told them, furthermore, to put entire trust in her talents, for she had read many books of chivalry and was well acquainted with the style in which distressed damsels were accustomed to beg their favors from knights-errant.

"Then all we need," said the curate, "is to put our plan into action; Fortune certainly seems to be propitious to our undertaking; it has unexpectedly begun to offer you, my friends, a glimmer of hope of ultimate success and has made our task easier as well."

Dorotea then took from her bundle a dress of rich woolen cloth and a short mantle of elegant green silk, and from a little casket she extracted a necklace and other jewels. With these she immediately adorned herself in such a way that she looked like a rich and goodly lady. All these things and more she said she had brought from home in case of need, but had never had any use for them till now. They were all delighted with her great elegance, wit, and beauty, and they agreed that Don Fernando must be a man of poor taste to have slighted such loveliness. But the most amazed one of all was Sancho Panza, who thought (and it was true) that never in his life had he seen so fair a creature. He earnestly begged the curate to tell him who the lady was and what she was doing in these out-of-the-way parts.

"This beautiful lady, brother Sancho," answered the curate, "is, to say the least, heiress in the direct male line of the great kingdom of Micomicón, who has come in search of your master to ask of him a boon, which is to redress a wrong or injury that a wicked giant has done her; and owing to the fame of your master, which has spread through all lands, this beautiful princess has come all the way from Guinea in quest of him."

"Happy search makes happy finds," said Sancho Panza; "especially if my master has the luck to undo the wrongs by wiping out the whoreson giant you mention; kill him he surely will if he meets him, unless he turns out to be a ghost, for against ghosts my master has no power. Now there is one thing among others that I particularly want to beg of you, Master Licentiate. Advise my master to marry this princess, otherwise he may suddenly get the notion of becoming an archbishop, which is what I fear. But if he's married, he will be incapable of receiving archbishop's orders and will come easily into his empire, and I shall get all I want, for I thought the whole matter over and have come to the conclusion that it would not suit me for my master to be an archbishop. I'm no good myself for the Church, seeing I'm a married man, and were I to go gadding about now picking up dispensations to hold church-livings, and me with a wife and children, I'd never see the end of the job. So it all hinges on my master marrying this lady straightaway, sir—I don't know her name yet, so I can't call her by it."

"Her name," replied the curate, "is Princess Micomicona; as her kingdom is called Micomicón, that obviously must be her name."

"There is no doubt about that," replied Sancho; "I've known many who take their titles and family names from the places where they were born, calling themselves Pedro of Alcalá and Diego of Valladolid, and I reckon the custom of queens taking the names of kingdoms must be the same over there in Guinea."

"So it must," said the curate, "and as to your master's marriage, I shall do my best to arrange it."

Sancho was quite as pleased with the answer as the curate was amazed at his simplicity and at seeing how firmly his master's ravings had taken root in his fancy. For he seemed seriously to believe that Don Quixote was going to become an emperor.

By this time Dorotea had mounted the curate's mule, and the barber had fixed the oxtail beard on his chin, so they told Sancho to guide them to Don Quixote, warning him on no account to say that he knew the curate and the barber, because whether his master became an emperor or not hinged on their not being recognized. Neither the curate nor Cardenio would go with them, the latter that he might not remind the knight of their quarrel, the former because his presence was not necessary for the moment; so they let the rest go on in front while they followed slowly on foot. The curate, however, did not neglect to give instructions to Dorotea on the part she had to play, but she replied that there was no cause for worry, for she would follow the books of chivalry to the letter. They had gone a little over two leagues when they came in sight of Don Quixote. They found him clothed, though without his armor, in a wild rocky spot. As soon as Sancho told Dorotea that this was Don Quixote, she whipped her palfrey, being closely followed by the well-bearded barber. When they reached the knight, the squire leaped from his mule to help his lady alight. Quickly dismounting, she threw herself on her knees before Don Quixote, and despite his efforts to raise her, she, still kneeling, addressed him as follows: "Never will I rise from this position, most valiant and invincible knight, until your goodness and courtesy shall grant me a boon that will not only redound to your honor and renown, but also benefit the most injured ' and disconsolate damsel that ever the sun beheld. And if the valor of your mighty arm be equal to what I have heard of your immortal fame, it is your bounden duty to succor a luckless woman who comes from a faraway country drawn by the scent of your great fame to seek from you a remedy for her misfortunes."

"Beauteous damsel," replied Don Quixote, "I will not answer one word nor hear anything of your matter until you rise from the ground."

"Sir knight, I will not rise," answered the afflicted damsel, "unless out of courtesy you grant me first the boon I ask."

"I do vouchsafe and grant it to you," replied Don Quixote, "provided it be nothing detrimental to my king, my country, or to her who keeps the key of my heart and liberty."

"No injury will be done to any of them, my good lord," answered the downcast damsel.

Then Sancho Panza went up and whispered softly in his master's ear, saying: "Your worship may well grant the request she asks, for it is a mere trifle; all that is required is to polish off a huge brute of a giant, and she who asks it is the Princess Micomicona, queen of the great kingdom of Micomicón in Ethiopia."

"Whoever she may be," said Don Quixote, "I will do my duty toward her." Then, turning to the damsel, he said: "Rise, most beautiful lady, for I grant you any boon you wish to ask of me."

"What I ask of you," said Dorotea, "is that you, O magnanimous gentleman, at once accompany me to where I shall conduct you and that you promise me not to undertake new adventures until you have avenged me on the traitor who, contrary to all human and divine law, has usurped my kingdom."

"I grant your request," said Don Quixote, "and therefore, lady, from this day on you can dispel the melancholy that

oppresses you and give new life and strength to your feeble
hopes, for with the help of God and my own, you shall see
yourself shortly restored to your kingdom and seated on the
throne of your great and ancient estate, despite all the knaves
and villains who would deny it. And now, all hands to the
task, for in delay, it is said, lies danger!"

The distressed damsel struggled to kiss his hands, but
Don Quixote, who was a most courteous knight, would not
permit it. He made her rise and embraced her with much
gentleness and courtesy. He then gave orders to Sancho to
tighten Rozinante's girths and help him to arm himself. Sancho took down the armor from a tree, where it hung like a
trophy, and girthing Rozinante, he accoutered his master
in a moment. And the knight, seeing himself armed, cried
out: "In God's name let us depart to assist this great lady!"

The barber was still on his knees, trying his best to hide
his laughter and to prevent his beard from falling off, for if
it had, their ingenious stratagem would perhaps have mis-
carried. Seeing that the boon was already granted and that
Don Quixote was diligently preparing to fulfill his promise,
he got up, and taking his lady by one hand, they both
assisted her to mount the mule. Then Don Quixote mounted
Rozinante, the barber his hack, and they were ready to start.
And Sancho, who was left to trudge along on foot, felt
again the aching grief for the loss of Dapple, but he bore it
cheerfully, reflecting that his master was well on the way
and just about to become an emperor. And he supposed without any shadow of a doubt that he would marry that princess
and become at least king of Micomicón. The only thing
that worried him was that this kingdom was inhabited by
Negroes and that his subjects would all be black. But then
his fancy supplied him with a fine remedy, and he said to
himself: "What do I care if my subjects are black? What
have I to do but ship them off to Spain, where I may
sell them for ready money with which I can buy some title
or some post in which I may live in clover all the days of
my life? No! I might as well go to sleep like a dunderhead
if I've not the gumption to sell thirty thousand Negroes
in the twinkle of an eye! By God I'll make them buzz, little
and big, and even if they are blacker than coal, I'll turn
them into white or yellow. Come on, all of you; I'm licking
my fingers already." After these reflections he went on in

such good spirits that he forgot to be tired of trudging along on foot.

Cardenio and the curate, who had been hiding in the bushes, observed all that happened and were now eager to join them. And the curate, who was a cunning schemer, presently devised an excellent expedient, for with a pair of scissors that he carried in a case he hastily cut off Cardenio's beard and dressed him in a gray cape and black cloak of his own, while he remained in his breeches and doublet, with the result that Cardenio would not have recognized himself had he looked in a mirror. While they were disguising themselves, the others had gone a good way ahead, but they easily reached the highroad before them because the thickets and the broken paths there did not allow those on horseback to travel as fast as those on foot. And so, at last they halted in the plain at the foot of the mountains, and as Don Quixote and his party came in view, the curate stared at the knight, pretending that he was trying to recognize him. After gazing earnestly at him for a good long while, he rushed up to him with open arms, crying out: "In a good hour have I found you, my countryman, the mirror of knighthood, Don Quixote of La Mancha, flower and cream of gallantry, protector of the needy, quintessence of knight-errantry." And saying this he embraced Don Quixote on his left knee.

The knight was startled by the man's words and behavior and looked at him attentively. Even when he finally recognized him he was still puzzled at finding him here, but made efforts to dismount. The curate, however, would not allow him to do so.

"Father," said Don Quixote, "you must allow me to alight; it is not right that I should remain on horseback and so revered a person as you travel on foot."

"I will on no account," replied the curate, "consent to your dismounting, for it was on horseback that your grace performed the mightiest exploits this age has witnessed. As for myself, an unworthy priest, I shall be satisfied if one of these gentlemen of your retinue will allow me to mount behind him, if they do not object. And I shall even fancy I am mounted on the charger Pegasus or on the Zebra or courser of the famous Moor Muzaraque, who even to this day lies enchanted on the great hill of Zulema, not far from the illustrious Compluto." [1]

"I did not think of that, revered father," answered Don Quixote, "but I know that my lady, the princess, will for my sake, order her squire to give you the saddle of his mule, for he can ride on the crupper if the beast will stand it."

"Yes, she will, I believe," said the princess, "and I am also sure that there will be no need for me to order my squire, for he is the last man to allow a priest to go on foot when he may ride."

"You may be certain of that," replied the barber. And immediately dismounting, he offered the curate the saddle, which the latter took without much pressing. But as ill luck would have it, when the barber was getting up from behind, the mule, which was a hired one and consequently a vicious jade, reared her hindquarters and gave two savage kicks, which had they caught Master Nicholas on the chest or on the head, he would have consigned the ramble after Don Quixote to the Devil. As it was, they gave him such a fright that he fell to the ground with so little care for his beard that it fell off. Finding himself without it, he could find no other remedy than to cover his face with both hands and cry out that his grinders were stove in. Don Quixote, seeing that huge mass of beard without jaws or blood lying a good distance away from the fallen squire's face, exclaimed: "By the living God, this is a great miracle! His beard has been wrenched and torn clean off his face as if he had been shaved."

The curate, who saw the risk they ran of their scheme being found out, rushed at once to pick up the beard and took it to where Master Nicholas lay, still moaning. Then hurriedly holding the barber's head to his chest, with one jerk he clapped the beard on, muttering over him some words that he said were an infallible charm for sticking on beards, as they would see. And when he had fixed it on, he withdrew, and the squire reappeared as well bearded and as sound as before. Don Quixote was dumbfounded at what he saw, and he begged the curate to teach him that charm when he had the time, for he felt confident that its curative powers must extend beyond the mere sticking on of beards, since it was obvious that the flesh must have been lacerated when the

1 Complutum was the old Latin name of Alcalá de Henares. The city was famous for its university, which was founded in 1507 by Cardinal Ximénez de Cisneros. It was also celebrated as the birthplace of Cervantes.

beard was torn off. But since the charm had healed everything, it would be a godsend for more than beards.

"That is so," said the curate, and he promised to explain it to him at the first opportunity.

They then agreed that the curate should be the first to ride, and after him the three by turns until they reached the inn, which must have been about two leagues from there. Now that the three of them were mounted—that is to say, Don Quixote, the princess, and the curate—and three were on foot—namely Cardenio, the barber, and Sancho Panza— Don Quixote said to the damsel: "Let your highness, madam, lead the way wherever it may please her."

But before she could reply, the curate said: "Toward what kingdom will your ladyship guide us? Will it be toward that of Micomicón? It must be so or I know little of kingdoms." She, being well versed in everything, knew that she had to answer yes, so she said: "Yes, sir, my way lies toward that kingdom."

"If it be so," said the curate, "you must pass through the village where I live, and from there you must take the road to Cartagena, where you may, with good fortune, embark. If there be a favoring wind, a calm sea, and no storm, you will come in the space of nine years in sight of the great Lake Meona—I mean, Meotis—which is a little more than a hundred days' journey on this side of your highness' kingdom."

"You are mistaken, good sir," said she, "for it is not two years since I departed from that place, and I assure you I have never had good weather, yet in spite of that, I have managed to see what I so longed for, the famous Don Quixote of La Mancha, whose glory reached my ears the moment I set foot in Spain and impelled me to seek him to commend myself to his courtesy and entrust my just cause to his invincible arm."

"No more," cried Don Quixote; "cease, I pray, these encomiums. I am a sworn enemy to flattery, and though I know that what you say is the truth, yet such discourses offend my chaste ears. What I can say, madam, is that whether I have courage or not, I will use it in your service, even if I were to lose my life. But, waiving all this for the moment, I beg the licentiate to tell me what has brought him to these parts, alone, without servants, and so lightly equipped that I am filled with amazement."

"To that," answered the curate, "I shall give a brief answer. Your worship should know that Master Nicholas, the barber, and myself traveled to Seville to collect certain sums of money that a relative of mine, who many years ago went to the Indies, had sent me, and it was not a small sum either, but over sixty thousand pesos, which is quite a windfall. And passing yesterday through these parts, we were set upon by four highwaymen, who stripped us to our very beards, and in such a manner that the barber thought fit to put on a false one; as for this youth who is with us (pointing to Cardenio) they made him a new man. And the best of it all is that it is rumored hereabout that those who robbed us are certain galley slaves who say that they were set at liberty, almost in this very spot, by a man so valiant that in spite of the commissary and the warders, he released them all. Doubtless he must be out of his wits or he must be as great a knave as they, or else some fellow devoid of soul and conscience, for he let loose the wolf among the sheep, the fox among the hens, the fly amid the honey. He had defrauded justice and rebelled against his king and natural lord, since he went against his just commands; he has, I say, robbed the galleys of their limbs and stirred up the Holy Brotherhood, which has been resting these many years. Finally, he has done a deed that may not be a gain to his body and will bring everlasting damnation to his soul."

Sancho had told the curate and the barber of the adventure of the galley slaves, which his master accomplished with so much glory, and therefore the curate laid stress upon it to see what Don Quixote would say or do. The knight, however, did not dare to say that he had been the liberator of those worthies, but his color changed with every word the curate said.

"These then," continued the curate, "were the fellows who robbed us, and may God out of His mercy pardon the man who stopped them from receiving the punishment they so richly deserved."

CHAPTER XXX

Of Dorotea's inventiveness, with other pleasing and entertaining matters

The curate had scarcely ended when Sancho burst out: "By my faith, your reverence, he who did that deed was my master, and not for want of warning, for I told him beforehand to mind what he was doing and that it was a sin to set them free, for they were all going to the galleys for being the most arrant rogues."

"Blockhead!" exclaimed Don Quixote. "It is not the duty of knights-errant to find out whether the afflicted, enslaved, and the oppressed whom they encounter on the roads are in evil plight and anguish because of their crimes or because of their good actions. Their concern is simply to relieve them because they are needy and in distress, having regard to their sufferings and not to their knaveries. I came across a number of poor unhappy wretches strung together like beads on a rosary, and I did for them what my religion demands of me. As for the rest, I am not concerned. If anyone sees something wrong in what I have done, excluding the presence of the reverend licentiate and his holy office, I say that he knows very little of the principles of chivalry and that, furthermore, he lies like a misbegotten son of a whore, and this I will ram down his throat with my sword, which can give him the answer at greater length."

Saying this, he steadied himself in his stirrups and slapped down his helmet, for the barber's basin, which he believed to be Mambrino's helmet, he carried hanging at his saddle-bow until he could repair the damage it had received from the galley slaves.

As Dorotea with her keen intelligence and sprightly wit already understood Don Quixote's crazy humor and saw that, with the exception of Sancho Panza, they all made fun of him, she resolved not to be left out. So, seeing him so enraged, she said to him: "Sir knight, be pleased to remember the boon you promised me; you are bound by it not to engage in any other adventure however urgent it may be; so, calm your wrath, for if his reverence had known that it was by your unconquered arm the galley slaves were freed, he would have put three stitches through his lips and even bitten his tongue thrice rather than have spoken a word of disparagement against you."

"That I dare swear," said the curate, "I would even have pulled out my moustache." [1]

"I will be silent, my dear lady," said Don Quixote, "and will restrain the just anger that has risen in my heart, and will remain quiet and peaceful until I have obtained for you the promised boon. But, in payment for this service I beg you to tell me, if it should not distress you, what is your grievance, and who, how many, and of what kind are the persons on whom I have to take due, sufficient, and entire revenge."

"I will do that willingly," said Dorotea, "if hearing of miseries and misfortunes will not make you angry."

"It will not," answered Don Quixote.

To which Dorotea replied: "If it is so, then your lordships will give all their attention."

At this Cardenio and the barber drew near to hear what kind of tale the wise and witty Dorotea would invent, and likewise did Sancho, who was as much deceived by her as his master. She, after settling herself comfortably on her saddle and with a preliminary cough and various other gestures, began with much charm to tell her story as follows: "In the first place, I would have you know, gentlemen, that my name is——"

Here she paused a moment, for she had forgotten the name the curate had given her. He, however, came to her rescue,

---

[1] In the day of Cervantes the clergy, who are nowadays clean-shaven, all wore moustaches and chin tufts. (Clemencín)

for he understood why she hesitated, and said: "It is no wonder that your highness should be troubled and embarrassed in telling your misfortunes. Those who suffer deeply are wont to lose their memories so that they even forget their own names, as seems to have happened to your ladyship, who has forgotten that she is called the Princess Micomicona, lawful heiress of the great kingdom of Micomicón. With this hint your highness may easily recall all she wishes to relate."

"'That is true," answered the damsel, "and from now I do not think it will be necessary to give me any more hints, for I shall be able to bring my truthful story to a safe conclusion. The king, my father, who was called Tinacrio the Sage, was very learned in what they call the magic arts. He discovered by his science that my mother, Queen Xaramilla, would die before him and that soon afterward he also would depart from this life and I be left an orphan, without father or mother. He used to say, however, that this did not trouble him as much as the knowledge that a certain mammoth giant called Pandafilando of the Malignant Eye—for it is a fact that although his eyes are set straight, he always squints out of pure malice to strike terror into all on whom he gazes—I say that my father knew that this giant, lord of a great island that almost touches our land, when he should hear that I was an orphan, would cross over with a mighty force into my kingdom and take it from me, without leaving me even a tiny village in which to take refuge, but that I could spare myself all this disastrous ruin if I married him. My father thought it highly unlikely that I should ever even consider such an unequal marriage; and he was right, for the thought never entered my mind of marrying that giant or any other, however huge and monstrous he might be. My father also said that after he was dead and I noticed that Pandafilando was about to enter into my kingdom, I should not defend myself, for that would be my destruction, but that I should abandon my kingdom without resistance if I would avert the death and total annihilation of my loyal subjects, for it would be impossible to defend myself against the satanic power of the giant. He urged me to embark at once for Spain with some of my people, for there I should find relief for my troubles by meeting a knight-errant whose fame at that time would extend through this whole kingdom and whose name, if I remember rightly, was to be Don Azote or Don Gigote."[2]

"Don Quixote you mean, lady," cried Sancho, "otherwise called the Knight of the Rueful Figure."

"You are right," replied Dorotea. "He also said that he would be tall of stature, with a withered face, and on his right side under the left shoulder, or near to it, he would have a gray mole with some hairs like bristles on it."

On hearing this, Don Quixote said: "Hold my horse, son Sancho, and help me to strip, for I wish to know if I am the knight of whom the wise king prophesied."

"Why do you wish to strip?" said Dorotea.

"To see if I have that mole of which your father spoke," answered Don Quixote.

"No need to strip," said Sancho, "for I know that your worship has a mole of that same kind in the middle of his backbone, which is a sign of being a sturdy man."

"That is enough," said Dorotea, "for among friends we should not be too particular. Whether it is on the shoulder or on the backbone is of little consequence; it is enough that there is a mole, and let it be where it please, since it is all one flesh. Without a doubt my good father was right in everything, and I am right in commending myself to you, Don Quixote, who are truly the one my father spoke of, for your face fits the description of that gentleman whose fame is widely known not only in Spain but throughout La Mancha.[3] For, indeed, the moment I landed at Osuna I heard of so many of your exploits that my heart at once told me you were the man I had come to seek."

"But, dear lady," said Don Quixote, "how did you land at Osuna, seeing that it is not a seaport?"

Before Dorotea could reply, the curate interposed and said: "Her highness meant to say that after she had landed at Málaga, Osuna was the first place where she heard news of your worship."

"That is what I meant to say," said Dorotea.

[2] *Azote* means a whip. *Gigote* (French *gigot*) meant, according to Covarrubias, the flesh of a sheep's leg. The word is applied to *quijote*—the thighpiece of an armor.

[3] Cervantes is being ironical, his favorite type of humor; see also the poems at the end of Part I by the "Academicians" of Argamasilla, this town being the least likely place for a university because of the illiteracy of its peasants.

"Now that we are all set fair," said the curate, "let your majesty continue."

"Nothing remains to be said," answered Dorotea, "except that having had the good fortune to meet the noble Don Quixote, I already consider myself queen and mistress of my whole kingdom, since he, out of his courtesy and generosity, has granted my request and will go wherever I may please to lead him. And I shall straightaway conduct him into the presence of Pandafilando of the Malignant Eye that he may kill him and restore to me all that he has so unjustly usurped. For all this must come to pass just as the wise Tinacrio, my father, has foretold. And he left it recorded in Chaldean or Greek letters—I cannot read them—that if the knight of the prophecy, after he has cut off the giant's head, should wish to marry me, I should at once consent without demur to become his lawful wife and should give him possession of my kingdom together with my person."

"What do you think of this, friend Sancho?" asked Don Quixote. "Did I not tell you so? See how we now have a kingdom to rule and a queen to marry."

"I'll swear to that," said Sancho. "May a pox take the whoreson knave who doesn't wed her the moment Sir Pandahilado's [4] weasand is slit! The queen's a poor-looking baggage, is she? Well I wish all the fleas in my bed were no worse!" And so saying he cut a couple of capers and showed every sign of delight. Then, catching the reins of Dorotea's mule and making her stop, he fell down on his knees before her and begged her to give him her hand to kiss in token that he acknowledged her as his queen and mistress. Who of those present would not have laughed upon seeing the madness of the master and the simplicity of the squire? Dorotea gave him her hands and promised to make him a great lord in her kingdom when Heaven should permit her to recover and enjoy it. Sancho then returned thanks in such glowing and farfetched terms that they all redoubled their laughter.

"This, gentlemen," continued Dorotea, "is my story, and it only remains to tell you that out of all the members of the suite I brought with me from my kingdom not a single one survives except this well-bearded squire, for they were all drowned in a great storm that caught us in sight of port. By a miracle he and I managed to float ashore on two planks;

---

[4] Pandahilado is Sancho Panza's distortion of Pandafilando, the giant whose name was coined by Dorotea.

and, indeed, the course of my life has been one continuous miracle and mystery, as you must have observed. And if I have been guilty of exaggeration, or have not been as accurate as I ought, lay the blame on what the reverend father licentiate said at the beginning of my story, to the effect that unending and overwhelming hardships deprive the victim even of memory."

"They shall not deprive me of mine, O illustrious and lion-hearted lady," cried Don Quixote, "however many I may suffer in your service and however great and unaccountable they may be. So, once again I confirm the boon I promised you, and swear to go with you to the end of the world, till I meet face to face that fierce enemy of yours whose proud head I intend, with God's help and my right arm, to cut off with the edge of this—I will not say good sword, thanks to Ginés de Pasamonte, who carried off my own." These last words he uttered in a low voice; then he continued: "When I have hewed it off and restored you to your realm in peace, it shall rest with your own will to dispose of your own person in whatever way you please. For so long as my memory is absorbed, my will captive, and my heart enslaved by her—I say no more; it is impossible for me to think of facing the thought of marriage, even if it were to the Phoenix itself."

Sancho was so disgusted at his master's refusal to marry that he raised his voice and cried out angrily: "Upon my soul, Don Quixote, I swear your worship is not in his right senses. How else is it possible that your worship should hesitate to marry so high a princess as this one here? Does he imagine that Fortune is going to offer him around every corner such a piece of good luck as she holds out now? Is my Lady Dulcinea more beautiful? By no means, not even by a half; and I am about to add that she doesn't come up to the shoe of this lady here. A fair chance I have of getting my grip on the courtship if you, sir, go fishing for mushrooms at the bottom of the sea.[5] Get married—get married at once, in the Devil's name, and clutch a hold of this kingdom that is dropping into your hands free, gratis, and for nothing. Then, when you are king, make me a marquess or a governor, and may the Devil take the rest!"

[5] *Pedir cotufas en el golfo* was a proverb meaning to seek for the impossible. *Cotufas* and *chufas* were the tubers of a kind of sedge which was a dainty in Valencia. It served to make the Spanish cooling drink *horchata,* which is still very popular in Spain in summertime.

Don Quixote, when he heard such blasphemies being said against his lady, could not bear it any longer; so, raising his lance, without speaking a word to Sancho or a by-your-leave, he gave him two such blows that he stretched him flat on the ground; and if Dorotea had not called out to him not to give the fellow any more, he would have killed his squire there and then.

"Do you imagine, foul villain," he said to him after a pause, "that you are always going to be allowed to take me by the breech and that all the sinning is to be on your side and the pardoning on mine? Then give up thinking so, you excommunicated rascal, for I am sure that is what you are because you have let your tongue rip against the peerless Dulcinea. Do you not know, rascally knave, that if it were not for the valor she infuses into my arm, I would not have the strength to kill a flea? Tell me, you mocker with the viperish tongue, who do you think has won this kingdom and cut off the head of this giant and made you marquess (for all this I consider already accomplished) if it be not the power of Dulcinea using my arm as the instrument of her deeds? She fights and conquers in me, and I live and breathe and have my life and being in her. O whoreson rascal, how ungrateful you are when you see yourself raised from the dust of the earth to be a titled lord, and you respond to such benefit by speaking ill of her who bestowed it upon you!"

Sancho was not so badly hurt that he could not hear what his master said. He jumped up nimbly and ran behind Dorotea's palfrey and from there said to his master: "Tell me, sir, if you are not going to marry this great princess, it is clear the kingdom will not be yours; and if it is not, what favors then will you be able to bestow on me? That is what I'm complaining of. Marry once and for all this queen, now that we have her here—rained down, as it were from the sky —and you may later on go back to my Lady Dulcinea, for there must be plenty of kings in the world who've kept mistresses. As to the matter of beauty, I've nothing to say on that score; but if you ask me the truth, I'm of the opinion that they are both fine, though I've never seen Lady Dulcinea."

"What do you mean you've never seen her, you blasphemous traitor?" cried Don Quixote. "Did you not just now bring me a message from her?"

"I mean," replied Sancho, "that I didn't see her long

enough to judge of her beauty and her good parts piece by piece; but in the lump she looked well enough."

"Now I forgive you," said Don Quixote; "and do you forgive my wrath toward you, for first impulses cannot be curbed at will."

"I see that only too clearly," answered Sancho, "and in my case the longing to talk is the first impulse; I can't help blurting out what comes to the tip of my tongue."

"Nevertheless," said Don Quixote, "take heed, Sancho, what you say, for the pitcher that goes so often to the well— I say no more."

"Well then," replied Sancho, "God is in Heaven, who sees all our trickery; He'll judge who does most harm, I, in not speaking well, or you, sir, in not doing so."

"No more of this," said Dorotea. "Go, Sancho, kiss your master's hand and beg his pardon. In the future be more cautious in your praises and in your disparagements. Speak no evil of this Lady Tobosa, whom I do not know except that I am her humble servant. Put your trust in Heaven and you will get an estate to live upon like a prince."

Sancho went up, his head bowed down, and begged his master's hand, who gave it with a grave air, and after he had kissed it, Don Quixote gave him his blessing and told him to go on a little ahead, for he had something to ask him about and things of great importance to discuss with him. Sancho did so, and the two going a little away from the rest, Don Quixote said: "Since your return I have had no time to question you concerning the message that you bore and the answer you brought back. Now that Fortune allows us time and place, do not deny me the happiness that you are able to give me by your good tidings."

"Ask me what you please, sir," answered Sancho. "I bet I'll get out as well as I got in; but I beg you, sir, not to be so full of revenge in the future."

"What do you mean, Sancho?" said Don Quixote.

"I mean," replied Sancho, "that the blows you gave me a moment ago were more on account of the quarrel the Devil raised between us the other night than for what I said against my Lady Dulcinea, whom I love and reverence like a relic, though she is nothing of the sort, only because she belongs to you."

"No more of this, Sancho," said Don Quixote, "for it

offends me. I pardoned you then, and you know the common saying: 'New sin, new penance.' "

Just at this moment they saw a man coming along the road toward them, a rider upon an ass, and as he came nearer, he appeared to be a Gypsy; but Sancho Panza, who, when he saw an ass, followed it with his eyes and heart, had no sooner caught sight of the man than he recognized Ginés de Pasamonte, and by the thread of the Gypsy he discovered the reel, his ass. This was the truth, for it was his Dapple on which Pasamonte was riding, who to avoid being recognized and to sell the ass had dressed himself up like a Gypsy, for he understood the language of that folk as well as many other tongues as if they were his own. Sancho saw and knew him, and no sooner had he recognized him than he called out loudly to him: "Ah, Ginesillo, you robber! Give up my jewel, let go my darling, don't rob me of my comfort! Return me my ass, give up my delight! Clear off, whoreson thief, and hand over what is not your own!"

There was no need for so many words and menaces, for at the very first Ginés jumped down, and making off at a racing speed, in a moment he fled away and disappeared. Sancho ran to his ass, and embracing him, cried: "How have you been, my darling Dapple of my eye, my sweet companion?" Then he kissed and fondled him as if he had been a human creature. The ass held his peace and allowed himself to be kissed and caressed by Sancho without answering a word. They all came up and congratulated him on having found his ass, especially Don Quixote, who told him that he would still give him the three ass foals, for which Sancho thanked him.

While the knight and his squire rode on ahead, the curate said to Dorotea that she had acted very cleverly both in the conciseness of her story and in its resemblance to the books of chivalry. She said that she had often amused herself by reading them but that she did not know where lay the provinces and seaports, and therefore she had made a guess when she said that she had landed at Osuna.

"So I understood," said the curate, "and therefore I hastened to set it right. But is it not strange to see how readily this unfortunate gentleman believes all these lying fictions merely because they resemble the style and manner of his foolish books?"

"It is," said Cardenio, "and so strange and unusual that I

don't know whether anyone who tried to invent such a character in fiction would have the genius to achieve success."

"There is another strange thing about it," said the curate. "If when you converse with this worthy gentleman you discuss other topics that have no bearing upon his madness, he speaks very reasonably and shows that he possesses a clear head and calm understanding. Indeed, provided one does not broach the subject of his chivalries, he could be considered a man of very sound judgment."

While they were conversing, Don Quixote was confabulating with Sancho, and he addressed him as follows: "Friend Sancho, let bygones be bygones; put away all angry and spiteful thoughts and tell me where, when, and how you found Dulcinea? What was she doing? What did you say to her? How did you talk to her? What answer did she make? How did she look when she read my letter? Who copied it for you? Tell me all, without adding a jot or lying to give me pleasure, for I wish to know everything."

"Master," replied Sancho, "if I must speak the truth, nobody copied out the letter, for I carried no letter at all."

"That is true," said Don Quixote, "for I found the little book in which it was written, two days after your departure. This troubled me greatly, for I did not know what you would do without the letter. I believed you would return as soon as you missed it."

"I would have done so," said Sancho, "had I not learned it by heart when your worship read it to me, so that I repeated it to a parish clerk, who copied it out of my head word by word. And he said that never in all his life, although he had read many letters of excommunication, had he read so pretty a letter as yours."

"Do you still remember it by heart?" asked Don Quixote.

"No, sir," answered Sancho, "for after I recited it, seeing it was of no further use, I let myself forget it. If I remember, it had 'Suffering,' I mean 'Sovereign, Lady' and the ending, 'Thine till death, the Knight of the Rueful Figure.' Between those two things I put in three hundred 'souls' and 'loves' and 'mine eyes.' "

CHAPTER XXXI

Of the delightful conversation between Don Quixote and his squire, and other happenings

"All this does not displease me, so continue," said Don Quixote. "You arrived; now, what was the queen of beauty doing? Surely you found her stringing pearls or embroidering some device with golden threads for this, her captive knight."

"No, that I did not," answered Sancho; "she was winnowing two bushels of wheat in a backyard of her house."

"Why, then," said Don Quixote, "you may reckon that each grain of wheat was a pearl when touched by her hands; did you note, my friend, the wheat, was it the white or brown sort?"

" 'Twas neither, but red," answered Sancho.

"Then I assure you," said Don Quixote, "that, winnowed by her hands, it made the finest white bread. But go on; when you gave her my letter, did she kiss it? Did she put it upon her head?[1] Did she use any ceremony worthy of such a letter? Or what did she do?"

"When I went to give it to her," answered Sancho, "she was all set on her job, winnowing away with a power of wheat in her sieve, and she said to me: 'Lay down that letter on that sack; I can't read it till I've sifted all that's here.' "

"Cunning lady!" cried Don Quixote. "She must have done that so that she might read and enjoy it at leisure; go on,

---

[1] To put a letter on the head before opening it signified to do the writer the greatest possible honor.

Sancho, and while she was working, what did she say to you? What did she ask about me? What did you answer? Hurry up and tell me everything; leave not a drop in the inkhorn."

"She asked me nothing," replied Sancho, "but I told her the state you were in for her sake, doing penance for her, naked from the waist up, shut up among these rocks like a savage, sleeping on the ground, eating bread without a table-cloth, never combing your beard, spending your time weeping and cursing your fortune."

"There you were wrong," said Don Quixote. "I do not curse my fortune, but rather bless it, for it has made me worthy of the love of so high a lady as Dulcinea of El Toboso."

"Aye, so high is she," answered Sancho, "that she's a good hand's breadth taller than I am."

"How is that, Sancho?" said Don Quixote. "Have you measured yourself with her?"

"It happened," answered Sancho, "that when I was helping her raise a sack of wheat onto an ass, we came so close together that I couldn't help seeing that she was taller than me by a good span."

"True," answered Don Quixote, "her stature is adorned with a thousand million graces of soul. Now, there is one thing you must not deny me, Sancho. When you approached her, did you not perceive a Sabaean odor, an aromatic fragrance, something sweet—I cannot find a name to describe it—a scent, an essence, as if you were in some dainty glover's shop." [2]

"All I can vouch for," said Sancho, "is that I got a whiff of something a bit mannish; this must have been because she was sweating and a bit on the run."

"It could not have been that," answered Don Quixote, "but you must have had a cold in your head or else smelled yourself, for I know well the scent of that rose among thorns, that lily of the fields, that liquid amber."

"That may be so," answered Sancho, "for many a time I've noticed the same smell off myself as I perceived off her ladyship Dulcinea; but there's no wonder in that, for one devil is the dead spit of another."

---

[2] It was the custom in those days for glovers to scent the gloves with amber.

"Well, then," continued Don Quixote, "now that she has done sifting her wheat and has sent it to the mill, what did she do when she read the letter?"

"She did not read it," answered Sancho, "for she said she could neither read nor write. She tore it up into tiny pieces, saying that she did not wish to give it to anybody to read for fear her secrets might be known all over the village. She said it was enough to hear what I had told her by word of mouth about your love for her and all you were doing for her sake, and finally she begged me to tell you, sir, that she kissed your hand and that she was more eager to see you than to write to you. And she begged and commanded you on sight of this present to leave these thornbushes, give up your mad foolishness, and set out at once on the road to El Toboso, unless something else of greater importance turns up, for she had mighty longing to see you. She laughed a good deal when I told her they called you the Knight of the Rueful Figure. I inquired whether that chap, the Biscayan, had been there with her. She said that he had and that he was a decent fellow. I asked also about the galley slaves, but she said she had not yet seen any of them."

"So far so good," said Don Quixote; "but tell me, what jewel did she bestow upon you at your departure as a reward for the news you had brought her? For it is a well-known, ancient custom among knights-errant and their ladies to give to their squires, damsels, or dwarfs who bring good tidings some rich jewel as a reward for the message."

"That may be so, and a good custom it was, I'm thinking; but it must have been in the days gone by, for nowadays it is only customary to give a chunk of bread and cheese, for that was what my Lady Dulcinea gave me over the palings of the yard when I took my leave of her; and, by the way, it was plain ewe's-milk cheese."

"She is wonderfully generous," said Don Quixote; "and if she did not give you a gold jewel, it was doubtless because she had none there with her; but as the proverb says, 'Sleeves are good even after Easter.'[3] When I see her, all will be right. Do you know, Sancho, what amazes me? The swiftness of your return; why, it seems to me as if you went and came back through the air, for you have been away only

---

[3] *Buenas son las mangas después de Pascua,* a proverb meaning better late than never.

a little more than three days, although El Toboso is more than thirty leagues from here. Therefore, I am convinced that the wise magician who takes care of my affairs and is my friend, for he necessarily must, and does, exist, or I wouldn't be a good knight-errant, must have helped you in your journey without your being aware of it. Remember there are wizards who snatch up a knight-errant sleeping in his bed, and without his knowing how, he awakes the next day more than a thousand leagues from the place where he fell asleep. If it were not for this, knights-errant would not be able to help one another in their perils as they do on all occasions. For one may be fighting in the mountains of Armenia with some dragon or a fierce serpent or some other knight, and when he is getting the worst of the battle and is at the point of death, then, just when he least expects it, he sees descend from somewhere on top of a cloud or from a chariot of fire another knight, his friend, who was shortly before in England and who helps him, delivers him from death, and returns him to his home in time for the evening meal; and between one place and the other there may be two or three thousand leagues. All this is done by the skill and wisdom of those wise enchanters who look after valorous knights. So, friend Sancho, I do not find it difficult to believe that you went to El Toboso and back, since, as I have said, some friendly wizard must have flown through the air with you without your being aware of it."

"That may be so," said Sancho, "for I give you my word that Rozinante went as if he had been a Gypsy's ass with quicksilver in his ears." [4]

"With quicksilver you say," answered Don Quixote, "aye, and with a legion of devils besides, for they are folk who travel and make others travel without being tired, as far as they please. But, to change the subject, what do you think I ought to do about my lady's order to go and see her? For although I perceive that I am bound to fulfill her behests, I find myself prevented by the boon I have granted to the princess who accompanies us, and the law of chivalry forces me to satisfy my pledge rather than my pleasure. On the one hand, my longing to see my lady disturbs and perplexes me; on the other, my plighted word and the glory I stand

---

[4] To put quicksilver in an animal's ear to make him go faster is still a Gypsy trick in Spain today.

to reap in this enterprise incite and spur me on. What I intend to do is to travel by rapid stages and quickly get to the place where the giant is. Then, when I reach the place, I will cut off his head, install the princess peaceably in her kingdom, and immediately return to the light that irradiates my senses; and I shall make such persuasive excuses that she shall even commend my delay, for she will realize that all contributes glamour to her glory and fame, since all I have achieved, am achieving, and shall achieve by force of arms in this life springs wholly from the favor she bestows on me and from the fact that I am hers."

"God save us, sir!" cried Sancho. "What a pitiful state your worship's poor brain must be in! Tell me, sir, do you intend to make this journey for nothing and let slip so rich and rare a match as this one, when they give you a kingdom as dowry? Why, I've heard it said that it's more than sixty thousand leagues around, that it's most abundant in the necessities of life, and that it's bigger than Portugal and Castile lumped together. Hush, for the love of God! Be ashamed of what you've said, and take my advice (pardon me) and marry her in the first village that has a parish priest. If not, there's our curate here who'll do the job to perfection; and take heed that I'm of age to give advice and that this one I'm giving you fits you well, for better sparrow in hand than a vulture on the wing [5] because he who has good and chooses ill has only himself to blame for his bad choice."

"Look here, Sancho," answered Don Quixote, "if you are advising me to marry so that I may be king when I have slain the giant and be able to bestow upon you the favors I promised, you must know that I can gratify your wishes without marrying, for I will impose an extra condition before going into battle, namely, that upon my coming off a conqueror, they shall give me as my fee a portion of the kingdom even if I do not marry the princess, and this I can give to anyone I please; to whom would you have me give it if not to you?"

"That is clear," answered Sancho; "but mind, sir, you select it toward the sea so that if the life doesn't suit me I may be able to ship away my black subjects and do with

[5] Our familiar equivalent is "a bird in the hand is worth two in the bush."

them what I said before. Don't worry yourself about going to see Lady Dulcinea just now, but go off and kill the giant, and let us make an end of the job, for I'm sure it will bring us great honor and profit."

"I tell you, Sancho," said Don Quixote, "that you are right and that I will follow your advice about going with the princess before I visit Dulcinea. But I warn you to say nothing to anyone about what we have been discussing and planning, not even to our companions. For since Dulcinea is so shy that she does not want her feelings known, it would not be seemly for me, or anyone acting for me, to disclose them."

"But if that's the case," said Sancho, "how is it, your worship, that you make everyone you conquer by your arm present himself to Lady Dulcinea, for that means you love her and that she's your sweetheart as clearly as if you'd written your signature to it. And since you force them to go down on their bended knees in her presence and to say that they come from your worship to offer their obedience, how can the feelings of the two of you remain hidden?"

"How doltish and stupid you are!" exclaimed Don Quixote. "Do you not see, Sancho, that all this redounds to her greater glory? You should know that according to our code of chivalry it is a great honor for a lady to have many knights-errant serving her, with no greater aim in life than that of serving her for what she is and without expectations of any rewards for their noble ideals than that she should be content to accept them as her knights."

"That's the sort of love," said Sancho, "I've heard them preach about, and they add that we ought to love Our Lord for Himself alone, without being driven to it by hope of glory or the fear of punishment; but speaking for myself, I'm all for serving Him for what He can do for me."

"The Devil take you for a clodhopper!" cried Don Quixote. "What wise things you say at times! One would think you had been to school."

"I swear on my faith that I cannot read," answered Sancho.

At this moment, Master Nicholas shouted to them to wait awhile, for they wanted to halt and drink at a small spring nearby. Don Quixote stopped, to Sancho's great relief, for he was by this time tired of telling so many lies and feared that his master would trip him with his own words, for although he knew that Dulcinea was a peasant lass of El Toboso, yet he had never seen her in all his life. In the meantime, Cardenio had put on the clothes that Dorotea was wearing when they met her, and although they were rather shabby, they were a great improvement on his own. They all dismounted near the fountain, and with the scanty provisions the curate had brought from the inn they satisfied as best they could their great hunger.

While they were thus engaged, a young lad passed by who looked very earnestly at all those who sat around the spring, and after a moment he ran up to Don Quixote, embraced his legs, and began to weep bitterly, saying: "Ah, my lord! Do you not know me? Look at me closely. I am Andrés, the boy whom you loosed from the oak tree to which I was tied."

Don Quixote recognized him at once, and taking him by the hand, he turned to those who were present and said: "To show you all how important it is to have knights-errant in the world to set right the wrongs and injuries that are done by insolent and wicked men, you must know that a few days ago, as I rode through a wood, I heard some cries and very piteous lamentations as of a person afflicted and in distress. I hastened instantly to the place, and there I found tied to an oak this boy whom you see here. This rejoices my heart, for he will check me if I do not speak the truth. I say that he was tied to an oak tree, naked from the waist up, and a doltish fellow, whom I afterward learned to be his master, was scourging him with the reins of his mare. As soon as I saw him, I asked the master the reason for his cruelty. The boor replied that he was flogging him because he was his servant and had been guilty of carelessness, due rather to rascality than stupidity. The lad then said: 'Sir, he beats me only because I ask him for my wages.' The master then made a number of speeches and excuses, which I heard but did not believe. I made him at once untie the boy and forced him to swear an oath that he would take him home and pay him every real upon the nail, aye, perfumed too. Is this not true, Andrés, my son? Did you not notice the authority with which I ordered him and how humbly he promised to do my bidding? Answer; do not hesitate. Tell these gentlemen what happened that they may learn how necessary it is to have knights-errant on the road."

"All that you say is very true, sir," answered the boy, "but the end of the business was very different from what you imagine."

"In what way different?" asked Don Quixote. "Did the boor not pay you then?"

"He not only did not pay me," answered the boy, "but no sooner had you gone out of the wood and we were alone again than he again tied me to the same tree and gave me so many lashes that left me flayed like Saint Bartholomew. And at each stroke he cracked some joke to make a mock of you, sir, and if I hadn't felt such pain, I'd have laughed at what he said. As a matter of fact, he left me in such a state that I have been in hospital ever since, getting myself cured of the injuries that the wicked villain did me. For all this you are to blame, sir, for if you had ridden on your own way and not meddled in other people's affairs, perhaps my master would have been content to give me one or two dozen lashes, and then he would have let me go and paid me what he owed me. But because you abused him so unreasonably and called him so many foul names, his anger rose, and because he could not revenge himself on you, as soon as he was alone, he let loose the storm upon me in such manner that I'm afraid I'll never again be a whole man as long as I live."

"The trouble was," said Don Quixote, "that I went away. I should not have departed until I had seen you paid, for I might well have known that no churl will keep his word if he finds it does not suit him to keep it. Nevertheless, Andrés, you do remember how I swore that if he did not pay you I would return and seek him out and find him, even if he should hide himself in the belly of a whale."

"That is true," replied Andrés, "but it was all of no use to me."

"You will see presently whether it is of use or not," said Don Quixote. And saying this, he got up hastily and commanded Sancho to bridle Rozinante, who was feeding while they ate. Dorotea asked him what it was he meant to do. He answered that he meant to go in search of the boor, punish him for his bad conduct, and make him pay Andrés to the last maravedi in spite of all the boors in the world. She answered that he should remember that he could not undertake any other adventure, according to his promise, until he had finished hers and that as he knew this better than anyone else, he would have to stifle his anger until he returned from her kingdom.

"That is true," answered Don Quixote; "and Andrés must have to have patience until I return, for once more I vow and promise never to rest until he is satisfied and paid."

"I don't believe these vows," said Andrés; "I'd sooner have enough money now to help me to get to Seville than all the revenge in the world. Give me something to eat and take with me, and may God be with you, sir, and with all knights-errant, and may they be as erring to themselves as they have been to me."

Sancho took out of his bag a chunk of bread and cheese, and giving it to the lad, said: "Take it, brother Andrés, for each of us has a share in your misfortune."

"What share have you in it?" asked Andrés.

"This share of bread and cheese that I give you," answered Sancho, "for God knows whether I shall have need of it or not. For I'd like you to know, my friend, that we squires to knights-errant suffer great hunger and bad luck, and other things that are better felt than told."

Andrés grabbed his bread and cheese, and seeing that nobody gave him anything else, he bowed his head and took the road in his hands, as the saying goes.

But before he went, he said to Don Quixote: "For the love of God, sir knight-errant, if you meet me again, even though you see me being cut to pieces, do not come to my aid, but leave me to my misfortunes. No matter how great they are, they will not be as great as those that spring from your help, and may God lay a curse on you and all the knights-errant that ever were born in the world."

Don Quixote jumped up to chastise him, but he set off running so fast that no one attempted to follow him. Don Quixote was much ashamed at Andrés' story, and the others made great efforts not to burst out laughing and put him to utter confusion.

CHAPTER XXXII

Of what happened to Don Quixote and all his company at the inn

As soon as their welcome repast was over, they saddled, and without any adventure of note they arrived next day at the inn, which was Sancho Panza's dread and terror; and though he would rather not have entered it, yet he could not avoid it. The landlord, the hostess, their daughter, and Maritornes, seeing Don Quixote and Sancho return, came out to welcome them with affection and joy. The knight received them with solemn courtesy and told them to prepare a better bed than they had the last time, to which the landlady replied that if he paid better than the last time she would give him one fit for princes. Don Quixote said that he would, and so they prepared him a reasonably good one, in the same cockloft where he had lain before. He went off to bed at once because he was tired and weary, both in body and mind. He had hardly locked himself in when the landlady rushed at the barber, and seizing him by the beard, she cried: "By the Cross, my tail will no longer be used for your beard; give me back my tail. My husband's thingummy is all about the floor, which is a disgrace; I mean his comb, which I used to stick in my tail."

The barber would not give it to her, though she tugged away until the curate told him to hand it over to her, for they no longer needed that disguise. The barber might now appear in his own shape and tell Don Quixote that after he had been robbed by the galley slaves, he had fled for refuge to this inn. As for the princess' squire, they could say that she had sent him on in advance to give notice to those of her kingdom that she was on her way back, bringing with her one who would give them all their freedom. On this the barber willingly gave up the tail to the landlady, together with the other things they had borrowed for Don Quixote's liberation.

All the people in the inn were struck by Dorotea's beauty and the handsome appearance of the shepherd boy Cardenio. The curate made them prepare the tastiest dinner the inn could provide, and the landlord in the hope of better payment got ready in a short time a reasonably good meal. All this was done while Don Quixote slept, and they were of the opinion that it was best not to wake him, for they thought it would do him more good to sleep than to eat. At table the company, consisting of the landlord, his wife, their daughter, and Maritornes, as well as the travelers, talked of the knight's strange craze and of the condition in which they had found him. The landlady told them of what had happened between him and the muleteers, and glancing around to see if Sancho was present and not seeing him, she told them the tale of the tossing in the blanket, to the great amusement of everyone.

The curate then said that it was the books of chivalry that had turned Don Quixote's head.

"I don't know how that can be," said the landlord, "for in my opinion there is no finer reading in the world, and I've two or three of them here, along with other papers, which have truly been a breath of life to me and to many others. When it is harvest time, the reapers often do gather here during the midday heat, and there is always someone who can read who takes up one of those books. Then, about thirty of us gather around him, and we sit listening to him with so much delight that it keeps off a thousand gray hairs. Speaking for myself, when I hear tell of those furious and terrible blows that the knights hand out, I long to be doing the same myself; I'd like to be listening to them day and night."

"I'm of the same opinion," said the landlady; "I never have a quiet moment in the house except when you are listening to the reading, for then you're so bemused that you forget to scold me."

"That's the honest truth," said Maritornes, "and I, too, love to hear those lovely goings-on, especially when they tell how a lady is lying under an orange tree wrapped in the arms of her knight, and the duenna keeping guard for them, dying of envy herself and all in a dither; I tell you, it is as sweet as honey."

"And what about you, young lady?" said the curate to the landlady's daughter.

"Ah, Father," said she, "I don't know. I also listen to them; and though I don't understand, I take pleasure in hearing them. But I don't like the blows that delight my father; only the lamentations that the knights make when they are away from their ladies sometimes make me weep, so much pity do I feel for them."

"Would you mend their sorrows, then, young gentlewoman," said Dorotea, "if they lamented for you?"

"I do not know what I would do," answered the girl. "I only know that some of those ladies are so cruel that their knights call them tigresses and lionesses and a thousand other foul names. But Lord save us! What kind of people are they? Can they be so heartless and unfeeling that they prefer to let an honorable man die or go mad rather than give him a kind look? I do not know why such coyness! If they pretend to be honest women, why don't they marry them, seeing that they long for nothing else?"

"Hold your tongue, child," said the landlady. "You seem to know a great deal of those matters, and it is not right for girls to know or to talk so much."

"His reverence," she answered, "asked me, and I couldn't help answering him."

"All right," said the curate, "bring me those books, my host; I should like to look through them."

"With pleasure," he replied, and going into his room, he brought out a little old trunk, fastened with a small chain, which he unfastened, and opening it, he showed three big books and some manuscript papers written in a very good hand. The first book he opened was *Don Cirongilio of Thrace*; the others, *Felixmarte of Hyrcania*[1] and *The His-*

[1] J. G. Lockhart in his commentary on this passage defends the innkeeper's taste against the sarcasm of the curate with an anecdote concerning Dr. Samuel Johnson. Bishop Percy informed Boswell that the doctor, when a boy, "was immoderately fond of reading romances of chivalry, and retained his fondness for them through life; so that, spending part of a summer at my parsonage-house in the country, he chose for his regular reading the old Spanish romance of Felixmarte of Hyrcania, in folio, which he read through." *Don Quixote*, tr. A. Motteux, Vol. I, p. 332, N. I. G. Bell, 1913.

tory of the Great Captain Gonzalo Hernández of Córdoba, together with *The Life of Don Diego García de Paredes*.

When he read the titles of the first two, the curate turned to the barber and said: "Our friend's housekeeper and his niece should be with us now."

"They are not needed," replied the barber; "I'm just as well able to carry them to the yard or to the fireplace, for truly there's a fine fire there this moment."

"What?" said the innkeeper. "Do you want to burn my books?"

"Only these two," replied the curate. "This *Don Cirongilio* and this *Felixmarte*."

"Are my books, then, heretic or phlegmatic," said the landlord, "that you wish to burn them?"

"Schismatic, you mean, my friend," said the barber, "not phlegmatic."

"Yes, yes," said the innkeeper, "but if you've a mind to burn any, let it be this one about the Great Captain and Diego García, for I'd rather let a child of mine be burned than either of the others."

"My friend," said the curate, "these two books are packed with lies, frenzies, and foolishness, but that about the Great Captain is a genuine history and relates the deeds of Gonzalo Hernández of Córdoba, who, on account of his many mighty exploits, merited to be called by all the world the Great Captain, an illustrious epithet that was earned by none but him. And that Diego García de Paredes was a noble gentleman, born in the city of Trujillo in Extremadura, a very valiant soldier and of such natural strength that with one finger he stopped a mill wheel turning at full speed. And once, when he stood armed with a broadsword at the entrance to a bridge, he prevented an entire army, vast in number, from entering. He did so many other deeds that if, instead of relating and describing them himself with the modesty of a knight and of one who is his own chronicler, another had written of them freely and dispassionately, his exploits would have cast those of the Hectors, Achilleses, and Rolands into oblivion."

"Tell that to my father!" said the innkeeper. "Fancy just stopping a mill wheel astonishing you! My God! You should see what I read about Felixmarte of Hyrcania, who with a single backhand cut five giants in two by the waist as if they had been tiny friars that children make out of beans.

And on another occasion he assailed a great and powerful army of more than one million, six hundred thousand soldiers, all in armor from head to foot, and routed them all as if they had been flocks of sheep. Then, what about the worthy Don Cirongilio of Thrace. The book describes how valiant and courageous he was when once a fiery serpent emerged from the water as he was sailing up a river. No sooner did he see it than he leaped upon it, sat astride its scaly shoulders, and squeezed its throat with both hands so hard that the monster, to save itself from being choked, had to dive to the bottom of the river, carrying the knight, who would not let go, along with it. And when they arrived below, he found himself in a paradise of wondrous palaces and gardens. There the serpent changed itself into an old man who spun him fantastic yarns. I tell you, sir, if you heard that book being read aloud, you would go mad with joy. I wouldn't give two figs for your Great Captain and that Diego García you brag about!"

Hearing this, Dorotea said in a whisper to Cardenio, "Our host is within an ace of playing understudy to Don Quixote."

"I agree," replied Cardenio. "To judge by his words, he takes every word in those books as Gospel truth, and barefoot friars themselves couldn't make him believe the contrary."

"Look here, friend," answered the curate, "there never existed such a person as Felixmarte of Hyrcania, or Don Cirongilio of Thrace, or any of the other knights described in those books of chivalry, for they are all fictions, invented by the idle brains who composed them, as you said just now, to pass the time as your reapers do in reading them. I swear to you that no such knights ever existed in the world and that such foolish feats never happened."

"Fling that bone to another dog," said the host; "as if I didn't know how many beans make five, or where my shoe pinches me. Don't try, your worship, to feed me with pap, for I wasn't born yesterday. You're a nice one to try to convince me that everything that those fine books say is lies and nonsense, for they were printed with the license of the lords of the Royal Council—as if they were people who would allow such a pack of lies to be printed, and such battles and enchantments as would drive a fellow out of his wits."

"I have told you already, my friend," answered the curate, "that this is done to beguile our idle moments. Just as in all well-ordered states there are certain games, such as chess, tennis, and billiards, for the entertainment of those who will not, may not, or cannot work, so these books are allowed to be printed in the fond hope that there can be no one so ignorant as to take any of them for true history. And if I were now permitted and my hearers more willing, I would point out the qualities that books of chivalry should contain in order to be good ones. These might perhaps make them of service, or even delight, to some people. But I hope that the day will come when I may explain my ideas to those who can turn them to account. In the meantime, my host, do believe what I am telling you; take your books and make up your own mind whether they are truth or lies, and much good may they do you! But I pray God you never go lame in the same foot as your guest Don Quixote."

"Not at all," replied the innkeeper; "I shan't ever be such a fool as to turn knight-errant, for I'm quite aware that it's not the fashion today to do as they did in the olden days when those famous knights are said to have roamed the world."

Sancho had come in during the conversation and was dumbfounded and depressed to hear them say that knights-errant were no longer in fashion and that all the books of chivalry were lies and nonsense; so, he decided in his own mind to wait and see how this expedition of his master turned out. If the result did not reach his expectation, he made up his mind to leave Don Quixote and go back to his wife, children, and usual occupation.

The innkeeper was taking away his trunk and the books when the curate said to him: "Wait; I would like to see what is in those papers that are written in such a good hand."

The host took them out and handed them to the curate, who found about eight sheets of manuscript that had at the beginning a title in large letters: "The Tale of Ill-Advised Curiosity." He then read three or four lines to himself and said: "Certainly the title of this tale appeals to me, and I have a mind to read it through."

"Your reverence," answered the innkeeper, "should read it, and I'll add that some of my guests who have read it here have enjoyed it very much and have asked me repeatedly to give it to them. But I wouldn't give it to them, for I intend to return it to him who left this trunk with these books and papers. The owner probably forgot them, but he is likely to return here some time. Although I know I'll miss them, I'll certainly give them back. I may be an innkeeper, but I'm still a Christian."

"You are right, my friend," said the curate, "but in spite of that, if I like the novel, you must let me copy it."

"Most willingly, friend," answered the host.

While the two were talking, Cardenio had taken up the tale and begun to read it. As he formed the same opinion of it as the curate, he begged him to read it aloud that all might hear.

"I would read it," said the curate, "but I believe it would be better to spend our time in sleeping than in reading."

"It will be enough rest for me," said Dorotea, "to while away an hour listening to a story, for my mind is not yet rested enough to permit me to sleep."

"In that case," answered the curate, "I'll read it, if only out of curiosity; perhaps it will be entertaining."

Master Nicholas also urged him to read it, and Sancho as well. So, seeing that it would please all of them and himself as well, the curate said: "Come now, listen to me, all of you, for this is how the novel begins."

CHAPTER XXXIII

In which "The Tale of Ill-Advised Curiosity" is told

"In Florence, a rich and famous Italian city in the province called Tuscany, lived Anselmo and Lotario, two wealthy noblemen, and such close friends that everyone who knew them called them 'the two friends.' They were both bachelors of the same age and the same habits, which was sufficient cause for the friendship that united them. It is true that Anselmo was a little more inclined to affairs of the heart than Lotario, who preferred the chase. But when the necessity arose, Anselmo would give up his pursuits and join Lotario's and Lotario his to take part in Anselmo's. Their minds, in fact, tallied so exactly with one another that no clock was more precise.

"Anselmo fell deeply in love with a fair damsel of that city, and as her ancestry matched her beauty, he decided (with his friend Lotario's approval, for without it he made no decision at all) to ask her parents for her hand, which he did. Lotario was the envoy, and it was he who negotiated and carried all to such a successful issue that in a short time Anselmo won the object of his desires. Camila was so overjoyed to have secured Anselmo as husband that she continually thanked Heaven and Lotario, the joint artificers of her present happiness. During the first few days, which as in all marriages were spent in feasting, Lotario continued to visit his friend Anselmo's house as he had done formerly and strove in every way possible to entertain him and to honor him. But as soon as the wedding excitements were over and the crowds of well-wishers and visitors had subsided, Lotario began purposely to stay away from Anselmo's house, for he believed (and all reasonable people would agree) that men should not be so often seen in the houses of their married friends as they used to be when they were bachelors. For though genuine friendship should be entirely devoid of suspicion, nevertheless a married man's honor is so delicate that it can be injured even by his own brother, still more by his friends.

"Anselmo noted the falling off in Lotario's visits and raised many complaints, saying that if he had imagined that marriage meant that he would no longer enjoy his friend's society, he would have never gone to the altar, and he entreated him not to allow the gratifying title of 'the two friends,' which they both had earned by their mutual devotion when bachelors, to sink into oblivion through caution carried to excess. He besought him, in fact, if such a word could be used among friends of such standing, to treat his house as his home again and to come and go as he had done before. He assured him, moreover, that his wife, Camila, had no other whim or wish except such as he wished her to have and that she was worried at Lotario's reserve, knowing what close friends they had been.

"Lotario answered all Anselmo's arguments so prudently and tactfully that the latter was convinced of his friend's sincerity, and they agreed that Lotario would dine with him twice a week and on feast days. But although this encouragement was made, Lotario decided to do no more than what he considered in the best interests of his friend's honor, for he valued Anselmo's good name more than his own. He used to say, and rightly, that a married man on whom Heaven has bestowed a beautiful wife should be as careful of the friends he brought to his house as of the women friends she mixed with every day. For though intrigues may not be openly arranged in marketplaces and churches or at public shows and church visits (things that husbands cannot always deny their wives), they may often be concocted or facilitated at the house of the very friend or relative in whom implicit trust is placed. Lotario also said that every married man needs to have a friend who will sound the note of warning if his behavior is not as good as it should be. For sometimes, owing to his great affection for his wife, a husband does not warn or tell her, for fear of troubling her, that certain things must, or must not, be done, for they may reflect either honor or dishonor upon him; and yet,

all this could be settled if he had a friend to advise him.
But where in the world could anyone find so staunch and
loyal a friend as Lotario demanded? Indeed, I do not know.
Lotario was the only one, for he protected his friend's honor
with so much vigilance that he tried to shorten his visits
to the house for fear idle gossips might criticize the visits
of a wealthy, highborn young man, possessing, as he did,
so many attractive qualities, to the house of so beautiful a
woman as Camila. Even though her good reputation might
suffice to curb malicious tongues, he did not wish her good
name or that of his friend to run the slightest risk. Therefore, he spent most of the days of the agreement in other
business and amusements, claiming that these were unavoid-
able, with the result that most of their meetings were spent
in mutual recrimination, the one in complaints and the other
in excuses.

"One day, when they both had gone for a stroll in the
fields outside the city, Anselmo said to Lotario: 'You may
think, my friend Lotario, that I am not grateful enough for
the favors that God has bestowed upon me in making me
the son of such parents and in giving me a plentiful supply
of nature's and of fortune's goods and for the greatest blessing of all, which was to give me Camila for a wife and you
for a friend, two treasures that I value as much as I
am capable of doing, if not as much as I should. Nevertheless, in spite of all these blessings, which usually are all
that any man could possibly desire, I am the most dissatisfied and peevish mortal in this world, because of late
I have been troubled by a whim that is so peculiar and so
unaccountable that I marvel at myself. I revile myself when
I am alone and I try to stifle it and banish it from my
thoughts, but in vain. In fact, it seems as if I intended all
along to proclaim it to the world. As it must come out in
the end, I should be grateful if you keep it hidden in the
archives of your mind. In that way and with your efforts
to relieve my anxieties, I am sure that I shall soon be freed
from the distress it causes me. I am confident that your
sympathy will enable me to become as happy as by my
own crazy foolishness I am now unhappy.'

"These words of Anselmo amazed Lotario, for he was at a
loss to understand where the long preamble was leading to,
and although he tried to guess what was the real cause of
his friend's anxiety, he was always wide off the mark. So,

to relieve the suspense, he replied that Anselmo was wronging their great friendship by adopting such a roundabout way of telling him his most secret thoughts, for he could rely on him either for advice or for help.

" 'That is true,' answered Anselmo. 'I know it, Lotario, and I shall tell you what distresses me. It is the question whether my wife, Camila, is as good and perfect as I think. I cannot be certain of the truth except by testing her by an ordeal that shall prove the purity of her virtue, as fire proves the purity of gold. For in my opinion, my friend, a woman is virtuous only in proportion to her temptations, and the very constant woman is one who does not yield to promises, gifts, tears, or the repeated importunities of insistent lovers.

" 'What reason,' said he, 'has one to thank a woman for being good if no one has tempted her to be bad? What merit is there in her being coy and modest, she who has no opportunity of going astray and who knows that she has a husband who will put her to death if he catches her lapse? For that reason I cannot have the same high regard for the woman who is virtuous out of fear or lack of opportunity as I have for the woman who, courted and pursued, emerges with the crown of victory. So, for these reasons and for many others that I could give you as support and confirmation of my opinion, I want Camila to pass through these ordeals, and be purified and tested by the fire of seeing herself courted and wooed by one who is worthy of her mettle. Then, if she emerges, as I believe she will, with the palm of victory, I shall consider myself the most fortunate of men. I shall be able to say that every desire of mine has been fulfilled and that I have been fated to possess the virtuous woman of whom the wise man says, "Who shall find her?" If things turn out contrary to my expectations and I have the satisfaction of knowing that I was right in my opinion, I shall not complain at having to endure the pain that such a costly experiment has brought me. Now, since nothing that you may say against my proposal will ever dissuade me from it, I want you, friend Lotario, to prepare yourself to act as the instrument that will enable me to accomplish my plan. I shall give you the opportunity of doing it, and I shall omit no means that seem to me necessary for wooing a woman who is chaste, honorable, reserved, and disinterested. What spurs me on to entrust this arduous enterprise to you is my certainty that if Camila is conquered by you, you will not carry your victory to the extreme limits, but only do what is laid down in our agreement. And so, I shall be dishonored only in intention, and the wrong done to me will remain buried in your honorable silence, which, I know, will be ·as eternal as death itself. Therefore, if you want me to have a life that I ·can tolerate, you must at once enter into this amorous battle, not with faint heart or sluggish courage but with all the earnestness and high spirit my plan requires and with the steadfast loyalty our great friendship presupposes.'

"Such were Anselmo's arguments, to which Lotario listened so attentively that he did not open his lips until his friend had finished. Then, after staring at him for some time as if he were gazing at some amazing and sinister object that he had never seen before, he replied: 'I cannot persuade myself, friend Anselmo, that what you have just been saying is not a joke. If I really thought you were in earnest, I would not have let you go so far, I should not have listened, and thus I would have cut short your long speech. I believe that either you do not know me or I do not know you. But no, I know very well that you are Anselmo, and you know that I am Lotario. The trouble is that I believe you are not the Anselmo you used to be, and you must have thought that I am not the Lotario I should be, for my friend Anselmo would never have spoken as you have done just now, nor would you have made the request you did of the Lotario you know. Good friends should prove and make use of their friends, as a poet said, *usque ad aras,* by which he meant that they must not use friendship in a manner that is hateful in the sight of God. And if such was the opinion of a heathen, how much more must a Christian believe it, knowing as he does that divine friendship must not be forfeited for a human one? When a friend goes to such extremities as to neglect his duty to God in order to help his friend, it must not be for trivialities and things of little consequence, but for something on which his friend's life and honor depend. Now tell me, Anselmo, is your life or your honor then in such peril that I must risk myself to satisfy you by doing the hideous action you ask of me? Neither, I am sure. On the contrary, if I understand you rightly, you are asking me to try hard to rob you, and to rob myself, of life and honor; for if I take your honor, it is clear that I take your life, since a man without honor

is worse than dead. If I become the instrument of such evil
as you wish, would I not end up dishonored and, in consequence, dead? Listen, Anselmo, my friend, and be patient
enough not to answer until I have finished telling you all
that I think about this request of yours. There will be time
enough after that for you to reply and for me to listen.'

" 'I agree,' said Anselmo; 'say what you like.'

"Lotario then continued: 'Your attitude of mind, Anselmo,
seems to me to be the same as that of the Moors, who
cannot be convinced of the errors of their sect by quotations from Holy Scripture or by arguments derived from
speculation or founded on the canons of faith, but one must
have examples that are simple, palpable, intelligible, and in-
dubitable, with irrefutable mathematical proofs such as: "If
equals be taken from equals, the remainders are equal." And
when they do not understand this in words, as in fact they
do not, then one has to show it to them with one's hands
and put it in front of their eyes. And even then no one
can convince them of the truth of our holy faith. So, I shall
be compelled to adopt similar methods with you, for this
new whim of yours is so preposterous that I believe it would
be waste of time to try and convince you of your simplemindedness, for that is what I would call it. Indeed, I have
a mind to let you wallow in your own foolishness as punishment for your evil intentions, but being a friend of yours,
I cannot bring myself to behave so cruelly toward you as to
leave you in such manifest danger of destruction. Now, to
explain matters, Anselmo, do tell me: did you not ask me
to court a modest woman? To tempt a chaste one? To beguile an honorable one? To woo a prudent one? Yes, that is
what you have asked me to do. But if you are certain that
you have a modest, chaste, honorable, and prudent wife,
what are you trying to find out? And if you are convinced
that she will emerge triumphant from all my assaults, as
no doubt she will, what titles do you intend to give her
afterward more glowing than those she already possesses?
What more will she be afterward than she is at the present
moment? Either you do not take her for what you say or
you do not know what you are asking. If you do not take
her for what you say, why do you insist on testing her instead of treating her straightaway as a bad woman and making her pay the penalty? But if she is really as virtuous
as you believe, it is foolish and irrelevant to experiment
with truth itself, for after you have done so, it cannot be

rated higher than it was before. It is therefore evident that to attempt things that will probably turn out more harmful than advantageous is the mark of one who is rash and devoid of reason, more so if he wants to conduct experiments that are not forced upon him and that show beforehand that to attempt them is madness. Man undertakes arduous enterprises for the sake of God, for the world's sake, or for both. The first are undertaken by the saints, who strive to live as angels in human form; the second are accomplished by men who sail the boundless ocean and endure the vagaries of climates as they rove through far-off lands in quest of what are called the goods of fortune; the third, which are those that are undertaken for the sake of God and man, are the achievements of staunch soldiers, who no sooner see a breach in the enemy's rampart made by a single cannonball than, shedding all fear of the perils that threaten them from all sides and soaring on the wings of the desire to conquer for their faith, for their country, and for their king, they hurl themselves forward into the jaws of death, which awaits them in a thousand guises.

" 'Such are the enterprises undertaken by man, and it is honor, glory, and profit to attempt them, no matter how laden they may be with difficulties and dangers; but the project you would now attempt will earn you neither heavenly glory, nor goods of fortune, nor fame among men. For even if you should be successful, you will be no happier, no richer, and no more honored than you are this moment; and if you fail, you will find yourself in the most desperate straits imaginable. And it will not profit you then to think that no one knows your misfortune, for it will be sufficient torture for you to be conscious of it yourself. To confirm this I shall quote a stanza of the celebrated poet Luis Tansilo from the end of the first part of his *Tears of Saint Peter*,[1] which goes as follows:

"In Peter's heart, as daylight at length came,
   The anguish grew, and he flushed deep for shame,
   Though no man was there to behold him sin,
   For now he recognized his own offence.
   A noble heart no witness ever needs

---

[1] This was a religious poem by Luigi Tansillo, written as an atonement in his late years for the erotic verse of his youth. It was translated into Spanish by Luis Gálvez de Montalvo, a close friend of Cervantes, and published in 1587.

To shame him, but is cowed by his own deeds,
Though only Heaven and earth watch in silence."

" 'So you will not relieve your sorrow by secrecy; instead you will have reason for unending lamentation, and even though your eyes shed no tears, your heart's blood will ooze drop by drop. So wept that simple doctor of whom our poet tells, who tasted the cup that the cautious Rinaldo wisely refused.[2] Even though that is a poetic fiction, it contains a hidden moral you should observe and follow. Furthermore, if you will pay heed to what I am now going to say, you will come to realize what a great error you are about to commit. Tell me, Anselmo, if Heaven or your good fortune had made you the lawful owner of a priceless diamond, and every jewel merchant who saw it was convinced of its excellence and quality, if everyone unanimously declared that it reached the utmost perfection in every respect, and you yourself believed them and had not the shadow of a suspicion to the contrary, would it be reasonable for you to pick up this diamond, put it between the anvil and the hammer, and there and then by dint of brutal battering prove whether it was as hard and as fine as they said? Suppose you put this plan into operation and the stone resisted such a nonsensical test, would it have any greater value or reputation? And if it broke, which might well happen, would not everything be lost? Yes, and its owner would be regarded by everyone as a fool.

" 'Now, consider Camila, Anselmo, my friend, as a priceless diamond, both in your estimation and in others', and reflect whether it is reasonable that she should be exposed to the risk of destruction, for even if she remains unshaken, she cannot rise to a greater value than she now possesses. But if she fails and does not resist the test, consider what your feelings would be without her and what motives you would have for self-reproach if you were the cause of her ruin and your own. Consider that there is no jewel in the world so precious as a chaste and virtuous woman and that all women's honor lies in their good name. And as your

[2] Cervantes derived the idea for "The Tale of Ill-Advised Curiosity" from cantos 42 and 43 of *Orlando Furioso*, where Rinaldo cautiously maintained that such an experiment would only produce evil results. When the host heard Rinaldo's comments, he burst into tears and told the sad story of his ill-advised curiosity.

wife's is the highest in the world, as you know, why do you insist on calling its truth into question? Remember, my friend, that woman is an imperfect creature and that one should not place obstacles that may trip her and make her fall, but rather clear the road of every stumbling block so that she may run free and unhampered to win the perfection she lacks, which consists of a virtuous life.

" 'Naturalists say that the ermine is a little animal with a fur of purest white, which prompts hunters to employ the following trick when they wish to catch it: When they have ascertained the places it usually haunts, they plug them up with mud and drive it that way, and when the little animal reaches the muddy barrier, it stands still and allows itself to be caught rather than pass through the filth and befoul and lose its whiteness, which it values more than its life and liberty. The chaste and virtuous woman is an ermine, and the virtue of chastity is whiter and more immaculate than snow; and he who does not wish her to lose it, but instead to treasure it, must not treat her like the ermine. He must not put in front of her the mud of the tempting wiles and flatteries of unfortunate lovers, for perhaps, no, certainly she has not the requisite spiritual strength to overcome and pass through those obstacles. Therefore, he must remove them from her path and set before her the purity of virtue and the beauty that is contained in a good name. For a good woman also resembles a mirror of clear shining glass, which may be dimmed and dulled by every breath that reaches it. A chaste woman must be trusted like holy relics, which are to be adored but not touched. A good woman should be guarded and tended like a beautiful garden full of fragrant flowers and roses whose owner never allows anyone to walk in it or touch the blooms; let them be content to enjoy its sweet scents and its beauty from afar through the iron railings. Finally, I want to quote you some verses I have just remembered, which I heard in a modern play; they seem to apply to our present problem. A shrewd old man advises another, the father of a young lady, to guard her, look after her, and keep her in the house; and among other reasons, he gives the following:

> "Woman must be made of glass;
> Hence no one ever ought to try,
> Whether she may break or no,

As all this may come to pass,
Since the odds are she will break,
Who but a crazy loon would dare
To risk a vessel that's so brittle?
Once shattered, she is past repair.
So I wish all men to cry 'true!'
To this, my sound opinion:
If Danaes abound today,
There are golden showers too."

" 'All I have said to you so far, Anselmo, concerns yourself, but now you must hear something that concerns me.
Pray forgive me for being so tedious, but the labyrinth in
which you have involved yourself and from which you wish
me to rescue you compels me to be long-winded. You look
upon me as your friend, yet you want to deprive me of my
honor, which is to repudiate friendship itself. And you even
go further than that, for you wish me to rob you of your
own honor as well. It is perfectly clear that you wish to deprive me of mine, for when Camila sees me wooing her, as
you ask, she is bound to take me for a man devoid of all
principles of honor, since I am trying to do something so
contrary to my obligations to myself and to you, who are
my friend. It is quite obvious that you wish me to rob you
of your own honor, for once Camila sees me wooing her, she
will immediately imagine that I have detected a touch of
frivolity in her that has encouraged me to reveal my lustful
desires. When she considers herself dishonored, her disgrace
is bound to reflect on you as a part of her. From this springs
a situation that is a familiar one to everyone: Although the
husband of an adulterous woman is not aware of her guilt
and has never given his wife an opportunity of being other
than she should be, and although he was not able to prevent
his misfortune, which is not the result of any carelessness or
lack of caution on his part, he is hounded with a vile, insulting name and to some extent regarded with contempt
rather than pity by those who know of his wife's guilt; and
thus misfortune strikes him down, not through any fault of
his but through the evil intentions of his guilty spouse. But
I now wish to emphasize the reason why the guilty woman's
husband is rightly dishonored, although he is not aware of
her wickedness and is not to blame and has no share in it

or has ever given her any excuse for her sin. Do not grow weary of listening to me; it will all be of great service to you.

" 'When God created our first father in the earthly paradise, Holy Scripture tells us that He caused a deep sleep to fall upon him, and while he was sleeping, he took one of the ribs of his left side and created our mother, Eve. And when Adam awoke and looked on her, he said: "This is flesh of my flesh and bone of my bones." And God said: "Therefore shall a man leave his father and his mother, and they shall be one flesh." Then was instituted the divine sacrament of matrimony, whose bonds only death can untie. This miraculous sacrament has such strength and virtue that it makes two different persons one single flesh; and with happily married couples it does even more, for though they have two souls, they have but a single will. Consequently, as the flesh of the wife is one with the flesh of the husband, the blemishes that are on her and the defects she acquires react upon the flesh of her husband, although, as I have said, he may not be the cause of the harm. For just as the whole body feels the pain of the foot or any of the other limbs because they are all one flesh and just as the head feels the ankle's pain although it is not the cause of it, so the husband shares in his wife's dishonor because he is one with her. Furthermore, as all honors and dishonors in this world originate from flesh and blood, the bad wife's being of this kind, part of them must inevitably fall to the husband's share, and he must be considered dishonored even though he is not aware of it. Reflect then, Anselmo, on the peril to which you expose yourself in seeking to disturb your good wife's peace of mind. Consider how vain and meddlesome you are to go prying and stirring up passions that lie dormant in your chaste wife's bosom. I warn you that what you stand to gain is little and what you will lose so much that I could not assess in words its value. However, if all I have said is not enough to make you renounce your evil plan, you must look for someone else to act as instrument of your misfortune and your infamy. I certainly do not intend to be your tool, even though by my refusal I lose your friendship, which is the greatest loss that I can imagine.'

"With these words the virtuous and wise Lotario ended his long harangue, leaving Anselmo so disquieted and reflective that he remained speechless for some time. At length

he replied: 'I have listened with close attention to all you
have said, my friend Lotario, and your arguments, examples,
and comparisons are a tribute to your great wisdom and perfect friendship. I see—and I confess it—that if I do not follow your opinion but go after my own, I shall be deserting
the good and pursuing the evil course. Yet, though I admit
this, you must realize that I am at present afflicted with an
illness that is common in women, which makes them long to
eat earth, chalk, coal, and other worse things that are foul to
look upon and still more loathsome to eat. Therefore, it is
necessary to discover some trick to cure me, and this may
easily be done if you will only start courting Camila, even
lukewarmly and hypocritically, for she cannot be so inexperienced that her virtue will collapse at the first encounter.
I shall be content with just a beginning, and you will then
have done what our friendship demands, for you will in this
way not only restore me to life, but also persuade me to retain my honor. There is one reason why you must do this
for me, and it is as follows: As I am resolved to put my
plan into practice, you cannot possibly allow me to reveal
my mad obsession to any other person and so imperil my
honor, which you are so anxious for me to preserve. Even if
your own does not loom as high in Camila's estimation as it
should while you are wooing her, that is of little moment,
for in a very short time, when we find in her the integrity
we expect, you will be able to tell her the unvarnished truth
about our scheme and then you will stand as high in her
esteem as ever before. Since you risk little and are able to
give me so much happiness, do not refuse to do this favor
even if it may prove still more troublesome for you, for, as
I said before, if you will only get it started, I shall count the
matter already settled.'

"Lotario, seeing that Anselmo's mind was already made
up, not knowing what further arguments to use and how to
dissuade him, and realizing to his dismay that his friend
would carry out his threat to entrust his wicked plan to someone else, resolved to give in to him and do his bidding in
order to prevent greater mischief. He intended, however, to
pilot the whole affair in such a way that Anselmo should be
satisfied at no cost to Camila's peace of mind. So, he begged
his friend not to breathe a word of his thoughts to a soul
and promised to undertake the plan and to start whenever
he wished. Anselmo embraced Lotario affectionately and

thanked him for his offer as if his friend had done him a great favor. Then the two agreed that the plan should be put into operation on the following day. Anselmo would give Lotario time and opportunity to speak to Camila alone and would supply him with money and jewels to offer as presents. He advised him to serenade her and to write verses in her praise; and if he should not want to take the trouble, he offered to write them himself. All this Lotario undertook, though his intentions were not those Anselmo reckoned upon, and on this understanding they returned to Anselmo's house, where they found Camila troubled and anxiously expecting her husband, for he was later than usual in coming home that day.

"Lotario went home, leaving Anselmo as highly satisfied as he himself was puzzled, not knowing what method he should adopt for extricating himself from this absurd situation. That night, however, he hit upon a plan for deceiving Anselmo without offending Camila, and next day he came to dine with his friend, and was welcomed by Camila, who always received him most cordially, knowing how fond her husband was of him. When they had finished dinner and the tablecloths were removed, Anselmo asked Lotario to stay with Camila while he went out on some urgent business from which he said he would return within an hour and a half. Camila begged him not to go, and Lotario offered to accompany him, but in vain, for Anselmo pressed Lotario all the more insistently to stay and wait for him, as he had some business of great urgency to discuss with him. He also told Camila not to leave Lotario alone till he returned. In fact, he played up so brilliantly the excuse of his absence that nobody could tell it was a lie.

"Anselmo went off, and Camila remained alone at table with Lotario, for the rest of the household had gone off to their dinner. So, Lotario found himself in the dueling lists as his friend desired, face to face with an enemy capable of routing a whole squadron of armed cavalry with her beauty alone. Lotario indeed had every reason to dread his fair enemy! But all he did was to lean his elbow on the arm of his chair and his hand on his cheek. Then, after begging Camila's pardon for his boorish manners, he said that he would like a short rest before Anselmo's return. Camila replied that he would rest more comfortably on the cushioned dais in the drawing room than in a chair, and she invited him to take a nap in there. But Lotario refused and stayed there sleeping until Anselmo returned. When his friend came back and found that Camila had retired to her room and that Lotario was asleep, he assumed that he had been so long away that the two had time to converse together and to sleep as well, and he could scarcely wait for Lotario to awake, so eager was he to go out with him and question him about his luck.

"Everything turned out as he wished. Lotario woke up, the two left the house, and in answer to Anselmo's questions Lotario replied that he had thought it inadvisable to show his hand the first time and so had merely praised Camila's beauty, saying that her loveliness and her intelligence were the sole theme of conversation throughout the whole city. This, he said, seemed like a good way of winning her confidence and making her inclined to listen to him with pleasure next time, a method the Devil uses when he is out to trick one who keeps both eyes on the alert for mischief from any quarter, for although he is an angel of darkness, he can transform himself into an angel of light and assume the cloak of virtue before he finally appears in his true colors. He said that it was a plan that usually succeeded, unless the deception was spied at the outset. This satisfied Anselmo, who said that he would give his friend the same opportunity every day but that he would, however, not leave the house, for they would be so busy there that Camila would never suspect his subterfuge.

"After that followed many days during which Lotario never spoke a word to Camila but told Anselmo that he had talked to her and that he never had been able to extract from her the slightest sign of encouragement or even the faintest shadow of hope. On the contrary, he said that she threatened him that she would have to inform her husband if he did not renounce his wicked designs.

" 'That is hopeful,' said Anselmo. 'Up to now Camila has resisted words, but we must now see how she resists deeds. Tomorrow I shall give you two thousand escudos in gold to offer her, and even to give to her, and the same amount to buy jewels to tempt her. Women, especially lovely women, are very fond of being elegantly dressed and making a striking effect, no matter how chaste they may be. If she resists this temptation I shall be satisfied and worry you no more.'

"Lotario replied that since he had started it, he would see

the business through to the end, although he felt that he
would emerge from it worn out and vanquished. On the
following day he received the four thousand escudos and
with them four thousand worries, for he did not know what
new lie to invent. In the end, however, he made up his mind
to tell Anselmo that gifts and offers made no more impression
on Camila's integrity than words had done and that there
was no point in his wearying himself further, as it was all
waste of time. But Destiny guided their affairs in another
way, for when Anselmo had left Lotario and Camila alone
as before, he shut himself up in a room and stood near the
keyhole to watch and listen to what went on between the
two. And when he observed that Lotario did not open his
lips to Camila in more than half an hour and would not have
done so if he had been there a century, he realized that all
his friend had said about Camila's answers was a tissue of
lies. To make sure of this he came out of the room, and calling Lotario apart, inquired what news he had and in what
kind of a mood was Camila. Lotario replied that he was not
going to take any further part in the business, for she had
spoken to him so rudely and given him such a dressing down
that he had not the courage to speak to her again.

" 'Oh, Lotario, Lotario,' cried Anselmo, 'how poorly you
fulfill your part of the bargain, though I had put all my trust
in you! I have been watching you through the keyhole of the
door, and I saw that you did not address a single word to
Camila; so, I can only suppose that you have still to break
the ice. If that is so, and I am sure it is, why are you deceiving me? Why are you trying with your tricks to wreck the
only chance I have of obtaining the satisfaction I so desperately crave.'

"Anselmo said no more, but this was enough to leave
Lotario ashamed and deeply mortified. Now that he had
been caught telling a lie, he felt as if his honor had been im-
pugned, and he swore to Anselmo that henceforth he would
guarantee to satisfy him and tell no more lies, as his friend
would see if he kept his vigilant eye on the alert; he added
that it would be unnecessary for him to go to any trouble,
for the plan he now intended to adopt would give entire
satisfaction and remove all suspicions. Anselmo believed
him, and to give him plenty of leeway he resolved to leave his
house for a week and go to a friend's who lived in a village
not far from the city. He arranged with this friend to send

for him urgently so that he might have an excuse to give to
Camila for his absence.

"Hapless and ill-advised Anselmo, what are you doing?
What plots and plans are you contriving? Consider that you
are acting against yourself, plotting your own dishonor, and
contriving your own perdition. Your wife, Camila, is a good
woman; in peace and tranquillity you possess her; no one in-
vades your privacy; your thoughts do not pass beyond the
walls of her house; you are her paradise upon this earth, the
goal of her desires, the sum total of her joys, and the
standard by which she measures her will, adapting it in every
way to yours and to that of Heaven. Then, since the mine of
her honor, beauty, modesty, and virtue yields to you without
any toil all the riches it contains and that you can desire,
why must you delve deep into the earth in quest of first
veins of new and unseen treasures? You are running the risk
that everything may suddenly collapse, as it is buttressed
only by the feeble props of her unstable nature. Remember
that by seeking the impossible you may justly be denied the
possible, as a poet has expressed it more lyrically:

> In death life is my quest,
> In infirmity I long for health,
> And in gaol freedom seems the best:
> I plan to shed my chains by stealth,
> And in a traitor place my trust,
> Alas my envious destiny,
> Which hitherto has frowned on me,
> Has with Heaven now decreed
> That possible things shall be denied
> Since for the impossible I've cried.'

"Next day Anselmo went to the village, telling Camila
that Lotario would come to look after the house and dine
with her while he was away and recommending her to treat
him as she would himself. Camila, being an honest and sensible woman, was dismayed by her husband's order and
pointed out that it was wrong for anyone to occupy his chair
while he was away. If he did this, she said, because he had
no faith in her capability of managing her house, let him
try for once and learn by experience that she was well able to
face even greater responsibilities. Anselmo replied that such
was his wish and that she had no other alternative but to bow

her head and obey. Camila said she would do what he said, but against her will. So, off went Anselmo, and next day Lotario came to his house and Camila gave him a kind and modest welcome, though she never gave Lotario an opportunity of finding her alone, but went about the house accompanied by her footman and maids, particularly by her own maid, Leonela, of whom she was very fond. The two had been reared together from childhood in Camila's parents' house, and when she had married Anselmo, she had brought the girl with her.

"For the first three days Lotario did not utter a word, though he had an opportunity when the tablecloth was removed and the servants went off to their own dinner, which, by Camila's orders, was to be a hurried meal. Camila, furthermore, insisted that Leonela should dine before she did and that she should never leave her side. The girl, however, who thought only of her own pleasure and needed plenty of time for her diversions, did not always follow her mistress' orders, with the result that she left the two alone together, as if she had been thus ordered. Camila's modest behavior and grave demeanor, however, were more than enough to put reins on Lotario's tongue.

"But whatever advantage was gained from Camila's many virtues, which had reduced Lotario to silence, led later to still greater trouble for both of them. For though his tongue was silent, his thoughts ran on, and he had time and leisure to contemplate, one by one, all Camila's mental and bodily perfections, and they were enough to inspire love in a marble statue, let alone in a heart of flesh. Lotario gazed at her all the time he should have been talking to her, thinking how worthy of being loved she was; and this thought began to encroach on his regard for Anselmo, and a thousand times he was on the point of leaving the city and going where Anselmo would never see him, nor he Camila, but his delight in gazing at her prevented him and delayed his departure. He struggled and battled with himself to banish and obliterate the joy he felt in looking at her. When he was alone, he cursed himself for his mad infatuation, calling himself a treacherous friend and even a bad Christian. He argued and made comparisons between himself and Anselmo, but he always ended up by convincing himself that Anselmo's folly and confidence were greater than his disloyalty and that if he could only excuse what he was about to do before God as well as he could in the eyes of men, he would have no fears of punishment for his crime.

"And so, Camila's beauty and goodness, added to the opportunity that the doltish husband had thrust into his hands, completely toppled over all Lotario's loyalty to his friend. After struggling desperately and unavailingly to resist his passion for three days after Anselmo had departed, he began to woo Camila with such vigor and with such amorous solicitude that Camila was astonished; she rose to her feet and without a single word retired at once to her room. But all her coldness did not dash Lotario's hopes, for hope always is twinborn with love. On the contrary, Camila soared still higher in his estimation. She, however, now that she was confronted by such an unexpected turn in Lotario's character, did not know what to do. But as she considered that it was dangerous and highly improper to give him a chance of speaking to her again, she decided to send one of her servants to Anselmo that same night with a letter in which she wrote as follows:

CHAPTER XXXIV

In which "The Tale of Ill-Advised Curiosity" is continued

" 'It is generally said that an army makes as poor an impression without its commander in chief as a castle does without its castellan, and I say that a young married woman makes even a poorer show without her husband, unless he is detained by business of the greatest urgency. I feel so lost and forlorn without you and so powerless to put up with your absence any longer that if you do not come quickly I shall have to go and stay at my parents' house, even though I leave yours unguarded. For the guardian you have left, if he is here in that capacity, is, I believe, more attentive to his own pleasures than to your best interests. As you are a man of good sense, I need say no more, nor is it right that I should do so.'

"When Anselmo received this letter, he realized that Lotario had already begun the enterprise and that Camila must have reacted as he himself had wanted all along. So, overjoyed at the news, he sent Camila a message in reply, telling her on no account to move from his house, as he would be back in a short time. Camila was dumbfounded at the reply, which threw her into greater confusion than ever. She did not dare to stay at home, and she was even more afraid to go to her parents', for if she remained, she would imperil her honor, and if she went, she would disobey her husband's orders. At last she decided to take what proved to be the wrong course, namely, to stay and not to avoid Lotario, lest she give her servants cause for gossip. Now she was sorry she had written as she had to her husband, and she worried lest he might imagine that frivolous behavior on her part might have encouraged Lotario to fail in the respect he owed her. Nevertheless, because she was sure of herself and trusted in God, she was confident that she could treat whatever Lotario might say to her with silent contempt. So she decided to say nothing more about the whole affair to her husband, so as not to involve him in any quarrel or unpleasantness. She even devised ways of excusing Lotario's conduct to Anselmo if he should ask what prompted her to write him that letter.

"Now that she had adopted this line of conduct, which was more innocent than suitable and advantageous, Camila stayed next day to listen to Lotario, and so persuasive was he that her steadfastness began to vacillate, and she had to employ all her reserves of modesty to protect her eyes from betraying signs of the compassion that Lotario's tearful pleas had stirred in her heart. All this Lotario observed, and his desires grew bolder. Finally, he felt the compelling urge to take full advantage of the opportunity that Anselmo's absence granted him and to intensify his blockade of the bastion. So he attacked her with praise of her beauty, for there is nothing that so quickly reduces and razes to the ground the towers and battlements of a beautiful woman's vanity than that same vanity when it is adulated by the tongue of flattery. In fact, he deliberately undermined the rock of her integrity with charges of such potency that Camila would have fallen even if she had been made of bronze. Lotario wept, beseeched, promised, feigned, flattered, and swore with such passion and with such signs of genuine feeling that he overwhelmed Camila, modesty and all, and won the triumph he most of all desired when he least expected it.

"Camila surrendered; yes, she surrendered; but can we wonder, when even Lotario's friendship could not stand its ground? Manifest proof that the passion of love can be vanquished only by flight and that it is vain to fight hand to hand with such a ruthless foe, for only superhuman powers can overcome those too human ones of love. Leonela alone knew of her mistress' fall, for this pair of treacherous lovers could not hide it from her. Lotario did not tell Camila of Anselmo's scheme or how he had given him the opportunity to do what he had done, lest she perhaps have a lower opinion of his love and think that it was by chance, not by set determination, that he had wooed her.

"A few days later Anselmo returned and failed to see that the treasure he thought little of, yet valued most of all, was missing. He immediately went to see Lotario, found him at home, and when they had embraced, asked him whether he had good or bad news to tell.

" 'The news I must give you, friend Anselmo,' said Lotario, 'is that you have a wife worthy to be called the model and crown of all virtuous women. The words I spoke to her were blown away by the breezes, my promises she treated with contempt, my gifts she refused, my feigned tears she mocked with scorn. In short, Camila is not only the epitome of all beauty but also the archive where honor resides and where dwell tenderness, modesty, and all the qualities that make an honest woman praiseworthy and fortunate. Take back your money, friend; here it is; I have no further need to touch it, for Camila's integrity will not surrender to such base things as gifts and promises. Be satisfied, Anselmo, and make no further trials. You have passed dry-shod over a sea of difficulties and have rid yourself of the suspicions that men have on the score of women. Do not reenter the tide of fresh anxieties or test with another pilot the goodness and strength of the ship that Heaven has allotted to you to bear you across the oceans of this world. Consider yourself now safe in harbor and moor yourself with the anchors of mutual respect and kindliness. Live in peace until they come to demand the debt that no human privilege can exempt you from paying.'

"Anselmo was overjoyed at Lotario's words and believed

them as firmly as if they had been uttered by an oracle. But he begged him nevertheless not to abandon the enterprise even if it was merely for the sake of curiosity and entertainment, although from then on he would not have to use such drastic methods as he had hitherto. All he wished his friend to do was to write some verses in her praise under the name of Chloris, and he would make Camila understand that his friend was in love with a lady to whom he had given that name so that he could celebrate her praises without hurting her modest susceptibilities. He added that if Lotario should not be willing to take the trouble to write the verses, he would do so himself.

" 'There will be no need of that,' replied Lotario. 'The muses are not so hostile to me that they do not visit me from time to time. Tell Camila of this imaginary love affair of mine. I shall write the verses, and if they are not as good as the subject deserves, at least they will be the best I can compose.'

"So the foolish husband and the treacherous friend agreed, and when Anselmo returned home, he asked Camila what had prompted her to write him the letter she had sent him. She was surprised he had not asked before, and she replied that Lotario had been somewhat bolder in his glances than when her husband was at home, but that she now realized that she had been mistaken and that it had been simply her imagination, for Lotario had then avoided seeing her and being alone with her. Anselmo said that she might now banish those suspicions because he knew that Lotario was in love with a noble maiden of the city, that he wrote verses to her under the name of Chloris, and that even if he were not, she had no reason to doubt Lotario's loyalty and his deep affection for them both. Now, if Camila had not been warned by Lotario that this love of his for Chloris was an invention and that he himself had told Anselmo about it so that he could occasionally write poems in praise of Camila, she would no doubt have fallen into the hopeless tangle of jealousy, but as she was forewarned, she survived this trouble unharmed.

"The next day, when the three of them were at table, Anselmo begged Lotario to recite some of the verses he had composed for his beloved Chloris. As Camila did not know her, he might safely say what he pleased.

" 'Even though she did know her,' replied Lotario, 'I should

conceal nothing, for when a lover praises his lady's beauty
and taxes her with cruelty, he does no injury to her good
name. But, be that as it may, I must tell you that I wrote a
sonnet yesterday on the ingratitude of this Chloris. It runs
like this:

Sonnet

> In the deep silence of the peaceful night,
> When mortal cares are wrapt in sweet repose,
> The paltry tale of my protracted woes
> To Heaven above and Chloris I recite.
> And when the sun with his reviving light
> Forth through the eastern gateways rose-hued goes,
> With sighs and groans provoked by constant throes
> I tell my ancient tale of grief and blight.
> And when proud Phoebus from his starry throne,
> Sends his rays down upon the thirsty soil
> Still my sighs grow and my groans fast increase.
> At nightfall I renew my gloomy toil,
> But though from morn to night I weep and groan,
> Chloris is deaf and will not grant me ease.'

"This sonnet pleased Camila very much, but Anselmo even
more. He praised it to the skies and said that the lady who
did not hearken to such patient truth was extremely cruel.
To this Camila replied: 'So everything that love-sick poets
say is true?'

" 'They do not say it as poets,' said Lotario, 'but as lovers
they are as reserved as they are truthful.'

" 'There is no doubt about that," answered Anselmo, eager
to back up Lotario's opinions before Camila, who had not
the faintest suspicion of Anselmo's trick, so deeply was she
in love with Lotario. Indeed, so delighted was she with everything he did that she took it for granted that his feelings
and verses were addressed to herself and that she was the
real Chloris; so she begged him to recite another sonnet or
poem if he knew one by heart.

" 'I do,' replied Lotario, 'but I do not think it is as good as
the first, or to put it more accurately, less bad; you can judge
for yourselves, for here it is:

Sonnet

Fair and ungrateful one; at last I know
I'm doomed, but Death with open arms I'll greet,
For when thou seest my body at thy feet,
That I was ever true thou shouldst allow.
I welcome now Oblivion's misty main,
I welcome too the loss of life and fame;
But thy beloved features and thy name
Deep graven on my heart shall still remain.
This relic may I keep until the day
Of sadness, when my tortured soul takes flight,
And flutters through the murky realms of night,
Chiding thy heart of granite as he wends his way.
Alas for him who drifts o'er stormy tides,
His lonely, loveless course no north star guides.'

"Anselmo praised this sonnet as he had the first. And so, in this manner he continued to add link on link to the chain that he was forging for his own dishonor, for the more Lotario dishonored him, the more he convinced himself of his spotless honor. And likewise, the deeper Camila sank in her gradual descent into infamy, the higher she rose in her husband's estimation toward the topmost pinnacles of virtue and renown. And on one occasion when she was alone with her maid, she said to her: 'I am ashamed, Leonela, to see how cheap I have made myself by not keeping Lotario guessing a good while before he could buy in full what I delivered to him so rapidly and readily. I am afraid that he must despise me for being such an easy prey and that he does not realize that he made such violent love to me that I could not resist him.'

"'Don't worry about that, my lady,' answered Leonela. 'It's not worthwhile; besides, there's no reason why a thing should lose its value because it's easily given, provided the gift be a valuable one in itself. Why, they even say that he who gives quickly gives twice over.'

"'Yes,' said Camila, 'but they also say that what costs little is little prized.'

"'That proverb does not apply to you,' answered Leonela, 'because love, I've heard it said, sometimes flies and sometimes walks; with one it runs and with another creeps; some its cools and some it burns; some it wounds and others it kills; in one instant it starts on its race of passion and in the same instant concludes and ends it; in the morning it will lay siege to a fortress and by evening it has weakened it, for there's no force that can resist it. That being so, what is it that frightens you and has you in such a dither? The very same thing must have happened to Lotario when love chose my master's absence as the instrument of your defeat. It was necessary, too, that love's plan of operations should be carried out in that time so as to avoid the possibility of the whole business being interrupted by the return of Anselmo. Remember that love has no better minister to carry out its desires than opportunity, and it makes use of opportunity in all its enterprises, especially at their outset. I know this all very well, more by experience than by hearsay, and one day I'll tell you, my lady, for I am flesh and young blood. What is more, Doña Camila, you would never have surrendered so soon if you had not first caught a glimpse of Lotario's entire soul in his eyes, his sighs, his declarations, his promises, and his gifts, and then judged from his qualities how worthy he was of your love. So if this be so, don't fill your head with scrupulous and priggish thoughts, but make sure that Lotario esteems you as highly as you do him and bless your stars that since you have slipped into love's trap, the man who clasps you in his arms is a man of integrity who not only possesses the four S's, which they say all good lovers should have,[1] but a whole ABC as well. Now listen to me and you will see that I know it by heart. He is, as I see it and as far as I can judge, amiable, bountiful, chivalrous, discreet, enamored, firm, gallant, honorable, illustrious, loyal, moderate, noble, open, prudent, quiet, rich, and the S's according to the saying. And then tender, valiant. X does not

---

[1] The four S's are: *Sabio, Solo, Solícito, Secreto* (wise, alone, attentive, secret) and Luis Barahona de Soto defines them in verses from his poem *Las Lágrimas de Angélica* (Granada, 1586):

> *Sabio en servir, y nunca descuidado,*
> *Solo en amar, y a otra alma no sujeto,*
> *Solícito en buscar sus desengaños,*
> *Secreto en sus favores y en sus daños.*
> (Wise in service, never thoughtless,
> Alone to love, subject to none,
> Tireless in seeking experience,
> Secret in his favors and penalties).

fit him because it is a harsh letter; Y I have already said it, Z, he is zealous of your honor.' [2]

"Camila laughed at her maid's ABC and concluded that she was more expert in love affairs than she admitted. In fact, the girl confessed as much by telling Camila that she was having a love affair with a young gentleman of the city. This disturbed her mistress, who feared that this might endanger her own honor. Camila questioned her closely to find out whether their affair had gone beyond mere words, and Leonela shamelessly and brazenly replied that it had. There is no doubt that ladies' failings cause their maids to lose all sense of shame; and when they see their mistresses trip, the maids think nothing of stumbling themselves and do not care if it is known. All Camila could do was to beg Leonela not to say anything to the young man she said was her lover about her affair and to manage her own with secrecy so that it should not come to the ears of Anselmo or Lotario. Leonela agreed, but her way of keeping her promise was enough to confirm Camila's fears that she would lose her reputation through her maid, for the shameless hussy Leonela, when she observed that her mistress' behavior was not what it used to be, had the imprudence to bring her lover into the house and keep him there, confident that her mistress would not dare to expose him even if she were to see him. This, incidentally, is one of the troubles that mistresses bring upon themselves by their sins, for thus they become the slaves of their own maids and are obliged to conceal their dishonorable behavior and loose conduct, as happened in Camila's case. For although she often ascertained that Leonela was with her lover in one of the rooms of the house, she not only did not dare to scold her but also gave her the opportunity to hide him and removed for her every obstacle, lest her husband might catch sight of him. But she could not prevent Lotario from seeing the lover come out on one occasion at daybreak. At first he did not know who he was and thought that he must be a ghost. When, however, he saw him walking away, carefully and cautiously wrapping himself in his cloak, he dropped this stupid notion for another, which would have been the ruin of them all if Camila had not found a remedy. Lotario did not

[2] The ABC of Love recalls the celebrated one in Lope de Vega's play *Peribañez y el Comendador de Ocaña*.

think that the man he had seen leave Anselmo's house at such a strange hour could possibly have gone in for Leonela's sake, for he did not even remember that such a person as Leonela existed. He only thought that Camila was behaving as frivolously and shamelessly with some other man as she had with him. Such are the consequences that follow the bad actions of a wicked woman. She loses her reputation for honor with the very man to whose prayers and entreaties she has surrendered, and he is convinced that she gives herself even more easily to others, and believes every idle suspicion that enters his head to be Gospel truth.

"There is no doubt that all Lotario's common sense failed him at this point, and all his wise arguments deserted him at a moment when he desperately needed them. Blind with jealous rage that gnawed at his entrails and dying to take vengeance on Camila, who had done him no wrong, he went straight to Anselmo, who was still in bed, and said to him: 'I must inform you, Anselmo, that I have been struggling for a long time with myself and violently reproaching myself for not telling you something that it is not possible or right for me to conceal any longer. You must know that Camila's fortress has now surrendered and is in my power for me to do what I will with it. If I have delayed in telling you the truth, it has only been to see whether it was merely a frivolous fancy on her part or if it was to test me and see whether my courting, which was done with your permission, was seriously meant. I believe, too, that if she was what she should be and what we both thought her to be, she would already have informed you of my wooing. Seeing, however, that she has not yet done so, I realize that the promises that she has given me are in earnest and that the next time you are absent from home she will speak with me in the closet in which you keep your jewels' (that, in fact, was the place where Camila generally received him). 'I do not want you to rush headlong into taking some sort of vengeance, for the sin has so far only been committed in intention, and perhaps between now and the time for action Camila will change her mind and show a beginning of repentance. Since you have always followed my advice, either wholly or only in part, take the advice I am going to give you now, so that you will be able to satisfy yourself, without any possibility of error, what your best course of action must be. Pretend that

you are going away for three days, as you have done before,
but arrange matters so that you can hide in your closet instead. The tapestries there and other possible coverings will
make this extremely easy. Then, you and I will see with
our own eyes what Camila will do, and if she is a guilty
woman, which is possible but not certain, you may then
silently, cautiously, and discreetly avenge your wrongs.'

"Anselmo was dumbfounded, amazed, and stunned by
Lotario's statements, for they caught him at a moment when
he least expected to hear them. Now he thought of Camila
as triumphant over Lotario's feigned assaults, and was beginning to enjoy the glory of her victory. He was silent for
some time and stared at the ground without moving an eye-
lash, but finally he said: 'Lotario, you have done all that I
expected of your friendship; I must follow your advice in
everything. Do what you please, but keep this matter secret,
for that is the only possible course in this unheard-of business.'

"Lotario promised he would, but by the time he left, he
had completely repented of what he had said and realized
how stupidly he had acted, since he might have revenged
himself on Camila in a less cruel and dishonorable way. He
cursed himself for his idiocy and his weak-kneed resolution,
but he was at a loss for a means of undoing the wrong he had
done or, at least, of producing a reasonable solution. In the
end he resolved to make a clean breast of everything to Camila, and as there were plenty of opportunities, that same
day he found her alone. But no sooner did she see him than
she said: 'Lotario, my friend, I have such palpitations that I
feel as if my heart will burst in my breast. Indeed, it will be
a miracle if it does not. Leonela's shamelessness has reached
such a pitch that she lets her lover into this house every
night and stays with him until morning. It will greatly harm
my reputation, for anyone who sees him come out of my
house at such an unusual hour will judge as he pleases. What
worries me is that I cannot punish her or scold her because
her close and intimate connection with our affairs puts a
bridle on my tongue, and I must not breathe a word about
her vagaries. I am very much afraid this will cause us all a
great deal of trouble.'

"Lotario's first reaction when Camila was telling her story
was that this was a subterfuge to make him believe that the
young man whom he had seen coming out of the house was

Leonela's lover and not hers. But when he saw her tears and her pitiable distress and when she besought him to come to her aid, he woke up to the truth and in a flash was overwhelmed with self-guilt and remorse. Nevertheless, he told Camila not to worry, for he would soon find a way to curb Leonela's insolence. He also told her what his mad rage of jealousy had driven him to say to Anselmo and how both had agreed that the latter should hide in the closet and witness her faithlessness to him. He begged her to pardon his foolish action and to advise him how to remedy it and find a way out of the twisted labyrinth in which he found himself as the result of his incredible stupidity.

"Camila was highly alarmed at Lotario's story and turned on him in a great fury, denouncing him, and justifiably so, for his dastardly suspicions and reproaching him for the wicked and foolish scheme he had contrived. But as women naturally possess a subtler talent for good and evil than men, though it fails them when they try to bring reason deliberately into their arguments, Camila immediately discovered a way of remedying this apparently irremediable affair. She told Lotario to get Anselmo to hide next day in the place he had spoken of, for she was sure she could turn his hiding to such good account that both of them might take their pleasure together without any fear of interruption or surprise. She didn't tell him all the details of her plan but warned him that as soon as Anselmo was hidden, he should come when Leonela called him and that he should answer any question she might ask him just as he would if he did not know that Anselmo was listening. Lotario tried hard to get her to tell him the whole of her scheme so that he might be able to act with more caution and circumspection.

"'I am certain,' said Camila, 'that there are no more precautions to take; just answer the questions I shall put to you.'

"Camila did not want to tell him of her schemes beforehand, because she was afraid that he would not follow the plan that seemed so excellent to her and that he might evolve on his own another that would not be as good.

"Lotario then departed, and next day Anselmo left, giving as an excuse that he was visiting his friend in the country. He then returned to hide, which he did with the greatest of ease, for Camila and Leonela had deliberately given him the opportunity.

"Anselmo was now hidden, and we can picture his state of anxiety, for now he expected to see the very heart of his dishonor laid bare before his own eyes. He saw himself actually on the point of losing the supreme treasure that he thought he possessed in his beloved Camila. As soon as Camila and Leonela were certain that Anselmo was hidden, they went into the closet; and Camila, on entering, heaved a deep sigh and said: 'Ah, Leonela, my friend, before I carry out my plan which I do not want you to know lest you might try to prevent me, would it not be better for you to take Anselmo's dagger, which I have asked you to bring, and plunge it into this infamous heart of mine? But do not do it; it would not be right for me to bear the burden of another's sin. First, I must know what it is that Lotario's rakish, lustful eyes saw in me to embolden him to reveal his wicked designs against his friend and against my honor. Stand at that window, Leonela, and call him. He is sure to be in the street, waiting to carry out his foul purpose. But first, I shall carry out mine, which shall be cruel, but honorable.'

"'Oh, my lady,' cried the sly and forewarned Leonela, 'what are you going to do with that dagger? Do you intend to take your own life, or Lotario's? Whichever you do will involve the loss of your honor and good name. Better to hide your wrong than to give that unkind man a chance to enter the house and find us alone. Think, my lady, how weak we women are. He is a man, and full of resolution. And as he comes with such a rascally purpose, he may in his blind passion do injury to you that will be worse than murder, before you have a chance of carrying out your plan. I blame my master Anselmo for making that shameless rascal so free of this house. But if you kill him, my lady, as I think you intend to do, what shall we do with him when he is dead?'

"'What then, my friend?' replied Camila. 'We shall leave him for Anselmo to bury, for it is only just that he should have the pleasant task of burying his own dishonor. Call him quickly; every moment I delay in taking righteous vengeance for my wrong, I am conscious of failing in the loyalty I owe to my husband.'

"Anselmo was listening to all this, and at each word that Camila uttered, his mind changed, but when he heard that she was bent on killing Lotario, he decided to emerge from his hiding place and reveal himself, for fear she might carry out her threat. But he restrained his impulse, so great was his desire to see how his wife's high-spirited and honorable resolution would end. So, he resolved to come out at the crucial moment to prevent the catastrophe.

"At this point Camila collapsed in a deep swoon, and Leonela, laying her on a bed that was there, began to weep more bitterly, saying: 'Oh, what a misfortune if she should die here in my arms, the fairest flower of chastity in the world, the crown of pure women, the model of virtue!' She ranted on in similar style to such an extent that anyone who overheard her would have sworn that she was the most affectionate and loyal maid in all the world and that her mistress was a second persecuted Penelope.[3]

"Camila was not long, however, in reviving from her faint, and as she came to, she said: 'Why do you not go, Leonela, and call that most disloyal of friends the sun ever saw or sight concealed? Quick, run, hurry, go, lest the fire of my anger be quenched by the delay and my just vengeance blow over in a storm of threats and curses.'

"'I'll go and call him at once, my lady,' said Leonela, 'but first you must give me that dagger, lest you do something desperate with it while I am away, which would leave all of us who love you crying our eyes out for the rest of our lives.'

"'Do not fear, friend Leonela, I shall not do it,' answered Camila, 'for though I may seem rash and bold in your eyes because I defend my honor, I shall not go to such lengths as Lucretia, who, it is said, killed herself, although she had committed no crime, without first slaying the man who was the cause of her dishonor. I shall die if I must, but I want to wreak my vengeance on the man who has brought me to this mournful state as the result only of his lustful insolence, for I was not at fault.'

"Leonela took a great deal of pressing before she went out to call Lotario. At last she went, and while awaiting her return, Camila spoke as to herself: 'Heavens help me! Would it

---

[3] Penelope, the wife of Ulysses, was the symbol of wifely fidelity. During the long absence of her husband at the Trojan War she was beleaguered by suitors whom she rejected by declaring that she must finish a robe for her aged father-in-law, Laërtes, before she could make up her mind. During the daytime she worked at the robe, but in the night she undid the work of the day.

not have been wiser to have sent Lotario away, as I have often done before, and not have permitted him, as I have now, to think me dishonest and abandoned if only for the little time I must wait before undeceiving him? It would certainly have been much better, but then I should not be revenged, nor would my husband's honor be vindicated, if he managed to wash his hands of it and get out free from the hole in which his wicked designs have placed him. Let the traitor pay for his lecherous desires with his life. Let the world know, if it ever does, that Camila not only kept faith with her husband, but avenged him on the man who dared to offend him. Perhaps it would be better to tell Anselmo of this, though I have already referred to it in the letter I sent to him in the country. As he was in no hurry to provide a remedy for the trouble I wrote about, I am convinced that he is so naïve and trustful that he could not believe, nor did he want to, that so staunch a friend could entertain even the slightest hint of a thought that was against his honor. I did not believe it myself then, nor for a long time, nor should I ever have believed it if his insolence had not grown to such proportions and his blatant bribes, his grand promises, and his repeated tearful entreaties had not made it clear to me. But why all these speeches now? Does a courageous determination need advice? No, indeed. Away with you traitors then! Now for vengeance! Let the false scoundrel enter; let him come; let him draw near; let him die, and good riddance to him, come what may! Pure I came into the possession of the husband Heaven gave me; pure I must go from him, even though I go bathed in my own chaste blood and in the impure blood of the falsest friend that ever lived.'

"As she talked on, she paced up and down the room with the dagger unsheathed, taking such wild, uneven strides and gesticulating in such a way that she seemed to be out of her wits. No delicate woman was she now, but a desperate virago.

"All the while Anselmo, hidden behind some tapestries, looked on in blank amazement. What he had already seen and heard seemed to him sufficient to allay even graver suspicions, and he would have been delighted to dispense with the proof of Lotario's arrival, for he feared some sudden disaster might be in the offing. But just as he was going to show himself and embrace and undeceive his wife, he paused, for Leonela returned, leading Lotario by the hand. No sooner

had Camila seen the latter than she traced with the dagger
a long line on the floor and said: 'Listen to me, Lotario. If
you dare to pass beyond this line here, or even to approach it,
I will plunge this dagger into my breast. And before you
say a word in answer, I want you to hear me speak. Afterward, you may answer what you will. First of all, Lotario,
I want you to tell me if you know my husband, Anselmo,
and what opinion you have of him. Next, I want to know
whether you know me. Answer me. Do not be confused or
delay your answers; I am not asking you riddles.'

"Lotario was not so doltish as not to have realized from the
very first moment what Camila's intentions were when she
told him to make Anselmo hide; so, he backed up her scheme
most efficiently and both of them made their imposture ring
truer than truth itself. So he answered her as follows: 'I did
not think, fair Camila, that you had summoned me to ask
me questions having so little bearing on my present purpose.
If your intention is to postpone granting the favor you promised, you might have postponed it from a greater distance,
for the closer we approach our hopes of possession, the more
we are tortured by our desire. But, in order that you may
not accuse me of not replying to your question, I shall
answer that I know your husband, Anselmo, and that we
have known one another since our tenderest years. Of our
friendship I shall not say anything, for you know all about
that and I do not wish to bear witness against myself. But it
is love, which excuses the greatest faults, that compels me
to do this wrong I am committing. You too I know, and I
value you as highly as he does. If that were not so, for
lesser qualities than yours I should not have broken the holy
laws of friendship, which I have now violated at the in-
stigation of that mighty enemy, love.'

" 'If you confess to that,' replied Camila, 'mortal enemy of
all that justly deserves to be loved, how can you have the
insolence to appear before the woman whom you know to be
his very mirror and reflection? If you would look at yourself
in her eyes, you would see what little excuse you have for
wronging him. But now, poor wretched woman that I am, I
know what has made you behave in a manner so unworthy
of yourself. It must have been some frivolity in me; I will
not call it immodesty, for it did not spring from deliberate
design but from one of those indiscretions into which women
unconsciously fall when they think that reserve is unneces-

sary. But tell me, traitor, when did I answer your entreaties with any word or sign that could awaken any shadow of hope in you of accomplishing your infamous desires? When were your words of love not rejected with bitterness and scorn? When did I accept your presents or credit your promises? As I know that no one can persevere in his wooing unless he is sustained by some hope, I shall take the blame for your insolence, for without doubt it is my carelessness that has made you persist in your suit so long. I shall, therefore, punish myself and inflict the penalty of your guilt upon myself. So that you may see that being so cruel to myself, I could not be anything but cruel to you, I have brought you here to witness the sacrifice I intend to make to the wounded honor of my most honored husband. By you he was injured with the greatest deliberation; by me, because of my lack of precaution in giving you an opportunity, if I did so, of furthering your base desires. What worries me most, however, is my suspicion that some thoughtlessness on my part kindled these rash thoughts in you, and this I fervently long to obliterate with these hands of mine, for were I to have any other executioner, my guilt would be more public. But before this happens, I want to kill as I die and take with me the man who will finally sate my desire for vengeance, for when I see from that place, wherever it may be, the punishment that impartial justice gives to the man who has reduced me to my present desperate plight, I shall be completely satisfied.'

"As she spoke she sprang upon Lotario with incredible strength and swiftness, flourishing the naked dagger and with such evident signs of wishing to bury it in his heart that he felt uncertain whether her demonstrations were false or true, for he had to use all his skill and strength to prevent her from stabbing him. So realistically did she perform her strange act of fraud that she even shed her own blood to give it the color of truth. Finding that she could not wound Lotario, or pretending that she could not, she said: 'Though Fate denies me complete satisfaction, at least she shall not be strong enough to prevent my attaining it in part.'

"Saying this, she wrenched her dagger hand free from Lotario's grasp, and pointing the blade where it could not wound her deeply, she stabbed herself, burying the weapon above her collarbone on the left side near the shoulder; she then let herself sink to the ground as if in a faint.

"Leonela and Lotario were dumbfounded at this unexpected turn of events and doubted their eyes when they saw Camila lying on the ground bathed in her own blood. Breathless and quivering with fear, Lotario rushed to pull out the dagger. But when he saw how small the wound was, his fears vanished, and he was amazed at the fair Camila's skill, poise, and ingenuity. To play his part, however, he began a long and doleful lament over her body, just as if she was dead, calling down great curses upon himself and upon the man who had been the cause of the whole catastrophe. And knowing that his friend Anselmo was listening, he spoke in such terms that anyone hearing him would have pitied him more than Camila, even if he had supposed that she was dead. Leonela took her in her arms and placed her on the bed, begging Lotario to go and find someone to attend to her in secret. She also asked him to advise her what they should say to Anselmo about her mistress' wound if he were to return before she was healed. He replied that they might say what they pleased, for he was no person to give useful advice. He only told her to try to stanch the blood, for he was going where no man should see him again. Then he left the house with a great show of sorrow and emotion, but no sooner was he alone and unobserved than he crossed himself in amazement at Camila's ingenuity and Leonela's excellent acting. He reflected on how positive Anselmo must be that his wife was a second Portia,[4] and longed to meet him so that they might rejoice together at the most plausible imposture imaginable.

"Leonela stanched her mistress' blood as she was told, though there was only just enough to make her performance convincing; then she washed the wound with a little wine and bandaged it as best she could, uttering such a litany of protests about her mistress as she cured her that even if nothing had been said before, that alone would have sufficed to convince Anselmo that in Camila he possessed the image of chastity. In addition to Leonela's protestations, Camila uttered lamentations, blaming herself for her cowardice and for lacking the courage to end her own life at the moment

---

[4] Portia, daughter of Cato Uticensis, the wife of Brutus, the assassin of Julius Caesar. She induced her husband, on the night before the Ides of March, to reveal to her the conspiracy against Caesar's life, and she wounded herself in the thigh to prove her courage and trustworthiness.

when it was most necessary, for life had become hateful to her. She begged her maid to advise her whether she ought to tell her beloved husband all that had happened or not, and Leonela strongly advised her on no account to do so, for this would oblige him to take vengeance on Lotario, which would involve him in no small risk. It was a good wife's duty to avoid giving her husband occasion for quarrels, but rather to save him from as many as she could. Camila replied that this was sound advice and that she would follow it, but they would in any case have to invent some explanation of her wound, for Anselmo was bound to see it. To this Leonela replied that she could not tell a lie, even as a joke.

" 'Then how could I, dear sister?' answered Camila. 'I should not have the courage to invent a lie or brazen it out even if my whole life depended on it. If we cannot find a way out of this fix, it would be better to tell him the naked truth than for him to catch us out in a lying tale.'

" 'Do not worry yourself, my lady,' replied Leonela; 'between now and tomorrow I'll think of something to say. As the wound is where it is, you may be able to cover it up so that he will not see it, and Heaven may be pleased to look kindly on the justice of our case. But calm yourself, my lady, and try to control your feelings so that my master may not find you all excited. And as for the rest, leave it all to me and to God, who always gives a helping hand to good intentions.'

"Anselmo with rapt attention had stood listening and watching this tragedy representing the death of his honor, performed by the players in such a strange and passionate manner that they seemed to transmute themselves into the characters they were acting. He longed for night, which would give him an opportunity of slipping out of his house and going to his friend Lotario to rejoice with him over the priceless pearl that he had discovered in the disclosure of his wife's virtue. The two women made certain that he was given an opportunity for getting away, and he took advantage of it and went in search of Lotario. Who could tell how many times he embraced his friend when he found him, what he said in his rapturous delight, and how he praised Camila to the skies? Lotario listened to all this without being able to show any external symptoms of joy, for he could not rid his mind of the bitter thought of how greatly his friend was deceived and how cruelly he himself had wronged him. But, although Anselmo observed that Lotario did not show any joy, he believed that it was because Camila had been wounded and he had been responsible. So, during their conversation he told him not to worry about Camila's accident, for the wound must be a slight one since they had both agreed to hide it from him. Lotario certainly had nothing to fear, he said, but should rejoice and show his happiness, for it was through his friend's help and scheming that he had been raised to the highest attainable peak of happiness. What was more, he would have no other recreation from that day on but to write verses in Camila's praise to immortalize her memory for future ages. Lotario praised his sentiments and promised to assist him to raise so noble a memorial.

"And so Anselmo henceforth remained the most delightfully deluded man in the whole world. He himself led home by the hand the man who had completely destroyed his good name in the firm belief that he had brought him nothing but glory. Camila received Lotario with seemingly sour glances, but with a smiling heart. This deception lasted for some days, until after a few months Fortune turned her wheel, their artfully concealed wickedness became public, and Anselmo's curiosity cost him his life."

CHAPTER XXXV

Of the fierce and monstrous battle that Don Quixote fought with certain skins of red wine, with the conclusion of "The Tale of Ill-Advised Curiosity"

Very little of the tale remained to be read when Sancho Panza in great alarm rushed in from the loft where Don Quixote was lying, shouting at the top of his voice: "Come quickly, sirs, and help my master, who is up to his neck in the toughest battle my eyes have ever seen. Lord save us, he has dealt the giant, the enemy of Princess Micomicona, such a slash that he has sliced his head clear off like a turnip."

"What are you saying, brother?" said the curate, leaving the rest of the tale unread. "Are you in your wits, Sancho? How the Devil can it be as you say, when the giant is at least two thousand leagues from here?"

Then they heard a great noise outside and Don Quixote shouting out: "Stand back, robber, rascal, rogue! Now I have you in my power. Your scimitar will not save you!" And it seemed as if he were slashing away at the walls.

Then Sancho said: "You shouldn't be standing here listening, but go in and stop the fight or help my master, although there'll be no need now, for I'm sure the giant is already dead and is giving an account to God of his wicked life. I saw his blood flood the floor, and his head cut off and topple on one side; why, it's as big as a great wineskin."

"Death and hell!" cried the landlord on hearing this. "If Don Quixote or Don Devil has not been slashing at one of the skins of red wine standing at the head of his bed,

363

and the wine that is spilled must be what this fellow takes for blood." [1]

Saying this, he rushed into the room, followed by the others, and they found Don Quixote in the strangest situation in the world. He was in his shirt, which was not long enough in front to cover his thighs and was six inches shorter behind; his legs were long, lanky, hairy, and none too clean. On his head he wore a little greasy red cap that belonged to the landlord. Around his left arm he had wrapped the blanket to which Sancho bore a grudge, and he knew why, and in his right hand he held his drawn sword, with which he was slashing about on all sides, shouting as if he were truly battling with a giant. And the strangest of all was that his eyes were closed, for he was still asleep and dreaming that he was in battle with the giant. His imagination was so intently fixed upon the forthcoming adventure that it made him dream that he had arrived at the kingdom of Micomicón and was already at war with his foe. And he had given so many slashes to the skins, thinking that he was giving them to his enemy, that the room was flooded with wine. At this sight the landlord flew into a towering rage and rushed at Don Quixote, and with clenched fists he began so to belabor him that if Cardenio and the curate had not pulled him off he would have finished the war for the giant. In spite of all this, the poor knight did not wake up until the barber brought a large bucket of cold water from the well and threw it all over his body. The shock awoke Don Quixote, but not so completely as to make him realize his plight. Dorotea, seeing how short and flimsy were his garments, would not go in to watch the fight between her champion and his rival. Sancho, meanwhile, was searching all over the floor for the head of the giant, and as he could not find it, he cried: "Now I'm sure that everything in this house is enchanted, for last time in this very spot where I am now, they gave me a rare pucking and pummeling without my being any wiser as to who gave them to me, for I couldn't see a soul. Now this head is nowhere to be seen, though I saw it cut off with my two eyes

[1] The adventure of the wineskins, as Lockhart reminds us, may be derived from *The Golden Ass* of Apuleius, when the hero, intoxicated after the bacchanalian festival of Momus, slashes three immense leather bottles of wine that he mistakes for robbers. In Spain wine in the inns and taverns is kept in large pigskins. The hairy side within is covered with pitch—a custom that is mentioned by the Hispano-Roman poet Martial.

and the blood streaming from the body like from a fountain."

"What blood or what fountain are you cackling about, you enemy of God and His saints?" said the landlord. "Can't you see, you scoundrel, that they are nothing else but the skins ripped open and all their red wine swimming in this room? May I see the soul of the one who ripped them open swimming in hell."

"All I know," answered Sancho, "is that if I'm so unlucky as not to find the head of the giant, why, my earldom will melt away like salt in water."

Sancho awake was worse than his master asleep, so greatly had the latter's promises turned his brain.

The landlord was in despair at seeing the crass stupidity of the squire and the mischief done by his master. He swore that it would not be as on the last occasion, when they went off without paying, that the privilege of knighthood would be no excuse for refusing to foot the bill for this time and the other, and that he would make them pay for the plugs that would have to be put on the slashed wineskins. The curate, meanwhile, was holding Don Quixote's hands, who, believing that he had finished the adventure and was in the presence of Princess Micomicona herself, fell on his knees before the curate and said: "Your highness, noble and beautiful lady, may live henceforth in safety, without any fear that this ill-born monster might do her harm. I, too, am liberated this day from the promise I made to you, for with the help of almighty God and through favor of the lady by whom I live and breathe, I have so well accomplished my task."

"Didn't I say so?" cried Sancho, hearing these words of his master. "To be sure, I wasn't drunk. Look now how my master has salted down the giant. The bulls are on their way; [2] my earldom is safe."

Who could refrain laughing at the follies of the two— master and servant? All of them did laugh except the landlord, who wished himself in hell. At length, however, the barber, Cardenio, and the curate managed with much ado to get Don Quixote to bed again, and he fell asleep at once, for he was utterly worn out. They let him sleep and went out to comfort Sancho Panza for not having found the giant's

---

[2] *Ciertos son los toros* is a phrase taken from the bullring and used proverbially. It expresses the feelings of relief of spectators when they see the preparations for the bullfight nearing completion.

head. As for the innkeeper, they had more difficulty in
pacifying him, for he was in despair at the sudden death of
his wineskins. And the landlady kept scolding and bawling:
"In an evil hour that knight-errant came into my house!
I wish to God my eyes had never seen him, for he has
cost me dear. Last time he went off with the price of a
night's supper, bed, straw, and barley for himself, his squire,
his horse, and his ass, saying that he was a knight-adventurer
—God send bad adventure to him and to all the adventurers there are in the world—and therefore wasn't bound to
pay a thing, for so it was written in the rules of knight-
errantry. Then, on his account, this other gentleman comes
along and takes away my tail, and now he has returned it
with more than a groatsworth of damage, the hair so scraped
off that it's of no further use to my husband. Then, to top it
all, he bursts my skins and spills my wine. May I see his
blood spilled! But don't let him think he'll get away with it,
for by the bones of my father and the soul of my mother,
they'll pay me every maravedi on the nail or my name is not
what it is and I'm not my father's daughter."

Thus the landlady went on in a great rage, and she was
abetted by the worthy Maritornes. As for the daughter, she
held her peace but now and then smiled. The curate at length
calmed the storm, promising to satisfy them as best he
could for their loss of wine and skins, and especially for the
damage to the tail of which they made so great a fuss.
Dorotea comforted Sancho Panza, telling him that if it should
turn out that his master had cut off the giant's head, she
promised, once she found herself peacefully settled in her
kingdom, to give him the best earldom she had. Sancho
was comforted by this, and he assured the princess that
she might depend upon it, for he had seen the head of the
giant, aye, and it had a beard that reached to the waist;
and if it could not be found, it was because everything that
took place in that house happened by enchantment, as he
had found out the last time he had stayed there. Dorotea
said that she believed him and that he should not worry, for
all would turn out to his heart's content.

When all was quiet, the curate insisted on finishing the
reading of the tale, for he saw there was little left. Cardenio,
Dorotea, and all the rest begged him to do so, and anxious to
please them all, besides wanting to read it himself, he went
on with the story as follows:

"So it came to pass that, owing to the satisfaction that Anselmo derived from Camila's goodness, he spent a happy and carefree life. And Camila purposefully glared at Lotario so that Anselmo should interpret her feelings for him in the opposite manner to what they really were. And to strengthen this delusion, Lotario asked permission not to come to the house any more, for he was aware how much Camila disliked seeing him. But the deluded Anselmo replied that he would not agree to this on any account. And so, in a thousand ways Anselmo was the architect of his own dishonor, while believing that he was creating happiness for himself. By this time, Leonela found herself so free and untrammeled in her own love affair that she threw all caution to the winds and pursued it without any restraint, confident that her mistress would offer her cover and even advise her how to carry it on with the minimum of risk. But at last one night Anselmo heard footsteps in Leonela's room, and when he tried to go in and see who it was, he found the door barred against him, which made him the more anxious to force it. He pushed so hard that he opened it, and as he rushed in, he caught sight of a man jumping out of the window into the street. When he ran quickly to catch him or see who he was, he could do neither, because Leonela clung to him, crying: 'Calm yourself, my lord, don't make a row. Don't follow the man who jumped out. It's my business; in fact, he's my husband.'

"Anselmo would not believe her, but blind with fury, he drew his dagger and tried to murder her, commanding her to tell him the truth or he would kill her. Then, out of fear and without realizing what she was saying, she cried out: 'Don't kill me, sir; I'll tell you something more important than you can imagine.'

" 'Tell me at once,' replied Anselmo, 'otherwise you'll die.'

" 'I can't just now,' said Leonela; 'I'm in such a dither. Leave it for tomorrow, and I'll tell you something that will dumbfound you. But I swear to you that the man who leaped out of this window is a young man of this city who has given me his word that he will marry me.'

"Anselmo was satisfied with this and agreed to wait the time she asked, for he never expected to hear her say anything against Camila, so absolutely sure was he of her virtue. So, he went out of the room, leaving Leonela locked up there and saying that she would not be let out until she had given him all the information she had promised.

"Then he went off to see Camila and told her all that had happened between him and her maid and of the latter's promise to tell him something of great importance. There is no need to say whether Camila was alarmed or not; indeed, she was in such a fright, believing as she did (and with good reason) that Leonela was going to tell Anselmo all she knew about her unfaithfulness, that she had not the courage to wait and see whether her suspicions were correct or not. That same night, when she thought Anselmo was asleep, she gathered together her finest jewels and some money, left the house without being seen, and went to Lotario's. She told him what had happened and begged him to find her a hiding place or to take her away to some place where they would both be out of Anselmo's reach. This threw Lotario into such confusion that he was unable to answer a single word, still less to make up his mind as to what to do. In the end, he decided to take Camila to a convent of which his sister was the prioress. Camila agreed to this, and with the rapidity that the situation demanded, Lotario took her and left her at the convent; then, he immediately left the city, informing no one of his departure.

"When the day broke, Anselmo was so eager to hear what Leonela was going to tell him that he did not notice Camila's absence from his side. He got up and went to the room where he had left the maid locked up. He opened the door and went in, but he could not find Leonela; all he found were some sheets tied to the window bars, a proof that she had climbed down and fled. Then he returned very downcast to tell Camila and was dumbfounded not to find her in bed or anywhere in the house. He asked the servants where she was, but none could answer his question. Then, by chance, as he was searching for her, he noticed that her boxes were open and most of her jewels missing. He now began to realize the extent of his calamity and that Leonela was not the cause of his misfortune. And so, just as he was, without troubling to finish dressing, he went sadly and pensively to tell his trouble to his friend Lotario. But when he found him gone and when his servants told him that their master had departed that night and had taken all the money he had with him, he thought he would go out of his mind. And to finish it all off, when he returned to his house he found not one of the servants there and the house silent and deserted.

"He did not know what to think, what to say, or what to do, but gradually his wits began to return. He reflected and saw himself in one instant wifeless, friendless, and servantless, left desolate, as it seemed, by Heaven above, and worst of all, deprived of his honor, for in Camila's disappearance he saw his own perdition. Finally, after a long while, he resolved to go to his friend in the country, with whom he had stayed when he had given the others their opportunity to contrive the whole disaster. He locked the doors of his house, mounted his horse, and in a stupor set out on his journey. But he had hardly gone halfway when, troubled by his thoughts, he was compelled to dismount and tie his horse to a tree, at the foot of which he lay down, heaving pitiful sighs. There he stayed almost till nightfall; then he saw a man coming on horseback from the city. After greeting him, he asked what news there was in Florence.

" 'The strangest news that has come to our ears for many a long day,' answered the townsman, 'is the general rumor that Lotario, Anselmo's great friend, the rich man who used to live at San Giovanni, carried off Anselmo's wife, Camila, last night and that Anselmo himself is also missing. All this was revealed by a maid of Camila's, whom the governor found last night letting herself down by a sheet from the window of Anselmo's house. I don't know exactly how the whole thing happened; I only know that the whole city is astounded at the news, for such a thing was most unexpected, considering the great and intimate friendship between these two men. It was so close that they used to be called "the two friends." '

" 'Do you know, by any chance,' asked Anselmo, 'what road Lotario and Camila have taken?'

" 'I've no idea,' replied the townsman, 'although the governor has been very active in looking for them.'

" 'God be with you, sir,' said Anselmo.

" 'And with you,' answered the townsman and rode off.

"At this disastrous news Anselmo was on the verge not only of losing his wits, but also of putting an end to his own life. He got up as best he could and reached the house of his friend, who had not yet heard of his misfortune; but when he saw him arrive, pale, worn out, and haggard, he realized that some serious mishap had befallen him. Anselmo at once begged him to help him to bed and to give him some writing materials. This he did; and Anselmo was left alone in bed with the door locked, just as he requested. Once alone, he was so overcome by the thought of his disaster that he clearly saw his life was drawing to an end. So, he decided to leave an account of the cause of his strange death. He began to write, but before he had finished putting down all he wished, his breath failed him and he gave up the ghost as the result of the sorrow that his ill-advised curiosity brought upon him. The master of the house, observing that it was late and that Anselmo had not called out, decided to go in and find out if he was any worse. He found him lying face down, half his body on the bed and the other half on the desk, and with the paper he had written unsealed and the pen still in his hand. Calling out to him and getting no response, and touching him and finding him cold, he realized that he was dead. Amazed and deeply grieved, he called his household to see the miserable end that had befallen Anselmo, and later he read the paper, on which Anselmo had written the following words:

"'A foolish and ill-advised desire has cost me my life. If news of my death should reach Camila's ears, let it be known that I forgive her, for she was not obliged to perform miracles, nor did I need to ask her to do so. So, as I was the one who fashioned my own dishonor, there is no reason why . . .'

"Anselmo had only written so far, and it was clear that his life had ended before he could finish his sentence. The next day his friend informed Anselmo's relations of his death. They already knew of his misfortunes and of the convent whither Camila had retired and where she was almost in a state to accompany her husband on his inevitable journey, not because of the news of his death, but from what she had heard of her absent lover. It was rumored that though she was a widow, she would not leave the convent, nor even less take the veil. But not many days later, news reached her that Lotario had died in a battle that took place between Monsieur de Lautrec and the Great Captain Gonzalo Hernández of Córdoba in the kingdom of Naples, where Anselmo's friend had retired to expiate in tardy repentance. When Camila heard this news, she became professed as a nun, and not long afterward she yielded up her life in sorrow and melancholy. Such was the end of these three, springing from such foolish beginnings."

"I like the tale," said the curate, "but I cannot convince myself that it is true; and if the author invented it, he did his work badly, for one cannot possibly believe that there could be a husband so foolish as to want to make the costly experiment Anselmo did. If this had been a case of a lover and his mistress, it might do; but between husband and wife there is something impossible about it. Nevertheless, the method of telling the story does not displease me at all."

CHAPTER XXXVI

Of other strange events that happened at the inn

Just then the landlord, who was standing by the inn door, cried out: "Here is a fine troop of guests coming. If they stop here, we may sing 'O be joyful!' "

"Who are they?" asked Cardenio.

"Four men on horseback," answered the landlord; "they're riding Moorish fashion,[1] with lances and targets, and all of them are wearing black masks on their faces. Along with them rides a woman in white on a sidesaddle, also with her face covered, and two lads on foot."

"Are they near?" asked the curate.

"So near," replied the landlord, "that they are now arriving."

Hearing this, Dorotea veiled her face, and Cardenio went into Don Quixote's room. They hardly had time to do this when the whole party of whom the landlord had spoken

---

[1] The Moorish mode of riding was *a la jineta,* with very short stirrups.

entered the inn. The four horsemen were of gallant bearing,
and having dismounted, they went to help the lady in the
sidesaddle to alight; and one of them, taking her in his
arms, placed her upon a chair that stood at the door of the
room into which Cardenio had entered. All this while neither
she nor they took off their masks or said a word; but the
lady, as she sank back in the chair, breathed a deep sigh
and let fall her arms as one who was sick and faint. The
footmen led the horses away to the stable.

As soon as the curate saw this, he was curious to learn
who they were that wore such strange attire and kept so
odd a silence; so he followed the footmen and asked one of
them what he wanted to know. The latter answered: "Egad,
your reverence, I can't tell you who they are, but they seem
to be people of no mean quality, especially he who took
in his arms the lady you're after seein'! This I'm saying, because the rest keep bowin' and scrapin' to him, and his word
is law to them."

"But the lady, who is she?" asked the curate.

"I can't tell you that either, Father," answered the footman, "for I've not caught a glimpse of her face the whole
journey. I've heard her many a time sighin' an' moanin' her
heart out. It's no wonder that we know no more than what
we've told you, for it's no more than two days that myself
and my comrade have been in their company, for they ran
across us on the road an' persuaded us to go with them to
Andalusia, promisin' to pay us well."

"Have you heard the name of any of them?" asked the
curate.

"No, Father," replied the lad, "for they travel in such silence that I wonder what's the cause. We hear nothin' but
the sighin' and sobbin' of the poor lady. It's our honest
belief that wherever she's goin', she's goin' against her wish.
I'd say by her dress that she is a nun or is goin' to become
one, which is more likely. Who knows? Perhaps she has no
leanin' toward bein' a nun, and that's what has her so
down in the mouth."

"That may be so," said the curate. Leaving them, he came
back to Dorotea, who, hearing the veiled lady sigh so and
moved by natural compassion, went up to her and said:
"What ails you, dear lady? If it is anything that women
have the power and experience to relieve, let me offer you
my service and goodwill."

To this the unhappy lady made no answer, and though Dorotea again spoke kind words to her, she remained silent, until the masked gentleman (the one whom the footmen had said the rest obeyed) came up and said to Dorotea: "Lady, do not trouble yourself to offer anything to that woman, for she never shows any gratitude, no matter what is done for her; and do not try to make her answer you unless you wish to hear some falsehood."

"I have never told one," said the lady, who till then had kept silence. "It is because I am so truthful and so averse to falsehood that now I find myself in this miserable state. And I call you to witness this, for it is my pure truth that causes you to be so false and lying."

Cardenio heard those words very clearly and distinctly, for he was close to her who uttered them, since the door of Don Quixote's room was all that separated them from one another. No sooner had he heard them than he cried out: "Heavens above! What is this I hear? What voice is that I hear?"

The lady, startled by his exclamation, turned her head, and as she could not see who uttered them, she rose to her feet and would have entered the room, but the gentleman stopped her and would not let her move a step. In the sudden commotion her mask fell off her face and showed a countenance of incomparable beauty, although pale and terror-stricken, for she rolled her eyes, looking here and there like one distracted, with such an expression of anguish that Dorotea and all who beheld her were moved to deep pity, though they did not know the cause. The gentleman held her firmly by the shoulders, and as he was thus occupied, he could not hold up his own mask, which fell from his face. As it did so, Dorotea, who also was holding the lady, raised her eyes and saw that he who held her in his arms was her own husband, Don Fernando. No sooner did she recognize him than, breathing out from the bottom of her heart a long and most pitiful *Oh*, she fell back in a faint, and if the barber had not by good fortune been close at hand, she would have fallen to the ground. The curate at once made haste to take off her veil and throw water on her face, and as soon as he uncovered it, Don Fernando— for it was he who was holding the other lady in his arms —recognized her and stood like one dead at the sight of her; nevertheless, he did not relax his hold of Luscinda. But she struggled to free herself from his arms, for she recognized Cardenio by his cry, and he had recognized her. Cardenio, who heard the groan that Dorotea uttered as she fell in a swoon, believing it was his Luscinda, ran out of the room in fear and trembling, and the first thing he saw was Don Fernando holding Luscinda in his arms. Don Fernando then recognized Cardenio. And all three, Luscinda, Cardenio, and Dorotea, stood in dumb amazement, scarcely knowing what had happened. They all gazed silently at one another: Dorotea at Don Fernando, Don Fernando at Cardenio, Cardenio at Luscinda, and Luscinda at Cardenio. Then, the first to break the silence was Luscinda, who addressed Don Fernando as follows: "Leave me, Don Fernando, for the sake of what you owe to yourself, if for no other reason. Let me cling to the wall of which I am the ivy, to the protection of one from whom neither your threats, your promises, nor your bribes could separate me. See how Heaven by mysterious and unaccountable ways has led me into the presence of my true husband, and well you know by a thousand costly proofs that only death can drive him from my memory. So let these unmistakable trials of experience convince you (since you have no alternative) to turn your love to fury, your affection to hatred, and to put an end to my life, for I shall consider it well lost provided I die before the eyes of my good husband. Perhaps my death will convince him that I kept my faith to him to the last act of my life."

By this time Dorotea had come to herself, and hearing Luscinda's words, she realized who she was, but seeing that Don Fernando did not yet release her from his arms nor yield to her entreaties, she roused herself as much as she was able, cast herself at his feet, shedding a flood of tears, and thus addressed him: "Ah, dear lord, if the beauty you now hold in your arms had not dazzled your eyes, you would have seen by this time that she who is kneeling at your feet is the forlorn, miserable Dorotea. I am that humble country girl to whom you promised marriage. I am she who lived a happy, innocent life until, seduced by your promises and by the apparent sincerity of your affection, opened the gates of her modesty and surrendered to you the keys of her freedom. How I am recompensed for such a gift is now clear by my being obliged to take refuge in the place where you find me, and by my seeing you as I do this moment. Do not, however, think that I have come here through ways of dishonor. Sorrow and despair alone have driven me since I found myself deserted by you. Remember, dear lord, that the matchless love I have for you may compensate for the beauty and high rank of her for whom you abandon me. You cannot be the fair Luscinda's, for you are mine; nor can she be yours, for she belongs to Cardenio. It would be easier, if you consider it, to make yourself love a woman who adores you than to command the love of a woman who hates you. You seduced my innocence, you played upon my simplicity, you were not blind to my condition, you know well how I submitted to your will; and so, you cannot plead that you were deceived. Since it is so, as it is, and since you are both a Christian and a gentleman, why do you put off making me as happy at last as you did at first? If you refuse to acknowledge me for what I am, your true and lawful wife, allow me at least to become your slave, for provided I be under your protection, I shall count myself fortunate. But do not abandon me to the vile gossip of the streets to my shame; do not bring sorrow on my aged parents, who have always been your faithful vassals. And should it seem to you that your blood will be tainted by mixing with mine, consider that there is little or no nobility in the world that has not run the same course, and that descent on the woman's side is not what counts in illustrious lineages. Moreover, true nobility consists in virtue, and if in this you fail, by denying me what is justly my due, I shall remain with higher claims to nobility than you. And now, my lord, all I wish to say in conclusion is that, whether you want it or not, I am your wife; witnesses are your oaths and vows, which must not and cannot be false if you claim to possess that honor and nobility whose lack you so despise in me. Witness too is your signature and Heaven, which you invoked so often to ratify your promises. And if all this should fail, your own conscience will not fail to murmur words of self-reproach and to disturb every enjoyment in your life."

These and other arguments the sorrowful Dorotea urged in so affecting a manner that all who were present, even those who had come with Don Fernando, could not help giving her their sympathy.

Don Fernando listened to Dorotea without saying a word until she had finished her speech and began to sigh and sob in such a way that all but a heart of bronze would have melted with pity. Luscinda stood gazing at Dorotea with no less compassion for her feelings than admiration for her charm and beauty; she would have liked to approach her and comfort her, had not Don Fernando's arms, which still held her tight, prevented her. As for Don Fernando, he gazed fixedly at Dorotea for a long time, but at last, over-whelmed with remorse and panic, he opened his arms, and setting Luscinda free, he cried: "You have conquered, fair Dorotea, you have conquered. Who could have the heart to deny so many truths together?"

Luscinda, who was still faint, would have fallen to the ground when Don Fernando released her, but Cardenio, who was standing near her and had placed himself behind Don Fernando so as not to be recognized, casting fear aside and daring all risks, ran up to support Luscinda, and clasping her in his arms, he said to her: "If it is the will of Heaven that you should have some rest at last, my faithful, con-stant, and lovely lady, nowhere, I believe, will you find it more securely than in these arms that now embrace you as they did once before when Fortune was pleased to let me call you mine."

At these words Luscinda raised her eyes to Cardenio, and having first assured herself by her eyes that it was he, al-most beside herself and abandoning all forms of decorum, cast her arms about his neck. Then laying her face close to his she said: "Yes, dear lord, you are the true master of this captive of yours, however unkind Fortune may oppose us and threaten this life of mine that only depends on yours." What a strange spectacle for Don Fernando and for the onlookers! They were dumbfounded at such an unforeseen incident. Dorotea thought that Don Fernando changed color and made a move to take revenge on Cardenio; she saw his hand reach for his sword. No sooner did the thought flash across her mind than she threw herself at his feet and em-braced his knees, kissing them and holding them so tightly that he could not move; then, without ceasing to weep, she said: "What is it you mean to do, my sole refuge in this unexpected crisis. Here at your feet is your wife, and the woman you desire is in her husband's arms. Reflect whether it would be right or possible for you to undo what Heaven has done, or whether it would not be better to decide to raise to your level the one who stands before you, stead-fast in her faith, despite all obstacles, and bathing her true

husband's bosom and face with tears of love. For God's sake
I beg you, and for your own sake I implore you, not to
allow this public disclosure to increase your anger, but rather
to calm it so that you may peacefully suffer these two lovers
to live happily all the years that Heaven may please to
grant them. If you do this, you will give proof of your
noble, generous soul, and the world will recognize that reason weighs more with you than passion."

While Dorotea was saying this, Cardenio, though he held
Luscinda in his arms, did not take his eyes off Don Fernando,
for he was resolved, if he saw him make a hostile move, to
defend himself and resist as best he could anyone who
should take sides against him, even if it should cost him his
life. But at this point, all those present—Don Fernando's
friends, the curate, the barber, and even the honest Sancho
Panza—gathered around Don Fernando and begged him to
yield to Dorotea's entreaties, for if she was speaking
the truth, as they believed she was, he should not allow her
hopes to be defrauded; they added that he should reflect that
it was the will of Heaven that had brought them together in
such an unexpected place. The curate told Don Fernando
that he should bear in mind that death alone could separate
Luscinda from Cardenio, and even though the edge of the
sword should divide them, they would consider theirs a most
happy death; that in irremediable cases it was wisest for
him to conquer himself and show a generous soul by allowing those two, of his own free will, to enjoy the blessing
that Heaven had granted them; that he should turn his eyes
toward the lovely Dorotea and he would see that few or
none could equal her, much less surpass her; that in addition to her beauty he should consider her modesty and her
very great love for him; that he should remember that if he
considered himself a gentleman and a Christian, he could
not do otherwise than fulfill his plighted word; that in doing
this he would be doing his duty to God and be approved
by all sensible men, for they know and recognize that it is
the privilege of beauty, so long as it is united to virtue, even
though in a humble subject, to rise to any dignity without
casting any shadow of disparagement on him who raises it
to a level with himself; and that when the strong laws of
passion prevail, no man can be blamed for obeying them,
provided there be no sin.

In short, to these they added so many other compelling

arguments that Don Fernando's manly heart at last softened
and allowed itself to be vanquished by those truths so forcibly urged. As proof that he had finally surrendered to the
sensible arguments that had been proposed to him, he bent
over, embraced Dorotea, and said: "Rise, my dear lady! It
is not right that she who is mistress of my soul should kneel
at my feet. If I have not until now given you any proof
of what I now say, surely it has been by the will of Heaven
so that I might learn to value you as I should, seeing how
loyal and constant is your love for me. What I beg of you
is that you should not upbraid me for my misconduct and
neglect, for the same cause and force that drove me to win
you compelled me to struggle against being yours. And to
convince you that this is true, turn and look at the eyes of
the now happy Luscinda. There you will find the excuse
for all my errors. And since she has found and achieved
what she desired and I have found in you what fulfills all
my wishes, let her live peacefully and contentedly many
long and happy years with her Cardenio, as I entreat Heaven
to grant me the same happiness with my Dorotea."

And saying this, he embraced her again and pressed his
face to hers with so much tender emotion that he had to
avail himself of all his composure to restrain his tears, which
would have been irrefutable proof of his love and repentance.
Cardenio, Dorotea, and almost all the onlookers were so
moved that they began to shed tears so copiously, some in
their own happiness, and some for that of others, that one
would have thought some grim calamity had befallen them.
Even Sancho Panza wept, though he said afterward that
he had cried only because he saw that Dorotea was not
Queen Micomicona, as he had believed, from whom he
expected so many favors. The surprise and general weeping
lasted for some time, but then Cardenio and Luscinda went
and knelt before Don Fernando and thanked him so courteously for the kindness he had done them that he was at a
loss what to reply; so, he raised them up and embraced them
with every mark of affection. Then, he asked Dorotea to
tell him how she had come to that place so far from her
home. She, in a few well-chosen words, told the story she
had told to Cardenio, and Don Fernando and his company
were so interested that they wished it had lasted longer,
such was the charm with which Dorotea described her sad
experiences.

Then, Don Fernando related what he had done after finding in Luscinda's bosom the paper in which she declared that she was Cardenio's wife and could not be his. He said that he wanted to kill her and would have done so if her parents had not prevented him and that he then left the house full of shame and rage, determined to avenge himself at the first opportunity; that next day he heard that Luscinda was missing from her parents' house and that no one knew where she had gone; that after a few months of inquiries he had learned that she was in a certain convent, intending to stay there all the days of her life if she could not spend them with Cardenio; that as soon as he heard this, he had chosen three gentlemen to help him and gone to the place where she was; that one day when the convent gate was open, while his men waited outside, he entered and found Luscinda in a cloister talking with a nun; and that he snatched her away without giving her time to resist, and from there he brought her to a certain village where they provided themselves with all they needed for carrying out the project. He said that when Luscinda found herself in his power, she lost all consciousness; that when she came to her senses, she did nothing but weep and sigh without speaking a word; and that so, in silence and in tears, they had come to this inn, which to him meant Heaven, where all the misfortunes of the world have their end.

CHAPTER XXXVII

*In which is continued the history of the famous
Princess Micomicona, with other pleasant adventures*

Sancho heard all this conversation with no small grief of
mind, for he saw that all his hopes of an earldom were
vanished like smoke, and that the lovely Princess Micomicona
was changed into Dorotea, the giant into Don Fernando,
while his master was sound asleep, careless of all that
happened. Dorotea could not believe that the happiness she
enjoyed was not a dream. Cardenio and Luscinda were of
the same mind, and Don Fernando gave thanks to Heaven
for the favor shown to him and for having extricated him
from that intricate labyrinth where he was on the point of
losing his honor and his soul. In a word, all in the inn were
contented and happy at the fortunate way in which those
desperate difficulties had been solved. The curate, who was a
man of sound sense, settled every matter satisfactorily and
congratulated each one upon his good fortune; but the most
jubilant person of all was the landlady, because Cardenio
and the curate had promised to pay for all the damage done
by Don Quixote.

Only Sancho, as we said before, was downcast, sorrowful,
and miserable, and so, he went with a melancholy face to his
master, who was then just awaking, and said: "Sir Rueful
Figure, you may sleep away till kingdom come without both-
ering to kill any giant or restore the princess to her country,
for all that is done and finished with."

"I can believe that," answered Don Quixote, "for I have
had the most terrific battle with the giant that ever I had
all the days of my life; but with one backstroke, swish, I
tumbled his head to the ground, and his blood gushed forth

in such profusion that it ran in streams along the earth, just like water."

"Like red wine, you might have said, sir," replied Sancho. "I want to tell you, your worship, if you don't know it already, that your dead giant is no other than a slashed wineskin, that the blood is a dozen gallons of red wine that were contained in its belly, and that the cutoff head is the whore that bore me, may the Devil roast it all."

"What are you saying, you mad fool?" answered Don Quixote. "Are you in your senses?"

"Please get up, sir," said Sancho, "and you'll soon see what a fine day's work you've done and what we'll have to pay; you'll see the queen transmogrified into a private lady called Dorotea, and many other things that will flabbergast you."

"I would marvel at nothing," replied Don Quixote. "If you remember rightly, on the last occasion we were here I told you that all that happened in this place was due to enchantment. It would be no wonder if the same were true now."

"I would believe every word," answered Sancho, "if my tossing in the blanket had been of that kind, but it was only too real and true; I saw the innkeeper, who's here this day, holding the end of the blanket and tossing me up to the sky, joking all the while with as much mirth as muscle. When it comes to knowing people, I'm of the opinion, though I may be a simple poor sinner, that there's precious little enchantment but a power of bruising and bad luck."

"All right," said Don Quixote, "God will remedy it. Come, give me my clothes; I want to see those transformations you speak of."

Sancho gave him his clothes, and while he was dressing, the curate told Don Fernando and the others of Don Quixote's mad pranks and of the trick they had used to get him out of Peña Pobre, where he imagined he was exiled through his lady's disdain. The curate also told them that since the good fortune of Lady Dorotea prevented them from continuing with their scheme, it was necessary to invent some other way of taking him home to his village. Cardenio offered to carry on what they had begun and said that Luscinda would act the part of Dorotea.

"No," cried Don Fernando, "it must not be so. I wish Dorotea herself to carry out her plan, and provided the worthy knight's home is not too far from here, I shall be very pleased to help in his cure."

"It is no more than two days' journey," said the curate.

"Even if it were more," replied Don Fernando, "I would be happy to travel there to accomplish so good a work."

At this moment Don Quixote sallied forth, clad in all his accouterments, with Mambrino's helmet, which was dented, on his head, his buckler on his arm, and leaning on his sapling, or lance. Don Fernando and his companions were spellbound by the knight's extraordinary appearance, for they saw his shriveled, yellow face, half a league long, and noticed the contrast between his arms and his grave courtly behavior, and they kept silence to hear what he would say. The knight, gazing fixedly at the fair Dorotea, with great gravity and calmness spoke as follows: "I am informed, beautiful lady, by this my squire, that thy grandeur has been annihilated and thy condition destroyed, for instead of being a queen and a mighty princess, thou art now become a private damsel. If this has been done by command of the necromancer-king, thy father, because he was afraid I could not give thee the necessary help, I say that he has not known, nor does he know, the half of his own art, and he has never understood the histories of chivalry. If he had read and studied them with as much attention and detail as I have, he would have found at every step that many knights of less fame than myself have accomplished much more difficult exploits than this one. Truly it is not a mighty deed to slay a paltry giant, no matter how arrogant he may be; why, not so many hours ago, I came to grips with him and— I will be silent, lest they may tell me that I lie. But time, which reveals all things, will tell all when we least expect."

"You came to grips with two wineskins, not with a giant," cried the landlord.

Don Fernando, however, told him to be silent and not to interrupt Don Quixote, who continued his speech thus: "In time, I say, noble and disinherited lady, if for the reason I have mentioned thy father has made this transformation in thee, do not trouble thyself, for there is no peril upon earth so great but my sword shall cut open a way through it, and by throwing thy enemy's head to the ground I shall set thy crown upon thine own head within a few days."

Don Quixote said no more and waited for the princess to

reply. She, knowing Don Fernando's wish that she should continue their plan of deception until Don Quixote had been led home to his village, answered gravely and pleasantly: "Whoever told you, valiant Knight of the Rueful Figure, that I had been altered and transformed did not speak truly, for I am the same today as yesterday. It is true that certain fortunate incidents have made some change in me, for they have given me my heart's desire; yet, for all that I have not ceased to be what I was before, and I still am resolved to avail myself of the aid of your doughty and invincible arm. Therefore, my good lord, restore to my father his honor and consider him wise and prudent, for by his magic he has found me so sure a remedy for all my misfortunes. For I am convinced, sir, that had it not been for you, I should never have attained the happiness I now enjoy. Most of these gentlemen here present will bear witness to the truth of my words. All that remains now is that tomorrow morning we set out on our journey, for today we shall not be able to travel far. As for the happy issue I expect, I put my trust in God and your invincible spirit."

Thus spoke the wise Dorotea, and Don Quixote, having heard her, turned to Sancho in great indignation, saying: "I tell you, Sancho, that you are the greatest rapscallion in all Spain. Tell me, you thieving gadabout, did you not say just now that this princess was turned into a damsel named Dorotea? And that the head I believed I had cut off a giant was the whore who pupped you, along with other follies that threw me into the greatest confusion I have ever known in all the days of my life? I swear" (he looked up to Heaven and gritted his teeth) "I have a mind to wreak such havoc upon you as will put some sense into the brains of all the lying knights-errant's squires there ever shall be in the world."

"I beg you, master, calm yourself," answered Sancho, "for I may well have been deceived about the changing of Princess Micomicona. But as regards the giant's head, or at least the ripping of the wineskins and the blood being red wine, I swear to almighty God I'm not deceived. Why, the skins are lying there slashed at the head of your bed, and the red wine has made a lake of the chamber. If you don't believe me, you'll see it when the eggs are fried, I mean, when his worship, the landlord, asks you for damages. As for the rest, I'm mighty glad the queen is as she was, for I'm as keen on my share as any neighbor's son would be."

"I now say, Sancho," replied Don Quixote, "you are a blockhead, but pardon me. We have had enough of this."

"Enough indeed," said Don Fernando, "and let no more be said. Since my lady, the princess, says she will go away tomorrow, and as it is too late to depart today, let us spend this night in pleasant conversation. Tomorrow we will all bear company to Don Quixote, for we wish to witness the valiant and amazing exploits that he is to perform in the course of this great adventure."

"It is I who shall serve you and bear you company," replied Don Quixote, "and I am very grateful for the favor you have done me and the good opinion you have of me, which I shall try to justify, or it shall cost me my life, and even more, if that were possible."

Many compliments and offers of service passed between Don Quixote and Don Fernando, but they were all silenced by a traveler who at that moment entered the inn. By his dress he appeared to be a Christian newly arrived from the land of the Moors. He wore a short blue-cloth tunic with half sleeves and no collar, his breeches were of blue linen, and he wore a cape of the same color. He had long boots, date-brown, and a Moorish scimitar slung on a strap across his breast. Behind him on an ass came a woman dressed in Moorish fashion, with her face covered and a veil on her head; she was wearing a little cap of gold brocade and was swathed in a cloak that enveloped her from her shoulder to her feet. The man was of a robust and comely figure, a little above forty years of age, somewhat swarthy of complexion, with long moustaches and a very well-trimmed beard. It was clear, in fact, from his appearance that if he had been well dressed, he would have passed for a person of birth and position.

On entering, he asked for a room and seemed to be vexed when they told him there was none in the inn; then, going up to his companion, who seemed from her dress to be Moorish, he lifted her down. Luscinda, Dorotea, the landlady, her daughter, and Maritornes, attracted by the novelty of the dress, which they had never seen before, gathered around the Moorish lady; and Dorotea, who was always gracious, courteous, and ready-witted, seeing that she and her escort were disappointed because there was no room available, said to her: "Do not be worried, my lady, because of the lack of accomodation here, for it is customary in inns not to have any, but all the same, if you would care to lodge with us" (pointing to Luscinda) "you will find it more comfortable here than in other places that you have stayed in on your journey."

The veiled lady made no answer; she simply rose from her seat, and crossing her hands on her breast and bowing her head, she bent her body from the waist in token of thanks. From her silence they concluded that she must surely be a Moor and that she did not know the Christian tongue. Presently, the captive, who up to then had been busy with other things, drew near, and seeing that they were all grouped around his companion and that she remained dumb to all their speeches, he said: "Ladies, this damsel scarcely understands my language and only speaks the tongue of her own country; that is why she has not replied to your questions."

"The only thing we have asked her," answered Luscinda, "is whether she will accept our company for tonight and share our sleeping quarters, where she shall have as much comfort as the accomodations will allow, an offer given with all the kindness and goodwill that we are bound to give all strangers, and especially when it is a woman who is in need."

"On her behalf and mine," he answered, "I kiss your hands, my lady, and appreciate your offer as highly as it deserves, for on such an occasion as the present and from such persons as your appearance shows, it is certainly a great favor."

"Tell me, sir," said Dorotea, "is this lady a Christian or a Moor? Her dress and her silence make us think that she is what we hope she is not."

"Moorish she is in body and dress, but in her soul she is a very devout Christian, for she is longing to become one."

"Then, she is not baptized?" inquired Luscinda.

"There has been no opportunity," he replied, "since we left Algiers, her country and her home, and up to now, she has not been in such instant peril of death as to be obliged to receive baptism without being first instructed in all the ceremonies Our Holy Mother the Church requires. But, please God that she soon be baptized with the formalities due to her rank, which is greater than her dress or mine shows."

This answer made all those who were listening curious to know who the Moorish lady and gentleman were. But no one cared to ask just then, for at that time of night it was better to help them get some rest than to ask questions about their lives. Dorotea took the Moorish lady by the hand, made her sit down beside her, and asked her to take off her veil. But the stranger looked toward her escort as if to ask him what they were saying and what she should do. He told her in Arabic that they were asking her to take off her veil, which she did, revealing a face so lovely that Dorotea thought her more beautiful than Luscinda, and Luscinda judged her lovelier than Dorotea, while the others were of the opinion that if any woman was the equal of those two in looks, it was the Moorish lady, and some of them even considered that in certain ways she was the loveliest of the three. And as it is beauty's privilege to win over all hearts and attract all minds, everyone yielded instantly to the desire of waiting on the lovely Moor.

Don Fernando asked her escort for her name, and he answered that it was Lela Zoraida, but when she heard his answer, understanding what the Christian had asked, she interrupted hastily and charmingly, though in some confusion: "No, no, Zoraida; María, María," making them understand that her name was not Zoraida but María.

Her words and the feeling with which she spoke brought tears to the eyes of some of her hearers, especially the women, who were naturally tender-hearted. Luscinda embraced her affectionately and said: "Yes, yes, María, María."

And the Moorish lady replied: "Yes, yes, María—Zoraida macange, that is to say, not Zoraida at all."

Meanwhile, night had fallen and under orders of Don Fernando's companions the innkeeper had striven to provide the best supper he could. So, when the hour arrived, they all sat down together at a long table such as one finds in a refectory, for there was not a round or square one in the inn. They gave the head and principal seat to Don Quixote, though he tried to refuse it, but when he had taken it, he insisted that the Lady Micomicona should sit by his side, for he was her champion. Then Luscinda and Zoraida sat down; opposite them sat Cardenio and Don Fernando, while the curate and the barber sat next to the ladies. And they all enjoyed a pleasant supper. Don Quixote added to their entertainment, for he now felt the same urge that had filled him with eloquence at the goatherds' supper in the Sierra Morena, and so, instead of eating, he addressed them as follows: "Truly, gentlemen, if we consider well, great and

unheard-of sights are witnessed by those who profess the
order of knight-errantry. What man living today who should
enter the gate of this castle and see us seated here would
judge and believe us to be what we are? Who would say that
this lady by my side is the great queen we all know her to
be and that I am that Knight of the Rueful Figure so celebrated abroad by the mouth of Fame? There is no doubt
that this art and profession surpasses all that men have ever
invented; it is all the more deserving of esteem as it is subjected to more dangers. Away with those who say that letters
win more fame than arms! Whoever they may be, I will tell
them they do not know what they are saying. The reason
that they generally give, and on which they rely, is that
the labors of the mind exceed those of the body and that
arms are exercised by the body alone, as though it were the
business of porters alone, requiring mere physical strength,
as though the profession of arms did not demand acts
of courage that call for a high intelligence, and as though
the mental powers of the warrior, who has to command an
army or defend a besieged city, were not called into play as
well as those of his body. Let it be seen whether bodily
strength will enable him to guess the designs and stratagems
of the enemy, to solve his problems, to overcome difficulties,
and to ward off the dangers that threaten. No, these are all
operations of the understanding in which the body has no
share. Seeing that arms require as much intelligence as letters,
consider which of the two minds is exerted most, the
scholar's or the warrior's. This will be determined by the
ultimate end and goal to which each directs his energies, for
the intentions most to be esteemed are those that have for
object the noblest end. The aim and goal of letters—I am not
now speaking of divine letters, whose sole aim is to guide
and elevate the soul of man to Heaven, for with that sublime end none can be compared—I speak of human letters,
whose end is to regulate distributive justice, to give every
man his due, to make good laws, and to enforce them
strictly: an end most certainly generous, exalted, and worthy
of high praise, but not so glorious as the aim of arms, which
is peace, the greatest blessing that man can enjoy in this
life. For the first good news that the world ever received
was brought by the angels on the night that was our day
when they sang in the skies: 'Glory be to God on High and
peace on earth to men of goodwill'; the salutation that the

blessed Master of Heaven and earth taught his disciples to say when they entered any house was 'Peace be to this house'; and many times He said to them: 'My peace I give unto you, My peace I leave you, peace be with you'—a precious legacy indeed, given and bequeathed by such a hand, jewel without which neither in Heaven nor on earth can there be any happiness. This peace is the true end of war, and by war and arms I mean the same thing. If we admit this truth, that the end of war is peace, and that in this it excels the end of letters, let us consider the physical toils of the scholar and of the warrior and see which are the greater."

Don Quixote uttered his discourse in such a rational manner that none who heard him could take him for a madman. On the contrary, as most of them were gentlemen who were connected with the profession of arms, they listened to him with great pleasure as he continued saying: "I say that the hardships of the student are, first of all, poverty (not that all are poor, but I wish to put their case as strongly as possible), and when I have said that he endures poverty, no more needs be said of his wretchedness, for he who is poor lacks every comfort in life. He suffers poverty in various ways: in hunger, in cold, in nakedness, and sometimes in a combination of all. Nevertheless, he does get something to eat, even though it may be later than at the accustomed hour, either from the scraps off the rich man's table or from the soupe at the convent gate, that last miserable resource, which the students call among themselves 'Going as a souper.' Nor do they fail to find some neighbor's brazier or ingle, which, if it does not warm them, at least diminishes the extreme cold; and so, they sleep tolerably well at night under cover. I will not descend to other more trivial details, such as the want of shirts, the lack of spare shoes, the scanty and threadbare clothing, the greedy guzzling they indulge in when good luck sets a banquet before them. This is the hard and rugged path they tread, stumbling here, then rising only to fall again over there, until they reach the eminence they covet. And after having escaped these Scyllas and Charybdises as though wafted onward by the wings of favorable Fortune, we have seen them rule and govern the world from an armchair, their hunger converted into feasting, their cold into refreshment, their nakedness into rich raiment, and their sleep on a mat to repose on fine linen and damask—the just reward for their virtuous efforts. But their hardships, when compared with those of the warrior, fall far short of them as I shall now show you."

CHAPTER XXXVIII

Of Don Quixote's curious discourse on arms and letters

Don Quixote, pursuing his discourse, said: "Since we began in the student's case by considering his poverty and its circumstances, let us see whether the soldier is any richer. We shall find that there is no one poorer in poverty itself, for he depends on his wretched pay, which comes late or never, or on what he grabs with his own hands at the imminent risk of his life and his conscience. Sometimes his nakedness is such that his slashed doublet serves him both for full dress and shirt; and in the midst of winter, in the open country, he has nothing to warm him against the rigors of the heavens but the breath from his mouth, which, as it issues from an empty place, must needs come forth cold against the law of nature. But let him wait till night comes, when he hopes to restore himself from those discomforts in the bed that awaits him. It will only be his fault if that bed prove too narrow, for he may measure out on the ground as many feet as he pleases and may toss himself thereon at will without fear of rumpling the sheets. And now, suppose the day and hour arrives for him to receive his degree, suppose the day of battle has come; then, they will put upon his head a tasseled doctor's cap [1] made of lint to heal some wound from a bullet that perhaps has passed through his temples or left him maimed of an arm or leg. And if this should not happen and Heaven in its mercy keep him safe and sound, he

---

[1] The tassel or *borla*, which was sewn on to the university cap, was the sign of a doctor's degree.

will probably remain as poor as ever. If he is to secure any promotion at all, he will need another and yet another engagement, and he must come off victorious in every one of them if he is to better himself; and such miracles are rare indeed.

"Now tell me, gentlemen, if you have ever considered it, how much fewer are those who have been rewarded by war then those who have perished in it? Without doubt you must answer that there is no comparison between them, for the dead are countless, whereas those who survive to win the rewards may be counted in numbers less than a thousand. The opposite is true of scholars, for by their salaries (I will not mention their perquisites) they have enough to provide for their needs; therefore, the soldier's reward is less though his toil is greater. It may be said in reply to this that it is easier to reward two thousand scholars than thirty thousand soldiers, for the former are rewarded by giving them employments that must necessarily be given to men of their profession, whereas the latter cannot be recompensed except from the property of the master whom they serve; and this impossibility adds greater weight to my argument, which is very difficult to decide. Let us take up again the question of the preeminence of arms over letters, which has never been settled, for the partisans of each can bring cogent arguments in support of their own side.

"It is said in favor of letters that arms could not subsist without them, for war also has its laws and is subject to them, and laws fall within the province of letters and men of letters. To this the partisans of arms reply that laws could not be maintained without them, for by arms, states are defended, kingdoms are preserved, cities are protected, roads are made safe, and seas cleared of pirates. Indeed, without arms, kingdoms, monarchies, cities, seaways, and landways would be subject to the ruin and confusion that war brings with it as long as it lasts and has license to use its privileges and powers. Besides, it is a well-established maxim that what costs most is, and ought to be, valued most. Now, to achieve eminence in letters costs a man time, vigils, hunger, nakedness, dizziness in the head, indigestion, and other inconveniences that I have already mentioned. But to arrive by grades to be a good soldier costs a man all that it costs the student, only in so much greater degree that there is no comparison between them, for at every step he is in danger of losing his life. What fear or poverty can threaten the student compared to that which faces a soldier who, finding himself besieged and stationed as sentry in the ravelin or cavalier of some beleaguered fortress, sees that the enemy is mining toward the place where he stands, yet he must not stir from there on any pretext or shun the danger that threatens him from so near? All that he can do is to give notice to his captain of what is happening, hoping that he may remedy it by some countermine, but he must quietly stand his ground in fear and momentary expectation of suddenly flying up to the clouds without wings and dashing down to the abyss against his will. And if this be thought a small danger, let us see if it is equaled or surpassed by the clash between two galleys, prow to prow, in mid ocean. Both of them locked and grappled together leave the soldier no more space than two feet of plank at the beak to stand upon; but, though he sees in front of him as many ministers of death threatening him as there are pieces of artillery pointing at him from the opposite ship, not farther than a lance's length from his body, and though he sees that a slip of his foot would land him in Neptune's bottomless gulf, nevertheless, with undaunted heart, inspired by the honor that spurs him on, he allows himself to be the mark for all their fire and endeavors to force his way by that narrow path into the enemy's vessel.[2] And what is most to be admired is that scarcely has one fallen, never to rise again until the end of the world, when another takes his place; and if he, too, drops into the sea, which lies in wait like an enemy, another and another succeeds without any time elapsing between their deaths. In all the perils of war there is no greater courage and boldness than this. Blessed were those ages that were without the dreadful fury of those diabolical engines of artillery, whose inventor, I truly believe, is now receiving in hell the reward for his devilish invention, by means of which a base and cowardly hand may deprive the most valiant knight of life. While such a knight fights with all the bravery and ardor that enkindle gallant hearts, without his knowing how or whence there comes a random bullet (discharged by one who

[2] This passage describing a soldier's experiences in seafighting is probably taken from Cervantes' own memory of that famous day of Lepanto in 1571, when he bore himself so gallantly on the most exposed part of the deck of the Spanish galleon *La Marquesa*.

perhaps ran away in terror at the flash of his own accursed machine) that cuts short and ends in an instant the life of one who deserved to live for centuries to come. When I consider this, I have a mind to say that I am grieved in my soul at having undertaken this profession of knight-errantry in so detestable an age as this we live in. For although no peril can daunt me, still it troubles me to think that powder and lead may deprive me of the chance of making myself famous and renowned for the strength of my arm and the edge of my sword over all the known earth. But Heaven's will be done! I shall win all the greater fame if I am successful in my quest, for the dangers to which I expose myself are greater than those that did beset the knights of past ages."

Don Quixote delivered this long harangue while the rest were eating their supper, and he forgot to raise a morsel to his mouth, though Sancho Panza more than once told him to eat, saying that afterward there would be time to talk as much as he pleased. Those who had listened to him felt sorry that a man who seemed to possess so good an understanding and such power of reason should lose them so entirely when dealing with his sinister and accursed chivalry. The curate told him that he was quite right in all he had said in favor of arms and that he himself, although a scholar and a graduate, was of the same opinion.

They then ended their supper, the tablecloths were removed, and while the hostess, her daughter, and Maritornes were tidying up Don Quixote of La Mancha's attic, where they arranged that the ladies should pass the night by themselves, Don Fernando asked the captive to tell them his life's story, for he was certain that it must be rare and entertaining, to judge by his having arrived in Zoraida's company. The captive replied that he would most willingly oblige, though he feared that his story would not entertain them as much as he would wish, but that he would tell it, such as it was, rather than disappoint them. The priest and all the others thanked him and pressed him to begin, and when he found them all so eager, he declared that such entreaties were unnecessary when a simple request sufficed. "So let your worships," said he, "give me their attention, and they will hear a true story, which I doubt could be equaled by the most fantastic fable composed by a master of the art of fiction." At these words they all sat down in perfect silence, and when he saw that they were quiet and expectant, he began to speak as follows, in a pleasant tone of voice:

CHAPTER XXXIX

In which the captive tells the story of his life and adventures

"My family originated in a village in the mountains of León, where Nature was kinder to them than Fortune, although in those poor villages my father was reputed to be a rich man, and indeed, he would have been if he had been as skillful in preserving his estate as he was in spending it. This tendency of his to be lavish and wasteful came from his having been a soldier in the years of his youth, for the soldier's profession is a school in which the niggard learns to be liberal and the liberal prodigal, for if there are any soldiers who are misers, they are, like monsters, rarely seen. My father passed the bounds of liberality and verged on those of prodigality, a trait that is by no means profitable to a married man with children who will inherit his name and rank. My father had three, all sons and all of an age to choose their way of life. Realizing, then, that he was unable, as he said, to bridle his nature, he resolved to deprive himself of the cause and means that made him a prodigal and a spendthrift, that is to say, to give up his estate, without which Alexander himself would have seemed a miser. One day, therefore, calling all three of us into a room alone, he addressed us more or less as follows: 'My sons, to impress upon you that I love you, it is enough to say that you are my sons, and to convince you that I do not love you, it is enough to say that I am incapable of controlling myself in order to preserve your fortune. But that you may in the future realize that I love you like a father and have no wish to ruin you like a stepfather, I intend to do something for you that I have been pondering over for a long time and that I have decided on after much consideration. You are now of an age

393

to take up a calling, or at least to choose some profession that
will bring you honor and profit in your riper years. My plan
is to divide my estate into four parts; three I shall bestow
upon you in equal shares, and the fourth I shall retain for
myself to live upon for as long as Heaven is pleased to preserve my life. But I want each one of you, once you have received your share of the estate, to follow one of the paths
that I shall indicate. There is a proverb in this Spain of ours
—a very true one I believe, as all of them are, for they are
but maxims gathered from long and wise experience. The
one I have in mind is: "The Church, the sea, or the king's
palace," which means that if you want to be powerful and
wealthy, follow the Church, or go to sea and become a merchant, or take service with kings in their palaces. For it is
said: "Better the king's crumb than the lord's plum." By
this I mean to express a wish that one of you should pursue
learning, another commerce, and the third should serve the
king in his wars, for it is difficult to obtain a place in his
household, and although war does not bring much wealth, it
gradually brings great fame and renown. Within a week I
shall give you each your share of the money in cash, as you
will see. Tell me if you are willing to follow my counsel and
take the advice I have proposed.'

"He called on me, the eldest, to answer, and after urging
him not to divest himself of his fortune, but to spend it as
freely as he pleased, for we were young men able to earn our
living, I finally said that I would comply with his wishes and
that my choice was to follow the profession of arms, thereby
serving God and the king. The second brother, after making
the same proposal, elected to go to the Indies and invest his
portion in merchandise. The youngest, and I think the wisest of us, said that he wanted to follow the Church or to
finish his studies at Salamanca.

"As soon as we had come to an understanding and had
selected our professions, my father embraced us all, and in
the short time he had mentioned, he carried out what he had
promised. When he had given each his share, which as well
as I can remember was three thousand ducats apiece in cash
(for an uncle of ours bought the estate and paid for it in
ready money so that it would stay in the family), we all three
on that same day said farewell to our good father. But as it
seemed to me inhuman to leave so old a man with such
scanty means of support, I induce him to take two of my

three thousand ducats, for the remainder would be enough
to provide me with everything a soldier needed. My two
brothers, moved by my example, gave him each a thousand
ducats, so that there was left for my father four thousand
ducats in cash, besides three thousand, the value of his
portion of the estate, which he was unwilling to sell and had
kept in land. At last, as I said, we took leave of him and of
the uncle I have mentioned, not without sorrow and tears on
both sides. They charged us to let them know, whenever we
had a chance to do so, how we fared, whether well or ill. We
promised to do so, and when he had embraced us and given
us his blessing, one set out for Salamanca, the other for
Seville, and I for Alicante, where I heard that there was a
Genoese ship taking in a cargo of wool for Genoa.

"It is now some twenty-two years since I left my father's
home, and in all that time I have heard no news whatever of
him or my brothers, although I have written several letters.
What my own adventures were during that period I shall
now relate briefly. I embarked at Alicante and reached
Genoa after a prosperous voyage. I proceeded, then, to
Milan, where I provided myself with arms and a military
uniform. From there I decided to go and take service in
Piedmont, but when I was already on the road to Alessandria
della Paglia, I received news that the great Duke of Alba
was marching into Flanders. So, I changed my plans, joined
him, served under him in the campaigns he made, was present
at the deaths of counts d'Egmont and Horn. I rose to be an
ensign under a famous captain from Guadalajara, Diego de
Urbina by name.[1] After I had been some time in Flanders,
news came out of the league that His Holiness Pope Pius V,
of blessed memory, had made with Venice and Spain against
the common enemy, the Turk, who just then with his fleet
had taken the famous island of Cyprus, which had been
subject to the Venetians, an unfortunate and lamentable
loss. It was known as a fact that the Most Serene Don Juan
of Austria, natural brother of our good king, Don Felipe, was
to be commander in chief of the allied forces, and there were
rumors of the great preparations that were being made. All
this aroused in me a great longing to take part in the coming

[1] He was captain of the company in the regiment of Diego de
Moncada in which Cervantes first served.

campaign, and though I had hopes and almost certain
prospects of being promoted to a captaincy as soon as the
occasion offered, I chose to forsake everything and go, as I
did, to Italy. It was my good fortune that Don Juan had
just arrived in Genoa on his way to Naples to join the
Venetian fleet, as he afterward did at Messina. Let me say,
in short, that I took part in that glorious expedition, promoted by then to be a captain of infantry, to which honorable post my good luck rather than my merits raised me.

"On that day, so fortunate for Christendom, for on it the
world and all the nations were disabused of the error that the
Turks were invincible on sea, on that day, on which Ottoman
arrogance and pride were broken forever, among all the
fortunate men—for the Christians who died there were more
fortunate than those who survived victorious—I alone was
unlucky, for instead of some naval crown, which I might
have expected, had it been in Roman times, I found myself
on the night that followed that famous day with fetters on
my feet and handcuffs on my hands. This is what took
place: Aluch Ali, king of Algiers, a daring and successful
corsair, had attacked and beaten the Maltese flagship, and
only three knights were left alive in her, and those three
badly wounded. Then, Juan Andrea's flagship, aboard which
I was with my company, came to the rescue, and doing what
was my duty in the circumstances, I leaped on board the
enemy's galley, which then detached itself from our attacking
ship, with the result that my men were prevented from following me, and so I found myself alone in the midst of my
enemies, unable to resist because they were in such numbers. In short, I was taken, covered with wounds. Now all
you gentlemen must have heard how Aluch Ali escaped with
his entire squadron; I remained a prisoner in his power, being
the only one sad man among so many who were free, for
there were fifteen thousand Christians, all at the oar in the
Turkish fleet, who regained their long coveted liberty on
that day. They carried me to Constantinople, where the
Grand Turk, Selim, made my master commander of the sea,
because he did his duty in that battle and carried off as evidence of his bravery the standard of the Order of Malta.
The following year, which was seventy-two, I found myself
at Navarino, rowing in the leading galley with the three lanterns,[2] and I saw and noted how the opportunity of cap-

---

[2] The distinguishing mark of the admiral's galley.

turing the entire Turkish fleet in that harbor was lost, for all
the marines and janissaries aboard were so certain they
would be attacked in the port itself that they had their kits
and their *passamaques*, which are their shoes, ready to flee
at once by land without waiting to be attacked, so great was
their fear of our fleet. But Heaven ordered it otherwise, not
for any fault or neglect of the general who commanded our
side, but for the sins of Christendom and because it is God's
will that there shall always be some scourge to chastise us.
In the end Aluch Ali took refuge at Modon, an island close
to Navarino, and throwing his men onshore, he fortified the
mouth of the harbor and lay quiet until Don Juan had retired. In this expedition the galley called *The Prize* was taken.
Her captain was a son of the famous pirate Barbarossa. It
was taken by the flagship of Naples, *The She-Wolf*, under
the command of the thunderbolt of war and father to his
soldiers, that successful and unbeaten captain Don Alvaro de
Bazán, marquess of Santa Cruz. I cannot help telling you
what took place at the capture of *The Prize*. The son of
Barbarossa was so cruel and treated his slaves so badly that
when those who were at the oars saw the galley *The She-Wolf*
bearing down upon them and about to board, they at once
dropped their oars and seized their captain, who was on the
stantrel shouting to them to row lustily, and passing him from
bench to bench, from the poop to the prow, they so bit him
that he had proceeded but little past the mast before his soul
had proceeded to hell, so great, as I said, was the cruelty
with which he treated them and so bitter the hatred they
bore him.

"We returned to Constantinople, and the following year,
which was seventy-three, it became known that Don Juan had
seized Tunis and had taken the kingdom from the Turks and
had placed Muley Hamet in possession, putting an end to
the hopes that Muley Hamida, the cruelest and bravest Moor
in the world, cherished of recovering the throne. The Grand
Turk took the loss very much to heart, and with the cunning
that is natural to all his race, he made peace with the
Venetians (who were much more eager for it than he was)
and the following year, seventy-four, he attacked the Goleta
and the fort that Don Juan had left half-built near Tunis.
While all these events were taking place, I was toiling and
moiling at the oar without any hope of liberty—at least I

had no hope of obtaining it by ransom, for I was determined not to send news of my misfortunes to my father.

"In the end the Goleta fell, the fort was lost. Attacking these strongholds were seventy-five thousand regular Turkish soldiers and more than four hundred thousand Moors and Arabs from all parts of Africa. In their train they carried such a quantity of munitions and materials of war and so many sappers that using their hands they might have buried both the Goleta and the fort with earth. The Goleta, which had been considered impregnable hitherto, was the first to fall. It was not through any fault of its garrison, for they did all they could and should have done, but because of the ease with which, as experience showed, entrenchments could be built up in that sandy desert, for although water could be found at the depth of sixteen inches, the Turks found none at five feet; and so, with many sacks of sand they raised their works high enough to command the walls of the fortress and fired from above so that no one was able to make a stand or put up a defense there.

"Most people agreed that our men should not have shut themselves in the Goleta but should have opposed the disembarkation in the open field. They who say this speak as armchair critics and with little experience of such matters. For as there were hardly seven thousand soldiers in the Goleta and the fort together, how could so small a number, however resolute, sally out and hold their own against such a host of the enemy? And how is it possible to avoid losing a fort that is not relieved, above all when surrounded by enemies so numerous, so determined, and so familiar with the territory? But many thought, and I thought so too, that it was a special favor and dispensation Heaven showed to Spain in permitting the destruction of that breeding place and cloak of iniquities, that glutton, sponge, and sink of the infinite amounts of money wasted there fruitlessly to no other purpose save to preserve the memory of its capture by the invincible Charles V, as if those wretched stones were needed to make his name eternal, as it is and ever shall be.

"The fort also fell, but the Turks had to win it little by little, for the soldiers who defended it fought so gallantly and stubbornly that the number of the enemy killed in twenty-two general assaults exceeded twenty-five thousand. Of the three hundred who were alive, not one was taken unwounded, a clear and manifest proof of their mettle and valor and of how sturdily they had defended themselves and held their position.

"A small fort or tower in the middle of a lake under the command of Don Juan Zanoguera, a gentleman of Valencia and a famous soldier, capitulated on terms. They captured Don Pedro Puertocarrero, commandant of the Goleta, who had done all in his power to defend the fortress and felt so much the loss of it that he died of grief on the way to Constantinople, where they were taking him as a prisoner. They also captured the commander of the fort, Gabriel Cervellón by name, a Milanese gentleman, a great engineer, and a most courageous soldier. In those two fortresses perished many persons of note, among whom was Pagano Doria, Knight of the Order of St. John, a man of generous disposition as was shown by his extreme generosity to his brother, the famous Juan Andrea Doria; what made his death the more sad was that he was slain by some Arabs to whom he entrusted himself when he saw that the fort was lost. They had offered to take him, disguised as a Moor, to Tabarca, a small seaport or station on that coast held by the Genoese who were engaged in coral-fishing. Those Arabs cut off his head and carried it to the commander of the Turkish fleet, who proved on them the truth of our Spanish proverb that says: 'Though treason pleases, the traitor displeases,' for it is said that he ordered those who brought him the present to be hanged for not having brought him alive.

"Among the Christians captured in the fort was one named Pedro de Aguilar, a native of some place in Andalusia. He had been an ensign in the fort, a soldier of great distinction and intelligence and particularly gifted in what is called poetry. I single him out because his destiny brought him to my galley and to my bench and made him slave to the same master, and before we left the port, this gentleman composed two sonnets by way of epitaphs, one on the Goleta and the other on the fort. I really must repeat them, for I know them by heart and I think they will give you pleasure rather than pain."

The moment the captive named Don Pedro de Aguilar, Don Fernando looked at his companions and they all three smiled; when he came to speak of the sonnets, one of them said: "Before your worship proceeds I wish he would tell me what became of this Don Pedro de Aguilar he spoke of."

"All I know," answered the captive, "is that after he had been two years in Constantinople, he escaped, disguised as an

Albanian, with a Greek spy. I do not know whether he got his liberty, but I suppose he did, for I saw that Greek a year later in Constantinople, though I could not ask him whether the escape had been successful."

"It was," replied the gentleman. "That Don Pedro is my brother, and he is at our house now, well, rich, married, and with three children."

"God be praised," said the captive, "for all the mercies He did him, for there is no joy on earth in my opinion that can compare with regaining one's lost liberty."

"What is more," added the gentleman, "I know the sonnets my brother wrote."

"Then recite them to us, sir," said the captive, "for you will be able to do it better than I."

"With pleasure," replied the gentleman. "I will first recite the one on the Goleta."

CHAPTER XL

In which the captive's story is continued

Sonnet

"Blest souls from this frail mortal husk set free,
  In guerdon of brave deeds beatified,
  Above this lowly earth of ours abide
  In Heaven's domes of immortality.
With glowing ardor and with ecstasy
  Your martial arts to battle you applied,
  And with your own blood and your foeman's dyed
  The sandy desert and the neighboring sea,
It was the ebbing life-blood first that failed,
  And wearied arms but stout hearts never quailed;
  Though vanquished yet you won the victor's crown.
Though tragic, still triumphant was your fall;
  For you who stood between the sword and wall
  There's glory in Heaven and on earth renown."

"That is the same way I learned it," said the captive.

"As for the one about the fort, if I remember correctly," said the gentleman, "it goes as follows:

SONNET

"Up from their barren battle-ridden sands,
  Where walls and battlements in ruin lie,
  Three thousand holy souls of soldiers fly
  Aloft to abodes of bliss in heavenly lands.
Against the fierce onslaught of countless foes
  Their peerless might of arm they showed in vain,

Though few and wearied they to the end were game,
Unflinching and unbeaten by their woes.
And this same barren earth hath ever been
The haunt of many tragic memories,
As well in our days as in days of yore;
But never yet to Heav'n she sent, I ween,
From her hard bosom purer souls than these,
Or braver bodies in her womb e'er bore."

The sonnets were not disliked, and the captive was delighted to hear the tidings they gave him of his comrade; so, continuing his tale, he went on to say: "After the surrender of the Goleta and the fort, the Turks gave orders for the dismantling of the Goleta. As for the fort, it was left in such a state that there was nothing left to level, and to do the work more quickly and easily, they mined it in three places, but nowhere could they blow up the part that seemed the least strong, namely, the old walls, whereas all that was standing of the new fortifications, the work of El Fratín, came to the ground with the greatest ease. Finally, the fleet returned to Constantinople, triumphant and victorious, and several months later my master Aluch Ali, otherwise Uchali Fartax, which in Turkish means 'the scabby renegade,' for that is what he was, died. Incidentally, it is customary among the Turks to name people by any defect, or by any good quality, they may possess; the reason for this is that there are among them only four surnames belonging to families that trace their descent to the Ottoman house, and the others, as I have said, take their names and surnames either from bodily blemishes or moral qualities. This scabby one had been at the oar as a slave of the Great Turk for fourteen years, and when over thirty-four years of age, his resentment at having been struck by a Turk while at the oar turned him renegade. He renounced his faith in order to be able to revenge himself; and such was his valor that without owing his advancement to the base ways and means by which most favorites of the Great Turk rise to power, he came to be king of Algiers, and afterwards general-on-sea, which is the third place of trust in the realm. He was a Calabrian by birth and a worthy man morally, and he treated his slaves with great humanity. He had three thousand of them, and after his death they were divided, as he directed in his will, between the Great Turk (who is heir of all who die and shares with the children of the deceased) and his renegades. I fell to the lot of a Venetian renegade who, when a cabin boy on board a ship, had been taken by Uchali and was so much beloved by him that he became one of his most favored youths. He came to be the most cruel renegade I have ever seen; his name was Hassan Agá,[1] and he grew to be very wealthy and became king of Algiers. I went there with him from Constantinople, rather glad to be so near Spain, not that I intended to write to anyone about my unhappy state, but because I wanted to see if Fortune would be kinder to me in Algiers than in Constantinople, from where I had attempted in a thousand ways to escape, but none found favor or fortune. In Algiers I intended to seek for other means of accomplishing what I so much desired, for I never abandoned the hope of obtaining my liberty. When in my plots and schemes and attempts the result did not come up to my expectations, I never gave way to despair, but at once I began to devise some new hope to support me, however faint or feeble it might be.[2]

"In this way I passed my life, shut up in a prison or house that the Turks call a bagnio, where they keep their Christian slaves, those of the king and those of private individuals and also those who are called the slaves of the *almacén*, that is to say, the slaves of the municipality, for they are employed in the public works of the city and in other services. These captives recover their liberty with great difficulty, for as they are held in common and have no particular master, there is no one with whom to bargain for their ransom, even if they have the money. To these bagnios, as I have said, private individuals of the town are in the habit of bringing their captives, especially when they are about to be ran-

[1] The history of Hassan Agá is also told in Diego de Haedo's *Topographia de Argel* (Valladolid, 1612). Diego de Haedo was archbishop of Palermo and captain general of the kingdom of Sicily in the latter years of Philip II; with the help of his nephew, Diego de Haedo took down day-by-day notes and records of Christian captives who came to his palace in Palermo. After the death of Philip, the nephew, who was made abbot of the Benedictine monastery of Frómista, incorporated his notes and those of his uncle in the Topography, which he finished in 1605. He was the first to establish Cervantes' birthplace at Alcalá de Henares.

[2] See also the two comedies of Cervantes, *The Algiers Affair* and *The Bagnios of Algiers*. In the latter play there are very nearly the same characters and adventures as we find in this tale.

somed, for there they can keep them in safety and at their ease until the money arrives. The king's captives that are to be ransomed do not go out to work with the rest of the gang, unless their ransom is delayed, in which case, to make them write for it more urgently, they force them to work and go for wood, which is no light labor.

"As it was known that I was a captain, I was held on ransom, and though I declared my scanty means and lack of wealth, nothing could dissuade them from adding me to the list of gentlemen and those waiting to be redeemed. They put a chain on me, more as a sign that I was to be ransomed than for safekeeping, and so, in that bagnio I spent my life with several other gentlemen and persons of quality, selected and held for ransom, and though hunger and scanty clothing vexed us at times—indeed almost always—nothing distressed us so much as hearing and seeing at every turn the unexampled and unheard-of cruelties my master inflicted upon the Christians. Every day he hanged a man, impaled another, cut off the ears of a third, and all with so little provocation or so entirely without any justification that even the Turks acknowledged that he did so for the sake of doing it and because he was murderously disposed toward the entire human race. The only one who fared at all well with him was a Spanish soldier, so-and-so de Saavedra by name, to whom he never gave a blow himself, or bade anyone else strike him, or even spoke a rough word to him, though the man did things that will live in the memory of the people there for many years to come. He did all these things to recover his lost liberty, and for the least of the many things he did, we all dreaded that he would be impaled, and he himself was in fear of it more than once. If time allowed I could describe some of the deeds done by that soldier that would fascinate and amaze you more than my own tale.[3]

[3] The most striking document extant referring to Cervantes' captivity in Algiers is the celebrated *Información*, which was drawn up officially at his own request by Pedro de Robirá, scrivener and notary apostolic, in the presence of Fray Juan Gil, our hero's liberator, before he would consent to leave on his homeward journey from captivity. The *Información* included evidence given by twelve witnesses of the behavior of Cervantes during captivity, of his great moral qualities and spiritual leadership. The document was signed and drawn up between the tenth and the twenty-second of October, 1580. It is the most precious document of all for those who would understand the biography of Cervantes

"To go on with my story, overlooking the courtyard of our prison were the windows of the house belonging to a wealthy Moor of high position. As one generally finds in Moorish houses, there were loopholes rather than windows, and these were covered with thick and close blinds. One day I happened to be on the terrace of our prison with three of my companions trying to kill time by seeing how far we could jump in our chains. We were all alone because all the other Christians had gone out to work. I chanced to raise my eyes, and all of a sudden I observed a cane with a handkerchief tied to the end of it emerging from one of those little closed windows I spoke of. The cane kept moving to and fro as if making signs to us to come and take it. We watched it, and one of those who were with me went and stood under the cane to see whether they would let it drop, but at once the cane was raised and moved from side to side as if those above meant to say *no* by a shake of the head. No sooner did the Christian move away than the cane was again lowered, making the same motions as before. Another of my companions went, and with him the same happened as with the first; when the third in his turn went forward, he had no more success than the first and second.

"Seeing this, I was determined to try my luck also, and no sooner did I stand under the cane than it was dropped and fell inside the bagnio at my feet. I hastened at once to untie the piece of cloth attached to it and perceived a knot in which were ten *zianies*, coins of pure gold used by the Moors, each worth ten of our reals. I need not tell you how my spirits rose at this windfall, but I wondered nonetheless how such good fortune should come upon us and upon me especially, for the refusal to drop the cane to anyone else was a clear sign that the favor was intended for me alone. I pocketed the money, broke the cane, returned to the terrace, and looking up, I observed a very white hand open and shut the window hastily. As from this we guessed that some woman living in that house had done us a kind deed, in token of our gratitude we made salaams in the Moorish fashion, bowing the head, bending the body, and crossing the

---

and his alter ego, Don Quixote of La Mancha. The power of Cervantes is also described by a fellow captive, Dr. Sosa, in the second of the dialogues printed by Padre Haedo in his *Topographia e Historia general de Argel*.

arm on the breast. Shortly afterward at the same window a small cross made of reeds was put out and immediately withdrawn. This sign made us believe that there must be a Christian slave in the house and that it was she who had done us this kindness, but the whiteness of her hand and the bracelets she wore dispelled this idea. Then we imagined that the hand must belong to some Christian renegade, one of those whom their masters often take for their lawful wives, and gladly, for they prefer them to the women of their own nation.

"In all our conjectures we were off the truth. From that day on, however, our sole occupation was to watch and stare at the window where the star of the cane, which had now become our polestar, had appeared. Over a fortnight passed before we saw any further sign of it. And although in that time we made every effort to ascertain who it was that lived in the house, nobody could tell us anything more than that he who lived there was a rich Moor of high position, Hadji Murad by name, former governor of Bata, one of their important posts. But when we least expected any further showers of *zianies* from that quarter, we saw the cane suddenly appear with another cloth tied in a larger knot to it, and this at a time when, as on the former occasion, the bagnio was deserted. We made the usual experiment, each of the three going before me, but only to me was the cane delivered; on my approach it was let fall. I untied the knot and found forty Spanish gold crowns and a paper written in Arabic, and at the end of the writing a large cross was drawn. I kissed the cross, pocketed the crowns, and returned to the terrace. We all made our salaams, the hand appeared at the window again, I made signs that I would read the letter, and then, the window was closed. We were all puzzled, though overjoyed, by what had taken place, and as not one of us understood a word of Arabic, our longing to know what was written in the paper was great, but greater was the difficulty of finding anyone to translate it for us. In the end I determined to confide in a renegade, a native of Murcia, who professed a very great friendship for me and had pledged himself never to reveal any secret of mine. It is, I must add, customary with some renegades, when they intend to return to the land of the Christians, to carry about them certificates from captives of standing, testifying, in whatever form they can, that such and such a renegade is a worthy man who has always shown kindness to Christians and is anxious to escape at the first opportunity that may present itself. Some obtain these testimonials with honest intentions. Others put them to a more casual and cunning use, for when they go to plunder in a Christian land, if they happen to be shipwrecked or taken captive, they produce their papers and say that such certificates explain the purpose of their journey, which was to settle in a Christian land, and that it had been with this intention that they had come on a raid with the Turks. In this way they hope to escape that first brunt and outburst of their captors and to make their peace with the Church before it does them any harm; then, when they see an opportunity, they return to Barbary to become what they were before. There are, however, others who procure these papers and make use of them honestly and remain on Christian soil.

"This friend of mine, then, was one of these renegades. He had certificates from all our companions in which we testified as strongly as we could in his favor; if the Moors had found those papers, they would have burned him alive. I knew that he understood Arabic very well and that he not only spoke it, but wrote it; however, before I revealed the whole matter to him, I asked him to read a paper that I had found by accident in a hole in my cell. The renegade opened the letter and examined it carefully for a long time, spelling it over and muttering between his teeth. I asked him if he understood it. He said that he did, perfectly, but that if I wanted him to give its meaning word by word, I must give him pen and ink that he might do it more accurately. We at once gave him what he required, and he set about translating it, bit by bit, saying when he had finished: 'All that is here in Spanish is what the Moorish paper contains, and you must bear in mind that when it says *Lela Marien,* it means Our Lady the Virgin Mary.'

"We read the paper and it ran as follows:

" 'When I was a child my father had a slave who taught me to pray the Christian prayers in my own language and who told me many things about *Lela Marien.* This Christian woman died, and I know that she did not go to the fire but to Allah, for I have seen her twice since and she told me to go to the land of the Christians to see *Lela Marien,* who had great love for me. I do not know how to go. I have seen many Christians from this window,

but none has seemed to me a gentleman but you. I am
young and beautiful and have plenty of money to take
with me. See if you can discover how we may go, and if
you succeed in doing this, you shall be my husband. But
if you refuse to marry me, it will not distress me, for
Lela Marien will find someone to marry me. I myself have
written this; take care to whom you give it to read;
trust no Moor, for they are all perfidious tricksters. I am
greatly troubled on this account and do not want you to
take anyone into your confidence because if my father
finds out, he will immediately throw me down a well and
cover me over with stones. I shall attach a thread to the
cane; tie the answer to it, and if you have no one to write
for you in Arabic, tell it to me by signs, for *Lela Marien*
will make me understand you. May she and Allah and
may this cross, which I often kiss as the captive bade me,
protect you.'

"Judge, gentlemen, whether we had reason for surprise
and joy at the contents of this letter. The renegade perceived that the paper had not been found by chance but
that it had been really addressed to one of us, and he
begged us that if what he suspected were the truth, we
should trust him and tell him all, for he would risk his life
for our freedom. Saying this, he took from his bosom a
metal crucifix and with many tears swore by the God the
image represented, in whom, though wicked and a sinner,
he truly and faithfully believed, to be loyal to us and to
keep secret whatever we chose to reveal to him. He declared prophetically that through the help of the lady who
had written that letter, he and all of us would regain our
liberty, and he himself would obtain what he so much desired, his restoration to Our Holy Mother the Church, from
which, through his own ignorance and sin, he had been
severed as a rotten limb. The renegade said this with so
many tears and such signs of repentance that we unanimously
agreed to tell him the truth of the matter, and so we gave
him a full account of all without hiding anything. We
pointed out to him the window from which the cane emerged,
and he resolved to ascertain who lived in it. We agreed
also that it would be advisable to answer the Moorish lady's
letter, and the renegade without a moment's delay took down
the words I dictated to him, which were exactly what I
shall repeat to you, for nothing of importance that took

place in this affair has escaped my memory, and never will as long as I live. This, then, was the answer I gave to the Moorish lady:

" 'The true Allah protect you, lady, and that blessed *Marien* who is the true mother of God and who has inspired your heart to go to the land of the Christians because she loves you. Pray to her that she may be pleased to teach you how you may put her commands into practice, for she is so good that she will surely do so. On my part and on that of all these Christians who are with me, I promise to do for you all that we are able, even unto death. Do not fail to write to me and inform me of what you intend to do. I shall always reply, for the great Allah has given us a Christian prisoner who can speak and write your language well, as you can judge from this letter. So, you must have no fear, for you can tell us anything you wish. As to your saying that you would be my wife if you were to reach the Christian land, I promise you as a good Christian that this shall be so. And remember that Christians fulfill their promises better than the Moors. May Allah and *Marien*, his mother, guard you, dear lady.'

"With this letter written and folded I waited two days until the bagnio was empty as before, and then I went to the accustomed place on the terrace to see if there were any sign of the cane, which was not long in making its appearance. As soon as I saw it, though I could not see who held it, I showed the letter as a sign that they should attach the thread, but I found it was already attached, and so I tied the letter to it. After a little while, our star appeared again with the white ensign of peace, the little bundle. It was dropped, and I picked it up and found in the bundle silver coins of all sorts and more than fifty gold crowns, which increased our joy fiftyfold and strengthened our hope of regaining our liberty. That very night our renegade returned and said that he had learned that it was, in fact, the Moor we had been told of who lived in that house, that his name was Hadji Murad, that he was enormously rich, that he had an only daughter, the heiress of all his wealth, that it was the general opinion throughout the city that she was the most beautiful woman in Barbary, that several of the viceroys who came there had sought her for a wife, but that she had always been unwilling to marry; he had learned, moreover, that she had had a Christian slave who was now dead. Everything agreed with the contents of the paper.

"We immediately took counsel with the renegade as to what means should be adopted in order to carry off the Moorish lady and bring us all to the land of the Christians. In the end it was agreed that for the present we should wait for a second communication from Zoraida (for that was the name of her who would now take the name of María), because we saw clearly that she and no one else could find a way out of all these difficulties. When we had decided upon this, the renegade bade us not to be uneasy, for he would lose his life to set us at liberty. For four days the bagnio was filled with people, for which reason the cane did not appear for four days, but at the end of that time, when the bagnio was once more deserted, it appeared with the cloth so pregnant as to promise a happy delivery. Cane and cloth came down to me, and I found another paper and a hundred crowns in gold without any other coin. The renegade was present, and in our cell we gave him the letter to read, which, he said, ran as follows:

"'I cannot think of a plan for our going to Spain, nor has *Lela Marien* shown me one, though I have asked her. All that can be done is for me to give you through this window plenty of money in gold. With it ransom yourself and your friends, and let one of you go to the land of the Christians to buy a vessel and come back for the others. He will find me in my father's garden, at the Barbizon gate, near the seashore, where I am to be all the summer with my father and my servants. You can carry me away from there by night without any danger and bring me away to the vessel. And remember you are to be my husband, else I shall pray to *Marien* to punish you. If you cannot trust anyone to go for the vessel, ransom yourself and go, for I know you will return more surely than another, for you are a gentleman and a Christian. Try to become acquainted with our garden, and when you are walking by here, I shall know that the bagnio is empty and I shall give you great sums of money. Allah protect you, my lord.'

"These were the contents of the second letter, and when we had all seen it, each one offered himself to be the ransomed man and promised to go and to return with scrupulous good faith; I myself offered to do the same. To all this the renegade objected saying that he would on no account consent to one going out free before all went together, for experience had taught him how ill those who have been set free keep the promises made in captivity. Captives of note had often tried this expedient, ransoming someone that he might go to Valencia or Majorca with money to equip a vessel and return for those who had ransomed him, but they never came back. Regained liberty and the dread of losing it efface from the memory all the obligations in the world. To prove the truth of what he said, he told us briefly what had happened to certain Christian gentlemen almost at that very time, the strangest case that had ever occurred even there, where astonishing and marvelous things were happening every instant. In short, he ended by saying that what could and ought to be done was that the money intended for the ransom of one of the Christians should be given to him for the purchase of a vessel there in Algiers under the pretense of becoming a merchant or trader in Tetuan and along the coast. Being master of the vessel, he could easily find a way for getting us out of the bagnio and taking us all on board, the more so if the Moorish lady gave, as she promised, money enough to ransom all, because once free it would be the easiest thing in the world for us to embark even at noon. The greatest difficulty was that the Moors do not allow a renegade to buy or to own a boat, unless it is a large ship to go pirating, because they are afraid that anyone who buys a small vessel, especially if he be a Spaniard, wants it only for escaping into Christian territory. This impediment he said he could get over by taking over a *tagarino* as partner with him in the purchase of the vessel and the profit of the cargo. Under cover of this he would become master of the vessel, in which case he looked upon all the rest as good as done. Though to me and my comrades it had seemed a better plan to send to Majorca for the vessel, as the Moorish lady suggested, we dared not oppose him, fearing that if we did not do as he said, he would denounce us, placing us in danger of losing our lives if the argument with Zoraida were revealed, for whose life we would all have sacrificed our own. We, therefore, put ourselves in the hands of God and the renegade. At the same time an answer was sent to Zoraida, telling her that we would do all that she advised, for she had

counseled us as if *Lela Marien* had breathed the words into
her ear and that it depended upon her alone whether we
were to postpone the project or carry it out at once. I renewed my promise to be her husband. And so, the next
day that the bagnio happened to be empty, she gave us at
different times by means of the cane and the cloth two thousand crowns in gold with a letter in which she said that
on the first *jumá*, that is to say, Friday, she was going to
her father's garden, but that before she went, she would give
us more money. If that were not sufficient, she added, we
were to let her know, for she would give us as much as we
needed, because her father had so much that he would not
miss it, especially as she had the keys of everything.

"We at once gave the renegade five hundred crowns to
buy the vessel. With eight hundred I ransomed myself, giving the money to a Valencian merchant who happened to be
in Algiers. He ransomed me from the king by pledging his
word that he would pay the sum due on the arrival of the
first ship from Valencia. Had he given the money at once,
it would have made the king suspect that my ransom money
had been for a long time in Algiers and that the merchant
for his own private gain had kept it secret. In fact, my
master was so difficult to deal with that I dared not on any
account pay down the money at once. The Thursday before the Friday on which the fair Zoraida was to go to the
garden, she gave us another thousand crowns and warned
us of her departure, begging me, if I were ransomed, to
find out her father's garden at once and to seize at all costs
an opportunity of going to see her there. I answered her
briefly that I would do so and bade her commend us to
Lela Marien with all the prayers the Christian slave had
taught her. After this was done, I gave orders to ransom
our three companions, so as to enable them to leave the
bagnio, for I was afraid that when they saw me ransomed
and themselves not (though the money was forthcoming),
they might become alarmed and the Devil might give them
the notion to do something that might endanger Zoraida.
Although their dispositions were of such a kind that I had
no need to be apprehensive, nevertheless, I wanted to avoid
running any risks in this matter. So, I had them ransomed
in the same way as I had been, and I handed over all the

money to the merchant so that he might with safety and confidence give security. However, we never disclosed our arrangement and secret to him, for it might have been dangerous.

CHAPTER XLI

In which the captive still continues his adventures

"Before a fortnight had passed our renegade had already purchased an excellent vessel capable of holding more than thirty persons, and to make the whole transaction safe and to lend color to it, he proposed to make, and in fact did make, a voyage to a place called Cherchel, about thirty leagues from Algiers toward Oran, where there is an extensive trade in dried figs. Two or three times he made this voyage in company with the *tagarino* I mentioned earlier. In Barbary they call the Moors of Aragón *tagarinos*, and those of Granada Mudéjares, but in the kingdom of Fez they call the Mudéjares *elches*, and those are the people the king chiefly employs in war. To proceed: every time he passed with his vessel, he anchored in a cove that was not two crossbow shots from the garden where Zoraida was waiting; then, the renegade, together with the two Moorish lads who rowed, used to station himself there deliberately, either going through his prayers or else rehearsing in jest what he meant to perform in earnest. Moreover, he would go to Zoraida's garden and ask for fruit, which her father gave him, not knowing him. But though, as he afterward informed me, he sought to have a word with Zoraida to tell her that he was the one who had been ordered by me to take her to the land of the Christians and that she should feel safe and happy, it was never possible for him to do so. Moorish women do not let themselves be seen by Moor or Turk, unless their husbands or their fathers bid them, whereas with Christian captives they allow freedom of intercourse and communication, even more than might be considered proper. I would have felt sorry if he had spoken to her, for perhaps she might have become alarmed at finding her affairs commented on by renegades. But God decreed otherwise, and our well-meaning renegade was not given the chance of carrying out his plan. But when he observed how safely he could travel to and from Cherchel and anchor where and how and when he pleased, when he noticed that his partner, the *tagarino*, saw eye to eye with him and had no will but his, and when he saw that I was already ransomed, he came to the conclusion that all that was left to do was to find some Christians to row the vessel. And so he urged me to find whatever men I wished to take with me, in addition to the ransomed men, and to mobilize them for the next Friday, which he fixed as the date of our departure. I therefore spoke to a dozen Spaniards, all lusty oarsmen and such as might easily leave the city. It was no easy task to find the men just then, for there were twenty ships out on a cruise and they had taken the rowers with them. My men would not have been available, were it not that their master remained at home that summer without going to sea in order to finish a small galley that they had upon the stocks. To those men I merely said that the following Friday, in the evening, they were to leave stealthily one by one and to muster in close proximity to Hadji Murad's garden, where they were to wait for me till I came. These directions I gave to each man separately, with orders that if they saw other Christians there, they were not to say anything to them, except that I had ordered them to hold themselves in readiness at the spot.

"Now that I had settled this preliminary, another still more necessary step had to be taken, which was to let Zoraida know how matters stood so that she might be prepared and on the alert, lest she be startled if we rushed in upon her before she thought the Christians' vessel could have returned. I, therefore, resolved to visit the garden and see if I could speak with her, and on the pretext of gathering some herbs I went there one day before our departure. The first person I met was her father, who addressed me in the language [1] that all over Barbary, and even in Constantinople, is the medium of communication between captives and Moors. It is neither Morisco, nor Castilian, nor of any other nation, but a medley of all languages, by means of which we can all understand one another. In this sort of language he asked me what I wanted in his garden and to whom I belonged. I replied that I was a slave of Arnaut Mamí (for I knew for certain that he was a great friend of his) and that I was looking for herbs to make a salad. He then asked me whether I were under ransom or not, and what my master demanded for me. While these questions and answers were proceeding, the fair Zoraida, who had not seen me for some time, came out of the garden house, and as Moorish women are not at all particular about letting themselves be seen by Christians, and as I have said before, are not coy in their presence, she did not hesitate to come to where her father stood with me. Moreover, her father, when he saw her approaching slowly, called her to his side.

"It would be beyond my power now to describe Zoraida's great beauty, her gentleness, and the rich, brilliant attire in which she appeared before me. I shall only say that more pearls hung from her fair neck, her ears, and her hair than she had hairs on her head. On her ankles, which, as is the Moorish custom, were bare, she wore *carcajes* (for so the Moors call the rings and bracelets for the feet) of the purest gold, set with many diamonds, which, she told me afterward, her father valued at ten thousand doubloons; those she had on her wrists were worth just as much. The pearls were in profusion and very fine, for the chief pride and display of Moorish women is to deck themselves with fine pearls and seed pearls, and of these there are, therefore, more among the Moors than among all other nations. Zoraida's father had the reputation of possessing a great many of the purest in all Algiers, and of possessing also more than two hundred thousand Spanish crowns. She, who once was mistress of all this, is now mine only. Judge how ravishing she must have looked in her days of dazzling splendor from the beauty that remains today after so many

[1] This was a *lingua franca*, described by the contemporary writer Haedo as "a mixture of various Christian tongues and of words chiefly Italian and Spanish with a sprinkling of Portuguese."

hardships. But remember that women's beauty has its time and seasons and is increased or diminished by chance causes; naturally emotions will heighten or impair it, though, alas, most frequently they destroy it. All I can say is that Zoraida then appeared so exquisitely attired and surpassingly lovely that, to me at least, she seemed the perfection of all I had ever beheld. When, in addition, I considered all that I owed her, I felt that some goddess from Heaven had descended on earth to bring me happiness and relief.

"As she approached, her father told her in his own language that I was a captive belonging to his friend, Arnaut Mamí, and that I had come for salad. She took up the conversation, and in the farrago of tongues I have spoken of she asked me if I was a gentleman and why I was not ransomed. I answered that I was already ransomed and that she could see by the price what value my master set on me, for he had given one thousand five hundred *sultanis* [2] for me; to which she replied: 'If you belonged to my father, I would certainly not have let him part with you for twice as much, for you Christians always tell lies about yourselves and make yourselves out poor to cheat the Moors.'

" 'That may be, lady,' I replied, 'indeed I dealt truthfully with my master, as I do and mean to do with everybody in the world.'

" 'And when do you go?' said Zoraida.

" 'Tomorrow, I think,' I replied, 'for there is a vessel here from France that sails tomorrow, and I think I shall go in her.'

" 'Would it not be better,' asked Zoraida, 'to wait until one comes from Spain and go in that instead of with the French, who are not your friends?'

" 'No,' I said, 'though if, as reported, a vessel were now coming from Spain, I might wait for her. However, it is more likely that I shall depart tomorrow, for my longing to return to my country and to those I love is so great that it will not allow me to wait for another opportunity, no matter how good it may be, if it be delayed.'

" 'No doubt you are married in your own country, hence you are anxious to go and see your wife.'

---

[2] A *sultan* or *soldan* meant a real, but according to Haedo they were of gold and were worth twenty-five *asperos* or square silver coins.

" 'I am not married,' I replied, 'but I have given my promise to marry on my arrival there.'

" 'And is the lady beautiful to whom you have given it?' asked Zoraida.

" 'So beautiful,' I said, 'that to describe her worthily and tell you the truth, she is very much like you.'

"At this her father laughed very heartily and said: 'By Allah, Christian, she must be very beautiful if she is like my daughter, who is the most beautiful woman in the whole kingdom. Look at her well and you will see I am telling you the truth.'

"Zoraida's father, as the better linguist, acted as interpreter for the greater part of this conversation, for although she spoke the bastard language that, as I have said, is employed there, she expressed her meaning more by gestures than by words. Then, while we were engaged in this conversation, a Moor came running up and shouted that four Turks had leaped over the fence or wall of the garden and were picking the fruit, though it was not yet ripe. The old man was alarmed, and Zoraida too, for all Moors have an instinctive dread of the Turks, especially of the soldiers, who are so insolent and overbearing to the Moors, their subjects, that they treat them worse than their slaves. So, her father said to Zoraida: 'Daughter, retire into the house and shut yourself in while I go and speak to these dogs; and you, Christian, pick your herbs and go in peace, and Allah bring you safe to your native land.'

"I bowed, and he went away to look for the Turks, leaving me alone with Zoraida, who pretended to retire as her father had bidden her, but the moment he was concealed by the trees of the garden, she turned to me with her eyes full of tears, saying: '*Amexi*, Christian, *amexi?*' This means: Are you going away, Christian, are you going away?

" 'Yes, lady,' I replied, 'but on no account without you. Expect me next *jumá*, and do not be alarmed when you see us, for we shall most certainly go to Christian lands.'

"I said this in such a way that she understood perfectly all that passed between us, and throwing one arm around my neck, she began with faltering steps to walk toward the house, but as Fate would have it (and it might have been very disastrous if Heaven had not ordained otherwise), just as we were moving on in this manner, her father, after getting rid of the Turks, returned and saw how we were

walking, and we knew that he saw. But Zoraida, ready and
quick-witted, took care not to remove her arm from my
neck; on the contrary, she drew closer to me and hid her
head on my breast, bending her knees a little and showing
all the signs and symptoms of fainting, while at the same
time I made it seem as though I were supporting her
against my will. Her father came running up to where we
were, and seeing his daughter in this state, he asked what
was the matter with her. As she gave no answer, he said:
'No doubt she has fainted in alarm at the entrance of those
dogs,' and taking her from mine, he clasped her to his own
breast. Then, she heaved a sigh, her eyes still wet with
tears, and said again: '*Amexi*, Christian, *amexi!*' This means:
Go, Christian, go.

"To this her father replied: 'There is no need, daughter,
for the Christian to go, for he has done you no harm, and
the Turks have now gone. Do not be alarmed; there is
nothing to hurt you, for as I have already told you, the
Turks, at my request, have gone back the way they came.'

" 'It was they who terrified her, as you have said, sir,'
I said to the father, 'but since she bids me go, I have no
wish to displease her; peace be with you, and with your
leave, I shall return to this garden for herbs if needs be, for
my master says there are nowhere better herbs for salad
than here.'

" 'Come as often as you please,' replied Hadji Murad. 'My
daughter does not speak thus because she is displeased with
you or any Christian; she only meant that the Turks should
go, not you, or that it was time for you to look for your herbs.'

"At this point I took my leave of both of them, and she
departed with her father, looking as if her heart would break.
Under pretense of looking for herbs, I made the round of
the garden at my ease and studied carefully all the approaches and outlets and the defenses of the house and
everything that might facilitate our task. This done, I returned and gave an account to the renegade and to my
companions of all that had passed, and I looked forward
with impatience to the hour when without fear I could enjoy
the prize that Fortune offered me in the fair and lovely
Zoraida. Time passed, and at length the appointed day we
so longed for arrived. As we all followed the arrangement
and plan that we had decided upon after careful considera-

tion and many a long discussion, we succeeded as fully as
we could have wished. On the Friday following the day
upon which I spoke to Zoraida in the garden, our renegade
anchored his vessel at nightfall almost opposite the spot
where she lived.

"The Christians who were to row were ready and hiding
in different places all around that area. They were waiting
for me, anxious, elated, and longing to attack the vessel
that lay before their eyes, for they did not know our renegade's plan and expected that they were to gain their liberty
by force of arms and by killing the Moors on board the
vessel. As soon, therefore, as my companions and I appeared,
all those who were in hiding, seeing us, came out and joined
us. It was now the time when the city gates were shut, and
there was not a soul to be seen in all the country about.
When we were all together, we were uncertain whether it
would be better first to go for Zoraida or to make prisoners of the Moors who rowed in the vessel. While we were
in this quandary, our renegade came up to us and asked
what delayed us, for it was now the time and all the Moors
were off their guard and most of them asleep. We told him
why we hesitated, but he said it was more important first
to secure the vessel, which could be done with the greatest
ease and without any danger, and then we could go for
Zoraida. We all approved of what he said, and so, without
further delay, guided by him, we made for the vessel. He
was the first to leap on board drawing his cutlass and crying
out in Morisco: 'Let no one stir from here if he does not
want it to cost him his life.'

"By this time almost all the Christians were on board,
and the Moors, who were fainthearted, hearing their captain speaking this way, were astounded, and without a single
one of them drawing a weapon—indeed, they had few or
none—they submitted without a word to be bound by the
Christians, who quickly secured them, threatening that if
they raised any kind of outcry, they would all be put to
the sword.

"When this was done and half our party had been left
to mount guard over the Moors, the rest of us, again taking
the renegade as our guide, hastened toward Hadji Murad's
garden, and as good luck would have it, on trying the gate,
it opened as readily as if it had not been locked. And, so
quite quietly and in silence we reached the house without

being seen by anyone. The beautiful Zoraida was watching
for us at a window, and as soon as she perceived that there
were people there, she asked in a low voice if we were
nizarani, that is to say, Christians. I answered yes and bade
her come down. As soon as she recognized me, she did not
delay an instant, for without answering a word, she came
down immediately, opened the door, and showed herself to
all, so beautiful and so richly attired that I cannot attempt
to describe her. The moment I saw her, I took her hand and
kissed it, and the renegade and my two companions did the
same, while the others, who did not understand the situation,
did as they saw us do, thinking only that we were giving her
thanks for our freedom. The renegade then asked her in
Morisco if her father was in the house. She answered that
he was and that he was asleep.

" 'Then we shall have to awaken him,' said the renegade, 'and carry him with us and all that is of value in this
lovely garden.'

" 'No,' she answered, 'my father must on no account be
touched. There is nothing more in this house than what I am
taking with me, which will be quite enough to enrich and
satisfy all of you. Wait a little and you shall see."

"With these words she went in again, telling us she would
return immediately and bidding us to keep quiet and make
no noise. I asked the renegade what had passed between
them, and when he told me, I bade him do nothing but what
Zoraida wished. She then returned with a little trunk so full
of gold crowns that she could scarcely carry it. Unfortunately,
her father awoke while this was going on, and hearing a
noise in the garden, he came to the window. Perceiving at
once that all those who were there were Christians, he
raised a prodigiously loud cry and began to call out in Arabic:
'Christians, Christians, thieves, thieves!' This outcry threw
us into the greatest consternation, but the renegade, seeing
the danger we were in and how important it was for him
to effect his purpose before we were heard, mounted with the
utmost speed to where Hadji Murad was, and with him went
some of our party. I, however, did not dare to leave Zoraida,
who had fallen in a swoon into my arms. To be brief, those
who had gone upstairs acted so promptly that in an instant
they came down carrying Hadji Murad with his hands tied
and a napkin in his mouth that prevented him from saying
anything, warning him at the same time that to attempt to

speak would cost him his life. When his daughter caught sight of him, she covered her eyes that she might not look upon him, while her father was stupefied, not knowing how willingly she had placed herself in our hands. But just then what we needed most was our legs; so, with the utmost caution and speed we ran toward the vessel, where those who had remained on board were already waiting anxiously for our return, fearing that we had met with some mishap.

"It must have been about two hours after night had set in before we were all aboard the vessel, when we untied Zoraida's father's hands and took the gag out of his mouth, but the renegade repeated his threat to kill the old man if he uttered as much as a word. When he saw his daughter there, however, he began to sigh piteously and the more when he saw how tightly I was clasping her and that she lay quiet without resisting or complaining or showing any reluctance. Nevertheless, he remained silent lest the renegade's threats might be put into effect.

"Zoraida, now that she found herself on board and saw that we were about to start rowing and that her father and the other Moors lay huddled on deck gagged and bound, bade the renegade ask me to do her the favor of releasing these Moors and of setting her father at liberty, for she would sooner throw herself into the sea than see that a father who had loved her so dearly was being carried away a captive before her eyes and on her account.

"The renegade repeated this to me, and I replied that I would gladly agree, but he answered that it was not advisable, because if they were left there, they would at once raise the country and stir up the city and lead to the dispatch of swift frigates in pursuit; so, we would be caught by sea or land without any chance of escape. All that could be done, he said, was to set them free at the first Christian ground we reached. On this point we all agreed, and Zoraida, to whom it was explained together with the reasons that prevented us from complying at once with her request, remained satisfied.

"In glad silence and with joyful alacrity each of our lusty rowers took his oar, and commending ourselves to God with all our hearts, we began to shape our course toward the island of Majorca, the nearest Christian land. Owing, however, to the freshening of the northerly Tramontana, with the sea growing somewhat rough, it was impossible for us to steer a straight course for Majorca, and we were compelled to hug the coast in the direction of Oran, not without great uneasiness on our part, lest we should be observed from the town of Cherchel, which lies on the coast not more than sixty miles from Algiers. Moreover, we were afraid of meeting on that course one of the small galleys that usually came with merchandise from Tetuan, though each of us for himself and all of us together felt that if a merchant galley were encountered, provided it were not a frigate, not only should we not be lost, but also we should capture a vessel in which we could more safely accomplish our voyage. And all the while we rowed, Zoraida kept her head in my hands that she might not see her father, and I felt that she was calling upon *Lela Marien* to help us.

"We must have made a good thirty miles when dawn found us some three musketshots off land, which seemed to us deserted and without anyone to see us. Yet for all that, we plied our oars as hard as we could to get farther out to sea, which was then a little smoother, and when we had gained about six miles, the order was given that only every fourth man should row, while we ate some food, with which the vessel was well provided. But the rowers said that this was no time to rest and that those who were not rowing should feed them, for they would not leave their oars on any account. This was done, but then a stiff breeze began to blow, which obliged us to leave off rowing and hoist the sail and to steer for Oran, as it was impossible to hold any other course. All this was done with great speed, and under sail we ran more than eight knots an hour without any other fear than that of falling in with some vessel that might prove to be a pirate. We gave the Moorish oarsmen food, and the renegade comforted them, telling them they were not captives, for we would set them free at the first opportunity.

"When Zoraida's father was addressed in the same terms, he replied: 'Anything else, Christians, I might hope or think likely from your generosity and humane ways, but do not think me so foolish as to imagine you will give me my liberty; you would never have risked the danger of depriving me of it, only to restore it to me so generously, especially as you know who I am and the sum you may expect to receive on restoring it. If you will but name that sum, I here offer you all you want for myself and for my unhappy daughter there, or else for her alone, for she is the greatest and most precious part of my soul.'

"As he said this, he began to weep so bitterly that he filled us all with compassion and Zoraida felt compelled to look at him, and when she saw him weeping, she was so distraught that she rose from my feet and ran to throw her arms around him, pressing her face to his. They both gave way to such an outburst of tears that many of us followed suit. But when her father saw how gaily dressed she was and how she was wearing all her jewels, he said to her in his own language: 'What does this mean, my daughter? Last night before this terrible disaster befell us, I saw you in your everyday and household dress, but now though you have had no time to attire yourself and though you have received no joyful tidings, why is this an occasion for adorning and beautifying yourself? I see you arrayed in the finest garments I could have given you when Fortune was more kind to us. Answer me this, for it causes me greater amazement and alarm than even this misfortune itself.'

"The renegade translated to us all that the Moor said to his daughter, but she did not answer a word. When, however, he observed in one corner of the vessel the little trunk in which she used to keep her jewels, which he knew he had left in Algiers and had not brought to the garden, he was still more astonished. He asked her how that trunk had come into our hands and what there was in it. To which the renegade, without waiting for Zoraida to reply, made answer: 'Do not trouble yourself, sir, to ask your daughter, Zoraida, so many questions, for the answer I give you will serve for all. I would have you know that she is a Christian, and it is she who has been the file for our chains and our deliverer from captivity. She is here of her own free will, as glad, I imagine, to find herself in this position as he who escapes out of darkness into light, out of death into life, out of suffering into glory.'

" 'Daughter, is what he says true?' cried the Moor.

" 'It is,' replied Zoraida.

" 'That you are actually a Christian,' said the old man, 'and that you have delivered your father into the hands of his enemies?'

"To which Zoraida answered: 'A Christian I am, but it is not I who has placed you in this position, for it never was my wish to do you harm, but only to do good to myself.'

" 'And what good have you done yourself, daughter?'

" 'That,' she replied, 'you must ask *Lela Marien*; she will be able to tell you better than I.'

"No sooner had the Moor heard these words than with incredible rapidity he flung himself headforemost into the sea, where no doubt he would have drowned if the long and cumbersome robes he wore had not kept him afloat in the water. Zoraida shrieked at us to save him, and we all hastened to help, and seizing him by his robe, we drew him in, half drowned and unconscious. Zoraida was in such distress that she kept weeping over him as piteously and bitterly as if he were really dead. We turned him face down and he voided a quantity of water, and at the end of two hours, he came to.

"Meanwhile the wind had changed and we were compelled to head for the land and ply our oars to escape being driven onshore; but by good luck we made it into a cove that lies on one side of a small promontory or cape called by the Moors the Cape of the Cava Rumía, which in our language means the wicked Christian woman, for there is a tradition among the Moors that in that spot is buried that Cava [3] through whom Spain was lost. *Cava* in their language means prostitute, and *rumía* Christian. Moreover, they consider it unlucky to anchor there except when necessity drives them, and they never do so otherwise. For us, however, it was not the shelter of the prostitute, but a haven of safety for our relief. Indeed, so rough had the sea become that we posted a lookout onshore and never let the oars out of our hands. We made a meal, however, of the stores the renegade had laid in, and we implored God and Our Lady with all our hearts to help us, protect us, and enable us to make a happy end after so prosperous a beginning. At Zoraida's entreaty, orders were given that her father and the other Moors, who were still bound, should be put ashore, for she found it more than her tender heart could bear to see her father bound and her fellow countrymen prisoners. We promised her to set them free at the moment of departure, for as the place was uninhabited, we ran no risk in leaving them there.

[3] In the ballads of the *Romancero*, "La Cava" is the name given to Florinda, daughter (or wife) of Count Julian. King Rodrigo, "the last of the Goths," seduced Florinda; Julian, to take revenge, conspired with the Moors against Rodrigo.

"Our prayers were not so vain as to be unheard by Heaven, for the wind immediately changed in our favor and the sea became calm, inviting us once more to resume our voyage with good heart. Seeing this, we untied the Moors and put them onshore one by one, at which they were amazed. But when came to land Zoraida's father, who had now completely recovered his senses, he said: 'Why do you think, Christians, that this wicked woman is glad that you have given me my liberty? Do you think it is out of pity for me? No, it is only because my presence would prevent her from gratifying her shameless desires. Do not imagine that she has been moved to change her faith because she believes that your religion is better than ours. No, it is only because she knows that immodesty is more freely practiced in your country than in ours.' Then, turning to Zoraida, while I and another of the Christians held him fast by both arms in case he might do something desperate, he cried: 'Infamous girl, misguided maiden! Whither are you drifting in your blind frenzy, now that you are in the power of these dogs, our natural enemies? Cursed be the hour when I begot you! Accused be the lavish luxury in which I reared you!'

"Seeing that he was not likely to end his tirade soon, I hurriedly put him ashore, and from there he went on shouting out his curses and lamentations, praying to Mohammed to beseech Allah to destroy, confound, and annihilate us. And when we had hoisted sail and could no longer hear his words, we saw his frantic gestures of despair: he plucked out his beard, he tore his hair, he crawled along the ground. But once he raised his voice to such a pitch that we were able to hear what he said: 'Come back, beloved daughter, come back to land. I forgive you all. Let those men have the money, for it is theirs now, and come back to comfort your father, who will perish on these desert sands if you forsake him.'

"All this Zoraida heard with sorrow and with tears, but all she could say in answer was: 'Allah grant that *Lela Marien*, who has made me become a Christian, give you comfort in your grief, beloved father. Allah knows that I could not do otherwise than I have done, and these Christians owe nothing to my will. Even if I had been unwilling to come with them and had wished to stay at home, it would have been impossible, so eagerly did my soul spur me on to accomplish this purpose, which I feel to be as good as to you it seems evil.'

"But neither could her father hear her, nor could we see him, when she said this. And so, while I consoled Zoraida, the rest turned their attention to our voyage, which a breeze from the night so favored that we were confident that the morrow at daybreak would find us off the coast of Spain. But since good seldom or never comes pure and undiluted without being accompanied or followed by some evil that spoils or disturbs it, our fortune, or perhaps the curses that the Moor had hurled at his daughter (for no matter what kind of father utters them, they are always to be dreaded), brought it about that when we were already in mid sea, the night about three hours spent, and when we were under full sail, the oars lashed, for the favoring breeze saved us the labor of using them, we saw by the light of the moon, which shone brilliantly, a square-rigged vessel in full sail a short distance away, luffing up and standing across our course, so close to us that we had to strike sail to avoid running foul of her, while her captain put the helm hard up to let us pass. Her crew came to the side of the ship to ask who we were, whither we were bound, and whence we came. As they asked in French, our renegade said to us: 'Let no one answer, for no doubt these are French corsairs who plunder all comers.' Acting on this warning, no one answered a word, but after we had gone a little ahead, their vessel now lying to leeward, suddenly they fired two guns, and apparently both were loaded with chain shot for the first shot cut our mast in half and brought down both it and the sail into the sea, and the other, discharged at the same moment, hit our vessel amidships, staving her in completely, but without doing any further damage. Finding ourselves sinking, we shouted for help and called upon those in the ship to pick us up, for we were filling. They then lay to, and lowering their cockboat, as many as a dozen Frenchmen, well armed with hatchlocks and their matches burning, piled into it and came alongside ours. Then, seeing how few we were and that our ship was sinking, they picked us up, saying that they had served us in that way for our incivility in not replying to them. Meanwhile, our renegade took the trunk with Zoraida's treasures and threw it into the sea, without anyone noticing what he was doing.

"Finally we went on board with the Frenchmen, who, after learning all they wanted to know about us, robbed us of everything we possessed as if they were our mortal enemies, and they even stripped Zoraida of the *carcajes* she wore on her feet. But the distress they caused her did not trouble me as much as my terror that after they had stolen her rich and precious jewels, they would proceed to rob her of the jewel she prized above all her possessions. The desires of such rascals, however, do not extend beyond money, and for this their lust is insatiable. On this occasion they went so far that they would have taken the clothes we wore as captives, had they been worth anything to them. Some of them even wanted to throw us all into the sea wrapped in a sail, for they intended to trade at some of the ports of Spain, pretending to be Bretons, and if they brought us alive, they would be punished as soon as the robbery was discovered. But the captain, the one who had plundered my beloved Zoraida, declared that he was content with the prize already obtained and that he would not touch at any Spanish port. He said he wanted to pass the Strait of Gibraltar by night, or as best he could, and head for La Rochelle, the port from which he had sailed. So, they agreed to give us the ship's cockboat and all that we required for the short voyage we still had to make. This they did next day on coming in sight of the Spanish coast, the sight of which made us forget all our sorrows and hardships so completely that they might never have occurred; such is man's joy at regaining his liberty.

"It must have been about noon when they put us into the cockboat, giving us two barrels of water and some biscuits. And just as the lovely Zoraida was departing, the captain, feeling some sense of pity, gave her about forty gold crowns and would not allow his men to strip her of the garments she is wearing now. We got into the cockboat after we had thanked them for their kindness, showing ourselves grateful rather than outraged. They stood out to sea and steered for the Strait. Having no other North Star than the land that lay before us, we plied our oars with such energy that by sunset we were so near that we might easily, we thought, land before night was too advanced. But as there was no moon and the sky was clouded, and as we did not know our whereabouts, we did not think it safe to make for the shore. Many of us, however, wished to make a landing, even among the rocks and far from any inhabited spot. In this way we would escape the attentions of the prowling vessels of the Tetuan pirates, who leave Barbary at nightfall and reach the Spanish coast by daybreak, where they generally pick up a prize and then go home to sleep in their own houses. Of the conflicting opinions the one that we adopted was to approach the shore slowly, if the sea was calm enough to allow it, and to land wherever we could. This we did, and a little before midnight we drew near to the foot of a large and lofty mountain, close enough to the sea to leave sufficient space for landing conveniently. We ran our boat up on the sand, and everyone sprang out and kissed the ground, and with tears of joyful satisfaction we gave thanks to the Lord God for all His incomparable goodness to us on our voyage. We removed from the boat the provisions it contained, we drew it up on the shore, and we then climbed a long way up the mountain, for even then we could not feel easy in our hearts, nor could we thoroughly convince ourselves that we really stood on Christian soil.

"Dawn came more slowly, I think, than we would have wished. We completed the ascent in order to see if from the summit we could perceive any village or shepherds' huts, but though we strained our eyes, we could see no house or person, no path or highway. However, we resolved to push on further, for we could hardly fail to find someone who could tell us where we were. What distressed me most was to see Zoraida trudging on foot over that rough ground, and though I once carried her on my shoulders, she was more distressed by my weariness than refreshed by the rest it gave her. So, she never again allowed me to undergo the exertion and walked on patiently and cheerfully while I led her by the hand. We had gone rather less than a mile when the tinkle of a little bell came to our ears, a clear proof that there were flocks nearby, and looking about carefully to see if there was a sign of anyone, we observed a young shepherd at the foot of a cork tree calmly and unsuspiciously whittling a stick with his knife. We hailed him, and he looked up and sprang nimbly to his feet, for, as we afterward learned, the first of us he caught sight of were the renegade and Zoraida, and seeing them in Moorish dress, he concluded that all the Moors of Barbary were after him. He plunged with astonishing rapidity into the thicket in front of him and began to raise a prodigious outcry, shouting: 'The Moors! The Moors have landed! To arms, to arms!'

"We were all thrown into confusion by these cries, and we did not know what to do; then, realizing that the lad's

shout would raise the country and that the horsemen that
guard the coast would come at once to see what was the
matter, we decided that the renegade should take off his
Turkish robes and put on a captive's jacket or coat, which one
of our party gave him at once though he was left in his
shirt. And so, commending ourselves to God, we followed
the same path that we saw the shepherd take, expecting any
moment that the coast guard would descend upon us. And
we were not wrong, for two hours had hardly elapsed when,
as we came out of the brushwood onto the plain, we perceived
some fifty horsemen riding toward us at a hard gallop. As
soon as we saw them, we stood still, waiting for them. When
they came close and saw a group of miserable Christians instead of the Moors they were expecting, they were taken
aback, and one of them asked if we were the cause of the
shepherd having raised the call to arms. I said yes, and as I
was about to explain to him what had occurred and whence
we came and who we were, one of the Christians of our party
recognized the horseman who had questioned us, and before I
could say anything more, he exclaimed: 'Thanks be to God,
sirs, for bringing us to such good quarters, for if I am not
mistaken, the ground we stand on is that of Vélez Málaga,
and you, sir, who inquire who we are, if my years of captivity
have not blotted you from my memory, are Pedro de Busta-
mante, my uncle.'

"The Christian captive had hardly uttered these words
when the trooper threw himself off his horse and ran to embrace the young man, crying: 'Nephew, my dear nephew! I
recognize you now. Long have we mourned you as dead—I,
my sisters, your mother, and all your relatives who are
still alive and whom God has been pleased to preserve that
they may enjoy the happiness of seeing you. We already
knew that you were in Algiers, and judging by your garments
and those of the rest of this company, I conclude that you
have had a miraculous deliverance.'

" 'That is so,' replied the young man, 'and there will be
plenty of time to tell you the whole story.'

"As soon as the horsemen realized that we were Christian
captives, they dismounted, and each one of them offered
us his horse to ride to the city of Vélez Málaga, which
was about one and a half leagues away. We told them where
we had left the boat, and some of them turned back to get it
and bring it along to the city. Others took us up behind them,

and Zoraida was placed on the horse of the young man's uncle. The whole town came out to meet us, for they had by this time heard of the arrival from one who had gone on in advance. They were not astonished to see liberated captives or Moorish captives, for people on that coast are well used to seeing both one and the other; but they were astonished by Zoraida's beauty, which was just then heightened both by the exertion of the journey and by the joy of finding herself on Christian soil with nothing more to fear. This brought such a glow to her face that unless I was then much deceived by my love, I would venture to declare that there was not a more beautiful creature in all the world, at least none that I had ever seen.

"We went straight to the church to give thanks to God for the mercies received, and as soon as Zoraida entered it, she said there were faces there like *Lela Marien's*. We told her they were images, and as well as he could, the renegade explained to her what they meant, that she might worship them as if each of them were the very same *Lela Marien* that had spoken to her. And she, who had a ready understanding and a quick and clear instinct, understood at once all he had said about them. From there they took us and distributed us all in different houses of the town, but as for Zoraida, the renegade, and myself, the Christian who came with us brought us to the house of his parents, who had a fair share of the gifts of fortune and treated us with as much kindness as they did their own son.

"We remained six days in Vélez, at the end of which the renegade, having laid his process in due form, set out for the city of Granada to restore himself to the sacred bosom of the Church through the medium of the Holy Inquisition. The other released captives took their departure, each the way that seemed best to him, and Zoraida and I were left alone with nothing more than the crowns that the courtesy of the Frenchman had bestowed upon Zoraida, out of which I bought the beast on which she rides. For the present I am attending her as her father and squire, not as her husband. We are now going to find out if my father is living, or if any of my brothers has had better fortune than mine has been, though as Heaven has made me the companion of Zoraida, I believe no other lot could be assigned to me, however happy, that I would rather have. The patience with which she endures the hardships that poverty brings with it and the eagerness she shows to be a Christian are such and so great that they fill me with admiration and bind me to serve her all the days of my life, although the happiness I feel in seeing myself hers and her mine is troubled and maimed by my not knowing whether I shall find a corner in my country for her shelter, and whether time and death have made such changes in the fortunes and lives of my father and brothers that I shall hardly find anyone that knows me, if they are not to be found.

"There is no more of my story, gentlemen, to be told. Whether it be strange and entertaining, let your better judgments decide. All I can say is that I would gladly have told it to you more briefly, though fear of wearying you has made me omit many a detail."

CHAPTER XLII

Which deals with further incidents at the inn and with many other things worthy of being known

With these words the captive held his peace, and Don Fernando said to him: "Indeed, captain, the way in which you have told your strange adventure has been as fascinating as the remarkable strangeness and novelty of the events themselves. The story is an unusual one and full of astonishing incidents that hold the listener in suspense; in fact, we have enjoyed it so much that we should be glad if we could hear it all over again, even if this meant listening till tomorrow."

After he had said this, Cardenio [1] and the rest offered to be of service in whatever way they could in such sincere terms that the captain was much gratified by their good-

---

[1] D. Antonio in the original, obviously a misprint.

will. Don Fernando, in particular, offered that if he would
return with him, he would get his brother, the marquess, to
become godfather at the baptism of Zoraida and that on his
own part he would provide him with the means of making
his appearance in his own country with all the credit and
comfort to which he was entitled. The captive expressed his
gratitude in courteous terms but would not accept any of his
generous offers.

By this time night had fallen, and when it was pitch
dark, a coach drove up to the inn accompanied by some men
on horseback, who demanded accommodation. The landlady answered that there was not the span of a hand in the
inn unoccupied.

"That may be so," said one of the horsemen who had
come in, "but a place must be found for his lordship, the
judge, who is on his way here."

At this name the landlady was taken aback, and said:
"Sir, the fact is that I have no beds, but if his lordship, the
judge, carries one with him, as no doubt he does, let him
come in and welcome. My husband and I will give up our
room to accommodate his worship."

"Very good, so let it be," said the squire.

By this time a man had alighted from the coach whose
dress proclaimed his dignity and office, for the long robe
with ruffled sleeves that he wore showed that he was, as his
servant said, a judge of appeal. He led by the hand a young
girl some sixteen years old, in traveling dress, but so gay and
winsome in appearance that all were captivated by her the
moment she appeared. If they had not already seen Dorotea,
Luscinda, and Zoraida at the inn, they would have doubted
whether she had her rival for beauty. Don Quixote was
present at the entrance of the judge with the young lady, and
as soon as he saw him, he said: "Your worship may with all
confidence enter and take your ease in this castle, for
though the accommodation be scanty and poor, there are
no quarters so cramped or uncomfortable that they cannot
make room for arms and letters, above all when arms and
letters have beauty for a guide and leader, as your worship's
learning does in the presence of this fair maiden, for whom
not only castles should open and reveal themselves, but also
rocks should split asunder, mountains cleave in two and
bow their towering peaks to give her welcome. Enter therefore, I pray, your worship, into this paradise, wherein you

will discover stars and suns to accompany the heaven your worship brings with him. Here shall he find arms at their zenith and beauty in its prime."

The judge was struck with amazement at the language of Don Quixote, and after scrutinizing him from head to foot, he was no less astonished by his figure than by his talk. But before he could find words to answer him, he had a fresh surprise when he saw standing before him Luscinda, Dorotea and Zoraida, who, having heard of the new guests and of the beauty of the young lady, had come to see her and welcome her. Don Fernando, Cardenio, and the curate, however, greeted him in simpler and more courtly style. In short, the judge made his entrance in a state of bewilderment both at what he saw and at what he heard, while the fair ladies of the inn gave the young damsel a cordial welcome. The judge could see that they all were people of quality, but Don Quixote's figure, countenance, and bearing had him at his wit's end. When all civilities had been exchanged and the problems of accommodation in the inn had been reviewed, it was arranged, as before, that all the women should retire to the garret that has already been mentioned and that the men should remain outside, as if to guard them. The judge, therefore, was very pleased to allow his daughter, for such the damsel was, to go with the ladies, which she did very willingly; and with part of the host's narrow bed and half of what the judge had brought with him, they made a more comfortable arrangement for the night than they had anticipated.

No sooner did the captive see the judge than his heart leaped within him, for he felt somehow that this was his brother, so he asked one of the servants in the judge's train what his master's name was, and whether he knew from what part of the country the latter came. The servant replied that he was called the Licentiate Juan Pérez de Viedma and that he had heard it said that he came from a village in the mountains of León. This information, together with what he himself had seen, confirmed him in the belief that this was his brother who by their father's advice had adopted the profession of learning. Excited and elated, he called Don Fernando, Cardenio, and the curate aside and told them how the matter stood, assuring them that the judge was his brother. Furthermore, the servant had informed him that the licentiate was now going to the Indies with the appoint-

ment of judge of the Supreme Court of Mexico. And he had
learned, likewise, that the young lady's mother had died in
giving birth to her and that he was very rich in consequence
of the dowry left to him with the daughter. He asked them to
advise him how to make himself known to his brother or how
to ascertain discreetly beforehand whether when he had made
himself known, his brother, seeing him so poor, would be
ashamed of him, or whether he would receive him with a
warm heart.

"Leave it to me to find out," said the curate, "though there
is no reason, captain, for supposing that you will not be
kindly received, because the good sense and wisdom that your
brother shows in his demeanor do not indicate that he will
prove arrogant or unfeeling or that he will not know how to
value the accidents of fortune for their proper worth."

"Still," said the captive, "I would not wish to make myself
known abruptly, but in some indirect way."

"I have told you already," said the curate, "that I will
manage it in a way to satisfy all sides."

By this time supper was ready, and they all took their
seats at the table, except the captive and the ladies, who
supped by themselves in their own room.[2] In the middle of
the supper the curate said: "I had a comrade of your
worship's name, sir judge, in Constantinople, where I was a
captive for several years, and he was one of the stoutest
soldiers and captains in the whole Spanish infantry, but he
had as large a share of misfortune as he had of gallantry
and courage."

"What was this captain's name, sir?" asked the judge.

"He was called Ruiz Pérez de Viedma," replied the
curate, "and he was born in a village in the mountains of
León. He once mentioned an incident that had happened to
him and his brothers that I should have set down as an old
wives' tale told over the fire in winter if it had not been related to me by a man so truthful as he was. He said that his
father had divided his property among his three sons and
had addressed words of advice to them sounder than those
of Cato. And I can say that the precept he followed of going
to the wars turned out so well for him that in a few years
by his valor and good conduct, and without any help except
his own merit, he rose to be captain of infantry and was

---

[2] Evidently Cervantes forgets that they had supped already.

well on the way of being given the command of a corps before long. But Fortune was against him, for when he might
have expected her favor, he lost it, and with it his liberty, on
that glorious day when so many recovered theirs, at the battle of Lepanto. I lost mine at the Goleta, and after a variety
of adventures, we found ourselves comrades in Constantinople. From there he went to Algiers, where I know he met
with one of the most extraordinary adventures that ever
befell anyone in this world."

The curate then went on to relate briefly his brother's
adventures with Zoraida, and to all of this the judge listened
more attentively than he had ever done before. The curate,
however, only went so far as to describe how the Frenchmen
plundered those who were in the boat, and the poverty and
distress in which his comrade and the fair Moor were left.
He added that he had not been able to learn what happened
to them, whether they had reached Spain or whether they
had been carried to France by the Frenchmen.

The captain, standing a little to one side, was listening
to all the curate said and watching every movement of his
brother. When the latter saw that the curate had come to
the end of his tale, he gave a deep sigh and said with his eyes
full of tears: "Oh, sir, if you only knew what news you have
given me and how deeply it touches me, obliging me to
show my feelings by these tears that spring from my eyes in
spite of all my worldly wisdom and self-restraint! That brave
captain you speak of is my eldest brother, who, being older,
bolder, and of nobler mind than I, chose the honorable and
worthy profession of arms, which was one of the three ca-
reers our father proposed to us, as your comrade mentioned
in what you believed was a fable. I followed that of letters,
in which God and my own exertions have raised me to the
position in which you see me. My younger brother is in
Perú,[3] so wealthy that with what he has sent to my father
and to me he has fully repaid the portion he took with him
and has even given my father enough to satisfy his natural
prodigality. Thanks to him, I have been able to follow my
studies in a more becoming and creditable fashion, and so
to reach my present position. My father is still alive, though

[3] Cervantes forgets that, according to the captive's story
(Chapter XXXIX), the youngest of the three brothers decided to
follow the Church and finish his studies at Salamanca.

dying with anxiety for news of his eldest son, and he prays
God unceasingly that death may not close his eyes until he
has looked upon those of his son. I am amazed, however,
that my brother, with all his common sense, should have
neglected to give news of himself, whether in his troubles
and sufferings or in his prosperity, for if his father or any
of us had known of his condition, he need not have waited
for that miracle of the cane to obtain his ransom. But now
I am anxious to know whether those Frenchmen set him
free or murdered him to hide the robbery. For this reason I
shall not continue my journey as joyfully as I began it, but
in melancholy and sadness. Oh, my dear brother! If I only
knew where you are now, I would hasten to seek you out
and deliver you from you hardships, even at the cost of my
own! If I could only bring news to our old father that you
are alive, even though perhaps you may be in the deepest
dungeon of Barbary, for even there his riches, my brother's,
and mine would rescue you! Oh, lovely, generous Zoraida,
who could ever repay your goodness to my brother! Oh, to be
able to be present at the birth of your soul and at your wedding, it would give us all such happiness!"

All this and more the judge uttered with such deep feeling after the news he had received of his brother that all
who heard him shared in it and showed their sympathy with
his sorrow. The curate, then, seeing how well he had succeeded in carrying out his purpose and the captain's wishes,
did not wish to keep them unhappy any longer; so, he rose
from the table and went into the room where Zoraida was,
and he led her out by the hand, followed by Luscinda,
Dorotea, and the judge's daughter. The captain was waiting
to see what the curate would do, which was to take him by
the other hand and advance with both of them to where
the judge and the others were. Then he said: "Dry your
tears, sir judge, for your wish will be crowned with all the
happiness you could desire. You have before you your worthy
brother and your good sister-in-law. He whom you see here
is Captain Viedma, and this is the fair Moor who has been
so good to him. The Frenchmen I told you of have reduced
them to the state of poverty in which you see them so that
you may show the generosity of your kind heart."

The captain ran to embrace his brother, who placed both
hands on his shoulders so as to have a good look at him, but
as soon as he had fully recognized him, he clasped him in

his arms so closely and shedding such tears of heartfelt joy that most of those there present had to keep him company with theirs. The words the brothers exchanged, the emotion they showed can scarcely be imagined, I fancy, much less put down in writing. There they told each other in a few words the events of their lives; there they showed the true warmth of brotherly love; there the judge embraced Zoraida, putting all his possessions at her disposal; there he made his daughter embrace her; there the fair Christian and the beautiful Moor drew fresh tears from every eye; and there stood Don Quixote observing all these strange proceedings attentively, without uttering a word, and ascribing them all to the chimeras of knight-errantry. Presently they agreed that the captain and Zoraida should return with his brother to Seville and sends news to his father of his having been delivered and found, so as to enable him to come and be present at the marriage and baptism of Zoraida, for it was impossible for the judge to put off his journey, as he was informed that in a month from that date the fleet would sail from Seville for New Spain, and to miss the passage would have been a great inconvenience to him. In short, everybody was pleased and glad at the captive's good future. As two-thirds of the night were already past, they resolved to retire to rest for the remainder of it. Don Quixote offered to mount guard over the castle lest they should be attacked by some giant or other dissolute scoundrel, covetous of the great treasure of beauty the castle contained. Those who understood him returned thanks for this service, and they gave the judge an account of his extraordinary humor, with which he was not a little entertained. Only Sancho Panza was fuming at the lateness of the hour for retirement, and he made himself more comfortable than any of them by throwing himself on the harness of his ass, which, as will be told further on, cost him very dear.

As the ladies, then, had retired to their apartments and the others were settling themselves with as little discomfort as possible, Don Quixote sallied out of the inn to act as sentinel of the castle as he had promised. A little before the approach of dawn the ladies heard a voice so sweet and musical that it forced them all to listen attentively, but especially Dorotea, who lay awake, and by whose side Doña Clara de Viedma, for so the judge's daughter was called, was sleeping. No one could imagine who it was who sang so sweetly, and the voice

was unaccompanied by any instrument. At one moment it
seemed to them as if the singer were in the courtyard, at
another in the stable; and while they were all attention, wondering, Cardenio came to the door and said: "Listen, whoever
is not asleep, and you will hear a muleteer singing, who as he
chants enchants."

"We are listening to him, sir," said Dorotea.

Upon this Cardenio went away, and Dorotea, with great
attention, made out the words, which were as follows:

CHAPTER XLIII

*In which the pleasant story of the muleteer is told,
with other strange happenings at the inn*

> Love's mariner am I
> On his deep ocean tossed;
> All hope of refuge lost,
> No haven is in sight.
>
> One star that shines on high
> I'm taking as my guide,
> One brighter far than all
> That Palinurus spied;
>
> Fearing to lose my way,
> At random I navigate,
> Watching ahead its ray,
> Careless yet full of care.
>
> Her chilling prudery,
> Her coyness that repels,
> Is a misty cloud that veils
> The face I long to see.

O Clara! Glittering star,
Dazzled I gasp for breath,
But when dimmed are thy beams
Then I am nigh to death.

The singer had reached this point in his song when it
struck Dorotea that it would be a pity if Clara missed hearing such a lovely voice; so, she shook the girl from side to
side until she awoke her, saying: "Forgive me, child, for waking you, but I do so want you to have the joy of listening to
the best voice you have ever heard, perhaps, in all your life."

Clara awoke quite drowsy and at first did not understand
what Dorotea said; so, she asked what it was, and Dorotea
repeated what she had said. Then the girl became attentive.
But she had hardly heard two lines of the song when she was
seized with a strange trembling as if she were suffering from
a severe attack of quartan ague, and throwing her arms
around Dorotea, she said: "Oh, my dear, dear lady! Why
did you awake me? The greatest kindness Fortune could do
me now would be to keep my eyes and ears tightly closed so
as neither to see nor to hear that unhappy musician."

"What are you talking about, child? Why, they say this
singer is a muleteer."

"No, no, he is not," replied Clara. "He is a lord of many
places, and the place he holds in my heart so firmly shall
never be taken from him, unless he be willing to surrender
it."

Dorotea was amazed at the passionate language of the
young girl, for it seemed to her far in advance of the experience of life that her tender years warranted; so, she said to
her: "You speak in such a way, Doña Clara, that I cannot
understand you. Explain yourself more clearly and tell me
what is this you are saying about hearts and places and this
musician whose voice has so moved you? But do not tell me
anything now; I do not want to lose the pleasure I get from
listening to the singer by giving my attention to your trans-
ports, for I think he is going to sing a new song with new
words and a new melody."

"Let him then, in Heaven's name," replied Clara; and
not to hear him she covered both ears with his hands, at
which Dorotea was again surprised, but turning her attention
to the song, she found that it ran in this fashion:

Sweet hope, be bold!
And through all obstacles and thickets break;
The path still hold
Firmly which thou didst plan and make;
Nor fear to see
Death ever by thy side awaiting thee.

The coward's heart
Fear-ridden will no joy of triumph know;
Unblest is he
That a bold front to Fortune does not show,
But yields his soul
And senses tamely to soft indolence.

If Love should sell
His glories dearly that is only fair,
For who could tell
The value of Love's pledges past compare?
And we all know,
What costeth little is but rated low.

The loving swain
Can mountains move if he is resolute,
And though my suit
Is beset by endless obstacles and pain,
I'll not despair,
But one day soar into the heavenly air.

Here the voice ceased and Clara's sighs began again, all
of which excited Dorotea's curiosity to know what could be
the cause of such sweet singing and such bitter weeping; so,
she again asked her to tell her what she had been about to
say before. Upon this Clara, afraid that Luscinda might hear
her, crept close to Dorotea, put her mouth so near the other's
ear that she could speak safely without fear of being heard
by anyone else, and said: "This singer, dear lady, is the son
of a gentleman of Aragón, lord of two villages, who lives
opposite my father's house in Madrid, and though my father
had the windows of his house covered with canvas in winter
and with lattices in summer, in some way (I do not know
how) this youth, who was pursuing his studies, saw me
(whether in church or elsewhere, I cannot tell) and, in fact,
fell in love with me, telling me of it from the windows of
his house with so many signs and tears that I came to believe

him, and even to love him, without knowing what he wished of me. One of the signs he used was to link one hand in the other, to show that he wished to marry me, and though I would be glad if that could be, being alone and motherless, I knew not whom I could confide in; and so, I left it as it was, showing no favor except (when my father was away from home and his father, too) to lift the canvas or blind a little bit and let him see me fully, at which he would be so enraptured that it seemed as if he were going mad.

"Meanwhile, the time for my father's departure arrived, which the youth ascertained though not through me, for I had never been able to tell him of it. He fell sick, of grief I suppose, and so the day we were going away I was not able to bid him good-bye, not even by a glance. But after we had been two days on the road, on entering an inn at a village one day's journey from here, I saw him at the door of the inn in the dress of a muleteer, and so well disguised that if I did not carry his image in my heart, I should have found it impossible to recognize him. I knew him, and I was surprised and delighted. He stole a glance at me, undetected by my father, from whom he always hides his face when he crosses my path on the road or in the inns where we halt, and as I know who he is, when I reflect that for love of me he makes this journey on foot and suffers all this hardship, I am ready to die of sorrow, and where he sets his foot, I set my eyes. I do not know his purpose in coming, or how he could have got away from his father, who loves him beyond measure, because he has no other heir and because he deserves it, as you will discover when you see him. Moreover, I can tell you that everything he sings is out of his own head, for I have heard them say he is a great scholar and poet, and what is more, every time I see him or hear him sing, I tremble all over and am terrified lest my father should recognize him and come to know of our loves. I have never spoken a word to him in my life, yet for all that, I love him so much that I cannot live without him. This, dear lady, is all I have to tell you about the musician whose voice has delighted you so much and from it alone you may easily see that he is no muleteer, but a lord of hearts and places as I have said."

"Say no more, Doña Clara," said Dorotea at this, at the same time kissing her countless times. "Say no more, I repeat, but wait till day dawns. I hope, with God's help, to set your affairs on the way toward the happy ending that such an innocent beginning deserves."

"Ah, lady, what ending can we expect," said Doña Clara, "when his father is so wealthy and important that he will not consider me fit to be his son's servant, much less his wife? And as to marrying without the knowledge of my father, I would not do it for all the world. I would not ask anything more than that this youth should go back and leave me. Perhaps with not seeing him and with the great distance we are going to travel, the pain I feel may be relieved, though I daresay the remedy I propose will do me very little good. I don't know by what devilment this has come about or how this love I feel got into me, seeing that I am such a young girl and he a mere boy, for I really believe we are of the same age, and I am not quite sixteen yet, nor shall be, my father says, till next Michaelmas."

Dorotea could not help laughing at Doña Clara's childish way of talking and said: "Let us go to sleep, dear lady, for we still have a little of the night left. God will soon send us the daylight, and all will be set right or it will go hard with me."

With this they fell asleep, and deep silence reigned throughout the inn. The only persons not asleep were the landlady's daughter and her maid, Maritornes. Since they both knew Don Quixote's weak points and that he was standing guard outside, fully armed and on horseback, they resolved to play some tricks upon him, or at any rate to amuse themselves for a while by listening to his nonsense.

Now, it so happened that there was no window in the inn on the side that overlooked the fields, but only a hole in the loft, out of which the straw was thrown. At this hole the two demimaidens took up their position and saw Don Quixote on horseback, reclining on his lance and heaving from time to time such deep and mournful sighs that it seemed as if each one would tear his soul asunder. And they heard him say in a soft, soothing, and amorous voice: "O my lady, Dulcinea of El Toboso, summit of all beauty, quintessence of discretion, treasury of charm, desposit of chastity, and finally, idea of everything that is beneficial, honest, and charming in this world! What may thy grace be doing at this moment? Art thou perchance thinking of thy captive knight, who for thy sake has subjected himself to so many perils?

Give me swift tidings of her, O three-faced luminary![1] Perhaps even now thou art gazing upon her, envious of her beauty, as she paces through some gallery of her sumptuous palace or leans over some balcony to consider how she may, without risking her virtue or dignity, calm the pangs that my poor aching heart endures for her, what glory she may bestow on my sufferings, what solace she may give to my cares, and finally, what life to my death, what guerdon to my long service. And thou, O sun, who now art busy saddling thy horses to sally forth betimes to see my lady, I beseech thee, when thou seest her, to salute her in my name. But beware that thou dost not kiss her on the face, or I shall be more jealous of thee than thou wert of that swift-footed, faithless Daphne, who made thee sweat and run over the plains of Thessaly, or by the banks of Peneus—I do not exactly remember where it was that thou didst run in thy jealous and amorous frenzy."

So far had Don Quixote proceeded in his mournful soliloquy when the innkeeper's daughter softly called to him, whispering: "Dear sir, come this way, if you please."

At this signal Don Quixote turned his head and saw by the light of the moon, which was then at its highest, that they beckoned him from the hole, which he imagined to be a window, and even with gilded bars suitable to such a castle as he conceived that inn to be. At once he believed in his strange fancy that again, as once before, the beautiful damsel, daughter of the lord of the castle, conquered by love of him, had come to tempt him. With this in mind and unwilling to show himself discourteous and ungrateful, he turned Rozinante about and came over to the hole, and when he saw the two girls, he said: "I take pity on you, beauteous lady, because you have fixed your love where it is not possible for you to meet with the response your great virtues and nobility deserve. Yet, you ought not to blame this miserable knight-errant, whom love has wholly disabled from paying his court to any other than to her whom, from the first moment, he made absolute mistress of his soul. Pardon me, therefore, good lady, and retire to your chamber and do not reveal your desires to me further, that I may not appear

---

[1] The three-faced luminary was Diana, goddess of the moon. This is an allusion to Virgil's *Aeneid* IV, 511.

yet more ungrateful. But if your love for me suggests to you any way wherein I may serve you other than by returning your passion, demand it straightaway, for I swear to you by that sweet absent enemy of mine to gratify you unconditionally, even if you were to demand a lock of Medusa's hair, which was all snakes, or even the beams of the sun enclosed in a vial."

"My lady needs none of that, sir knight," said Maritornes.

"What does she want then, wise duenna?" asked Don Quixote.

"Only one of your beautiful hands," said Maritornes, "that she may satisfy the longing that brought her to this window, putting her honor in such danger that if her lord and father came to know it, the least he would do would be to slice off her ear."

"I should like to see him do it!" answered Don Quixote. "He had best beware of what he does, unless he wishes to have the most disastrous end that ever a father had in this world for having laid violent hands on the delicate limbs of his enamored daughter."

Maritornes, not doubting that Don Quixote would give up his hand as she had requested and having made up her mind what to do, descended from the loft and went to the stable, from where she took the halter of Sancho Panza's ass and hastened back with it to the hole, just as Don Quixote had stood upon Rozinante's saddle that he might more easily reach the barred window at which he thought the love-sick damsel was standing. As he stretched out his hand to her, he cried: "Take, lady, this hand, or as I should rather say, this lash of evildoers. Take this hand I say, which no other woman has ever touched, not even she herself who holds complete possession of my whole body. I give it to you, not that you may kiss it, but that you may behold the contexture of the sinews, the knitting of the muscles, the large and swelling veins, from which you may learn how mighty is the force of that arm to which belongs such a hand."

"We'll soon see," said Maritornes. Then, making a running knot in the halter, she cast it on his wrist, and descending from the hole, she tied the other end very tightly to the bolt of the hayloft door.

Don Quixote, feeling the roughness of the halter about his wrist, exclaimed: "My lady, you seem rather to rasp than to clasp my hand; I pray you not to handle it so roughly, since it is not to blame for what you suffer through my adverse inclinations, nor is it right that you should vent all your displeasure on so small a part of me. Consider that those who love well do not so ill avenge."

But there was no one to give heed to those words of Don Quixote, for as soon as Maritornes had him tied up, she and the other one, almost bursting with laughter, ran away and left him fastened in such a manner that it was impossible for him to loose himself. He was standing, as we said before, on Rozinante's saddle, with his whole arm stuck through the hole and tied to the bolt of the door, and he was in great fear that if Rozinante budged ever so little on either side, he would be left hanging by the arm. Therefore, he did not dare to make the least movement, though he might well have expected from Rozinante's patience and mild temper that he would stand without stirring for a whole century. Finding that he was trussed up and that the ladies had vanished, Don Quixote began to imagine that all this had been done by way of enchantment, as the time before when the enchanted Moor of a muleteer had drubbed him in that same castle. Then he cursed himself for his foolishness in venturing to enter the castle a second time after his bad experience on the first occasion, for it was a maxim with knights-errant that when they had attempted an adventure and had not come well out of it, it was a sign that it was reserved not for them, but for some other, and therefore they were not bound to attempt it a second time. Yet for all this, he pulled his arm to see if he might release himself, but he was so well tied that all his efforts were in vain. It is true that he pulled his arm cautiously, lest Rozinante should stir, and although he longed to get down into his seat on the saddle, he could only stand upright or wrench off his arm.

Many a time he wished for the sword of Amadis, against which no enchantment had power; then he began to curse his stars; then reflected on how his presence would be missed in the world during the time he remained there enchanted, as he believed he was; then he again remembered his beloved Dulcinea of El Toboso; many a time he would call on his good squire, Sancho Panza, who, buried in sleep and stretched out upon his packsaddle, did not even dream of the mother who bore him; then he summoned to his aid the

sages Lirgandeo and Alquife; [2] then he invoked his good
friend Urganda to succor him; at last, the morning found him
so full of despair and confusion that he bellowed like a bull,
for he had no hope that the day would bring him any cure
for his sufferings, which would be everlasting, seeing that he
was enchanted. He was all the more convinced of this inas-
much as Rozinante had not budged ever so little, and he concluded that he and his horse would remain in that state,
without eating, drinking, or sleeping, until the evil influences
of the stars had passed or some great magician had disenchanted him.

In this he was greatly deceived, for scarcely did day begin
to break when there arrived four horsemen at the inn door,
well equipped, with firelocks on their saddlebows. They
knocked loudly on the inn door, which was still shut, and
Don Quixote, hearing from where he still stood guard, cried
out in a loud and arrogant voice: "Knights, or squires, or
whoever you may be, you have no right to knock at the
gates of this castle, for it is more than clear that at such an
hour as this either those who are within are sleeping or else
are not in the habit of opening their fortress until the sun
has spread his beams over the whole land. Therefore, stand
back and wait until it be clear day, and then we will see
whether it be right or not to open our gates to you."

"What the hell castle or fortress is this," cried one of them,
"that makes us observe such ceremonies? If you are the innkeeper, tell them to open the door, for we are travelers who
only want to feed our horses before moving on; we're
riding posthaste."

"Do you think, gentlemen, that I look like an innkeeper?"
answered Don Quixote.

"I don't know what you look like," replied the other, "but
I'm sure you're talking nonsense in calling this inn a castle."

"It is a castle," said Don Quixote, "and one of the best
in this province, and it has people inside who have had a
scepter in their hand and a crown on their head."

"You should have said it the other way around," said the
traveler, "the scepter on their head and the crown on their

---

[2] Lirgandeo was the tutor of the Knight of the Sun; Alquife
was the chronicler of Amadis of Greece, the Knight of the Flaming Sword.

hand.[3] Probably, if we get down to facts, there is a company of players within; they often wear those crowns and scepters you're speaking of. But I don't believe people worthy of crown and scepter would lodge in so paltry an inn, where they keep such silence as they do here."

"You know little of the world," replied Don Quixote, "for you ignore the chances that are wont to happen in knight-errantry."

The companions of the man who asked the questions, being wearied of this discourse, began again to knock furiously at the door, and this time to such effect that they waked not only the innkeeper, but also all the guests. The former, then, got out of bed and inquired who was knocking.

In the meantime it happened that one of the horses on which the four strangers rode came sniffing around Rozinante, who stood melancholy and sad, with his ears down, bearing without budging his outstretched master. But being, after all, made of flesh, though he seemed to be of wood, he could not help feeling sympathy and turning to smell him who made these advances. But scarcely had he moved one step when Don Quixote's two feet, which were close together, slipped, and the knight slid from the saddle and would have fallen to the ground had he not remained hanging by the arm. This caused him so much pain that he felt as though his wrist was being cut away or his arm was being pulled out, for he hung so near to the ground that he touched it with the tips of his toes. This increased his misery because, feeling how little was wanted to set his feet flat on the ground, he strained himself desperately to reach it, like those who are undergoing the torture of the strappado. They hover between touching and not touching, and they themselves aggravate their own sufferings owing to their eagerness to stretch themselves under the delusion that with a little more stretching they will reach the ground.

[3] This is a reference to the custom in those days of branding criminals on the hand with the crown.

CHAPTER XLIV

In which the unprecedented adventures at the inn are continued

In fact, so great was the outcry made by Don Quixote that the landlord hastily opened the inn door and ran out to see who it was that roared so loud. Maritornes, whom the cries had also awakened, guessing what it was, ran to the hayloft, and without anyone seeing her, she untied the halter that held up Don Quixote. He fell to the ground in the sight of the landlord and the four travelers, who came up to him and asked him what made him roar so loud. Without answering, he slipped the halter from his wrist, and rising to his feet, he leaped on Rozinante, braced on his shield, couched his lance, and wheeling around the field, rode back at a half gallop, crying out: "Whoever shall dare to say that I have been justly enchanted, provided my lady, Princess Micomicona, will give me leave to do it, I say that he lies and I challenge him to single combat."

The new arrivals were astounded at Don Quixote's words, but the innkeeper told them not to mind him, for he was out of his wits. They then asked the landlord whether by any chance a lad of about fifteen years, dressed as a mule boy, had come to his inn, and they gave a description of him that tallied with that of Doña Clara's lover. The landlord replied that there were so many people in the inn that he had not noticed the man they asked for, but one of them, seeing the coach in which the judge had come, exclaimed: "He must be here without doubt, for this is the coach they say he was following. Let one of us stay at the door and the rest go in to look for him; it would even be wiser for one of us to ride around the inn, in case he should get away over the yard wall."

"That we shall certainly do," replied another of them. Then, two went inside, one stayed by the door, and the fourth rode around the inn. The landlord watched all this and could not make out why they were taking all these pains, though he guessed they were looking for the lad whom they had described to him.

By now it was broad daylight, and for that reason and because of the noise Don Quixote had made, they were all awake and getting out of bed, especially Doña Clara and Dorotea, who had been unable to get much sleep that night: the former through excitement at having her lover so near her, and the other through eagerness to see him.

Don Quixote, when he saw that none of the four took any account of him or answered his challenge, was ready to burst with rage and fury; if he could have found in the ordinances of his chivalry that a knight-errant could undertake another enterprise after he had pledged his word and faith not to attempt any until he had finished what he had promised, he would have attacked them all and made them answer against their will. But as it did not seem to him proper or expedient to begin a new enterprise until he had installed Micomicona in her kingdom, he had to remain quiet and hold his peace to see what would be the result of the traveler's searches. One of them finally found the youth they were looking for fast asleep by the side of a mule boy, unaware that anyone was hunting for him, still less of being discovered. The man shook him by the arm saying: "Certainly, Don Luis, the clothes you are wearing sit well on one of your rank, and the bed I find you on accords no less with the comforts you received at your mother's knee!"

The lad rubbed his sleepy eyes, and staring for a while at his captor, he recognized him at last as one of his father's servants. So astounded was he that for a long time he could not utter a word. And the servant went on, saying: "There is nothing you can do now, Don Luis, but submit patiently and come back home if you don't want to drive your father, my master, to the tomb, for I'm very much afraid that's what will happen, so upset is he by your absence."

"Why, how did my father know," said Don Luis, "that I traveled this road and in this disguise?"

"A student whom you told your plans to was the one who let the cat out of the bag, so moved was he by the despair of your father when he missed you. So, the master sent four of us servants in search of you, and here we are at your service, more delighted than you can imagine that we can return so quickly and restore you to your father, who loves you so dearly."

"That shall be as I please or as Heaven decrees," replied Don Luis.

"What can you wish or Heaven decree except to consent to come back with us? There is no other course open to you."

The mule boy who had been lying next to Don Luis overheard this conversation; so, he got up and went to tell Don Fernando, Cardenio, and the rest, who were already dressed, of what was going on. He mentioned that the man had called the lad *Don* and repeated what he had said and how he had urged the boy to return to his father's house, but the lad would not. This, added to what they knew about the fine voice that Heaven had bestowed upon him, made them all most eager to know who he was, and even to help him if the men tried to do him any violence. So, they went to the place where he was, and they found him still arguing with his servant.

Dorotea then came out of her room, and behind her, Doña Clara, much alarmed. Dorotea called Cardenio aside and told him in a few words the story of the singer and of Doña Clara, and he told her what had occurred when his father's servants had come to look for him. But he did not speak softly enough, for Doña Clara overheard him and became so agitated that she would have fallen to the ground if Dorotea had not run to support her. Cardenio then told Dorotea to take the girl back to their room, for he would try and set everything straight, and they retired.

All four men who were trailing Don Luis were now inside the inn and standing around the youth, urging him to come back at once without delaying a moment to comfort his father, but he replied that on no account could he do so until he had concluded an affair in which his life, his honor, and his heart were at stake. The servants then insisted, saying that they would under no circumstances return without him and that they would carry him away whether he agreed or not.

"That you will not do," replied Don Luis, "unless you carry me away dead; whatever way you take me I shall be lifeless."

By this time all the others who were in the inn had gathered to hear the dispute, notably Cardenio, Don Fernando, his companions, the judge, the priest, the barber, and Don

Quixote, who then thought that there was no more need of guarding the castle. Cardenio, who already knew the youth's story, asked the servants what motive they had for carrying that lad away against his will.

"Our motive is," replied one of the four, "that we may save his father's life, for he is in danger of losing it because of this gentleman's absence."

To this Don Luis replied: "There is no reason why I should give an account here of my affairs. I am free; I shall go back if I please; if not, none of you will force me."

"Reason will compel you," answered the man, "and if that is not sufficient, it's sufficient to make us do our duty; that's why we are here."

"Let us know what is at the bottom of all this business," said the judge at this point.

The man, who recognized him as a neighbor, then answered: "Do you, my lord judge, not know this gentleman? Why, he's your neighbor's son, who has run away from his father's house in a disguise most unsuitable to his quality, as your worship can see."

The judge then looked at the lad more closely, recognized him, and embraced him, exclaiming: "What childish folly is this, Don Luis? What overmastering reason can you have had for coming here in this manner and in this dress that is so unbecoming to your rank?"

Tears came into the youth's eyes, and he could not answer a word to the judge. The latter then bade the four servants calm down, for all would be well, and taking Don Luis by the hand, he led him aside and asked him the reason for his being there.

While the judge was putting these and other questions to him, they heard a great noise at the door of the inn. The cause of this was that two guests who had lodged there the night before, seeing all the people occupied with the new guests, had tried to slip away without paying what they owed. But the landlord, who paid more attention to his own than to other people's business, laid hold of them as they were going out the door and demanded his money. Furthermore, he abused them for their dishonest conduct in such terms that they answered with their fists, which they did with such vigor that the poor landlord was obliged to shout for help. The landlady and her daughter did not see anyone unoccupied who might give help except Don Quixote, to whom the daughter shouted: "Help! Sir knight, by the power that God gave you, help my poor father, whom two scoundrels are thrashing like a bundle of corn."

Don Quixote answered deliberately and with great gravity: "Beauteous damsel, your prayers cannot at the present time be granted, for I am not permitted to engage in any new adventure until I have finished the one I have promised to carry through. All I can do to serve you is what I will say to you: Run and tell your father that he must fight on as best he can and that he must not allow himself to be conquered, while I ask permission from Princess Micomicona to help him in his distress. If she will give me leave, you may be sure that he will be delivered."

"As I am a sinner," cried Maritornes, who was standing nearby, "before you get the leave you mention, my master will be in the next world."

"Allow me, lady, to get the leave I speak of," replied Don Quixote, "and it will matter little whether he be in the next world or not, for I will bring him back again in spite of the next world, or at least, I will so revenge myself on those who shall have sent him there that you will be more than satisfied."

Without saying more, he went in and knelt before Dorotea, asking her in knightly and courtly phrases that she be pleased to give him leave to go and help the governor of the castle, who was in grave distress.

The princess granted him leave very willingly, and he, buckling on his shield and laying hand on his sword, ran to the inn door, where the two guests were still mauling the landlord. But as he arrived, he stopped and stood still although Maritornes and the landlady asked why he delayed in assisting their master and husband.

"I delay," said Don Quixote, "because it is not lawful for me to lay hands upon my sword against squire like men who are not dubbed knights. But call my squire, Sancho, for his duty is to take up this defense and vengeance."

All this took place outside the inn door, where blows and buffetings were being bandied about with gusto, all to the cost of the landlord and the rage of Maritornes, the landlady, and her daughter, who were in despair at having to witness the cowardice of Don Quixote and the ill-treatment their master, husband, and father was suffering.

But let us leave him there, for he will always find a helper,

and if none appears, let him suffer and hold his tongue for
being so foolhardy as to risk himself in what is more than
his strength warrants, and let us move back fifty paces and
hear what was the answer Don Luis gave to the judge,
whom we left asking the lad privately the cause of his coming on foot and being so shabbily dressed. The lad, then,
clasping him strongly with both hands, as a token that some
great sorrow was wringing his heart, and shedding tears in
great profusion, answered: "I can tell you nothing, dear sir,
but that from the moment when Heaven made us neighbors
and I saw Doña Clara, your daughter and my lady, I made
her mistress of my heart, and if you, my true lord and
father, do not hinder it, this very day she shall be my
wife. For her I left my father's house; for her I put on this
dress, to follow her wherever she might go, as the arrow
does the mark or the mariner the North Star. She knows no
more of my passion than what she has been able to deduce the
few occasions she saw from afar tears in my eyes. You, sir,
know that my parents are wealthy and noble and that I am
their sole heir. If you think that these are sufficient endowments, I beseech you to make me completely happy and receive me now for your son. Though my father may have
other designs of his own and may not be pleased with this
blessing I have been able to find for myself, time has more
power to alter and transform things than human will."

Saying this the love-sick youth was silent, and the judge
was astonished and perplexed. He was no less impressed by
Don Luis's naïve manner of disclosing his private feelings
than he was amazed at finding himself in such an unexpected
predicament. All he answered, therefore, was to bid Don Luis
to calm himself for the moment and to arrange with his servants not to go back that day. He would then have time
to consider what was best for all. At this Don Luis kissed
his hands and moistened them with his tears, which would
have melted a heart of stone, let alone the judge's. Being a
practical man, he was already aware of the advantages of
such a match for his daughter, though he hoped it would be
possible for it to be concluded with the consent of Don
Luis's father, who he knew aspired to have his son made a
noble man of title.

By this time there was peace between the guests and the
landlord, for through Don Quixote's persuasion and fair
words, more than through menaces, they had paid him for

everything. Don Luis's servants were waiting for the end
of the judge's conversation and for their master to make his
decision. All now would have been well if the Devil, who
never sleeps, had not so ordered that another traveler arrived
at the inn. This was none other than the barber from whom
Don Quixote had taken Mambrino's helmet and Sancho Panza
the ass's harness, which he had exchanged for his own.
And while this barber was leading his beast to the stable, he
happened to catch sight of Sancho Panza mending some part
of the packsaddle. As soon as he saw him, he recognized him
and at once rushed at him, crying: "Ah, mister thief, I've
nabbed you! Give up my basin and my harness and everything
you stole from me!"

Sancho, finding himself attacked so suddenly and hearing
those rough words, with one hand clutched the packsaddle and
with the other gave the barber such a buffet that he bathed
his teeth in blood. But for all that the barber held fast his
grip of the saddle and cried out so loud that all the people
in the inn ran out, hearing the noise and the scuffle.

"Help here, in the name of the king and justice," shouted
the barber; "this thief and highwayman wants to kill me because I'm trying to get back my own goods."

"That is a lie," cried Sancho; "I'm no highwayman. My
master, Don Quixote, won these spoils in fair battle."

Don Quixote was already there and very glad to see how
well his squire defended himself and attacked the enemy, and
from that time on, he took him to be a man of courage and
resolved to have him dubbed knight at the first opportunity
offered, for he thought that the order of knighthood would
be well bestowed on him.

Among the many things that the barber said in his argument, he cried: "Gentlemen, this packsaddle is as surely mine
as the death that I owe to God, and I know it as well as if
I had brought it into the world, and there is my ass in the
stable who won't let me lie; if not, try it on him, and if it
doesn't fit him to the hair, call me an infamous rascal. And
what's more, on the very day when they took my packsaddle,
they robbed me also of a new brass basin that had never
been used and was worth a crown."

Here Don Quixote could no longer contain himself, and
thrusting himself between the two combatants to separate
them, he deposited the packsaddle on the ground that it
might be in sight of all until the dispute would be decided;

then he said: "Gentlemen, see clearly and manifestly the error into which this worthy squire has fallen, for he calls a basin what was, is, and always shall be, the helmet of Mambrino, which I won from him by force in fair battle and made myself lord of it by right and lawful possession. In regard to the packsaddle I do not interfere; but I can say that my squire, Sancho, asked my leave to take away the trappings from the horse of this vanquished coward that he might adorn his own with them. I gave him leave, and he took them. As to these being turned from a horse's trappings into an ass's packsaddle, I can give no other reason but the common one, namely, that these transformations are wont to take place in the affairs of chivalry. To confirm the truth of my words, run, friend Sancho, and bring the helmet that this good fellow declares to be a basin."

"Faith, master," said Sancho, "if we have no better proof of our story than what you say, the helmet of Mambrino is as much a basin as this fellow's trappings are a packsaddle."

"Do what I command," replied Don Quixote, "for it cannot be that all things in this castle are governed by magic."

Sancho went for the basin and brought it, and as soon as Don Quixote saw it, he took it in his hands and said: "See, gentlemen, with what face can this squire declare that this is a basin and not the helmet that I have mentioned. I swear to you, by the order of chivalry that I profess, that this is the very same helmet that I won from him. Nothing has been added or taken away from it."

"There is no doubt about that," said Sancho, "for since my master won it till now, he only fought one battle in it, when he freed that unlucky chain gang. Indeed, if it hadn't been for that same basin-helmet, he'd not have escaped as free as he did, for there was a lot of stone throwing in that tussle."

CHAPTER XLV

In which the controversy of Mambrino's helmet and the packsaddle is decided, with other happenings, all quite true

"Now, gentlemen," cried the barber, "what do you think of those who still hold that this is not a basin but a helmet?"

"If anyone says the contrary," said Don Quixote, "I will make him know, if he is a knight, that he is lying, and if he's a squire, that he is lying a thousand times."

Our own barber, who was present all this time, knew Don Quixote's humor, and he had a mind to encourage his folly and carry the jest further' to make them laugh; so, he addressed the other barber as follows: "Sir barber, or whoever you are, know that I am also of your profession, that I hold a certificate for more than twenty years, and that I am well acquainted with all the instruments of the barber's art, every one of them. Moreover, in my youth I was a soldier, and I know what a helmet is like, and a morion, and a close-casque, and other kinds of soldier's gear. Therefore, I say, always subject to better judgment, that this piece before us, which this good gentleman holds in his hand, not only is not a barber's basin, but is as far from being one as black is from white and truth from falsehood. It is a helmet, though, in my opinion, not a complete one."

"No, truly," said Don Quixote, "it lacks half, namely, the beaver."

"That's true," said the curate, who perceived his friend's intention, and Cardenio, Don Fernando, and his companions affirmed likewise. Even the judge would have taken part in the prank if he had not been so preoccupied with Don Luis's affair, but he was so immersed in his thoughts that he paid little or no attention to these trivialities.

"Lord save us!" cried the befooled barber. "Is it possible that so many honorable gentlemen should say this is not a basin but a helmet? Sure, this is enough to strike a whole university dumb with amazement, no matter how wise it be. Enough said; if this basin is a helmet, then this pack-saddle must be a horse's trappings as this man has said."

"To me it looks like a packsaddle," said Don Quixote, "but I have already said that I will not interfere in the matter."

"Whether it be a packsaddle or trappings," said the curate, "it is only Don Quixote who can say, for in these matters of chivalry all these gentlemen and myself bow to his knowl-edge."

"By Heaven, gentlemen," said Don Quixote, "so many strange and unaccountable things have befallen me in this castle on the two occasions I have stayed here that I would not dare to make a positive affirmation concerning anything contained in it, for I imagine that everything here works by enchantment. On the first occasion, a Moorish magician in the castle troubled me greatly, and Sancho suffered at the hands of certain of his followers, and last night I was left hanging by this arm for close on two hours, without knowing how or why I fell into that mischance. Therefore, it would be rash on my part to interfere in so perplexing a business. For those who say this is a basin and not a helmet I have given my answer, but I will leave it for others to decide whether this be a packsaddle or the trappings of a horse. Perhaps, as none of you have been dubbed knights, the spells in this place may have no effect on you, your under-standing will be free, and you will be able to judge of the affairs of this castle as they really and truly are, and not as they appear to me."

"There is no doubt," Don Fernando replied, "that Don Quixote has spoken very wisely in saying that the decision in this case rests with us, and so that it may proceed in sound foundations, I shall take the votes of these gentlemen in secret and give you a full and clear account of the result."

All this was the subject of great laughter to those who knew Don Quixote's humor, but to those who did not, it seemed the greatest nonsense in all the world, especially to the four travelers who had arrived at the inn early in the morning and to three others who had just arrived and who had the appearance of officers of the Holy Brotherhood, as in fact they were.

But he who despaired most of all was the barber whose basin had been transformed before his very eyes into the helmet of Mambrino and whose packsaddle would doubtless turn into the rich trappings of a horse. All of them laughed to see how Don Fernando took their votes whispering in their ear so that they might declare in secret if that precious object they had quarreled so much about were a packsaddle or horse trappings.

After he had taken the votes of those who knew Don Quixote, he said in a loud voice: "The truth is, my good man, that I am tired of asking so many opinions, for no sooner do I ask what I want to know than they answer me that it is absurd to say that this is an ass's packsaddle and not the trappings of a horse—and of a well-bred horse at that. So, you must have patience; in spite of you and your ass, this is not a packsaddle but horse trappings, and you have conducted your case very badly."

"May I never have a share in Heaven," cried the barber, "if all you gentlemen be not deceived! Likewise may my soul appear to God as this packsaddle appears to me a packsaddle and not horse trappings. But laws go as kings will; I'll say no more, and in truth I'm not drunk, nor have I broken my fast, sinner though I be."

The barber's simplicity made them laugh as merrily as did the vagaries of Don Quixote, who then said: "There is nothing more to be done here except for everyone to take his own, and let Saint Peter bless what the Lord has given."

One of the travelers now spoke saying: "If this be not a planned joke, I can't for the life of me understand why men of sense, as everyone here seems to be, can have the face to say that this is not a basin and that is not a packsaddle. I'll swear by" (here he hurled a round oath) "that all the people on earth will not convince me that this is no basin and this no jackass' packsaddle."

"Perhaps it might be a she-ass's," said the curate.

"It is all the same," said the traveler. "The only point is whether it is or is not a packsaddle, as you say."

Then one of the three troopers of the Holy Brotherhood, who had heard the dispute and the question, exclaimed indignantly: "It is as much a packsaddle as my father is my father, and he who says, or shall say, to the contrary must be sodden with drink."

"You lie like a baseborn knave!" answered Don Quixote.

Then raising his lance, which he had never let out of his hand, he aimed such a blow at the trooper's head that had he not jumped aside, it would have laid him flat on the ground. The lance was broken into splinters against the ground, and the other troopers, seeing their companion so roughly handled, raised the hue and cry, shouting for help in the name of the Holy Brotherhood. The landlord, who was one of that body, ran at once for his staff of office and his sword and took his place beside his companions. Don Luis's servants surrounded him lest he escape in the confusion. The barber, seeing the house was turned topsy-turvy, laid hold again of his packsaddle, and Sancho did the same. Don Quixote set hand to his sword and attacked the troopers. Don Luis screamed at his servants to leave him alone and to go and help Don Quixote, Cardenio, and Don Fernando, for they all had taken sides with Don Quixote. The curate kept shouting; the landlady was screaming; her daughter was weeping; Maritornes was howling; Dorotea stood frightened; Luscinda was perplexed; and Doña Clara fainted away. The barber drubbed Sancho; Sancho mauled the barber; Don Luis, whom one of his servants dared to hold back, hit him so hard that his teeth were bathed in blood; Don Fernando knocked one of the troopers down and trampled him underfoot to his heart's content; the landlord bawled at the top of his voice again for help to the Holy Brotherhood. Thus the whole inn was nothing but wails, shouts, screams, dismay, confusion, alarms, disasters, slashes, cudgeling, kicks, and spilling of blood.

In the midst of all this chaos, tumult, and uproar, Don Quixote suddenly imagined that he was launched hell for leather into the discord of Agramante's camp,[1] and so he cried aloud in a voice that thundered through the inn: "Hold back, all of you! Sheath all your swords! Keep the peace and listen to me, if you wish to live!"

At the sound of his mighty voice they all stopped fighting, and he continued, saying: "Did I not tell you, gentlemen, that this castle was enchanted and that some legion of demons must live here? As proof of what I say, note with your own eyes how the discord of Agramante's camp has been transplanted among us. Here they fight for the sword, yonder for

---

[1] Proverbial for a fierce battle. From *Orlando Furioso*, CXXVII.

the horse, there for the eagle, here for the helmet, and we
are all of us fighting, and not one of us understands the
other. Come, therefore, sir judge, and you, sir curate; one of
you can play the part of King Agramante and the other that
of King Sobrino; make peace between us, for by almighty
God it is great wickedness that so many gentlemen of quality
here should kill one another for such trivial matters."

The troopers, who did not understand the language of Don
Quixote and found themselves ill-used by Don Fernando,
Cardenio, and their comrades, would not be pacified; the
barber, however, gave in, for both his beard and his packsaddle had been pulled to bits in the fight; Sancho, as a
good servant, was attentive to the slightest hint of his master;
Don Luis's four servants, seeing that little could be gained
by not doing so, held their peace; the landlord alone insisted
that they had to punish the insolent behavior of that madman who was continually creating a hubbub in his inn. At
last, the row died down for the moment; the packsaddle remained a horse trapping until the day of judgment, the basin
a helmet, and the inn a castle in the imagination of Don
Quixote.

When they all had calmed down and had made peace
with each other through the intercession of the judge and
the curate, Don Luis's servants began again to argue that he
should return with them at once. While Don Luis argued
with them, the judge told Don Fernando, Cardenio, and the
curate what should be done, repeating the reasons that Don
Luis had told him. Finally it was agreed that Don Fernando
tell Don Luis's servants who he was and how he would be
pleased if Don Luis were to accompany him to Andalusia,
where his brother, the marquess, would receive Don Luis in
the manner that his rank deserved, for it was obvious that
Don Luis did not intend to go to his father just then, even
if he were cut to pieces. The servants, having understood
the determination of Don Luis's resolution and impressed
by Don Fernando's rank, decided among themselves that three
of them should return to tell their master what was going on
and that the fourth should stay to serve Don Luis and to
keep an eye on him until they come back to get him or to tell
him what his father ordered.

Thus that jumble of arguments and quarrels was calmed
down by the authority of Agramante and the prudence of
King Sobrino. But the enemy of concord and the adversary

of peace, finding himself despised and mocked and with
nothing but a scanty profit from the chaos in which he had
involved them all, resolved to try his hand once more and
stir up fresh quarrels. It happened then that the troopers,
when they heard the quality of their adversaries in the brawl,
retired from the fray, believing that no matter what happened, they would get the worst of it. But one of them, the
one who had been drubbed and kicked by Don Fernando,
suddenly remembered that among the warrants in his possession he had one against Don Quixote, whom the Holy Brotherhood had ordered to be taken into custody for liberating
the galley slaves, thus confirming what Sancho had rightly
feared. No sooner did this thought come into his mind than
he tried at once to ascertain whether the description of Don
Quixote on the warrant tallied with the man who stood before him. He took from his bosom a parchment scroll and
began to read it slowly, for he was no good at reading, and
at every word he came to, he fixed his eyes on Don Quixote,
comparing the details in his warrant with those of the
knight's face. He found that this, beyond all manner of
doubt, was the very man described in the warrant. As soon
as he felt sure of this, he folded his parchment, held the warrant in his left hand, while with the right he seized Don
Quixote by the collar with so tight a grip that the knight
could hardly breathe; at the same time he cried aloud: "Help
for the Holy Brotherhood! To show you that I'm asking for
it in earnest, let this warrant be read, which states that this
highway robber is to be arrested."

The curate took the warrant and saw that all the trooper
said was true and that the description therein applied to Don
Quixote. The knight, however, finding himself ill-used by that
baseborn knave, felt his choler rising to such heights that all
the bones in his body began to creak. He caught the trooper
by the throat with both hands so that if he had not been
rescued by his companions, he would have given up the
ghost there and then before the knight would have given up
his prey. The landlord, who was under the obligation of
helping those of his office, rushed at once to take his part.
The landlady, seeing her husband engaged again in battle,
raised a fresh outcry, in which Maritornes and her
daughter swelled the chorus, invoking the help of Heaven
and all the company.

Sancho, when he saw what was afoot, cried out: "God

almighty! It's true what my master says of the enchantments of this castle; it's not possible for a man to live here an hour in peace and quiet."

Don Fernando parted the trooper and Don Quixote, and to the relief of both of them, he unlocked their grip on one another. Nevertheless, the troopers kept on demanding their prisoner and calling on the company to help them, in accordance with the laws of the king and the Holy Brotherhood.

When he heard them say these words, Don Quixote laughed and exclaimed: "Come hither, filthy, baseborn crew! Do you call me a highway robber because I liberated those in chains, freed those who were bound, aided those who were wretched, raised the fallen, and succored the needy? O infamous brood! Your understanding is too mean and base for you to deserve that Heaven should communicate to you the power that lies in knight-errantry. You are even unworthy to be shown the sin and ignorance in which you wallow, when you refuse to revere the shadow, much more the actual presence, of a knight-errant. Come hither, ye that are not troopers but thieves in a troop, highway robbers with license from the Holy Brotherhood! Tell me, who was the idiot who signed a warrant for the arrest of such a knight as I am? Who was he who did not know that knights-errant are free from all jurisdiction, that their law is their sword, their charters their courage, their statutes their own will? Who is the blockhead, I say again, who is not aware that there exists no patent of nobility with so many privileges and exemptions as the one that a knight-errant acquires the day he is dubbed a knight and devotes himself to the stern exercise of chivalry? What knight-errant ever paid poll tax, customs, queen's patten money, king's tribute, toll, or impost? What tailor ever took money from him for a suit of clothes? What castellan ever lodged him in his castle and made him pay his scot? What king did not seat him at his own table? What maiden did not fall in love with him and surrender herself to his will and pleasure? And, lastly, what knight-errant was there, is there, or shall there be in the world who has not the courage, single-handed, to give four hundred cudgelings to four hundred troopers, should they dare to confront him."

CHAPTER XLVI

Of the notable adventure of the officers of the Holy Brotherhood and the great ferocity of our good knight Don Quixote

While Don Quixote was uttering this oration, the curate was trying to persuade the troopers that the knight was out of his wits, as they could perceive by his words and his actions, and that even if they did arrest him, they would have to release him afterward as a madman. To this the trooper who had the warrant answered that he was not there to pass judgment on Don Quixote's madness; he just had to carry out the orders of his superior officer. Once he was arrested, they could let him out three hundred times for all he cared.

"Nevertheless," said the curate, "this time you must not take him away; nor do I believe that he will let himself be taken."

In fact, the curate brought forth so many arguments and Don Quixote himself did so many eccentric things that the troopers would have had to be as mad as he was not to recognize the knight's infirmity. At last, they were convinced, and they even agreed to act as arbiters and make peace between the barber and Sancho Panza, who still nursed their quarrel with great bitterness. They, being officers of justice, mediated and arbitrated the affair in such a way that both parties were, if not totally pleased, at least partially satisfied, for they ordered them to exchange the saddle pads, but not the girths and the halters. As for Mambrino's helmet, the curate, secretly and unperceived by Don Quixote, gave eight reals for the basin, and the barber wrote out a receipt in token of the settlement, promising not to say that he had been deceived, now and forever and ever, amen.

Those two disputes being settled, which were the gravest and the most urgent, nothing remained but for Don Luis's servants to agree that three of them should go back, leaving one to accompany their master wherever Don Fernando wished to take him. And as by now their lucky stars had begun to remove all obstacle and smooth over difficulties in favor of the lovers and the brave people in the inn, so Fortune was pleased to carry the matter through and crown it with a happy issue, for the servants consented to do what Don Luis wished, at which Doña Clara was so overjoyed that no one could look into her face without noticing the radiance in her heart.

Zoraida, although she did not fully understand the incidents she had witnessed, was sad and cheerful by turns, according to the expressions she saw on each one's countenance, especially her Spaniard, on whom she always had her eyes fixed in complete submission. The landlord, however, had not turned a blind eye on the compensation that the curate had paid to the barber; he demanded Don Quixote's scot as well as payment for the damage to his skins and the loss of his wine, and he swore that neither Rozinante nor Sancho's Dapple would budge from the inn until he had been paid to the last farthing. Everything was settled by the curate and paid by Don Fernando, although the judge had willingly offered to pay, and everybody rested in peace and tranquillity so that the inn no longer resembled the discord of Agramante's camp, as Don Quixote had said, but the peace and quiet of the Augustan age. And it was generally agreed that they had to thank the goodwill and eloquence of the curate and the unexampled generosity of Don Fernando for everything.

Don Quixote, finding himself free from all quarrels, both his own and his squire's, thought that it was high time for him to continue the journey he had begun and to bring to an end the great adventure for which he had been called and chosen. Therefore, with firm resolution he went and cast himself upon his knees before Dorotea, who would not allow him to utter a word until he rose; so, to obey her, he stood up and said to her: "It is a well-known proverb, beauteous lady, that diligence is the mother of good luck, and in many grave matters experience has shown us that the solicitude of the suitor brings about a good conclusion to a doubtful suit; but in nothing is this truth more clearly shown than in the affairs of war, in which rapidity of action forestalls the designs of the enemy and snatches the victory before the adversary has time to be on the defensive. All this I say, high and worthy lady, because it seems to me that our stay in this castle is without profit and may turn out to our disadvantage, as we may find out some day. For who knows but your enemy, the giant, may have already learned by spies how I intend to destroy him, and our delay may give him the opportunity of fortifying himself in some impregnable castle against which even the might of my untiring arm will be of little avail? Therefore, dear lady, let us by our diligence hinder his plans, and let us depart quickly with good fortune on our side."

Don Quixote said no more and awaited calmly for the answer of the beautiful princess. She, with a lordly air and in a style adapted to Don Quixote's, replied as follows: "I thank you, sir knight, for the desire you show to assist me in my great need, so like a knight whose function is to protect the orphans and the distressed. Heaven grant that your desires and mine may succeed so that you may see that there are grateful women on earth. As for my departure, let it be at once, for I have no other will than yours. Therefore, dispose of me as you will, for she who has given you the defense of her person and has committed into your hands the recovery of her estates will not contradict what your wisdom should order."

"By the hand of God," cried Don Quixote, "since a lady thus humbles herself to me, I will not lose the opportunity of raising her up and setting her upon the throne she has inherited from her sires. Let us depart immediately, for my wishes are spurring me on to the journey, and there is a saying that in delay there is danger. Since Heaven has never created, nor hell ever seen, one to frighten or intimidate me, go saddle Rozinante, Sancho, and get ready your ass and the queen's palfrey; let us take leave of the castellan and these gentlemen and depart instantly."

Sancho, who was present during all this, said, wagging his head from side to side: "O master, master! There's a great deal more mischief done in the village than is noised about; with all due deference to the honest people, I'm saying it."

"What can be noised about in any village or in any of the cities of the world to my discredit, your bumpkin?"

"If you get into a rage, master," answered Sancho, "I'll hold my tongue and omit saying what I'm bound as a good squire and an honest servant to tell you."

"Say what you will," replied Don Quixote, "provided your words are not intended to rouse fears in me. You, when you fear, behave like yourself; whereas I behave like myself when I fear not."

"As I'm a sinner," answered Sancho, "that's not it. But I'm certain and positive that this lady who calls herself queen of the great kingdom of Micomicón is no more a queen than my own mother. If she were what she says, she wouldn't at every head's turn and behind every door be nuzzling with somebody of the present company."

Dorotea blushed at Sancho's words, for it was true that her husband, Don Fernando, had every now and then, on the sly, gathered with his lips part of the prize his love had earned. Sancho had noticed this and he thought such wanton behavior rather became a courtesan than the queen of a great kingdom. Dorotea was neither able nor willing to answer him, but rather to let him continue, which he did as follows: "I'm telling you this, master, because if after we have traveled highways and byways and endured bad nights and worse days, he that is disporting himself in this inn is to steal the fruit of our labors, there's no need to tire myself saddling Rozinante, harnessing Dapple, or getting ready the palfrey. In fact, we'd be wiser to stay still and to leave every whore to her spinning, and let us be off to our dinner."

Heavens above! What a mighty rage surged in Don Quixote's bosom when he heard his squire utter those unmannerly words! It was so great that, with faltering voice and stammering tongue, with fire blazing from his eyes, he said: "O baseborn scoundrel! Ill-mannered, vulgar, ignorant, ill-spoken, foul-tongued, insolent, and audacious backbiter! Do you dare to utter such words in my presence and in the presence of these distinguished ladies? How dare you conceive such rude and insolent thoughts in your muddled imagination? Leave my presence, monster of nature, treasury of lies, storehouse of deceits, depository of rascalities, inventor of mischiefs, publisher of follies, enemy of the respect due to royalty! Begone! Never appear before me, on pain of my wrath."

Saying this, he arched his brows, puffed out his cheeks,

glared about him on every side, and stamped his right foot on the ground, thus showing his pent-up rage.

At these words and furious gestures Sancho fell into such a fit of cowering and cringing that he would have been glad if the earth had opened that instant beneath his feet and engulfed him. He was at a loss what to say or do, so he turned his back to hasten out of the presence of his angry master. But the tactful Dorotea, who understood perfectly the humors of Don Quixote, said the following words to pacify him: "Do not be offended, Knight of the Rueful Figure, at the idle words your good squire has spoken. Perhaps he said them not without some cause, for considering his good sense and Christian understanding, we could not suspect him of wishing to slander or accuse anyone falsely. We must, therefore, believe without a doubt that as you have yourself said, sir knight, in this castle all things are subject to enchantment, and Sancho must have seen, through that diabolical illusion, what he believes he saw, so much to the prejudice of my honor."

"I swear by almighty God," said Don Quixote, "that your highness has hit the mark, and some evil specter must have appeared to this sinner Sancho, which made him see what he could not have seen except by magic, for I know too well the goodness and the innocence of this poor unhappy wretch, who is incapable of bearing false witness against a living soul."

"So it is, and so it shall be," said Don Fernando; "therefore, Señor Don Quixote, you must pardon him and restore him to your bosom, *sicut erat in principio*, before these apparitions drove him out of his senses."

Don Quixote said he pardoned him, and the curate went for Sancho, who came in very crestfallen, and after falling down on his knees, he humbly begged his master's hand. The latter gave him his hand, and after letting him kiss it, he gave him his blessing, saying: "Now, Sancho, my son, you will be thoroughly convinced of the truth of what I have told you many times, namely, that all things in this castle come about by means of enchantment."

"I do believe so," said Sancho, "except that business in the blanket, which really happened by ordinary means."

"Do not believe it," answered Don Quixote; "if it had been so, I would have avenged you then, and even now. But neither then nor now could I see anyone on whom I could take vengeance for that injury."

Everyone wanted to know what was this business of the blanket, and the landlord gave them a full account of Sancho Panza's flight through the air, at which they all laughed not a little and at which Sancho would have been no less ashamed if his master had not assured him again that it was enchantment.

In spite of this, Sancho's folly never reached such a pitch that he could believe it was not the absolute truth, without any shadow of doubt, that he had been tossed in a blanket by persons of flesh and bone, and not by visionary phantoms, as his master believed and affirmed.

The illustrious company had already been two days in the inn, and thinking it was time to depart, they considered how, without giving Dorotea and Don Fernando the trouble of accompanying Don Quixote back to his village, on the pretext of restoring Princess Micomicona, the curate and the barber might take him with them and get him cured at home. This was the plan they decided upon. They made a bargain with a wagoner who happened to be passing by with his team of oxen to carry our knight in the following manner: They made a kind of cage of trellised poles, large enough to hold Don Quixote in it comfortably; then, Don Fernando and his companions, together with the troopers, Don Luis's servants, and the landlord, under the direction of the curate, covered their faces and disguised themselves so that they might appear to Don Quixote to be different persons than any he had seen in the castle. This being done, they silently entered the room where he lay sleeping and seizing him forcibly, they tied up his hands and feet very firmly so that when he awoke with a start he could not move nor do anything but stare and wonder at the strange faces he saw before him. And straightaway his disordered imagination suggested to him that these were the phantoms of that enchanted castle and that without any doubt he was enchanted, for he could neither move nor defend himself. All this turned out exactly as the curate, the inventor of the scheme, had anticipated. Sancho alone, of all who were present, was in his right mind as well as in his own clothes, for though he was well-nigh infected with his master's infirmity, yet he could not help knowing who all these counterfeit phantoms were, but he did not dare to unseal his lips until he should see what would be the result of this assault and seizure of his master. The latter, likewise, did not say a word, but submissively awaited the outcome of his misfortune.

The outcome was that they brought in the cage and shut him in, nailing the bars so well that they could not easily be burst open. They then hoisted him on their shoulders, and as he was carried out of his chamber, a voice was heard, as dreadful a voice as the barber could muster (not the pack-saddle barber, by the way) that said: "O Knight of the Rueful Figure, be not downcast at thy imprisonment, for so it must be in order that the adventure to which thy bravery has committed thee may be more speedily accomplished. It shall be accomplished when the furious spotted Manchegan lion shall mate with the white dove of El Toboso after they have humbled their stately necks beneath the soft yoke of matrimony. From this unheard-of union there shall come forth to the light of day doughty whelps who shall rival the ramping talons of their valiant sire. And this shall come to pass ere the god who pursues the fleeting nymph shall twice have visited in his swift and natural course the bright constellation. And thou, O most noble and obedient squire who ever had sword in belt, beard on chin, and smell in nose, be not dismayed nor discontented to see the very flower of knight-errantry carried away before thine eyes, for in a short time, if it pleases the great artificer of the world, thou shall see thyself so exalted and sublimated that thou shalt not know thyself, and thou shalt not be cheated of the promises that thy good lord has made to thee. I assure thee, on behalf of the sage Mentironiana,[1] that thy wages shall punctually be paid to thee, as thou shall see in due course. Follow, therefore, the steps of the brave, enchanted knight, for it is right that ye should go where ye will both remain. I am not allowed to say any more; so, farewell. I now return whither I alone know."

As he finished the prophecy, the barber raised his voice in pitch and then modulated it in such a soft, pathetic tone that even those who knew the plot almost believed that what they heard was real. Don Quixote was comforted by this prophecy, for he at once understood its whole meaning and saw that it promised him the fortune of being wedded to his

---

[1] Mentironiana, a name coined by Cervantes. *Mentira* means "lie."

beloved Dulcinea of El Toboso, from whose womb would spring the whelps, his sons, to the eternal glory of La Mancha. Being convinced of the sincerity of the prediction, he lifted up his voice, and sighing deeply he said: "O thou, whoever thou art, who hast foretold this great happiness for me, I beg thee to entreat the wise magician who directs my fortunes not to allow me to perish in this prison wherein they have now put me until I see accomplished the incomparable promises they have made me. If this come to pass, I shall glory in the chains that bind me, and this pallet on which I lie will be no hard field of battle, but a soft bridal bed of down. And as concerns my squire, Sancho Panza, I trust in his goodness of heart and conduct that he will not abandon me in good or evil fortune. For, though it should happen through his or my hard lot that I may not be able to bestow on him the island that I have promised him, yet at least he shall not lose his wages, for in my will, which is already made, I have set down what he is to have."

Sancho Panza bowed respectfully and kissed both his master's hands, for he could not kiss only one since they were tied together. Then the phantoms hoisted the cage onto their shoulders and placed it on the ox wagon.

CHAPTER XLVII

Of the strange manner in which Don Quixote of La Mancha was enchanted, with other notable incidents

When Don Quixote found himself cooped up in that manner in the cart, he said: "Many learned histories have I read of knights-errant, but never have I read, nor seen, nor heard, that they carried enchanted knights in this manner and as slowly as these lazy animals seem to go. They are usually carried through the air with amazing rapidity, enveloped in some thick, dark cloud, or in a chariot of fire, or mounted upon a hippogriff or some such animal. To be carried off in an ox cart! By the living God, it fills me with shame! Perhaps, however, the chivalries and enchantments of our day follow a different road from that followed by the ancients. As I am a new knight and the first to revive the forgotten exercise of knight-errantry, perchance new ways of enchantment and new methods of carrying the enchanted have come into fashion. What do you think, Sancho, my son?"

"I don't know what to think," answered Sancho, "for I'm not so well up in the scriptures-errant. But still, I'd swear that the ghosts we've seen are not too Catholic."

"Catholic?" answered Don Quixote. "My sainted father! How can they be Catholic when they are all devils who have put on weird shapes to accomplish their purpose and put me in this state? If you wish to convince yourself, touch them and feel them, and you will find that they have no bodies and that they are made of air; they only exist to our eyes."

"By God, sir," replied Sancho, "I've touched them already, and this devil who's so busy is as plump as a partridge and has another characteristic very different from what you'd find in devils, for I've heard it said that devils stink of sulphur and other foulness; but this one smells of amber half a league

471

off." Sancho said this of Don Fernando, who, being a fine gentleman, must have smelled as Sancho said.

"Do not wonder at this, friend Sancho," answered Don Quixote. "I tell you, the devils are very cunning, and though they carry smells about them, they do not smell, for they are spirits. And if they do smell, it is not of good things, but of such as are foul and fetid. The reason is that wherever they are, they take hell with them, and there is no relief for them from its torments. Because a sweet smell is something that delights and makes people happy, it is impossible for them to smell of sweet things. Therefore, if you think that this devil you speak of smells of amber, either you are deceiving yourself or he is deceiving you by making you believe he is not a devil."

All this conversation took place between master and servant. Don Fernando and Cardenio, fearing that Sancho would discover their stratagem, for he had already suspected that something was afoot, resolved to hasten their departure. They called the landlord aside and ordered him to saddle Rozinante and put the packsaddle on Sancho's ass. This was done without delay. The curate had already concerted with the troopers that they would accompany them to the village for so much a day. Cardenio hung on one side of Rozinante's saddlebow the buckler and on the other side the basin, made signs to Sancho to get up on his ass and take Rozinante by the bridle, and placed the two troopers on each side of the cart. But before the cart began to move, the landlady, her daughter, and Maritornes came out to say farewell to Don Quixote, and they pretended to shed sorrowful tears at his misfortunes. The knight addressed them as follows: "Do not weep, good ladies; all these misfortunes are the lot of those who profess what I profess. If these disasters did not befall me, I would not consider myself a famous knight-errant, for such mishaps do not happen to knights of small repute, whom nobody remembers. But courageous knights do suffer such misfortunes, for there are many princes and many other knights who are envious of their virtues and who plan to destroy them by evil means. However, Virtue is so powerful that, all by herself and in spite of all the black magic of Zoroaster, its inventor, she will emerge victorious from any situation and will shine on earth as the sun does in the sky. Forgive me, fair ladies, if unwittingly I have given you any cause for an-

noyance, and pray to God that I may be delivered from the
fetters that some evil-minded magician has cast about me. If
ever I am freed from them, never shall I forget to requite the
favors you have bestowed upon me in this castle."

While this was taking place between the ladies of the
castle and Don Quixote, the curate and the barber took leave
of Don Fernando and his companions, of the captain and his brother, and of all those very contented ladies,
especially of Dorotea and Luscinda. They all embraced one
another and promised to send one another their news. Don
Fernando told the curate where he was to write to inform him
of what became of Don Quixote. He assured him that nothing
would give him more pleasure than to hear of it, and he
promised to send the curate any news that might please him
about his own marriage and Zoraida's baptism, or Don Luis's
affairs and Luscinda's homecoming. The curate undertook to
comply with all his requests most punctually. Once more they
embraced, and once more they exchanged offers of service.
The landlord went up to the curate and gave him some papers,
saying that he had discovered them in the lining of the trunk
in which he had discovered "The Tale of Ill-Advised Curiosity." He told him that he could take them all away as the
owner had never returned and that as he could not read,
he did not want them himself. The curate thanked him, and
opening the papers at once, he saw written at the beginning
of the manuscript: "The Tale of Rinconete and Cortadillo," [1]
from which he assumed that this was another story, and he
imagined that it would be a good one, since "The Tale of Ill-
Advised Curiosity" had been, and both were probably by the
same author. So, he kept it, intending to read it when
he had an opportunity.

Then, he and his friend the barber, both wearing their
masks so that they would not be recognized by Don Quixote,
mounted and set out after the cart. The order of their march
was as follows: first went the cart, driven by its owner; on
either side marched the officers, as we have said, with their
firelocks; then followed Sancho Panza upon his ass, leading
Rozinante by the bridle; behind all this rode the curate and
the barber upon their powerful mules with their faces cov-

---

[1] This is one of the exemplary novels published in 1613. See
The Deceitful Marriage and Other Exemplary Novels (Signet
CT157).

ered as has been said, with a grave and sober air, traveling no faster than the slow pace of the oxen permitted. Don Quixote was seated in his cage with his hands tied and his legs stretched out, leaning against the bars, as silent and patient as if he were not a man of flesh but a statue of stone. And silently and slowly they journeyed for about two leagues when they came to a valley that the wagoner thought to be a suitable place for resting and feeding his oxen. He told the curate of his plan, but the barber was of the opinion that they should advance a little further, for he knew that behind a hill that loomed in view a short distance away there was a valley with more plentiful and better grass than where they wished to halt. They took the barber's advice and resumed their journey.

At this moment the curate, looking around, saw six or seven men on horseback, well mounted and equipped, who quickly overtook them, for they were not riding at the slow and loitering pace of oxen, but as people mounted on canon's mules and eager to forge ahead and take their siesta in the inn, which seemed to be less than one league away. The swift travelers overtook the laggards, and there were courteous greetings on both sides. Then one of the former, who turned out to be a canon from Toledo and master of the rest, seeing the orderly procession with the cart, the troopers, Sancho, Rozinante, the curate, and the barber, and especially Don Quixote cooped up in his cage, could not help asking what they meant by carrying a man in that manner, although having already seen the badge of the officers, he had supposed that the man must be some criminal highwayman or other malefactor, whose punishment concerned the Holy Brotherhood. One of the officers whom the canon questioned replied: "We, sir, haven't a notion what this all means, but the gentleman himself may be able to tell you."

Don Quixote, overhearing these conversations, replied: "Are you gentlemen, perchance, well versed and skilled in matters of knight-errantry? If you are, I will communicate my misfortunes to you; if not, there is no reason why I should weary myself relating them."

By this time the curate and the barber, observing that the travelers were talking to Don Quixote of La Mancha, had come up to answer for him, so that their plot might not be discovered. But the canon, whom Don Quixote had addressed, replied: "Truly, brother, I know more about books of chivalry than about Villalpando's 'Summaries';[2] so, if that is all there is to it, you can safely tell me whatever you please."

"Then by God's hand," replied Don Quixote, "since it is so, I would have you know, sir, that I am traveling in this cage under a spell because of the envy and treachery of evil enchanters, for virtue is more persecuted by the wicked than it is cherished by the good. I am a knight-errant, not one of those whose names Fame has never seen fit to perpetuate in her records, but one who, despite and in defiance of envy itself and of all the magicians of Persia, all the Brahmans of India, all the gymnosophists of Ethiopia, shall inscribe his name in the temple of immortality to serve as a pattern and example to future ages, wherein knights-errant may see what steps they have to follow if they would reach the peak of heroism and the pinnacle of arms."

"The knight Don Quixote of La Mancha speaks the truth," said the curate at this juncture, "for he is traveling in this cart under a spell, not through his own faults and mistakes, but owing to the malignity of those who hate virtue and frown on heroism. This, sir, is the Knight of the Rueful Figure, for you already must have heard men speak of him. His valorous exploits and mighty deeds will be engraved on lasting brass and everlasting marble, no matter how unwearying be the attempts of malice and envy to dim and obscure them."

When the canon heard the prisoner and the free man talk in this style, he almost crossed himself with astonishment, for he could not understand what had happened, and all his companions likewise were amazed.

Just then, Sancho Panza, who had edged closer to hear the conversation, thought fit to clarify matters by remarking: "Look here, gentlemen, whether you agree or don't agree with what I'm going to say, the fact is that Don Quixote is no more enchanted than my mother. He is as sound as a bell in all his faculties; he eats and drinks and does his business like all other men, just as he did yesterday before they clapped him in the cage. As this is how matters stand, how do they expect me to believe he is enchanted? For I've heard many people say that those who are bewitched neither eat, nor sleep, nor

---

[2] Las Súmulas by Gaspar Cardillo de Villalpando, published at Alcalá de Henares in 1557, was the university textbook for students of dialectic.

speak, whereas my master, if they slacken the rein, will out talk thirty lawyers." Then, turning around and peering at the curate, he continued: "O Master Curate, Master Curate. Do you think I don't recognize you? And do you imagine that I don't spot what you're up to and that I don't see through these newfangled enchantments? Of course I know you, even though you've a mask on your face, and I can guess what you're after, no matter how you try to bamboozle me with your lies. In short, virtue cannot live where envy rules, nor can generosity where rules miserliness. Bad luck to the Devil! If it were not for your reverence, by this time my master would have been married to the Infanta Micomicona, and I'd have been a count at least, for how could I expect any less when I consider the generosity of my master, the Knight of the Rueful Figure, and the greatness of my services. But I now know how true the saying is that they're fond of quoting in these parts, that Fortune's wheel turns swifter than a mill wheel, and he who was up on top yesterday is crawling on the ground today. Mind you, I'm sorry for my wife and my children, for just when they might have expected to see their father walk in the door a governor or a viceroy of some island or kingdom, they'll see him come in a stableboy. I've said all this, your reverence, just to prick your conscience and remind you of how badly you treat my master; take heed that God doesn't call you to account in the next life for this caging of my master and charge against you all the succors and benefits that my lord, Don Quixote, leaves undone all this time he is shut up."

"Fiddle-de-dee!" cried the barber. "Are you also, Sancho, of your master's fraternity? I swear to God I'm beginning to think that you'll have to bear him company in his cage and that you'll remain as enchanted as he is, for you've caught a touch of his humor and chivalry. That was an unlucky hour when you became impregnated with his promises, and worse still when that island you crave entered your brain."

"I'm not in child by anyone," retorted Sancho, "nor am I the kind of man who would let myself be put in pod by even the king himself, for though I'm poor, I'm an old Christian and I don't owe anything to anyone; and if I'm set on getting islands, others are set on worse, for everyone of us is the son of his own deeds. Seeing that I'm a man, I may even come to be pope, much more governor of an island, and especially as my master is capable of winning so many that he may have no one to give them to. Mind how you speak, Master Barber, for shaving beards is not all, and there is a great difference between Pedro and Pedro. I say this for we all know one another, and there'll be no passing false dice on me. As to this business of enchanting my master, God knows the truth; so let sleeping dogs lie, for it is worse to stir it."

The barber did not want to answer him, for fear that Sancho might in his simplicity reveal what the curate and he were trying so hard to conceal. The curate, with the same fears in his mind, invited the canon to ride with him a little ahead, promising to reveal the mystery of the cage and other things that would amuse him. The canon agreed, and going ahead with his servants, he listened attentively to all that the curate told him about Don Quixote's character, life, madness, and habits. He told him briefly of the origin of his madness and the whole course of his adventures up to his confinement in that cage and the plan they had arranged for taking him home to see if they could in any way find a cure for his madness. The canon and his servants were again astonished at hearing Don Quixote's strange history, and having heard it, he said: "Truly, sir priest, my personal belief is that those so-called books of chivalry are most harmful to the commonwealth, and although I have read, out of idleness and bad taste, the beginnings of almost all that have been printed, I never could bring myself to read any of them right to the end, for they all seem to me more or less the same, and there is no more in one than in another. Besides, I think that this kind of writing falls under the heading of Milesian fables, which are fantastic tales whose purpose is to amaze but not to instruct, contrary to the fables called apologues, which delight as well as instruct. And even though the chief aim of such books is to please, I do not understand how they ever succeed, seeing that they are a hodgepodge of outlandish absurdities. For the delight that the soul receives must arise from the beauty and harmony it perceives in the things that the eye or the imagination sets before it, and nothing that is ugly or deformed in itself can ever give us any pleasure. But what beauty or what structural harmony can there possibly be in a book or story where a youth of sixteen gives one slash of his sword at a giant as tall as a steeple and slices him in two halves as tidily as if he was made of almond paste? And when they wish to describe a battle, they tell us that there are a million fighting men on the enemy's side, and if

the hero of the book is to face them, they compel us to
believe, in spite of our protests, that such and such a knight
obtained the victory by the valor of his doughty arm alone.
Then, what shall we say of the ease with which a queen- or
empress-to-be sinks into the arms of an unknown wandering
knight? How could any mind that is not wholly barbarous
and unlettered be entertained by reading that a massive tower
filled with knights sails over the sea like a ship with favoring
breezes and tonight docks in Lombardy and dawns next day
in the land of Prester John of the Indies or in some other
country Ptolemy never discovered nor Marco Polo saw? If
they reply that the men who compose such books write them
as fiction and that they are not obliged to rack their brains
over finer points and unities, I would answer that the more
truthful it appears, the better it is as fiction, and the more
probable and possible it is, the more it captivates. Works of
fiction must match the understanding of those who read them,
and they must be written in such a way that, by toning down
the impossibilities, moderating the excesses, and keeping their
readers in suspense, they may astonish, stimulate, and entertain so that admiration and pleasure go hand in hand. But no
writer will achieve this who shuns verisimilitude and imitation of nature, in which lie the highest qualities of literature.
I have never seen a book of chivalry with a whole body for a
plot, with all its members complete, so that the middle
corresponds to the beginning and the end to the beginning
and the middle. Instead, they are composed of so many
limbs that they seem rather to have been intended to form a
chimera or a monster than a well-proportioned figure. Moreover, they are uncouth in style, their adventures are incredible, their amours licentious, their compliments absurd,
their battles boring, their speeches doltish, their travels ridiculous, and finally, they are devoid of all art and intelligence
and therefore deserve to be expelled from a Christian republic
as a useless race."

The curate listened to him with great attention, for he
recognized him as a man of good sense and agreed with all
that he had said. So, he told him that, being of his opinion
and bearing such a grudge against the books of chivalry,
he had burned all those belonging to Don Quixote, which were
many. He proceeded to give the canon an account of the inquisition that he had held upon them and to say which he had
condemned to the fire and those whose lives he had spared,

at which the canon had a great laugh. He said that in spite of all he had said against them, he discovered one good thing in them, namely, the opportunity that they offered a good intellect to display itself. For they presented a wide and spacious field through which the pen might run without any obstacles, describing shipwrecks, storms, clashes, and battles; portraying a brave captain with all the qualities needed for such a part, showing him cautious in forestalling the craftiness of his enemies and eloquent in persuading or dissuading his soldiers, prudent in counsel, prompt in resolution, as courageous in awarding as in delivering an attack; depicting now a tragic and lamentable incident, now a joyful and unexpected event; here a beautiful lady, chaste, intelligent, and modest, there a Christian knight, brave and gentle; in one place a monstrous, barbarous braggart, in another a courteous prince, valiant and wise; representing the goodness and loyalty of vassals, the greatness and generosity of noblemen. "The author might at times show his knowledge of astrology, or his proficiency in cosmography and music, or his experience in affairs of state; and sometimes, if he pleased, he might find an opportunity of proving his skill in necromancy. He may display the wiles of Ulysses, the piety of Aeneas, the prowess of Achilles, the misfortunes of Hector, the treachery of Sinon, the friendship of Euryalus, the generosity of Alexander, the courage of Caesar, the clemency and truthfulness of Trajan, the fidelity of Zopyrus, the prudence of Cato, and in short, all those attributes that contribute to create the model hero, sometimes placing them in one single man, at other times sharing them out among many. And if all this is done in a pleasant style with an ingenious plot, keeping as near as possible to the truth, the author will, without doubt, weave a web of such variegated and beautiful threads that, when finished, it will show such beauty and perfection that it will achieve the end that is the aim of all those works, which is, as I have said, to instruct as well as to entertain. For the loose structure of those books gives the author the chance of displaying his talent in the epic, the lyric, the tragic, the comic, and all the qualities included in the pleasing sciences of poetry and rhetoric, for the epic may be written in prose as well as in verse."

CHAPTER XLVIII

In which the canon pursues the subject of books of chivalry, with other matters worthy of his intelligence

"What you say, sir canon, is true," replied the curate, "and for that reason the writers of such books are all the more deserving of blame, for until now they have written them without paying heed to good sense, art, or to the rules. Had they been guided by them, they might have become as famous in prose as the two princes of Greek and Latin poetry are in verse."

"I, for one," said the canon, "have been tempted to write a book of chivalry, observing all the points I mentioned, and to tell you the truth, I have written more than a hundred sheets; to ascertain whether they come up to my opinion of them, I have shown them to learned and judicious men, very fond of that kind of reading, as well as to others who are ignorant and only wish to be entertained by listening to absurdities, and from all of them I met with flattering approval. Nevertheless, I have proceeded no further, not only because I considered it a task unbecoming my profession, but also because I found that the number of the ignorant exceeded that of the wise, and though it is better to be praised by the few wise and jeered at by the many fools, yet I do not want to subject myself to the muddled judgment of the capricious crowd, who are mostly given to reading such books. But what made me drop the work and even banish all thoughts of finishing it was an argument that I drew from the plays that are being performed nowadays. For I said to myself: if those now in fashion, whether fictitious or historical, are all, or most of them, notorious absurdities without head or tail; if the rabble listens to them with pleasure and approves of them and reckons them good when they are so far from being so;

480

if the authors who write them and the managers who put them on and the actors who play them say that they must be good because the crowd likes them that way and not otherwise, that authors who have a plan and follow the plot as the rules of drama require serve only to please the three or four men of sense who understand them, while all the rest cannot make head or tail of their subtleties, and this being so, the managers prefer to earn their daily bread from the many than a reputation from the few: such would have been the fate of my book, after scorching my eyebrows in a desperate attempt to keep the rules I mentioned before, and it would have been love's labor lost. At times, I have striven to persuade the managers that their judgments are wrong and that they would draw a bigger audience and gain greater fame by putting on plays that follow the rules instead of these extravagant pieces, but so hidebound and so obstinate are they that no argument or proof in the world would shift them from their opinion. I remember on a certain occasion saying to one of these stubborn fellows: 'Tell me, do you not remember that a few years ago three tragedies written by a famous poet of this country were played with such gusto that all who heard them, the learned and the unlettered, the rabblement and the highbrows, cheered them to the echo, and that those three plays alone earned the players more money than thirty of the best that have been produced ever since?'

" 'I suppose,' replied the manager I am speaking of, 'your worship means the *Isabella*, the *Phyllis* and the *Alexandra*.' [1]

" 'Those are the three,' I said, 'and did they not stick carefully to the rules of drama, and did that hinder them from being successes and pleasing all the public? So, the

---

[1] The three plays are by Lupercio Leonardo de Argensola (1559–1613). He and his brother Bartolomé (1562–1631) were praised by Cervantes and Lope de Vega. The latter said that the two brothers had come from Aragón to reform the poets of Castile, who had corrupted by their neologisms the Castilian language. Lupercio was the secretary of the Conde de Lemos and the Empress María of Austria. He went to Naples with the Conde as secretary when the latter was appointed viceroy. It was a deep disappointment to Cervantes that his Maecenas, the Conde de Lemos, did not appoint him to a post in Naples. Nevertheless, so prejudiced was he in favor of the classical precepts of drama that he praised the three tragedies of his rival, Argensola, which are devoid of any outstanding merit.

fault does not lie with the public for demanding absurdities, but with those who cannot stage anything else. Yes, there is no absurdity in *Ingratitude Avenged*, nor in *Numantia*. And you will find none in *The Merchant Lover*, nor in *The Friendly Enemy*,[2] nor in a number of others written by several good poets to their own triumph and renown and to the profit of the players.' To these I added other arguments, and I departed leaving him somewhat perplexed, but not so satisfied or convinced as to retract his mistaken opinions."

"You have broached a subject, sir canon," said the curate at this juncture, "that rouses in me an ancient grudge I bear against the plays they act today. It is as deep-seated as the grudge I bear against the books of chivalry. For though drama, according to Tully, should be a mirror of human life, a pattern of manners, and an image of truth, the plays that are staged nowadays are mirrors of absurdity, patterns of folly, and images of lewdness. For what greater absurdity can there be in the subject we are treating than for a child to appear in the first scene of the first act in swaddling clothes and in the second to enter as a bearded man? What could be more ridiculous than to portray for us a valiant dotard and a young coward, an eloquent lackey, a statesman like a page, a king as a porter, and a princess as a kitchen maid? And what shall I say of their method of observing the time and place in which the actions they represent can or should happen? I have seen a play whose first act opened in Europe, the second in Asia, and its third ended in Africa; if there had been four acts, the fourth would have ended in America, and so it would have been played in all the quarters of the globe. If imitation be the chief aim of the drama, how is it possible to satisfy any average intelligence, when an action claims to take place in the days of King Pepin and Charlemagne, yet they make the principal character in it the Emperor Heraclius, who enters Jerusalem bearing the Cross and wins the Holy Sepulcher, like Godefroi de Bouillon, although a whole age had passed between one event and the other? And when the play is based on a fictitious story, they introduce historical facts and mingle with them incidents that happened to different persons at different times with no at-

---

[2] *Ingratitude Avenged* is by Lope de Vega; *Numantia* is by Cervantes; *The Merchant Lover* is by Gaspar Aguilar; *The Friendly Enemy* is by Agustín Tárraga.

tempt at realism, but with blatant errors that are inexcusable. The worst of it is that there are blockheads who say that this is the perfect art and to look for anything else is to go fishing for dainties. And what about sacred dramas? What a number of false miracles they represent! What apocryphal and unintelligible incidents—the miracles of one saint ascribed to another! Why, even in their profane plays they make no bones about dragging in miracles without rhyme or reason, merely because they think some miracles, or 'scenic shows' as they call them, will be effective and serve to attract the ignorant public who will crowd into the theater and applaud. All this is prejudicial to the truth, detrimental to history, and puts our Spanish genius in a shameful light before foreigners, who scrupulously observe the rules of the drama and look upon us as uncouth barbarians when they see the nonsense and absurdities of the plays we write. And it is not enough excuse to say that the chief reason why well-ordered states allow stage plays to be acted is to entertain the common people with an honest pastime that will divert the evil humors that idleness at times engenders and that, since any play can do that, whether it is good or bad, it is no use imposing laws or compelling playwrights and actors to write their plays as they should be written, because, as I have said, they can achieve their purpose with any kind of a play. To this I would reply that their purpose could be better achieved, beyond all comparison, by plays that are good than by those that are not so, because the public, after seeing a well-written and well-constructed play, would come away delighted by the comic part, instructed by the serious, intrigued by the plot, enlivened by the witty quips, warned by the tricks, edified by the moral, incensed against vice, and enamored of virtue. A good play will produce all those effects upon the mind of an audience however obtuse and uncouth, and a play possessing all these qualities is bound to amuse and entertain, please and satisfy, much more than one that is devoid of them, as are most of those that nowadays are played. It is not the fault of the poets who write them, for some of them recognize where they go astray and know extremely well what they ought to do, but as plays have become a marketable commodity, they say, and say rightly, that the managers would not buy them if they were not of the usual kind. So, the poet tries to conform to what is required by the manager who pays him his salary. The

truth of this may be proved by the infinite number of plays
written by a most fortunate genius of this country with so
much splendor and so much charm, with such elegant verses,
with such choice language, and finally with such eloquence
and noble style, that the world is full of his renown. And
yet, because he is willing to suit the taste of the managers, not
all his plays have reached, as some have, the requisite pitch
of perfection. Others write their plays with so little heed of
what they are doing that, after the show is over, the actors
have to take to their heels and hide for fear of being punished,
as they often have been, for acting scenes offensive to kings
or libelous to some family.

"All these evils, and many more of which I shall not
speak, would cease if there were some intelligent and judicious person at court to examine all plays before they are
acted, not only those that are to be acted in the capital, but
also all that are to be performed anywhere in Spain.[3] In that
case no magistrate in any town would permit any play to be
put on without that official's sanction, under hand and seal.
Thus, the managers would be careful to send their plays to
Madrid and would then be able to play them with safety.
And the playwrights, too, would take more trouble in writing their comedies, fearing the rigorous examination they
would have to pass at the hands of someone who knows his
job. In this way good plays would be produced, and the
aims of dramatic art would be successfully attained, which
are not only public entertainment, but also the fair fame of
Spanish genius, the profit and security of the actor's profession, and the saving of the time and trouble now spent in
chastising them. And if the same official, or someone else,
were entrusted with the task of examining the books of

[3] Through the mouths of the canon of Toledo and the curate
Cervantes gets in some shrewd digs at the dramatic methods of
his rival, Lope de Vega, whom he accuses of writing for the gallery. The latter, however, revenged himself when an advance copy
of *Don Quixote, Part I,* came his way in 1604, for writing to a
friend, he said: "Of the poets I do not speak, but there is none
so bad as Cervantes; nor is anyone so foolish as to praise *Don
Quixote.*" Though Cervantes was reactionary in his doctrines on
the drama, he revised them in later years, and in the eight plays
he published in 1615 he followed the technique of Lope de Vega,
especially in *Pedro de Urdemalas.* He recants his views in *El
Rufián Dichoso.* Lope de Vega in his *New Art of Making
Comedies* (1609) expresses the same views that are attacked here.

chivalry that are to be published in the future, no doubt some would appear with the perfection you have spoken about, thus enriching our language with the gracious and precious treasure of eloquence and leading to the eclipse of the old ones by the radiant presence of the new. They would furnish honest entertainment not only for the idle, but also for the busiest of men, for the bow cannot remain forever bent nor can our frail human nature bear up without its moments of lawful recreation."[4]

The canon and the curate had reached this point in their conversation when the barber, spurring forward, said to the priest: "Here, sir licentiate, is the place I told you of, where our oxen can have plenty of fresh pasture while we enjoy our siesta."

"So it seems to me," said the curate. The canon, when he learned their intentions, was attracted by the sight of the pleasant valley nestling below and decided to stay with them. And wishing to enjoy it as well as the conversation of the curate, for whom he had taken a liking, and to hear more details of Don Quixote's adventures, he ordered some of his servants to go to the inn, which was not far off, and bring them enough food for all, for he was resolved to rest there that afternoon. One of the servants answered that the sumpter mule, which by that time was at the inn, carried sufficient provisions and that they would need nothing from there but barley.

"Since that is so," said the canon, "take all our mounts there and bring back the sumpter mule."

While this was taking place, Sancho Panza, seeing that the curate and the barber, whom he regarded as suspicious persons, were not at his elbow, went up to his master's cage and said: "Master, I must unburden my conscience and tell you what's happening about this enchantment of yours: it is that the two who are riding along with us here,

---

[4] Cervantes in his Prologue to the *Exemplary Novels* (1613) made a similar plea for honest entertainment in literature: "My intention has been to place in the marketplace of our commonwealth a billiard table, at which everyone can entertain himself without threat to body or soul, for innocent recreation does good rather than harm. It is so, because people cannot always be at church, or always saying their prayers, or unceasingly engaged in their business, however well qualified they may be for it. There are hours of recreation when the wearied spirit needs repose."

their faces masked, are the curate and the barber of our village. I think that they've played this trick of carrying you in this manner out of pure envy of you, sir, because you outdid them in famous deeds. Now, if I'm right in this, it follows that you're not enchanted but hoodwinked and befooled. To prove this, I'd like to ask you one question; if you answer me as I think you will, you'll put your finger on this trick, and you'll find that you're not enchanted but gone daft in the head."

"Ask what you will, Sancho, my son," replied Don Quixote. "I will answer all your questions. But when you say that those who accompany us are our townsmen and acquaintances, the curate and barber, it may well be that they look like them, but you must not believe for an instant that they really and truly are so. What you must believe and understand is that if they are like them, as you say, it must be that those who have enchanted me have assumed their likeness, for it is child's play for magicians to take on any appearance they please. And they must have assumed the likeness of our friends to give you cause to think as you do and to whirl you into a maze of fancies, out of which not even the clue of Theseus could extricate you. They must have done this, I suppose, to muddle my brain and make me incapable of guessing the causes of my disaster. For if, on the one hand, you tell me that our village curate and barber bear me company, and if on the other, I find myself caged—and I know that only superhuman power could coop me up in this way, for no human force would be sufficient—what would you have me say or think, except that the mode of my enchantment surpasses all I have ever read in all the histories that treat of knights-errant who have been enchanted? So, you may calm yourself and give up your notion that they are those you say, for they are no more the curate and the barber than I am a Turk. As to your queries, make them, for I will answer you even if you continue questioning me until tomorrow morning."

"Blessed Virgin!" cried Sancho in a loud voice. "Is it possible, master, that you're so thick-skulled and brainless? Can't you believe that it's the honest truth I'm telling you and that there's more roguery than magic in this confinement of yours? I'll clearly prove to you how you are not enchanted. Now, what I want is for you, sir, to answer me one question, so may God deliver you from this trouble, and may you, when you least expect it, find yourself in the arms of Lady Dulcinea——"

"A truce to your conjuring," cried Don Quixote, "and ask what you will, for I have already told you I will faithfully answer all your questions."

"That's what I want," said Sancho, "and what I wish is for you to tell me the whole truth, without adding or subtracting anything, as it is expected of those who, like your worship, make a profession of arms under the title of knights-errant——"

"I tell you I will lie in nothing," answered Don Quixote. "Make an end of your questions, for, in truth, I am weary of your oaths, your supplications, and your preambles, Sancho."

"I'm certain my master's a good man and tells the truth, and so I'll ask you one question that is very much to the point. Speaking respectfully, can you tell me whether since you have been cooped up—or as you call it, enchanted—in this cage, you have had any longing to make great or little waters, as the saying goes."

"I do not understand what you mean by 'making waters,' Sancho. Explain your meaning if you want me to answer correctly."

"Is it possible, sir, that you do not know what making great or little waters is? Why, children at school are suckled on it. It means whether you feel inclined to do what nobody else can do for you."

"Ah! Now I understand you, Sancho. Yes, I have often had the inclination, and I have it at the present moment. Help me out of this strait; all is not clean with me."

CHAPTER XLIX

Which deals with the shrewd conversation between Sancho Panza and his master, Don Quixote

"Ah!" cried Sancho. "Now I've caught you! This is what I longed to know with all my heart and soul. Come now, sir, can you deny what everyone says in these parts when a person is in the dumps: 'I don't know what's the matter with so-and-so; he doesn't eat, nor drink, nor sleep, nor answer pat when you ask him a question; surely he must be enchanted.' So, it's as plain as a pikestaff that those who don't eat, nor dine, nor sleep, nor do the natural doings I speak of, are enchanted. But they who have the longing you have, and eat, and drink, when they can get it, and answer questions, are not enchanted."

"You are right, Sancho," replied Don Quixote, "but I have told you that there are many kinds of enchantment and perhaps they change with the times from one kind to another. It may be that enchanted persons nowadays do the things I do, even though they did not do them before. I know, and I am convinced, that I am enchanted, and that is enough for the peace of my conscience. If I were not enchanted, I would be greatly perturbed to think that I had let myself be cooped up in this cage like a lazy coward when there are, this very moment, so many distressed in the world who are in extreme need of my protection."

"For all that," replied Sancho, "you should try and get out of this prison. I'll guarantee to help you and release you from it so that you may mount again your good Rozinante; he's so crestfallen, he must be enchanted too. But once we've done this, let us try our luck once more and go off in search of adventures, and if all doesn't turn out well, there'll be time enough to return to the cage.

And I promise you, on the faith of a true and loyal squire, to shut myself up along with your worship if your worship were so unlucky or I so stupid."

"I'm content to do as you say, brother Sancho," replied Don Quixote, "and when you see an opportunity of arranging my deliverance, I will obey you unconditionally. But you will see, Sancho, how mistaken you are in your judgment of my misfortune."

Our knight-errant and ill-errant squire entertained themselves with this conversation until they reached the place where the priest, the canon, and the barber had dismounted and were awaiting them. The wagoner then unyoked his oxen from the cart and turned them loose in that green and pleasant place whose freshness invited not only enchanted persons like Don Quixote, but also so rational and sensible a fellow as his squire. Sancho then begged the curate to allow his master to leave the cage for a short while, for that prison could not remain as clean as the decency of such a knight as his master required. The curate understood and said that he would be very willing to grant his request if he were not afraid that Don Quixote, finding himself free, would play one of his pranks and go off where no one would ever find him.

"I'll go bail for his not running away," replied Sancho.

"And I, and for any sum," said the canon, "especially if he gives me his word as a knight not to leave without our consent."

"I give it," answered Don Quixote, who was listening to all they said, "the more so because any enchanted person, as I am, is not at liberty to do with his body as he pleases. For his enchanter can make him unable to stir for three centuries, and if he were to escape, he would be brought back flying through the air." Since this was the case, he added that they might well release him, especially as it would be to everyone's advantage: indeed, if they did not let him out, he could not refrain from offending their noses, unless they withdrew to some distance.

The canon took him by one of his hands, although they were tied, and on his pledged word, they uncaged him, and he, finding himself outside his jail was overjoyed. The first thing he did was to stretch himself, and then he went up to Rozinante and gave him a few slaps on the haunches, saying: "I still put my faith in God and in His Blessed Mother,

O flower and mirror of steeds! I trust that soon we two shall find our wish fulfilled: you with your master on your back, and I on top of you, exercising the function for which God sent me into the world."

Saying this, Don Quixote went with Sancho to a remote spot from where he returned much relieved and with a still greater wish to carry out the designs of his squire.

The canon gazed at him and wondered at his strange craziness and at how he showed such good sense in all his speeches and answers, only losing his stirrups, as we have said before, when the subject of his knight-errantries came up. And so, when they were all seated on the green grass waiting for the sumpter, the canon, moved by compassion, said to him: "Is it possible, my good sir, that the idle and unlucky reading of books of chivalry has affected you and turned your brain awry to such an extent that you have come to believe that you are under a spell and other things of the sort that are as far from being true as falsehood itself is from the truth? How is it possible for human reason to convince itself of the existence of all that infinity of Amadises, of that multitude of renowned knights, and of so many emperors of Trebizond? Who in the world could possibly believe so much in Felixmarte of Hyrcania, so many palfreys, so many wandering damsels, so many serpents, so many dragons, so many giants, so many unheard-of adventures, so many kinds of enchantments, so many battles, so many fierce encounters, so many bizarre costumes, so many love-sick princesses, so many titled squires, so many dwarfs, so many compliments and love letters, so many valiant ladies, and finally, so many and such monstrous absurdities as are contained in the books of chivalry? For myself, I can say that when I read them, they give me a certain pleasure as long as I do not begin to reflect that they are all lies and childish foolishness. But when I realize what they are, I hurl the very best of them against the wall, and I would pitch them into the fire if I had one close at hand. They certainly deserve such a punishment for being liars, impostors, and beyond the bounds of common nature, for being founders of new sects and new ways of life, and for causing the ignorant masses to believe and hold as Gospel truth the follies they contain. They even have the audacity to muddle the minds of intelligent and wellborn gentlemen, as may well be seen by what they have done to your wor-

ship, for they have brought you to such a pass as to make
it necessary to shut you up in a cage and carry you on an
oxcart, as they transport a lion or a tiger from town to
town to exhibit it for money. Come, Don Quixote, take
pity on yourself; come back into the bosom of common
sense and learn to use the generous share of it that Heaven
has been pleased to bestow upon you by applying your rich
intellect to some other kind of reading that may benefit
your soul and increase your honor. But if you are still obsessed by books of adventures and chivalry, read the book
of Judges in Holy Scripture, where you will find great and
genuine exploits that are as heroic as they are true. Lusitania
had its Viriathus, Rome had its Caesar, Carthage its Hannibal, Greece its Alexander, Castile its Count Fernán
González, Valencia its Cid, Andalusia its Gonzalo Fernández, Extremadura its Diego García de Paredes, Jérez
its Garci Pérez de Vargas, Toledo its Garcilaso, Seville its
Manuel de León: their doughty deeds will entertain, instruct, delight, and amaze the highest intellects that read
them. This reading will truly be worthy of your excellent
mind, my dear Don Quixote, from which you will rise
learned in history, enamored of virtue, instructed in goodness, bettered in manners, valiant without rashness, bold
without vacillation, and all this to the honor of God, your
own profit, and the glory of La Mancha, from where, as I
have learned, you derive your birth and origin."

Don Quixote listened very attentively to the canon's arguments, and when he saw that he had finished, having gazed
at him for some time, he said: "Sir, it seems to me that
your discourse was aimed at convincing me that there have
never been knights-errant in the world, that all books of
chivalry are false, lying, harmful, and unprofitable to the
republic, and that I have done wrong to read them, and
worse to believe in them, and worst of all to imitate them
by setting myself to follow the rigorous profession of knight-
errantry that they teach. And furthermore, you deny that
there have ever been in the world Amadises, either of Gaul
or Greece, or any of all the true knights of whom the writings are full."

"What you say was precisely what I meant," replied the
canon.

To which Don Quixote answered: "You also added that
such books have done much harm, for they have turned my

brain and put me in a cage, and that it would be better for me to amend my ways and change my reading to other books more truthful, entertaining, and instructive."

"That is so," said the canon.

"Why then," retorted Don Quixote, "in my judgment, it is you who are crazy and enchanted for daring to blaspheme against an institution so universally acknowledged and so respected that he who would deny it, as you do, would merit the same punishment that you say you inflict on the books when you read them and they displease you. For to try to convince anyone that there never was an Amadis in the world nor any of the other knights-adventurers so often recorded in the histories would be the same as trying to persuade him that the sun does not shine, nor the frost chill, nor the earth yield sustenance. Where could we find an intellect in the world capable of persuading another that the story of the Infanta Floripes [1] and Guy of Burgundy was not true? Or the adventures of Fierabrás at the Bridge of Mantible, which took place in the time of Charlemagne and which I swear is as true as it is now daylight. And if that is a lie, then it follows that no Hector existed, nor Achilles, nor the Trojan War, nor the Twelve Peers of France, nor King Arthur of England, who is roaming about the world to this day transformed into a raven and is expected in his kingdom any day. And they will also dare to say that the story of Guarino Mezquino is false, as well as the quest for the Holy Grail, and that the loves of Sir Tristram and the Queen Iseult and those of Guinevere and Lancelot are fictitious, although there are persons who can almost remember having seen the Lady Quintañona, who was the finest cupbearer Great Britain ever had. And this is so true that I remember that a grandmother of mine, on my father's side, used to say to me when she saw an old lady in her stately headdress: 'That woman, my boy, is very like the Lady Quintañona,' from which I gather that she must have known her, or at least must have seen some portrait of her. Then, who can deny that the story of

[1] Floripes was the sister of Sir Fierabrás and married Guy of Burgundy, the nephew of Charlemagne. Sir Fierabrás also slew the huge giant who guarded the celebrated Bridge of Mantible, which consisted of thirty arches of black marble.

Pierre [2] and the fair Magalona is true, since even to this day one may see in the king's armory the peg with which he guided the wooden horse on which he used to ride through the air and which is a little higher than the pole of a coach. And near this peg is Babieca's saddle and at Roncesvalles is Roland's horn, which is the size of a great beam; from which we may infer that there were Twelve Peers, that there were Pierres, that there were Cids and other such knights of the kind usually termed adventurers. If that is denied, I shall be told it is not true that the brave Lusitanian Juan de Merlo was a knight-errant who went to Burgundy and fought in the city of Arras with the famous lord of Charny, Monseigneur Pierre, and after that with Monseigneur Henri de Remestan in the city of Basle, emerging victorious from both enterprises and crowned with honor and glory. They will also deny the adventures and challenges achieved in Burgundy by the valiant Spaniards Pedro Barba and Gutierre Quixada—from whose stock I am descended in the direct male line—when they vanquished the sons of Count St. Pol. Let them deny me likewise that Don Fernando de Guevara went in quest of adventures in Germany, where he fought with Messire Giorgio, a knight of the duke of Austria's house. Let them say that the jousts of Suero de Quiñones of the Honorable Pass of Arms [3]

[2] Pierre was Pierre de Brecemont, Sieur de Charny. The story of the magic horse and the peg comes from the *Arabian Nights*.

[3] The Honorable Pass of Arms was held on the bridge of Orbigo in the summer of 1434 by Suero de Quiñones and his knights. For thirty days they defended the bridge against all the knights who passed along the road of Saint James, and three hundred lances were broken off at the haft in the joustings. Pedro Barba and Gutierre Quixada were two Castilian knights who also took part in the Honorable Pass of Arms; the former was son of the judge who had presided over the jousts, the other had taken part in them as a knight-adventurer. Suero de Quiñones defeated Gonzalo de Castañeda—one of Gutierre Quixada's companions—who loudly proclaimed the valor of Suero de Quiñones and rejoiced to have been defeated by so valiant a knight. Gutierre Quixada, however, resented that one of his nine champions had been defeated and vowed revenge. Twenty-four years later he was to find his opportunity. One day in 1458, in the open field between Castroverde and Barcial de la Loma in Navarra, Quixada again came face to face with Suero de Quiñones. The two knights armed cap-a-pie charged each other with lances couched. There

were a fable, as well as the exploits of Sir Luis de Falces against the Castilian knight Don Gonzalo de Guzmán, and many other deeds performed by Christian knights of these and foreign kingdoms, so genuine and true, I repeat, that he who denies them must be devoid of all reason and right understanding."

The canon was amazed to hear the hodgepodge Don Quixote made of truth and lies and to see the knowledge he possessed of everything in any way concerned with the exploits of his knight-errantry; and so, he replied to him as follows: "I cannot deny, sir, that there may be some truth in what you have said, especially in what you say of the Spanish knights-errant, and I am also willing to admit the existence of the Twelve Peers of France, but I will not believe that they did all the things Archbishop Turpin writes of them, for the truth of it is that they were knights chosen by the kings of France and were called peers as being all equal in worth, in rank, and in valor; or at least, if they were not, they should have been. They were an order like the present-day Order of Santiago, or of Calatrava, whose professing knights are presumed to be, or should be, worthy, valiant, and wellborn. As we now speak of the Knights of St. John, or of Alcántara, so they spoke in those days of the Knights of the Twelve Peers, because they were twelve equals, chosen as members of that order. As for the Cid, there is no doubt about him, and even less about Bernardo del Carpio, but there is very great doubt whether they per-

---

was a clash of armor and one of the knights fell from his charger and lay motionless. He was dead. It was Suero de Quiñones. Don Quixote was proud of his ancestor Gutierre Quixada and boasts of his adventures and challenges in Burgundy. It is interesting to note that the most recent biographer of Cervantes, Astrana Marín, in Vol. IV of his monumental work suggests that the model for Don Quixote may have been one of the Quixada family at Esquivias, a certain Alonso Quixada who lived in the first third of the sixteenth century. Alonso Quixada was the third son of Juan Quixada and María, the great-aunt of Doña Catalina, the wife of Cervantes. Alonso Quixada entered the Benedictine Order and lived in the monastery of Saint Augustine in Toledo. He became so absorbed in books of chivalry that he believed that the deeds told of Amadis and his knights in those lying books were Gospel truth. He was, however, not mad but eccentric. Cervantes, in case his wife's family might take exception, changed the name of his hero from Quixada to Quixano.

formed the deeds told of them. As to the other thing you speak of, the peg of Count Pierre and its standing next to Babieca's saddle in the king's armory, I confess, my son, that I am so ignorant or so shortsighted that although I have seen the saddle, I have never hit upon the peg, though it is as big as you say it is."

"Yet, there it is, without any question," answered Don Quixote, "and what is more, they say it is kept in a case of neat's leather to prevent it rusting."

"That is very probable," answered the canon, "yet, by the holy orders I received I do not remember having seen it. But granted that it is there, there is no reason why I should have to believe the tales of all those Amadises, nor those of that multitude of knights we are told about, nor is it reasonable that a man like you, of such fine intellect and reputation, should accept all the extravagant absurdities in those nonsensical books of chivalry as genuinely true."

CHAPTER L

Of the learned arguments between Don Quixote and the canon, with other incidents

"That is a fine joke indeed!" answered Don Quixote. "Books that are printed by royal license and with the approbation of those to whom they are submitted, books that are read with general delight and celebrated by great and small, by rich and poor, by the learned and the ignorant, by plebeians and gentlefolk—in short, by all kinds of persons of every condition—could they be lies and at the same time bear such an appearance of truth? Do they not inform us of the father, the mother, the country, the family, the time, the place, and the deeds, step by step and day by day, that such and such a knight or knights performed? Be silent, sir; do not utter such blasphemies. Believe me, I advise you to behave like a man of sense: read these books and you will see what pleasure you get from them. For, tell me, is there anything more delightful than to see this very moment before our eyes, as it were, a great lake of pitch, boiling hot, and swimming and writhing about in it, a swirling mass of serpents, snakes, lizards, and many other kind of grisly and savage creatures, and then to hear a dismal voice from the lake crying: 'You knight, whoever you are, you who stare at this awful lake, if you wish to reach the guerdon hidden beneath these black waters, show the valor of your dauntless heart and plunge into the midst of this dark seething flood, for if you do not do so, you will not be worthy to see the mighty marvels hidden within the seven castles of the seven fairies who dwell beneath these murky waters?' No sooner has the knight heard this grim voice than without further thought for himself, without pausing to consider the peril to which he is exposed, and without relieving himself of his weighty armor, he commends himself to God and his lady and casts himself into the middle of the seething pool; there, when he least expects it and when he knows not when it will end, he finds himself amid flowered meadows whose beauty far exceeds the Elysian fields. There the sky seems to him more transparent and the sun to shine with fresher radiance. He sees before him a pleasant wooded glade of green and leafy trees whose verdure rejoices his eyes, while his ears are lulled by the gentle and spontaneous song of tiny, painted birds that are amid the interlacing branches. Then he discovers a little stream whose clear waters, like liquid crystal, glide over fine sand and white pebbles that resemble sifted gold and purest pearl. There he perceives a fountain wrought of mottled jasper and polished marble; here another, roughly fashioned, where small mussel shells with the twisted white and yellow houses of the snail, set in disordered order and alternating with fragments of glittering crystal and counterfeit emeralds, combine to create so varied a composition that Art, imitating Nature, seems here to surpass her. Then, all of a sudden, in the distance appears a strong castle or sightly palace, whose walls are of beaten gold, its turrets of diamonds, and its gates of jacinth; it is so admirably built, in fact, that though the materials of which it is built are nothing less than diamonds, carbuncles, rubies, pearls, gold, and emeralds, the workmanship is even more precious. And after this, could one see a fairer sight than a goodly train of damsels sallying forth from the castle gate in such gay and gorgeous attire that if I were to try to describe it as the histories do, I should never finish? And then to see the leader of them all take by the hand the dauntless knight who plunged into the burning lake and silently conduct him into the rich palace or castle and bathe him in lukewarm water and then anoint him all over with sweet-smelling ointments and put on him a shirt of finest samite, all fragrant and perfumed, while another damsel hastens to throw over his shoulders a mantle that they say is worth at least the price of a city, and even more?

"What could be more fascinating than when they tell us that after all this they lead him into another hall, where he finds the tables laid in such style that he is filled with wonder? And to see him sprinkling on his hands water distilled with ambergris and sweet-smelling flowers? And to see him

seated on a chair of ivory? And to see all the damsels wait
upon him, preserving their miraculous silence and bringing
him such a varied profusion of delicacies so deliciously
cooked that his appetite does not know toward which of
them to stretch his hand? What pleasure then to hear the
music that plays while he is at table, without his knowing
who makes it or from where it comes! And when the dinner
is ended and the tables cleared, for the knight to recline
upon his chair, perhaps picking his teeth as the custom is,
when suddenly another damsel, more beautiful than the
first, enters through the door of the hall and sits down by
the side of the knight and begins to tell him what manner
of castle that is, how she lives there under enchantment,
and other things that surprise the knight and amaze the
readers of his tale.

"I will enlarge on this no further, for you can gather from
what I have said that any passage from any story of knight-
errantry is bound to rouse both wonder and delight in any
reader, whoever he may be. Believe me then, good sir, and
as I have told you before, read those books and you will
see how they banish your melancholy and improve your
temper, if perchance it be bad. I declare that ever since I
have become a knight-errant, I am valiant, courteous, liberal,
well bred, generous, polite, bold, gently patient, and an en-
durer of toils, imprisonments, and enchantments. And although it is so short a while since I found myself shut up
in a cage like a madman, I expect through the might of my
arm, if Heaven favors and Fate does not thwart me, to
find myself in a few days king of some kingdom in which I
can display the gratitude and liberality contained in this
bosom of mine, for by my faith, sir, a poor man is incapacitated from showing the virtue of liberality toward
anyone, though he may possess it in the greatest degree;
and gratitude that consists merely of desire is a dead thing,
as faith without works is dead. For this reason I wish that
Fortune would speedily offer me an opportunity of making
myself an emperor so that I might show my genuine desire
to do good to my friends, especially to this poor Sancho
Panza, my squire, who is the best fellow in the world, for
I should like to bestow upon him the earldom I promised
him a long while ago, although I fear he will not have the
capacity to govern his estate."

Sancho, who overheard these last words of his master,

exclaimed: "Get to work, Don Quixote, and get me that earldom you have promised me so often and I have waited for so long. I promise you that I have the ability for governing; and if I lacked it, I have heard of men who take over noblemen's estates, giving them so much a year; they see to the management, while the lad himself lies in clover, enjoying the rent they pay him without a care in the world. I will do the same, and I won't start haggling over anything more or less but hand it all over at once and enjoy my income like a duke, and the Devil take the rest!"

"That, brother Sancho," said the canon, "applies to the enjoyment of the revenues, but there is the administration of justice, which must be attended to by the lord of the estate. And here is where capacity and sound judgment come in, and above all, an honest intention to do right. If that is lacking at the outset, all will go wrong in the middle and the end, and God usually helps the good intentions of the simple but thwarts the designs of the cunning."

"I don't know a thing about those philosophies," answered Sancho Panza; "I only wish I were as sure of getting the earldom as I am of being a good governor, for I have as great a soul as my neighbor and as tough a body as the best of them, and I'd be as much the king of my estate as anyone is of his. And this being so, I'd do as I liked; and doing as I liked, I'd do my pleasure; and doing my pleasure, I'd be content; and being content, there's nothing more to wish for; and when there's nothing more to wish for, it's all over. So, for Christ's sake, let the estate come, and then we'll see, as one blind man said to another."

"These are not bad philosophies, as you say, Sancho," said the canon, "but all the same there is plenty to be said on the subject of earldoms."

To this Don Quixote replied: "I do not know what more can be said. I am guided by the example of the great Amadis of Gaul, who made his squire count of the Firm Isle. So I may make a count of Sancho Panza without my conscience pricking me, for he is one of the best squires a knight-errant ever had."

The canon was astonished at the well-reasoned nonsense uttered by Don Quixote (if nonsense can ever be well reasoned), at his description of the adventures of the Knight of the Lake, and at the impression produced upon him by the deliberate lies of the books he had read. He marveled, too, at Sancho's simplicity in desiring so ardently to obtain the earldom his master had promised him.

By this time the canon's servants, who had gone to the inn for the sumpter mule, had returned; so, making their table of a carpet and the green grass of the meadow, they sat down in the shade of some trees and took their meal there so that the wagoner might take advantage of the pasture there, as has already been said. While they were eating, they suddenly heard a loud noise and the tinkle of a little bell from some brambles and thick bushes that grew nearby, and at the same time they saw a beautiful she-goat, speckled with black, white, and gray. After her came a goatherd calling to her as herders do, bidding her to stop and return to the fold. But the truant goat, frightened and trembling, ran up to the company as though for protection, and there stayed still.

The goatherd came up, caught her by the horns, and said to her as though she were capable of speech and reason: "Gadabout! Gadabout! You speckled wanton! How you've been limping lately! What wolves have scared you, darling? Won't you tell me what it is, my pretty one? It must be because you're a woman and can't keep still! Hell take your temperament and the temperament of all like you! Come back, come back, darling; even if not so happy, you'll at least be safer in your fold or with your companions; and if you, who have to guard them and guide them, go gallivanting guideless and astray, what will become of them?"

The goatherd's words amused his hearers, especially the canon, who said to him: "Come, come, brother, calm down, I pray, and don't be in such a hurry to take this she-goat back to her fold; since she is a woman, as you say, she must follow her natural instinct in spite of all your pains to stop her. Take this mouthful and drink a drop with us; it will cool you down, and the goat can rest for a while."

As he said this, he handed him on the point of his knife the hindquarter of a cold rabbit. The goatherd took it and thanked him, and when he had drunk and rested for a while, he said: "I don't want your worships to take me for a simpleton for talking to this animal so sensibly, for, in truth, the words I spoke are not devoid of mystery. I am a peasant, but not so much that I do not understand how one should converse with men and with beasts."

"That I can well believe," replied the curate, "for I already know by experience that mountains nurse scholars and the sheepfolds house philosophers."

"At least, sir," rejoined the goatherd, "they harbor men who have learned by experience. And to convince you and to give you an example of it, though it maybe seems that I am inviting myself without being asked, if it doesn't bore you, gentlemen, and if you will lend me a patient ear for a little while, I will tell you a true tale that will confirm that gentleman's words" (pointing to the curate) "as well as my own."

To this Don Quixote answered: "Seeing that this matter has a slight shadow of knightly adventure about it, I will listen to you, my brother, most willingly, and all these gentlemen will do likewise, for they are men of good sense and fond of strange narratives that surprise, entertain, and charm the senses, as I am sure your story will do; so, begin, friend, for we shall all listen."

"Count my ear out," said Sancho, "for I'm going with this pasty to that stream, where I'm going to gorge myself for three days, for I've heard my master, Don Quixote, say that a knight-errant's squire has to eat, when he gets a chance, till he can eat no more, for they may by accident enter a wood that's so entangled that they can't for the life of them find a way out in six whole days, and if a man doesn't go in with his belly well lined or his wallet well stored there he may stay, as often happens, till he turns into a mummy."

"You are quite right, Sancho," said Don Quixote. "Go wherever you will and eat what you can. As for me, I am already satisfied, and all I need is refreshment for the mind, and this I shall give it by listening to this good man's story."

"And we shall give the same to ours," said the canon, who then begged the goatherd to begin what he had promised to tell.

The goatherd gave the goat, which he was holding by the horns, a few slaps on the back, saying: "Lie down by my side, speckle; we'll have time enough to return to the fold."

The goat seemed to understand him, for when the master sat down, she stretched herself quietly by his side, and looking up into his face, she seemed to say that she was ready to listen to the goatherd, who began his story thus:

CHAPTER LI

*What the goatherd related to those who were carrying
Don Quixote*

"Nine miles from this valley is a town that although small
is one of the richest in all these parts. There lived a farmer
who was held in the greatest esteem, and though it is usual
for the wealthy to be respected, yet he was more considered
for his native virtue than for the wealth he possessed. But
his greatest treasure, he used to say, was his daughter, a
girl of such superlative beauty, rare intelligence, charm, and
virtue that everyone who knew her, or even set eyes on her,
wondered at the extraordinary qualities with which Heaven
and nature had endowed her. As a child she was pretty,
and as she grew older she increased in good looks, until at
the age of sixteen she was exceedingly beautiful. The fame
of her loveliness began to spread among the adjoining villages—but why do I say through the adjoining villages? It
spread to remote cities and even made its way into the
palaces of kings and into the ears of all kinds of people,
who would come to see her from everywhere as if she were
a rare sight or a wonder-working image. Her father guarded
her carefully, and she guarded herself, for there are no
locks, bolts, or bars that protect a maiden better than those
of her own modesty. The father's wealth and the daughter's beauty led many, both townsmen and strangers, to ask
her in marriage; but he who had the disposal of so rich
a jewel was greatly perplexed and was unable to decide
upon which of her innumerable wooers to bestow her. Among
the multitude who desired her I was one, who entertained
many sanguine hopes of success, not only because I was
known to her father, but also because I was a native of
their town, of unblemished blood, in the flower of my age,

with rich and worldly goods, and no less well endowed in mind. But a fellow villager with all the same qualifications also sought her hand, with the result that the father put off his decision and kept everything hanging in the balance, for it seemed to him that either of us would be a good match for his daughter. To be rid of this difficulty, he resolved to refer it to Leandra (for that is the name of the rich maid who has plunged me into such misery), thinking that as we two were equal, it was best to leave to his beloved daughter the right to choose according to her own liking, a course that should be followed by all fathers with children to marry. I do not mean that they should let them choose from base or evil persons, but that they should put the good before them and let them choose among them according to their taste. I do not know what choice Leandra made; I only know that her father put us both off on the score of his daughter's extreme youth in general terms that neither bound him nor released us. My rival is called Anselmo, and I Eugenio, for you should know the names of the persons involved in the tragedy whose end is still in suspense, though it is fairly obvious that it is bound to be disastrous.

"About this time there came to our town one Vicente de la Roca, son of a poor local farmer. He had returned from Italy and other places where he had been soldiering. A captain who happened to be passing through the village with his company had carried him off when he was a lad of about twelve years, and twelve years later he returned as a young man in a soldier's uniform, sporting countless bright colors and adorned with innumerable crystal gewgaws and fine steel chains. One day he would put on one piece of finery, and the next day another, but all of them were flimsy, showy, of little weight and less worth. The country people, who are malicious by nature—and when idleness gives them leisure, they are malice itself—noted and took an exact count of his gewgaws and frippery, and they discovered that he had only three suits of different colors, with stockings and gaiters to match; but he so transformed and varied them that if no one had counted them, one would have sworn that he had shown off ten suits of clothes and more than twenty plumes of feathers. But do not, I pray you, consider these details about his clothes a superfluous digression, for they play a chief part in my story.

"He used to sit on a bench under a great poplar tree in our marketplace, and there he would keep us gaping open-mouthed, hanging upon the exploits he described to us. There was no country in the whole world he had not visited and no battle he had not taken part in. He had killed more Turks than there are in Morocco and Tunis and engaged in more single combats, according to his account, than Gante and Luna, García de Paredes, and a thousand others whom he named, and from every one of them he had emerged victorious, without losing a drop of blood. Then, again, he would show scars of wounds, which, though they were not visible, he would persuade us they were the result of musket shots received in various actions and skirmishes. Finally, with unparalleled arrogance he would address his equals patronizingly in familiar speech,[1] even those who knew him and declared that his right arm was his father, his deeds his lineage, and that, as a soldier, he owed nothing even to the king himself. In addition to these pretensions, he was a bit of a musician and could thrum a guitar with such skill that some people said he could make its strings speak. But his talents did not stop there, for he had also that of the poet, and he would write a ballad a mile and a half long upon every trifling thing that happened in the town.

"This soldier, then, whom I have just described, this Vicente de la Roca, this braggart, this charlatan, this musician, this poet, was often seen and admired by Leandra from a window of her house that looked onto the market-place. She was captivated by the bright tinsel of his clothes, bewitched by his ballads, for he would give away twenty copies of every one he composed; the exploits that he had told of himself came to her ears, and in the end—for so the Devil must have ordered it—she fell in love with him before the presumptuous idea of wooing her entered his mind. And as no love affair is more easily brought to an issue than the one which has on its side the lady's desire, Leandra and Vicente came to an understanding without any difficulty, and before any of her numerous suitors could suspect her inclinations, she had already satisfied it by leaving the home of her dear and beloved father (she had no

---

[1] Instead of addressing them as *Vuestra Merced*, he used *vos*, which was only used with those of inferior category or with those with whom one was on terms of great intimacy.

mother) and by eloping from the village with the soldier, who came off with more triumph from this enterprise than from all the many others he had claimed. This event filled the whole village with amazement, and everyone else who heard of it. I was confounded, Anselmo thunderstruck, her father afflicted, her relatives ashamed, justice aroused, and the officers on the watch. They scoured the roads, they searched the woods and everywhere they could, and at the end of three days, they found the giddy Leandra in a mountain cave, clad only in her shift and without the large sums of money and the precious jewels that she had brought away with her. They took her back into the presence of her heartbroken father and questioned her about her plight. And she confessed without hesitation that Vicente de la Roca had deceived her; that under the promise of becoming her husband, he had persuaded her to leave her father's house, telling her that he would take her to the richest and most luxurious city in all the world, which was Naples; that she had been so ill-advised and worse deceived as to believe him; that after robbing her father, she had put herself under his care the same night she was missed; and that he had taken her to a wild mountain and shut her in the cave where they had found her. She also related how the soldier, though he had not robbed her of her honor, had stolen everything she had and how he had taken her to the cave and gone away: a fact that revived the wonder of all.

"It was difficult, sir, to believe in the young man's restraint, but she affirmed it so persistently that she partly consoled her father, who set no store in the valuables they had taken so long as his daughter was left in possession of the jewel that, once lost, is beyond all hope of recovery. The very day Leandra appeared, her father removed her from our sight; he took her and shut her up in a convent in a town not far from here, hoping that time would obliterate some part of the disgrace she had brought upon herself. Leandra's youth served as some excuse for her bad behavior, at least for those who had nothing to gain from proving her good or bad, but those who knew that she was an intelligent girl and possessed of considerable shrewdness attributed her fault not to ignorance, but to frivolity and the failings natural to women, the majority of whom are wont to be unsteady and ill balanced.

"Now that Leandra was shut up, Anselmo's eyes became

blind, or at least there was no sight that gave him any
pleasure, and my own were in darkness, without a light to
guide them toward joy. In Leandra's absense our sorrow
increased, our patience diminished, and we cursed the
soldier's finery and abused her father's lack of precaution.
In the end Anselmo and I agreed to leave the village and
come to this valley, where he grazes a flock of his own
sheep and I a large herd of goats, also my own. And so we
spend our lives among the trees, and here we give vent to
our feelings, sometimes singing in unison the praises or
dispraises of the lovely Leandra, at other times breathing
our sighs separately and alone and confiding our complaints
to Heaven. Many others of Leandra's suitors have followed
our example and have come to these wild mountains to take
up the same employment, and so many are they that this
spot is transformed into the pastoral Arcadia, for it is so
crowded with shepherds and sheepfolds that there is no
corner in which one does not hear the name of the fair
Leandra. One man curses her and calls her fickle, incon-
stant, immodest; another denounces her as forward and
frail; one absolves and pardons her, another tries her and
sentences her; one utters paeans to her beauty, another
vilifies her character; in fact, all disparage her and all
adore her, and the madness extends so far that some complain of her disdain without ever having spoken to her,
and some moan their fate and suffer the maddening disease
of jealousy for which she never gave anyone any cause, for,
as I have said, her sin was discovered before her infatuation
was known. There is not a hollow rock, nor riverbank, nor
shade of a tree, that is not occupied by some shepherd telling
his misfortunes to the winds; and echo repeats Leandra's
name whenever it can· sound. The hills ring with Leandra,
the streams murmur Leandra, and Leandra keeps us all
distracted and enchanted, hoping without hope and fearing
without knowing what we fear.

"Of all these distracted men the one who shows the least
and has the most sense is my rival Anselmo, who, though
he has so many other things he might complain of, complains only of her absence and sings his lament in verses
that show his excellent talents to the sound of a fiddle,
which he plays admirably. I follow an easier and, in my
opinion, a wiser path, which is to curse the fickleness of
women, their inconstancy, their double-dealing, their broken

promises, their broken faith, and last of all, the lack of judgment they show in their choice of objects for their desires and affections. And that was the reason, gentlemen, for the words I addressed to this goat on my arrival here; because she is a female, I despise her, though she be the best of all my herd.

"This is the story I promised to tell you. If I have been tedious in my tale, I shall not be brief in serving you. Near here is my cottage, where I have fresh milk, an excellent cheese, and various fruits of the season, no less pleasant to the sight than to the taste."

CHAPTER LII

Of the quarrel that Don Quixote had with the goatherd, with the rare adventure of the disciplinants, which he successfully achieved with the sweat of his brow

The goatherd's tale much delighted all who heard it, especially the canon, who was particularly taken by the manner of telling it, for the narrator seemed more like a polished courtier than a rustic goatherd, and he admitted that the curate was right when he had said that mountains nurse scholars. The whole company offered their services to Eugenio, but the one who was most liberal in this respect was Don Quixote, who said to him: "I declare, brother goatherd, that if I were free to undertake any new adventure, I would instantly set out to bring yours to a fortunate conclusion. I would deliver Leandra from the convent (where I am sure she must be detained against her will) in spite of the abbess and all who might oppose me, and I would place her in your hands for you to deal with according to your will and pleasure, observing, however, the laws of chivalry, which ordain that no violence be done to any damsel. Yet,

I trust in Our Lord, God, that a wicked enchanter shall not exercise so much sway that another more beneficial enchanter may not prevail over him. When that time comes, I promise you my favor and assistance, as I am bound to do by my profession, which is none other than to succor the helpless and the destitute."

The goatherd stared at him, and observing that Don Quixote was so tattered and gaunt, he was surprised and said to the barber, who was seated next to him: "Sir, who is this strange-looking man who talks in such an odd manner?"

"Who should it be," replied the barber, "but the famous Don Quixote of La Mancha, the redresser of injuries, the righter of wrongs, the protector of damsels, the terror of giants, and the winner of battles?"

"That seems to me," answered the goatherd, "like what we read in books about knights-errant, who did all the things you say this man does, though I take it that your worship is joking, or the gentleman must have a couple of rooms in his brain vacant."

"You are an arrant rascal," cried Don Quixote at this; "and it is you who is vacant and deficient, for I am much fuller than ever was the whore's daughter who gave you birth."

As he spoke, he caught up a loaf of bread that lay near him and hit the goatherd full in the face with it with such force that he flattened his nose. But the goatherd did not appreciate the joke, and seeing that he was being mishandled in earnest, without a thought for the carpet, or the table-cloth, or the diners around it, he sprang upon Don Quixote, and seizing him by the throat with both hands, he would have strangled him if Sancho Panza had not at that moment come to the rescue. Sancho grabbed the goatherd by the shoulders and threw him back upon the table, breaking plates, smashing the cups, spilling and upsetting everything that was upon it.

Don Quixote, finding himself free, rushed to get on top of the goatherd, who, with his face smeared with blood after having been kicked and pummeled by Sancho, was on all fours groping about for a knife off the table to take some bloody vengeance; but this the canon and the curate prevented. Nevertheless, the goatherd, seconded by the barber, got Don Quixote under him and rained upon him such a shower of blows that the poor knight's face poured blood as copiously as his own. The canon and curate were bursting with laughter, the troopers danced for joy, and everyone hallooed them on as men do when two dogs are fighting. Sancho Panza alone was in despair, because he could not break loose from one of the canon's servants who prevented him from helping his master. At last, while all were enjoying the sport, except the two combatants, who were mauling one another, they heard the sound of a trumpet, so doleful that it made them turn their faces toward the place from which it seemed to come. But the one who was most excited at the sound was Don Quixote, who, though he lay under the goatherd sorely against his will, pretty well bruised and battered, cried to his adversary: "Brother demon, for you surely can't be anything else, since you have power and strength enough to subdue mine, I pray you, let us call a truce for just one hour, for the mournful sound of that trumpet that reaches our ears seems to summon me to some new adventure."

The goatherd, who was now tired of pummeling and being pummeled, let him go at once, and Don Quixote stood up, turned his face in the direction of the sound, and suddenly saw a number of men, dressed in white after the fashion of disciplinants, descending a little hill.

It so happened that year that the clouds had denied the earth their moisture; so, throughout the valleys of that region, processions, public prayers, and penances were ordered to beseech Heaven to open the flood gates of its mercy and send them rain. It was for this purpose, therefore, that the people of a neighboring village were coming in procession to a holy shrine that stood on a hill at the edge of the valley. Don Quixote, as soon as he saw the strange attire of the disciplinants, did not pause to recall the many occasions on which he had seen a similar sight before but immediately imagined that it was some kind of adventure that was reserved for him alone as knight-errant. He was all the more confirmed in his opinion by mistaking an image that they carried all swathed in mourning for some noble lady whom those ruffians and unmannerly churls were carrying away against her will. No sooner did this thought flash through his mind than he rushed over to Rozinante, who was grazing nearby, and taking off the bridle and buckler that hung from the pommel of the saddle,

he bridled him in an instant. Then, asking Sancho for his
sword, he mounted Rozinante, and bracing his buckler, he
cried in a loud voice to all those present: "Now, valiant
company, ye shall see how necessary it is that there be in
the world knights who profess the order of knight-errantry;
now, I say, shall ye see, in the restoration of that captive
lady to liberty, whether knights-errant ought to be valued!"

Saying this, he clapped his heels to Rozinante (for spurs
he had none), and at a half gallop (for nowhere in all this
truthful history can one read that Rozinante ever went at
full speed) he advanced to encounter the disciplinants,
though the curate and the barber tried to stop him. But all
their efforts were in vain, nor could he be stopped by the
screams of Sancho, who shouted: "Master, where are you
going? What devils in your heart are driving you on to attack our Catholic faith? Mind, sir! Bad'cess to it! That is a
procession of disciplinants and the lady they're carrying on
the bier is the most blessed image of the Immaculate Virgin.
Take heed, sir, what you're doing; this time I can assure
you that it's not what you think."

Sancho wasted his breath, for his master was so set
upon encountering the sheeted ones and upon freeing
the lady in black that he heard not a word, and even if he
had, he would not have turned back though the king himself had commanded him. When he reached the procession,
he stopped Rozinante, who already wanted to rest a little,
and in a hoarse, angry voice he cried out: "You there, who
cover up your faces probably because you are evil, halt
and pay heed to my words!"

The first to halt were those who were carrying the image.
Then, one of the four priests who chanted the litanies,
noticing the strange appearance of Don Quixote, the leanness of Rozinante, and other ludicrous details, answered
him, saying: "Brother, if you have anything to say, say it
quickly, for these brethren are scourging their flesh, and we
cannot, nor is it right that we should, stop to listen to anything that may not be said in two words."

"I will say it in one," replied Don Quixote. "You must
instantly free that beauteous lady whose tears and sad appearance show clearly that you are bearing her away against
her will and that you have done her some grievous wrong.
But I, who came into the world to redress such injuries,
will not allow you to move one single step forward till you

have restored to her the liberty she desires and deserves."

From these words all who heard them concluded that Don Quixote must be some madman, and they began to laugh heartily. But their laughter only served to add gunpowder to the knight's fury, for without another word he drew his sword and attacked the litter. One of those who carried it, leaving the burden to his comrades, stepped forward to encounter Don Quixote, brandishing a forked pole on which they propped the litter while resting, and with it he parried the heavy stroke that the knight aimed at him. The force of the stroke snapped the pole in two, but with the remaining stump that was left in his hand he dealt the knight such a thwack on the shoulder of his sword-arm that his buckler was unable to shield him against the rustic onslaught, and down came poor Don Quixote to the ground in a bad way. Sancho, who came panting after him, seeing him fall, called out to his assailant not to strike him again, for he was a poor enchanted knight who had done nobody any harm all his life. The peasant stopped, not, however, on account of Sancho's appeal, but because he saw that Don Quixote stirred neither hand nor foot. And, believing that he had killed him, he hastily tucked up his habit to his girdle and set off, racing like a deer across the country.

By that time everyone in Don Quixote's company had reached where he lay, but when the men in the procession saw them running in their direction and with them troopers of the Holy Brotherhood with their crossbows, they feared some trouble. So, they clustered in a circle about the image: the penitents lifted their hoods and grasped their lashes; the priests brandished their tapers, and all waited for the attack with the firm resolve to defend themselves, and if they could, to take the offensive against their aggressors. But Fortune arranged matters better than they expected, for Sancho did nothing but cast himself upon the body of his master, making over him the most sorrowful and drollest lament in the world, for he truly believed that Don Quixote was dead. Our curate was recognized by one of the priests in the procession, and this calmed the apprehension of both sides. Our curate in a few words told the second curate of Don Quixote's condition; then, he and the whole crowd of disciplinants went to see whether or not the poor knight was dead, and heard Sancho Panza proclaim with tears in his eyes: "O flower of chivalry, one single blow of a cudgel has finished the course of your well-spent years! O glory of your race, honor and credit to all La Mancha, and even to the whole world, which, now that you are gone, will be overrun with evildoers, who will no longer fear punishment for their iniquities! O liberal above all the Alexanders, since for a mere eight months' service you have given me the best island that the sea surrounds! O humble to the haughty and arrogant to the humble! Resister of perils, sufferer of affronts, lover without cause, imitator of the good, scourge of the wicked, enemy of the base! In a word, knight-errant, which is the highest thing anyone could say!"

At the cries and groans of Sancho, Don Quixote revived, and the first words he said were: "He who lives absent from thee, sweet Dulcinea, endures far greater sufferings than these. Help me, friend Sancho, to lift myself into the enchanted cart, for I am no longer in a condition to press the saddle of Rozinante; this shoulder of mine is broken to pieces."

"That I'll do with all my heart, dear master," replied Sancho, "and let us go back to our village in the company of these gentlemen, and there we will make schemes for another sally that may be more profitable to us."

"You speak well, Sancho," answered the knight. "It is prudent for us to wait until the evil influence of the stars that now reigns passes away."

The canon, the curate, and the barber approved this resolution, and after they had enjoyed Sancho Panza's fooleries to the full, they placed Don Quixote on the cart as before. The procession resumed its former order and went on its way. The goatherd took his leave of them all, and as the troopers refused to go any further, the curate paid them what he owed them. The canon then begged the curate to let him know what might happen to Don Quixote (whether he recovered from his madness or remained in it), and with this he took his leave. Thus they all parted and went their several ways.

The party now consisted only of the curate, the barber, Don Quixote, Sancho, and good Rozinante, who bore all the ups and downs as patiently as his master. The wagoner yoked his oxen, and having laid Don Quixote on a bundle of hay, plodded his way at his usual calm, deliberate pace, following the directions of the curate; and at the end of six days they reached Don Quixote's village. They made their entrance at noon, and as it happened to be Sunday, all the people were in the marketplace when the wagon passed through. Everyone rushed to see who was in it, and when they recognized their townsman, they were amazed. A boy ran off at full speed to give the news to his housekeeper and his niece that their master and uncle was coming home lean and yellow, stretched out on a bundle of hay in an oxcart. It was a pathetic thing to hear the cries of the two ladies, the blows they gave themselves, the execrations they uttered afresh against the books of chivalry, all of which were repeated when they saw Don Quixote enter the door of his house.

As soon as she received news of Don Quixote's arrival, Sancho Panza's wife ran there, and as soon as she saw Sancho, her first inquiry was whether the ass had come home in good condition. Sancho replied that he was in better health than his master.

"Thanks be to God," said she, "for this great favor. Now tell me, husband, what good have you got from your squireship? What petticoat have you brought for me? What dainty shoes for your children?"

"I've brought you nothing of the kind, dear wife," said Sancho, "but I've other things of more consequence."

"I'm glad to hear so," answered the wife. "Show me those things of more consequence. I'm dying to see them to gladden my heart, for I've been mournful and down in the mouth all those ages you've been away."

"I'll show them to you at home, wife," said Sancho. "For the present, hold your soul in patience. Please God we may sally out another time in search of adventures and you'll soon see me count or governor of an island, and not one of those around here, but the finest that can be found."

"May the Lord be pleased to grant it, husband, for we're in sore need of it. Tell me now; what's all this about islands? I don't catch your meaning."

"Honey is not for an ass's mouth," answered Sancho. "You'll see in good time, wife, aye, and you'll be all agape at hearing yourself called ladyship by all your vassals."

"What are you prating about ladyships, islands, and vassals?" cried Juana Panza, for that was the name of Sancho's wife, not because they were relatives, but because in La Mancha it is customary for wives to take their husbands' last name.

"Don't fret yourself, Juana, and be in such a hurry to know everything at once; it's enough for you to know that I'm tell-

ing the truth, so mum's the word; but I can tell you one
thing by the way, namely, that there's nothing in this world
so pleasant as for an honest man to be squire to a knight-
errant on the prowl for adventures. It's true that most of
those we encountered were not as comfortable as a body
would wish, for out of a hundred adventures, ninety-nine
usually turned out cross and crooked. I know by experience, for from some I came off blanketed and from others
bruised and battered, but when all's said and done, it's a fine
thing to be gadding about spying for chances, crossing mountains, exploring woods, climbing rocks, visiting castles, lodging in inns at our own sweet will, with devil a maravedi to
pay."

While this conversation was passing between Sancho
Panza and Juana Panza, his wife, Don Quixote's housekeeper and niece received the knight, undressed him, and
put him into his old bed. He looked at them with squinting
eyes, for he could not make out where he was. The curate
told the niece to take very good care of her uncle and to be
very watchful lest he should make another sally, telling her
the trouble it had cost to get him home. The two women
began their lamentations once more, again execrating the
books of chivalry and imploring Heaven to plunge the
authors of so many lies and absurdities into the bottomless
abyss. In fact, they were at their wits' end, for they were
afraid they might lose their master and uncle the moment
he felt a little better. And events turned out as they feared.

But though the author of this history has eagerly and
diligently inquired after Don Quixote's exploits on his third
sally, he has not been able to discover any account of them,
at least from any authentic documents. Only tradition has
preserved in the memory of La Mancha that the third time
Don Quixote left his home he went to Saragossa, where he
took part in some famous jousts in that city, and that he had
adventures there worthy of his valor and of his sound intelligence. Nor would our author have been able to discover any
details of his death, nor would he even have heard of it, if
Fortune had not thrown in his path an aged physician who
had in his possession a leaden box that he said he had discovered among the ruined foundations of an ancient hermitage that was being rebuilt. In this box he had found certain
parchments written in the Gothic script, but in Castilian verse,
which contained many of his exploits and emphasized the

beauty of Dulcinea of El Toboso, the shape of Rozinante, the fidelity of Sancho Panza, and the burial of Don Quixote himself, with various epitaphs and eulogies on his life and character. Such as could be deciphered and interpreted the trustworthy author of this original and matchless history has set down here, and he asks no recompense from his readers for the immense pains it has cost him to ransack all the archives of La Mancha to drag it into light. All he asks is that they should give it as much credit as sensible men are wont to give to the books of chivalry, which are held in such high esteem in the world. With this he will reckon himself well paid and satisfied, and he will be encouraged to go in search of other histories, perhaps less truthful than this one, but at least as inventive and entertaining.

The first words written on the parchment scroll found in the leaden box were these:

The Academicians of Argamasilla,
A Town of La Mancha, On the Life and Death
Of the Valiant Don Quixote of La Mancha,
Hoc scripserunt.
"Priggish," [1] Academician of Argamasilla.
Upon the Tomb of Don Quixote

Epitaph

The dunderhead who for La Mancha won
More trophies than bold Jason for his Creta; [2]
The wiseacre whose belfry bore a vane,
Sharp-pointed, when a blunter barb were meeter;
The arm that from distant Cathay to Gaeta
Extended o'er the world his mighty name;
The Muse, as hideous as she is discreet,
Who carved on brazen plates the poet's line;
He who the Amadises far outshone
And made famed Galaor appear a fool,
Outstripping both of them in love and war,

[1] These nicknames of all the academicians have burlesque significations.

[2] Jason, who set sail in the *Argo* in quest of the Golden Fleece, had no connection with Crete; error (perhaps voluntary) on the part of Cervantes.

E'en making both the Belianises quail;
He who on Rozinante erring went
Now lies in this cold marble monument.

"TOADY," ACADEMICIAN OF ARGAMASILLA, IN LAUDEN DULCINEAE OF EL TOBOSO

Sonnet

She whom you see, this lusty, plump-cheeked lass,
High bosomed, mannish like a grenadier,
Is El Toboso's queen, fair Dulcinea,
For whom great Don Quixote wished to pass
His life in penance in the Brown Sierra
And wearied trod on foot, when his steed was lame,
The plains of Montiel, until he came
To Aranjuez's green lawns and her bubbling fountains:
The fault was Rozinante's. O hard doom
Of this Manchegan damsel and her errant knight
Unconquered! But, alas, in her youthful bloom
Death came with stealthy tread and quenched her light,
And he, whose glory many marvels proved,
Could not escape the storms and wiles of love.

"CROTCHETY," A VERY WITTY ACADEMICIAN OF ARGAMASILLA, IN PRAISE OF ROZINANTE, DON QUIXOTE OF LA MANCHA'S STEED

Sonnet

On the imposing throne of adamant
Trodden by mighty Mars's bloody heel,
The mad Manchegan doth his standard plant,
Hoisting his arms and his fine-tempered steel,
With which he pierced and hacked and cleft in twain:
New feats of arms for which art must devise
A style to suit new heroes on campaign.

And if Gaul sings the praise of Amadis,
Whose sons and grandsons have ennobled Greece
With many a triumph and increased its fame,
Now Don Quixote wears Bellona's crown,
And 'tis La Mancha's turn to praise the name,
Of Rozinante, the world's noblest steed,
And make his deeds to future ages known.

"PLAYBOY," ACADEMICIAN OF ARGAMASILLA, TO SANCHO PANZA

Sonnet

Here's tubby Sancho Panza, who is small,
But yet—strange miracle—his valor's great:
No simpler squire was ever known to all,
Nor one more guileless ever served a knight.
Within an ace he came to being an earl,
But this grim, churlish age conspired with fate
To insult and belabor him, for an ass
Always gets kicks and buffets from a churl.
An ass he rode—this I with shame must mention—
Our simple squire as he came trudging on
Behind mild Rozinante and his knight:
How vain the fondest hopes of mankind seem!
How tempting all their promises of rest
And yet they fade away in smoke and dream.

"HOBGOBLIN," ACADEMICIAN OF ARGAMASILLA, ON THE TOMB OF DULCINEA OF EL TOBOSO

Epitaph

The valiant knight lies here below,
Well beaten and ill-errant, he
Was borne by faithful Rozinante
O'er fair and evil paths, I trow.
Rustic Sancho Panza's laid
Beside his master in the grave;
No one truer ever gave
His life to the squirish trade.

"DING-DONG," ACADEMICIAN OF ARGAMASILLA, ON DON QUIXOTE'S TOMB

EPITAPH

Here fair Dulcinea's laid,
Once so buxom and so lusty,
Now by ugly death she's made
A pile of ashes cold and dusty.

Of good honest stock she came,
Was quite a lady, many cried:
She was Don Quixote's flame,
And her town's chief joy and pride.

These were all the verses that could be deciphered. The rest, as the characters were worm eaten, were handed to an academician to puzzle out their meaning. We are informed that he has done so at the cost of many sleepless nights and much labor and that he intends to publish them; so, we may hope for the third sally of Don Quixote.

Forse altri canterà con miglior plettro.[3]

[3] "Perhaps another may sing with a sweeter tone" From Ariosto's *Orlando Furioso* XXX, 16, a work that profoundly influenced Cervantes.

PART II

APPROBATION

By assignment and order of Dr. Gutierre de Cetina, Vicar General of this city of Madrid, Court of His Majesty, I have seen this book, the *Second Part of the Ingenious Knight Don Quixote of La Mancha* by Miguel de Cervantes Saavedra. I do not find in it anything prejudicial to Christian zeal or lacking the decency that is compatible with good example and moral integrity; but rather do I find much learning and profitable lessons in its well-developed theme, which aims both at extirpating the vain and lying books of chivalry, whose infection had corrupted more than was right, and in its polished Castilian language, untainted by vain and studied affectation (a vice abhorred by all men of good sense). While correcting these vices, so witty and pointed are its arguments, so prudent and Christian its method of reprimanding that anyone stricken by the infirmity it claims to cure will imbibe with such pleasure the author's nostrum that when he least expects it he will grow to detest his former vice, and so find himself well satisfied and with profit from his lesson too.

There have been many writers who have not known how to mingle the useful with the pleasant, and in consequence their work has come to nought, in spite of all their toil. As they are unable to imitate Diogenes as philosopher or scholar, they go to the opposite extreme and blindly and licentiously try to imitate him as cynic. They go in for defamation and invent cases that never took place in order to render more sinister the vice they attack so bitterly; and probably they discover ways hitherto unknown for tracking down that vice, with the result that they end up as masters of it. They make themselves odious to all sensible men and their works lose all credit with the people (if they ever had any) and the vices they so imprudently wished to correct are reduced to a worse state than before. For not every abscess should be cauterized, and sometimes it reacts much better to milder remedies, through whose application a wise doctor cures more effectively than by making drastic use of the knife.

How differently our nation and foreign countries too feel about the writings of Miguel Cervantes! Why, Spain, France, Italy, Germany, and Flanders look upon him as a miracle and long to see him in the flesh. I can truly state that on February 25 of this year, 1615, when His Eminence don Bernardo de Sandoval y Rojas, Cardinal Archbishop of Toledo, paid a return visit to His Excellency the French Ambassador, who had come to Spain to negotiate the marriages between the royal houses of France and Spain, many French gentlemen of the ambassador's suite, who were connoisseurs of literature, came up to me and to other chaplains of the Cardinal eager to know what were the best books in Spain at the moment, and what one did I happen to be censoring at the moment. No sooner did they hear the name Cervantes than they began to talk excitedly among themselves and to sing the praises of an author whose works were so universally admired, not only in France but also in neighboring countries. One of them knew most of *La Galatea* by heart, and the first part of the present work, and the *Exemplary Novels*. So warm was the praise that I offered to take them to see the author—an invitation that they accepted with great enthusiasm. They asked many questions about his age, his pursuits, his condition, and his fortune. I was obliged to say that he was old, a soldier, and poor. To which one of them replied in these very words: "How is it that Spain has not made such a man very rich? How is it that she does not support him out of the public exchequer?" Another member of the party then wittily remarked: "If necessity obliges him to write, please God that he never attains to wealth, so that while he himself remains poor, he may enrich the world by his works."

I am inclined to think that as censor I have rather exceeded my limits, and some may say that what I have written verges on flattery. Nevertheless the truth of this short report of mine will convince critics and so tranquilize my conscience. Besides, in these days nobody flatters anyone who has not the wherewithal to grease his palm in return, and benevolent though such insincerities may be, they have to be materially rewarded.

Madrid, February 27, 1615
The Licentiate Márquez Torres [1]

[1] Francisco Márquez Torres, the censor of Part II of *Don Quixote* and author of the *Approbation,* was a fervent admirer of Cervantes. In the *Approbation* he refers to the visit of the French Ambassador, Noël Brûlart de Sillery, to Madrid to negotiate the double marriage between the French and Spanish royal families, for Louis XIII was about to marry the Infanta Anne of Austria, the daughter of Philip III, and the Infante Philip (the future Philip IV) was to marry Isabel, the daughter of Henry IV of France. Noël Brûlart de Sillery was keenly interested in the work of Cervantes because Part I of *Don Quixote,* translated in its entirety by César Oudin, had appeared in 1614 (two years after the English translation by Thomas Shelton). Márquez Torres, who was born in Baza (province of Granada) in 1574, after being a curate in his native town came to Madrid in 1613 and entered the service of Cardinal don Bernardo de Sandoval y Rojas, Archbishop of Toledo, as chaplain and master of pages, in addition to his duties as censor. After the death of the Cardinal in 1618 Márquez Torres was appointed chaplain in the Royal Chapel in Granada, where he remained until 1629, when he was transferred to the Cathedral of Guadin, where he died in 1656. See F. Rodríguez Marín, *Don Quixote de la Mancha, Nueva edición crítica* (Madrid, 1928), pp. 265–268.

TO THE COUNT OF LEMOS

Some days ago when I sent Your Excellency my plays, printed before they were played, I said, if I remember correctly, that Don Quixote was waiting with his boots already spurred to go and pay his respects to Your Excellency. Now I announce him booted and on the road, and if he arrives, I think I shall have done Your Excellency some service, for from countless directions I have been goaded into sending him out, in order to purge the disgust and nausea caused by another Don Quixote who has been roaming through the world masquerading as the second part.

But the personage who has manifested the greatest longing for him is the Emperor of China, who dispatched to me a month ago a letter by express messenger, begging, or rather imploring, me to send the knight to him, for he wanted to found a college for the teaching of Castilian, and intended *The History of Don Quixote* to be the textbook used there. Furthermore, he informed me that I was to be the rector of the college. I asked the bearer whether His Majesty had given him any money to defray my expenses. He replied that His Majesty had not given a thought to it.

"Then, brother," I answered, "you may return to your China at ten o'clock, or twenty o'clock, or at whatever hour you can start, for my health is not good enough for me to undertake so long a journey. Besides, in addition to being unwell I am confoundedly short of money, and emperor for emperor and monarch for monarch I stand by the great Count of Lemos in Naples. Without all such paltry college appointments and rectorships he protects me and confers upon me more favors than I can desire."

With this I dismissed him, and with this I take my leave, offering Your Excellency *The Toils of Persiles and*

Sigismunda, a book that I shall finish within four months, *Deo volente*, and that will surely be either the worst or the best written of books of entertainment in our language—but I must say that I repent of having said the worst, for according to the judgment of my friends, it will attain the highest excellence. Come, Your Excellency, with all the health we can wish you; Persiles shall be at hand to kiss your hands, and I your feet, as Your Excellency's servant, which I am.

From Madrid, the last day of October, 1615.

Your Excellency's servant,

Miguel de Cervantes Saavedra

Prologue

God bless me, how eagerly you must be awaiting this prologue, illustrious, or perhaps plebeian, reader, expecting to find in it vengeance, quarrels, and abuse against the author of the second *Don Quixote*—I mean the one they say was begotten at Tordesillas and born at Tarragona.[1] But, to tell the truth, I am not going to give you that satisfaction, for though injuries stir up anger in the meekest hearts, in my case this rule must suffer exception. You would like me to call him an ass, a fool, and a bully, but I have no intention of doing so. Let his sin be his punishment—let him eat it with his bread, and there let it be. What I cannot help resenting is that he charges me with being old and maimed, as if it had been in my power to halt the passage of time, as if the loss of my hand had occurred in some tavern and not

[1] A reference to the apocryphal *Don Quixote* that claimed to be the continuation of Cervantes' work; it was published at Tarragona in 1614 by a certain Alonso Fernández de Avellaneda, native of Tordesillas. Cervantes never found out who Avellaneda was, and we today know even less than Cervantes, though scholars for centuries have exausted their ingenuity in inventing countless theories.

on the greatest occasion that present, past, or future ages have ever seen or can ever hope to see. If my wounds do not shine in the eyes of those who look on them, they are at least respected by those who know where they were acquired, for a soldier looks better dead in battle than safe in flight. And so convinced am I of this that even if now I could achieve the impossible, I would still rather have taken part in that prodigious engagement than now be whole of my wounds without ever having fought there. The wounds a soldier shows on his face and on his chest are stars to guide others to the heaven of honor and to inspire them with a noble emulation; and we should remember that one does not write with gray hairs, but with the mind, which grows more mellow with the years. I also resented his calling me envious and explaining to me, as to an ignoramus, what kind of thing envy is; though of the two kinds of it, I know only the righteous, noble, and well-meaning kind. And since this is the case, I am not likely to persecute any priest, above all if he happens to be a familiar of the Holy Office into the bargain. And if he wrote what he did on behalf of a certain person, he is wholly mistaken, for I adore that man's genius, I admire his works and his ever virtuous way of life.[2] But, indeed, I am grateful to this author for saying that my novels are more satirical than exemplary, though they are good, for they could not be good if they were not so in everything.

I am sure you are saying that I am behaving with great restraint and keeping within the bounds of modesty, because I know that one should not heap affliction on the afflicted, and the vexations that this gentleman suffers must be great indeed, for he does not dare to appear in the open field and under a clear sky, but hides his name and disguises his country, as if he had committed the crime of high treason. If by any chance you come to know him, tell

---

[2] The prologue reflects the rage and mortification of Cervantes at Avellaneda's spurious sequel to Part I and his personal abuse against the author of the true *Don Quixote*. The accusation that he had slandered Lope de Vega was a dangerous one, for who knew what important person might be at the back of Avellaneda? Lope de Vega, moreover, was a Familiar of the Holy Office and caution was the best policy in answering. For this reason he declares his admiration for Lope's genius but adds in his most ironic vein: ". . . his ever virtuous way of life." He knew the scandals that had arisen concerning Lope's private life, which are fully revealed in the private correspondence between the great dramatist and his patron, the Duke of Sessa.

him from me that I do not consider myself aggrieved, because I know only too well what the temptations of the Devil are, and that one of his most sinister is to give a man the notion that he is able to write and print a book by which he will gain as much fame as money. To prove my point, I should like you, with your usual wit and charm, to tell him the following story:

There was a madman in Seville who had the craziest notion that ever entered a madman's brain. He made a tube out of a cane, sharpened it at the end, and picked up a dog in the street or elsewhere. He would then hold down one of the animal's hind legs with one foot and lift up the other with his hand. Next, inserting his tube in the right place, he would blow into it, as hard as he could till he had blown the dog up as round as a ball. Then, holding it up in this way, he would give it a couple of slaps on the belly and let it go, saying to the bystanders—and there were always plenty of them: "Your worships perhaps think that it is an easy thing to blow up a dog?" Does your worship think it is an easy thing to write a book?

And if my story does not suit him, you can tell him this one, dear reader, which is also about a madman and a dog:

In Córdoba there was another madman whose habit was to carry in his hand a piece of marble or stone of no light weight, and when he met with an unwary dog, he would go up close to him and let the weight fall plump on top of him. The dog, in a panic, would yelp and bark up three streets without stopping. It so happened once that among his victims was a hatter's dog of whom his master was very fond. The stone came down, struck his head, and the battered beast uttered a dismal howl. His master saw the deed, flew into a rage, picked up a yard measure and rushed out after the madman, and beat him until he had not a whole bone in his body. At every blow he gave him, he shouted: "Dog thief! My pointer! Didn't you see, cruel brute, that my dog was a pointer?" And repeating many times the word 'pointer,' he sent the madman away beaten to a pulp. The madman learned his lesson and went off, and for over a month he did not appear in public. But at the end of this time he reappeared with an even heavier weight, and he would go up to a dog, and staring at him from head to foot, not caring or daring to let the stone fall, he would say: "This is a pointer! Beware!" In short, all the dogs he met, whether mastiffs or curs, he called pointers; so, he never dropped his stone again. Perhaps the same may happen to this story-teller, who will not risk discharging any more the load of his wit in books, for bad books are harder than rocks. Tell him too that I do not care a straw for his threat to deprive me of my profit by means of his book, for adapting the words of the famous farce of *La Perendenga,* I reply: "Long live my master, the alderman, and Christ for us all. Long live the Count of Lemos, whose Christian charity and well-known liberality protect me against all the blows of my scant fortune. And long live the supreme benevolence of His Eminence of Toledo, Don Bernardo Sandoval y Rojas, even though there may be no more printing presses in the world, and even though more books be printed against me than there are letters in the couplets of Mingo Revulgo." [3] These two princes, without receiving adulation or any other kind of flattery from me, but out of their good heart alone, have undertaken to do me kindnesses and favors for which I consider myself luckier and richer than if Fortune had placed me on her highest pinnacle by the ordinary way. The poor man may attain to honor, but not the wicked. Poverty can cloud nobility, but not obscure it altogether. If virtue show some glimmer of light, even though it be through the straits and chinks of penury, it will come to be valued by lofty and noble spirits. Say no more to him, and I will say no more to you than to bid you to take note that this second part of *Don Quixote,* which I offer you, is cut by the same craftsman's hand and from the same cloth as the first, and that in it I present Don Quixote at greater length, and in the end, dead and buried. Let no one, therefore, presume to raise new testimonies to him, for the past ones are sufficient; let it also suffice that an honest man has told the story of these witty follies and has no wish to go into them again, for however good things may be, a surfeit of them brings down the price, and scarcity, even in bad things, confers a certain value. I forgot to tell you that you may look out for *Persiles,* which I am just finishing, and the second part of *Galatea.*

---

[3] *Coplas de Mingo Revulgo,* a poetical dialogue between two shepherds, Gil Arrebato and Mingo Revulgo, satirizing King Henry IV of Castile and his favorite, Don Beltrán de la Cueva, and giving rules for good government. The first edition of Lisbon (without date) is believed to be anterior to 1485.

CHAPTER I

What passed between the curate, the barber, and Don Quixote regarding the knight's infirmity

Cide Hamete Benengeli in the second part of this history concerning Don Quixote's third sally relates that the curate and the barber remained nearly a month without seeing him, in order not to revive past events and bring them back to his memory. But this did not prevent them from visiting his niece and his housekeeper, whom they charged to be careful to treat him well and give him to eat such food as was comforting and good for heart and brain, for they had every reason to believe that all his misfortunes proceeded from that quarter. The two women declared that they were doing so and that they would continue to lavish care and affection on their master, for they had noticed that he gave signs at times of being in his right mind. This news gave the curate and the barber great satisfaction, for it seemed to prove that they had done right in bringing him back enchanted in the ox wagon, as has been related in the last chapter of the first part of this great and accurate history. So, they resolved to visit him and test his recovery, though they thought that was scarcely possible, and they agreed not to touch in any way on knight-errantry, so as not to run the risk of ripping open wounds that were still so tender.

They paid him a visit at last and found him sitting up in his bed, dressed in a green-baize jacket and a red Toledo cap and so lean and shriveled that he looked as if he had been turned into a mummy. He welcomed them cordially and to their questions about his health he replied intelligently in very well-chosen words. In the course of conversation they discoursed on so-called affairs of state and systems of government, correcting this abuse and condemning that, reforming one practice and abolishing another, each one of the three setting himself up as a new lawgiver, a modern Lycurgus, or a brand-new Solon. And to such a degree did they re-model the state that they might as well have cast it into a furnace and forged a new one. And Don Quixote spoke with such good sense on all the subjects they treated that the two examiners believed, without shadow of doubt, that he was quite recovered and in full possession of his wits. The niece and the housekeeper were present at the conversation and could not find adequate words to thank God when they saw that their master was so clear in his mind. The curate, however, changed his original plan, which was not to touch on the subject of chivalry, and resolved to test Don Quixote's recovery thoroughly to see whether it was genuine or not; so, changing from one subject to another, he came at last to talk of some news that had come from the capital. Among other things he said that they had it for certain that the Turk was descending with a powerful fleet, but no one knew what his designs were or where the mighty storm would burst. And owing to this fear, which almost every year rouses men to arms, all Christendom was on the alert, and His Majesty had made provision for the defense of the coast of Naples, Sicily, and the island of Malta.

"His Majesty has acted like a most prudent warrior," replied Don Quixote, "in fortifying his realms in time, so that the enemy may not find him unprepared; but if he would take my advice, I would counsel him to take one precaution of which His Majesty is not aware at the present moment."

No sooner did the curate hear this than he said to himself: "God protect you, my poor Don Quixote, for it looks to me as if you are tumbling from the pinnacle of your madness into the deep abyss of your simplemindedness."

But the barber, who already had the same suspicions as the curate, asked Don Quixote what kind of measures he thought they should adopt, for perhaps they might be added to the long list of unpractical projects usually offered to princes.

"Mine, Mr. Scrapebeard," said Don Quixote, "are not unpractical but highly practical."

"No harm meant," replied the barber, "but experience has shown that all or most of the projects presented to His

Majesty are either impossible, absurd, or damaging to the king and the country."

"But mine," rejoined Don Quixote, "is neither impossible nor ridiculous, but the easiest, the justest, the readiest, and the simplest that could enter the mind of any thinking man."

"Your worship is slow in telling us about it, Don Quixote," said the curate.

"I do not wish to tell it now," said Don Quixote, "and have it reach by tomorrow morning the ears of the lords of the Council, and for someone else to get the thanks and the reward for my pains."

"As for me," said the barber, "I give my word here and before God that I'll not repeat what you say to king, or rook, or earthly man,[1] an oath I learned from the ballad of the priest, who in the prologue warns the king against the thief who had robbed him of a hundred doubloons and his ambling mule."

"I do not know the story," said Don Quixote, "but I know that the oath is a good one, because I believe that the barber is an honest man."

"Even if he were not," said the curate, "I will go bail for him and vouch that he'll speak as much as a dumb man, under pain of any penalty imposed by the court."

"And who will go bail for your reverence?" said Don Quixote.

"My profession," replied the curate, "which is to keep secrets."

"Bless my heart!" exclaimed Don Quixote. "What else has His Majesty to do but to order by public crier all the knight-errants who are wandering about Spain to assemble at the capital on a certain day, and even if no more than half a dozen came, might there not be one among them who alone would be strong enough to annihilate the whole army of the Turk? Let your worships give me your attention and follow me. Is it, mark you, an unheard-of exploit for a single knight-errant to cut to bits an army of two hundred thousand men as if all together had but one throat or were made of almond paste? Now tell me, how many histories are there full of such marvels? If there were living today—to my misfortune, though I shall not say to anyone else's—the famous

[1] A metaphor from chess. Rook or *roque* later was called Tower.

Don Belianís or any one of those of the innumerable
offspring of Amadis of Gaul! If any of them were living today
and were to face the Turk, I would not be in the latter's
shoes. But God will take care of his people and will provide
someone who, if not as resolute as the knights-errant of old,
will at least not be behind them in spirit. God understands
me, and I say no more."

"Alas!" cried the niece, at this point. "Strike me dead if my
master doesn't want to turn knight-errant again."

To which Don Quixote replied: "A knight-errant I shall
die, and let the Turk make his descent or ascent whenever he
will and with whatever power he can. I say once more
that God understands, and I say no more."

At this the barber chimed in: "Allow me, your worships,
to tell you a short tale about something that took place at
Seville, for as it fits this situation like a glove, I'm dying to
tell it."

Don Quixote and the curate gave him leave, and the
others pricked up their ears; so, the barber began as follows:
"In the madhouse at Seville was a certain man whose relations had put him there because he had lost his wits. He had
graduated in common law at Osuna, but even if it had been
at Salamanca, many think he would have been just as mad.
This graduate, at the end of some years of confinement, convinced himself that he was sane and in his right mind, and
in this frame of mind he wrote to the archbishop, imploring
him earnestly and in convincing terms to order his release
from the misery in which he lived, for his relatives kept him
there in order to enjoy his share of the estate, and in spite
of the clearest evidence, they wished to have him stay
mad till his death. The archbishop, impressed by his many
sensible and well-reasoned letters, ordered one of his chaplains to ascertain from the governor of the madhouse whether
what the licentiate wrote was true. He asked him to speak to
the madman, and if he seemed to be in his senses, to set him
at liberty. The chaplain did so, and the governor informed
him that the man was still mad, and that though he often
talked like a person of great intelligence, in the end he would
break out into wild tirades as crazy and exaggerated as his
previous talk had been sensible, as he would find out by
speaking to him. The chaplain wished to do so, and when he
visited the madman, he talked with him for an hour and more,
and in all that time he never said a queer or crazy word but

spoke so sensibly that the chaplain was obliged to believe him sane. Among other things that the madman said was that the governor had an edge against him because he did not want to lose the bribes his relations paid him for declaring that he was still mad, though with lucid intervals. The greatest obstacle he had to deal with in his misfortunes, he said, was his great wealth, for in order to enjoy it his enemies misjudged him and cast doubts upon the mercy that Our Lord had done him by turning him from a beast into a man. In short, he spoke so convincingly as to throw suspicion on the governor and to make his relatives appear covetous and inhuman and himself so sane that the chaplain resolved to take him away with him, so that the archbishop might see him and verify the truth for himself. In all good faith, then, the worthy chaplain begged the governor to give orders for the licentiate to be given back the clothes in which he had arrived. But the governor once more bade him mind what he was doing, for the licentiate undoubtedly was still mad. However, the governor's warning could not prevail upon the chaplain to leave the madman behind; so, seeing that the archbishop had given the order, the governor obeyed, and the madman was given back his clothes, which were new and decent. When he found himself stripped of his lunatic's dress and clothed in the garb of sanity, he begged the chaplain out of charity to allow him to bid farewell to his mad companions. The chaplain told him he would like to accompany him and see the inmates who were lodged there. So they went upstairs, accompanied by some other people who were present, and the madman went up to a cage in which was a raging maniac who happened to be calm and quiet at the time, and said to him: 'My brother, see if you have any commands for me. I am going home, for God in His infinite mercy and goodness has been pleased to restore me to my senses, though I don't deserve it. Now I am sane and in my right mind, for to God's power nothing is impossible. Put great hope and trust in Him; since He has restored me to my former state, He will restore you too, if you have faith in Him. I will send you some dainties to eat, and be sure you eat them, for I must tell you that I am convinced, as one who has gone through it, that all our madness proceeds from our having our bellies empty and our brains full of wind. Take heart! Have courage! For despondency in our misfortunes weakens our health and hastens death.'

"Another madman in another cage opposite the raging lunatic's overheard all that the graduate said, and rising from an old mat on which he was lying stark naked, he asked in a loud voice who this man was who was going away cured and sane. The graduate replied: 'It is I, brother, who am going. I have no need to stay here any longer, for which I give infinite thanks to Heaven, which has done me this great favor.'

" 'Mind what you say, graduate, and don't let the Devil deceive you,' answered the madman. 'Rest your feet and stay snugly and quietly at home, and you'll spare yourself the return journey.'

" 'I know that I am well,' rejoined the graduate, 'and shall not have to go the rounds again.'

" 'You well?' cried the madman. 'Good! We shall see. God be with you, but I vow to Jupiter, whose majesty I represent on earth, that for the sin that Seville is committing today in releasing you from this house and treating you as a sane man, I shall inflict such punishment on her as shall be remembered for centuries and centuries to come, amen. Do you not know, you mean little graduate, that I have the power to do so? For let me tell you, I am Jupiter the thunderer and hold in my hands the flaming thunderbolts with which I can and do threaten to destroy the world. But with one punishment alone I mean to chastise this ignorant city. For three whole years I will not rain on it and on all the surrounding districts, and the time is to be reckoned from the instant I utter this threat. You free, you sane, you in your right senses? And I mad and sick and in chains? I would as soon think of raining as hang myself.'

"The madman's loud burst of oratory attracted the attention of the bystanders, but our graduate, turning to our chaplain and seizing him by the hands, cried: 'Don't be concerned, my dear sir; take no notice of what this lunatic says, for if he is Jupiter and will not rain, I am Neptune, the father and god of the waters, and I will rain as often as I please and whenever it is necessary.'

"To which the chaplain replied: 'All the same, Lord Neptune, it would not be right to annoy Lord Jupiter. Your worship may remain at home, and we will come back for you another day when we have more time.'

"The governor and the bystanders burst out laughing, and the chaplain was half ashamed at their jeering. The graduate was stripped and clapped in his cage, and that is the end of my story."

"So that, Master Barber, is the story," said Don Quixote, "that suited our situation so well that you had to tell it? O Master Scrapebeard! How blind is he who cannot see through a sieve! Is it possible that your worship does not know that comparisons between wit and wit, valor and valor, beauty and beauty, birth and birth, are always hateful and cause resentment? I, Master Barber, am not Neptune, the god of the waters, and I am not setting myself up as a wise man when I am not. I only strive to convince the world of its errors in not reviving that most fortunate age in which the order of chivalry flourished. But our depraved age does not deserve to enjoy so great a blessing as did those in which knights-errant undertook and burdened their shoulders with the defense of kingdoms, the protection of damsels, the relief of children and orphans, the chastisement of the proud, and the rewarding of the humble. Most of our knights nowadays prefer to nestle in the damasks, brocades, and other rich silks they wear than in armored coats of mail. There are now no knights who sleep in the fields, exposed to the rigor of the heavens in full armor from head to foot. There is no one now who snatches a nap, as they say, resting on his lance and with his feet on the stirrups as knights-errant did of old. There is no one now to sally forth from this wood and enter that mountain, and from there to go to a wasted and deserted shore of the sea, most often stormy and tempestuous and to find there on the beach a little boat without oars, sail, mast, or tackle, and with undaunted heart to fling himself in and entrust himself to the implacable waves of the deep sea, which at one moment toss him up to the sky, and at another engulf him in the abyss. Then, exposing his chest to the irresistible tempest, he finds himself, when he least expects it, more than nine thousand miles from the place where he embarked; and leaping on to a remote and unknown shore, he undergoes experiences worthy to be inscribed not on parchment, but on brass. Today sloth triumphs over industry, idleness over labor, vice over virtue, arrogance over bravery, and theory over the practice of arms, which only lived and flourished in the Golden Age and among knights-errant. If I am not right, tell me, who was more virtuous and valiant than the renowned Amadis of Gaul? Who was wiser than Palmerin of England? Who more pleasant

and dexterous than Tirante the White? Who more gallant than
Lisuarte of Greece? Who a greater slasher or more slashed
than Don Belianís? Who more undaunted than Perión of
Gaul, or more eager to face peril than Felixmarte of Hyrcania? Or more sincere than Esplandian? Who more impetuous than Cirongilio of Thrace? Who more fearless than
Rodamante? Who more prudent than King Sobrino? Who
bolder than Rinaldo? Who more invincible than Orlando?
And who more high-spirited and courteous than Ruggiero,
from whom are descended today the dukes of Ferrara, according to Turpin's cosmography? All these knights and
many more I could mention, Master Priest, were knights-
errant, the light and glory of chivalry. These, and such as
these, I should wish to take part in my project, and if
they did, His Majesty would find himself well served at
great saving of expense, and the Turk would be left tearing
his beard. Therefore I wish to remain at home, since the
chaplain is not taking me out, and if Jupiter, as the barber
has said, will not rain, here am I who will rain whenever I
please. This I say so that Master Basin may see that I understand him."

"Really, Don Quixote," said the barber, "that wasn't why
I told you the tale. I meant well by it, so help me God, and
your worship shouldn't take offense."

"I know best whether I took offense or not," replied Don
Quixote.

The curate then remarked: "Although I've hardly said a
word up to now, I should like to relieve myself of a scruple
that is gnawing and scraping at my conscience upon hearing
Don Quixote's last remarks."

"The curate has license for other more solemn matters,"
answered Don Quixote, "so, he can declare his scruple, for
it is unpleasant to go about with scruples on one's conscience."

"Well, with your leave," replied the curate, "I shall reveal my scruple. It is that I am unable to convince myself
in any way, Don Quixote, that all this crew of knights-errant
your worship has mentioned have really and truly been people
of flesh and blood living in this world. On the contrary, I
think that it is all fiction, fable, and lies, dreams told by
men awake, or rather half asleep."

"That is another mistake," replied Don Quixote, "into
which many have fallen who do not believe that such knights

have ever existed. Often with different people and at different times I have tried to expose this almost universal error to the light of truth. On some occasions I have not succeeded in my purpose; on others I have, supporting my argument with evidence so infallible that I might say I have seen Amadis of Gaul with my own eyes. He was a man tall of stature and fair of face, with a well-trimmed black beard, and his looks were half mild and half severe. He was short of speech, slow to anger, and quickly appeased. Now in the same manner in which I have portrayed Amadis, I could, I believe, paint and describe all the knights-errant who wander in the histories, for I have absolute faith that they were exactly as the histories tell us, and my knowledge of their deeds and their characters makes it possible for me by sound philosophy to make out their features, their complexions, and their statures."

"How big then, my dear Don Quixote," inquired the barber, "would the giant Morgante have been in your worship's opinion?"

"As to the existence of giants," replied Don Quixote, "there are various opinions. But Holy Scripture, which cannot depart from the truth by so much as an inch, proves that they existed by telling us the story of that great Philistine, Goliath, who was seven cubits and a half tall, which is a prodigious height. There have been also found in the island of Sicily shinbones and shoulder blades of a size that shows that their owners were giants and as tall as great towers; geometry proves this beyond a doubt. Nevertheless, I am unable to say with certainty what was the size of Morgante, although I imagine he could not have been so very tall, and I am inclined to this opinion by discovering in the history where special emphasis is laid upon his deeds that he often slept under a roof, and since he found houses to contain him, it is clear that his size was not excessive."

"That is true," said the curate, who, delighted to hear him talk such nonsense, then asked him what he felt about the features of Rinaldo of Montalbán and of Orlando and the other Peers of France, for they all were knights-errant.

"Of Rinaldo," replied Don Quixote, "I make bold to say that he was broad in face, red-complexioned, with rolling and rather prominent eyes, very thin-skinned and choleric, friendly to robbers and to vagabonds. About Roland, or Rotolando, or Orlando—for histories give him all these names—I am positively convinced that he was of middle

stature, broad-shouldered, rather bowlegged, dark-complex-
ioned, and red-bearded, with a hairy body and a threatening
appearance, abrupt in speech, but very polite and well bred."

"If Orlando was no more of a gentleman than your worship
has made out," said the curate, "it was no wonder that the
lady Angélica the Fair rejected him for the gaiety, the
dash, and the charm of the downy-cheeked Moorling to whom
she gave herself. She showed good sense in falling in love
with Medoro's gentleness rather than with the roughness of
Orlando."

"That Angélica, sir priest," answered Don Quixote, "was
a giddy, wanton damsel, and a trifle flighty, and she left
the world as full of her indiscretions as of her famous
beauty. She scorned a thousand lords—a thousand valiant
and a thousand wise lords—and contented herself with a
smooth-faced little chit of a page with no other fortune than
the reputation he gained by his loyalty to his friend. The
great singer of her beauty, the celebrated Ariosto, did not dare,
or perhaps did not care, to relate what happened to this lady
after her base surrender—for no doubt her conduct was
not too chaste—and left her with these lines:

'And how she won the scepter of Cathay,
   Another bard will sing to a mellower lay.'

"This, no doubt, was a kind of prophecy, for poets are
also called *vates,* which means diviners. This truth can be
plainly seen, for since then a famous Andalusian poet has
wept and sung about her tears, and another celebrated and
unique Castilian poet has sung her beauty." [2]

"Tell me, Don Quixote," interposed the barber, "has there
been no poet who has made some satire on this lady
Angélica, among all those who have praised her?"

"I truly believe," replied Don Quixote, "that if Sacripante
or Orlando had been poets, they would have given the damsel
a trouncing, for it is right and natural for poets who have
been scorned or not accepted by their ladies, either fictitious
or modeled on those they have chosen as mistresses of

[2] The Andalusian poet is Luis Barahona de Soto (1548–1595),
author of *La Primera Parte de la Angélica.* The Castilian
is Lope de Vega (1562–1635), author of *La Hermosura de
Angélica.*

their thoughts, to revenge themselves in satires and lampoons, a vengeance assuredly unworthy of generous hearts. But up to now there has come to my notice no defamatory verse against the lady Angélica, who turned the whole world topsy-turvy."

"A miracle," exclaimed the curate.

But at this point they heard the housekeeper and the niece, who had withdrawn from their conversation, making an outcry in the yard, and they all ran out to see what the noise was about.

CHAPTER II

Which deals with the notable quarrel between Sancho Panza and Don Quixote's niece and housekeeper, with other amusing incidents

The story tells that the noise Don Quixote, the curate, and the barber heard were the niece and the housekeeper screaming indignantly at Sancho Panza, who was struggling to get in and see Don Quixote, while they were holding the door against him.

"What does that feckless gadabout want in this house? Off with you to your own haunts, brother, for it's you and none other who deludes my master and leads him gallivanting over hill and dale."

To which Sancho replied: "Housekeeper of Satan! I'm the one who is deluded and led gallivanting over hill and dale, and not your master; it is he who led me on a jaunt all over the world, and you are wide off the mark. It was he who tricked me away from home, with his colloguing, promising me an island, and I'm still waiting for it."

"May those foul islands choke you," replied the niece, "damn you, Sancho. And what are those isles of yours? Are they something to eat, you glutton and gormandizer?"

"They are not anything to eat," answered Sancho, "but to

govern and rule, and better than any four cities and richer than four judgeships at court."

"You shan't come in here, all the same," said the housekeeper, "you bag of mischief, you sack of villainies! Go and govern your house, till your plot, and rid your empty pate of isles and islands."

The curate and the barber were greatly amused to hear this conversation of the three, but Don Quixote was afraid Sancho would blurt out a whole heap of mischievous nonsense and touch upon points that might not be wholly to his credit. So, he called to him and bade the two women to hold their tongues and let him enter. Sancho went in, and the curate and the barber took their leave of the knight. They despaired of his cure, for they saw how fixed he was in his crazy notions and how deeply absorbed by his accursed nonsensical knight-errantry. And so the curate said to the barber: "You will see, my friend; when we least expect it, our knight will be off bush-ranging."

"I've no doubt of that," replied the barber, "but I'm less surprised at the knight's madness than at the squire's foolishness in believing the story of the isle, for I'm sure that all the disappointments imaginable will not drive it out of his head."

"May God help them," said the curate, "and let us keep our eyes open and see what comes of this crazy alliance of knight and squire. Both of them seem to be cast in the same mold, and the master's eccentricities would not be worth a farthing without the squire's foolishness."

"That's true," said the barber, "and I should be very glad to know what the two of them are talking about this moment."

"I dare wager," replied the curate, "that the niece or the housekeeper will tell us by and by, for they are not the kind to refrain from listening."

In the meantime Don Quixote had shut himself in his room with Sancho, and when they were alone, he said: "I am deeply grieved, Sancho, that you have said and still say that it was I took you from your cottage, when you know that I myself did not stay at home. We set out together, together we lived, together we wandered. One and the same fortune, one and the same destiny has fallen upon us both; if they tossed you in a blanket once, they have beaten me a hundred times, and this is the one advantage I have over you."

"That is quite right," answered Sancho, "for as your worship says, disasters belong rather to knights-errant than to their squires."

"You are mistaken, Sancho," said Don Quixote. "Remember the saying: *quando caput dolet,* etc." [1]

"I understand no language but my own," replied Sancho.

"I mean," said Don Quixote, "that when the head aches, all the limbs feel pain; and so, as I am your lord and master, I am your head, and you are a part of me because you are my servant; and for that reason the evil that touches me, or shall touch me, should hurt you, and yours should hurt me."

"So it should be," said Sancho, "but when they tossed me, the limb, in the blanket, my head was outside the wall, watching me fly through the air and not feeling any pain. But since the limbs have to suffer the head's pain, the head should also be made to suffer for the limbs."

"Do you mean to suggest, Sancho," replied Don Quixote, "that I felt no pain when they were tossing you? If that is what you say, you are wrong. You should not even think such a thing, for my I felt more pain then in my spirit than you did in your body. But let us put that aside for the present, for there will be a time when we can consider the matter and come to a proper conclusion. Now tell me, Sancho, my friend, what do they say about me in the village? What opinion of me have the common people and the gentry and the knights? What do they say of my valor, of my deeds, and of my courtesy? How do they speak of the enterprise I have undertaken to revive and restore to the world the forgotten order of chivalry? In short, Sancho, I want you to tell me all that has come to your ears. You must answer me without exaggerating praise or mitigating blame. For it is the duty of loyal vassals to speak the truth to their lords without exaggerating it through flattery or lessening it through vain deference. And I would have you know, Sancho, that if the naked truth reached the ears of princes without the trappings of flattery, these times would be different, and other ages would more fitly be reputed iron than ours, which I reckon to be of gold. Take this warn-

---

[1] *Quando caput dolet, caetera membra dolent* (when the head hurts, the other limbs hurt) is the complete proverb.

ing, Sancho, and discreetly and faithfully give me the true answer to the questions I have asked you."

"I'll do so with all my heart, sir," replied Sancho, "on condition that your worship does not get angry at what I say, for you want me to tell you the naked truth and not to dress it in any clothes, except those I found it in."

"On no account shall I be angry," answered Don Quixote. "You can speak freely, Sancho, without beating about the bush."

"Then the first thing I'll say is that the common people take your worship for a mighty great madman, and they think I'm no less of a simpleton. The gentry say that you're not content with being a country gentleman and that you have turned yourself into a don and thrust yourself into knighthood with no more than a few miserable vinestocks and two acres of land,[2] with a tatter behind and another in front to bless your name. The knights say they don't relish seeing the petty gentry setting themselves up against them, especially those squireens who black their shoes and darn their black stockings with green silk."[3]

"That," said Don Quixote, "has nothing to do with me, for I am always well dressed and never patched. Ragged I may be, but ragged more from the wear and tear of my armor than from time."

"As to your worship's valor, courtesy, and exploits," continued Sancho, "there are different opinions. Some say, 'mad but droll'; others, 'valiant but unfortunate'; others, 'courteous but saucy'; and so they go sticking their noses into this and that until they don't leave a whole bone either in your body or in mine."

"Observe, Sancho," said Don Quixote, "that whenever virtue is found in an eminent degree, it is persecuted. Few or none of the famous heroes of old have escaped being slandered by malicious tongues. Julius Caesar, a most high-spirited, most prudent, and most valiant captain, was branded as ambitious and not too clean either in his garments or in his morals. Alexander, whose exploits achieved for him the name of Great, was said to have been somewhat of a drunk-

[2] *Dos yugadas* (two yokes) was the amount of land a team of oxen could plow in a day.

[3] Shoe polish was unknown in those days, and they used printer's black dissolved in oil or water.

ard. And Hercules, the hero of the many labors, according
to gossips was lascivious and effeminate. Don Galaor, the
brother of Amadis of Gaul, is rumored to have been over-
lecherous and his brother to have been a sniveler. So, Sancho,
seeing that there is so much slander against good men, what
they say about me may pass if it is no more than what
you have told me."

"Ah, but there's the rub, body of my father!" replied
Sancho.

"Is there anything more then?" asked Don Quixote.

"Faith an' we still have to skin the tail,' said Sancho.
"Why, up to now it has been tarts and fancy bread, but if
your worship wants to know all about the calumnies they
fling at you, I'll bring you here presently one who will tell
you the lot of them without missing an atom, for last night
Bartolomé Carrasco's son arrived from studying at Salamanca, where he was made a bachelor. And when I went up to
welcome him, he told me that the history of your worship is
already told in a book by the name of *The Ingenious Gentleman Don Quixote of La Mancha*. And he says that they also
mention me in it by my own very name of Sancho Panza,
and Lady Dulcinea of El Toboso, too, and many a thing
that happened to us in private, which made me cross myself in amazement to think how the history writer could
have got wind of what he wrote."

"You may be sure, Sancho," said Don Quixote, "that the
author of our history is some wise enchanter, for nothing can
be hidden from them."

"But if the author of this history was a wise enchanter,"
replied Sancho, "how comes it about that according to the
bachelor Sansón Carrasco—for that's the man's name—
the author of our history is called Cide Hamete Berengena?" [4]

"That is a Moor's name," rejoined Don Quixote.

"So it may be," answered Sancho, "for I have heard that
Moors for the most part are very fond of eggplants."

"You must be mistaken, Sancho," said Don Quixote, "in
the name of this Cide, which in Arabic means lord."

"Very likely," replied Sancho, "but if you would like to
have me bring the bachelor here, I'll go for him like a shot."

"You will do me a great favor, my friend," said Don

[4] The Arabic manuscript was found at Toledo, where the inhabitants were jokingly called *berengeneros* (the eggplanters).

Quixote. "What you have told me makes me anxious, and I shall not eat a mouthful that will do me good until I am informed of everything."

"Then I'll go to fetch him," answered Sancho.

So, leaving his master, he went off to find the bachelor, with whom he returned in a short while. And between these three a most entertaining conversation took place.

CHAPTER III

Of the ridiculous conversation that passed between Don Quixote, Sancho Panza, and the bachelor Sansón Carrasco

Don Quixote remained very pensive, waiting for the bachelor Sansón Carrasco, from whom he expected to hear how he had been put into a book, as Sancho had told him. He could not convince himself that such a history could exist, for the blood of the enemies he had slain was hardly dry on the blade of his sword, yet they were already saying that his high deeds of chivalry were in print. Nevertheless, he imagined that some sage, either friend or enemy, by his magic art had given them to the press; if a friend, to magnify and exalt them above the most renowned feats of any knight-errant; if an enemy, to annihilate them and place them below the meanest ever written of some base squire, although, he said to himself, the deeds of squires were never written of. If, however, it were true that such history was in existence, seeing that it was about a knight-errant, it must of necessity be grandiloquent, lofty, distinguished, and true. This thought consoled him somewhat, but he was worried to think that its author was a Moor, as the name Cide suggested, for he could expect no truth from the Moors, since they are all impostors, forgers, and schemers. He also dreaded that his love affairs might be treated indelicately, which might lead to the disparagement and prejudice of Lady Dulcinea of El Toboso's good name. For he was anxious that it should be made quite clear that he had always been faithful to her and had always shown her respect, turning a blind eye to all queens, empresses, and damsels of every degree for her sake. And so, Sancho, when he returned with Carrasco, found him rapt and absorbed in these and countless other fancies, but the knight received the new guest with courtesy.

The bachelor, though his name was Sansón, was no giant in stature, but was a very great wag. He was of sallow complexion, very sharp witted, about twenty-four years of age, with a round face, a flat nose, and a large mouth—all signs of a mischievous disposition and of one who is fond of joking and making fun, as he showed straightaway, for no sooner did he see Don Quixote than he dropped to his knees before him, saying: "Let your mightiness give me your hands to kiss, Sir Don Quixote of La Mancha. By the habit of St. Peter [1] that I wear—though I've taken no more than the first four orders—your worship is one of the most famous knights-errant there has ever been or ever shall be in all the rotundity of the earth. Blessings on Cide Hamete Benengeli, who has written the history of your doughty deeds, and double blessings on the connoisseur who took the trouble to have it translated from Arabic into our Castilian vulgar tongue for the universal entertainment of mankind."

Don Quixote made him rise and said: "So it is true that there is a history of me and that it was a Moor and a wise man who wrote it."

"So true is it," said Sansón, "that I believe there are today in print more than twelve thousand volumes of the said history. For proof you have only to ask Portugal, Barcelona, and Valencia, where they have been printed, and it is rumored that it is being printed at Antwerp, and I am

[1] This was the ecclesiastical dress worn by university students: soutane, cloak, college cap.

convinced that there is not a country or language in the world in which it will not be translated." [2]

"One of the things," said Don Quixote in reply, "which shall give the greatest pleasure to a virtuous and eminent man is to see himself in his lifetime printed and in the press, and with a good name on people's tongues, a good name, I repeat, for were it the contrary, no death could be so bad."

"If it is a question of a good reputation and a good name," said the bachelor, "your worship singly carries off the palm from all knights-errant, for the Moor in his language and the Christian in his have taken great pains to portray for us, quite realistically, your worship's gallantry, your great courage in facing perils, your patience in adversity and in sufferings, whether because of misfortunes or because of wounds, and the chastity and continence in the platonic loves of your worship and my lady, Doña Dulcinea of El Toboso."

"Never," butted in Sancho at this point, "have I heard Lady Dulcinea called doña, but plain Lady Dulcinea of El Toboso. So, history has gone astray."

"That's not an important objection," replied Carrasco.

"No, surely," replied Don Quixote, "but tell me, Master Bachelor, which of my deeds are most highly praised in this history?"

"About that point," answered the bachelor, "opinions vary as tastes vary. Some favor the adventure of the windmills, which seemed to your worship to be Briareuses and giants; others, the adventure of the fulling mills. One is all for the description of the two armies, which afterward turned out to be two flocks of sheep; another praises the one of the corpse they were carrying to Segovia for burial. This one declares that the best of all is the freeing of the galley slaves, that one says that none equals that of the Benedictine giants and the combat with the valiant Biscayan."

"Tell me, Master Bachelor," cried Sancho, "does the adventure with the Yanguesans come in, when our good

---

[2] If Cervantes, as is believed, wrote this chapter in 1612–1613, Sansón is not exaggerating, for before those dates the following editions had been published: three editions in Madrid (1605 and 1608); two in Lisbon (1605); two in Valencia (1605); two in Brussels (1607 and 1611); and one in Milan (1610)—in total ten editions, which would make, as Rodríguez Marín calculates, a total of fifteen thousand.

Rozinante had the notion of looking for mushrooms at the bottom of the sea?"

"The sage left nothing in the inkhorn," answered Sansón. "He tells everything and touches on every point, even the capers that the worthy Sancho cut on the blanket."

"I cut no capers on the blanket," answered Sancho, "but in the air I did, and more than I would have liked."

"In my opinion," said Don Quixote, "there is no human history in the world which has not its ups and downs, especially those that deal with knight-errantry. They can never be full of lucky incidents alone."

"For all that," replied the bachelor, "some who have read your history say that they would have been glad if the author had omitted some of the countless drubbings that were given Don Quixote in his various encounters."

"Ah! There's where the truth of the story comes in," rejoined Sancho.

"Yet, they might in all fairness have kept quiet about them," said Don Quixote, "for there is no point in writing about actions that do not change or affect the truth of the story, if they tend to diminish the stature of the hero. Aeneas, I am sure, was not as pious as Virgil made him out to be, nor Ulysses as prudent as he is described in Homer."

"That is true," replied Sansón, "but it is one thing to write as a poet, and another as a historian. The poet can tell or sing of things, not as they were, but as they ought to have been; the historian must relate them not as they should have been, but as they were, without adding to or subtracting from the truth."

"Well, if this Moor is out for truth," said Sancho, "then my beatings will be found there as well as my master's, for they never took measure of his worship's shoulders without measuring my whole body. But there's no wonder in that, for that same master of mine says that the limbs must take their fair share of the head's pain."

"You're a cunning rogue, Sancho," answered Don Quixote, "I swear your memory never fails you when you want to remember something."

"Even if I wanted to forget the cudgelings I got," said Sancho, "devil a bit would the bruises let me, for they're still as plain as paint on my ribs."

"Be quiet, Sancho," said Don Quixote, "and don't interrupt the bachelor, who, I hope, will now tell me what they say of me in this history he has referred to."

"And of me," said Sancho, "for I'm told that I am one of the principal presonages in it."

"*Personage*, not *presonages*, Sancho, my friend," said Sansón.

"So, here we have another word corrector!" rejoined Sancho. "If it goes on like this, we'll never come to the end of it in this life."

"May I be blowed, Sancho," replied the bachelor, "if you're not the second person in the history! Why, there are some who prefer to hear you talk than the best parts in the whole book, though, to be sure, there are others who say you were much too credulous in taking as Gospel truth that island Don Quixote has promised you."

"The sun is still shining on the thatch," said Don Quixote, "and in the meantime, as Sancho is growing older and riper in experience, wit, and years, he will become fitter and more able for the post of governor than he is at present."

"By God, sir," said Sancho, "any island I can't govern at my age, I'll never govern, even if I live to be as old as Methuselah. The worst of it is that this isle of yours keeps itself hidden away the Lord knows where, and not that I haven't brains enough to govern it."

"Commend it to God, Sancho," said Don Quixote, "and all will be well, perhaps better than you think, for not a leaf stirs on a tree without God's will."

"That is true," said Sansón, "for if God is willing, Sancho will not lack a thousand isles, much less one."

"I have seen governors about here," said Sancho, "who, in my opinion, don't come up to the sole of my shoe. Yet, for all that they're called lordship and served on silver."

"Those are not governors of isles," answered Sansón, "but of other governments that are easier handled. Governors of isles must at least be grammarians."

"I'll deal with the *gram*," said Sancho, "but as to the *marians*, I'll let them be, for I don't understand them. But leaving this matter of a governorship in God's hands—may He put me where I can serve Him best—let me say, Master Bachelor, that I'm mighty glad the author of this history has spoken of me in such a way that the things told of me don't give offense, for as I'm a good squire, if he'd said any derogatory things about me, not becoming the old

Christian I am, our quarrel would reach the ears of the deaf."

"That would be to work miracles," said Sansón.

"Miracles or no miracles," said Sancho, "let everyone mind how he speaks or writes about persons, and not jot down helter-skelter the first thing that comes into his noddle."

"One of the blemishes they find in this history," said the bachelor, "is that the author has inserted in it a novel called 'The Tale of Ill-Advised Curiosity'—not that it is bad or badly told, but that it is out of place and has nothing to do with the history of his worship, Don Quixote."

"I'll bet," rejoined Sancho, "that the son of a dog has made a pretty kettle of fish of everything."

"Now I am sure," said Don Quixote, "that the author of my story is no sage but some ignorant prater who set himself blindly and aimlessly to write it down and let it turn out anyhow, like Orbaneja, the painter of Ubeda, who, when they asked him what he was painting, used to answer: 'Whatever it turns out.' Sometimes he would paint a cock in such a way and so little like one that it was necessary to write beside it in Gothic characters: 'This is a cock.' And so it must be with my history, which will need a commentary to be understood."

"No," replied Sansón, "for it's so plain that there is nothing in it to cause any difficulty. Children finger it, young people read it, grown men know it by heart, and old men praise it. It is so thumbed and read and so familiar to all kinds of people that no sooner do they catch sight of a lean hack than they cry out: 'There goes Rozinante.' Those who are most given to reading it are pages, for there's no lord's antechamber in which you will not find a *Don Quixote*. When one lays it down, another picks it up; some grab at it, others beg for it. This story, in fact, is the most delightful and least harmful entertainment ever seen to this day, for nowhere in it can one detect even the shadow of an indelicate expression or an uncatholic thought."

"To write in any other way," said Don Quixote, "would be to write not truths but lies, and historians who resort to lying ought to be burned like coiners of false money. But I do not know what induced the author to make use of novels and irrelevant tales when he had so much to write of in mine. No doubt he felt bound by the proverb: 'With straw or with hay, what odds we say!' For really if he had confined himself to my thoughts, my sighs, my tears, my righteous desires, and my enterprises, he could have compiled a volume greater than all the works of El Tostado, or at least as big.[3] So, my conclusion is, Master Bachelor, that one needs good judgment and ripe understanding to write histories or books of any sort whatsoever. To be witty and write humorously requires great genius. The most cunning part in a comedy is the clown's, for a man who wants to be taken for a simpleton must never be one. History is like a sacred text, for it has to be truthful, and where the truth is, there is God. But in spite of this, there are some who write books and toss them off into the world as though they were pancakes."

"There is no book so bad," said the bachelor, "that there is not something good in it." [4]

"No doubt of that," replied Don Quixote, "but it often happens that authors who have deservedly reaped and won great fame by their books have lost it all, or at least lessened it, when they have given them to the press."

"The reason of that is," answered Sansón, "that printed books are viewed at leisure, and so their faults are easily noticed, and the greater the fame of their authors, the more closely they are examined. Celebrated men of genius, great poets, and famous historians are always, or as a rule, envied by those who make it their pleasure and special pastime to judge the writings of others, without having published anything of their own."

"That is no wonder," said Don Quixote, "for there are many theologians who are no good in the pulpit, but excellent at recognizing the faults or excesses of those who preach."

"All that is so, Don Quixote," said Carrasco, "but I would be happy if those censors would be more merciful and less scrupulous and if they refrained from pitilessly stressing the specks on the bright sun of the work they are crabbing. For if *aliquando bonus dormitat Homerus*,[5] let them reflect

---

[3] Alonso de Madrigal, Bishop of Avila, known as El Tostado, gave rise to the proverb: *escribe más que el Tostado* (he writes more than El Tostado). His works were printed in 13 volumes in Venice (1569).

[4] This celebrated adage comes from Pliny the Elder; *Dicere solebat, nullum esse librum tam malum, ut non aliqua parte prodesset. Epistles* of Pliny the Younger, Book III.

[5] Worthy Homer sometimes nods. Horace, *Ars Poetica*, 359.

how long he stayed awake to give us the light of his work
with the least possible shadow. And it is possible that what
seem to be faults to them are moles, which at times heighten
the beauty of the face that has them. And so, I say that
he who prints a book runs a very great risk, for it is absolutely impossible to write one that will satisfy and please
every reader."

"The one that treats of me," said Don Quixote, "must
have pleased but few."

"Rather the opposite, for as there are an infinite number
of fools in the world, an infinite number of people have enjoyed that history. But there are some who have found
fault and assailed the author's memory for forgetting who
it was who robbed Sancho of his ass, for it is not then
stated and it is only from the context that we infer that it
was stolen. Yet, a little later on we find Sancho riding on
this same ass, and we are never told how he turned up
again. They also say that he forgot to put down what
Sancho did with the hundred crowns he found in the leather
bag in the Sierra Morena, for they were never mentioned
again. Many people want to know what he did with them
and how did he spend them, for it is one of the major
omissions in the work."

"I'm not prepared now, Master Sansón," replied Sancho,
"to go into details or accounts, for I feel faint in the
stomach and if I don't cure it with a few swigs of the old
stuff, it will put me on St. Lucy's thorn.[6] I have a drop at
home, and my old woman is waiting for me. When I've had
my dinner, I'll come back and answer all your worship's
questions, and all the world's, whether it's about my losing the ass or spending the hundred crowns."

Then, without waiting for an answer or saying another
word, he went home.

Don Quixote begged and prayed the bachelor to stay
and take potluck with him. He accepted the invitation and
stayed for the meal, and a pair of pigeons were added to
the usual fare. Knight-errantry was discussed at table, and
Carrasco was careful to humor the knight. When the meal
was over, they took their siesta until Sancho returned, when
their discussion was resumed.

[6] This expression meant to feel the pangs of hunger. Santa Lucía
of Sicily cured those suffering from sore eyes.

CHAPTER IV

In which Sancho Panza satisfies the doubts and questions of the bachelor Sansón Carrasco, with other matters worthy of being known and related

Sancho returned to Don Quixote's house, and resuming the previous conversation, he said: "Since Master Sansón said he wanted to know who stole my ass and how and when, I'd like to state in reply that the same night the pair of us were running away from the Holy Brotherhood into the Sierra Morena, after the luckless adventure with the galley slaves and the one with the corpse they were carrying to Segovia, my master and I got into a thicket. My master rested on his lance and I on my ass. Bruised and worn out after our recent affrays, we settled down to sleep as soundly as if we were lying on four feather mattresses. As for me, I slept so heavy a sleep that whoever it was had a chance to creep up and prop me up on four stakes, which he put under the four corners of my packsaddle in such a way as to leave me mounted on it and stole my ass from under me without my feeling it."

"That is an easy trick," said Don Quixote, "and there is nothing new in it, for the same thing happened to Sacripante at the siege of Albraca when that famous thief Brunelo took away his horse from between his legs by the same device." [1]

"Dawn came," continued Sancho, "and no sooner did I stretch myself than the stakes gave way and down I fell plump to the ground with a great fall. I looked for my ass and didn't find him. The tears gushed from my eyes, and I made such a great wailing that if the author of our history

[1] The theft of Sacripante's horse is described in Ariosto's *Orlando Furioso*, Canto XXVII, stanza 84.

hasn't put it in, you can reckon that he has missed a good thing. At the end of I don't know how many days, when we were traveling with the lady Princess Micomicona, I recognized my ass, and who do you think was riding on him but that notorious trickster and evildoer Ginés de Pasamonte, disguised as a Gypsy, the jailbird whom my master and I freed from the galley chain."

"The mistake is not there," replied Sansón, "but when the author says that Sancho was riding on this same dapple, before the ass turned up again."

"I don't know how to answer that," said Sancho. "All I can say is that perhaps the history writer was wrong, or it may have been a slip of the printers."

"That is it, I am sure," said Sansón, "but what was done with the hundred crowns? Did they fade away?"

"I spent them on myself and on my wife and children. It was because of them that my wife has been so patient about my rovings and ramblings in the service of my master, Don Quixote, for if I had come back home assless and penniless, I should have expected a bleak welcome. Now, if there's anything else you want to know, here I am, and I'll answer the king himself in person, though it's nobody's business to meddle in whether I took them or I didn't, and whether I spent them or not. For if the blows I got on that journey had to be paid in cash, even if they were rated at no more than four maravedis apiece, a hundred crowns more wouldn't pay me for half of them. Let every man lay his hand on his breast and not go calling white black and black white, for everyone is as God made him, and often a great deal worse."

"I'll take care," said Carrasco, "to warn the author of this history, if he reprints it, not to forget what our worthy Sancho has said, for it would enhance its merit a great deal."

"Is there anything else to amend in this work, Master Bachelor?" inquired Don Quixote.

"Yes, there must be," he answered, "but nothing as important as what has been mentioned."

"Does the author," asked Don Quixote, "by any chance promise a second part?"

"Yes, he does," replied Sansón, "but he says he has not found it, nor does he know who has it. And so, we are in doubt whether it will come out or not. And therefore, because some say: 'Never have second parts been any good,' and others: 'Enough has been written about Don Quixote,' it is doubtful whether there will be a sequel, though those who are rather of a jovial than of a saturnine temperament say: 'Let us have more Quixoteries; let Don Quixote charge and Sancho talk, and come what may, we'll be content.' "

"What is the author's intention then?"

"Why," replied Sansón, "as soon as he has found the history, which he is now searching for with extraordinary pains, he will straightaway give it to the press, influenced rather by the profit he will draw from doing so than by any praise."

At this point, Sancho observed: "So, the author looks for money, does he? It'll be a wonder if he hits the nail on the head, for there'll be nothing but hurry, hurry, like a tailor on Easter Eve, and works done in a hurry are never finished as tidily as they should be. Let this Mister Moor, or whatever he is, keep his eye on what he is doing, for myself and my master will give him so much in the matter of adventures and different incidents that he could contrive not only one second part but a hundred. The good man evidently believes we are lying asleep here in the straw, but let him hold our feet for the shoeing and he'll soon find which foot we limp on. What I mean to say is that if my master would take my advice, we should already be in the fields undoing wrongs and righting injuries, as is the usage and custom of good knights-errant."

Sancho had hardly finished uttering these words when the neighing of Rozinante reached their ears, which neighing Don Quixote took for a happy omen, and he resolved to make another sally in three or four days from that time. Announcing his intention to the bachelor, he asked advice as to where he should start his expedition. The bachelor replied that in his opinion he ought to go to the kingdom of Aragón and the city of Saragossa, where in a few days certain solemn jousts would be held at the festival of Saint George, at which he might win fame over the Aragonese knights, which would mean that he would win it over all the knights in the world. He praised Don Quixote's most honorable and valiant resolution but warned him to be more cautious in affronting perils, seeing that his life did not belong to him, but to all those who needed him to protect them in their misfortunes.

"This is just what I object to, Master Sansón," said Sancho at this point. "My master attacks a hundred armed men as a greedy boy would half a dozen watermelons. Body of the world, Master Bachelor! There are surely times for attacking and times for retreating, and we don't want it always to be 'Saint James and at 'em, Spaniards!' [2] Besides, I've heard it said (I think it was my master himself, if I remember correctly) that the middle course of valor lies between the extremes of cowardice and rashness. If this is so, I don't want him to run away without good reason, or to make an attack when the odds require the opposite. But above all, I warn my master that if he takes me with him, it must be on condition that he does all the fighting and that I'm not to be obliged to do anything but look after his person in what concerns cleanliness and comfort. In this I am ready to dance attendance on him; but to think that I have to lay hand on the sword, even against rascally churls of the baser kind with their hatchets, is a foolish thought. I, Master Sansón, don't expect to win the fame of a fighting man, but only that of the best and most loyal squire that ever served knight-errant, and if my master, Don Quixote, in return for my many faithful services should be pleased to give me some island of the many he says he is bound to meet with in these parts, I'll be profoundly grateful. And if he should not give it to me, I'm just as I came into the world, and a man must not live on the favors of anyone but God. Moreover, my bread will taste as well, aye, and even better, without a government than with one. For, how do I know that in these governorships the Devil may not have laid a trap for me to make me stumble, fall, and break my grinders? Sancho I was born, and Sancho I mean to die. Nevertheless, if Heaven, fairly and squarely, without trouble or risk, were to hand me an island or something like it, I am not such a fool as to fling it away, for it is said: 'When they give thee a heifer, run with the halter,' and 'When good luck comes thy way, take it home with thee.' "

"Brother Sancho," said Carrasco, "you have spoken like a professor, but put your trust in God and in your master, Don Quixote, for he will give you not an island but a kingdom."

[2] This was the battlecry of the Spaniards in the Middle Ages.

"It is all the same, be it the greater or the lesser," answered Sancho, "though I can tell Master Carrasco that the kingdom my master gives me will not be flung into a sack full of holes, for I've felt my own pulse and I find myself healthy enough to rule kingdoms and govern islands, and I have told my master as much long before now."

"Take care, Sancho," said Sansón, "for titles change manners, and perhaps when you find yourself governor, you will not recognize the mother who bore you."

"That may be true," replied Sancho, "of those who are born in a ditch among the mallows, but not of those who have four finger's depth of old Christian fat on their souls, as I have.³ No, just take a look at my disposition; do you think that is likely to show ingratitude to anyone?"

"God grant it may not," said Don Quixote. "We shall see this when the governorship comes along; I seem to see it already."

With these words he begged the bachelor, if he were a poet, to do him the favor of composing some verses on the subject of his intended departure from his lady, Dulcinea of El Toboso, and to put one letter of her name at the beginning of each line so that when the poem was complete, by taking these first letters together, they might read *DULCINEA OF EL TOBOSO*.

The bachelor replied that although he was not one of the famous poets of Spain, who, as they say, were no more than three and a half, he would not fail to compose such verses. He found, however, that there was a great difficulty in the composition because the name contained eighteen letters, and if he were to make four stanzas of four lines each, there would be two letters over, and if he were to write four of those five-line stanzas, which are called *décimas* or roundelays, they would be two letters short. Nevertheless, he would try to squeeze in two letters, as best he could, so as to get the name into four stanzas.

"That you must do, whatever way you can," said Don Quixote, "because if the name is not there, plain and manifest, no woman would believe that the verses had been made for her."

³ Sancho was very proud of being an old Christian (*Cristiano viejo rancio*), that is to say, without any mixture of Jewish or Moorish blood.

This matter was settled, and also that they should set out in eight days. Don Quixote charged the bachelor to keep it a secret, especially from the curate and Master Nicholas, the barber, and from his niece and housekeeper, lest they should prevent him from carrying out his laudable and valiant purpose. All this Carrasco promised and then departed, charging Don Quixote to keep him informed, whenever possible, of his good or evil fortunes. And so, they said farewell to each other, and Sancho went off to make the necessary preparations for their expedition.

CHAPTER V

Of the shrewd and humorous conversation between Sancho Panza and his wife, Teresa Panza, and other matters worthy of happy record

The translator of this history, when he reaches the fifth chapter, declares that he considers it apocryphal because in it Sancho talks in a style that is far superior to what one would expect from one of so limited an understanding, and he makes such subtle comments that they seem beyond the range of his intelligence. However, in order to fulfill the duty he owed to his office, he was unwilling to omit translating it, so he proceeds as follows:

Sancho went home in such high spirits that his wife noticed his glee a bowshot away, so much so that she asked him: "What are you bringing, Sancho friend, that you are so merry?"

To which he replied: "Wife, if God were willing, I'd be very glad to be less merry than I am this instant."

"I don't get your meaning, husband," said she, "and I don't know what you are at when you say that you would be glad, if God were willing, not to be happy, for though I'm a fool, I don't know how a body can be happy for not being so."

"Listen, Teresa," replied Sancho; "I'm merry because I'm determined to go back to serve my master, Don Quixote, who wants to go out a third time to look for adventures, and I'm going with him again, for my needs will have it so, and also the hope that cheers me with the thought of finding another hundred crowns like those we have spent. Mind you, I'm sad at having to leave you and the children, and if God would be pleased to give me my daily bread dry-shod and at home, without dragging me over byways and crossroads—and He could do it for a mere song by merely willing it—no doubt my happiness would be stronger and more enduring, for now it is mixed with sorrow at parting. So, I was right in saying I would be glad, God being willing, not to be so happy."

"Look here, Sancho," answered Teresa, "since you've become a limb to a knight-errant you talk so roundabout that nobody can understand you."

"It is enough if God understands me, wife," replied Sancho, "for He is the Understander of all things, that's all I need say. But mind, sister, you must look after Dapple for the next three days so that he may be fit to bear arms. Double his feed and have an eye to the packsaddle and the rest of his harness, for it's no wedding we are going to, but around the world to engage in the game of give-and-take with giants and dragons and monsters, and to hear hissings and roarings and bellowings. And all this would be mere lavender if we hadn't to deal with Yanguesans and enchanted Moors."

"I'm quite ready to believe, husband," answered Teresa, "that squires-errant don't eat their bread for nothing; so, I'll be always praying to Our Lord to deliver you quickly from all those hard knocks."

"I tell you, wife," answered Sancho, "that if I did not feel convinced that I'll see myself governor of an island before very long, I would drop dead on the spot."

"Not that, husband," said Teresa. "Let the hen live though it be with the pip; live, and let the Devil take all the governments in the world. Without one you came out of your mother's belly, without one you've lived till now, and without one you'll go or be carried to your grave when it should please God. How many are there in the world who live without a government, yet they continue to exist all the same and they are counted in the number of the people? The best

sauce in the world is hunger, and as the poor are never without that, they always eat with gusto. But take heed, Sancho,
if you're lucky and find yourself with some government on
your hands, don't forget me and your children. Remember
that your son, Sanchico, is now turned fifteen, and it's reasonable that he should go to school if his uncle, the abbot,
intends to put him into the Church. Remember, too, that
your daughter, Marisancha, will not die if we get her wed,
for I have a shrewd suspicion that she's every bit as keen
to get a husband as you are to see yourself governor, and
when all's said and done, a daughter looks better badly married than well kept."

"By my faith," answered Sancho, "if God brings me any
kind of government, my dear wife, I'll marry Marisancha so
high that they'll not reach her without calling her your
ladyship."

"Not on your life, Sancho," replied Teresa; "marry her
to her equal, that's the safest plan, for if you take her out
of clogs and put her into high-heeled shoes, if you change
her gray-flannel petticoat into hoops and silk gowns, and if
out of plain Marica and *tu* you transform her into Doña So-
and-so and my lady, the poor girl won't know whether she's
on her head or her heels, and at every turn she'll fall into a
thousand blunders, showing the thread of her coarse homespun."

"Silence, you foolish woman," said Sancho; "all she has to
do is to practice it for two or three years, and then the ladylike airs and dignity will come naturally to her; and suppose
they don't, what does that matter? She will be her ladyship
come what may."

"Measure yourself by your equals, Sancho," answered
Teresa. "Don't try to raise yourself higher and remember
the proverb that says: 'Wipe your neighbor's son's nose and
take him into your house.' Surely it would be a fine business to marry our María to some countling or a grand gentleman, who, when he felt inclined, would treat her like dirt,
calling her country Joan, clodhopper's child, and spinning
sister. Not on my life, husband; not for that have I brought
up my daughter all these years, I tell you. You, Sancho, bring
the money, and leave the marriage business to me. Why,
there's Lope Tocho, Juan Tocho's son, a lusty, live lad whom
we know; I've seen him making eyes at the girl, and I know
she'll be well matched to him, for he's our equal. We'll have

her always under our eyes so that we'll all be one family, parents and children, grandchildren and sons-in-law. Why, the blessing of God will be with the lot of us. So, I won't have you marrying her in those courts and grand palaces where they won't know what to make of her, nor will she know what to make of herself."

"Come here, blockhead and wife for Barabbas," cried Sancho. "What do you mean by trying, without why or wherefore, to hinder me from marrying my daughter to one who'll give me grandchildren who'll be treated as lordships? Look here, Teresa, I've always heard my elders say that he who doesn't know how to enjoy good luck when it's nigh shouldn't grumble when it passes him by; and now that it's knocking at our door, we should not shut it out. Let us spread our sails before the favoring breeze."

It was this style of speech and Sancho's remarks further on that made the translator, so he says, take the chapter to be apocryphal. "Can't you see, you dolt," continued Sancho, "that it will be best for me to clap myself into some profitable governorship that will lift our feet out of the mud and marry Marisancha to whom I please? Then you'll see how they'll call you Doña Teresa Panza and seat you in church on rugs, cushions, and finery right in the face of the highborn ladies of the town. No, no, stay as you are, neither growing nor waning, like a tapestry figure! Well, mum's the word for the present. Sanchica will be a countess whether you like it or not."

"Do you know what you are saying, husband?" replied Teresa. "I am afraid that this countess business will be the ruin of my daughter. However, do as you please, make her a duchess or a princess; I tell you it will not be with my will and consent. I've always been a lover of equality, brother, and I can't stand people giving themselves airs when they should not. They christened me Teresa, a plain, simple name, without any of those additions or tags or ornaments of dons and doñas. Cascajo was my father's name, and as I'm your wife they call me Teresa Panza, though strictly they ought to call me Teresa Cascajo. But 'Kings go as the laws will,' and I'm satisfied with this name without sticking a doña on the top of it to make it so heavy that I cannot carry it. I don't want to make people gossip about me when they see me all dolled out as a countess or a governor's wife. 'Look at the airs Lady Slut gives herself!' they'll say.

'Only yesterday she was not above stretching a hank of flax, and she went to Mass with the tail of her skirt over her head instead of a cloak; and today she struts in a farthingale, with her brooches and swagger, as if we didn't know her!' If God preserves me in my seven senses, or five, or as many of them as I have, I've no intention of letting them see me make such a show. You, brother, be off and become a government of an island, and swagger to your heart's content; by the years of my mother, neither my daughter nor myself will stir a foot from our village, for the honest woman is the one with the broken leg who stays at home, and to be doing her bit is as good as a feast for the decent girl. Be gone with your Don Quixote to your adventures, and leave us to our misadventures, for God will mend them provided we be good, and I'm sure I don't know who put the don on him, for neither his father nor his grandfather had it."

"I declare," cried Sancho, "you must have some devil in that body of yours. God bless us, woman, what a power of things you have strung together, one after the other, without head or tail! What have Cascajo, the brooches, the proverbs, and the airs to do with what I'm saying? Listen, dolt and nincompoop (I'm right to call you this, seeing that you don't grip my meaning and you go tearing away from good fortune), if I said that my daughter had to throw herself down from a tower or go gallivanting all over the world as Doña Urraca [1] wished to do, there would have been some reason for not submitting to my will; but supposing that in an instant and in less than the twinkling of an eye I clamp the doña and your ladyship to her back and fetch her out of the stubble and place her under a canopy, on a pedestal, and on a couch with more velvet cushions on it than there are

[1] Doña Urraca, the daughter of King Ferdinand I of Castile, when she heard that her father had divided his realms among his four sons and had left her nothing, declared that she would roam like a loose woman through the world and would give her body to the Moors for money and gratis to the Christian warriors. Moved by such a threat, the King gave her Zamora, which in consequence became the scene of many a bloody battle. The incident is described in one of the ancient ballads with which Sancho, as a true Manchegan peasant, was familiar.

Moors in the clan of the Almohades,[2] why won't you agree
and fall in with what I wish?"

"Do you know why, husband?" answer Teresa. "Because
of the proverb that says: 'Who covers thee, discovers thee.'
All give the poor man a hasty glance, but they keep their eyes
glued on the rich man, and if the said rich man was once
poor, then you will hear the sneering and the gossiping and
the continued spite of the backbiters in the streets, swarming
as thick as bees."

"Look here, Teresa," said Sancho, "and pay heed to what
I'm going to tell you, for maybe you've never heard it all
your life. And remember that I'm not airing my own opinions, but those of the reverend father who preached in this
village last Lent and who said, if I remember correctly, that
all present things that our eyes behold make a stronger impression on us and remain more vividly in our memories
than things past." (These remarks of Sancho are another
reason for the translator's former statement that this chapter
is apocryphal, for they are beyond the mental capacity of our
honest Sancho.) "Hence it happens," he continued, "that
when we see someone dressed up in all his finery with a
great train of servants, we feel obliged to pay him respect,
though our memory at the moment may remind us of the
lowly state in which we once saw him. For the disgrace of
poverty or humble birth, once it is in the past, does not exist,
and the only things that exist are those we see in the present.
So if a person whom Fortune has raised from his lowly
state to the height of his present prosperity—these were the
words of the preacher—be well bred, liberal, and courteous to
all and if he does not seek to vie with those who were noble
from ancient times, rest assured, Teresa, that no one will remember what he was, and all will respect him for what he
is—that is to say, all except the envious, from whom no
prosperous fortune is safe."

"I can't make head or tail of you, husband," answered
Teresa. "Do what you will, and don't break my head with
your orating and speechifying. And if you have revolved to
do what you say——"

"*Resolved* you should say, woman," said Sancho, "not
revolved."

[2] Sancho makes a play upon the word *almohadas* (cushions)
and Almohades (a Moorish dynasty that succeeded the Almorá-
vides in South Spain in 1145).

"Don't start argufying with me, husband," said Teresa. "I speak as God pleases, and I am content to call a spade a spade, and I say that if you're set on having a government, take your son, Sancho, with you and teach him from this day how to hold one, for sons should inherit and learn the trades of their fathers."

"As soon as I get it," said Sancho, "I will send for him by post, and I will send you money, of which I'll have plenty, for you'll always find people ready to lend it to governors when they have none. And mind you dress him so as to hide what he is and make him look what he has to be."

"You send the money," said Teresa, "and I'll dress him up as gawdy as a branch on Palm Sunday."

"Then we both agree that our daughter is to be a countess," said Sancho.

"The day I see her a countess," replied Teresa, "I'll feel that I'm burying her; but once again I say, do as you please, for such is the burden we women receive at birth, to be obedient to our husbands no matter how doltish they may be."

And with this she began to weep in real earnest as though she already saw Sanchica dead and buried. Sancho consoled her by saying that since he would have to make her a countess, he would postpone doing it as long as he could. So ended their conversation, and Sancho went back to see Don Quixote and make arrangements for their departure.

CHAPTER VI

*Of what happened to Don Quixote with his niece and
his housekeeper, one of the most important chapters
in all this history*

While Sancho Panza and his wife, Teresa Cascajo, held
their irrelevant conversation, the niece and the housekeeper
of Don Quixote were not idle, for by a thousand signs they
began to perceive that their uncle and master intended to
break away the third time and to return to his, for them, ill-
errant chivalry. They tried every method of diverting him
from his unlucky notion, but they might as well have
preached in the desert or hammered on cold iron. Among
many other arguments they used, the housekeeper said to
him: "Truly master, if you do not stay still and quiet at
home, and cease rambling over hill and dale like a restless
spirit, looking for what they call adventures, but which I call
misfortunes, I shall have to call upon God and the king to
send some remedy."

To which Don Quixote replied: "I know not what answer
God will give to your complaints, housekeeper, nor what
His Majesty will answer either. I do, however, know that if
I were king, I would refuse to answer the innumerable peti-
tions that are presented to him every day, for one of the
greatest of the many troubles kings have is being obliged to
listen to all and to answer all, and therefore, I would not
wish that my affairs should worry him."

Whereupon the housekeeper said: "Tell us, master, are
there no knights at His Majesty's court?"

"There are plenty of them," answered Don Quixote, "and
it is right there should be for the adornment of the princely
dignity and the exaltation of the monarchy."

"Then, why should your worship not be one of those who

serve their king and lord in his court, without moving a step?" said she.

"Look here, dear lady," said Don Quixote, "all knights cannot be courtiers, nor can all courtiers be knights-errant, nor ought they be. There must be all sorts in the world, and even though we may all be knights, there is a vast difference between one and another, for the courtiers, without leaving their chambers or the threshold of the court, roam all over the world by looking at the map, without spending a farthing and without suffering heat or cold, hunger or thirst. But we, the true knights-errant, in sun, in cold, in the open, exposed to the wrath of the heavens by night and by day, on foot and on horseback, we measure the whole earth with our own feet. Nor is it only enemies in pictures that we know, but in their own real bodies, and on every occasion, no matter how great the risk, we attack them, without minding childish details or the laws of the duel: whether one carries or does not carry a shorter sword or lance, whether one bears on his person relics or any hidden subterfuge, whether the sun has to be divided and shared between the combatants or not, and other ceremonious rites of the sort that are observed in single combats of man to man, which you know nothing about, but I do.[1] And I would have you know, also, that the true knight-errant, though he should see ten giants, who not only touch the clouds with their heads but pass through them, each of whom walks on two huge towers instead of legs, whose arms are like the masts of mighty vessels, and whose eyes are like great mill wheels, burning fiercer than a glass furnace, must on no account be frightened by them. Rather with gallant courage and fearless heart he must attack them, and if possible, vanquish and lay them low in one instant; even if they be armed with the shells of a certain fish, which, they say, are harder than diamonds, and even if instead of

[1] These remarks of Don Quixote are an echo of ancient chivalry, which established a rigid code of knightly behavior. It was a cardinal rule that the combatants should be equally mounted, that their lances and swords should be of the same length, and that in duels the sun should be equally divided between them—that is to say, that the rays should fall sideways between them, so that neither should have the sun at his back. A chivalrous knight would have scorned taking an unfair advantage over his adversary in those days—before Satan invented high explosives and totalitarian war.

swords they wield trenchant blades of Damascus steel or clubs studded with spikes of the same metal, such as I myself have seen more than twice. All this I have said, housekeeper, that you may see the difference that exists between one kind of knight and another; and it would be well if every prince gave more value to the second, or more properly speaking, first kind of knights-errant, for as their histories tell us, some among them have been the salvation, not merely of one kingdom, but of many."

"Ah master," cried the niece, "remember that all you say about knights-errant are fables and lies. Their histories, if they are not burned, certainly deserve each of them to be wrapped in a sanbenito [2] or to bear some mark by which they might be known as infamous and corrupters of good manners."

"Now, by almighty God who sustains me," cried Don Quixote, "if you were not my own sister's daughter, I would chastise you so for the blasphemous words you have uttered that the whole world would resound with it. What! Is it possible that a young hussy who can scarcely manage a dozen bobbins of lace should have the impudence to wag her tongue and make disparaging remarks about the histories of knights-errant? What would Amadis say if he heard such a thing? He, no doubt, would forgive you, for he was the most meek and courteous knight of his time, and moreover, a great protector of damsels. But others might have heard you who would not have let you escape so easily; all are not courteous and well mannered, some are vain, swaggering rascals. Nor are all who call themselves gentlemen to be taken at their own valuation, for some are of gold, others are of base alloy, and all look like gentlemen, but not all are able to stand the touchstone of truth. There are low men who blow themselves up to bursting point to appear gentlemen, and others of exalted rank who seem to be dying to pass for men of the vulgar herd. The former rise through ambition or virtue; the latter sink through indolence or vice. And it is necessary to have knowledge and discernment in order to distinguish between these two kinds of gentlemen, so alike in name and so different in actions."

---

[2] The *sanbenito,* short for *saco benedicto,* was the garment worn by penitents under sentence by the Inquisition. It was a short yellow shirt with a red cross in front.

"God save us!" cried the niece. "To think that you, uncle, should know so much that if need be, you could mount a pulpit or go preaching through the streets, and yet to see you so blind and deluded as to consider yourself valiant when you are old, strong when you are sick, a straightener of crooked ways when you yourself are bent with age, and above all, a knight when you are not one, for though the gentry may be so, the poor cannot!"

"There is much reason in what you say, niece," answered Don Quixote, "and I could tell you things about birth that would astonish you, but for fear of mingling sacred with profane subjects, I refrain. Look, friends, and take note. All the pedigrees in the world can be reduced to four kinds, which are the following: The first are those who from humble beginnings went on extending and expanding until they reached supreme greatness; the second are those who had high beginnings, continued to preserve them, and do still maintain them in their pristine dignity; others, though they were great at first, have dwindled and declined until they ended in nothingness, like the point of a pyramid, which compared to its base or seat is nothing; there are others, and they are the most numerous, who had neither good beginnings nor a respectable development, and are bound to end without a name, as does the lineage of plebeian and common folk. Of the first, those who have risen from humble origins to their present greatness, the Ottoman house may serve as an example, for though it sprang from the lowly and mean shepherd who founded it, it now stands on the pinnacle we see it. Of the second lineage, which had its origin in greatness and maintained its state without increasing it, we have many princes to serve as examples. Princes by succession, they preserve their inheritances without increasing or diminishing them, containing themselves peacefully within the boundaries of their estates. Of those who began great and ended in a point there are thousands of examples, for all the pharaohs and Ptolemies of Egypt, the Caesars of Rome, with all that herd—if I may call them thus—of countless princes, monarchs, lords, Medes, Assyrians, Persians, Greeks, and Barbarians—all these lineages and lordships have ended in a point and in nothingness, like those who gave them birth, for it would be impossible now to find any of their descendants, and if we were to find them, it would be in some low or humble station. Of the plebeian stock all I can say is that it serves only to swell the number of living men whose great deeds merit no other fame or eulogy. I want to impress upon you, my dear simpletons, that there is great confusion among lineages and that only those appear great and illustrious that show themselves so by the virtue, wealth, and generosity of their owners. I spoke of virtue, wealth, and generosity, because a great man who is vicious will only be a great doer of evil, and a rich man who is not liberal will only be a miserly beggar, for the possessor of wealth is not made happy by possessing it, but by spending it, and not by spending it as he pleases, but by knowing how to spend it well. To the poor gentleman there is no other way of showing that he is a gentleman than by virtue, by being affable, well bred, courteous, and helpful, not haughty, arrogant, or censorious, but above all by being charitable, for by two maravedis given with a cheerful heart to the poor, he will show himself as liberal as he who distributes alms to the sound of a bell. And no one who sees him adorned with the virtues I have mentioned will fail to recognize and judge him, though he know him not, to be of good stock. Indeed, it would be a marvel if this was not so, for praise has always been virtue's guerdon, and those who are virtuous cannot fail to be praised.

"There are two roads, my daughters, by which men can travel and reach wealth and honor: one is the way of letters, the other the way of arms. As for myself, I have more of arms than of letters, and I was born, to judge by my inclination to arms, under the influence of the planet Mars. I am, therefore, almost forced to follow that road, and by it I have to travel in spite of the whole world, and it will be useless for you to weary yourselves in persuading me that I should resist what Heaven wills, Fortune ordains, reason demands, and above all, my own inclination dictates. Knowing as I do the innumerable toils that are the accompaniments of knight-errantry, I know, too, the infinite benefits that are its guerdon. I know that the path of virtue is very narrow and the road of vice broad and spacious. I know that their ends and goals are different, for that of vice, though wise and spacious, ends in death, and that of virtue, narrow and full of toils, in life, not life that has an ending but in the one that has no end. I know, as our great Castilian poet says:

" 'By these rough paths we mount,
   Toward the heights of immortality,
   Which none can reach who have descended.' "

"Ah, woe is me!" cried the niece. "My uncle is a poet, too! He knows everything, and there's nothing he cannot do; why, I'll bet if he had a mind to turn mason, he could build a house as easily as a cage."

"I promise you, niece," answered Don Quixote, "that if these knightly thoughts did not monopolize all my faculties, there would be nothing I could not do, nor any handicraft I could not acquire. even so far as making birdcages and toothpicks."

Just then, a knocking at the door was heard, and when they inquired who was there, Sancho Panza answered that it was he. No sooner did the housekeeper hear who it was than she ran away to hide herself so as not to see him, so much did she hate him. The niece opened the door, and his master, Don Quixote, welcomed him with open arms, and the two shut themselves up in his room, where another conversation ensued every bit as good as the last.

CHAPTER VII

*Of the discussion between Don Quixote and his squire,
with other most notable incidents*

When the housekeeper saw that Sancho Panza was locking
himself in with her master, she guessed what was afoot, and
feeling certain that the result of their conference would be
a third sally, she snatched her cloak, all full of trouble and
anxiety, and set off in search of the bachelor Sansón Carrasco, thinking that as he was a well-spoken person and a
new acquaintance of her master, he might be able to convince him to abandon his mad enterprise. She found the
bachelor walking to and fro in the courtyard of his house,
and straightaway, perspiring and all aflutter, she threw herself at his feet. Carrasco, seeing how distressed she was, said
to her: "What is this, Mistress Housekeeper? What has happened? You look as if you were heartbroken."

"Nothing, Señor Sansón," said she, "only that my master
is breaking out—breaking out for sure."

"Whereabouts is he breaking out, señora?" asked Sansón.
"Has he broken any part of his body?"

"He is not breaking out," she replied, "unless it be through
the door of his madness. I mean, dear Master Bachelor,
that he is about to break out again (this will be the third
time) to hunt all over the world for what he calls ventures,[1]
though I can't make out why he calls them thus. The first
time he was brought back to us slung across the back of an
ass, drubbed all over; the second time he came home in an
oxcart, shut up in a cage in which he convinced himself
he was enchanted, and the poor fellow was in such a state

---

[1] A play on the double meaning of *ventura*: good fortune and
a venture or risk.

that the mother who bore him would have not known him, so lean and yellow was he, with his eyes deep sunk in the recesses of his skull. To bring him back to a shadow of his former self cost me more than six hundred eggs, as God knows, and all the world, and my hens, which won't let me tell a lie."

"I can believe you," replied the bachelor, "for they are so good, so fat, and so well fed that they would not say one thing for another even if they burst for it. In short, then, Mistress Housekeeper, is there nothing else, or is there any further trouble in addition to what we are afraid Don Quixote may do?"

"No, señor," said she.

"Well, then," answered the bachelor, "don't worry; go home in peace and get something hot ready for my lunch, and while you are walking along, say the prayer of St. Apollonia,[2] that is, if you know it. I'll follow presently and you'll see marvels."

"Poor me!" answered the housekeeper. "Do you want me to say the prayer of St. Apollonia? That would be grand if it was a toothache my master had, but it's in his brains only that he has it."

"I know what I'm saying, Mistress Housekeeper; be off and don't start arguing with me. You know I am a bachelor of Salamanca, and no one can bachelorize more than that," replied Carrasco.

With this the housekeeper departed, and the bachelor immediately went to look for the curate to make certain arrangements that we shall relate in due time.

While Don Quixote and Sancho were locked in together, a conversation took place between them that is recorded in the history with great precision and truthful detail. Sancho said to his master: "Sir, I have perverted my wife to let me go with your worship wherever you please to take me."

"*Converted* you should say, Sancho," said Don Quixote, "not *perverted.*"

"I've begged your worship once or twice, if I'm not mistaken, not to mend my words; if you don't understand what I mean by them, just say when you don't understand: 'Sancho,

---

[2] A joke of the bachelor. St. Apollonia was the patron of those who suffered from toothache. The Manchegans today still recite spells to her to relieve their aching molars.

or Devil, I don't understand you,' and if I don't make myself clear then, you can correct me, for I am so focile——"

"I don't understand you, Sancho," Don Quixote said, "for I do not know what *so focile* means."

"So focile means," replied Sancho, "that I am so-so."

"I understand less now," said Don Quixote.

"Well, if you can't understand me," answered Sancho, "I don't know how to say it. I can't say any more, God help me."

"Now, now I understand," cried Don Quixote. "You mean to say that you are so docile, meek, and tractable that you will take what I say to you and do as I teach you."

"I'd like to bet you grasped my meaning from the beginning," said Sancho, "but wished to put me in a dither in order to hear me make another two hundred blunders."

"Maybe so," replied Don Quixote; "well, now come to the point. What does Teresa say?"

"Teresa says," replied Sancho, "that with your worship it should be 'Fast bind, fast find'; that now's the time for more writing and less talking, for 'He who settles doesn't tangle'; and that 'A bird in hand is better than two in the bush.' And I say that 'A woman's counsel is bad, but he who won't take it is mad.' "

"And so say I," answered Don Quixote. "Speak, friend Sancho, go on; today pearls are dropping from your lips."

"The fact is," answered Sancho, "that as your worship knows, we are all of us mortal, 'Here today and gone tomorrow,' and 'The lamb goes as soon as the sheep,' and nobody can promise himself more hours of life in this world than God wishes to give him, for 'Death is deaf, and when he comes to knock at our life's door, he is always in a hurry, and neither prayers, nor force, nor scepters, nor miters can delay him,' as the common saying goes and as they tell us from the pulpits."

"That is quite true," said Don Quixote, "but I don't know what you are getting at."

"What I'm getting at," said Sancho, "is that you should settle some fixed salary to be paid to me monthly while I'm in your service and that this salary be paid out of your estate, for I don't want to trust rewards that arrive late or never; God help me with what is my own. In short, I want to know what I'm earning, whether it is much or little, for upon one egg set the hen, and 'many a mickle makes a muckle,' and provided one gains something, nothing is lost. To be sure, if it should happen (which I neither believe nor expect) that your worship would give me the island that has been promised me, I'm not the one to be ungrateful or grasping, and I would be willing to have the said island valued and taken out of my wages, cat for quantity." [3]

"Friend Sancho," said Don Quixote, "sometimes a cat is as good as a rat."

"I see," replied Sancho; "I'll bet I ought to have said *rat* and not *cat*, but it doesn't matter, for your worship understood me."

"I understand you," answered Don Quixote, "and I have penetrated the depth of your thoughts, and I know the mark you are shooting at with the countless arrows of your proverbs. Listen, Sancho, I would willingly fix your wages if I could discover an instance in any of the histories of knights-errant that would give even the faintest hint of what their squires used to get by the month or by the year. But I have read them all, or most of them, and I cannot remember reading that a knight-errant gave fixed wages to his squire. I only know that they served for a reward and that when they least expected it, if their masters were lucky, they found themselves rewarded with an island or something equivalent, and at least they were given a title and a lordship. And so, if such hopes and inducements, Sancho, persuade you to return to my service, you are welcome, but it is ridiculous to imagine that I am going to turn topsy-turvy the ancient usage of knight-errantry. Go back to your home, Sancho, and expose my intentions to your Teresa, and if she is willing and you are willing to be on reward with me, *bene quidem*; if not, we remain friends as before, for 'If the dovecote does not lack food, it will not lack pigeons'; and remember, my son, that 'A good hope is better than a poor holding, and a good complaint than bad pay.' I speak in this way, Sancho, to show you that I, too, can pour out as thick a shower of proverbs as you can. In short, I mean to say that if you don't want to come on reward with me and run the same chances as I run, God be with you and make a saint of you. I shall find plenty of squires more obedient and willing, and not as thickheaded and talkative as you."

When Sancho heard his master's firm and resolute words,

[3] Sancho means rate for quantity.

the sky became clouded for him and the wings of his heart drooped, for he had believed that his master would never go without him for all the wealth in the world. While he stood there moody and dejected, Sansón Carrasco arrived with the housekeeper and the niece, who were eager to hear what arguments he would employ to dissuade their master from setting out in quest of adventure. Sansón, a consummate wag, went up and embraced him as before, saying in a loud voice: "O flower of knight-errantry! O shining light of arms! O honor and mirror of the Spanish nation! May it please almighty God in His infinite power to grant that the person or persons who hinder or disturb your third sally may lose their way in the labyrinth of their schemes and never accomplish what they most desire."

Then, turning to the housekeeper, he said: "Mistress Housekeeper, you may well give up saying the prayer of St. Apollonia, for I know that the spheres have positively determined that Don Quixote should put into operation his new and lofty enterprises, and I should lay a heavy weight upon my conscience did I not urge this knight not to curb his strong arm, for as long as he remains inactive, he is defrauding those who have been injured of the means of having their wrongs redressed. Forward, then, my lord Don Quixote, and let your worship and highness set out today rather than tomorrow. If anything is needed in order to pursue your design, here am I to supply it with my person and estate; and if it were necessary that I should attend upon your magnificence as squire, I should consider it the height of good fortune."

At these words Don Quixote turned to Sancho and said: "Did I not tell you, Sancho, that there would be squires in plenty? Take note that he who offers his services is no other than the renowned bachelor Sansón Carrasco, the perpetual joker and diverter of the Salamantine schools, sound of body, nimble of his extremities, reserved, sufferer of both heat and cold as well as of hunger and thirst, endowed with all those things that are required of a knight-errant's squire. But Heaven forbid that in order to follow my inclinations he should shake the foundations of letters, shatter the cup of science, and break the palm of liberal arts. Let this new Sansón stay in his own country, and in honoring it, let him bring honor to his venerable parents, for I will be content with any squire now that Sancho does not deign to come with me."

"But I do deign," said Sancho, with his eyes full of tears. "Never will they say of me, master, 'the bread partaken, the company forsaken.' Sure, I don't spring from any ungrateful stock, for all the world knows, and especially my village, who were the Panzas from whom I descend. Besides, I have learned through word and deed of your worship's desire to do me favor, and if I have been a bit of a bargainer on the score of my wages, it was only to please my wife, for when she takes it into her head to press a point, no hammer drives in the hoops of a cask as she drives a man to do what she wants. But, after all, a man must be a man, and a woman a woman, and as I am a man anywhere in the world, which I can't deny, I'll be one in my own house, in spite of anybody. So, there's nothing else to do but for your worship to draw up your will with its codicil so that it can't be provoked, and let us hit the road so that Master Sansón's soul may not suffer, for he says that his conscience dictates that he must persuade your worship to go out a third time into the world; so, I again offer to serve you faithfully and loyally, as well as and better than any squire has served knight-errant past or present."

The bachelor was amazed to hear the style and manner of Sancho Panza's speech, for though he had read the first history of the latter's master, he had never believed that Sancho was as droll as he was described there. But when he heard him say: "will with its codicil so that it can't be *provoked*," instead of "will with its codicil so that it can't be *revoked*," he believed all he had read, and reckoned him as one of the most downright dunderheads of our age, saying to himself that two such lunatics as master and servant could not be found in all the wide world. At last, Don Quixote and Sancho embraced and made friends, and with the advice and approval of the great Carrasco, who henceforth became their oracle, it was decided that in three days they should depart. In the interval they would have an opportunity to provide for the journey and to look for a proper helmet, which Don Quixote insisted he must have. Sansón offered him one, for he knew that a friend of his who had one would not refuse it to him, though it was all dingy from rust and moldy instead of clean and shining like polished steel. The curses that the housekeeper and the niece hurled at the bachelor cannot be told. They tore their hair, they clawed their faces, and they raised a moaning dirge just as hired keeners used to do, as if they were mourning the death of their master instead of his departure.

When Sansón had persuaded Don Quixote to set out once again, he had his own eye on a plan of action that will be described further on in our history, and it was a plan about which he had taken advice from the curate and the barber, with whom he had previously been in consultation.

During those three days Don Quixote and Sancho provided themselves with what they considered necessary, and when Sancho had placated his wife and Don Quixote his niece and his housekeeper, they set out at nightfall on the road to El Toboso without being seen by anyone but the bachelor, who wished to keep them company for a couple of miles from the village. Don Quixote was mounted on his good Rozinante and Sancho on his old Dapple, his wallets stored with eatables and his purse full of money, which his master gave him in case of need. Sansón, after embracing the knight, returned to the village, and the pair went on their way to the great city of El Toboso.

CHAPTER VIII

In which we learn what happened to Don Quixote on his way to see his lady, Dulcinea of El Toboso

"Blessed be mighty Allah," says Hamete Benengeli at the beginning of this eighth chapter. "Blessed be Allah!" he repeats three times, and he declares that he utters these blessings finding that he has already got Don Quixote and Sancho Panza into the field, and that the readers of his delightful history may reckon that from this point the exploits and humor of the knight and his squire begin. He begs them to forget the past knight-errantries of the ingenious gentleman and to fix their eyes on those that are to come and are now beginning on the road to El Toboso, as the others began on the Plain of Montiel. He asks but little, considering all that he promises; and thus he goes on to say:

Don Quixote and Sancho were left alone, but scarcely had they said farewell to Sansón when Rozinante began to neigh and the ass to sigh, which both knight and squire took as a good sign and a most lucky omen, though to tell the truth the sighs and brays of Dapple were louder than the neighings of the horse, whence Sancho concluded that his good fortune was to exceed and overtop that of his master, basing his arguments upon some kind of fortune-telling that he had learned goodness only knows where, for the history does not say. Only he was heard to say, when he stumbled or fell, that he wished he had not left his home, for by stumbling or falling he could get nothing but a torn shoe or a broken rib, and I must say that though he may have been a fool, he was not wide off the mark on this point.

Don Quixote said to him: "Sancho, my friend, night is coming on and we shall be unable to reach El Toboso by daylight, for there I am determined to go before I undertake any other adventure and there I shall receive the blessing and the kind permission of the peerless Dulcinea. When she gives it to me, I feel sure that I shall bring to a fortunate conclusion every perilous enterprise, for nothing in this life makes knights-errant more valiant than finding themselves favored by their ladies."

"So I believe," replied Sancho, "but I think it will be difficult for your worship to speak with her or see her, much less to receive her blessing, unless she flings it over the wall of the stable yard where I saw her the first time when I took the letter that told the news of the mad follies your worship was doing in the Sierra Morena."

"Did you really think those were stable-yard walls, Sancho," said Don Quixote, "where you saw that never-sufficiently-celebrated grace and beauty? They must have been the galleries, corridors, or porticoes, or whatever they call them, of some rich and royal palace."

"That may be so," answered Sancho, "but to my eyes they looked like mud walls, unless, of course, my memory cheats me."

"In any case, let us go there, Sancho," answered Don Quixote. "Provided I see her, it is the same to me whether it be over a wall, at a window, or through the chinks and gaps in a garden fence, for any beam from the sun of her beauty that reaches my eyes will light up my understanding and strengthen my heart so that I shall be supreme and unequaled in wisdom and valor."

"To tell you the truth, master," said Sancho, "when I saw the sun of Lady Dulcinea of El Toboso, it was not bright enough to throw out beams. This must have been because her worship was winnowing that wheat I spoke to you about, and the heap of dust she raised clouded her face and darkened it."

"What! Do you still insist," cried Don Quixote, "on believing and maintaining that my lady, Dulcinea, was winnowing wheat—a task and occupation utterly at variance with what is done by ladies of rank, who are reserved for other pursuits that will display, a bow shot away, their refinement and quality? You fail to remember, O Sancho, the lines of our poet in which he paints for us the labors of the four nymphs in their crystal dwellings, who rose from their beloved Tagus and seated themselves upon the verdant meadow to embroider those rich stuffs that the ingenious poet describes as woven and interwoven with gold, silk, and pearls.[1] In like manner must my lady have been busied

[1] A reference to Garcilaso de la Vega's *Third Eclogue* 1, 53 sq.

when you saw her, only that the envy that some wicked enchanter bears against me transforms all things that give me pleasure into shapes different from their own. For this reason, if the history of my deeds, which they say is now in print, was written by some wise man who was an enemy of mine, I am afraid he may have mingled a thousand lies with one truth and turned aside to relate idle tales that have nothing to do with the course of truthful history. O envy, root of countless evils and cankerworm of the virtues! All the vices, Sancho, bring certain pleasures with them, but envy brings nothing but discord, rancor, and rage."

"That is what I say, too," answered Sancho, "and I suspect that in that legend or history, which the bachelor told us he had seen about us, my reputation goes all topsy-turvy, jolting up and down, here and there, helter-skelter, sweeping the streets, as the saying goes. Nevertheless, on the faith of an honest man, I never said a bitter word about any enchanter, nor am I well off enough to be envied. To tell you the truth, I am a bit roguish and I've a streak of malice in me, but it is all covered by the broad cloak of my simplicity, which is always natural and never put on. Why, if I'd nothing else to my credit but my believing as I do believe firmly and truly, in God and the Holy Catholic Roman Church and my being a mortal enemy of the Jews, as I am, the historians ought to have mercy on me and treat me well in their writings. Well, let them have their say, for naked I was born, naked I am, I neither lose nor win; and if I do find myself put into books and bandied about all over the world, I don't care a fig. Let them say what they like about me."

"That reminds me, Sancho," said Don Quixote, "of what happened to a famous poet of these days who, having written a malicious satire against all courtesans, failed to mention in it the name of a particular lady, because there was some doubt whether she was or not. And when she saw that she was not on the list, she complained to the poet, asking what fault he had discovered in her that caused him to omit her, and insisting that he should expand his satire and put her in the sequel, or take the consequences. The poet accordingly did so, and with duennalike malice he left her without a shred of reputation. And she was gratified to see herself infamously famous. There is also the story they tell of the shepherd who set fire and burned down the celebrated temple of Diana, considered one of the seven wonders of the

world, simply in order that his name might be remembered
for centuries to come; although it was forbidden to speak of
him, or even to mention his name by word of mouth or in
writing, so that his ambition might not be fulfilled, it is
nevertheless known that he was called Erostratus.

"A similar thing happened in the case of the great emperor
Charles V and a certain gentleman in Rome. The emperor
wished to see the Rotunda, a famous temple that in ancient
days was called the Temple of All the Gods and today is
more appropriately named All Saints'.[2] Of all the pagan
buildings in Rome this is the one that preserves most completely the grandeur and majesty of those who built it. It is
constructed in the shape of half an orange and is very large
and well lighted, although the only illumination comes
through one window, or rather a round skylight at the top.
It was from this point of vantage that the emperor gazed
down on the building. By his side stood a Roman gentleman
who explained to him all the beauties and fine points of the
vast and intricate architecture of the famous edifice. After
they had descended from the skylight, the gentleman turned
to the emperor and said: 'A thousand times, Your Sacred
Majesty, I longed to clasp Your Majesty and throw myself
down from that skylight so that I might win for myself
eternal fame in the world.'

"'I thank you,' the emperor replied, 'for not having
yielded to so evil an impulse. But henceforth I shall see to
it that you have no further opportunity to put your loyalty
to the test, and so I command you never to speak to me or
to appear where I am.' And with these words he gave him a
handsome present.

"What I mean to say, Sancho, is that the desire of winning
fame is a powerful incentive. What was it, do you think, that
drove Horatius, clad in full armor, to cast himself down from
the bridge into the depths of the Tiber? What burned
Mutius' arm and hand? What impelled Curtius to hurl himself into the deep abyss that yawned in the middle of Rome?
What was it that made Julius Caesar cross the Rubicon, in
spite of all the omens that had warned him against it? And

[2] Charles V visited Rome, according to his biographer Fray
Prudencio de Sandoval (1536), "in disguise, so as to be better
able to appreciate its ancient grandeur." The temple is the
Pantheon, which today is not called All Saints' but Santa María
della Rotonda.

to come down to more modern times, what scuttled the ships and left the valiant Spaniards, led by the most courteous Cortes, isolated in the New World? [3] These and many other great deeds of various kinds are, were, and shall continue to be a manifestation of that love of fame that mortal men desire to win by notable exploits as their share of immortality. We, Christian and Catholic knights-errant, on the other hand, have more to hope from the glory that in future ages we shall enjoy in the ethereal and celestial regions than from the vanity of fame that is to be achieved in this present finite time, for however long such fame may endure it must finally end with the world itself, which has its fixed term. And so, Sancho, our deeds must not transgress those limits laid down for us by the Christian religion that we profess. We must slay pride by killing giants, envy by our generous and noble bearing, anger by our calm behavior and equanimity, gluttony and drowsiness by fasting and long vigil, self-indulgence and lust by steadfast loyalty to those whom we have made the mistresses of our heart, and sloth by roaming everywhere in the world in quest of opportunities of becoming famous knights as well as Christians. Such, Sancho, are the means by which we must win the highest praise that fame bestows."

"All that your worship has said to me so far," said Sancho, "I've understood very well, but I wish you could rarefy one doubt that has just occurred to me."

"*Clarify* is what you mean to say Sancho," replied Don Quixote. "Speak out, for I will try to answer you as best I can."

"Tell me, sir," continued Sancho, "those Julys or Augusts, and all those knights you mentioned who were always doing deeds and who are dead, where are they now?"

"The heathen ones," said Don Quixote, "are no doubt in Hell. The Christians, if they were good Christians, are either in purgatory or in Heaven."

"That's all right," said Sancho; "but now tell me this. Those tombs where the bodies of the great lords lie, have

---

[3] Hernán Cortes was called by his contemporaries *el hijo de la cortesía* (the son of courtesy). He scuttled his ship at the beginning of the conquest of Mexico, in order to kill in his followers all desire of returning to Spain and to show them that there was no other alternative to conquest.

they silver lamps in front of them, or are the walls of their chapels adorned with crutches, shrouds, locks of hair, legs, and eyes made of wax? Or if not, what kind of decorations do they have?"

"The tombs of the heathens," answered Don Quixote, "were mostly sumptuous temples. Julius Caesar's ashes, for example, were placed upon a stone pyramid of huge size, which in the Rome of today is known as St. Peter's Needle. Emperor Hadrian's burial place was a castle as big as a fair-sized town and was called the Moles Hadriani, which is now the Castle San Angelo at Rome. Queen Artemisia buried her husband, Mausolus, in a tomb that was reckoned one of the seven wonders of the world. But none of these tombs nor those many others that the pagans built were adorned with shrouds nor with any other offerings and tokens to show that those buried in them were saints."

"I'm coming to that," said Sancho. "Tell me now, which is the greater thing: to bring a dead man to life or to kill a giant?"

"The answer is obvious," replied Don Quixote. "To bring the dead to life, of course."

"Ah," said Sancho, "that is where I've caught you. Then, the fame of those who resurrect the dead, who give sight to the blind, who heal cripples and bring health to the sick, who have lamps burning in front of their tombs, and whose chapels are thronged with devout people kneeling and adorning their relics will be a better one in this life and in the next than the fame of all the heathen emperors and knights-errant in all the world."

"I'll grant you that one also," replied Don Quixote.

"Well then," continued Sancho, "as this fame, the favors, these privileges, or whatever you call them, belong to the bodies and relics of the saints, who with the approval and permission of Our Holy Mother the Church, have lamps, candles, shrouds, crutches, paintings, locks of hair, eyes, legs, to spread their Christian fame abroad. Kings carry the bodies or relics of the saints on their shoulders, kiss the pieces of their bones, and decorate and enrich the chapels and their favorite altars with them."

"What do you mean to infer, Sancho, from all that you have said?" asked Don Quixote.

"I mean to say," replied Sancho, "that we might set about becoming saints. Then we shall get the good name we're after all the sooner. You may remember, sir, that yesterday or the day before—it was so recently that we may say this—they canonized or beatified two little barefoot friars, and now people think it very lucky to kiss and touch the iron chains with which they girt and tormented their bodies. Those chains, they say, are held in greater veneration than Orlando's sword in the armory of the king, God bless him. So, dear master, it's better to be a humble little friar of any order you like than a valiant knight-errant. A couple of dozen lashings will carry more weight with God than a couple of thousand lance thrusts, whether they be given to giants, dragons, or other monsters."

"I agree with all that," said Don Quixote, "but we cannot all be friars and there are many paths by which God takes his own to Heaven. Chivalry is a religion, and there are sainted knights in His glory."

"Yes," replied Sancho, "but I have heard it said that there are more friars than knights-errant in Heaven."

"That," replied Don Quixote, "is because the number of the religious is greater than the number of knights."

"There are plenty of errant ones," said Sancho.

"Many," answered Don Quixote, "but few are those who deserve the names of knights."

In these and similar discussions they spent that night and the following day, without encountering anything worth noting, much to Don Quixote's mortification; but at last, the next day at nightfall, they came in view of the great city of El Toboso, at the sight of which Don Quixote's spirits rose and Sancho's sank, for he did not know Dulcinea's house, nor in all his life had he ever seen her, any more than his master. Thus they were both anxious—one to see her, and the other because he had not seen her—and Sancho could not imagine what he would do when his master sent him into El Toboso. At last, Don Quixote made up his mind to enter the city when night had fallen, and they waited among some oak trees near the city. When the time finally came, they entered the city, where many things did indeed happen to them.

CHAPTER IX

In which is told what therein shall be seen

It was on the stroke of midnight, a little more or less, when the knight and his squire left the wood and entered El Toboso. The town lay in deep silence, for all the inhabitants were asleep, resting at full length, as the saying goes. The night was fairly clear, though Sancho wished it had been quite dark so that he might find in the darkness an excuse for his folly. Not a sound was heard all over the town but the barking of dogs, which deafened Don Quixote's ears and disturbed the heart of Sancho. Now and then an ass brayed, pigs grunted, cats meowed, and the various noises grew in intensity in the stillness of the night. All this the enamored knight regarded as an evil omen. Nevertheless, he said to Sancho: "Sancho, my son, lead on to the palace of Dulcinea, perchance we may find her awake."

"Body of the sun, what palace am I to lead on to," answered Sancho, "when the one I saw her highness in was only a tiny house?"

"She must have retired then," said Don Quixote, "to some little apartment of her palace to enjoy herself with her damsels, as is customary among great ladies and princesses."

"Sir," said Sancho, "if your worship insists, in spite of me, that Lady Dulcinea's house is a castle, is this an hour, think you, to find the door open? And is it fitting for us to be knocking till they hear us and open the door, thus putting the whole household in an uproar and confusion? Do you think that we are visiting the houses of our wenches like rakes who come and knock and enter at any hour, no matter how late it is?"

"Let us first make sure of finding the palace," answered Don Quixote, "and then I will tell you what it is right for us to do. But look, Sancho, either my eyesight is bad, or that great dark mass of shadows that can be seen from here should be caused by Dulcinea's palace."

"Let your worship lead the way," said Sancho, "perhaps it may be so; though I see it with my eyes and touch it with my ends, I'd believe it as much as I believe it's now daylight."

Don Quixote led the way, and after advancing about two hundred paces, he came upon the mass that caused the shadow, and found that it was a great tower. He then knew that the building was no castle, but the principal church of the village. So he said: "It is the church we have lighted upon, Sancho."

"So I see," replied Sancho. "God grant that we may not light upon our graves, for it's not a good sign to find oneself gadding about in a graveyard at this time of the night, and what's more, I told your worship, if I remember right, that this lady's house is in a blind alley."

"May God curse you, blockhead!" cried Don Quixote. "Where have you have found castles and royal palaces built in blind alleys?"

"Sir," answered Sancho, "every land has its customs. Perhaps it is usual here in El Toboso to build palaces and grand houses in blind alleys. I beg you, therefore, to let me have a look about these streets and alleys here; perhaps in some corner or other I may butt into this palace, and may I see the dogs devouring it for dragging us into this goose chase!"

"Speak respectfully, Sancho, of the affairs of my lady," said Don Quixote; "let us keep our feast in peace, and not throw the rope into the well after the bucket."

"I'll keep my peace," answered Sancho, "but how can I have the patience to listen to your worship saying that you want me, after only one glimpse of my lady's house, to recognize it always and to find it in the middle of the night, when you yourself can't find it, though you must have seen it thousands of times?"

"You will drive me to despair, Sancho," said Don Quixote. "Look here, you heretic; have I not told you a thousand times that never once in my life have I seen the peerless Dulcinea, nor have I ever crossed the threshold of her palace? I am enamored only by hearsay and owing to the great reputation she possesses for beauty and wit."

"I agree now," answered Sancho, "and I'll add that if you've never seen her, neither have I."

"That cannot be," replied Don Quixote, "for you yourself told me that you saw her winnowing wheat when you brought back an answer to the letter that I sent by you."

"Don't worry about that, master," said Sancho. "I must tell you that my glimpse of her and the answer I brought you back were by hearsay too. I can no more tell who Lady Dulcinea is than I can punch the sky above."

"Sancho, Sancho," said Don Quixote, "there are times for joking and times when jokes are out of place. If I say that I have neither seen nor spoken to the lady of my soul, there is no reason why you should say that you have not spoken to her or seen her, when you know that the opposite is true."

While the two were thus conversing, they saw a man with a pair of mules approaching, and from the noise the plow made as it was dragged along, they judged him to be a laborer who had risen before dawn to go to his work. Such was the case. The laborer came along singing the ballad that says:

> " 'Twas an evil day befell the men of France
>   In the chase of Roncesvalles." [1]

"May I be slain, Sancho," cried Don Quixote, when he heard the words, "if any good will come to us this night. Do you hear what he is singing?"

"Yes, I do," said Sancho, "but what has the chase of Roncesvalles to do with what we have to do? It would be no different if it was the ballad of Calaínos."

When the laborer came up, Don Quixote asked him: "Can you tell me, good friend, and may God speed you, where is the palace of the peerless princess Doña Dulcinea of El Toboso?"

"Sir," replied the fellow, "I'm a stranger here myself and I have been only a few days in the village doing a bit of farm work for a rich farmer. In that house opposite, the curate and the sacristan live, and both or either of them will give your worship an account of this princess, for they have a list of all the folk of El Toboso. All the same, I don't believe there's a single princess in the length and breadth of

---

[1] The beginning of a ballad of the Carolingian cycle: *Mala la hubistes, franceses, en esa de Roncesvalles.*

the village. There are many ladies, sure enough, and of quality, too, and each one of them may well be a princess in her own house."

"Then, my friend, the lady I am seeking must be one of those," said Don Quixote.

"That may be," answered the laborer. "God be with you, for here comes the daylight." Without waiting to hear any more questions, he whipped his mules and moved on.

Sancho, seeing that his master was perplexed and somewhat dissatisfied, said to him: "Master, the day will be soon upon us, and it will not be wise for the sun to find us in the street. It will be better for us to leave the city and for your worship to hide in some neighboring wood, and I'll return by day and search in every corner for the house, castle, or palace of my lady. I'll be mighty unlucky if I don't find it, and as soon as I have found it, I'll speak to her ladyship and tell her where your worship is waiting for her directions as to how you may visit her without any damage to her honor and reputation."

"Sancho," replied Don Quixote, "you have uttered a thousand words of wisdom in a few brief sentences. I willingly accept the advice you have given me. Come on, son, let us look for a place where I may hide, while you return to see and speak with my lady, from whose discretion and courtesy I expect not only favors but even miracles."

Sancho was in a fever to get his master out of the village, lest the latter discover the lie about the answer that he had brought to him in the Sierra Morena on Dulcinea's behalf, so he hastened their departure, and two miles from the village they found a grove in which Don Quixote hid himself while Sancho returned to the city to speak with Dulcinea. On that mission things happened to him that demand renewed attention and power of belief.

CHAPTER X

In which is related the device that Sancho adopted to enchant Lady Dulcinea, and other incidents as absurd as they are true

When the author of this great history comes to relate the events of this chapter, he says that he would have liked to pass them over in silence, through fear of not being believed, for the delusions of Don Quixote here reach the greatest heights and limits imaginable, and even exceed those, great as they are, by two bow shots. However, he wrote them down finally, although not without fear and misgiving, just as they occurred, without adding or subtracting one atom of the truth from the history, or heeding any objection that might be brought against him as a liar. And he was right, for truth, though it may run thin, never breaks, and it always flows over the lie as oil over water. And so, continuing his story he says that as soon as Don Quixote had hidden himself in the thicket, oak wood, or grove near great El Toboso, he bade Sancho to go back to the city and not to return to his presence without first speaking to his lady on his behalf, begging her to be so good as to allow herself to be seen by her captive knight and to deign to bestow her blessing on him so that he might hope to win the highest success in all his arduous enterprises. Sancho agreed to do as he ordered and to bring his master as good an answer as he had on the first occasion.

"Go, my son," said Don Quixote, "and do not let yourself be dazzled when you find yourself before the light of the sun of beauty you are going to seek. Fortunate you are above all the squires in the world! Bear in your mind and do not let it escape you: how she receives you; whether she changes color while you are giving her my message;

whether she is restless or troubled when she hears my name; whether she moves from her cushion if you by chance should find her seated on the rich dais of her authority, and if she is standing, observe whether she rests now on one foot, now on the other; whether she repeats her answer to you two or three times; whether she changes from soft to harsh, from bitter to affectionate; whether she raises her hand to her hair to smooth it, although it is not untidy. In a word, my son, watch all her actions and movements, for if you describe them to me as they were, I shall ascertain what she keeps stored in the recesses of her heart and discover how my love is prospering. For I want you to know, Sancho, if you do not know already, that between lovers the outward actions and movements they display when their loves are discussed are the surest messengers that carry news of what is taking place in their innermost souls. Go, friend, and may better fortune than mine guide you and send you better success than I expect, as I hover between fear and hope in this bitter solitude where you leave me."

"I'll go and come back in a flash," said Sancho. "Cheer up that little heart of yours, dear master, which this very moment must be no bigger than a hazelnut. Remember the saying that 'A stout heart breaks bad luck,' and 'When there are no flitches, there are no hooks'; and they say, too, 'When you're least aware, out jumps the hare.' I say this because though last night we didn't find the palaces or castles of my lady, now that it's day, I'm hoping to find them where I least expect. And once they're found, leave me to deal with her."

"Well, Sancho, your proverbs are so felicitous and so relevant to our present business that I hope God will send me as much good luck in my desires."

At these words Sancho turned away, gave Dapple the stick, and set off, leaving Don Quixote behind, seated on his horse, resting in his stirrups, and leaning on his lance, filled with sad and troubled fancies. There we shall leave him while we follow Sancho Panza, who took leave of his master in no less anxious and meditative a frame of mind, so much so, indeed, that as soon as he had left the grove, he looked around, and seeing that Don Quixote was out of sight, he dismounted from the ass and sat down at the foot of a tree, where he began to converse with himself, saying: "Now, tell us, brother Sancho, where your worship is going. Are you

in search of some ass you've lost? Not at all. Then, what
are you looking for? I'm looking for a mere nothing, a
princess, and in her for the sun of beauty and the whole
sky together. And where do you expect to find what you
mention, Sancho? Where? In the great city of El Toboso.
Very well, and on whose behalf are you going to look for
her? For the famous knight Don Quixote of La Mancha,
who rights wrongs, gives food to them who are hungry and
drink to them who are thirsty. That's all very well, but do
you know her house, Sancho? My master says it must be
some royal castle or magnificent palace. And have you caught
a stray glimpse of her? Neither I nor my master ever saw
her. And do you think it would be fair and proper if the
people of El Toboso, once they found that you were here
with the intention of snaffling their princesses and meddling
with their ladies, were to come and batter your ribs with
cudgels and leave not a whole bone in your body? Indeed,
they would be perfectly in their rights if they refused to
admit that I am under orders, and that:

> " 'A messenger, my friend, thou be,
>   No penalty may fall on thee.'

"Don't you put your trust in that, Sancho, for the Manchegan folk are as hotheaded as they are honest, and they
won't let a soul touch them on the raw. By God, if they
smell your purpose, you're in for a bad time, I tell you.
To hell with it, you whoreson rogue! Let the bolt fall on
someone else! Not at all, I am not going looking for a cat
with three feet to please another, for when all's said and
done, tracking Dulcinea up and down El Toboso will be as
bad as looking for a needle in a haystack or for a scholar
in Salamanca. The Devil, the Devil has landed me into
this and no one else!"

Such was the conversation Sancho held with himself, and
the only result of it was that he continued the conversation as follows: "Well, there's a cure for everything except
death, under whose yoke we all have to pass, whether we
like it or not, when our time is up. I've seen by a thousand
signs that this master of mine is a madman and fit to be
tied, and as for myself, I follow him and serve him since I'm
not far behind him if there is a word of truth in the proverb
that says: 'Tell me the company you keep and I'll tell you

what you are,' and the other: 'Not with whom you are bred,
but with whom you are fed.' Now if he is mad, as he truly
is, and if his madness is such that most of the time he
believes one thing to be another and says that white is
black and black is white, as was the case when he said the
windmills were giants, the friars' mules dromedaries, the
flocks of sheep armies of enemies, and many other things to
the same tune, it will not be very hard to make him believe
that the first peasant wench I come across here is Lady
Dulcinea. And if he doesn't believe it, I'll swear on oath,
and if he swears, I'll swear again; and if he persists, I'll
persist the more, and in this way, no matter what happens,
my word will always top the mark. Perhaps if I hold out in
this way, I shall put an end to his sending me on messages
of this kind another time. On the other hand, perhaps he
will think, as I imagine he will, that one of the wicked
enchanters who, he says, have a grudge against him has
changed her shape to do him an injury."

With these thoughts Sancho lulled his conscience and considered his business as good as settled. He stayed there until
the afternoon, so as to make Don Quixote think that enough
time had elapsed for him to have gone to El Toboso and back.
And all turned out so luckily for him that when he rose to
mount Dapple, he saw three peasant girls coming from
El Toboso toward him, mounted on three ass-colts or fillies—
our author, incidentally, does not tell us which, though it is
more probable that they were she-asses, as these were the
usual mounts of village women. However, as this is neither
here nor there, there is no need to stop and verify the
detail. In short, no sooner did Sancho see the girls than he
rode back at a canter to look for his master, Don Quixote,
and found him sighing and uttering a thousand amorous
lamentations.

When Don Quixote saw him, he said: "What news, friend
Sancho? Am I to mark this day with a white stone or a
black one?"

"Your worship," replied Sancho, "had better mark it with
red ocher as they do the names on the professors' chairs [1]
so that the lookers-on may read them clearly."

---

[1] This is a reference to those who had received the degree of
doctor in Spanish universities. Their names were painted on the
walls in red.

"So, you bring good news," said Don Quixote.

"So good," answered Sancho, "that your worship has nothing to do but clap spurs to Rozinante and ride out into the open country. There you'll see Lady Dulcinea, who, with two of her damsels, is coming to visit your worship."

"Holy God! What are you saying, Sancho, my friend?" said Don Quixote. "Mind you do not deceive me and try to beguile my real sadness with false joys."

"What advantage would I get by deceiving your worship," answered Sancho, "especially when my truth is about to unfold itself? Spur on, master, and you'll see the princess, our mistress, coming robed and adorned, in fact, like herself. Her ladies and she are all one shimmer of gold, all clusters of pearls, all diamonds, all rubies, all brocade of more than ten folds; their hair flowing down their shoulders like so many sunbeams playing with the wind; and above all, they're coming along mounted on three piebald nackneys, the finest you'd see anywhere."

"*Hackneys,* you mean to say, Sancho," said Don Quixote.

"Well," said Sancho, "hackneys and nackneys are much the same. But let them come as they will; there they are, the finest ladies you could wish for, especially my lady, the Princess Dulcinea, who dazzles one's senses."

"Let us go, Sancho, my son," replied Don Quixote, "and as a reward for bringing me these tidings, which are as welcome as unexpected, you may have the best of the spoils of my next adventure. If this is not enough, I'll bequeath you the fillies I shall get from my three mares, which, as you know, are in foal on our town common."

"I'll stick to the foals," replied Sancho, "for I'm not so sure that the spoils of the first adventure will be good ones."

By this time they had come out of the wood and saw the three village lasses close at hand. Don Quixote gazed along the road toward El Toboso, and seeing nobody but the three peasant girls, he was all disturbed and asked Sancho whether he had left them outside the city.

"Outside the city?" answered Sancho. "Are your worship's eyes in the back of your head that you can't see them coming along toward us, and there she is shining like the sun itself at noon?"

"I see nothing, Sancho," said Don Quixote, "but three peasant girls on three asses."

"God save me from the Devil," replied Sancho. "Is it possible that your worship mistakes three hackneys, or whatever they're called, which are as white as driven snow, for asses? By the Lord, I'd pluck my beard out by the roots if that were the case."

"Well, I must say, Sancho, my friend," said Don Quixote, "that they are as truly jackasses or jennies as I am Don Quixote and you Sancho Panza; at least, that is how they appear to me."

"Silence, master!" exclaimed Sancho. "Don't say that, but skin your eyes and come and do homage to the lady of your thoughts, who is now close at hand."

With these words he rode on to welcome the three village lasses, and dismounting from Dapple, he caught hold of one of the asses of the girls by the halter, and sinking on both knees to the ground, he said: "Queen and princess and duchess of beauty, may it please your arrogance and greatness to receive into your favor and good disposition this captive knight of yours who is standing there turned into marble stone, all worried and unnerved at finding himself in the presence of your magnificence. I am Sancho Panza, his squire, and he is the much-wandered knight Don Quixote of La Mancha, otherwise called the Knight of the Rueful Figure."

Don Quixote had now sunk on his knees beside Sancho, and with eyes starting out of his head, he kept staring at her whom Sancho called queen and lady. As he saw in her nothing but a village lass, not even good-looking at that, for she was moon faced and snub nosed, he was perplexed and confounded, without even daring to open his lips. The girls, too, were thunderstruck at seeing those two men, so different in appearance, on their knees, trying to prevent their companion from passing on. She, however, who had been stopped, broke silence and exclaimed in a coarse, angry voice: "Get out of the way, bad 'cess to you, and let us pass, we're in a hurry."

To which Sancho replied: "O princess and universal lady of El Toboso, how comes it that your magnanimous heart is not softened by the sight of the pillar and support of knight-errantry on his knees before your sublimated presence?"

One of the others, when she heard these words, cried: "Whoa there, you! I'll currycomb you like my father-in-law's she-ass! Look how the bits of gentlemen try to make fun of us village girls, as if we weren't as good a hand at cracking

jokes as themselves. Be off on your way and let us be off
on ours; you'd better, I'm telling you."

"Get up, Sancho," said Don Quixote at this, "for I see
that Fortune, 'unsated with the evil she hath done me,' [2]
has seized possession of all the ways by which any comfort
could reach the wretched soul imprisoned in my fleshly body.
And thou, O loftiest perfection of all virtue that can be
desired, extremity of human courtesy, sole relief of this
afflicted heart that adores thee, now that a wicked enchanter persecutes me, bringing clouds and cataracts into my
eyes, transforming thy unequaled loveliness and changing thy
features into those of a poor laboring girl—who knows, too,
if he has not at the same time turned mine into those of
some monster to make them abominable in thy sight?—do
not refuse to look upon me with loving tenderness and consider that, by kneeling thus to thy deformed beauty, I am
giving the surest token of my soul's humble adoration of
thee."

"Come, come, tell it to my grandfather!" cried the girl.
"It's little I care for your saucy love palaver! Get out of the
way and let us go, and we'll be grateful."

Sancho drew aside to let her go, delighted at having so
successfully extricated himself from his intrigue. No sooner
did the girl who had acted Dulcinea find herself free than
she pricked her *nackney* with a spike she had at the end of a
stick and started to gallop across the field. The ass, however,
feeling the point of the spike more acutely than usual, began
to curvet and caper in such a way that it flung Lady Dulcinea
to the ground. Don Quixote, seeing this, rushed over to raise
her up, while Sancho tightened up the packsaddle, which had
slipped under the ass's belly. When the saddle was fixed,
Don Quixote wished to lift his enchanted lady in his arms
and set her upon the ass, but drawing back a little, she
took a short run, and placing both hands on the ass's rump,
she sprang into the saddle lighter than a falcon and landed
astride like a man.

"Long live Roque!" cried Sancho. "Our lady is swifter
than a falcon and can teach the cleverest Cordoban or Mexi-
can how to mount in Moorish fashion. In one leap she
sprang over the crupper of the saddle, and without spurs she

---

[2] A quotation from the third eclogue of Cervantes' favorite
poet, Garcilaso de la Vega.

is making the hack race like a zebra. Why, the rest of her damsels are also all flying like the wind."

This was the truth, for as soon as they saw Dulcinea in the saddle, they all pricked on after her and dashed away at full speed, without looking behind them for more than half a league. Don Quixote gazed after them, and when they had disappeared, he turned to Sancho and said: "Sancho what do you think now? How enchanters must loathe me! See how far their spite and hatred go when they try to deprive me of the happiness of seeing my lady in her own proper form. Truly was I born to be an example of misfortune and a target at which the arrows of adversity are aimed. Notice, too, Sancho, that those traitors were not satisfied merely to change and transform my Dulcinea, but they changed and transformed her into a shape as low and ugly as that of that village girl. And not content with that, they deprived her of something that is the property of ladies of quality, to wit, the fragrant perfume that always emanates from those who spend their lives amid sweet amber and flowers. For I must confess, Sancho, that when I approached to lift Dulcinea upon her hackney (as you say it was, though I thought it was a she-ass), she gave me such a whiff of raw garlic that my very soul reeked of the pestiferous odor."

"O vile, spiteful enchanters!" cried Sancho at this. "Would that I could see the lot of you strung by the gills like pilchards on a twig! You know much, you have the power to do much, but you do much more! It should have been enough for you, rogues, to have changed the pearls of my lady's eyes into cork galls, her hair of purest gold into the bristles of a red oxtail, and in short, all her features from good to bad, without interfering with her smell, for even by that alone we might have guessed what was hidden under that ugly skin, though to tell the honest truth, I never noticed her ugliness but only her beauty, which was enhanced in value by a mole that she had above her right lip, like a moustache, with seven or eight red hairs like threads of gold and more than a span in length."

"Now," said Don Quixote, "since the moles of the face always correspond to those of the body, Dulcinea must have another mole on the broad of her thigh corresponding to the side on which she has one on her face. All the same, hairs of such a length as you have mentioned are very long for moles."

"I surely can tell you, master, that they were there as plain as the day for the eye to see."

"I believe it, friend," answered Don Quixote, "for nature bestowed on Dulcinea nothing that was not perfect and well finished. Wherefore, if she had a hundred moles similar to the one you have described, they would not be moles but moons and glittering stars. But tell me, Sancho, about that packsaddle (for so it seemed to me when you were fixing it) was it a flat saddle or a sidesaddle?"

"It was nothing but," replied Sancho, "a jennet-saddle [3] with a field-covering of such value that it was worth half a kingdom."

"Again I say," cried Don Quixote, "and I shall say it a thousand times, that I am the most unfortunate man in the world not to have seen all this!"

The roguish Sancho had more than enough to do to hide his mirth at hearing the crazy ravings of his master, whom he had so nicely deceived. At last, after much further talk, they remounted their beasts and took the road to Saragossa, where they expected to arrive in time to be present at a solemn festival that is held annually in that illustrious city. But before they arrived there, things happened to them, so many, so important, and so novel that they deserve to be recorded and read, as will be seen further on.

[3] The *silla a la jineta* was a saddle adapted for ladies riding with high pommel, cantle, and short stirrups. However, in La Mancha today it is still the custom for women to ride astride.

CHAPTER XI

Of the strange adventure that befell the valorous Don Quixote with the cart or wagon of the Parliment of Death

Don Quixote went on his way mightily dejected, for he kept meditating on the cruel trick the enchanters had played upon him in changing Lady Dulcinea into the mean shape of a village girl, and he could not think of any method by which he might restore her to her original form. So absorbed was he in these reflections that without being aware of it, he loosened his hold on Rozinante's reins, who, noticing the liberty granted to him, stopped at every step to crop the fresh grass that abounded in that plain.

Sancho Panza roused him from his reverie by saying: "Master, sadness was made for men, not for beasts, but if men let themselves give way too much to it, they turn into beasts. Your worship must pull yourself together and be your old self again. Come, grip hold of Rozinante's reins, rouse yourself, and show that spirit that knights-errant ought to have. What the devil is all this? Are we here or in France? Let the Devil run away with all the Dulcineas in the world, for the health of a single knight-errant is worth more than all the enchantments and transmogrifications on earth."

"Hush, Sancho," said Don Quixote in a more hopeful tone, "hush, I repeat, and cease uttering blasphemies against that enchanted lady, for I alone am to blame for her misfortune and calamity. They spring from the envy the wicked bear against me."

"So say I," replied Sancho. "What heart, having seen her before, wouldn't weep to see her as you saw her now?"

597

"You may well say that, Sancho," replied Don Quixote, "for you saw her in all the glory of her loveliness, for the enchantment did not go so far as to disturb your eyesight or conceal her beauty from you. Against me alone and against my eyes is directed the power of their venom. Nevertheless, Sancho, one thing comes to my mind: you portrayed her beauty poorly, for if I remember rightly, you said she had eyes like pearls, and eyes that look like pearls are rather those of a sea bream than of a lady. In my belief Dulcinea's eyes must be green emeralds, large and full, with twin rainbows that serve her for eyebrows. As for those pearls, take them from her eyes and transfer them to her teeth, for I am sure, Sancho, you got them mixed up and took her teeth for her eyes."

"All's possible," answered Sancho, "for her beauty dumbfounded me as her ugliness did your worship. But let us leave it all in God's hands, for He knows what's happiness in this vale of tears, in this wicked world of ours, where there's scarcely anything to be found without its tinge of mischief, trickery, and rascality. But there's one thing, master, that has me more worried than all the rest: blessed if I know what we're to do when your worship conquers some giant or another knight and orders him to go and present himself before the loveliness of Lady Dulcinea. Where is he to find her, that poor giant or that poor wretched conquered knight? I fancy that I'm seeing them wandering all over El Toboso, gaping like half-wits, looking everywhere for Lady Dulcinea; and even if they meet her in the middle of the street, they won't recognize her any more than they would my father."

"Perhaps, Sancho," replied Don Quixote, "the enchantment will not extend so far as to deprive the vanquished and presented knights of the power of recognizing Dulcinea. In any case, we shall try the experiment whether they see her or not on one or two of the first ones I conquer and send to her, ordering them to return and give me a report of how they have fared in this matter."

"Your plan, sir," said Sancho, "seems a good one to me, for by this trick we shall find out what we want to know. If it proves that she is disguised only for your worship, the misfortunes will be more yours than hers, but provided that Lady Dulcinea is well and happy, we over here will get on as best we can, seeking our adventures and leaving

Time to shift for herself, for she's the best of all doctors for such and worse ailments."

Don Quixote was about to answer Sancho Panza, but he was prevented by a cart that passed across the road, laden with the strangest figures that could be imagined. He who drove the mules and acted as carter was a hideous demon. The cart was open to the sky, without wicker tilt or awning. The first figure that presented itself to Don Quixote's eyes was that of Death himself with a human face; next to him was an angel with large painted wings; at one side was an emperor with a crown, apparently, on his head; at the feet of Death was the god called Cupid, without the bandage over the eyes but with his bow, quiver, and arrows. There was also a knight armed cap-a-pie, except that he wore no morion or helmet but only a hat adorned with plumes of varied colors. With these there were others of different faces and costumes. At this unexpected encounter Don Quixote became somewhat disturbed, and Sancho was struck with terror. But on second thought Don Quixote rejoiced, for he believed that some new perilous adventure was at hand; so, under this impression and with the firm intention of facing any danger, he halted in front of the cart and cried in a loud threatening voice: "Carter, coachman, or devil, or whatever you are, be quick to tell me who you are, where you are going, and who are the people you are carrying in your coach, which resembles rather the boat of Charon than an ordinary cart."

To which the Devil, stopping the cart, answered courteously: "Sir, we are players of Angulo el Malo's [1] company; we have been acting the play, *The Parliament of Death*, this morning in a village behind that hill, seeing that it is the octave of Corpus Christi,[2] and we have to act it this evening

[1] Angulo el Malo was a well-known manager of a theatrical company in the days of Cervantes. He is referred to also in *The Dogs' Colloquy*. See *The Deceitful Marriage and Other Exemplary Novels* (Signet CT157), p. 304.

[2] Ever since the Middle Ages it was customary in Spain to perform on the feast of Corpus Christi short religious dramas called *autos sacramentales*. They were performed in the open streets on carts drawn by oxen. The most famous writer of these plays was Calderón, to whom Shelley bore tribute by his reference to the "starry *autos* of Calderón." The actors in Spain traveled from town to town in open carts as here described. The Church abolished *autos sacramentales* in 1765.

in that village that can be seen from here; and because it is so near at hand and to save ourselves the trouble of undressing and dressing again, we go in the costumes in which we play. That lad there goes as Death, the other as the Angel; that lady, who is the manager's wife, is the Queen; this man plays a soldier; that one the Emperor, and I am the Devil, one of the leading characters, for I always have leading parts in this company. If there's something else you wish to know about us, ask me, and I'll know how to answer to the point, for since I'm the Devil, I'm up to everything."

"By the faith of a knight-errant," answered Don Quixote, "when I saw the cart, I imagined that some great adventure was at hand, but I do declare that one must touch with the hand what appears to the eye, if one would be undeceived. God speed you, good people, and carry on your festival. Remember, if there is anything in which I may be useful to you, I will do it willingly, for from childhood I have always been fond of the masquerade, and in my youth I had a craving for the stage."

While they were talking, Fortune willed that one of the company who was clad in motley, with a great number of bells, and bearing on the end of a stick three ox bladders fully blown, came up to them. This clown, then, sidling up to Don Quixote, began twirling his stick and banging the ground with his bladders and capering with shrill jingling of bells. At the sight of this weird apparition Rozinante began to shy so violently that Don Quixote was unable to hold him in, and taking the bit between his teeth, the horse set off at a canter across the plain with greater speed than the bones of his anatomy ever gave promise of. Sancho, thinking that his master was in imminent danger of being thrown, jumped off his Dapple and ran in haste to help him, but by the time he reached him, he was already stretched on the ground and Rozinante was lying beside him, for he had fallen with his master—the usual end of his frisky exploits.

And no sooner had Sancho left his beast to go to the help of Don Quixote than the impish dancer with the bladders leaped upon the ass, and buffeting him with them, the fear and the clatter, more than the smart of the blows, made him fly across the country toward the village where they were going to hold their festival. Sancho saw the flight of Dapple and the fall of his master, and he did not know which of the two disasters he should attend to first; but in

the end, like a good squire and a good servant, he let his
love for his master prevail over his affection for his ass,
though every time he saw the bladders rise in the air and
fall upon the hindquarters of his ass he felt the grippings
and terrors of death, and he would rather have had those
blows fall upon the apple of his own eyes than upon the least
hair of Dapple's tail. In such turmoil and perplexity he came
to where Don Quixote lay in a sadder plight than he would
have wished. After helping him to mount Rozinante, he said:
"Sir, the Devil has carried off Dapple."

"What devil?" asked Don Quixote.

"The one with the bladders," answered Sancho.

"Then I will get him back," said Don Quixote, "even if
he were shut up with him in the deepest and darkest
dungeons of hell. Follow me, Sancho, for the cart goes
slowly, and I will take the mules as payment for the loss of
Dapple."

"There's no need to worry, master," said Sancho; "let you
keep your anger in check, for I see now that the Devil has
already let Dapple go, and he's going off to his haunts."

And so, indeed, it turned out, for the Devil, after falling
with the ass in imitation of Don Quixote and Rozinante,
set off on foot to the village, and the ass returned to his
master.

"Nevertheless," said Don Quixote, "it will be well to make
one of those in the cart pay for the Devil's discourtesies,
even if it were the emperor himself."

"Drive such a thought out of your mind, master," replied
Sancho. "Follow my advice and never meddle with actors, for
they're favored folk. I myself have seen an actor arrested for
for two murders, and yet get off scot-free. Remember that
because they're rollicking folk of pleasure, everyone favors
and protects them, and helps and treats them with consideration, especially when they are members of the royal companies and with a charter, for almost everyone of them
dresses and makes up as a prince."

"In spite of all that," said Don Quixote, "the player devil
is not going to go away boasting, even if the whole human
race favors him."

Saying this, he turned toward the cart, which was now
near the village, and shouted loudly as he rode: "Stay! Halt,
you merry, festive band! I want to teach you how to treat
asses and animals that serve the squires of knights-errant!"

So loud were the shouts of Don Quixote that the folk in the cart heard and understood the purpose of him who had uttered them. Death in a trice leaped from the cart, and after him the Emperor, the Devil carter and the Angel; nor did the Queen and the god Cupid lag behind. They all armed themselves with stones and drew themselves up in a line, ready to receive Don Quixote with the edges of their pebbles. Don Quixote, when he saw them drawn up in such a gallant squadron, with their arms raised ready to let fly a massive discharge of stones, reined in Rozinante and began to consider in what manner he could assail them with the least danger to his person. As he halted, Sancho came up, and seeing that he was about to attack such a well-drawn-up squadron, he said to him: "It would be raving madness to engage upon such an enterprise. Remember, dear master, that against 'gutter ammunition,' [3] aye, and there's plenty of it too, there is no defensive armor in the world unless you shut yourself up in a bronze bell; besides, you should remember that it is rash rather than brave for a single man to attack an army where Death takes part, and emperors fight in person, with good and wicked angels to lend a hand. And if this reflection will not make you keep quiet, perhaps you will do so when you know for certain that among all those people over there, though they look like kings, princes, and emperors, there's not one single knight-errant."

"Now, indeed," said Don Quixote, "you have hit the point that can and should turn me from my resolve. I cannot and should not draw my sword, as I have many a time told you, against one who is not dubbed a knight. It is for you, Sancho, if you care, to take vengeance for the injury that has been done to the ass, and I from here will help you by shouting out salutary advice."

"There is no reason to take vengeance on anybody," answered Sancho, "for a good Christian never takes it for wrongs; besides, I'll make my ass submit his wrong to my will, which is to live in peace as long as Heaven grants me life."

"Since that is your resolve," replied Don Quixote, "good Sancho, wise Sancho, Christian Sancho, honest Sancho, let us leave these phantoms alone and go off in search of worthier adventures, for I see that this country will not fail to provide us with many marvelous enterprises."

[3] Slang phrase for pebbles.

He then turned about; Sancho went to catch Dapple; Death and all his flying squadron returned to their cart and continued their journey. Thus the terrifying adventure of the cart of Death ended happily, thanks to the wise advice that Sancho Panza gave his master. And to the latter, next day, there came another adventure with a love-stricken knight-errant, no less exciting than the last.

CHAPTER XII

Of the strange adventure that befell the gallant Don Quixote with the brave Knight of the Mirrors

Don Quixote and his squire spent the night following their encounter with Death beneath some tall and shady trees, and the former, at Sancho's persuasion, partook of the food from the store carried by Dapple. While they were at supper, Sancho said to his master: "Sir, what a fool I should have been if I had chosen for my reward the spoils of the first adventure accomplished by your worship, instead of the foals of the three mares! Well, well, a sparrow in the hand is better than a vulture on the wing."

"Nevertheless, Sancho," replied Don Quixote, "if you had let me attack as I wished, the Empress' gold crown and Cupid's painted wings would have fallen to you as spoils, for I would have seized them by force and put them into your hands."

"The scepters and crowns of stage emperors," answered Sancho Panza, "are never made of real gold, but only of brass or tinfoil."

"That is true," said Don Quixote, "the ornaments of the drama should not be real, but only make-believe and fiction like the drama itself. Indeed, Sancho, I want you to turn a kindly eye upon the play and in consequence upon those who represent and compose it, for they are all productive of much good to the state, placing before us at every step a mirror in which we may see vividly portrayed the action of human life. Nothing, in fact, more truly portrays us as we are and as we would be than the play and the players.[1] Now tell me, have you never seen a play acted in which kings, emperors, pontiffs, knights, ladies, and divers other characters are introduced? One plays the bully, another the rogue; this one the merchant, that the soldier; one the wise fool, another the foolish lover. When the play is over and they have divested themselves of the dresses they wore in it, the actors are all again upon the same level."

"Yes, I've seen it," answered Sancho.

"Well, then," said Don Quixote, "the same happens in the comedy and life of this world, where some play emperors, others popes, and in short, all the parts that can be brought into a play; but when it is over, that is to say, when life ends, death strips them all of the robes that distinguished one from the other, and all are equal in the grave."

"A brave comparison!" said Sancho. "Though not so new, for I've heard it many a time, as well as that one about the game of chess: so long as the game lasts, each piece has its special office, and when the game is finished, they are all mixed, shuffled, and jumbled together and stored away in the bag, which is much like ending life in the grave."

"Each day, Sancho," said Don Quixote, "you are becoming less doltish and more wise."

"Yes, master, for some of your wisdom must stick to me," said Sancho, "just as land that is of itself barren and dry will eventually, by dint of dunging and tilling, come to yield a goodly crop. What I mean to say is that your worship's talk has been the dung that has fallen upon the barren soil of my poor wit and that the time during which I have served you and enjoyed your company has been the tillage. With the help of this I hope to yield fruit that are like blessings and such that will not slide away from the paths of good breeding that you have made in my shallow understanding."

---

[1] Compare Hamlet's speech to the players in Act 3, Sc. 2. "The purpose of playing, whose end, both at the first and now, was and is, to hold, as 'twere, the mirror up to nature; to show virtue her own feature, scorn her own image, and the very age and body of the time his form and pressure."

Don Quixote laughed at Sancho's affected style of speech and perceived that what he said about his improvement was true, for from time to time he spoke in a way that astonished him; though on most occasions when Sancho tried to talk in argument and in a lofty style, his speech would end by toppling down from the peak of his simplicity into the abyss of his ignorance. And where he showed his culture and his memory best was in his use of proverbs, no matter whether they came pat to the subject or not, as must have been seen already and noted in the course of this history.

In such a conversation they spent a great part of the night, but Sancho felt a wish to let down the hatches of his eyes, as he used to say when he wanted to sleep. So, having unharnessed Dapple, he left him free to crop the abundant pasture. He did not take the saddle off Rozinante, as his master's express orders were that as long as they were in the field or not sleeping under a roof, Rozinante was not to be unsaddled; it was, by the way, an ancient custom, established and observed by knights-errant, to take off the bridle and hang it on the saddlebow; but to remove the saddle from the horse—never on your life! Sancho observed this rule and gave him the same liberty he had given Dapple, whose friendship for Rozinante was so unequaled and so close that a tradition handed down from father to son says that the author of this true history wrote some chapters on the subject that, in order to preserve the propriety and decorum due to so heroic a history, he did not include. At times, however, he forgets this resolve and describes how, as soon as the two beasts were together, they would scratch one another, and how, when they were tired or satisfied, Rozinante would lay his neck across Dapple's more than half a yard beyond, and the pair would stand in that position, gazing thoughtfully at the ground, for three days, or at least, as long as they were left alone and hunger did not compel them to look for food.

It is said that the author left on record a comparison between their friendship and that of Nisus and Euryalus, and of Pylades and Orestes, and if this is true, it can be understood how steadfast must the friendship of these two animals have been to the wonder of the world and to the shame of humankind, who fail so lamentably to preserve friendship for one another.[2] Because of this it has been said:

> Friend to friend no more draws near,
> And the jouster's cane has become a spear.

And that other song that goes:

> Says friend to friend: "Here's mud in your eye!"

But let no one imagine that the author went off the tracks when he compared the friendship of these animals to that of men, for men have received many lessons from dumb beasts and learned many things of value, as for example: from storks the enema, from dogs vomiting and gratitude, from cranes watchfulness, from ants thrift, from elephants chastity, and loyalty from the horse.

At last, Sancho fell asleep at the foot of a cork tree, and Don Quixote dozed under a robust oak. But a short time had elapsed when a noise he heard behind awoke the latter, and standing up, he gazed in the direction the noise came from, and spied two men on horseback, one of whom, letting himself slip from the saddle, said to the other: "Dismount, friend, and take the bridles off the horses, for this spot seems to me both rich in grass for them and in silence and solitude for my love-sick thoughts."

Saying this, he stretched himself upon the ground, and as he flung himself down, the armor he wore clattered—a manifest proof by which Don Quixote knew him to be a knight-errant—and going over to Sancho, who was fast asleep, he pulled him by the arm, and after rousing him with no small difficulty, he said to him in a low voice: "Brother Sancho, we have an adventure."

"God send us a good one," said Sancho, "and where, master, may Mistress Adventure be?"

"Where, Sancho?" answered Don Quixote. "Turn your eyes and there you will see stretched a knight-errant, who, I believe, is not too happy, for I saw him fling himself off his horse and throw himself on the ground with signs of dejection, and as he fell, his armor clattered."

---

[2] Nisus and Euryalus were the two friends who accompanied Aeneas to Italy and perished in a night attack against the Rutulian camp. Orestes, the son of Agamemnon and Clytemnestra, after his father's death went to the court of the King of Phocis, where he formed a close friendship with Pylades, the latter's son.

"But how does your worship make out that this is an adventure?" said Sancho.

"I do not insist," answered Don Quixote, "that this is a full adventure, but it is the beginning of one, for this is the way adventures begin. But listen, for he seems to be tuning a viol or lute, and by the way he is spitting and clearing his throat, he must be preparing to sing something."

"Faith and so he is," answered Sancho. "He must be a love-sick knight."

"There is no knight-errant who is not," said Don Quixote. "Let us listen to him, for if he sings, by that thread we shall gain a clue to his thoughts, for the tongue speaks out of the abundance of the heart."

Sancho was about to reply to his master, but the voice of the Knight of the Wood, which was neither very bad nor very good, prevented him, and the two, listening attentively, heard the following sonnet:

> O cruel one, bestow on me
> Some token of your sovereign sway,
> Which I may follow earnestly,
> And never from its precepts stray.
> If you would have me fade away
> In silence, then account me dead,
> But if you'd hear my ancient lay,
> Then Love himself my cause shall plead.
> My soul to contraries inured
> Is made of wax and adamant,
> And well prepared for Cupid's law.
> Whether soft or hard my heart is yours,
> To grave it leave to you I'll grant,
> And to your will I'll bow with awe.

With a sigh that seemed to spring from the depths of his heart, the Knight of the Wood ended his song, and after a short pause he exclaimed in a sad and sorrowful voice: "O most beautiful and ungrateful woman in all the world! Is it possible, most serene Casildea of Vandalia, for thee to allow thy captive knight to be consumed and to perish in perpetual wandering and in harsh and unkind labors? Is it not enough that I have compelled all the knights of Navarra, of León, of Tartessus, Castile, and all the knights of La Mancha as well, to acknowledge thee to be the most beautiful lady in the world?"

"Not so," cried Don Quixote at this, "for I am of La Mancha, and I have acknowledged no such thing, nor could I, nor ought I, acknowledge anything so prejudicial to the beauty of my mistress. This knight, as you can see, Sancho, is raving. But let us listen; perhaps he will give himself away still more."

"That he will surely," answered Sancho, "for he seems the kind who'll go on mourning and groaning for a month on end."

This was not so, however, for the Knight of the Wood, overhearing voices nearby, proceeded no further with his lamentations, but sprang to his feet and called out in a loud but courteous voice: "Who goes there? Who are you? Are you by any chance one of the band of the happy or of the afflicted?"

"Of the afflicted," answered Don Quixote.

"Then come to me," replied the Knight of the Wood, "and you will come to the very fountainhead of sorrow and affliction."

Don Quixote, when he heard such gentle and courteous words, went over to him, and Sancho likewise. The melancholy knight then took Don Quixote by the arm and said: "Sit down here, sir knight. Now that I know that I have found you in this place, where solitude and the night dews, the natural couch and proper dwelling of knights-errant, keep you company, I need no further proof that you belong to their number."

To which Don Quixote answered: "I am a knight, and of the order you mention; and although sorrows, misfortunes, and disasters keep their abode in my soul, they have not scored away my compassion for the misfortunes of others. From what you were singing a moment ago I gathered that yours are amorous woes—I mean, of the love you have for that ungrateful beauty whom you named in your lament."

While this conversation was proceeding, they were seated side by side upon the hard sward, in peace and good company, not in the manner of men who at break of day would have to break one another's heads.

"Are you, sir knight, perchance, in love?" inquired the Knight of the Wood.

"To my woe, I am," answered Don Quixote, "though the sorrows arising from well-placed affections should be accounted blessings rather than calamities."

"That is true," replied he of the Wood, "provided disdain does not unbalance our reason and understanding, for if exaggerated, it resembles vengeance."

"I was never disdained by my lady," said Don Quixote.

"No, surely not," said Sancho, who stood close by, "my lady is as meek as a yearling ewe and softer than butter."

"Is this your squire?" asked he of the Wood.

"Yes, he is," said Don Quixote.

"This is the first time I have ever seen a squire," said he of the Wood, "who dared to speak while his master was speaking. Anyhow, there is mine over there, who is as tall as his father, and it cannot be proved that he has ever opened his lips when I was speaking."

"By my faith," said Sancho, "I have spoken and am fit to speak before one as great, and even— But let it be, it'll be worse to stir it about."

The squire of the Wood then took Sancho by the arm, saying: "Let us two go where we can talk squirelike together, and leave these gentlemen, our masters, to butt at each other, telling the story of their loves. I wager the day will find them at it without having settled anything."

"With all my heart," said Sancho, "and I'll tell your worship who I am so that you may judge whether I deserve to be counted among the number of most talkative squires."

The two squires then withdrew to one side, and a dialogue passed between them as droll as that of their masters was serious.

CHAPTER XIII

In which the adventure of the Knight of the Wood is continued, with the wise, novel, and agreeable conversation between the two squires

The knights and squires were separated, the latter telling the stories of their lives, the former of their loves; but the history tells first of the conversation between the servants, and then follows with that between their masters. And so, it relates that he of the Wood, when they had drawn a little aside, said to Sancho: "It's a wearisome life we lead, sir, those of us who are squires to knights-errant. We certainly eat our bread in the sweat of our brows, which is one of the curses God laid on our first parents."

"It may be said, too," added Sancho, "that we eat it in the chill of our bodies, for who suffers the heat and the cold worse than the wretched squires of knight-errantry? It wouldn't be so bad if we had something to eat, for sorrows are lighter when there's bread to eat, but there are times when we go a day or two without breaking our fast, unless it be on the wind that blows."

"All that can be put up with," said he of the Wood, "when we have hopes of a reward, for unless he serves an especially unlucky knight-errant, a squire is sure after a little time to find himself at least rewarded with a handsome government of some island or a tidy countship."

"I have told my master already," said Sancho, "that I'll be content with the government of some island, and he's so noble and generous that he has promised it to me many a time."

"As for me," said he of the Wood, "I'll be content with a canonry for my services, and my master has already assigned me one."

"Your master," said Sancho, "must then be a knight in the ecclesiastical line and can grant such favors to his good squire, but mine is only a layman, though I do remember some wise, but in my opinion, intriguing folks who tried to persuade him to have himself made archbishop. He, however, would be nothing but an emperor, and I was trembling all the time lest he should become bitten with the fancy of going into the Church, for I didn't consider myself suitable to hold offices in it. In fact, I may as well tell you that, though I look like a man, I'm just a beast as far as the Church is concerned."

"Ah! That's where you are wrong," said he of the Wood. "Those insular governorships are not all plain sailing. Some are twisted, some poor, some dreary, and in short, the loftiest and best regulated brings with it a heavy load of worry and trouble, which the unlucky wight to whose lot it has fallen bears upon his shoulders. Far better would it be for us who profess this plague-stricken service to return to our homes and there spend our days in more pleasant occupations, such as hunting and fishing, for where in the world would you find a squire so poor as not to have a hack, a couple of grey-hounds, and a fishing rod with which to while away the time in his own village?"

"I'm not short of any of these things," said Sancho. "It's true I've no hack, but I've an ass that is worth twice as much as my master's horse. God send me a bad Easter, and may it be the next one, if I would swap him, even if I got four bushels of barley to boot. You'll laugh at the value I'm putting on my Dapple, for dapple is the color of my ass. As for greyhounds, I'm in no want, for there are plenty of them in my home town, and surely the finest sport of all is where it's at other people's expense."

"Truly and earnestly, sir squire," said he of the Wood, "I've made up my mind to give up the drunken frolics of these knights of ours and go back to my village and bring up my children, for I've three like three oriental pearls."

"I've two," said Sancho, "fit to be presented to the Pope in person, especially a girl whom I'm rearing to be a countess, please God, though against her mother's wishes."

"And how old is this lady who is being brought up to be a countess?" inquired he of the Wood.

"Fifteen years, more or less," replied Sancho, "but she's as

tall as a lance and as fresh as an April morning and as
strong as a porter."

"Those qualities," said he of the Wood, "make her fit to
be not only a countess but a nymph of the greenwood. Ah,
the frisky whore! What spunk the jade must have!"

To this Sancho replied somewhat sulkily: "She's no whore,
nor was her mother, nor will either of them be, please God,
so long as I'm alive. And do keep a civiller tongue on you.
Considering that you've been reared among knights-errant,
who are the last word in courtesy, I don't think your language is becoming."

"Oh, how little you understand the language of compliments, sir squire," answered he of the Wood. "Do you mean
to tell me that you don't know that when a horseman lands
a good lance thrust at a bull in the square, or when anyone
does anything very well, the people are accustomed to say:
'How well the whoreson rogue has done it!' and what seems
to be insulting in the phrase is high praise? Come, sir, let
you disown the sons or daughters whose actions don't earn
their parents such compliments."

"Yes, I do disown them," answered Sancho, "and in the
same way you may heap the whole of whoredom straightaway on me, my wife, and my children, for all they do and
say is over and above deserving of like praise. And that I
may see them again, I pray God deliver me from mortal
sin, which is the same as delivering me from this dangerous
squire business into which I've fallen for the second time,
baited and bribed by a purse with a hundred ducats in it
that I found one day in the heart of the Sierra Morena.
And I tell you the Devil is always putting before my eyes,
here, there, and everywhere, a bag full of doubloons, which
I'm forever turning over with my hand and hugging it and
carrying it home with me to make investments and settle
rents and live like a prince. So long as I think of this, I
don't care a fig for all the toils I endure with this fool of a
master of mine, whom I know to be more of a madman
than a knight."

"Hence the common saying that 'covetousness bursts the
bag,'" said he of the Wood; "but if you mean to talk of
such men, let me tell you that there is no greater in the
world than my master, for he is one of those of whom it is
said: 'Care for his neighbor kills the ass,' for he makes a
madman of himself in order that another knight may recover

the wits he has lost, and he goes about looking for what, were he to find it, may, for all I know, hit him in the snout."

"Is he by any chance in love?" asked Sancho.

"He is," said he of the Wood, "with a certain Casildea of Vandalia, the rawest and most hard-boiled lady in the world, but it is not on the score of rawness that he limps, for he has other greater plans rumbling in his belly; you'll hear him speak of them before long."

"No matter how smooth the road, there's sure to be some rut or hollow in it," said Sancho. "In other houses they cook beans, but in mine it is by the potful; madness has always more followers and hangers-on than wisdom; but if the common saying is true, that 'to have a friend in grief gives some relief,' I may draw consolation from you, for your master is as crazy as mine."

"Crazy but valiant," answered he of the Wood, "and more roguish than crazy or valiant."

"Mine is not like that," replied Sancho. "I mean, he has nothing of the rogue in him. On the contrary, he has a soul as simple as a pitcher; he could do no harm to anyone, but good to all, nor has he any malice in him; why, a child would convince him it is night at noonday, and it is on account of this simplicity that I love him as I love the cockles of my heart, and I can't invent a way of leaving him, no matter what piece of foolishness he does."

"Nevertheless, brother and sir," said he of the Wood, "if the blind lead the blind, both are in danger of falling into the ditch. It is better for us to retire quickly and get back to our dens, for those who seek adventures don't always find good ones."

Sancho kept spitting from time to time, and as the charitable Squire of the Wood noticed that his spittle was gluey and somewhat dry, he said: "It seems to me that all this talk of ours has made our tongues stick to our palates, but I have a loosener, hanging from the saddlebow of my horse, which is quite good." And getting up, he came back a moment later with a large skin of wine and a pasty half a yard long, which is no exaggeration, for it was composed of a domestic rabbit so big that Sancho, as he held it, took it to be a goat, not to say a kid, and gazing at it, he said: "Is this what you carry along with you, sir?"

"What were you thinking then?" said the other. "Am I perchance some homespun, water-drinking squire? I carry better food supplies on my horse's crupper than a general does when he is on the march."

Sancho fell to, without any need of pressing. In the dark he gobbled lumps as large knots on a tether, observing as he ate: "You are indeed a trusty and a loyal squire, round and sound, grand and gorgeous, as is proved by this feast, which, if it has not come here by magic, seems like it at least; and not like me, poor devil, who am only carrying in my saddlebags a scrap of cheese so hard that you could brain a giant with it, and to keep it company, a few dozen carob pods and as many filberts and walnuts. Thanks to the poverty of my master and the idea he has and the rule he follows that knights-errant must not feed on anything except dried fruits and the herbs of the field."

"By my faith," replied he of the Wood, "my stomach is not made for thistles or wild pears from the woods. Let our masters keep to their opinions and laws of chivalry, and eat what is prescribed. As for me, I carry my meat baskets and this wineskin slung from my saddlebow, whether they like it or not, and I'm so devoted to her, aye, and so arrantly fond of her, that hardly a minute passes without my giving her a thousand kisses and hugs."

Saying this, he put the skin into Sancho's hands, who, raising it up, pressed it to his mouth and remained gazing at the stars for a quarter of an hour. When he had finished his drink, he let his head fall on one side, and heaving a deep sigh, he exclaimed: "Whoreson rogue, what a tip-top liquor it is!"

"There you are," said he of the Wood when he heard Sancho's exclamation. "See how you have praised my wine by calling it 'whoreson.'"

"Well," said Sancho, "I confess that I'm aware it's no dishonor to call somebody whoreson when we mean to praise him. Now tell me, sir, by the life you love best, is this Ciudad Real wine?"

"O peerless wine taster!" said he of the Wood. "From there and from nowhere else has it come, and it is a few years old, too."

"Trust me in that," said Sancho. "I knew I'd make a successful guess as to where it came from. Would you believe me, sir, when I tell you that I've such a great natural instinct in testing wines that no sooner do I smell one of them than I tell its country, its kind, its flavor and age, the changes it will undergo, and every detail concerning the wine. But you needn't wonder, for I've had in my family, on my father's side, the two finest wine tasters La Mancha has known for many a long year, and to prove what I'm saying, I'll tell you what happened to them. They were both given wine from a cask to try, and they were asked their opinion about its condition, quality, goodness or badness. One of them tested it with the tip of his tongue, the other did no more than hold it to his nose. The first said that the wine tasted of iron; the second that it had a flavor of cordovan leather. The owner declared that the cask was clean, and that the wine had no blending that could have imparted a taste of iron or leather. Notwithstanding this, the two famous wine tasters stuck to their point. Time went by, the wine was sold, and when the cask was cleaned, a small key was found in it hanging to a cordovan thong. Consider now whether one who comes of such a stock is able to give an opinion in such matters."

"Since that is so," said he of the Wood, "let us give up going in search of adventures; and since we have loaves, don't let us go looking for tarts, but return to our cots, for there God will find us if it be His will."

"I'll serve my master till he gets to Saragossa," said Sancho, "then maybe we'll come to an understanding."

Finally, the two worthy squires talked so much and drank so much that they had need of sleep to tie up their tongues and allay their thirst, for to quench it was impossible. And so the pair of them, clinging to the now nearly empty wineskin and with half-chewed morsels in their mouths, fell fast asleep; and there we will leave them for the present to relate what took place between the Knight of the Wood and him of the Rueful Figure.

CHAPTER XIV

In which the adventure of the Knight of the Wood is continued

Among the many speeches that passed between Don Quixote and the Knight of the Wood, our history tells us that the latter said to Don Quixote: "In a word, sir knight, I wish you to know that my destiny, or rather my choice, led me to become enamored of a certain lady, the peerless Casildea of Vandalia. I call her peerless, because she has no peer in bodily stature, rank, or beauty. This Lady Casildea repaid my honorable desires by forcing me, as his stepmother did Hercules, to engage in many perilous exploits, promising me at the end of each that, with the end of the next, I should obtain the object of all my hopes. But my labors have gone increasing link by link until they are past counting, nor do I know which is to be the one that will finally announce the accomplishment of my honorable wishes. On one occasion she ordered me to go and challenge that famous giantess of Seville known as the Giralda,[1] who is as valiant and strong as if made of brass, and though never stirring from one spot, is the most changeable and volatile woman in the world. I came, I saw, I conquered, and I made her keep still and on one point, for none but north winds blew for more than a week. On another occasion she made me go and

[1] This is the brass statue of Faith, fourteen feet in height, which was perched on the spire of the great tower of the Cathedral of Seville; it serves as a weathercock. The tower was erected by the Moors in the thirteenth century, and afterward was transformed into a belfry.

weigh the mighty Bulls of Guisando,[2] an enterprise that
should have been recommended to porters rather than to
knights. Another time she commanded me to fling myself
into the pit of Cabra,[3] an unheard-of peril, and bring her
back a detailed account of what is hidden in its abyss. I
stopped the motion of the Giralda; I weighed the Bulls of
Guisando; I descended into the pit and drew to the light of
day the secrets of its abyss; yet my hopes are as dead as
dead can be, and her orders and disdains as much alive
as ever. And now her last command is for me to go through
all provinces of Spain and compel all the knights-errant
wandering about to confess that she is the most beautiful
woman alive today and that I am the most valiant and the
most enamored knight on earth. In accordance with her
demand I have already traveled over the greater part of
Spain and have vanquished many knights who have had the
presumption to gainsay me. But my greatest pride and boast
is that I have conquered in single combat that so famous
knight Don Quixote of La Mancha, and made him confess
that my Casildea is more beautiful than his Dulcinea. By
this victory alone I consider that I have conquered all the
knights in the world, for the said Don Quixote has vanquished them all, and since I have vanquished him, his glory,
his fame, and his honor are forthwith transferred to my
person, and his innumerable exploits are now set down to
my account and have become mine."

Don Quixote was astounded to hear such words from the
Knight of the Wood, and he was a thousand times on the
point of telling him he lied and had the *you lie!* on the
tip of his tongue, but he restrained himself as best he could
in order to make him confess the lie out of his own mouth.
So, he said to him calmly: "I say nothing about your worship, sir knight, having vanquished most of the knights of
Spain, and even of the world, but I doubt that you have
conquered Don Quixote of La Mancha. Perhaps it may have
been some other knight who resembled him, though, indeed,
there are few like him."

"How! Not vanquished him?" said he of the Wood. "By

[2] The Bulls of Guisando are four rough granite figures of
animals in the district of Ávila.

[3] The pit of Cabra in the district of Córdoba is traditionally
supposed to be the shaft of an ancient mine.

Heaven above us, I fought Don Quixote and vanquished
him and overcame him. He is a man of tall stature, gaunt
features, lanky shriveled limbs; his hair is turning gray, his
nose is aquiline and a little hooked, and his moustaches are
long, black, and drooping. He goes into battle under the
name of the Knight of the Rueful Figure, and he has for
squire a peasant called Sancho Panza. He presses the back
and curbs the reins of a famous horse called Rozinante, and
finally, he has for mistress of his will a certain Dulcinea
of El Toboso, once upon a time known as Aldonza Lorenzo,
just as mine, whose name is Casildea and who comes from
Andalusia, I call Casildea of Vandalia. If all these tokens
do not suffice to vindicate the truth of my words, here is
my sword, which will compel incredulity itself to give
credence to it."

"Softly, sir knight," said Don Quixote, "and listen to what
I am about to say. You must know that this Don Quixote
you speak about is the greatest friend I have in the world;
in fact, I may say that I regard him as I would my very
self, and by the precise tokens you have given of him
I am sure that he must be the same whom you vanquished.
On the other hand, I see with my eyes and feel with my
hands that it is impossible for him to be the same, unless,
perhaps, that particular enemy of his, who is an enchanter,
may have taken his shape in order to allow himself to be
vanquished so as to cheat him of the fame that his noble
exploits as a knight have won him throughout the world.
To confirm this I must tell you that only two days ago
these said enchanters, his enemies, changed the shape and
person of the fair Dulcinea of El Toboso into a vulgar and
mean village lass, and in the same manner they must have
transformed Don Quixote. If all this does not suffice to
convince you of the truth of my words, here stands Don
Quixote himself: he will maintain it by arms, on foot or on
horseback or in any way you wish."

With these words he stood up and grabbed his sword,
waiting for the decision of the Knight of the Wood, who in
a voice equally calm replied: "A good prayer needs no
sureties. He who managed to vanquish you once when transformed, Señor Don Quixote, may well hope to conquer you
in your person. But since it is not right for knights to perform their deeds in the dark like highwaymen and bullies,
let us wait till daylight, that the sun may look down on

our achievements. And it must be a condition of our battle that the vanquished shall remain entirely at the mercy of the conqueror, provided that what is imposed shall be becoming a knight."

"I am more than satisfied with these conditions," answered Don Quixote.

And so saying, they went to seek their squires, whom they found snoring in the same posture as when sleep first waylaid them. They roused them and ordered them to prepare the steeds, for at sunrise the two knights would engage in bloody single combat. When Sancho heard the news, he was thunderstruck, fearing for the safety of his master, because of the tales that he had heard the Squire of the Wood tell of his knight's powers. Without saying a word, however, the two squires went off in search of their beasts, for the three horses and the dapple had smelled each other and were by this time all together.

On the way, he of the Wood said to Sancho: "You must know, brother, that fighting men from Andalusia are accustomed, when they are seconds in any combat, not to stand idle with their hands folded while their champions are engaged. I'm saying this to remind you that while our masters are fighting, we, too, must have a fight and knock one another to splinters."

"That custom, sir squire," replied Sancho, "may be current among the bullies and fighting men you mention, but never in any circumstances among the squires of knights-errant. At least I have never heard my master speak of such a custom, and he knows all the rules of knight-errantry by heart. But even if it is an express rule that squires should fight while their masters are fighting, I don't intend to follow it, but to pay the penalty that might be imposed on peacefully minded squires like myself, for I'm sure it will not be more than a couple of pounds of wax.[4] I would prefer to pay that, for I know it will cost me less than the plasters I'll need to heal my head, which I already reckon to be smashed in two pieces. Furthermore, I cannot fight, for I've no sword and never in my life carried one."

"I know a good remedy for that," said he of the Wood. "I've here two linen bags of the same size; you take one

---

[4] Religious confraternities imposed such a fine upon their members for trifling offenses.

and I'll take the other, and we'll have a bout of bag-blows on equal terms."

"If that's the way it goes," answered Sancho, "I'm game, for such a fight will beat the dust off us rather than hurt us."

"That mustn't happen," replied the other, "for we'll put in the bags, to keep the wind from blowing them away, half a dozen fine smooth stones, all of the same weight. In this way we'll be able to pound one another without doing much damage."

"Body of my father," said Sancho, "what a nice kind of sable skins and pads of cotton wool he's putting into the bags to save breaking our heads and mashing our bones to powder! But even if they were filled with pads of raw silk, I tell you, my dear sir, there's to be no fighting for me. Let our masters fight and take their medicine, but let us eat, drink, and be merry, for Time is anxious enough to snatch away our lives from us without our going out in search of appetizers to finish them off before they reach their season and drop off the tree for very ripeness."

"Still," said he of the Wood, "we must fight, if only for half an hour."

"Not on your life," replied Sancho; "I'm not going to be so churlish or ungrateful as to pick any quarrel, no matter how trifling, with one whom I have eaten and drunk with; besides, who the devil could manage to fight in cold blood, without anger or annoyance?"

"I'll provide a remedy for that," said he of the Wood. "Before we start fighting I'll walk nicely and gently up to your worship and give you three or four buffets that will land you at my feet. By this means I'll rouse your choler though it be sleeping sounder than a dormouse."

"I've a trick against yours that's just as good," replied Sancho. "I'll take up a stout cudgel, and before your worship gets near enough to raise my choler, I'll send yours to sleep with such sound whacks that it will not awake unless it be in the next world, where all know that I am not the kind of man to let my face be messed about by anyone. Let each man watch out for his own arrow, though, mind you, the better way would be for everyone to let his choler sleep in peace, for no one knows the heart of his neighbor, and many a man comes for wool and goes back shorn; and God always blessed the peacemakers and cursed the peace-breakers; for if a baited cat who's shut in turns into a lion, God knows what I, who am a man, shall turn into. So, from now on I warn you, Mister Squire, that I'll put down to your account all the harm and damage that may come of our quarrel."

"I agree," said he of the Wood; "God will send the dawn and all will be as right as rain."

And now a thousand kinds of little painted birds began to warble in the trees, and with their blithe and jocund notes they seemed to welcome and salute the fresh Aurora, who already was showing her beautiful countenance through the gates and balconies of the East, shaking from her tresses countless liquid pearls. The plants, bathing in that fragrant moisture, seemed likewise to shed a spray of tiny white gems, the willow trees distilled sweet manna, the fountains laughed, the brooks murmured, and the meadows clad themselves in all their glory at her coming. But hardly had the light of the day allowed things to be seen and distinguished, when the first object that Sancho Panza caught sight of was the Squire of the Wood's nose, which was so big that it almost overshadowed his whole body. It is said, indeed, that it was of huge size, hooked in the middle, all covered with warts, and of a mulberry color like an eggplant, and that it hung down two fingers' length below his mouth. The size, the color, the warts, and the hook of the aforesaid nose made its owner's face so hideous that Sancho, as he gazed at it, began to shudder hand and foot like a child in a fit of epilepsy, and he resolved in his heart to let himself be given two hundred buffets rather than to allow his choler to provoke him into attacking that monster.

Don Quixote looked at his adversary and found that he already had his helmet on, with the visor down, so that he could not see his face, but he noticed that he was a muscular man, though not very tall in stature. Over his armor he wore a surcoat or cassock of a cloth that seemed to be of the finest gold, all bedizened with many little moons of glittering mirrors, which gave him a most gallant and showy appearance. Above his helmet fluttered a great cluster of green, yellow, and white plumes, and his lance, which was leaning against a tree, was very long and thick and had a steel point more than a palm in length.

Don Quixote noticed everything, and from what he saw he inferred that the said knight must be very powerful; but for all that he did not fear as Sancho did, but with noble courage he addressed the Knight of the Mirrors, saying: "If your great longing to fight, sir knight, has not exhausted your courtesy, I would beg you earnestly to raise your visor a little that I may see if the gallantry of your countenance corresponds with that of your accouterment."

"Whether you are vanquished or victor in this enterprise, sir knight," answered he of the Mirrors, "you will have more than enough time and opportunity to see me. If I do not now satisfy your request, it is because, in my opinion, I should wrong the beauteous Casildea of Vandalia by wasting time in raising my visor before forcing you to confess what you know I demand."

"Well," said Don Quixote, "while we are mounting our steeds you can surely tell me if I am the Don Quixote whom you said you vanquished."

"To that we answer," said he of the Mirrors, "that you are as like the knight whom I vanquished as one egg is like another, but as you say that enchanters persecute you, I dare not say whether you are the aforesaid or not."

"That is enough," said Don Quixote, "to convince me of your deception; however, to relieve you of your misapprehensions, let our horses be brought, and in less time than you would take in raising your visor, if God, my lady, and my arm prevail, I shall see your face, and you shall see that I am not the vanquished Don Quixote you consider me to be."

Therefore, cutting short further words, they mounted their horses, and Don Quixote turned Rozinante's reins in order to take up the requisite ground for charging back upon his rival, while he of the Mirrors did the same; but Don Quixote had hardly gone twenty paces when he heard himself called by the Knight of the Mirrors, who said, when each had returned halfway: "Remember, sir knight, that the condition of our battle is that the vanquished, as I said before, shall be at the disposal of the victor."

"I know it already," answered Don Quixote, "but there is a proviso that what is commanded and imposed upon the vanquished must not transgress the bounds of chivalry."

"That is understood," replied he of the Mirrors.

Just at this moment the amazing nose of the squire presented itself to Don Quixote's view, and he was no less astonished to see it than Sancho had been, so much so that he took him for some monster or else for a human being of some new species that is rarely seen on the face of the earth. Sancho, seeing his master go off to take his ground, did not want to remain alone with the nosy individual, for he was afraid that one flick of that nose on his own would end the battle as far as he was concerned and leave him stretched on the ground either because of the blow or because of fright; so, he ran after his master, holding on to one of Rozinante's stirrups, and when he thought it was time to turn about, he said: "I beg your worship, master, before you turn to charge, to help me climb up on that cork tree, from where I may witness your gallant encounter with this knight at better ease and comfort than from the ground."

"I am rather of the opinion, Sancho," said Don Quixote, "that you would even mount a scaffold to see the bulls without danger."

"To tell you the truth," replied Sancho, "the fearsome nose of that squire has me all in a dither and full of terror, so that I dare not stay near him."

"It is, indeed, such a one," said Don Quixote, "that were I not what I am, it would strike fear in me, too. So, come, I will help you to climb up where you will."

While Don Quixote stopped to let Sancho climb into the cork tree, he of the Mirrors took as much ground as he considered necessary, and thinking that Don Quixote had done likewise, without waiting for any sound of trumpet or other signal to direct them, he wheeled his horse, which was no swifter or better-looking than Rozinante, and at his top speed, which was no more than an easy trot, advanced to meet his foe, but noticing that he was busy hoisting Sancho up into the tree, he drew reins and halted midway, for which his steed was profoundly grateful, for it was unable to move. Don Quixote, imagining that his rival was careering down on top of him, drove his spurs vigorously into the lean flanks of Rozinante and made him dash along in such a way that, as the history relates, this was the one occasion when he was seen to make an attempt to gallop, for on all others he did no more than plain easy trotting; and with this unheard-of fury he charged at him of the Mirrors, who was digging the spurs into his horse up to the buttons, without being able to make him stir an inch from the spot where he had halted in his career. At this critical moment did Don Quixote bear down upon his adversary, who was in difficulties with his horse and embarrassed with his lance, for he could neither manage it nor was there time to put it into the rest. Don Quixote, however, paid scant heed to such embarrassments, but in perfect safety and without taking any risk crashed into him of the Mirrors with such force that in spite of himself, he threw him to the ground over the horse's rump and so great was the fall that he lay apparently dead, not stirring hand or foot. No sooner did Sancho see him fall than he slid down the cork tree and ran at top speed to where his master was, who, after dismounting from Rozinante, stood over the Knight of the Mirrors. Unlacing his helmet to see if he was dead and to give him air if haply he were alive, he saw— Who can say what he saw without arousing the wonder, astonishment, and awe of all who hear it? He saw, the history says, the very face, the very figure, the very aspect, the very physiognomy, the very effigy, the very image of the bachelor Sansón Carrasco. As soon as he saw him, he cried out in a loud voice: "Come, Sancho, and behold what you have to see but not to believe; make haste, my son, and learn what wizards and enchanters are able to accomplish."

Sancho came up, and when he saw the face of the bachelor Carrasco, he began to cross himself a thousand times and bless himself as many more. All this time the prostrate knight showed no signs of life, and Sancho said to Don Quixote: "In my opinion, master, you should stick your sword into the mouth of this one who looks like the bachelor Carrasco, and perhaps in him you will kill one of your enemies, the enchanters."

"That is good advice," said Don Quixote, "for the fewer enemies, the better."

Then, drawing his sword, he was about to put into operation Sancho's advice, when the Squire of the Mirrors came up, now minus the nose that had made him so hideous, and cried out in a loud voice: "Mind what you are doing, Señor Don Quixote, for that man lying at your feet is your friend the bachelor Sansón Carrasco, and I am his squire."

"And what about the nose?" said Sancho, seeing him without his former hideous appendage.

"I have it here in my pocket," said the latter, and sticking his hand into his right pocket, he drew out a clownish nose of varnished pasteboard of the kind we have already described.

Sancho, then, after peering at him more and more closely, exclaimed in a loud voice of amazement: "Holy Mary, protect us! Isn't it Tomé Cecial, my neighbor and comrade?"

"Who else would I be?" replied the unnosed squire. "Tomé Cecial I am, comrade and friend, Sancho Panza, and I'll tell you presently of the means, the vagaries, the schemings, that brought me here; but in the meantime, beg and beseech your master not to touch, maltreat, wound, or kill the Knight of the Mirrors, whom he has lying at his feet, for without doubt he is the bold and ill-advised bachelor Sansón Carrasco, our compatriot."

At this moment he of the Mirrors came to his senses, and Don Quixote no sooner saw it than he held the naked point of his sword to his face, saying: "You are a dead man, knight, unless you confess that the peerless Dulcinea of El Toboso surpasses your Casildea of Vandalia in beauty; besides, you have to promise that if you survive this combat and fall, you will go to the city of El Toboso and present yourself before her on my behalf, letting her do with you what she pleases. And if she leaves you to your own devices, you must return and look for me (the trail of my deeds will guide you in my direction) and tell me all that has taken place between her and you. These are conditions that do not depart from the terms of knight-errantry."

"I confess," said the fallen knight, "that the torn and dirty shoe of Lady Dulcinea of El Toboso is better than the ill-combed though clean beard of Casildea, and I promise to go and return from her presence to yours and give you a complete and detailed account of what you ask me."

"You have also to confess and believe," added Don Quixote, "that the knight you vanquished was not, nor could be, Don Quixote of La Mancha, but somebody else who resembles him, just as I confess and believe that you, though you appear to be the bachelor Sansón Carrasco, are not he, but another like him, and that my enemies have conjured you up before me in his shape that I may restrain and moderate my impetuous wrath and make humane use of my glorious victory."

"I confess, judge, and consider everything to be as you confess, judge, and consider it," answered the crippled knight. "Let me rise, I pray you, if the shock of my fall will allow it, for I am indeed in a very bad way."

Don Quixote helped him to rise, with his squire Tomé

Cecial, off whom Sancho never for an instant took his eyes and whom he questioned incessantly, proving thereby to his own satisfaction that the latter was truly the Tomé Cecial he said he was. But Sancho was so impressed by what his master had said about the enchanters having changed the figure of the Knight of the Mirrors into that of the bachelor Sansón Carrasco that he was unable to believe the truth of what he saw with his own eyes. In the end, both master and man remained under their delusion; and so, he of the Mirrors and his squire, feeling down in the dumps and out of tune with the world, took their departure from Don Quixote and Sancho, intending to look for some place where the knight's ribs might be plastered and strapped.

Don Quixote and Sancho continued to make their way toward Saragossa, and the history leaves them at this point in order to give an account of who were the Knight of the Mirrors and his nosy squire.

CHAPTER XV

In which is told who the Knight of the Mirrors and his squire were

Don Quixote rode onward in great spirits. He was extremely pleased, elated, and vainglorious at having won a victory over such a valiant knight as he imagined him of the Mirrors to be, and from his knightly word he expected to learn whether his lady still continued to be enchanted, for the said vanquished knight was bound, on pain of ceasing to be one, to return and give him a report of what took place between himself and her. But if Don Quixote was thinking of one thing, he of the Mirrors was certainly thinking of another. In fact, the latter had no other thought at the moment than to find some place where he might get poulticed, as we have said before.

The history then says that when the bachelor Sansón Carrasco counseled Don Quixote to resume his relinquished knight-errantry, he did so in consequence of a conference he had previously held with the curate and the barber upon the measures to be taken to induce Don Quixote to stay at home in peace and quiet, without exciting himself over his accursed adventures. At that conclave it was decided by the unanimous vote of all, and at the special instance of Carrasco, that Don Quixote should be allowed to set out, as it was impossible to restrain him, that Sansón should sally forth as a knight-errant, join battle with him, for which a pretext could readily be found, and vanquish him—an easy matter they thought—and that it should be agreed and regulated that the one conquered should remain at the mercy of his conqueror. And once Don Quixote was vanquished, the knight-bachelor would order him to go back to his village and home and not leave it for two years or until some other command was imposed upon him, all of which conditions Don Quixote would carry out without fail rather than break the laws of chivalry. During the period of his seclusion, he might possibly forget his foolish notions, or else an opportunity might be found of discovering a sure remedy for his madness.

Carrasco undertook the task, and Tomé Cecial, Sancho's comrade and neighbor, a merry, scatterbrained fellow, offered his services as squire. Sansón armed himself as has been described, and Tomé Cecial, to avoid being recognized by his comrade when they met, fitted on over his natural nose the false one already mentioned. And so they followed the same road as Don Quixote and very nearly reached him in time to be present at the adventure of the cart of Death, and at last they met in the wood, where everything that the wise reader has read took place. And if it had not been for the extraordinary fancies of Don Quixote, who took it into his head that the bachelor was not the bachelor, Master Bachelor would be forever incapacitated from taking his degree as licentiate, because he did not find nests where he expected to find birds. Tomé Cecial, seeing how badly their plans had turned out and what a wretched end their expedition had come to, said to the bachelor: "For sure, Master Sansón Carrasco, we've met with our deserts. It's easy to plan and start an enterprise, but most times it's hard to get out of it safe and sound. Don Quixote is mad, and we are sane, but he comes off safe and in high spirits, while you, master, are left drubbed and downcast. Tell us, now, who is the greater madman, he who is so because he can't help it, or he who is so of his own free will?"

To which Sansón replied: "The difference between these two madmen is that he who is so perforce will be one forever, but he who is so of his own accord can leave off being one whenever he likes."

"That being so," said Tomé Cecial, "I was mad of my own accord when I agreed to become your squire, and of my own accord, I wish to leave off being one and go back home."

"You may please yourself," replied Sansón, "but to imagine that I am going home before I have given Don Quixote a beating is an absurdity, and it is not my wish to make him recover his wits that will drive me to hunt him now, but a lust for revenge, for the aching of my ribs will not let me form a more charitable resolve."

The two conversed in such a manner until they reached a town where by good fortune they found a bone-setter who cured the hapless Sansón. Then, Tomé Cecial went home, leaving the bachelor behind nursing his revenge. Our history will return to him at the proper time, but now it must frolic along with Don Quixote.

CHAPTER XVI

Of what happened when Don Qixote met a wise gentleman of La Mancha

Don Quixote continued his journey full of the joy, satisfaction, and high spirits we have described, fancying himself, owing to his late victory, the most valiant knight-errant in the world. All the adventures that might happen to him from that day on he reckoned as already successfully accomplished; he despised enchanters and enchantments; he gave no thought to the innumerable beatings he had received in the course of his knight-errantry, nor to the stoning that had knocked out half his teeth, nor to the ingratitude of the galley slaves, nor to the bold insolence of the Yanguesans who had belabored him with their staves. Finally he said to himself that if he could only discover a method of disenchanting his Lady Dulcinea, he would not envy the highest good fortune that the most fortunate knight-errant of past ages ever achieved or could achieve.

He was riding along entirely absorbed in these fancies when Sancho said to him: "Isn't it strange, master, that I've still before my eyes that monstrous and hugeous nose of my comrade Tomé Cecial?"

"Can it be, Sancho, that you really believe that the Knight of the Mirrors was the bachelor Sansón Carrasco, and his squire, Tomé Cecial, your comrade?"

"I don't know what I'm to say to that," answered Sancho. "I only know that the details he gave me about my house, my wife, and my children, no one but himself could have given me; and as for his face, once he had removed the nose, it was the very face of Tomé Cecial, for I've often seen him in my village—there was but a wall between my house and his—and the tone of his voice was just the same."

"Let us be reasonable, Sancho," replied Don Quixote. "Now tell me, how it can be argued that the bachelor Sansón Carrasco would come as a knight-errant, armed with arms offensive and defensive, to do battle with me? Have I, perchance, ever been his enemy? Have I ever given him cause to have a grudge against me? Am I his rival, or does he make profession of arms that he should envy the fame I have earned in them?"

"But what shall we say, master," replied Sancho, "about that knight, whoever he was, being the very image of the bachelor Carrasco, and his squire the dead spit of my comrade Tomé Cecial? And if that is enchantment, as your worship says, was there no other form in the world for them to take the likeness of?"

"It is all," said Don Quixote, "an artifice and trick of the malignant magicians who persecute me and who, guessing that I was to be victorious in the conflict, settled that the vanquished knight should display the face of my friend the bachelor in order that my affection for him might intervene to halt my sharp blade and restrain my mighty arm and moderate the righteous indignation of my heart, so that he who sought to rob me of my life by trickery should save his own. And in proof, you know already, Sancho, through experience, which cannot lie or deceive, how easy it is for enchanters to change some countenances into others, making the beautiful ugly and the ugly beautiful, for not two days ago you saw with your own eyes the beauty and elegance of the peerless Dulcinea in all its perfection and natural grace, while I saw her in the ugly and mean form of a course country wench, with cataracts in her eyes and a stinking breath from her mouth. Seeing that the perverse enchanter caused such a wicked transformation, it is no wonder that he effected that of Sansón Carrasco and of your comrade in

order to snatch away my victory. Nevertheless, I console myself, because when all is said and done, I have been victorious over my enemy, no matter what shape he took."

"God knows the truth of it all," answered Sancho. Knowing
as he did that the transformation of Dulcinea had been a
device and trick of his own, he was not at all pleased by his
master's wild fancies; but he did not like to reply, for fear of
saying anything that would reveal his trickery.

While they were conversing, they were overtaken by a man
who was riding on the same road behind them, mounted on a
very handsome gray mare and dressed in an overcoat of fine
green cloth slashed with tawny velvet and a hunting cap of
the same to match. His mare's trappings were rustic and for
riding with short stirrups, and were also of purple and green.
He wore a Moorish scimitar hanging from a broad baldric of
green and gold, and his leggings were of the same make. His
spurs were not gilt but covered with green lacquer and so
glossy and burnished that, because they matched the rest
of his apparel, they looked better than if they had been made
of pure gold. When the stranger overtook them, he greeted
them courteously and would have pressed on ahead, had not
Don Quixote accosted him, saying: "Gallant sir, if your worship is taking the same road as ourselves and if haste is not
your object, I should be grateful if we could ride together."

"Indeed," replied the man on the mare, "I should not have
passed on ahead of you if I had not been afraid that your
horse would be disturbed by my mare's company."

"You may, sir," answered Sancho, "in all safety rein in
your mare, for our horse is the most modest and well behaved in the world. He has never misconducted himself on
such an occasion as this, and the only time he didn't behave,
my master and I paid for it seven times over. Your worship,
I repeat, may pull up, if you wish; why, if they served your
mare to him between two courses, our horse wouldn't even
look her in the face, I assure you."

The traveler drew rein and gazed with amazement at the
figure and face of Don Quixote, who was riding without
his helmet, which Sancho carried like a wallet on the
pommel of Dapple's saddle. And the more did the man in
green stared at Don Quixote, the more did Don Quixote stare
at the man in green, who seemed to him a man of substance.
He appeared to be about fifty years of age; his gray hairs
were few, his face aquiline, his expression between cheerful

and grave—in short, his dress and general appearance stamped him as a man of fine endowments. What the man in green thought of Don Quixote was that he had never seen a man of that kind or physiognomy; he was amazed at his long scrawny neck, his tall body, his gaunt sallow face, his armor, his gestures and his carriage, a figure and image not seen in those parts for many a year.

Don Quixote observed how attentively the traveler was staring at him and assumed that his astonishment was due to his curiosity. So, being courteous and eager to oblige everybody, he anticipated the latter's questions and said to him: "I should not wonder if your worship were surprised at my appearance, which is both strange and out of the ordinary. But you will cease to do so when I tell you, as I do now, that I am a knight

> 'Of those, as people say, who ride
> In quest of valiant enterprise.'

I have left my native country; I have pledged my estate; I have forsaken my comfort and delivered myself into the arms of Fortune to lead where she will. I have sought to revive the now extinct order of knight-errantry, and for many a day, stumbling here, falling there, flung down in one place and rising up in another, I have been accomplishing a great part of my design, succoring widows, protecting maidens, and relieving wives, orphans, and young children, the proper and natural office of knights-errant; and so, by my many valiant and Christian deeds I have been found worthy to appear in print in almost all, or at least most, of the nations of the earth. Thirty thousand volumes of my history have been printed, and it is on the way to be printed thirty thousand times more, if Heaven does not prevent it. In fact, to sum up all in a few words, or in one word, I must tell you that I am Don Quixote of La Mancha, otherwise called the Knight of the Rueful Figure. And though to praise oneself is degrading, I am compelled at times to sound my own, though naturally only when there is no one present to sound them. So, gentle sir, neither this horse, nor this lance, nor this shield, nor this squire, nor all these arms together, nor the sallowness of my face, nor my lanky limbs, should henceforth astonish you, now that I have informed you who I am and what profession I follow."

After saying this Don Quixote remained silent, and the man in green delayed so long in answering that he seemed unable to find words, but after a while he said: "You rightly guessed my thoughts, sir knight, when you noted my amazement, but you have not managed to dispel the wonder the sight of you causes in me. Though you say that it should be removed once I know who you are, it has not done so. On the contrary, now that I know, I am all the more perplexed and astounded. What! Is it possible that there are knights-errant in the world today and that histories are printed about real knight-errantries? I cannot persuade myself that there is anyone on earth today who favors widows, protects maidens, honors wives, and succors orphans, and I would not have believed it had I not seen it in your worship with my own eyes. Blessed be Heaven for that history of your noble and authentic chivalries, which your worship says is in print, for it will cast into oblivion the innumerable books of counterfeit knights-errant with which the world is filled, that do such harm to good morals and such damage and discredit to genuine history."

"There is much to be said," answered Don Quixote, "on this point of whether the stories of knight-errant are fictions or not."

"But is there anyone who doubts their falsity?" asked the man in green.

"I doubt it," replied Don Quixote, "but there let the matter rest. If our journey lasts, I hope, with God's help, to convince your worship what you have done wrong in going along with the stream of those who declare that they are not true."

From this last remark of Don Quixote the traveler began to suspect that he must be some crazy fellow, but he waited for further evidence to confirm his suspicions. But before they could broach any other subject, Don Quixote begged him to say who he was, since he had told him already something about his way of life.

To which the man in green replied: "I, Knight of the Rueful Figure, am a gentleman and native of a village where, please God, we shall go to dine today. I am more than moderately rich, and my name is Don Diego de Miranda. I spend my life with my wife, my children, and my friends. My pursuits are hunting and fishing, but I keep neither hawk nor hounds, but only a quiet pointer and a saucy ferret or two. I have about six dozen books, some in Spanish and some in Latin, some historical and some devotional, but books of chivalry have never even crossed my threshold. I read profane books more than devotional, provided they give me honest entertainment, delight me by their language, and startle and keep me in suspense by their plots, though there are very few of this kind in Spain. Sometimes I dine with my neighbors and friends, and very often they are my guests. My table is clean, well appointed, and never stinted. I take no pleasure in scandal and allow none in my presence; I do not pry into my neighbors' lives, nor do I spy on other men's actions. I hear Mass every day; I share my goods with the poor, without boasting of my good works, lest hypocrisy and vainglory worm themselves into my heart, for they are foes that subtly waylay even the wariest. I try to make peace between those I know to be at loggerheads. I am devoted to Our Lady and always put my trust in the infinite mercy of Our Lord."

Sancho listened most attentively to the account of the gentleman's life and occupation, and he said to himself that it was a good and holy life and that the man who led it must be able to work miracles. So, flinging himself off Dapple and hastily seizing the gentleman's right stirrup, devoutly and almost in tears he kissed his feet again and again.

At this the gentleman exclaimed: "What are you doing, brother? Why these kisses?"

"Let me kiss you," answered Sancho, "for I do believe your worship's the first saint I've seen riding with short stirrups in all the days of my life."

"I am no saint," replied the gentleman, "but a great sinner. But you, brother, must be good; your simplicity proves it."

Sancho regained his saddle, after having succeeded in extracting a laugh out of his melancholy master and causing fresh amazement in Don Diego. Don Quixote then asked the gentleman how many children he had and said that the ancient philosophers, who were devoid of the true knowledge of God, held that the highest good lay in the gifts bestowed by Nature and Fortune, and in the number of friends and good children.

"I, Don Quixote," rejoined the gentleman, "have one son, and if he did not exist, perhaps I might count myself more fortunate than I do at present, not because he is wicked, but because he is not as good as I would wish. He is eighteen years old; he has been for six years in Salamanca studying Latin and Greek, and when I wished him to proceed to the study of other sciences, I found him so steeped in the one of Poetry—if it can be called a science—that there was no way of getting him to take cheerfully to Law, which I would like him to study, or to the queen of all the sciences, Theology. I wish him to be a credit to his family, for we live in an age when our princes highly reward virtuous and deserving learning, for learning without virtue is like pearls on a dunghill. All his day he spends in discussing whether Homer expressed himself well or ill in such and such verse of the *Iliad*; whether Martial was indecent or not in some epigram; whether such and such verses of Virgil are to be understood in this way or in that. In short, all his conversation concerns the books of those poets, and those of Horace, Persius, Juvenal, and Tibullus, for he has no high opinion of modern writers in Spanish. Yet, in spite of his dislike for poetry in the vernacular, his thoughts are now absorbed in making a gloss on four verses they have sent him from Salamanca, which, I believe, refer to some literary competition."

To all this Don Quixote replied: "Children, sir, are part of their parents' bowels, and so we must love them, whether they are good or bad, as we love the souls that give us life. It is the duty of their parents to guide them from infancy along the paths of virtue, good breeding, and Christian behavior, so that, grown up, they may be the staff of their parents' old age and the glory of their posterity. But when it comes to forcing them to study this or that science, I consider it unwise, although there may be no harm in persuading them; and seeing that they are in no need of studying to earn their daily bread, as the student is lucky enough to be endowed by Heaven with parents who spare him that, my advice is that they should be permitted to pursue the branch of learning to which they are most inclined. And although that of Poetry is less useful than it is pleasurable, it is certainly not one of those that dishonor their votary. Poetry, my dear sir, I would compāre to a tender, young, and ravishingly beautiful maiden, whom many other maidens, namely, all the other sciences, strive to enrich, to polish, and to adorn. And she has to exact service from all, and all of them can only become exalted through her. But this maiden refuses to be manhandled, or dragged through the streets, or exposed to the public at the market corners or in the ante-chambers of palaces, for she is fashioned of an alchemy of such power that anyone who knows how to treat her will transmute her into purest gold of inestimable price. He who possesses her must keep her within bounds, not letting her descend to base lampoons or impious sonnets; she must not be displayed for sale, unless in heroic poems, in mournful tragedies, or in merry and artificial comedies. She must not suffer herself to be handled by buffoons, nor by the vulgar mob, who are incapable of recognizing or valuing the treasures she enshrines. Do not imagine, sir, that by vulgar I mean only the common and humble people, for everyone who is ignorant, be he a prince or a lord, can and should be included in the category of the vulgar; so anyone with the qualifications I have mentioned who takes up and treats Poetry will become famous and his name will be held in esteem among all the civilized nations of the world. As to what you say, sir, of your son not appreciating the poetry in our Spanish tongue, I am convinced that he is wrong there, and the reason in this: the great Homer did not write in Latin because he was a Greek, nor Virgil in Greek because he was a Latin. In short, all the ancient poets wrote in the tongues they sucked with their mother's milk, and they did not go out in quest of strange ones to express the greatness of their conceptions; and this being so, it is only reasonable that the fashion should extend to all nations, and the German poet should not be undervalued because he writes in his language, nor the Castilian, nor even the Biscayan, who writes in his. But your son, sir, as I believe, does not dislike the poetry in the vulgar tongue, but only the poets who are merely vernacular and know no other tongues or other sciences to adorn, jog, and stimulate their natural inspiration. And yet, even in this we may be mistaken, for according to true belief, the poet is born—that is to say, the natural poet sallies forth from his mother's womb a poet, and with that impulse that Heaven has given him, without further study or art, he composes things that prove the truth of the saying: *est Deus in nobis*,[1] etc. Let me also say that the natural poet who makes use of art will improve himself and be

---

[1] This comes from Ovid, Fasti VI, 5. *Est deus in nobis, agitante calescimus in illo.* ("There is a god in us, he stirs and lo! we feel his fire.")

much greater than the poet who relies only on his knowledge of the art. The reason is clear, for art is not better than nature, but merely perfects her. So, nature combined with art and art with nature will produce a most perfect poet. To conclude my speech, noble sir, your worship should allow your son to go where his star calls him, for if he is as good a student as he should be and if he has successfully mounted the first step of learning, which is that of the languages, he will ascend of his own accord to the summit of humane letters, which so well become a gentleman of leisure, and adorn, honor, and exalt him as miters do bishops or robes learned doctors of law. But your worship should chide your son if he writes lampoons to the prejudice of the characters of others, and punish him and tear them up; but if he writes satires after the manner of Horace, reproving vice in general terms and as elegantly as the Roman did, praise him, for a poet may lawfully castigate envy and upbraid the envious in his verses and flagellate other vices, too, provided he does not single out any particular person, though there are poets who run the risk of banishment to the Isles of Pontus for the sake of uttering one malicious jibe.[2] If the poet, however, is chaste in his morals, he will be chaste also in his verses. The pen is the tongue of the soul, and the thoughts begotten there will burgeon in whatever he writes. And when kings and princes behold the miraculous science of Poetry in subjects who are wise, virtuous, and grave, they honor, esteem, and reward them, and even crown them with the leaves of the tree that lightning never strikes, as a warning that no one should attack men whose temples are honored and adorned by such crowns."[3]

The man in green was lost in amazement at Don Quixote's reasoning, so much so that he began to alter the opinion he had formed of the knight's craziness. But in the middle of the conversation, which was not much to his taste, Sancho had strayed from the road to beg a little milk from some shepherds who were milking their ewes close by; and just as the gentleman was about to renew the conversation, highly

[2] Ovid, who enjoyed the favor of Augustus for a number of years, was suddenly banished to Tomi on the Euxine, near the mouths of the Danube. The pretext of his banishment was his licentious poem on the art of love, *Ars Amatoria*.

[3] This refers to the laurel tree.

delighted with Don Quixote's wisdom and good sense, the
latter, lifting his head, saw a cart decorated with the king's
colors coming along the road by which they were traveling.
Imagining that this must be some new adventure, he shouted
to Sancho to come and bring him his helmet. Sancho, hearing himself called, left the shepherds, and spurring on Dapple, hastened toward his master, whom befell a stupendous and fearful adventure.

CHAPTER XVII

*In which is set forth the highest point that Don
Quixote's unheard-of courage ever reached, with the
happily terminated adventure of the lions*

Our history relates that when Don Quixote called Sancho
to bring him his helmet, the latter was buying some curds
from the shepherds, and being flustered by his master's pressing call, he did not know what to do with them nor how to
carry them. So, in order not to lose them, as he had already
paid for them, he thought it best to pour them into his master's helmet, and using this clever shift, he turned back to see
what his master needed. Don Quixote cried out to him: "Give
me that helmet, my friend, for either I know precious little
of adventures, or what I see yonder is one that should,
and does, require me to arm myself."

The man in green heard this and gazed around in all directions without seeing anything but a cart coming toward
them with two or three small flags, which made him think
that it was carrying the king's treasure, and so he told Don
Quixote. But the knight did not believe it, for he always
firmly imagined that everything that befell him must be adventures and still more adventures. So, he replied: "Forewarned is forearmed. Nothing is lost by taking precautions,

for I know by experience that I have enemies visible and invisible, and I never know when or where, nor in what moment, nor in what shape they may attack me."

And turning to Sancho, he asked him for his helmet, and as the squire had no time to take out the curds, he had to give it to him as it was. Don Quixote took it, and without noticing what was in it, he clapped it on his head hastily, and as the curds were pressed and squeezed, the whey began to pour down over Don Quixote's face and beard, which gave him such a start that he exclaimed to Sancho: "What's this, Sancho? I think my head is softening, or my brains are melting, or else I am sweating from head to foot. But if I am sweating, it is certainly not from fear, though I am truly sure the adventure I have to face is a terrible one. Give me something to wipe myself with, for this copious sweat is blinding my eyes."

Sancho held his tongue and handed him a cloth, thanking God that his master had not found out the truth.

Don Quixote wiped himself and took off the helmet to see what it was that made his head feel cool, and seeing the white mess inside the helmet, he put it up to his nose, and sniffing he said: "By my Lady Dulcinea of El Toboso, these are curds you have put here, your treacherous, impudent, ill-favored squire!"

To which with calm composure Sancho replied: "If they are curds, master, give them to me, and I'll eat them; but let the Devil eat them, for it must be he who put them there! How could you ever imagine that I would have the impudence to soil your worship's helmet? Indeed, you must already know the culprit! In faith, master, from the understanding which God has given me, I am convinced that I, too, must have enchanters who persecute me as a creature and limb of your worship, and they must have put that nasty mess there in order to rouse your patience to anger and make you drub my ribs as you are wont to do. But this time they have missed their mark, for I put my trust in my master's good sense; he must have considered that I have no curds or milk, or anything of the kind, and if I had, it is in my belly I would put them and not in the helmet."

"That may be," replied Don Quixote.

The gentleman had observed all with amazement, especially when Don Quixote, after wiping clean his head, face, beard, and helmet, put it on again, stood up in his stirrups, and feeling for his sword and grasping his lance, cried: "Now, come what may, I stand ready to face Satan himself in battle."

At this moment the cart with the flags approached. In it was nobody but the carter, who rode one of the mules, and a man who was seated in front. Don Quixote stood in front of it and said: "Whither are you going, brothers? What cart is this? What have you got in it? What flags are those?"

To this the carter replied: "The cart is mine, but in it is a fine pair of caged lions that the general is sending from Oran as a present to His Majesty, and the flags are of the king, our master, which signify that what is inside the cart is his property."

"Are the lions big?" asked Don Quixote.

"So big," said the man at the door of the cart, "that none bigger, or even as big, have ever crossed from Africa into Spain. I am the keeper and I've carried many, but never a pair like these. They are male and female; the male is in the front cage, and the female in the one behind. They are now very hungry, for they've eaten nothing today; so it would be best for your worship to stand aside, for we must make haste to reach the place where we may give them their feed."

To this Don Quixote answered, smiling slightly: "Lion cubs to me? To me lion cubs? At such a time, too? Then, by God, those gentlemen who send them here will soon see whether I am the man to be frightened by lions. Dismount, my good man, and since you are the keeper, open the cages and drive out those beasts. In the midst of this open field I will let them know who Don Quixote of La Mancha is, in spite of the enchanters who have sent them to me."

"Goodness gracious!" muttered the gentleman in green at this. "Our good knight is giving me proof of his nature. The curds, no doubt, have softened his skull and mellowed his brains."

At this point Sancho came up to him and exclaimed: "Sir, for God's sake, try and stop my master fighting with these lions; if he fights them, they'll tear us all to pieces."

"Is your master so crazy," the gentleman replied, "that you actually fear and believe he will really fight those furious beasts?"

"He's not crazy," replied Sancho, "but foolhardy."

"I'll make him stop," said the gentleman. And going up to Don Quixote, who was pressing the keeper to open the cages, he said: "Sir knight, knights-errant should engage in enterprises that hold out some prospect of success, but not in those that are entirely devoid of it, for valor that verges on temerity has more of madness about it than bravery. Moreover, these lions have not come against you, nor do they dream of doing so. They are going to be presented to His Majesty, and it is not right to detain them or hinder their journey."

"Get you gone, my dear sir," answered Don Quixote, "and look to your tame partridge and your spry ferret, and let every man look to his own duty; this is mine, and I know whether these gentlemen, the lions, are coming against me or not." Then turning to the keeper, he said sharply: "I swear, sir rascal, that if you don't open the cage at once, I'll stitch you to the cart with this lance."

The carter saw the armed phantom's grim determination and said to him: "Please, sir, for charity's sake, let me unhitch the mules and place myself in safety along with them before the lions are unleashed, for if they kill my beasts, I'm ruined for life, seeing that all I possess is this cart and the mules."

"O man of little faith!" replied Don Quixote. "Get down and unyoke, and do what you will; soon you will see that your toils were in vain and that you might have spared yourself the trouble."

The carter got down and in haste unyoked, and the keeper called out in a loud voice: "Bear witness, all who are here, how against my will and under compulsion I open the cages and let loose the lions. And I protest to this gentleman that all the harm and mischief these beasts shall do will be put to his account, together with my wages and dues as well. You, sir, take cover before I open; as for myself, I am sure they will do me no harm."

Once more the gentleman in green entreated the knight not to commit such an act of madness, for to engage in such freakish folly was to tempt Providence, but Don Quixote answered that he knew what he was up to. The gentleman warned him once more to mind what he was doing, for he was surely mistaken.

"Well, sir," replied Don Quixote, "if your worship does not wish to witness what you believe is about to be a tragedy, clap spurs to your gray mare and retire to safety."

Hearing this, Sancho besought his master with tears in his

eyes to give up such an enterprise, compared with which the adventure of the windmills and the fearsome one of the fulling mills and, in fact, all the deeds his master had attempted in the whole course of his life were nothing but cakes and fancy bread. "Look sir," said he, "here there is no enchantment nor anything of the kind, for through the chinks and bars of the cage I have seen the claw of a live lion, and I'm sure that a lion with such a claw must be bigger than a mountain."

"Fear, at any rate," answered Don Quixote, "will make it seem bigger to you than half the earth. Retire, Sancho, and leave me. If I die here, you know our old compact. You will go straight to Dulcinea; I say no more."

Other words he added to those declarations that took away all hope that he would give up his insane purpose. The man in green would have resisted him, but not being so well armed, he thought it would be imprudent to fight with a madman, for he now was convinced that the knight was stark, staring mad. Don Quixote then went on pressing the keeper and repeating his threats, which gave the gentleman a chance to spur his mare, Sancho to prod Dapple, and the carter his mules—all trying to get away from the cart as far as possible before the lions erupted from their cages. Sancho wept for his master's death, for this time he truly believed he would perish at the claws of the lions. He cursed his luck and the unlucky hour when he took it into his head to return to his service. Nevertheless, in spite of all his tears and groans, he took good care to flog up Dapple so as to drive him farther away from the cart. Then, when the keeper saw that those who had fled were far enough away, he again entreated and warned Don Quixote as he had done before, but the knight replied that he heard him but would listen to no more warnings or entreaties and bade him make haste. While the keeper was opening the first cage, Don Quixote was considering whether it would be better to do battle on foot or on horseback, and in the end he decided to fight on foot, for he was afraid Rozinante would take fright at the lions. He, therefore, sprang off his horse, flung his lance aside, and braced his buckler on his arm. Then, unsheathing his sword with marvelous valor and undaunted heart, he advanced at a leisurely pace and posted himself in front of the cart, commending his soul to God and then to his lady, Dulcinea.

We now must observe that when the author of our true history came to this point, he exclaimed: "O brave and incomparably courageous Don Quixote of La Mancha! Mirror wherein all the valiant may behold themselves! You second Don Manuel of León,[1] who was the honor and glory of Spanish knights! With what words shall I describe this most fearful exploit, or how make it credible to future ages? What praises can be unfitting and unmeet for you, though hyperbole he piled on hyperbole? You on foot, you alone, you bold and undaunted with only a simple sword and no trenchant Toledo blades of the little dog make,[2] with a shield of not very bright and shining steel, you stand watchful and ready for the two fiercest lions ever bred in African forests! Let your deeds themselves, valiant Manchegan, extol you; here I leave them in all their glamor, for I lack words to glorify them."

Here the author broke off his apostrophe and proceeded to take up the thread of his history, saying:

The keeper, seeing that Don Quixote had taken up his position and that it was impossible to avoid letting loose the male lion without falling under the rage of the wrathful and undaunted knight, opened wide the doors of the first cage, containing, as we have said, the male lion. The beast was now seen to be of extraordinary size and of grim and awful aspect. The first thing he did was to turn around in the cage in which he lay and to extend his claws and stretch himself out to his full length. Then, he opened his mouth and yawned very leisurely, and with about two palms' lengths of tongue, which he put out, he licked the dust from his eyes and washed his face. When this was done, he put his head out of the cage and gazed all around with eyes like blazing coals, a sight that would have struck terror in temerity itself. Don Quixote alone stood looking at him intently, longing for him to leap out of the cart and come to close grips with him, when he hoped to hack him to pieces. Up to such a point did his unheard-of madness raise him. The noble lion, how-

[1] Don Manuel of León was a knight of the time of Ferdinand and Isabella, and took part in the seige of Granada. He is the hero of Robert Browning's poem "The Glove."

[2] The little dog was the trademark of the celebrated armorer of Toledo, Julián del Rey.

ever, more courteous than arrogant, took scant notice of such childish bravado, and after looking around about him, as we have said, he turned his back and showed Don Quixote his hind parts, after which coolly and calmly he flung himself down in the cage. Seeing this, Don Quixote ordered the keeper to prod him and tease him to make him come out.

"I will not do so," replied the keeper, "for if I excite him, the first he will tear to pieces will be myself. Be content, sir, with what you have done, which leaves no more to be said on the score of courage, and don't try to tempt Fortune a second time. The lion has the door open; he's free to come out or not; since he hasn't come out up to now, he won't come out all day. Your worship's sturdy heart has been already shown to the world; no gallant champion, to my way of thinking, is bound to do more than to challenge his enemy and wait for him in the field. If his rival doesn't come, to him sticks the disgrace, and the man who waits his ground carries off the crown of victory."

"That is true," replied Don Quixote; "so, shut the door, my friend, and give me a sworn statement of what you have seen me do here, in the best form you can; to wit, that you did open for the lion, that I waited for him, that he did not come out, that still I waited for him, that still he did not come out, and that he lay down again. I am not bound to do more. Away with enchantments and God protect right, truth, and true chivalry! Shut the door, friend, while I signal to the fugitive and absent to return that they may learn of this exploit from your lips."

The keeper did so, and Don Quixote, sticking on the point of his lance the cloth with which he had wiped the shower of curds off his face, began to signal to those who were still continuing to flee, though looking around at every step, urged on by the gentleman in green. Sancho, happening to notice the signal of the white cloth, exclaimed: "May I be blowed if my master had not conquered the wild beasts, for he's calling us!"

They all stopped, and seeing that it was Don Quixote who was making the signals, losing some of their fear, they approached little by little until they clearly heard the voice of Don Quixote calling to them. At length they reached the cart, and as they came up, Don Quixote said to the carter: "Yoke your mules once more, my friend, and continue your journey, and you, Sancho, give him two gold crowns for himself and for the keeper as a compensation for the delay they have had through me."

"I'll give them with a heart and a half," said Sancho; "but what has happened to the lions? Are they alive or dead?"

Then the keeper gave a detailed account of the encounter, praising to the skies the power and valor of Don Quixote, at whose sight the cowed lion dared not to come out of his cage, though he had held the door open a good while, and that it was only because he had told the knight that it was tempting Providence to excite the lion and force him to come out, as he wanted him to do, that the knight had, against his will, allowed him to close the door.

"What do you think of this, Sancho?" said Don Quixote. "Are any enchantments able to prevail against true valor? The enchanters may be able to rob me of good luck, but of courage they cannot."

Sancho gave them the gold crowns, the carter yoked up, the keeper kissed Don Quixote's hands for the guerdon received and promised him to give an account of the brave exploit to the king himself as soon as he saw him at court.

"Then," said Don Quixote, "if His Majesty should happen to ask who performed it, you must say that it was the Knight of the Lions, for it is my wish that from this day on there may be changed, altered, and transformed the name that till now I have borne of the Knight of the Rueful Figure. In this I follow the ancient custom of knights-errant, who changed their names when they pleased or when it suited them."

The cart went on its way and Don Quixote, Sancho, and the gentleman in the green coat continued theirs.

All this while Don Diego de Miranda had not opened his mouth, so carefully was he watching and noting every word and action of Don Quixote, who appeared to him to be at once a sane man turned mad and a madman who had glimmers of sanity. The first part of this history had not yet come to his notice, for if he had read it, he would have ceased to wonder at the knight's deeds, since he would have ascertained the nature of his madness. But as he did not know it, he sometimes took him for sane, sometimes for mad. For what Don Quixote said was consistent, elegant, and well expressed, but what he did was eccentric, rash, and absurd. "What could be madder," he reflected, "than to put on a helmet full of curds and believe that enchanters had melted one's brains? And what could be rasher and more absurd than to insist on fighting with lions?"

Don Quixote interrupted his soliloquy by saying: "No doubt, Don Diego de Miranda, your worship regards me as both foolish and mad. And it would be no wonder if you did, for my actions can have no other interpretation. Nevertheless, I wish your worship to note that I am not so mad or foolish as I must have appeared to you. It is a fine sight to see a gallant knight under the eyes of his king give effective lance thrusts at a brave bull in the midst of a great square; it is a fine sight to see a knight, all armed in burnished armor, pace the lists in merry jousts before the ladies; and it is a fine sight to see all those knights who in military exercises or the like entertain, cheer, and if one may say so, honor the courts of their princes. But finer than all these is to see a knight-errant roaming through deserts and solitudes, by crossroads and forests and mountains, in quest of perilous adventures, in order to bring them to a happy and fortunate conclusion only for the sake of glory and lasting renown. It is a finer sight, I say, to see a knight-errant succoring a widow in some lonely waste than a courtier knight dallying with a maiden in the cities. All knights have their particular offices; let the courtier serve the ladies, lend pomp and circumstance to the royal court by his gay liveries, support poor knights at his beautiful table, arrange jousts, maintain tourneys, and show himself generous, liberal and lavish, and a good Christian above everything, for in this way he will fulfill his precise obligations. But let the knight-errant explore the corners of the world, penetrate the most intricate labyrinths, encounter at every step the impossible, brave the scorching rays of the sun in midsummer on high and unpeopled deserts, and in winter the grim inclemency of the winds and frosts; let no lions daunt him, nor hobgoblins scare him, nor dragons terrify him, for to seek them, attack them, and conquer them all are his principal duties. And as the lot has fallen on me to be of the number of knights-errant, I cannot then fail to attempt everything that seems to me to fall within the bounds of my duty. So, it was strictly my right to attack these lions whom I attacked just now, although I knew it to be rash temerity, for I know well what valor is, namely, a virtue that is situated between the two vicious extremes, which are cowardice and rashness. But it is far better for the brave man to mount to the height of rashness than to sink into the depths of cowardice, for just as it is easier for the generous than for the miser to be prodigal, so it is easier for the daring than for the cowardly to become truly valiant. And in the matter of encountering adventures, let your worship, Don Diego, believe me that it is better to lose the game by a card too much than by one too little, for 'this knight is rash and foolhardy' sounds better in the hearer's ears than 'such a knight is timid and cowardly.' "

"Let me admit, Don Quixote," replied Don Diego, "that all that your worship has said and done is adjusted by the balance of reason itself, and I believe that if the laws and ordinances of knight-errantry had been lost, they would be found in your worship's heart, as in their right repository and archive. But let us hurry on, for it is growing late, and let us reach my village and home. There you may rest yourself after your recent labors, for though they may not have been physical, they must have been of the mind, and those too sometimes lead to weariness of the body."

"I accept the offer as a great favor and kindness, Don Diego," answered Don Quixote. And spurring on faster than before, at about two o'clock in the afternoon they arrived at the village and home of Don Diego, whom Don Quixote called the Knight of the Green Cloak.

CHAPTER XVIII

Of what happened to Don Quixote in the castle or house of the Knight of the Green Cloak, with other eccentric matters

Don Diego de Miranda's house, Don Quixote found, was spacious in a village style: with his coat of arms in rough stone above the street door, the buttery in the front yard, the wine cellar in the porch, and several earthenware jars about, which, as they were from El Toboso, revived his memories of his enchanted and transmogrified Dulcinea. So heaving a sigh, regardless of what he said and in whose presence he was, he exclaimed:

"Sweet pledges, now discovered to my woe,
Joyous and sweet, when Heaven willed it so!

O Tobosan jars, how you recall the sweet pledge of my great bitterness!"

The student poet, Don Diego's son, who had come out with his mother to welcome the knight, heard him say this, and mother and son stood amazed at his eccentric appearance. And he, alighting from Rozinante, went very courteously to beg her hands to kiss, while Don Diego said: "Madame, pray receive with your accustomed hospitality Don Quixote of La Mancha, whom you have before you; he is a knight-errant, and the wisest and most valiant in all the world."

The lady, whose name was Doña Cristina, greeted him with marks of great affection and civility, and Don Quixote reciprocated with a number of judicious and polite phrases. He also addressed the same compliments to the student, who on hearing him speak took him for a man of wit and sense.

Here the author describes in detail Don Diego's home, whose contents were those of a wealthy farmer's house, but the translator of this history thought fit to pass over in silence these and similar particulars, seeing that they have little to do with the main purpose of the history, which draws its strength rather from truth than from dull digressions.

They led Don Quixote into the hall, where Sancho took off his arms, leaving him in his Walloon breeches and chamois leather doublet, all stained with the grime of his armor. His Vandyke collar was of student cut, unstarched and without lace, his buskins were date-colored, and his shoes waxed. His good sword was girt on, hanging from a baldric made of sealskin, for he had, it is believed, a long-standing affection of the kidneys, and over all he wore a cloak of honest gray homespun.[1] But first of all he had washed his head and face with five or six buckets of water, though there is some difference of opinion about the number, but the water remained always the color of whey, thanks to the gluttony of Sancho and the purchase of those foul curds that so whitewashed his master. In such a garb and with a gay and gallant air, Don Quixote walked into another hall, where the student was waiting to entertain him while the table was being laid, for Doña Cristina, on the arrival of so noble a guest, was eager to show that she was well able to kill the fatted calf for any guest who came to her home. While Don Quixote was taking off his armor, Don Lorenzo—for this was the name of Don Diego's son—found an opportunity of saying to his father: "Who on earth is this knight, father, whom you have brought home? His name, his appearance, and his calling himself a knight-errant certainly puzzles both my mother and myself."

"I don't know what to say, son," replied Don Diego. "All I can tell you is that I have seen him act like the craziest madman in the world, and yet to talk so wisely as to blot out and efface his deeds. Speak to him yourself and feel the pulse of his understanding, and as you are shrewd, make up your mind whether he is in his wits or not, though I

[1] It was an ancient superstition that a belt or baldric of sealskin cured a kidney affection. Gonzalo Fernández de Oviedo refers to it in Vol. I of his *Historia de las Indias*.

must confess that I think he is more mad than sane."

Lorenzo then went to meet Don Quixote, as we have said, and during their conversation Don Quixote said to him: "Don Diego de Miranda, your father, has told me about your rare talents and subtle wit, and above all that you are a great poet."

"A poet perhaps," replied Don Lorenzo, "but by no means a great one. It is true that I am rather fond of poetry and of reading the good poets, but not to such an extent that I can give myself the title of great, as my father says."

"I approve of your humility," said Don Quixote, "for there is no poet who is not arrogant and does not consider himself the greatest in the world."

"There is no rule without exceptions," answered Don Lorenzo, "and there may be some who are, and yet not think so."

"Few," said Don Quixote, "but tell me, what are these verses that you have in hand at present, which, according to your father, make you rather restless and pensive? If it is some gloss, I understand something myself of this art of glossing, and I should like to hear them. If they are for a literary contest, try to win the second prize, for the first is always won by favor or by the person's high standing. The second goes by pure merit; so, the third should be the second, and the first should be the third on this reckoning, like the degrees that are given in the universities. Nevertheless, the first is, in name at any rate, a great personage."

"Until now," said Don Lorenzo to himself, "I cannot take you for a fool; let us go on." And he said to Don Quixote: "Sir, you seem to have attended the schools. What sciences did you study?"

"Knight-errantry," replied Don Quixote, "which is as good as poetry, and even two fingers' breadth better."

"I do not know what that science is," rejoined Don Lorenzo, "and up till now it has not come to my notice."

"It is a science," replied Don Quixote, "that includes within it all or most of the sciences of the world, since he who proposes it must be a jurist and know the laws of justice, as regards distribution and exchange, in order to give each one what is his own and what is due. He must be a theologian so that he may give reasons for the Christian rule he professes, clearly and distinctly, whenever he may be asked. He must be a physician, and especially a herbalist, that he

may recognize in the midst of wilderness and deserts the
herbs that have the virtue of curing wounds, for the knight-
errant cannot at every step go looking for someone to cure
him. He must be an astronomer, that he may know by the
stars how many hours of the night have passed, and in
what part and climate of the world he is. He must know
mathematics, for at any time he may be in need of them.
In addition, not mentioning that he must be adorned with
all the virtues, theological and cardinal, and descending to
other more minute details, I say that he must be able to
swim as well as they say Fish Nicholas or Nicolao did. [2]
He must know how to shoe a horse and mend a saddle and
bridle. Moreover, to return to higher matters, he must keep
faith with God and his lady; he must be chaste in thought,
a man of his word, generous in action, valiant in deed,
patient in adversity, charitable to the needy, and finally, a
maintainer of the truth, although its defense may cost him
his life. All these parts, great and small, go to make up a
good knight-errant. Therefore, Don Lorenzo, consider whether
it is a snivelling science that the knight learns who studies
and professes it, and whether the highest taught in colleges
and schools can be compared to it."

"If that is so," replied Lorenzo, "I agree that this science
excels all the others."

"How, if that is so?" rejoined Don Quixote.

"What I mean to say," replied Don Lorenzo, "is that I
doubt whether there are, or ever have been, knights-errant
with so many virtues."

"I now repeat," replied Don Quixote, "what I have said
many times before, that the majority of people in this world
believe that knights-errant have never existed, and I hold
that unless Heaven miraculously convinces them of the truth
—that there were and that there are—any labor that I may
undertake for that purpose must be in vain, as experience
has so often shown me. So, I shall not stop now to deliver
you from the error you hold in common with the multitude.
What I intend to do is pray to Heaven to deliver you from

[2] According to Benedetto Croce the legendary exploits of
Nicolao the Fishman were celebrated in Messina and Naples. He
used to swim to and fro from Sicily to the mainland of Italy.
He was supposed to possess the secret of rejuvenating old women.
B. Croce, "Il viaggio ideale di M. de Cervantes a Napoli nel
1612," in *Bollettino del Comune di Napoli*, Vol. I, pp. 280–2.

it and to make you see how beneficial and necessary knights-errant were to the world in past ages and how useful they would be today if they were in fashion. But now the sins of mankind—sloth, idleness, gluttony, and luxury—are triumphant."

"Our guest has broken loose," said Don Lorenzo to himself at this point, "but for all that, he is a gallant madman, and I should be a crack-brained fool not to see that."

Here their conversation ended, for they were called to dinner. So, when Don Diego asked his son what opinion he had formed of their guest's wits, he replied: "All the physicians and good scribes in the world could not give a clear account of his ailment. He is mad in patches, full of lucid intervals."

They sat down to dinner, and the fare was, as Don Diego had said on the road, of the kind he generally gave to his guests, namely, clean, plentiful, and tasty. But what delighted Don Quixote most was the marvelous silence that reigned throughout the whole house, which seemed like a Carthusian monastery. So, when the cloth had been removed, grace said, and their hands washed, Don Quixote earnestly begged Don Lorenzo to recite his poem for the literary contest, to which the latter replied: "In order not to appear like those poets who refuse when they are asked to read their verses, but spew them forth when they are not asked, I shall recite my gloss, for which I expect no prize as I have written it only to exercise my wits."

"A wise friend of mine," answered Don Quixote, "was of the opinion that no one should weary himself by writing glosses, and the reason, he used to say, was that the gloss could never come near the text, that often, or most times, the gloss was far from the intention and purpose of the theme to be glossed, and furthermore, that the rules for glossing were too stringent, for they allowed no interrogations, nor *said he*, nor *shall I say*, nor making verbs of nouns, nor changing the sense, with other restrictions and impediments with which glossers are hampered, as you must know."

"Truly, Don Quixote," said Don Lorenzo, "I should love to catch your worship tripping in some serious blunders, but I cannot, for you slip through my hands like an eel."

"I do not understand what you say or mean about my slipping."

"I will explain," replied Don Lorenzo, "but now listen, I beg you, to the gloss and to the theme, which runs as follows:

> " 'If my was *should be turned to* is
> *Without the hope of what shall be,*
> *Or that the time should come again*
> *Of what hereafter is to be.'*

THE GLOSS

"As all things fade and pass away,
So Fortune's favors will not stay;
And though once she gave me all,
Now she will not heed my call.
For ages at thy feet I've lain,
Stern Fortune, hoping, but in vain;
What happiness for me, what bliss
If my was should be turned to is.

I wish no other prize or glory,
No other victory or palm,
But to regain once more the calm
Where lack disturbs my memory;
If thou wilt give me back thy boon,
My restless craving will be spent,
The more, if thou wilt give it soon,
For then I'll rest and be content
Without the hope of what shall be.

Like a fool I call upon the past,
And beg it to return in vain:
No power on earth can call back Time,
For it will never come again.
It races on with nimble wing;
And he is wrong who hopes to bring
By his cries all the past again,
Or that the time should come again.

To live in such perplexity,
Forever poised 'twixt hope and fear,
Is not life; better death in verity;
If by this way I could get clear
Of all my woes, then this were bliss;
But reason whispers in my ear
Of what hereafter is to be."

When Don Lorenzo had finished reciting his poem, Don Quixote rose to his feet and grasped the young man's right hand, crying in a loud voice, which was like a shout:

"Praise be to High Heavens, noble youth, for you are the best poet in the world, and you deserve to be crowned with laurel, not by Cyprus or by Gaeta, as the poet said (whom God forgive!), but by the academies of Athens, were they still surviving, and by those still in existence as Paris, Bologna, and Salamanca.[8] Would to Heaven that the judges who should deny you the first prize might be shot to death by the arrows of Phoebus, and may the Muses never darken the thresholds of their homes! Recite to me, sir, if you would be so good, some of your greater poems, for I should like to feel at all points the pulse of your admirable genius."

Is it necessary to say that Don Lorenzo was highly gratified by the praise of Don Quixote, although he considered him a madman? O power of flattery! How far you extend, and how wide are the bounds of your amiable jurisdiction! This truth Don Lorenzo vindicated by complying with Don Quixote's request and reciting to him the following sonnet on the fable of Pyramus and Thisbe:

SONNET

The fair maiden the cruel wall doth break
That had been cleft by Pyramus' manly heart.
Straightway from his Cyprian home doth Cupid start
To see the prodigious rift that love did make.
There no voice enters, only silence spake,
For souls though dumb may not be kept apart,

[8] According to Rodríguez Marín the poet referred to here possibly was Juan Bautista de Bivar, to whose talents in improvizing verses Cervantes also pays tribute in the "Canto de Caliope" in Book VI of *La Galatea*.

Perforce they'll speak, and Love has still the art
A crafty enemy to subjugate.
But the rash maiden's passion goes awry,
And haste makes her woo death instead of love.
The hapless pair together: tragic story!
Are both united in their common doom:
One sword, one sepulcher, one memory
Slays, covers, crowns with immortality.

"Blessed be God," cried Don Quixote when he had heard
Don Lorenzo's sonnet, "that among the infinite number of
poetasters I have seen one consummate poet, for that you
are, sir, as the skill and artifice of this sonnet informs me."

For four days Don Quixote was hospitably entertained in
Don Diego's house, at the end of which he begged
leave to depart, saying that he thanked his host for the
favors and good cheer he had received in his house, but
that since it was not right for knights-errant to give up many
hours to ease and luxury, he wished to go and fulfill his
duty, seeking adventures, in which he was told that the land
abounded. He said that in this way he hoped to pass the
time till the day of the jousts at Saragossa, which was his
direct route, and that he had first to enter the cave of
Montesinos, of which so many astonishing stories were
told in those parts, and also to investigate and learn the
origin and true sources of the seven lagoons, commonly
called the Lakes of Ruidera. Don Diego and his son commended his noble purpose and bade him take all that he
fancied from their house and farm, for they would most
gladly serve him, as they were bound by his personal worth
as well as his honored profession.

The day of his departure came at last, bringing joy to
Don Quixote but sadness and melancholy to Sancho Panza,
who had fared very well on the plenty of Don Diego's house
and who grudged returning to the hunger that prevails in
forests and deserts and to the scantiness of his ill-furnished
wallets. Nevertheless, he filled and stored them with all that
he thought he needed.

On taking leave, Don Quixote said to Don Lorenzo: "I
do not know whether I have told your worship before, but
if I have, I will repeat it, that if you would save labor and
pains in climbing to the inaccessible peak of the temple of

Fame, you have only to quit the rather narrow road of poetry and follow the narrowest path of all, that of knight-errantry, which is sufficient to raise you to be an emperor in the twinkling of an eye."

With these words Don Quixote settled the question of his madness, and still more when he said: "God knows I should like to take Don Lorenzo with me to teach him how to spare the humble and subdue and trample upon the proud, accomplishments proper to the profession I follow. But since his youth does not warrant it, nor his commendable pursuits allow it, I content myself with advising him that as a poet he will be able to acquire fame, if he is guided more by other's opinions than by his own. For there is no father or mother to whom their children seem ugly, and this delusion is even more prevalent where the children of the brain are concerned."

Father and son were once more amazed at Don Quixote's mixture of wise and foolish arguments and at his obstinacy in running through the gamut of his luckless adventures, which were the aim and end of all his desires. They repeated their offers and their compliments, and then taking leave of the lady of the castle, Don Quixote and Sancho departed upon Rozinante and the ass.

CHAPTER XIX

Of the adventure of the enamored shepherd, with other truly pleasant incidents

Don Quixote had not left Don Diego's village far behind him when he met two men, either priests or students, and two peasants, all mounted on four asses. One of the students carried, wrapped up in a piece of green buckram, what seemed like a small white cloth and two pairs of stockings of rough homespun, while the other carried nothing but two new fencing foils with their buttons. The peasants were laden with other things that showed that they came from some large town where they had bought them and that they were taking them home to their village. The peasants as well as the students were struck with the same amazement that all felt who saw Don Quixote for the first time, and they were dying to know who this strange individual, so unlike other men, could be. Don Quixote greeted them, and after finding out that their road was the same as his, he offered them his company and begged them to slacken their pace as their ass-fillies traveled faster than his horse. Then, to oblige them he told them in a few words who he was and the office and the profession he followed, which was that of knight-errant, seeking adventures all over the earth. He told them that his name was Don Quixote of La Mancha, and his title the Knight of the Lions.

All this was Greek or gibberish to the peasants, but not so to the students, who at once noticed what was wrong with the brain of Don Quixote. Nevertheless, they regarded him with wonder and respect; and one of them said to him: "If your worship, sir knight, has no fixed road, following

as you do the example of those who seek adventure, come
with us and you will see one of the finest and richest weddings
that up to this day has ever been celebrated in La Mancha,
or for many leagues around."

Don Quixote then asked if it was some prince's to deserve such ceremonies.

"It is not," replied the student, "but for a farmer and a
farmer's daughter; he is the richest in all this country, and
she is the fairest beauty men have ever seen. The celebration will be rare and extraordinary, for the bridal ceremonies
will be held in a meadow adjoining the village of the bride,
whom they call Quiteria the Fair, and the bridegroom is
called Camacho the Rich. She is eighteen years of age, and
he is twenty-two, and they are a well-matched pair, though
those who know by heart all the pedigrees in the world
would say that the family of the beautiful Quiteria is better
than Camacho's. Nevertheless, no one gives a thought to
that nowadays, for riches can solder many a crack. In any
case, Camacho is free with his money, and he has taken
the fancy of screening the whole meadow with boughs and
covering it overhead, so that the sun will find it difficult to
get in to reach the grass that covers the soil. He has or-
ganized dances also, both of swords and of little bells, for
there are in his village folk who can jingle and clatter the
bells to perfection. I won't mention clog dancers, for he has
engaged a host of them. But none of those, nor the many
things I have omitted to mention, will make this wedding
more memorable than those that I suspect the unfortunate
Basilio will do there.

"This Basilio is a youth from the same village as Quiteria
and he dwelt in the house next door to that of her parents,
a circumstance that gave Cupid the opportunity of reviving
in the world the long forgotten loves of Pyramus and Thisbe,
for Basilio loved Quiteria from his tender years and she responded to his passion with countless innocent demonstrations of affection. And so, the loves of the two children,
Basilio and Quiteria, were the talk of all the village. As
they grew up, the father of Quiteria resolved to deny to
Basilio his accustomed entrance to his house, and to avoid
all doubts and suspicions, he arranged to marry his daughter
to the rich Camacho as he did not approve of marrying her
to Basilio, who had not such a plentiful share of Fortune's
as of Nature's gifts, for, speaking truthfully and without

envy, he is the most athletic youth we know, a great thrower of the bar, a first-rate wrestler, and a fine ball player; he runs like a deer, leaps like a goat, bowls over the ninepins as if by magic; he sings like a lark, plays the guitar so that he makes it speak, and above all, wields a sword like the best of them."

"For that one accomplishment alone," said Don Quixote at this, "the youth deserves to marry, not only the fair Quiteria, but Guinevere herself, were she alive today, in spite of Lancelot and of all who should try to prevent it."

"Say that to my wife," said Sancho Panza, who up to this had listened in silence, "for she won't allow anyone to marry save with his equal, sticking to the proverb that says: 'Every ewe with its mate.' What I would like is that this worthy Basilio (I'm taking a fancy to him already) should marry Lady Quiteria, and eternal life and rest—I meant to say the opposite—to those who try to prevent those who love one another from marrying."

"If all who love one another well were to marry," said Don Quixote, "parents would lose the right to marry their children when and to whom they choose, and if the daughters were allowed to choose their husbands as they wished, one would pick her father's groom, and another some passer-by in the street whom she fancies to be a fine and gallant fellow, though he might be a good-for-nothing swashbuckler; for love and fancy easily blind the eyes of understanding, which are so necessary when choosing one's state. And the state of matrimony runs a great risk from errors, and one needs plenty of circumspection and the particular favor of Heaven to make a good choice. When anyone wishes to make a long journey, if he is prudent, he looks for a safe and agreeable travel companion before he takes to the road. Then, why should he not do the same when he has to travel all the days of his life to the resting place of death, and especially if the companion has to consort with him in bed and at the table and everywhere, as the wife has to do with her husband? The companionship of one's own wife is not mere merchandise that, once bought, can be returned, bartered, or exchanged, for marriage is an inseparable union that lasts as long as life. It is a noose that becomes a Gordian knot once we put it around our neck. And if Death's scythe does not cut it, there is no untying it. I could say much more on this subject if I were not prevented by my desire to know whether Master Licentiate has anything more to tell us concerning the story of Basilio."

To this the student, bachelor, or licentiate, as Don Quixote called him, replied: "There is nothing more to say except that from the moment Basilio heard that the fair Quiteria was to be married to Camacho the Rich he has never been seen to smile, or heard to speak a rational word; he always goes about full of sadness, talking to himself and giving clear tokens that he has lost his wits. He eats and sleeps little; when he eats, it is nothing but fruit, and when he sleeps, it is in the fields on the hard earth like a brute beast. From time to time he gazes at the sky, and at other times he fixes his eyes on the ground in such a distracted way that he resembles a clothed statue with its drapery billowing in the wind. Indeed, he shows such signs of a heart overwhelmed by passion that we who know him are convinced that when tomorrow the fair Quiteria says *yes* will be his death sentence."

"God will find a better way," exclaimed Sancho, "for God, who gives the sore, gives the plaster. Nobody knows what's in store. There are many hours between now and tomorrow, and in one, even in a minute, the house topples down; I've seen the rain falling and the sun shining at the same time. Many's the time a fellow goes to bed hale and hearty and can't budge an inch the next day. And tell me now, is there anyone who can boast that he has put a spoke in the wheel of Fortune? Not on your life; and between a woman's *yes* and *no*, I'd not risk putting a pin's point, for there wouldn't be room for it. If you tell me Quiteria loves Basilio heart and soul, then I'll give him a bag full of good luck, for I've always heard that love looks through spectacles that make copper seem gold, poverty riches, and teardrops pearls."

"When are you going to stop, Sancho, a plague on you?" said Don Quixote. "When you begin to string together your proverbs and tales, only Judas himself would understand you —may he seize you. Tell me, blockhead, what do you know about spokes, or wheels, or anything else?"

"Well, if you don't understand me," rejoined Sancho, "it's no wonder that my opinions are taken for nonsense. But no matter; I understand myself, and I know that I haven't said many foolish things in my comments, only your worship is always an incensory of my sayings and even of my doings."

"*Censor,* you should say," replied Don Quixote, "and not *incensory;* confound you for a perverter of good language!"

"Don't be cross with me, master," answered Sancho, "for you know I wasn't reared at court nor trained at Salamanca to learn whether I'm adding or subtracting a letter from the words I use. God help me! You mustn't expect a Sayagan to speak like a fellow from Toledo, and who knows but there may be Toledans who aren't so pert at this business of talking polite." [1]

"That is true," said the student, "for those who have been brought up in tanneries and the Zocodover [2] cannot talk like those who stroll about all day in the cathedral cloisters, and yet they are all Toledans. The pure, proper, elegant, and clear language may be found among the educated people of the court, even though they may have been born at Majalahonda. I said educated, for there are many who are not so, and wisdom is the grammar of good language, and comes from practice. I, sirs, for my sins, have been a student of canon law at Salamanca, and I pride myself on expressing my thoughts in clear and significant language."

"If you hadn't taken more pride in your skill with those foils you carry than in your skillful use of language," said the other student, "you would have come out at the top in your degree examination instead of at the bottom."

"Look here, bachelor," replied the first student, "you have the most mistaken opinion in the world about skill with the sword if you think it useless."

"It is not my opinion," retorted Corchuelo, for that was the name of the second student, "but a well-known fact, and if you wish me to prove it to you here and now, you have the sword there, and now we have an opportunity. I have a steady wrist and a strong arm, which with my courage will make you confess that I am not wrong. Dismount and try out your measured steps, circles, angles, and science, for I hope to make you see stars at noon with my rough-and-ready art, in which, next to God, I put my trust. There is no one alive who will make me turn back, and not a living man whom I will not force to give ground."

---

[1] The people of Toledo had the reputation in those days of speaking the finest Castilian. In the thirteenth century Alfonso el Sabio cited them as models of good speech.

[2] The square at Toledo, which was the meeting place of picaroons and peasants.

"As regards turning your back or not," answered the former, "I don't concern myself, though who knows but the very spot where you first plant your feet may be the opening of your grave—I mean that you might lie dead there as a result of the swordsmanship you despise."

"We shall see presently," replied Corchuelo, and alighting briskly from his ass, he snatched one of the foils that his companion carried on his.

"This is not the way to settle the affair," said Don Quixote at this point. "I want to be the umpire of this fencing bout, and judge of the oft undecided question." Then, dismounting from Rozinante and grasping his lance, he planted himself in the middle of the road at the moment when the student who was expert at fencing advanced against his adversary with easy and graceful step, while Corchuelo rushed on, darting fire from his eyes, as the saying goes.

The two peasants of the company, without alighting from their asses, served as spectators of the mortal tragedy. The slashes, lunges, downstrokes, backstrokes, and wrist strokes that Corchuelo dealt were innumerable and came thicker than hailstones. He attacked like a raging lion, but met a blow on the mouth from the button of his adversary's foil that stopped him in his mad onrush, and he was made to kiss it as though it were a relic, though not with as much devotion as relics are wont to be kissed.

The licentiate finally counted off with lunges every one of the buttons of the short cassock that Corchuelo wore, tearing the skirts into strips, like the tentacles of an octopus. Twice he knocked off his hat, and so bedeviled and bamboozled him that out of sheer rage and vexation he took his foil by the hilt and hurled it away with such force that one of the peasants present, a scrivener, who went to fetch it, testified later that it went about three-quarters of a league away from him, a testimony that has served and still serves to prove incontestably how brute force is conquered by skill.

Corchuelo sat down worn out, and Sancho went up to him, saying: "By my faith, sir bachelor, if you'll take my advice, you'll never challenge anyone to fence again, but only to wrestle and throw the bar, for you've the youth and sinews for that; but as for those so-called fencers, I have heard that they can put the point of a sword through the eye of a needle."

"I'm satisfied with having tumbled off my ass,"[3] Corchuelo replied, "and with having learned through experience a truth of which I was so ignorant."

With these words he got up and embraced the licentiate, and they became better friends than ever. Without waiting for the scrivener who had gone for the sword, as they thought he would be a long time, they determined to push on so as to arrive early at Quiteria's village, to which they all belonged.

During the remainder of the journey the licentiate held forth on the virtues of swordsmanship, using such conclusive arguments and so many figures and mathematical demonstrations that they all became convinced of the value of the art and Corchuelo was cured of his obstinacy.

It was nightfall, but before they reached the village, it seemed to them all as if in front of it there was a sky filled with countless glittering stars. At the same time they heard sweet, confused sounds of various instruments, such as flutes, tambourines, psalteries, pipes, tabors, and timbrels, and when they drew near, they saw that the trees of a bower that had been erected at the entrance of the village were all filled with illuminations, which were undisturbed by the wind, for it blew so softly that it had not even the strength to rustle the leaves of the trees. The musicians were the funmakers at the wedding, for they roamed through that gay pleasure ground in bands, some dancing, others singing, and others playing the various instruments we have already mentioned. Indeed, it seemed as though mirth and gladness were frisking and gamboling all over the meadow. Some others were briskly erecting platforms, from which people might more comfortably see the plays and dances that were to be performed the next day on the spot dedicated to the celebration of the marriage of the rich Camacho and the obsequies of Basilio. Don Quixote refused to enter the village, though the peasant and the bachelor urged him to do so, giving what he thought was a most valid excuse, that it was the custom of knights-errant to sleep in the fields and woods in preference to populated places, even though it might be under gilded roofs, and so he turned aside from the road, much against Sancho's will, for he had still lingering memories of the good lodgings he had received in Don Diego's house or castle.

[3] A proverb meaning to be undeceived.

CHAPTER XX

In which an account is given of the wedding of Camacho the Rich, with the adventure of Basilio the Poor

Scarcely had fair Aurora given shining Phoebus time to dry up the liquid pearls on her golden hair with the heat of his rays when Don Quixote, shaking off sloth from his limbs, sprang to his feet and hailed his squire, Sancho, who still lay snoring. Before awaking him, Don Quixote addressed him saying: "O fortunate one above all who inhabit the face of the earth, since without envying or being envied you sleep with mind at rest. Neither enchanters harass you nor enchantments frighten you. Sleep, I say again and a hundred times, for no jealousy of your lady holds you in everlasting vigil, nor do thoughts of how to discharge your debts keep you awake; nor of what you must do tomorrow to feed yourself and your small straitened family. Ambition does not disturb you, nor the vain pomps of the world worry you, for the limits of your desires extend no further than care for your ass. The care of your person you have laid on my shoulders, a burden and compensation that nature and custom have imposed on masters. The servant sleeps and his master watches, thinking how he will sustain, better, and favor him. Anguish at seeing the sky turn to bronze without shedding on earth the needful dew does not afflict the servant but the master, who in barrenness and famine must sustain the man who served him in fertility and abundance."

To all this Sancho made no reply, since he was asleep, nor would he have awakened so soon as he did, had not Don Quixote roused him to his senses with the butt-end of his lance. He awoke at length, drowsy and lazy, and looking around on all sides, he exclaimed: "Unless I'm mistaken there comes from that bower a steam and a reeking a great deal more of fried rashers than of thyme and rushes. A wedding that begins with such odors, by my sainted soul, must have lashings and plenty in store."

"Stop, you glutton," said Don Quixote; "come, let's go and watch this ceremony and see what the forlorn Basilio will do."

"Let him do what he pleases," replied Sancho. "He would be poor, and he would marry Quiteria. Fancy wanting to marry in the clouds when one hasn't a penny to bless one's name! By my faith, sir, it's my opinion that the poor fellow should be content with what he can get, and he shouldn't be ferreting for dainties at the bottom of the sea. I'd bet my arm Camacho could cover Basilio in gold pieces, and if it is so, as it must be, Quiteria would be daft to throw away the jewels and the finery Camacho must have given, and can give her, and choose instead Basilio's bar pitching with his bad luck. Why, they won't give you a pint of wine in a tavern for a good throw of the bar or a clever trick with the sword. Skills and graces that aren't salable, better leave them to Count Dirlos, but when such talents fall to one who has good cash, then let me change places with him. On a good foundation you can build a solid house, and the best foundation and ground work in the world is money."

"For God's sake, Sancho," cried Don Quixote at this, "stop your speechifying. I do believe that if you were left to follow every notion that comes to your mind, you would have no time left for eating or sleeping; you would waste it all in talking."

"If your worship had a good memory," answered Sancho, "you'd remember the articles of our agreement, made before we left home this last time. One of them was that I should be allowed to talk as much as I pleased, so long as I didn't speak against my neighbor or your worship's authority. And I don't think I've violated that article so far."

"I do not remember any such article, Sancho," said Don Quixote, "and supposing it were true, I want you to hold your tongue and come along with me, for the instruments we heard last night are beginning to gladden the valleys once more, and no doubt the nuptials will be celebrated in the cool of the morning and not in the heat of the afternoon."

Sancho obeyed his master, and after putting the saddle on Rozinante and the packsaddle on Dapple, the two mounted and rode leisurely toward the bower of the trees. The first thing that caught Sancho's eye was a whole steer spitted on a whole elm tree, and in the fire over which it was roasting there was burning a good-size mountain of firewood; six earthenware pots that were around the blaze had not been made in the common mold, for they were six medium-sized vats, and each could hold a whole slaughterhouse of meat. Whole sheep were swallowed up and hidden in them as if they had been mere pigeons. Innumerable were the hares already skinned and chickens plucked, which hung on the trees ready for burial in the pots; countless too were the birds and game of divers kinds hanging from the branches that the air might cool them. Sancho counted more than sixty wine-skins of more than eight gallons each, and all filled, as it afterward turned out, with generous wines. There were also rows of loaves of the whitest bread, like heaps of wheat piled up on the threshing floors; the cheeses, arranged like open brickwork, formed a wall, and two caldrons full of oil, bigger than dyer's vats, served to fry the fritters, which, when fried, were drawn out with two mammoth shovels and plunged into another caldron of prepared honey that stood nearby. There were more than fifty cooks male and female, all of them clean, busy, blithe, and buxom. In the swollen belly of the steer were twelve tender little suckling pigs, sewn up within to give the meat a delicious flavor. As to the spices of different kinds, they seemed to have been bought not by the pound but by the quarter, and all lay open to view in a big chest. Indeed, the preparations for the wedding, though in rustic style, were plentiful enough to feed an army.

Sancho noticed all, inspected all, and fell in love with all. At first the fleshpots caught his fancy, from which he would most willingly have extracted a fair helping of stew; then the wineskins monopolized his attention; and lastly the fritters in the pan, if indeed one could call those bloated caldrons pans. And so, unable to resist his impulses any longer, he went up to one of the cooks and in civil though hungry words begged leave to soak a crust of bread in one of the pots. To which the cook answered: "Brother, this is not a day over which hunger holds sway, thanks to Camacho the Rich. Dismount and look if there is a ladle handy, and skim off a hen or two; and much good may they do you."

"I don't see one," said Sancho.

"Wait," cried the cook; "well, blast me for a sinner, but you're a dainty and bashful customer!" And saying this, he seized a pot, and dipping it into one of the huge half jars, he drew out in it three hens and a couple of geese, saying to Sancho: "Eat, my friend, and break your fast on these mere skimmings until dinnertime comes."

"I've nothing to put it into," said Sancho.

"Then take pot and all," said the cook, "for the wealth and joy of Camacho supply all demands."

While Sancho was thus busily engaged, Don Quixote was watching the entrance through one part of the bower of about twelve peasants mounted on twelve beautiful mares richly caparisoned, with a number of little bells jingling on their breastplates. The peasants, who were all clothed in festive garments, gathered together in a marshaled troop and ran many races over the meadow, shouting jubilantly as they ran: "Long live Camacho and Quiteria! He is as rich as she is fair, and she is the fairest in the world!"

Hearing this, Don Quixote said to himself: "It is clear that these people have never seen my Dulcinea of El Toboso. If they had, they would moderate their praises of this Quiteria."

Soon afterward various companies of dancers began to enter at different points the leafy enclosure. Among them was one of sword dancers, about twenty-four youths of gallant bearing, all dressed up in the whitest linen and with headdresses of different colors embroidered in fine silk. One of the peasants on the mares asked the leader, an athletic youth, if any of the dancers had hurt himself.

"Up to the present, thank God," said he, "none of us are hurt: we are safe and sound." And he began at once to wheel and twist with the rest of his troop in such skillful fashion that although Don Quixote was accustomed to see similar dances, he thought he had never seen any as good as this. He also admired another of twelve beautiful maidens, none of whom seemed to be less than fourteen or more than eighteen years of age. They were clad in green stuff, their locks were partly plaited and partly flowing loose, but all so golden that they rivaled with sunbeams, and over them they wore garlands of jasmine, roses, amaranth, and honeysuckle. They were led by a venerable old man and an ancient matron who were more active and athletic than one would have expected from their years. A Zamoran bagpipe gave them music, and they, with modesty in their glances and nimbleness in their feet, proved themselves the best dancers in the world.

Behind them there came a masque of the kind they call "speaking dances." It was made up of eight nymphs grouped in two rows; of one row Cupid was leader, and of the other Interest. The former was adorned with wings, bow, quivers, and arrows; the latter was clad in a rich dress of gold and colored silks. The nymphs who followed Cupid carried on their backs white parchments on which their names were written in big letters. The first one was Poetry, the second Discretion, the third Good Lineage, the fourth Valor. Those who followed Interest were marked in the same way. Liberality was the first one's name, Gifts the second's, Treasure the third's, and Peaceful Possession the fourth's. In front of all the nymphs there came a castle of wood drawn by four savages, clad in ivy and hemp dyed green, and so lifelike that they almost frightened Sancho. On the front of the castle and on each of the four sides it bore the inscription: "Castle of Modesty." Four skillful tambourine and flute players made sweet music, and when the dance had opened, Cupid, after executing two figures, lifted his eyes and bent his bow against a solitary maiden who stood between the turrets of the castle. He addressed her as follows:

> "I am the mighty god;
> The sky and earth obey,
> The seas bend to my nod;
> The powers of hell I sway.

> Fear I never knew,
> What I will I can do,
> And none can say me nay;
> I bid, forbid, and take away."

The verse ended, Cupid discharged an arrow over the top of the castle and returned to his place. Then Interest came out and performed other figures. The drums stopped and he spoke:

> "I'm Interest, and kind to few,
>   But none can do without me;
> Yet all in all to thee I'm true
>   For all eternity."

Then Interest retired, and Poetry came forward, and after performing her figures like the others, she said, fixing her eyes on the lady of the castle:

> "I, my lady, am sweet Poetry,
>   Decked in fancy and many a fad;
> All my heart I send to thee,
>   In a thousand sonnets clad.
>
> If, perchance my earnest pleas
>   Don't vex thee when I importune,
> Be thou envied of thy sex,
>   When I raise thee above the moon."

Poetry went aside, and from the side of Interest, Liberality sallied forth, and after dancing her tunes, she said:

> "Liberality we always call
>   The gift that shuns the extreme
> Between the rash and prodigal,
>   And what is timorous and mean.
>
> But I'll exceed in praising thee.
>   Though 'tis a sin with gifts to make,
> I intend a prodigal to be,
>   Since only giving proves my love."

In this way all the figures in the two bands came forward and retired, each one going through her motions and reciting her verses, some of which were elegant and some ridiculous, though Don Quixote only remembered (and he had a good memory) those that have been quoted. Presently they all mingled together, forming chains and dissolving again with spontaneous joyous rhythm, and whenever Cupid passed in front of the castle, he shot his arrows up at it, while Interest broke golden balls against it. At length, after they had danced a good while, Interest drew out a large purse, made out of a brindled catskin, which seemed to be full of coins, and flung it at the castle; such was the force of the blow that the planks fell asunder and left the damsel exposed and defenseless. Interest then advanced accompanied by his band, and throwing a big golden chain over her neck, he made a show of leading her away a prisoner.

No sooner was this seen by Cupid and his followers than they tried to rescue her, and their actions they mimicked in the form of a dance, accompanying them with the tambourine. The savages made peace between them, and after skillfully readjusting the planks of the castle, the damsel once again shut herself up in it, and the dance ended amid the great applause of the bystanders.

Don Quixote asked one of the nymphs who had composed and arranged the dance. She replied that it was a curate of that village, who had a great talent for such masques.

"I will wager," said Don Quixote, "that the said curate or bachelor is a greater friend of Camacho than of Basilio and that he is better at writing satire than at Vespers, for he has fitted most cleverly the talents of Basilio and the riches of Camacho into the dance."

Sancho, who was listening to all that was said, exclaimed: "The king is my cock;[1] I'll stick by Camacho."

"It is indeed easy to see," said Don Quixote, "that you are a boor, and one of those who always cheer for the winner."

"I don't know what kind I am," replied Sancho, "but I know very well that I'll never get such elegant skimmings off Basilio's fleshpots as these I've got off Camacho's." And showing him the pot full of geese and pullets, he snatched up one and began to eat with great gusto, saying: "A fig for the talents of Basilio! What you have is what you're worth. As my grandmother used to say, there are only two families in the world, the Haves and the Havenots; and she always stuck to the Haves, and to this day, master, people prefer to feel the pulse of Have than of Know. An ass covered with gold looks better than a horse with a packsaddle. So, once more I say that I stick by Camacho, from whose pots come the

---

[1] Metaphor from cock-fighting. The victorious cock was called the king.

plenteous skimmings of geese and hens, hares and rabbits. But from Basilio's, if any come to hand or to feet, they'll only be cask-rinsings."

"Have you finished your harangue, Sancho?" said Don Quixote.

"I'll soon have finished it," replied Sancho, "for I see you receive it with annoyance; if it were not for that, there would have been enough work cut out for three days."

"Please God, Sancho," said Don Quixote, "that I may see you dumb before I die."

"At the speed we're going," replied Sancho, "before you die, master, I shall be chewing clay, and then, perhaps, I'll be so dumb that I won't say a word until the end of the world, or at least, until the day of judgment."

"Even if that should happen, Sancho," said Don Quixote, "your silence will never make up for all you have talked, are talking, and will talk all your life. Besides, it is only natural that my death will come before yours, so I never expect to see you dumb, not even when you are drinking or sleeping, and what more can I say?"

"In good faith, master," replied Sancho, "it is no use trusting the fleshless one, I mean Death, who devours the lamb as well as the sheep, and as I've heard our curate say, she tramples with equal feet upon the lofty towers of kings and the lowly huts of the poor. This dame is more powerful than dainty; she not at all squeamish; she devours all and does for all, and she packs her saddlebags with people of all kinds, ages, and ranks. She is not a reaper who sleeps her siestas, for she reaps at all hours and cuts down the dry grass as well as the green. She does not appear to chew, but to bolt and gobble all that is put before her, for she has a dog's hunger, which is never satisfied. And though she has no belly, she seems to have the dropsy and to be thirsty to drink the lives of those who live, as one who drinks a jug of cold water."

"Say no more, Sancho," said Don Quixote; "don't spoil it and risk a fall, for truly what you have spoken about in your rustic speech is what a good preacher might have said. I tell you, Sancho, that if your wisdom was equal to your mother wit, you could take to the pulpit and go preaching your fine sermons through the world."

"He preaches well who lives well," replied Sancho, "and I know no other theologies than that."

"You don't need them," said Don Quixote. "But I cannot make out how it is that, the fear of God being the beginning of wisdom, you, who are more afraid of a lizard than of Him, should know so much."

"Let you, master," replied Sancho, "judge your chivalries and stop meddling with the fears and fancies of others, for I'm as proper a God-fearing man as any neighbor's son. Now let me mop up these skimmings, for all the rest is nothing but idle talk for which we'll have to give an account in the next life."

With these words, he began a fresh attack upon his pot with such hearty gusto that he even aroused the appetite of Don Quixote, who no doubt would have helped him if he had not been prevented by something that must be told further on.

CHAPTER XXI

The continuation of Camacho's wedding, with other enjoyable adventures

While Don Quixote and Sancho were engaged in the conversation reported in the last chapter, they heard loud shouts and a great turmoil raised by the men on the mares as they galloped shouting to welcome the bride and the bridegroom, who were approaching, surrounded by countless musical instruments and festive pageantry and accompanied by the priest, the relatives of both, and the notabilities from the neighboring villages, all dressed up in their finery. When Sancho saw the bride, he cried: "By my faith, she's not dressed like a farmer's daughter but like a fine court lady! Lord bless us, as far as I can make out, the necklace she's wearing is of rich coral, and her green Cuenca stuff is thirty-pile velvet; and mark the trimming of white linen, I swear

it's satin! Now have a look at her hands—are they not
adorned with jet rings? May I be struck dumb if they're not
rings of gold, genuine gold, and set with pearls as white as
curdled milk, every one of them worth an eye out of one's
head! Whoreson wench, what tresses she has! If they're not
false, I've never seen longer or more golden all the days of
my life. Now see how gallantly she carries herself, and
mark her figure! Wouldn't you compare her to a palm tree
moving along laden with bunches of dates? That's what the
baubles that she's wearing look like, dangling from her hair
and her throat. Upon my soul, I swear she's a pretty lass;
she'll sail on an even keel through the shoals of Flanders."

Don Quixote laughed at Sancho's naïve and rustic words
of praise, but he thought that, with the exception of his
lady, Dulcinea of El Toboso, he had never seen a more
beautiful woman. The fair Quiteria looked a little pale,
probably on account of the bad night that brides always
spend preparing themselves for their wedding on the following day.

The procession advanced toward a theater that stood on
one side of the meadow, adorned with carpets and boughs,
where they were to plight their troth and from which they
were to witness the dances and masques. Just as they arrived at the spot, they heard a loud outcry behind them
and a voice crying: "Tarry a moment, thoughtless and hasty
people."

At these cries they all turned their heads and saw the man
who had uttered them. He was dressed in a black garment
slashed with crimson patches like flames. He was crowned
(as they saw presently) with a garland of mournful cypress,
and he carried in his hand a long staff. As soon as he drew
near, they all recognized him as the gallant Basilio, and they
all anxiously waited to see what the end of his words would
be, for they feared that some catastrophe might take place,
owing to his appearance at such a moment. He approached
at last, wearied and breathless, and planting himself in front
of the bridal pair, he dug his staff, which had an iron spike
at the end, into the ground; then, turning pale and gazing
fixedly at Quiteria, he addressed her in a hoarse, trembling
voice as follows: "Well dost thou know, faithless Quiteria,
that according to the holy law that binds us, thou canst take
no husband as long as I am alive, nor art thou ignorant
either that I while I waited for time and my industry to im-

prove my fortunes, I never failed to observe the respect due
to thy honor; but thou, after casting behind thee all thy obligations to my love, art resolved to surrender what is mine
to another whose wealth gives him not only good fortune
but also happiness. Long live the rich Camacho! May he live
many happy years with the ungrateful Quiteria, and let poor
Basilio die, Basilio whose poverty clipped the wings of his
happiness and brought him to the tomb."

With these words he seized the staff that he had stuck in
the ground, and leaving half of it in the ground, he showed
that it served as a scabbard to a fair-sized rapier that was
enclosed within. Then, planting what might be called the
hilt in the ground, with an agile spring and with calm, deliberate purpose he threw himself upon it. In an instant the
blood-stained point and half the blade appeared at his
back, and the hapless man lay stretched on the ground,
bathed in blood, pierced by his own weapon.

His friends at once ran up to his assistance, filled with
sorrow at his pathetic fate, and Don Quixote, leaving
Rozinante, hastened also to help, and taking him up in his
arms, he found that he had not yet expired. They wanted to
draw out the rapier, but the priest who was present was of
the opinion that they should not extract it until he had confessed him, for if they drew it out, he would die at once.
Basilio, however, reviving slightly, said in a faint, sorrowful
voice: "If thou, cruel Quiteria, wouldst only consent in this
last fatal moment to give me thy hand as my bride, I might
still imagine that my rashness could be pardoned, since
by its means I reached the bliss of being thine."

The priest, when he heard this, said that he should attend
to the salvation of his soul rather than to the lust of the body
and that he should beg God's pardon for his sins and for
his act of desperation. To this Basilio replied that he was
resolved not to confess unless Quiteria first gave him her
hand in marriage, for that happiness would strengthen his
will and give him breath for confession.

Don Quixote, hearing the wounded man's petition, cried
out in a loud voice that Basilio's request was just, reasonable, and easy to comply with, and that Señor Camacho
would be no less honored in receiving Lady Quiteria as the
widow of the valiant Basilio than if he received her from her
father. "All that is needed in this case," said he, "is a mere
yes, and no other consequence can come from pronouncing it,

for the nuptial couch of this marriage must be the grave."

Camacho listened to all this in perplexity and bewilderment, and he knew not what to do or say, but the pleas of Basilio's friends were so urgent, as they besought him to allow Quiteria to give her hand to Basilio lest the latter's soul be lost, leaving this life so wickedly, that they compelled him to say that, provided Quiteria was willing, he would agree, since it was to delay only for a moment the fulfillment of their desires. Then, they all ran up to Quiteria, and some with entreaties and others with tears and others with cogent arguments begged her to give her hand to poor Basilio. But she, harder than marble and more immovable than a statue, seemed to be either incapable or unwilling to utter a single word; nor would she have answered if the priest had not told her to make up her mind quickly, for Basilio was about to give up the ghost and there was no time to wait for irresolute minds. At last, without answering a word, sad and distracted in appearance, the fair Quiteria advanced to where Basilio lay with eyes upturned and breathing painfully, muttering her name between his teeth, and as it seemed, about to die like a heathen and not like a Christian. Kneeling by him, she asked for his hand more by signs than by words. Basilio, opening his eyes and gazing fixedly at her, said: "O Quiteria, thou hast become compassionate when thy pity can but serve as a knife to end my life! I have no more strength to bear the glory thou art giving me by selecting me as thine nor can I alleviate the pain that is so swiftly veiling my eyes with the ghastly shadow of Death. I now entreat thee, fatal star of mine, not to give me out of complaisance thy hand, not to deceive me again. I beseech thee to confess and say that without forcing thy will, thou art giving me thy hand as thy lawful husband, for it is not right that thou shouldst deceive me in a state like this, nor play tricks upon one who has always been so loyal to thee."

As he said these words he began to swoon away, and the bystanders thought that each fainting fit would carry away his soul. Quiteria, full of modesty and bashfulness, taking hold of Basilio's right hand with her own, said: "No force could bend my will, and therefore, of my own free will I give thee the hand of a lawful wife, and take thine if thou dost give it freely, being untroubled by the calamity thy hasty act has brought upon thee."

"Yes, I give it," said Basilio, "with the clear understanding that Heaven has been pleased to grant me, and thus I give myself to be thy husband."

"And I," replied Quiteria, "give myself to be thy wife, whether thou livest many years or they carry thee from my arms to the grave."

"I'm thinking," said Sancho at this point, "that for one so badly wounded this young gentleman talks too much. They should make him stop his wooing and attend to his soul; to my way of thinking, he has more of it on the tip of his tongue than between his teeth."

When Basilio and Quiteria had joined hands, the priest with tears in his eyes pronounced his blessing upon them and prayed Heaven to grant good repose to the soul of the newly wedded man. But, no sooner had he received the blessing than he sprang swiftly to his feet and with surprising agility drew out the rapier that had been sheathed in his body. All the bystanders were astounded, and some, more simple than inquisitive, began to shout: "A miracle, a miracle!"

But Basilio replied: "No miracle, no miracle; but a stratagem, a stratagem!"

The priest, perplexed and amazed, hastened to examine the wound with both hands and found that the knife had passed not through Basilio's flesh and ribs, but through a hollow iron tube fitted to that place, full of blood so prepared (as was afterward ascertained) as not to congeal. In short, the priest and Camacho and all the bystanders realized that they had been fooled and deceived. The bride showed no trace of displeasure at the trick, but on the contrary, when she heard people saying that the marriage, being fraudulent, would not be valid, she declared that she confirmed it afresh, from which they all inferred that the two had planned the whole affair secretly together. As a result, Camacho and his supporters became so enraged that they turned to vengeance, and unsheathing many swords, they attacked Basilio, but in a moment an equal number were drawn in his defense, while Don Quixote, leading off on horseback, with his lance couched and his shield as cover, made them all give way. Sancho, who never derived any pleasure from such deeds, straightaway took refuge among the fleshpots from which he had drawn his delicious skimmings, for he was sure that such a place would be respected as sacred. Don Quixote in a loud voice kept crying: "Hold, gentlemen, hold! You have no right to exact vengeance for the wrongs that love does to us. Remember that love and war are the same thing, and since it is permissible in war to make use of stratagems to overcome the enemy, so in the contests of love the tricks and wiles employed to achieve the desired end are allowable, provided they do not bring injury or dishonor on the beloved one. Quiteria belonged to Basilio and Basilio to Quiteria according to the just and benevolent dispensation of Heaven above. Camacho is rich and can purchase his pleasure when, where, and how he pleases. Basilio has nothing but this one ewe lamb, and no one, however powerful he may be, shall take her from him. Those two whom God hath joined together man cannot put asunder, and he who attempts it must first pass the point of this lance."

Saying this, he brandished the lance so fiercely that he struck terror into all who did not know him.

So deep an impression did Quiteria's disdain produce upon Camacho that it caused him to banish her from his thoughts in an instant. The persuasive words of the priest, who was a man of wisdom and good sense, prevailed upon him, and in this way he and his followers were pacified. They put away their swords and blamed Quiteria's inconstancy more than Basilio's ingenuity. Camacho reflected that if Quiteria as a maiden loved Basilio, she would still love him after marriage, and so he should rather give thanks to Heaven for having taken her away from him than for having given her to him.

As Camacho and his group were consoled and pacified, all those in Basilio's calmed down, and the rich Camacho, to show that he felt no resentment at the trick that had been played upon him, insisted that the festivities should continue as if he were really getting married. Neither Basilio, however, nor his wife, nor their followers would take any part in them, and they departed for Basilio's village, for even the poor, if they are virtuous and wise, have those who will follow, honor, and uphold them, just as the rich have their minions and flatterers. They took Don Quixote away with them, for they considered him a man of courage and mettle. Sancho alone was downcast at not being able to take part in the magnificent feast and festival of Camacho, which lasted until nightfall. Dejected and despondent he followed his master, who joined Basilio's party; and he left behind him the fleshpots of Egypt, though in his heart he carried them along with him, and the skimmings in the pot, which by now were almost consumed, evoked in his mind the glory and abundance of the good cheer he was losing. And so, sulkily and pensively, though not hungrily, he followed on Dapple in the wake of Rozinante.

CHAPTER XXII

In which is given an account of the great adventure of the cave of Montesinos, in the heart of La Mancha, which our gallant Don Quixote brought to a happy conclusion

The newlyweds lavished many favors upon Don Quixote, for they felt themselves under an obligation to him for the zeal he had shown in defending their cause, and they lauded his wisdom not less than his valor, considering him a Cid in arms and a Cicero in eloquence. Worthy Sancho enjoyed three days of hospitality at the expense of the pair, from whom he learned that the sham wound was not a stratagem arranged with the fair Quiteria, but one planned by Basilio, who foresaw the result they had witnessed. It is true, nevertheless, that he had informed some of his friends of his designs, that they might, at the right moment, back up his plan and ensure the success of his trick.

"Trick it should not be called," said Don Quixote, "seeing that it aimed at virtuous ends. The marriage of lovers is a most excellent end, for the greatest enemy of love is hunger and continuous want. Love is all gaiety, enjoyment, and happiness, especially when the lover possesses the beloved object, and poverty and want are their declared foes." All this he said in order to persuade Basilio to give up practicing the talents he was skilled in, for though they brought him fame, they earned him no money, and to set himself to acquiring a livelihood by lawful and industrious means, which are always within the possibilities of prudent and painstaking men. The poor man who is a man of honor (if indeed a poor man can be a man of honor), when he posssesses a beautiful wife, has a jewel, and if she is taken from him, his honor is taken and slain. The beautiful and honorable wife whose husband is poor deserves to be crowned with the laurels and the crowns of victory and triumph. Beauty by itself attracts the desires of all those who recognize it, and the royal eagles and birds that soar on high swoop down upon it as upon a tasty lure; but if to this beauty be joined want and penury, then the crows, the kites, and other birds of prey also attack it, and she who stands firm against such trials deserves indeed to be called the crown of her husband.

"Remember, O wise Basilio," add Don Quixote, "that a certain sage, I know not who, held that there was not more than one good woman in all the world, and he advised everyone to think and believe that this one good woman was his own wife, and so he would live happy. I myself am not married, nor, so far, has it even come into my mind to be so; nevertheless, I would dare to give advice to anyone who might ask it, as to the mode in which he should seek a wife to marry. The first thing I would advise him is to pay more attention to reputation than to fortune, for the good woman does not win a good name solely by being good, but by appearing so, for looseness and public frivolity do greater injury to a woman's honor than secret misdeeds. If you bring a good woman to your house, it will be an easy matter to keep her good, and even improve her in that goodness. But if you bring home a bad one, you will find it a hard task to mend her ways, for it is not easy to pass from one extreme to another. I do not say it is impossible, but I consider it difficult."

Sancho, who had been listening to all this, said to himself: "Whenever I say a word that has a bit of marrow and substance about it, this master of mine straightway says that I ought to take a pulpit in my hand and roam the world preaching fine sermons; but I say of him that when he starts stringing sentences and giving counsels, not only might he take a pulpit in his hand, but two on each finger, and go into the marketplaces with the cry, 'Who'll buy my wares?' on his lips. Devil take him for a knight-errant, what a number of things he knows! I used to think to myself that the only things he knew had to do with chivalry, but there's not a thing he doesn't peck at nor dip his spoon into."

Sancho kept mumbling to himself so loud that his master overheard him and asked: "What are you muttering about, Sancho?"

"I'm not saying or murmuring anything," said Sancho, "only saying to myself that I wish I had heard what your worship has just said before I got married. Perhaps I'd say now: 'The ox that's loose licks himself well!' "

"Is Teresa so bad then, Sancho?" said Don Quixote.

"She's not too bad," replied Sancho, "but she's not very good; at least, she's not as good as I would like her to be."

"You do wrong, Sancho," said Don Quixote, "to speak ill of your wife, for she is the mother of your children."

"We don't owe each other a thing," answered Sancho, "for she speaks ill of me when she's got the whim, especially when she's jealous; then Satan himself couldn't stomach her." her."

They remained three days with the newlyweds by whom they were treated and served as royalty. Don Quixote asked the nimble licentiate to get them a guide to conduct them to the cave of Montesinos, of which so many wonderful things were related in those parts, for he had a great wish to explore it and to see with his own eyes if the wonders reported were true. The licentiate replied that he would get him a cousin of his own, a famous scholar, one much given to reading books of chivalry, who would be very glad to guide him to the mouth of the cave and would show him the lagoons of Ruidera, which were also famous all over La Mancha, and even all over Spain. He also said that Don Quixote would enjoy his kinsman's company, who was well versed in writing books and in dedicating them to princes.

The cousin arrived later on, with a she-ass in foal, whose packsaddle was covered with a many-colored rug or sackcloth. Sancho saddled Rozinante, harnessed Dapple, and stocked his saddlebags, to which we should add those of the cousin, which likewise were well supplied. And so, commending themselves to God and taking leave of all, they set out on the road leading to the famous cave of Montesinos.[1]

---

[1] The road to the cave of Montesinos passes through the Plain of Montiel by the lagoons of Ruidera in La Mancha. The cave is deep and according to the local Manchegans it continues for several kilometers and ends in the feudal castle of Rochefrías.

On the way Don Quixote asked the cousin of what kind were his pursuits, his profession, and studies. To which he replied that his profession was that of a humanist, and his pursuits and studies were to write books for publication, all of great profit and no less entertainment to the state; that one of them was entitled *The Book of Liveries,* in which he described seven hundred and three devices, with their colors, mottoes, and ciphers, from which the gentlemen at court could select and use whichever they pleased on the occasion of festivals and revels, without having to beg them from anybody or rack their brains, as they say, to invent them to suit their wishes and purposes.

"For," he said, "I give appropriate devices to the jealous, the scorned, the forgotten, and the absent, which fit them like a glove. I have another book as well, which I mean to call *Metamorphoses,* or *The Spanish Ovid,* a new and most original work in which, while parodying Ovid, I describe the Giralda of Seville, the Angel of the Magdalen, the Gutter of Vecinguerra at Córdoba, and the Bulls of Guisando, the Sierra Morena, the fountains of Leganitos and Lavapiés in Madrid, not forgetting that of the Piojo, that of the Golden Gutter, and that of the Priora; and all these with such allegories, metaphors, and transformations that they will entertain, astonish, and instruct at the same time. I also have another book that I call the *Supplement to Polydore Virgil,*[2] which deals with the invention of things. It is a work of deep learning and research, because I clarify and verify in most elegant style the subjects of great importance that Polydore omitted. He forgot to tell us who was the first man who ever had catarrh and who was the first to use ointments to cure himself of the French pox. All this I explain with the utmost precision on the testimony of twenty-five authorities. So your worship may judge whether I have not worked well, and whether this book will not be indispensable to the whole world."

Sancho, who had been listening carefully to the cousin's narrative, said to him: "Tell me, sir, and best of luck with the printing of your books, but can you inform me—of course you can, as you know everything—who was the first man who scratched his head? I'm of the opinion that it must have been our father Adam."

[2] Polydore Virgil, author of a treatise *De rerum inventoribus* on inventions of all kinds, was imitated by many Italian and Spanish authors in the seventeenth century.

"Yes, it must have been," answered the cousin, "for there is no doubt Adam had a head and hair; and that being so, and as he was the first man in the world, he must sometimes have scratched himself."

"So I believe," answered Sancho; "tell me now, who was the first tumbler in the world?"

"Frankly, brother," replied the cousin, "I am not able to solve that at present, until I have gone further in my studies. I shall look into the matter when I get back to my books, and I'll answer you when we meet again, for this must not be the last time."

"Look here, sir," answered Sancho, "don't go to any trouble about it, for I've hit upon the answer to my question. The first tumbler in the world, let me tell you, was Lucifer, for when they threw or pitched him out of Heaven, he went tumbling into the pit of hell."

"You are right, my friend," said the cousin.

"That question and answer," said Don Quixote, "are not yours, Sancho. You have heard them from someone else."

"Whist, sir," answered Sancho, "for if I start questioning and answering, I shan't be done till tomorrow morning. Yes, for if it's just a matter of asking idiotic questions and giving silly replies, I needn't go begging help from the neighbors."

"You have said more than you know, Sancho," said Don Quixote, "for there are some people who tire themselves out learning and proving things that, once learned and proved, don't matter a straw as far as the mind or memory is concerned."

That day was spent in such pleasant discussions, and at night they put up in a little village that the cousin told Don Quixote was no more than six miles from the cave of Montesinos. He added that if he was determined to enter it, he would need to provide himself with ropes so that he might be tied up and lowered into its depths.

Don Quixote said that even if it reached to the abyss, he was determined to see where it ended. So, they bought about a hundred fathoms of rope, and next day at two o'clock in the afternoon they arrived at the cave. Its mouth is wide and spacious, but full of thorns and wild fig bushes and brambles and briars, so thick and intertwined that they completely close it up.

When they caught sight of it, the cousin, Sancho, and Don Quixote dismounted, and the first two straightaway tied up the latter very firmly with the ropes, and while they were binding him and winding them around him, Sancho said: "Mind what you're doing, master; don't bury yourself alive, or put yourself where you'll be like a flask lowered down into a well to cool. Surely it's no affair of yours to be exploring this place, which must be worse than an underground dungeon."

"Tie me up and hold your peace," replied Don Quixote. "Such an enterprise as this has been reserved for me."

The guide then said: "I pray you, Señor Don Quixote, to note and examine with a hundred eyes all that is inside the cave. Perhaps there may be things that I may include in one of my books."

"The drum is in hands that will know well how to beat it," said Sancho.

When Don Quixote's binding was complete, which went over his doublet but not over his armor, he said: "It was remiss of us not to have provided ourselves of a little bell to be tied on the rope close to me. By the sound you would know that I was still descending and was alive. However, since that is impossible, let God's hand guide me."

Saying this, he fell upon his knees, and in a low voice he offered up a prayer to Heaven, beseeching God to help him and give him success in his new perilous adventure. Then, in a loud voice he cried: "O mistress of my actions and movements, most illustrious and peerless Dulcinea of El Toboso, if it is possible for the prayers and the supplications of thy venturesome lover to reach thy ears, by thy incomparable beauty I beseech thee to listen to them, for they do but beg thee not to refuse me thy favor and protection at this moment when I need them so urgently. I am about to plunge, to engulf, and to sink myself in the abyss that yawns at my feet, only to make the world recognize that if thou dost favor me, there is no impossible feat that I may not accomplish."

With those words he approached the cavern, and finding that it was not possible to let himself down or make an entrance unless by force of arm or by cutting a passage, he drew his sword and began to cut away the brambles at the mouth of the cave. At the noise he made, a great number of crows and jackdaws fluttered out so thickly and with such a rush that they knocked Don Quixote down, and if he had

been as superstitious as he was a good Catholic, he would
have taken it for an evil omen and would have refused to
bury himself in such a place. At last, he rose to his feet,
and seeing that no more crows came out, or night birds such
as bats, which had flown out at the same time as the crows,
he let the cousin and Sancho give him rope, and he began to
lower himself into the depths of the dreaded cave. As he
entered it, Sancho gave him his blessing and made a thousand signs of the Cross over him, saying: "May God and
the Rock of France and the Trinity of Gaeta [3] guide you, O
flower, cream, and skimming of knights-errant! There you
go, you bully of the world, heart of steel, and of arm of
bronze. Once more, may God guide you and bring you back
safe and sound to the light of this world of ours you are
leaving to bury yourself in darkness."

The cousin likewise offered up similar prayers and supplications.

Don Quixote, as he descended, called out for more and
more rope, and they gave it to him little by little. When his
shouts, which sounded from the cave as through a funnel,
could not be heard, they had already uncoiled the hundred
fathoms of rope. They were of the opinion that they should
pull up Don Quixote, for they had no more rope to give
him. They waited, however, for about half an hour and then
began to gather in the rope with great ease and without any
weight, a sign that made them believe that Don Quixote had
remained inside. Sancho, when he realized this, wept bitterly
and pulled away in great haste in order to learn the worst.
But when they came to about eighty fathoms, they felt a
weight, which cheered them up considerably. At last, at
ten fathoms they saw Don Quixote clearly, and Sancho
shouted to him, saying: "Welcome back, master, we fancied
you were staying down there to found a family."

Don Quixote answered not a word, and when they had
pulled him all the way up, they saw that his eyes were shut
and that he appeared to be fast asleep.

They laid him on the ground and untied him, but still he
did not awake. Then, they turned him over this way and

[3] The Rock of France is an allusion to the statue of the
Virgin discovered in the fifteenth century. A Dominican monastery was erected there and the site became the center of a celebrated pilgrimage. The chapel of the Holy Trinity of Gaeta was
north of Naples.

that, and so shook him and rolled him about that at last he came to himself and stretched himself as if he had just awakened from a deep sleep. Looking around him from one side to another like one who had great fear on him, he cried: "God forgive you, friends; you have snatched me from the most delightful vision that any human being has ever beheld. Now indeed I know that all the pleasant things of this life pass away like a shadow and a dream, or wither like the flowers of the field. O hapless Montesinos! O sorely wounded Durandarte! O unlucky Belerma! O tearful Guadiana, and ye luckless daughters of Ruidera, who show by your waters the tears your eyes did shed!"

The cousin and Sancho listened with great attention to the words of Don Quixote, who uttered them as though they were torn from his very bowels. They besought him to explain what he meant and to tell them what he had seen in the hell below.

"Hell do you call it?" said Don Quixote. "Do not call it thus, for it does not deserve such a name, as you will see presently."

He then begged them to give him something to eat, for he was very hungry. They spread the cousin's saddlecloth on the grass, visited their saddlebags, and seated together in good brotherly fellowship, they lunched and supped at the same time.

Then, when the saddlecloth was removed, Don Quixote said: "Let no one stir. Now, my sons, give me all your attention."

CHAPTER XXIII

Of the wonderful things that the consummate Don Quixote said he had seen in the deep cave of Montesinos, whose impossibility and immensity has caused this adventure to be considered apocryphal

It was then about four o'clock in the afternoon when the sun veiled itself behind clouds and shone with subdued light, so that Don Quixote was enabled to relate without heat and discomfort what he had seen in the cave of Montesinos to his two illustrious auditors. He began as follows: "About twelve or fourteen fathoms down in the depth of this dungeon, on the right hand, there is a recess big enough to contain a large cart with its mules. A tiny ray of light enters through some chinks or crevices that are open to the earth's surface. This recess I saw when I was weary and downcast at finding myself dangling in the air by the rope and traveling down through that dark region below without any clear idea of where I was going; so, I determined to enter it and rest for a moment. I shouted to you not to let out more rope until I should ask for it, but you must not have heard me. I then gathered in the rope you were letting down, and after making a coil of it, I sat down upon it, meditating all the while on what I ought to do in order to lower myself to the bottom of the cavern, seeing that I had no one to hold me up. While I was thus perplexed, suddenly and without warning a deep sleep fell upon me, and without knowing the why or the wherefore, I awoke and found myself in the midst of the most delightful meadow that Nature could create or the most vivid imagination visualize. I opened my eyes, I rubbed them, and I found that I was not asleep but wide awake. Nevertheless, I felt my head and my heart to make sure that I myself was there and not some vain specter, but the touch, the feeling, the discourse I held with myself, proved to me that I was the same then as I am here at this moment. Then I saw before me a sumptuous royal palace or castle, with walls that seemed to be made of clear, transparent crystal, and through two great doors that opened I saw a venerable old man come toward me, clad in a long cloak of purple-colored serge that trailed on the ground. He wore over his shoulders and breast a scholar's green-satin hood, and his head was covered with a black Milanese cap, and his snow-white beard fell below his waist. He carried no arms at all, only a rosary of beads that were bigger than fair-sized walnuts—indeed, each tenth bead was like a moderate-sized ostrich egg. His bearing, his gait, his gravity, and his imposing presence, each thing by itself and all of them together, held me spellbound with admiration. He came up to me, and the first thing he did was to embrace me closely. Then he said: 'For many an age, valiant knight Don Quixote of La Mancha, we who inhabit these enchanted solitudes have waited to see you, that you may announce to the world what lies buried in the deep cavern that you have entered, called the cave of Montesinos, an exploit reserved for your invincible heart and spirit. Come with me, illustrious sir, for I wish to show you the wonders that this transparent palace contains, whereof I am the governor and perpetual chief warden, for I am Montesinos himself, after whom the cave is named.'

"No sooner had he said that he was Montesinos than I asked him if the story told in the world above was true, that he had cut the heart of his great friend Durandarte out of his breast with a little dagger and carried it to Lady Belerma, in accordance with Durandarte's instructions at the point of death. He replied that the story was correct in all particulars save in the matter of the dagger, for it was not a dagger, nor little, but a burnished poniard sharper than an awl."

"That same poniard," said Sancho, "must be one of those made by Ramón de Hoces, the Sevillian."

"I do not know," said Don Quixote, "but it could not have been made by that poniard maker, for Ramón de Hoces lived yesterday, whereas the affair of Roncesvalles, where this misfortune took place, was many years ago. But this matter is not of importance; it does not disturb or alter the truth of the story."

"You are right," said the cousin. "Pray proceed, Señor Don Quixote, for I am listening to you with the greatest pleasure in the world."

"And I am no less pleased to tell the story," said Don Quixote. "Well, to continue, the venerable Montesinos led me into the palace of crystal, where in a lower hall, all made of alabaster and extremely cool, there stood an elaborately carved marble tomb, on top of which I saw a knight stretched out full length, not of bronze or marble, but of actual flesh and bone. He had his right hand (which to my eyes appeared somewhat hairy and sinewy, a sign that its owner was of great muscular strength) placed over his heart, but before I could question Montesinos, he, seeing me gaze in amazement at the tomb, said: 'This is my friend Durandarte, flower and mirror of the true lovers and valiant knights of his time. He is kept enchanted here, as I am myself and many other men and women, by that Gallic enchanter Merlin, who, they say, was the Devil's son; but, in my opinion, he is no Devil's son, for he knows, as the saying goes, a deal more than the Devil. How or why he enchanted us, no one knows, but time will reveal the reason at no distant date. What amazes me is that I know as surely as that it is now day that Durandarte ended his life in my arms and that after his death I extracted his heart with my own hands; indeed, it must have weighed a couple of pounds, for according to scientists, he who has a large heart is endowed with greater valor than he who has a small one. Now since the knight did really die, how comes it that he moans and complains from time to time as if he were alive?'

"As he said these words that wretched Durandarte cried aloud:

> " 'O my cousin Montesinos!
>   Heed, I pray, my last request:
>   When thou seest me lying dead
>   And my soul from my corpse has fled,
>   With thy poniard or thy dagger
>   Pluck the heart from out my breast,
>   And hie thee with it to Belerma.'

"On hearing these words the venerable Montesinos sank upon his knees before the hapless knight, and with tears in his eyes, he exclaimed: 'Long since, Sir Durandarte, my dearest cousin, have I done what you bade me on the rueful day when I lost you. I took out your heart as best I could, without leaving the slightest piece of it in your breast; I wiped it with a lace handkerchief; I went off with it by the road to France, after having first laid you in the bosom of the earth with tears so plentiful that they sufficed to wash and cleanse my hands of the blood that stained them when I groped in your bowels. Then, O cousin of my soul, as further proof, at the first place I reached after leaving Roncesvalles, I sprinkled a few pinches of salt on your heart that it might not smell badly and that I might bring it, if not fresh, at least pickled, into the presence of Lady Belerma, whom, along with you and me, and Guadiana, your squire, and the duenna Ruidera and her seven daughters and two nieces, and other friends, Merlin the Wizard keeps here enchanted these many years. And though five hundred years have passed, not one of us has died. Ruidera and her daughters and nieces alone are missing, for Merlin, pitying them for the tears they had shed, changed them into so many lagoons, which now in the world of the living and in the province of La Mancha the people call the lagoons of Ruidera.[1] The seven daughters belong to the kings of Spain and the two nieces to the knights of a very holy order, called the Order of St. John. Guadiana, your squire, who also was bewailing your fate, was changed into a river of his own name, but when he reached the surface of the earth and saw the sun of another Heaven, so great was his sorrow at finding that he was leaving you that he plunged into the bowels of the earth. Nevertheless, as he cannot avoid following his natural course, from time to time he comes forth and shows himself to the sun and the world. The lagoons I have mentioned supply him with their waters, and with their help and the help of many others he enters Portugal in all his pomp and glory. But wherever he goes he shows his sadness and melancholy and takes no pride in breeding choice and tasty fish, but only coarse and tasteless kinds, very dif-

---

[1] La Ruidera (or Roydera) was in reality a Moslem castle in the neighborhood of the lakes to which it gave its name. It was captured from the Moors in 1215.

ferent from those of the golden Tagus. All this, my cousin,
I have told you many times before, but since you make me
no answer, I am afraid you do not believe me, or do not
hear me, which greatly distresses me, as God knows. Now
I have news to give you, which, while it may not alleviate
your sorrows, will by no means increase them. Learn that you
have here before you (open your eyes and you will see
him) that great knight about whom the magician Merlin has
prophesied so many things; that Don Quixote of La Mancha,
I say, who once again and to better purpose than in the past
has revived in the present the already forgotten order of
knight-errantry. By his aid and favor we may be disenchanted, for great deeds are reserved for great men.'

"'And if this does not take place," replied the hapless
Durandarte in a swooning voice; 'if this may not be, then,
O cousin, I say: patience and shuffle the cards.' And turning
over on his side, he relapsed into his former silence without
speaking another word.

"And now a great outcry and lamentations arose, accompanied by deep groans and pitiful sobbings. I turned around
and saw through the walls of crystal in another hall a procession of two lines of fair damsels all clad in mourning,
with white turbans of Turkish fashion on their heads. Behind, in the rear of the procession, walked a lady, for so her
dignity proclaimed her to be, also clothed in black, with a
white veil so long and ample that it kissed the ground. Her
turban was twice as large as the largest of any of the others;
she had eyebrows that met, and her nose was rather flat;
her mouth was large, but her lips were red; her teeth, which
at times she showed, were few and not well set, though as
white as peeled almonds. She carried in her hands a fine
handkerchief, and in it, as well as I could make out, a mum-
mified heart, for it was all dried up and pickled. Montesinos
said that all those in the procession were servants of Durandarte and Belerma, who were enchanted there with their
master and mistress, and that the last one, she who bore
the heart wrapped up in the handkerchief, was the Lady
Belerma, who with her damsels, four days a week, walked in
that procession and sang, or rather wept, her sorrowful
dirges over the body and wretched heart of his cousin. He
added that if she appeared to me somewhat ugly, or at least,
not as beautiful as fame reported, it was because of the bad
nights and the worse days she spent in that enchantment, as

I could see by the great dark circles around her eyes and her sickly complexion. 'And,' said he, 'her sallowness and the rings around her eyes do not come from the periodical ailment common to women, for it is many months, and even years, since it has appeared at her gates, but from the grief her own heart suffers for that object that she continually holds in her hands; it brings back to her memory the misfortune of her luckless lover. If it were not for this, scarcely would the great Dulcinea of El Toboso, so renowned in all these parts, and even in all the world, equal her in beauty, charm, and wit.'

" 'Go slow, Don Montesinos,' said I. 'Tell your story rightly, for you are aware that all comparisons are odious, and there is no reason to compare one person with another. The peerless Dulcinea of El Toboso is what she is, and Doña Belerma is what she is and has been, and there let the matter rest.'

"To which he answered: 'Forgive me, Don Quixote, for I confess that I was wrong in saying that Lady Dulcinea could scarcely equal Lady Belerma, for it was enough for me to learn, I know not by what indications, that you are her knight, to make me bite my tongue rather than compare her to anything but Heaven itself.' After this satisfaction that the great Montesinos gave me, my heart recovered from the shock it had received at hearing my lady compared to Belerma."

"And yet I'm amazed," cried Sancho, "that your worship did not jump upon the old fellow and kick every bone in his body and tear out his beard, without leaving a hair in it."

"No, Sancho, my friend," said Don Quixote, "it would not have been right for me to do so, for we are all bound to show respect to the aged, even though they be not knights, but especially to those who are and who become enchanted. I am certain that I owed him nothing in the matter of the many questions and answers that passed between us."

At this point the cousin remarked: "I cannot understand, Don Quixote, how in so short a space of time as you were down below you were able to see so many things and to say and answer so much."

"How long is it since I went down?" asked Don Quixote.

"A little more than an hour," replied Sancho.

"That cannot be," answered Don Quixote, "for night came when I was down there, and then morning, and again a night and a morning three times, so that, by my reckoning, I have been three days in these remote regions hidden from the upper world."

"My master must be right," said Sancho, "for since everything that has happened to him is by enchantment, perhaps what seems an hour to us would seem three days and nights down there."

"That must be so," said Don Quixote.

"Did you, dear sir, eat anything all that time?" asked the cousin.

"I have not broken my fast," answered Don Quixote, "nor did I feel hunger, even in my imagination."

"Do the enchanted eat?" inquired the cousin.

"They do not eat," answered Don Quixote, "nor do they void excrement, but it is thought that their nails, hair, and beard grow."

"And do the enchanted ones sleep, master?" asked Sancho.

"Certainly not," replied Don Quixote, "at any rate, during the three days I spent with them no one closed an eye; neither did I."

"This is a point," said Sancho, "where the proverb comes pat: 'Tell me the company you keep and I'll tell you what you are.' You, master, kept company with enchanted fellows who were fasting and watching. What wonder, then, that you neither ate nor slept while you were with them? But forgive me, master, if I tell you that of all you've said up to the present, God seize me—I was just going to say the devil—if I believe a single word."

"What!" cried the cousin. "Could Don Quixote tell a lie? Why, even if he wished to do so, this was no time for him to invent such a load of lies."

"I don't believe my master tells lies," answered Sancho.

"If not, what do you believe?" asked Don Quixote.

"I believe," said Sancho, "that this fellow Merlin, or these enchanters who bewitched the whole crew your worship says you saw and talked to down below, has piled your imagination with all that hodgepodge you have been telling and with everything else that you still have to tell."

"That might be, Sancho," replied Don Quixote, "but as a matter of fact, it is not so, for all that I have told you I saw with my own eyes and touched with my own hands. Now, what will you say when I tell you that among the countless marvelous things Montesinos showed me, he pointed out three peasant girls who were capering and frisking like she-goats over those delightful fields, and no sooner had I caught sight of them than I recognized one as the peerless Dulcinea of El Toboso and the other two as the same country wenches that were with her and to whom we spoke on the road from El Toboso? I asked Montesinos if he knew them. He answered that he did not, but that he thought they must be some enchanted ladies of quality, for it was but a few days since they had made their appearance in those meadows. He added that I should not be surprised at that, because many ladies of past and present times were enchanted there in various strange shapes, and among them he recognized Queen Guinevere and her duenna, Quintañona, who poured out the wine for Lancelot 'When from Brittany he came.' " [2]

As soon as Sancho Panza heard his master say this, he thought he would lose his wits, or else die with laughter, for since he knew the truth about the pretended enchanting of Dulcinea and had been himself the enchanter and the concocter of all the evidence, he made up his mind, beyond all shadow of a doubt, that his master was out of his wits and mad as a March hare. So, he said to him: "It was a bitter day, dear master, when you went below to the other world, and it was an unlucky moment when you met Señor Montesinos, who has so transmogrified you for us. Up here, master, you were in your full senses, just as God has given you, uttering your maxims and giving counsels at every turn, and not as you are now, blabbing the greatest balderdash that ever was known."

"I know you, Sancho," replied Don Quixote, "so, I pay no heed to your words."

"No more do I to yours," said Sancho, "even though you beat me or kill me for those I've spoken or mean to speak if you don't correct and mend your own. But tell me, now that we're at peace, what made you recognize the lady our mistress? If you did speak to her, what did you say, and what did she say in reply?"

"I recognized her," said Don Quixote, "because she wore the same clothes as when you showed her to me. I spoke to her, but she did not answer a word, but only turned her back on me and fled, and she ran at such a pace that an arrow would not have overtaken her. I wanted to follow

[2] From the ballad on Lancelot that Don Quixote quoted in the first adventure in the inn (Part I, Ch. II).

her and would have done so if Montesinos had not advised me not to weary myself in doing so, for it would be vain, especially as the hour was approaching when it would be necessary for me to leave the cave. He told me, moreover, that in time he would tell me how he, Belerma, Durandarte, and all who were there were to be disenchanted. What pained me most of all was that while Montesinos was speaking to me, one of the two attendants of the hapless Dulcinea came up to me without my having seen her coming, and with tears in her eyes, she said to me in a low agitated voice: 'My Lady Dulcinea of El Toboso kisses your worship's hand and beseeches you to let her know how you are; because she is in great need, she also entreats your worship as earnestly as she can to be so good as to lend her, upon this new dimity petticoat I have here, half a dozen reals, or as many as you have, which she promises to repay in a very short time.' Such a message amazed me; so, turning to Montesinos, I said: 'Is it possible, Señor Montesinos, that persons of quality who are enchanted can suffer need?' He replied: 'Believe me, Don Quixote of La Mancha, what is called want is the fashion all over the world; it extends throughout, touches everyone, and doesn't even spare the enchanted. And since Lady Dulcinea of El Toboso sends to borrow the six reals, and the security is apparently good, there is nothing to do but to give them to her, for she must no doubt be in sore straits.'

" 'I will not take a pledge for her,' I replied, 'nor can I yet give her what she asks, for all I have is four reals,' which I gave her (they were those that you, Sancho, gave me the other day to hand as alms to the poor I met on the road), and I said: 'Tell your mistress, my dear friend, that I am distressed to hear of her troubles and that I wish I were a Fúcar [3] to relieve them; I would have her know that I cannot be, and ought not to be, in good health, seeing that I lack her pleasant company and witty conversation. So, I beseech her as earnestly as I can to allow herself to be seen and greeted by this her captive and foot-weary cavalier. You must tell her also that when she least expects

[3] Fúcar is the Spanish form of Fugger, the name of famous bankers at Augsburg, who became the Rothschilds of the sixteenth century. They helped Charles V in his wars and rose to great eminence in Spain. *Ser un Fúcar* (to be a Fúcar) was a proverbial saying, meaning to be a Croesus.

it, she will hear that I have made a vow, like the one that the Marquess of Mantua made to avenge his nephew Baldwin when he found him dying on the mountainside, which was not to eat bread off a tablecloth, with some other trifles he added, until he had avenged him. And I will do the same: not to rest, and to wander over the seven regions of the earth more diligently than the Infante Don Pedro of Portugal,[4] until I have freed her from her enchantment.'

"'All that and more, your worship should do for my lady,' said the damsel in answer, and taking the four reals, instead of making me a curtsy she cut a caper that lifted her two yards up into the air."

"Holy God!" shouted Sancho at this point. "Is it possible that such things can happen in the world and that enchanters and enchantments can have the power to change the good of my master into such crazy folly? O master, master, for God's sake, mind yourself, consider your honor and give no credit to this empty balderdash that has destroyed your senses."

"You talk this way, Sancho, because you love me," said Don Quixote, "and because you are inexperienced in the affairs of the world. Everything that presents points of difficulty appears to you impossible. But after time has passed I shall tell you about some of the things I saw below that will make you believe what I have related, for its truth admits no reply or question."

[4] Don Pedro of Portugal was the second son of John of Portugal and brother of Prince Henry the Navigator. The account of his travels in the East between 1416 and 1428, published in 1554, was celebrated in Spain.

CHAPTER XXIV

In which a thousand trifles are recounted, as nonsensical as they are necessary to the true understanding of this great history

The translator of this great history from the original written by its first author, Cide Hamete Benengeli, says that when he came to the adventure of the cave of Montesinos, he found written in the margin, in the hand of Hamete, these words: "I am unable to understand or to persuade myself that all that is written in the previous chapter literally happened to the valiant Don Quixote. The reason is that all the adventures until now have been feasible and probable, but this one of the cave I can find no way of accepting it as true, seeing that it exceeds all reasonable bounds. Nevertheless, I cannot possibly believe that Don Quixote, who was the most truthful gentleman and the noblest knight of the times, could tell a lie; why, he could not lie, even if they riddled him with arrows. On the other hand, when I consider the minute and detailed manner in which he has spoken, I find it still more impossible to believe that he could have fashioned such a tissue of absurdities in so short time.

"So, if this adventure seems apocryphal, it is not I who am to blame, for I write it down without vouching its truth or falsity. You, cautious reader, as you are wise, must judge for yourself, for I cannot, and should not, do more. One thing, however, is certain, that finally he retracted it on his deathbed and confessed that he had invented it, since he believed that it fitted in well with the adventures he had read of in his histories."

After that the author continues: The cousin was amazed

at Sancho's boldness no less than at the forbearance of his master, and he concluded that the calmness he showed arose from his joy at seeing his lady, Dulcinea of El Toboso, even though enchanted. For if this were not so, Sancho's speeches and arguments would have earned him a drubbing, since in reality, the scholar thought, the squire had been a little too impudent with his master, whom he addressed as follows: "Don Quixote, I reckon as well spent the day I have passed with you, for in it I have gained four things. First of all, my acquaintance with your worship, which I consider most fortunate. The second one, an explanation of the secret that is contained in this cave of Montesinos, of the transformations of Guadiana and of the lagoons of Ruidera, all of which will serve me in the *Spanish Ovid* I have in hand. The third, the discovery of the antiquity of playing cards, which were in use at least in the days of the Emperor Charlemagne, as may be gathered from the words that your worship attributes to Durandarte, when at the end of the long talk Montesinos had with him, he woke up and said: 'Patience and shuffle the cards.' The enchanted one could not have learned this phrase and form of speech under a spell, but in France and in the time of the Emperor when he was not enchanted. And this discovery comes just in the nick of time for the other book I am writing, which is the *Supplement to Polydore Virgil on the Inventions of Antiquity*, and I believe that in this he has forgotten to include the invention of cards, but I shall do so now, for it is of great importance, particularly as I shall be able to quote so serious and truthful an authority as Sir Durandarte. The fourth one is to have learned for certain the source of the river Guadiana, hitherto unknown to me."

"You are right," said Don Quixote, "but I should like to know, if by God's favor they grant you a license to print these books (which I doubt), to whom you intend to dedicate them."

"There are lords and grandees in Spain," replied the cousin, "to whom they might be dedicated."

"Not many," answered Don Quixote, "not because they are not deserving of the honor, but because they do not like to receive it, lest they be obliged to give to the authors the satisfaction to which they are entitled for their labor and

courtesy.[1] I know a prince who can supply the defects of
all the rest with such advantages that if I were rash enough
to mention them, I should arouse the jealousy of more than
one generous soul.[2] But let this matter lie fallow until a
more auspicious occasion, and let us go in search of somewhere to lodge tonight."

"Not far from here," said the cousin, "is a hermitage
where lives a hermit who is said to have been a soldier
once and who has the reputation of being a good Christian,
very wise, and also charitable. Near his hermitage he has a
small cottage that he has built at his own cost, but though
it is small, it is big enough to receive guests."

"Does this hermit by any chance keep chickens?" asked
Sancho.

"Few hermits are without them," replied Don Quixote,
"for those you find today are not like those of the Egyptian
deserts, who clothed themselves in palm leaves and ate roots
of the earth. Don't imagine that because I speak well of the
latter, it is at the expense of the hermits of today. I only
mean to say that present-day penances do not equal the
rigor and asceticism of ancient days; but nonetheless, they
are all of them good, at least I consider them good, and if
worse comes to worst, the hypocrite who pretends to be
good does less harm than the public sinner." [3]

While they were talking they saw a man on foot coming
toward them, walking fast and prodding with his stick a
mule loaded with lances and halberds. On coming up, he
greeted them and passed on. Don Quixote, however, cried:
"Stop, good fellow! You seem to be going faster than the
mule wants to."

"I can't stop, sir," replied the man, "for these weapons
you see me carrying are needed for tomorrow. So, I'm compelled to press on. Good-bye; but if you want to know the
reason why I'm carrying these things, I mean to put up to-

---

[1] This is a veiled reference to the miserliness of the Duke of
Béjar and other literary patrons.

[2] In the days of Cervantes the grandees were often called
princes. The reference here is to our author's generous Maecenas,
the Count of Lemos.

[3] This is summed up in the characteristic Spanish proverb:
Pecado encelado, medio perdonado. Cervantes had already discussed this doctrine in "The Dogs' Colloquy."

night at the inn beyond the hermitage. If you're traveling the same way, you'll find me there, and I'll tell you some wonders. So, good-bye once more."

And he prodded his mule on so fast that Don Quixote had no time to ask him what wonders he had to tell them. But as he was curious and always possessed by the desire to learn something new, he decided that they should press on at once, so as to spend the night at the inn, and not stop at the hermitage where the scholar wanted them to stay. So, all three mounted and took the straight road to the inn, which·they reached a little before nightfall. On the way the cousin suggested to Don Quixote that they should call at the hermitage to get a drop to drink, and when Sancho heard him, he turned Dapple in that direction, and Don Quixote and the scholar took the same way. But, as Sancho's ill luck would have it, the hermit was not at home, as they were told by an underhermitess whom they found in the hermitage. They asked for a drop of the best wine,[4] but she answered that her master did not keep it, but if they would have water gratis, she would give them some most willingly.

"If I had a water thirst," answered Sancho, "there are wells on the road where I could have quenched it. O Camacho's wedding and the plenty of Don Diego's house! How often I miss you!"

They left the hermitage and spurred on toward the inn, and a little farther on they came across a youth who was plodding along in front of them at so slow a pace that they quickly caught up with him. He carried a sword over his shoulder, and slung on it, a bundle or parcel of his clothes; as it seemed, it probably contained his breeches, a cloak, and a shirt, for he had on just a short velvet jacket that was frayed and glossy like satin in spots, and his shirt was sticking out. His stockings were of silk, and his shoes were square-toed like those worn at court.[5] He was about eigh-

[4] In the days of Cervantes there were two classes of tavern-keepers in Madrid: those selling *vin ordinaire* (*los de lo barato*) and those selling the higher quality of wine (*los de lo caro*) as well as the lower. Of the latter class there were only eight in the seventeenth century.

[5] The dictator in the days of Philip III was the Duke of Lerma, who was responsible for moving the court from Madrid to Valladolid. As he suffered from enlarged bunions he wore square-toed shoes. Out of servility the courtiers introduced the fashion of wearing the square-toed shoes.

teen or nineteen years of age—a blithe and merry-faced lad, and to all appearance, of an active disposition. He went along singing seguidillas to enliven the boredom of his journey. And as they reached him, he was just finishing one, which the cousin learned by heart and which ran thus:

> I'm off to the wars for the want of pence,
> If I had any money I'd show more sense.

The first to speak to him was Don Quixote, who said: "You travel very lightly, gallant sir. Whither are you bound, may we ask, if it pleases you to tell us?"

The youth answered: "The heat and my poverty are the reasons for my traveling so lightly, and it's to the wars I'm going."

"How poverty?" asked Don Quixote. "The heat I can understand."

"Sir," replied the youth, "in this bundle here I carry a pair of velvet breeches to match the jacket I'm wearing. If I wear them out on the road, I shall not be able to cut an honorable figure in the city, and I've not a penny with which to buy others. And so, I travel along in this fashion to keep cool, until I overtake some companies of infantry that are less than forty miles from here, with whom I shall enlist, and after that there will be plenty of baggage wagons in which to travel to the port of embarkation, which they say is Cartagena. I would rather have the king as lord and master and serve him in the war than some seedy pauper at court."

"Do you get a bounty,[6] by any chance?" asked the cousin.

"If I had served some Spanish grandee or some distinguished personage," replied the lad, "I wager I would get one, for that is what happens to those who serve good masters, for from the servants' hall they rise to be ensigns and captains, or to get a good pension allowance. But I unluckily have always served job-hunting fellows—the kind whose keep and wages were so paltry and wretched that half

---

[6] This was an extra pay above the ordinary pay. As the common soldier's pay was very small, it was usual for youths of good family, who enlisted, to receive an extra gratuity from their commander. Cervantes was rewarded in this way by Don John of Austria, on account of his valiant conduct at Lepanto.

of it would be spent on starching a ruff; indeed, it would be a miracle if a fortune-hunting page [7] could ever come by any good fortune whatever."

"Now tell me, for goodness' sake," said Don Quixote, "is it possible that all the time you served you never were able to get a livery?"

"They gave me two," replied the page, "but as the man who leaves a religious order before being professed is stripped of his habit and receives his own clothes in return, so my masters gave me back my own, for once their business at court was over, they returned to their homes and took back the liveries they had given simply for show."

"What remarkable *spilorceria*, as the Italian say!" [8] rejoined Don Quixote. "Nevertheless, you are lucky to have left the court with so worthy an intention, for there is nothing on earth more honorable or more profitable than, first of all, to serve God, and then your king and natural lord, especially in the profession of arms, by which is won, if not more wealth, at least more honor than by letters, as I have said many a time. Granted that more great families have been founded by letters than by arms; arms have a certain advantage over letters because they possess a certain splendor with which nothing else can compare. Now see that you remember what I am going to tell you as it will be of great profit and relief to you in your hardship: do not allow your mind to dwell upon the troubles that may befall you, for the worst of them is death, and if it be an honorable death, it is the best fortune of all. When they asked Julius Caesar, that brave Roman emperor, what the best death was, he replied: 'The one that comes unexpectedly, suddenly, and unforeseen'; and although he was a heathen and ignorant of the true God, his reply was right from the human point of view. Suppose that they kill you in the first attack or trap you, that you are hit by a cannon ball or blown up by a mine, what odds? You die, and that is the end of the matter. As Terence says, the soldier who dies in battle looks better than the one who lives and seeks safety in flight; and the

[7] Cervantes speaks of his own early experience as page-adventurer and soldier through the medium of this dashing young soldier of fortune.

[8] The Accadémia della Crusa defines *spilorceria* as extreme miserliness.

soldier who is most obedient to his commanders wins the highest fame. And mark my words, my son: it is better for a soldier to smell of gunpowder than of civet, and when old age descends upon you in this honorable profession, even though you may be full of wounds and crippled or lame, at least it will not come upon you without honor, such as poverty will not be able to lessen, especially as they are now making an order that all old and crippled soldiers should be supported and relieved.[9] It is not well to treat such men after the fashion of those who emancipate their Negro slaves when they are old and unable to work, for after casting them out of their houses with the name of freeman, they make them slaves to hunger, from which they cannot hope to be emancipated except by death. For the present I will say no more; but get up behind me on my horse till we come to the inn, and there you shall dine with me. Tomorrow you shall continue your journey, and may God reward you as your intentions deserve."

The page did not accept the invitation to mount, but he did that to dine at the inn, and at this point they relate that Sancho muttered to himself: "God save you for a master! Is it possible for a man who can say so many good things as he has to maintain just now, that he saw the impossible tomfooleries that he relates about the cave of Montesinos? Well, well, time will tell."

It was about nightfall when they arrived at the inn, and Sancho was pleased to note that his master took it for a real inn and not for a castle, as he usually did. And no sooner had they entered than Don Quixote asked the landlord about the man with the lances and halberds. He replied that he was in the stable attending to his mule. The cousin and Sancho likewise went out to the stable to see to their beasts, giving Rozinante the best manger and the best stall in the stable.

[9] These words were used by Cervantes, the wounded ex-serviceman, in an ironical sense. During the reign of Philip II, after the glorious battle of Lepanto, Spain was thronged with poor discharged soldiers who roamed through the country living by their wits like the heroes of Alemán and Quevedo. It was only 150 years after the death of Cervantes that a pension for ex-servicemen was introduced.

CHAPTER XXV

Of the adventure of the braying and the entertaining meeting with the puppet-showman, with the memorable prediction of the prophetic ape

Don Quixote's loaf was all dough, as the saying goes, so impatient was he to hear the wonders that the man with the weapons had promised him. So, he went out to look for him where the innkeeper said he was, and when he had found him, he begged him for an answer to the questions they had asked him on the road.

"I can't tell you the tale of my wonders standing up," answered the man; "I need more time. Let me finish giving my beast his feed, good sir, and I'll tell you things that will amaze you."

"Don't let that trouble you," replied Don Quixote; "I'll help you."

And so he did, sifting the barley and clearing out the manger, and these humble services induced the man to tell him willingly what he wanted to hear. So, sitting down on a stone bench with Don Quixote beside him, and with the cousin, the page, Sancho Panza, and the innkeeper as senate and audience, he began as follows: "Your worships should know that in a town about fourteen miles from this inn, it happened that an alderman lost an ass through the deceitful trick of a maidservant of his (it is a long story to tell), and although the alderman made every effort to find him, he could not. A fortnight or so passed, so the story goes, since the ass was missing, when, as the alderman-loser was standing in the marketplace, another alderman of the same town came up to him and said: 'Give me a reward for good news, friend, your ass has turned up.'

" 'That I will and with gusto, friend,' replied the other, 'but tell me where he has appeared.'

" 'On the mountain,' answered the finder, 'I saw him this morning without a packsaddle or gear of any kind, and so lean that he was a pitiful sight. I wanted to catch him and bring him to you, but he is now so wild and shy that when I approached him, he galloped off and plunged into the thick of the wood. We'll go back together to look for him, if you like; just let me take this she-ass home, and I'll be back directly.'

" 'You'll do me a great favor,' said the man who had lost his ass. 'I'll try to repay you in the same coin.'

"Everybody who is acquainted with the truth of the matter tells the story with these details just as I'm telling you. To be brief, the two aldermen went off hand in hand and on foot to the mountain, but when they reached the exact place where they expected to find the ass, they did not find him, nor was there a sign of him anywhere in those parts, in spite of all their searching. Seeing then that he was not to be found, the alderman who had seen him said to the other: 'Look, my friend, I've just thought of a plan by which we shall certainly discover the animal, even if he's hidden in the bowels of the earth, not to say the mountain. It is this: I can bray marvelously, and if you can do a little in that line, the thing is as good as done.'

" 'A little do you say, my friend?' said the other. 'By God, I'll take odds from nobody, not even from the asses themselves!'

" 'Now we'll see,' answered the second alderman, 'for my plan is that you should go in one side of the wood, and I on the other, so as to make a complete circuit of it. At intervals you'll bray, and I'll bray, and the ass is sure to hear us and bray back at us if he is in the wood.'

" 'I think your plan is excellent,' said the owner of the ass, 'and worthy of our great intellects.'

"There they separated, as agreed, but as chance would have it, both brayed almost at the same instant, and each, deceived by the bray of the other, ran up to look for him, believing that the ass had turned up. When they came in sight of each other, the owner of the lost beast said: 'Is it possible, friend, that it wasn't my ass who brayed?'

" 'It was only I,' replied the other.

" 'Then let me tell you, friend,' said the owner, 'that as far as braying goes there is not a bit of difference between you and an ass, for I've never in my life seen or heard anything more natural.'

" 'Such praises and compliments,' answered the author of the plan, 'apply more accurately to you than to me, my friend. I declare to God that you can give odds of two brays to the greatest and most expert brayer in the world. Your tone is loud, your pitch is up to the mark, your note well sustained, and your cadences dense and rapid. In fact, I acknowledge myself beaten; I yield you the palm and present you with the colors for this rare accomplishment.'

" 'Now let me say,' replied the owner, 'that henceforth I'll rise in my own estimation and reckon I know a thing or two, since I have a talent, for though I thought I could bray well, I never imagined I was as good as you say.'

" 'And I'll add,' replied the second one, 'that there are uncommon talents that are lost to the world because they are wasted on the wrong men who haven't the sense to profit by them.'

" 'Except in cases like this,' said the owner; 'ours are not of much value, but now, please God, they may come in useful.'

"They then separated once more and resumed their braying, but at every turn they deceived themselves and came back to one another, until at last they arranged to give each other, as a countersign, two brays at a time, so that each might understand that it was the other and not the ass. With this double braying they again made the circuit of the wood without meeting with any response, even by signs, from the lost ass. But how could the poor hapless beast have replied? They discovered him in the thickest part of the wood devoured by wolves. When he saw him, the owner exclaimed: 'I was really astonished he did not reply, for if he had been alive, he would have brayed if he had heard us, or he'd have been no ass. But the trouble I've had looking for him was well worth it, even though I found him dead, seeing that I've heard you, my friend, bray so charmingly.'

" 'We're both birds of a feather,' answered the other, 'for if the abbot sings well, the altar boy's not far behind.'

"With this, disconsolate and hoarse, they returned to their village, where they told their friends, neighbors, and acquaintances all that happened in their quest of the ass, each praising to the skies the other's gift for braying.

"The story was the tidbit of the village gossips, and soon it spread to the neighboring villages. And the Devil, who never sleeps, as he is fond of sowing heartburnings, strewing discord everywhere, raising calumnies in the wind, and weaving chimeras out of nothing, ordered it that the people of the other villages no sooner caught sight of anyone from ours than they immediately would begin to bray as if to slap our faces with our aldermen's braying propensities. Then the boys took to it, which is to say that all the demons in hell joined in the game, and the braying kept spreading from one village to another to such an extent that the natives of our braying village are well known and as easily marked down as blacks from whites. And this unlucky jest has been carried so far that many times the mocked ones have sallied out with arms in their hands and in regular array do battle with the mockers without either king or rook, or fear or shame being able to prevent it. Tomorrow or the next day, I believe, the people of my village, the brayers, are to take the field against another village about six miles from ours, one of those that persecutes us most. And to be well prepared for them, I have bought those lances and halberds that you have seen. These are the wonders I said I had to tell you of, and if they don't appear so to you, I know no other."

With this the worthy man ended his tale, and just then, there came through the inn door a man all clad in chamois leather, hose, breeches, and doublet, who cried out in a loud voice: "Master Landlord, have you room? Here's the fortune-telling monkey, and the puppet show, 'The Releasing of Melisendra.'"

"By my faith!" cried the landlord. "Here's Master Pedro! That means there's a grand night in store for us."

(I forgot to say that the said Master Pedro had his left eye and nearly half his cheek covered with a patch of green taffeta, a sign that there was something wrong with all that side of his face.)

"You're welcome, Master Pedro," said the landlord; "but where are the ape and the puppet show? I don't see them."

"They're not far off," replied he of the chamois leather; "but I came on in advance to find out if there was any room."

"I'd put the Duke of Alba [1] himself out to make room for Master Pedro," said the landlord. "Bring in the ape and the puppets. There are folk in the inn this night who'll pay to see them and the tricks of the monkey."

"May luck come of it," answered he of the patch, "and I'll lower the price and be well satisfied if I only pay my expenses. I'll go back and speed up the cart with the ape and the puppet theater."

With that he went out of the inn. Don Quixote then asked the landlord who Master Pedro was, and what show and what ape he had with him. The landlord answered:

"This is a famous puppet-showman who for a good while has been roaming about Mancha de Aragon,[2] exhibiting the show of Melisendra liberated by the famous Don Gaiferos, one of the best and best-acted stories that have been seen in this part of the kingdom for many a year. He also has with him an ape with the most amazing gift ever seen among apes or imagined among men. For if you ask him anything, he listens attentively to the question and then jumps upon his master's shoulders; then, drawing close to his ears, he tells him the answer, and Master Pedro immediately proclaims it. He says far more about past events than about things to come, and though he does not give the correct answer in all cases, he generally makes no mistake, so that he makes us believe that he has the Devil in his inside. He charges two reals for every question if the monkey answers, I mean, if his master answers for him after he has whispered into his ear. And so, it is believed that this same Master Pedro is very rich. He is a gallant man, as they say in Italy, and a boon companion, and leads the finest life in the world; he talks more than six men, drinks more than a dozen—all at the cost of his tongue, his ape, and his puppet show."

At this point Master Pedro returned, and in a cart followed the show and the ape—a big animal, without a tail,

---

[1] This refers to the Great Duke of Alba, the conqueror of Portugal and hero of Garcilaso de la Vega, whose name was on the lips of every Spaniard in the days of Cervantes. It was one of the duke's family—a prior of the Order of St. John—who had founded Don Quixote's so-called birthplace, Argamasilla de Alba. The Great Duke had died in 1583.

[2] This was hilly country between Belmonte and the Sierra of Cuenca.

with buttocks like felt, but not an ugly face. As soon as
Don Quixote saw him, he questioned him: "Tell me, Master
Fortune-teller, what fish do we catch, and what is to be-
come of us? See, here are my two reals."

He then ordered Sancho to give them to Master Pedro,
and the latter answered for the ape: "Sir, this animal does
not answer or give information about things that are to
come. Of things that are past, he knows something, of the
present a little."

"By God," said Sancho, "I wouldn't give a farthing to
learn what's over and done with me, for who knows that
better than I do myself? And it would be mighty foolish for
me to pay for what I know. Nevertheless, seeing that he
knows things present, here are my two reals, and tell me,
most monkeyish sir, what my wife, Teresa Panza, is doing
now and how is she enjoying herself?"

Master Pedro refused to take the money, saying: "I'll not
take payment in advance until the service has been given."
And after he had given with his right hand a couple of
slaps on his left shoulder, the ape with one leap perched
himself upon it, and putting his mouth to his master's ear,
he began to chatter his teeth rapidly. After keeping this
up for the space of a credo, with another leap he skipped
to the ground. At the same instant Master Pedro ran over
and sank on his knees before Don Quixote, embracing his
legs as he exclaimed: "These legs I embrace as I would the
two pillars of Hercules! O illustrious reviver of the now-for-
gotten knight-errantry! O never sufficiently celebrated knight,
Don Quixote of La Mancha, courage of the swooning, but-
tress of those about to fall, arm of the fallen, staff and
consolation of the unfortunate!"

Don Quixote was astounded, Sancho agape, the cousin
speechless, the page astonished, the landlord puzzled; in
short, everyone was amazed by the words of the puppet-
master, who continued: "And you, good Sancho Panza, the
best squire to the best knight in the world, be of good
cheer, for your good wife, Teresa, is well, and she is at this
present moment carding a pound of flax, and as further
proof she has at her left hand a jug with a broken spout
that holds a tidy amount of wine with which she cheers herself at her work."

"That I can well believe," said Sancho. "She's a lucky one,
and if she weren't jealous, I wouldn't exchange her for the

giantess Andandona,[3] who, according to my master, was a very clever and decent woman. My Teresa is one of those who won't let themselves want for anything, even though their heirs should have to foot the bill."

"Now I say," cried Don Quixote, "that he who reads much and travels much, sees much and knows a great deal. I say this because who could persuade me that there are apes in the world that can divine, as I have now seen with my own eyes? For I am that very Don Quixote of La Mancha this worthy animal has spoken of, though he has exaggerated somewhat my virtues. But whatever I may be, I give thanks to Heaven, which has endowed me with a soft and compassionate heart, always inclined to do good to all and harm to no one."

"If I had money," said the page, "I would ask Master Monkey what will happen to me in the peregrination I am making."

To this Master Pedro, who had risen from Don Quixote's feet, replied: "I have already said that this little beast does not answer questions about the future, but if he did, not having money would not matter, for to oblige Don Quixote here present I would renounce all the profits in the world. And now, since I am indebted to him, and to please him, I will set up my puppet show and entertain all who are in the inn, without any charge whatever."

As soon as he heard this news the landlord, delighted beyond measure, pointed out a place where the show might be erected, which was done at once.

Don Quixote was not very pleased with the ape's divinations, as he did not think it right that an ape should divine things past or future. And so, while Master Pedro was preparing his show, he retired with Sancho into a corner of the stable, where, without being heard by anyone, he said to him: "Listen, Sancho, I have considered carefully the extraordinary talent of this ape, and I myself am convinced that without doubt this Master Pedro must have made a pact, tacit or express, with the Devil."

"If the packet is express from the Devil," said Sancho, "it must be a very dirty one, but what good is it to Master Pedro to have such packets?"

"You do not understand me, Sancho," said Don Quixote.

[3] The giantess of *Amadis of Gaul*.

"I only mean to say that he must have made some bargain with the Devil to impart this power to the ape so that he may earn his living, and after he has grown rich, he will hand over to him his soul, for this is the aim of the universal enemy of mankind. What makes me believe this is that I observe that the ape only answers about things past or present, and the Devil's knowledge extends no further, for the future he knows only by conjecture, and then not always, for God alone knows the times and the seasons. For Him there is neither past nor future, all is present. Since this is so, it is clear that the ape speaks in the style of the Devil, and I am astonished that they have not denounced him to the Holy Office and questioned him and extracted from him by whose power he divines. For surely this ape is no astrologer, nor his master either, nor do they know how to cast a horoscope, such as is so much a fashion in Spain that there is not a wench or page or old cobbler who does not claim to set up a figure as easily as pick up a knave of cards from the ground, bringing to nothing, with their lies and their ignorance, the wonderful truth of science. One lady, I know, asked one of those astrologers whether her little lapdog would be in pup and would bring forth, and how many and what color the pups would be. The astrologer, after casting his horoscope, said that the bitch would be in pup and would bring forth three pups, one green, another scarlet, and the third mottled, provided that the said bitch would be covered between eleven and twelve o'clock, by day or night, and that it should be on a Monday or a Saturday. What actually happened was that two days later the bitch died of indigestion, and the astrologer won the reputation in that town of being a famous planet-ruler."

"Nevertheless," said Sancho, "I wish, master, you would tell Master Pedro to ask his ape if what happened to you in the cave of Montesinos is true. As for me, with all respect to your worship, I hold that it was all moonshine and lies, or at least dreams."

"That may be," replied Don Quixote, "but I shall follow your advice, though I have some scruples about doing so."

At this point Master Pedro came to look for Don Quixote and tell him that the puppet show was now in order and that his worship should come to see it, for it was well worth seeing. Don Quixote told him what was in his mind and asked him to inquire from the ape whether the things that had taken place in the cave of Montesinos were imaginary or real, for in his opinion they seemed to partake of both. Master Pedro, without answering, went to fetch the ape, and placing him before Don Quixote and Sancho, he said: "Listen, Master Ape, this gentleman wishes to know whether certain things that happened to him in the cave of Montesinos were false or true."

Making the usual signs, the ape jumped on his left shoulder and appeared to whisper in his ear. Then Master Pedro said: "The ape says that the things your worship saw or that happened to you in that cave were part false and part true. That is all he knows on this question, but if your worship wishes to know more, he will answer on Friday next all that you ask him, for his power is now exhausted and will not return until Friday, as he has said."

"Did I not say, master," said Sancho, "that I could not believe the truth of all the stories you told me, nor even half of them?"

"The future will tell, Sancho," answered Don Quixote. "Time, the discoverer of all things, leaves nothing that it does not drag into the light of the sun, even though it be buried in the bosom of the earth. But enough of that, let us go and see Master Pedro's show, for I am sure it must contain some novelty."

"*Some,* do you say?" said Master Pedro. "This show of mine has sixty thousand novelties in it. Let me tell Don Quixote that this is one of the things most worth seeing in the whole world, but *operibus credite et non verbis,*[4] and let us set to work, for it's growing late, and we have a lot to do and to say and to show."

Don Quixote and Sancho obeyed him and went to where the show was set up and uncovered, plentifully supplied on all sides with lighted wax tapers that gave it a gay and festive air. Master Pedro took his place inside it, for it was he who had to work the puppets, and a boy, a servant of his, stood outside to act as interpreter and explain the mysteries of the show. He held a wand in his hand to point out the figures as they emerged upon the stage. All those who were in the inn were already seated in front of the show, and some were standing, but Don Quixote, Sancho, the page, and the cousin were given the best places. The interpreter then began to say what the hearer or the reader of the following chapter will hear or see.

---

[4] *Operibus credite et non verbis* (Let deeds speak, not words), John 10:38.

CHAPTER XXVI

In which is continued the diverting adventure of the puppet-showman, with other truly entertaining incidents

"Here Tyrians and Trojans, all were silent." [1] I mean that all who looked on were hanging on the lips of the interpreter of the marvels of the show, when drums and trumpets were heard within and the sound of cannon. When the noise ceased, the boy lifted up his voice and cried: "This true story that is here represented before your worships is taken word by word from the French chronicles and from the Spanish ballads that are in the mouths of the folk and in the mouths of the boys who roam the streets. It tells of the release by Señor Don Gaiferos of his wife, Melisendra, who was a captive in Spain, in the power of the Moors in the city of Sansueña, for so they called the city that is now named Saragossa. Let your worships see there how Don Gaiferos is playing at backgammon, according to what they are singing:

Gaiferos is at tables [2] playing,

For now Melisendra is forgotten.

[1] The first line of Virgil's *Aeneid*, Bk. 2.
[2] The game of *tablas,* or tables, was a very ancient game resembling our backgammon. It was played with dice.

"And that character who appears over there with a crown on his head and a scepter in his hands is the Emperor Charlemagne, the supposed father of Melisendra, who, being angered at his son-in-law's idleness and negligence, comes forth to chide him. Note, good folks, with what vehemence he scolds him; why, you would fancy he was going to give him half a dozen raps with his scepter. Indeed, there are authors who say that he did give them and that they were well laid on, too; and after saying many a thing about endangering his honor for not trying to release his wife, he said, so they say: 'I have said enough, look to it!' [3]

"Take notice, gentlemen, how the emperor turns his back and leaves Don Gaiferos fuming and frothing; see now how in a blaze of choler he flings the board and the pieces from him and calls in haste for his armor, begging his cousin Don Roland for the loan of his sword, Durindana. And Don Roland refuses to lend it and offers him his company in the difficult enterprise that he is undertaking. But the valiant, choleric hero will have none of it, saying that he alone suffices to rescue his wife, even though she were hidden in the deepest bowels of the earth. Thereupon he departs to arm himself and start at once upon his journey. Turn your eyes, gentlemen, to that tower, which you must imagine to be one of the towers of the alcazar of Saragossa, now called the Aljafería. That lady who appears on the balcony, dressed in Moorish fashion, is the peerless Melisendra, who many a time used to look out from there upon the road to France and console herself in her captivity by turning her imagination toward Paris and her consort. Note, too, a new incident that now takes place, one such as, perhaps, was never seen before. Can you not see that Moor who stealthily on tiptoe, with his finger to his mouth, creeps up at the back of Melisendra? See how he gives her a kiss right in the center of her lips and how she hastens to spit and wipe them with the white sleeve of her smock. Look how she weeps and tears her lovely hair, as though it were to blame for the trespass. See, too, that stately Moor who stands in the corridors over there; he is King Marsilio of Sansueña, who, having seen the other Moor's insolence, at once orders him to be arrested (though he was a relative and a great favorite), to be given

[3] This phrase became a proverb and we find it in a play by Lope de Vega, El guante de Doña Blanca, Act II.

two hundred lashes, and to be led through the most crowded
streets of the city with criers going before and the officers of
the law behind. And there you see them come out to execute
the sentence, though the crime has hardly been committed,
for among the Moors there are neither indictments nor re-
mands, as among us."

At this point Don Quixote cried out in a loud voice: "Boy,
boy, go on straight ahead with your story and don't go off
into curves and crossways, for proof after proof is needed if
we would establish a truth."

"Boy, do as the gentleman bids you and don't go in for
variations," cried Master Pedro from within, "and you'll always be right. Stick to your plain song and don't trouble
about counterpoints, for they are liable to break down from
being too subtle."

"I'll do so," replied the boy; then he continued saying,
"This figure you see here on horseback, clad in a Gascon
cloak, is Don Gaiferos himself. His wife (now that she has
been avenged of the insolent behavior of the amorous Moor),
standing on the battlements of the tower with calmer and
more tranquil mien, converses with her husband, thinking
him to be some stranger, and addresses him in the words
recorded in the ballad that says:

> Sir Knight, if you to France are bound,
> Pray ask for my spouse, Don Gaiferos.

"The rest I'll not repeat, because prolixity begets weariness. It is enough to see how Don Gaiferos makes himself
known to her and how Melisendra by her joyful gestures
makes it plain to us that she has recognized him, and more so
now when we see her let herself down from the balcony and
place herself on the crupper of her good husband's horse.
But alas, hapless lady, the lace of her underpetticoat has
caught on one of the iron bars of the balcony, and there she
is, dangling in the air without being able to reach the ground.
But watch how merciful Heaven sends aid in our sorest
needs. Don Gaiferos approaches, and without minding to
see whether her rich petticoat is torn or not, he seizes her
and by force pulls her to the ground. Then, with one leap
he sets her on the crupper of his horse, astride like a man,
and bids her hold on tight and clasp her arms around his
neck, so as to cross them on his breast, to avoid falling off,

for Lady Melisendra was not accustomed to such a way of riding. See also how the neighing of the horse shows his joy at the gallant and beautiful burden he carries, his lord and lady! See how they wheel around and leave the city and merrily gallop along the road to Paris! Go in peace, O peerless pair of true lovers! May you reach in safety your longed-for fatherland, and may Fortune place no hindrance to your lucky journey; may the eyes of your friends and kinsmen see you enjoying in peace and tranquillity the remaining days of your life, and may they be as many as those of Nestor!" [4]

Here Master Pedro once more cried: "Keep it plain and simple, boy, don't go in for high flights; all affectation is bad."

The interpreter made no answer, but went on: "There was no lack of idle eyes, which see everything, to see Melisendra descend and mount the horse. Straightaway they ran with the news to King Marsilio, who at once ordered them to sound the alarm. See how quickly it is done and how the whole city shakes with the booming and pealing of the bells from the towers of the mosques."

"Not so," said Don Quixote at this point. "In this point of the bells Master Pedro is altogether wrong, for bells are not used among the Moors, but drums and a kind of shawm like our clarion. It is surely a great absurdity to ring bells in Sansueña."

On hearing this, Master Pedro stopped ringing and said: "Don't single out trifles, Don Quixote, and don't expect a perfection that is impossible to find. Do they not play in these parts almost every day a thousand comedies full of a thousand absurdities, and in spite of that, they run their course successfully and are listened to, not only with applause, but with admiration and all the rest? [5] Go on, boy, and let them have their say. Provided I fill my moneybags, let them show more absurdities than there are motes in the sun."

"That is the truth," replied Don Quixote.

[4] 'The years of Nestor' was a proverb. Nestor was supposed to have lived three centuries, but Homer in the *Iliad* said he had lived and governed for three generations, which, according to Herodotus, meant a hundred years.

[5] Another sarcastic reference to the drama of the day.

The boy continued: "See what a numerous and shining cavalcade rides out from the city in pursuit of the two Catholic lovers! What a number of trumpets are blaring! What a number of clarions ringing! Listen to the drums and timbrels beating! I'm afraid they'll overtake them, and we'll see them brought back tied to the tail of their own horse, which would be a horrifying spectacle."

Don Quixote, seeing such an array of Moors and hearing such a strident din, thought it was his duty to help the fugitives; so, springing to his feet, he cried in a loud voice: "Never as long as I live will I allow an outrage to be committed in my presence upon so famous a knight and so gallant a lover as Don Gaiferos. Halt, baseborn rabble! Follow him not, nor pursue him, or with me you do battle!"

And suiting the action to the word, he drew his sword, and with one bound he planted himself by the show. Then, with extraordinary speed and violence he began to shower blows upon the puppet Moors, knocking over some, beheading others, maiming this one, and demolishing that. And among many more, he delivered one downstroke, which, if Master Pedro had not ducked, huddled, and sidestepped, would have sliced off his head as easily as if it had been made of almond paste. Master Pedro kept shouting, "Stop, Don Quixote! Look and you'll see that those you are knocking over and killing are not real Moors, but only little pasteboard figures! See, sinner that I am, how you're wrecking and ruining my whole livelihood."

Don Quixote, however, did not stop raining slashes, downstrokes, cuts, and backstrokes, and at last, in less than the time required for saying two credos he knocked the whole show to the ground, with all its fittings cut to pieces, King Marsilio severely wounded, the Emperor Charlemagne with his crown and head slit in two. The whole assembly of listeners was thrown into confusion; the ape fled to the roof of the inn; the cousin was afraid; the page was crouching with fear; even Sancho Panza himself was in a state of great alarm, for as he swore after the squall had passed, he had never seen his master in such a mad passion.

The complete destruction of the show being accomplished, Don Quixote became somewhat calmer and said: "I wish I had here before me at the present moment all those who do not, or will not, believe how useful knights-errant are in the world. Consider, if I had not been here present, what would

have become of the valiant Don Gaiferos and the fair
Melisendra? I wager that by this time those curs would
have overtaken them and done them some terrible wrong.
Wherefore, long live knight-errantry above everything that
lives on earth this day!"

"Let it live and welcome," said Master Pedro in a faint
voice, "and let me die, for I'm so unlucky that I may say
with King Rodrigo:

> 'Yesterday I was the Lord of Spain;
> Today there's not a battlement
> That I may call my own.' [6]

"Hardly half an hour ago, barely a moment ago, I saw
myself lord of kings and emperors, with my stables, my
chests and bags full of countless horses and innumerable gay
dresses, but now I see myself forlorn and desolate, poor and
a beggar, and above all, without my ape, for I swear my teeth
will have to sweat before I am able to catch him again. And
all this has happened because of the rash fury of this knight
here, who, they say, protects orphans, redresses wrongs, and
does other charitable deeds. In my case alone his noble intentions have failed, blessed be the loftiest thrones of Heaven!
Indeed, Knight of the Rueful Figure he must be, for he has
disfigured mine."

Sancho Panza was moved by Master Pedro's words and
said to him: "Don't cry and complain, Master Pedro, you're
breaking my heart. I want you to know that my master, Don
Quixote, is so Catholic and scrupulous a Christian that if he
once realizes that he has done you any wrong he will pay up
and make it up to you to your advantage."

"If only Don Quixote pays me for some part of the
damage he has done me, I'll be well satisfied, and his worship
will salve his conscience, for there's no salvation for one
who keeps what belongs to another against the will of the
owner and makes no restitution."

"That is true," said Don Quixote, "but up to the present I
am not conscious of having anything that belongs to you,
Master Pedro."

[6] These lines are reminiscent of the ancient ballad of King
Rodrigo's loss of Spain in the *Cancionero de romances de Amberes,* fol. 127 Vto.

"What!" cried Master Pedro. "And these relics strewn about the hard, sterile ground—what scattered and annihilated them but the invincible force of that mighty arm of yours? Whose are those corpses but mine? With whom did I earn my livelihood if not with them?"

"Now I am fully convinced," said Don Quixote, "of what I have often believed, that these enchanters who persecute me are forever conjuring up before my eyes figures like these, and then they turn and transform them into what they please. Truly I declare to you, gentlemen who hear me, that all that has taken place here seemed to me to happen really: that Melisendra was Melisendra, Don Gaiferos Don Gaiferos, Marsilio Marsilio, and Charlemagne Charlemagne. It was for this reason that my anger rose within me, and in order to be loyal to my profession of knight-errant I wished to give aid and protection to those who were fleeing, and with this virtuous intention I did what you have seen. If the result has been the opposite, it is not my fault, but that of the wicked beings who persecute me. Nevertheless, I am willing to condemn myself in costs for my error, though it did not proceed from malice. Let Master Pedro see what he wants for the damaged figures, for I offer to pay him for them in good and current money of Castile."

Master Pedro bowed to him, saying: "I expected no less from the unique Christian spirit of the valiant Don Quixote of La Mancha, the true helper and protector of all needy and distressed vagabonds. The innkeeper here and the great Sancho Panza shall be arbiters and assessors between your worship and me of what these damaged figures are worth or might be worth."

The landlord and Sancho agreed to act, and then Master Pedro lifted from the ground King Marsilio of Saragossa, minus the head, and said: "You can see how impossible it is to restore this king to his former state; therefore, I think, subject to your better judgment, that I should receive for his decease, end, and demise the sum of four and a half reals."

"Go on," said Don Quixote.

"Well, for this slash from top to bottom," continued Master Pedro, taking up in his hands the cleft Emperor Charlemagne, "it would not be too much to ask five reals and a quarter."

"That's no small sum," said Sancho.

"Nor too much," replied the landlord. "Let us settle the

difference and give him five reals."

"Give him the five and a quarter," said Don Quixote. "In such a great misfortune as this, a quarter more or less makes precious little difference; but conclude the business quickly, Master Pedro, for the supper hour approaches and I am somewhat hungry."

"Now, for this puppet," said Master Pedro, "which is the fair Melisendra and is minus its nose and eye, I want—mind you I'm being fair to you—two reals and twelve maravedis."

"It must be the work of the Devil," cried Don Quixote, "if Melisendra and her husband are not at least at the French frontier, for the horse they rode seemed to me to fly rather than gallop, so there is no reason to sell me a cat for a hare by showing me a noseless Melisendra, when she is now, if all went well, enjoying herself to her heart's content in France with her husband. May God give everyone his deserts, Master Pedro, and let us play fair and square. Proceed."

Master Pedro, perceiving that Don Quixote was swerving from the path of reason and returning to his old craze, was determined not to let him escape; so he said: "This must not be Melisendra but one of her handmaidens. So, just give me sixty maravedis and I'll be content and count myself well paid."

In this manner he continued to put a price on the many shattered puppets, which afterward the two arbitrators reduced to the satisfaction of both sides. The total reached the sum of forty reals and three quarters, and in addition to this sum, which Sancho straightaway paid, Master Pedro asked two reals for his trouble in catching the ape.

"Give them to him, Sancho," said Don Quixote, "not to catch the monkey but to get monkey drunk.[7] I would willingly give two hundred this instant as reward for good news to anyone who could tell me for certain that Lady Melisendra and Don Gaiferos are now in France among their own folk."

"No one can tell us that better than my ape," said Master Pedro, "but there's no devil can catch him now. However, I expect affection and hunger will make him search for me tonight. Anyhow, God's dawn will soon be here and we shall see."

[7] *Mona* (she-monkey) is a slang expression for a drunken orgy.

And so the puppet-show squall passed, and all took supper in peace and good fellowship at Don Quixote's expense, for he was of a most liberal disposition.

Before dawn the man with the lances and halberds departed and soon after the student and the page took leave of Don Quixote. The former set off for home, and the latter continued his journey, toward which Don Quixote contributed a dozen reals. Master Pedro did not want to enter into any more arguments with Don Quixote, whom he knew only too well, so he rose before the sun, and collecting together the remains of his show and his ape, he also went off in search of his adventures. The landlord, who did not know Don Quixote, was no less amazed by the knight's generosity than by his madness. Finally, after Sancho, by his master's orders, had paid him very well, the two said farewell to him and left the inn at about eight o'clock in the morning for the open road, where we shall leave them, for this is a fitting moment for relating other matters pertaining to this famous history.

CHAPTER XXVII

In which we are told who Master Pedro and his ape were, with Don Quixote's misfortune in the braying adventure, which did not end as he wished or expected

Cide Hamete, the chronicler of this great history, opens this chapter with these words: "I swear as a Catholic Christian." On this his translator comments that Cide Hamete by swearing as a Catholic Christian, when he doubtlessly was a Moor, meant only that as the Catholic Christian, when he swears, swears or ought to swear the truth and observe it in all he says, so he would tell the truth, as if he had sworn like a Christian Catholic, in writing of Don Quixote, especially in explaining who Master Pedro was and who was the ape that astounded all the villages by his prophecies. He then goes on to say that those who had read the first part of this history would clearly remember that Ginés de Pasamonte, whom Don Quixote set free with other galley slaves in the Sierra Morena, a good turn for which he was scurvily thanked and worse requited by that malignant and ill-conditioned crew. This Ginés de Pasamonte, whom Don Quixote called Ginesillo de Parapilla,[1] was he who robbed Sancho Panza of his Dapple. As the time and manner of the theft was omitted from the first part through the negligence of the printers, many readers have attributed the omission to the author's faulty memory. But, in a word, Ginés it was who stole the ass, while Sancho Panza was asleep on its back, adopting the cunning trick used by Brunelo when he abstracted Sacripante's steed from between his legs at the siege

---

[1] It was not Don Quixote, but the commissary who called Ginés de Pasamonte Ginesillo de Parapilla.

of Albraca. And later Sancho recovered him, as has been related. This Ginés, then, was afraid of being caught by the
officers of the law, who were on the hue and cry after him to
punish him for his crimes and rascalities, which were so
numerous and outrageous that he even wrote a whole volume
to describe them. He, therefore, resolved to pass into the
kingdom of Aragon. So, putting a patch over his left eye, he
took up the trade of puppet-showman, for at this and at the
sleight of hand he was a wizard.

Later on he bought the ape from some released Christians
who had returned from Barbary, and taught it to jump on
his shoulder when he made a certain signal and to mutter,
or appear to mutter, in his ear. Thus prepared, before entering a village with his ape and puppet show, he would ascertain in the neighboring village, or from anyone he could,
what particular incidents had taken place in such and such a
village and what people had been concerned in them. After
committing these to memory, the first thing he would do was
to stage his puppet play, which sometimes was about one
story, sometimes about another, but all bright, amusing, and
familiar to the audience. Once the performance was over,
he would announce the ape's accomplishments, telling the
people the beast could divine all the past and the present,
though he had no skill in things to come. For the reply to
each question he asked two reals, though for some he made
it cheaper, according as he felt the pulses of the questioners;
and sometimes he would put up at the homes of people
whose stories he knew, and if they asked him no questions,
as they were unwilling to pay, he would make a sign to the
ape and then say that he had been told of such and such
things, which tallied exactly with what had happened. In
this way he gained an immense reputation, and everyone
followed him. At other times he was cunning enough to
adapt his answers to suit the questions, and as no one cross-
examined him or pressed him to say how his ape did his di-
vining, he made apes of them all and filled his leather
pouches. Thus, no sooner did he arrive at the inn than he
recognized Don Quixote and Sancho, and knowing them, he
was easily able to astound the two of them and all the rest
who were present. But it would have cost him dear if Don
Quixote's hand had descended a little lower when he sliced
off the head of King Marsilio and played havoc with all his
chivalry, as has been mentioned in the previous chapter.

This is all there is to say of Master Pedro and his ape.

To return to Don Quixote of La Mancha, I say that after leaving the inn, he determined first to visit the banks of the river Ebro and all that neighborhood before entering the city of Saragossa, since there was time for this before the jousts began. With this intention he continued his journey and traveled for two days without meeting with anything worth recording. The third day, however, as he was mounting the slope of a hill, he heard a great noise of drums, trumpets, and musketry. At first he thought that a regiment of soldiers was passing that way, and to get a sight of them, he spurred on Rozinante and ascended the hill. But when he reached the top, he saw below him more than two hundred men armed, as he reckoned, with different sorts of weapons, such as spears, crossbows, partisans, halberds, and pikes, as well as some muskets and many bucklers. Descending the hill, he drew so near to the array that he distinctly saw their banners and could make out the different colors and devices they bore, especially one on which upon a standard or pennon of white satin was a lifelike painting of an ass of the small Sardinian breed, with its head up, its mouth open, and its tongue out, in the very act and posture of braying, around which were written in large letters these two lines:

> They brayed not in vain
> Our gallant bailiffs twain.

From this device Don Quixote concluded that these must be the people of the braying village, and so he told Sancho, informing him of what was inscribed on the standard. He said also that the man who had given them an account of the affair had been wrong in saying that they were two aldermen who brayed, for according to the verses on the standard they were bailiffs.

Sancho answered: "Don't worry about that, sir; it may well be that the aldermen who then brayed have come in time to be bailiffs of their village, and so they can be called by both titles; what's more, it doesn't make any difference to the truth of the story whether the brayers are aldermen or bailiffs; a bailiff's as good at braying as an alderman."

They then realized that the mocked village had come out to fight another that had mocked it more than was reasonable or neighborly.

Don Quixote rode up to them to Sancho's great dismay, for he did not relish finding himself mixed up in such forays. The men in the battalion received him in their midst, thinking that he was one of their party. Don Quixote then raised his visor with noble air and bearing and advanced to the ass-standard, where all the chiefs of the army gathered around to look at him, struck with the same amazement that fell on all who saw him for the first time. And seeing them staring at him so intently without anyone speaking or asking him a question, he determined to profit by that silence, and so breaking his own, he lifted up his voice and said: "My good sirs, I beseech you most earnestly not to interrupt a speech that I wish to deliver to you until you find that it either vexes or wearies you. Should this happen, at the slightest hint you give, I shall clap a seal on my mouth and a gag on my tongue."

They all urged him to say what he pleased, for they would most willingly listen to him. So, with their permission Don Quixote proceeded, saying: "I, dear sirs, am a knight-errant, whose calling is arms and whose profession is to succor those who need succor and to relieve the distressed. I heard some days ago of your misfortune, and the cause that drives you to take up arms with such frequency against your foes, and having pondered over your affairs not once but many times, I find that according to the rules of dueling, you are mistaken in considering yourselves affronted, for one individual cannot affront an entire village, unless he charge it collectively with treason, because he does not know who in particular has committed the treason that is the subject of the charge. An example of this we have in Don Diego Ordóñez de Lara, who challenged the whole city of Zamora because he was not aware that Vellido Dolfos alone had committed the treason of killing his king. So, it was he who challenged them all, and the vengeance and the answer were the concern of all, though it is true that Don Diego went a little too far and even greatly exceeded the correct limits of a challenge, for he was not obliged to challenge the dead, the waters, the bread, the unborn children, or the other objects that are listed there.[2] But a truce to that, for once anger

---

[2] This is a reference to the *Crónica del Cid,* or to the ballad in the *Cancionero de Amberes,* which describes the results of the murder of the king by the traitor Vellido Dolfos in the siege of Zamora. It is translated by J. G. Lockhart:

overflows its banks, neither father, governor, nor bridle can muzzle its tongue. Then, since one man alone cannot affront a kingdom, a province, a city, a republic, or a whole population, there is no need to go out and take up the challenge for such an affront, for it is not one. And it would be a fine thing, indeed, if the people of Clock Town were to be forever at daggers drawn with anyone who called them by that name, nor should the ladlers, or the eggplant-lovers, or the whalers or the soap boilers, or others whose names and nicknames are forever in the mouths of boys and the rabble. A fine thing, indeed, if all those famous towns were to become enraged, revenge themselves, and perpetually go about unsheathing and sheathing their swords, like pulling and pushing the tubes of a sackbut, in every petty squabble. No, no, God does not will or permit that. Prudent men and well-ordered states must take up arms, unsheath their swords, and imperil their persons, their lives, and their goods for four reasons. Firstly, to defend the Catholic faith; secondly, in self-defense, which is permitted by natural and divine law; thirdly, in defense of honor, family, and estate; fourthly, in the service of the king in a just war; and if we wish to add a fifth (which can be included in the second), in defense of one's country. To these five principal causes we can add others that are just and reasonable and compel one to take up arms. But he who rushes to arms for childish trifles and for things that should be regarded as laughable and highly diverting rather than as an affront, is, in my opinion, completely devoid of common sense. Besides, to take unjust vengeance—and no vengeance can be just—goes directly against the sacred law we profess, which commands us to do good to our enemies and to love those who hate us, a commandment that, though it may seem rather difficult to obey, is only so for those who have less of God than of the world and more of the flesh than of the spirit. For Jesus Christ, God and true man, who never lied, nor could, nor can lie, for He is our lawgiver, said that His yoke was easy and His burden light. He would not then have commanded us to do anything that was impossible to perform. So, my dear sirs, you are bound by laws both divine and human to keep the peace."

Thrice loud and long he shouted, "False City, hear my cry,
I curse thee, sinful Zamora, I curse and I defy."

"The Devil take me," said Sancho to himself at this point, "if this master of mine isn't a thologian; and if he isn't one, he's as like as one egg to another."

Don Quixote took a little breath, and seeing that they were still giving him their attention, he determined to go on with his speech. And he would have done so, if Sancho with his irrepressible sharpness had not intervened, for seeing his master pause, he piped up for him: "My master, Don Quixote of La Mancha, formerly called the Knight of the Rueful Figure and now the Knight of the Lions, is a very discreet gentleman who knows both Latin and the vernacular like a bachelor, and in all he deals with or counsels, he acts like a very good soldier. He has all the laws and rules of what they call the duel at his fingertips, so there is nothing more to do but to follow his advice. Put the blame on me if it leads you astray, all the more so since it's said that it's foolish to fly into a rage merely for hearing a fellow braying. I remember that when I was a boy I used to bray whenever I had the fancy, without anyone tipping me the wink, and I did it so prettily and naturally that when I brayed all the asses in the village brayed too. But that didn't prevent me from being the son of my parents, who were decent, honest people; and though more than one of the stiff-necked toffs in the place envied me my talent, I didn't care two farthings. And to show you that I'm speaking the truth, wait and listen, for this trick's like swimming: once learned you never forget it."

Then, putting his hands to his nose, he began to bray so uproariously that all the neighboring vallies echoed. But one of the villagers standing near him, thinking he was making fun of them, raised a pole he was carrying and dealt him such a blow with it that Sancho was knocked to the ground without more ado. Don Quixote, seeing his squire so maltreated, went for his assailant with his lance in his hand, but so many of them intervened that it was impossible to take his vengeance. On the contrary, finding that a shower of stones rained down upon him and that a thousand leveled crossbows and no less a number of muskets threatened him, he turned Rozinante's reins and departed from them as fast as he could gallop, beseeching God with all his heart to be delivered from that peril and fearing at every step that a bullet would enter his back and come out through his chest; and every moment he fetched a breath to see whether it failed him. But the band of villagers were glad to see him

flee and did not shoot at him. As for Sancho, they set him
upon his ass, scarcely conscious, and let him go after his
master, not that he had sense enough to guide the beast, but
Dapple followed in Rozinante's traces, for he could not
bear to be separated from him. Now that Don Quixote had
gone a good distance, he turned his head and saw Sancho
coming. Then, seeing that no one was pursuing him, he waited
for him.

The village band stayed there till night, and then, since
their enemies had not come out to battle, they went back to
their village, rejoicing and exulting, and had they known
the ancient custom of the Greeks, they would have raised
there on that spot a trophy.[3]

CHAPTER XXVIII

*Of things that Benengeli says the reader will learn if
he reads them with attention*

When a valiant man flees, it is obvious that there is foul
play, and it is a wise man's duty to reserve himself for a
better occasion. This truth was verified in Don Quixote, who,
giving way to the fury of the villagers and the evil intentions of that indignant band, took to his heels, and without
thinking of Sancho or of the peril he was in, he withdrew as
far as he thought necessary for safety. Sancho followed him,
lying across his ass, as has been said. He caught up with his
master at last, already having recovered his senses, and when
he overtook him, he let himself fall at the feet of Rozinante,
all sore, bruised, and beaten. Don Quixote dismounted to

---

[3] After a victory the Greeks always raised a trophy, which
consisted in piling their arms.

examine his wounds, but finding him sound from head to foot, he said to him very angrily: "It was an evil hour that you learned to bray, Sancho! And when did you find it a good idea to mention a rope in the hanged man's house? What counterpoint could you expect for your braying music but cudgelings? Give thanks to God, Sancho, that instead of blessing you with a stick, they did not make the sign of the Cross over you with a cutlass."

"I'm in no state now to answer," replied Sancho, "for it's like speaking through my shoulders. Let us mount and get away out of here, and I'll silence my brayings. But I can't help telling how knights-errant take to their heels and leave their good squire to be milled like privet or wheat at the hands of their enemies."

"Retreat is not flight," said Don Quixote, "you must know, Sancho, that courage that is not based upon prudence is called rashness, and the achievements of the rash are rather to be ascribed to good luck than courage. So, I confess that I retired but I did not fly; and in this I have imitated many valiant persons who have reserved themselves for better times. The histories are full of such examples, which I shall not quote now, for they would be neither of profit to you nor of pleasure to me."

By this time Sancho was once more mounted, with the help of Don Quixote, who in his turn got upon Rozinante, and at a leisurely pace they proceeded toward the shelter of a grove of poplars that appeared in sight about a mile away. From time to time Sancho uttered deep sighs and painful groans, and when Don Quixote asked him the cause of his anguish, he replied that from the base of his spine to the nape of his neck he was in such pain that it was driving him out of his senses.

"The cause of your pain, I am sure," said Don Quixote, "must be that as the stick with which they beat you was long and slender, it reached the whole of your back, where the aching parts lie. If it had caught more of you, the pains would have been worse."

"I swear to God," cried Sancho, "your worship has cleared up a great mystery in a pretty fashion! Hang it! Was it so difficult to find the cause of my pain that you have to tell me that the aching parts are just the ones basted by the stick? If my ankles were sore, you might have had cause to wonder why they pained me, but that I should ache where they drubbed me, there's precious little mystery about that. To tell you the truth, my dear master, another man's aches hang by a hair, and every day I'm more forcibly reminded of how little I can expect from keeping company with your worship, for since this time you let me be beaten, we shall come back again and again to the blanketings of old and other such follies, and if it's my back that pays the penalty today, next time it'll be my eyes. I should do much better —only I'm just an uncouth yokel and shan't get any wiser in all the days of my life—I should do much better, I repeat, to go back home and support my wife and bring up my children with whatever God may be pleased to give me, instead of gallivanting after your worship over trackless roads and nonexistent paths, drinking badly and eating worse. Then, take sleeping! Count out, brother squire, seven feet of earth, and if you want more, count as much again; as you pay the piper, you may stretch yourself out to your heart's content. May I see the knight who first started knight-errantry burning in Hell and ground to dust, or at least the first who was willing to be squire to such a pack of idiots as the knights-errant of old must have been. Of the ones today I'll say nothing, for because your worship is one of them and because I'm certain you know a point more than the Devil about all you talk and think about, I hold them in respect."

"I would lay a good wager with you, Sancho," said Don Quixote, "that now that you are talking with no one to stop you, you don't feel an ache in all your body. Say, my son, all that comes into your mind and into your mouth, for provided it relieves you of your pain, I shall willingly restrain the resentment your foolish ranting causes me. And if you are so eager to return home to your wife and children, God forbid that I should hinder you. You have money of mine. Reckon how long it is since we left our village on this third expedition,[1] reckon how much you are owed every month, and pay yourself out of hand."

"When I served Tomé Carrasco," answered Sancho, "the father of the bachelor Sansón Carrasco, whom your worship knows well, I got two ducats a month, besides my food. I don't know what I should earn with your worship, but I know that a knight-errant's squire has more work to do than

---

[1] Cervantes forgets that this was Sancho's second sally, not his third. He did not accompany Don Quixote on the first sally.

a farmer's man. The fact of the matter is that we who work for farmers, however much we have to toil by day and whatever ill may happen, have a stew for supper by night and a bed to sleep in. But I haven't slept in a bed since I've been in your worship's service, and except for the short while we stayed in Don Diego de Miranda's house, and the outing I had with the skimmings from Camacho's pots, and what I ate, drank, and slept at Basilio's, all the rest of the time I've slept on the hard ground, in the open air, subject to what they call the inclemencies of heaven, sustaining myself on scraps of cheese and crusts of bread, and drinking water now from the brooks, now from the springs in the byways we travel."

"I confess, Sancho," said Don Quixote, "that all you say is true. How much do you think I should give you more than Tomé Carrasco did?"

"I think," said Sancho, "if your worship gave me two reals more a month, I should be satisfied. That is so far as wages for my work go. But when we come to the matter of your solemn promise to grant me the governorship of an island, you should in all fairness add another six reals for compensation, which would make thirty reals in all."

"That is well," replied Don Quixote, "according to the wages you have assigned to yourself, it is twenty-five days since we left the village. Calculate proportionally, Sancho, and see what I owe you. Then pay yourself, as I have said, by your own hand."

"God bless us and save us!" cried Sancho. "Your worship's far out in your calculation, for in the business of the promised island you must count from the day your worship promised it to this present hour."

"Well, how long is it since I made the promise, Sancho?" asked Don Quixote.

"If I remember rightly," answered Sancho, "it must be more than twenty years, and three days more or less."

Don Quixote gave himself a great slap on the forehead and began to laugh heartily, saying: "Why, I scarcely traveled two months in the Sierra Morena or in all the course of our sallies; yet, how can you say, Sancho, that it is twenty years since I promised you the island? I think you want to liquidate in your wages all the money of mine you have. If this is so and it pleases you to do so, I grant it here and now, and much good may it do you, for rather than have so bad a squire I shall be glad to be left poor and penniless. But tell me, perverter of the squirely ordinances of knight-errantry, where have you ever seen or read that a knight-errant's squire has bargained with his master, saying, 'You will have to give me so much a month for serving you?' Embark, embark, scoundrel, rogue, monster, for you seem to be all three —embark, I say, on the *mare magnum* of their histories, and if you find that any squire has said or thought as you have spoken, you may nail it on my forehead and seal fool on my face with your five fingers as well. Turn your reins on your ass's bridle and go back home, for you shall not go one step further with me. O ill-requited bread! O ill-placed promises! O man more beast than human! Now, when I was intending to set you up in state, and in such a state that they would call you lord despite your wife, now do you leave me? Are you going now when I had reached the firm and mighty resolve to make you lord of the best island in the world? Well, as you have said again and again, the honey is not . . . etc. An ass you are, an ass you needs must be, and an ass you will end when the course of your life is run, for I really believe that it will reach its last turn before you realize and admit that you are a beast."

Sancho looked fixedly at Don Quixote while he was uttering these reproaches, and he was so stricken with remorse that the tears came into his eyes, and in a weak and doleful voice he cried: "Master, I confess that all I need to be a complete ass is the tail. If your worship would care to put one on me, I'll reckon I have deserved it and would serve you as an ass the rest of my life. Pardon me, your worship, take pity on my youth, consider that I know but little and that if I talk a lot, it springs from weakness rather than from malice. But who errs and mends himself to God commends."

"I should have been surprised, Sancho, if you had not mingled a bit of a proverb with your speech. Well, I pardon you, on condition that you mend your ways and show yourself in the future less fond of your own interests, but try instead to widen your mind, pluck up courage and spirit to hope for the fulfillment of my promises, for though there may be delays it is not impossible."

Sancho promised to do his utmost, even if it meant drawing strength out of weakness. Then they entered the wood, where Don Quixote settled himself at the foot of an elm and Sancho at the foot of a beech, for such trees have

feet but no hands. Sancho spent the night in pain, for the
beating made itself more felt with the night dew. But Don
Quixote passed it in his everlasting meditations, though for
all that, they both closed their eyes in sleep. When dawn
broke, they continued their journey in search of the banks
of the famous Ebro, where an adventure befell them that
will be related in the coming chapter.

CHAPTER XXIX

Of the famous adventure of the enchanted boat

Following their regular course, two days after leaving the
poplar wood, Don Quixote and Sancho came to the river
Ebro, the sight of which greatly rejoiced Don Quixote as he
contemplated and gazed upon the clarity of its waters, the
charm of its banks, the serenity of its course, and the
abundance of its liquid crystal. The sight of the river, in
fact, renewed a thousand amorous thoughts in his mind, and
especially he mused on what he had seen in the cave of
Montesinos. Although Master Pedro's ape had told him that
part of it was true and part false, he inclined rather to its
being true than false, the very opposite of Sancho, who considered it all one great lie. As they were jogging along in
this way, there appeared in sight a little boat without oars of
any kind or any sort of gear, made fast to the trunk of a
tree that stood on the bank.

Don Quixote looked in all directions, and seeing no one,
at once without more ado he dismounted from Rozinante
and ordered Sancho to do likewise from Dapple and to tie
up both beasts close together to the trunk of a poplar or
willow growing there. And on Sancho's inquiring the reason
for this sudden dismounting and tethering, Don Quixote replied: "I must tell you, Sancho, that this boat, directly and

without any possibility of there being an error, summons me to embark and travel in it to succor some knight or other person of rank in distress, who must certainly be in great peril. For such is the style of the books of chivalry and such the practice of the enchanters who figure in them. When any knight is involved in any peril and can only be delivered by the hand of another knight, though they may be six or nine thousand miles apart, they either snatch him up on a cloud, or provide him with a boat in which he embarks, and in less than the twinkling of an eye they bear him either by air or by sea wherever he pleases and where his help is needed.[1] So, Sancho, this boat is put here for that very purpose, and this is as true as it is now day. But before this happens, tie Dapple and Rozinante together, and may God's hand guide us, for no one will prevent me from embarking, even if barefooted friars entreated me."

"Since it is so," replied Sancho, "and your worship insists on plunging at every step into these fooleries—I don't know what else to call them—there's nothing for it but to obey and bow one's head, heeding the proverb: 'Do what your master bids and sit down with him at his table!' But all the same, for my conscience's sake I must warn your worship that I don't think this boat belongs to any of your enchanted folk, but to some fishermen of this river, for they catch the best shad in the world here."

This Sancho said as he was tying up the beasts, leaving them to the care and protection of the enchanters, with great sorrow in his heart. But Don Quixote bade him not to worry about abandoning the animals, for he who was to lead them through such longinquous ways and regions would not fail to provide for them.

"I can't make head or tail of your *logiquous*," said Sancho; "I never heard such a word in all my life."

"*Longinquous*," replied Don Quixote, "means remote, and it is no wonder you do not understand it, for you are not obliged to know Latin, like some who pretend to know it and don't."

"They are tied up," replied Sancho. "What have we to do now?"

---

[1] This passage is taken from *Amadis of Gaul*. Amadis one day perceived a little bark drifting toward shore; he immediately embarked, and was carried off to champion the cause of Lady Galvioletta of Brittany.

"What?" said Don Quixote. "Why, cross ourselves and weigh anchor; I mean, embark and cut the rope by which the bark is fastened."

And leaping into it, with Sancho after him, he cut the rope, and the boat drifted away slowly from the banks. When Sancho found himself a matter of two yards away on the river, he began to tremble, fearing that he was lost, and nothing gave him more pain than to hear Dapple bray and to see Rozinante struggling to get loose. And he said to his master: "The ass brays bewailing our absence, and Rozinante is trying to get free to throw himself in after us. O dearest friends, rest in peace, and may the folly that carries us away from you be turned to repentance and bring us back to your presence!"

And with this he began to weep so bitterly that Don Quixote said to him sternly and angrily: "Of what are you afraid, you coward? Why do you weep, you butter-heart? Who is pursuing you, soul of a town mouse? What do you lack, you who would be needy in the very bowels of abundance? Are you by any chance plodding on foot and shoeless over the Scythian mountains? No, you are seated on a bench like an archduke, on the peaceful current of this agreeable river, from where in a short while we shall emerge into the open sea. But we must already have emerged and traveled at least two thousand miles, or more. If I had only an astrolabe here with which I could take the height of the pole, I would tell you how far we have gone, though either I know little or we have passed, or shall soon pass, the equinoctial line that divides and cuts the opposite poles at equal distance."

"And when we get to this noxious line your worship speaks of," asked Sancho, "how far shall we have gone?"

"A long way," replied Don Quixote, "for when we come to the line I mentioned, we shall have covered the half of the three hundred and sixty degrees of earth and water the globe contains, according to the computation of Ptolemy, who was the best cosmographer known."

"By God," said Sancho, "but your worship has got me a nice fellow as a witness of what you say, this gaffer with his whorish amputation or I know not what."

Don Quixote burst out laughing at the interpretation Sancho had given to the name, the computation, and the reckoning of the cosmographer Ptolemy and said: "You must learn,

Sancho, that according to the Spaniards and those who embark at Cádiz to go to the East Indies, one of the signs by which they know that they have passed the equinoctial line I mentioned is that the lice die on everyone aboard ship. Not one remains alive, and you could not find one in the whole vessel if you were to be paid its weight in gold. So you might pass a hand over your thigh; if you catch anything living, we shall have no doubts on this point; if nothing, then we have passed."

"I don't believe a word of that," answered Sancho, "but I'll do what your worship orders all the same, though I don't know why we need to make these experiments, for I can see with my own eyes that we haven't moved more than five yards from the bank. We haven't shifted two yards away from where the animals are, for there are Rozinante and Dapple in the very place we left them, and taking a look around as I do now, I vow we are not stirring nor moving at an ant's pace."

"Make the investigation I have told you, Sancho, and do not bother about the others, for you know nothing about the colures, lines, parallels, zodiacs, ecliptics, poles, solstices, equinoxes, planets, signs, and points, which are the measures of which the celestial and terrestrial spheres are composed. But if you knew these things, or any part of them, you would see how many parallels we have sailed through, how many signs we have beheld, and what constellations we have left and are now leaving behind. Again I say to you, feel and fish, for I am sure you are as clean and pure as a sheet of white paper."

Sancho felt himself, and reaching his hand gently and cautiously to his left ham, he raised his head and looked at his master, saying: "Either the test is false, or we have not arrived at the place your worship says, not by many miles."

"Well, why?" asked Don Quixote. "Have you found anything?"

"More than that," replied Sancho. And shaking his fingers, he washed his whole hand in the river, down which the boat was softly gliding in midstream, without any occult intelligence to move it, or any hidden enchanter, but only the current of the water, which was calm and smooth there.

At that moment they came in sight of two great water mills in the middle of the river, and no sooner did Don Quixote see them than he exclaimed in a loud voice: "Do you see? There, my friend, stands the city, castle, or fortress. In it must lie some persecuted knight, or some queen, infanta, or princess in distress, for whose succor I have been brought here."

"What the devil city, fortress, or castle does your worship speak of, sir?" cried Sancho. "Can't you see that these are water mills, standing in the river, where they grind wheat?"

"Be silent, Sancho!" said Don Quixote. "They may seem to be water mills, but they are not. I have already told you that spells transform all things and change them from their natural shapes. I do not mean that they actually change them, but they appear to, as we learned by experience in the transformation of Dulcinea, sole refuge of my hopes."

By this time the boat had reached the middle of the stream and had begun to travel rather less slowly than before. The millers, seeing it drifting down the river and on the point of being sucked into the rapids caused by the wheels, rushed out with long poles to stop it. And because they came all covered with flour, their faces and clothes powdered with meal, they were a sinister-looking lot of ruffians. They shouted loudly: "Where are you going, you devils? Are you out of your mind? Do you want to drown or be dashed to pieces on these wheels?"

"Did I not tell you, Sancho," exclaimed Don Quixote, "that we had reached a place where I have to show the strength of my arm? Look what demons oppose me! Look at those ugly faces grimacing at us! Now you shall see, rascals!"

And standing up in the boat he began to threaten the millers with loud cries, exclaiming: "Foul and ill-conditioned rabble, release and set at liberty the prisoner you hold under duress, whether he be highborn or lowly or to whatever degree he may belong! For I am Don Quixote of La Mancha, otherwise called the Knight of the Lions, for whom by Heaven's high ordinance the happy termination of this adventure is reserved."

As he spoke he grasped his sword and began to flourish it in the air at the millers, who, hearing but not understanding these crazy rantings, set to work with their poles to halt the boat, which was now entering the rapids of the millrace.

Sancho went down on his knees and prayed to Heaven to deliver him from this impending peril, which it did through the prompt and energetic efforts of the millers, who planted their poles against the boat and stopped it, but not skillfully enough to prevent its capsizing and throwing Don Quixote and Sancho head over heels into the water. Luckily for the knight that he could swim like a duck, though the weight of his armor made him sink twice to the bottom, and had it not been for the millers, who dived into the water and rescued and dragged them both bodily out, it would have been Troy for both of them. When they were brought to land, more drenched than droughty, Sancho fell upon his knees, and with hands joined and eyes staring up to Heaven, he implored God in a long and devout prayer to deliver him from all his master's rash designs and enterprises in the future.

By this time the fishermen who owned the boat, which had been broken to pieces by the mill wheels, had arrived, and seeing it smashed, they manhandled Sancho and began to strip him, clamoring meanwhile to Don Quixote for payment. He, with great calmness, as if nothing had happened, told the millers and the fishermen that he would foot the bill most willingly, provided that they would release, without fail, the person or persons who were held prisoners in that castle.

"What persons or what castle are you talking about, madman?" replied· one of the millers. "Do you want to carry away those who come to have their wheat ground in these mills?"

"Enough," said Don Quixote to himself. "One might as well preach in the desert as try to induce this rabble by prayers to do any virtuous act. In this adventure two powerful enchanters must have been at loggerheads, the one thwarting the other in his designs. So, when one furnished me with a boat, the other capsized me. God help us! All this world is nothing but trickery and stratagem, one against the other." And raising his voice and gazing at the water mills, he continued saying: "Friends, whoever you are, who lie captive in this prison, forgive me. Unfortunately for myself and for you, I cannot deliver you from your misery. This adventure must remain reserved for another knight."

Saying this, he accepted the fishermen's terms and paid them fifty reals for the boat, which Sancho handed over to them with great reluctance, saying: "Two boatings like this one will sink our whole fortune to the bottom."

The fishermen and the millers gazed in amazement at those two figures, so unlike other men in appearance, and were completely unable to understand the drift of Don Quixote's words and questions. But concluding that both knight and squire were mad, they left them and departed, the millers to their mills, the fishermen to their huts. Don Quixote and Sancho went back to their beasts and their beastlike existence,[2] and such was the end of the adventure of the enchanted boat.

[2] Here Cervantes speaks coldly and cynically of his hero and looks at him through the eyes of the seventeenth century, without any of the idealism and refinements that the modern reader gives to the two heroes of the novel.

CHAPTER XXX

Of what befell Don Quixote with a fair huntress

Knight and squire, when they returned to their animals, were decidedly melancholy and out of humor, especially Sancho, whose soul was afflicted because of the losses inflicted on their stock of money, for he thought that with every penny taken he was being robbed of the very apples of his eyes. At length, without speaking a word to each other, they mounted and went away from the famous river, Don Quixote buried in thoughts of his love and Sancho in those of his preferment, which just then, it seemed to him, he was far from getting, for though he was a fool, he was quite well aware that all or most of his master's actions were extravagant, and he was looking around for an opportunity when, without going into accounts or farewells, he might one day give his master the slip and go home. But Fortune ordered matters contrary to his worst fears.

It so happened that next day, at sunset, as they came out of a wood, Don Quixote gazed over a green meadow and at the other end noticed some people. When he drew near, he saw that they were a hawking party.[1] He came closer and perceived among them an elegant lady on a palfrey or milk-white nag caparisoned with green trappings and a silver side-saddle. The lady herself was clad in green of so rich and

[1] Covarrubias, the lexicographer of the seventeenth century, tells us in his *Tesoro* that *caza de altanería* did not signify ordinary hawking, but higher game, of which the heron was the choicest victim. "This kind of chase," he adds, "is reserved only for princes and great lords."

gorgeous texture that comeliness seemed to be personified in her. On her left hand she bore a hawk, a token by which Don Quixote knew that she must be some great lady and the mistress of all those hunters, which was true; so, he said to Sancho: "Run, Sancho, my son, and say to that lady of the palfrey with the hawk that I, the Knight of the Lions, kiss the hands of her noble beauty, and if her excellency grants me leave, I will go myself to kiss them, and serve her to the best of my power and as her highness shall command. Mind, Sancho, how you speak, and be careful not to intrude any of your proverbs into the message."

"You've got a fine intruder here!" said Sancho. "Leave that to me! Sure, this is not the first time in my life that I have carried messages to high and full-blown ladies."

"Except for the message you carried to Lady Dulcinea," said Don Quixote, "I am not aware that you ever carried any other, at least in my service."

"That is true," replied Sancho, "but a good paymaster needs no sureties, and when there's plenty in the house, the supper's soon ready—I mean, there's no need to warn or tip me the wink about anything, for I'm a match for all, and I know a wee bit about everything."

"I am sure of that, Sancho," said Don Quixote. "Good luck on your journey, and God guide you."

Sancho went off at top speed, spurring Dapple out of his usual pace, and came to where the fair huntress was; and dismounting, he knelt before her, saying: "Fair lady, that knight over there, called the Knight of the Lions, is my master, and I'm his squire, and at home they call me Sancho Panza. This same Knight of the Lions, who was called a short while ago the Knight of the Rueful Figure, sends by me to say that your greatness be pleased to give him leave that, with your good pleasure and consent, he may come and carry out his wishes, which are, as he says and I do believe, nothing else than to serve your lofty nobility and beauty, and if you give it, your ladyship will do something that will redound to your honor, and he will receive a most marked favor and contentment."

"Truly, good squire," answered the lady, "you have delivered your message with all the details and formalities that such embassies require. Rise up from the ground, for it is not meet that the squire of so great a knight as he of the Rueful Figure, of whom we have heard a great deal, should remain on his knees. Rise, my friend, and tell your master that I welcome him to the services of myself and my husband, the duke, in a country house we have here."

Sancho got up, delighted as much by the beauty of the good lady as by her high breeding and courtesy, and above all, by what she had said about having heard of his master, the Knight of the Rueful Figure, and if she did not call him Knight of the Lions it must have been because he had only recently taken the title. "Tell me, brother squire," asked the duchess (her title is yet unknown),[2] "this master of yours, is he not one of whom a history is in print called *The Ingenious Gentleman Don Quixote of La Mancha,* who has for the mistress of his heart a certain Dulcinea of El Toboso?"

"He's the very same, my lady," answered Sancho, "and that squire of his, who figures, or ought to figure, in the said history and whom they call Sancho Panza, is myself, if they haven't changed me in the cradle—I mean, in the press."

"I'm delighted to hear all this," said the duchess. "Go, brother Panza, and tell your master that he is welcome to my estates and that nothing could happen that could give me more pleasure."

Sancho returned to his master in high spirits with this agreeable answer and told him all the great lady had said to him, praising to the skies, in his rustic speech, her great beauty, her charm, and her courtesy. Don Quixote preened himself in his saddle, set his feet taut in the stirrups, fixed his visor, dug his spurs into Rozinante, and with easy bearing advanced to kiss the hands of the duchess. She had sent for her husband and told him, while Don Quixote was approaching, all about the message. The duke and the duchess had read the first part of this history and were, therefore, well aware of Don Quixote's crazy humor; so, they awaited his coming with the greatest eagerness, for they intended to follow his humor and treat him as a knight-errant as long as he stayed with them, with all the accustomed ceremonies

[2] According to the commentator Pellicer, Cervantes drew the duke and duchess from real life. The originals were Don Carlos de Borja and María Luisa de Aragón, Duke and Duchess of Villahermosa, and the castle where all the adventures took place was theirs in the neighborhood of Pedrola. In 1905 the Duchess of Villahermosa, their descendant, gave festivities in Pedrola in celebration of the third centenary of the publication of Part I of the immortal work. See Juan Antonio Pellicer, *Don Quixote,* 5 vols. (Madrid, 1797).

that they had read about in the books of chivalry, of which
they were very fond.

Don Quixote approached with visor raised, and as he made
signs of wishing to dismount, Sancho hastened to hold his
stirrups, but in getting down off Dapple, he was unlucky
enough to catch his foot in one of the ropes of the packsaddle in such a way that he could not free it but remained
hanging by it with his face and chest to the ground. Don
Quixote, who was unused to dismount without having the
stirrups held for him, imagining that Sancho had by this
time caught hold of it, shot his body off with a lurch and
brought with him Rozinante's saddle, which no doubt was
badly girthed, with the result that both saddle and he came
to earth, not without discomfiture to him and plenty of curses
that he mumbled against the luckless Sancho, who still lay
prone with his foot tangled in the halter. The duke ordered
his huntsmen to go to the aid of the knight and squire,
and they raised Don Quixote, who, though badly shaken by
his fall, limped along as best he could and knelt before their
graces. But the duke would not permit it; on the contrary,
he dismounted from his horse and went over to embrace
Don Quixote, saying: "I am sorry, Sir Knight of the Rueful
Figure, that your entry into my estate should have been so
unfortunate, but the carelessness of squires is often the cause
of worse accidents."

"That which has befallen me in meeting you, valiant
prince," replied Don Quixote, "cannot be unfortunate, even
if my fall had dragged me down into the bottomless abyss,
for the glory of having seen you would have raised and
rescued me from it. My squire, God's curse upon him, is
more skilled at loosening his tongue to utter impertinences
than in tightening the girths of a saddle to keep it steady.
But wherever I may be, fallen or risen, on foot or on horseback, I shall always be at your service and at that of my
lady, the duchess, your worthy consort, worthy mistress of
beauty and universal princess of courtesy."

"Gently, my lord Don Quixote of La Mancha," said the
duke, "for where my lady Doña Dulcinea of El Toboso
is, it is not right that other beauties should be praised."

Sancho, who was now released from his noose, was standing close by and put in his word before his master could
answer, saying: "There's no denying—in fact, we must as-
sent emphatically—that Lady Dulcinea of El Toboso is very

beautiful, but the hare jumps up where one least expects it, and I've heard tell that what we call Nature is like a potter who makes vessels of clay, and he who makes one fine vase can just as well make two, or three, or a hundred. I say this, because my lady the duchess is no whit behind my mistress, Lady Dulcinea of El Toboso."

Don Quixote turned to the duchess, saying: "Your highness may consider that no knight-errant in the world ever had a more droll or talkative squire than I have. And he will prove the truth of my words if your loftiness is pleased to accept my services for a few days."

To this the duchess made answer: "I value the worthy Sancho highly for being droll, because it is a sign that he is shrewd, for drollery and humor, as you, Don Quixote, are well aware, are not housed in dullards. And since good Sancho is droll and humorous, henceforth I set him down as shrewd."

"And talkative," added Don Quixote.

"So much the better," said the duke; "for one cannot utter many witty things in few words; so, not to waste time in mere talk, come, great Knight of the Rueful Figure——"

"Of the Lions, your highness should say," said Sancho, "for now there is no rueful figure."

The duke continued: "Let the figure be a lion, then. Now let the Knight of the Lions come to a castle of mine that is nearby, where he shall be welcomed as befits his exalted state."

By then Sancho had girthed Rozinante's saddle, and Don Quixote having mounted, the duke sprang on to his own fine horse, and with the duchess between them, they set out for the castle. The duchess insisted that Sancho ride by her side, for she took infinite pleasure in hearing his shrewd comments. Sancho needed no pressing; he mingled with the three and made a fourth in the conversation, to the great amusement of the duchess and the duke, who considered themselves fortunate indeed to welcome to their castle so noble a knight-errant and so aberrant a squire.

CHAPTER XXXI

Which treats of many and great matters

Sancho was overjoyed at finding himself, as he thought, in favor with the duchess, for he imagined that he would find in her castle what he had found in Don Diego's house and in Don Basilio's; he was always fond of good living and grasped any opportunity by the forelock, whenever it presented itself.

Our history relates that before they reached the manor house or castle, the duke rode on in advance and gave orders to his servants how they were to behave to Don Quixote; therefore, when the latter came up to the castle gates with the duchess, two lackeys or grooms, clad from head to foot in what they called morning gowns of fine crimson satin, ran out and caught Don Quixote in their arms almost before he could see or hear them, saying: "Let your highness go and help my lady the duchess to dismount from her horse."

Don Quixote did so, and great compliments passed between the two over the business, but in the end the duchess' determination prevailed, and she would not dismount from her palfrey except in the arms of the duke, saying that she did not consider herself worthy of laying so useless a burden upon so great a knight. At length the duke came out to take her down, and as they entered a great courtyard, two beautiful maidens approached and threw over Don Quixote's shoulders a long mantle of the finest scarlet cloth [1] and

---

[1] A scarlet mantle lined with ermine was the customary garment worn by knights when they had put off their armor.

in a moment all the galleries of the court were thronged with men and women servants of the duke and duchess crying: "Welcome, flower and cream of knights-errant." Then all poured little vials of perfumed water over Don Quixote and the duke and duchess. All this astonished Don Quixote, and for the first time he felt thoroughly convinced that he was a knight-errant in fact and not in imagination, for he saw himself treated in the same way as he had read that such knights were treated in past ages.

Sancho, forsaking Dapple, attached himself to the duchess and entered the castle, but his conscience pricked him at having left his ass forlorn; so, he went up to a grave duenna who had sallied out with the rest to receive the duchess, and in a low voice said to her: "Mistress González,[2] or whatever your worship's name may be——"

"My name is Doña Rodríguez de Grijalba," answered the duenna. "What is your will, brother?"

To which Sancho replied: "I wish your worship would do me the favor to go out to the castle gate, where you'll find a dappled ass of mine; please give orders for them to put him in the stable, or put him there yourself, for the poor fellow is easily scared and can't stand being left alone."

"If the master is as wise as the servant," said the duenna, "we're in a nice fix. Off with you, brother, and bad luck to you and him who brought you here! Go mind your own ass; we duennas are not used to jobs of that kind."

"I've heard my master tell," answered Sancho, "and mind you, he's a wizard for stories—of how Lancelot, when he came from Britain, 'Ladies waited on him, and duennas on his steed'; when it comes to my ass, I wouldn't swap him for Sir Lancelot's horse."

"If you are jester, brother," said the duenna, "keep your jokes for the right occasion where they'll be paid for; from me you'll get nothing but a fig."

"In that case," replied Sancho, "it's sure to be a ripe one, and if years count, you certainly won't lose the trick by too few points."

"You son of a whore," said the duenna, blazing with anger, "if I'm old or not, that is God's business, not yours, you garlic-stuffed rascal." She said all this in such a loud

---

[2] It was common in the sixteenth century to give duennas the name González, and pages the name Álvarez.

voice that the duchess heard it, and turning around and seeing the duenna so heated and her eyes so flaming, she asked her with whom she was bickering.

"With this fine fellow here," said the duenna, "who respectfully requests me to go and put an ass of his that is at the castle gate into the stable. And he brings it up as an example that they did the same I don't know where, when some ladies waited on a certain Lancelot and duennas on his nag, and what is more serious, he ends up by calling me an old woman."

"That I would consider," replied the duchess, "the greatest insult that anyone could inflict upon me." Then to Sancho she said: "Remember, Sancho, my friend, that Doña Rodríguez is quite a young lady, and that headdress she wears more by authority and custom than because of years."

"May the rest of mine be unlucky," replied Sancho, "if I said it with that intention. I only said it because I've so great a fondness for my ass, and I thought I couldn't commend him to a more kindhearted soul than the lady Doña Rodríguez."

Don Quixote, who was listening, then said to him: "Is this suitable conversation, Sancho, for such a place?"

"Master," replied Sancho, "everyone must speak out his need wherever he may be; here I remembered Dapple, and here I spoke of him. Had I thought of him in the stable, I would have spoken of him there."

The duke then remarked: "Sancho is quite right, and there is no reason why he should be blamed. Dapple will receive fodder in plenty. Sancho may set his mind at rest, for the ass shall be treated as he himself would be."

While this conversation, amusing to all except Don Quixote, was going on, they went upstairs and led the knight into a hall hung with rich cloth of gold and brocade. Six maidens relieved him of his armor and waited on him as pages, all of them trained by the duke and duchess as to what they had to do and how they were to treat Don Quixote so that he might believe that he was being tended as a knight-errant. After his armor had been removed, he stood there in his tight-fitting breeches and chamois-skin doublet, a long, lean, lanky figure, with cheeks that kissed each other on the inside; a figure that would have excited the handmaidens to outbursts of merriment, had they not taken care to hide their laughter (which was one of the strict orders they had received from their master and mistress). They asked him to let himself be stripped that they might put a shirt on him, but he would not allow it, for he said that modesty was as becoming to knights-errant as valor.[3] However, he told them to give the shirt to Sancho, and after shutting himself alone with him in a room where there was a rich bed, he said to him: "Tell me now, you clown of today and noodle of yesterday, do you think it was right of you to offend and insult a duenna so worthy of reverence and respect as that one? Was that the time to think of your Dapple, or are these lordly gentlemen the kind who would let the beasts go hungry when they treat their owners in such elegant style? For God's sake, Sancho, keep an eye to yourself, and do not show the yarn, for fear that they see what coarse, brutish stuff you are spun of. Remember, you sinner, that well-bred and honorable servants cause their masters to be respected and that one of the greatest advantages that princes possess over other men is that they have servants as good as themselves to wait on them. Do you not see, you unlucky bane of mine, that if they find out that you are a coarse clodhopper or a clownish loony, they will think that I am some roaming quack or huckstering knight?[4] No, no, Sancho, my friend, shun such pitfalls, for he who trips into being a droll chatterbox at the first stumble drops into a despised clown. Bridle your tongue, reflect and chew the cud before you let your words escape from your mouth, and remember that we have arrived at a point whence, by the help of God and the strength of my arm, we shall come forth greatly advanced both in fame and fortune."

Sancho promised his master faithfully that he would sew up his mouth and bite off his tongue rather than utter a word that was not fitting and well considered, and he told him not to be anxious about the point in question, for no one would ever discover through him who they were.

Don Quixote then dressed himself, put on his baldric with

---

[3] In the romances of chivalry it was customary for damsels to undress the knights who visited the castle and clothe them in fresh garments.

[4] These diatribes of Don Quixote suggest that the knight was slightly nettled at the praise lavished on Sancho by the duke and duchess for his sallies. Perhaps the knight may have felt a touch of jealousy at the prominence accorded to Sancho by his hosts, who had already read and enjoyed the Part I of the great book.

his sword, threw the scarlet mantle over his shoulders, placed
on his head a hunting cap of green satin that the maidens
had given him, and thus arrayed, sallied into the great hall,
where he found the damsels drawn up in two rows, half on
one side and half on the other, all of them with vessels
for washing the hands, which they presented with many
curtsies and ceremonies. Then came twelve pages with a
seneschal to conduct him to dinner, for his host and hostess
were already awaiting him. Placing him between them, they
led him with much pomp and circumstance into another hall,
where there was a sumptuous table laid with but four
covers. The duchess and the duke came out to the door of
the dining hall to receive him, and with them one of those
grave ecclesiastics who rule noblemen's houses; one of those
who, not being born princes themselves, never know how to
teach those who are how to behave as such; who would
measure the greatness of grandees by their own narrowness
of mind; who, trying to teach their pupils to practice economy, end by making them miserly. One of this kind, I
say, was the grave prelate who came out with the duke and
duchess to receive Don Quixote.[5]

Many courtly compliments were exchanged, and at last,
placing Don Quixote between them, they took their places
at the table. The duke invited Don Quixote to sit at the
head of the table, and though he refused, the host was so
pressing in his request that the knight had to take it. The
ecclesiastic sat opposite to him, and the duke and duchess at
the sides. All this time Sancho stood by, gaping with amazement at the honor paid to his master by these princes; and
observing all the ceremonies and formalities that passed between the duke and his master to persuade the latter to take
his place at the head of the table, he said: "If your wor-

[5] Some commentators say that the portrait of this ecclesiastic
is drawn from the confessor to the Duke of Béjar, who nearly
succeeded in persuading the duke to refuse the dedication of the
first part of *Don Quixote*. Others say it refers to Bartolomé
Leonardo de Argensola the poet. He and his brother Lupercio
prevented the Count of Lemos from dispensing patronage to other
writers. There are, however, frequent references in Spanish literature of the sixteenth and seventeenth centuries to the despotic
behavior of confessors in noblemen's houses.

ships would give me leave, I'll tell you a tale of what happened in my village about this matter of seats."

No sooner had Sancho said this than Don Quixote trembled, for he was sure that his squire was about to deliver himself of some piece of tomfoolery. Sancho looked at him, and straightaway understood, so he said: "Don't be afraid, master, that I'll go astray or say anything that won't hit the nail on the head. I haven't forgotten the advice your worship gave me a while ago about talking much or little, well or ill."

"I remember nothing of it, Sancho," answered Don Quixote; "say what you want, but say it quickly."

"Well, what I'm going to say," said Sancho, "is true, as my master, Don Quixote, will not let me lie."

"As far as I am concerned, Sancho, you may lie to your heart's content; I will not put an obstacle in your way, but take heed what you are going to say."

"I've so heeded and reheeded it," said Sancho, "that I'm as safe and sound as the bell ringer in the watchtower, as you'll see from the story."

"I should advise your highnesses to give orders for the removal of this idiot," exclaimed Don Quixote, "for he will utter a thousand absurdities."

"By the life of the duke," said the duchess, "let no one attempt to take Sancho from me. I am very fond of him, for I know he is very wise."

"Wise may the days of your holiness be," said Sancho, "for the good opinion you have of me, though I don't deserve it. This is my story. A gentleman of my village sent an invitation—a wealthy man he was, and of quality too, for he was one of the Alamos of Medina del Campo and married Doña Mencía de Quiñones, the daughter of Don Alonso de Marañón, knight of the Order of Santiago, who was drowned in the Herradura [6] and about whom there was that quarrel, years ago, in our village, in which, as far as I can understand, my master Don Quixote was mixed up, and out of which little Thomas, the scapegrace, received a wound; the son of Balbastro, the blacksmith, he was— Isn't

[6] Sancho here refers to a shipwreck that took place in 1562 in the port of La Herradura, about 25 miles from Vélez Málaga during a fierce storm. More than four thousand men perished along with their general Don Juan Mendoza.

all this true, my dear master? By your life say so; otherwise these lords here may take me for a lying chatterbox."

"So far," said the ecclesiastic, "I take you more for a chatterbox than a liar, but later on, I do not know what I shall take you for."

"You quote so many witnesses and proofs, Sancho," said Don Quixote, "that I have to admit that you must be telling the truth; go on and shorten the story, for at the rate you are going it will take you two days to finish it."

"He must not shorten it," said the duchess. "On the contrary, to please me, he should tell it in his own way, even though it takes him six days to finish it. They would, indeed, be the best I ever spent in my life."

"Well, then, gentlemen, I say," continued Sancho, "that this said gentleman, whom I know as well as I do my own hands, for it's but a bowshot from my house to his, invited a poor but decent laborer——"

"Get on, brother," cried the ecclesiastic; "at the rate you are going you will not stop your story till the next world."

"I'll stop less than halfway, please God," said Sancho. "And so I say that this laborer, arriving at the house of the aforesaid gentleman who had invited him—God rest his soul, for he's now dead; and more by token, they say, he had an angel's death, although I wasn't there, for just at that time I had gone off to reap at Tembleque——"

"By your life, my son," cried the ecclesiastic, "come back quickly from Tembleque and finish your story without burying the gentleman, unless you want to have more funerals."

"Well, it so happened," said Sancho, "that as the two of them were, as I said, about to sit down to table—sure, I fancy I can see them clearer than ever—"

The duke and duchess were highly amused at the irritation displayed by the worthy ecclesiastic at Sancho's pauses and long-winded manner of telling his story. As for Don Quixote, he was chafing with wrath and vexation.

"Well, as I was saying," continued Sancho, "as the two were about to sit down to table, as I said, the laborer insisted that the man should take the head of the table, and the gentleman insisted upon the laborer taking it, for in his own house the other should do as he was bid, but the laborer, who prided himself on his politeness and good breeding, would not allow it. The gentleman, therefore, out of sheer exasperation, put both his hands on his guest's shoulders and forced him to sit down saying: 'Sit down, you clod-hopper, for where I sit, that is the head of the table!' There's the story, and I think it comes pat here."

Don Quixote turned a thousand colors, and his tanned face looked like jasper. The duke and duchess suppressed their laughter, lest Don Quixote get in a temper, once he saw through Sancho's mischievous meaning. So, to change the conversation and to keep Sancho from uttering further absurdities, the duchess asked Don Quixote what news he had of Lady Dulcinea and if he had sent her lately any presents of giants or evildoers, for he must have conquered many.

To which Don Quixote replied: "Señora, my misfortunes, though they had a beginning, will never have an end. I have conquered giants, and I have sent her miscreants and evil-doers, but where could they find her if she is enchanted and transformed into the ugliest peasant wench that can be imagined?"

"I don't know," said Sancho, "to me she seems the most beautiful creature in the world; at any rate in agility and in leaping she's the equal of any tumbler. In good faith, señora, she leaps from the ground onto an ass like a cat."

"Have you seen her enchanted, Sancho?" asked the duke.

"Have I seen her!" answered Sancho. "Who the devil was it but myself who first thought of the enchantment business? She's as much enchanted as my father."

The ecclesiastic, when he heard them speaking of giants and evildoers and enchantments, suspected that this must be Don Quixote of La Mancha, whose history the duke was continually reading; and he himself had often taken him to task, telling him how foolish it was to read such follies, and convincing himself of the truth of his suspicion, he addressed the duke, very angrily saying: "Your excellency, my lord, will have to give an account to God for what this good man is doing. This Don Quixote, or Don Idiot, or whatever you call him, is not, to my mind, so big a blockhead as your excellency would have him be when you encourage him to continue his extravagant absurdities." Then turning to Don Quixote, he said: "And you, numskull, who put it into your head that you are a knight-errant and that you conquer giants and capture miscreants? Go on your way, with good luck to you as my parting words. Go back to your home and rear your children, if you have any, and look after your estate and give up roaming through the world, swallowing wind and making yourself the laughingstock of those who know you, and those who do not. Where in heaven's name have you found that there are or ever were knights-errant? Where are there giants in Spain, or marauders in La Mancha, or enchanted Dulcineas, or all the medley of daft deeds that they tell about you?"

Don Quixote listened attentively to the words of the revered gentleman, and no sooner did he perceive that the latter had done talking than, regardless of the presence of the duke and duchess, he jumped to his feet, blazing with fury and indignation, and said— But his reply deserves a chapter to itself.

CHAPTER XXXII

Of Don Quixote's reply to his reprimander, with other incidents, grave and gay

So, springing to his feet and trembling from head to foot like a man dosed with mercury, Don Quixote said in an excited, stammering voice: "The place where I am, those in whose presence I find myself, the respect I have and have always had for the profession to which your reverence belongs, bind the hands of my just indignation. For this reason and because I know, as all know, that the weapon of gownsmen is the same as that of women, namely, the tongue, so with mine I will enter into equal combat with your reverence, from whom we might have expected good counsels rather than infamous abuse. Pious and well-intentioned reprimands require different behavior and other methods. In any case, by rebuking me publicly and in such bitter terms you have exceeded the bounds of just rebuke, for that should consist of gentleness rather than of rudeness. And it is not right, without knowing anything of the sin that is reproved, to call the sinner blockhead and idiot. Now tell me, your reverence, for which of the follies that you have noticed in me do you condemn and abuse me, and bid me go home and look after my house and wife and children, without knowing whether I have any? Is nothing else needed than to slip into other men's houses by hook or by crook and rule over the masters, and after having been reared in the straitened circumstances of some seminary and without having ever seen more of the world than is contained within twenty or thirty leagues around, to proceed to lay down the law for chivalry and pass judgment on knights-errant? Is it, perchance, a vain business, or is the time ill-spent, which is spent in roaming the world, not seeking its pleasures but its hard toils, by which good men ascend to the abode of immortality? If knights, if grandees, if nobles, and if men of high birth considered me an idiot, I should consider it as an irreparable affront; but I do not care a mite if clerks who have never entered or trodden the paths of chivalry should mark me down as an idiot. Knight I am and knight I will die, if it pleases almighty God. Some choose the broad road of proud ambition, some that of mean and servile flattery, some that of deceitful hypocrisy, and a small number that of true religion; but I, influenced by my star, follow the narrow path of knight-errantry, and in practicing that calling I despise wealth but not honor. I have redeemed injuries, righted wrongs, chastised insolence, conquered giants, and trampled on monsters. I am in love for no other reason than that it is an obligation for knights-errant to be so; but though I am, I am no lustful lover, but one of the chaste, platonic kind. My intentions are always directed toward virtuous ends, to do good to all and evil to none. If he who so intends, so acts, and so lives deserves to be called an idiot, it is for your highnesses to say, most excellent duke and duchess." [1]

"By God, that's great," cried Sancho. "Say no more, dear lord and master, in your defense, for there's no more in the world to be said, thought, or persevered in, and besides, when this gentleman denies, as he has done, that there are or ever have been knights-errant in the world, can we wonder that he knows nothing of what he has been talking about?"

"Are you by any chance, brother," said the ecclesiastic, "the Sancho Panza they talk about, to whom your master has promised an island?"

"Yes, so I am," replied Sancho, "and I'm the one who deserves it as well as anyone else. I'm one of the 'Stick to the

---

[1] Don Quixote's refutal of the arrogant cleric, as Unamuno tells us, recalls the Cid's reply to the monk Bernardo, who dared to address him in the presence of King Alfonso VI during a conversation in the monastery of San Pedro de Cardeña: "Who told you, worthy friar, you with your cowl, to meddle in councils of war? Go up to the pulpit, pray God that they win, and not Joshuah, save by the order of Moses. I the banner will bear to the port. Take you your cape to the choir . . . 'tis smeared, not with blood, but with grease." M. de Unamuno, *The Life of Don Quixote and Sancho*, trans. by H. P. Earle (New York, 1917), p. 205.

good and you'll be one of them,' and I'm of the 'Not with whom you're bred, but with whom you've fed' tribe, and of the 'He who leans on a good tree, good shelter has he.' I've leaned on my master, and many a month I've been going in his company, and please God, I'll turn out just such another as he; long life to him and long life to myself, for he'll have no lack of empires to command, nor I of islands to govern."

"No, Sancho, my friend, certainly not," said the duke, "for I, in the name of Don Quixote, confer upon you the governorship of an odd one of mine, which is of no mean quality."

"Kneel down, Sancho," said Don Quixote, "and kiss his excellency's feet for the boon he has conferred upon you."

Sancho did as he was told, but on seeing this, the ecclesiastic rose from the table in a rage, exclaiming: "By the habit I wear, I must say that your excellency is as fooled as those two sinners. Is it a wonder that they are mad, when we see sane people sanctioning their madness? Let your excellency stop with them, but as long as they remain in this house I shall stay in mine and save myself the trouble of rebuking what I cannot remedy." And without saying another word or eating another morsel, he went off, in spite of all the entreaties of the duke and duchess. It must be admitted, however, that the duke did not say much, owing to his amusement at the uncalled-for rage.

When he had finished laughing, he said to Don Quixote: "You have answered for yourself so nobly, Knight of the Lions, that there is no need to demand further satisfaction, for this, though it appears an offense, is not one at all; for, as women can give no offense, no more can ecclesiastics, as you yourself know better than I."

"That is true," said Don Quixote, "and the reason is that he who cannot be offended can offend no one. Women, children, and ecclesiastics, because they are unable to defend themselves, even though they may be attacked, cannot be affronted. For between an offense and an affront there is this difference, as your excellency knows better than I. An affront comes from one who is capable of giving it, and gives it and upholds it, but an offense can come from anyone without carrying an affront with it. Take as an example: a man is standing carelessly in the street; ten men with arms in their hands come up and strike him; he draws his sword and does his duty, but the number of his adversaries prevents him and will not let him achieve his purpose, which is to avenge himself; this man is offended but not affronted. Another example will confirm the same thing: a man has his back turned; another comes and strikes him, and after striking him, he does not wait but runs away; the other pursues but does not overtake him; he who received the blows suffered an offense, but not an affront, because an affront has to be maintained. If the striker, even if he struck foully, had drawn his sword and stood facing his enemy, he who was beaten would remain both aggrieved and affronted; aggrieved because he received a treacherous blow, affronted because he who gave it maintained his deed, standing his ground without turning his back. And thus, according to the laws of the accursed duel, I may be wronged, but I am not affronted, for children cannot wound and women do not generally do so, and so they have no call to maintain their position. The same applies to those in the religious profession, for these three classes of people lack arms offensive and defensive, and so, although by nature they are obliged to defend themselves, they have not the power to offend anyone. But though I said a little while ago that I might have been aggrieved, now I say that I cannot be in any way, for one who cannot receive an affront can still less give one. Wherefore I should not resent, and do not resent, what that worthy man said to me. I only wish he had stayed a little longer, so that I could have convinced him of his error in believing and stating that knights-errant have never existed in the world. If Amadis or one of his countless descendants had heard his words, I am sure it would not have gone well with his reverence."

"I'll swear it wouldn't," said Sancho. "Why, they would have given him a slash that would have slit him from top to bottom like a pomegranate or an overripe melon. They were not fellows to stand such jokes! By my faith, I'm sure that if Rinaldo of Montalbán had heard the words of the little man, he would have landed him such a clout on the mouth that he wouldn't have spoken for the next three years. Let him have a scrap with them and he'll see how he'll get out of their hands!"

The duchess, as she listened to Sancho, was ready to die with laughter, and in her mind she considered him a funnier fool and a greater madman than his master, and there were many there who were of the same opinion.

Don Quixote at length became appeased, and the dinner came to an end. When the cloth was removed, four maidens came in, one holding a silver basin, another a jug also of silver, a third with two fine white towels on her shoulder, and the fourth with her arms bared to the elbow and in her white hands (they certainly were white) a round ball of Neapolitan soap. The girl with the basin approached and with grace and charm shoved it under Don Quixote's beard. Though he was mystified by such a ceremony, he said not a word, for he supposed that it was a custom of that country to wash beards instead of hands, and so he stretched out his own as far as he could; at the same instant the jug began to pour water upon it, and the maiden with the soap rubbed his beard rapidly, raising snowflakes, for the lather was no less white, not only over the beard, but also all over the face and eyes of the submissive knight, who was obliged to keep them tightly shut. The duke and duchess, who had not been informed of this ceremony, waited to see how this strange washing would end. The barber-maiden, when she had covered him with a handful of lather, pretended there was no more water and told the girl with the jug to go for some more, while Don Quixote remained there, the strangest and most laughable figure imaginable. All present, and there were many, stood watching him, and when they saw him there with half a yard of neck, and that exceedingly brown, his eyes shut, and his beard full of lather, it was a marvel of discretion that they were able to stifle their laughter. The damsels who were in the joke kept their eyes lowered, not daring to look at their master and mistress; the latter felt anger and laughter surging within them, and they knew not what to do, whether to punish the girls for their impudence or to reward them for the amusement they derived from seeing Don Quixote in such a plight. At last the maiden with the jug returned and they finished washing Don Quixote; then, the girl with the towels wiped him and dried him thoroughly, and all four together, after making a deep curtsy, were about to depart, when the duke, who was afraid Don Quixote might see through the joke, called the maid with the jug, saying: "Come and wash me, and mind there is enough water."

The girl, who was quick-witted and active, came and placed the basin for the duke as she had done for Don Quixote, and in a trice they had him well soaped and washed.

After wiping and drying him, they made their curtsy and departed. It was known later that the duke had sworn that if they had not washed him as they had washed Don Quixote, he would have punished them for their saucy impudence, which they had cleverly atoned for by soaping him as well.

Sancho observed the ceremony of the washing with deep attention, and he said to himself: "God bless us! If it were only the custom in this country to wash the beards of squires as well as of knights! For, by God and my soul, I've sore need of it, and I'd take it as a kinder favor if they were to give us a bit of a scrape with the razor."

"What are you muttering to yourself, Sancho?" asked the duchess.

"I was saying, my lady," he replied, "that in the courts of other princes I've always heard tell that when the cloth is removed they give water for the hands but not suds for the beards. And so it's good to live much to see much, though, to be sure, they also say that he who lives a long life must face much strife. Still, to face one of these same washings must be rather pleasure than pain."

"Do not worry, friend Sancho," said the duchess; "I will make my maids wash you, and even put you in the bath if necessary."

"I'll be content with the beard," said Sancho, "at any rate, for the present. As for the future, it's God's will what'll happen."

"Carry out the worthy Sancho's request, seneschal," said the duchess, "and do exactly what he wishes."

The seneschal replied that Señor Sancho would be served in everything, and with that he went off to dinner, taking Sancho with him, while the duke and duchess and Don Quixote remained at table talking of many and various things, but all touching on the profession of arms and knight-errantry.

The duchess begged Don Quixote to describe the beauty and features of Lady Dulcinea of El Toboso, for by her reputation abroad, she must be the fairest creature in the world, even in La Mancha. Don Quixote sighed when he heard the duchess' request, and he said: "If I could tear out my heart and lay it on a plate on the table before your highness' eyes, I would spare my tongue the trouble of saying what can hardly be thought of, for your excellency would see her portrayed in full. But why should I now attempt to describe feature by feature the beauty of the peerless Dulcinea? That is a burden worthy of other shoulders than mine, an enterprise that should occupy the pencils of Parrhasius, of Timanthus, and of Apelles, and the chisels of Lysippus, to paint and to carve her on wood, on marble, and in bronze.[2] It would require the Ciceronian and Demosthenian rhetoric as well to praise her."

"What does *Demosthenian* mean, Don Quixote?" asked the duchess. "It is a word I have never heard in all the days of my life."

"*Demosthenian* rhetoric," replied Don Quixote, "is as much as to say the rhetoric of Demosthenes, as Ciceronian is Cicero's, who were the two greatest rhetoricians in the world."

"That is so," answered the duke, "and you have shown your ignorance by asking such a question. But nevertheless, Don Quixote would give us great pleasure if he would portray her for us, for surely even in a rough sketch or outline she will emerge so fair that the fairest will envy her."

"I would do it, certainly," said Don Quixote, "had the mishap that befell her lately not blurred her in my mind's eye, a mishap that makes me ready to weep for her rather than describe her. For your highnesses must know that a few days ago when I went back to kiss her hands and receive her blessing and permission for this third sally, I found her enchanted and transformed from a princess into a peasant girl, from fair to foul, from angel to devil, from fragrant to pestiferous, from well-spoken to boorish, from gentle to tomboyish, from light to darkness—in short, from Dulcinea of El Toboso into a coarse Sayagan wench."[3]

[2] Parrhasius, a native of Ephesus, practiced his art chiefly at Athens, circa 400 B.C. He was a rival of Zeuxis.

Timanthus, painter of Sicyon. His masterpiece was the "Sacrifice of Iphigenia," circa 400 BC.

Apelles, born at Colophon in Ionia, contemporary of Alexander the Great; his greatest picture "Aphrodite rising from the sea" was brought by Augustus to Rome.

Lysippus of Sicyon, great Greek sculptor, contemporary of Alexander the Great. His statue "Opportunity" gave rise to the proverb, "Take time by the forelock."

[3] Sayago, in the province of Zamora, was where Castilian was worst spoken; the people there were considered very uncouth and rustic.

"God bless me!" exclaimed the duke in a loud voice at this moment, "who can it be who has done the world such wrong? Who was it who robbed it of the beauty that was its joy, of the grace that was its charm, and the modesty that was its distinction?"

"Who," replied Don Quixote, "who can it be but some malignant enchanter, one of the many envious ones who persecute me—that accursed race born unto the world to obscure and obliterate the exploits of the good and to light up and exalt the deeds of the wicked. Enchanters persecute me and will persecute me until they sink me and my exalted chivalries in the deepest abyss of oblivion. They damage and wound me where they see I feel it most, for to rob a knight-errant of his lady is to rob him of the eye with which he sees, of the sun by which he is lighted, and of the prop by which he is sustained. Many other times I have said it, and now I say it again, a knight-errant without a lady is like a tree without leaves, a house without foundations, and a shadow without the body by which it is caused."

"There is no more to be said," replied the duchess, "but yet, if we are to give credit to the history of Don Quixote, which has lately been given to the world, amidst the general applause of mankind, we gather from it, if I remember right, that your worship has never seen Lady Dulcinea, and that this lady does not exist on earth but as a fantastical mistress whom your worship has begotten and brought forth in your mind, and painted with all the graces and perfections you desired."

"On that point there is much to say," replied Don Quixote. "God knows whether Dulcinea exists on earth or not, or whether she is fantastical or not. These are not matters where verification can be carried out to the full. I neither engendered nor bore my lady, though I contemplate her in her ideal form, as a lady with all the qualities needed to win her fame in all quarters of the world. These are: beauty without blemish, dignity without haughtiness, love with modesty, good manners springing from courtesy, courtesy from good breeding, and lastly, high lineage, because over good blood beauty shines and glows with greater perfection than among fair ones humbly born."

"That is true," remarked the duke, "but Don Quixote must give me leave to say what the history of his exploits, which I have read, compels me to say. From them we infer that there is a Dulcinea, in El Toboso or out of it, and that she is beautiful in the highest degree, as your worship portrays her. Nevertheless, in the matter of high lineage she does not compare with the Orianas, the Alastrajareas, the Madásimas, and others of that breed, of whom the histories, your worship knows so well, are full."

"As to that," replied Don Quixote, "I can answer that Dulcinea is the child of her own works, that virtues adorn blood, and that the virtuous and humble are to be more highly regarded and esteemed than the wicked of high rank. Moreover, Dulcinea has an element in her that may raise her to be a queen with crown and scepter, for the merit of one lovely and virtuous woman is enough to perform even greater miracles, and if not formally, at least potentially she possesses within a store of greater fortunes."

"I notice, Don Quixote," said the duchess, "that you are exceedingly cautious in all you say and that you proceed, as the saying goes, with plummet in hand. Henceforth I shall believe, and make my whole household believe—and even the duke, my husband, if it is necessary—that there is a Dulcinea in El Toboso, that she is living today, and that she is beautiful, nobly born, and deserving that such a knight as Don Quixote should serve her. Indeed, I can pay her no higher compliment. There is, however, one doubt that still perplexes me, and I cannot help feeling somewhat of a grudge against Sancho Panza. My doubt arises from the fact that in the aforesaid history it is related that the same Sancho Panza, when he carried on your worship's behalf a letter to the said Lady Dulcinea, found her winnowing a sack of wheat, and by the token, the story says it was red wheat, a thing that makes me doubt the greatness of her lineage."

To this Don Quixote replied: "My lady, your highness must know that everything or almost everything that happens to me exceeds the ordinary limits of what happens to other knights-errant, whether it is ruled by the inscrutable will of destiny or by the malice of some envious enchanter. Now, since it is an established fact that of all or most of the famous knights-errant, one is endowed with immunity from enchantment, another has flesh so impenetrable that he cannot be wounded, as had the famous Roland, one of the Twelve Peers of France, of whom it is told that he could only be wounded in the sole of his left foot, and even so only with the point of a stout pin, and with no other kind of weapon at all. So,

when Bernardo del Carpio slew him at Roncesvalles, finding
that he could not wound him with the sword, he lifted him
from the ground in his arms and strangled him, thus recalling
the death that Hercules inflicted on Antaeus, that fierce giant
who, they said, was a son of Earth. I mean to infer from
what I say that I perhaps may also have some gift of this
kind. It is certainly not that of being invulnerable, for on
many occasions experience has proved to me that I am of
tender flesh not at all impenetrable. Neither is it the gift of
being immune against enchantment, for I have already seen
myself cast into a cage into which the whole world would
not have been powerful enough to put me, save by force of
enchantment. But since I managed to free myself from that,
I am inclined to believe that there is no other power that
can harm me. And so, these enchanters, seeing that they
cannot use their vile magic upon my person, revenge themselves upon what I love most and try to rob me of my life
by ill-treating that of Dulcinea, for whom I live. And so, I
am convinced that when my squire carried my message to
her, they changed her into a peasant girl, engaged in so mean
an occupation as winnowing wheat, though I have already
said that this wheat was neither red wheat nor wheat at all,
but grains of Orient pearl. As a proof of all this, I must tell
your highnesses that when I passed by El Toboso a little
while ago, I could not for the life of me find the palace of
Dulcinea, and the next day, though Sancho, my squire, saw
her in her proper shape, which is the most beautiful in the
world, to me she appeared as a coarse, ugly peasant wench,
and by no means well spoken, she who is the paragon of
wisdom. Now since I am not and cannot be enchanted according to sound reason, it is she who is enchanted, injured,
changed, altered, and transformed. Through her my enemies
have avenged themselves upon me, and for her I shall mourn
perpetually till I see her in her former state.

"All this I have told you, for fear any should mind what
Sancho said about Dulcinea's winnowing, for as they changed
her to me, it is no wonder if they changed her to him.
Dulcinea is noble, wellborn, and of one of El Toboso's distinguished families, which are many, ancient, and excellent;
and no doubt the peerless Dulcinea has no small share of
their stock, for through her, her town will be famous and
memorable in future ages as Troy has been for Helen and

Spain for La Cava, though she will have a greater claim to fame.

"On the other hand, I want your highnesses to understand that Sancho Panza is one of the drollest squires that ever served a knight-errant. Sometimes he is so acutely simple that it is no small enjoyment to guess whether he is simple or cunning; he has roguish tricks that condemn him as a knave and blundering ways that confirm him a fool. He doubts everything and yet believes everything; when I imagine that he is crashing headforemost into folly, he bobs up with some shrewd or witty thing that sends him shooting up to the skies. In fact, I would not exchange him for another squire, even if they were to give me a city to boot, and for this reason I am in doubt whether it will be well to send him to the government your highness has conferred upon him, though I perceive that he possesses a certain talent for this business of governing. With a little trimming of his understanding he should manage his governorship as successfully as the king does his taxes, especially as we know by long experience that to be a governor does not require much cleverness or book learning, for there are a hundred about here who can hardly read and yet govern as ruthlessly as gerfalcons. The main point is to mean well and to desire to do right in everything, for they will never lack men who will advise and direct them in their actions, like those governors, men of the sword and unlettered, who pronounce sentences through assessors. I would advise him neither to take bribes nor to lose his due, and other smaller matters that lie heavy on my chest but will be mentioned in due time for Sancho's benefit and to the advantage of the isle he is to govern."

The conversation between the duke, the duchess, and Don Quixote had reached this point when they heard many voices and a great din in the palace. All of a sudden Sancho burst abruptly into the hall, in a scare, with a straining cloth for a bib, and followed by a number of lads, or rather kitchen scullions and other underlings, one of whom carried a small pail full of water, which from its color and dirt was evidently dishwater. The lad with the pail pursued him and chased him hither and thither, trying hard to shove it under his beard, and another one of the scullions made an attempt to wash it.

"What does this mean, brothers?" asked the duchess.

"What do you want to do to this good man? What! Do you not know that he is governor elect?"

To which the barber-scullion replied: "The gentleman won't let himself be washed, as the custom is, and as the duke, my master, was washed and the gentleman, his master."

"Yes, I will," answered Sancho in a blaze of wrath, "but I'd like it to be done with cleaner towels, with cleaner lye, and with hands not so dirty, for there's not so much difference between me and my master that he should be washed with angel's water [4] and me with devil's lye. The customs of the countries and the palaces of princes are only good when they do not cause annoyance, but the custom of the washing that is followed here is worse than that of the flogging of penitents.[5] I'm clean in the beard and I don't need such refreshings. And whoever tries to wash me or touch a hair of my head—I mean, of my beard—speaking with all due respect, I'll give him such a puck that my fist will be rammed in his skull, for such cirimonies and soapings look more like horseplay than entertainment."

The duchess was ready to die with laughter when she saw the rage of Sancho and heard his words, but Don Quixote was not pleased to see his squire so vilely adorned with the spotted towel and surrounded by the kitchen underlings. So, after making a low bow to the duke and duchess, as though he begged for permission to speak, he addressed the rabble in a dignified tone: "Ho there, gentlemen! Leave this lad alone and go back to where you came from, or wherever else you will; my squire is as clean as any other person, and these little pails are as irritating to him as a narrow-mouthed drinking cup would be. Take my advice and leave him alone, for neither he nor I understand this joking business."

Sancho caught the word from his master and continued: "Just let them come and play their jokes on the loutish clodhopper; I'll suffer it as sure as it's now nighttime! Let them bring me a comb here, or whatever they please, and curry this beard of mine, and if they get anything out of it that offends against cleanliness, let them clip me crosswise." [6]

[4] Water scented with rose, thyme, and orange.

[5] In Holy Week it was customary for penitents (*disciplinantes*) to flog themselves as they walked in procession through the streets. To cleanse oneself thus from sin was called by the folk *jabonadura* (soaping).

[6] This was the punishment meted out to blasphemers and usurers in ancient times.

At this the duchess, laughing all the while, said: "Sancho Panza is right in all he has said and will be right in all he shall say. He is clean, and as he says himself, he does not need to be washed; if our ways do not suit him, his soul is his own. Besides, you ministers of cleanliness have been exceedingly remiss and thoughtless, I do not know whether I should not say audacious, to bring pails, wooden utensils, and kitchen dish-clouts, instead of basins and jugs of pure gold and towels of holland, to such a person and such a beard. Indeed, you are a low, ill-bred crew, and since you are rascals, you cannot help showing the grudge you bear against the squires of knights-errant."

The roguish scullions, and even the seneschal who was with them, believed that the duchess was speaking in earnest, so they took the straining cloth off Sancho's chest, and all full of confusion they fled from the hall.

Sancho, when he found himself released from what, in his opinion, was a great peril, threw himself on his knees before the duchess and said: "From great ladies we expect great favors. I cannot repay what your ladyship has done for me this day but by longing to see myself dubbed a knight-errant so that I might spend all the days of my life serving so high a lady. I'm a laboring man, my name is Sancho Panza, I'm married, I've children, and I'm serving as a squire. If in any of those ways I can serve your highness, I'll be no longer in obeying than your ladyship in commanding."

"It is easy to see, Sancho," said the duchess, "that you have learned to be courteous in the very school of courtesy. It is easy to see, I mean, that you have been reared in the bosom of Don Quixote, who is, of course, the cream of compliments and the flower of ceremonies, or *cirimonies* as you say. May such a master and such a servant be fortunate! One is the cynosure of knight-errantry and the other is the star of squirely loyalty. Rise, friend Sancho; I will repay your courtesy by making the duke, my lord, grant as soon as he can the favor of the governorship that was promised."

And so the conversation ended. Don Quixote went away to take his siesta, but the duchess begged Sancho, if he was not eager to sleep, to come and spend the afternoon with her and her damsels in a very cool chamber. Sancho replied that though it was true that he usually slept four or five hours in the heat of the summer days, to serve her excellency he would try his hardest not to snooze even a single hour that

day and would come in obedience to her command. And so
he left the hall. The duke then gave fresh orders to his
servants to treat Don Quixote as a knight-errant, without
deviating in any way from the style in which it is reported
that knights of old were treated.

CHAPTER XXXIII

*Of the amusing conversation that passed between the
duchess, her maids, and Sancho Panza, which deserves
to be read and noted*

The history then relates that Sancho did not take his
siesta that afternoon, but visited the duchess after eating,
as he had promised, and that she was so delighted to listen
to his talk that she made him sit down beside her on a low
seat, though Sancho, out of pure good breeding, wanted not
to sit down.

The duchess, however, told him he was to sit down as
governor and talk as squire, for in both respects he deserved
even the throne of the Cid Rui Díaz, the Campeador.
Sancho shrugged his shoulders, obeyed, and sat down, and
all the damsels and duennas of the duchess crowded around
him, listening in deep silence to what he would say. But it
was the duchess who was the first to speak.

"Now that we are alone," said she, "and there is no one
here to hear us, I wish that the governor would resolve
some doubts I have, rising out of the history of the great
Don Quixote that is now in print. One of these doubts is that
since the good Sancho never saw Dulcinea, I mean, Lady
Dulcinea of El Toboso, nor took Don Quixote's letter to her,
for it was left in the memorandum book in the Sierra
Morena, how did he dare to invent the answer and all that
about finding her winnowing wheat, seeing that the whole
story was a joke, a lie, so much to the prejudice of the

peerless Dulcinea's reputation and so injurious to the quality and loyalty of a good squire?"

When he heard these words, Sancho, without answering, got up from his chair; with noiseless steps, his body hunched up and a finger placed over his lips, he went all around the room lifting the hangings, after which he returned to his seat and said: "Now, my lady, that I've seen there is not a soul listening to us on the sly, only the bystanders, I'll answer what you have asked me without fear or dread. And the first thing I'll say is that I consider my master, Don Quixote, to be stark raving mad, though at times he says things that, to my mind and even to everybody who hears him, are so wise and run in such a straight furrow that Satan himself could not have said them better. Nevertheless, truly and without question I'm convinced that he's daft. Now, since I've got this fixed in my head, I can risk making him believe things that have no head nor tail, like that business about the answer to the letter, and the other of six or eight days ago, which is not yet written out in history, namely, the enchantment of my Lady Dulcinea, for I made him believe she's enchanted, though there's no more truth in it than over the hills of Ubeda." [1]

The duchess begged him to tell her about the enchantment or joke, and Sancho told her everything exactly as it had happened, from which the listeners received no little pleasure. Then, continuing her conversation, she said: "Owing to what worthy Sancho has told me, a doubt keeps springing up in my mind, and a kind of whisper reaches my ears that says: 'If Don Quixote is mad, crazy, and cracked, and if Sancho Panza, his squire, knows it, and yet serves and follows him and relies on his vain promises, there is no doubt that he is more of a madman and a fool than his master. Since that is so, it will be bad for you, my lady duchess, if you give the said Sancho an island to govern, for how can he who does not know how to govern himself be able to govern others?'"

"By God, my lady," said Sancho, "that doubt of yours had a timely birth. But your ladyship should speak out

---

[1] *Ir por los cerros de Ubeda* was a proverbial expression meaning to go off the track. It is said of something that is irrelevant. As the modern Spanish poet, Antonio Machado, tells us, there are no hills near Ubeda. Cervantes, too, who had wandered all over La Mancha, likewise knew that those hills did not exist.

plain and clear. I know what you say is the honest truth,
and if I had a head on my shoulders, I'd have left my
master this long time. But this is my fate and my bad luck;
I can't help it. I must follow him, we are from the same village, I've eaten his bread, I love him well, he is grateful, he
gave me his ass foals, and above all, I'm faithful; therefore,
it's quite impossible for anything to separate us except the
man with the pickaxe and shovel.[2] And if your highness
does not want to give me the government you promised,
God made me without it, and perhaps if you don't give it
to me, it will be all the better for my conscience, for though
I'm a fool I know the proverb, 'To her hurt the ant grew
wings,'[3] and maybe Sancho the squire will get to Heaven
sooner than Sancho the governor. 'They bake as good bread
here as in France'; and 'By night all cats are gray'; and
'It's hard luck on the man who hasn't broken fast by two
in the afternoon'; and 'No stomach's a hand's breadth bigger than another,' but if it is, it can be filled 'with straw or
hay,' as the saying goes; and 'The little birds of the field
have God to feed them'; and 'Four yards of Cuenca cloth
keep a man warmer than four of Segovia broadcloth';[4] and
"On leaving this world and going under, the prince travels
as narrow a path as the journeyman'; and 'The Pope's body
fills no more feet of soil than the sacristan's'; and no matter
if the one is higher than the other, for when we go into the
pit, we all have to shrink and make ourselves small, or they
make us shrink in spite of us, and then—goodnight to us.
And I say again that if your ladyship does not want to give
me the island because I'm a fool, I'll know how to care
nothing about it because I'm a wise man. I've heard it said
that 'Behind the Cross stands the Devil,' and that 'All that
glitters is not gold,' and that from among the oxen, the
plows, and the yokes, Wamba, the husbandman, was made
king of Spain, and from among the brocades, jollities, and

[2] As Covarrubias says in his *Tesoro,* the pick and the shovel
signify death.

[3] Because when she flew the birds gobbled her up. The proverb warns those who rise through luck to a position above their
deserts. They meet with the ruin they would have avoided had
they remained in obscurity.

[4] Cuenca coarse cloth was the cheapest, and Segovia material
was the finest and most expensive.

riches, Rodrigo was taken to be devoured by snakes, if the verses of the old ballads don't lie." [5]

"To be sure they don't lie," cried Doña Rodríguez, the duenna, who was one of the listeners. "There's a ballad that says they put King Rodrigo alive into a tomb full of toads, snakes, and lizards and that two days later the king cried out from within the tomb in a low, plaintive voice:

> " 'They nibble me now, they nibble me now,
> In the part where I most did sin.'

According to that, the gentleman here is quite right in wishing to be a laboring man rather than a king, if he is to be eaten by vermin."

The duchess could not restrain her laughter at her duenna's simplicity, nor from marveling at the language and proverbs of Sancho, to whom she said: "Worthy Sancho knows that what a knight once promises he tries to fulfill, even at the cost of his own life. The duke, my lord and husband, though he is not a knight-errant, is none the less a knight; therefore, he will keep his word about the promised island, in spite of the envy and malice of the world. Be of good heart, Sancho; when you least expect it, you will find yourself seated on the throne of your island, and you will grasp firm hold of your governorship, and you may even expect to exchange it for another of three-bordered brocade.[6] But I charge you to mind how you govern your vassals, for I warn you they are all loyal and wellborn."

"About that business of governing them well," said Sancho, "there's no need to charge me to do it, for I'm naturally charitable and full of pity for the poor, and I don't go stealing the fire from him who kneads and bakes; and by the sign of the Cross they're not going to load the dice against me. I'm an old dog, so I know all about their whistle; I can keep my eyes skinned, if need be, and I don't let black

---

[5] Refers to the ancient ballads describing the fate of Rodrigo, the last king of the Visigoths.

[6] This phrase means that Sancho will exchange his governorship at a later date for one that is more profitable. In La Mancha it is a common saying, when a child appears in a new suit of clothes, for his relations to greet him and wish him luck in the words: "May you reject it for another of finer stuff" (*que le deseche con otro de tela superior*).

spots flicker before my eyes, for I know where the shoe pinches. I'm saying this, because I'll be always ready to give the good a helping hand, but I won't let the bad put a foot near me. Besides, my view is that in this business of governing the beginning is what counts, and maybe after being governor for a fortnight, I'll lick my fingers for such a tasty job and know more about it than about plowing and reaping, for which I was reared."

"You are right, Sancho," said the duchess, "for no one is born educated, and bishops are made out of men and not out of stones. But let us return to the subject we were discussing a short while ago, namely, the enchantment of the Lady Dulcinea. I am convinced that your idea of deceiving your master by making him believe that the peasant girl was Dulcinea, and that if he did not recognize her it must have been because she was enchanted, was all a contrivance of one of the enchanters who persecute Don Quixote. For I know from a good source that the coarse country wench who leaped on the ass was and is Dulcinea of El Toboso, and that you, my good Sancho, though you fancy yourself the deceiver, are the one who is deceived. And remember that we, too, have enchanters here who wish us well and tell us clearly and unmistakably what happens in the world; so, believe me, Sancho, that leaping country lass was and is Dulcinea of El Toboso, who is as much enchanted as the mother who bore her. When we least expect it, we shall see her in her own proper figure, and then Sancho will come out of the delusion in which he lives."

"That may well be," said Sancho Panza, "and now I'm willing to believe what my master says about what he saw in the cave of Montesinos, where he says he saw Lady Dulcinea of El Toboso in the dress that I said I had seen her in when I enchanted her all at my own sweet will. Now, it must have been all the reverse, as your ladyship says, for it cannot be supposed that I could with my weak and feeble wits contrive so clever a trick in a moment, nor do I think my master is so mad as to believe that I could do so. But, my lady, your excellency must not think me ill-natured, for a blockhead like me is not bound to understand the wicked plots of those wicked enchanters. I contrived all that to avoid a scolding from my master, Don Quixote, but not with any intention of injuring him. If the whole business has gone awry, there is a God in heaven who judges our hearts."

"That is true," said the duchess, "but tell me, Sancho, what is this you say about the cave of Montesinos, for I should be glad to know."

Sancho then told her, word for word, what we have already related about that adventure, and upon hearing it the duchess said: "From this incident we may infer that, since the great Don Quixote says he saw there the same peasant wench whom Sancho saw on the way from El Toboso, she is, no doubt, Dulcinea, and that there are very active and interfering enchanters about here."

"That's what I say," said Sancho, "and if my Lady Dulcinea of El Toboso is enchanted, that will be so much the worse for her. It's not my job to engage in a brawl with my master's enemies, who must be many and evil. The honest truth is that the one I saw was a peasant wench, and I took her for a peasant wench. And if that was Dulcinea, do not blame me and raise a fuss about it. Nevertheless, there they are blathering at me every instant, saying: 'Sancho said it, Sancho did it, Sancho come, Sancho go!' As if Sancho was a nobody and not that same Sancho who's now roaming all over the world in books, according to Sansón Carrasco, and he for sure is one bachelored by Salamanca, and fellows of that kind surely don't tell lies, except when the whim bites them or when it's well worth their while. So there's no reason why anybody should barge into me. Besides, I've a good reputation, and I have heard my master say that 'A good name's worth more than great riches.' If they only shove me into this government, they'll see wonders, for he who has been a good squire will be a good governor."

"All that the worthy Sancho has just said," observed the duchess, "are Catonian aphorisms, or at least drawn from the very heart of Michael Verino himself, *florentibus occidit annis*.[7] Well, well, if we may speak in Sancho's own style, 'You'll often find a good drinker under a bad cloak.'"

"In truth, my lady," replied Sancho, "I've never in my

[7] The full epigram runs *Verinus Michael florentibus occidit annis* (Michael Verinus died in the prime of life, or prematurely). The epigram was written by Angelo Poliziano in praise of Miguel Verino from Minorca, the author of a celebrated volume of Latin epigrams often reprinted. It was entitled *Libri Distichorum*, Salamanca, 1496.

life had the vice of drink. Out of thirst, may be, for I'm no
hypocrite. I drink when I have the mind to do so, and when
I haven't and they hand me a drink, I take it not to appear
finical or boorish. And when it's a toast to a friend, who'd
be so hardhearted as to refuse to pledge a friend? But though
I wear breeches, I don't soil them, all the more as the squires
of knights-errant nearly always drink water, for they're forever traipsing through forests, woods and meadows, and
mountains and crags, without ever finding a beggarly sop
of wine, even if they'd give one of their eyes for it."

"So I believe," replied the duchess. "And now let Sancho
go and rest. Later on we shall talk at greater length, and
give orders for him to go off soon and be, as he says, shoved
into this governorship."

Sancho again kissed the duchess' hand and besought her
to grant him the favor of seeing that good care was taken
of Dapple, for he was the light of his eyes.

"What dapple is this?" asked the duchess.

"My ass," replied Sancho. "Instead of giving him that
name, I usually call him Dapple. I asked this duenna here
to take care of him when I entered the castle, but she flew
into a temper, as if I had called her old or ugly, though it
should be more natural for duennas to feed asses than to
give orders in halls. God bless us and save us! What an
edge a certain gentleman of my village had against those
ladies!"

"He must have been some gross fellow," said Doña
Rodríguez, the duenna. "If he had been a gentleman, he
would have set them above the horns of the moon."

"Now let us have no more of this," said the duchess.
"Hush, Doña Rodríguez, and you, Señor Panza, calm
yourself and leave Dapple to my charge. As he is Sancho's
treasure, I'll put him on the apple of my eye."

"Provided he's in the stable, I'm satisfied," replied Sancho,
"for neither he nor myself is worthy to remain one instant
on the apple of your eye. I'd prefer to stick daggers into myself than agree to it, for although my master says that in
matters of courtesy it is better to lose by overdoing than by
underdoing, in equine and asinine matters it is better to
keep the rhythm under control and take the middle road."

"Take him on your governorship, Sancho," said the
duchess, "and there you'll be able to entertain him as you
like and even pension him off."

"Don't think, my lady, that you've exaggerated," said Sancho, "for I've seen more than two asses go to governorships, and there's nothing strange in my taking mine with me."

Sancho's words made the duchess laugh again, and after sending him off to bed, she went away to report to the duke the conversation that had passed between herself and the squire.

With the duke she plotted and arranged to play a joke upon Don Quixote that would be unusual and in accordance with knight-errantry style. And they certainly invented many, so ingenious and characteristic that they are among the best adventures this great history contains.

CHAPTER XXXIV

Which tells of the information received for the disenchantment of the peerless Dulcinea of El Toboso, which is one of the famous adventures in this book

The duke and duchess took great pleasure in conversing with Don Quixote and Sancho Panza, and as they were resolved to carry out their intention to play some tricks on them that might bear some appearance of being adventures, they took a hint from what Don Quixote had told them of the cave of Montesinos, and from it they prepared a famous one. What astonished the duchess more than anything else was the credulity of Sancho, who had come to believe as an infallible truth that Dulcinea was enchanted, whereas it was he himself who had been the enchanter and the playboy in all that affair. Accordingly, she and the duke gave orders to their servants as to how they should behave, and six days later they took Don Quixote on a hunting party with as great an array of huntsmen and beaters as any crowned king could muster.

They gave Don Quixote a hunting suit and Sancho one of the finest green cloth; but Don Quixote refused to put his on, saying that he would soon have to return to the hard exercise of arms and could not carry wardrobes and stores with him. As for Sancho he took what they gave him, intending to sell it as soon as he had an opportunity.

When the appointed day arrived, Don Quixote put on his armor and Sancho his new suit, and the squire, riding on Dapple, whom he would not leave behind even though they offered him a horse, joined the band of beaters. The duchess came out magnificently dressed, and Don Quixote, courteous and gallant as always, held the rein of her palfrey,[1] though the duke did not wish to allow it. At last they reached a wood between two high mountains, where, after arranging hiding places and snares and scattering the people to their various beats, the hunt began with great noise, shouting, and tallyho, so that with the barking of the hounds and the blaring of the horns they could not hear one another speak. The duchess dismounted and with a sharp hunting spear in her hand took up her station in a place where she knew the wild boars were accustomed to pass.[2] The duke and Don Quixote likewise dismounted and posted themselves by her side. Sancho took up a position behind all of them, without dismounting from Dapple, whom he did not dare to leave lest some mishap befall him.

Scarcely had they taken their places on foot in line with their retainers, when they saw a gigantic boar, pressed by the hounds and followed by the huntsmen, careering toward them, gnashing his teeth and tusks, and foaming at the mouth. As soon as he saw him, Don Quixote braced his shield on his arm, drew his sword, and advanced to meet him; the duke with his hunting spear did likewise, but the duchess would have gone in front of all of them, had the duke not prevented her. Sancho alone, when he saw the beast at bay, jumped off Dapple, took to his heels as hard as he could, and in sheer desperation tried in vain to scramble up a tall oak tree. But halfway up, while he clung to a branch trying to reach the top, as bad luck would have it, the branch snapped, and in his fall he was caught by a stump of the tree and remained suspended in the air, unable to reach the ground. Finding himself in this position and feeling his suit was beginning to rip and thinking that the ferocious beast would reach him if he came that way, he began to bellow for help so lustily that all who heard and did not see him believed that some wild animal had his teeth in him. In the end the tusked boar fell pierced by the many spears that pressed upon him, and Don Quixote, turn-

[1] This was the highest token of respect a knight could give to a lady.

[2] By a law of 1611 firearms were prohibited in hunting. Two years after the publication of Part II of *Don Quixote*, firearms were permitted. F. Rodríguez Marín, *op. cit.*, Vol. V, pp. 209–210.

ing around at the shouts of Sancho, saw him hanging from the oak head downward, and Dapple, who did not forsake him in his calamity, standing close beside him. Cide Hamete says that he rarely saw Sancho without Dapple, or Dapple without Sancho, such was the friendship and good faith between them. Don Quixote went over and unhooked Sancho, who, when he found himself free and on the ground, examined the rent in his hunting suit, and was deeply grieved, for he thought that suit was worth an inheritance to him.

They laid the mighty boar upon a sumpter mule, and having covered it with sprigs of rosemary and branches of myrtle, they bore it away as the spoils of victory to some large field tents that had been pitched in the middle of the wood. There they found the tables laid and dinner served in such sumptuous style that it was easy to see the greatness and magnificence of the host and hostess. Sancho, as he showed the rents in his torn suit to the duchess, remarked: "If it had only been hunting hares or little birds, my suit wouldn't be in such a pickle; I can't see what pleasure there is in lying in wait for an animal that may murder you with his tusk if he gets a go at you. I remember once hearing an old ballad that says:

> " 'By bears be you devoured
> Like Favila of old.' "

"That was a Gothic king," said Don Quixote, "who, when following the chase, was eaten by a bear."

"That's just what I'm saying," answered Sancho, "and I'd sooner kings and princes didn't expose themselves to such dangers for the sake of a pleasure that, in my opinion, should not be one at all, for it consists in killing an animal that has done no harm to anyone."

"You are mistaken, Sancho," replied the duke, "for hunting is the most suitable and necessary exercise of all for kings and princes. The chase is the image of war; it has its stratagems, wiles, ambushes, by which one can overcome the enemy in safety; in it we have to bear extreme cold and intolerable heat; indolence and sleep are scorned; bodily strength is invigorated; the limbs of one who takes part in it are made supple; indeed, it is an exercise that can be taken without harm to anyone and with pleasure to many.

And the best point about it is that it is not for everybody, as other kind of sports are, except hawking, which is also reserved for kings and great lords. Therefore, O Sancho, change your opinion, and when you are governor, follow the chase and you will soon find that one loaf will do you as much good as a hundred." [3]

"By no means," replied Sancho, "a good governor should have a broken leg and keep at home. Wouldn't it be a fine thing if people came to see him on business, footweary, and he's away in the woods enjoying himself? Sure, that way the government would go to hell altogether! By my faith, sir, hunting and amusements are more for lazybones than for governors. My bit of amusement will be a game of trumps [4] at Easter and bowls on Sundays and holidays. Huntings and the like don't suit my temper or my conscience."

"God grant it may be so," said the duke, "for 'There's many a slip 'twixt cup and lip.' "

"Come what may," answered Sancho, " 'A good payer needs no sureties,' and 'God's help is better than rising at dawn', and 'It's the belly carries the feet, not the feet the belly'; I mean that if God helps me and I do what I ought to do honestly, there's no doubt I'll govern better than a gerfalcon. [5] Just let them stick a finger in my mouth and see if I bite or not."

"May the curse of God and His saints light upon you, Sancho," cried Don Quixote. "When will the day come, as I have often told you, when I shall hear you to speak a single connected sentence without proverbs? I beseech you, my lord and lady, pay no heed to this idiot; he will grind your souls, not between two but between two thousand proverbs, which he drags in as much in season and as much to the purpose as— God grant as much health to him as to me if I wish to hear them!"

"Sancho Panza's proverbs," said the duchess, "may be more numerous than those of the Greek commander, yet

---

[3] This is an old slang phrase meaning "You will be a hundred times the better for it."

[4] An old game called *Triunfo envidiado,* the ancient English country card game of Brag.

[5] To govern like a gerfalcon *mejor que un gerifalte* was a slang phrase meaning "like a thief."

they are no less valuable for their conciseness, and I for one confess that they give me more pleasure than others that are more to the purpose and more reasonably introduced."

As they conversed in this entertaining manner they sallied forth from the tent into the wood, and they spent the day visiting the hunters' posts and ambushes. Then night fell, which was not as clear or calm as might have been expected at such a season (for it was then midsummer), but bringing with it a strange dim light that greatly helped the scheme of the duke and duchess. And so when it began to be dusk, a little after twilight, suddenly the whole wood seemed to be on fire and from far and near countless trumpets and other military instruments sounded and resounded as if many squadrons of cavalry were passing through the wood. The blaze of the fire and the noise of the martial clarions almost blinded the eyes and deafened the ears of all those who were in the wood. Soon all heard innumerable *lelilíes*, or cries such as the Moors utter when they ride into battle; trumpets and clarions blared, drums rattled, fifes skirled, so unceasingly and so fast that he could not have had any senses who did not lose them at the confused din of so many instruments. The duke was dumbfounded, the duchess astonished, Don Quixote wondered, Sancho trembled; in fact, even those who were in the know were frightened. Through fear, they kept silence when a postilion, disguised as a devil, passed in front of them, blowing, instead of a bugle, a huge hollow horn that bellowed a harsh, terrifying sound.

"Ho there, brother courier!" said the duke. "Who are you? Where are you going? What warriors are those who seem to be passing through the wood?"

To which the courier answered in a deep, horrifying voice: "I am the Devil; I am searching for Don Quixote of La Mancha; those who come yonder are six troops of enchanters who are bringing on a triumphal car the peerless Dulcinea of El Toboso. She is enchanted and comes together with the gallant Frenchman Montesinos, to give instructions to Don Quixote as to how she is to be disenchanted."

"If you were the Devil, as you say and as your appearance shows," said the duke, "you would have recognized the said knight, Don Quixote of La Mancha, for he stands before you."

"By God and my conscience," replied the Devil, "I did

not notice him, for my mind is so busy with so many things that I forgot the main reason for my presence here."

"This surely must be an honest kind of devil," said Sancho, "and a good Christian into the bargain, for if he wasn't, he wouldn't swear by God and his conscience. I'm certain that even in hell itself there must be some good folks."

The Devil then, without dismounting, turned to Don Quixote and said: "To thee, the Knight of the Lions (may I see thee in their claws), the unlucky but valiant knight Montesinos sends me, bidding me to tell thee to wait for him on the very spot where I may find thee, for he is bringing with him the lady called Dulcinea of El Toboso to show thee how thou mayst disenchant her. Now, since there is no further reason for my coming, I shall stay no more. May devils of my kind remain with thee, and good angels with these noble lords and ladies."

After these words he blew his monstrous horn, turned his back, and went away without waiting for an answer from anyone.

They all felt fresh wonder, especially Sancho and Don Quixote; Sancho, because in spite of the truth, they insisted that Dulcinea was enchanted; Don Quixote, because he was unable to convince himself whether all that had taken place in the cave of Montesinos were true or not. While he was pondering deeply over these problems, the duke said to him: "Do you mean to wait, Señor Don Quixote?"

"Why not?" replied the knight. "Here will I wait, fearless and steadfast, though all hell should assail me."

"Well, if I see another devil and hear another horn like the last one, I'll wait here as much as in Flanders," said Sancho.

By now night had closed in more completely, and many lights began to flicker through the wood, just as the dry exhalations from the earth, which look like shooting stars to our eyes, flit through the heavens. At the same instant a frightful noise was heard, like that made by the massive wheels of ox wagons, which, it is said, put to flight even wolves and bears, so harsh and continuous is their creaking. In addition to this din, there was a further tumult that made the company feel as if in the four corners of the wood four separate battles were going on at the same time: in one quarter resounded the heavy thunder of artillery; in another countless muskets were crackling; close at hand could be

heard the shouts of men fighting hand to hand; while in the
distance they could hear the echoing Moorish war cries. In a
word, the bugles, horns, clarions, trumpets, drums, cannon,
musketry, and above all, the hideous creaking of the wagons
made up so confused and terrifying a din that Don Quixote
had to harden his heart to face it. Sancho, however, gave
way and fell down in a faint on the hem of the duchess'
skirts, but she sheltered him and ordered her servants to
throw water on his face. This was done, and he came to his
senses just as one of the cars with the screeching wheels
reached the spot where he lay. It was drawn by four plodding oxen, all covered with black trappings; on each horn
they had fixed a large blazing torch of wax. On the top of
the wagon a raised seat had been constructed, on which
was seated a venerable old man with a beard whiter than
the very snow and so long that it fell below his waist. He
was clad in a long robe of black buckram, for, as the cart
was furnished with a host of candles, it was easy to make
out everything that was in it. Guiding it were two ugly
devils, also clad in buckram with faces so hideous that
Sancho, having caught one glimpse of them, shut his eyes
tight so as not to see them again. When the wagon had
come up to them, the venerable old man rose from his lofty
seat, and standing up, he cried out in a loud voice: "I am
the sage Lirgandeo." And the cart passed on without his
saying another word. Behind it came another wagon of the
same form, with another man enthroned, who, when the
cart stopped, said in no less solemn a tone: "I am the sage
Alquife, the great friend of Urganda the Unknown." And
the wagon passed on. Then a third cart appeared of the
same sort, but the man seated on the throne was not old
like the rest, but robust and of forbidding aspect. When he
stood up like the others, he cried out in a voice that was
hoarser and more devilish: "I am Arcalaús the Enchanter,
the mortal enemy of Amadis of Gaul and all his kin." And
the wagon passed on. The three wagons, after moving on a
short distance, halted, and the jarring screech of their wheels
ceased. Then they heard nothing but the sound of sweet
concerted music, which gladdened the heart of Sancho, for
he took it to be a good omen, and he said to the duchess,
from whom he did not stir a step: "My lady, where there's
music there can't be mischief."

"Neither where there are lights and brightness," replied the duchess.

To which Sancho answered: "Fire gives light, and bonfires give brightness, as we see by those that surround us, and perhaps they may burn us; but music is always the sign of feasting and merriment."

"Time will tell," said Don Quixote, who was listening to all. And he was right, as the following chapter will tell.

CHAPTER XXXV

The continuation of Don Quixote's instructions for the disenchantment of Dulcinea, with other wonderful events

Keeping time to the pleasing music, they saw advancing toward them what is called a triumphal car, drawn by six gray mules, caparisoned with white linen, on each of which was mounted a torch-bearing penitent,[1] also clad in white, with a large lighted white wax taper in his hand. The car was twice and even three times as large as the former ones, and in front of it and on the sides stood twelve more penitents, white as snow, all with their lighted tapers, a sight that aroused fear as well as wonder; on a raised throne was seated a nymph clad in a thousand veils of silver lamé, with countless leaves of gilded tinsel that made her appear, if not richly, at least showily appareled. She had her face covered with a fine transparent veil, in such a way that its folds did not prevent the beautiful features of the maiden from being distinguished, while the multitude of lights enabled all to judge her beauty and her years, which seemed not to have reached twenty nor to be under seventeen. Beside her came a figure swathed in a trailing robe of state[2] that reached to the ground, and with his head

[1] In ancient days in Spain there were two classes of penitents at Seville: (1) torch-bearing penitents (*disciplinantes de luz*), who carried lighted tapers in the processions; (2) blood penitents (*penitentes de sangre*), who flagellated themselves in the procession so that their blood spurted over their white habits.

[2] Robes of state worn by persons of distinction were called trailers (*rozagantes*) because they reached to the ground.

enveloped in a black veil. As soon as the car arrived in front of the duke, the duchess, and Don Quixote, the music of the clarion ceased and soon that of the harps and guitars on the car also. Then the figure in the robe stood up, and throwing his folds apart and removing the veil from his face, disclosed plainly before all the figure of Death, fleshless and hideous. At this sight Don Quixote felt uneasy, Sancho alarmed, and the duke and duchess made a show of nervousness. This living Death, standing up, spoke in a sluggish, sleepy voice as follows:

"Merlin I am, miscalled the devil's son
In lying annals authorized by time;
Of magic prince, of Zoroastric art
Monarch and archive, with a rival eye
I view the efforts of the age to hide
The doughty deeds of errant cavaliers
Who are, and ever have been, dear to me.

Enchanters and magicians and their folk
Are always harsh, austere, malevolent,
But not so mine—soft, tender, amorous
My nature, my joy doing good to all.
In the dim caverns of the gloomy Dis,
Where now my soul abides amid my spells,
My mystic squares and characters, there came
Unto my pitying ears the plaintive voice
Of peerless Dulcinea, Tobosan maid.

I learned of her enchantment and sad fate,
How she from noble dame became transformed
To peasant wench; and touched with tender pity,
I searched the volumes of my devilish craft,
Closing my soul in this grim skeleton,
And hither have I come to give relief
To woe so great, and break the cursed spell.
O lady! Thou, glory and pride of all
Who case their limbs in steel and adamant!
Light, lantern, pilot, star, and cynosure
Of those who scorn the sloth of feather beds,
And seek the hardy toils of bloodstained arms!

To thee, I speak, great hero, ever praised,
Spain's boasted pride, La Mancha's peerless knight,
Don Quixote wise and brave, to thee I say,
For peerless Dulcinea of El Toboso,
Her pristine form and beauty to regain,
Needful it is that thy squire, Sancho Panza,
Three thousand and three hundred stripes should lay
On both his brawny buttocks bar'd to heaven,
Such as may sting and tease and hurt him well:
The authors of her woes have thus decreed,
And therefore, lords and ladies, I am here."

"Faith and skin!" cried Sancho at this. "Three thousand
lashes indeed! I'd as soon give myself three stabs in the belly
with a dagger as these stripes. The Devil take this method
of disenchanting! I don't see what my arse has to do with
enchantings! By God, if Master Merlin hasn't found another
way for disenchanting Lady Dulcinea of El Toboso, she may
go enchanted to her burial."

"I will take you, Don Clown, gorged with garlic," cried
Don Quixote, "and tie you to a tree naked as when your
mother bore you, and not three thousand and three hundred,
but six thousand and six hundred lashes will I give you, so
well laid on that three thousand and three hundred hard tugs
shall not tug them off. And answer me not a word, else
will I tear out your heart!"

Hearing this, Merlin said: "This must not be so, for
the stripes that the good Sancho has to receive must be of
his own free will and not by force, and at whatever time
he pleases, for no term is fixed. And furthermore, he is
allowed, if he wishes, to commute by half the infliction of
this whipping; he may let it be done by another's hand, even
though it be somewhat weighty."

"Neither another hand nor my own, nor one weighty or
for weighing, shall touch my bum! Did I by any chance
bring Mistress Dulcinea of El Toboso into the world, that
my bottom should pay for the sins her eyes have committed.
My master, yes—he's a part of her, for isn't he always calling her 'my life' and 'my soul' and 'my stay and prop'; he
may and ought to whip himself for her, and bear all the
pains needed for her disenchanting. But imagine me whipping myself! Not on your life, I pronounce."

Hardly had Sancho ceased speaking when the silvery nymph who was beside the ghost of Merlin stood up, and removing the thin veil off her face, disclosed one that was extraordinarily beautiful; and with masculine assurance and in no very ladylike voice she addressed Sancho Panza in the following words: "O wretched squire, soul of an empty pail, heart of a cork tree, and bowels of flint and pebbles, if they had ordered you, brazen-faced sheep stealer, to throw yourself headlong from some tall tower; if, enemy of mankind, they had asked you to swallow a dozen toads, two dozen lizards, and three dozen snakes; if they had requested you to butcher your wife and children with some sharp murderous scimitar, 'twere no marvel had you shown yourself squeamish and pigheaded. But to make such a song about three thousand and three hundred lashes, which every poor sniveling charity-boy gets every month, it is enough to amaze, confound, and stupefy the compassionate bowels of all who hear it, and even of all who will hear it in the course of time. Turn, wretched, hardhearted animal, turn, I say, your startled owl's eyes upon these pupils of my eyes, which have been compared to glittering stars, and you will see them weeping tears, drop by drop, trickle by trickle, making furrows, tracks, and paths over the fair meadows of my cheeks. Let it move you, sly, ill-conditioned monster, to see my blooming youth—still in its teens, for I am nineteen and have not reached twenty—withering and wasting beneath the coarse shell of a rude peasant wench; and if I now do not look like one, it is because of a special favor granted to me by Lord Merlin, here present, solely that my beauty may soften you, for the tears of beauty in affliction turn rocks into cotton wool and tigers into sheep. Lay on, lay on those fleshy globes of yours, you loutish, untamed beast; revive from sloth your lusty vigor, which only urges you to eat and eat, and restore me the silken softness of my skin, the gentleness of my disposition, and the beauty of my face. And if for me you will not relent or come to reason, do so for the sake of that poor knight who is beside you, your master, I mean, whose soul I see even at this instant sticking crosswise in his throat, not ten inches from his lips, waiting only for your harsh or gentle answer either to fly out of his mouth or go back again into his stomach."

Don Quixote, when he heard this, felt his throat and turned

to the duke, saying: "By God, my lord, Dulcinea speaks truly, for I have my soul stuck crosswise in my throat, like the nut of a crossbow."

"What do you say to this, Sancho?" asked the duchess.

"I say, my lady," replied Sancho, "what I said before, that as for the lashes, I pronounce them."

"*Renounce* you should say, Sancho, and not as you say it," said the duke.

"Leave me alone, your worship," answered Sancho; "I'm in no mood at present to go quibbling and hairsplitting about niceties or a letter more or less, for these lashes they have to give me, or I have to give myself, have put me in such a dither that I don't know what I'm saying or doing. But I'd like to know from the lady here, my Lady Dulcinea of El Toboso, where she learned this way of begging that she has. She comes to ask me to lay open my flesh with lashes, and she calls me 'soul of an empty pail' and 'loutish, untamed beast' and a whole string of bad names, which the Devil is welcome to. Is my flesh made of brass? Do I care a hang whether she is enchanted or not? What hamper of white linen, shirts, kerchiefs, or socks—not that I wear them—does she bring with her to coax me? No, nothing but one piece of abuse after another, though she must remember the old saying that 'An ass with a load of gold goes lightly up a mountain,' and that 'Gifts break rocks,' and that 'Praying devoutly but hammering stoutly,' and that 'A bird in hand is worth two in the bush.' Then there's my master, who, instead of stroking my neck and petting me to make me turn to wool and carded cotton, says that if he catches me, he'll tie me naked to a tree and double the ration of lashes. These tenderhearted gentlemen should have been aware of what they were doing; it's not a mere squire but a governor they're ordering to whip himself, just as if it was a case of 'Drink with cherries.' [3] Let them learn—curses upon them —let them learn how to beg, how to ask, and how to behave themselves, for there's a time for all things, and people are not always in a good humor. At the present instant I'm bursting with grief at seeing my green suit all torn, and here

---

[3] To drink with cherries (*beber con guindas*) is a proverbial phrase used ironically in the sense of putting one good thing upon another. Clemencín compares it to the phrase "honey upon a jam tart." We might compare it with our phrase "to paint the lily."

they are coming to ask me to whip myself of my own free will, when I've as little stomach for it as I would for becoming an Indian chieftain."

"Well, the truth is, Sancho, my friend," said the duke, "that if you don't become softer than a ripe fig, you shall not get the government. A nice thing it would be for me to send my islanders a cruel governor with flinty bowels who won't hearken to the tears of afflicted damsels, or to the prayers of wise, imperious, and antique enchanters and sages. In short, Sancho, either you must whip yourself, or they must whip you, or you shan't be governor."

"My lord," replied Sancho, "won't you give me two days' time to examine what's best for me?"

"No, certainly not," said Merlin. "Here, at once and in this place, the matter must be settled. Either Dulcinea will return to the cave of Montesinos and to her former state of peasant wench, or else in her present form she will be carried off to the Elysian fields, where she will wait until the number of lashes is completed."

"Come, dear Sancho," said the duchess, "pluck up good courage and show some return for the bread you have eaten off Don Quixote. We are all bound to serve him and please him for his kind nature and noble chivalry. Say yes, my son, to this whipping; leave the Devil to his own devices, for 'Faint heart never breaks bad luck,' as you know so well."

To this Sancho replied with irrelevant words, which he addressed to Merlin: "Well, your worship, Lord Merlin, tell me this: when that devilish courier came here with a message from Señor Montesinos, he ordered my master to wait here for him, for he was coming to arrange how Lady Dulcinea of El Toboso was to be disenchanted, yet up to the present we have not seen Montesinos, nor anyone like him."

To which Merlin replied: "The Devil, friend Sancho, is a blockhead and a great rascal. I sent him in search of your master, not with a message from Montesinos, but from me, for Montesinos is in his cave expecting, or rather waiting for, his own disenchantment, for in his case the tail has yet to be skinned. [4] If he owes you anything or if you have any business to transact with him, I will bring him to you and put him where you please. But, for the present,

---

[4] Meaning that the most difficult part of the business has yet to be done.

make up your mind to agree to this whipping penance, and believe me, it will be of much profit both to your soul and your body: to your soul, because of the charity with which you perform it; to your body, because I know that you are of a sanguine complexion, and it will do you no harm to draw a little blood."

"There are many doctors in the world—even the enchanters are doctors," replied Sancho, "but since they all tell me so, though I personally don't see it, I say I am willing to give myself three thousand and three hundred lashes, provided I may give them whenever I please, without any fixing of days or times. I'll try to wipe off the debt as soon as possible, that the world may enjoy the beauty of Lady Dulcinea of El Toboso, for it now appears, contrary to what I believed, that she is truly beautiful. I insist, too, on a further condition, namely, that I am not to be bound to draw blood from myself with the whipping and that if any of the lashes happen to be fly swatters, they are to count. Item, that if I make a mistake in the reckoning, Lord Merlin, as he knows all, shall make it his business to keep count and let me know how many fall short or are over the number."

"There will be no need to let you know about those that are over," said Merlin, "for the moment you reach the exact number Lady Dulcinea will at once become disenchanted and will come full of gratitude to give thanks to the good Sancho, and even rewards for his good work. So, you need not be particular about too many or too few lashes. Heaven forbid that I should cheat anyone, even by a hair of his head."

"Well, then, in God's hands let it be," said Sancho, "I abide by my hard fortune. I say that I accept the penance, with the conditions we have agreed."

Hardly had Sancho uttered these last words when the music of the clarions struck up once more, and again a host of muskets were discharged, and Don Quixote hung on Sancho's neck, giving a thousand kisses on his forehead and on his cheeks. The duke and duchess and all the bystanders expressed the greatest satisfaction, and the car began to move on. As it passed, the fair Dulcinea bowed to the duke and duchess and made a low curtsy to Sancho.

And the joyous smiling dawn came on apace; the tiny flowers of the field revived and raised their heads, and the crystal waters of the brooks, murmuring over the white and gray pebbles, flowed along to pay their tribute to the expectant rivers; the glad earth, clear sky, pellucid air, calm light, each and all together, gave manifest tokens that the day that came treading on the skirts of the dawn would be fine and unclouded. The duke and duchess, pleased with their hunt and with having carried out their plans so successfully, returned to the castle, resolving to continue their joke, which gave them more amusement than anything in the world.

CHAPTER XXXVI

*Of the strange and inconceivable adventure of the
Doleful Duenna, alias Countess Trifaldi, with a letter
that Sancho Panza wrote to his wife, Teresa Panza*

It was a steward of the duke's establishment, a comical
fellow of nimble wit, who had played the part of Merlin
and had arranged the whole plan of the last adventure. He
had also written the verses and made the page play Dulcinea, and now with the collaboration of his master and
mistress he prepared another trick, the most amusing and the
strangest imaginable.

Next day the duchess asked Sancho whether he had made
a beginning with his penance for disenchanting Dulcinea.
He said that he had and that he had given himself five
stripes the same night. The duchess then asked him what he
had given them with, and he replied, with his hand.

"That," said the duchess, "is more like giving oneself
slaps than stripes. I am sure that the sage Merlin will not
be satisfied with such softness. Worthy Sancho, you must
make a scourge of thorns, or a knotted cat-o'-nine-tails,
which will make you smart, for it is with blood that the letter enters,[1] and the freeing of so great a lady as Dulcinea
will not be granted so cheaply; take heed, Sancho, that works
of charity that are performed halfheartedly are without merit
and of no avail." [2]

---

[1] This was an ancient proverb adopted as a motto by the
flagellants and those who mortified the flesh. It corresponded to
our phrase "there is no argument like the stick."

[2] The last clause (*Y advierta, Sancho, que las obras de caridad
que se hacen tibia y flojamente, no tienen mérito ni valen nada*),
which appears in the first edition of 1615, was ordered to be ex-
purgated by the Holy Inquisition in 1619, though no objections
were made to all the rest of the work.

To this Sancho answered: "If your ladyship will give me a scourge or proper rope's end, I'll lam myself with it, provided it does not hurt too much, for I must tell you that though I'm a rustic, there's more cotton wool than tough hemp in my flesh, and it won't do for me to play hell with myself for the good of anybody else."

"By all means," replied the duchess. "Tomorrow I will give you a scourge that will be just the thing for you, for it will adapt itself to the tenderness of your fleshy parts, as if they were two sisters."

"Then," said Sancho, "I must tell your highness, dear lady of my soul, that I've written a letter to my wife, Teresa Panza, giving her an account of all that has happened to me since I left her. I have it here in my bosom, and all it needs is the address. I'd be grateful if your discretion would read it, for I think it runs along in the governor style, I mean, in the way governors ought to write."

"But who dictated it?" asked the duchess.

"Who indeed but myself, sinner that I am?" replied Sancho.

"And did you write it yourself?" asked the duchess.

"Not I," answered Sancho, "for I can neither read nor write, though I can make my mark."

"Let us see it," said the duchess, "for I'll dare wager you show in it the quality and quantity of your wit."

Sancho took out an open letter from his bosom, and handing it to the duchess, she saw that it ran as follows:

SANCHO PANZA'S LETTER TO HIS WIFE, TERESA PANZA

Well whipped maybe I was, but it's a fine mount I have. If a good governorship I have, a good hiding it cost me. This you will not understand now, Teresa, but by and by it'll become clear to you. I want to tell you, Teresa, that I mean for you to ride in a coach, for that is only right, seeing that every other way of going is like cats on all fours. You are a governor's wife; see if anybody is backbiting you. I send you here a green hunting suit that my lady the duchess gave me; alter it so as to make a petticoat and bodice for our daughter. Don Quixote, my master, I hear tell in these parts, is a sensible madman and a droll blockhead, and I am by no means behind him. We have been in the cave of Montesinos, and the sage Merlin has laid hands on me to help him for disenchanting Dulcinea of El Toboso, who is called Aldonza Lorenzo over there.

With three thousand and three hundred stripes, less five, that I'm to give myself, she will be left as disenchanted as the mother that bore her. Say not a word of this to a soul, for mention your business to folks, and some will say that it's white, others that it's black. I'll be starting hence in a few days for my governorship, and I'm going there with the greatest wish to make money, for they do tell me that all new governors start out with the same wish. I'll feel the pulse of it and will let you know if you are to come and be with me or no. Dapple is well and sends his humblest wishes. I'm not leaving him behind though they carry me off to be Grand Turk. My lady the duchess kisses your hands a thousand times; mind you send her back by return two thousand, for nothing costs less nor is cheaper than civilities, as my master says. God has not been good enough to give me another bag with another hundred crowns, like the one the other day; but don't let that vex you, Teresa dear, for he who sounds the bell is safe, and it will all come out in the wash—I mean, the governorship; only it worries me greatly what they tell me, that once I get the taste of it, I'll eat my hands after it, and if that's so, it will not turn out cheap for me; though to be sure, maimed and crippled beggars pick up a pretty benefice of their own in the alms they beg. So, by one way or another you will be rich and in luck. God give it you as He can and keep me to serve you. From this castle, the 20th of July, 1614.

Your husband, the governor,

Sancho Panza.

When she had finished reading the letter, the duchess said: "On two points the worthy governor goes a little astray. One is in saying, or letting it be understood, that this governorship has been bestowed upon him for the lashes that he has to give himself, when he knows (and he cannot deny it) that when my lord, the duke, promised it to him, no one dreamed that there were lashes in the world. The other is that he shows himself here to be very covetous, and I don't want him to turn out the opposite of what I expected, for 'Greediness bursts the bag,' and the covetous governor misgoverns justice."

"That's not my meaning, lady," said Sancho, "and if you think the letter doesn't run as it should, there's nothing to

do but tear it up and make a new one, and maybe it will
be a worse one if it's left to my gumption."

"No, no," replied the duchess, "this one is all right; I'll
show it to the duke."

They went out into the garden where they were to dine,
and the duchess showed Sancho's letter to the duke, who
was highly delighted with it.

They dined, and when the cloths were removed and they
had enjoyed themselves a good while listening to Sancho's
amusing sallies, they suddenly heard the doleful sound of a
fife and the harsh beating of an untuned drum. They all
seemed disturbed by this chaotic, warlike, and dismal harmony, especially Don Quixote, who could hardly sit calmly
in his chair for pure excitement. Of Sancho we can only
say that fear took him to his accustomed refuge, which was
by the duchess' side or in her skirts, for really and truly
the sound they heard was most tragic and lugubrious. And
as they were all waiting in suspense, they saw entering the
garden in front two men clad in mourning robes, so long
and flowing that they trailed along the ground; they were
beating two big drums draped in black. By their side walked
the fifer, also pitch black, and these three were followed
by a personage of gigantic stature, cloaked rather than clad
in a jet-black gown with a monstrously long train. Over his
gown he wore a broad baldric, also black, from which hung
a huge scimitar with black sheath and hilt. His face was
hidden under a transparent black veil, through which showed
a very long beard, white as snow. He kept step to the drum-
beats with portentous gravity and composure. In short, his
stature, his swaggering gait, his blackness, and his escort were
well calculated to produce the amazement they did on all
who saw him and did not know who he was. With ponderous
and ceremonious pace he advanced and knelt before the
duke, who, with everyone else there, awaited him standing.
But the duke would not allow him to speak until he had
risen up. The prodigious scarecrow then rose, and towering
over all, he raised the mask from his face and disclosed the
longest, whitest, and bushiest beard that human eyes had
ever seen. And then, from his brawny and expanded chest
he squeezed out and bellowed forth a grim and sonorous
voice, fixing his eyes on the duke as he spoke: "Most high
and mighty lord, my name is Trifaldín of the White Beard.
I am squire to the Countess Trifaldi, otherwise called the

Doleful Duenna, on whose behalf I bear a message to
your highness. It is that your magnificence should be pleased
to grant her faculty and license to enter and tell you of her
plight, which is one of the strangest and most amazing that
any distressed imagination in the world could imagine. But
first she desires to know if in your castle there abides the
valorous and unconquered knight Don Quixote of La Mancha,
in quest of whom she has come on foot and fasting from
the kingdom of Candaya to this your realm, a journey that
can or should be considered miraculous or the result of enchantment. She is waiting at the door of this fortress or
country house, and she awaits only your good pleasure to
enter. I have spoken."

Then he coughed and stroked his beard from top to bottom with both hands, and with great composure he stood
waiting for the duke's response, who said: "It is now many
days, good squire Trifaldín of the White Beard, since we
heard of the distress of my lady the Countess Trifaldi,
whom the enchanters have caused to be called the Doleful
Duenna. You may gladly tell her to enter, stupendous squire,
and that the valiant knight Don Quixote of La Mancha is
here, from whose generous nature she may safely expect aid
and protection. And likewise you may say to her on my
behalf that if my help is necessary, it shall not be lacking,
for I am bound by my knighthood to help her. By it I am
compelled to favor every sort of women, in particular widowed matrons in sorrow and distress, such as her ladyship
must be."

On hearing this Trifaldín bent a knee to the ground,
and then giving a sign to the fife and drums to strike up,
he departed from the garden to the same music and at the
same pace as he had entered, leaving them all amazed at
his presence and figure.

Turning to Don Quixote, the duke exclaimed: "Thus, renowned knight, the darkness neither of malice nor of ignorance can cover and obscure the light of valor and of virtue.
This I say, because, virtuous sir, though you have hardly
been six days in this castle, already the sorrowful and the
afflicted come to seek you from far-off lands, and not in
coaches or on dromedaries, but on foot and fasting, confident that they will find in that mighty arm the remedy
for their distresses and troubles, thanks to your great deeds
that cover and circle the whole earth."

"I wish, sir duke," replied Don Quixote, "that blessed man of religion were here, who showed such distaste for knights-errant and so malignant a grudge against them, that he might see with his own eyes whether such knights are needed in the world. He would, at any rate, come to realize that those deeply afflicted and desolate, in desperate cases and appalling disasters, do not go to seek their remedy in the houses of scholars, nor in those of village sacristans, nor from the knight who has never ventured beyond the boundaries of his town, nor from the lazy courtier who prefers to look for news to repeat and tell than to attempt to perform deeds and exploits for others to relate and write down. Remedy for distresses, relief in hardship, succoring of maidens, and consoling of widows are nowhere so readily to be obtained as from knights-errant. I give infinite thanks to Heaven that I am one, and I regard as well spent whatever troubles or hardships I may have to suffer in this most honorable profession. Let the duenna come in and ask what she will, for I will seek her relief by the strength of my arm and the dauntless resolution of my courageous spirit."

CHAPTER XXXVII

In which is continued the famous adventure of the Doleful Duenna

The duke and duchess were extremely delighted to see how well Don Quixote responded to their plan. But here Sancho put in his words, saying: "I for one shouldn't like this lady to lay any stumbling block in the way of my promised government, for I once heard a Toledo apothecary say—and he talked like a linnet—that where duennas meddled there could be nothing but muddle. Heavens above, what an edge that apothecary had against them! So, I gather that since all duennas are meddlers and mischief makers, whatever their kind or quality may be, what will they be like when they're doleful as they say this Countess Three Skirts or Three Tails is? In my country skirts and tails, tails and skirts, are all one."

"Peace, Sancho, friend," said Don Quixote, "for since this duenna comes from such distant lands in quest of me, she cannot be one of those listed by the apothecary, particularly as she is a countess, and when countesses serve as duennas, it must be in the service of queens and empresses, for in their own houses they are high ladies and are served by other duennas."

At this point Doña Rodríguez, who was present, piped up: "My lady the duchess has duennas in her service who might well be countesses if fortune had pleased, but laws go as kings will. Let no one speak ill of duennas, particularly when they are old and unwed, for though I am not one, yet I can easily see and appreciate the advantage that

796

a maiden duenna has over a widow, and the man who clipped us still has the shears in his hands."

"All the same," answered Sancho, "there's so much to shear in those duennas, according to my barber, that it would be better not to stir the rice, even though it sticks."

"Squires are always our enemies," replied Doña Rodríguez, "for seeing that they are the demons of the antechambers and see us at every turn, such times as they are not saying their prayers (which are many) they spend in gossiping about us, digging our bones up and burying our good names. But let me tell those moving logs that we shall live in the world and in the houses of the great in spite of them, though we die of hunger and cover our bodies, delicate or otherwise, with a nun's black habit, as a dunghill is sometimes covered up with a sheet on the day of a procession. On my faith, if I were allowed and if the time were ripe, I would let them know—not only the present company, but the whole world—that there is not a single virtue you will not find in a duenna."

"I believe," said the duchess, "that my good Doña Rodríguez is right, and very much so. But she must wait until the time is ripe to stand up for herself and the other duennas, to refute the bad opinion given her by that rascally apothecary and to obliterate it entirely from the mind of the great Sancho Panza."

To which Sancho replied: "Since I've had a sniff at a governorship I've blown away all squirish vapors, and I don't care a wild fig for all the duennas in the world."

They would have kept up this duenna controversy, had they not heard the fife and drums strike up again to announce the approach of the Doleful Duenna. The duchess asked the duke whether it would be right to go and receive her, seeing that she was a countess and a lady of rank.

"In so far as she's a countess," interjected Sancho before the duke could reply, "I'm for your highnesses going out to receive her, but in so far as she's a duenna, I'm of the opinion you shouldn't budge."

"Who asked you to meddle in this?" asked Don Quixote.

"Who, sir?" answered Sancho. "I meddle, and I've a perfect right to meddle, as a squire who has learned the laws of courtesy in your worship's school. For you're the most courteous and well-bred knight there is in all courtiership, and in these matters, as I've heard your worship say, you

may lose as much by a card more as by a card less, and
good ears need few words."

"It is as Sancho says," replied the duke. "Let us see what
the countess is like, and by that we shall measure the courtesy due to her."

At this the drums and fife came in as before, and here the
author brought this chapter to an end and began another,
pursuing the same adventure, one of the most notable in
the history.

CHAPTER XXXVIII

In which the Doleful Duenna relates her misfortune

In the wake of the mournful musicians there began to appear, in the garden beyond, some dozen duennas, divided
into two files, all dressed in ample nun's habits, apparently
of milled serge, with white wimples of fine Indian muslin, so
long that only the hem of their habits showed. Behind
them came Countess Trifaldi, whom the squire Trifaldín
of the White Beard led by the hand, clothed in finest black
baize, unnapped, for had it been napped every grain would
have shown up as big as a good Martos chickpea. Her tail
or skirt, or whatever they call it, ended in three trains,
which were borne by three pages, also in mourning and
making a handsome mathematical figure with the three acute
angles formed by the three trains. Hence it was concluded
that because of it she was called Countess Trifaldi, as one
might say the Countess of the Three Skirts. This, according
to Benengeli, was true, for her proper title was Countess
Lobuna, because of the many wolves bred in her country,
and if they had been foxes instead of wolves, she would
have been called Countess Zorruna, for it was a custom in
those parts for the proprietors to take their names from

the thing or things in which their estates most abounded. The countess, however, to celebrate the new fashion of her skirt, dropped Lobuna and took the name of Trifaldi.

The lady and her twelve duennas advanced at a procession pace, their faces covered with black veils, not transparent like Trifaldín's, but so thick that nothing showed through them. As soon as this squadron of duennas appeared, the duke, the duchess, and Don Quixote stood up, as did all who were watching the slow procession. The twelve duennas halted and made a lane, through the middle of which the Doleful One advanced without letting go the hand of Trifaldín. At this the duke, the duchess, and Don Quixote advanced about twelve paces to welcome her. Then, sinking on her knees to the ground, she cried in a voice that was coarse and rough rather than soft and delicate: "May it please your highnesses not to offer so much courtesy to this your waiting man—woman, I should say—for as I am the Doleful One I cannot respond as I ought, since my strange and unheard-of misfortune has carried off my wits I know not where, but it must be very far off, for the more I look for them the less I find them."

"He would indeed be witless, lady countess," replied the duke, "who did not at once discover your personal worth. Without any further examination you deserve all the cream of courtesy and the flower of courtly ceremony." And raising her by the hand, he took her over to sit beside the duchess, who also received her with much politeness. Don Quixote remained silent, and Sancho was dying to see the faces of the countess and of some of her many ladies; but this was not possible till they unveiled themselves of their own accord.

All kept quiet and stood by in silence, waiting to see who should break it, and the Doleful Duenna did in these words: "I am confident, most powerful lord, loveliest lady, and most distinguished company, that my extreme affliction will find in your most valiant hearts a reception no less pleasing than generous and compassionate, for it is one that could melt marble, soften adamant, and even melt the steel of the most hardened hearts in the world. But before it is made public to your hearing, not to say your ears, I should like to ascertain whether there is in this body, circle, and company that most stainless of knights, Don Quixote of La Manchísima ¹ and his squireliest Panza."

"The Panza," said Sancho before anyone else could reply, "is here and the Don Quixotísimo likewisisimo; therefore, Dolefullest Duenisima, you may say what you wishisimo, for we are all ready and preparedisimo to be your servantisimuses."

Therefore Don Quixote rose to his feet, and addressing the Doleful Duenna, said: "If your distresses, anguished lady, can promise you any hope of relief through any valor or might of any knight-errant, here are mine, which, though small and feeble, shall all be employed in your service. I am Don Quixote, whose business it is to succor the distressed of all kinds; since this is so, you have no need, lady, to beg for favors or to hunt for preambles; you must tell of your misfortunes plainly and without circumlocutions, for your hearers will know, if not how to relieve them, at least to condole with them."

Hearing this, the Doleful Duenna gave every indication that she would fling herself at Don Quixote's feet, and indeed she did throw herself down and strove to embrace them, crying: "Before these feet and these legs I prostrate myself, O unconquered knight, for they are the pedestals and columns of knight-errantry. I would kiss these feet, on whose steps hangs the entire remedy of any misfortune. O valiant errant whose veritable deeds outstrip and eclipse the fabulous prowess of the Amadises, Esplandians and Belianises!"

Then, leaving Don Quixote, she turned to Sancho Panza, and seizing him by the hands, she exclaimed: "O most loyal squire that ever served knight-errant in past or present ages, whose goodness stretches further than the beard of Trifaldín, my attendant here present! Well may you pride yourself that in serving the great Don Quixote you are serving the sum total of all the knights who ever handled arms in the world! I conjure you by all you owe to your essential goodness to be my kind intercessor with your master, that he may immediately favor this, the humblest and most dejected of countesses."

To this Sancho replied: "To say, my lady, that my goodness is as long and large as your squire's beard means pre-

¹ The superlative Manchísima, a sign of affectation.

cious little to me. May my soul be bearded and whiskered
when I leave this life, that is the point, but I wouldn't
give two farthings for beards down here. But without such
artful tricks or prayers I'll ask my master—and I know he
loves me well, especially now that he has need of me in a
certain business—to favor and aid your grace in whatever
he can. So, your grace should unload your troubles, tell us
your tale, and leave us to do the rest, for we all understand one another."

The duke and duchess were bursting with laughter at this
tirade, and so was everyone else who had divined the scope
of this adventure, and in their hearts they praised the shrewd
and dissembling wiles of La Trifaldi, who returned to her
seat and said: "Queen Doña Maguncia was ruler of the
famous kingdom of Candaya, which lies between great
Trapobana and the Southern Sea, six miles beyond Cape
Comorín. She was the widow of the King Archipiela, her
lord and husband, by which marriage they had as issue the
Infanta Antonomasia, heiress of the kingdom, who was
bred and grew up under my tutelage and teaching, for I was
her mother's chief and most ancient duenna. It happened
then that, as the days came and went, the girl Antonomasia
reached the age of fourteen and to such a high pitch of
loveliness that nature could not raise her higher. And I
would not say her wit was childish; on the contrary, she was
as witty as she was beautiful. She was truly the loveliest
girl in the world, and is so still, if the envious Fates and
the three cruel sisters have not cut the thread of her life. But
they have not done that, for Heaven could not allow such
evil to be done on earth, and a cluster from the fairest vine
in the vineyard to be snapped off unripe. Her beauty, which
my dull tongue has insufficiently praised, inflamed the hearts
of countless native and foreign princes, and among those
who dared to aspire to such heavenly loveliness there was a
knight of low degree at court who relied on his youth and
gallantry, his many accomplishments and charm, his ease of
manners and his sparkling wit. And in addition, I would
have your highnesses know, if I do not weary you, that he
could play a guitar so well that he made it speak. And what
is more, he was a poet and a great dancer and was so good
at making bird cages that he could have earned his living
by their manufacture, had he been in extreme need. All such
talents and graces are more than sufficient to move a moun-

tain, let alone a delicate maiden. But all his graces and
charms, all his endowments and accomplishments would have
been of little or no avail against the fortress of my child's
honor, if the shameless rascal had not resorted to the expedient of storming me first. The malign and heartless vagabond first tried to win my goodwill and bribe my consent,
so that I, like a bad custodian, might deliver to him the keys
of the fortress I was guarding. In short, he cajoled me and
suborned me by the trifles and trinkets he gave me. But
what really turned my head and brought me to the ground
were some verses that I heard him sing one night from a
barred window that looked on to a narrow street where he
was standing, running, if I remember rightly, as follows:

> " 'An arrow wounds me to the soul
>   Wing'd by my sweetest enemy,
>   Yet greater still my misery,
>   For I must dumbly fear my dole.'

"The song seemed pearls to me and his voice syrup, and
after that, I mean, from that time till now, considering the
harm I fell into by these and other such verses, I have
been of the opinion that poets should be banished from good
and well-ordered states, as Plato advised, at least the lewd
ones, for the verses they write are not like the ballads of
the Marquess of Mantua, which charm and bring tears to
the eyes of women and children, but are pointed lines,
which like smooth thorns pierce your soul and wound you
there like lightning, leaving your clothes untouched.

"On another occasion he sang:

> " 'Come, Death, so stealthily to me,
>   That I thy coming may not know,
>   And so rejoice at dying so
>   That, Life, I'll no more cling to thee.'

And many other little songs and refrains that enchant when
sung and astonish when read. Then, suppose they humble
themselves to compose a kind of verse formerly fashionable
in Candaya, called seguidillas? There you should have seen
the pirouetting of souls, the frolicking laughter, the jigging
of bodies, and in short, all the senses rioting like quicksilver.
And so, I say, gentlemen, that such minstrels ought strictly
to be exiled to the Islands of the Lizards. It is not they

who are to blame, however, but the simpletons who praise
them and the foolish women who believe them. If I had
been the good duenna I ought to be, his stale conceits would
not have moved me nor could I have believed that he spoke
the truth when he said: 'Dying I live, in frost I burn, in fire
I tremble, I hope without hope, I go and stay,' and other
absurdities of that kind of which their writings are full.
And then, when they promise the Phoenix of Arabia,
Ariadne's crown, the horses of the Sun, the pearls of the
South, the gold of Tibar, the balsam of Pancaya? It is here
that they stretch their pen farthest, for it costs them little to
promise what they never intend nor are able to perform.
But whither am I digressing? Alas, how unhappy I am!
What madness, what folly leads me to recite the faults of
others, when I have so much of my own to speak out? How
unlucky I am, I repeat! For it was not the verses that were
my undoing but my own guilelessness. It was not the music but my own frivolity that seduced me. My great ignorance
and lack of caution opened the road and made easy the path
to the approaches of Don Clavijo, for that is the name of
the gentleman I mentioned. And so, since I was the go-
between, he found his way, not once but many times, to
Antonomasia's room, though under promise of marriage, for
although I was a sinner, I would never have allowed him to
come near the sole of her slipper without being her husband. No, no, not that! Marriage must always be the condition for any business of the kind I arrange. The only hitch
in this affair was difference of rank, for Don Clavijo was
a private gentleman and the Infanta Antonomasia was
heiress, as I have said, of the kingdom. For some days the
matter was hidden and cloaked by the ingenuity of my subtle
precautions, until I realized that a certain swelling of
Antonomasia's belly was rapidly revealing everything, and
this fear brought the three of us together to have counsel.
We decided that before the ill-wanted burden came to light,
Don Clavijo should ask for Antonomasia's hand before the
vicar, on the strength of a contract of marriage that the
princess had made him, worded by my ingenuity and in
such strong terms that Samson himself could not break it.
Our plan was put into operation, and the vicar examined the
contract and took the lady's confession. She confessed all
openly, and he ordered her to be put under the custody of a
bailiff of the court, a most honorable man——"

Here Sancho interrupted, saying: "So in Candaya, too,

there are court bailiffs, poets, and seguidillas? I take my oath, it makes me realize that the whole world is one. But do please hurry up, my lady Trifaldi, for it's late and I'm dying to know the end of this long story."

"Of course I will," replied the countess.

CHAPTER XXXIX

In which La Trifaldi continues her stupendous and memorable story

Every word Sancho spoke delighted the duchess as much as it vexed Don Quixote, but bidding him to be silent, the Doleful One proceeded, saying: "At last, after much cross-examining, as the princess stuck obstinately to her determination without wavering or departing from her first declaration, the vicar gave judgment in favor of Don Clavijo and delivered her to him as his lawful wife, at which the Queen Doña Maguncia, Princess Antonomasia's mother, was so annoyed that within three days we buried her."

"She must have died, no doubt," exclaimed Sancho.

"That is clear," answered Trifaldín, "for in Candaya we do not bury the living but the dead."

"It has been known to happen before now, sir squire," rejoined Sancho, "that they bury someone who has fainted, believing him to be dead, and it seemed to me that Queen Maguncia was bound to faint rather than die, for with life much can be remedied, and the Infanta's slip wasn't so serious as to force them to feel so sore about it. If this lady had married one of her pages or some other servant of the house, as many have done, so I've heard tell, the damage could not have been repaired. But to have married a clever and gentle knight as has been described to us, really and truly, though it was foolishness, it was not as bad as they think. For according to my master's rule, who is here present and won't let me lie, just as they make bishops of lettered men they can make kings and emperors of knights, especially if they're errants."

"You are right, Sancho," said Don Quixote, "for a knight-errant, if he has two grams of luck, has every possibility of becoming the greatest lord in the world. But let the Doleful Lady continue, for it is evident to me that the bitter part of this story, till now so sweet, remains to be told."

"The bitter part certainly is to come," answered the countess, "and so bitter that bitter apple is sweet and oleander tasty in comparison. As the queen was dead, not fainting, we buried her. But no sooner had we covered her with earth and said our last farewell to her, when—*quis talia fando temperet a lacrymis?* [1]—there appeared on top of the queens's grave the giant Malambruno mounted on a wooden horse. He was a first cousin of Maguncia, and he was not only cruel but an enchanter, and to avenge his cousin's death, to punish Don Clavijo for his audacity, and to spite Antonomasia's frivolity, he held them spellbound on the very grave itself. She was changed into a brass monkey and he into a hideous crocodile of some unknown metal, and between them stands a column, also of metal, with some characters written in Syriac tongue, which, when translated into Candayan and then into Castilian, contain this sentence: 'These two rash lovers shall not recover their former shape until the valiant Manchegan shall come to fight me in single combat, since the Fates reserve this unparalleled adventure for his great valor.'

"This done he drew from its sheath a broad and formidable sword, and seizing me by the hair, he made a feint of slitting my throat and shearing off my head at a blow. I was frantic; my voice stuck in my throat; I became all limp with terror. But nevertheless, I recovered myself as best I could, and speaking to him in doleful tones, I made such a piteous plea that he suspended the execution of his cruel sentence. Finally, he ordered all the duennas of the palace to be brought before him, all those who are here at present, and

[1] From Virgil, *Aeneid*, Bk. II. Who would not weep to tell of such sorrow?

after enlarging upon the enormity of our fault and abusing the duennas, their evil practices, and their wicked schemings, loading on to all of us the guilt that was mine alone, he said that he would not inflict capital punishment on us but other protracted pains that would be a perpetual social death. Then, at the very instant that he finished speaking we all felt the pores of our faces open and as if all over them we were pricked with the points of needles. At once we clapped our hands to our faces and found ourselves in the state that you will now see."

Then the Doleful One and the other duennas raised the veils with which they had been covered, and disclosed their faces, all bushy with beards—some fair, some black, some white, some grizzled. At this sight the duke and duchess gave signs of being wonder-struck, Don Quixote and Sancho were dumbfounded, and all the spectators scared.

"Thus," continued La Trifaldi, "did that ill-intentioned rascal Malambruno punish us by covering our smooth, soft skins with those rough bristles. Would to God he had cut off our heads with his huge scimitar, instead of shading the light of our faces with this fleece that covers us, for if we consider the matter, dear gentlemen—and what I am going to say now I should say with my eyes cascading tears, but the thought of our misfortune and the seas that they have already wept keep them devoid of moisture and dry as ears of corn, and therefore I shall speak without tears—where, I ask you, can a duenna go with a beard? What mother or father will take pity on her? Who will give her aid? And if even when she has a soft skin and tortures her face with a thousand sorts of lotions and cosmetics, she can scarcely find anyone to like her, what is she to do when she discloses a face like a jungle? O duennas, my companions, in an unlucky moment were we born, in an evil hour did our parents beget us!"

And as she spoke she gave signs of fainting away.

CHAPTER XL

Of matters concerning this adventure and this memorable history

Really and truly, all who enjoy stories of this kind should show their gratitude to Cide Hamete, its original author, for the meticulous care he has observed in recording its minutest details, leaving nothing, however trivial, that he does not bring to light distinctly. He depicts thoughts, discovers intentions, answers unspoken questions, clears up doubts, resolves objections; in short, he elucidates the tiniest points the most carping critic could raise. O most renowned author! O fortunate Don Quixote! O famous Dulcinea! O droll Sancho Panza! May you jointly and singly live infinite ages to the delight and general enjoyment of mankind!

The history goes on to tell that when Sancho saw the Doleful One in a faint, he said: "On the faith of an honest man and the memory of all my ancestors, the Panzas, I swear I've never heard or seen, nor has my master ever related to me, nor even imagined, an adventure like this one. A thousand devils take you; I would not abuse you, Malambruno, for the enchanter and giant you are! Could you not find another kind of punishment to inflict on these except bearding them? Wouldn't it have been better and more fitting to have cut off half their noses from the middle upward, even if it made them talk with a snuffle rather than to stick beards on them? I'll bet they have not the money to pay for being shaved."

"That is the truth, sir," replied one of the twelve. "We have not the means to cleanse ourselves. So, as a thrifty remedy, some of us have taken to using pitch or sticky plasters, and by clapping them to our chins and pulling them off with a jerk, we remain bare and smooth as the bottom of a stone mortar, for though there are women in Candaya who go from house to house removing body hair, plucking eyebrows, and composing lotions and elixirs that women use, we, being my lady's duennas, would never allow them admittance, for most of them, not being ladies of quality, have the unsavory reputation of go-betweens who are no longer principal parties. So, if we are not relieved by Don Quixote, with beards we shall be carried to the grave."

"I would pluck mine out," said Don Quixote, "in the land of the Moors if I could not relieve you of yours."

La Trifaldi by then had recovered from her faint and said: "The tinkling of that pledge, valiant knight, reached my ears in the midst of my swoon and helped to bring me around and restore my senses. So, once more I beseech you, illustrious errant and indomitable sir, to put your gracious promise into operation."

"There will be no delay on my account," replied Don Quixote. "Think what it is I am to do. My heart is most ready to serve you."

"The case is this," replied the Doleful One, "that from here to the kingdom of Candaya, if one goes by land, it is fifteen thousand miles more or less. But if you go by air and in a straight line, it is nine thousand six hundred and eighty-one. Malambruno, I must tell you, said that when Fortune should provide me with a knight to deliver us, he would send him a mount much better than your hired hacks, and with less vices, for it will be the same wooden horse on which the valiant Pierres carried off the fair Magalona. That horse is guided by a peg in his forehead that serves as a bridle, and he flies through the air with such speed that the devils themselves seem to bear him. This horse, according to the ancient tradition, was fashioned by the sorcerer Merlin. He lent it to Pierres, who was his friend and made long journeys on him, stole the fair Magalona as I have said, and bore her on his crupper through the air, leaving all who watched them from the earth staring like fools. He lent the horse only to those he liked or who paid him best, and from the great Pierres' time till now we know of no one who has ridden him. Since then Malambruno by his arts has captured him, holds him in his power, and uses him on the voyages he makes from time to time through different parts of the world. Today he is here, tomorrow in France, and the day after in Potosí. And the best of it is that the horse neither eats, nor sleeps, nor costs anything in shoeing, but ambles at such a pace through the skies without having wings that his rider can carry a cup of water in his hands without ever spilling a drop, so calmly and easily does he travel, for which reason the fair Magalona greatly enjoyed riding him." [1]

"For smooth and easy going," interjected Sancho, "give me my Dapple. Granted he doesn't travel by air, but on land I'll back him against any ambler in the world."

Everyone laughed, and the Doleful Lady continued: "And this same horse, if Malambruno intends to bring our troubles to an end, will be here in our presence within half an hour of nightfall, for he notified me that the sign by which I should know that I had found the knight I was seeking would be his sending me the horse with all convenience and dispatch to the place where that knight might be."

"How many does this horse carry?" asked Sancho.

"Two persons," the Doleful One answered, "one in the saddle and the other on the crupper. Generally these two are knight and squire, when there is no stolen maiden."

"I should like to know, Doleful Lady," said Sancho, "what this horse is called."

"His name," replied the lady, "is not that of Bellerophon's horse, who was called Pegasus, nor of Alexander the Great's Bucephalus, nor of the raving Roland's, whose name was Brillador, nor yet Bayard, who belonged to Rinaldo of Montalbán, nor Frontino like Ruggiero's, nor Bootes, nor Pirithous, which they say were the names of the horses of the Sun. Nor is he called Orelia either, like the horse on which the unfortunate Roderick, last king of the Goths, rode into battle in which he lost his life and his kingdom."

"I'll bet," said Sancho, "that as they've not given him any of these famous names of horses, they haven't given the name of my master's mount, Rozinante, either, though it would suit a great deal better than any of those you've mentioned."

[1] The story of Pierres and the fair Magalona was very popular. Orginally French, it was translated into Spanish by Felipe Camus and published in Toledo in 1526. The wooden horse figures in the story.

"You are right," replied the bearded countess, "but yet his name suits him well, for he is called Clavileño the Nimble, a name that fits him because he is wooden, because of the peg he has in his forehead, and because of the speed at which he travels. So, as far as his name is concerned, he can easily compete with the famous Rozinante."

"I don't dislike the name," replied Sancho, "but what sort of bridle or halter do you have to guide him by?"

"I have already told you," answered La Trifaldi, "by the peg, for by turning it in one or the other direction the rider can make him go where he will, through the air, or brushing and almost sweeping the earth, or in the midregion, which is the proper course to be kept to in all well-ordered actions."

"I should like to see him," said Sancho, "but to imagine that I'll ride him, either in the saddle or in the crupper, is to look for pears off an elm tree. A fine thing it would be for me, who can hardly keep on the back of Dapple and on a packsaddle softer than silk itself, to get up on a wooden crupper without so much as a pillow or a cushion! By God, I've no mind to bruise myself to take off anybody's beard. Let everyone be shaved as best he can, for I don't intend to accompany my master on his long journey. Besides, I've nothing to do with this business of the shaving of these beards, as I'm in on the disenchanting of Dulcinea."

"Yes, friend, you are," said La Trifaldi, "and so much so that without your presence I understand we shall do nothing."

"In the name of all the kings," cried Sancho, "what have squires to do with their master's adventures? Are they to get the fame for their successes and we to bear the burden? Marry, come up! Supposing that the historians were to say: 'Such a knight carried through such and such an adventure, but with the help of so-and-so, his squire, without whom it would have been impossible to complete it.' But that they should write merely: 'Don Paralipómenon of the Three Stars carried through the adventure of the six hobgoblins,' without ever mentioning the person of his squire, who was present all through, just as if he had never been born! Now, sirs, I repeat that my master is welcome to go alone, and much good may it do him. But I shall stay here in the company of my lady the duchess, and maybe when he comes back, he'll find Lady Dulcinea's case improved by a third or a fifth, for I intend in my idle and leisure moments to give myself a bout of whipping on my pelt."

"All the same, you must accompany him, good Sancho," remarked the duchess, "if it is necessary, for those who will beg you to go are worthy people, and the faces of these ladies must not be left bristly because of your pitiful fears, which would surely be a shame."

"In the name of all the kings, again say I," rejoined Sancho, "if this charitable action were done for some modest maidens or some orphan girls, a fellow might risk his skin, but that I should suffer to rid duennas of their beards! Blast it! I'd rather see the lot of them bearded from the tallest to the tiniest, from the prettiest to the plainest."

"You are hard on duennas, Sancho, my friend," said the duchess, "and your opinion of them is no higher than that of the Toledan apothecary. But believe me, you are unfair, for in my house there are duennas who might serve as models of their kind, and here is my Doña Rodríguez, who will not let me say otherwise."

"Let your excellency say even more," said La Rodríguez, "for God knows the truth of everything, and good or bad, bearded or beardless though we be, yet our mothers bore us like all the rest of our sex. Since God cast us into the world, He knows the reason why, and I stick to His mercy and to no one's beard."

"That is enough, Lady Rodríguez," said Don Quixote. "Lady Trifaldi and company, I wait for Heaven to look with kindly eyes on your misfortunes. Sancho shall do what I command him. Let Clavileño come and let me find myself facing Malambruno, for I know there is no razor that could shave your graces more easily than my sword will shave Malambruno's head from his shoulders, for God suffers the wicked, but not forever."

"Ah," cried the Doleful One, "may all the stars of the celestial firmament look down upon your greatness with benignant eyes, valiant knight, and infuse into your spirit all prosperity and valor to be a shield and protection to the downtrodden race of duennas, hated by apothecaries, back-bitten by squires, and bamboozled by pages! Woe to the wretch who in the flower of her years did not choose to be a nun rather than a duenna! What an unhappy lot we duennas are, for even though we were descended in the direct male line from Hector of Troy himself, our mistresses would

never cease flinging a haughty *vos* at us, as though they
thought that made them queens. O giant Malambruno, although you are an enchanter, we can rely on your promise.
Send us at once the peerless Clavileño that our misfortunes
may be ended, for if the heat wave sets in and these beards
of ours remain, we shall indeed be out of luck!"

La Trifaldi spoke with such feeling that she drew tears
from the eyes of all the bystanders, and even filled Sancho's
to the brim; he resolved in his heart to accompany his master
to the very end of the earth, if this was necessary to rid
those venerable faces of their wool.

CHAPTER XLI

*Of the coming of Clavileño and the conclusion of this
protracted adventure*

Night had descended by this time, and with it the appointed moment for the arrival of the famous horse
Clavileño, whose delaying kept Don Quixote on tenterhooks,
for he imagined that Malambruno's delay in sending it meant
either that he was not the knight for whom that adventure
was reserved, or that the giant did not dare to meet him in
single combat. But suddenly there entered through the garden four savages all clad in green ivy, bearing upon their
shoulders a great wooden horse. They set him on his feet, and
one of them cried: "Let the knight who has courage for it
mount this machine."

"I'm not mounting then," said Sancho, "for I haven't the
courage and I'm no knight."

The savage went on to say: "Let the squire, if there is one,
climb up on the crupper and trust the valiant Malambruno,
for except by his sword he will be injured by no other, nor
by the malice of any other person. There is no more to do

than to twist this peg on the horse's neck and he will bear them through the air to where Malambruno awaits them. But in case the height and distance should cause giddiness, they must keep their eyes blindfolded till the horse neighs, which will be a sign that they have completed their journey."

This said, they retired gracefully by the way they had come, leaving Clavileño. The Doleful One, as soon as she saw the horse said to Don Quixote, almost in tears: "Valiant knight, Malambruno has kept his promise; the horse is here, our beards are growing, and each one of us beseeches you by every hair to shave and shear us; nothing remains to be done but to mount with your squire and make a happy start on your strange journey."

"That shall I do, Countess Trifaldi, with good heart and better spirits, without even stopping to find a cushion or clap spurs on my heels, so eager am I to see you, lady, and all these duennas shorn and smooth."

"That I won't do," said Sancho, "neither with good nor ill will, nor in any way. And if this shaving can't be done without my climbing on the crupper, my master may look out for another squire to keep him company and these ladies for another method of smoothing their faces, for I'm no wizard to relish traveling through the air. And what will my islanders say when they hear that their governor goes tripping down the winds? And here's another point: it is nine thousand and nine miles from here to Candaya, and supposing the horse should tire or the giant get angry, we might be half a dozen years in getting back, and there would be no island nor islanders who would recognize me. And as it is commonly said that 'Theres danger in delay,' and 'When they give you the calf, run with the halter,' with all due respect to these ladies' beards, Saint Peter is all right in Rome; I mean to say that I'm nice and comfortable in this house, where they've done me so many favors and from whose master I look forward to the great benefit of finding myself governor."

"Friend Sancho," replied the duke, "the island I have promised you can neither move nor fly, and it has such deep roots struck into the depths of the earth that it cannot be tugged or shifted from where it is with a couple of pulls. And I am aware, as you must realize, that there is not a single post of the highest rank that is not gained by some kind of bribe, more or less, so the price I mean to get for this governorship is that you accompany your master, Don Quixote, and complete and crown this memorable adventure. And whether you return on Clavileño with the speed we expect from his swiftness, or meet with adverse fortune and return on foot like a pilgrim from tavern to tavern and inn to inn, you will always find your island, when you return, where you left it, and your islanders just as eager to welcome you as their governor as they have ever been. My goodwill, too, will always be the same. Do not have any doubts on this score, friend Sancho; otherwise you would sadly misunderstand my desire to serve you."

"Not another word, sir," cried Sancho. "I'm just a poor squire and I can't carry such a load of favors on my back. Let my master mount, let them blindfold these eyes of mine; commend me to God and let me know whether I'll be able to commend myself to Our Lord or call upon the angels to favor me when we're soaring through the skies." [1]

"Sancho," replied La Trifaldi, "you may safely commend yourself to God or to whom you please, for Malambruno, though an enchanter, is a Christian and works his enchantments with great shrewdness and wisdom, without meddling with a soul."

"Well then," said Sancho, "God help me and the Holy Trinity of Gaeta!"

"Since the memorable adventure of the fulling mills," said Don Quixote, "I have never seen Sancho in such fear as now, and if I were as superstitious as some are, his pusillanimity would cause me some heartthrobbing. But come here, Sancho, for with these gentlemen's leave, I should like to have a word or two with you in private."

And drawing Sancho aside among some of the garden trees and seizing both his hands, he said: "Now you see, Sancho, what a long journey awaits us, and God knows when we shall return, or what opportunities or leisure our affairs will afford us. Therefore, I want you now to retire to your room, as if you were going to look for something needed on the journey, and give yourself in the same breath, say five hundred on account of the three thousand and three hundred

[1] Sancho seems to be referring to the tradition among witches of invoking the names of saints and angels when they anointed their armpits with the magic salve and mounted their broomsticks by night to fly to their sabbat or *aquelarre* in the cave of the black he-goat. See "The Dogs' Colloquy" in *The Deceitful Marriage and Other Exemplary Novels* (Signet CT157).

lashes you owe. They will stand to your credit, for a thing begun is already done."

"Heavens above!" said Sancho. "Your worship must be crazy; why not say: 'You see me in a hole and you ask if I'm a virgin.' Now that I've to sit on a bare board, your worship wants me to flay my buttocks? Hang it all, it isn't playing the game. Let's go now and shave these duennas; when we get back, I promise you, as I'm here I'll be in such a hurry to wipe out my debt that your worship'll be very pleased. I'll say no more."

"With that promise, good Sancho," replied Don Quixote, "I am comforted, for though you are foolish, you are certainly a veracious man."

"My skin's not verdant but brown," said Sancho, "but even if I were a mongrel, I'd keep my word."

With that they came back to mount Clavileño, and as he climbed on, Don Quixote said: "Blindfold yourself, Sancho, and mount, Sancho! For he who sends for us from such distant lands will not deceive us, seeing the scant glory he would gain from defrauding one who trusts him. But even supposing that everything should turn contrary to my expectation, no malice can obscure the glory of our having attempted this enterprise."

"Let's go, sir," said Sancho, "for these ladies' beards and tears are stuck in my heart, and I shan't eat my food with gusto till I see them as smooth as they were at birth. Get on, your worship, and blindfold yourself first, for if I have to go on the crupper, it's clear that he on the saddle has to mount first."

"That's true," replied Don Quixote, and taking a handkerchief from his pocket, he begged the Doleful One to cover his eyes carefully. But after they were bandaged, he uncovered them again and said: "If I remember rightly, I have read in Virgil of the Trojan Palladium, which was the wooden horse that the Greeks presented to the goddess Pallas and which was pregnant with armed knights who afterward wrought the total destruction of Troy. So, first it would be well to see what Clavileño carries in his stomach."

"There is no need," said the Doleful One. "I will answer for him, for I know that Malambruno has nothing malicious or treacherous about him. You may mount, Don Quixote, without any fear, and on my shoulders be it if any harm befalls you."

It seemed to Don Quixote that anything he might say in reply concerning his own safety would be to the prejudice of his valor. So, without further discussion he mounted Clavileño and tried the peg, which turned easily, and as he had no stirrup and his legs hung down, he looked like nothing so much as a figure in a Flemish tapestry, painted or woven, riding in some Roman triumph. Slowly and gingerly Sancho managed to get up, and making himself as comfortable as he could on the crupper, he found it somewhat hard and not at all pleasant. So he begged the duke, if it were possible, to oblige him with a cushion or pillow, even one from his lady the duchess' dais or off some page's bed, for the croup of that horse felt more like marble than wood.

To this La Trifaldi replied that Clavileño would suffer no kind of trappings on him, but what he could do was to sit sidesaddle like a woman and then he would not feel the hardness so much. Sancho did so, and bidding them farewell, he let them blindfold his eyes, though after they had been bandaged he uncovered them again, and looking tenderly on everyone in the garden, he begged them to aid him in his peril with a couple of paternosters and as many Ave Marias, that God might provide someone to say the same for them when they were in a similar predicament.

On which Don Quixote said: "Are you then on the gallows, thief, or at your last gasp, to resort to such prayers? Are you not, you soulless and dastardly coward, on the very same seat the fair Magalona occupied, from which she descended, not to her grave, but to be queen of France, if the histories do not lie? [2] And I, who am beside you, cannot I compare with the valiant Pierres, who pressed on the same spot that I now press? Blindfold yourself, blindfold yourself, you spiritless beast, and do not let the fear that overrides you pass your lips, at least not in my presence."

"Let them blindfold me," answered Sancho, "but since they won't let me commend myself or be commended to God, why wonder if I'm afraid that there may be some band of devils hereabout who will carry us off to Peralvillo?" [3]

They blindfolded themselves, and Don Quixote, feeling that all was in order, touched the peg. No sooner did he put his

[2] Pierres was king of Naples, not of France.

[3] Peralvillo was a town near Ciudad Real where the Holy Brotherhood tried and punished evildoers.

fingers on it than the duennas and everyone else present raised their voices and cried: "God guide you, valiant knight! God be with you, dauntless squire! Now you are in the air already, cleaving it more swiftly than an arrow! Now you are beginning to mount and soar to the astonishment of all of us below. Hold on, valiant Sancho, you are tottering; be careful not to tumble off, your fall would be worse than that of the rash youngster who tried to drive the chariot of the Sun, his father!" [4]

Sancho heard their shouts, and pressing closer to his master, with his arms around him, he asked: "Sir, how can they say we're flying so high when their voices reach us here? They seem to be speaking just beside us."

"Pay no attention to that, Sancho, for as these flights are out of the ordinary course of things, you will see and hear what you please a thousand miles away. And do not hug me so tight or you will upset me. For the life of me I cannot make out what is so worrying and frightening you, for I swear to you that never in all the days of my life have I ridden an easier-paced mount. We seem not to be moving from one spot. Banish all fear, my friend, for this business is really going as it should, and we have the wind astern."

"That's true enough," answered Sancho, "for on this side there is such a breeze buffeting me that there might be a thousand bellows blowing."

And Sancho was right, for they were blowing air on him from several large bellows. Indeed, the scheme had been so well planned by the duke, the duchess, and their steward that not a single detail was missing to make it perfect. And Don Quixote, feeling the wind blowing on him, said: "There can be no doubt, Sancho, that we have come to the second region of the air, where the hail and snow are born. Thunder, lightning, and thunderbolts are engendered in the third region. If we go on climbing at this rate, we shall soon hit the region of fire, and I do not know how to manage this peg so as not to mount so high that we shall be scorched."

Just then, with some pieces of wick hanging from a cane, easily lit and quenched, they warmed the riders' faces from

---

[4] This alludes to the mythical story of Phaeton, son of the god Helios, who requested his father to allow him to drive the chariot of the Sun across the heavens. The boy was too weak; the horses bolted out of their track; and Zeus killed him with a flash of lightning.

a distance, and Sancho, feeling the heat, exclaimed: "Bless me if we are not already in, or near, the hot place, for a great piece of my beard has been singed. And, sir, I'm all for taking off the bandage and seeing where we are."

"Do no such thing," replied Don Quixote. "Remember the true story of Dr. Torralba, whom the devils carried flying through the air riding on a broomstick, with his eyes shut.[5] In twelve hours he reached Rome and got down at the Torre di Nona, which is a street in that city, and saw all the tumult and the attack and the death of Bourbon, and by morning he was back in Madrid, where he gave an account of all he had seen. He also said that as he was going through the air, the Devil bade him open his eyes, which he did and found himself, as it seemed to him, so near the body of the moon that he could have taken hold of it with his hands; he did not dare to look down for fear of turning giddy. So, Sancho, there is no reason for us to uncover our eyes, for he in whose change we are will take care of us. Now, perhaps, we are tacking and climbing so that we may swoop down on the kingdom of Candaya like a hawk or a falcon on a heron, to snare it better for his mounting. And although it seems to us scarcely half an hour since we left the garden, believe me, we must have traveled a great distance."

"I know nothing about that," replied Sancho Panza. "I can only say this, that if Lady Magallanes, or Magalona, was happy on this crupper, her flesh couldn't have been very tender."

All this conversation between the two heroes was overheard by the duke, the duchess, and those in the garden, and it gave them great amusement. But wishing to bring this strange and well-contrived adventure to a close, they set fire to Clavileño's tail with a wick, and suddenly the horse, being filled with firecrackers, flew into the air with a tremendous bang and threw Don Quixote and Sancho Panza to the ground, half scorched.

By this time the whole troop of bearded duennas had vanished from the garden, La Trifaldi and all, and those who remained lay stretched on the earth as if in a faint. Don Quixote and Sancho rose up in a sorry state, and looking in all directions, they were amazed to find themselves in the

---

[5] Dr. Torralba was a celebrated magician who was tried by the Inquisition in 1528.

same garden they had started from and to see such a number of people lying on the ground. Their wonder increased when they saw a tall lance planted in one corner of the garden, and hanging from it by two green silk cords a smooth white parchment on which was written in large gold letters:

The illustrious Don Quixote of La Mancha has ended and achieved, by merely attempting it, the adventure of Countess Trifaldi, otherwise called the Doleful Duenna. Malambruno is content and satisfied. The chins of the duennas are now smooth and clean; their majesties, Don Clavijo and Antonomasia, are restored to their former state. And once the squirely whipping is completed, the white dove will see herself free from the pestiferous gerfalcons who persecute her, and in the arms of her loving mate. For thus it is ordained by the sage Merlin, protenchanter of enchanters.

When Don Quixote read the letter on the parchment, he clearly understood that they referred to Dulcinea's disenchantment, and giving thanks to Heaven for the achievement of so great a deed with so little peril and for restoring to their former bloom the faces of the venerable duennas, who were nowhere to be seen, he approached the duke and duchess, who had not yet come to their senses. Grasping the duke by the hand, he said to him: "Well, my good lord, courage, courage! It is all nothing. The adventure is achieved without any damage to anyone, as is clearly shown by what is written on that scroll."

The duke came to himself gradually, like someone waking from a hearty sleep, and so did the duchess and all the others who were lying about the garden, and with such tokens of wonder and alarm as almost to persuade one that what they had learned so well to act in jest had happened in earnest. The duke read the scroll with his eyes half closed, and then, with open arms he went to embrace Don Quixote, declaring that he was the bravest knight ever seen in any age. Meanwhile, Sancho went to look for the Doleful One, to see what her face was like without her beard and whether she was as beautiful without it as her graceful figure promised. But

they told him that as soon as Clavileño came flaming down
from above and struck the ground, the whole troop of duennas, and La Trifaldi with them, had disappeared and that
they had gone, shaved clean and without a bristle.

The duchess asked Sancho how he had fared on the
journey, and he replied: "I felt, lady, that we were going, as
my master said, flying through the fire region, and I wanted
to uncover my eyes a bit, but when I asked my master's
leave to take off the bandage, he wouldn't allow me. But as
I have some sparks of curiosity in me and want to know what
is forbidden and denied me, quietly and stealthily I pushed
the handkerchief that covered my eyes just a little bit up on
my nose and looked down toward the earth. And the whole
of it seemed to me no bigger than a grain of mustard seed
and the men walking on it no bigger than hazelnuts. So, you
can see how high we must have been then."

At which the duchess remarked: "Sancho, my friend, consider what you are saying. Evidently you did not see the
earth or the men going about on it. It is clear that if the
earth appeared to you like a grain of mustard seed and each
man like a hazelnut, one man alone would have covered
the whole earth."

"That's true," answered Sancho, "but all the same, I looked
through one little corner and saw the whole of it."

"Take care, Sancho," said the duchess, "for we do not see
the whole of what we look at from one little corner."

"I don't understand your lookings," answered Sancho. "I
only know that your ladyship would do well to realize that
as we flew by enchantment, by enchantment I might well see
the whole earth and all the men on it from wherever I looked.
And if you don't believe this, your grace won't believe that
when I moved the bandage up to my eyebrows I saw myself
so near the sky that there wasn't a hand a half between
me and it; and I can swear to you, my lady, it was mighty
big, too. We happened to be going by the place where the
seven she-goats are, and by God, as I was a goatherd in my
country when I was young, as soon as I saw them I felt a
longing to play with them for a bit. And if I hadn't done so,
I think I would have burst. I hem and haw. I'm here, I'm
there—so what do I do? Without a word to a soul, not even
to my master, softly and gently I skip down from Clavileño
and have a frolic with the kids—they're just like ordinary
gilly flowers—for about three quarters of an hour, and
Clavileño didn't budge from the spot nor move on."

"And while honest Sancho was playing with the goats," inquired the duke, "how was Don Quixote amusing himself?"

To which Don Quixote replied: "As all these matters and all such happenings are outside the order of nature, it is no wonder that Sancho says what he does. I can only answer for myself that I did not uncover myself either above or below, nor did I see sky, earth, sea, or sands. It is true that I felt myself passing through the regions of air, and even touching the region of fire, but I am unable to believe that we passed beyond it. As the region of fire is between the atmosphere of the moon and the farthest region of air, we could not have reached the sky, where the seven kids are that Sancho speaks of, without being scorched. So, seeing that we are not burned, either Sancho is lying or Sancho is dreaming."

"I'm neither lying nor dreaming," replied Sancho. "If I do, you just ask me about the marks of those she-goats, and by that you will see whether I'm telling the truth or not."

"Tell me, Sancho," said the duchess.

"Two of them," replied Sancho, "are green, two scarlet, two blue, and one mottled."

"That is a new kind of goat," said the duke, "for in our region of the earth such colors are not usual—I mean, she-goats of such colors."

"That's clear enough," said Sancho, "for there certainly should be a difference between the she-goats of heaven and those of earth."

"Tell me, Sancho," asked the duke, "did you see by any chance a buck among those she-goats?"

"No, sir," answered Sancho, "but I've heard tell that not one buck has passed the horns of the moon."

They preferred not to ask him any more about his journey, for Sancho evidently was in the mood for roaming through all the heavens and giving an account of everything in them, although he had not stirred from the garden. In conclusion, this was the end of the adventure of the Doleful Duenna, which gave the duke and duchess cause for laughter, not only at the time, but also for all their lives, and Sancho a subject of talk for centuries, if he would have lived so long.

Don Quixote went up to Sancho and whispered in his ear: "Sancho, if you want me to believe what you saw up in the sky, I wish you to accept my account of what I saw in the cave of Montesinos. I say no more."

CHAPTER XLII

Of Don Quixote's advice to Sancho Panza before he went to govern his island, with other serious matters

The duke and duchess were so delighted with the amusing results of the adventure of the Doleful One, that they decided to carry on with their jests, seeing how apt a subject they had to take them in earnest. So, having laid down the plan and having given their servants and retainers instructions how they were to act toward Sancho in the matters of the governorship of the promised island, the day after Clavileño's flight the duke told Sancho to prepare and put himself in readiness to go and be governor, for his islanders were longing for him as for water in May. Sancho made his bow and said: "Ever since my journey through the sky, when from its lofty height I gazed on the earth and saw it so small, my great desire to be a governor has somewhat cooled. For what greatness is there in governing on a grain of mustard seed? What dignity or power in commanding half a dozen men the size of hazelnuts? For as far as I could see there were no more than that on the whole earth. If your lordship would be so kind as to give me a teeny-weeny bit of the sky, even a mile would do, I would rather have it than the biggest island in the world."

"Look here, friend Sancho," replied the duke, "I cannot give anyone a portion of the sky, not even so much as a fingernail of it, for such favors and rewards are reserved for God alone. What I can give, I will give to you, and that is an island, ready-made, round and sound, exceedingly fertile and plentiful, where, if you know anything of management, you may with the riches of the earth purchase an inheritance in Heaven."

"Well, then," replied Sancho, "let me have the island, and I'll do my best to be such a governor that, in spite of knaves, I'll fly up to Heaven. And, mind you, it's not covetousness that makes me forsake my cottage and set myself as a somebody, but the longing I have to taste what it's like being a governor."

"Once you taste it," said the duke, "you will eat your hands off after it, so sweet is it to command and be obeyed. And I am certain that when your master becomes an emperor (this is bound to happen as his affairs proceed so well), it would be impossible to tear his power from him, and his only regret will be that he was not made one sooner."

"Sir," answered Sancho, "I imagine it must be pleasant to govern, though it were no more than a flock of sheep."

"May I be buried with you, Sancho," replied the duke, "if you don't know something about everything, and I hope you will be as good a governor as your wisdom leads me to believe. But enough of this for the present; tomorrow you will surely depart to your island, and this evening you shall be provided with suitable apparel and with all things necessary for your journey."

"Clothe me as you will," said Sancho, "I'll still be Sancho Panza."

"That is true," said the duke, "but clothes should always be suitable to the office and rank that is held; it would not be well for a lawyer to dress like a soldier, or a soldier like a priest. You, Sancho, are to be dressed partly like a lawyer and partly like a captain, for in the government I am giving you arms are as necessary as letters, and a man of letters as needed as a swordsman."

"As for letters," replied Sancho, "I've precious few, for I scarcely know my ABC; but still, if I can remember my Christ-Cross,[1] it's enough to make me a good governor; as for my arms, I'll handle those they give me till I fall, and God be my support."

"With such intentions," said the duke, "Sancho cannot go astray."

Don Quixote then arrived, and after hearing the news that Sancho was immediately to depart to his government, with the

---

[1] The cross which is put at the beginning of the alphabet.

duke's leave he took him aside to give him some good advice concerning his conduct in the discharge of his office. And when he entered his chamber, he shut the door and almost forced Sancho to sit beside him. Then, in a quiet, deliberate voice he said: "I give Heaven infinite thanks, Sancho, my friend, that even before I have met with response to my fondest hopes, good fortune has gone out to welcome you. I, who trusted in my own success for the reward of your good services, find myself at the beginning of my advancement, while you, before your time and beyond all reasonable expectation, have crowned your wishes. Some bribe, importune, solicit, rise early, pray, insist, and yet at the end do not obtain what they desire, while another comes and without knowing why or wherefore finds himself spirited into a position of rank and authority that many others had sought in vain. There is indeed much truth in the saying that 'Merit does much, but fortune more.' You, who in my eyes are the veriest blockhead, without burning the midnight oil or rising betimes, without any toil or trouble, by simply breathing the air of knight-errantry, find yourself the governor of an island in a trice, as if it were a mere trifle. All this I say, Sancho, to let you know that you should not attribute the favor you have received to your own merits, but give thanks, first to Heaven, which disposes things so kindly, and then to the essential greatness of the profession of knight-errantry. When you are convinced of what I have already told you, pay heed, my son, to me, your Cato,[2] who will be your guide, your counselor, and your North Star to steer you safely into port out of that stormy sea on which you are about to embark, for, mark you, Sancho, a post of influence and deep responsibilities is often no better than a bottomless gulf of confusion.

"First of all, O my son, fear God, for to fear Him is wisdom, and if you are wise, you cannot err.

"Secondly, consider what you are and try to know yourself, which is the most difficult study in the world. From knowing yourself you will learn not to puff yourself up like the frog that wished to rival the ox; and when you remember having been a swineherd in your own country, that

[2] He refers to the famous *Disticha Catonis,* a book of aphorisms that served as text in all the schools and was called The Cato.

thought will be in the flushed exaltation of your pride like the peacock's ugly feet." [3]

"That is true," said Sancho, "but it was when I was but a slip of a lad. When I grew up to be a bit more of a man, I drove geese, not hogs. But all this doesn't seem to me to fit the case, for all governors don't come of royal stock."

"That is true," replied Don Quixote, "wherefore those who are not of noble descent must grace the dignity of the office they bear with mildness and civility, which when accompanied with prudence will enable them to escape the malicious mischief makers from which no estate is exempt.

"Show pride, Sancho, in your humble origins, and do not scorn to say that you spring from laboring men, for when men see that you are not ashamed, none will try to make you so; and consider it more deserving to be humble and virtuous than proud and sinful. Countless are those who, though of low extraction, have risen to the highest posts of Church and State.

"Remember, Sancho, that if you make virtue your rule in life and if you pride yourself on acting always in accordance with such a precept, you will have no cause to envy princes and lords, for blood is inherited, but virtue is acquired, and virtue in itself is worth more than noble birth.

"Seeing that this is so, if by chance one of your poor relations comes to visit you in your land, do not reject or affront him, but on the contrary, welcome and entertain him, for this way you will please God, who insists that none of the beings created by Him should be scorned. If you send for your wife to be with you (for it is not right that those appointed to governments should be long separated from their spouse), teach, instruct, and refine her native coarseness, for all that a wise governor can accomplish is often thrown away and brought to nothing by an ill-bred, foolish woman.

"If you should become a widower (as may well happen), and your position entitles you to a better match, do not choose one who will serve you as a hook and fishing-rod, or as one who cries, 'I will not take it, but throw the coin in my hood,' for, believe me, whatever the judge's wife re-

---

[3] This refers to the proverb: *Mírate a los pies y desharás la rueda* (Look at your feet and you'll fold up your tail). The vain peacock spreads out his tail, but when he sees his ugly feet, he folds it again.

ceives, the husband must account for at the final judgment, when he shall be made to pay fourfold for all that he has not accounted for during his life.

"Never let arbitrary law rule your judgment; it is the vice of the ignorant who make a vain boast of their cleverness.

"Let the tears of the poor find more compassion, but not more justice, from you than the pleadings of the wealthy.

"Be equally anxious to sift out the truth from among the offers and bribes of the rich and the sobs and entreaties of the poor.

"Whenever equity is possible and is called for, let not the whole rigor of the law press upon the guilty party, for a rigorous judge has not a better repute than the one who is compassionate.

"If by any chance your scales of justice incline to one side, let pity weigh more with you than gold.

"If you should have to give judgment in the case of an enemy of yours, forget your injuries and concentrate upon the true facts of the case.

"Don't let passion blind you in another man's case, for the mistakes you will commit are often without remedy and will cost you both reputation and fortune.

"When a beautiful woman appears before you to demand justice, blind your eyes to her tears, deafen your ears to her lamentations, and give deep thought to her claim, otherwise you may risk losing your judgment in her tears and your integrity in her sighs.

"When you have to punish a man, do not revile him, for the penalty the unhappy man has to suffer is sufficient without the addition of abusive language.

"When a criminal is brought before you, treat him as man subject to the frailties and depravities of human nature, and as far as you can, without injuring the opposite party, show pity and clemency, for though one attribute of God is as glorious as another, His mercy shines more brightly in our eyes than His justice.

"If you follow these precepts, Sancho, your days will be long and your renown eternal, your rewards will be without number and your happiness unimaginable. You shall marry your children to your heart's content, and they and your grandchildren shall receive titles. You will live in peace and cherished by all men, and when, after a gentle, ripe old age, Death steals upon you, your grandchildren's children with their tender and pious hands shall close your eyes.

"The instructions I have given you so far are to adorn your soul. Listen now to some that will serve you for the adornment of your body."

CHAPTER XLIII

Of Don Quixote's further advice to Sancho Panza

Who, after listening to Don Quixote's last speech, would not have taken him for a very wise person, whose wisdom was exceeded only by his excellent intentions? For as it has often been remarked in the course of this great history, the knight only went astray when he touched upon chivalry, but in every other topic he showed that he possessed a clear-sighted and unbiased mind, with the result that his actions belied his judgment, and his judgment his actions, at every step. In these further instructions that he gave Sancho, however, he displays a lively humor and carries to a high pitch both his good sense and his madness. Sancho listened to him with the utmost attention and tried his best to commit his counsels to memory, intending to preserve them for future use and so bring the pregnancy of his government to a happy delivery.

"Now let us consider," Don Quixote continued, "the regulation of your person and your domestic concerns.

"In the first place, Sancho, I want you to be clean in your person. Keep your fingernails pared, and do not allow them to grow as some do, who in their ignorance imagine that long nails embellish their hands, whereas such long fingernails are rather the claws of a lizard-hunting kestrel—a swinish and unsightly abuse.

"Do not wear your clothes baggy and unbuttoned, Sancho, for a slovenly dress is proof of a careless mind, unless, as in the case of Julius Caesar, it may be attributed to cunning.

"Investigate carefully the income of your office, and if you can afford to give liveries to your servants, supply them with garments that are decent and durable rather than garish and gaudy; and give what you save in this way to the poor. That is to say, if you have six pages to clothe, clothe three and give what remains to three poor youths. Thus you will have attendants both in Heaven and earth. This original way of giving liveries has never been followed by the vainglorious of this world.

"Do not eat either garlic or onions, lest the stench of your breath betray your humble birth.[1]

"Walk slowly and gravely; speak with deliberation, but not so as to give the impression that you are listening to yourself, for all affectation is hateful.

"Eat little at dinner, and still less at supper, for the health of the whole body is forged in the stomach.

"Drink with moderation, for drunkenness neither keeps a secret nor observes a promise.

"Be careful, Sancho, not to chew on both sides of your mouth at once and do not on any account eruct in company."

"Eruct," said Sancho, "I don't know what you mean by that."

"To eruct," said Don Quixote, "means *to belch,* but since this is one of the most beastly words in the Castilian language, though a most significant one, polite people, instead of saying *belch,* make use of the word *eruct,* which comes from Latin, and instead of *belchings* they say *eructations.* And though some do not understand these terms, it does not much matter, for in time use and custom will make their meanings familiar to all. It is by such means that languages are enriched."

---

[1] In the ancient times garlic had a worse reputation among aristocratic Spaniards than it has today. Alfonso El Sabio fulminated against it in his *Siete Partidas* in an unavailing attempt to break his Castilian knights of the habit. Queen Isabel the Catholic loathed the smell and even the taste of garlic, and refused to eat parsley because it had grown in close vicinity to garlic, saying, *"Disimulado venía el villano vestido de verde"* (The yokel came disguised in green). A strange proverb, according to Rodríguez Marín, is current in Andalusia concerning garlic: *Los mejores ajos se siembran con maldiciones* (The best garlic is sowed with curses).

"Truly, master," said Sancho, "I shall make a special point of remembering your advice about not belching, for to tell you the honest truth, I'm mighty given to it."

"*Eructing*, Sancho, not belching," said Don Quixote.

"From now on," replied Sancho, "I'll say *eructing*, and please God I'll never forget it."

"Furthermore, Sancho, you must not overload your conversation with such a glut of proverbs, for though proverbs are concise and pithy sentences, you so often drag them in by the hair that they seem to be maxims of folly rather than of wisdom."

"God alone can remedy that," answered Sancho, "for I know more proverbs than would fill a book, and when I talk, they crowd so thick and fast into my mouth that they struggle to get out first. And the tongue starts firing off the first that comes, haphazard, no matter if it is to the point or no. However, in the future I'll take good care to say only those that are beneficial to the dignity of my place, for 'Where there's plenty, the guests can't be empty'; and 'He that cuts doesn't deal'; and 'He's safe as a house who rings the bells'; and 'He's no fool who can spend and spare.'"

"There, there you are, Sancho!" said Don Quixote. "On you go, threading, tacking, and stitching together proverb after proverb till nobody can make head or tail of you! With you it is a case of 'My mother whips me yet I spin the top!' Here am I warning you not to make such an extravagant use of proverbs, and you then foist upon me a whole litany of old saws that have as much to do with our present business as over the hills of Ubeda. Mind, Sancho, I do not condemn a proverb when it is seasonably applied, but to be forever stringing proverbs together without rhyme or reason makes your conversation tasteless and vulgar.

"When you ride on horseback, do not throw your body back over the crupper, nor keep your legs stiff and straddling from the horse's belly, nor yet so loose, as if you were still riding Dapple. Remember that the art of riding a horse distinguishes a gentleman from a groom.

"Be moderate in your sleep, for he who rises not with the sun enjoys not the day; remember, O Sancho, that diligence is the mother of good fortune and that sloth, her adversary, never accomplished a good wish.

"There is one final piece of advice that I wish to give you, though it has nothing to do with the adornment of

your body. I would have you remember it carefully, for I
believe that it will not be less profitable than any of those
that I have already given you. It is this. Never allow yourself to discuss lineage or the preeminence of families, for
if you compare them, one is sure to be better than the other,
and he whose claim you have rejected will hate you, and
he who is preferred will not reward you.

"Now with regard to your dress, you should wear breeches
and hose, a long coat, and a cloak somewhat longer; as for
trunk hose, do not think of them, for they are not becoming
either to gentlemen or to governors.

"This is all the advice I can think of giving you for the
present. As time goes on, if you let me know the state of
your affairs, I shall give you further instructions as the occasions warrant."

"Master," said Sancho, "I know that all you have told
me is mighty wholesome and profitable, but what good can
they be to me when I can't remember one of them? I grant
you, I'll not forget that about paring my nails and about
marrying again, but as for all the rest of that tangled hodgepodge, I can't remember, nor will I remember, any more of
them than of the clouds of yesteryear. So, you must give them
to me in black and white. It's true that I can't write or
read, but I'll give it to my father confessor for him to hammer them into my noddle so that I'll remember them at
the right moment."

"As I am a sinner," said Don Quixote, "it is a scandal
for a governor not to be able to read or write! For I must
tell you, Sancho, that when a man cannot read or is left-
handed, it means one of two things: either that he comes of
very humble parents, or that he was of so wayward a nature
that his teachers could get no good of him. This is, indeed,
a grave defect in you, and therefore I want you to learn
to write at least your name."

"I can sign my name well enough," said Sancho, "for
when I was steward of the Brotherhood in my village, I
learned how to scrawl a kind of letters, like what they mark
on bales of cloth, which, they told me, spelled my name.
Besides, I can always let on that my right hand is lame,
and so another can sign for me, for there's a remedy for
all things but death. And now that I've the staff of office
in my hand I'll do as I please, for as the saying goes, 'He

whose father is mayor . . .';[2] and am I not governor,
which is more than mayor, I think? So, let them backbite
and bedevil my name, they'll come for wool and I'll send
them home shorn, for 'His home tastes good whom God
loves'; and, 'The rich man's follies pass current for wise
deeds'; and I, being rich and a governor, and as free-handed
as I intend to be, there'll be no fault to find in me. It is
always so: 'Plaster yourself with honey and you'll have
flies in plenty'; as my grandmother used to say: 'Tell me
what you have and I'll tell you what you're worth,' and
'There's no taking vengeance on a well-rooted man.' "

"A curse upon you, Sancho!" cried Don Quixote. "May
sixty thousand devils take you and your proverbs! For the
past hour you have been stringing them and choking me
with them. Take my word for it, those proverbs will one
day bring you to the gallows; they will drive your people
in sheer desperation into open rebellion. Tell me, in God's
name, where in the world do you rake them up? Who taught
you to apply them? As for me, I sweat as if I were digging
and delving before I utter one and apply it properly."

"By God, master," replied Sancho, "you complain about
mere trifles. Why in the Devil's name should you mind if
I make use of my own goods and chattels? I've no other
stock; proverbs and still more proverbs, that's all there is
to my name; and just now I've four on the tip of my tongue,
all pat and purty like pears in a pannier. But I won't say
them, for silence is Sancho's name."

"That Sancho is not you then," said Don Quixote, "for
you are all tittle-tattle and stubbornness. Still, I would fain
know these four famous proverbs that come so pat to the
purpose, for though I keep rummaging my memory, which
is a pretty good one, I am thankful to say I cannot for the
life of me call one to mind."

"Where would you find any better than these?" said Sancho. " 'Between two grinders never place your thumbs';
and 'When a man says, "Get out of my house, what would
you have with my wife?" there's no more to be said'; and
'Whether the pitcher hits the stone, or the stone hits the

---

[2] The full proverb is: *El que tiene el padre alcalde seguro va
a juicio* (a mayor's son's case is as good as won).

pitcher, 'tis the worse for the pitcher.' All those, master, fit
to a hair. Let no one meddle with his governor or his deputy,
or he'll rue it, like him who places a finger between two
grinders, and even if they're not grinders, it's enough that
they be teeth. Next, it's no good giving any response to a
governor, any more than arguing with a man who says, 'Get
out of my house, what business have you with my wife?'
And as for the stone and the pitcher, even a blind man
may see that. So, he who sees a splinter in another man's
eye should first look to the beam in his own, that people
may not say of him, 'The dead woman was afraid of the
one with her throat cut'; besides, master, you know that 'A
fool knows more in his own house than a wise person in
another man's.' "

"That is not so, Sancho," replied Don Quixote, "for the
fool knows nothing, either in his own or in any other house,
for no substantial knowledge can be erected upon so bad a
foundation as folly. But let the matter rest, Sancho, for if
you govern badly, though the fault will be your own, the
shame will be mine. However, I am comforted by the thought
that I have done my duty in giving you the best counsel in
my power. Thus I am relieved of my obligation and promise. God speed you, Sancho, and direct you in your government, and may He deliver me from the anxiety I feel, that
you will turn that hapless island topsy-turvy, which, indeed,
I might prevent by letting the duke know what you are by
telling him that your potbellied, paunchy little carcass is
nothing else but a bag full of proverbs and sauciness!"

"Listen, master," answered Sancho, "if you think I'm not
fit for this government, I'll renounce it from now on, for I'm
fonder of a black nail paring of my soul than of my whole
body, and as plain Sancho I can continue to live as well
upon bread and onions as Governor Sancho upon capon and
partridge. Besides, when we're asleep, we're all alike, great
and small, rich and poor. And if you, master, would call
to mind who first put this whim of government into my
noddle, who was it but yourself? As for me, I know no more
about governing islands than a vulture, and if you think the
Devil will collar me when I become governor, remember
that I'd rather go up to Heaven as plain Sancho than down
to hell as governor."

"By Heaven, Sancho," said Don Quixote, "these last words
of yours are enough to prove you worthy to govern a thou-

sand islands. You have a good disposition, without which knowledge is valueless. Commend yourself to God and try never to go wrong in your intention; I mean, strive with determination to do right in whatever business occurs, for Heaven always favors good desires. And now let us go to dinner, for I believe their highnesses are waiting for us."

CHAPTER XLIV

How Sancho Panza was taken to his governorship, and of the strange adventure that befell Don Quixote in the castle

They say that in the original version of this history it states that when Cide Hamete came to write this chapter, his interpreter did not translate it as it was written, owing to the complaint the Moor made against himself for having undertaken so dry and limited a story as this one of Don Quixote. For it seemed to him that he was always having to speak of the knight and Sancho, without ever daring to indulge in digressions and episodes of a more serious and entertaining character. He noted that to have his mind and pen forever confined to a single subject and to have to speak through the mouths of a few characters only was intolerable and unprofitable drudgery to an author. To avoid this difficulty, he had in the first part resorted to the device of short tales like "Ill-Advised Curiosity" and "The Captive's Story," which are, as it were, detached from the story, though the rest of the tales are incidents that happened to Don Quixote himself and could not be omitted. He also felt, as he says, that many readers, carried away by their interest in the knight's exploits, would be inclined to neglect these tales, passing over them either hastily or with boredom, thereby failing to notice their elegance and fine craftsmanship, which

would have been clearly manifest if they had been published
by themselves and not joined to Don Quixote's lunacy and
Sancho's fooleries. And therefore, in this second part he
resolved not to insert any tales, either detached or interwoven with the narrative, but only some episodes like them,
arising naturally out of the actual course of events, and
even these should be used sparingly and with no more words
than necessary to explain them. And seeing that he confines
himself closely within the boundaries of the narrative, although he has the skill, the knowledge, and the capacity
to deal with the whole universe for his theme, he asks that
his pains be not undervalued, but that he be commended
not for what he writes, but for what he has refrained from
writing.

The author then proceeds with his story, saying that after
supper on the evening of the day when Sancho received his
instructions, Don Quixote handed him a written copy of them,
telling him to get somebody to read them to him. But the
squire had no sooner received them than he dropped them,
and they fell into the hands of the duke, who showed them
to the duchess, and the pair of them were again amazed at
the madness and good sense of Don Quixote. And so, continuing the jest, they sent Sancho that afternoon with a
numerous retinue to the place that was to be his island.
He who was in charge of the matter happened to be a
steward of the duke, a very shrewd and humorous fellow
(for there can be no humor without shrewdness), and it was
he who had played the part of Countess Trifaldi so amus-
ingly, as has already been described. Thus qualified and thoroughly instructed by his lord and lady in the behavior he
should adopt toward Sancho, he was marvelously successful in carrying out his design.

Nevertheless, it so happened that the moment Sancho laid
eyes upon this steward, he fancied he was gazing on the
very face of La Trifaldi, and turning to his master, he said:
"Sir, may the Devil carry me off this very instant, righteous
man and Christian as I am, if your worship doesn't agree
that this steward of the duke's here is the spitting image of
the Doleful One."

Don Quixote scrutinized the steward carefully and said
to Sancho after inspecting him: "There is no reason why the
Devil should carry you off, Sancho, either as righteous man
or Christian—though I do not know what you mean—for

the Doleful One's face is just like the steward's; yet for
all that, the steward is not the Doleful One, for if this were
so, it would imply too great a contradiction. However,
this is not the time for going into all that, as it would involve us in an endless labyrinth. Believe me, friend, we must
pray very earnestly to Our Lord to deliver us from wicked
sorcerers and enchanters."

"It's no joke, sir," replied Sancho, "for a while ago I
heard him speak, and I fancied it was La Trifaldi's voice
ringing in my ears. Well, I'll hold my tongue, but I'll keep
my eyes open in the future, in case I spot some other signs
that'll tell me if I'm right or wrong in my suspicions."

"That you must do, Sancho," said Don Quixote, "and keep
me advised about the matter and of all that happens to you
in your government, too."

Sancho set out at last accompanied by a numerous train.
He was dressed like a man of the law and wore over the
long robe a loose, slashed coat of watered camlet and a cap
of the same stuff. He was mounted upon a mule, which he
rode with short stirrups in the Moorish fashion, and behind
him, by the duke's order, went Dapple, caparisoned with
gaudy trappings of silk, which so delighted Sancho that every
now and then he turned his head to gaze upon him, and
thought himself so lucky that now he would not have changed
fortunes with the emperor of Germany. He kissed the duke's
and the duchess' hands at parting, and when it was time to
receive his master's blessing, the Don wept and the squire
blubbered outright.

Now, amiable reader, let the worthy Sancho depart in
peace and in a happy hour. When we come to describe his
conduct in office, you may well expect over two bushels of
laughter, but for the moment let us hearken to what befell
his master that night. And if this does not make you hold
your sides laughing, at least you will grin like a monkey,
for the noble knight's adventures are always bound to create
either surprise or merriment.

As soon as Sancho had departed, Don Quixote felt an
acute sense of loneliness, and had it been in his power to
cancel the commission and deprive Sancho of his government,
he would have done it there and then. The duchess, perceiving his mélancholy, inquired the cause of it, adding that
if it was because of Sancho's absence, she had plenty of

squires, duennas, and damsels, all ready to serve him to his heart's content.

"It is true, my lady," answered Don Quixote; "I miss Sancho, but that is not the principal cause of my apparent sadness. I must decline all of your grace's kind offers, except the goodwill with which they are tendered. Furthermore, I entreat your excellency to allow me to wait upon myself in my own apartment."

"In truth, Don Quixote," said the duchess, "I cannot allow that. You shall be served by four of my maidens, all as blooming as roses."

"To me," replied Don Quixote, "they will not be roses, but thorns pricking my very soul. They will no more enter my chamber than fly. If your grace wishes to confer further favors upon me, unworthy as I am, I beseech you to suffer me to be alone and leave me without attendants in my chamber, that I may keep a wall between my passions and my modesty. I will not abandon this rule of mine for all your grace's liberality to me. Indeed, I would rather sleep in my clothes than allow anyone to undress me."

"Enough, enough, Don Quixote," answered the duchess, "I will give orders that not so much as a fly shall enter your chamber, much less a damsel. I am not so inconsiderate as to urge anything that would cripple the exquisite sense of decency of Don Quixote, for I am well aware that the most conspicuous of all his virtues is modesty. You shall undress and dress by yourself, your own way, how and when you please. No one shall molest you, and in case some natural necessity might oblige you to open your door during the night, care shall be taken to supply your room with the needed vessels. And may the great Dulcinea of El Toboso live a thousand centuries, and may her name be extended all over the earth's circumference, since she has merited the love of so valiant, so chaste, and so honorable a knight, and may the kindly heavens inspire the heart of our governor, Sancho Panza, to finish his flogging penance speedily, that the world may again enjoy the beauty of so noble a lady."

"Your highness' words," replied Don Quixote, "truly reflect your character, for no evil can come from the lips of virtuous ladies. Dulcinea will be more fortunate and more celebrated in the world because of your highness' commendation, than for all the praises the most eloquent in the land could bestow on her."

"Well now, Don Quixote," said the duchess, "it is supper time and the duke must be waiting. Come, your worship, let us sup, and you shall retire early, for the journey you took yesterday to Candaya was not so short as not to have caused you some fatigue."

"No, I feel none, my lady," answered Don Quixote, "for I dare swear to your excellency that never in my life have I ridden a quieter or better-paced beast than Clavileño. I do not know what could have induced Malambruno to get rid of so swift and gentle an animal and to burn him in that way for nothing at all."

"We may suppose," answered the duchess, "that out of repentance for the wrong he had done La Trifaldi and company and other persons, and for the crimes he must have committed as sorcerer and enchanter, he resolved to do away with all the instruments of his art; as Clavileño was the chief of them and caused him the most anxiety in his wanderings from land to land, he burned him, so that his ashes and the trophy scroll might immortalize the valor of the great Don Quixote of La Mancha."

Don Quixote returned thanks to the duchess, and after supper he retired to his chamber, not allowing anybody to attend him, lest he feel inclined to transgress the bounds of chaste decorum that he always observed toward his Lady Dulcinea, thus emulating the chastity of Amadis, flower and mirror of knights-errant. He closed the door, and by the light of two wax candles he started to undress. But, alas, as he was striving to pull off his hose (O misery unworthy of such a person), then fell not sighs or anything to tarnish the luster of his breeding, but about four-and-twenty stitches in one of his stockings gave way, which made it look like a lattice window. The good knight was extremely afflicted and would have given there and then an ounce of silver for a dram of green silk—I say green, because his stockings were of that color.

At this point Benengeli could not forbear exclaiming: "O poverty, poverty, I know not what moved that great Cordoban poet to call you 'holy but misprized gift.' Although I am a Moor, I know well from my dealings with Christians that sanctity consists of charity, humility, faith, obedience, and poverty; however, fully aware of all this, I say that he who is happy being poor must have a lot of God in him, unless it be that kind of poverty of which one of the great saints of the Church says: 'Possess all things but act as if you had them not,' and this is called poverty in spirit. But you, secondary poverty (and it is you I speak of), why do you insist on persecuting gentlemen and wellborn souls more than other people? Why do you force them to smoke their shoes for lack of wax, and wear on the same threadbare garment odd buttons of silk, hair, and even glass? Why must their ruffs be, for the most part, pleated and not starched?" This shows how ancient was the use of starch and pleated collars. But to continue: "Wretched is the poor gentleman who, to ginger up his honor, starves his body and fasts unseen and with his door locked, and then, putting on a brave face, sallies forth into the street picking his teeth, though that is an honorable hypocrisy, seeing that he has eaten nothing and thus has nothing to pick! [1] Wretched is he, I repeat, whose honor is so extremely shy as to fancy that at a league's distance people may see the patch on his shoe, the sweat stains on his hat, the threadbareness of his clothes, and even the cravings of his famished belly!"

Such were the melancholy reflections that Don Quixote recalled as he gazed at the rent in his stocking. However, he consoled himself when he found that Sancho had left him a pair of traveling boots, which he resolved to put on the next day. At last he went to bed, pensive and heavyhearted, being no less depressed at the absence of Sancho than at the misfortune of his stocking, which he would have darned, even with silk of another color, one of the most significant tokens of gentlemanly poverty.

He then put out the candles, but it was hot and he could not sleep, so he got out of the bed and slightly opened a window with an iron grille that looked on to a beautiful garden. No sooner had he opened it than he heard people walking and talking below. He listened attentively, and as those below raised their voices he could hear these words: "Do not press me to sing, Emerencia, for you know that ever since this stranger came to our castle and my eyes beheld him, I cannot sing; I can only weep. Besides, my lady does not sleep soundly, and I would not let her find us here for all the treasures in the world. And even if she slept and did not wake, my singing would be all in vain if this new Aeneas

---

[1] This description closely resembles that of the penniless nobleman in *Lazarillo de Tormes*.

who has come into my land but to mock and then abandon me should sleep and not awaken to hear these words."

"Do not worry, dear Altisidora," someone answered. "No doubt the duchess and everybody in the house are asleep, except the lord of your heart and disturber of your soul, for I heard him open the window a moment ago, so he must be awake. Sing, my poor darling, in a low and gentle voice to the sound of your harp, and if the duchess hears, we can blame the heat of the night."

"That is not the point, Emerencia," replied Altisidora. "I do not want my song to lay bare my heart, for then I should be taken for a frivolous, wanton girl by those who have no knowledge of love's mighty power. But whatever happens, better a blush on the face than a stain on the heart."

Then a harp was heard playing very softly, and Don Quixote was spellbound as he listened, for there arose in his memory innumerable adventures, similar to this, of windows, lattices and gardens, serenades, love-songs, sighs and swoonings, which he had read of in his vanished books of chivalry. He at once imagined that one of the duchess' maidens had fallen in love with him and that her modesty compelled her to keep her love a secret. He trembled at the thought that he might give in, but determined in his mind not to allow himself to be overcome. So, commending himself with heart and soul to his lady, Dulcinea of El Toboso, he resolved to listen to the music. And to let them know he was there, he pretended to sneeze, which greatly delighted the maids, for they desired nothing better than for Don Quixote to hear them. Then after the tuning and preluding on the harp, Altisidora struck up the following ballad:

"Wake up, knight, wake up, I say,
Sleep in holland sheets no more;
Love is knocking at the door,
And two suns turn night to day.

Listen to this lonesome maid,
Well nourished but unfortunate;
Her soul seeks you for her mate,
Let no cruel word be said.

You your own adventures follow,
But find instead another's woe;
You wound your victims, yet I'm sure
You never give a healing cure.

Tell me, knight, who cast the spell
And cursed you with such evil luck?
Was it some serpent gave you suck,
Or some she-dragon out of Hell?

El Toboso's Dulcinea,
That plump apple-cheekèd lass,
May boast that she has snared at last,
And tamed a tiger's heart from Libia.

From this she'll reap fame and glory
From Jarama to Henares,
From Tagus to the Manzanares,
From Pisuerga to Arlanza.

I wish I were in her shoes;
I'd give my petticoat or skirt,
The one with golden fringès girt,
The gayest of them all I'd choose.

I wish it were my luck just now
To linger close beside your bed;
I'd gently currycomb your head,
And brush the scurf away like snow.

I ask too much, I don't deserve
So great a boon; my only wish
Is just to give your legs a rub;
Even a humble girl can serve.

Fine tasseled nightcaps I would make,
Rich slippers of chased silver too,
And silken hose of elegant hue,
And cloaks of cambric, for your sake.

I would buy you many a pearl,
Each as big as an oaken gall,
Which if it had not a rival,
Might be called 'the Only Pearl.'

From your Tarpeian rock don't gaze
Upon the fire that scorches me;
Manchegan Nero of the world,
Don't add fuel by your rage.

I'm a tender, budding maid,
And I've not yet reached fifteen;
I'm just three months over fourteen;
I swear, the honest truth I've said.

I'm neither limp nor lame from birth,
Nor am I twisted anywhere;
Bright as lilies shines my hair,
And my tresses sweep the earth.

Though my mouth is aquiline,
And my nose a trifle flat,
My topaz teeth make up for that
And lift my charm to the sublime.

If you listen when I sing,
Mine's the sweetest voice, you'll vote;
And my bust and shape, I hope,
Is the sum of everything.

These and all my other graces
Fall as trophies to your quiver:
I'm one of the palace flora,
And my name's Altisidora."

Here ended the song of the love-sick Altisidora, and here
began the dread of the courted knight, who said to himself,
heaving a deep sigh: "Why am I so unhappy a knight that
no damsel can gaze at me without falling in love? Why is

the peerless Dulcinea so unlucky that she may not be permitted to enjoy alone my incomparable constancy? Queens, what do you want from her? Empresses, why do you persecute her? Maidens of fifteen, why do you plague her? Let her triumph, enjoy, and entertain herself with the fate that Love wished to give her by surrendering to her my heart and my soul. Take notice, enamored band, that to Dulcinea alone I am paste and sweetmeats, and to all others flint; to her I am honey, and to you all I'm gall. In my estimation Dulcinea alone is beautiful, discreet, honest, noble, and wellborn; all others are ugly, foolish, flighty, and baseborn. I was born to be hers and no one else's. Let Altisidora weep or sing, let the lady despair on whose account I was drubbed in the castle of the enchanted Moor, for I must be Dulcinea's roasted or boiled, clean, wellborn and chaste, in spite of all the powers of sorcery in the world."

With this he hastily closed the window and threw himself upon his bed, feeling as gloomy and out of sorts as if some misfortune had befallen him. There we shall leave him for the present, for the great Sancho Panza is calling us, as he wishes to make a beginning of his famous government.

CHAPTER XLV

Of how the great Sancho Panza took possession of his island, and the way in which he began to govern

O perpetual discoverer of the Antipodes! Torch of the world! Eye of heaven! Sweet stirrer of wine coolers! Here Thymbraeus, there Phoebus! Now archer, now physician! Father of poetry, inventor of music, you who always rise and, though you seem to, never set! On you I call, O Sun, by whose aid man engenders man. On you I call to favor me and to illuminate the darkness of my understanding, that I may be able scrupulously to describe the great Sancho Panza's government, for without you I feel weak, dejected, and perplexed.

I say then that Sancho and all his suite came to a village of about a thousand inhabitants that was one of the best the duke possessed. They gave him to understand that it was called the island of Barataria, either because Barataria was really its name, or because he had obtained it at so cheap a rate.[1] When he arrived at the gates of the town (for it was walled), the chief officers of the town council came out to welcome him; the bells were rung, and with popular demonstrations of joy and with pomp and circumstance the people conducted the new governor to the church to give thanks to Heaven. After some ludicrous ceremonies, they gave him the keys of the town and consecrated him as perpetual governor of the island of Barataria. The garb, the beard, the plumpness, and the squatness of the new governor surprised

---

[1] Manchegan folklorists, including Pellicer, locate the island of Barataria in Alcalá de Ebro, which is practically surrounded by the great river. *Barato* means cheap; in old Spanish it also meant jest.

all who were not in the secret, and even those (and there were many) who knew about it were inclined to wonder.

At last, after leaving the church, they carried him to the Court of Justice and placed him on the throne, and the duke's steward said to him: "My Lord Governor, it is an ancient custom in this island that he who takes possession must answer some difficult and intricate questions that are put to him, and by his answers the people feel the pulse of his understanding and thus judge whether they ought to rejoice or to be sorry for his coming."

While the steward was saying this to Sancho, the latter was gazing at an inscription in large letters on the wall opposite his seat, and as he could not read, he asked what was the meaning of that which was painted on the wall.

"Sir," said someone, "it is there written on what day your excellency took possession of this island, and the inscription says: 'This day, such a date of such a month, in such a year, Don Sancho Panza took possession of this island; may he enjoy it for many years.' "

"Now tell me, who is this man they call Don Sancho Panza?"

"Your lordship," answered the steward, "for we know of no other Panza in this island but the one seated on this throne."

"Well, take note, brother," said Sancho, "that the don does not belong to me, nor did it ever belong to any of my family. I'm called plain Sancho, and my father was called Sancho, and so was my grandfather, and all of us have been Panzas, without any dons or doñas added to our names. I'll bet there are more dons than stones in this island. But I'll say no more, God understands me, and perhaps, if my government lasts four days, I'll weed out those swarms of dons that for sure must be plaguesome as mosquitoes. Come on with your questions, Master Steward, I'll answer as best I can, whether the town be sorry or not."

Just then two men came into the court, one dressed as a country fellow, the other like a tailor, with a pair of shears in his hands. "My Lord Governor," said the tailor, "I and this farmer here are appearing before your worship because yesterday this honest man came to my shop (begging your pardon, I'm a licensed tailor, thanks be to God) and putting a piece of cloth in my hands, he asked me: 'Sir, is there enough of this to make me a cap?' So I measured the stuff and answered that there was. Now, as I see it, he must have fancied that I was out to steal some of his cloth, for he was a bad-natured cuss, and we tailors have a bad repute. 'Tell me kindly' said he, 'might thereb e sufficient for two caps' I guessed his thoughts and told him yes. Then, sticking to his knavish intentions, he went on increasing the number of caps, and I saying yes all the time till we reached five caps. Just now he has come for them; I gave them to him. And what did he do then? He refused to pay me for the making and says that I must either give him back his cloth or pay for it."

"Is all this true, brother?" asked Sancho.

"Yes, sir," answered the man, "but let your worship make him show you the five caps he made for me."

"With pleasure," replied the tailor, and bringing his hand from under his cloak, he showed the five caps on the ends of his fingers, saying: "Here are the five caps this good man ordered me to make, and by God and my conscience, none of the cloth is left, and I'm ready to submit the work to the judgment of the trade inspectors."

All those present laughed at the number of the little caps and the strangeness of the claim. Sancho reflected for a moment and then said: "I am of the opinion that there's no need of long delay in this suit, for it may be decided without ado on an equitable basis. And so, I give judgment that the tailor lose the making and the countryman the stuff, and that the caps be given to the prisoners in jail. Let there be no more of this."

If this provoked the laughter of the bystanders, the next one aroused their admiration. For after the governor's order was executed, two old men appeared before him, one with a cane in his hand that he used as a staff; the other, who had no stick, said to Sancho: "My lord, some time ago, I lent this man ten crowns of gold to oblige and serve him, on condition that he should return them on demand. I did not ask him to pay them back for a good while, lest he be put in greater straits to pay me than he was in when I had lent them. At length, thinking that he neglected to pay me, I asked for them back, not once but many times. Not only does he not repay me, but he also denies the debt and says that I never lent him such a sum, or if I did, that he has already paid me. I have no witness to the loan, nor has he of the pretended payment, and for that reason I would beseech your worship to put him on his oath. Yet, if he will swear before your worship that he has returned the money, I will this instant forgive him before God and man."

"What do you say to this, old gentleman with the staff?" said Sancho.

"I confess, my lord," replied the old man, "that he did lend me the money, and if your worship will be pleased to lower your rod of justice, since he leaves it to my oath, I'll swear that I have really and truly returned it to him."

The governor then lowered his rod, and the old man gave the staff to his creditor to hold, as though it hindered him while he was swearing; then, taking hold of the cross of the rod, he swore it was true that the other had lent him the ten crowns, but that he had restored them to him into his own hand, and that having forgotten this, he was continually asking him for them. As soon as the great governor heard this, he asked the creditor what he had to say in reply to the statement just heard. The latter replied that he submitted, that he could not doubt that his debtor had spoken the truth, for he believed him to be an honest man and a good Christian, and that as his memory had played him false, he would ask for his money no more. The debtor then took his staff again, and after making a low bow to the governor, he left the court.

Sancho had observed the defendant take his staff and walk away, and he had noticed also the resignation of the plaintiff. He bent his head over his chest, laid the forefingers of his right hand upon his forehead, and continued for a short time apparently in deep meditation. Then, raising his head, he ordered the old man with the staff to be called back, and when he had returned, the governor said: "Honest friend, hand me that staff of yours; I'll be needing it."

"Certainly," answered the old man, "here it is." And he delivered it into his hands.

Sancho took it and passed it over to the other old man, saying: "There, take that, and go in God's name, for you are now paid."

"How, sir?" answered the old man. "Is this cane worth ten gold crowns?"

"Yes," said the governor, "if not, I'm the greatest blockhead in the world, and all will now see whether or not I've the head to govern a whole kingdom."

He then ordered the cane to be split in front of everyone

there. As soon as this was done, ten crowns of gold were found within it. All the spectators were amazed and considered the new governor to be a second Solomon. They asked him how he had discovered that the ten crowns were in the cane. He replied that, having noticed how the defendant gave the cane to the plaintiff to hold while he took the oath and how he then swore that he had returned him the money into his own hands, afterward taking back his cane from the plaintiff, he then took it into his head that the money in question must be inside the cane. From this, he added, they might learn that though sometimes those who govern are blockheads, yet it often pleases God to direct them in their judgment, for he had heard the curate of his village tell of a similar case; and he had such a great memory that if he didn't forget what he wanted to remember, there would be no other memory to equal his throughout the island.

At last, the two old men departed, one crestfallen and the other with his money in his pocket, while the spectators were once again amazed. He who recorded Sancho's words, deeds, and gestures could not make up his mind whether to consider him a fool or a wise man.[2]

This trial was no sooner over than a woman entered the court, hauling after her a man dressed like a rich grazier.

"Justice, my Lord Governor, justice!" cried she in a loud voice. "And if I can't get it on earth, I'll surely get from Heaven! Lord Governor of my soul, this wicked scoundrel caught hold of me in the middle of a field and took advantage of my body as if it were a stinking dishrag. Woe is me! He has robbed me of that which I've kept intact these three-and-twenty years, saving it from Moors and Christians, natives and foreigners. Tough as a cork tree I was, and I preserved myself as entire as a salamander in fire or as wool in a thornbush, and yet here is this fine fellow who comes with his clean hands to maul and mangle me to my ruin!"

"We have still to decide," said Sancho, "whether this swain's hands are clean or not." Then turning to the grazier, he said, "What do you say in answer to this woman's complaint?"

The grazier, full of confusion, replied: "Gentlemen, I'm a poor drover and a pig-dealer, and this morning I left the

[2] This story was probably taken from the chapter on St. Nicholas of the *Legenda Aurea* by Jacobus de Voragine.

town after selling, begging your worship's pardon, four of
my pigs, and what with the dues and tricky ways of the government inspectors I had to hand them over for less than
the beasts were worth. As I was walking along the road
home, I met this woman here; and the Devil, who sticks
his finger in every pie, tempted us and made the two of us
yoke together. Then, your worship, I gave her money, it was
enough, I tell you, to have quieted any sensible woman, but
she started cursing and argufying, and with that, she
grabbed me and wouldn't let go till she landed in this court
before your worship. She says that I did force her, but by the
sacred oath I'm taking or hope to take, I swear she's lying.
And this, your worship, is the honest truth, every scrap of
it."

Then the governor asked him if he had any silver money
about him; he answered that he had about twenty ducats in
a leather purse. Sancho ordered him to take it out and to
give it, money and all, to the plaintiff. The grazier did as he
was told, trembling; the woman took the purse and dropped
a thousand curtsies to the assembly, invoking many blessings of God upon the good governor, who took such special
care of poor orphan children and wronged virgins. Then out
of the court she nimbly tripped, holding the purse tight with
both hands, though first she peeped into it to see if the money
in it was really silver.

No sooner had she left the room than Sancho said to
the grazier, who was already in tears, for his eyes and his
heart, too, were off on the trail of his purse: "Honest man,
run after that woman and take the purse from her, whether
she will or not, and bring it back here."

The grazier, who was neither deaf nor a dullard, did not
need to be told twice. Instantly he was away like a streak of
lightning to do what he was bidden. All present were in a
state of mighty expectancy, for they longed to know the issue
of this suit.

In a few minutes the man and the woman came back,
clinging and clutching at one another even more desperately
than on the first occasion: she with her petticoat tucked up,
and the purse lapped up in it, and he striving and struggling
to take it from her, but in vain, so stoutly did she defend it.
"Justice from God and the world!" she bawled at the top of
her lungs. "See, my Lord Governor, the shameless impudence of this ruffian, who in the open street tries to rob me of

the purse your worship commanded to be given to me."

"Has he got it from you?" asked the governor.

"Got it!" cried the woman. "I'd sooner let him take my life than my purse. A nice baby I'd be indeed! It would need other cats to claw my beard, and not this measly, mangy cur. Pincers and hammers, crows and chisels won't wrench it from my clutches, no, not even the claws of a lion. Sooner would I let them strip my soul from my body."

"She is right," said the man; "I agree she has me beaten. I confess that I haven't the strength to lift it off her." So saying, he let go his hold.

Sancho then addressed the woman: "Hand me that purse, chaste and valiant woman."

The woman gave it to him, and he returned it to the man. Then he said to the violent but not violated woman: "My dear sister, if you had shown the same or even half as much courage and resolution to defend your body as you have done to defend your purse, the strength of Hercules could not have violated you. Go in God's name and a plague upon you! Don't let me find you in this island, or within six leagues of it, on pain of two hundred lashes; away with you this instant, I say, you trickstering, brazen-faced hedge whore!"

The woman, in a terrible fright, slunk away, bending her head in shame and disappointment.

"Now, my good man," said the governor, "in God's name go back to your home with your money, and in the future, if you don't want to ruin yourself, don't yoke with such heifers."

The countryman stammered out his thanks in a rough fashion and went his way, leaving the whole court in astonishment at their new governor's judgments and decrees. An account of the entire proceedings was noted down by the appointed chronicler and immediately forwarded to the duke and duchess, who waited for it with the utmost impatience.

But here let honest Sancho rest. His master bids us hasten to his side, as he is greatly excited by the singing of Altisidora.

CHAPTER XLVI

Of the terrifying cat-and-bell scare experienced by Don Quixote in the course of his wooing by the enamored Altisidora

We left the great Don Quixote rapt in the meditations aroused in him by the music of Altisidora, the love-sick maiden. No sooner did he go to bed with them than, like fleas, they plagued him, not letting him sleep a wink, and mingled in his brain with the disaster of his stocking. But as time is swift and no barrier can stop it, he galloped over the hours, and the morrow quickly arrived. When he saw the dawn, he forsook his downy bed, put on his chamois suit, and drew on his riding boots to hide the rent in his hose. Next he flung the scarlet mantle over his shoulders and clapped on his head the green-velvet cap trimmed with silver lace. His sharp and doughty sword he slung over his shoulder by its belt, and picking up a large rosary, which he always carried with him, he strutted along with great pomp and solemnity toward the antechamber where the duke and duchess expected him. As he passed through a gallery, he encountered Altisidora and her companion, who had purposely awaited his coming. No sooner did Altisidora see him approaching than she feigned a swooning fit and straightaway sank into the arms of her friend, who hastily began to unfasten her bodice. When Don Quixote saw this, he turned to the damsel, saying: "I now know the meaning of this swooning."

"You know more than I do," replied the damsel, "for Altisidora is the most healthy lady in all the house, and I have never heard her utter a single sigh since I have known her. A curse upon all knights-errant who are so ungrateful! Pray, Don Quixote, depart, for this poor young girl will not revive as long as you are near."

"Madam," replied the knight, "I beseech you to order a lute to be left in my chamber this night, and I will console as best I can this love-sick lady's grief. In these first blossomings of love prompt undeceiving usually is an effective remedy."

So saying he went off to avoid being observed by those who might see him there, but he was no sooner gone than the fainting Altisidora came to her senses and said to her companion: "We must put a lute there for him. Evidently Don Quixote proposes to give us some music, and if it is his own, it won't be too bad."

When they related this last incident to the duchess and when they told her of Don Quixote's request for a lute, she was delighted beyond measure and planned with the duke and her maids a new trick that would be more laughable than hurtful, and they looked forward to the night, which was no longer in coming than the day. The duke and duchess, meanwhile, spent the interval in pleasant conversation with Don Quixote, and it was on this same day that the duchess really and truly dispatched one of her pages, the youth who had taken the part of the enchanted Dulcinea in the wood, to Teresa Panza with the letter from her husband, Sancho Panza, and the bundle of clothes he had left to be forwarded, charging him to bring back an exact account of all that passed with her.

After this—it was by now eleven o'clock at night—Don Quixote found a guitar in his room. He thrummed it and opened the window. Then, hearing people walking in the garden, he ran his fingers over the strings, tuned as best he could, and after spitting and cleaning his throat, began to sing in a harsh, though not unpleasant, voice the following ballad, which he had composed himself:

"Amorous passions often do
　　Unhinge souls and drive them awry;
　　Idleness is their best ally,
But sloth is instrumental, too.

　　Stitching or some useful hobby
　　That keeps a girl a busy bee,
　　To the sweet poison may well prove
　　The antidote and cure for love.

A girl who's modest and demure—
Her one longing is to wed—
Chastity's her richest dower,
Nothing gives her greater power.

Gallant knights who go to war,
And gallants of the court who tarry
Wanton lights-o'-love pursue,
But the modest girls they marry.

Often loves 'twixt host and guest
In the morning are begun,
But at parting they are ended,
In the evening with the sun.

Love that is so lightly bred
Blooms today, tomorrow's gone,
Leaving no image, no, not one
Stamped on the soul for evermore.

Portrait after portrait painted
Meets with neither sign nor favor;
Once the first damsel comes in,
Then the second cannot win.

Toboso's peerless Dulcinea,
So deeply graven in my soul,
Forever holds me in her thrall:
Her name forever I'll extol.

All lovers say that constancy
Is the most valued quality,
For by it Love works prodigies,
And through it lovers soar to Heaven."

Don Quixote had reached this point in his song, which
was heard by the duke and duchess, Altisidora, and almost
all the people in the castle, when suddenly from a corridor
above his window a rope was let down, to which over a hundred tiny tinkling bells were fastened.

Immediately after that, a huge sackful of cats, all with
smaller bells tied to their tails, was emptied out the window.
The jingling of the bells and the meowing of the cats made
such a deafening din that the duke and duchess, though they
had been the inventors of the jest, were scared. Don Quixote

himself was panic-stricken. Unluckily two or three cats
leaped in through the bars of his window and darted up
and down the room as if a whole legion of devils had been
flying to and fro. In a moment they put out the candlelights
in their frantic efforts to escape from the chamber. Meanwhile
the rope with the bigger bells kept ceaselessly bobbing up and
down, scaring the majority of those who were not in the
secret of the plot. Don Quixote then jumped up, and seizing
his sword, he began to fence about him and to make thrusts
at the window, shouting: "Out, malicious enchanters! Away,
hoggish scum! I am Don Quixote of La Mancha, against
whom your vile intentions are of no avail." Then, turning his
attention to the cats that were scampering up and down the
room, he laid about him furiously as they made desperate
attempts to get out of the window. At last, they made their
escape, all but one of them, which, finding itself hard pressed
by Don Quixote, sprang at his face, and burying its claws
and teeth in his nose, caused him such agonizing pain that
he roared at the top of his voice. When the duke and duchess
heard the outcry, they guessed the cause and rushed at once
to his assistance, and having opened the door of his chamber
with a master key, they found the poor gentleman writhing
in his efforts to disentangle the cat from his face. By the
lights they carried they saw the unequal combat. The duke
hastened to intervene and remove the beast, but Don Quixote
shouted: "Let nobody take him; let me fight hand to hand
with this devil, this wizard, this necromancer! I'll make
him understand what it means to deal with Don Quixote of
La Mancha."

The cat, however, paid no heed to these bloodcurdling
threats and hung on like grim death until at last the duke unhooked its claws and flung it out of the window.

Don Quixote's face was all crisscrossed with scratches, and
as for his nose, it was in no healthy a condition; nevertheless,
he was extremely indignant because they had not allowed
him to bring to a victorious end his battle with the rascally
enchanter. Immediately, orders were given for oil of
Hypericum to be brought, and Altisidora herself with her
lily-white hands bound up his wounds. While she was dressing him, she whispered in his ear: "Hardhearted knight,
these misadventures have befallen you as a just punishment
for your willful obstinacy and disdain. Please God that your
squire, Sancho, may forget to whip himself, that your be-

loved Dulcinea may never be delivered from her enchantment, and that you never be blessed with her embraces in the bridal bed—at least as long as I, who love you, shall be alive."

Don Quixote made no answer to this tirade, but he sighed deeply and then stretched himself out on his bed after he had thanked the duke and duchess, not because he was afraid of that caterwauling, bell-jingling crew of enchanters, but because he was grateful for their kindness in coming to his assistance.

The duke and duchess left him to rest and went away grieved at the depressing result of their joke, for they had not imagined that the adventure would have turned out so disastrous and costly to Don Quixote. For it cost him five days of confinement in his room and in bed, where another adventure befell him, more pleasant than the last. His chronicler will not tell it now, as he has to visit Sancho Panza, who was proved to be very busy and very amusing in his government.

CHAPTER XLVII

In which the account of how Sancho Panza behaved in his government is continued

The history tells us that Sancho Panza was conducted from the Court of Justice to a sumptuous palace, where in a great hall a magnificent banquet was prepared.

As soon as Sancho entered, he was greeted by the sound of many instruments, and four pages waited on him with water to wash his hands, which he did with great gravity. The music then ceased, and Sancho sat down to dinner at the head of the table, for there was but one seat and the cloth was only laid for one. A certain personage, who, as it afterward appeared, was a physician, stood by his side with a rod of whalebone in his hand. They then took off the beautiful white cloth that covered dishes of fruit and a great variety of viands. One who looked like a student said grace; a page put a lace-edged bib under Sancho's chin; another who performed the service of butler set a plate of fruit before him. But scarcely had he tasted it when the man with the rod touched the plate, and it was instantly snatched away by a page. The butler then put in its place another containing meat. Yet, no sooner did Sancho try to taste it than the physician with the rod touched it, and a page whisked it away as speedily as the plate of fruit.

Sancho was astonished at this proceeding, and looking around him, he asked if this dinner was to be a conjuring game. He with the rod replied: "My Lord Governor, your meals here will follow the same usage and fashion as in other islands where there are governors. I am a physician, and I am paid a salary in this island to look after the gover-

nor of it, and so I am more careful of his health than my
own. I study night and day, examining his constitution, that
I may know how to cure him when he falls ill. The principal
thing I do is always to attend him at his meals, to see that
he eats what is good for his system and avoids whatever I
fancy may be prejudicial to his health and injurious to his
stomach. That is why I ordered the plate of fruit to get
removed, because it is too watery, and the other dish because it is too hot and overflavored with spices, which increase a man's thirst; for he who drinks much, destroys and
consumes the radical moisture that is the fuel of life."

"In that case," said Sancho, "this dish of roasted partridge, which seems to me well-flavored, will do me no manner of harm."

"Stop," replied the physician, "as long as I am alive my
Lord Governor shall not eat them."

"Why so?" said Sancho.

"Because," answered the doctor, "our great master Hippocrates, the North Star and luminary of medicine, says in one
of his aphorisms: *Omnis saturatio mala, perdicis autem pes-
sima*, which means, 'All surfeit is bad, but that of partridges
is worst of all.'"

"If that is so," said Sancho, "please, doctor, give an eye
to the dishes here on the table and see which of them will
do me the most good or the least harm, and let me eat of
that without whisking it away with your wand, for by the
life God grants me as governor, I'm perishing with hunger,
and to deny me belly fodder—say what you will, doctor—
is the way to shorten, not to lengthen, my life."

"Your worship is right," replied the doctor, "and so I am
of the opinion that you should not eat these stewed rabbits,
for that is a furry kind of diet. And I wouldn't touch a
morsel of that veal if I were you; had it not been roasted
and condimented, you might, perhaps, have a taste, but as it
is, certainly not."

"Well, then," said Sancho, "what about that huge dish
that is piping hot? I think it's an olla podrida; seeing that
it is a hodgepodge of many meats, surely I'm bound to light
upon something that'll be wholesome and tasty."

"*Absit,*" said the doctor, "far from us be such a thought.
Olla podrida indeed! There is no dish in the world more
injurious. Leave mixed stew to canons, college rectors, or
lusty gluttons at country weddings, but never let them be

seen on the tables of governors, where delicacy and daintiness should be the order of the day. The reason is that simple medicines are usually more highly valued than compounds, for with simple medicines you cannot go wrong, whereas with compounds you err by altering the amount of the ingredients. Therefore, what I would at present advise my lord governor to eat in order to preserve his health is a hundred or so rolled-up wafers, with a few thin slices of quince that will sit lightly on the stomach and help the digestion."

When Sancho heard this, he leaned back in his chair and stared at the doctor from top to toe. Then in a solemn tone he asked him what his name was and where he had studied. The latter said in reply: "My Lord Governor, my name is Doctor Pedro Recio de Agüero; I am a native of a place called Tirteafuera, which lies between Caracuel and Almodóvar del Campo, on the right hand, and I have taken my doctor's degree in the University of Osuna." [1]

"Then listen to me," cried Sancho in a rage, "Doctor Pedro Recio of Evil Augury, native of Tirteafuera, lying between Caracuel and Almodóvar del Campo, on the right hand, graduate of the University of Osuna, take yourself out of here at once! If not, I swear by the sun above that I'll take a cudgel, and starting with yourself, I'll so belabor all the doctors in the island that not one of them will be left—I mean, of those like yourself whom I know to be ignorant quacks, for those who are wise and prudent I'll set on high and honor them like so many angels. Once more, clear out of here, Pedro Recio; if not, I'll take the chair I'm sitting on and I'll crack it on your skull. Let them call me over the coals for it when I give up my office, and they'll discharge me when I tell them that I did God's service by killing off a bad physician who's a public executioner. Now, give me something to eat; if not, let them take back their government, for an office that doesn't feed its master isn't worth a couple of beans."

The doctor quaked with fear when he saw the governor in such a rage, and he would have acted up to his name and taken himself away, but just then the sound of the post horn was heard in the street. "It's an express courier from

[1] *Recio de agüero* means positive of omen. *Tirteafuera* means take thyself away.

my lord the duke," said the butler, after he had looked out
the window. "It must be some important dispatch."

The courier entered, sweating and in great agitation. Pulling a packet out of his bosom, he handed it to the governor,
who gave it to the steward, telling him to read the superscrip-
tion, which ran as follows: "To Don Sancho Panza, Governor
of the island of Barataria. To be delivered to him or to his
secretary."

"Who is my secretary?" said Sancho.

"It is I, my lord," answered one who was present, "for I
can read and write, and I am a Biscayan." [2]

"With that last qualification," said Sancho, "you may well
be secretary to the emperor himself. Open the letter and see
what it says."

The new secretary did so, and after having perused the
dispatch, he said that it was a business that could be told
only in private.

Sancho then ordered all the company to leave the room
except the steward and the butler. When the hall was cleared,
the secretary read the following letter:

It has come to my notice, Don Sancho Panza, that some
of our enemies intend to deliver a fierce attack upon your
island one of these nights. You ought, therefore, to be
watchful and stand upon your guard that you may not be
caught unawares. I have also learned through reliable
spies that four men have got into the town in disguise to
murder you because they are afraid of your intelligence.
Keep a strict watch; watch carefully before you admit
strangers to audience; eat nothing that is set before you. I
will take care to send you assistance if you are in want
of it. I rely upon your judgment. From this castle, the
16th day of August, at four in the morning.

Your friend,
The Duke.

Sancho was dumbfounded at the news, and the rest appeared to be no less so. And turning to the steward, he
said: "The first thing we have got to do, and do quickly,

---

[2] The office of secretary was frequently entrusted to Basques
on account of their reputation for loyalty.

is to shove Doctor Recio into prison, for if anybody intends to kill me, it must be he, and that by a lingering death, the worst of all, starvation."

"Nevertheless," said the butler, "I think your worship should not eat any of the food here upon the table, for it was sent in by some nuns, and as the saying goes, 'Behind the Cross stands the Devil.' "

"I don't deny it," replied Sancho, "so, for the present give me a chunk of bread and about four pounds of grapes; they won't poison me. For, when all's said and done, I can't go on without eating, and if we've got to get ready for the battles that threaten us, we need to be well-fed. Remember, it's the belly that keeps the heart up, and not the heart the belly. Meanwhile, secretary, do send the duke an answer and tell him that his commands shall be carried out on the nail. Remember me kindly to my lady the duchess and beg her not to forget to send a special messenger with my letter and bundle to my wife, Teresa Panza. Tell her I'll take this as a special favor and that I'll serve her to the best of my power. And, by the way, you might as well include a salutation to my master, Don Quixote of La Mancha, that he may see that I'm always grateful to the hand that fed me. The rest I'll leave to you as a good secretary and a sturdy Biscayan. Now clear away the cloth and bring me something to eat. Then you'll see how I'm able to deal with all the spies, cutthroats, and wizards who dare to put their nose near me and my island."

At that moment a page came into the room and said to the governor: "My Lord, there is a countryman outside who wishes to have a word with your lordship about some very important business."

"It's mighty strange," cried Sancho, "how these men of business keep plaguing us! How is it that they're such blockheads as not to understand that this is not the time for business? Do they imagine that we governors and judges are made of iron and marble and that we have no need of rest and refreshments like other folks of flesh and bone? By God and my conscience, if my government lasts (I've a shrewd suspicion that it won't), I'll give some of those men of business a leathering. Now tell that good man to come in, but mind you make sure first that he isn't one of those spies or one of my murderers."

"He isn't, sir," replied the page. "He seems a harmless

fellow, and if I'm not mistaken, he's as good as good bread."

"There's nothing to fear," said the steward, "for we're all here."

"Would it be possible, steward," asked Sancho, "for me to have something of weight and substance to eat, now that Doctor Pedro Recio has gone, even if it were only a bit of bread and an onion?"

"Tonight at supper we shall make up for the shortcomings of your dinner, and your lordship shall be more than satisfied."

"God grant it," said Sancho.

At this the peasant came in, who was of fine presence and as decent and honest a soul as you could see a mile away. His first words were: "Who is the Lord Governor here?"

"Who should he be," answered the secretary, "but the one seated in the chair?"

"Then I humble myself in his presence," said the countryman, and sinking to his knees, he begged the governor for his hand to kiss.

But Sancho refused it and bade him to rise and say what he wanted. The peasant did so, saying: "I'm a laboring man, sir, a native of Miguel Turra, a village six miles from Ciudad Real."

"We've another Tirteafuera here!" exclaimed Sancho. "But speak on, friend, for I can tell you that I know Miguel Turra very well. It's not very far from my own village."

"This is the matter, sir," continued the countryman. "I am by the grace of God married with the license and blessing of the Holy Roman Catholic Church. I have two sons, both students; the younger is studying for a bachelor and the elder for a licentiate. I am a widower, for my wife died, or rather a wicked doctor killed her by purging her when she was pregnant; and had God pleased that another child of hers should see the light and had it been a boy, I would have put him to study for a doctor, so that he might not be envious of his brothers, the bachelor and the licentiate."

"So," said Sancho, "if your wife hadn't died or been killed, you wouldn't be a widower now."

"No, sir, by no means," replied the peasant.

"We're getting on like a house on fire," said Sancho. "Get a move on, brother, for it's the hour for sleep rather than for business."

"Well, to continue," said the countryman, "this son of mine, who is to be a bachelor, fell in love with a young lady in our village, called Clara Perlerino, daughter of Andrés Perlerino, a very wealthy farmer; and this name of Perlerino doesn't come to them by descent or ancestry, but because everyone in the family is paralytic, and to make it sound better, they call themselves Perlerines. Though to tell the honest truth, the young maid is like an oriental pearl. When you look at her from the right side, she's like a flower of the field; on the left side, however, she's not so good, for she's short of the eye she lost from smallpox. But though there are many pockmarks on her face, and big ones among them, too, those who love her say that they aren't pockmarks but graves in which the souls of her lovers lie buried. She's so clean that to avoid soiling her face she carries her nose so cocked up that they say it looks as if it were running away from her mouth. Mind you, for all that she's a fine handsome lass, for she has a large mouth, and but for the loss of ten or a dozen teeth and grinders, it would top the score as the most shapely of its kind. Blessed if I know what to say about her lips, for they are so thin and delicate that if it were the fashion to wind lips, one might make a skein of them; but as they have a different color from ordinary lips, they look marvelous, for they are mottled blue, green, and purple. Forgive me, Lord Governor, for describing so minutely the features of the young lady, but seeing that some day or other she will be my daughter, I like the lass and to me she seems not half bad."

"Go on describing her till kingdom come," cried Sancho, "for I'm relishing your portrait, and if I had dined, your portrait would be the finest dessert one could have to top a meal."

"That I've still to serve you," replied the countryman, "but the time may come when we may get to it, if we do not now. And I tell you, sir, that if I could paint that doxy's elegance and the height of her body, it would surely astound you, but that's just what I can't do because she is bent and shrunken, and her knees knock her mouth, yet for all that it's quite clear that if she could stand upright her head would touch the ceiling. She would by now have given my bachelor son her hand in marriage, only she cannot stretch it out, for it is shriveled up, though from her long furrowed nails you can tell how finely modeled it is."

"All right," said Sancho, "but rest assured, brother, that you have painted the girl from head to foot. What is it you want now? Why not come to the point without all these turnings and windings and with less beating about the bush and all these odds and ends."

"I should like your worship to do me a favor," replied the countryman, "and give me a letter of recommendation to the girl's father, begging him to be good enough to allow this marriage to take place, since we're not unequal in fortune's or in nature's gifts. For, to tell you the honest truth, sir, my son's possessed, and there's not a day that passes that the devils don't give him three or four fits; and owing to having fallen into the fire on one occasion, his face is all creased and crinkled like parchment and his eyes are moist and oozing rheum, but his temper's angelic. Indeed, if he didn't bang and batter hell out of himself, he would be a saint."

"Do you want anything else my good fellow?" asked Sancho.

"There's just one other thing I'd like," said the countryman, "only I dare not mention it. But I must get it off my chest, come what may, otherwise it'll be going bad inside me, so I'll tell you, sir. I'd like your worship to give me three hundred or six hundred ducats to help toward my bachelor son's dowry. I have a mind, sir, to help him set up house and home, for after all, they'll have to live on their own and not be subject to the prying interference of their parents."

"Is there anything else you'd like?" said Sancho. "Don't let shame or shyness hinder you from asking."

"No, nothing at all," answered the countryman.

No sooner did he answer than the governor jumped to his feet and seized the chair on which he had been sitting, shouting: "I swear to God, Don Clodhopper, tatterdemalion, mudlark that you are, that if you don't make yourself scarce this instant and fade from my sight, I'll crack and split that skull of yours with this chair! Whoreson rogue, Satan's painter! So, you've the nerve to come asking me for six hundred ducats? Where am I to get them? And why should I give them to you even if I had them, you stinking cur? What the hell do I care about Miguel Turra and the whole clan of Perlerines? Clear out, and if you don't, I swear by the duke, my master, that I'll do what I said! You are not from Miguel Turra; you're some flibbertigibbet sent by Hell to tempt me. What, you godless villain? It's not a day and a half that I'm holding the governorship and you expect me to have six hundred ducats, do you?"

The steward made signs to the countryman to go out of the hall, which he did, hanging his head, evidently terrified that the governor might carry out his threat; but the rogue knew well how to act his part.

Let us, however, leave Sancho in his rage, and peace to all the company, and go back to Don Quixote, whom we left with his face all bandaged and under treatment for his cattish wounds, which took over a week to heal. On one of those days an incident occurred that Cide Hamete promises to tell as truthfully and accurately as he always relates the details of his history, no matter how minute they may be.

CHAPTER XLVIII

*Of Don Quixote's adventure with Doña Rodríguez,
the duchess' duenna, with other incidents worthy of
record and of eternal remembrance*

Don Quixote was extremely peevish and melancholy with
his face bandaged and marked, not by the hand of God,
but by the claws of a cat: such are the misfortunes attendant
on knight-errantry. For six days he did not appear in public,
but on one of those nights, as he lay awake and watchful,
brooding over his misfortunes and over Altisidora's persecu-
tion, he heard someone opening the door of his room with
a key. Immediately he imagined that the love-sick maiden
was coming to ambush his chastity and inveigle him into
betraying the fidelity he owed to his lady, Dulcinea of El
Toboso.

"No," he murmured in an audible voice, fully trusting
his imagination, "the greatest beauty on earth shall not prevail upon me to cease to adore the lady whom I hold engraved and imprinted in the center of my heart and in my
innermost entrails. Even if you are transformed, my lady,
into an onion-reeking country doxy, or a nymph of the golden
Tagus, weaving tresses of twisted silk and gold, or if Merlin
and Montesinos detain you where they please, wherever you
may be, you are mine; everywhere I have been or shall be,
I am yours."

As he finished saying this, the door opened. He stood up
on the bed, wrapped from head to foot in a yellow satin
quilt, a nightcap on his head, and his face and moustaches
in bandages—his face because of his scratches, and his
moustaches to prevent them drooping and falling. In this

864

getup he looked the strangest phantom imaginable. He stared
fixedly at the door, but when he expected to see the love-
stricken and forlorn Altisidora come in, he saw a most
venerable duenna, with a white plaited veil, so long that it
covered and cloaked her from head to foot. In the fingers
of her left hand she carried a lighted candle, and with her
right she shaded her face to keep the light from her eyes,
which were covered by a pair of enormous spectacles. She
advanced with noiseless steps, moving her feet very softly.

Don Quixote gazed at her from his watchtower, and when
he noted her attire and her silence, he was sure that she
was some witch or sorceress coming to do him some bad
turn, and began to cross himself most energetically. The
apparition, meanwhile, drew closer, and when it reached the
middle of the room, it raised its eyes and saw the energy
with which Don Quixote was blessing himself. And if he
was frightened at the sight of such a figure, she was no
less startled by his appearance, so that no sooner did she
see him so tall and yellow, in his quilt and in the grotesque
bandages that disfigured him, than she let out a loud scream,
crying: "Jesus! What do I see!"

With the sudden shock, the candle fell from her hands,
and finding herself in the dark, she turned around to take
to her heels, and in her alarm she tripped over her skirt
and came down with a mighty thud. Then the frightened
Don Quixote began to say: "I conjure you, phantom, or
whatever you are, to tell me your name and to say what
you want of me. If you are a soul in torment, tell me, for
I will do everything in my power for you. I am a Catholic
Christian and love to do good to all the world. It was with
that purpose I took up the order of knight-errantry that
I profess, whose offices extend even to doing good to souls
in purgatory."

The bewildered duenna, hearing herself thus exorcized,
guessed that Don Quixote was no less frightened than she
was and replied in a low plaintive voice: "Don Quixote, if
perhaps your worship is Don Quixote, I am no phantom or
specter or soul in purgatory, as your worship seems to think,
but Doña Rodríguez, duenna of honor to my lady the
duchess. I am in such a distress as it is your worship's
custom to relieve."

"Tell me, Doña Rodríguez," cried Don Quixote, "do
you come to me on an errand of mediation and love? For I

must inform you that I am good for no one, thanks to the peerless beauty of my lady, Dulcinea of El Toboso. I say in all frankness, Doña Rodríguez, that if you put aside all love messages you may go and relight your candle and come back, and we shall converse on any subject you wish or suggest, with the exception, as I say, of all incitements to love."

"I with a message from anyone, sir!" replied the duenna. "Little does your worship know me! I certainly am not so stale and decrepit that I have to resort to such childish foolery. Thanks be to God, I have still a soul in my body and all my teeth and molars in my mouth, but for a few I lost to the catarrh, which is so common in this land of Aragon. But wait a moment, your worship, I shall go out and light my candle and come back directly to tell my troubles to the reliever of all the troubles in the world."

Without waiting for a reply she went out of the room, where Don Quixote remained calmly and thoughtfully awaiting her. But presently a thousand thoughts about this new adventure crowded into his mind, and it struck him that he had judged and acted wrongly in putting himself in danger of breaking his pledged faith to his lady.

"Who knows," he said to himself, "whether the Devil, who is cunning and crafty, may not be trying to deceive me with a duenna, though he has failed to do so with empresses, queens, duchesses, or countesses. For I have often heard very wise men say that if he can, he would rather give you a flat-nosed than a hawk-nosed woman. And who knows whether this solitude, this opportunity, and this silence may not arouse my slumbering desires and cause me, after all these years, to fall where I have never stumbled? In such cases it is better to take to flight rather than await the battle. Yet, I cannot be in my senses if I think and utter such nonsense, for it is impossible for a white-veiled, fat, bespectacled duenna to move or arouse any lecherous thoughts in the most depraved heart in the world. Is there by chance in all the world a single duenna with wholesome flesh? Is there one of them in the world who is not impertinent, affected, and prudish? Out, you breed of duennas, useless for any human pleasure! How wise was that lady who, they say, had two dummy ones at the head of her dais, with spectacles, sewing cushions, and all, as if they were working; she found such stuffed figures just as effective for preserving the dignity of her hall as a pair of duennas of flesh and blood!"

With these words he leaped out of bed with the intention of shutting the door and preventing Doña Rodríguez from entering, but when he went to close it, the lady was already on her way back with a lighted candle of white wax. But when she saw Don Quixote at close quarters, wrapped in his quilt with his bandages and his nightcap or bonnet, her fears arose afresh, and stepping back a few paces, she said: "Am I safe, sir knight? I don't consider it a sign of modesty that your worship has got out of bed."

"That is the very question I would ask you, lady," replied Don Quixote. "Tell me whether I shall be safe from assault and ravishment."

"From whom or of whom do you ask for this assurance, sir knight?" asked the duenna.

"From you and of you," answered Don Quixote, "for I am not made of marble, nor you of brass, nor is it now ten o'clock in the morning, but midnight, or even a little after, I think. We are, besides, in a room more close and secret than that cave must have been where the bold, traitorous Aeneas enjoyed the favors of the lovely and submissive Dido. But give me your hand, lady, for I want no greater security than my conscience and modesty and the guarantee that reverend veil affords me."

Saying this, he kissed his right hand and seized hers, which she gave him with equal ceremony.

Here Cide Hamete puts in a parenthesis and swears by Mohammed that he would give the better of two cloaks he had to have seen those two walk from the door linked arm in arm.

At last Don Quixote got into bed, and Doña Rodríguez remained seated in a chair a little way from his bedside, without taking off her spectacles or putting down her candle. Don Quixote huddled down amid the bedclothes and muffled himself completely, leaving only his face uncovered, and when the two were settled, the first to break the silence was Don Quixote, who said: "You may now unburden and unbosom yourself of all that you nurse within your sorrowful heart and afflicted bowels. It shall be listened to by me with chaste ears and relieved by compassionate deeds."

"So I believe," replied the duenna; "from your worship's gentle and agreeable appearance no less Christian an answer

could be expected. The case is, Don Quixote, that though
you see me seated in this chair and in the middle of the
kingdom of Aragon and in the habit of a decayed and forlorn duenna, I am a native of Asturias, of Oviedo and of a
family that is related to many of the best in that province.
But my ill luck and the improvidence of my parents, which
led to their untimely impoverishment, brought me, I do not
know how or why, to the court of Madrid, where, for the
sake of peace and to save me from further misfortunes, my
parents placed me in service as waiting-maid to a lady of
quality. And I would have your worship know that no one
has ever surpassed me at hemstitching and plain needlework
in the whole of my life. My parents left me in service and
returned to their country, and a few years afterward they
went—it must have been to Heaven, for they were good
people and Catholic Christians. I was left an orphan and
limited to the wretched wages and scanty favors that are
usually paid to such servants in a palace. About this time,
a squire of the house fell in love with me, without my giving him the slightest cause for it. He was a man already
advanced in years, bearded and a fine-looking man, and what
is more, as wellborn as the king, for he came from the
mountains.[1] We did not manage our love affair secretly
enough to keep it from the notice of my lady, and she, to
save us from scandalmongers, had us married with the license and approbation of Our Holy Mother the Church,
from which marriage was born a daughter. She put an end
to my good fortune, if I had any, not because I died in
childbirth, for the delivery was easy and at the proper time,
but because shortly afterward my husband died of a shock
he received, which if I only had time to tell you about it,
would astonish your worship."

At this point she began to weep piteously and said: "Forgive me, Don Quixote, for I cannot help it; every time I remember my unfortunate husband my eyes fill with tears.
God help me! How proudly he used to carry my lady behind
him on the crupper of a stout mule, black as jet itself! In
those days they did not use coaches or chairs, as they say
is the fashion now, and ladies rode behind their squires. I
can't help giving you this detail so that you may note the

---

[1] The inhabitants of the highlands of Santander (La Montaña)
always boasted of their nobility.

good breeding and punctilious behavior of my good husband. At the entrance of the street of Santiago in Madrid, which is somewhat narrow, a judge of the court happened to be coming out with two of his officers before him, and no sooner did my good squire see him than he turned his mule's reins, as if he meant to wait upon him. My lady, who rode on the crupper, said to him in a low voice: 'What are you doing, you wretched fellow, don't you see that I am here?'

"The judge out of politeness pulled up his horse and said: 'Go on your way, sir, it is I who should wait upon Lady Casilda,' for that was my mistress' name. However, my husband, cap in hand, insisted on waiting upon the judge. Seeing this, my lady, full of rage and spite, drew out a large pin—or, I believe, a bodkin—out of its sheath and ran it into his loin, whereupon my husband gave a loud cry and his body writhed so violently that he tumbled to the ground with his lady. Two of her grooms ran to pick her up, and the judge and his officers ran to her, too. The Guadalajara Gate [2] was in an uproar—I mean, the idlers who were lounging about. My mistress went away on foot and my husband ran into a barber's shop, crying that his bowels were pierced through and through. My husband's courteousness became so proverbial in the city that boys would run after him in the streets, and because of this and because he was somewhat shortsighted, my lady dismissed him. The sorrow this caused him, without any doubt, hastened the calamity of his death. I was left a widow, without protection and with a daughter on my hands who went on growing in beauty like the foam of the sea. At last, as I had the fame of being a great seamstress, my lady the duchess, who had lately married the duke, offered to bring me with her to their kingdom of Aragon, and my daughter with me. Here in the course of time, my daughter grew up, and with all the graces in the world. She sings like a lark, dances as fast as a thought, reads and writes like a schoolmaster, and reckons like a miser. I don't mention her cleanliness, for running water is not cleaner; now she should be sixteen, five months, and three days, more or less. In short, this girl of mine fell

[2] The Guadalajara Gate was one of the principal entrances of Madrid. It was the most scandalous spot in the whole city because in its vicinity were situated the licensed brothels of the city.

in love with the son of a very rich farmer who lives in one of the duke's villages, not very far from here. I can't tell you how it all happened, but these two came together, and he deceived her under promise of marriage. Now he refuses to keep his word, and although the duke, my master, knows it, for I have complained to him, not once but many times, and besought him to order this farmer to marry my daughter, he turns a deaf ear and will hardly listen to me. And the reason is that this playboy's father is wealthy, lends him money, and sometimes goes surety for him in his pranks; so, the duke doesn't like to displease him or worry him in any way.

"Therefore, my dear sir, I want your worship to undertake the charge of redressing this wrong, either by entreaty or by arms, for as all the world says, your worship was born to right wrongs, to redress injuries, and to protect the unfortunate. Think of my daughter's orphan state, your worship, her good breeding, her youth, and all the virtues I have told you she possesses. By Heaven and my conscience there's not one among all my lady's maids who reaches up to the sole of her shoe. And as for that one they call Altisidora, whom they consider the gayest and the freest, if you compare her with my daughter, she doesn't come within six miles of her. For I want you to know, dear sir, that all is not gold that glitters, for this same Altisidora has more boldness than beauty and more freedom than modesty. Moreover, she is not very wholesome, for she has a certain taint in her breath, with the result that nobody can bear being near her for a moment. And even my lady the duchess—I must be silent, for they say that walls have ears."

"On my life, Doña Rodríguez, what ails my lady the duchess?" asked Don Quixote.

"As you are so pressing," answered the duenna, "I cannot refuse to answer your question with the whole truth. Do you note, Don Quixote, the beauty of my lady the duchess, the bloom of her complexion that resembles a smooth and burnished sword, those two cheeks of milk and carmine that hold the sun in one and the moon in the other, and that airy elegant way she walks, as if she scorned the earth? Doesn't she seem to shed health on all sides wherever she goes? But let me enlighten your worship by saying that she owes all that to God in the first place, and in the next to two issues she has, one in each leg, through which she discharges all the ill humors of which the doctors say she is full." [8]

"By all that is holy!" exclaimed Don Quixote. "Can my lady the duchess really have two such drains? I should not have believed it of the barefoot friars, had they told me, yet since Doña Rodríguez says so, it must be so. But such issues and in such a place must distill not humors but liquid ambergris. I really believe that this opening of issues must be an important matter for the health."

Scarcely had Don Quixote finished this sentence when the door of the room burst open with a great bang, and with the shock the candle fell out of Doña Rodríguez' hand, leaving the room dark as the wolf's maw, as the saying goes. Then the poor duenna felt her throat so tightly gripped by two hands that she could not scream, and someone else, without a word, very swiftly lifted her skirts and began to lay on her bare buttocks so unmercifully with what was apparently a slipper that it was a piteous sight to watch. And though Don Quixote felt this, he did not budge from his bed, not knowing what was the matter. He stayed quiet and still, for he feared that it might soon be his turn for a beating. It was no idle fear, for leaving the well-drubbed duenna, who did not dare to scream, the silent executioners fell on Don Quixote, and pulling off his sheet and quilt, they pinched him so hard and so often that he was compelled to defend himself with his fists, and all this in a mysterious silence. The battle lasted almost half an hour. Then the phantoms departed, and Doña Rodríguez gathered up her skirts and went out of the door moaning her disaster, but without saying a word to Don Quixote. He, mournful and pinched, perplexed and pensive, remained alone.

There we shall leave him, longing to know who was the malign enchanter who had brought him to such a pass. But that will be told in good time, for Sancho Panza calls us and the order of this history demands that we go to him.

[8] In the seventeenth century, issues like leeches and blood-letting were fashionable and many kept them open for years even without necessity. Cristóbal Hayo wrote against this abuse: *Parecer del doctor sobre el abuso de las fuentes* (Salamanca, 1635).

CHAPTER XLIX

Of what happened to Sancho Panza on the rounds of his island

We left the great governor vexed and angry with that portrait-painting rogue of a peasant, who had been tutored by the steward, as the steward was by the duke, to make a fool of him. But he held his own against them all, ignorant, coarse, and boorish though he was, and he said to those with him and to Doctor Pedro Recio, who had come back into the hall once the private matter of the duke's letter had been settled: "It is clear as daylight to me that judges and governors ought to be made of brass to be able to last out against those businessmen who take heed of none but themselves and insist on being listened to at all hours and at all times, and if the wretched judge don't think fit to give an ear to their business, then they start backbiting and gossiping against him, until they gnaw the very flesh off his bones and rake up a power of muck about his ancestors. Now, Mr. Businessman, you're a fool and a blockhead! Don't be in such a hurry! Just keep your patience and wait for a fit moment to make your application; don't come at dinner time or when a man is dropping off to sleep, for, by your leave, I'd have you know that we judges are made of flesh and bones like yourselves, and we must allow nature what nature requires—unless it be myself, for I'm forbidden to eat, thanks to Doctor Pedro Recio Tirteafuera, here present, who wants me to die of hunger and yet swears on oath that this kind of dying is life. God grant such a life to him and to all his crew—I mean, the quacks, for the good physicians deserve palms and laurels."

All who knew Sancho Panza were amazed at the elegance

of his speech, which they could not account for, unless it be that offices and responsible positions sharpen some men's minds and stupefy others.

At length, Doctor Pedro Recio Agüero de Tirteafuera promised the governor he should sup that night, though he transgressed all the aphorisms of Hippocrates. With this promise the governor was satisfied, and he waited with great impatience for the hour of supper, and though time, as he thought, stood still, yet the longed-for moment came at last. They served him cold beef hashed with onions and some calves' feet, somewhat stale. He tucked into this fare with more gusto than if they had given him Milanese godwits, Roman pheasants, Sorrento veal, Morón partridges, or Lavajos geese.

In the midst of his supper he turned to the doctor and said: "Listen, Master Doctor, from now on don't fash yourself giving me dainties and tidbits, for that'll make my belly go all contrary, seeing that it's used to nothing but good, honest beef, bacon, pork, goat's meat, turnips, and onions; and if you give it palace fare it will turn queasy and sicken at them. Now what the butler might do is serve me one of them so-called spicy hodgepodges, for the more gamey they are, the better they smell, in my opinion, and you can stuff them with anything you will, provided it be eatable, for I'll appreciate it and pay you back some day. So, let nobody play tricks on me, for either we are or we aren't, and let us all live and break a crust together in peace and good fellowship, for when God sends the morn, it's morn for all. I'll govern this island fair and square without any greasing of palms; so, let everyone keep his eye skinned and mind his own business, for the Devil's in Cantillana,[1] and if you give me half a chance, I'll show you wonders. No, make yourselves honey and the flies will eat you."

"Indeed, my Lord Governor," said the butler, "your worship is quite right in all that you've said, and I can assure you in the name of all the islanders that they will serve your worship with loyalty, love, and goodwill, for the gentle way of governing you have shown from the outset gives us

---

[1] The full proverbial phrase is: *El diablo esta en Cantillana y el obispo en Brenes* (The Devil is in Cantillana and the bishop in Brenes). It corresponds to our phrase: there'll be wigs on the green.

no cause to think or do anything to the disadvantage of your worship."

"I'm sure of it," replied Sancho, "and arrant fools they'd be if they did or thought otherwise. So, I repeat once more, see that you take good care of my food, and Dapple's also, for that is the main point in all this business. When it's the right time for it we'll go our rounds, for I'm dead set on clearing this island of all kinds of rubbishy wasters, tramps, and sharpers, for I want you to know, friends, that lazy loungers in a state are like drones in a hive of bees; they eat up the honey the worker bees gather. I intend to encourage the laboring men, preserve the privileges of the gentry, reward the good, and above all things, reverence religion and honor holy men. What do you think of my plan, good friends? Am I talking sense or simply cracking my brains to no purpose?"

"My Lord Governor, your worship speaks so well," answered the steward, "that I stand in admiration to hear a man devoid of letters, as you are (for I believe you cannot read), utter so many weighty sayings, so far beyond what we expected from you when we came hither. Every day sees a fresh marvel in the world; jests turn out to be in earnest, and the biters are bit."

That night, when the governor had supped, with Doctor Recio's sanction, they prepared for going the rounds. He set out accompanied by the steward, the secretary, the butler, the chronicler who was to record his deeds, and a few constables and notaries, altogether making up a middle-sized battalion. It was indeed a goodly sight to see our governor marching in the midst of them, armed with his rod of office. They had hardly passed through a couple of streets when they heard the clashing of swords, and hastening to the place from where the noise came, they found two men fighting, who stopped when they saw the officers of the law approaching. One of them said: "Help, in the name of God and the king! Are people to be attacked and robbed in the open street?"

"Hold, my good man," cried Sancho, "and tell me what's the reason for this brawl, for I'm the governor."

"My Lord Governor," interrupted the other party, "let me tell shortly what occurred. Your worship should know that this gentleman has just come from the gambling house that is across the street, where he has won over a thousand reals,

God knows how, except that I happened to be present, and against my conscience, gave judgment for him in more than one doubtful throw. He got up, and when I expected that he would give me at least a paltry crown in gratuity,[2] as is the custom among gentlemen of quality like myself, who are always ready in an emergency to back unreasonable claims and to prevent quarrels, he pocketed his money and left the gambling house. Being vexed at such conduct, I followed him and requested him civilly to give me at least eight reals, for he knew that I was a man of honor, without employment or pension, seeing that my parents had brought me up to no profession. But the knave, who is as great a thief as Cacus and a worse sharper than Andradilla, refused to give me more than a measly four reals. Think, my Lord Governor, how shameless a fellow he must be! I swear, if your worship had not come on the scene, I would have made him spew out his winnings and taught him how to balance his accounts."

"What's your answer to this?" said Sancho to the other. He admitted that what his antagonist had said was true; that he meant to give him no more than four reals, for he was tipping him continually; that those who expect gratuities should be civil, take graciously what is given them, and not look a gift horse in the mouth unless they know for certain that the winners are common cheats and have won unfairly; and that the proof that he was a man of honor and no cheat was that he had refused the other's request, for cheats are always in the fee of the bystanders who are their accomplices.

"That is very true," said the steward. "It is for you to say, my Lord Governor, what is to be done with these two men."

"This is what must be done," replied Sancho. "You, sir, the winner, whether by fair or foul play, give immediately a hundred reals to your bully-brack here, and shell out an extra thirty for the poor prisoners. And as for you, sir, who have neither office nor pension and are a drag on this island, take your hundred reals, and some time tomorrow be sure to clear out of this island, and don't set foot in it for ten years, unless you would finish your banishment in the

[2] Those who took part in gaming were expected to give a gratuity from the common pile or from their own gains to the employers of the establishment and even those who watched the game. This gratuity was called *barato*.

next world, for if you disobey my order, I'll have you swing-
ing from a gibbet, or at least, the hangman will do the job
for me. And if anyone gives any backchat he'll feel the
weight of my hand."

Thereupon the one disbursed and the other received; this
one went home and that one went out of the island. As for
the governor, he commented as follows: "It won't be my
fault if I don't get rid of those gambling houses, for I've a
shrewd suspicion that they're highly injurious to the state."

"As regards that house," said one of the notaries, "I'm
sure your worship will not be able to do away with it, for it
is owned by a person of great influence, who loses a great
deal more year in and year out at cards than he gains. Your
worship may show your authority against other gambling
houses of less note that do more harm and shelter more
abuses than those frequented by the gentry, for in them
the notorious cardsharpers don't dare to play their tricks.
Furthermore, since the vice of gambling has become a common practice, it is better to play in the houses of people
of quality than in those of the lower classes, where after
midnight poor fools are gulled and fleeced of everything they
have in the world."

"Well, notary," said Sancho, "I know there's a great deal
to be said on the subject."

Just then a constable came up with a youth in custody,
and said: "Lord Governor, this young man was coming toward us, but no sooner did he catch sight of the Law than
he turned tail and began to run like a stag, a sign that he's a
criminal. I raced after him, and if he hadn't stumbled and
fallen, I should never have caught him."

"Why did you run away, man?" asked Sancho.

"Sir, to avoid answering all the questions the constables
ask," answered the youth.

"What is your trade?"

"A weaver."

"What do you weave?"

"Iron heads for lances, by your worship's leave."

"So you're joking, eh? Fancy yourself as a comic? Right
you are! Where were you going just now?"

"To take the air, sir."

"Where do you take the air in this island?"

"Where it blows."

"Good! You answer to the point. You're a smart fellow,

my lad, but kindly get it into your head that I'm the air, that I blow astern of you, and that I'll blow you into jail. Ho there! Seize him and take him away; I'll make him sleep there this night out of the air."

"By God," said the youth, "your honor can no more make me sleep in jail than make me king!"

"Why can't I make you sleep in prison?" asked Sancho. "Haven't I power to arrest you and discharge you whenever and as often as I please?"

"However much power your worship may have," said the youth, "it won't be enough to make me sleep in prison."

"Why not?" demanded Sancho. "Take him at once where he'll see his mistake with his own eyes, and in case the jailer should use his interested liberality on your behalf, I'll make him go bail for two thousand ducats that he won't let you stir a step from prison."

"This is all most laughable," replied the youth. "The point is that no man living shall make me sleep in jail."

"Tell me, devil," said Sancho, "have you any angel to deliver you and free you from the fetters in which I'll order you to be clapped?"

"Now, governor," replied the youth with a charming smile, "let us reason together and come to the point. Suppose your worship orders me to be taken to prison, and has me loaded with fetters and chains there and put in a cell, laying the jailer under heavy penalties to carry out your orders and not let me out; all the same if I don't wish to sleep and stay awake all night without closing an eyelid, will your worship with all your power be able to make me sleep if I don't choose to?"

"No, of course not," said the secretary, "the man has made his case."

"You would stay awake then," asked Sancho, "only because it's your own will, and with no intention of going against mine?"

"None, sir," said the youth, "none at all."

"Then away with you then, in God's name!" cried Sancho. "Go and sleep at home, and may God send you sound sleep. I don't want to deprive you of it, but I'd advise you in the future not to pull the leg of the Law, or you may meet someone who'll answer your joke with a crack on your head."

The youth went off, and the governor continued his

rounds, and after a little while two constables came up with a man in custody.

"My Lord Governor," said they, "this person who seems to be a man is, in fact, a woman, and not an ugly one either." They then held two or three lanterns up to her face, by the light of which they discovered the face of a girl about sixteen years of age. She was as fair as a thousand pearls, with her hair put up in a snood of gold and green silk. They noted that her stockings were of flesh-colored silk, her garters of white taffeta, fringed with gold and seed pearls; her breeches were green and gold, her close-fitting jacket of the same, under which she wore a doublet of fine white and gold stuff, and her shoes were white and like those worn by men. She had no sword, but a very richly wrought dagger, and her fingers were covered with a quantity of valuable rings. Everyone was struck by the maiden's beauty, but nobody knew her. Those who were in the secret of the jests to be played on Sancho were more puzzled than the rest, for they had not planned this incident, and therefore, they were eager to see how it would turn out.

Sancho was thrilled by the young lady's beauty, and he asked her who she was, where she was going, and why she had dressed up in those clothes.

With downcast eyes she modestly answered: "I cannot, sir, answer so publicly what I wish so much to be kept a secret. You may, however, rest assured that I am no thief or criminal, but an unhappy maiden whom the spur of jealousy has driven to violate the laws of decorum."

The steward, hearing this, said: "Be pleased, my Lord Governor, to order your retinue to retire, that this young lady may speak out her mind more freely." The governor did so, and they all departed, except the steward, the butler, and the secretary.

"I, sirs, am the daughter of Pedro Pérez Mazorca, a dealer in wool in this village, who visits my father's house quite often——"

"That will not pass, lady," said the steward, "for I know Pedro Pérez very well, and he doesn't have any children, male or female. Moreover, you said that he is your father, and then you added that he visits your father quite often."

"I had already noticed that," said Sancho.

"Sirs, I am all mixed up, and I don't even know what I'm saying," answered the maiden. "But the truth is that I am the daughter of Diego de la Llana, whom all of you must know."

"That will pass," replied the steward, "for I know Diego de la Llana. I also know that he is a wealthy and honest gentleman, that he has a son and a daughter, and that since he became a widower, there isn't a soul in this village who can say that he has seen the daughter's face, for he keeps her so locked up that even the sun cannot see her. Yet, for all that, rumor has it that she is extremely beautiful."

"That is true," replied the maiden. "And I am that daughter. Whether the rumor about my beauty is true or not, you can judge for yourselves, sirs, for you have seen me." And with this she started to weep piteously.

The secretary, noticing everything, approached the steward and whispered in his ear: "Something serious has evidently befallen this poor damsel, to cause such an elegant lady to wander away from home in such a disguise and at such an hour."

"No doubt about that," replied the steward, "besides, her tears confirm that suspicion."

Sancho consoled her as best as he could and asked her to tell them what had happened, for they all would earnestly try to help her by every means possible.

The young lady then continued: "The truth is, gentlemen, that since the death of my mother ten years ago, my father has kept me in close confinement. At home we have a small but richly ornamented chapel where we hear Mass. So, in all these years I have seen nothing but the sun in the heavens by day and the moon and the stars by night. I know nothing about the streets, squares, or churches, or about men, except my father, my brother, and Pedro Pérez, whom, because he usually comes to our house, I would have passed on you as my father, that I might conceal the right one. For many days and months I have felt deeply depressed owing to this confinement, and I have constantly longed to see the world, or at least the town where I was born, and I convinced myself that my longing was not unbecoming or unseemly in a highborn lady. When I heard people talking of bullfights, tourneys, and theatrical shows, I asked my brother, who is a year younger than I am, to tell me about them and about many other things I had never seen. He described them as best he could, but it only made me more curious to see them. At last, to shorten the story of my undoing, I prayed and besought my brother, would that I had never prayed nor besought him——"

At this point she broke down and wept bitterly.

"Pray, my lady, continue your story," said the steward. "Your words and tears keep us all in anxious suspense."

"The words I have to add are few," answered the maiden, "but the tears I have to shed will be many, for ill-advised wishes cannot bring with them anything but tears."

The steward, smitten by the maiden's beauty, raised his lantern to see her again. It seemed to him that the tears she shed were mother of pearl or meadow dew, and to extol them he even compard them to pearls from the Orient, and he prayed that her misfortunes were not as serious as her tears and sighs led him to believe.

The governor was impatient at the young lady's delay in telling her story, and he bade her cease keeping them in suspense, for it was late and he had still much of the town to cover.

The young lady, sobbing and sighing as she spoke, said: "To my misfortune I entreated my brother to lend me some of his clothes and to take me out one night to see all the town while our father was asleep. Finally, giving in to my entreaties, he consented, and having lent me his clothes, he put on mine, which fitted him exactly, as he has no trace of beard on his face, he makes a mighty pretty lady. So, we slipped out of the house and took a ramble all over the town, but as we were going home, we perceived a crowd of people coming our way. And my brother said: 'Sister, this must be the governor's round; quicken your step and put wings on your feet. Run after me, for if we are recognized, it will be worse for us.' With that he started, not to race, but to fly. But before I had gone six paces I was so frightened that I fell down, and the constables caught me and dragged me before your worships, who must surely consider me a shameless hussy."

"So is that all your trouble, young lady," said Sancho, "and was it not jealousy then that drove you out of your home, as you said at the beginning of your story."

"Nothing has befallen me, and I was not driven out by jealousy, but simply by the desire to see the world, which in my case did not extend beyond the streets of this village."

The truth of the girl's story was confirmed by the arrival

of two other constables, who had seized the brother as he sped away. The female dress of the youth was only a rich petticoat and a cloak of blue damask edged with embroidery of gold; on his head he wore no wig and no ornament but his own hair, which looked like ringlets of gold.

The governor, the steward, and the butler took him aside, and making sure that his sister could not hear, they asked him why he was wearing that dress. He, with no less shame and bashfulness, told the same thing that his sister had related, much to the delight of the enamored steward.

The governor then addressed them as follows: "Now, my young people, this seems to me to be nothing but a childish frolic, and there was no need of all these tears and tantrums. By saying that you were so-and-so, who had left your parent's home with the desire to look around, merely out of curiosity and with no other design, the matter would have been closed without all this weeping and wailing."

"That is true," said the maiden, "but I would have your worships know that the scare I've suffered has been so great that it made me forget all the rules of decorum."

"There's no harm done," Sancho replied. "Come along with me, and we'll see you home to your father's and perhaps he won't be any the wiser. But remember to be more careful in the future and don't be so childish and eager to go gadding abroad, for 'The modest maid stays at home, as if she had a leg broken'; and ''Tis roaming ruins the hen and the maid'; and 'She that longs to see, longs also to be seen.' I'll say no more."

The youth thanked the governor for his kindness, and so they both went home under an escort. When they came to the house, the young man threw a pebble up at a grated window, and presently a maid servant, who had been watching out for them, came down and opened the door. They entered, leaving everyone amazed, not only by their good breeding and their beauty, but also by their strange wish to see the world at night without leaving the village. But they attributed this to their youth.

The steward's heart had been pierced by love, and he resolved to ask for the maiden's hand in marriage, for he was sure that her father would not refuse, seeing that he was the duke's steward. And Sancho had a mind to arrange a match between the young man and his daughter, Sanchica, and he resolved to bring it about as soon as possible, for he thought no man's son would refuse to wed a governor's daughter. And so his round ended for that night, and within two days his governorship, by which all Sancho's designs were cut short and erased, as shall be seen later.

CHAPTER L

Which reveals who the enchanters and executioners were that beat the duenna and pinched and scratched Don Quixote, with the adventure of the page who bore the letter to Teresa Panza, Sancho Panza's wife

Cide Hamete, that most precise investigator of every detail of this true history, says that at the time when Doña Rodríguez left her room to go to Don Quixote's apartment, another duenna who slept with her heard her go. And as all duennas are fond of prying, peering, and sniffing, she went after her so silently that the worthy Rodríguez did not notice her. No sooner did this duenna see the other enter Don Quixote's room than, anxious lest she fail in the general custom of all duennas, which is tale-bearing, she rushed off to inform her mistress the duchess that Doña Rodríguez was in Don Quixote's bedroom. The duchess told the duke and asked his permission for herself and Altisidora to go and see what that lady wanted with Don Quixote. The duke agreed, and the two of them cautiously and silently crept step by step and took up their position behind the doors of the room, so close that they overheard every word spoken inside. But when the duchess heard La Rodríguez let out the secret of her garden of fountains, neither she nor Altisidora could stand it any longer. So, bouncing into the room in a towering fury and lusting for revenge, they pinched Don Quixote and slapped the duenna in the manner already described. For insults directed at the beauty and pride of women raise them to the highest pitch of anger and kindle their desire for vengeance. The duchess told the duke what had taken place, at which he was much entertained.

Then, following her plan for amusing herself at Don Quixote's expense, the duchess sent the page who had played the part of Dulcinea in the artifice for her disenchantment—which Sancho in all his business of governing had clean forgotten—to his wife, Teresa Panza, with her husband's letter and another from herself, also a string of rich corals as a present.

The history says that the page was a bright, intelligent lad, and being eager to please his lord and lady, he set off in high spirits for Sancho's village. When he came near his destination, he saw a group of women washing in a stream, and he asked them if they could inform him whether there lived in that village a woman whose name was Teresa Panza, wife to one Sancho Panza, squire to a knight called Don Quixote of La Mancha. No sooner had he asked the question than a young wench who was washing among the rest got up and said: "That Teresa Panza is my mother, that Sancho is my own father, and the same knight our master."

"In that case, damsel," said the page, "lead me straight to your mother; I've a letter and a present here for her from your father."

"That I will with a heart and a half, sir," said the girl, who looked about fourteen years of age, and leaving the clothes she was washing to one of her companions, without pausing to tidy her hair or put on her shoes, she raced ahead of the page's horse, barelegged and all disheveled.

"Come on, sir," said she, "for our house is by the entrance to the village, and my mother is at home; but she's very sad, not having heard for many days what happened to my father."

"Well," said the page, "I bring tidings that will make her give thanks to God, I warrant."

At last, after leaping, running, and jumping, the girl reached the village, and before entering into the house, she shouted at the top of her voice: "Come out, mother, come out, come out! Here's a gentleman who brings letters and presents from my good father."

Hearing the shouts, Teresa Panza came out spinning a lock of coarse flax. She was wearing a russet skirt that was so short that it seemed to have been chopped off at the placket, "to her shame";[1] her bodice was of the same russet stuff and her shirt was open and messy. She was not old, although she seemed to have passed forty, but she was strongly built, hale, and buxom. Seeing her daughter and the page, she said: "What is it, daughter? Who's the gentleman?"

"A servant of your ladyship's," answered the page. As he spoke, he dismounted and knelt humbly before Lady Teresa, saying: "Give me leave to kiss your ladyship's hand, seeing that you are the only legitimate spouse of Don Sancho Panza, lawful governor of the island of Barataria."

"Come, come, sir, no more o' this, get up from there, I pray," replied Teresa, "for I'm no court dame but a plain unvarnished country woman, daughter of a humble clod-beater, and wife of a squire-errant, but not a governor."

"Your ladyship," answered the page, "is the most worthy wife of a thrice worthy archgovernor, and as proof of this truth, take this letter and this present." And he took out of his pocket a string of coral beads set in gold and fastened it around her neck, saying: "This letter is from the governor, and another that I have for you, together with these beads, comes from my lady the duchess, who sends me to your ladyship."

Teresa was dumbfounded, and her daughter likewise. The girl then said: "I'll be hanged if our master, Don Quixote, hasn't something to do with this; he must have given my father the government or earldom he so often promised him."

"That is so," replied the page, "and it is out of respect for Don Quixote that Don Sancho is now governor of the island of Barataria, as you may see by the letter."

"Good gentleman," said Teresa, "read it out to me, for though I can spin, I can't read a scrap."

"No more can I," added Sanchica, "but wait here a moment and I'll run and fetch one who can, either the bachelor Sansón Carrasco, or the priest himself, who'll be leaping to hear news of my father."

"You may save yourself the trouble. I can read, though I cannot spin, and I will read it to you." And he read all of it to them, but as its contents have already been given, it is not repeated here.[2] He then produced the letter from the duchess, which read as follows:

---

[1] Frivolous women were punished in this way.
[2] It is given in Chapter XXXVI.

"Friend Teresa,

The good qualities of your husband, Sancho, honesty and good sense, obliged me to persuade my husband, the duke, to make him governor of one of the many islands in his possession. I am informed that he is as sharp as a hawk in his government, for which I am very glad, and the duke likewise. I give thanks to Heaven that I have not been deceived in my choice of him for that office. For I must tell you, Lady Teresa, that it is mighty difficult to run across a good governor in this world of ours, and may Heaven make me as good as Sancho shows himself in his government.

I herewith send you, my dear friend, a string of coral beads set in gold; I wish they were oriental pearls, but as the saying goes, 'Whoever gives you a bone won't wish you dead.' The day will come when we shall get to know each other, and then God knows what may come to pass. Remember me to your daughter, Sanchica, and tell her from me to get herself ready, for I mean to make a big match for her when least she expects it. They tell me that you have fine large acorns in your village; pray send me two dozens of them, for I shall value them all the more as coming from your hands. And, please write me a nice long letter to let me know about the state of your health and your welfare, and if you want anything, you have only to gape and I shall guess your meaning. Heaven protect you. From this castle,

Your friend, who wishes you well,
The Duchess."

"Lord bless us!" said Teresa when she heard the letter. "What a good, plain, and humble lady she is, to be sure! Let them bury me with such ladies as this, and not with the haughty madams we have in our village, who, because they are gentlefolks, think the wind musn't blow upon them; they go flaunting in style to church as if they were very queens! They turn up their noses in scorn to look on a poor peasant woman, and yet, here is a good lady, who, though a duchess, calls me her friend and treats me as if I were as high as herself. Please God that I see her some day as high as the highest steeple in La Mancha. As for the acorns, sir, I'll send her ladyship a peck of them, and of such huge a size that people will come from far and near to see and wonder. And now, Sanchica, give a hearty welcome to the gentleman;

take care of his horse and fetch some fresh eggs from the stable, slice some rashers of bacon, and let us feed him like a prince, for his good news and his handsome face deserve no less. Meanwhile, I'm off to tell the glad news to the neighbors, especially to our good priest and Master Nicholas, the barber, for they are, and have been all along, good friends of your father."

"I'll do as you say," replied Sanchica. "But listen, mother, you must give me half the beads, for I'm sure her ladyship was not so foolish as to send them all to you."

"They're all for you, daughter," replied Teresa, "but let me wear them a few days around my neck, for they truly cheer my very heart."

"You will be still more cheered," said the page, "when you see what I have got in my portmanteau, for it is a fine suit of green cloth that the governor wore only one day at a hunt, and he has sent it all to my lady Sanchica."

"May he live a thousand years!" cried Sanchica. "And the fine gentleman who brought it likewise, and even two thousand, if need be!"

Teresa went out of the house with the letters in her hands and the beads around her neck, and as she went along, her fingers played on the papers as if they had been a tambourine. Meeting by chance the curate and the bachelor Carrasco, she began dancing and capering before them. "By my faith," cried she, "we're no poor relations now, for we've got a bit of a government! Now let the proudest painted ladyship among them turn up her nose at me and I'll paint her afresh."

"What is this, Teresa Panza?" said the curate "What madness is this? And what papers have you here?"

"No madness at all," replied Teresa, "but these are letters from duchesses and governors, and the beads I'm wearing are fine coral; the Ave Marias and the paternosters are of beaten gold; and I'm a governor's lady."

"Heaven be our witness, there's no understanding you, Teresa; we don't know what you mean."

"These will tell you," replied Teresa, handing them the letters.

The curate read them aloud to Sansón Carrasco, and then both stared at one another in amazement. The bachelor asked who had brought the letters. Teresa said that if they would come home with her, they should see the messenger, who was a fine, handsome young man, and that he had brought her

another present worth twice as much. The curate took the
string of corals from her neck and examined it again and
again, and being convinced that they were genuine, he wondered still more and said: "By the cloth I wear, I don't know
what to say or think of these letters and presents! On the
one hand I see and feel the fineness of these corals; on the
other I read that a duchess sends to ask for two dozens of
acorns."

"Make all this fit if you can," said Carrasco, "but let us
go and see the messenger; perhaps he can explain the difficulties that puzzle us."

They then returned with Teresa and found the page sifting
a little barley for his horse, and Sanchica cutting rashers to
fry with eggs for the page's dinner. The appearance and behavior of the youth made an excellent impression upon both
the curate and the bachelor, and after the usual exchange
of civilities, Sansón asked him to give them some news of
Don Quixote and Sancho Panza, for though they had read
a letter from the latter to his wife and another from the
duchess, they were completely puzzled, and they could not
for the life of them imagine what was meant by Sancho's
government, especially government of an island, for they
were well aware that all or most of the islands in the
Mediterranean belonged to the king.

"Gentlemen," replied the page, "there is no doubt about
Señor Sancho Panza being governor, but I am not going
to say whether it is an island or not; I only know it is a place
that has above a thousand inhabitants. As to that business
about the acorns, I tell you that the duchess is so plain and
so humble that there's no wonder in her sending to a peasant
woman for a few; why, I've known her send to borrow a comb
from one of her neighbors. For I must tell you, gentlemen,
that the ladies of Aragon, though as high in rank, are not
as punctilious and ceremonious as the ladies of Castile; they
treat their people with greater familiarity."

Sanchica came in with her lap full of eggs. "Tell me, sir,"
said she to the page, "now that my father is a governor,
does he wear trunk hose?" [3]

"I never noticed," replied the page, "but I suppose he
does."

_____

[3] Trunk hose (calzas atacadas) were only worn by old-
fashioned gentlemen in the second half of the sixteenth century.

"God save us!" answered Sanchica. "What a sight my father must be in tights! Isn't it funny that ever since I was born, I've longed to see my father in trunk hose."

"You'll certainly have that pleasure, my lady, if you live," replied the page. "By heavens, if his government only lasts two months, you'll see him traveling the roads with a winter mask against the cold." [4]

The curate and the bachelor saw clearly that the page was speaking ironically, but the fineness of the corals and the hunting suit sent by Sancho (which Teresa had already shown them) perplexed them.

Meanwhile, they could not help smiling at Sanchica's fancies, and still more when her mother said: "Your reverence, do keep a sharp lookout to see if any of our neighbors are going to Madrid or Toledo. I want them to buy me a farthingale, a round, well-made one of the newest fashion, and the best that is to be had, for as true as I'm telling you, I mean to be a credit to my husband's government as far as I can; and if I get vexed, I'll go myself to that court and flaunt a coach, too, as well as the best of them, for she who has a governor for husband may well afford to have a coach."

"You're right, mother!" said Sanchica. "I wish to Heaven it would be today rather than tomorrow, though folks who saw me perched in our coach beside my lady mother would jeer, saying: 'Take a look at the trollop, the garlic-guzzler's daughter. Look how she's lolling and airing herself in the coach like she was a she-pope.' But, let them jeer away and tread along in the muck, so long as I'm riding in my coach with my feet well above the ground. A bad year and a bad month to all the backbiting bitches in the world! While I go warm, let them laugh till they burst. Am I not right, dear mamma?"

"Of course you are, child!" replied Teresa. "And indeed my good Sancho foretold me all this, and even greater luck; you shall see, daughter, it won't stop till it has made me a countess. In luck it's the beginning that matters, and as I've many a time heard your dear father say (who, as he's yours, so he's the father of proverbs), 'When they give you a heifer make haste with the halter'; when they give you a government, grab it; when they give you an earldom, snatch it;

---

[4] Persons of quality, especially those who were of delicate constitution, used to wear cloth masks or hoods against the cold.

when they whistle for you with a fine fat gift, gobble it up; if not, fall asleep, and when good luck raps at the door, give it the go by."

"What do I care if they say," added Sanchica, "when they see me preening myself and stepping it stately: 'When the mongrel saw himself wearing breeches . . .' and all the rest of it?" [5]

"I'm forced to believe," said the curate, "that the whole race of Panzas were born with their bellies bunged up with proverbs, for I never knew one of them that didn't spurt them out at all hours, no matter what the conversation was about."

"I agree," said the page, "for the governor utters them at every turn, and though many are wide of the mark, they give great joy to the duchess and the duke."

"Do you still mean to assure us," said the bachelor, "that this tale of Sancho's government is true and that there is a duchess who sends these letters and presents? For though we touch the presents and have read the letters, we don't believe it and think that this is one of the adventures of our compatriot Don Quixote, and so a matter of enchantment. Indeed, I've a mind to touch you and feel you to find if you are a man of flesh and bone and not a magic messenger."

"As for myself," replied the page, "I can only say that I am really a messenger, that Don Sancho Panza is actually a governor, and that the duke and the duchess can give and have given him the said government, which, I'm told, he administers in admirable fashion. Whether this is the result of enchantment or not, I leave to you to argue out, but I swear by the lives of my parents, who are living and whom I love dearly, I know nothing else about the matter."

"It may be so," replied the bachelor, "but *dubitat Augustinus.*"

"It doesn't matter who doubts," said the page. "I've told you the truth, and truth will always prevail over falsehood and rise to the top as oil does over water, but if you will not believe me, *operibus credite, et non verbis.* Come with me, one of you, and you'll see with your eyes what you will not believe by your ears."

[5] The full proverb is: "When the mongrel saw himself wearing breeches, he wouldn't recognize his friend" (*Vióse el perro en bragas de cerro, y no conoció a su compañero*). It corresponds to our phrase, "beggars on horseback."

"That's the jaunt for me," said Sanchica. "Come on, sir, take me behind you on your nag, for I've a great longing to see my father."

"The daughters of governors should not travel unattended, but in coaches and litters and with a great train of servants."

"Glory be to God!" said Sanchica. "I could just as well go on an ass as in a coach; I'm a nice one to be namby-pamby and particular."

"Silence, girl," said Teresa, "you know not what you are saying; the gentleman is right, for 'According to reason, each thing in its season.' When it was plain Sancho, it was plain Sancha; but now that he's governor, you are a lady. Aren't I in the right?"

"My lady Teresa says more than she thinks," said the page. "But now give me a bite of dinner and let me go as soon as possible, for I mean to return home this night."

"Well then, sir," said the curate, "do come with me and share a humble meal in my house, for Madam Teresa has more goodwill than good cheer to entertain so worthy a guest."

The page made a gesture of refusal, but at length he felt that it would be best to comply; the curate was very pleased to have his company, for thus he would be able to question him at leisure about Don Quixote and his exploits.

The bachelor offered Teresa to write the answers to her letters, but she would on no account let him meddle in her affairs, for she considered him a bit of a mocker. And so, she gave a roll and a couple of eggs to a young novice who could write, and he wrote two letters for her, one to her husband and the other to the duchess, both dictated by herself and perhaps not the worst in this great history, as we shall see by and by.

CHAPTER LI

Of the progress of Sancho Panza's government, with other matters such as they are

The day dawned after the night of the governor's round. The steward could not sleep a wink, so smitten was he by the face, the charm, and the beauty of the disguised damsel, while the secretary spent what remained of it writing down for his master and mistress all of Sancho's sayings and doings, so amazed was he by the squire's mixture of shrewdness and simplicity.

At length the governor rose, and by order of Doctor Pedro Recio, they served him for breakfast a little preserved fruit and a few glasses of cold water, which Sancho would have willingly exchanged for a piece of bread and a bunch of grapes. But finding that he was compelled to conform and had no choice, he submitted to it, though grieved in his heart and mortified in his stomach, because Pedro Recio convinced him that scanty and delicate fare sharpened the intellect, which was most essential for persons appointed to commands and high positions of authority requiring strength of mind rather than brawn and muscle. By this sophistry Sancho was induced to suffer such pangs of hunger that in his heart he cursed his government and even the giver of it. However, with his hunger and his preserved fruit, he sat in judgment that day, and the first case that came before him was a question submitted by a stranger, in the presence of the steward and the rest of the fraternity. It was as follows:

"Sir, a deep river divides a certain lord's estate into two parts—listen carefully, your worship, for the case is an important one and rather difficult. I must tell you, then, that over this river there was a bridge and at one end a gallows and a sort of courthouse in which there usually sat four judges to administer the law imposed by the owner of the river, the bridge, and the estate. It ran as follows: 'Before anyone crosses this bridge from one side to the other, he must first swear whither and for what he is going. If he shall swear truly, let him pass; if he shall tell a lie, let him die for it, hung on the gallows there put up, without any remission.' With the knowledge of his law and the rigorous conditions imposed, many passed, and as it appeared that they swore truly, the judges let them pass freely. Now it happened that they once put a man on his oath, and he swore that he was going to die on the gallows there—and that was all.

"After due deliberation the judges pronounced as follows: 'If we let this man pass freely, he will have sworn a false oath, and according to the law, he must die; but he swore that he was going to die on the gallows, and if we hang him that will be the truth, so by the same law he should go free.' We ask your worship, governor, what the judges ought to do with this man, for they are still perplexed and undecided. When they heard of your worship's great wisdom and acuteness, they sent me to beg you for your opinion on this intricate and doubtful case."

"Really, these worthy judges who sent you to me might have saved themselves the trouble," replied Sancho, "for I'm dull-witted rather than smart; but all the same, repeat the matter to me once more, so that I may understand it, and maybe I'll hit the nail on the head."

The questioner repeated what he said at first, and Sancho said: "I think I can resolve this business in a jiffy, and it is like this: The man swears that he is going to die on the gallows; and if he does die, his oath was true, and by the law as it stands he deserves to go free and cross the bridge. But if they don't hang him, he swore to a lie and by that same law deserves to be hanged."

"The governor is quite correct," said the messenger, "and as regards his understanding and his interpretation of the case, there is no more question or doubt."

"But let me continue," replied Sancho. "They must let that part of the man that swore truly cross the bridge, and hang the part that swore to a lie, and in that way the conditions of passage will be fulfilled to the letter."

"Then, lord governor," said the questioner, "this man will have to be divided into two parts, the lying part and the truthful part; and if he's divided, he's bound to die. Thus, no part of the law's demands is fulfilled, and it's absolutely necessary for us to comply with it."

"Look here, sir," said Sancho, "either I am a blockhead, or there is just as much reason for this passenger you mention to die as to live and cross the bridge, for if the truth saves him, the lie equally condemns him. And this being so, as it is, I am of the opinion that you should tell all these gentlemen who sent you to me that since the reasons for condemning him and absolving him are in an equal balance, they should let him pass freely, for it's always more praiseworthy to do good than to do wrong. This decision I would give under my own signature, if I knew how to sign; and in this case I have not spoken out of my own head, for there came to my mind a precept, among the many, that my master, Don Quixote, gave me the night before I came to be governor of this island; it was that when justice is in doubt, I should draw back and resort to mercy. And God has seen fit that I should now remember it, and it fits this case like a glove."

"So it does," replied the steward, "and for my part, I'm sure that Lycurgus, who gave laws to the Lacedeamonians, could not give a better decision than that which the great Sancho Panza has given. And so let this morning's session be brought to an end. I shall give orders for the governor to be given a dinner that will more than satisfy him."

"That's all I ask, and fair play," said Sancho. "Once they give me a bite of food, they may shower me with cases and questions, for I'll blow them into smoke in the twinkling of an eye."

The steward kept his word, for his conscience was uneasy at the idea of killing so wise a governor by hunger. Besides, he intended to finish him off that night by playing him the last trick he was commissioned to play.

It happened that the governor dined that day contrary to all the rules and aphorisms of Doctor Tirteafuera, and when the cloths were removed a courier arrived with a letter for him from Don Quixote. Sancho ordered the secretary to read it to himself, and if he discovered nothing in it that should be kept secret, to read it aloud. The secretary obeyed, and after glancing over it, he said: "It may well be read aloud. What Don Quixote writes to your worship deserves to be inscribed and engraved in letters of gold. This is what he says:

LETTER OF DON QUIXOTE OF LA MANCHA TO SANCHO PANZA, GOVERNOR OF BARATARIA ISLAND

"When I expected, friend Sancho, to hear news of your blunders and folly, I have heard tidings of your wise actions, for which I gave special thanks to Heaven, which can raise the poor from the dunghill and turn fools into wise men.[1] They tell me that you govern like a man, yet as a man you might as well be a dumb beast so humbly do you behave. But I wish you would take note, Sancho, that it is often fitting and necessary for the authority of one in office to go counter to his natural humility. For the correct behavior of a person appointed to an office of responsibility must conform to the requisites of that office and not to those suggested by his humble disposition. Dress well, for a stick well adorned does not look like a stick. I do not say that you should wear finery or trinkets, or that being a judge, you should clothe yourself as a soldier, but that you should wear the clothes that your office requires, so long as it is neat and well made.

"To gain the goodwill of the people you govern two things among others you must do: the first is to be civil to everyone (though I have told you this already on one occasion); the other, to provide an abundance of the necessities of life, for nothing so vexes the hearts of the poor than hunger and want.

"Do not make many statutes; but if you do, endeavor to make good ones, and above all, see that they are kept and fulfilled, for statutes not kept might as well not exist. Rather, they show that the prince who had the wisdom and authority to make them had not the courage to have them observed. And laws that intimidate but are not carried out come to be like the log that was king of the frogs. At the beginning he frightened them, but in time they despised him and climbed upon his back.

"Be a father to virtues and a stepfather to vices. Do not always be harsh or always mild; choose the mean between two extremes, for here lies the point of wisdom.

[1] Psalm CXII.

"Visit the prisons, the slaughterhouses, and the markets, for the presence of the governor in such places is of much importance. It comforts the prisoners who expect a speedy liberation; it is a bugbear to butchers, who for a time have to use accurate weights; and it is a terror to the market saleswomen for the same reason.

"Do not appear covetous (even if you are so, which I do not believe) or given to women and gluttony, for if the people and those who deal with you get to know of your prevailing tendency, they will open a barrage of fire on you on that side until they have brought you down to the depths of perdition.

"Consider and reconsider, view and review the counsels and instructions I gave you in writing before you left here for your government and you will discover in them, if you still have them, an additional help to ease you over the troubles and difficulties that governors have to face at every step.

"Write to your lord and lady and show them your gratitude, for ingratitude is the daughter of pride and one of the greatest sins known, and the person who is grateful to his benefactors gives token that he will be so to God also, who has bestowed and continues to bestow so many blessings on him.

"The duchess has dispatched a messenger with your suit and another present to your wife, Teresa Panza. Any moment we expect an answer. I have been a little indisposed from a certain cat-clawing that befell me, somewhat to the detriment of my nose. But it was nothing, for if there are enchanters who victimize, there are also those who defend me. Let me know whether the steward who is with you had anything to do with the business of La Trifaldi as you suspected. Do keep me advised of everything, for the distance is short, particularly as I intend soon to leave this idle life I am living at present, for I was not born for it.

"A certain matter has arisen that I believe will involve me in disgrace with the duke and duchess. But though it concerns me, it does not affect my decision at all, for after all, when it comes to the point, I must comply with my profession rather than with their pleasure, for as the saying goes, *Amicus Plato, sed magis amica veritas.* I say this in Latin, for I suppose that since you have become a governor you have learned it.

"So farewell, and God keep you from all harm.

Your friend,
Don Quixote of La Mancha."

Sancho listened very attentively to the letter, which was praised for its good sense by all who heard it. He then rose from the table, and calling the secretary, he shut himself up with him in his chamber, wishing at once, without more delay, to reply to his master, Don Quixote. He told the secretary to write what he dictated, without adding or omitting a word, which he did, and the answer was as follows:

SANCHO PANZA'S LETTER TO DON QUIXOTE OF LA MANCHA

The pressure of my business is so great that I have no time to scratch my head, or even to cut my nails, and so I wear them long, God help me. This I say, beloved master, that your worship may not be surprised if I have given you no account till now of my good or evil fortune in this government, in which I suffer from worse hunger than when we two were gallivanting in the woods and wilds.

My lord the duke wrote to me the other day, giving me notice that certain spies had come into this island to kill me. But so far the only one I have discovered is a certain doctor in this town who gets a salary for killing all the governors who come here. His name is Doctor Pedro Recio, and he is a native of Tirteafuera. From that name your worship can judge whether or not I have reason to fear dying at his hands. This same doctor boasts that he does not cure existing maladies but that he prevents them from coming. The medicines he uses are diet and still more diet, till he has reduced his patient to skin and bone, as if leanness were not a worse sickness than fever. In short, he is killing me of hunger, and I am dying of vexation, and instead of coming to this government, as I thought, to get hot food and cool drinks and to refresh my body between holland sheets and upon feather pillows, I have come to do penance like a hermit, and as I am not doing it willingly, I am afraid that the Devil will get me in the end.

Up to now I have not touched a fee or taken a bribe,

and I cannot imagine when this is to end, for they have told me here that the governors who usually visit this isle take a great deal of money either in gifts or in loans from the people of the town before entering, and that this is the ordinary custom among newly created governors, and not only here.

Going the rounds the other night, I came across a most lovely damsel in men's clothes and a brother of hers dressed as a woman. My steward fell in love with the girl and has a mind to make her his wife, so he says, and I have chosen the boy for my son-in-law. Today the pair of us are going to make our intentions known to the father of them both, who is one Diego de la Llana, a gentleman and as old a Christian as you could wish.

I visit the markets as your worship counsels me, and yesterday I found a saleswoman who was selling fresh hazelnuts, and I discovered that she had mixed with one bushel of fresh nuts another of old, worthless, and rotten ones. I impounded them all for the charity boys, who will know how to pick the good from the bad, and I sentenced her not to enter the market for a fortnight. They have told me that I did well, and what I can say to your worship is that the general report in this town is that there are no worse people than the saleswomen. They are all shameless, godless, brazen hussies all of them, and I can believe it from what I have seen in other towns.

I am mighty glad that my lady the duchess has written to my wife, Teresa Panza, and sent her the present your worship speaks of, and will try to show myself grateful at the proper time. Kiss her hands for me and tell her that I say that she has not thrown it into a torn sack, as will be seen in due course. I would not like your worship to have any unpleasant tiffs with my lord and lady, sir, for if you quarrel with them, I shall certainly suffer for it; and it would not be right, since you advise me to be grateful, not to be so yourself after all the favors they have done you and the hospitality they have given you in their castle.

I cannot make out that cat-clawing business, but I imagine it must be one of those tricks the wicked enchanters are always playing on your worship. I shall learn about it when we see one another.

I would like to send your worship something, but I don't know what to send, unless it is some enema tubes to be used with bladders—strange objects that they manufacture in this island. But if my office lasts, I will find something to send you, by hook or by crook.

If my wife, Teresa Panza, should write to me, pay the carriage and send me the letter, for I have a great longing to hear how things are with my house, my wife, and my children.

And so, may God deliver your worship from ill-intentioned enchanters and bring me safe and sound out of this government, which I doubt, for from the way Doctor Pedro Recio is treating me I do not expect to leave with more than my life.

> Your worship's servant,
> Sancho Panza, the Governor.

The secretary sealed the letter and dispatched the courier at once. Those who were playing the joke on Sancho met and planned among themselves how to make an end of his government. That evening Sancho spent in drawing up some ordinances concerning the good government of what he fancied was an island. He decreed that there should be no regraters of provisions in the state and that wine could be imported from anywhere they pleased, on condition that they declared the place from which it came, in order to fix the price according to its value, goodness, and reputation, and that he who watered it or changed the name should lose his life for it. He lowered the price of all footwear, especially of shoes, the current prices of which he deemed exorbitant. He fixed the rate of servants' wages, which were increasing unchecked at a headlong pace. He imposed the heaviest penalties on those who sang loud and disorderly songs, whether by night or by day. He decreed that no blind man should sing of miracles in ballads unless he could bring authentic evidence of their being true, because most of their tales were, in his opinion, fictitious and brought discredit upon the genuine ones. He created and appointed a constable for the poor—not to persecute them, but to examine whether they were in good faith, for under the disguise of feigned poverty and counterfeit sores go sturdy thieves and hale and hearty drunkards. In short, so good were the laws he ordained that they are preserved in that place to this day under the name of "The Constitutions of the Great Governor Sancho Panza."

CHAPTER LII

In which is recorded the adventure of the second Doleful or Distressed Duenna, otherwise called Doña Rodríguez

Cide Hamete relates that Don Quixote, being already cured of his scratches, decided that the life he led in that castle was the complete negation of all the rules of knighthood, which he professed, so he resolved to beg the duke and duchess' leave to depart for Saragossa, as the date drew near of the festival at which he hoped to win the armor that is offered as the prize for jousting. As he was one day at table with his hosts and on the point of carrying out his intention and asking for leave, suddenly there entered through the door of the great hall two women, as they later proved to be, clad in mourning from head to foot. One of them ran up to Don Quixote and threw herself prostrate on the ground, pressing her lips to his feet and uttering such sad and melancholy groans that all who saw and heard her were in consternation. Even the duke and duchess, though they had a strong suspicion that this was some new trick that their servants had devised for Don Quixote, were perplexed at the heartfelt sincerity of the lady's grief. Don Quixote, moved to compassion, raised her from the floor and made her take her veil from her tearful face. She did so, and to their utter amazement the face disclosed was that of Doña Rodríguez, the duenna of the house, and the other in mourning was her daughter, who had been deceived by the son of the rich farmer. All those who knew her were astonished, and the duke and duchess most of all, for they considered her a bit of a ninny and too timid to play such crazy pranks.

Doña Rodríguez, at last, turned toward her master and mistress and said: "I beseech your excellencies to be so good as to allow me to retire a moment with this knight, for this I must do if I am to extricate myself from a situation into which I have been brought by the impudence of an out-and-out rascal."

The duke said that she might retire with Don Quixote for as long as she pleased, and she then turned to the knight saying: "Some days ago, valiant knight, I told you how treacherously and cruelly a wicked farmer had used my dearly beloved daughter, who is the unfortunate lady here before you, and you promised me to champion her cause and redress the injury she has suffered. But now I am informed that you wish to depart from the castle in quest of good ventures—may God send them your way! And so, I want you, before you steal away into the highways, to challenge this stubborn rustic and compel him to marry my daughter, in fulfillment of his promise of marriage to the girl before he lay with her. To expect that the duke, my master, will do me justice is to ask for pears off an elm tree for the reason which I have told your worship privately. And so may Our Lord grant you good health and not leave us defenseless."

Don Quixote with much gravity and solemnity replied to the duenna's pleas: "Good duenna, moderate your tears, or rather dry them, and be sparing of your sighs. I shall undertake the charge of redressing your daughter's wrong, though it would have been wiser of her not to have put such easy trust in a lover's promises, for most of them are quick to promise but mighty slow to perform. Therefore, by leave of the duke, I shall set out immediately in search of this profligate young man; I will find him, challenge him, and slay him, should he refuse to fulfill his plighted word, for the chief business of my order is to spare the humble and chastise the proud; I mean, to succor the wretched and destroy their oppressors."

"There is no need," replied the duke, "for your worship to take any trouble in looking for the rustic of whom this worthy lady complains, and you need not ask my leave to challenge him, for I consider him already duly challenged, and I engage to inform him of this challenge and to make him accept it and come to answer for himself to this castle of mine, where I will provide you both with a fine field, observing all the conditions that in such affairs are customary and securing justice equally to each, as all princes are obliged to do who offer free field to those who do battle within the boundaries of their domains."

"With that assurance and with your highness' good leave," replied Don Quixote, "I declare that I hereby for this occasion waive my rank as gentleman, and lower and level myself to the lowliness of the offender, and make myself equal with him, thus qualifying him for the right of combat with me. Thus, though absent, I defy and challenge him because he did wrong in defrauding this poor girl, who was a maiden and now through his fault is one no longer, and he shall fulfill the promise he gave to be her lawful husband, or he shall die in the ordeal."

Then, taking off a glove, he flung it into the middle of the hall, and the duke picked it up, repeating what he had already said, that he accepted the challenge in his vassal's name, and fixing the date at six days hence, and the place in the castle courtyard, and the arms those customary among knights—lance and shield and coat of mail with all the accouterments of armor, without deceit, trickery, or any talisman or amulet, inspected and examined by the judges of the test. "But," said the duke, "first of all this good duenna and this bad maiden must place the justice of their cause in the hands of Don Quixote, for in no other way can anything be done or this same challenge be put into effect."

"Yes, I do place it there," replied the duenna.

"And I, too," added the daughter, all tearful, ashamed, and most grudgingly.

When these formalities had been settled and the duke had thought out what he intended to do in this case, the two mourners went away. The duchess gave orders that they were henceforth to be treated not as her servants, but as lady adventurers who had come to the castle to demand justice. So, they were given a room to themselves and were waited on as strangers, to the amazement of the other servants, who could not fathom where the folly and effrontery of Doña Rodríguez and her unfortunate daughter would end.

At this point, as a climax to the feast and a fitting conclusion to the dinner, who should enter the hall but the page who had taken the letters and presents to Teresa Panza, the wife of the governor Sancho Panza. His arrival delighted the duke and the duchess, who were eager to hear news of

his journey. The page replied to their questions that he could
not answer publicly or in a few words, and he begged their
excellencies to wait until they were alone. In the meantime
they might find amusement in the letters, two of which he
brought out and handed to the duchess. One bore the heading: "Letter for my lady the duchess of I do not know
where," and the other: "To my husband, Sancho Panza,
Governor of the Island of Barataria, whom may God prosper
more years than me."

The duchess' cake, as the saying goes, would not bake until
she had read her letter. So she eagerly opened it, and after
hastily running her eye over it, finding nothing secret in it,
she read it aloud to the duke and the bystanders:

TERESA PANZA'S LETTER TO THE DUCHESS

"My Lady,
    The letter your grace wrote me made me right glad, for
I mightily longed for it. The string of corals is very fine,
and the hunting suit of my husband doesn't fall short of
it. All our village is very pleased that your honor has made
my husband a governor, though not a soul will believe it,
especially the curate and Master Nicholas, the barber, and
Sansón Carrasco, the bachelor. But I don't care, for so
long as the thing is true, as it is, let each one say what
he wills; though, to tell the truth, if I had not seen the
corals and the suit, I would not have believed it, for the
folks in this village take my husband for a dolt, and they
can't for the life of them imagine what kind of government he's fit for, unless it's over a herd of goats. Well, God
help him and guide him in the way He thinks best for His
children. As for me, dear lady, I am resolved, with your
kind permission, to make hay while the sun shines, and
go to court, taking my ease in a coach and making my
friends, who are envious enough already, stare their eyes
out when they see me riding by. And therefore, I pray
your excellency to bid my husband send me a tidy sum of
money, and let it be sufficient, for I'm sure living at court
is expensive; bread there costs a real, and a pound of
meat thirty maravedis, which is as bad as the day of
judgment. If he doesn't want me to go, let him warn me
in time, for my feet are itching to be on the road; and,
besides, my friends and neighbors keep telling me that if

I and my daughter strut about the court stately and stylishly, my husband will be better known by me than I by him; for men would be bound to ask: 'What ladies are those in that coach?' And my footman will reply: 'It's the wife and daughter of Sancho Panza, governor of the island of Barataria.' Thus will my husband be known, and I made much of, for 'All's to be found at Rome.'

"I am as sorry as sorry can be that around here there has been no gathering of acorns this year; however, I'm sending your highness about half a peck that I picked one by one with my own hands, and they were the biggest I could find—I wish they were as big as ostrich eggs.

"Pray let your pomposity not forget to write to me, and I'll be sure to send you an answer, and let you know how I am in health, and give you the news of our village, where I'm waiting and praying the Lord to preserve your excellency and not to forget me. My daughter, Sanchica, and my son kiss your ladyship's hands.

"She who wishes rather to see you than to write to you,
Your servant,
Teresa Panza."

This letter amused all the company, especially the duke and duchess, and the latter then asked Don Quixote whether it would be right to open the governor's letter, for she was sure it must be a very good one. The knight told her that he would open it to satisfy her curiosity. Accordingly he did so, and found that it was as follows:

TERESA PANZA'S LETTER TO HER HUSBAND, SANCHO PANZA

"Dearest Husband,

"I received thy letter, Sancho of my soul, and I vow and swear to thee, as I am a Catholic Christian, that I was within two fingers' breadth of going stark raving mad for joy. Look here, my darling, when I heard that thou wert made a governor, I thought I'd fall down dead with the gladness, for thou knowest how they say that sudden joy will kill as soon as great sorrow. As for thy daughter, Sanchica, she wet herself unbeknown to herself for sheer pleasure. There before my eyes was the suit thou didst send me, and the corals my lady the duchess sent was around my neck, and the letters in my hands, and the young fellow who brought them standing by my side. Yet, for all that, I thought that what I was seeing and feeling was only a dream, for who could have thought that a goatherd would come to be a governor of islands? My mother used to say: 'He who would see much must live long.' I say this because, if I live longer, I hope to see more. I'll never rest content till I see thee a tax collector or a collector of customs, for though they be offices that send those who use them badly to the Devil, they always have plenty of money. My lady the duchess will tell thee the longing I have to go to court. Think it over and let me know thy mind, for I want to bring credit on thee by riding in a coach.

"Neither the curate, the barber, the bachelor, nor even the sacristan will believe that thou art a governor, and they say that it's all humbug or enchantment like all the affairs of thy master, Don Quixote; and Sansón says that he will go and find thee out, and drive this government out of thy noddle, and Don Quixote's madness out of his brainpan. But I only laugh at them, and look at my string of coral beads, and think of how to make thy suit of green into a gown for thy daughter. I sent my lady the duchess some acorns, but I wish they were of gold. Do send me some strings of pearls, if they are worn in thy island.

"The news from our village is that La Berrueca has married her daughter to a poor kind of a painter who came here offering to paint the King's Arms over the town hall; he asked them two ducats for the job, which they paid in advance; so he fell to work and spent eight days daubing away, but at the end of that time he made nothing of it, and he said that he couldn't paint such trumpery; he handed back the money, and in spite of all this, he married with the name of a good workman. The truth is, he has left his paintbrushes and taken up the spade, and he goes to the field like a gentleman. Pedro de Lobo's son has taken orders and shaven his crown, meaning to be a priest. Minguilla, Mingo Silvato's granddaughter, heard of it, and she is suing him for breach of promise of marriage. Bad tongues try to hint that he has put her in the family way, but he swears by all that's holy he had nothing to do with it. We have no olives this year, and there's not a drop of vinegar to be found in the village. A company of soldiers passed through here and carried along with them three wenches out of the village; I don't tell your their names, for perhaps they'll come back, and there are sure to be fellows who will marry them, for better or for worse. Sanchica is making bone lace; she gets eight maravedis a day clear, which she drops into a money box to help her buy household stuff, but now that she's a governor's daughter, you must give her a dowry so that she need not work. The fountain in the marketplace is dried-up; a thunderbolt fell upon the gibbet, and there may the lot of them end. I expect an answer to this, and thy decision as to whether I'm to go to court or not. God grant thee more years than myself, or as many, for I wouldn't like to leave thee behind me.

Thy Wife,
Teresa Panza."

The letters caused much applause, merriment, and admiration; as a finishing touch, the courier returned, bringing Sancho's answer to Don Quixote. This was publicly read, and made all who had thought the governor a fool reconsider their opinion.

The duchess retired to hear from the page the account of his journey to Sancho's village, which he gave her in detail, without omitting a single circumstance. He also brought her the acorns and a cheese that Teresa had given him. Now let us leave the duchess and the page to record the end of the government of the great Sancho Panza, the flower and mirror of all island governors.

CHAPTER LIII

Of the violent end of Sancho Panza's government

"To think that the affairs of this life will always remain in
the same state is a vain presumption; indeed they all seem to
be perpetually changing and moving in a circular course.
Spring is followed by summer, summer by autumn, and
autumn by winter, which is again followed by spring, and
so time continues its everlasting round. But the life of man
is ever racing to its end, swifter than time itself, without hope
of renewal, unless in the next, which is limitless and infinite."
So says Cide Hamete, the Mohammedan philosopher, for
many by natural instinct, without the light of faith, have
understood the swiftness and instability of this present life,
and the duration of the eternity to come. In this context,
however, our author alludes only to the instability of Sancho's
fortune and the brief duration of his government, which so
suddenly ended, ceased, dissolved, and vanished like smoke
into the air.

It was the seventh night of our governor's administration,
and he was in bed, fed up not with bread and wine, but with
judging cases, giving opinions, and making statutes and proclamations. Just at the moment when sleep, in spite of the
pangs of hunger, was beginning to close his eyes, all of a
sudden he heard such a din of bells and shouting that he
really thought the island was sinking. He sat up in bed, listening intently to try and find out, if possible, the cause of
such an uproar. But far from discovering it, a great number
of drums and trumpets added their beating and blaring to the
former noise, and such a dreadful alarm ensued that he began
to quake with fear. Up he leaped from his bed and put on his

slippers, on account of the damp floor, and without a stitch on him but his shirt, he ran and opened the door of his chamber. He saw about twenty men running along the galleries with lighted torches in their hands and their swords drawn, all shouting: "To arms, governor, to arms! A host of enemies has got into the island, and we are lost unless your courage can save us." Bawling at the tops of their voices and brandishing their swords, they rushed up to where Sancho stood scared and stupefied by what he saw and heard.

"Arm this instant, my lord," cried one of them, "otherwise you'll be destroyed and the whole island with you."

"What's the good of my arming?" replied Sancho. "Do I know a thing about arms or relief tactics? Why don't you send for Don Quixote, my master? He'll deal with them in the twinkling of an eye and retrieve our fortunes. Alas, as I'm a sinner, I know nothing about these sudden attacks!"

"How so, my lord," said another, "what's the meaning of this faintheartedness? See, here we bring you defensive and offensive arms; arm yourself and come with us to the marketplace. Be our leader and our captain, for that is your duty, since you are our governor."

"Well, then, arm me and wish me good luck," said Sancho. Instantly they brought him two big shields, which they had provided for the occasion. Without letting him put on his other clothes, they clapped the shields over his shirt; one they tied on in front, the other behind. They pushed his arms through holes they had made in the shields, and fastened them so tightly together with cords that the poor governor remained cased and walled up as stiff and straight as a spindle, without being able to bend his knees or stir a single step. They put a lance in his hands, with which he propped himself up as best he could, and they urged him to march and lead them on and put spirit into the whole people, for, they added, there would be no doubt of victory since he was their polestar, their lantern, and their morning star.

"How can I march," said the governor, "when I can't stir my knee joints with these planks digging so hellishly deep into my flesh? What you should do is to carry me in your arms and place me, slantwise or standing up, at some gate, which I'll defend with this spear or with my body."

"Come, come, my lord," said another, "it's fear rather than shields that hinders your marching. Hurry and get a move on;

it is high time, the enemy grows stronger, and danger threatens."

The poor governor, urged and upbraided, tried to totter forward, but down he fell with such a bump that he thought he had broken every bone in his body. There he lay like a huge tortoise in its shell, or like a flitch of bacon sandwiched between two boards, or like a boat keeled over on the shore. But those jesting fellows, though they saw him lying prone, did not show him the least compassion; on the contrary, having put out their torches, they renewed their shouting and alarms, and clattered their arms unceasingly, and trampled upon the unfortunate Sancho, and slashed away at the shields so continuously that if he had not ducked his head between the bucklers, it would have gone hard with him. Indeed, the poor governor, huddled up in his narrow shell, sweated with terror and prayed with all his heart and soul to God for deliverance from such a horrible danger. Some butted into him, others fell on top of him, and one among them leaped upon his body and stood there for a long time, as if he were on a watchtower giving orders to the troops. "This way, my men," he bawled in a stentorian voice, "this way the enemy is charging thickest; guard that gate over there; close that other gate; knock down those scaling ladders; bring grenades, burning pitch, resin, and kettles of boiling oil; barricade the streets with mattresses!" In short, he called for all the instruments of death and all the gear used in the defense of a city besieged.

Sancho, bruised and battered, listening to all that was taking place, kept saying to himself: "If only the blessed Lord would be pleased to allow this island to be captured, and if I could only see myself either dead or delivered from this anguish!"

Heaven heard his prayers, and when he least expected it, he heard the shouts: "Victory, victory! The enemy is vanquished. Rise, governor, and make ready to enjoy the conquest and to divide the spoils your invincible army has snatched from the enemy."

"Lift me up," said Sancho in a plaintive tone, and when they had set him on his legs, he said: "As to all the enemies I may have killed, let them be nailed to my forehead. I want no dividing of spoils, but I beg and entreat some friend, if I have any, to give me a sup of wine, for I'm choking with the drought, and to help me dry up the sweat that's pouring off me, for I'm turning to water."

They wiped him, gave him wine, and untied the shields. Then, when he sat down on the bed, what with his fright, his agony, and his suffering, he fainted away, and those responsible for the scene began to repent that they had carried the joke so far. However, their anxiety passed away when they saw Sancho recover after a short time. He asked them what time it was, and they told him it was daybreak. He said no more, but began to put on his clothes in silence, while the rest looked on, wondering why he was in such haste to dress.

At length, having put on his clothes and creeping along, a step at a time, because he was too much bruised to hurry, he wended his way to the stable, followed by all the company. Then, going up to Dapple, he embraced him and gave him a kiss of peace on his forehead. "Come hither," said he with tears in his eyes, "my friend and partner of my toils and troubles; when you and I consorted together and had no other care in the world but mending your harness and feeding that little carcass of yours, happy were my hours, my days, and my years; but since I forsook you and mounted the towers of ambition and pride, a thousand woes, a thousand torments, and four thousand tribulations have entered my soul."

While he was speaking, he set about saddling the ass, without anyone interrupting him. When this was done, he mounted with great difficulty, and then addressing the steward, the secretary, the butler, Pedro Recio, and many other bystanders, he said: "Make way, gentlemen, and let me return to my former liberty. Let me go in search of the life I left, and rise again from this present death. I was not born to be a governor, or to defend islands or cities from enemies who wish to attack them. I know more about plowing, digging, pruning, and planting vines than about making laws or defending cities and kingdoms. 'St. Peter is all right at Rome,' I mean to say that a man does best the job for which he was born. In my hand a sickle is better than a governor's scepter; and I'd rather stuff my belly with *gazpacho* [1] than submit to an impertinent doctor who starves me to death. I'd rather

---

[1] *Gazpacho* is an Andalusian dish, a cold soup made of biscuit, oil, onions, vinegar, and garlic.

rest under a shady oak in the summer and wrap myself up in a rough sheepskin in winter, at my own sweet will, than lie down, with the slavery of a government, in holland sheets and dress myself up in richest sables. God be with you, gentlemen, and tell my lord the duke that naked was I born, and naked I am now; I neither lose nor win, for without a penny I came to this government, and without a penny I leave it, quite the opposite to what governors of other islands are wont to do when they leave them. Let me go, gentlemen; I must plaster myself, for I don't believe I have a single rib unbroken, thanks to the enemies who have trodden on me all night long."

"This must not be so, my lord," said Dr. Recio. "I'll give your worship a potion against falls and bruises, which will give you back your former vigor. As to your diet, I promise your honor to turn over a new leaf and let you eat whatever you please."

"You've chirped too late," replied Sancho. "I'd as soon turn Turk as not go. No, no! 'Once bitten twice shy,' as far as this is concerned. By God, you might as soon make me fly up to Heaven without wings as get me to take this or any other government, even though it were served in a covered dish. I'm of the stock of the Panzas, and every man of us is stubborn as a mule. Once we cry 'Odd,' odd it's got to be, against the whole world, even though it be even. I'll leave behind in this stable the ant wings that made me soar through the air only to be eaten by martlets and other birds; I'll walk again on firm ground, for he who doesn't look good in cordovan pumps can still wear rope sandals. No, let every sheep to her mate; never stretch your feet beyond the sheet; so, let me be on my way, for it's getting late."

"My Lord Governor," said the steward, "we would not presume to hinder your departure, although we are sorry to lose you because of your wise and Christian conduct, but your worship knows that every governor, before he leaves his government, is required to render an account of his administration. Render to us an account of your ten days as governor and depart with God's blessing."

"No man can require that of me," replied Sancho, "save my lord the duke. To him I go, and to him I'll give a fair and square account, and since I depart as bare as I do, there's no further token needed to show that I've governed like an angel."

"By God, the great Sancho is right," said Dr. Recio. "I think that we should let him leave, for the duke will be most pleased to see him."

And so they all agreed to let him go, and they offered to supply him with whatever he might need on his journey. Sancho told them that all he required was a little barley for Dapple and half a cheese and half a loaf for himself, for in such a short journey nothing more would be necessary. Then they all embraced him, and he with tears in his eyes embraced them and departed, leaving them in admiration both of his good sense and of his unshakable determination.

CHAPTER LIV

Which deals with matters relating to this history and not to any other

The duke and duchess resolved that Don Quixote's challenge to their vassal for the cause already mentioned should go forward, and as the youth was in Flanders, where he had fled rather than have Doña Rodríguez for his mother-in-law, they arranged to put in his stead a Gascon lackey called Tosilos, first instructing him very carefully in all he had to do. Two days afterward the duke told Don Quixote that his opponent would come in four days and present himself in the field, armed as a knight, and maintain that the damsel had lied by half a beard—even by a whole beard—if she affirmed that he had given her a promise of marriage. Don Quixote received the news with great satisfaction, promising himself to do wonders on the occasion and considering it most fortunate that he would have an opportunity of displaying the power of his mighty arm before the duke and duchess. Therefore, with much content and complacency he waited for the four days, which seemed like four centuries, so eager was he to enter the fray.

Let us, however, leave them for the present, as we leave other things, and go to bear Sancho company, whose feelings were a mixture of gladness and sadness. He rode along on Dapple in the direction of his master, whose company pleased him more than being governor of all the islands in the world.

He had not gone far from his island, city, or town (for he had never troubled himself to find out what it was) when he saw six pilgrims plodding along the road with their staves, foreigners as they turned out to be, of the class that beg for alms in song. As they approached they lined up and began their song in the language of their country, but all that Sancho could understand was one word that clearly signified alms, whence he guessed that begging was the burden of their chant. Being extremely charitable, according to Cide Hamete, he took out of his saddlebags the half loaf and half cheese and gave it to them, making signs that he had nothing else to give. They received his gift eagerly, saying: *"Guelte, guelte."* [1]

"I don't understand you," replied Sancho. "What do you want, good folks?"

One of them pulled out of his bosom a purse and showed it to Sancho, making him understand that it was money they wanted. Sancho, putting his thumb to his throat and shaking his hand with his four fingers upward, made a sign that he had not a penny in the world. Then, clapping heels to Dapple, he broke through them, but as he passed, one of them, who had been gazing at him most earnestly, caught hold of him, and throwing his arms around his waist, cried out loud in excellent Spanish: "God save us! What do I see? Is it possible that I'm holding in my very arms my dear friend and worthy neighbor Sancho Panza? I'm sure it is, for I'm neither drunk nor dreaming."

Sancho, who was astonished to hear his name called and to be embraced by the pilgrim stranger, stared at him without speaking, but stare as he would, he could not remember him.

---

[1] German *geld*. Cervantes spells it *guelte* or *güellte*.

"Is it possible, brother Sancho Panza, that you don't recall your neighbor Ricote, the Morisco shopkeeper of your village."

Then Sancho, after giving him another close look, began to call him to mind; at last, he remembered him perfectly, and without dismounting, he hugged him around the neck, saying: "Ricote, who the devil could recognize you in this costume? Tell me now, who has frenchified you in this way? How is it you dare to come back to Spain? Why, if they find you out, you'll be in for a bad time."

"If you don't give me away, Sancho," replied the pilgrim, "I'm safe enough, for not a soul would know me in this getup. Now let us retire to that wood yonder, where my companions mean to dine and have a nap, and you'll dine with us. They are decent, peaceable folk, I assure you, and I'll have an opportunity to tell you how I spent my time since I was forced to leave our town in obedience to the king's edict, which, as you know, so severely threatens the people of my unfortunate nation." [2]

Sancho accepted the invitation, and after Ricote had spoken to the rest of the pilgrims, they all turned into the poplar wood, which was a good distance from the main road. Then they threw aside their staves, took off their pilgrims' habits, and remained naked. They were all good-looking youths, with the exception of Ricote, who was well on in years. Each had his own wallet, which, as it soon appeared, was well furnished, at least with peppery and spicy victuals such as would raise a raging thirst two leagues away. They stretched themselves on the ground, and using the green grass as their tablecloth, they spread out on it bread, salt, knives, nuts, cheese, and some ham bones, which, though they had precious little to pick on them, could at least be sucked with relish. They also brought out a kind of black delicacy that is called caviar, made of the roes of a fish, still better to tempt a man to pluck the leather. Even olives were not missing, and though a bit dry and unseasoned, they were most tasty. But the champion of the whole feast was six bottles of wine, for each pilgrim possessed one as his share; even honest Ricote, who from a Morisco had become a German or

---

[2] Between 1609 and 1613 proclamations were made ordering the expulsion from Spain of the Moriscos, who, though outwardly converted, secretly practiced their religion.

a Hollander, grabbed his bottle, which in size was a match for the other five. They began their banquet in good humor and at a leisurely pace, for they dwelt upon each morsel with the utmost relish, spiking but a snippet of each dainty at a time on the end of their knife in order to make the most of it. Then after a pause, with one accord they all raised their arms and wineskins aloft into the air, and joining their mouths to the mouths of the bottles, with their eyes fixed upward as if taking aim at the heavens, they remained in this posture a good while, letting the heart's blood of the vessels gurgle into their bellies as they wagged their heads from side to side in token of their rapturous ecstasy.

Sancho beheld all this, and not a complaint did he utter; on the contrary, wishing to comply with the good old proverb, "When in Rome do as the Romans do," he asked Ricote for his bottle, and taking his aim as the rest had done, he showed no less satisfaction. Four times the wineskins were tilted upward with good effect, but the fifth was to no purpose, for the skins by then were flabby and as dry as a rush, a circumstance that somewhat damped their rollicking spirits. From time to time one of the pilgrims would take Sancho by the right hand, saying: "Spanish and German here all one: goot companion." Sancho would echo in response: "Goot companion, I swear to God," then he would burst into a fit of laughter lasting almost an hour. And from that moment all memories of his past misfortunes faded away, for anxieties have little power over men during the time that is spent in eating and drinking. In short, no sooner was the wine finished than a deep sleep seized them, and they lay snoring beside the leftovers of their feast, all except Sancho and Ricote, who had indeed eaten more but drunk less. So, the two friends, leaving the pilgrims buried in their sweet sleep, went a short distance away and sat down in the shade of a beech tree, and Ricote, without once stumbling into his Morisco jargon, spoke in pure Castilian as follows:

"You are well aware, Sancho Panza, my friend, how terrified all of our race were when the edict of His Majesty was proclaimed. It certainly produced such fear and dread upon me that I almost imagined that the law had already been executed upon me and my children before the time limit for our departure had expired. In my opinion I acted like a prudent man, the way that he who knows that by a set date his house is going to be taken away would have acted. Accord-

ingly I left our village by myself and went to seek some place
beforehand, where I might conveniently convey my family
without the hurry and confusion that prevailed when the rest
set out, for I knew, and so did the elders of my race, that
the edicts were no mere threats, as some said, but genuine
laws that would be put into force within a determined time.
I was all the more inclined to believe this, being aware that
our people were continually plotting against the State, and I
could not but think that His Majesty was inspired by Heaven
to take so gallant a resolution. It is true that we were not all
guilty; some of us were sturdy and steadfast Christians, but
we were so few in number that we were no match for those
who were otherwise, and it was not safe for Spain to nurse
the serpent in its bosom. And so the banishment was just
and necessary, a punishment that some might consider a
mild and pleasant fate, but to us it seems the most disastrous
calamity that could befall us. Wherever in the world we are,
we weep for Spain, for, after all, there we were born, and it
is our fatherland. Nowhere can we find the compassion that
our misfortunes crave; in Barbary and other parts of Africa,
where we expected to be welcomed and cherished, it is there
that they treat us with the grossest inhumanity. We did not
know our happiness until we had lost it. The longing that
most of us have to return to Spain is such that the majority
of those who speak the language as I do, who are many, come
back hither, leaving their wives and children over there in
penury; so strong is their love for their native land! Now I
know by experience the truth of the saying, 'Sweet is the love
of one's own fatherland.'

"When I left our village, I went to France, and though I
was well treated there, I wished to roam the world. From
France, therefore, I passed into Italy, and thence into Germany, where I thought one might live in greater freedom, for
the inhabitants are not overparticular, and as there is liberty
of conscience, everyone lives his own way. There I took a
house in a village near Augsburg and joined these pilgrims,
who are accustomed to come to Spain in great numbers every
year to visit its sanctuaries, which they regard as their Indies
and their surest and most profitable source of income. They
roam over the whole country, and there is not a village where
they are not certain to get food and drink in plenty, and at
least a real in money. As a rule, they manage by the end
of the journey to clear more than a hundred crowns, which

they change into gold and hide either in the hollow of their staves, or between the patches of their cloaks, or in some secret way. And thus they carry them off safely to their country, in spite of the numerous inspectors and other officers who search them before they leave.

"Now, Sancho, my real object in coming here is not to collect alms but to carry off the treasure that I left buried when I went away. As it lies in a place outside the village, I'll be able to fetch it without danger to myself. As soon as that is done, I intend to write or cross myself from Valencia to my wife and daughter, who are, I know, in Algiers. I'll find some means to get them over to a port in France, and thence carry them into Germany, where we will wait and see what God has in store for us. Francisca, my wife, I know is a good Catholic Christian, and my daughter, Ricota, also. Though I myself am not so far on as they are, yet I am more of a Christian than a Mohammedan, and I pray constantly to almighty God to open the eyes of my understanding and make me know how I can best serve Him. I am, however, surprised that my wife and daughter should have preferred to go to Barbary rather than to France, where they might have lived as Christians."

"Listen, Ricote," said Sancho, "that must not have been their choice, for Juan Tiopieyo, your wife's brother, carried them off, and as he's a cunning Moor, he went where there was most money to be got. And I'll add one thing more, namely, that you may be wasting your time looking for your hidden treasure, for I heard it said that many pearls and gold coins had been seized from your brother-in-law and your wife by the inspectors."

"That may be," replied Ricote, "but I know, Sancho, that they did not touch my hidden nest egg, for I never told them where I hid it, for fear of some accident. Now, if you'll come along with me and help me to rescue this money, I'll give you two hundred crowns to help you meet your obligations, for I now you've got many."

"I'd do it," answered Sancho, "but I'm not at all covetous. If I had been so, would I have left this morning an employment that might have given me enough to build the walls of my house with beaten gold, and before six months were over you'd find me eating off silver plates? For this reason and because, to my way of thinking, it would be treason to the king if I were to help his enemies, I won't go with you, even if you were to offer me twice as much cash down."

"Now tell me," said Ricote, "what kind of job have you left?"

"I've left off being governor of an island, such an island as I swear you wouldn't find if you were to search the world."

"Where is it?" asked Ricote.

"Two leagues from here," replied Sancho, "and it's called the island of Barataria."

"Hush, Sancho," said Ricote; "islands lie out in the sea; there are none of them on the mainland."

"Why not?" replied Sancho. "I tell you, Ricote, my friend, that I came from there this morning. And yesterday there I was governing it at my own sweet will, proud and haughty as a highwayman on his last ride. Yet, for all that, I turned it down, because I think that a governor's job is mighty dangerous."

"What did you get from your governorship?" asked Ricote.

"I got," answered Sancho, "experience enough to know that I'm no hand at governing anything but a herd of cattle, and that the wealth a fellow earns by such governorships has got to be paid in hard labor, loss of sleep, and in hunger, too, for governors of islands must eat next to nothing, especially if they have physicians to look after their health."

"I can make neither head nor tail of this," said Ricote; "in fact, it all seems nonsense to me, for who in Heaven's name would give you islands to govern? Were they so badly off for brainy men that they had to choose you? Hold your tongue, Sancho, and come back to earth, and consider whether you'll come with me and help me carry off my hidden treasure. Indeed, I may well call it treasure, seeing there's so much of it, and I'll give you a tidy sum to live on, as I said before."

"I told you, Ricote," replied Sancho, "that I'm not willing. But set your mind at ease, rest, for I'll not give you away. Now go your way, and let me go mine, for I know only too well that 'Well-got wealth may meet disaster, but ill-got wealth destroys its master.'"

"Sancho, my friend, I won't press you any longer," said Ricote. "But tell me now, were you by chance in our village when my wife, my daughter, and my brother-in-law went off?"

"Yes, I was there," replied Sancho, "and I can tell that your daughter looked so handsome that the whole village turned out to see her, and all said that she was the fairest creature on God's earth. She kept crying all the way and embracing all her friends and acquaintances; she begged all who came to see her off to pray to Our Lady for her, and that in so piteous a manner that she even made me cry, and I'm no blubberer. By my faith, there were many who had a good mind to kidnap her on the road and hide her away, but the fear of the king's order had them cowed. He who carried on most passionately was Don Pedro Gregorio, that rich young heir you know. They say that he was daft about her, and since she has left, he hasn't shown himself in our village. We all thought that he had gone after her, to kidnap her, but we've heard nothing up to the present."

"All along I suspected that this young fellow was courting my daughter, but I always put my trust in my Ricota's virtue, so it didn't worry me to know that he loved her. You must have heard say, Sancho, that Moorish women seldom or ever marry old Christians for love, and I'm sure that my daughter, who, I believe, minded her Christian religion more than love, would pay scant heed to the courting of this young heir."

"God grant it," replied Sancho, "otherwise it would be the worse for both of them. Now, friend Ricote, it's time to say farewell, for I want to reach my master, Don Quixote, this night."

"God be with you, brother Sancho, I see my companions are stirring, and it's time for us to continue our journey."

The two then embraced, Sancho mounted Dapple, Ricote picked up his pilgrim staff, and thus they parted.

CHAPTER LV

Of what happened to Sancho on the road, and other matters, the best that can be

Sancho had spent so much time conversing with Ricote that he was unable to reach the duke's castle that day, though he was within a mile and half of it when night fell. It was rather dark and cloudy, but as it was summertime, he felt no uneasiness and turned off the highway intending to wait till morning. But as ill luck would have it, in searching for a place to shelter, he and Dapple all of a sudden fell into a deep hole that yawned amid some old ruins. As he was falling, he commended his soul to God, not expecting to stop till he came to the bottom of the pit. But this did not happen, for when he had fallen a little more than eighteen feet, Dapple struck ground, and he found himself still on his back, unbruised and unscathed. Sancho felt himself all over and held his breath, wondering whether he was still safe and sound and without a bone broken. When he found himself whole and sound in wind and limb, he could never give adequate thanks to Heaven for his miraculous preservation. He then groped about the walls of the pit to try, if it were possible, to climb out without help, but he found them all smooth, and without any footing. This grieved him exceedingly, and to increase his depression, Dapple began to groan piteously and dolefully, and the poor beast did not lament without good cause, for in truth he was in a woeful plight.

"Alas," cried Sancho, "what unexpected mishaps occur at every step to those who live in this miserable world! Who would have thought that he who but yesterday saw himself

seated on the throne as island governor, with servants and
vassals at beck and call, should today find himself buried
in a pit without a soul to relieve him or a servant or vassal
to come to his aid? Here we shall perish of hunger, my ass
and I, if we don't die before that, he from his bruises and
broken bones, and I of the doldrums. At least I won't be
as lucky as my master, Don Quixote of La Mancha, when
he went down below into the cave of that enchanted Montesinos, where he found someone to treat him better than if
he had been at home, for it appears that he found a table
laid and his bed made. There he saw beautiful and delightful
visions, but here I'm sure to see toads and snakes. What an
unhappy wretch I am! Look where my crazy ravings have
landed me! They'll be digging my bones out of here, clean,
white, and scraped, when it's Heaven's will that I be found,
and my good Dapple's with them; and from them, who
knows, they'll discover who we are, at any rate those who
have been told that Sancho Panza never parted from his
ass, or his ass from Sancho Panza. Once more, I say,
wretched the pair of us! Our rotten luck wouldn't let us
die in our own country and among our own. There, if no
relief could be found for our calamity, at least there would
always be someone to mourn it and to close our eyes when
we were breathing our last. O my comrade and friend! What
a scurvy return I've made you after all your good services!
Forgive me and pray to Fortune as best you can to get us
out of this wretched plight in which we find ourselves, and
I promise I'll place on your head a crown of laurels that'll
make you pass for poet laureate, and give you a double feed."

In this way did Sancho mourn over his misfortune, and his
ass listened to what he said, but not a word did he answer,
so great was the anguish and distress of the poor beast. At
length, after a whole night of miserable lamentations, daylight came, and by its radiance and glory, Sancho realized
that there was not the remotest possibility of their getting
out of that pit without help, and he began to shout as
loud as he could, in the hope that somebody would hear
him. But his was 'A voice crying in the wilderness,' as not
a living soul was within hearing. He then gave himself up
for dead. Seeing that Dapple was lying on the ground, he
set to work to get him up on his legs, and with great difficulty he did so, though the poor animal could hardly stand.
Then he took out of his saddlebags, which had shared their

fate in the fall, a piece of bread and gave it to the ass, who relished it. "Better a fat sorrow than a lean one," said he to the ass, as if the latter understood him.

After a time he noticed at one side of the cavern a crevice large enough for a man to squeeze through if he stooped. Having crawled through on all fours, he found that it led into a vault, and by a ray of sunlight that came through the roof, he saw was large and spacious; he noted that it led into another vault of equal size. After this discovery he went back to the ass, and picking up a stone, he began digging away to remove the earth from the hole; in a short time he made it large enough for Dapple to pass. Then, leading the ass by the halter, he went along through the various vaults to see if he could find a way out on the other side. Sometimes he was in the dusky gloom, sometimes in pitch darkness, but always in fear and trembling.

"Almighty God protect me!" said he to himself. "This is all misfortune to me, but my master, Don Quixote, would take it as a rare adventure. He'd look upon these caves and dungeons as lovely gardens and gorgeous palaces of Galiana,[1] and he'd feel sure that they would end in some flowering meadow or other. But here am I, a poor, feckless, chickenhearted loon, who am forever fancying that the earth is going to open all of a sudden under my feet and swallow me up. Welcome, bad luck, if you come alone."

Such were Sancho's despairing laments as he cautiously groped his way through the vaults, until at last, after going somewhat more than a mile and a half, he saw a glimmering light, like that of day, shining through an aperture above, which he looked upon as an entrance to another world. Here Cide Hamete Benengeli leaves him for an instant and returns to Don Quixote, who with joy and satisfaction was looking forward to the appointed time of the battle that he had to fight for the honor of Doña Rodríguez' daughter.

The knight happened that morning to be out in the country exercising his steed, and Rozinante, in one of his curvetings, pitched his feet so near the brink of a deep cave that had not Don Quixote pulled in his reins sharply, he would

---

[1] Galiana was a Moorish princess whose father, King Haxen of Toledo, built her a magnificent palace on the Tagus, which the Toledans traditionally called the palace of Galiana. Her garden was called *La huerta del rey* (the garden of the king).

inevitably have tumbled into it. Having managed to check
his horse in time, he wheeled him around, rode up to the
edge, and gazed earnestly down into the yawning chasm.
All at once he heard a noise down in the depths, and listening intently, he was able to distinguish the following words:
"Hello! Above there! Is there any Christian to hear me? Is
there no charitable gentleman to take pity on a sinner buried
alive, a poor governor without a government?"

Don Quixote fancied it was Sancho's voice he heard, and
this amazed him, so he shouted as loudly as he could:
"Who are you below there? Who is it that cries for help?"

"Who should be here shouting for help but miserable Sancho Panza, governor for his sins and for his accursed misfortune of the island of Barataria, formerly squire to the
famous knight Don Quixote of La Mancha?"

At these words Don Quixote's wonder and alarm increased, for he then imagined that Sancho was dead and
that his soul was there doing penance. With this fancy in
his mind, he said: "I conjure you as a Catholic Christian
to tell me who are; if you are a soul in purgatory, let me
know what you want me to do for you. Since my profession
is to assist and succor all who are afflicted in this world,
I shall also be ready to relieve and aid the distressed in
the world below who cannot help themselves."

"In that case," said he from below, "you who are speaking
to me must be my master, Don Quixote; by the tone of
your voice I know it's none else."

"My name is Don Quixote," replied the knight, "and I
think it is my duty to assist the dead as well as the living.
Tell me, then, who you are, for I am astounded at what I
hear. If you are my squire, Sancho Panza, and are dead,
and if the Devil has not carried you off and through God's
mercy you are in purgatory, Our Holy Mother the Roman
Catholic Church has enough suffrages to redeem you from
the pains you suffer; I will solicit her on your behalf, as
far as my estate will allow. So, proceed and tell me who
you are."

"Well, then," replied the voice, "I swear by whatever you
will that I'm Sancho Panza, your squire, and that I never
died in all the days of my life, but having left my government for reasons that I'll need more time to tell you, I fell
into this cave, where I'm standing now, and Dapple with me,
who won't let me lie—as a further proof here he is by me."

Then, as if the ass had understood what his master said and wanted to back up his evidence, he began to bray so loudly that the whole cavern echoed and reechoed.

"That is a prime witness," said Don Quixote. "I know his bray as well as if I was his parent, and I know your voice, too, dear Sancho. Wait for me; I'll hasten off to the duke's castle, which is nearby, and get people to pull you out of the pit where your sins, doubtless, have cast you."

"Make haste, I pray you, sir," said Sancho, "and for God's sake, come back quick, for I can't bear being buried alive, and I'm dying of fear."

Don Quixote left him and hastened to the castle to tell the duke and duchess about Sancho's mishap. They were very astonished, though they knew that he might easily have fallen down into the pit, which had been there from time immemorial. They could not, however, understand how he came to give up his government without their having been notified of his coming. They straightaway sent their servants with ropes and cables to draw him out, and at the cost of many hands and much toil they pulled up Dapple and his master from the dark realms to the light of the sun. A certain student saw him and exclaimed: "That's how all bad governors should come out of their governments, just as this sinner comes out of this deep abyss, pale, famished, and as far as I know, penniless."

Sancho heard his remark and replied: "Listen here to me, backbiter, it's only eight or ten days since I started to govern the island that was given to me, and in all that time I never once had my belly full, except once; physicians have persecuted me, enemies trodden on me and battered my bones, and I've not had a moment to take bribes or to receive what was owing to me. When all this is taken into account, I didn't deserve by a long way to end up this way. But 'Man proposes and God disposes,' and He knows what's best and right for every one of us; and we should take time as it comes, and our lot as it falls; don't let anyone say, 'I'll drink no more of this water,' for 'Where one thinks to find a flitch, there's never a stake to hang it on'; God knows my mind and that's enough; I won't say another word, although I could."

"Be not angry, Sancho, nor troubled at what is said," said Don Quixote, "otherwise you will never have a moment's peace. Provided your conscience is clear, let the world say what it will, for you might as well put up gates in the open country as tie up the tongues of slanderers. If a governor returns rich from his government, they say he has been a robber; if poor, then they say he was a worthless fool."

"In that case," replied Sancho, "I'm sure they'll all take me for a fool rather than a robber."

Such was their discourse as they walked along toward the castle, surrounded by a crowd of boys and others. When they arrived, they found the duke and duchess waiting for them in the gallery. Sancho refused to go up to see the duke until he had stabled Dapple and given him his feed, for, said he, the poor beast had had a poor night's lodging. When that was done, he went up to the duke and duchess and knelt down before them, saying: "My lord and lady, not through any merit of mine, but because your grandeurs wished it, I went off to govern your island, Barataria. I entered it naked, and naked I came away. I neither won nor lost. Whether I governed well or badly, there were witnesses who'll say what they please. I've settled problems, decided law-suits, always perishing with hunger, for that was the wish of Dr. Pedro Recio of Tirteafuera, physician-in-ordinary to insular governors. Enemies made a set against us in the night, and after landing us into great danger, the people of the island say they were saved and won the victory by the strength of my arm. May God help them insofar as they speak the truth. In that time I bore all the burdens this business of governing brings with it, and I found them, by my account, too heavy for my shoulders or my ribs to bear—they are, in fact, not the arrows for my quiver. And so, before the government could knock me all of a heap, I resolved to knock it all of a heap; accordingly, yesterday morning I left the island as I found it, with the same streets, the same houses, the same roofs it had when I entered it. I've neither asked for a loan, nor set myself to make a pile. Though I intended to issue some wholesome laws, I made none of them, for I was afraid that they would not keep them, and that's the same as making none at all. I left the island, I repeat, without any company but my Dapple; I fell into a pit and groped my way through it, till this morning by the light of the sun I saw the way out, but it was no easy matter, for if Heaven hadn't sent my master, Don Quixote, to rescue me, I'd have stayed there till doomsday. So now, my lord duke and my lady duchess, here's your governor Sancho Panza again, who in a mere ten days' government has learned that he wouldn't give a fig to be a governor, not only of an island, but even of the whole wide world. Admitting this, and kissing your excellencies' feet, and copying boys at play when they cry, 'You leap and I'll follow,' I give a leap out of the government back into my old master's service again; for after all, though with him I often eat my daily bread in fear and trembling, at least I eat my bellyful; and as far as I'm concerned, if only that's well stuffed, it's all the same whether it be with carrots or partridges."

Here Sancho ended his long speech, and Don Quixote, who was always anxious lest his squire utter a thousand absurdities, gave thanks to Heaven when he saw that he had ended with so few. The duke embraced Sancho and told him that he was grieved that he had left his government so soon, but that he would give him some other less troublesome and more profitable post. The duchess, too, embraced him and gave orders that he should be taken care of, for he seemed to be badly bruised and in a bad way.

CHAPTER LVI

Of the prodigious and unparalleled battle that took place between Don Quixote of La Mancha and the lackey Tosilos, in the defense of Doña Rodríguez' daughter

The duke and the duchess did not repent of the trick they had played on Sancho Panza by giving him his governorship, especially as the steward came the same day and gave them a detailed description of all that Sancho had said and done during those days. In conclusion, he gave them a dramatic account of the attack on the island, of Sancho's fear, and of his departure, from which they received no little entertainment.

After this our history relates that the time for the battle arrived. Even though the duke had again and again instructed his lackey Tosilos how he was to deal with Don Quixote so as to overthrow him without killing or wounding him, he ordered the steel heads to be taken off the lances, telling Don Quixote that his Christian feelings, on which he prided himself, would not allow the battle to be fought with peril to life and limb. He was content to give them a fair field on his ground, although he was infringing a decree of the Holy Council that prohibited such duels, but he did not wish the affair to be carried to extremities. Don Quixote said that his excellency might arrange matters as he pleased and that he would obey him in everything. At last the dreaded day arrived, and as the duke had given orders for the erection of a spacious platform in front of the castle square, on which the judges of the lists, the appellant duennas, mother and daughter, might take their places, a huge crowd of people poured in from all the towns and villages of the neighborhood to witness this unusual contest, for within the memory of living man, no one had seen or heard of anything like it.

The first to enter the lists was the marshal of the ceremonies, who surveyed the ground and paced it all over, in case there might be any foul play there, or any hidden object that might cause one of the contestants to stumble and fall. Then the duennas entered and took their seats, hooded to their eyes and even to their bosoms, and they showed signs of concern when Don Quixote presented himself in the lists. Shortly after, heralded by many trumpets, there appeared on one side of the square the great lackey Tosilos, who had his visor down and was entirely encased in a stout and shining suit of armor. His horse was clearly a Frisian, a massive, grizzled animal, with at least a quarter of a hundredweight of hair on each of his fetlocks. The doughty combatant advanced, following the precise instructions of his master on how he was to behave toward the valiant Don Quixote of La Mancha, being warned on no account to slay him, but to try and avoid his first onslaught, for fear of meeting his death, which was certain if they clashed headlong. He paced the square, and coming to where the duennas were seated, he stopped for a while to gaze at the lady who sought him in marriage. Then the marshal of the field summoned Don Quixote, who had already presented himself in the lists, and side by side with Tosilos he spoke to the duennas, asking whether they consented to Don Quixote's championing their right. They replied that they did and that they would accept all he did in that cause as well done, valid, and final. By this time the duke and duchess had taken their places in a gallery overlooking the lists, which were crowded with people expecting to see that grim encounter. A condition imposed on the combat was that if Don Quixote conquered, his antagonist must marry Doña Rodríguez' daughter, and if he were conquered, his opponent was to be free of the promise exacted of him and need not give further satisfaction.

The marshal of the ceremonies divided the sun between them and stationed each of them in the place where he was to stand. The drums beat, the air resounded with the flourish of trumpets, the earth trembled under their feet; the hearts of the gazing crowd were in suspense, wondering what would be the issue of the affair, some in hope, others in fear. At length, Don Quixote, commending himself with all his heart

to Our Lord and to Lady Dulcinea of El Toboso, stood
waiting for them to give him the preconcerted signal for the
outset. Our lackey, however, had very different thoughts, and
what worried him I will now tell you.

It seems that as he looked upon his fair enemy, she appeared to him to be the most beautiful woman he had seen
in all his life, and the little blind urchin who in these quarters is generally called Love could not lose such an opportunity of triumphing over a lackey's heart and adding it to
the list of his trophies. And so, coming up to him softly
and unseen, he ran a six-foot dart into the lackey's left
side and pierced his heart through and through, which he
could do quite safely, as Love is invisible and comes and
goes where he wills without anyone calling him to account
for his deeds.

So, when the signal for the outset was given, our lackey
was so bewitched by the beauty of the lady whom he had
made mistress of his heart, that he took no notice of the
trumpet's sound. Don Quixote, on the other hand, charged
the moment he heard it, and rushed against his enemy at
the utmost speed that Rozinante could muster. And Sancho
Panza, his good squire, when he saw him sally forth, cried
aloud: "God guide you, cream and flower of knights-errant!
God send you victory, for you have right on your side!"

And although Tosilos saw Don Quixote coming at him,
he did not stir a step from his post, but called loudly to
the marshal of the lists, saying to him, as he came up to
see what he wanted: "Sir, is this not a battle to decide
whether or not I'm to marry that lady?"

"That is so," was the answer.

"Then," said the lackey, "my conscience pricks me, and
I would lay too much of a burden on it if I went on with
this battle; so, I declare myself beaten, for I'm willing to
marry that lady at once."

The marshal of the lists was astonished at Tosilos'
speech, and as he was one of those in the secret of the plot,
he was completely at a loss as to what to reply. Don Quixote
halted in midcareer, seeing that his enemy was not attacking. The duke could not understand why they were not
going on with the battle, but the marshal of the lists went
up and told him what Tosilos had said, at which he was
much surprised and extremely angry. While this was going
on, Tosilos went up to where Doña Rodríguez was sitting

and said in a loud voice: "Madam, I wish to marry your daughter, and I do not want to use strife and quarreling to obtain what I am able to get peacefully and without peril of death."

When Don Quixote heard this, he exclaimed: "Since this is so, I am free and absolved from my promise. Let them marry, in God's name, and since Our Lord has given her to him, may Saint Peter give her his blessing."

The duke descended to the castle square and went up to Tosilos, saying: "Is it true, knight, that you yield yourself vanquished and that your cowardly conscience bids you marry that lady?"

"Yes, sir," replied Tosilos.

"Upon my word, that's wisely said," piped up Sancho at this juncture, "for if you give the cat what you have to give the mouse, you'll be quit of your troubles."

Tosilos went off to unlace his helmet, begging them to give him urgent assistance, for his breath was failing him and he could not bear being so long immured in that straitened space. They released him from his confinement with all speed, and when the lackey's face was revealed, both Doña Rodríguez and her daughter cried out aloud: "This is a cheat! This is a cheat! They have put Tosilos, the duke's lackey, in place of my real husband! Justice from God and the king for this trickery—or rather this villainy."

"Do not be grieved, ladies," said Don Quixote, "this is neither trick nor villainy. And if it is, it is not the duke who is the cause, but the wicked enchanters who persecute me, and as they were jealous lest I win glory by this victory, they have transformed your husband's face into this man's, who, you say, is the duke's lackey. Take my advice and marry him, in spite of the malice of my enemies, for there is no doubt that he is really the man you desire for your husband."

When the duke heard this, he was ready, in spite of his anger, to burst out laughing, and he said: "Such extraordinary things happen to Don Quixote that I am inclined to think that this is not my lackey. But let us adopt the following plan: Let us postpone the marriage for a fortnight, if they are willing, and keep this person about whom we are doubtful under lock and key. During that time perhaps he will return to his original shape, for the grudge the enchanters bear Don Quixote cannot last so long, especially

as these tricks and transformations are of so little avail to
them."

"Oh, sir," cried Sancho, "these rascals make a regular
habit of changing anything that has to do with my master
from one shape into another. A knight he conquered in
days gone by, called the Knight of the Mirrors, they changed
into the shape of the bachelor Sansón Carrasco, a native
of our village and a close friend of ours; and my lady,
Dulcinea of El Toboso, they have turned into a rustic peasant wench; and so I imagine this lackey will die and live a
lackey all the days of his life."

At this Doña Rodríguez' daughter put in her say: "I
don't care who he may be who asks for my hand, I'm grateful to him, and I'd rather be the lawful wife of a lackey
than a gentleman's cast-off mistress, though my seducer's
no gentleman."

The final result of all these tales and goings-on was that
Tosilos was locked up to see what would come of his transformation. Everyone adjudged the victory to Don Quixote,
but most of the spectators were disappointed and depressed
because the eagerly awaited combatants had not hacked one
another to pieces, just as boys are sorry when the man they
are expecting is not brought out to be hanged because he is
pardoned either by the injured party or by the judge.

The people went off, the duke and duchess returned to
the castle, Tosilos was locked up, Doña Rodríguez and
her daughter were very glad to know that by one way or
another the whole business would end in matrimony, and
Tosilos hoped for no less.

CHAPTER LVII

Which tells how Don Quixote took leave of the duke and of his adventure with the witty and wanton Altisidora, the duchess' maid-in-waiting

Don Quixote thought it high time to leave the idle life he led in the castle, for he felt that he was much to blame for allowing himself thus to be shut up and for living indolently amid the tempting dainties and delights provided for him, a knight-errant, by the duke and duchess.

He believed, too, that he would have to give a strict account to Heaven for leading a life so opposed to the active ideals of his profession. Accordingly, he besought their graces to grant him permission to depart; they yielded to his request, though they showed him plainly that they deeply regretted his going. The duchess gave Sancho Panza his wife's letters, which he wept over.

"Who would have thought," cried he, "that all the mighty hopes with which my wife puffed herself up at the news of my government should come to this at last, and that it should be my fate to return to the rambling adventures of my master, Don Quixote of La Mancha! However, I'm thankful that my Teresa was like herself in sending the acorns to the duchess; if she hadn't sent them and had showed herself an ungrateful woman, upon my word, I'd be mighty sad. It's a comfort that no man can say that the gift was a bribe, for I had my government before she sent it, and it's right that those who receive a benefit should show themselves thankful, even though it be only a gaudy gewgaw. Naked I went into the government, and naked I came out, and so I can say with a clear conscience—and that's no

small matter—naked I came from my mother's womb, and
naked I am this moment; I neither win nor lose."

Such were Sancho's sentiments on the day of his departure. As for Don Quixote, he had taken leave of the duke
and duchess the night before, and early next morning he
sallied forth from his apartment in full armor and descended
into the courtyard. The surrounding galleries were thronged
with the people of the castle, and the duke and duchess were
there to see him set out on his adventures. Sancho was
mounted upon Dapple, with his saddlebags, his wallet, and
his provisions. He was most pleased because the steward,
the one who had played La Trifaldi, had given him, unbeknown to Don Quixote, a purse containing two hundred
gold crowns to defray the expenses of the journey. And
while everyone was gazing at Don Quixote, all of a sudden
the pert and witty Altisidora raised her voice from amid
the crowd of duennas and damsels of the duchess and addressed the knight in a piteous voice, saying:

> "Hear then, wicked knight,
>   Check your reins awhile;
> Weary not the flanks
> Of your spavin'd beast,
> False one, you are fleeing
> From no poison'd snake,
> But a tender lambkin,
> Not quite grown to sheep.
> Monster, you've deceived
> The sweetest maid that ever
> Diana on her hills has seen,
> Or Venus watched within her groves.
> *Perjur'd Vireno, fugitive Aeneas!*
> *Go, monster, join your peer Barabbas!*
>
> Impious one, you're bearing off
> In your ruthless clutching paws
> The palpitating heartstrings
> Of a tender, loving maid!
> Three kerchiefs you have stolen
> And two garters white and black
> Off a pair of legs that vie
> With white marble for their gloss;
> Two thousand sighs as well
> Which, if fire, would soon I bet

Set alight two thousand Troys,
If there were two thousand Troys.
Perjur'd Vireno, fugitive Aeneas!
Go, monster, join your peer Barabbas!

May the heart of your squire, Sancho,
Turn so black and stony cold
That your lady, Dulcinea,
May forever be enchanted.
Let her sadly rue your guilt,
For sometimes the just must pay
While sinners joyfully make hay.
May your very best adventures
Into misadventures turn,
Your hopes all vanish into dreams,
Your staunchness into oblivion.
Perjur'd Vireno, fugitive Aeneas!
Go, monster, join your peer Barabbas!

And may they all call you false
    From Seville to Marchena;
And from Loja to Granada,
And from London to all England.
And if you ever play *reinado*,
At piquet or else *primera*,
May you never draw a king,
Or ever see an ace or seven.
And when you try to cut your corns
May your blood then flow in streams;
And when they pull your grinders out
May the stumps cling to your gums.
Perjur'd Vireno, fugitive Aeneas!
Go, monster, join your peer Barabbas!

While the doleful Altisidora was making her complaint, Don Quixote stood gazing at her, and without a word of reply, he turned to Sancho and said: "By the life of your forefathers, Sancho, I conjure you to tell me the truth. Tell me, have you by any chance got the three kerchiefs and the garters this love-sick girl is talking about?"

"Yes," replied Sancho, "I have the three kerchiefs, but as for the garters, they are over the hills and far away."

The duchess was surprised at Altisidora's impudence, for though she knew that she was bold, frolicsome, and even wanton, she would not have imagined her capable of acting in such a blatant manner, and as she had not been told of this joke, her wonder grew the more.

The duke, however, who wished to carry the sport further, then said: "Sir knight, it does not look well that after all the hospitable treatment you have received in this castle of mine, you should make bold to carry off at least three kerchiefs, not to mention a pair of garters belonging to my maid. These are indications of a false heart and are not becoming to your fair name. Return her the garters, or I challenge you to mortal combat, without any fear of your rascally enchanters transforming me or changing my face as they did that of Tosilos, my lackey, who entered into battle with you."

"God forbid," replied Don Quixote, "that I should unsheathe my sword against your most illustrious person, from whom I have received so many favors. The kerchiefs I shall return, for Sancho says he has them. As for the garters, it is impossible, for neither he nor I have ever taken them. If this maid of yours would look in her hiding places, she will find them, I am sure. I, my lord duke, have never been a thief, and I never mean to be one as long as I live, if God does not let me out of His care. This maid speaks, as she admits, like one love-sick, for which I am not to blame. And so I have no reason to ask pardon of her or of your excellency, whom I beseech to have a better opinion of me and to give me leave once more to pursue my journey."

"May God send you a good journey, Don Quixote," cried the duchess, "and may we always hear good news of your exploits. Go, and God bless you, for the longer you stay, the greater the fire you kindle in the bosoms of the damsels who look upon you. And as for this maid of mine, I shall punish her so that she shall not trangress in the future either with her eyes or with her tongue."

"One word only I beseech you to hear, valiant Don Quixote," said Altisidora, "and it is this: I beg your pardon for saying you had stolen my garters, for by God and my soul I have them on, and I have fallen into the same blunder as the man who went searching for the ass he was riding on."

"Didn't I say so?" cried Sancho. "A fine hand I am at hiding stolen things! If I had wanted to, I'd have had a wonderful opportunity in my government."

Don Quixote bowed his head and made obeisance to the duke, the duchess, and all the bystanders. Then, he turned Rozinante's rein, and with Sancho following him on Dapple, he left the castle, directing his course toward Saragossa.

CHAPTER LVIII

Which tells of how adventures poured on Don Quixote so thick and fast that they gave no room to one another

As soon as Don Quixote found himself in open country, safe and sound and free from Altisidora's endearments, he fancied himself in his own element and felt all his old chivalric impulses revive. Turning to Sancho, he said: "Liberty, Sancho, my friend, is one of the most precious gifts that Heaven has bestowed on mankind; all the treasures the earth contains within its bosom or the ocean within its depths cannot be compared with it. For liberty, as well as for honor, man ought to risk even his life, and he should reckon captivity the greatest evil life can bring. I say this, Sancho, because you were a witness of the luxury and plenty that we enjoyed in the castle we have just left; yet, in the midst of those seasoned banquets and snow-cooled liquors, I suffered, or so it seemed to me, the extremities of hunger, because I did not enjoy them with the same freedom as if they had been my own. The obligations that spring from benefits and kindnesses received are ties that prevent a noble mind from ranging freely. Happy the man to whom Heaven has given a morsel of bread for which he is obliged to thank Heaven alone." [1]

"Nevertheless," said Sancho, "we should feel grateful for two hundred gold crowns that the duke's steward gave me

---

[1] This sentiment has a double meaning here, for it applies both to Don Quixote and to his creator, Cervantes, whose struggle and self-denial in the cause of freedom were the source of all his troubles.

in a little purse, which I carry next my heart as a restorative and comfort in case of need, for we'll not always run across hospitable castles; instead, we'll be more likely to meet inns where we'll be drubbed."

Our knight- and squire-errant were conversing in such fashion as they jogged along when, after riding a little more than three miles, they saw about a dozen men dressed like laborers who were taking their dinner in a little green meadow with their cloaks spread out on the grass. Close by them they had what looked like white sheets that covered certain objects underneath, some upright and some lying flat, at short distances from each other. Don Quixote rode up to those who were eating, and after first saluting them courteously, he asked them what lay under their linen covers. One of them answered: "Sir, under these linen cloths are some images, sculptured in relief, which are to be placed in a show we are presenting in our village. We carry them covered up so that they don't get tarnished, and on our shoulders so that they may not be broken."

"If you would be so kind," replied Don Quixote, "I should like to see them, for images that are carried so carefully must surely be good ones."

"Yes, they are," said the other, "seeing what they cost, for there's not one of them that didn't cost more than fifty ducats, and to prove that it's true, your worship, wait and see with your own eyes."

And rising up, he left his meal and went to take the covering off the first image, which proved to be of Saint George, mounted on horseback with his lance thrust through the mouth of a serpent that was twined about his feet, with all the ferocity with which he is usually depicted. The whole image looked one blaze of gold, as they say, and when Don Quixote saw it, he said: "This knight was one of the best of the errants the army of Heaven ever had; he was called saint, and he was also a defender of maidens. Let us see this other one."

The man uncovered it, and it proved to be Saint Martin, mounted on a horse, dividing his cloak with a poor man. And no sooner did Don Quixote see him than he exclaimed: "This knight, too, was one of the Christian adventurers, and I believe he was even more generous than valiant, as you can see, Sancho, by his dividing his cloak with the poor man and giving him half. It must surely have been winter at the time, for if it had not been, he would have given him all of it, since he was so charitable."

"That couldn't have been the reason," said Sancho; "he must rather have been following the old proverb that says, 'To give and to keep has need of brains.'"

Don Quixote laughed and begged them to take off another of the cloths, beneath which was revealed the image of the patron of Spain on horseback with bloody sword, trampling down Moors and treading on their heads. And when he saw him, Don Quixote said: "This is a knight, indeed, and of Christ's squadrons. He is called Saint James the Moor-killer, one of the most valiant saints and knights the world ever had or Heaven has."

Then they uncovered another statue, which showed Saint Paul fallen from his horse, with all the usual details that are included in paintings of his conversion. Seeing that it was so lifelike that one might have said that Christ was speaking and Saint Paul replying, Don Quixote said: "This was the greatest enemy Our Lord's Church had in its time, and the greatest defender it will ever have—a knight-errant in his life and a peaceful saint in his death, an untiring laborer in the vineyard of the Lord and teacher of the Gentiles. Heaven was his school, and Jesus Christ himself his professor and master."

There were no more images, so Don Quixote bade them cover them up again, saying to those who were carrying them: "I consider it a good omen, brothers, to have seen what I have seen, for these saints and knights professed what I profess, which is the calling of arms. The only difference there is between me and them is that they were saints and fought in the heavenly manner, and I am a sinner and fight in the human way. They conquered Heaven by force of arms, because Heaven suffers violence, but up to now I do not know what I conquer by force of my labor. But should my Dulcinea of El Toboso be released from the pains she suffers and my fortunes be improved and my mind set aright, who knows but I may direct my steps along a better road than that which I am now following."

"May God hear you, and may sin be deaf," rejoined Sancho to this.

The men were as amazed at Don Quixote's appearance as at his words, for they did not understand one half of what he meant by them. As they had finished their dinner, they shouldered their images, and bidding farewell to Don Quixote, they proceeded on their journey. Sancho was again struck with wonder at his master's knowledge, as if he had never known him before, for he believed that there was no history or event in the world that he had not at his finger's end and stamped in his memory. So he said to him: "Really, master, if what happened to us today can be called adventure, it has been one of the mildest and gentlest that has befallen us in all the course of our wanderings, for we have come out of it without beatings and without any fear. We haven't laid hands to our swords, or thumped the earth with our bodies, or even been left empty-bellied. Blessed be God that I've seen all this with my own two eyes!"

"You are right, Sancho," answered Don Quixote, "but you must consider that times are wont to vary and change their course, and what the common people call omens, since they are not founded upon any cause in nature, ought to be reckoned as happy accidents by one who is wise. One of such omen-mongers may get up early one morning, and as he leaves his house, he may meet a friar of the Order of the Blessed Saint Francis; then he will turn his back as if he had encountered a griffin, and go back home again. Another, a Mendoza, spills the salt on his table, and immediately melancholy spills on his heart as if nature were obliged to give signs of approaching disasters by things so unimportant as these. The wise Christian should not pry too inquisitively into the counsels of Heaven. Scipio lands in Africa and stumbles as he leaps ashore. His soldiers take it for a bad omen, but he embraces the ground and cries: 'You cannot escape, Africa, for I have you clasped in my arms.' So, Sancho, my meeting with these images has been for me a most fortunate event."

"I can well believe it," answered Sancho, "and I wish your worship would tell me the reason why Spaniards, when they're going into battle, call on that Saint James, the Moor-killer: 'Saint James and close Spain!' Is Spain perhaps open, that she has to be closed? Or what is this ceremony?"

"You are a very simple, Sancho," replied Don Quixote. "Now consider that God has given Spain as her patron and protector this great knight of the Red Cross, especially in those desperate contests that the Spaniards have had with the Moors, and so they invoke and call upon him as their defender in all their battles, and many a time they have seen him there present, unhorsing, trampling, destroying, and slaughtering the hosts of Hagar. I could produce for you many examples that are recorded in truthful Spanish history."

Sancho changed the subject and said to his master: "I am amazed, sir, at the boldness of Altisidora, the duchess' maid-in-waiting. The creature they call Love must have wounded and pierced her cruelly. They say that he's a blind urchin, but though he's blear-eyed, or rather without sight, even if he takes the tiniest heart as his target, he scores a direct hit and pierces it right through with his arrows. I've heard tell, too, that Love's darts are blunted and dulled by the coyness and modesty of young maids. But in this Altisidora surely they must have been more whetted than blunted."

"Take note, Sancho," said Don Quixote, "that Love heeds no restraints and keeps no rules of reason in his goings-on. He is just the same as Death, who attacks the lofty palaces of kings as well as the humble cottages of shepherds. And no sooner does he take possession of a heart than he straightaway forces it to shed all timidity and shame. So, Altisidora, being shameless, proclaimed her desires, which roused in my heart more confusion than compassion."

"Such shameful cruelty!" cried Sancho. "Such unheard-of ingratitude! Speaking for myself, I would have thrown up the sponge and would have become her slave if there had been the slightest sign of a loving word from her. Why, your heart's of marble, and your guts of brass, and your soul of plaster! But I can't for the life of me imagine what it is that girl can have seen in your worship to make her give way and submit like this. What grace was it, what gallant air, what charm, what looks, which of all these was it, or was it all of them together, that did the trick? For, honestly speaking, I often pause to look at your worship from the sole of your boot to the topmost hair on your head, and I see more things in you to scare me than bewitch me. And as I've heard, too, that beauty is the first and chief quality that breeds love, I don't know what the poor thing fell in love with, since your worship has none."

"Remember, Sancho," answered Don Quixote, "that there are two kinds of beauty: one of the soul and the other of the body. That of the soul displays its radiance in intelligence, in chastity, in good conduct, in generosity, and in good breeding, and all these qualities may exist in an ugly man. And when we focus our attention upon that beauty, not upon the physical, love generally arises with great violence and intensity. I, Sancho, am well aware that I am not handsome, but I also know that I am not deformed, and it is enough for a man of worth not to be a monster for him to be dearly loved, provided he has those spiritual endowments I have spoken of."

As they conversed, they passed into a wood that lay beyond the road, and suddenly and unexpectedly Don Quixote found himself entangled in some nets of green thread that were stretched from a tree. As he was unable to imagine what they could be, he said to Sancho: "In my opinion, Sancho, the affair of these nets must be one of the strangest adventures imaginable. May I die if the enchanters who persecute me do not want to entangle me in them and halt my journey, as if in vengeance for my cruelty to Altisidora. But I will teach them that, though these nets were made of hardest adamant instead of green threads, were even stouter than those that enmeshed Venus and Mars, I would break them as easily as I would rushes or cotton yarn."

As he was trying to push forward and break through the nets, all of a sudden there appeared ahead from between the trees two most lovely shepherdesses—at least two were clad like shepherdesses, except that their bodices and skirts were of finest brocade; their skirts, I mean, were petticoats of luxurious golden silk. The gold of their hair, which fell loosely over their shoulders, could vie with the rays of the sun, and they were crossed with garlands of green laurel and red amaranth. Their age seemed not to be less than fifteen or more than eighteen. This was a sight to dazzle Sancho, astound Don Quixote, and make the sun stop in its course to watch them. All four of them stood still in wondering silence. At last one of the shepherdesses was the first to speak; she said to Don Quixote: "Stop, sir knight, and do not break these nets, which are not spread here for your harm but for our pastime. As I know that you will ask why they are placed here and who we are, I shall tell you in few words. In a village about six miles from here live many people of quality, gentle and rich folk, some of whom have arranged with their sons and daughters and their friends to make up a party and to come to enjoy themselves in this spot, which is one of the most charming in all this region. Here we have formed among ourselves a new pastoral Arcadia and the girls have dressed as shepherdesses and the youths as shepherds. We have learned two eclogues by heart, one by the famous poet Garcilaso and the other by the most excellent Camoëns, in his own Portuguese tongue, which till now we have not represented. Yesterday was the first day of our coming here. We have pitched our tents—they are called field tents—among these bushes on the banks of a flowing brook that waters all these meadows. Last night we stretched these nets among the trees to trap the silly little birds, intending to drive them into the nets by our noise. If you please, sir, to be our guest, you will be liberally entertained, for there will be no melancholy or sadness at our party."

She stopped and said no more, and Don Quixote replied: "Surely, fairest lady, Actaeon could not be more astonished when unawares he spied Diana bathing in the waters, than I am at the sight of your beauty. I applaud your plan of diversions and thank you for your invitation. And if I can serve you, you may command me with the certainty that you will be obeyed, for my profession bids me show myself complaisant and benevolent to all kinds of people, especially to those of the rank to which you happen to belong; and if these nets, which occupy only a small space, were to cover the whole circumference of the globe, I would seek new worlds to pass through to avoid breaking them. And so that you may believe these extravagant words of mine, learn that it is Don Quixote of La Mancha, no less, who makes this promise, if by chance this name has reached your ears."

"Ah, dear friend!" then cried the other shepherdess. "What good fortune is ours! Do you see this gentleman who stands before us? Well, you must know that he is the most valiant, the most love-sick, and the most courteous knight in all the world, unless the history of his exploits, which I have read in print, lies and deceives us. I would wager that this worthy fellow who accompanies him is a certain Sancho Panza, his squire, who is unrivaled for his drolleries."

"That is the truth," said Sancho, "I am the droll fellow and the squire your grace speaks of, and this gentleman is

my master, the same Don Quixote of La Mancha historified
and aforesaid."

"Oh!" cried the other shepherdess. "Let us beg him to
stay, dear, for our families will be delighted to welcome him.
I have also heard of his valor and of his great charm. He
is said to be the staunchest and most constant lover ever
known, and they say that his lady is a certain Dulcinea of
El Toboso, to whom in all Spain they award the guerdon of
beauty."

"And she has a right to it," said Don Quixote, "unless,
indeed, your matchless beauty places it in doubt. But do not
trouble to detain me, for the urgent duties of my profession
leave me no opportunity for rest."

At this moment the brother of one of the shepherdesses
approached, dressed also as a shepherd, and as richly and
splendidly as his sister, who informed him that the gentleman with them was the valiant Don Quixote of La Mancha,
and the other his squire, Sancho, of whom he had heard, for
he had read their history. The elegant shepherd offered
his greetings and begged the knight to accompany him to
their tents. And Don Quixote had to give in and comply.
Then the beaters came up, and the nets were filled with different kinds of birds, which, deceived by the color of the
meshes, fell into the danger they tried to avoid.

More than thirty persons gathered in that spot, all elegantly dressed as shepherds and shepherdesses. They were informed at once who Don Quixote and his squire were, and
they were no little delighted, for they knew him already
from his history. They withdrew to the tents, where they
found the tables sumptuously and elegantly laid. They honored Don Quixote by putting him at the head, and they all
gazed at him in wonder. At length, when the cloth was removed, the knight with gravity lifted up his voice, saying:
"Though we are told that pride is man's greatest sin, I say
it is ingratitude, and I base my belief on the common saying: 'Hell is full of the ungrateful.' This sin I have tried to
avoid from the moment that I had the use of reason, and if
I cannot requite the benefits I receive with other benefits, I
put in their stead my wish to repay them. And when that
is not enough, I proclaim them, for he who declares and
proclaims the benefits that he receives would likewise repay
them if he could, because for the most part those who receive

are inferior to those who give. Thus God is above us all, for He is a greater giver than any; so, man's gifts cannot equal those of God in quality because of the infinite distance between them. But this meagerness and inadequacy, however, may be somewhat compensated by gratitude.

"I am grateful for the favors you have done me, but as I am unable to respond in like manner, owing to the limits imposed on me by my restricted means, I can only offer what little is in my power. Therefore, I declare that for two whole days I shall maintain in the middle of this highroad that leads to Saragossa that these two ladies, here disguised as shepherdesses, are the most beautiful and most courteous ladies in the world, excepting only the peerless Dulcinea of El Toboso, sole mistress of my thoughts, without offense, be it said, to all of either sex who are listening to me."

At these words Sancho, who had been listening with great attention, exclaimed loudly: "Is it possible that there's anyone in the world who'd dare to say and swear that this master of mine is not right in his head? Tell me, gentlemen shepherds, is there any village priest living, no matter how wise and learned he may be, who could speak as my master has spoken? Or is there any knight-errant, no matter how renowned he may be for bravery, who could make such an offer as he has made?"

Don Quixote, in a blaze of anger and flushing to the root of his hair, turned on Sancho, saying: "Is it possible, Sancho, that there is anyone in all the face of the world who would not say that you are a dolt, lined with the same crass doltishness and with who knows what extra trimmings of downright knavery and mischief? Who told you to poke your nose in my affairs and inquire whether I am sane or crazy? Hold your tongue and shut your mouth; saddle Rozinante, if he is unsaddled, and let us go and put my offer into effect. Since reason is on my side, you can count all who would gainsay me as vanquished already."

And then, in a fury and with indignant gestures he rose from his seat, leaving the company astounded and wondering whether to take him for a sane man or a lunatic. They, however, tried to dissuade him from exposing himself to such a test, and they declared that they were all so well aware of his sentiments of gratitude that no further demonstrations of his valorous spirit were necessary.

Nevertheless, Don Quixote persisted in his resolution, and bracing his shield and couching his lance, he planted himself on Rozinante in the middle of a highway, not far from that green meadow. Sancho followed him on Dapple, together with all those of the pastoral flock, curious to see the result of his arrogant and extravagant challenge.

And then, taking up his position, as I've said, in the middle of the road, Don Quixote rent the air with such words as these: "You, passengers and wayfarers, knights, squires, men on foot or on horseback who pass along this road, or who will pass in the next two days! Know that Don Quixote, knight-errant, is posted here to maintain that there is no beauty or courtesy in the world greater than that of the nymphs inhabiting these woods and meadows, not counting the mistress of my soul, Dulcinea of El Toboso. Therefore, let anyone of contrary opinion come forward, for here I await him."

Twice he repeated these same words, and twice they were unheard by any adventurer. But Fortune, who continued to advance his affairs from better to better, ordained that after a short interval there appeared on the road a crowd of men on horseback, many of them with lances in their hands, riding all jumbled together and at a great pace. And no sooner did those with Don Quixote catch sight of them than they turned tail and got out of the road, perceiving that if they stood their ground they might run into danger. Only Don Quixote with undaunted heart stood still, while Sancho Panza took cover behind Rozinante's hindquarters. The troop of spearmen came up and one of them who rode ahead began to shout at Don Quixote: "Out of the way, devil mend you, or these bulls will make mincemeat of you!"

"Go, vile rabble!" replied Don Quixote. "I don't care a rap for bulls, not even for the fiercest ever bred on the banks of the Jarama! Confess, you rascally herd, all of you, that what I have proclaimed is true; otherwise do battle with me."

Neither did the herdsmen have time to answer, nor Don Quixote to get out of the way, even if he had so desired. And so, the troop of wild bulls and tame bullocks, and the crowd of herdsmen and others who were taking them to be enclosed in a neighboring town, where next day they were to be fought, passed over Don Quixote and over Sancho, Rozinante and Dapple, overthrowing them all and rolling them on the ground. There lay Sancho trodden upon, Don Quixote stunned, Dapple trampled, and Rozinante in poor shape. After a while they all rose, and Don Quixote set off in great haste, staggering and stumbling, after the herd, shouting at the top of his voice: "Halt! Stop, you rascally rabble! One knight alone awaits you, one who scorns the wretched coward's adage: 'For a fleeing enemy build a silver bridge.'"

But this did not stop the runaways, who took no more notice of his threats than of last year's clouds. Weariness halted Don Quixote, and more enraged than avenged, he sat down on the road, waiting for Sancho, Rozinante, and Dapple to come up. They arrived; master and man remounted, and without turning to take leave of the feigned or counterfeit Arcadians, they continued their journey with more shame than satisfaction.

CHAPTER LIX

In which is recorded the extraordinary event that might pass for an adventure of Don Quixote.

A clear and limpid spring that they discovered in a shady clump of trees relieved Don Quixote and Sancho of the dirt and weariness resulting from the uncivil behavior of the bulls, and there by its edge the forlorn pair, master and man, sat down to rest, letting Rozinante and Dapple loose, without headstall and bridle. Sancho turned to the larder in his saddlebags and brought out what he was pleased to call his belly timber. He rinsed his mouth, and Don Quixote washed his face, and after that refreshment their spirits rose somewhat. Don Quixote, however, out of pure vexation would not touch a morsel, and Sancho out of pure politeness did not dare to tuck into the food before him, waiting for his master to taste the first bit. But as he saw that the latter was so rapt in his meditations that he forgot to raise the bread to his mouth, the squire silently and in defiance of all the rules of good breeding began to cram into his belly the bread and cheese before him.

"Eat, Sancho, my friend!" said Don Quixote. "Sustain life, for you have more need of it than I, and let me die a martyr to my thoughts and a victim of my misfortunes. I, Sancho, was born to live dying, and you to die eating, and to prove the truth of my words, look at me. Here am I, printed in histories, famous in arms, courteous in my actions, respected by princes, courted by maidens; yet, after all, when I looked for palms, triumphs, and crowns, won and deserved by my valorous exploits, I have seen myself this morning trampled, kicked, and trodden upon by herds of unclean and filthy animals. This refection blunts my teeth, dulls my grinders, benumbs my hands, and entirely robs me of my appetite, so that I think I may let myself die of hunger, the most cruel of all deaths."

"At that rate," said Sancho without stopping his rapid munching, "your worship will not approve of the proverb that says: 'Let Marta die, but die with her belly full.' As for myself, I've no intention of killing myself; no, I'll do like the cobbler who stretches the leather with his teeth till he makes it reach as far as he wants. I'll stretch the span of my life by eating as far as Heaven will let it run. Consider, master, that there's no greater foolishness in the world than for a man to despair. Take my advice, and after you've eaten, throw yourself down and have a bit of a snooze on the green grass here, which is as soft as a feather mattress. When you awake, I guarantee that you'll find yourself another man."

Don Quixote followed Sancho's advice, for he was convinced the squire spoke more like a philosopher than a fool; but before doing so he said to him: "Ah, Sancho! If you would only do for me what I am now going to propose, my sorrows would be lessened and my relief more certain. All that I want you to do is this: While I follow your advice and try to sleep, do go a short distance away and expose your bare skin to the open air. Then, take the reins of Rozinante and give yourself three or four hundred lashes as payment on account of the three thousand and odd that you are bound to give yourself in order to disenchant Dulcinea, for truly it is no small shame that the poor lady should remain enchanted owing to your carelessness and neglect."

"There's a great deal to be said on that," said Sancho, "but for the present let us both sleep, and then, God knows what may happen. Remember, sir, that this lashing oneself in cold blood is a tough business, all the more when the stripes fall on a body so thinly covered and worse lined as mine is. Let my Lady Dulcinea be patient, and one day, when she least expects it, she'll see my pelt turned into a regular sieve with the belting. 'While there's life there's hope,' which is just as good as saying, 'A promise is always a promise.' "

Don Quixote thanked him and ate sparingly; but Sancho gorged himself. They both then lay down to sleep, leaving Rozinante and Dapple, those inseparable companions and friends, to crop at their own discretion the rich grass abounding in that meadow.

They awoke rather late in the day, mounted again, and continued their journey, hurrying toward an inn that seemed to be about a league away. I say it was an inn, because Don Quixote himself called it so, contrary to his usual procedure, which was to take inns for castles. When they arrived, they asked the landlord if he had any lodgings.

"Yes," he replied, "and as good accommodation as you'd find in Saragossa itself."

They dismounted, and Sancho put his baggage in a room, of which the host gave him the key. Then he put Rozinante and Dapple in the stable, fed them, and returned to receive Don Quixote's orders, whom he found seated on a stone bench. Sancho kept thanking Heaven that his master had not mistaken the inn for a castle.

As suppertime was near, Sancho asked the host what there was to eat. "Whatever you will," he replied; "you may make your choice; soaring birds of the air, earth-bound birds,[1] fishes from the open sea, there's nothing this inn can't provide."

"We don't need all that," said Sancho. "A couple of roasted chickens will do us well, for my master is delicate and has a small appetite, and I myself am no gluttonous trencherman."

"We've no chickens," replied the innkeeper, "for the kites have eaten them."

"Well, then," said Sancho, "roast us a pullet, but mind it's a tender one."

"Lord bless us! A pullet!" replied the innkeeper. "As true as I'm telling you, I sent over fifty yesterday to be sold in town. But, setting aside pullets, you may ask for anything else."

"In that case, there's sure to be a fine joint of veal or kid."

"Veal or kid, you say?" said the host. "I'm afraid there's none just now; it's all finished. Next week there'll be enough and to spare."

"Much help that'll be to us," answered Sancho. "I'll lay a bet that you can make up all these deficiencies with lashings of eggs and bacon."

"Hold on!" cried the host. "My guest must be a sly one

---

[1] To ask for birds of the air (*pedir las pajaritas del aire*) was to ask for the daintiest fare.

and no mistake! I've told him I have neither pullets nor hens, and yet he expects me to have eggs! Mention some other delicacies, but don't ask for hens."

"Body of me!" said Sancho. "Let us come to something; tell me what you have and don't make me rack my brains any longer."

"Now what I really and truly have," said the host, "is a pair of cow heels that look like calves' feet, or a pair of calves' feet that look like cow heels, dressed with onions, peas, and bacon. They are just ready and crying out, 'Come eat me, come eat me.'"

"Mark them down as mine at once," said Sancho, "and let no one touch them. I'll give more for them than anybody else. In my opinion, there's nothing better in the world; give me cow heels and you can keep your calves' feet."

"Nobody shall touch them," said the host, "for my other guests are so genteel that they bring their cook, their butler, and their larder along with them."

"If you're talking about genteel folks," said Sancho, "I'll say there's no genteeler person than my master, but his profession doesn't allow for any larders and butteries; we just squat down in the middle of a field and fill our bellies with acorns or medlars."

This was the extent of the conversation that passed between Sancho and the innkeeper, for Sancho would not answer when the innkeeper asked what was his master's occupation or profession.

As supper was now ready and Don Quixote was still in his chamber, the innkeeper brought it to him there, and he sat down comfortably to his meal. The room next to that occupied by Don Quixote was separated from it only by a thin partition, and he could hear distinctly the voices of the persons inside.

"Don Jerónimo," said one of them, "I beseech you, till supper is brought in, let us read another chapter of the second part of *Don Quixote of La Mancha*."

No sooner did the knight hear his name mentioned than he sprang to his feet, and listening with attentive ears, he heard the said Don Jerónimo answer: "Why, Señor Don Juan, do you want to read such absurdities? Whoever has read the first part of *Don Quixote of La Mancha* cannot possibly enjoy the second part." [2]

"Nevertheless," said Don Juan, "it would be better to read it, for no book is so bad as not to have something good in it. What displeases me most about this second part is that the author describes Don Quixote as no longer in love with Dulcinea."

As soon as he heard these words, Don Quixote, full of rage and indignation, raised his voice and said: "Whoever shall say that Don Quixote of La Mancha has forgotten, or ever can forget, Dulcinea of El Toboso, I will make him know, with equal arms, that his words stray far from the truth. Neither can the peerless Dulcinea be forgotten, nor can Don Quixote ever forget her. His motto is constancy, and his profession to preserve it staunchly and without constraint."

"Who is that speaking to us?" replied one of persons in the next room.

"Who should it be, indeed," said Sancho, "but Don Quixote of La Mancha himself, who'll make good all he has said and all he has to say, for 'A good payer needs no sureties.'"

At these words two gentlemen rushed into the room, and one of them, throwing his arms about Don Quixote's neck, said: "Your presence does not belie your name, and your name cannot fail to give credit to your presence. You are, indeed, the true Don Quixote of La Mancha, polestar and morning star of knight-errantry, in spite of him who has attempted to usurp your name and annihilate your exploits, as the author of this book, which I deliver to you, has tried to do in vain."

Don Quixote, without making a reply, took up the book, and after turning over some of the pages, he laid it down, saying: "In glancing at this volume I have noticed three things for which the author deserves to be rebuked. First, I object to certain words in his prologue; in the second place,

[2] While Cervantes was writing this chapter, or intending to do so, he received news of the publication of the second part of *Don Quixote*, written by the so-called Alonso Fernández de Avellaneda and printed in Tarragona in 1614. As a result, Cervantes determines to alter his hero's course. His original intention had been to bring Don Quixote and the bachelor Sansón Carrasco together at the tournament in Saragossa, for the latter knew that the knight planned to go there. From now on Cervantes draws humorous toll from his rival's libel.

his language is Aragonese, for he sometimes omits the article; the third and most damaging objection is that he strays from the truth in an essential point of the history, for he says that the wife of my squire, Sancho Panza, is called Mari Gutiérrez, whereas her name is Teresa Panza, and he who errs in so important a circumstance may well be suspected of errors all through the book."

At this point Sancho butted in, saying: "He's a fine history-maker, and no mistake! A fat lot he knows of our adventures when he calls my wife, Teresa Panza, Mari Gutiérrez! Turn over a few more pages, master, and see whether I'm there, and if they've changed my name, too."

"By your words, friend," said Don Jerónimo, "I infer that you are Sancho Panza, squire to Don Quixote."

"I am so," replied Sancho, "and I'm proud of it."

"In that case," said the gentleman, "this new author does not treat you as civilly as he ought. He makes you out a glutton and a fool, without a tittle of humor and very different to the Sancho described in the first part of your master's history."

"God forgive him," said Sancho; "he might have left me in my corner, for 'He who knows the fiddle should play on it'; and 'St. Peter is well at Rome.' "

The two gentlemen begged Don Quixote to go to their chamber and sup with them, as they well knew that the inn had nothing fit for his entertainment. Don Quixote, who was always courteous, accepted their invitation, and Sancho remained with full powers over the pot. He sat down at the head of the table with the innkeeper for company, for he was no less a devotee of cow heels than the squire.

In the course of the meal Don Juan asked Don Quixote what news he had of Lady Dulcinea of El Toboso, whether she had married, whether she had been brought to bed or was pregnant, and whether she was still a virgin, and while preserving her chastity and good name, still heeded Don Quixote's loving salutations. To which he replied: "Dulcinea is a virgin, my desires are more constant than ever, our intercourse as unfruitful as formerly, and her beauty transformed into that of a coarse peasant wench."

And he began to tell them in detail of Lady Dulcinea's enchantment, the events in Montesinos' cave, and the instructions of the sage Merlin for her disenchantment, which was through Sancho's flogging. Great was the pleasure the two gentlemen took in hearing Don Quixote relate his extraordinary adventures, and they were as much amazed at his eccentricities as at his elegant manner of describing them. At one moment they took him for a wise man, at another he veered into craziness, without their being able to settle what grade to give him between sanity and madness.

Sancho finished his supper, and leaving the innkeeper in a fuddled state, he came into the room where his master was, saying as he entered: "May I be hanged, gentlemen, if the author of that book your worships have got a hold of has any wish to be hail fellow well met with me, but though he calls me a glutton, as you say, I hope he doesn't call me a drunkard, too."

"Yes, he does call you so," said Don Jerónimo, "though I don't remember the exact words. But I know they were insulting ones, and false as well, as I can plainly see on the physiognomy of honest Sancho here before me."

"Believe me, gentlemen," said Sancho, "the Sancho and the Don Quixote of that history must be different people from those who appear in the one written by Cide Hamete Benengeli. In the latter you'll find the pair of us: my master, valiant, wise and a lover, and I, simple and droll, but not a glutton or a drunkard."

"I believe you," said Don Juan, "and if it were possible, there should have been a law that no one should dare to write of the affairs of the great Don Quixote except Cide Hamete, his first historian, just as Alexander decreed that no one should dare paint his portrait except Apelles."

"Let anyone portray me who will," replied Don Quixote, "but let him not abuse me; patience often stumbles when they pile on too many injuries."

"None can be done to Don Quixote," said Don Juan, "which he cannot avenge, unless he wards it off with the shield of his patience, which I believe is mighty and great."

In such conversation they spent a great part of the night, and although Don Juan would have liked Don Quixote to read more of the book to see where it was false, they could not prevail upon him to do so. He said that he took it as read and concluded that it was wholly stupid. And furthermore, he did not wish its author to flatter himself that he had read it, even if he should happen to hear that he had held it in his hands, for filthy and obscene subjects should be shielded from our thoughts, and much more from our eyes.

The two gentlemen asked Don Quixote which way he was traveling. He told them he was going to Saragossa, to be present at the tournament held in that city every year for the prize of a suit of armor.[3] Don Juan told him that the spurious second part of his history described how Don Quixote, whoever he was, had been at Saragossa at a public running at the ring, of which the author gives a measly account, defective in contrivance, mean in style, wretchedly poor in devices, and rich only in absurdities.

"For that reason," said Don Quixote, "I will not set foot in Saragossa, and so the forgery of this new historian shall be exposed to the eyes of the world, and mankind will be convinced that I am not the Don Quixote of whom he speaks."

"You are wise to act thus," said Don Jerónimo; "besides, there is another tournament in Barcelona, where you may display your valor."

"So I intend," replied Don Quixote, "and now, gentlemen, I crave permission to leave you, for it is time to retire to rest; pray rank me among the number of your best friends and most loyal servants."

"Include me, too," said Sancho; "who knows, I may be good for something."

Don Quixote and Sancho then retired to their chamber, leaving the two gentlemen surprised at the medley of good sense and madness they had observed in the knight, but fully convinced that these two persons were the genuine Don Quixote and Sancho and that those the Aragonese author had described were not.

Don Quixote rose early next morning and rapped at the partition of the next room to bid his new friends farewell. Then Sancho paid the innkeeper royally and advised him either to boast less of the provisions of his inn or to keep it better supplied.

[3] The knights of Saragossa belonged to the confraternity of their patron, St. George, and they were obliged to hold three jousts and tournaments every year, which were called *justas del arnés* (jousts for armor).

CHAPTER LX

What happened to Don Quixote on the way to Barcelona

The morning was cool, and it gave promise that the day would be so, too, when Don Quixote rode out of the inn, after first informing himself which was the most direct way to Barcelona without touching at Saragossa, such was his eagerness to prove the new historian a liar, for he understood that he had grossly slandered him. It so happened that nothing worth recording befell him for more than six days. At the end of that time, however, he lost his way, and night overtook them in a thick forest of oaks or cork trees, for on this point Cide Hamete does not observe his usual precision. Master and man dismounted and lay down at the foot of the trees.

Sancho, who had already eaten his supper, in an instant let himself be wafted through the gates of sleep, but Don Quixote, being a prey to his fancies rather than to hunger, could not close his eyes. His thoughts flashed here, there, and everywhere; at one moment he thought himself in the cave of Montesinos; at another he saw his Dulcinea, who had been transformed into a peasant wench, leap upon her ass; the next moment he thought he heard the sage Merlin proclaiming the conditions required for disenchanting her. He was in despair when he remembered Sancho's uncharitable negligence, for he believed that he had given himself only five lashes, a small number, indeed, when compared with the great number that still remained. This reflection drove him into such a state of exasperation that he reasoned with himself as follows: "If Alexander the Great cut the Gordian knot, saying: 'To cut is just the same as to untie,' and became in that way the ruler of all Asia, why should I not try the same method now in the disenchantment of Dulcinea and decide to whip Sancho myself, whether he will or not? For if the condition of this remedy consists in Sancho's receiving the three thousand and odd lashes, what does it matter to me whether he gives himself those stripes or another gives them to him, since the essential point is that he should receive them from whatever hand they may come?"

With this idea in his mind he came up to the sleeping Sancho, after having first taken the reins of Rozinante and adjusted them in such a way that he might use them as a whip. He then started to undo the tapes that upheld Sancho's breeches, though it is said that the squire had only the one in front to hold them up. Hardly had he begun his operations when Sancho awoke and was instantly on the alert. He cried out: "What's the matter? Who is trying to undo my breeches?"

"It is I," replied Don Quixote, "who have come to atone for your negligence and to find a remedy for my torments; I have come to whip you, Sancho, and discharge, at least in part, the debt that you did engage yourself to pay. Dulcinea is perishing; you live on without caring what becomes of her; I am dying with longing; so, let down your breeches of your own free will, for I am determined in this lonely place to give you at least two thousand lashes."

"No, master, not on your life," said Sancho, "hands off, or by God, the deaf will hear us. The lashes I am bound to give myself must be given of my own free will and not under compulsion; at present I'm not in the humor for flogging. Be content that I promise to flog and flay myself when I'm so inclined."

"It is useless to leave it to your courtesy, Sancho," said Don Quixote, "for you are hardhearted, and though a peasant, your flesh is tender."

So saying, he strove with all his might to undo the squire's breeches, but Sancho jumped to his feet, and making for his master, he gripped him, tripped him, and laid him flat on his back, whereupon, setting his right knee upon his chest, he held his hands fast so that he could scarcely stir or draw his breath.[1] Don Quixote kept crying out: "How, traitor!

---

[1] In the days of Cervantes the men of La Mancha had the reputation of being excellent wrestlers, even when the sport had declined in Spain.

Do you dare to raise a hand against your master and against the hand that feeds you?"

"I neither mar king nor make king," [2] replied Sancho. "I only defend myself, who am my lord. If you promise me, master, that you'll let me alone and not try to whip me, I'll set you free; if not,

> " 'Here now thou diest traitor,
> Enemy of Doña Sancha.' " [3]

Don Quixote gave him his word and swore by the life of all he held most dear never to touch even a hair on Sancho's coat, but leave the whipping entirely to his discretion.

Sancho got up and moved off to another place, a good distance away; but as he was going to lie down under another tree, he felt something touch his head. Lifting up his hands, he found it to be a man's feet, with shoes and stockings on, which were dangling to and fro. Quaking with fear, he moved on to another tree, but there he found a similar pair of dangling feet. He then shouted out to his master for help. Don Quixote came up, and Sancho told him that all the trees were full of human legs and feet. Don Quixote felt them, and immediately guessing what it meant, he said to his squire: "Be not afraid, Sancho, these must be the legs of robbers and bandits who have been strung up for their crimes; here it is customary for officers of the law to hang them in bands of twenties and thirties when they can catch them. From this circumstance I gather that we are not far from Barcelona." As it happened, Don Quixote was right, for when the day began to break, they raised their eyes and saw the fruit of the trees, which were the bodies of bandits.

---

[2] A very old proverb dating from the fourteenth century. It refers to the meeting between King Pedro the Cruel and his bastard brother Enrique de Trastamara in the tent of the French knight Du Guesclin. Pedro and Enrique struggled together, and when Enrique was getting the worst of the fight Du Guesclin, according to one tradition, helped him by saying: *"Ni quito ni pongo rey; pero ayudo a mi señor"* (I neither raise up king nor pull him down, but I defend my lord).

[3] These are the two last lines of an ancient ballad on the Infantes de Lara (*Cancionero de Amberes*). The words are uttered by the bastard Mudarra when he is about to slay the enemy of his father's house and so revenge the slaughter of the seven infants of Lara. Sancho here puns on his own name as he quotes the lines.

If the knight and his squire were unnerved by these dead bandits, how much more did they quake when they suddenly found themselves surrounded by more than forty living bandits who ordered them in the Catalan tongue to halt and not to move till their captain arrived? Don Quixote happened to be on foot, his horse unbridled, his lance leaning against a tree some distance away; in short, being defenseless, he thought it best to cross his hands, bow his head, and reserve himself for a better opportunity. The bandits made haste to rifle Dapple, and in a trice they seized everything they could find in the saddlebags or in the wallet. It was lucky for Sancho that he had hidden in his sash the duke's gold pieces and those he had brought from home; but for all that, these worthy fellows would certainly have prodded, pryed, and peered all over him, sparing not even what lurked between his flesh and skin, had they not been interrupted by the arrival of their captain. He seemed to be about thirty-four years of age, of sturdy physique, his stature tall, his face austere, and his complexion swarthy. He rode a strong horse, wore a coat of mail, and carried two pistols on each side. Noticing that his squires (for so men of that profession are called in those parts) were about to strip Sancho, he commanded them to stop; he was instantly obeyed, and thus the sash escaped untouched. He was surprised to see a lance leaning against a tree, a shield on the ground, and Don Quixote in armor and pensive, with the saddest and most melancholy face that sadness itself could devise.

Walking up to him, he said: "Do not be downhearted, my good man, for you have not fallen into the hands of some cruel Osiris, but into those of Roque Guinart,[4] whose nature is more compassionate than cruel."

"My sadness," replied Don Quixote, "does not arise from having fallen into your hands, O valiant Roque, whose fame reaches the ends of the earth, but from my negligence in allowing your followers to surprise me with my horse un-

[4] Roque Guinart was a celebrated bandit whose exploits made him the terror of Catalonia in the early days of the seventeenth century. His real name was Perot Roca Guinarda and he came from near Vich. During the years 1607–1611, he became a kind of Robin Hood figure in the popular imagination. He fought for the partisans known as the Niarros against the Cadells. In 1611 he was pardoned and was appointed captain of a *tercio* of regular troops in Naples.

bridled. According to the tenets of the order of knight-
errantry that I profess, it was my duty to be continually on
the alert, and at all hours to be my own sentinel, for I would
have you know, great Roque, that had they found me on
horseback with my lance and my shield, they would have
found it no easy task to vanquish me, for I am Don Quixote
of La Mancha, he whose exploits echo throughout the
world."

Roque Guinart straightaway realized that Don Quixote's
infirmity had more of madness than of valor in it, and
though he had from time to time heard men speak of him,
he had never believed that what was said of him was true,
and he did not imagine that such a humor could exist in any
man. He was, in consequence, delighted to meet him, as he
now had an opportunity to investigate for himself.

"Valiant knight," said he, "do not vex yourself or exclaim
against your destiny, for who knows whether by this
stumbling you may now rectify your twisted fortunes. Indeed, Heaven, by strange and unaccountable ways beyond
man's comprehension, is wont to raise the fallen and enrich
the poor."

Don Quixote was just going to thank him when they heard
behind them a noise as of a troop of horses, though it turned
out to be only one, upon which there came riding at full
gallop a youth who seemed to be about twenty years of age,
clothed in green damask laced with gold, breeches, and a
loose coat, with a hat turned up in the Walloon fashion, waxed
tight-fitting boots, and gilt spurs, dagger, and sword. In his
hand he carried a small firelock and two pistols by his sides.
At the noise Roque turned his head and saw this handsome
figure, who called out as he drew near to him: "I was coming in search of you, valiant Roque, to find in you, if not a
cure, at least a relief for my affliction. And not to keep you
in suspense, for I see that you have not recognized me, I
shall tell you who I am. I am Claudia Jerónima, daughter of
Simón Forte, your particular friend and a sworn enemy of
Clauquel Torrellas, who is also yours, as he is one of the
opposite faction. Now you know that this Torrellas has a
son called Don Vicente Torrellas, or at least was so called
two hours ago. He, then— To cut short the story of my misfortune, I shall tell you briefly the trouble he brought upon
me. He saw me and courted me; I listened to him and fell in
love with him, unknown to my father, for there is no woman,

however retiring or modest she may be, who cannot find time enough to carry her passionate desires into effect. In short, he promised to be my husband and I gave him my word to be his wife, though we went no further than that. I learned yesterday that he had forgotten his obligations to me, and was going to marry another, and that the ceremony was to take place this morning. The news drove me distraught, with the result that I lost my patience. So, as my father was not in town, I had the notion of putting on the dress you see, and spurring on my horse, I overtook Don Vicente about three miles from here. Then, without pausing to reproach him or to listen to his excuses, I fired this gun at him, and these two pistols into the bargain. I believe I must have lodged more than two bullets in his body, and in this way I have washed my honor clean in his blood. And there I left him, surrounded by his servants, who did not, or could not, interfere in his defense. Now I have come to ask you to pass me over to France, where I have relations with whom I can live, and also to beg you to defend my father, so that Don Vicente's many friends may not venture to wreak cruel revenge on him."

Impressed by the fair Claudia's gallant bearing and courage no less than by her handsome figure and strange story, Roque said: "Come, lady, and let us see if your enemy is dead. Afterward, we shall consider what is the best course for you."

But Don Quixote, who had been listening eagerly to Claudia's words and Roque Guinart's reply, exclaimed: "No one needs to trouble himself to defend this lady, for I take it upon myself. Let them give me my horse and arms and await me here, for I will go to seek this gentleman. Dead or alive I shall compel him to fulfill the word he has pledged to this beautiful lady."

"Let no one doubt that," said Sancho, "for my master's a master at matchmaking, for it's not so many days ago that he made another man marry, who'd also refused to keep his promise to a maiden. And if it hadn't been for the enchanters who plague him and changed his true shape into a lackey's, that maiden would have ceased to be one by this time."

Roque, who was more concerned with the fair Claudia's adventure than with the speeches of master and servant, paid no heed to them. He commanded his squires to give back to Sancho all that they had plundered from Dapple, and he ordered them to return to the place where they had been stationed the night before. Then, he immediately set off with Claudia, in great haste, to look for the wounded or dead Don Vicente.

They came to the spot where Claudia had met him, and they found nothing there but newly spilled blood. Looking about in all directions, however, they observed some people on the side of a hill and concluded correctly that it must be Don Vicente, whom his servants were carrying, either alive or dead, to heal or to bury him.

They made haste to overtake them, and as the procession was going slowly, they easily did so. They found Don Vicente in the arms of his servants, beseeching them in a feeble voice to leave him there to die, for the pain of his wounds would not allow him to go any further.

Claudia and Roque jumped down from their horses and went to him. The servants were frightened at Roque's presence, and Claudia was troubled at the sight of Don Vicente. She went up to him, and seizing his hands, she said in a tone that was both tender and severe: "If you had given me those hands and kept our compact, you would not have come to such a pass."

The wounded gentleman opened his eyes, which were almost closed, and recognizing Claudia, he replied: "Now I see, fair and deluded mistress, that it was you who killed me, a punishment I never deserved, for neither by my desires nor by my actions could I ever wish or do you wrong."

"Then, is it not true," cried Claudia, "that you were going this morning to marry Leonora, rich Balvastro's daughter?"

"No, indeed," replied Don Vicente. "It must have been my ill luck that brought you this news, that you might through your jealousy deprive me of my life. But I consider my lot fortunate since I relinquish it in your arms. And to prove to you that this is true, hold my hand and take me for your husband, if you will, for I have no other satisfaction to give you for the injury you fancy you have received from me."

Claudia pressed his hand, and her heart was so oppressed that she fell in a faint upon Don Vicente's bleeding breast, while he was seized by the death spasm. Roque was perplexed and did not know what to do. The servants ran for water to throw in their faces and returned to sprinkle them with it. Claudia recovered from her faint, but not Don Vicente from his paroxysm, for his life was ended. When

Claudia perceived this and became aware that her sweet spouse no longer lived, she rent the air with her sobs, wounded the heavens with her lamentations, tore her hair, tossing it to the winds, disfigured her face with her hands, and showed all the signs of grief and sorrow that could be expected from a wounded heart.

"Come, thoughtless woman!" she cried. "How easily were you driven to carry out your evil purpose! Jealousy, you raging fury, to what a desperate end you bring her who harbored you in her bosom! O husband of mine, whose hapless fate has brought you from the bridal bed to the grave, because of your pledge to me!"

So pathetic were Claudia's lamentations that they brought tears to Roque's eyes, though he was little used to shed them on any occasion. The servants wept, Claudia fainted again and again, and all around was a scene of grief and desolation. At length Roque Guinart ordered Don Vicente's servants to take his body to his father's place, which was nearby, to give him burial. Claudia told Roque that she would retire to a convent where an aunt of hers was abbess, and there she intended to end her days in the company of a better and more eternal spouse. Roque commended her pious resolution and offered to accompany her wherever she pleased and to defend her father from Don Vicente's relations and from all the world, if they should seek to injure him. Claudia would on no account accept his company, but after thanking him for his offer in the best way she could, she took her leave of him in tears. Don Vicente's servants lifted the body, and Roque returned to his men. So ended the loves of Claudia Jerónima. But what wonder when we realize that cruel and invincible jealousy wove the web of her doleful story.

Roque Guinart found his squires where he had commanded them to be, and Don Quixote among them, mounted on Rozinante and making them a speech in which he urged them to give up their way of life, as perilous for the soul as well as the body. But as the majority were Gascons, a rough and lawless people, Don Quixote's harangue did not much impress them. When Roque arrived, he asked Sancho Panza whether his men had restored to him the jewels and effects they had taken from Dapple. Sancho replied that they had, but that three kerchiefs were missing, worth three cities.

"What's that you say, man?" cried one of them. "I have them, and they're not worth three reals."

"That is true," said Don Quixote, "but my squire values them at the price he mentioned for the sake of the person who gave them to me."

Roque Guinart ordered them to be immediately restored; then, commanding his men to form a line, he bade them produce before him all the clothing, jewels, money, and everything else that they had stolen since the last handout. Then, making a rapid evaluation and reducing whatever could not be divided into its money value, he shared it all out among his band with such careful impartiality that he neither exceeded nor fell short of strict distributive justice by a single point. And after this handout, which left everyone satisfied and in the best of spirits, Roque said to Don Quixote: "If I were not so scrupulous with these fellows it would be impossible to live with them."

Whereupon Sancho remarked: "According to what I see here, justice must be a mighty fine thing, for it has to be practiced among thieves."

One of the squires who happened to overhear Sancho's remark raised the butt of his musket and would doubtlessly have split open Sancho's skull if Roque Guinart had not roared at him to stop. Sancho was scared and resolved to open his lips no more as long as he was in that company.

At this moment one or more of the squires posted on the road as scouts to watch all travelers came running up with information for the chief. "Sir," said the scout, "there's a great troop of people not far off, on the road to Barcelona."

"Have you noticed," said Roque, "whether they're such as look for us, or such as we look for?"

"Such as we look for," answered the scout.

"Off with you then," said Roque, "and bring them here; see that none escape."

The order was immediately obeyed, and the bandits went off; Don Quixote, Sancho, and the chief waited to see what they would bring. Meanwhile Roque addressed Don Quixote as follows: "I am sure, Don Quixote, that this life of ours must appear strange to you, with its constant sequence of adventures and accidents, all of them perilous. I don't wonder that it seems so to you, for I must confess that no manner of life compares with ours for hazards and anxieties. I was driven into it by a lust for vengeance, which is strong enough to sway even those whose natures are calm and peaceable. By temperament I am gentle and humane, but as I have said

before, no sooner do I feel the wish to avenge a wrong that
has been done to me than all my good intentions fall to the
ground. And once I have given way to my evil nature, I feel
that I must go on, even in spite of my better designs; and as
one fall is followed by another fall and sin is added to sin,
my resentments and acts of vengeance have linked themselves
together in such an uninterrupted chain that I find myself
bearing the burden of other men's crimes as well as my
own. Nevertheless, with the help of God, I hope to extricate
myself from this entangled maze and bring a peaceful end
to my misfortunes."

Don Quixote was surprised to hear Roque utter such sound
and sensible words, for he did not expect such qualities from
one whose occupation was robbing and killing. "Señor
Roque," said he, "once a man recognizes his infirmity and
consents to take the medicines prescribed by his physician,
he has taken the first great step toward health. You are sick;
you know your infirmity, and God, our physician, will apply
medicines that, provided you give them time, will certainly
heal you. For sinners who are men of understanding more
easily mend their ways than fools, and as your superior
sense is manifest, be of good heart and trust in your recovery.
If you wish to take the shortest way toward your salvation,
come with me and I will teach you to be a knight-errant; it
is a profession full of toils and troubles, no doubt, but if you
look upon them as penances for your misdeeds, you will
save your soul in the twinkling of an eye."

Roque smiled at Don Quixote's naïve counsel, and changing the subject, he related Claudia Jerónima's tragic story,
which moved Sancho deeply, for he had been quite attracted
by the girl's beauty, boldness, and spirit.

By this time Roque's company of bandits had returned
with their captives, who consisted of two gentlemen on horseback, two pilgrims on foot, a coach full of women, attended
by half a dozen servants, some on foot and some on horseback, and two muleteers who belonged to the two gentlemen.
They were surrounded by the victorious squires, who, as
well as the vanquished travelers, stood in profound silence
awaiting the sentence of the great Roque. First of all he
asked the gentlemen who they were, where they were going,
and what money they carried.

One of them answered: "We are captains of the Spanish infantry, sir; we are going to join our companies at Naples; and thus we intend to embark at Barcelona, where four galleys are about to sail for Sicily. We carry about two or three hundred crowns, which we thought a tidy sum for men of our profession, who seldom carry well-lined purses."

The same question was put to the pilgrims, who said that they intended to embark for Rome and that they had between them about sixty reals.

Roque then questioned the travelers in the coach, and one of the horsemen answered that the persons within were Doña Guiomar de Quiñones, wife of the regent of the vicarship of Naples, her little daughter, a maidservant, and an old duenna, together with six servants, and that their total sum of money amounted to six hundred crowns.

"So then," said Roque Guinart, "we have here nine hundred crowns and sixty reals; I think I have about sixty soldiers here. See how much falls to each, for I'm a bad accountant."

Hearing this, the highwaymen shouted: "Long live Roque Guinart and damn the dogs who seek his ruin!"

The officers looked crestfallen, the lady very dejected, the pilgrims in no way pleased, at seeing their goods confiscated. Roque held them for a while in suspense, but he did not wish to prolong their melancholy, which was visible at a bow shot's distance; so, turning to the captains, he said: "Do me the favor, gentlemen, to lend me sixty crowns, and you, lady, oblige me with eighty as a small gratification for these worthy gentlemen of my squadron, for 'The abbot who sings for his meat must eat.' You may then depart and continue your journey without hindrance, for I'll give you a pass in case you run across any other squadrons of mine that are scattered about this region. It is not a practice of mine to interfere with soldiers, and I have no intention of failing in my respects toward the fair sex, especially, madam, when they are ladies of quality."

The captains gave cordial thanks to Roque for his courtesy and generosity, for they considered it a generous gesture of him to allow them to keep their money. Doña Guiomar de Quiñones wanted to throw herself out of the coach to kiss his feet and his hands, but Roque would not permit it; he even begged her pardon for the injury he was forced to do in compliance with the duties of his office. The lady then ordered one of her lackeys to pay the eighty crowns, and the captains settled their share of the debt; as for the pilgrims, they were about to offer their "widow's mite," but Roque told them to wait a little. Then, turning to his men, he said: "Each man will get two crowns as his share of the pool, which means that there are twenty over. Let ten be given to these pilgrims, and the remaining ten be given to this honest squire, so that he may say a good word about us hereafter."

Then, taking pen, ink, and paper, he wrote out a passport directed to the chiefs of his various squadrons, and wishing them good luck, he let them go their way. They departed fully convinced that such a gallant, generous chief was an Alexander the Great rather than a notorious robber.

When the travelers had gone, one of the bandits mumbled in his Catalan language: "This captain of ours would do better as a friar than as a bandit. In the future, if he must be openhanded, let it be with his own money."

The poor wretch spoke low, but Roque heard him, and drawing his sword, he almost cleft his skull in two, saying: "That's how I chastise mutiny."

The rest were dumbfounded and said not a word, so great was their obedience to his authority. Roque then withdrew and wrote a letter to a friend at Barcelona, to let him know that the famous Don Quixote of La Mancha was with him, that this knight was the most amusing and the most sensible man in the world, and that as the knight was on his way to Barcelona, he would be sure to see him there on St. John the Baptist's day, parading the strand in full panoply, on his steed Rozinante, and followed by his squire, Sancho Panza, upon an ass. He bade him give notice of this to his friends the Niarros so that they might amuse themselves with him, but he wanted his enemies the Cadells to miss that pleasure, though that was impossible, for Don Quixote's deeds of madness and good sense and the drolleries of his squire, Sancho Panza, were bound to give entertainment to the entire world. Roque dispatched this letter by one of his squires, who exchanged the highwayman's dress for a peasant's and went into Barcelona to deliver it to the person to whom it was addressed.

CHAPTER LXI

Of what happened to Don Quixote upon entering Barcelona, with other matters containing more truth than wisdom

Don Quixote spent three days and three nights with Roque, and had he tarried with him three hundred years, he might have still found plenty to observe and admire in that kind of life. They bivouacked at dawn on this side of the country, only to take their evening meal at the opposite side. Sometimes they fled from they knew not whom, at other times they lay in wait for they knew not whom, often forced to snatch a nap standing and every moment liable to be disturbed in haste by the approach of danger. They were always on the watch, sending out spies, questioning sentries, blowing the matches of their firelocks, though they had but few, for they were chiefly armed with flintlocks. Roque passed his nights apart from his men, letting nobody know where his hiding place was to be found; secrecy was vitally necessary owing to the continual proclamations issued against him by the viceroy of Barcelona, and as a consequence, he feared to trust even his own men lest one of them betray him to the authorities for the price of his head. His was, indeed, a nerve-racking and unhappy life.

At last, after pursuing a hazardous journey by unfrequented roads, shortcuts, and secret bypaths, Roque, Don Quixote, and Sancho, attended by six squires, set out for Barcelona. They reached the strand of Barcelona on St. John's Eve at night, and Roque embraced Don Quixote and Sancho, giving the latter the ten crowns he had promised, but not handed over until then, and he left them with cordial offers of services on both sides. Roque turned back, and Don Quixote remained waiting for daybreak, mounted as he was. And it was not long before the pale of face of Aurora began to peep through the balconies of the earth, rejoicing the flowers and plants in the fields, while at the same time the ears of men were cheered by a gay rousing sound of pipes, kettledrums, and jingling bells, mingled with the "Tramp, tramp! Make way, make way!" of horsemen and pedestrians who appeared to be leaving the city. Aurora gave way to the Sun, whose face, broader than a buckler, gradually rose from below the horizon. Then Don Quixote and Sancho gazed about them and descried the sea, which they had never seen before. To them it seemed a very great expanse, far greater than the lakes of Ruidera, which they had seen in La Mancha. They saw the galleys bobbing at anchor off the shore, which, when their awnings were removed, appeared covered with flags and pennants that flickered in the wind and sometimes kissed and swept the surface of the water. From within them they heard the sound of trumpets, hautboys, and clarions filling the air with martial music. Soon afterward the galleys began to glide over the calm sea and engage in a kind of naval skirmish; at the same time numerous cavaliers, in rich uniforms and gallantly mounted, rode out from the city and completed the warlike tourney by their movements on the shore. The marines discharged repeated volleys from the galleys, which were answered by those on the ramparts and forts of the city walls, and thus the air was rent by the thunder of this mimic battle, which echoed and reechoed far and wide. The sea sparkled, the land was gay, the sky serene in every quarter save where wisps of smoke clouded it for an instant; indeed, it seemed as if everything in the smiling scene contributed to gladden the heart of man.

Sancho, though, could not imagine how those hulks that moved on the sea could have so many feet; and as for Don Quixote, he stood gazing in silent amazement upon the scene. Presently the band of cavaliers in bright uniforms came galloping up to him, whooping and shouting in the Moorish manner, and one of them—the person to whom Roque had written—cried in a resounding voice to the knight: "Welcome to our city, O mirror, beacon, and North Star of knighterrantry! Welcome, I repeat, O valiant Don Quixote of La Mancha, not the false, spurious, and apocryphal one sent to us in lying histories, but the true, legitimate, and loyal one described by Cide Hamete Benengeli, the flower of all historians."

Don Quixote made no answer, nor did the cavaliers wait for any; they wheeled about and pranced around the knight and his squire. Don Quixote, seeing all this, turned to Sancho and said: "They have, indeed, recognized us. I bet that they have read our history, and even the one that the Aragonese has recently published."

Then the gentleman who had spoken before addressed Don Quixote, saying: "Be pleased, sir knight, to come with us, for we are all devoted friends of Roque Guinart."

And Don Quixote replied: "If courtesy begets courtesy, then yours, kind sir, is akin to that of the great Roque; lead me where you wish, for my will is yours, especially to serve you."

The gentleman answered in no less polite and refined a fashion, and all of them then enclosed the knight and proceeded toward the city accompanied by the martial music of trumpet and hautboys. But at the entrance, the father of mischief himself, along with some boys, who are the very Devil, so ordained it that two of their number, bolder than the rest, managed to wriggle their way through the crowd of horsemen until they reached Don Quixote and his squire. One lifted up Dapple's tail, and the other that of Rozinante, and they shoved a handful of briars under each of them. The poor animals, feeling such unusual spurs, clapped their tails closer, which so increased their pain that they began to curvet and plunge and kick so violently that their riders were thrown to the ground. Don Quixote, abashed and nettled at the affront, made haste to remove the sting from the tail of his long-suffering steed, and Sancho performed the same office for his Dapple. The escorts would have chastised the offenders, but the young scapegraces darted away with lightning rapidity and disappeared in the crowd that followed the procession. The knight and the squire mounted again, and amid the blare of music and loud acclamations, they proceeded on their way until they came to their guide's house, a stately mansion that proclaimed the owner to be a man of wealth. There we shall leave them for the present, for such is the will of Cide Hamete.

CHAPTER LXII

*Which treats of the adventure of the enchanted head,
with other childish matters that cannot be omitted*

Don Quixote's host, who was called Don Antonio Moreno,
was a wealthy gentleman of cheerful disposition, always
ready to enjoy a good-humored jest. Now that he had the
knight in his house he resolved to extract as much innocent
amusement as he could from his guest's whimsical infirmity
without offense to his person, for jests that cause pain are
not jests, and pastimes that inflict an injury upon one's neighbor are unworthy of the name. The first thing he did was
to make Don Quixote take off his armor; he then led him
to a balcony that looked out into one of the principal streets
of the city, and there in his tight-fitting chamois doublet,
he exposed him to the populace, who gathered below and
stood gaping at him as if he had been some strange baboon.
The horsemen in uniform careered before him once more,
as though they had put on their finery for him alone, and
not in honor of that day's solemnity. And Sancho was
highly delighted, for he thought that somehow or other he
had landed into another Camacho's wedding, another house
like Don Diego de Miranda's, another castle like the duke's.

Don Antonio that day had some of his friends to dinner,
and they all did honor to Don Quixote, treating him like a
knight-errant, at which he became so puffed up with vanity
that he could scarcely contain himself for pleasure. As for
Sancho, his waggish drolleries came so fast that all the servants in the home and everyone who heard him hung upon
his lips. When they sat down to dine, Don Antonio said
to Sancho: "We have heard here, worthy Sancho, that you

have such a fondness for breast of chicken, cream of rice, and forcemeat balls that if you have any left, you keep them in your shirt pocket for another day." [1]

"No, sir, that's not true," replied Sancho. "In fact, I'm more tidy than greedy in my habits, and my master, Don Quixote, who is here present, knows well that with just a handful of acorns or nuts we two often go for eight days together. It's true that sometimes if they chance to give me the heifer, I run with the rope; I mean to say that I eat what I'm given and make hay while the sun shines. But you can take it from me that anyone who says that I'm a gluttonous and untidy eater is wide off the mark, and I would say it in another way but for my respect for the honorable beards here present."

"I assure you," said Don Quixote, "that Sancho's abstemiousness and tidiness at table might be engraved on tablets of brass to remain a perpetual memorial for future ages. It is true that when he is hungry he appears somewhat ravenous, for he eats fast and chews on both sides of his mouth. But he is a scrupulously tidy eater, and during the time he was governor he learned to eat so delicately that he used to eat grapes and even pomegranate seeds with a fork."

"What!" exclaimed Don Antonio. "Has Sancho been a governor?"

"Yes," answered Sancho, "of an island called Barataria. I governed it for ten days as well as anyone could wish, and during that time I lost my rest and learned to despise all the governorships in the world. I ran away from it and fell into a cave; I thought I was dead, and it was only by a miracle that I came out alive."

Don Quixote related in detail the whole episode of Sancho's governorship, which vastly entertained his hearers. Then, when the cloths were removed, Don Antonio took the

---

[1] Breast of chicken and cream of rice (*manjar blanco*), according to a cooking book of the period, was a very popular dish; those who sold it in the streets were called *manjarblanqueros* or blancmange-sellers. Diego Granado, *Libro del Arte de Cozina*, Luis Sánchez, (Madrid, 1599). The reference to forcemeat balls (*pelotillas de carne*) is an intentional thrust at Avellaneda's spurious continuation of *Don Quixote*. Avellaneda describes how the glutton Sancho seized the forcemeat balls off the dish and hid them in his pocket.

knight by the hand and led him into a private room where there was no other furniture than a table, evidently of jasper, supported by a leg of the same material, on which stood a bust apparently of bronze, in the style of the heads of the Roman emperors. Don Antonio paced up and down the room with Don Quixote, taking several turns around the table, and after a while he said: "Now that I am sure, Don Quixote, that no one is listening or can hear us, and the door is closed, I shall tell you of one of the strangest adventures, or rather wonders, that could be imagined, on condition that what I shall say to you be kept a profound secret."

"I take my oath," replied Don Quixote, "and I will even throw a flagstone over it to make quite sure. And I would have you know, Don Antonio," (by now he had learned his host's name) "that you are talking to one who, though he has ears to hear, has no tongue to speak. So you may with safety convey what lies in your breast into mine, and reckon that you have consigned it to the depths of silence."

"On the faith of that pledge," answered Don Antonio, "I shall at once fill you with amazement and give myself some relief from the disappointment I feel at having nobody to whom I may communicate my secrets, for they should by no means be confided to all."

Don Quixote was perplexed and waited to see what would be the outcome of all these precautions. Then Don Antonio took hold of the knight's hand, passed it over the bronze head and along the table and down the jasper pedestal on which it stood, and said: "This head, Don Quixote, was made by one of the greatest enchanters and wizards the world has ever known. I believe he was a Pole by race and a disciple of the famous Escotillo,[2] of whom they relate so many marvels. He was here in my house, and at the price of a thousand crowns he constructed this head, which has the virtue and property of answering any questions spoken into his ear. He took the bearings, he traced the characters, he studied the stars, he marked the minutes,

[2] Luis Zapata (1526–1595) in his *Miscelánea* (1592) tells many anecdotes of the wizard Escotillo, who converted gold doubloons into slates and vice versa, and horses into cows. In the *Disquisiciones Magicae* (1604) of Martín del Río we find similar stories.

and he perfected his work, as we shall see tomorrow, for on Fridays it is mute, and as today is Friday, we shall have to wait until tomorrow. During that time you will be able to decide what question you will ask, and I know by experience that its answers will be true."

Don Quixote was amazed at this description of the head; he was inclined not to believe Don Antonio, but seeing how little time there was for making a trial, he preferred to say nothing except merely to thank his host for revealing so great a secret to him. They then left the room, Don Antonio locked the door, and they went into the hall where the other gentlemen were sitting. In the meanwhile Sancho had told the company many of the adventures and incidents that had befallen his master.

That same afternoon they took Don Quixote for a stroll through the city, clad not in armor, but in street dress, a long coat of tawny cloth that would have made even ice itself sweat at that season. They gave their servants orders to entertain Sancho and on no account to let him leave the house. Don Quixote rode, not upon Rozinante, but upon a tall, easy-stepping mule, very richly caparisoned. They put the long coat on him, and at the back, without his seeing it, they stitched a parchment to his back on which they had written in large letters: "This is Don Quixote of La Mancha." No sooner did they begin their parade than the scroll became the attraction of everyone in the streets, and as a great number of passersby read it, Don Quixote was astonished to find how many people recognized him and greeted him by name. So, he turned to Don Antonio, who rode by his side, saying: "There is a great prerogative in knight-errantry, since it makes those who profess it known and celebrated right to the end of the earth, for look, Don Antonio, even the boys of this city know me, though they have never seen me before."

"That is so, Don Quixote," replied Don Antonio, "for just as fire cannot be hidden and confined, virtue cannot help being known, and that which is achieved by the profession of arms outshines and excels all others."

Now, as Don Quixote was riding along amid the acclamations we have described, a certain Castilian who happened to read the scroll on his back exclaimed in a loud voice: "The Devil take Don Quixote of La Mancha! What! How have you got here alive after all the drubbings you've received? You're a madman, and if you had been crazy in private and behind the doors of your folly, you would have done less harm. But you have the peculiar capacity of turning everyone who has to do with you into dolts and madmen. Just look at these gentlemen riding with you! Go back home, idiot, and look after your estate, your wife, and your children; quit these trifling vanities that rot your brain and blight your understanding."

"Brother," said Don Antonio, "go your way and don't offer your advice when it is not wanted. Don Quixote is a man of good sense, and we who ride with him are no fools. Virtue must be honored wherever it is found. Go away and bad luck to you; don't meddle where you're not wanted."

"Indeed, you're right, your worship," answered the Castilian, "for to offer this worthy man advice is to kick against the pricks. But it grieves me all the same that the good sense they say this blockhead has in all things should run to waste along the channel of knight-errantry. But bad luck to me and all my descendants if from now on, should I live longer than Methuselah, I offer advice to anyone, though he pester me for it."

The advice-monger then went off, and the parade continued, but so great was the crowd of boys and people reading the scroll that Don Antonio had to take it off, under the pretense of doing something else. When night fell, they returned to the house, where a ball took place, for Don Antonio's wife, who was a lady of distinction, gay, handsome, and intelligent, had invited some of her friends to come and honor her guest and to join in the diversion created by his eccentric humor. A great number came, and after a sumptuous banquet, the dance began at about ten o'clock at night. Among the ladies there were two of a roguish and frolicsome humor, who, although they were very modest, were not unwilling to engage in a little innocent flirtation to amuse the company. These two were so insistent on getting Don Quixote out to dance that they wore him out in body and in soul. He was, indeed, a sight to see, with his long, lean, lanky figure, his yellow complexion, and his close-fitting doublet and hose; an awkward figure too, and by no means light-footed at a saraband. The roguish ladies fussed and flattered, and more than once they gave him private hints of their inclinations, but he as often repelled them and told them no less secretly that he was in-

different to their charms. At last, their teasing so exasperated
him that he cried aloud: *"Fugite, partes adversae!* [8] Leave
me in peace, unwelcome thoughts! Away, ladies! Play your
amorous pranks with someone else, for the peerless Dulcinea
is the sole queen of my soul."

With these words he sat down on the floor in the middle
of the room, for he was utterly worn out by so much dancing. Don Antonio gave orders that he was to be carried up
to bed, and the first who came to lend a helping hand was
Sancho, who said: "Lord bless us and save us, master! What
did you mean by dancing? Do you think that all brave men
are dancers and that all knights-errant must be cutting
capers? If you do, you're wrong; there's men who would
sooner slay a giant than cut a caper. Had you been on for
the clog dance, I'd have been your man, for I can slap
and tap away like a falcon; but as for any of your fine
dancing, I can't work a stitch of it."

The company was highly amused at Sancho's observations.
He led away his master and put him to bed, leaving him
well muffled up to sweat away the efforts of his dance.

The next day Don Antonio decided to make the experiment with the enchanted head, and with Don Quixote, Sancho, two other friends, and the two ladies who had tormented the knight at the dance and who had stayed that
night with Don Antonio's wife, he locked himself up in the
room that contained the head. After explaining its properties,
he pledged them to secrecy, saying that this was the first
day on which the virtue of the said enchanted head was to
be put to the test. No other person except Don Antonio's
two friends knew of the mystery of the enchantment, and if
Don Antonio had not first revealed it to them, they would
have been as astonished as the rest, for it was impossible
not to be impressed, so ingeniously and artfully had it been
contrived. The first who went up to the ear of the head
was Don Antonio himself, who said in a subdued voice, yet
not so softly that he could not be heard by all: "Tell me,
head, by the virtue contained in you, what are my thoughts
this moment?"

And the head replied without moving its lips in a clear
and distinct voice: "I have no knowledge of your thoughts."

[8] This expression is used in ecclesiastical exorcisms. (Flee,
my enemies.)

On hearing this they were all struck with amazement, especially as there was no human being in all the room or near the table who could have answered.

"How many are we?" asked Don Antonio again.

And the answer came in the same quiet tone: "There are you and your wife, two friends of yours and two of hers, and a famous knight called Don Quixote of La Mancha and his squire, Sancho Panza by name."

Here again was fresh cause for astonishment, and everyone's hair stood on end in fear. Don Antonio then moved away from the head and said: "This is enough to convince me that I was not cheated by the man who sold you to me, learned head, talkative head, answering head, marvelous head! Let someone else come and ask it what he wishes."

And as women are generally impatient and inquisitive, the first to go at it was one of Don Antonio's wife's two friends, and her question was: "Tell me, head, what shall I do to be very beautiful?"

And the reply was: "Be very chaste."

"I have no more to ask," said the questioner.

Then her companion went up and said: "I should like to know, head, if my husband loves me or not."

And the answer was: "Consider what he does for you, and you will know."

The married woman moved away and said: "I might have spared it that question, for a man's actions certainly proclaim his feelings."

Then one of Don Antonio's two friends went up and asked: "Who am I?"

And the reply came: "You know."

"That does not answer my question," replied the gentleman. "I asked you to tell me whether you knew me."

"Yes, I know you," answered the voice. "You are Don Pedro Noriz."

"I don't want to know anymore, for that's enough to convince me, O head, that you know everything."

Then he moved away, and the other friend went up and asked: "Tell me, head, what are the desires of my son and heir?"

"I have already said," came the answer, "that I have no knowledge of wishes, but I can tell you all the same that your son would like to bury you."

"That," said the gentleman, "is 'What I see with my eyes,

I touch with my fingers,' and I ask no more."

The wife of Don Antonio then went up and said: "I don't know, head, what to ask you; I would only like to know whether I shall enjoy married life for many years."

And the answer came: "Yes, you will, for his good health and his temperance promise him long years of life, which many cut short by their intemperance."

Next came Don Quixote, who said: "Tell me, you who answer, was it the truth or a dream my account of what happened to me in the cave of Montesinos? Will the whippings of Sancho, my squire, be fulfilled? Will the disenchantment of Dulcinea be accomplished?"

"With regard to the cave," was the answer, "there is much to be said; it has something of both. Sancho's whippings should go on slowly. Dulcinea's disenchantment will be duly accomplished."

"I wish to know no more," said Don Quixote, "for when I see Dulcinea disenchanted, I shall reckon that all the good fortune I can desire has come to me at once."

The last to ask was Sancho, and his question was: "Shall I ever get another governorship? Shall I quit this hungry squire's life? Shall I see my wife and children again?"

To which the answer came: "You will govern in your own house, and if you go home, you will see your wife and children, and by giving up service you will cease to be a squire."

"By God, that's rich," cried Sancho Panza. "I could have told myself all that; the prophet Perogrullo couldn't do better." [4]

"Beast!" cried Don Quixote. "What answer do you expect? Is it not enough that the replies this head gives correspond to the questions asked it?"

"Yes, it's enough," replied Sancho, "but I wish it would be plainer and tell me more."

With this the questions and answers were brought to an end, but there was no end to the amazement of all present, except Don Antonio's two friends, who were in the secret. This Cide Hamete Benengeli wished to explain at once, for fear of keeping the whole world in suspense, believing that some magic or strange mystery was hidden in this head.

---

[4] The prophecies of Perogrullo (*Profecías de Perogrullo*) like the French *Vérités de la Pallisse* meant truisms or platitudes. Even Quevedo did not disdain to include lists of them in his *Visita de los chistes*.

He says that Don Antonio Moreno, in imitation of another head that he had seen at Madrid, designed by a die-cutter, manufactured this one at home for his own entertainment and to puzzle the ignorant. Its construction was as follows: The top of the table was of wood, painted and varnished to look like jasper, and the pedestal on which it stood was of the same material, with four eagle's claws protruding from it to support the weight more firmly. The head, which looked like a bust and figure of a Roman emperor, of the color of bronze, was all hollow, and equally so was the top of the table, into which it fitted so exactly that no sign of a junction was visible. The stand of the table likewise was hollow, to correspond with the throat and chest of the bust, and the whole was made to communicate with another room that was underneath the one in which the table stood. Through all these hollow channels in the stand, the table, the throat, and the chest of the said bust, ran a tin pipe, very neatly adjusted, so that it was not visible to anybody. In the room below, corresponding to the one above, was stationed the man who had to answer with his mouth applied to this same pipe, so that the voice from above came down and the voice from below sounded above in clear articulate words, as in an ear-trumpet. And so it was impossible to discover the deception. One of Don Antonio's nephews, a bright and witty youth, was the answerer, and after being informed by his uncle of those who were to enter the chamber of the head with him that day, it was easy for him to answer promptly and accurately the first question. The rest he answered by guesswork, and as he was a clever youth, cleverly. And Cide Hamete goes on to say that this oracular machine continued to exist for ten or twelve days, but when the rumor spread through the city that Don Antonio had in his house an enchanted head that answered all the questions asked of it, he was afraid that its fame might reach the ears of those watchful sentinels of our faith. So he gave an account of the matter to the inquisitors, who ordered him to take it apart and use it no further, lest the ignorant masses be scandalized. But in Don Quixote and Sancho Panza's opinion the head was still enchanted and oracular, which gave more satisfaction to Don Quixote than to Sancho.

The gentlemen of the city, to please Don Antonio and to entertain Don Quixote and give him an opportunity of displaying his eccentricities, arranged a tilting at the ring for six days later, but it did not take place owing to an accident that shall be described later.

Don Quixote wished to go for a stroll through the city without ceremony and on foot, for he feared that the boys would persecute him if he went on horseback. So, he and Sancho, with two other servants Don Antonio gave him, went out for a walk. As they were going down a street, Don Quixote lifted his eyes and saw inscribed over a door in very large letters, "Books printed here," which greatly pleased him, for he had never before seen any printing and longed to know how it was done. He went in with all his followers and saw them drawing off the sheets in one place, correcting the proofs in another, setting up the type in this, and revising in that—in short, all the processes that are to be seen in a large printing house. Don Quixote went up to one department and asked what they were doing there. The workmen duly explained, and he watched with wonder and passed on. Then he approached another man and asked him what he was doing, and the workman replied: "Sir, that gentleman you see there," and he pointed out a fine-looking fellow of dignified appearance, "has translated an Italian book into our Castilian tongue, and I am setting it up for the press."

"What is the title of the book?" asked Don Quixote.

"Sir," replied the author, "the book in Italian is called *Le Bagatelle.*

"And what corresponds to *Le Bagatelle* in our Castilian?" asked Don Quixote.

"*Le Bagatelle,*" said the author, "is, we might say, trifles in our tongue, and though this book is humble in its title, it has good solid things in it."

"I know a little Italian," said Don Quixote, "and pride myself on singing some of Ariosto's stanzas. But tell me, sir—and I do not ask this to test your knowledge—have you ever come across the word *pignata* in your reading?"

"Yes, often," replied the author.

"And how do you translate it into Castilian, sir?" asked Don Quixote.

"How else," answered the author, "but by stew?"

"Bless me!" exclaimed Don Quixote. "How advanced you

are in the Tuscan tongue! I would lay a good wager that when the Tuscan tongue has *piace*, you say 'please,' and when it has *piu*, you say 'more,' and you translate *su* by 'above' and *giu* by 'beneath.'"

"Yes, so I translate them, certainly," said the author, "for these are their proper equivalents."

"Yes, I'll dare swear that you are not appreciated by the world, which is forever loath to reward intellect and merit. What abilities are lost here! What talents neglected! What virtues unappreciated! But yet, it seems to me that translating from one tongue into another, unless it be from those queens of tongues, Greek and Latin, is like viewing Flemish tapestries from the wrong side, for although you see the pictures, they are covered with threads that obscure them so that the smoothness and the gloss of the fabric are lost. And translating from easy languages does not signify talent or power of words, any more than does transcribing or copying one paper from another. By that I do not wish to imply that this exercise of translation is not praiseworthy, for a man might be occupied in worse things and less profitable occupations. I except from this observation two famous translators; the one, Doctor Cristóbal de Figueroa for his *Pastor Fido*, and the other Don Juan de Jáuregui for his *Aminta*, for they leave you doubting which is the translation and which the original. But tell me, sir, is the book printed on your own account or have you sold the copyright to a bookseller?"

"I am printing it on my own account," replied the author, "and I expect to gain a thousand ducats at least from this first edition of two thousand copies. At six reals apiece they'll be all sold in the twinkling of an eye."

"You are mighty clever at reckoning," said Don Quixote, "but it is quite clear that you do not know the tricks of the printing trade or the arrangements printers make with one another. When you find yourself saddled with two thousand copies of a book, you will find your shoulders so sore, I wager, that it will scare you, especially if the book is a bit off the beaten track and without a touch of spice in it."

"What then?" exclaimed the author. "Do you want me to hand it over to a bookseller who will give me three maravedis for the copyright and will even think that he does me a favor in giving me that? I do not print my books to win renown in the world, for I am already known by my works. I want profit, for fame isn't worth a mite without it."

"God send you good luck," answered Don Quixote, and he passed on to another department, where he saw they were correcting a sheet of a book entitled *Light of the Soul,* and when he saw it he said: "Books like this, numerous though they be, are the kind that ought to be printed, for there are many sinners nowadays, and infinite light is needed for so many in the dark."

He went on farther and saw them also correcting another book, and when he asked its title, they replied that it was *The Second Part of the Ingenious Gentleman Don Quixote of La Mancha,* composed by someone or other, native of Tordesillas.

"I have heard of this book already," said Don Quixote, "but truly, I thought that it had been burned by now and reduced to ashes for its presumption. But as every hog has its Martinmas,[5] so it will have its day. Works of invention are only good insofar as they touch the truth or the semblance thereof, and true stories are better the more authentic they are."

With these words he left the printing house with looks of annoyance. That same day Don Antonio arranged for him to be taken to see the galleys lying off the strand, which delighted Sancho greatly because he had never seen any in all his life. Don Antonio informed the commodore that he was going to bring him a guest that afternoon, the famous Don Quixote of La Mancha, of whom he and all the inhabitants of the city had heard. But what happened on that occasion shall be told in the following chapter.

[5] A proverbial phrase meaning that every book has its day of reckoning. The metaphor refers to pigs who have their day of slaughter on St. Martin's day.

CHAPTER LXIII

Of the disaster that befell Sancho Panza on his visit to the galleys, and the strange adventure of the Moorish girl

Deep as Don Quixote's meditations were over the enchanted head's replies, none of them hit on the deception, but all centered on Dulcinea's promised disenchantment, which he regarded as certain. To that he returned again and again and rejoiced in his heart in the belief that he would see it speedily accomplished. As for Sancho, though he loathed being a governor, as has been said, he still had a longing to rule once more and to be obeyed, for such is the evil effect that authority, even mock authority, brings in its train.

That afternoon Don Antonio Moreno, their host, and his two friends accompanied Don Quixote and Sancho to the galleys. The commodore had been warned of their arrival, and as the celebrated pair reached the strand, all the galleys struck their awnings and sounded their clarions.

Then immediately a pinnace was launched covered with rich carpets and cushions of crimson velvet, and no sooner did Don Quixote set foot aboard than the captain's galley fired her midship gun and all the rest followed suit. And as Don Quixote climbed the starboard ladder, the whole crew saluted him with three cheers, as is the custom when an important person boards a galley. The general, for so we shall call him, who was a Valencian gentleman of quality, gave Don Quixote his hand and embraced him, saying: "I shall mark today with a white stone, for I do not expect to spend a better one in all my life than this day when I meet Don Quixote of La Mancha—a day and a mark to signify that he is one who epitomizes all the valor of knight-errantry."

Don Quixote replied in no less courteous terms, being delighted beyond measure at finding himself treated in such noble fashion. They all went on to the poop, which was very gaily decorated, and sat down on the side benches. Then the boatswain passed along the gangway and gave the signal on his whistle for the crew to strip off their shirts, which they did in an instant. Sancho was startled to see so many men in their bare skin, and even more so when he saw them set the awning so quickly that it seemed to him as if all the devils were at work. But this was mere tarts and gingerbread to what was to follow. Sancho was sitting on the stantrel, next the aftermost oarsman on the starboard side. The latter, following his instructions, seized Sancho and hoisted him up in his arms, and then the whole crew, standing ready, starting from the starboard side, sent him flying along from hand to hand and from bench to bench, so that poor Sancho lost the sight of his eyes and evidently believed that the devils of hell were carrying him off. And they did not stop until they had sent him up the larboard side and put him down again in the poop. The unfortunate fellow was left battered, panting, and all in a sweat, unable to make out what had happened to him. Don Quixote, when he saw Sancho's flight without wings, asked the general if such ceremonies were usual with those who came on board the galleys for the first time, for if by any chance this were so, he, who had no intention of being initiated in them, desired not to take part in such exercises, and he swore to God that if anyone tried to take hold of him to make him fly, he would kick his heart out. He then arose and laid his hand on his sword.

At that precise moment they struck the awning and with a tremendous din they let fall the lateen yard from aloft. Sancho thought the sky was slipping off its hinges and was crashing down on his head, so he ducked in great fear and stuck it between his legs. Don Quixote did not find it much to his liking either, for he, too, began to tremble and shrink his shoulders, and he turned visibly paler. The crew hoisted the yard with the same speed and clatter as they had lowered it, and all this in silence, as if they had neither voice nor breath. The boatswain gave the signal to weigh anchor, and leaping into the middle of the gangway, he began to sting the crew's backs with his whip, and gradually they put out to sea. When Sancho saw so many red feet—for such he thought the oars to be—moving as one, he said to himself: "Here things are really and truly enchanted, but the things my master talks of are not. What have these wretches done that they flog them so? And how does this single man, who goes whistling about here, have the audacity to flog so many people? Here I say is hell itself, or at least purgatory."

Don Quixote, who noted the attention with which Sancho watched what was taking place, said to him: "Ah, friend Sancho, how quickly and at what little cost you could, if you would, strip your body naked from the middle upward, take your place among these gentlemen, and finish off the disenchantment of Dulcinea! For amid the torment and pain of so many you would not much feel your own. Besides, it may be that the sage Merlin will reckon each of these lashes, laid on with goodwill, as the equivalent of ten of those which in the end you will have to give yourself."

The general would have inquired what lashes these were and what was the disenchantment of Dulcinea, when a seaman called out: "Monjuí is making signals that there is a vessel with oars on the coast to westward."

Hearing this, the general leaped on to the gangway and cried: "Pull away, my sons! Don't let her escape; this must be some brigantine of the Algerine corsairs that the shore fort signals to us."

The other three galleys then came up to the flagship for orders. The general commanded two of them to stand out to sea, intending to keep along the coast himself with the third, for that way the vessel could not escape them. The crew plied their oars, driving the galleys forward with such fury that they seemed to be flying. When the galleys that had put out to sea were about two miles off, they sighted a vessel that they took to be one of about fourteen or fifteen banks or oars, and so it was. The vessel, as soon as she sighted the galleys, beat a retreat, hoping to escape by her speed. But she fared badly, for the flagship was one of the fastest craft sailing the seas, and gained upon her so fast that the crew of the brigantine clearly perceived that they could not escape. Therefore, their commander wished his men to stop rowing and surrender, so as not to exasperate the captain who commanded our galleys. But Fortune ordained otherwise, and when the flagship had approached so near that those in the brigantine could hear the shouts summoning to surrender, two Toraquis—that is to say, two drunken Turks —who were on the vessel with some dozen others, fired their muskets and killed two soldiers on our forecastle. At this the general swore not to leave a single man in the brigantine alive, but as he began to attack furiously, she slipped away under the flagship's oars. The galley shot ahead some distance, and when the pirates saw that they escaped, they made sail while the galley was turning, and once more set off in flight with sail and oar. But despite their efforts, their rash attempt was their undoing, for the flagship overtook them within a little more than half a mile, clapped her oars on them, and took them all alive. By this time the other two galleys had come up, and all four, with the prize, returned to shore, where a vast number of people were waiting, curious to see what they had captured. The general cast anchor near the land, and perceiving that the viceroy of the city was on the strand, he ordered the skiff to be launched to bring him on board. Then he ordered the lateen yard to be lowered so as to hang the captain of the brigantine out of hand and the other Turks he had caught in the vessel, about thirty-six in number, all tough fellows, and the majority, Turkish musketeers. The general asked who was master of the brigantine, and he was answered in Castilian by one of the captives, who afterward turned out to be a Spanish renegade: "This young man here, sir, is our master."

And he pointed to a lad of hardly twenty years of age, one of the handsomest and most gallant that human imagination could portray. The general then questioned him: "Tell me, ill-advised dog, what made you kill my soldiers, since you saw that it was impossible for you to escape? Is this the respect you owe to a captain's galley? Do you not know that rashness is not bravery? Faint hopes should make men bold, but not rash."

The master would have replied, but the general could not then attend to his answer, for he had to go and receive the viceroy, who was just then coming on board the galley, and with him some of his attendants and several people of the city.

"It has been a fine chase, general," said the viceroy.

"So fine," replied the general, "that your excellency will shortly see them hanging from that yardarm."

"How so?" asked the viceroy.

"Because," replied the general, "they have killed two soldiers of mine, contrary to all law and contrary to all rights and usages of war; and I have sworn to hang every man I have captured, and this youth in particular who is the master of the brigantine." And he pointed to the youth who already had his hands tied and the rope around his neck, awaiting death.

The viceroy looked at the youth, and when he saw him so handsome, so gallant, so resigned to his fate, his beauty instantly secured him a reprieve, for the viceroy felt an urgent desire to save him from death.

"Tell me, captain," he inquired, "are you a Turk by race, or a Moor, or a renegade?"

And the youth replied in the same Castilian tongue: "I am neither Turk, Moor, nor renegade."

"Then what are you?" asked the viceroy.

"A Christian woman," answered the youth.

"A woman and a Christian? In such dress and in such a plight? This is amazing but scarcely credible."

"Well then, gentlemen," said the youth, "suspend my execution, for you will not lose much by deferring your vengeance while I tell you the story of my life."

Who could be so hardhearted as not to be moved by those words, at least to the extent of listening to what that sad, pitiable youth had to tell? The general bade her say what he would, but not to expect to be pardoned for her flagrant offense.

With this permission the youth began to speak as follows: "I was born of that unhappy, unwise nation on which a sea of misfortune has lately fallen, the child of Morisco parents. In the course of their misfortune I was carried off to Barbary by two of my uncles, and although I declared I was a Christian, which I am, and no pretended or feigned one either, but a genuine Catholic, it availed me nothing. All my protests had no influence upon those who were in charge of our miserable banishment, and my uncles would not believe me. They took it as a lie and a tale that I had invented in order to stay in the land where I was born. And

so, against my will they compelled me to go with them. I
had a Christian mother and a wise and Christian father,
too; I sucked the Catholic faith with my mother's milk. I
was brought up with good principles, and neither in my
speech nor in my customs did I ever, I believe, show any
signs of being a Moor. Along with my virtues, for so I consider them, grew such beauty as I have, and though my reserve and seclusion were great, they did not prevent my
being seen by a young gentleman called Don Gaspar
Gregorio, the eldest son of a gentleman whose estate adjoins our village. How he saw me, how we conversed, how
he lost his heart to me, and how I was no gainer through
him, would be too long to tell, particularly at this moment
when I am afraid that the cruel rope that threatens me may
cut short my story. So I will only say that Don Gregorio
wished to accompany me in my exile. He mixed with the
Moriscos who came from other places, for he knew the
language very well, and on the voyage he made friends
with my two uncles, with whom I was traveling, for my
cautious and farsighted father had left the place as soon
as he heard the first proclamation of our banishment, and
gone in quest of some spot in foreign lands that might afford us shelter. He left a number of pearls and precious
stones of great price, with some money in Portuguese
crusadoes and gold doubloons, buried in a hiding place only
known to me. He bade me on no account to touch the
treasure he left behind, in the event of our being expelled before his return. I obeyed him, and with my uncles, as I
have said, and other relatives and friends, I passed over
into Barbary. The spot where we settled was Algiers, and indeed, we might as well have chosen hell itself. The king got
news of my beauty and rumor informed him of my wealth,
which in certain ways proved to my advantage. He summoned me before him and asked me from what part of
Spain I came and what money and jewels I had with me. I
told him the place, and that the jewels and money were still
buried there, but could easily be recovered if I were to go
back for them myself. All this I said, hoping that his covetousness might blind him more effectively than his lust for my
beauty. While he was talking to me, however, news reached
him that one of the handsomest and most gallant youths
imaginable had come with me. I realized at once that they
were speaking of Don Gaspar Gregorio, whose good looks

were past extolling. I was alarmed at the thought of Don
Gregorio's danger, for among those barbarous Turks a handsome boy or youth is more highly prized than the most
beautiful woman. The king immediately commanded him to
be brought before him so that he might see him, and asked
me whether what they said of this youth was true. Then, inspired, as I believe, by Heaven, I said that it was but that
he must be aware that it was no man but a woman like myself. And I besought him to let me go and dress her in
natural clothes, that she might display her full beauty and
appear in his presence with less bashfulness. He agreed and
postponed until the next day the discussion of my return to
Spain to bring back the hidden treasure. I talked with Don
Gaspar and told him what danger he ran in appearing as a
man. Then I dressed him as a Moorish woman, and that
same evening I brought him into the presence of the king,
who was struck with admiration at the sight of him and decided to keep this maiden as a present for the Great Turk.
And to avoid the danger she might run in his own women's
seraglio, he ordered her to be placed in the house of Moorish ladies of rank who were to guard her and wait on her.
Don Gregorio was taken there immediately. What both of
us felt—for I cannot deny that I love him—I leave to the
imagination of all lovers who are parted. The king presently
devised a scheme for my returning to Spain in this brigantine,
accompanied by two Turks—they were the pair who killed
your soldiers. This Spanish renegade came with me as well."
She pointed to the man who had first spoken. "And I know
for certain that he is secretly a Christian and that he has
resolved to remain in Spain and not return to Barbary. The
rest of the brigantine's crew are Moors and Turks, who are
there only to serve at the oars. But so greedy were those
insolent Turks that they violated their orders, that as soon
as we touched Spain this renegade and I should be put
ashore in Christian dress, with which we came provided.

They decided first to sweep the coast and take a prize, if
they could, fearing that if they landed us first, we might
meet with some accident that would make it known that the
brigantine was at sea, and then they might be taken, if
there happened to be any galleys on that coast. Last night
we sighted this shore, and as we did not know of these four
galleys, we were discovered, and you have seen what has

befallen us. The end of it is that Don Gregorio remains in
woman's dress among the Moors, in manifest peril of his life,
and that I am here with my hands bound, expecting, or
rather fearing, to lose my life, of which I am already weary.
This, gentlemen, is the conclusion of my doleful story, as
true as it is unfortunate. What I beseech you is that you
let me die like a Christian woman, since, as I have told you,
I have not in any way been guilty of the crime into which
those of my race have fallen."

She ceased, and the tears that filled her lovely eyes drew
many from those of her audience. Then the viceroy, who
was much moved, went up to her and with his own fingers
loosed the rope that bound the Moorish girl's lovely hands.

While the Christian Moor was telling her strange tale, an
ancient pilgrim who had gone on board the galley with the
viceroy kept his eyes fixed on her, and no sooner had she
ended the story than he flung himself at her feet, and clasping hold of them, he said to her in words broken by countless sobs and sighs: "O Ana Félix, my unhappy daughter!
I am your father, Ricote, returned to seek you, for I cannot
live without you, who are my soul."

At these words Sancho opened his eyes and raised his
head, which he had kept lowered as he brooded on his recent unhappy mishandling. And when he looked at the pilgrim, he recognized him as the same Ricote whom he had
met on the day he left his government, and he was convinced that this was his daughter. She no sooner was un-
bound than she rushed to embrace her father, mingling
her tears with his. And he, turning to the general and the
viceroy, said: "This, gentlemen, is my daughter, less happy
in her fate than in her name. She is called Ana Félix, with
the surname of Ricote, and she is as famous for her beauty
as for her father's wealth. I left my country to seek in
foreign lands a place to shelter us and give us refuge, and
when I found it in Germany, I returned in pilgrim's habit
in company with other Germans to look for my daughter
and dig up the great riches that I had left buried. I did
not find my daughter, though I did my treasure, which I
have with me. But now by the strange turns of fortune
you have witnessed I have found a treasure that enriches
me incalculably more, which is my beloved daughter. If our
innocence and my daughter's tears and mine can induce

your strict justice to allow the gates of mercy to be opened, do extend it to us, who have never thought of wronging you, or in any way have been party to the designs of our people, who have been justly expelled."

Sancho then raised his voice saying: "I know Ricote well and I am quite certain that what he says of Ana Félix being his daughter is true, but as regards the other trifles of going and coming and having good or bad intentions, it's none of my business."

While all present were struck with wonder at this strange case, the general declared: "Your tears, I assure you, will prevent my fulfilling my oath. Live, Ana Félix, all the years of the life that Heaven has allotted to you. But those arrogant and desperate men should pay the penalty for their crime."

Then he immediately gave orders for the two Turks who had slain his two soldiers to be hanged from the yardarm. But the viceroy earnestly besought him not to hang them, for their action arose rather from frenzy than arrogance. The general did what the viceroy asked him, for it is not good to take vengeance in cold blood. They then sought to devise a plan for delivering Don Gaspar Gregorio from his perilous situation, and Ricote offered toward the plan more than two thousand ducats that he had in pearls and jewels. They discussed many schemes, but the most practical proposal came from the Spanish renegade, who proposed to return to Algiers in a small vessel of about six banks of oars manned by Christian rowers, for he knew where, how, and when he could disembark, and he also knew where Don Gaspar was lodged. The general and the viceroy were in doubt whether to rely on the renegade and to entrust him with the care of a Christian crew. But Ana Félix and her father vouched for him. Ricote undertook to pay the Christians' ransoms, if by chance they were betrayed.

When they had agreed on this plan, the viceroy returned on shore and Don Antonio Moreno took the Moorish girl and her father along with him, with the viceroy's recommendations to welcome them and make as much of them as he could. And for his own part he offered whatever was in his house for their entertainment, such kindliness and warmth of feeling did Ana Félix's beauty rouse in his heart.

CHAPTER LXIV

*Of the adventure that gave Don Quixote more sorrow
than any that had ever befallen him*

Our history tells us that Don Antonio Moreno's wife was
delighted to welcome Ana Félix to her house. She received
her with great kindness, for she had fallen as much in love
with her beauty as with her intelligence, for the Moorish
girl excelled in both. And all the people in the city flocked
to see her, as if responding to the tolling of bells.

Don Quixote told Don Antonio that their scheme for
rescuing Don Gregorio was not a good one, for there was
more danger than advantage in it. It would be wiser, he
thought, for them to put him ashore in Barbary with his
horse and his arms, for he would deliver him in spite of all
Moordom, as Don Gaiferos had done his wife, Melisendra.

"Consider, your worship," said Sancho on hearing this,
"that when Don Gaiferos rescued his wife and took her to
France, it was all done on dry land, but here, if we do perhaps deliver Don Gregorio, we have no way of bringing
him to Spain, for there's the sea between."

"There is a remedy for everything except death," replied
Don Quixote. "We only need a vessel off the shore, and the
whole world would not prevent our boarding it."

"Your worship paints so good a picture that it sounds
easy," said Sancho, "but 'There's many slip 'twixt cup and
lip,' and I'm pinning my faith on the renegade, who seems
to me to be a stout fellow and able to take care of himself."

Don Antonio replied that if the renegade did not succeed
in his plan, they would adopt the expedient of the great
Don Quixote's crossing over to Barbary.

Two days later the renegade set sail in a light vessel of twelve oars with a very brave and seasoned crew, and after another two days the galleys sailed for the Levant, and the viceroy promised the general to keep him informed of the fortunes of Don Gregorio and Anna Félix.

One morning when Don Quixote was riding out for an airing on the strand, armed cap-a-pie—for, as he often said, "my ornaments are arms, my rest the battle fray," and he was never a moment without them—he spied a knight riding toward him, armed like himself from head to foot, with a shining moon painted on his shield, who, when he came within hearing, called out to him: "Illustrious knight and never-enough-renowned Don Quixote of La Mancha, I am the Knight of the White Moon, whose unheard-of exploits perchance may have reached your ears. I come to enter into combat with you and to compel you by sword to own and confess that my mistress, whoever she may be, is incomparably more beautiful than your Dulcinea of El Toboso. If you will fairly confess this truth, you will spare your own life and me the trouble of taking it. If you are resolved to fight and if victory be mine, my terms require that you relinquish arms and the quest of adventures and retire to your home for the space of one year, where you shall live quietly and peaceably, without laying hand to your sword, for thus you will improve your temporal and spiritual welfare. But should you vanquish me, my head shall be at your mercy, my arms and my steed shall be yours, and the fame of my deeds shall be added to yours. Consider what is best for you and give me your answer without delay, for this day must decide the issue of this affair."

Don Quixote was surprised, not to say dumbfounded, as much by the arrogance of the Knight of the White Moon's challenge, as at the subject of it; so, with solemn gravity and composure he replied: "Knight of the White Moon, whose exploits have not yet come to my ears, I will make you swear that you have never set eyes upon the illustrious Dulcinea, for if you had done so, I am confident that you would never have made this claim, since the sight of her perfections must have convinced you that there never was, or ever can be, beauty comparable to hers. And so, without calling you a liar, I declare that you are mistaken and accept your challenge upon the spot, this very day. Further-

more, I accept all your conditions, with the exception of
the transfer of your exploits, for they are unknown to me;
I must remain contented with my own, such as they are.
Choose, then, your ground and I shall do the same, and may
St. Peter bless him whom God favors."

Meanwhile the viceroy, who had been informed of the
arrival of the Knight of the White Moon and of the conversation that he was holding with Don Quixote, hastened
to the scene of action accompanied by Don Antonio and
others, firmly convinced that this must be some new jest invented by Don Antonio Moreno or by some other gentleman of the city. They arrived just as Don Quixote was
wheeling Rozinante about to take his ground, and perceiving that they were on the point of attacking one another,
the viceroy intervened and asked what was the reason for
such a sudden encounter. The Knight of the White Moon
replied that it was a question of preeminence in beauty,
and then he briefly told what he had said to Don Quixote
concerning the conditions of the duel. The viceroy then went
up to Don Antonio and asked him in a whisper if he knew
who the Knight of the White Moon was, or whether it was
some trick they wished to play upon Don Quixote. Don
Antonio answered that he did not know who he was, or
whether the challenge was in earnest or not. The viceroy was
troubled by that answer and wondered whether he ought or
ought not to let the battle continue. At length, by dint of
persuading himself that it was some jest, he withdrew, saying: "Gentlemen, if there be no other remedy than confession or death, and if Don Quixote is stubborn in his resolve,
and you, Knight of the White Moon, are obstinate likewise,
then in God's name go to it."

The Knight of the White Moon in courteous and well-
chosen words thanked the viceroy for what he had done,
and Don Quixote did likewise. And after recommending
himself to Heaven and to his Dulcinea, he retired to take a
longer compass of ground, for he saw his opponent do the
same; then, without any flourish of trumpets or any other
martial instrument to give the signal for the outset, they
both turned their horses around at the same instant. But
he of the White Moon, who was mounted on the fleeter
steed, met Don Quixote two-thirds down the course and
hurtled into him with such a fierce onslaught that, without
touching him with his lance, which he seemed purposely to
hold aloof, he brought both horse and rider to the ground.

He then sprang upon him and said as he clapped his lance to his opponent's visor: "Knight, you are vanquished and a dead man if you don't confess in accordance with the conditions of our challenge."

Don Quixote, who was bruised and stunned, without lifting his visor and as though speaking from the tomb, said in a faint low voice: "Dulcinea of El Toboso is the most beautiful woman in the world, and I am the most unfortunate knight on earth, and it isn't just that my weakness should discredit this truth. Go on, knight, press on with your lance and take away my life, since you have robbed me of my honor."

"That I shall certainly never do," said he of the White Moon. "Long may the fame of Lady Dulcinea of El Toboso's beauty live and flourish! All I demand is that the great Don Quixote should retire to his village for one year, or for a period to be fixed by me, in accordance with the agreement drawn up before this battle."

The viceroy, Don Antonio, and many others witnessed all that passed, and they heard Don Quixote promise that he would fulfill all the terms of their engagement like a genuine and punctilious knight, provided nothing was required to the prejudice of Lady Dulcinea. When this declaration was made, he of the White Moon turned about his horse, and after bowing to the viceroy, he rode at a half gallop into the city.

The viceroy commanded Don Antonio to go after him and to ascertain by all possible means who he was. Then, they raised Don Quixote from the ground, and uncovering his face, they found him pale and bathed in sweat. Rozinante was in such a plight that he was unable to stir for some time. As for Sancho, he was so sorrowful and cast down that he knew not what to say or do; he fancied that all had taken place in dreams and that the whole business was the result of enchantment. He saw his master overthrown and bound to lay aside his arms for a whole year. He imagined that his master's glory had been finally eclipsed and his own hopes from the latter's recent promises vanished like smoke in the wind. He was afraid that Rozinante might be crippled forever and his master's bones be permanently knocked out of joint, though it would be no small blessing if his madness were knocked out of him. In the end they carried the knight into the city on a hand-chair that the viceroy had sent for. The viceroy himself returned, eager to ascertain who was this Knight of the White Moon who had left Don Quixote in such a piteous state.

CHAPTER LXV

Which reveals who the Knight of the White Moon was, with the liberation of Don Gregorio and other incidents

Don Antonio Moreno rode after the Knight of the White Moon, and a great number of boys also followed, pestering him until he took refuge in an inn inside the city. Don Antonio entered there, too, as he was eager to make his acquaintance. A squire came forward to receive him and take off his armor, and he shut himself up in a lower room, where he was followed by Don Antonio, who was on tenterhooks to know who he was. Then, when the Knight of the White Moon found that the gentleman would not leave him, he said: "I know very well, sir, what you have come here for: to find out who I am. As it happens, there is no reason for me to conceal myself; so, while my servant is taking off my armor, I shall tell you the whole truth of my story, without omitting a single detail. You must know sir, that I am called the bachelor Sansón Carrasco; I come from the same town as Don Quixote of La Mancha, whose madness and folly have been the cause of deep sorrow to his friends and neighbors. I myself felt particular sympathy for his sad case, and as I believed his recovery to depend upon his remaining quietly at home, I earnestly endeavored to accomplish that end. And so, about three months ago I sallied forth myself as a knight-errant, calling myself the Knight of the Mirrors and intending to fight and vanquish him without doing him any harm and to impose as the condition of our combat that the vanquished should be at the mercy of the conqueror. Feeling certain of my success, I expected to send him home for twelve months, hoping that during that time he might be restored to health. But Fortune willed otherwise, for it was he who vanquished me; he unhorsed me, and my scheme was of no avail. He continued his journey, and I returned home vanquished, ashamed, and injured by my fall. Nevertheless, I did not abandon my scheme, as you have seen this day, and as he is so punctilious and so particular in observing the laws of knight-errantry, he is sure to perform his promise. This, sir, is my whole story, and I beseech you not to reveal me to Don Quixote, in order that my good intentions may produce their fruit and that the worthy gentleman may recover his sense, for when he is freed from the follies of chivalry, he is a man of excellent understanding."

"O sir!" replied Don Antonio. "May God forgive you for the wrong you have done in robbing the world of the most diverting madman who was ever seen. Is it not plain, sir, that his cure can never benefit mankind half as much as the pleasure he affords by his eccentricities? But I feel sure, sir, that all your art will not cure such deep-rooted madness; were it not uncharitable, I would express the hope that he may never recover, for by his cure we would lose not only the knight's good company, but also the drollery of his squire, Sancho Panza, which is enough to transform melancholy itself into mirth. All the same, I shall hold my peace and not breathe a word to him, to see whether I am right in suspecting that all Mister Carrasco's efforts will have no effect."

The bachelor answered that the business in any case was far advanced and that he was confident there would be a favorable result. And so, after Don Antonio had offered to follow the latter's instructions, the bachelor took his leave that same day. He had his armor tied on a mule; he mounted the charger on which he had done battle and left the city for home, meeting no adventure on the way worthy of mention in this true history.

Don Antonio told the viceroy everything that Carrasco had said. The viceroy was not too pleased by it, for Don Quixote's retirement would mean a loss to all those who were entertained by the tales of his mad adventures.

For six days Don Quixote was confined to his bed, dejected, melancholy, thoughtful, out of humor, and full of bleak reflections on his luckless overthrow. Sancho strove hard to comfort him, saying: "Raise your head, master, cheer up and thank your stars that you've come off without even a broken rib. Remember, sir, that 'They that give must take'; and that 'Where there are hooks there aren't always flitches.' Come now, sir, a fig for the doctor! You've no need of him. Let us be off for home, and give up this gallivanting up and down in search of adventures in lands and places, God knows where. And when you come to think of it, I'm the one who's the greater loser by this, though it's your worship who is in a worse pickle. Though with my government I gave up all desire of being a governor again, I've never lost the hankering to be a count. But I may as well say good-bye to all that if your worship gives up trying to be a king and resigns your profession of chivalry! So all my hopes end in smoke."

"Be quiet, Sancho. Do you not see that my seclusion and retirement need only last a year? After that I shall return to my honored calling, and I am bound to win a kingdom, and some countship or other for you."

"God grant you may," said Sancho, "and let sin be deaf, for I've always heard that good hopes are better than poor holdings."

They were still arguing when Don Antonio entered, crying out joyfully: "A reward for good news, Don Quixote! Don Gregorio and the renegade who went to fetch him are in port. In port, do I say? Why, they're already at the viceroy's and will be here in a moment."

Don Quixote was a little cheered at this news, and said: "As a matter of fact, I was just going to say that I should have been delighted if it had fallen otherwise, for then I should have had to cross into Barbary, where by the force of my arm I would have freed not only Don Gregorio, but also all the Christian captives in Barbary. But what am I saying, poor wretch? Have I not been conquered? Have I not been unhorsed? Am I not forbidden to take up arms for a year? Then, what am I promising? What am I bragging about, when I am more fitted to handle a distaff than a sword?

"Stop that, sir," said Sancho; "let the hen live, even if she has the pip. Today it's your turn and tomorrow mine. There's no need to fash yourself about all those knocks and shacks! Today you're moping, but tomorrow you'll be hopping, unless you've a mind to stay in bed; I mean, to show the white feather, instead of plucking up courage for fresh fights. So now, your worship, stand up on your two legs and welcome Don Gregorio, for it sounds to me as if the folks here are all aflutter, so he must already be in the house."

And such was the case, for Don Gregorio and the renegade had already given the viceroy an account of their voyage there and back, and so eager was Don Gregorio to see his Ana Félix that he rushed to Don Antonio's with his rescuer. Although he had been in woman's dress when they took him away from Algiers, he had changed it in the boat for that of a captive who had escaped with him. But no matter what dress he had worn, his appearance would have won him respect, admiration, and envy, for he was exceedingly handsome and evidently about sixteen or seventeen years of age. Ricote and his daughter went out to meet him, the father with tears and the daughter with blushes. They did not, however, embrace, for people whose love is deep do not usually express their feelings openly. All present were struck with admiration and wonder at the handsome pair, for though they did not speak to one another, their eyes were tongues that unveiled their modest and radiant happiness. The renegade described his stratagem and the means he had employed for liberating Don Gregorio, and the latter told of the perils and conflicts he had to face among the women with whom he had stayed, and though his was not a long story, his few well-chosen words showed that his discretion was in advance of his years. In conclusion, Ricote liberally rewarded the renegade as well as the men who had rowed the rescue boat. The renegade was reconciled and restored to the Church, and a rotten limb was thus made clear and whole through penance and repentance.

Two days later the viceroy discussed with Don Antonio how permission could be obtained for Ana Félix and her father to stay in Spain, for they thought that it was only right that so Christian and evidently so right-minded a daughter and a father should remain in Spain. Don Antonio offered to go to the capital to arrange the matter, as he had of necessity to go there on other business, and pointed out that at court many similar problems could be solved by means of favors and bribes.

"No," said Ricote, who was present at their discussion. "There's nothing to hope for from favors or bribes, for the great Don Bernardino de Velasco, Count de Salazar, to whom

His Majesty has entrusted our expulsion, will not be swayed
by prayers, promises, gifts, or even pity. Although it is true
that he tempers justice with mercy, he believes that the entire
body of our race is tainted and rotten; consequently he applies to it the burning cautery rather than the soothing
balm. Therefore, by prudence, wisdom, and diligence as well
as by terror, he has carried upon his sturdy shoulders the
weight of this vast project to its due execution, and our
arts, stratagems, intrigues, and wiles have no power to blind
his Argus eyes, which are forever watchful. Hence, there is
not one of our people left behind to lie concealed and sprout
like a hidden root in days to come and bear poisoned fruit
in Spain, which is today cleansed and freed from the terror
that our members caused her. Truly it was a heroic impulse
of Philip the Third and an unheard-of wisdom to entrust its
execution to this Bernardino de Velasco!"

"At any rate," said Don Antonio, "when I am there I shall
strive with all the means in my power, and leave God to
decide. Don Gregorio shall come with me to relieve the anxiety that his parents must feel at his absence. Ana Félix
shall remain with my wife at my house, or in a convent,
and I know that the viceroy will be glad to have the worthy
Ricote stay with him till he sees how I manage."

The viceroy consented to all that was proposed, but when
Don Gregorio heard what was afoot, he declared that on no
account could he, or would he, leave Doña Ana Félix.
Finally, however, he agreed with the arrangements, for he
reflected that he might manage to return for her when he
had seen his parents. So Ana Félix stayed with Don Antonio's wife, and Ricote in the viceroy's house.

At last the day came for Don Antonio's departure, and
two days later for that of Don Quixote and Sancho, for the
knight's fall did not allow him to take the road any sooner.
When Don Gregorio and Doña Ana Félix said farewell,
there were tears, sighs, sorrowing, and sobbing. Ricote offered Don Gregorio a thousand crowns if he wanted them,
but he refused to take more than five, which he borrowed
from Don Antonio, promising to repay them in the capital.
With this the two departed, and afterward Don Quixote and
Sancho, as we have said—Don Quixote unarmed and in
traveling dress, and Sancho on foot, for Dapple was loaded
with the armor.

CHAPTER LXVI

Which treats of what the reader shall see or the listener hear

As he rode out of Barcelona Don Quixote cast his eyes on the spot where he had been overthrown, saying: "Here stood Troy! Here my unhappy fate, and not my cowardice, despoiled me of the glories I had won! Here Fortune made me feel her fickle changes! Here my deeds were eclipsed! Here, in fine, fell my happiness nevermore to rise again!"

Then Sancho said to him: "Great hearts, my dear master, should be as patient in adversity as they are joyful in prosperity; that's surely my own experience, for when I was made a governor I was as blithe and merry as a lark, and now that I'm only a poor footslogging squire, I am not sad. I've heard say that she they call Fortune is a drunken, freakish drab, and above all, blind, so that she doesn't see what she's doing, and she does not know whom she raises or whom she pulls down."

"You are much of a philosopher, Sancho," said Don Quixote, "and I wonder how you come to talk so sensibly. But I must tell you that there is no such thing as Fortune in the world. Nothing that happens here below, whether of good or evil, comes by chance, but my the special disposition of Providence, and that is why we have the proverb: 'Every man is the maker of his own fortune.' I, for my part, have been the maker of mine, but because I did not act with all the prudence necessary, my presumptions have brought me to my shame. I should have remembered that my poor, feeble Rozinante could never withstand the strongly built horse of the Knight of the White Moon. However, I risked everything for adventure; I did my best, and was overthrown, and though it cost me my honor, I did not lose, nor could I lose my integrity, and I can still fulfill my promise. When I was a knight-errant, bold and valiant, my actions gave luster to my exploits, and now that I am no more than a dismounted squire, I can still prove the validity of my word. Trudge on, then, friend Sancho, and let us hie us home to pass our year's novitiate. In our retirement we shall gather fresh strength to return to the profession of arms, which I can never forget."

"This footslogging is not so pleasant as to tempt me to go tramping on long journeys, master," replied Sancho. "Let us hang up these arms of yours upon some tree in place of one of those bodies that dangle from the branches in these parts, and when I am sitting on my dapple's back with my feet up, we'll make whatever journeys your worship pleases. But there's little sense in thinking I can traipse along on my two feet mile after mile."

"You are right, Sancho," answered Don Quixote. "Hang my armor up as a trophy, and underneath them or about them we shall carve on the bark of the trees the inscription that was written on the trophy of Roland's arms:

> 'Let no one dare these arms displace
> Who would not valiant Roland face.' "

"That's the very thing for me," said Sancho, "and were it not that we'll be needing Rozinante on the road, it would be a good idea to hang him up too."

"On second thought," replied Don Quixote, "neither the armor nor the horse shall be treated thus. I don't want men to say, 'For good service bad guerdon.' "

"Your worship is right," said Sancho, "for I've heard wise men say that the ass's fault must not be laid on the packsaddle, and since you're to blame for this kettle of fish, you should punish yourself and not vent your anger upon your armor, which is all battered and bloody already, or upon poor meek Rozinante, or upon my tender feet, wanting to make them trudge more than is fair."

In these arguments and discussion they spent the whole of

that day, and the next four as well. But on the fifth day, as they were coming into a village, they found a crowd of people around the inn door enjoying themselves, for it was a holiday. And As Don Quixote approached them, a peasant raised his voice and said: "One of these two gentlemen coming this way shall decide our bet, for they don't know the parties concerned."

"That I will do surely," answered Don Quixote, "and with all fairness, if I can manage to understand it."

"The case is this, then, good sir," said the peasant. "A man of this village who is so fat that he weighs eleven arrobas has challenged a neighbor of his who only weighs five to run a hundred-yard race with him, on condition that they run at even weights. And when the challenger was asked how the weights were to be equalized, he said that the challenged man, who weighs five arrobas, must carry six arrobas of iron on his back, and so they would be equal at eleven arrobas."

"That is not right," interrupted Sancho before Don Quixote could answer. "It's up to me to settle this question, seeing that only a few days ago I gave up the job of governor and judge, as all the world knows."

"Do so, and welcome, friend Sancho," said Don Quixote, "for I am not fit to give crumbs to a cat, my wits are so shaken and confused."

With this permission Sancho said to the peasants who crowded around, with mouths agape, awaiting his decision: "Brothers, the fat man's demand is unreasonable and hasn't the shadow of justice in it. For if what they say is true, that the man challenged may choose the weapons, it isn't right for his opponent to choose for him weapons that would hinder him and prevent his winning the victory. So, my judgment is that the fat challenger should prune, trim, pare, and remove six arrobas off his flesh, from whatever part of his body he pleases, and when reduced to five arrobas in weight, he will be on equal terms with his opponent. Then they will be able to run even."

"God's truth," cried one of the countrymen who heard Sancho's decision. "This gentleman has spoken like a saint and given judgment like a canon. But I'd make a shrewd guess that the fat fellow won't be keen to part with an ounce of his flesh, let alone six arrobas."

"The best way would be for them not to run at all," chimed in another; "then the lean chap won't break down under his load, and the fat fellow won't lose his flesh. Let half of the wager go in wine, and let's take these gentlemen to the tavern that has the best. And the cloak be on me when it rains." [1]

"I thank you, gentlemen," said Don Quixote, "but I cannot stop a moment, for sorrowful thoughts and disasters compel me to appear discourteous and to travel in haste."

And so, spurring Rozinante, he passed on, leaving them astonished at the appearance of his strange figure and at the wisdom of his servant, for such they judged Sancho to be. And another of the countrymen said: "If the servant is so wise, what must the master be? If they're going to study at Salamanca, I bet they'll be judges at court in the twinkling of an eye. It's all a game; nothing but study and more study, then with favor and good luck a man finds himself, when he least expects it, with a scepter in his hand or a miter on his head."

Master and man spent that night in the open field under the bare, open sky, and when they pushed on next day, they saw a man coming on foot toward them with a wallet around his neck and a javelin or pike in his hand, evidently a foot-courier. As the man drew near to Don Quixote he quickened his pace, and coming up to him half running, he clasped him around the right thigh, for he could reach no higher, and exclaimed with signs of great joy: "O my lord Don Quixote of La Mancha, how overjoyed my lord and master the duke will be when he hears that your worship is returning to his castle, for he is still there with the duchess."

"I do not recognize you, friend," answered Don Quixote, "and I cannot guess who you are, if you do not tell me."

"I, sir," replied the courier, "am Tosilos, the lackey of the duke, who would not fight with you about marrying Doña Rodríguez' daughter."

"God save us!" cried Don Quixote. "Is it possible that you are the man whom my enemies, the enchanters, transformed into a lackey to defraud me of the honor of that battle?"

"Silence, my good sir," answered the courier; "there was neither enchantment nor transformation, and I was as much the lackey Tosilos when I entered the lists as I was Tosilos,

[1] i.e. I'll pay the bill.

the lackey, when I came out. I meant to marry without fighting, for the girl caught my fancy, but my plan turned out
otherwise, for no sooner did you leave our castle than the
duke ordered me a hundred stripes for disobeying the order
that he had given me before going into the battle, and it all
ended with the wench becoming a nun and Doña Rodríguez returning to Castile. And I'm now on my way to
Barcelona to deliver a bundle of letters from my master to
the viceroy. If your worship would like a little drink, pure
though warmish, I've a wineskin full of the best and a few
slices of Tronchón cheese, which will help to rouse your
thirst if it happens to be sleeping."

"I like the offer," said Sancho, "but you can cut out the
rest of the compliment; so, pour away, my dear Tosilos, and
to hell with all the enchanters in the Indies."

"I do declare, Sancho," said Don Quixote, "that you are
the greatest glutton in the world and the greatest booby on
the face of the earth if you cannot be persuaded that this
courier is enchanted and this Tosilos transformed. But stay
with him and drink your fill. I will go on slowly and wait
for you to catch up with me."

The lackey burst out laughing, unsheathed his gourd, and
unpacked his package. Then he took out a little loaf, and
he and Sancho sat down on the green grass and in peace
and good comradeship rapidly consumed the wallet's entire
store with such hearty appetite that they even licked the
packet of letters because it smelled of cheese. At length
Tosilos said to Sancho: "There's no doubt, friend Sancho,
that this master of yours ought to be reckoned a madman."

"Why ought?" replied Sancho. "He owes nothing to anybody, for he always pays his debts, especially when the coin
is madness. I see it all quite plain, and I tell him about it
plainly enough, I assure you, but what's the use? Particularly now that he's done for, for he's been beaten by the
Knight of the White Moon."

Tosilos asked him to tell what had happened, but Sancho
replied that it would be uncivil to keep his master waiting
for him. There would, however, be time for the story some
other day, if they met. So, getting up and shaking the crumbs
from his beard and his clothes, he said good-bye to Tosilos
and left him. Then, driving Dapple before him, he overtook
his master, who was waiting for him in the shade of a tree.

CHAPTER LXVII

Of Don Quixote's determination to become a shepherd and lead a pastoral life till the year of his pledge had expired, with other truly entertaining incidents

If Don Quixote was greatly troubled in mind before his overthrow, he was infinitely more so after it. He lay in the shade of a tree, as we have said, and there his thoughts, like flies around honey, settled on him and stung him. Some of them dwelt upon Dulcinea's disenchantment and others on the life he must lead in his enforced retirement. Then Sancho came up and was loud in his praises of the lackey Tosilos' liberal disposition.

"Is it possible, Sancho," asked Don Quixote, "that you still think that he is a real lackey? You seem to have forgotten how you saw Dulcinea of El Toboso turned and transformed into a peasant wench and the Knight of the Mirrors into bachelor Carrasco—all works of the enchanters who persecute me. But tell me now, did you ask that Tosilos, as you call him, what has been the fate of Altisidora; whether she has wept for my absence or already cast into oblivion those amorous desires that tormented her in my presence?"

"My thoughts," replied Sancho, "were then too busily employed to have time to ask such foolish questions. Heavens above, sir! Is your worship now in a fit state to inquire about other people's desires, especially amorous ones?"

"Look here, Sancho," said Don Quixote, "there is a great deal of difference between acts that are done out of love and those done out of gratitude. A knight may well not be in love, but strictly speaking, he must never be ungrate-

ful. Altisidora, to all appearances, loved me deeply; she gave
me the three kerchiefs you know of; she wept at my departure; she cursed me; she abused me; and in spite of shame,
she complained of me publicly—all certain proofs that she
adored me, for lovers' anger usually vents itself in such
maledictions. I had neither hopes to give her, nor treasures
to offer her, for my hopes are pledged to Dulcinea, and the
treasures of a knight-errant are as fleeting and fictitious
as fairy gold. All I can devote to her are the memories I
have of her, without prejudice, however, to those I have of
Dulcinea, whom you are wronging by your delay in scourging yourself and chastising that flesh of yours—may I see
the wolves devour it—which you would rather preserve for
the worms than for the relief of that hapless lady."

"Sir," answered Sancho, "to tell you the truth, I can't
persuade myself that the flogging of my bottom has anything to do with the disenchanting of the enchanted. It's
like saying: 'If your head hurts, anoint your knees.' At least,
I'd like to wager that there isn't a single instance of disenchantment by lashes in all the histories of knight-errantry
your worship has read. But whether there is or not, I'll
whip myself when the time suits and I've a mind to punish
myself."

"God grant it," answered Don Quixote, "and may Heaven
give you the grace to realize your obligation to succor my
lady, who is yours too, since you are my servant."

Thus discoursing, they were plodding their way when they
reached the very place where they had been trampled by
the bulls. Don Quixote recognized it and said to Sancho:
"This is the field where we fell in with the merry shepherdesses and the gallant shepherds who here had a mind to
revive another pastoral Arcadia. The conceit was as novel
as it was ingenious, and if you are agreeable, Sancho, we
shall imitate their example and turn shepherds, at least for
the time I have to live in retirement. I shall buy some sheep
and all the rest of the things that are needed for the pastoral
vocation. I shall call myself the shepherd Quixotiz and you
the shepherd Panzino. We shall wander through the mountains, woods, and meadows, singing here, lamenting there,
drinking of the liquid crystals of the spring, or the limpid
brooks, or the swelling rivers. The oaks shall give us of
their sweetest fruit with bountiful hand; the trunk of the

hard cork trees shall offer us seats; the willows, shade; the roses, perfume; the spacious meadows, carpets embellished with a thousand colors; the air, clear and pure, shall supply us breath; the moon and the stars, light, in spite of the darkness of night; song shall give us delight, and tears, gladness; Apollo, verses and love conceits whereby we shall be able to win eternal fame, not only in the present age but also in those to come."

"By God," cried Sancho, "but that kind of life squares entirely with me, corners and all; what's more, no sooner will the bachelor Sansón Carrasco and Master Nicholas, the barber, catch sight of us than they'll want to go in for it too and turn shepherds with us. But God grant that the curate doesn't take it into his head to enter the fold as well; he's so frolicsome and fond of his fun."

"You have spoken very well," said Don Quixote, "and the bachelor Sansón Carrasco, if he joins the pastoral company, as no doubt he will, could call himself the shepherd Sansonino or Carrascón; the barber could call himself Niculoso, as old Boscán called himself Nemoroso.[1] I do not know what name we could give the curate, unless it be one derived from his calling, such as Curiambro. As for the shepherdesses whose lovers we are to be, we can pick and choose their names like pears, and since that of my mistress goes as well with that of a shepherdess as of a princess, there is no need to weary myself in seeking another to fit her better. You, Sancho, shall call your shepherdess by whatever name you please."

"The only name for mine," replied Sancho, "will be Teresona; that'll suit her plumpness excellently and her name, for she's called Teresa. It'll sound well when I sing of her in my verses and reveal my chaste desires, for I'm not one to go fooling about in other men's houses in search of better bread than is made of wheat. As for the curate, he had better not go taking a shepherdess, for good example's sake; but should the bachelor have a mind to get one, that's his own doing."

[1] According to Menéndez y Pelayo, Cervantes is mistaken in calling Boscán (Garcilaso de la Vega's tutor) Nemoroso. Francisco Saa de Miranda's fifth eclogue (Lisbon, 1595), dedicated to Garcilaso de la Vega, calls him Nemoroso. Garcilaso, as a matter of fact, calls himself both Salicio and Nemoroso.

"God bless me!" exclaimed Don Quixote. "What a life we shall lead, Sancho, my friend! What flageolets shall enchant our ears! What Zamoran bagpipes, what tambourines, what timbrels, what rebecs! And if perhaps among those various kinds of music we hear the *albogues*, there we will have almost all the pastoral instruments."

"What are *albogues*?" asked Sancho. "I've never heard of them or seen one in my life."

"*Albogues*," replied Don Quixote, "are thin brass plates, like candlesticks, that are struck one against the other on the hollow side, and make a sound that, though not pleasing or harmonious, blends well with the rustic tone of the bagpipe and the tambourine. This word *albogue* is Moorish, like all words beginning with *al* in our Castilian language; such as *almohaza, almorzar, alhombra, alguacil, alhucema, almacén, alcancía*, and others like them. Our language contains only three words from the Moorish that end in *i*. They are *borceguí, zaquizamí* and *maravedí. Alhelí* and *alfaquí* can be recognized as Arabic both by their initial *al* and by their final *i*. This I mention incidentally, since it has come to my mind through my happening to mention *albogues*. One circumstance that will greatly assist us in perfecting ourselves in our new profession is that I am a bit of a poet, as you know, and the bachelor Sansón Carrasco is a very good one. I do not mention the curate, but I will wager that he has some smack and tricks of the poet, and Master Nicholas has it as well, I am sure, for all or most barber are guitarists and rhymers. I shall moan about absence; you shall praise yourself as a constant lover; the shepherd Carrascón shall complain of scorn; the curate Curiambro of whatever he likes; and so we shall go on to our heart's content."

"But I'm so unlucky, sir," answered Sancho, "that I'm afraid I shall never see the time when I can follow this calling. What smooth spoons I shall make when I'm a shepherd! What fried bread crumbs, what cream cheeses, what garlands and shepherd's knickknacks! They may not win me the name of a wise one, but they won't fail to get me a name for wit. Sanchica, my daughter, shall bring us our dinner to the fold. But look out, for she's a buxom wench, and there are shepherds who are more malicious than simple, and I shouldn't like her to go for wool and come back shorn; for loving and lustful desires are quite as common in the fields as in the cities, and you find them in shepherd's cabins as well as in royal palaces. So, 'Take away the opportunity and you take away the sin'; and 'What the eye doesn't see, the heart doesn't grieve for'; and 'A leap over the hedge is better than good men's prayers.' "

"No more proverbs, Sancho," said Don Quixote, "for any one of those you have quoted is enough to explain your meaning. Many a time I have warned you not to be so prodigal with proverbs and to restrain yourself in uttering them, but I suppose this is like preaching in the desert, and 'My mother beats me and I whip the top.' "

"Your worship," said Sancho, "reminds me of the saying: 'The pot called the kettle black.' You are scolding me for quoting proverbs, yet you string them together in pairs yourself."

"Observe, Sancho," replied Don Quixote, "that I introduce proverbs to the purpose, and when I quote them, they fit like a ring on the finger. But you bring them in by the hair. You drag them, instead of guiding them. And, if I remember rightly, I have told you before that proverbs are brief maxims drawn from the experience and observations of the wise men of old, and a proverb ill-applied is not wisdom but arrant nonsense. But let us leave the subject, and as darkness is coming on, go a little off the highway to some place where we can spend the night. God knows what tomorrow will bring."

They left the road and supped late and badly, much to the dismay of Sancho, who was reminded of the hardships of knight-errantry, suffered among woods and forests, though sometimes plenty reigned in castles and homes, as at Don Diego de Miranda's, and at the rich Camacho's wedding, and at Don Antonio Moreno's, but he reflected that it would not be always day or always night; and so, that night he spent in sleeping and his master in watching.

CHAPTER LXVIII

Of the bristly adventure that befell Don Quixote

The night was rather dark, for although the moon was in the sky, she was nowhere to been seen, for sometimes Lady Diana goes for a ramble in the Antipodes and leaves the mountains dark and the valleys gloomy. Don Quixote yielded to nature and slept his first sleep without giving way to the second; quite the reverse of Sancho, who never had a second, for his first lasted him from night till morning, which showed his sound constitution and his freedom from anxiety. But Don Quixote's cares kept him so wide awake that he eventually roused Sancho by saying: "I am amazed, Sancho, at your utter lack of sensibility. Why, I do believe you are made of marble or solid brass and have not a trace of emotion or feeling in you. I watch while you sleep; I weep while you sing; I faint from fasting while you wallow in sloth and can hardly breathe from gluttony. It is the duty of good servants to share their masters' pains and feel their sorrows, even for the sake of appearances. Look how serene this night is, and how lonely is this place, which invites us to vary one slumber with a little watching. Get up, in Heaven's name! Withdraw a little distance away from here and willingly and cheerfully give yourself three or four hundred lashes on account of those for Dulcinea's disenchantment. This I entreat you as a favor, for I do not wish to have a tussle with you as I did on the last occasion, since I know that your muscles are strong. When you have done we shall spend the rest of the night in singing—I my severance, you your constancy—and thus we shall make our start in the pastoral calling we are to follow in our village."

"Sir," replied Sancho, "I am no monk to get up in the middle of my sleep and flog myself, much less do I think that it's easy to suffer the aches of whippings one moment and sing like a lark the next. Let me doze off, your worship, and don't worry me about this whipping business, or you'll drive me to swear that I'll never touch a hair on my coat, much less my flesh."

"O heart of stone! O squire devoid of pity, ungrateful for my bread and thankless after all the favors I have done you in the past and hope to do in days to come! Through me you became a governor; through me you in all likelihood will become a count or obtain some other equivalent title. And all this, mind you, with no more delay than just this present year, for *post tenebras spero lucem*.[1]

"Bless me if I can understand that!" cried Sancho. "I only know that while I sleep I have neither fear, nor hope, nor trouble, nor glory. Good luck to him who invented sleep, the cloak that covers all of man's thoughts, the food that takes away all hunger, the water that quenches all thirst, the fire that warms the cold, the cold that cools heat, the general coin, in short, with which all things are bought, the balance and weight that levels the shepherd with the king and the fool with the wise man. There is only one bad thing about sleep, as I have heard say, and it is that it looks like death, for between one sleeping and one dead there's mighty little difference."

"Never, Sancho," said Don Quixote, "have I heard you speak so eloquently as now; it makes me realize the truth of the proverb you are so fond of repeating: 'Not with whom you are bred but with whom you are fed.' "

"By my faith, master," replied Sancho, "it's not I who am stringing proverbs now! Why, they are falling from your worship's lips also, in pairs, faster than from mine. There's only this difference between yours and mine, that yours come pat and timely and mine are out of season; but anyhow, they're proverbs all the same."

They were at this point when they heard a harsh deafening noise that spread through all the valleys around. Don Quixote

[1] *Post tenebras spero lucem* (After darkness I await the light), Job 17. Juan de la Cuesta, the printer of both parts of *Don Quixote*, stamped on the cover of both volumes the emblem of the hooded falcon with these Latin words around it.

started to his feet and clapped his hand to his sword. Sancho crouched under Dapple's belly, pushing the bundle of armor on one side of him and fortifying the other with the ass's packsaddle, and there he lay shivering, as full of fears as his master of surprise. Meanwhile the din was growing louder and louder as it drew nearer to the two tremblers, or to one at least, for the other's valor is well known by now. Now what had happened was as follows: Some farmers were driving a herd of over six hundred swine to a certain fair, and such was the din that the beasts made with their grunting and squealing that Don Quixote and Sancho were almost deafened by it, and they could not understand what it could be.

At length the huge grunting herd came on pell-mell, and paying scant heed to Don Quixote or Sancho, it rode roughshod over them, knocking down Sancho's entrenchments and not only tumbling Don Quixote over, but also sweeping along Rozinante. The thronging, the grunting, the pace at which the filthy animals came on, routed packsaddle, armor, Dapple, Rozinante, Sancho, and Don Quixote, and left chaos in their wake.

Sancho raised himself up as best he could, and asked his master for his sword, saying he wanted to kill half a dozen of that unmannerly swinish herd, for he had now discovered what they were.

"Let them be, friend," said Don Quixote, "this affront is the punishment that Heaven inflicts upon my guilty head, for it is just that jackals should devour, wasps sting, and hogs trample on a vanquished knight-errant."

"And it's Heaven's chastisement, too, I suppose," answered Sancho, "that sends the gnats to sting, the bee to bite, and hunger to famish us squires for attending on vanquished knights-errant. If we squires were the sons of the knights we serve, or their very close relatives, it would not be unreasonable to expect that we should share in their punishment even up to the fourth generation. But what have the Panzas to do with the Quixotes? Well, let us get things settled again and get a little sleep out of what is left of the night. Tomorrow will be another day."

"You may sleep, Sancho," replied Don Quixote, "for you were born to sleep, but I was born to watch. And in the little time that is left till dawn I shall give rein to my thoughts and vent them in a little madrigal that tonight, unknown to you, I composed in my head."

"To my mind," replied Sancho, "those thoughts that give room for the making of verses can't be so very serious. But let your worship go ahead and versify to your heart's content, and I'll sleep as long as I can."

Then, taking up as much ground as he wanted, he curled himself up and slept as sound as a top, undisturbed by bonds, or debts, or troubles of any kind. Don Quixote, leaning against a beech or a cork tree—Cide Hamete Benengeli does not mention what kind of tree it was—sang in this strain to the music of his own sighs:

"Love, when I try to seek release
From wounds that you inflict on me,
It drives me to death; in agony
I hope that thus my pains will cease.

To such a pass when I arrive,
The haven in my sea of ills,
Death with such joy my bosom fills,
I cannot die, I am alive.

Alas, thus by life I am slain;
An evil to mix life with Death,
For living I die; then the breath
Of Death comes, and I live again.

Each line he accompanied with sighs and many tears, groaning like one whose heart was pierced through and through by grief of defeat and by his absence from Dulcinea.

By then the dawn appeared, and the sun darted his beams into Sancho's eyes. He awoke and uncurled, shaking and stretching his drowsy limbs. Then, gazing at the havoc that the hogs had made of his store, he cursed the herd and even more. At length the pair resumed their journey, and at dusk they saw coming toward them some ten horsemen with four or five men on foot. Don Quixote's heart was thrilled with excitement and Sancho's quailed with terror, for the people who were coming up to them bore lances and shields, and were advancing in very warlike formation. Don Quixote turned toward Sancho and said: "Ah, Sancho, if I could use my arms and if my promise had not tied my hands, I would reckon this array coming against us as mere tarts and gingerbread. But perhaps it may not be what we fear."

By this time the horsemen had come up, and raising their spears, they surrounded Don Quixote without a single word, pointing them at his back and breast and threatening him with death. Then one of those on foot, putting his finger to his lips as a sign for him to be silent, seized Rozinante's bridle and led him off the road. The rest of the men followed on foot in the steps of Don Quixote's captors, driving Sancho and the dapple from behind, and all of them preserving a marvelous silence. Two or three times the knight was on the point of asking where they were taking him and what they wanted, but no sooner did he begin to open his lips than they made as if to close them with the points of their spears. The same thing happened to Sancho, for as soon as he was about to open his mouth one of the footmen pricked him with a goad, doing the same to Dapple as if he too wanted to speak. Night closed in; they quickened their pace; the fears of the two prisoners increased, more so when they heard their captors cry from time to time: "Get on, troglodytes! Silence, barbarians! Pay up, anthropophagi! Don't complain, Scythians! Don't open your eyes, murderous Polyphemuses, man-eating lions!" and many other such names with which they tortured the ears of the wretched master and his servant. Sancho went along muttering to himself: "What, call us turtledoves? Us barbers and poppycocks! And say shush to us as if we were lap dogs? I don't like the sound of those names at all; this is an evil wind blowing none of us any good. All our troubles are coming to roost together like kicks on a dog. Pray God that it may stop at threats, this misadventurous adventure."

Don Quixote rode on dazed, unable to guess the meaning of all those abusive epithets addressed to them, though he gathered enough to know that they boded no good and that he might expect plenty of trouble. About an hour after dark they reached a castle, which Don Quixote recognized as the duke's, where he had been staying a little while ago.

"God bless me!" he cried, as soon as he recognized the mansion. "What can this be? In this house surely there is courtesy and good entertainment, but for the vanquished all good turns to evil and evil to worse."

When they arrived at the main court of the castle, they saw that it was decorated and set out in a manner that increased their amazement and doubled their fears, as will be seen in the following chapter.

CHAPTER LXIX

Of the rarest and strangest adventure that befell Don Quixote in the whole course of this history

The horsemen dismounted, and with those on foot, they caught Don Quixote and Sancho violently and bodily in their arms and took them into the courtyard, around which blazed about a hundred torches set in their sconces. Around the galleries of the court were more than five hundred lamps so that in spite of the night, which was rather dark, the scene was as bright as day. In the center of the court was raised a tomb about two yards above the ground, covered all over with a spacious canopy of black velvet, around which, along the steps, tapers of white wax were burning upon more than a hundred silver candlesticks. On the top of the tomb was displayed the corpse of a damsel, so lovely that by her beauty she seemed to make death itself beautiful. She lay with her head upon a pillow of brocade, crowned with a garland woven of various sweet-smelling flowers, her hands crossed upon her bosom, and between them a branch of yellow victor's palm. On one side of the court a stage had been erected, and seated upon two chairs were two personages who, as they had crowns on their heads, appeared to be kings, either real or pretended. By the side of this stage, to which two steps gave access, were two other seats on which their captors seated Don Quixote and Sancho, still in complete silence and making them understand by signs that they must likewise keep silent. But they would have done so without any signs, for amazement at what they saw kept their tongues tied. Two persons of quality then mounted the stage with a great retinue, and Don Quixote at once recognized them as his hosts, the duke and the duchess. They sat on two richly ornamented chairs by the side of the two who looked like kings. Who would not have been wonder-struck at the sight when in addition to it Don Quixote recognized the dead body that lay on the tomb as that of the lovely Altisidora? As the duke and duchess ascended the stage, Don Quixote and Sancho rose and made them a profound obeisance, which the ducal pair acknowledged with a curt nod of the head. Then an officer came across, and going up to Sancho, he threw over him a robe of black buckram all painted with flames of fire, and taking off Sancho's cap, he placed on his head a pasteboard miter like those worn by penitents of the Holy Office, whispering in his ear that he must not open his lips, or they would clap a gag on him or take his life.[1] Sancho looked at himself from top to toe and saw that he was all ablaze, but as they did not burn him, he did not care two raps for them. He took off the miter and saw that it was painted with devils. Then he put it on again, saying to himself: "Well, the flames don't scorch and the devils don't carry me off."

Don Quixote also gazed at Sancho, and though fear kept his senses numbed, he could not help laughing at his squire's figure. And then, from beneath the bier, as it seemed, a soft melodious music of flutes began to rise, which sounded soft and amorous, though unbroken by any human voice, for even silence itself in that place was mute. Then there suddenly appeared close to the pillow of this seeming corpse, a beautiful youth clad in Roman dress, who sang in a sweet and clear voice to a harp, which he himself played, the following two stanzas:

> Until Altisidora slain
> By cruel Quixote shall return
> To life, whilst at the fairy court
> In somber sackcloth ladies mourn;
> And whilst my lady clothes her maids

---

[1] According to contemporary accounts of *autos de fé* in the sixteenth century, the Inquisition made those condemned wear miters and sanbenitos with devils and flames painted on them, if they died persisting in their error. Those who renounced their error before death wore miters and sanbenitos painted with flames alone. Here as a joke Sancho wears the sanbenito of a persistent heretic.

In serge and sorrow's gloomy baize,
So long I'll sing her sad disgrace
In tones that rival those of Thrace.[2]

Nor think that death shall end my song,
Or my heart's tears shall cease to flow;
For still, though dead, my poet's tongue
Shall pay in song the debt I owe;
And when my soul from prison freed
Shall wander along the Stygian shore,
You still it will celebrate and sing
Until oblivion's waters ring.

"No more," cried one of the two who looked like kings at this point; "no more, divine singer; it would be an unending task to recall to us the death and charms of the peerless Altisidora, not dead, as the ignorant world believes, but living on the tongues of fame and in the penance that Sancho Panza, here present, must undergo to restore her to the light. Therefore, O Rhadamanthus,[3] you who judge with me in the gloomy cavern of Dis, as you know all that the inscrutable Fates have decreed concerning the restoration of this damsel to life, speak and declare it now, so that the happiness we expect from her return may be delayed no longer."

Hardly had Minos, the fellow judge of Rhadamanthus, spoken these words when the latter rose to his feet and said: "Here, officers of this house, high and low, great and small! Come here, one and all, and mark Sancho's face with twenty-four thwacks. Give him a dozen pinches and six pinpricks on his arms and loins, for on this ceremony Altisidora's restoration depends."

On hearing this Sancho broke silence and cried out: "Confound it! I'd sooner turn Moor than let my face be marked or my cheeks be fingered. God's truth! What has this messing about my face to do with this young lady's resurrection? The

[2] This refers to Orpheus (born in Thrace), who tamed wild beasts by his song.

[3] The three judges of the underworld, according to the ancient Greeks, were three: Minos, Rhadamanthus, and Aeacus. Cervantes (like Machiavelli in his novella *Belphagor*) omits Aeacus.

old wife had such a craving for spinach, she left neither
green nor dry.[4] They enchant Dulcinea and whip me to
disenchant her. Altisidora dies of some disease God chose
to give her, and to revive her I'm to get twenty-four thwacks
in the face, my body pitted with pinpricks and my arms
black and blue with pinches. Try those games on your brother-
in-law; I'm too old a dog and I'll turn a deaf ear to your
whistle."

"You shall die," cried Rhadamanthus in a loud voice.
"Relent, tiger! Humble yourself, proud Nimrod! Suffer in
silence, for nothing impossible is demanded of you. Do not
start raising difficulties in this business. Snicked you must
be, pricked you must be, and pinched until you groan. Ho
there, officers! Obey your orders, or else, on my word as an
honest man, you will see for what you were born!"

At this point some six duennas appeared and crossed the
court in a procession, one behind the other, four of them
with spectacles and all with their right hands raised and
four inches of their wrist bare to make their hands seem
larger, as is now the fashion.[5] No sooner did Sancho see
them than he bellowed like a bull: "I'd let the whole world
manhandle me, but to let those duennas touch me, never!
Claw my face as they did my master's in this very castle; run
me through the guts with sharp-edged daggers, tear my arms
with red-hot pincers. I'll bear it with patience to oblige these
gentlefolks; but let the Devil carry me off to hell if I ever
allow one of those duennas to lay a hand on me."

Then Don Quixote also broke silence, saying to Sancho:
"Have patience, my son, and oblige these gentlemen, and
give thanks to Heaven for having granted such virtue to your
person that by its martyrdom you can disenchant the enchanted and resuscitate the dead."

[4] The full proverb is: *regostóse la vieja a los bledos, ni dejó
verdes ni secos.* The more usual form of the proverb is: *Gustó
la vieja los berros, y lamióse los dedos* (the old woman liked
watercress so much she licked her fingers).

[5] In those days it was the fashion for ladies to expose their
wrists, hence the short sleeves they wore. The poets of the time
tell us that long fingers and plump white hands were the most admired.

By this time the duennas had surrounded Sancho, and he calmed down and became more resigned. He settled himself firmly in his chair and presented his face and beard to the first one, who gave him a well-marked thwack and then made him a deep curtsy.

"Less courtesy and make up, my lady duenna," said Sancho, "for I'm damned if your hands don't stink of vinegar."

In short, all the duennas slapped him, and many others of the household pinched him, but what he could not stand was the pinpricking. And so, he jumped out of his chair all in a fury, and seizing a lighted torch that was close by, he dashed after the duennas and the rest of his tormentors, shouting: "Away with you, monsters of hell! Do you suppose that I'm made of brass and can stand these tortures of the damned?"

At this, Altisidora, who must have been tired of having lain on her back so long, turned on her side, at which sight the bystanders all cried out almost with one voice: "Altisidora is alive! Altisidora lives!"

Rhadamanthus bade Sancho calm his rage, for their object was now achieved. When Don Quixote saw Altisidora begin to move, he went and knelt before Sancho, saying: "Now is the time, son of my loins—my squire no more—to give yourself some of those lashes to which you are pledged for disenchanting Dulcinea. Now is the time, I repeat, when your virtue is seasoned and effective for achieving the good work that is expected of you."

To which Sancho replied: "This is more like trick upon trick than honey upon pancakes. A fine business, indeed, after all the pinchings and smackings and prickings to look forward to the lashes! After that nothing more remains but to take a big stone, tie it round my neck, and toss me into a well, which I wouldn't much mind if I'm to be made the heifer at the wedding feast to cure other folk's ailments.[6] Leave me alone, or by God, I'll use the thirteen-letter word [7] and run amuck, even if I spoil the market!"

---

[6] The heifer at the marriage feast (*la vaca de la boda*) was the victim of the feast in the ring. It also could mean the man who foots the bill for the revels or the one to whom all look for urgent advice and help.

[7] This was a phrase popularly used in the marketplace (*echarlo todo a doce o trece*) and meant "to run amuck or risk all." The words often used were *desbarajuste* (confusion) or *vociferación*, which have 12 letters.

Here Altisidora sat up on her tomb, and at the same moment the clarions sounded, accompanied by flutes and by a general shout of "Long live Altisidora! Long live Altisidora!"

The duke, the duchess, and the kings, Minos and Rhadamanthus, got up, and all in a body, with Don Quixote and Sancho, went to receive Altisidora and bring her down from the tomb. And she, pretending to be faint, bowed to the duke and duchess and to the kings, and looking across at Don Quixote, she said to him: "God forgive you, loveless knight; because of your cruelty I have been, as it seems to me, nine thousand years in·the other world. But you, most compassionate squire in all the world, I thank for the life I now possess. From this day forth, friend Sancho, you may dispose of six of my smocks, which I bequeath to you to make six shirts for yourself, and if they are not whole, at least they are clean."

Sancho kissed her hands for the gifts, kneeling on the ground with the miter in his hand. The duke gave orders that he be relieved of this, that his cap be returned to him, and also that his overcoat be put on him instead of the robe of flames. But Sancho begged the duke to give him the robe and the miter, which he would like to carry away to his own village as a keepsake to remind him of that amazing adventure. The duchess replied that he should certainly keep them, for he must surely be aware how much she esteemed him. The duke gave orders to clear the courtyard and all to retire to their own rooms, and Don Quixote and Sancho to be taken to the apartments that they knew of old.

CHAPTER LXX

*Which follows the sixty-ninth and deals with matters
indispensable for the clear understanding of this
history*

Sancho slept that night in a truckle bed in the same room with Don Quixote, a thing that he would have avoided if he had been able, for he knew well that with questions and answers his master would not let him sleep. And he himself was in no mood for talking, for he was still smarting from the pain of his recent martyrdom, which prevented him from speaking, and he would have preferred to sleep in a hovel than in that rich room with company. His fears and suspicions were only too well founded, for no sooner did his master get into bed than he said: "What do you think, Sancho, of this evening's adventure? Great and powerful are the powers of love scorned, and with your own eyes you have seen Altisidora dead, slain by no other arrows, by no other sword, by no other warlike weapon or lethal poison, than the cruelty and scorn with which I have always treated her."

"She might have died when and how she pleased, and welcome," replied Sancho, "and left me alone to myself, since neither did I love her nor did I disdain her in all my life. I don't know and I can't think what the health of Altisidora, that silly, capricious young girl, has to do with the torture of Sancho Panza. Now, indeed, I see plainly that there are enchanters and enchantments in the world, from whom may God deliver me, for I can't deliver myself. All the same, I beg your worship to let me sleep and ask me no more questions if you don't want me to throw myself out the window."

"Sleep, Sancho, my friend," replied Don Quixote, "if the

pinpricks and pinches and slappings you have received will
let you."

"No pain," answered Sancho, "equals the insult of that
slapping, if only because I suffered it at the hands of duennas, blast them! But I beg your worship once more to let me
sleep, for sleep is the remedy of all our miseries when
awake."

"So be it," said Don Quixote, "and God be with you."

The two fell asleep, and Cide Hamete, the author of this
great history, during this interval wished to give an account
of what it was that prompted the duke and duchess to devise
the elaborate contrivance that has just been described. He
says that the bachelor Sansón Carrasco, remembering how
as the Knight of the Mirrors he was beaten and overthrown
by Don Quixote, a defeat and overthrow that played havoc
with all his schemes, decided to try his hand again, hoping for
a more fortunate issue than the last time. So when he learned
from the page who brought the letter and the present to
Sancho's wife, Teresa Panza, where Don Quixote was, he
looked for a different horse and armor and painted a white
moon on his shield, carrying it all upon a mule that was led
by a peasant, not by Tomé Cecial, his old squire, lest he be
recognized by Sancho or by Don Quixote. He came, then, to
the duke's castle, and that nobleman informed him of Don
Quixote's departure, of the road he had chosen, and of
his intention to take part in the jousting at Saragossa. The
duke also described the tricks played at the knight's expense
and the scheme for Dulcinea's disenchantment at the expense
of Sancho's posteriors. Finally, he gave him an account of
the trick that Sancho had played upon his master, making
him believe that Dulcinea was enchanted and transformed
into a country wench, and how his wife, the duchess, had
convinced Sancho that it was he himself who had been mistaken and that Dulcinea really was enchanted. All this greatly amused and surprised the bachelor, thinking of Sancho's
cunning and simplicity as well as of Don Quixote's extraordinary madness. The duke begged him, if he should come
across the knight, to return that way, whether he vanquished
him or not, and let him know what had happened. The
bachelor promised that he would and set off on his quest, but
not finding Don Quixote at Saragossa, he went on and met
with the adventure that has been related. He returned by
the duke's castle and gave him an account of everything,

with the conditions of the combat and how Don Quixote was returning to fulfill, like a good knight-errant, his pledge of retiring to his village for a year. During which time, added the bachelor, he might possibly be cured of his madness. It was this motive, in fact, that had induced him to assume his disguise, for it was a pitiful thing that a gentleman so intelligent as Don Quixote should remain a lunatic. Whereupon he took leave of the duke and returned to his village to wait there for Don Quixote, who was following him. From all this the duke took the opportunity of playing this last trick, such delight did he take in the vagaries of Sancho and Don Quixote. He distributed a number of his retainers on foot and on horseback, on all the roads around the castle, far and near, by which he imagined that Don Quixote was to return, with orders to bring him to the castle, willingly or by force, if they should locate him. And when they did find him, they gave notice to the duke, who had already arranged what was to be done. As soon as he got word of Don Quixote's arrival, he ordered them to light the torches and the lamps in the courtyard and to place Altisidora upon the tomb, with all the apparatus that has been described, the whole farce so well acted and so lifelike that it was but little removed from reality. In fact, Cide Hamete says that he considers the hoaxers to be as mad as their victims, for the duke and duchess came within a hair's breadth of looking like fools for taking such immense trouble to play tricks on a pair of fools.

Day caught the pair, one of them sound asleep, the other wide awake with his unbridled fancies, and with it came the desire to rise, for the featherbed of sloth made scant appeal to Don Quixote, whether victor or vanquished. Then Altisidora (in Don Quixote's opinion having returned from death to life), continuing the humor of her master and mistress, came into Don Quixote's room crowned with the same garland she had worn on the tomb, and clad in a tunic of white taffeta flowered with gold, her hair loose upon her shoulders, leaning on a black staff of finest ebony. At her presence Don Quixote, troubled and abashed, shrank down and completely covered himself under the sheets and quilts of his bed, dumbfounded and unable to utter a single word of greeting. So, Altisidora sat down in a chair beside the head of his bed, and after heaving a deep sigh, she said to him in a tender

and feeble voice: "When women of quality and modest
maidens tread honor underfoot and give their tongues leave
to break through every impediment, revealing to the public the
secrets buried in their hearts, they are indeed reduced to a
state of desperation. I, Don Quixote of La Mancha, am one
of these—smitten, vanquished, and lovelorn—but still patient
and modest; indeed, so much so that my heart burst through
my silence and I lost my life. For two days ago, through
grief at your inhuman treatment, O harder than marble to
my plaints, you stubborn knight, I lay dead, or at least was
believed to be by those who saw me and were it not that
Love took pity on me and entrusted my recovery to the sufferings of this good squire, there I should have remained in
the other world."

"Love might just as well have entrusted it to my ass,"
said Sancho, "and I should have thanked him for it. But tell
me, lady—and may Heaven accommodate you with a kinder
lover than my master—what did you see in the other world?
What's it like in hell? For who dies in despair is sure to end
up there."

"To tell you the truth," answered Altisidora, "I couldn't
have been dead outright, for I never went to hell; once I had
put foot in there, I shouldn't have been able to get out when
I wished. The truth is that I arrived at the gate, where about
a dozen devils were playing tennis, all in their breeches and
doublets, with their collars trimmed with Flanders lace and
with ruffles of the same that served for cuffs, with four inches
of arm bare to make their hands seem longer. In their hands
they had rackets of fire, and what surprised me was that, instead of balls, they used what looked like books stuffed with
wind and fluff, an astonishing sight! But that did not astound
me so much as to see that all the players there were grumbling and snarling and cursing one another, whereas it's usual
in games for the winners to be glad and the losers sorry."

"That's no wonder," observed Sancho, "for whether they're
playing or not playing, devils can't be glad, winning or
losing."

"That's probably so," answered Altisidora, "but there's another thing that astonishes me too—I mean, that astonished
me then—and that was that after the first volley, there wasn't
a ball left whole or fit to be used a second time, so they
whirled away books, old and new, which was a wonderful

sight. To one of these volumes, brand new and smartly bound, they gave such a whack, that they knocked its guts out and scattered all the leaves about. Then one devil said to another: 'Look, what book is that?'

"And the other devil replied: 'This is the second part of *The History of Don Quixote of La Mancha*, not composed by Cide Hamete, its original author, but by an Aragonese who calls himself a native of Tordesillas.'

" 'Away with it out of here,' answered the other devil, 'and plunge it into the pit of hell and never let me set eyes on it again.'

" 'Is it so bad?' asked the other.

" 'So bad,' replied the first, 'that if I myself were deliberately to try to make it worse I should not succeed.'

"They continued their game, tossing about other books, and I, because I heard them name Don Quixote, whom I so much love and adore, retained this vision in my mind."

"A vision it must have been undoubtedly," said Don Quixote, "for there is no other person of that name in the world, and that history is passing from hand to hand even now, though it stays in none, for they all kick it away. I have not been troubled to hear of myself passing like a phantom body through the shades of hell or through the light of the earth, for I am not he of whom that history treats. If it were good, faithful, and true, then it would have centuries of life; but if it is bad, its passage will be short from its birth to its burial."

Altisidora was about to proceed with her complaint of Don Quixote, when the knight said to her: "I have told you many times, madam, how distressed I am that you should fix your affections on me, for all I can do is acknowledge them, not relieve them. I was born to belong to Dulcinea of El Toboso. The Fates, if they exist, have dedicated me to her, and to think that any other beauty can occupy the place she holds in my heart is to imagine the impossible. This should be sufficient disillusion to make you retreat within the limits of your chastity, for no one can be obliged to do the impossible."

On hearing this, Altisidora, pretending to be angry and upset, cried out: "My God, Don Codfish, pestle-pounder, date stone, you're more obstinate and hardhearted than a clodhopper when he's aiming at the target! I'll tear your

eyes out if I can get at you! Do you really imagine, Don Vanquished, Don Cudgeled, that I died for you? All you've seen
tonight has been pretense; I'm not the sort of woman to let
myself grieve the black dirt of a fingernail for such a camel
—much less die for one!"

"That I can well believe," said Sancho, "this dying for
love's all a joke; they may talk about it, but as for doing it,
let Judas believe it."

While they were thus talking, the singer and poet who
had sung the two stanzas already noted came in and said to
Don Quixote with a deep bow: "Reckon me, sir knight, among
your most faithful servants; I have been deeply devoted to
you for a long time, for your fame as well as for your deeds."

"Tell me, sir," Don Quixote answered, "who you are, that
my courtesy may respond to your deserts." The youth replied that he was the musician and panegyrist of the previous
night.

"Certainly," answered Don Quixote, "you have a beautiful
voice, though what you sang did not seem to me much to
the point, for what have the stanzas of Garcilaso to do with
this lady's dying?"

"Do not wonder at that," answered the singer. "With the
unshorn poets of our age it is the custom for each to write as
he wishes and to steal from whom he will, whether it be
much to the point or not, and there is nothing they sing or
write so stupid that they do not ascribe to poetic license."

Don Quixote was about to reply, but he was prevented by
a visit from the duke and duchess, with whom he had a
long and agreeable conversation, during which Sancho uttered
so many drolleries and showed such shrewdness that he left
his hosts more astonished than ever at his mixture of simplicity and sharpness. Don Quixote begged them for leave
to depart that same day, since it was more fitting for a vanquished knight like himself to live in a pigsty than in a royal
palace. They gladly granted him his request, and the duchess
asked him whether Altisidora remained in his good graces.

"Madam," he replied, "your ladyship should know that
this damsel's malady proceeds from idleness. The remedy
for that is honest and continuous occupation. She has just
informed me that they wear lace in hell, and since she must
certainly know how to make it, let it never be out of her

hands. When she is busily working her bobbins, the image or images of her desires will not work in her imagination. That is the truth, and that is my opinion and advice."

"And mine too," added Sancho, "for never in all my life have I seen a lacemaker who died for love. Maidens who have work to do devote their thoughts more to finishing their tasks than to thinking of their loves. I speak from experience, for while I am digging, I don't think of my darling—I mean, my Teresa Panza—though I love her better than my eyelashes."

"You are right, Sancho," exclaimed the duchess, "and I shall see that my Altisidora is kept busy in the future with some kind of needlework, for she does it extremely well."

"There is no need, my lady, to resort to that remedy," said Altisidora, "for the very thought of the cruelty with which this vagabond scoundrel has treated me will blot him from my memory forever without any other help. And now, with your highness' permission, I shall retire from here, so as no longer to have before my eyes his rueful figure—I mean, his ugly, abominable face."

"This reminds me," said the duke, "of the common saying: 'He who rails will soon forgive.' "

Altisidora made a pretense of wiping her tears with her handkerchief, and with a curtsy to her master and mistress she left the room.

"Poor girl!" exclaimed Sancho. "You've bad luck, say I, very bad luck! For you've had to do with one whose soul's as dry as a rush and whose heart's as tough as oak. Faith, if you had to deal with me, another kind of cock would crow for you."

The conversation ended. Don Quixote dressed himself and dined with the duke and duchess, and departed that afternoon.

CHAPTER LXXI

*Of what befell Don Quixote and Sancho, his squire,
on the way to their village*

The vanquished and wayworn Don Quixote rode along
very melancholy on one count, and very cheerful on another. His sadness arose from his defeat, and his cheerful-
ness from his appreciation of Sancho's virtue as he had
shown in the resurrection of Altisidora, although he was
somewhat reluctant to believe that the lovelorn maiden had
really died. But Sancho was by no means cheerful. He was
sad because Altisidora had not kept her promise of giving
him her smocks. And turning this over and over in his
mind, he said to his master: "Really, sir, I am the un-
luckiest doctor in the whole world. There are physicians
who kill their patients and seek to get paid for their trouble,
though all they do is sign a slip of paper for medicines
that the apothecary makes up for them, and hey presto,
the trick is done! As for myself, whom the cursing of that
girl cost drops of blood, thwacks in the face, pinches, pricks,
and whippings, I don't get a mite. But I swear here and
now that if they put another sick person in my hands, they'll
have to grease my palm before I cure him, for 'The abbot
dines by what he chants,' and I can't believe that Heaven
has bestowed on me the virtue I have for me to communicate it to others free, gratis, and for nothing."

"You are right, Sancho," replied Don Quixote, "and
Altisidora has acted very wrongly in not giving you the
promised smocks, though your virtue was *gratis data*, and has
not cost you any more study than learning how to endure
tortures in your person. As for myself, I can tell you that if

it is payment you want for your whipping on account of
Dulcinea's disenchantment, I would long ago have given
you what was fair. But I do not know whether payment
will go well into the cure, and I should not wish the reward to hinder the medicine. All the same, I think that
nothing would be lost by trying. So, consider, Sancho, how
much you want, and down with your breeches. You may
pay yourself cash down with your own hand, for you have
all my money in your keeping."

At this offer Sancho opened wide his eyes and ears, and
consenting in his heart to give himself a hearty flogging,
he said to his master: "Well now, sir, I'm ready to put
myself at your disposal and satisfy your worship's desires,
for my own profit. And if I appear mercenary, it is my
love for my wife and children. So, tell me, your worship,
how much you will give me for every lash I give myself?"

"If I had to pay you, Sancho," replied Don Quixote, "in
proportion to the greatness and importance of the service
rendered, not all the wealth of Venice or the silver mines
of Potosí [1] would suffice to recompense you. Reckon up
what you have of mine, and put a price on each stroke."

"They are three thousand three hundred and odd," said
Sancho, "of which I have given myself about five. The
rest are to come. Let those five count as the odd ones and
let us come to the three thousand and three hundred, which,
at a quarter of a real apiece—and I wouldn't for the world
take less—come to three thousand three hundred quarter-
reals. The three thousand quarter-reals make one thousand
five hundred half-reals, which are seven hundred and fifty
reals. The three hundred quarter-reals make one hundred
and fifty half-reals, which go to seventy-five reals. Adding
these to the seven hundred and fifty, it comes to eight hundred and twenty-five reals. These I'll subtract from the cash
of your worship's I have on me, and I'll go home all gaudy
and gladhearted, though well whipped, for, as they say, 'He
who goes fishing shouldn't fear a wetting.' I'll say no more."

"O blessed Sancho! O kindly Sancho!" cried Don Quixote.
"How solemnly shall we be bound, Dulcinea and I, to serve
you, all the days that Heaven shall grant us. If she returns
to her former self, as she must, her misfortune will turn to

---

[1] The silver mines of Potosí in the Andes symbolized for the
Spaniards limitless wealth.

good fortune, and my defeat shall turn to triumph. Come, Sancho, tell me, when will you begin your flogging? If you hasten it, I shall add a hundred reals."

"When? Tonight without fail," Sancho replied. "Just you order that we spend it in the fields under the open sky, and I'll lay open my flesh."

At last the night came for which Don Quixote had longed with all the impatience in the world, for it seemed to him that the wheels of Apollo's car had broken and that the day was of more than its customary length, just as lovers feel who can never adjust the time to their desires. Finally, they entered among some pleasant trees that stood a little way off the road. And then, after they had emptied Rozinante's saddle and the dapple's packsaddle, they lay down on the green grass and supped off Sancho's stores. Then, after having made a strong and flexible whip out of the dapple's halter and headstall, Sancho retired about twenty paces from his master among some beeches. When Don Quixote saw him go off so briskly and resolutely, he remarked: "Mind you do not lash yourself to pieces; give time for one stroke to await another; you should not set off at too furious a pace, lest your breath fail you halfway—I mean, do not lay on so fiercely that you might kill yourself before reaching the required number. And in case you lose by a card too many or too few, I shall stand close by and count the lashes on my rosary beads. May Heaven prosper your pious undertaking."

" 'A good payer needs no sureties,' " answered Sancho. "I'm all set on giving myself a fine decent whipping, but I suppose I needn't kill myself to work the miracle."

With that, he stripped himself to the waist, and seizing the whip, he began to lay on the lashes, while Don Quixote counted the strokes. But by the time that Sancho had applied six or eight lashes to his bare back, he felt that the joke had gone too far, and he began to feel that he had made too cheap a bargain. So, he paused for a while and called out to his master, saying that the bargain was off, for such stripes as he was giving himself were worth at least half a real, not a quarter.

"Go on, Sancho, my friend, and do not be fainthearted," said Don Quixote. "I will double the price of the strokes."

"In that case," answered Sancho, "God's will be done and let it rain lashes."

But the cunning rogue gave up lashing his own back and began to flog the trees, every now and then giving forth such dismal groans that it sounded as if he was at death's door. As Don Quixote was naturally tenderhearted, he was afraid that Sancho might put an end to his life, and in that case his squire's imprudence might prevent him from attaining his purpose, so he cried out: "By your life, friend, let the matter lie in abeyance for the present, for this physic seems mighty severe, and it would be wiser to take it in gentler doses. After all Rome was not built in a day. You have given yourself a thousand lashes, if I have not counted wrongly. Let that do for the present, for as the homely phrase goes: 'The ass will carry a load, but not a double load.'"

"No, no, sir," replied Sancho, "it must not be said of me: 'The money paid, the work delayed.' Stand by a little longer, and let me give myself another thousand lashes, at any rate, for in two rounds I'll settle the whole job and have plenty to spare."

"Well, since you are in the humor," said Don Quixote, "may Heaven help you; stick to it, for I shall withdraw."

Sancho returned to his task and flayed the trees so furiously that he soon had stripped their barks off, so severely did he lash them. And once, raising his voice and dealing a smashing blow on a beech tree, he cried out: "Die Samson and all your kith and kin!"

At the sound of that piteous cry and the swish of the remorseless whip Don Quixote ran up and seized the twisted halter that had served Sancho as a whip, saying: "Heaven forbid, friend Sancho, that you should lose your life for my pleasure, for it must help to support your wife and children. Let Dulcinea wait until a more auspicious occasion presents itself, and I shall live in hopes that when you have regained new strength, this business may be concluded to the satisfaction of all parties."

"Since your worship wishes it so," replied Sancho, "I'll stop, and gladly, too. Throw your cloak over my shoulders, for I'm sweating and don't want to catch cold, which is a danger that new flagellants run."

Don Quixote did so, and remaining in his doublet, he covered up Sancho, who fell asleep until the sun awoke him, and then they continued their journey, which they ended for the day at a village, nine miles further on. They dismounted at an inn, which Don Quixote recognized as such, and not as a castle with deep moat, turrets, portcullises, and drawbridge as he generally fancied, for since his defeat he spoke on all subjects with sounder judgment, as we shall see presently. They lodged him in a basement that was hung with old painted fabrics, such as one often sees in villages. One of them represented the story of Helen of Troy when Paris stole her away from her husband, Menelaus, but it was painted by a wretched dauber. Another had the story of Dido and Aeneas: she was on the top of a tower, waving a sheet to her runaway guest, who was fleeing over the sea in a frigate or brigantine. Don Quixote noted, however, in the two pictures that whereas Helen was not by any means unhappy at going away, for she had a roguish smile on her face, Dido really did show her grief, for the tears she shed were painted as big as walnuts. He made the following observation: "Those two ladies were most unfortunate not to have been born in the present age, and I am even more unlucky not to have been born in theirs. I would have faced these gentlemen and saved Troy from being burned and Carthage from being destroyed; why, by killing Paris alone, all these disasters could have been prevented."

"I'll lay you a wager," said Sancho, "that before long there will not be an inn, tavern, or barber shop in the whole country that has not painted our lives and deeds along the walls. All the same, I'd prefer a better painter than the blockhead who has done these daubs."

"You are right, Sancho," said Don Quixote. "That painter puts me in mind of Orbaneja, a painter from Ubeda, who, when he was asked what he was painting, would answer: 'Whatever comes out,' and if he happened to draw a cock, he would write underneath: 'This is a cock,' lest people think it was a vixen. Of such a kind, Sancho, must have been that painter or writer—for it is all one—who published the history of this new Don Quixote that has come out. He must have written whatever came out. Or he must have been like a certain poet at court years ago, called Mauleón,[2] who used to answer offhand any question put to him. When

[2] Mauleón was a well-known wag in Toledo in the days of Cervantes.

someone asked him the meaning of *Deum de Deo*,[3] he replied: 'Let him give when he will.' But leaving that aside, tell me truly, Sancho, are you in the mood for another round of flogging tonight? Would you like to do it indoors or in the open air?"

"Well, master," said Sancho, "a flogging is a flogging, whether it's indoors or outdoors, but I prefer it among trees, for I feel that they bear me company and help me to endure my sufferings."

"Well, friend Sancho, then it must not be," replied Don Quixote. "You must recover your strength, so we shall reserve it for our village, where we shall arrive the day after tomorrow at the latest."

Sancho answered that his master might decide as he pleased but that he, for his part, wanted to finish the business off out of hand, in hot blood, and while the mill was grinding, for 'There is always danger in delay'; and 'It is best to pray to God and wield the hammer'; and 'One *I take* is better than two *I'll give you*'; and 'A bird in hand is worth two in the bush.'

"No more proverbs, for God's sake, Sancho," cried Don Quixote. "You are reverting to *sicut erat in principio*. Speak plainly and don't be complicated, as I have told you so often, and you will see how 'One loaf is as good for you as a hundred.'"

"I don't know what cursed luck is mine," rejoined Sancho, "but I cannot talk sense without slipping in a proverb, and I cannot utter one that doesn't seem to me to the point. Still I'll mend my ways if I can."

And with that their conversation ended for the time being.

---

[3] *Deum de Deo* was a phrase originally used by a preacher in a sermon and distorted by ignorant members of the congregation who had no Latin into *dé donde diere* (let him give when he will).

CHAPTER LXXII

How Don Quixote and Sancho arrived at their village

Don Quixote and Sancho spent the rest of that day in the inn, expecting the return of the night, the one to have an opportunity of ending his penitential flogging in the open air, the other to see the penance performed, since this would lead to the accomplishment of his desires.

Just then a gentleman came riding up to the inn with three or four servants, and one of them addressed him who appeared to be the master: "Don Álvaro Tarfe, your worship should spend the heat of the day here. The inn seems cool and clean."

Don Quixote, remembering the name Tarfe, turned to his squire, saying: "Mark my words, Sancho, I think I met this same Álvaro Tarfe before when I turned over the pages of that so-called second part of my history." [1]

"That is quite possible," said Sancho, "but just let him dismount, and then we'll question him."

The gentleman alighted, and was given by the landlady a ground-floor room facing Don Quixote's apartment, hung with other painted cloths like those in the knight's apartment. When the stranger had changed into light summer garments, he came out to the porch of the house, which was large and airy, and found Don Quixote walking up and down.

"Pray, sir, which way are you traveling?" said he to our knight.

"To a village not far away, where I was born," answered

---

[1] Don Álvaro Tarfe is one of the principal characters of Avellaneda's *Don Quixote*.

Don Quixote; "and pray, sir, which way are you bound?"

"To Granada, sir," replied the gentleman, "the land where I was born."

"And a fine country it is," said Don Quixote. "But do tell me, sir, I beg you, your name, for it is more important for me to know it than I can conveniently tell you."

"My name is Álvaro Tarfe," answered the gentleman.

"Then surely," said Don Quixote, "you are the same Don Álvaro Tarfe whose name occurs in the second part of Don Quixote of La Mancha's history that was lately published by a modern author."

"I am the very man," answered the gentleman, "and that very Don Quixote, the principal subject of that book, was my closest friend; it was I who drew him away from his home, or at least, I persuaded him to travel in my company to Saragossa to see the tournament; as it turned out I behaved as a true friend, for had it not been for my intervention, his arrogant impudence would have exposed him to a flogging at the hands of the public hangman."

"But pray tell me, sir," said Don Quixote, "am I in any way like that Don Quixote of yours?"

"Not in the least," answered the stranger.

"And had Don Quixote," said our knight, "a squire, one Sancho Panza?"

"Yes," said Don Álvaro, "but though he was reported to be a comical fellow, I never heard him say a witty thing."

"To be sure," said Sancho, "for it's not every Tom, Dick, or Harry that can crack a joke or say witty things; and that Sancho you mention must be some paltry pilferer, a thief, and a liar. For I myself am the true and genuine Sancho Panza; I'm brimful of God's wit! Just you try me for one year only, and you'll find that scarcely a minute goes by without my pouring forth such a flood of quips and cracks; why, half the time I am unaware of my own waggery, and yet all who hear me say my jokes will be the death of them. And as for the true Don Quixote, there you have him before you; he is the celebrated, the staunch, the wise, the loving Don Quixote of La Mancha, the righter of wrongs, the protector of orphans, the mainstay of widows, the killer of maidens, he whose one and only sweetheart is the peerless Dulcinea of El Toboso; here he stands and here am I, his squire. All other Don Quixotes and all other Sancho Panzas are but shams and tales of a tub."

"By God, I believe what you have said," cried Don Álvaro, "for the few words you have just uttered have more humor than · all that I ever heard the other Sancho Panza say; he was too much of a glutton to be entertaining, for he carried his brains in his belly. For my part, I believe that the enchanters that persecute the good Don Quixote sent the bad one to persecute me. Indeed, I do not know what to make of the whole matter, for though I can swear on my oath that I left one Don Quixote under surgeon's hands at the Nuncio's house in Toledo, yet here pops up another Don Quixote entirely different from mine."

"For my part," said Don Quixote, "I do not claim to be the good, but I may venture to say that I am not the bad one; and as a proof of it, sir, I can assure you that I have never in the course of my life been in Saragossa; indeed, so far from it, that hearing that this spurious usurper of my name had appeared there at the tournament, I refused to go near it, being determined to expose to the world his imposture. And so, I bent my course directly to Barcelona, the home of courtesy, the sanctuary of strangers, the refuge of the poor, the fatherland of patriots, the avenger of the wronged, the residence of true friendship, and unique in the world for its beauty and its location. And though some accidents that befell me there are unpleasant to recall and mortify me deeply, yet I find relief from my misfortune in my memories of that city. In conclusion, Don Álvaro Tarfe, I am the Don Quixote of La Mancha whom fame has celebrated, and not the paltry wretch who has usurped my name and tried to arrogate to himself my honorable ambitions. I beg you, sir, as a gentleman, to be so good as to depose before the mayor of this village, that you never saw me in all your life till this day, that I am not the Don Quixote mentioned in that second part, and that Sancho Panza, my squire, is not the person you formerly knew."

"With all my heart," said Don Álvaro; "but I must confess that I am extremely puzzled to find at the same time two Don Quixotes and two Sancho Panzas, so alike in name and so different in behavior. Indeed, I must repeat that I did not see what I did see, and all that happened to me did not happen."

"Quite so," said Sancho. "Your worship must have been bewitched the same as Lady Dulcinea of El Toboso; and if it were feasible to disenchant your worship as well as her by giving myself three thousand and odd lashes on my behind, I'd do so with a heart and a half; and what is more, they would not cost you a maravedi."

"I do not understand what you mean by those lashes," said Don Álvaro.

Sancho replied that it was a long story, but that if they were traveling the same way, he would gladly tell it to him.

As it was now dinnertime, Don Quixote and Don Álvaro dined together. The mayor of the village happened to come into the inn with a public notary, so Don Quixote requested him to take the deposition that Don Álvaro Tarfe, there present, was ready to give, stating that the said deponent did not have any knowledge of Don Quixote of La Mancha, there present, and that the said Don Quixote was not the same person mentioned in a certain book entitled *The Second Part of Don Quixote of La Mancha*, written by a certain Avellaneda, native of Tordesillas. In short, the mayor drew up an affidavit, and the declaration was completed in due form, much to the satisfaction of Don Quixote and Sancho, for they gave undue importance to the document, not realizing that their words and actions were more than enough to make the distinction apparent between the two Don Quixotes and the two Sanchos. Many compliments and offers of service passed between Don Álvaro and Don Quixote, in which the great Manchegan showed so much discernment that he convinced Don Álvaro that he had been deceived. The latter even suspected that he must have been under a spell, since he had touched with his hand two different Don Quixotes.

They started on their journey toward the evening, and about half a league from the village the road divided into two, one way leading to Don Quixote's village and the other to Don Álvaro's destination. Don Quixote in that short interval let him know the misfortune of his defeat, with Dulcinea's enchantment, and the remedy prescribed by Merlin, at which Don Álvaro's wonder increased. After embracing the knight and his squire, he left them on their way and followed his own.

Don Quixote spent that night among the trees to give

Sancho the opportunity to end his penance, but the crafty knave adopted the same methods as the night before. The barks of the beech trees paid for all, and Sancho took such good care of his back that a fly would not have been flicked off if it had chanced to alight there. But all the while Don Quixote kept counting up the strokes, and he did not miss one of them. He reckoned that with those of the preceding night they amounted to the sum of three thousand and twenty-nine. The sun, which apparently rose with more than ordinary haste to see the sacrifice, gave them the light to continue their journey, which they did, both commenting on Don Álvaro's mistake and what a good idea it had been to take his affidavit in due form before the notary.

They spent that day on the road, and that night Sancho completed his task, to the great joy of his master, who waited impatiently for the moment when he might meet his lady, Dulcinea, in the disenchanted state; and as he went along he scrutinized every woman he met to see whether she was Dulcinea of El Toboso, such implicit faith had he in Merlin's promises, which to him were infallible.

With these hopes and fancies in his mind they reached the top of a hill from which they could see their village in the distance. Sancho had no sooner caught a glimpse of it than he fell on his knees and said: "Open your eyes, beloved home of mine, and behold your son Sancho Panza come back again, if not very rich, at least very well whipped. Open your arms and welcome your son Don Quixote too, who, though he was conquered by another, nevertheless conquered himself; that is the best kind of victory a man can wish for, and I have his own word for it. However, though I've had my fill of flogging, it's a fine mount I have this day."

"A truce to your foolish prattle," said Don Quixote, "and let us step with our right foot foremost as we enter our native village, where we shall give our imaginations play and lay down the plans for our intended pastoral life."

With these words they came down the hill and went directly to their village.

CHAPTER LXXIII

Of the omens that Don Quixote met at the entrance to his village, with other incidents that embellish and accredit this great history

As they entered the village, Cide Hamete informs us, Don Quixote noticed two boys pummeling one another on the threshing floor, and heard one say to the other: "Don't fash yourself, Periquillo, for you'll never see her in all the days of your life."

Don Quixote, overhearing this, said to Sancho: "Did you catch what the boy said, 'You'll never see her in all the days of your life.' "

"Well," rejoined Sancho, "what does it matter what the boy said."

"What?" retorted his master. "Don't you realize that such words, when applied to my affairs, clearly portend that I shall never see my Dulcinea?"

Sancho was about to answer again, but was hindered from so doing by a great hue and cry of hounds and huntsmen in full pursuit of a hare, which was so hard pressed that she came and squatted for shelter just between Dapple's feet. Immediately Sancho laid hold of her and presented her to Don Quixote, but the knight kept muttering to himself: *"Malum signum! Malum signum!* A hare runs away, hounds pursue her, and Dulcinea does not appear."

"You are a strange man, sir," said Sancho. "Let us suppose that poor bunny here is Mistress Dulcinea, the greyhounds that followed her are the wicked enchanters who transmogrified her into a country lass; she races away, I catch her and hand her safe and sound to your worship,

1039

and you hold her in your arms and pet her: what harm is there in this, and what bad omen is this?"

By this time the two boys who had been fighting came up to see the hare, and when Sancho inquired why they had been fighting, he was answered by the boy who had uttered the ominous words, that he had snatched from his play-mate a cage full of crickets, which he would not give back to him again. Sancho pulled a threepenny piece out of his pocket and gave it to the boy for his cage; and giving it to Don Quixote, he said: "There you are, sir; all the tokens of bad luck have been brought to nothing, and though I am a blockhead, I'm convinced all these things have no more to do with our affairs than the clouds of yesteryear. And if I remember right, I've heard the curate of our village say that no decent self-respecting Christian should give ear to such foolishness; and I've heard you yourself, master, say not many days ago that all those Christians who troubled their heads with fortune-telling rubbish were no better than nincompoops. So, without more ado let us make straight for our homes."

By now the huntsmen had come up and asked for their hare, which Don Quixote delivered up to them. They passed on, and just as they were entering the town, they perceived the curate and the bachelor Sansón Carrasco at their devotions in a small field. We must add that Sancho had thrown over Dapple and the bundle of arms, as a cover, the buckram robe painted with flames of fire that they had put on him in the duke's castle on the night when Altisidora rose from the dead. He had also fitted the miter on Dapple's head, and this ornament transformed him as strangely as ever an ass was transformed in all the world. The curate and the bachelor recognized them at once and hastened toward them with open arms. Don Quixote dismounted and embraced them affectionately. Meanwhile the boys, who are as sharp-eyed as lynxes and miss no detail, sighted the ass's miter and rushed up to look at it, saying: "Have a look, boys! Here is Sancho's ass gaudier than Mingo, and Don Quixote's hack leaner than ever." [1]

Surrounded by the boys of the town and attended by the curate and the bachelor, they moved toward the house of

---

[1] This is a reference to the popular fifteenth-century poem of *Mingo Revulgo,* in which Mingo is dressed in his blue smock and red doublet.

Don Quixote, where they found the housekeeper and his niece, who had heard of their arrival, waiting for them on the doorstep. News had also reached Teresa, the wife of Sancho Panza, and she came running half-naked and with her hair all tousled, leading by the hand her daughter, Sanchica. But when she found that her husband was not quite dressed up to her notions of what a governor should wear, she said: "What's all this, husband? You look as if you'd plodded all the way on shanks's mare! You look more misgoverned than governor, I'm thinking."

"Whisht, Teresa!" said Sancho. "Many a time there's a hook but devil a flitch on it. First of all, let us go home, and then I'll tell you wonders. I've money, and after all, that is what counts, and I made it by my own labors without harming a soul."

"Bring home the money, my dear," said Teresa, "no matter how or where you've earned it; after all there's nothing new in that."

Sanchica then hugged her father and asked what he had brought her, for she longed for his return as the flowers do for the dew in May. So, she caught hold of her father's waistband with one hand and pulled Dapple after her by the halter with the other, and her mother took Sancho by the arm on the other side, and away they all went to his cottage, leaving Don Quixote in his own house under the care of his niece and housekeeper with the curate and the bachelor to keep him company.

Don Quixote drew the last two aside, and without observing time or season, he gave them a short account of his defeat and the obligation he lay under of remaining in his village for a year, which, like a true knight-errant, he was determined to observe most faithfully. He added that he intended to become a shepherd and spend that year in the solitude of the fields and woods, giving rein to his amorous thoughts and practising the virtues of the pastoral life. Furthermore, he begged them, if more important duties were not a hindrance, to become his companions, and he assured them that he would furnish them with sufficient sheep and cattle to enable them to belong to such a profession. He let them know that the principal part of the business was already done, for he had planned names that would fit them exactly. The curate asked him what they were, and Don Quixote replied that he was to call himself the shepherd Quixotiz, the bachelor the shepherd Carrascón, the curate the shepherd Curiambro, and Sancho Panza the shepherd Panzino. They were all astonished at Don Quixote's new strain of madness, but considering that this might be a means of preventing him from wandering from home and hoping at the same time that within the year he might be cured of his mad knight-errantry, they applauded his pastoral folly as a wise idea and offered to become his companions in carrying it out.

"Better still," said Sansón Carrasco, "as all the world is now aware that I am a very celebrated poet, I shall compose pastoral or courtly verses at every turn, or such as may best assist our cause, so that we may entertain ourselves in the lonely wastes where we may have to wander. But what is most important, gentlemen, is for each one of us to choose the name of the shepherdess he intends to celebrate in his verses, and not to have a single tree, no matter how tough its bark, on which her name is not inscribed and cut on it, as is the custom of love-sick shepherds."

"That is quite right," answered Don Quixote, "though for myself I have no need to seek for the name of any imaginary shepherdess, for I have the peerless Dulcinea of El Toboso, glory of these banks, ornament of these meadows, the prop of beauty, the cream of grace, and in short, the cynosure of all praise, however exaggerated it may be."

"That is true," said the curate, "but we must look around for indulgent shepherdesses who are easy to manage, and we may have to trim their angles if they don't square with us."

"And if they should fail," added Sansón Carrasco, "we'll give them the names in print that are known to all the world: Phyllidas, Amaryllises, Dianas, Fleridas, Galateas, and Belisardas; since they're for sale in the markets, we can easily buy them and keep them for our own. If my lady—my shepherdess, I should say—by chance be called Ana, I'll celebrate her under the name of Anarda; if Francisca, I'll call her Francenia; and if Lucía, Lucinda: that is all it will come to. And if Sancho Panza is to enter our confraternity, he can celebrate his wife, Teresa Panza, under the name Teresaina."

Don Quixote smiled at the application of the name and the curate extolled his chaste and honorable resolution, repeating his offer to bear him company for as long as he could spare from compulsory duties. With this they took leave of him, advising him to take care of his health and to adopt a healthy diet.

As luck would have it, the housekeeper and the niece heard the conversation between the three on the subject of the pastoral life, and no sooner had the priest and the bachelor gone than they both burst into Don Quixote's room, and the niece cried: "Mercy on us, uncle! What does this mean? We thought that you had come to stay at home and live here like a quiet, honest gentleman, and here you are longing to wander off into fresh labyrinths, becoming a 'gentle shepherd, come and go.' In truth, uncle, the straw is too old to make pipes of."

"Heaven help us, sir!" added the housekeeper. "How will your worship be able to stand the summer's heat, the winter's frost, and the howling of the wolves in the open country? Pray, sir, you mustn't think of it; it's a business for strong men who are born and bred to it from the days when they were babes in arms. And if it comes to worst, better to be a knight-errant than a shepherd. Mark my words, master, and heed my counsel; I'm not full of food and drink, but fasting, and I'm no chicken, but fifty years of age, and I say to you: Stay at home, look after your property, go to confession often, do good to the poor, and let me take the blame if you go wrong."

"My dear girls, do cease your prating," Don Quixote answered. "I know best what I have to do; only help me to my bed, for I do not feel very well. Remember that whether I be a knight-errant or an errant shepherd, you will always find me ready to provide for you, and you may rely on my good faith."

And his affectionate daughters—for so the niece and the housekeeper undoubtedly were—undressed him, put him to bed, where they brought him something to eat, and made him as comfortable as possible.

CHAPTER LXXIV

*Of how Don Quixote fell ill, of the will he made, and
of his death*

As all human things, especially the lives of men, are not
eternal, and even their beginnings are but steps to their end,
and as Don Quixote was under no special dispensation of
Heaven, he was snatched away by death when he least expected it. Whether his sickness was caused by his melancholic
reflections on his defeat, or whether it was so preordained by
Providence, he was stricken down by a violent fever that
confined him to his bed for six days. All that time his good
friends, the priest, the bachelor, and the barber, often visited
him, and his trusty squire, Sancho Panza, never left
his bedside. They were convinced that his sickness was
due to his sorrow at having been defeated and his disappointment in the matter of Dulcinea's disenchantment; and
so, they tried in every way to cheer him up. The bachelor begged him to pluck up his spirits and get up from his
bed so that they might begin their pastoral life, adding that
he had already written an eclogue that would put Sannazaro's [1] nose out of joint, and that he had bought with his
own money from a shepherd of Quintanar two pedigreed dogs
to watch the flock, one called Barcino and the other
Butrón. But this had no effect, for Don Quixote continued
to mope as before. A physician was sent for, who, after
feeling his pulse, took a rather gloomy view of the case and
told him that he should provide for his soul's health, for that
of his body was in dangerous condition. Don Quixote re-

[1] Jacopo Sannazaro (1456–1533) was famous for his pastoral
novel, *Arcadia*.

ceived the news calmly and serenely, but his niece, his
housekeeper, and his squire began to weep as bitterly as if
he had been laid out already. The physician was of the
opinion that melancholy and mortification had brought him
to death's door. Don Quixote then asked them to leave him
for a little while, as he wished to sleep. They retired, and he
slept at a stretch, as they say, for more than six hours, and
the housekeeper and the niece were afraid that he might not
waken from it. At length he did awaken and cried out in a
loud voice: "Blessed be the Almighty for this great benefit
He has granted me! Infinite are His mercies, and undimin-
ished even by the sins of men."

The niece, who was listening very attentively to these words
of her uncle, found more sense in them than there was in his
usual talk, at least since he had fallen ill, and she questioned
him: "What do you mean, uncle? Has anything strange taken
place? What mercies and what sins of men are you talking
about?"

"Mercies," answered Don Quixote, "that God has just this
moment granted to me in spite of all my sins. My judgment
is now clear and unfettered, and that dark cloud of ignorance
has disappeared, which the continual reading of those detestable books of knight-errantry had cast over my understanding. Now I see their folly and fraud, and my sole regret
is that the discovery comes too late to allow me to amend my
ways by reading others that would enlighten my soul. I find,
dear niece, that my end approaches, but I would have it
remembered that though in my life I was reputed a madman, yet in my death this opinion was not confirmed. Therefore, my dear child, call my good friends, the priest, the
bachelor Sansón Carrasco, and Master Nicholas, the barber,
for I wish to make my confession and my will."

There was no need for the niece to go to the trouble, for
presently all three arrived at the house, and Don Quixote
no sooner saw them than he said: "My dear friends, welcome
the happy news! I am no longer Don Quixote of La Mancha,
but Alonso Quixano, the man whom the world formerly
called the Good, owing to his virtuous life. I am now the
sworn enemy of Amadis of Gaul and his innumerable brood;
I now abhor all profane stories of knight-errantry, for I know
only too well, through Heaven's mercy and through my own

personal experience, the great danger of reading them."

When his three friends heard him talk thus, they concluded that he was stricken with some new madness. Sansón then said to him: "What does all this mean, Don Quixote? Now that we have just received news that Lady Dulcinea is disenchanted, and now that we are just about to become shepherds and spend our days singing and living like princes, you talk about turning yourself into a hermit. No more foolish tales, I beg you, and come back to your senses."

"Those foolish tales," replied Don Quixote, "that up to now have been my bane may with Heaven's help turn to my advantage at my death. Dear friends, I feel that I am rapidly sinking; therefore, let us put aside all jesting. I want a priest to hear my confession, and a notary to draw up my will. At such a moment a man must not deceive his soul; therefore, I beg you to send for the notary while the priest hears my confession."

Don Quixote's words amazed his hearers, but though they were at first skeptical about the return of his sanity, they were forced to take him at his word. One of the symptoms that made them fear he was near the point of death was the suddenness with which he had recovered his intellect, for after what he had already said, he conversed with such good sense and displayed such true Christian resignation that they believed his wits had been restored at last. The curate, therefore, told the company to leave the room, and he confessed Don Quixote. In the meantime the bachelor hastened to fetch the notary, and presently he returned with him and with Sancho Panza. The latter (who had already heard from the bachelor the news of his master's plight), finding the niece and the housekeeper in tears, began to make wry faces and finally burst out crying. After the priest had heard the sick man's confession, he came out saying: "There is no doubt that Alonso Quixano is at the point of death, and there is also no doubt that he is in his entire right mind; so, we should go in and enable him to make his will."

These sad tidings burst open the floodgates of the housekeeper's, the niece's, and the good squire's swollen eyes; their tears flowed fast and furious, and a thousand sighs rose from their breasts, for, indeed, as it has been noted, the sick gentleman, whether as Alonso Quixano the Good or as Don Quixote of La Mancha, had always been so good-natured and so agreeable that he was beloved not only by his family, but by all who knew him.

The notary, with the rest of the company, then went into the sick man's chamber, and Don Quixote stated the preamble to the will, commending his soul to Heaven and including the customary Christian declarations. When he came to the legacies he said:

"Item, I give and bequeath to Sancho Panza, whom in my madness I made my squire, whatever money he has of mine in his possession; and whereas there are accounts and reckonings to be settled between us for what he has received and disbursed, my will and pleasure is that he should not be required to furnish any account of such sums, and whatever may remain due to me, which must be but little, be enjoyed by him as my free gift, and may he prosper with it. And as when I was mad, he was through my means made governor of an island, I would now, in my right senses, give him the government of a kingdom, were it in my power, for his honesty and his faithfulness deserve it.

"And now, my friend," said he, turning to Sancho, "forgive me for making you appear as mad as I was myself, and for drawing you into my errors and persuading you that there have been and still are knights-errant in the world."

"Woe is me!" cried Sancho all in tears. "Don't die on me; but take my advice and live on for many a year; the maddest trick a man can play in his life is to yield up the ghost without more ado, and without being knocked on the head or stabbed through the belly to mope away and die of the doldrums. Shame on you, master; don't let the grass grow under your feet. Up with you this instant, out of your bed, and let us put on our shepherd's clothing and off with us to the fields as we had resolved a while back. Who knows but we may find Lady Dulcinea behind a hedge, disenchanted and as fresh as a daisy. If it's your defeat that is tearing your heart, lay the blame on me and say that it was my fault in not tightening Rozinante's girths enough, and that was why you were unhorsed. You must remember, too, sir, from your books on knight-errantry how common it was for knights to jostle one another out of the saddle, and he who's lying low today may be crowning his victory tomorrow."

"Just so," said Sansón; "there is good sense in what honest Sancho says."

"Go softly, I pray you, gentlemen," replied Don Quixote; "one should never look for birds of this year in the nests of yesteryear. I was mad, but I am now in my senses; I was once Don Quixote of La Mancha, but I am now, as I said before, Alonso Quixano the Good, and I hope that my repentance and my sincere words may restore me to the same esteem as you had for me before. So now proceed, Mr. Notary.

"Item, I declare and appoint Antonia Quixano, my niece, here present, sole heiress of all my estate, both real and personal, after all my just debts and legacies have been paid and deducted out of my goods and chattels; and the first charges on the estate shall be salaries due to my housekeeper, together with twenty ducats over and above her salary wages, which I leave and bequeath her to buy a gown.

"Item, I appoint the curate and the bachelor Sansón Carrasco, here present, to be the executors of this my last will and testament.

"Item, it is my will that if my niece Antonia Quixano should wish to marry, it will be with none but a person who, upon strict investigation, shall be found never to have read a book of knight-errantry in his life; but if it should be ascertained that he is acquainted with such books and she still insists on marrying him, she is then to lose all rights to my bequest, which my executors may then distribute in charity as they think fit.

"Item, I entreat the said executors that if at any time they happen to meet with the author of a certain book entitled *The Second Part of the Exploits of Don Quixote of La Mancha*, they will in my name most heartily beg his pardon for my having been unwittingly the cause of his writing such an amount of folly and triviality as he has done. Indeed, as I depart from this life my conscience troubles me that ever I was the cause of his publishing such a book."

After finishing the will, he swooned away and stretched his body to its full length in the bed. The company were alarmed and ran to his assistance; but these fainting attacks were repeated with great frequency during the three days that he lived after he had made his will. The household was in grief and confusion; and yet, after all, the niece continued to eat her meals, the housekeeper drowned her sorrows in wine, and Sancho Panza puffed himself up with satisfaction, for the thought of a legacy possesses a magic power to remove, or at least to soothe, the pangs that the heir should otherwise feel for the death of his friend.

At length Don Quixote's last day came, after he had received all the sacraments and expressed his abhorrence of books of knight-errantry. The notary, who was present, said that he had never read of any knight who ever died in his bed so peacefully and like a good Christian as Don Quixote. And so, amid the tears and lamentations of his friends, who knelt by his bedside, he gave up the ghost, that is to say, he died. And when the priest saw that he had passed away, he bade the notary give him a certificate stating that Alonso Quixano the Good, commonly known as Don Quixote of La Mancha, had died a natural death. This he desired lest any other author, except Cide Hamete Benengeli, take the opportunity of raising him from the dead and presume to write endless histories of his pretended adventures.

Such was the death of that imaginative gentleman Don Quixote of La Mancha, whose native place Cide Hamete did not wish to ascertain, with the intention that all the towns and villages in La Mancha should vie with one another for the honor of having given him birth, as the seven cities of Greece did for Homer. We shall omit the lamentations of Sancho and those of the niece and the housekeeper, as well as the epitaphs that were composed for his tomb, and we shall only quote the following, which the bachelor Sansón Carrasco inscribed on it:

> Here lies the noble fearless knight,
> Whose valor rose to such a height;
> When Death at last did strike him down,
> His was the victory and renown.
> He reck'd the world of little prize,
> And was a bugbear in men's eyes;
> But had the fortune in his age
> To live a fool and die a sage.

And said the most prudent Cide Hamete to his pen: "Here you shall rest, hanging from this rack by this copper wire, my quill. Whether you are well cut or badly pointed here you

shall live long ages, unless presumptuous and unworthy historians take you down to profane you. But before they touch
you, warn them in as strong terms as you are able:

> Beware, beware, all petty knaves,
> I may be touched by none:
> This enterprise, my worthy king,
> Is kept for me alone.

For me alone Don Quixote was born, and I for him. He knew
how to act, and I knew how to write. We two alone are as
one, despite that fictitious and Tordesillescan scribe who
has dared, and may dare again with his coarse and ill-trimmed
ostrich quill, to write the exploits of my valorous knight.
This is no burden for his shoulders, no subject for his frost-
bound muse; and should you by chance get to know him, do
warn him to let Don Quixote's weary and moldering
bones rest in the grave, and not seek, against all canons
of death, to carry him off to Old Castile, compelling him to
leave the tomb where he really and truly lies stretched out full
length, powerless to make a third expedition [2] and new
sally. Surely his two, which have met with approval and have
delighted all the people who knew about them, both here
and abroad, are enough to make a mockery of all the innumerable sallies undertaken by all the countless knights-
errant. Thus you will comply with your Christian profession
by offering good advice to one who wishes you ill, and I
shall be proud to be the first author who ever enjoyed wit-
nessing the full effect of his writing. For my sole aim has
been to arouse men's scorn for the false and absurd stories
of knight-errantry, whose prestige has been shaken by this
tale of my true Don Quixote, and which will, without any
doubt, soon crumble in ruin. Vale."

[2] This should be "fourth expedition." Cervantes errs in this
passage; Don Quixote set out on his adventures three times, once
alone and twice accompanied by Sancho.

SIGNET CLASSIC   MENTOR
(0451)

Classic Tales of Medieval Chivalry

Tales of Romance & Adventure

A TALE OF TWO CITIES *Charles Dickens*   526562
With traumatic eloquence, Dickens brings to life the "Reign of Terror" which followed the French Revolution. Here, in the "times which try men's souls," Dickens tells a tale of heroism, love, and sacrifice.

THE SCARLET PIMPERNEL *Baroness Orczy*   527623
Set in France just after the Revolution, this is the classic story of swash-buckling adventure and romance. The Pimpernel, a mysterious masked hero who saves unfortunate nobles and beautiful maidens from the Revolutionary authorities, is relentlessly pursued across Europe by the vengeful and unforgiving authorities.

THE PHANTOM OF THE OPERA *Gaston Leroux*   524829
Filled with the color and theatrical spectacle of the Paris Opera House, this classic work of horror and suspense remains a riveting story of adventure, desire, and mystery.

TARZAN OF THE APES *Edgar Rice Burroughs*   524233
This is the story of the young Lord Greystoke. Orphaned in the African jungle, raised by the great apes, he teaches himself to read, discovers his true identity and rescues those adventurers who somehow came to rescue him.

To order call: 1-800-788-6262

Thought-provoking tales
of the human condition

The Pilgrim's Progress John Bunyan
523997
Bunyan began this classic work of Christian allegory while imprisoned for his Nonconformist preaching. Follow his hero, Christian, as he flees the City of Destruction and travels the Straight and Narrow, through Vanity Fair, into the Slough of Despond, and beyond. This is not only the story of an allegorical pilgrim on his way to salvation, but the story of everyone striving to remain true to themselves in a devious, contentious, and hostile world.

The Canterbury Tales: A *Selection* Geoffrey Chaucer
524004
This unique edition maintains much of the middle English text, while at the same time incorporating normalized contemporary spellings to produce a text which is both easy to read, and faithful to the sound and sense of Chaucer's original. This volume contains all of the most famous tales, from the mirthful to the bawdy to the profoundly moral, reflecting not only the manners and mores of medieval England, but indeed the full comic and tragic dimensions of life.

The Decameron Giovani Boccaccio; trans. Mark Musa
627466
Similar to Chaucer's CANTERBURY TALES, THE DECAMERON is a series of tales told by a group of diverse individuals in an attempt to help pass the time....But these storytellers are not on a pilgrimage, they have locked themselves in a castle in an attempt to escape the plague.

To order call: 1-800-788-6262

Epic Poems from Ancient Times

☐ GILGAMESH: A Verse Narrative
    translated by Herburt Mason   627180
Dating from the 3rd millennium, this is the oldest story known. It tells
the tale of Gilgamesh, King of Uruk, his defiance of the gods, and his
friendship with Enkidu, the wild man who lived among the animals.
It is a moving tale of heroic achievement, human frailty, and mortali-
ty. It also contains the first written reference to the Biblical flood.

☐ THE ILIAD *translated by W.H.D. Rouse*   527372
This very readable prose translation tells the tale of Achilles, Hector,
Agamemnon, Paris, Helen, and all Troy besieged by the mighty
Greeks. It is a tale of glory and honor, of pride and pettiness, of
friendship and sacrifice, of anger and revenge. In short, it is the
quintessential western tale of men at war.

☐ THE ODYSSEY *translated by W.H.D. Rouse*   527364
Kept away from his home and family for 20 years by war and
malevolent gods, Odysseus returns to find his house in disarray. This
is the story of his adventurous travels and his battle to reclaim what is
rightfully his.

READ THE TOP 25 SIGNET CLASSICS

TO ORDER CALL: 1-800-788-6262